BY HARRY TURTLEDOVE

The Guns of the South

THE WORLDWAR SAGA
Worldwar: In the Balance
Worldwar: Tilting the Balance
Worldwar: Upsetting the Balance
Worldwar: Striking the Balance

COLONIZATION
Colonization: Second Contact
Colonization: Down to Earth
Colonization: Aftershocks

Homeward Bound

THE VIDESSOS CYCLE
The Misplaced Legion
An Emperor for the Legion
The Legion of Videssos
Swords of the Legion

THE TALE OF KRISPOS
Krispos Rising
Krispos of Videssos
Krispos the Emperor

THE TIME OF TROUBLES SERIES
The Stolen Throne
Hammer and Anvil
The Thousand Cities
Videssos Besieged

A World of Difference
Departures
How Few Remain

THE GREAT WAR
The Great War: American Front
The Great War: Walk in Hell
The Great War: Breakthroughs

AMERICAN EMPIRE
American Empire: Blood and Iron
American Empire: The Center Cannot Hold
American Empire: The Victorious Opposition

SETTLING ACCOUNTS
Settling Accounts: Return Engagement
Settling Accounts: Drive to the East
Settling Accounts: The Grapple
Settling Accounts: In at the Death

Every Inch a King

the

TALE OF KRISPOS

the

TALE OF KRISPOS

Harry Turtledove

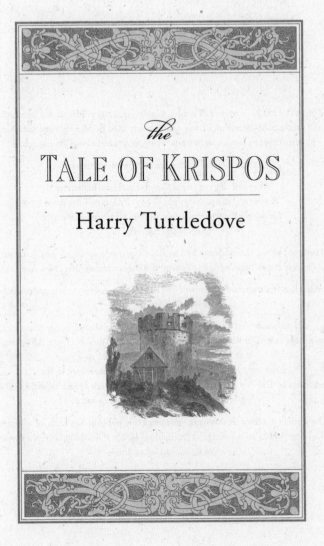

Ballantine Books DEL REY   NEW YORK

2007 Del Rey Books Trade Paperback Edition

Published in the United States by Del Rey Books, an imprint of The Random House Publishing Group, a division of Random House, Inc., New York.

DEL REY is a registered trademark and the Del Rey colophon is a trademark of Random House, Inc.

Krispos Rising and *Krispos of Videssos* originally published in paperback in the United States by Del Rey Books, an imprint of The Random House Publishing Group, a division of Random House, Inc., in 1991.
Krispos the Emperor originally published in paperback in the United States by Del Rey Books, an imprint of The Random House Publishing Group, a division of Random House, Inc., in 1994.

The stories contained in this work were originally published in separate volumes by Del Rey Books, an imprint of The Random House Publishing Group, a division of Random House, Inc.

ISBN 978-0-345-46720-1

Printed in the United States of America

www.delreybooks.com

2   4   6   8   9   7   5   3   1

Text design by Laurie Jewell

CONTENTS

VIDESSOS
AND THE
SURROUNDING LANDS
IN THE
TIME OF KRISPOS

N

PARDRAYA

MYLASA RIVER

DEGIRD RIVER

MYLASA

SEA

KOUPHIS R.

OLOS RIVER

MAKURAN

MASHIZ.

VIDESSIA
SEA

PATRODOTO
RESAINA
GARSA

RHAMNOS R.

EMPIRE

ITHOME R.

ARANDOS R.

SEA
OF
SALT

SAILORS'

AUTHOR'S NOTE

The three books that comprise *The Tale of Krispos* are set in the same universe as the four books of *The Videssos Cycle: The Misplaced Legion, The Legion of Videssos, An Emperor of the Legion,* and *Swords of the Legion.* The events described in *The Tale of Krispos* take place about five hundred years before those chronicled in *The Videssos Cycle.* Thus the preceding map is different from the one in front of the books of *The Videssos Cycle.* So, too, are some of the customs that appear here: nations, even imaginary ones, do not stand still over five hundred years.

Book I

KRISPOS RISING

This one is for Rebecca
(who arrived during Chapter V)
and for her grandmothers,
Gertrude and Nancy.

Chapter I

THE THUNDER OF HOOFBEATS. SHOUTS IN A HARSH TONGUE.
Krispos opened one eye. It was still dark. It felt like the middle of
the night. He shook his head. He did not like noise that woke him up
when he should have been asleep. He closed the eye and snuggled down
between his mother and father on the straw palliasse he and they and his
little sister used for a bed.

His parents woke, too, just when he was trying to go back to sleep.
Krispos felt their bodies stiffen on either side of him. His sister Evdokia
slept on. *Some people have all the luck,* he thought, though he'd never
thought of Evdokia as particularly lucky before. Not only was she three—
half his age—she was a *girl.*

The shouts turned to screams. One of the screams had words: "The
Kubratoi! The Kubratoi are in the village!"

His mother gasped. "Phos save us!" she said, her voice almost as shrill
as the cries of terror in the darkness outside.

"The good god saves through what people do," his father said. The
farmer sprang to his feet. That woke Evdokia, where nothing else had. She
started to cry. "Keep her quiet, Tatze!" Krispos' father growled. His
mother cuddled Evdokia, softly crooned to her.

Krispos wondered whether he'd get cuddled if he started crying. He thought he'd be more likely to get his father's hand on his backside or across his face. Like every farm boy from anywhere near the town of Imbros, he knew who the Kubratoi were: wild men from north of the mountains. "Will we fight them, Father?" he asked. Just the other day, with a stick for a sword, he'd slain a dozen make-believe robbers.

But his father shook his head. "Real fighting is for soldiers. The Kubratoi, curse 'em, are soldiers. We aren't. They'd kill us, and we couldn't do much in the way of fighting back. This isn't play, boy."

"What *will* we do, Phostis?" his mother asked above Evdokia's sniffles. She sounded almost ready to cry herself. That frightened Krispos more than all the racket outside. What could be worse than something bad enough to frighten his mother?

The answer came in a moment: something bad enough to frighten his father. "We run," Phostis said grimly, "unless you'd sooner be dragged north by the two-legged wolves out there. That's why I built close to the forest; that's why I built the door facing away from most of the houses: to give us a chance to run, if the Kubratoi ever came down again."

His mother bent, rose again. "I have the baby."

In her arms, Evdokia said indignantly, "Not a baby!" Then she started to cry again.

No one paid any attention to her. Krispos' father took him by the shoulder, so hard that his flimsy nightshirt might as well not have stood between man's flesh and boy's. "Can you run to the trees, son, fast as you can, and hide yourself till the bad men go away?"

"Yes, Father." Put that way, it sounded like a game. Krispos had played more games in the forest than he could count.

"Then run!" His father threw open the door. Out he darted. His mother followed, still holding Evdokia. Last came his father. Krispos knew his father could run faster than he could, but his father didn't try, not tonight. He stayed between his family and the village.

Bare feet skimming across the ground, Krispos looked back over his shoulder. He'd never seen so many horses or so many torches in his life before. All the horses had strangers on them—the fearsome Kubratoi, he supposed. He could see a lot of villagers, too. The horsemen rounded up more of them every second.

"Don't look, boy! Run!" his father said. Krispos ran. The blessed trees drew nearer and nearer. But a new shout was up, too, and horses drummed their way. The sound of pursuit grew with horrid quickness. Breath sobbing in his throat, Krispos thought how unfair it was that horses could run so fast.

"You stop, or we shoot you!" a voice called from behind. Krispos could hardly understand it; he had never heard Videssian spoken with any accent but the country twang of his own village.

"Keep running!" his father said. But riders flashed by Krispos on either side, so close he could feel the wind from their horses, so close he could smell the beasts. They wheeled, blocking him and his family from the safety of the woods.

Still with the feeling it was all a game, Krispos wheeled to dash off in some new direction. Then he saw the other horsemen, the pair who had gone after his father. One carried a torch, to give them both light to see by. It also let Krispos clearly see them, see their fur caps, the matted beards that seemed to complement those caps, their boiled-leather armor, the curved swords on their hips, the way they sat their mounts as if part of them. Frozen in time, the moment stayed with Krispos as long as he lived.

The second rider, the one without a torch, held a bow. It had an arrow in it, an arrow drawn and pointed at Krispos' father. That was when it stopped being play for the boy. He knew about bows, and how people were supposed to be careful with them. If these wild men didn't know that, time someone taught them.

He marched straight up to the Kubratoi. "You turn the aim of that arrow aside this instant," he told them. "You might hurt someone with it."

Both Kubratoi stared at him. The one with the bow threw back his head and howled laughter. The wild man *did* sound like a wolf, Krispos thought, shivering. He wished his voice had been big and deep like his father's, not a boy's squeak. The rider wouldn't have laughed then.

The rider probably would have shot him, but he did not think of that until years later. As it was, the Kubrati, still laughing, set down his bow, made an extravagant salute from the saddle. "Anything you say, little khagan, anything you say." He chuckled, wiping his face with the back of his hand. Then he raised his eyes to meet those of Krispos' father, who had hurried up to do what he could for the boy. "Not need to shoot now, eh, farmer-man?"

"No," Krispos' father agreed bitterly. "You've caught us, all right."

Along with his parents and Evdokia, Krispos walked slowly back to the village. A couple of horsemen stayed with them; the other two rode ahead so they could get back to doing whatever Kubratoi did. That, Krispos already suspected, was nothing good.

He remembered the strange word the rider with the bow had used. "Father, what does 'khagan' mean?"

"It's what the Kubratoi call their chieftain. If he'd been a Videssian, he would have called you 'Avtokrator' instead."

"Emperor? That's silly." Even with his world coming apart, Krispos found he could still laugh.

"So it is, boy," his father said grimly. He paused, then went on in a different tone, as if beginning to enjoy the joke himself: "Although there's said to be Vaspurakaner blood on my side of the family, and the Vaspurs all style themselves 'prince.' Bet you didn't know your father was a prince, eh, son?"

"Stop it, Phostis!" Krispos' mother said. "The priest says that nonsense about princes is heresy and nothing else but. Don't pass it on to the boy."

"Heresy is what the priest is supposed to know about," his father agreed, "but I won't argue about the nonsense part. Who ever heard of a prince going hungry?"

His mother sniffed, but made no further answer. They were inside the village by then, back where other people could hear them—not good, not if they wanted to talk of heresy. "What will they do with us?" was a safer question to ask, though not one, necessarily, with a surer answer. The villagers stood around under the bows of the Kubratoi, waiting.

Then more riders came up, these leading not people but the village's herds and flocks. "Are the animals coming with us, Father?" Krispos asked. He had not expected the Kubratoi to be so considerate.

"With us, aye, but not for us," was all his father said.

The Kubratoi started shouting, both those who spoke Videssian and those who did not. The villagers looked at one another, trying to figure out what the wild men meant. Then they saw the direction in which the cattle and sheep were going. They followed the beasts northward.

For KRISPOS, THE TREK TO KUBRAT WAS THE BEST ADVENTURE he'd ever had. Tramping along all day was no harder than the chores he would have been doing had the raiders not descended on his village, and he always had something new to see. He'd never imagined, before, how big the world was.

That the march was forced hardly entered his mind. He ate better on it than he had at home; the Kubrati he'd defied that first night decided to make a pet of him and brought him chunks of roast lamb and beef. Soon other riders took up the game, so the "little khagan" sometimes found himself with more than he could eat.

At his father's urging, he never let on. Whenever the Kubratoi did not insist on having him eat in front of them, he passed their tidbits on to the rest of the family. The way he made the food disappear earned him a reputation as a bottomless pit, which only brought more his way.

By the end of the third day on the road north, the raiders who had descended on his village met with other bands bringing captives and booty back to Kubrat. That took Krispos by surprise. He had never given any thought to the world beyond the fields he knew. Now he saw he and his family were caught up in something larger than a local upheaval.

"Where are those people from, Father?" he asked as yet another group of bewildered, bedraggled peasants came stumbling into the larger stream.

His father shrugged, which made Evdokia giggle—she was riding on his shoulders. "Who can say?" Phostis answered. "Just another village of farmers that happened to be unlucky like ours."

"Unlucky." Krispos tasted the word, found it odd. He was enjoying himself. Sleeping under the stars was no great handicap, not to a six-year-old in summer. But his father, he could tell, did not like the Kubratoi and would have hit back at them if he could. That made Krispos ask another question, one he had not thought of till now. "Why are they taking farmers back to Kubrat?"

"Here comes one." His father waited till the wild man rode by, then pointed at his back. "Tell me what you see."

"A man on a horse with a big bushy beard."

"Horses don't have beards," Evdokia said. "That's dumb, Krispos."

"Hush," their father told her. "That's right, son—a man on a horse. Kubratoi hardly ever come down from their horses. They travel on them, go to war on them, and follow their flocks on them, too. But you can't be a farmer if you stay on your horse all the time."

"They don't want to be farmers, though," Krispos said.

"No, they don't," his father agreed. "But they need farmers, whether they want to farm themselves or not. Everybody needs farmers. Flocks can't give you all the food you need and flocks won't feed your horses at all. So they come down into Videssos and steal folk like—well, folk like us."

"Maybe it won't be so bad, Phostis," Krispos' mother said. "They can't take more from us than the imperial tax collectors do."

"Who says they can't?" his father answered. "Phos the lord of the great and good mind knows I have no love for the tax collectors, but year in, year out they leave us enough to get by on. They shear us—they don't flay us. If the Kubratoi were so fine as all that, Tatze, they wouldn't need to raid every few years to get more peasants. They'd be able to keep the ones they had."

There was a commotion among the captives that night. Evidently a good many of them agreed with Krispos' father and tried to escape from the Kubratoi. The screams were far worse than the ones in the village the night the wild men came.

"Fools," Phostis said. "Now they'll come down harder on all of us."

He was right. The men from the north started traveling before dawn and did not stop to feed the peasants till well after noon. They pushed the pace after the meager meal, too, halting only when it got too dark for them to see where they were going. By then, the Paristrian Mountains loomed tall against the northern skyline.

A small stream ran through the campsite the Kubratoi had picked. "Shuck out of your shirt and wash yourself," Krispos' mother told him.

He took off his shirt—the only one he had—but did not get into the water. It looked chilly. "Why don't you take a bath, too, Mama?" he said. "You're dirtier than I am." Under the dirt, he knew, she was one of the best-looking ladies in his village.

His mother's eyes flicked to the Kubratoi. "I'm all right the way I am, for now." She ran a grimy hand across her grimy face.

"But—"

The swat of his father's hand on his bare behind sent him skittering into the stream. It was as cold as it looked, but his bottom still felt aflame when he came out. His father nodded to him in a strange new way, almost as if they were both grown men. "Are you going to argue with your mother the next time she tells you to do something?" he asked.

"No, Father," Krispos said.

His father laughed. "Not until your backside cools off, anyway. Well, good enough. Here's your shirt." He got out of his own and walked down to the stream, to come back a few minutes later wet and dripping and running his hands through his hair.

Krispos watched him dress, then said carefully, "Father, is it arguing if I ask why you and I should take baths, but Mama shouldn't?"

For a bad moment he thought it was, and braced himself for another smack. But then his father said, "Hmm—maybe it isn't. Put it like this— no matter how clean we are, no Kubrati will find you or me pretty. You follow that?"

"Yes," Krispos said, although he thought his father—with his wide shoulders, neat black beard, and dark eyes set so deep beneath shaggy brows that sometimes the laughter lurking there was almost hidden—a fine and splendid man. But, he had to admit, that wasn't the same as pretty.

"All right, then. Now you've already seen how the Kubratoi are thieves. Phos, boy, they've stolen all of us, and our animals, too. And if one of them saw your mother looking especially pretty, the way she can—" Listening, she smiled at Krispos' father, but did not speak. "—he might want to take her away for his very own. We don't want that to happen, do we?"

"No!" Krispos' eyes got wide as he saw how clever his mother and father were. "I see! I understand! It's a trick, like when the wizard made Gemistos' hair turn green at the show he gave."

"A little like that, anyhow," his father agreed. "But that was real magic. Gemistos' hair really *was* green, till the wizard changed it back to brown again. This is more a game, like when men and women switch clothes sometimes on the Midwinter's Day festival. Do I turn into your mama because I'm wearing a dress?"

"Of course not!" Krispos giggled. But that wasn't supposed to fool anyone; as his father said, it was only a game. Here, now, his mother's prettiness remained, though she was trying to hide it so no one noticed. And if hiding something in plain sight wasn't magic, Krispos didn't know what was.

H E HAD THAT THOUGHT AGAIN THE NEXT DAY, WHEN THE WILD men took their captives into Kubrat. A couple of passes opened invitingly, but the Kubratoi headed for neither of them. Instead, they led the Videssian farmers down a forest track that seemed destined only to run straight into the side of the mountains.

But it did not run into the mountains—rather, into a narrow defile the trees and a last spur of hill screened from view. Though the sky stayed blue overhead, everything in the gorge was lost in shadow, as if it were twilight. Somewhere a nightjar hooted, thinking its time had come.

Strung out along the bottom of that steep, twisting gorge, people and animals could move but slowly. True evening came when they were only part of the way through the mountains.

"It's a good trick," Krispos' father said grudgingly as they settled down to camp. "Even if imperial soldiers do come after us, a handful of men could hold them out of this pass forever."

"Soldiers?" Krispos said, amazed. That Videssian troopers might be riding after the Kubratoi had never crossed his mind. "You mean the Empire cares enough about us to fight to get us back?"

His father's chuckle had little real amusement in it. "I know the only time you ever saw soldiers was that time a couple of years ago, when the harvest was so bad they didn't trust us to sit still for the tax collector unless he had archers at his back. But aye, they might fight to get us back. Videssos needs farmers on the ground as much as Kubrat does. Everybody needs farmers, boy; it'd be a hungry world without 'em."

Most of that went over Krispos' head. "Soldiers," he said again, softly. So he—for that was how he thought of it—was so important the Avtokrator would send soldiers to return him to his proper place! Then it was as if—well, almost as if—he had caused those soldiers to be sent. And surely that was as if—well, perhaps as if—he were Avtokrator himself. It was a good enough dream to fall asleep on, anyhow.

When he woke up the next morning, he was certain something was wrong. He kept peering around, trying to figure out what it was. At last his eyes went up to the strip of rock far overhead that the rising sun was painting with light. "That's the wrong direction!" he blurted. "Look! The sun's coming up in the west!"

"Phos have mercy, I think the lad's right!" Tzykalas the cobbler said close by. He drew a circle on his breast, itself the sign of the good god's sun. Other people started babbling; Krispos heard the fear in their voices.

Then his father yelled "Stop it!" so loudly that they actually did. Into that sudden silence, Phostis went on, "What's more likely, that the world has turned upside down or that this canyon's wound around so we couldn't guess east from west?"

Krispos felt foolish. From the expressions on the folk nearby, so did they. In a surly voice, Tzykalas said, "Your boy was the one who started us hopping, Phostis."

"Well, so he was. What about it? Who's the bigger fool, a silly boy or the grown man who takes him seriously?"

Someone laughed at that. Tzykalas flushed. His hands curled into fists. Krispos' father stood still and quiet, waiting. Shaking his head and muttering to himself, Tzykalas turned away. Two or three more people laughed then.

Krispos' father took no notice of them. Quietly he said, "The next time things aren't the way you expect, son, think before you talk, eh?"

Krispos nodded. He felt foolish now himself. One more thing to remember, he thought. The bigger he got, the more such things he found. He wondered how grown people managed to keep everything straight.

Late that afternoon, the canyon opened up. Green land lay ahead, land not much different from the fields and forests around Krispos' home village. "Is that Kubrat?" he asked, pointing.

One of the wild men overheard him. "Is Kubrat. Is good to be back. Is home," he said in halting Videssian.

Till then, Krispos hadn't thought about the raiders having homes—to him, they had seemed a phenomenon of nature, like a blizzard or a flood. Now, though, a happy smile was on the Kubrati's face. He looked like a man heading home after some hard work. Maybe he had little boys at that home, or little girls. Krispos hadn't thought about the raiders having children, either.

He hadn't thought about a lot of things, he realized. When he said that out loud, his father laughed. "That's because you're still a child. As you grow, you'll work through the ones that matter to you."

"But I want to be able to know about all those things now," Krispos said. "It isn't fair."

"Maybe not." No longer laughing, his father put a hand on his shoulder. "But I'll tell you this—a chicken comes out of its egg knowing everything it needs to know to be a chicken. There's more to being a man; it takes a while to learn. So which would you rather be, son, a chicken or a man?"

Krispos folded his hands into his armpits and flapped imaginary wings. He let out a couple of loud clucks, then squealed when his father tickled his ribs.

The next morning, Krispos saw in the distance several—well, what were they? Neither tents nor houses, but something in between. They had wheels and looked as if animals could pull them. His father did not know what to call them, either.

"May I ask one of the Kubratoi?" Krispos said.

His mother started to shake her head, but his father said, "Let him, Tatze. We may as well get used to them, and they've liked the boy ever since he stood up to them that first night."

So he asked one of the wild men trotting by on his pony. The Kubrati stared at him and started to laugh. "So the little khagan does not know of yurts, eh? Those are yurts you see, the perfect homes for following the flocks."

"Will you put us in yurts, too?" Krispos liked the idea of being able to live now one place, now another.

But the horseman shook his head. "You are farmer folk, good only for raising plants. And as plants are rooted to the ground, your houses will be rooted, too." He spat to show his contempt for people who had to stay in one spot, then touched the heels of his boots to his horse's flanks and rode off.

Krispos looked after him, a little hurt. "I'll travel, too, one day," he said loudly. The Kubrati paid no attention to him. He sighed and went back to his parents. "I *will* travel!" he told his father. "I will."

"You'll travel in a few minutes," his father answered. "They're getting ready to move us along again."

"That's not what I meant," Krispos said. "I meant travel when *I* want to, and go where *I* want to."

"Maybe you will, son." His father sighed, rose, and stretched. "But not today."

JUST AS CAPTIVES FROM MANY VIDESSIAN VILLAGES HAD JOINED together to make one large band on the way to Kubrat, so now they were taken away from the main group—five, ten, twenty families at a time, to go off to the lands they would work for their new masters.

Most of the people the Kubratoi told to go off with the group that included Krispos' father were from his village, but some were not, and some of the villagers had to go someplace else. When they protested being broken up, the wild men ignored their pleas. "Not as if you were a clan the gods formed," a raider said, the same scorn in his voice that Krispos had heard from the Kubrati who explained what yurts were. And, like that rider, he rode away without listening to any reply.

"What does he mean, gods?" Krispos asked. "Isn't there just Phos? And Skotos," he added after a moment, naming the good god's wicked foe in a smaller voice.

"The Kubratoi don't know of Phos," his father told him. "They worship demons and spirits and who knows what. After they die, they'll spend forever in Skotos' ice for their wickedness, too."

"I hope there are priests here," Tatze said nervously.

"We'll get along, whether or not," Phostis said. "We know what the good is, and we'll follow it." Krispos nodded. That made sense to him. He always tried to be good—unless being bad looked like a lot more fun. He hoped Phos would forgive him. His father usually did, and in his mind the good god was a larger version of his father, one who watched the whole world instead of just a farm.

Later that day, one of the Kubratoi pointed ahead and said, "There your new village."

"It's big!" Krispos said. "Look at all the houses!"

His father had a better idea of what to look for. "Aye, lots of houses. Where are the people, though? Hardly any in the fields, hardly any in the village." He sighed. "I expect the reason I don't see 'em is that they're not there to see."

As the party of Kubratoi and captives drew near, a few men and women did emerge from their thatch-roofed cottages to stare at the newcomers. Krispos had never had much. These thin, poorly clad wretches, though, showed him other folk could have even less.

The wild men waved the village's new inhabitants forward to meet the old. Then they wheeled their horses and rode away . . . rode, Krispos supposed, back to their yurts.

As he came into the village, he saw that many of the houses stood empty; some were only half thatched, others had rafters falling down, still others had chunks of clay gone from the wall to reveal the woven branches within.

His father sighed again. "I suppose I should be glad we'll have roofs over our heads." He turned to the families uprooted from Videssos. "We might as well pick out the places we'll want to live in. Me, I have my eye on that house right there." He pointed to an abandoned dwelling as dilapidated as any of the others, set near the edge of the village.

As he and Tatze, followed by Krispos and Evdokia, headed toward the home they had chosen, one of the men who belonged to this village came up to confront him. "Who do you think you are, to take a house without so much as a by-your-leave?" the fellow asked. Even to a farm boy like Krispos, his accent sounded rustic.

"My name's Phostis," Krispos' father said. "Who are you to tell me I can't, when this place is falling to pieces around you?"

The other newcomers added their voices to his. The man looked from them to his own followers, who were fewer and less sure of themselves. He lost his bluster as a punctured bladder loses air. "I'm Roukhas," he said. "Headman here, at least until all you folk came."

"We don't want what's yours, Roukhas," Krispos' father assured him. He smiled a sour smile. "Truth is, I'd be just as glad never to have met you, because that'd mean I was still back in Videssos." Even Roukhas nodded at that, managing a wry chuckle. Phostis went on, "We're here, though, and I don't see much point in having to build from scratch when there're all these places ready to hand."

"Aye, well, put that way, I suppose you have a point." Roukhas stepped backward and waved Phostis toward the house he had chosen.

As if his concession were some sort of signal, the rest of the longtime inhabitants of the village hurried up to mingle with the new arrivals. Indeed, they fell on them like long-lost cousins—as, Krispos thought, a little surprised at himself, they were.

"They didn't even know what the Avtokrator's name was," Krispos' mother marveled as the family settled down to sleep on the ground inside their new house.

"Aye, well, they need to worry about the khagan more," his father answered. Phostis yawned an enormous yawn. "A lot of 'em, too, were born right here, not back home. I shouldn't be surprised if they didn't even remember there *was* an Avtokrator."

"But still," Krispos' mother said, "they talked with us as we would with someone from the capital, from Videssos the city—someone besides the tax man, I mean. And we're from the back of beyond."

"No, Tatze, we just got there," his father answered. "If you doubt it, wait till you see how busy we're going to be." He yawned again. "Tomorrow."

Life on a farm is never easy. Over the next weeks and months, Krispos found out just how hard it could be. If he was not gathering straw for his father to bind into yealms and put up on the roof to repair the thatch, then he was fetching clay from the streambank to mix with roots and more straw and goat hair and dung to make daub to patch the walls.

Making and slapping on the daub was at least fun. He had the chance to get filthy while doing just what his parents told him. He carried more clay for his mother to shape into a baking oven. Like the one back at his old village, it looked like a beehive.

He spent a lot of time with his mother and little sister, working in the vegetable plots close by the houses. Except for the few still kept up by the handful of people here before the newcomers arrived, those had been allowed to run down. He and Evdokia weeded until their hands blistered, then kept right on. They plucked bugs and snails from the beans and cabbages, the onions and vetch, the beets and turnips. Krispos yelled and screamed and jumped up and down to scare away marauding crows and sparrows and starlings. That was fun, too.

He also kept the village chickens and ducks away from the vegetables. Soon his father got a couple of laying hens by doing some timber cutting for one of the established villagers. Krispos took care of them, too, and spread their manure over the vegetables.

He did more scarecrow duty out in the fields of wheat and oats and barley, along with the rest of the children. With more new arrivals than boys and girls born in the village, that time in the fields was also a time of testing, to see who was strong and who was clever. Krispos held his own and then some; even boys who had two more summers than he did soon learned to give him a wide berth.

He managed to find time for mischief. Roukhas never figured out who put the rotten egg under the straw, right where he liked to lay his head. The farmer and his family did sleep outdoors for the next two days, until their house aired out enough to be livable again. And Evdokia ran calling for her mother one day when she came back from washing herself in the stream and found her clothes moving by themselves.

Unlike Roukhas, Tatze had no trouble deducing how the toad had got into Evdokia's shift. Krispos slept on his stomach that night.

Helping one of the slower newcomers get his roof into shape for the approaching fall rains earned Krispos' father a piglet—and Krispos the job of looking after it. "It's a sow, too," his father said with some satisfaction. "Next year we'll breed it and have plenty of pigs of our own." Krispos looked forward to pork stew and ham and bacon—but not to more pig-tending.

Sheep the village also had, a small flock owned in common, more for wool than for meat. With so many people arriving with only the clothes on their backs, the sheep were sheared a second time that year, and the lambs, too. Krispos' mother spent a while each evening spinning thread and she began to teach Evdokia the art. She set up a loom between two forked posts outside the house, so she could turn the spun yarn into cloth.

There were no cattle. The Kubratoi kept them all. Cattle, in Kubrat, were wealth, almost like gold. A pair of donkeys plowed for the villagers instead of oxen.

Krispos' father fretted over that, saying, "Oxen have horns to attach the yoke to, but with donkeys you have to fasten it round their necks, so they choke if they pull hard against it." But Roukhas showed him the special donkey-collars they had, modeled after the ones the Kubratoi used for the horses that pulled their yurts. He came away from the demonstration impressed. "Who would have thought the barbarians could come up with something so useful?"

What they had not come up with was any way to make grapes grow north of the mountains. Everyone ate apples and pears, instead, and drank beer. The newcomers never stopped grumbling about that, though some of the beer had honey added to it so it was almost as sweet as wine.

Not having grapes made life different in small ways as well as large. One day Krispos' father brought home a couple of rabbits he had killed in the field. His mother chopped the meat fine, spiced it with garlic—and then stopped short. "How can I stuff it into grape leaves if there aren't any grape leaves?" She sounded more upset at not being able to cook what she wanted than she had over being uprooted and forced to trek to Kubrat; it made the uprooting hit home.

Phostis patted her on the shoulder, turned to his son. "Run over to Roukhas' house and find out what Ivera uses in place of grape leaves. Quick, now!"

Krispos soon came scampering back. "Cabbage," he announced importantly.

"It won't be the same," his mother said. It wasn't, but Krispos thought it was good.

Harvest came sooner than it would have in the warmer south. The grown men cut first the barley, then the oats and wheat, going through the fields with sickles. Krispos and the rest of the children followed to pick up the grains that fell to the ground. Most went into the sacks they carried; a few they ate. And after the grain was gathered, the men went through the fields again, cutting down the golden straw and tying it into sheaves. Then the children, two to a sheaf, dragged it back to the village. Finally, the men and women hauled buckets of dung from the middens to manure the ground for the next planting.

Once the grain was harvested, it was time to pick the beans and to chop down the plants so they could be fed to the pigs. And then, with the grain and beans in deep storage pits—except for some of the barley, which was set aside for brewing—the whole village seemed to take a deep breath.

"I was worried, when we came here, whether we'd be able to grow enough to get all of us through the winter," Krispos' father said one evening, taking a long pull on a mug of beer. "Now, though, Phos the lord of the great and good mind be praised, I think we have enough and to spare."

His mother said, "Don't speak too soon."

"Come on, Tatze, what could go wrong?" his father answered, smiling. "It's in the ground and safe."

Two days later, the Kubratoi came. They came in greater numbers and with more weapons than they'd had escorting the new villagers away from the mass of Videssian captives. At their shouted orders, the villagers opened one storage pit in three and loaded the precious grain onto packhorses the wild men had brought with them. When they were done, the Kubratoi trotted off to plunder the next village.

Krispos' father stood a long time, staring down into the empty yard-deep holes in the sandy soil back of the village. Finally, with great deliberation, he spat into one of them. "Locusts," he said bitterly. "They ate us out just like locusts. We would have had plenty, but we'll all be hungry before spring comes."

"We ought to fight them next time, Phostis," said one of the younger men who had come from the same village as Krispos and his family. "Make them pay for what they steal."

But Krispos' father sadly shook his head. "I wish we could, Stankos, when I see what they've done to us. They'd massacre us, though, I fear. They're soldiers, and it's the nature of soldiers to take. Farmers endure."

Roukhas was still Phostis' rival for influence in the village, but now he agreed with him. "Four or five years ago the village of Gomatou, over a couple of days west of here, tried rising up against the Kubratoi," he said.

"Well? What happened to it?" Stankos asked.

"It's not there anymore," Roukhas said bleakly. "We watched the smoke go up into the sky."

No one spoke of rebellion again. To Krispos, charging out against the Kubratoi with sword and lance and bow and driving them all back north over the Astris River to the plains from which they'd come would have been the most glorious thing in the world. It was one of his playmates' favorite games. In truth, though, the wild men were the ones with the arms and armor and horses and, more important still, both the skill and will to use them.

Farmers endure, Krispos thought. He didn't like just enduring. He wondered if that meant he shouldn't be a farmer. What else could he be, though? He had no idea.

THE VILLAGE GOT THROUGH THE WINTER, WHICH WAS FIERCER than any Krispos remembered. Even the feast and celebrations of Midwinter's Day, the day when the sun finally turned north in the sky, had to be forgotten because of the blizzard raging outside.

Krispos grew to hate being cooped up and idle in the house for weeks on end. South of the mountains, even midwinter gave days when he could go out to play in the snow. Those were few and far between here. Even a freezing trip out to empty the chamber pot on the dung heap or help his father haul back firewood made him glad to return to the warm—if stuffy and smoky—air inside.

Spring came at last and brought with it mud almost as oppressive as the snow had been. Plowing, harrowing, sowing, and weeding followed, plunging Krispos back into the endless round of farm work and making him long for the lazy days of winter once more. That fall, the Kubratoi came to take their unfair share of the harvest once more.

The year after that, they came a couple of other times, riding through the fields and trampling down long swathes of growing grain. As they rode, they whooped and yelled and grinned at the helpless farmers whose labor they were wrecking.

"Drunk, the lot of 'em," Krispos' father said the night after it happened the first time, his mouth tight with disgust. "Pity they didn't fall off their horses and break their fool necks—that'd send 'em down to Skotos where they belong."

"Better to thank Phos that they didn't come into the village and hurt people instead of plants," Krispos' mother said. Phostis only scowled and shook his head.

Listening, Krispos found himself agreeing with his father. What the Kubratoi had done was wrong, and they'd done it on purpose. If he deliberately did something wrong, he got walloped for it. The villagers were not strong enough to wallop the Kubratoi, so let them spend eternity with the dark god and see how they liked that.

When fall came, of course, the Kubratoi took as much grain as they had before. If, thanks to them, less was left for the village, that was the village's hard luck.

The wild men played those same games the next year. That year, too, a woman who had gone down to the stream to bathe never came back. When the villagers went looking for her, they found hoofprints from several horses in the clay by the streambank.

Krispos' father held his mother very close when the news swept through the village. "*Now* I will thank Phos, Tatze," he said. "It could have been you."

One dawn late in the third spring after Krispos came to Kubrat, barking dogs woke the villagers even before they would have risen on their own. Rubbing their eyes, they stumbled from their houses to find themselves staring at a couple of dozen armed and mounted Kubratoi. The riders carried torches. They scowled down from horseback at the confused and frightened farmers.

Krispos' hair tried to rise at the back of his neck. He hadn't thought, lately, about the night the Kubratoi had kidnapped him and everyone else in his village. Now the memories—and the terror—of that night flooded back. But where else could the wild men take them from here? Why would they want to?

One of the riders drew his sword. The villagers drew back a pace. Someone moaned. But the Kubrati did not attack with the curved blade. He pointed instead, westward. "You come with us," he said in gutturally accented Videssian. "Now."

Krispos' father asked the questions the boy was thinking: "Where? Why?"

"Where I say, man bound to the earth. Because I say." This time the horseman's gesture with the sword was threatening.

At nine, Krispos knew more of the world and its harsh ways than he had at six. Still, he did not hesitate. He sprang toward the Kubrati. His father grabbed at him to haul him back, too late. "You leave him alone!" Krispos shouted up at the rider.

The man snarled at him, teeth gleaming white in the torchlight's flicker. The sword swung up. Krispos' mother screamed. Then the wild man hesitated. He thrust his torch down almost into Krispos' face. Suddenly, astonishingly, the snarl became a grin. The Kubrati said something in his own language. His comrades exclaimed, then roared laughter.

He dropped back into Videssian. "Ha, little khagan, you forget me? Good thing I remember you, or you die this morning. You defy me once before, in Videssos. How does farmer boy come to have man's—Kubrati man's—spirit in him?"

Krispos hadn't recognized the rider who'd captured him and his family. If the man recognized him, though, he would turn it to his advantage. "Why are you here? What do you want with us now?"

"To take you away." The scowl came back to the Kubrati's face. "Videssos has paid ransom for you. We have to let you go." He sounded anything but delighted at the prospect.

"Ransom?" The word spread through the villagers, at first slowly and in hushed, disbelieving tones, then louder and louder till they all shouted it, nearly delirious with joy. "Ransom!"

They danced round the Kubratoi, past hatred and fear dissolved in the powerful water of freedom. It was, Krispos thought, like a Midwinter's Day celebration somehow magically dropped into springtime. Soon riders and villagers were hoisting wooden mugs of beer together. Barrel after barrel was broken open. Little would be left for later, but what did that matter? They would not be here later. A new cry took the place of "Ransom!"

"We're going home!"

Evdokia was puzzled. "What does everyone mean, Krispos, we're going home? Isn't this home?"

"No, silly, the place Mother and Father talk about all the time is our real home."

"Oh." His sister barely remembered Videssos. "How is it different?"

"It's . . ." Krispos wasn't too clear on that himself, not after almost three years. "It's better," he finished at last. That seemed to satisfy her. He wondered if it was true. His own memories of life south of the mountains had grown hazy.

The Kubratoi seemed in as big a hurry to get rid of their Videssian captives as they had been to get them into Kubrat in the first place. Evdokia had trouble keeping up; sometimes Krispos' father had to carry her for a stretch, even if it shamed her. Krispos made the three days of hard marching on his own, but they left his feet blistered and him sleeping like a dead man each night.

At last the villagers and hundreds more like them reached a broad, shallow valley. With an eye rapidly growing wiser to the ways of farming, Krispos saw that it was better land than what his village tilled. He also saw several large and splendid yurts and, in the distance, the flocks by which the Kubratoi lived. That explained why the valley was not farmed.

The wild men herded the Videssians into pens much like those in which the peasants kept goats. They posted guards around them so no one would even think of clambering over the branches and sneaking off. Fear began to replace the farmer's jubilation. "Are we truly to be ransomed," someone shouted, "or sold like so many beasts?"

"You keep still! Big ceremony coming tomorrow," yelled a Kubrati who spoke Videssian. He climbed up onto the fencing of the pen and pointed. "See over there. There tents of Videssos' men, and Empire's banner, too. No tricks now."

Krispos looked in the direction the man's arm had given. He was too short to see out of the pen. "Pick me up, Father!"

His father did, then, with a grunt of effort, set the boy on his shoulders. Krispos saw the tops of several square tents not far from the yurts he'd noticed before. Sure enough, a sky-blue flag with a gold sunburst on it snapped in front of one of them. "*Is* that Videssos' banner?" he asked. Try as he would, he could not recall it.

"Aye, it's ours," his father said. "The tax collector always used to show it when he came. I'm gladder to see it now than I was then, I'll tell you that." He put Krispos down.

"Let me see! My turn! Let me see!" Evdokia squealed. Phostis sighed, then smiled. He picked up his daughter.

THE NEXT MORNING, THE PEASANTS GOT FAR BETTER FARE THAN they'd had on the trek to the valley: roasted mutton and beef, with plenty of the flat wheatcakes the Kubratoi baked in place of leavened bread. Krispos ate till his belly felt like bursting from joy and he washed down the meat with a long swig from a leather bucket of mare's milk.

"I wonder what the ceremony the wild man talked about will be like," his mother said.

"I wish we could see more of it," his father added. "Weren't for us, after all, it wouldn't be happening. Not right to leave us penned up while it's going on."

A little later, the Kubratoi let the farmers out of the pens. "This way! This way!" the nomads who spoke Videssian shouted, urging the crowd along toward the yurts and tents.

Krispos spotted the wild men he had yelled at on the day he was captured and on the day he started back to freedom. The Kubrati was peering into the mass of peasants as they walked by him. His eye caught Krispos'. He grinned. "Ho, little khagan, I look for you. You come with me—you part of ceremony."

"What, me? Why?" As he spoke, though, Krispos cut across the flow of people toward the Kubrati.

The now-dismounted rider took him by the shoulder, as his father did sometimes. "Khagan Omurtag, he want some Videssian to talk to envoy from Empire, stand for all you people in magic, while envoy paying gold to get you back. I tell him about you, how bold you are. He say all right."

"Oh. Oh, my!" Excitement ousted fear. Khagan Omurtag, in Krispos' imagination, was nine feet high, with teeth like a wolf's. And an envoy from the Avtokrator should be even more magnificent—tall, handsome, heroic, clad in gilded chain mail, and carrying an enormous sword. . . .

Reality was less dramatic, as reality has a way of being. The Kubratoi had built a little platform of hides stretched across timbers. None of the four men who stood on it was nine feet tall, none wore gilded chain mail. Then the wild man lifted Krispos, and he was on the platform, too.

"Pretty boy," murmured a short, sour-faced man in a robe of green silk shot through with silver threads. He turned to the Kubrati standing across from him. "All right, Omurtag, he's here. Get on with your miserable heathen rite, if you think you must."

Krispos waited for the sky to fall. No matter that the khagan of Kubrat was neither especially tall nor especially lupine—was, in fact, quite an ordinary-looking Kubrati save that his furs were of marten and sable, not fox and rabbit. He was the khagan. Talking that way to him had to cost a man his head.

But Omurtag only threw back his head and laughed. "Sweet as always, Iakovitzes," he said. His Videssian was as smooth and polished as the envoy's, and a good deal more so than Krispos'. "The magic seals the bargain, as well you know."

"Phos watches over all bargains from above the sun." Iakovitzes nodded to the man in a blue robe behind him. Dim memories stirred in Krispos. He'd seen such men with shaved heads before, though not in Kubrat; the fellow was a priest.

"So you say," Omurtag answered. "My *enaree* here knows the spirits of ground and wind. They are closer than any lofty god above the sun, and I trust them further."

The *enaree* was the first grown man Krispos had ever seen who cut off his beard. It made him look like an enormous little boy—till one looked into his eyes. They saw farther than boys' . . . farther than men's had any business seeing, too, Krispos thought nervously.

The khagan turned to him. "Come here, lad."

For a split second, Krispos hung back. Then he thought that he had been chosen for his boldness. He straightened his back, put his chin up, and walked over to Omurtag. The tight-stretched hides vibrated under his feet, as if they were an enormous drumhead.

"We have your people," Omurtag intoned, taking hold of Krispos' arm with his left hand. His grip was firm and hard. His right hand plucked a dagger from his belt, set it at the boy's throat. Krispos stood very still. The khagan went on, "They are ours, to do with as we will."

"The Empire has gold and will pay for their safe return." Iakovitzes sounded, of all things, bored. Krispos was suddenly sure he'd performed this ceremony many times before.

"Let us see that gold," the khagan said. His voice was still formal, but anything but bored. He stared avidly at the pouch Iakovitzes withdrew from within a fold of his robe.

The Videssian envoy drew out a single bright coin, gave it to Omurtag. "Let this goldpiece stand for all, as the boy does," Iakovitzes said.

Omurtag passed the coin to the *enaree*. He muttered over it; the hand that was not holding it moved in tiny passes. Krispos saw the Videssian priest scowl, but the man held his peace. The *enaree* spoke in the Kubrati tongue. "He declares it is good gold," Omurtag said to Iakovitzes.

"Of course it's good gold," Iakovitzes snapped, breaking the ritual. "The Empire hasn't coined anything else for hundreds of years. Should we start now, it would be for something more important than ransoming ragged peasants."

The khagan laughed out loud. "I think your tongue was stung by a wasp one day, Iakovitzes," he said, then returned to the pattern of the ceremony. "He declares it is good gold. Thus the people are yours." He gently pushed Krispos toward Iakovitzes.

The envoy's touch was warm, alive. He moved his hand on Krispos' back in a way that was strange and familiar at the same time. "Hello, pretty boy," Iakovitzes murmured. Krispos recognized the tone and realized why the caress had that familiarity to it: his father and mother acted like this with each other when they felt like making love.

Having lived all his life in a one-room house with his parents, having slept in the same bed with them, he knew what sex was about. That variations could exist, variations that might include him and Iakovitzes, had not occurred to him before, though. Now that it did, he found he did not much care for it. He moved half a step away from the Avtokrator's envoy.

Iakovitzes jerked back his hand as if surprised to discover what it had been up to. Glancing at him, Krispos doubted he was. His face was a mask that must have taken years to perfect. Seeing Krispos' eye upon him, he gave a tiny shrug. *If you don't want it, too bad for you,* he seemed to say.

Aloud, the words he spoke were quite different. "It is accomplished," he said loudly. Then he turned to the crowd of peasants gathered in front of the platform. "People of Videssos, you are redeemed!" he cried. "The Phos-guarded Avtokrator Rhaptes redeems you from your long and horrid captivity in this dark and barbarous land, from your toil under the degrading domination of brutal and terrible masters. Masters? No, rather let me call them robbers, for they robbed you of the liberty rightfully yours . . ."

The speech went on for some time. Krispos was at first impressed and then overwhelmed with the buckets of big words Iakovitzes poured over the heads of the farmers. *Over our heads is right,* the boy thought. He was missing one word in three, and doubted anyone else in the crowd was doing much better.

He yawned. Seeing that, Omurtag grinned and winked. Iakovitzes, caught up now in the full flow of his rhetoric, never noticed.

The khagan waggled a finger. Krispos walked back over to him. Again Iakovitzes paid no attention, though Krispos felt the eyes of both priest and *enaree* upon him.

"Here, lad," Omurtag said—softly, so as not to disrupt Iakovitzes' speech. "You take this, as a reminder of the day." He handed Krispos the goldpiece Iakovitzes had given him to symbolize the Videssians' ransoming.

Behind Iakovitzes, the blue-robed priest of Phos jerked violently, as if a bee had stung him. He made the circular sun-sign over the left side of his breast. And Omurtag's own *enaree* grabbed the khagan and whispered harshly and urgently into his ear.

Omurtag shoved the seer aside, so hard that the *enaree* almost tumbled off the edge of the platform. The khagan snarled something at him in the Kubrati tongue, then returned to Videssian to tell Krispos, "The fool says that, since this coin was used in our ceremony here, with it I have given you the Videssian people. Whatever will you do with them, little farmer boy?"

He laughed uproariously at his own wit, loud enough to make Iakovitzes pause and glare at him before resuming his harangue. Krispos laughed, too. Past tunic and sandals—and now this coin—he had never owned anything. And the idea of having a whole people was absurd, any-how.

"Go on back to your mother and father," Omurtag said when he had control of himself again. Krispos hopped down from the platform. He kept tight hold of the goldpiece Omurtag had given him.

"THE SOONER WE'RE OUT OF KUBRAT AND THE FASTER WE'RE BACK in civilization, the better," Iakovitzes declared to whoever would listen. He pressed the pace back to Videssos harder than the Kubratoi had when they were taking the peasants away.

The redeemed Videssians did not leave by the same winding, narrow pass through which they had entered Kubrat. They used a wider, easier route some miles farther west. An old graveled highway ran down it, one that became broad and well maintained on the Videssian side of the mountains.

"You'd think the Kubrati road used to be part of this one here," Krispos remarked.

Neither of his parents answered. They were too worn with walking and with keeping Evdokia on her feet to have energy left over for speculation.

But the priest who had gone to Kubrat with Iakovitzes heard. His name, Krispos had learned, was Pyrrhos. Ever since Omurtag gave the boy that goldpiece, Pyrrhos had been around a good deal, as if keeping an eye on him. Now, from muleback, the priest said, "You speak the truth, lad. Once the road was one, for once the land was one. Once the whole world, near enough, was one."

Krispos frowned. "One world? Well, of course it is, sir priest. What else could it be?" Trudging along beside him, Phostis smiled; in that moment, son sounded very much like father.

"One world ruled by Videssos, I mean," Pyrrhos said. "But then, three hundred years ago, on account of the sins of the Videssian people, Phos suffered the wild Khamorth tribes to roll off the Pardrayan plain and rape away the great tracts of land that are now the khaganates of Thatagush, Khatrish—and Kubrat. Those lands remain rightfully ours. One day, when Phos the lord of the great and good mind judges us worthy, we shall reclaim them." He sketched the sun-symbol over his heart.

Krispos walked a while in silence, thinking about what the priest had said. Three hundred years meant nothing to him; Pyrrhos might as well have said *a long time ago* or even *once upon a time*. But sin, now—that was interesting. "What sort of sins?" the boy asked.

Pyrrhos' long, narrow face grew even longer and narrower as his thin-lipped mouth pursed in disapproval. "The same sins Skotos"—he spat in the roadway to show his hatred of the dark god—"always sets forth as snares for mankind: the sin of division, from which sprang civil war; the sin of arrogance, which led the fools of that time to scorn the barbarians till too late; the sin of luxury, which made them cling to the great riches they had and not exert themselves to preserve those riches for future generations."

At that, Krispos' father lifted his head. "Reckon the sin of luxury's one we don't have to worry about here," he said, "seeing as I don't think there's above three people in this whole crowd with a second shirt to call their own."

"You are better for it!" the priest exclaimed. "Yet the sin of luxury lives on; doubt it not. In Videssos the city, scores of nobles have robes for each day of the year, sir, yet bend all their energy not to helping their neighbors who have less but rather only to acquiring more, more, and ever more. Their robes will not warm them against the chill of Skotos' ice."

His sermon did not have the effect he'd hoped. "A robe for each day of the year," Krispos' father said in wonder. Scowling angrily, Pyrrhos rode off. Phostis turned to Krispos. "How'd you like to have that many robes, son?"

"That sounds like too many to me," Krispos said. "But I would like a second shirt."

"So would I, boy," his father said, laughing. "So would I."

A day or so later, a company of Videssian troopers joined the returning peasants. Their chain-mail shirts jingled as they came up, an accompaniment to the heavy drumroll of their horses' hooves. Iakovitzes handed their leader a scroll. The captain read it, glanced at the farmers, and nodded. He gave Iakovitzes a formal salute, with clenched right fist over his heart.

Iakovitzes returned the salute, then rode south at a trot so fast it was almost a gallop. Pyrrhos left the peasants at the same time, but Iakovitzes' horse quickly outdistanced his mule. "My lord, be so good as to wait for your servant," Pyrrhos called after him.

Iakovitzes was so far ahead by then that Krispos, who was near the front of the band of peasants, could barely hear his reply: "If you think I'll crawl to the city at the pace of a shambling mule, priest, you can bloody well think again!" The noble soon disappeared round a bend in the road. More sedately, Pyrrhos followed.

Later that day, a dirt track from the east ran into the highway. The

Videssian captain halted the farmers while he checked the scroll Iakovitzes had given him. "Fifteen here," he told his soldiers. They counted off the fifteen men they saw, and in a moment fifteen families, escorted by three or four horsemen, headed down that track. The rest started south again.

Another stop came before long. This time, twenty families were detached from the main group. "They're treating us just like the Kubratoi did," Krispos' mother said in some dismay.

"Did you expect we'd get to go back to our old village, Tatze?" his father said. She nodded. "I didn't," he told her. "We've been gone a good while now. Someone else will be working our fields; I suppose we'll go to fill some holes that've opened up since."

So it proved. The next morning, Phostis was one of a group of thirty peasant men told off by the Videssian soldiers. Along with the others and their kinsfolk, he, Tatze, Krispos, and Evdokia left the main road for a winding path that led west.

They reached their new village late that afternoon. At the sight of it, even Phostis' resignation wore thin. He glared up at one of the troopers who had come with the farmers. "The Kubratoi gave us more to work with than this," he said bitterly. Krispos watched his father's shoulders slump. Having to start over from nothing twice in three years could make any man lose heart.

But the Videssian soldier said, "Take another look at the fellows waiting there for you, farmer. Might be you'll change your mind."

Phostis looked. So did Krispos. All he'd noticed before was that there weren't very many men in the village. He remembered arriving at the one in Kubrat. His father was right: more people had been waiting there than here. And he saw no one out in the fields. So what good could this handful of men be?

Something about the way they stood as they waited for the newcomers to reach them made Krispos scratch his head. It was different from the way the villagers in Kubrat had stood, but he could not put his finger on how.

His father could. "I don't believe those are farmers at all," he said slowly.

"Right the first time." The trooper grinned at him. "They're pensioned-off veterans. The Avtokrator, Phos bless him, has established five or six like them in every village we're resettling with you people."

"But what good will they be to us, save maybe as strong backs?" Phostis said. "If they're not farmers, we'll have to show them how to do everything."

"Maybe you will, at first," the soldier said, "but you won't have to show 'em the same thing twice very often, I'll warrant. And could be they'll have a thing or two to teach you folk, as well."

Krispos' father snorted. "What could they teach us?"

He'd meant that for a scornful rhetorical question, but the horseman answered it. "Bow and sword, spear and shield, maybe even a bit of horse-work. The next time the Kubratoi come to haul you people away, could be you'll give 'em a bit of a surprise. Tell me now, wouldn't you like that?"

Before his father could answer, Krispos threw back his head and howled like a wolf. Phostis started to laugh, then stopped abruptly. His hands curled into fists, and he bayed, too, a deep, solid underpinning to his son's high yips.

More and more farmers began to howl, and finally even some of the soldiers. They entered the new village like a pack at full cry. *If the Kubratoi could only hear us,* Krispos thought proudly, *they'd never dare come south of the mountains again.*

He was, after all, still a boy.

Chapter II

FOR SOME YEARS, THE KUBRATOI DID NOT RAID INTO VIDESSOS. Sometimes, in absent moments, Krispos wondered if Phos had heard his thought and struck fear into the wild men's hearts. Once, when he was about twelve, he said as much to one of the retired veterans, a tough gray-beard called Varades.

Varades laughed till tears came. "Ah, lad, I wish it were that easy. I'd sooner spend my time thinking bad thoughts at my foes than fighting, any day. But more likely, I reckon, is that old Omurtag still hasn't gone through all the gold Rhaptes sent him to buy you back. When he does—"

"When he does, we'll drive the Kubratoi away!" Krispos made cut-and-thrust motions with the wooden sword he was holding. Grown men, these days, practiced with real weapons; the veterans had been issued enough for everyone. A spear and a hunting bow hung on the wall of Krispos' house.

"Maybe," Varades said. "Just maybe, if it's a small band bent on robbery instead of a full-sized invasion. The Kubratoi know how to fight; not much else, maybe, but that for certain. You farmers won't ever be anything but amateur soldiers, so I wouldn't even try taking 'em on without a good advantage in numbers."

"What then?" Krispos said. "If there's too many, do we let them herd us off to Kubrat again?"

"Better that than getting killed to no purpose and having them herd off your mother and sisters even so."

Krispos' second sister, Kosta, had just turned two. He thought of her being forced to trek north, and of his mother trying to care for her and Evdokia both. After a moment, he thought of his mother trying to do all that while mourning his father and him. He did not like any of those thoughts.

"Maybe the Kubratoi just won't come," he said at last.

Varades laughed again, as boisterously as before. "Oh, aye, and maybe one of the village jackasses'd win all the hippodrome races down in Videssos the city. But you'd better not count on it." He grew serious. "I don't want you to mistake my meaning, boy. Sooner or later, they'll come. The whoresons always do."

B y THE TIME KRISPOS WAS FOURTEEN, HE WAS CLOSE TO BEING as tall as his father. The down on his face began to turn dark; his voice cracked and broke, generally at moments when he least wanted it to.

He was already doing a man's work in the fields. Now, though, Varades and the other veterans let him start using real arms. The wire-wound hilt of a steel sword felt nothing like the wooden toy he'd swung before. With it in his hand, he felt like a soldier—more, like a hero.

He felt like a hero, that is, until Idalkos—the veteran who had given him the blade—proceeded to disarm him half a dozen times in the next ten minutes. The last time, instead of letting him pick up the sword and go on with the lesson, Idalkos chased him halfway across the village. "You'd better run!" he roared, pounding after Krispos. "If I catch you, I'll carve hams off you." Only one thing saved Krispos from being even more humiliated than he was: the veteran had terrorized a good many people the same way—some of them Phostis' age.

Finally, puffing, Idalkos stopped. "Here, come back, Krispos," he called. "You've had your first lesson now, which is that it's not as easy as it looks."

"It sure isn't," Krispos said. As he walked slowly back toward Idalkos, he heard someone giggle. His head whipped around. There in her doorway stood Zoranne the daughter of Tzykalas the cobbler, a pretty girl about Krispos' age. His ears felt on fire. If she'd watched his whole ignominious flight—

"Pay the chit no mind," Idalkos said, as if reading his thoughts. "You did what you had to do: I had a sword and you didn't. But suppose you didn't have room to run. Suppose you were in the middle of a whole knot of men when you lost your blade. What would you do then?"

Die, Krispos thought. He wished he could die, so he wouldn't have to remember Zoranne's giggle. But that wasn't the answer Idalkos was looking for. "Wrestle, I suppose," he said after a moment.

"Would you?" Krispos put down the sword. He set himself, leaning forward slightly from the waist, feet wide apart. "Here, I'm an old man. See if you can throw me."

Krispos sprang at him. He'd always done well in the scuffles among boys. He was bigger and stronger than the ones his own age, and quicker, too. If he could pay back Idalkos for some of his embarrassment—

The next thing he knew, his face was in the dirt, the veteran riding his back. He heard Zoranne laugh again and had to fight back tears of fury. "You fight dirty," he snarled.

"You bet I do," Idalkos said cheerfully. "Want to learn how? Maybe you'll toss me right through a dung heap one fine day, impress your girl there."

"She's not my girl," Krispos said as the veteran let him up. Still, the picture was attractive—and so was the idea of throwing Idalkos through a dung heap. "All right, show me what you did."

"A hand on the arm, a push on the back, and then you twist—so—and take the fellow you're fighting down over your leg. Here, I'll run you through it slow, a couple of times."

"I see," Krispos said after a while. By then they were both filthy, from spilling each other in the dirt. "Now how do I block it when someone tries to do it to me?"

Idalkos' scar-seamed face lit up. "You know, lad, I've taught my little trick to half a dozen men here, maybe more. You're the first one with the wit to ask that question. What you do is this. . . ."

That was the start of it. For the rest of that summer and into fall, until it got too cold to spend much time outside, Krispos learned wrestling from Idalkos in every spare moment he had. Those moments were never enough to suit him, not squeezed as they were into the work of the harvest, care for the village's livestock, and occasional work with weapons other than Krispos' increasingly well-honed body.

"Thing is, you're pretty good, and you'll get better," Idalkos said one chilly day in early autumn. He flexed his wrist, winced, flexed it again. "No, that's not broken after all. But I won't be sorry when the snow comes, no indeed I won't—give me a chance to stay indoors and heal up till spring."

All the veterans talked like that, and all of them were in better shape than any farmer their age—or ten years younger, too. Just when someone started to believe them, they'd do something like what Idalkos had done the first time they wrestled.

So Krispos only snorted. "I suppose that means you'll be too battered to come out with the rest of us on Midwinter's Day," he said, voice full of syrupy regret.

"Think you're smart, don't you?" Idalkos made as if to grab Krispos. He sprang back—one of the things he'd learned was to take nothing for granted. The veteran went on, "The first year I don't celebrate Midwinter's Day, sonny, you go out to my grave and make the sun-sign over it, 'cause that's where I'll be."

SNOW STARTED FALLING SIX WEEKS BEFORE MIDWINTER'S DAY, the day of the winter solstice. Most of the veterans had served in the far west against Makuran. They complained about what a hard winter it was going to be. No one who had spent time in Kubrat paid any attention to them. The farmers went about their business, mending fences, repairing plows and other tools, doing woodwork . . . and getting ready for the chief festival of their year.

Midwinter's Day dawned freezing but clear. Low in the south, the sun hurried across the sky. The villagers' prayers went with it, to keep Skotos from snatching it out of the heavens altogether and plunging the world into eternal darkness.

As if to add to the light, bonfires burned in the village square. Krispos ran at one, his hide boots kicking up snow. He leaped over the blaze. "Burn, ill-luck!" he shouted when he was right above it. A moment later, more snow flew as he thudded down.

Evdokia came right behind him. Her wish against bad luck came out more as a scream—this was the first year she was big enough to leap fires. Krispos steadied her when she landed clumsily. She grinned up at him. Her cheeks glowed with cold and excitement.

"Who's that?" she said, peering back through the shimmering air above the flames to see who came next. "Oh, it's Zoranne. Come on, let's get out of her way."

Pushed by his sister, Krispos walked away from the fire. His eyes were not the only ones in the village that followed Zoranne as she flew through the air over it. She landed almost as heavily as Evdokia had. If Evdokia hadn't made him move, he thought, he could have been the one to help Zoranne back up.

"Younger sisters really are a nuisance," he declared loftily.

Evdokia showed him he was right: she scooped up a handful of snow and pressed it against the side of his neck, then ran away while he was still writhing. Bellowing mingled outrage and laughter, he chased her, pausing a couple of times to make a snowball and fling it at her.

One snowball missed Evdokia but caught Varades in the shoulder. "So you want to play that way, do you?" the veteran roared. He threw one back at Krispos. Krispos ducked. The snowball hit someone behind him. Soon everyone was throwing them—at friends, foes, and whoever happened to be in the wrong place at the right time. People's hats and sheepskin coats were so splashed with white that the village began to look as if it had been taken over by snowmen.

Out came several men, Phostis among them, wearing dresses they must have borrowed from a couple of the biggest, heaviest women in the village. They put on a wicked burlesque of what they imagined their wives and daughters did while they were out working in the fields. It consisted of gossiping, pointing fingers while they gossiped, eating, and drinking wine, lots of wine. Krispos' father did a fine turn as a tipsy lady who was talking so furiously she never noticed falling off her stool but lay on the ground, still chattering away.

The male spectators chortled. The women pelted the actors with more snowballs. Krispos ducked back into his house for a cup of wine for himself. He wished it was hot, but no one wanted to stay indoors and tend a pot of mulled wine, not today.

The sun set as he came back to the square. The village's women and girls were having their revenge. Dressed in men's short tunics and doing their best not to shiver, several of them pretended to be hunters bragging about the immense size of their kill—till one of them, fastidiously holding it by the tail, displayed a mouse.

This time, the watching women cheered and most of the men jeered and threw snow. Krispos did neither. One of the female "hunters" was Zoranne. The tunic she wore came down only to mid-thigh; her nipples, stiff from the cold, pressed against its thin fabric. As he looked and looked, he felt a heat grow in him that had nothing to do with the wine he'd drunk.

At last the women skipped away, to thunderous applause. More skits came in quick succession, these mocking the foibles of particular villagers:

Tzykalas' efforts to grow hair on his bald head—in the skit, he raised a fine crop of hay—Varades' habit of breaking wind, and more.

Then Krispos watched in dismay as a couple of farmers, plainly intended to be Idalkos and him, practiced wrestling. The embrace in which they ended was more obscene than athletic. The villagers whooped and cheered them on.

Krispos stamped away, head down. He was at an age where he could laugh at others, but could not bear to have them laugh at him. All he wanted to do was get away from the hateful noise.

Because he was not watching where he was going, he almost ran into someone coming back toward the center of the village. "Sorry," he muttered and kept walking.

"What's wrong, Krispos?" He looked up, startled. It was Zoranne's voice. She'd changed back into her own long skirt and a coat, and looked a good deal warmer for it. "What's wrong?" she said again.

"Those stupid jokers back there, that's what," he burst out, "making as if when Idalkos and I wrestle, we don't just wrestle." Half his rage evaporated as soon as he said out loud what was bothering him. He began to feel foolish instead.

Zoranne did not help by starting to laugh. "It's Midwinter's Day, Krispos," she said. "It's all in fun." He knew that, which only made matters worse. She went on, "Anything can happen on Midwinter's Day, and no one will pay any mind to it the day after. Am I right?"

"I suppose so." He sounded surly, even to himself.

"Besides," she said, "it's not as if what they made out was true, is it?"

"Of course not," he said, so indignantly that his changing voice left the last word a high-pitched squeak. As if from nowhere, the memory of Iakovitzes' hand on his back stirred in his mind. Maybe that was part of why the skit had got under his skin so.

She did not seem to notice. "Well, then," she said.

Back by the bonfires, most of the villagers erupted in laughter at some new skit. Krispos realized how quiet it was out here near the edge of the village, how alone he and Zoranne were. The memory of how she'd looked capering in that brief tunic rose again. Without his conscious mind willing it, he took a step toward her.

At the same moment, she was taking a step toward him. They almost bumped into each other. She laughed again. "Anything can happen on Midwinter's Day," she said softly.

When Krispos fled that embarrassing skit, he hadn't worried about picking a direction. Perhaps not surprisingly, he'd ended up not far from his own house; as usual, his father had preferred one on the outskirts of the village. Suddenly that seemed like a blessing from Phos. Krispos gathered his courage, reached out, and took Zoranne's arm. She pressed herself to his side.

His heart hammering, he led her to his doorway. They went inside together. He quickly shut the door behind them to keep the heat from the firepit in the middle of the floor from getting out.

"We'd better hurry," he said anxiously.

Just then, more laughter came from the center of the village. Zoranne smiled. "We have some time, I think." She shrugged off her coat, got out of her skirt. Krispos tried to undress and watch her at the same time, and almost fell over. Finally, after what seemed much too long, they sank to the straw bedding.

Krispos soon learned what everyone must: that knowing how man and woman join is not enough to keep that first joining from being one surprise after another. Nothing he thought he knew made him ready for the taste of Zoranne's soft skin against his lips; the feel of her breast in his hand; the way the whole world seemed to disappear but for her body and his.

As it does, it returned all too quickly. "You're squashing me," Zoranne said. Brisk and practical, she sat up and picked bits of straw from her hair, then from his.

Given a little more time and a little less nervousness, he might have enjoyed that. As it was, her touch made him spring up and scramble into his clothes. She dressed, too—not with that frantic haste, but not taking her time, either.

Something else he did not know was whether he'd pleased her, or even how to find out. "Will we . . . ?" he began. The rest of the question seemed stuck in his mouth.

Zoranne did not help much. "I don't know. Will we?"

"I hope so," Krispos blurted.

"Men always hope so—that's what women always say, anyhow." She unbent a bit then. "Well, maybe we will—but not now. Now we ought to get back to where everyone else is."

He opened the door. The freezing air outside hit him like a blow. Zoranne said, "We should go back separately. The grandmothers have enough to gossip about already."

"Oh." Krispos had wanted to shout it from the housetops. If Zoranne didn't . . . "All right." He could not keep the disappointment out of his voice, though.

"Come on," she said impatiently. "I told you this wouldn't be the last time." As a matter of fact, she hadn't quite said that before. Thus encouraged, Krispos willingly shut the door again and watched Zoranne slip off into the night.

SHE KEPT HER WORD, IF NOT AS OFTEN AS KRISPOS WOULD HAVE liked. Every taste he had of her, every time the two of them managed not to be busy and to be able to find privacy, only made him want her more. Not knowing a better name, he thought of that as love.

Then, for a while, his own afternoons were occupied: Varades taught him and a couple of younger boys their letters. He learned them without too much trouble; being able to read and write his own name was almost as exciting, in its own way, as sporting with Zoranne.

He would have liked it even more had the village had anything much to read. "Why did you show us our letters if we can't use them?" he complained to Varades.

"To give myself something to do, as much as any other reason," the veteran answered frankly. He thought for a moment. "Tell you what. We might beg a copy of Phos' scripture the next time a blue-robe comes around. I'll go through it with you, best I can."

When Varades asked him, a couple of weeks later, the priest nodded. "I'll have one copied out for you straightaway," he promised. Krispos, who was standing behind Varades, felt like cheering until the man went on, "You understand, it will take a few months. The monasteries' scriptoria are always behind, I'm sorry to say."

"Months!" Krispos said in dismay. He was sure he would forget everything before the book arrived.

But he did not. His father made him scratch letters in the dirt every day. "High time we had somebody in the family who can read," Phostis said. "You'll be able to keep the tax man from cheating us any worse than tax men always do."

Krispos got another chance to use his skill that spring, before either the scripture or the tax collector arrived. Zoranne's father Tzykalas had spent the winter months making half a dozen pairs of fancy boots. When the roads dried out enough to be passable, he took them to Imbros to sell. He came back with several goldpieces—and portentous news.

"The old Avtokrator, Phos guard his soul, has died," he declared to the men he met in the village square.

Everyone made the sun-sign. The passing of an Emperor was never to be taken lightly. Phostis put into words what they were all thinking: "His son's but a boy, not so?"

Tzykalas nodded. "Aye, about the age of Krispos here, I'd say, judging by his coin." The cobbler dug it out of his pouch to show the other villagers the new portrait. "His name is—"

"Let me read it!" Krispos exclaimed. "Please!" He held out his hand for the goldpiece. Reluctantly Tzykalas passed it to him. It was only a little wider than his thumbnail. All he could make out from the image was that the new Avtokrator was, as Tzykalas had said, too young to have a beard. He put the coin close to his face so he could make out the tiny letters of its inscription. "His name is Anthimos."

"So it is," Tzykalas said grumpily. He snatched the goldpiece out of Kripsos' hand. Too late, it occurred to the youth that he had just stolen a big part of Tzykalas' news. *Too bad,* he thought. No matter how he felt about Zoranne, he'd never been fond of her father. That was one reason he hadn't proposed to her: the idea of having the cobbler as a father-in-law was anything but appealing.

What he wanted to do was go home and dig up the goldpiece he'd got from Omurtag so he could read it. He'd buried it beside the house for luck when his family came to this new village, and they'd never been desperate enough to make him dig it up and spend it. But no, he decided, not now; if he did leave, Tzykalas would only think him ruder yet.

"A boy for Avtokrator?" someone said. "That won't be good—who'll keep the plow's furrow straight till he learns how to guide it?"

"That I can tell you," Tzykalas said, sounding important again. "The talk in Imbros is that Rhaptes' brother Petronas will be regent for his nephew until Anthimos comes of age."

"Petronas, eh? Things won't be too bad, then." Drawn by the sight of several men standing around talking, Varades had come up in time to hear Tzykalas' last bit of news. The veteran went on, "I fought under him against Makuran. He's an able soldier, and no one's fool, either."

"What if he seizes the throne for himself, then?" Krispos' father said.

"What if he does, Phostis?" Varades said. "Why would it matter to the likes of us, one way or the other?"

Krispos' father thought about it for a moment. He spread his hands. "There you have me, Varades. Why indeed?"

ZORANNE STOOD IN THE DOORWAY OF TZYKALAS' HOUSE. SHE shook her head. "No."

"Why not?" Surprised and irritated, Krispos waved his hand to show

how empty the village was. "Everyone's in the farther fields for the rest of the day, and probably tomorrow, too. Even your father's gone off to buy some new awls, you said. We've never had a better chance."

"No," she repeated.

"But why not?" He put a hand on her arm.

She didn't pull away, not physically, but she might as well have. He let his hand fall. "I just don't want to," she said.

"Why?" he persisted.

"Do you really want to know?" She waited till she saw him nod. "All right, I'll tell you why. Yphantes asked me to marry him the other day, and I told him yes."

The last time Krispos had felt so stunned and breathless was when Idalkos kicked him in the pit of the stomach one day while they were wrestling. He'd never paid any particular attention to Yphantes before. Along with everyone else in the village, he'd been sad when the man's wife died in childbirth a couple of years before, but . . . "He's old," Krispos blurted.

"He's years away from thirty," Zoranne said, "and he's already well set up. If I had to wait for you, I'd be past twenty myself by the time you were even close to where Yphantes is now, and that's too long a time."

"But—but then you, but then you and he—" Krispos found he could not make his mouth work the way it was supposed to.

Zoranne understood anyway. "What if we were?" she said defiantly. "You never gave me any promise, Krispos, or asked for one from me."

"I never thought I needed to," he mumbled.

"Too bad for you, then. No woman wants to be taken for granted. Maybe you'll remember that next time with someone else, and end up happier for it." Her face softened. "Krispos, we'll probably live here together in this village the rest of our lives. No point in us hating each other, is there? Please?"

For want of anything better to say, he said, "All right." Then he turned and quickly walked away. If he had any tears, Zoranne was not going to see them. He owned too much pride for that.

That evening he was so quiet that his sister teased him about it, and then he was quiet through the teasing, too. "Are you feeling well, Krispos?" Evdokia asked, real worry in her voice; when she could not get a rise out of him, something had to be wrong.

"I'm all right," he said. "I just want you to leave me alone, that's all."

"I know what it is," she said suddenly. "It's something to do with Zoranne, isn't it?"

He very carefully put down the bowl of barley and turnip soup from which he had been eating; had he not been so deliberately careful with his hands, he might have thrown it at her. He got up and stamped out of the house, off into the woods.

He took longer than he should have to realize that sitting by himself among the trees wasn't accomplishing anything, but after a while he did figure it out. It was quite dark when he finally came home. Then he almost turned around and went back; his father was waiting for him, a few steps outside the door.

He kept on. He would have to deal with his father sooner or later; better sooner, he thought. "I'm sorry," he said.

His father nodded, the motion barely visible in the gloom. "You should be." Phostis hesitated a moment before he said, "Evdokia was right, I gather—you've had some trouble with your girl?"

"She's not my girl," Krispos said sullenly. "She's going to marry Yphantes."

"Good," his father said. "I hoped she would. I told Yphantes as much, earlier this year. In the long run, it'll save you trouble, son, believe me."

"When you what?" Krispos stared at him, appalled. That moment of shock also let him notice something he'd missed before: both his father and his sister knew about Zoranne. "How did you find out about us? We were so careful—"

"Maybe you think so," Phostis said, "but I'd bet the only person in the village who doesn't know is Tzykalas, and he would if he weren't a fool who'd sooner talk than see. I'd be just as well pleased not to have a marriage connection with him, I can tell you."

Krispos had been angry at his father often enough. Till now, he'd never imagined wanting to hate him. In a voice like ice, he asked, "Is that why you egged Yphantes on?"

"That's part of the reason, aye," Phostis answered calmly. Before Krispos' rage could overflow, he went on, "But it's not the biggest part. Yphantes needs to marry. He needs a wife to help him now and he needs to get an heir to carry on. And Zoranne needs to marry; at fourteen, a girl's a woman, near enough. But you, son, you don't need to marry. At fourteen, a man's still a boy."

"I'm not a boy," Krispos snarled.

"No? Does a man pitch a tantrum when he's teased? You were acting the way Kosta does when I tell her I won't carry her piggyback anymore. Am I wrong or am I right? Think before you answer me."

That last sentence kept Krispos from blowing up in fury. He *did* think; in cold—or at least cooler—blood, what he'd done seemed foolish. "Right, I suppose, Father, but—"

"But me no buts. Finding a girl who'll say yes to you is wonderful; Phos knows I don't deny it. Why, I remember—" His father stopped, laughed a small, self-conscious laugh. "But never mind me. Just because she says yes doesn't mean you want to live with her the rest of your life. That should take more looking than just one girl, don't you think?"

Krispos remembered his own misgivings about Tzykalas the day before. Without much wanting to, he found himself nodding. "I guess so."

"Good." His father put a hand on his shoulder, the way he'd been doing since Krispos was a little boy. "What you have to remember is, bad as you feel today, today's not forever. Things'll feel better inside you after a while. You just have to learn the patience to wait till they do."

Krispos thought about that. It made sense. Even so, though . . . "It sounds like something that's easier to tell someone else than to do," he said.

"Doesn't it just?" Phostis laughed that small laugh again. "And don't I know it?"

Greatly daring, Krispos asked, "Father, what was she like?"

"She?"

"The one you talked about—sort of talked about—a few minutes ago."

"Oh." Phostis walked farther away from the house. He glanced back toward it before going on more quietly, "Her name was Sabellia. Your mother knows of her. Truly, I don't think Tatze'd mind my speaking about her, save only that no woman ever really takes kindly to her man going on about times before he was with her. Can't say I blame her; I'm as glad she doesn't chatter on about her old flames, too. But Sabellia? Well, I must have been right around your age when I met her . . ."

Krispos rubbed his chin. Whiskers rasped under his fingers, not the fuzz he'd had since his voice started changing but the beginnings of a real man's crop. *About time,* he thought. A couple of fifteen-year-olds grew beards as good as his, though he'd had two more summers in which to raise his.

He rubbed again. A beard, even a thin one, was a useful thing to be thoughtful with. Last time out in the woods, somewhere not far from here, he'd spotted an elm branch that had exactly the right curve for a plow handle. He would have paid more attention to it had he not been with a girl.

That oak looked familiar, or so he thought till he got close to it. He walked on. He didn't remember the hazel tree beyond the oak. Sighing, he kept walking. By now he was sure he had come too far, but he didn't want to go back, either. It would have been too much like an admission of failure.

Faint in the distance, he heard noise ahead. He frowned. Few villagers came this far east of home. He'd brought Likinia out here precisely because he had felt sure they'd get to be alone. He supposed men from the next village over could be doing some lumbering, but they'd have to drag the wood a long way back if they were.

The noise didn't sound like lumbering, anyhow. He heard no axes, no sounds of falling branches or toppling trees. As he moved closer, a horse neighed softly. That confused him worse than ever. A horse would have been handy for hauling timber, but there was no timber.

What did that leave? His frown deepened—the most obvious answer was bandits. He hadn't thought the nearby road had enough traffic to support a robber band, but he could have been wrong. He kept moving toward the noise, but now with all the caution he could muster. He just wanted to see if these really were bandits and then, if they were, to get back to the village and bring as many armed men here as he could.

He was flat on his belly by the time he wriggled up to the last brush that screened him from the noisemakers, whoever they were. Slowly, slowly, he raised his head until he could peer between two leafy branches whose shadows helped hide his face.

"Phos!" His lips shaped the word, but no sound came from between them. The men relaxing by the side of the road were not bandits. They were Kubratoi.

His lips moved silently again—twelve, thirteen, fourteen Kubratoi. The village had not had any word of invasion, but that meant nothing. The first word of trouble they'd had when he was a boy was the wild men howling out of darkness. He shivered; suddenly, reliving the terror of that night, he felt like a boy again.

The remembered fear also told him what he had wondered before— why the Kubratoi were sitting around taking their ease instead of storming straight for the village. They would hit at night, just as that other band had. With the advantage of surprise, with darkness making them seem three times as many as they really were, they would be irresistible.

Krispos gauged the shadows around him as he slithered backward even more carefully than he had approached. The sun was not far past noon. He could deal with the Kubratoi as he'd intended to treat the bandits. The villagers had learned weapons from the veterans settled with them to be ready for just this sort of moment.

Soon Krispos was far enough away from the wild men to get back to his feet. Fast and quiet as he could, he headed toward the village. He thought about cutting back to the road and running down it. That would be quickest—if the Kubratoi didn't have a sentry posted somewhere along there to make sure no one gave the alarm. He decided he could not take the chance. Through the woods it would have to be.

He burst out of the forest an hour and a half later, his tunic torn, his arms and face scratched. His first try at a cry of alarm yielded only a rusty croak. He rushed over to the well, drew up the bucket, and drank deep. "The Kubratoi!" he shouted, loud as he could.

The men and women who heard him spun and stared. One of them was Idalkos. "How many, boy?" he barked. "Where?"

"I saw fourteen," Krispos told him. "Down at the edge of the road . . ." He gasped out the story.

"Only fourteen, you say?" A fierce light kindled in Idalkos' eyes. "If that's all there really are, we can take 'em."

"I thought so, too," Krispos said. "You get the people here armed. I'll go out to the fields and bring in the rest of the men."

"Right you are." Idalkos had been an underofficer for many years; when he heard orders that made sense, he started carrying them out without worrying about where they came from. Krispos never noticed he'd given an order. He was already running toward the largest group of men that he saw, shouting as he ran.

"The Kubratoi!" someone said fearfully. "How can we fight the Kubratoi?"

"How can we not?" Krispos shot back. "Do you want to go back to the other side of the mountains again? There's only a dozen or so of them, and they won't be expecting us to hit first. With three times as many men as they have, how can we lose? Idalkos thinks we can win, too."

That brought around some of the farmers who stood there indecisively. Soon they all went pounding back toward the village. Idalkos and a couple of other men were already passing out weapons when they got there. Krispos found himself clutching a shield and a stout spear.

"We go through the woods?"

Idalkos made it sound like a question, but Krispos did not think he was really asking. "Aye," he said. "If they have someone watching the road, he could ride back and warn the rest."

"Right you are," Idalkos said again. He went on, "And speaking of warning—Stankos, you saddle up one of those mules and ride for Imbros, fast as you can, cross-country. If you see the whole landscape crawling with Kubratoi, come back. I'm not sending you out to get yourself killed.

But if you think you can make it through, well, I wouldn't mind seeing a few garrison soldiers up this way. How about the rest of you lads?"

Nods and nervous grins showed him his guess was good. The villagers had nerved themselves to fight, but they were not eager.

Or most of them, the older, more settled farmers, were not. They kept looking back at the fields; their homes; their wives and daughters, who crowded round the knot of would-be warriors, some just standing silently, others wringing their hands and trying not to weep.

Krispos, though, was almost wild with excitement. "Come on!" he shouted.

Some of the other young men also raised a cry. They pelted after Krispos into the woods. The rest of the villagers followed more slowly. "Come on, come on, if we all fight we can do it," Idalkos said. He and Varades and the rest of the veterans kept their amateur companions moving.

Before long, Idalkos had pushed his way up beside Krispos. "You're going to have to lead us, at least till we get to the buggers," he said. "You're the one who knows where they are. It'd be good if we tried to get as quiet as we could *before* we're close enough that they're likely to hear us."

"That makes sense," Krispos said, wondering why he hadn't thought of it himself. "I'll remember."

"Good." Idalkos grinned at him. "Glad you're not too proud to use a notion just on account of somebody else thought of it."

"Of course not," Krispos said, surprised. "That would be stupid."

"So it would, but you'd be amazed how many captains are idiots."

"Well, but then I'm no cap—" Krispos paused. He seemed to be leading the villagers, if anyone was. He shrugged. It was only because he'd been the one to find the Kubratoi, he thought.

He was still a mile away from the wild men when he walked past the elm with the curving branch he'd been looking for. He tried to note just where the tree was. Next time, he told himself, he'd find it on the first try.

A few minutes later, he stopped and waited for everyone to catch up. Only then did he think to wonder if there would be a next time after the fight ahead. He sternly suppressed that thought. Turning to the farmers, he said, "It isn't far. From here on out, pretend you're hunting deer—quiet as you go."

"Not deer," Varades said. "Wolves. The Kubratoi have teeth. And when we hit 'em, we all yell 'Phos!' That way nobody has any doubts about who's who. Nothing to make you want to piss your breeches faster'n almost getting killed by your own side."

The villagers stole forward. Soon Krispos heard men chattering, heard a horse snort. His comrades heard, too, and looked at one another. The Kubratoi were making no secret of where they were. "Quiet as we can now," Krispos whispered. "Pass it along." The whisper traveled through the group.

Try as they would, the farmers could not keep their presence secret as long as they wanted. They were still more than a hundred yards from the Kubratoi when the buzz of talk from the wild men suddenly changed. Idalkos bared his teeth, as if he were a fox realizing a rabbit had taken its scent. "Come on, lads," he said. "They know we're here. Phos!" The last word was a bellowed war cry.

"Phos!" The villagers shouted, too. They crashed through the brush toward the Kubratoi. "Phos!" Krispos yelled as loud as anyone. The idea of rushing into battle was enormously exciting. Soon, he thought, he would be a hero.

Then the brush was gone. Before Krispos could do more than catch sight of the Kubratoi, an arrow hissed past his face and another grazed his arm. He heard a meaty *thunk* as a shaft pierced a man beside him. The farmer fell, shrieking and writhing and clawing at it. Fear and pain suddenly seemed realer than glory.

Whether for glory or not, the fight was still before him. Peering over the top of his shield, he rushed at the nearest wild man. The Kubrati snatched for an arrow. Perhaps realizing he could not shoot before Krispos was upon him, he threw down the arrow and grabbed his sword.

Krispos thrust with his spear. He missed. The Kubrati closed with him. As much by luck as by skill, he turned the fellow's first slash with his shield. The Kubrati cut at him again. He backpedaled, trying to get room to use the spearhead against the wild man. The Kubrati pursued. Feinting with the sword, he stuck out a foot and tripped Krispos.

He managed to keep his shield above him as he went down. Two villagers drove the wild man away before he could finish Krispos. Krispos scrambled to his feet. A couple of Kubratoi were down for good, and two or three villagers. He saw a man from north of the mountains trading sword strokes with Varades. Fighting a veteran, the wild man was fully occupied. He never noticed Krispos until the youth's spear tore into his side.

The wild man grunted, then stared in absurd surprise at the red-dripping spearpoint that burst out through his belly. Then Varades' sword bit his neck. More blood sprayed; some splashed Krispos in the face. The Kubrati folded in on himself and fell.

"Pull your spear out, boy!" Varades yelled in Krispos' ear. "You think they're going to wait for you?" Gulping, Krispos set a foot on the wild man's hip and yanked the spear free. The soft resistance the Kubrati's flesh gave reminded him of nothing so much as butchering time. *No, no glory here,* he thought again.

All across the small field, the villagers were swarming over the Kubratoi, two against one here, three against one there. Individually, each Kubrati was a better warrior than his foes. The wild men seldom got the chance to prove it. Soon only four or five of them were left on their feet. Krispos saw one look around, heard him yell something to his comrades.

Though he'd never learned the Kubrati tongue, he was sure he knew what the wild man had said. He shouted, "Don't let them make it back to their horses! They still might get away."

As he spoke, the Kubratoi broke off combat and ran toward the tethered animals. Along with the rest of the villagers, Krispos dashed after them. He wondered why they hadn't mounted and fled when they first heard the villagers coming; probably, he supposed, because they'd imagined farmers would be easy meat. That had been true a decade ago. It wasn't true anymore.

Krispos speared one of the Kubratoi in the back. The man flung his arms wide. Three villagers piled onto him. His scream cut off. In a moment, the rest of the Kubratoi were dragged down and slain. A couple of villagers took cuts in the last frantic seconds of the fight, but none seemed serious.

Krispos could hardly believe the little battle had ended so abruptly. He stared this way and that for more wild men to kill. All he saw was farmers doing the same thing. "We won!" he said. Then he started to laugh, surprised at how surprised he sounded.

"We won!" "By Phos, we won!" "We beat 'em!" The villagers took up the cry. They embraced, slapped one another on the back, showed off cuts and bruises. Krispos found himself clasping hands with Yphantes. The older farmer wore an enormous grin. "I saw you get two of the bastards, Krispos," he said. "By the good god, you made me jealous. I think I wounded one, but I'm not even sure of that."

"Aye, he fought well," Idalkos said.

Praise from the veteran made Krispos glow. He also found he did not mind praise from Yphantes. Whether or not the man who had married Zoranne was jealous of Krispos, Krispos was no longer jealous of him. Zoranne remained special in his memory, but only because she had been his first. What he'd felt for her at fourteen seemed very far away after three years of growth and change.

Such thoughts fled as Krispos saw his father coming up with right hand clutched to left shoulder. Blood trickled between Phostis' fingers and splashed his tunic. "Father!" Krispos exclaimed. "Are you—"

Phostis cut him off. "I'll live, boy. I've done worse to myself with a sickle more than once. I've said often enough that I'm not cut out for this soldiering business."

"You're alive. That's what counts," Idalkos said. "And while you may not want to soldier, Phostis, your boy here has the knack for it, I'd say. He sees what needs doing and he does it—and if it's giving an order, men listen to him. That's Phos' own gift, nothing else—I've seen officers without it. If ever he wanted to head to Videssos the city, the army'd be glad to have him."

"The city? Me?" Krispos had never even imagined traveling to the great imperial capital. Now he tasted the idea. After a moment, he shook his head. "I'd sooner farm. It's what I know. Besides, I don't fancy killing any more than my father does."

"Neither do I," Idalkos said. "That doesn't mean it isn't needful sometimes. And, like I told you, I think you'd make a good soldier."

"No, thanks. All I really want to make is a good crop of beans this year, so we don't go hungry when winter comes." Krispos spoke as firmly as he could, both to let Idalkos know he meant what he said and to reinforce that certainty in his own mind.

The veteran shrugged. "Have it your way. If you want to go on being a farmer, though, we'd best make sure these were the only Kubratoi operating around here. The first thing we'll do is strip the bodies." Some of the villagers had already started taking care of that. Idalkos went on, "The cuirasses and the bows are better than what we already have. The swords are more for fighting from horseback like the Kubratoi do than afoot, but we'll still be able to use 'em."

"Aye, but what about the wild men now?" Krispos demanded. "We were both worried they'd have a scout close to the village. If he got away and warned another, bigger band—"

"Then the swords and arrows we're gathering won't matter, because we don't have enough men to hold off a big, determined band. So if there is a scout, he'd best not get away." Idalkos cocked his head. "Well, brave captain Krispos, how would you go about making sure he doesn't?"

In a tone of voice only slightly different, the veteran's question would have been mockery. As it was, though, he seemed rather to be setting Krispos a problem, the way Varades sometimes had when he gave the youth a long, hard word to spell out. Krispos thought hard. "If most of us march down the road toward the village," he said at last, "anybody would be sure to notice us. A rider could get away easy enough by going wide around us, but he'd come back to the road after he did, to find out what had happened to his friends. So maybe we ought to set some archers in ambush just up ahead there, before the bugger could round that bend and see what we've done to the rest of the wild men."

"Maybe we should." Grinning, Idalkos gave Krispos a Videssian military salute, clenched fist over heart. He turned to Phostis. "Skotos take you, man, why couldn't you have raised a son who was discontented with following in his father's footsteps?"

"Because I raised one with sense instead," Krispos' father said. "Better to be turning up the ground than to have it tossed on top of you on account of you've been killed too young."

Krispos nodded vigorously. Idalkos sighed. "All right, all right. It's a good scheme, anyhow; I think it'll work." He started yelling to the villagers. A couple of them cut branches and vines to make travois on which to drag back their dead and the three or four men hurt too badly to walk. They left the horses of the Kubratoi for the ambush party to fetch back, and the wild men's corpses for ravens' meat.

When Krispos watched his plan unfold, he felt the same awe that seeing the seeds he had planted grow to maturity always gave him. Just as he'd guessed, a lone Kubrati was sitting on his horse a couple of miles closer to the village than his comrades had rested. The rider started violently at the sight of spear-waving Videssians bearing down on him. He kicked his horse to a trot, then to a gallop. The villagers gave chase, but could not catch him.

As Krispos had expected, the Kubrati rode back to the road. The youth and Idalkos grinned at each other as they watched the column of dust the wild man's horse kicked up fade in the distance. "That should do for him," Krispos said happily. "Now we can head for home."

They arrived not long after sunset—a little before the raiders would have hit the village if they still lived. In the fading light, Krispos saw women and children waiting anxiously outside their homes, wondering whether husbands, fathers, sons, and lovers would come back again.

As one, the returning men shouted, "Phos!" Not only was it a cry no Kubratoi would make, their loved ones recognized their voices. Shouting themselves, they rushed toward the victorious farmers. Some of their glad cries turned to wails as they saw not all the men had come home safe. For most of them, though, it was a time of joy.

Embracing his mother, Krispos noticed how far he had to stoop to kiss her. Stranger still was the kiss he got from Evdokia. In the passage from one day to the next, he'd paid scant heed to the way his sister had grown, but suddenly she felt like a woman in his arms. He needed a moment to realize she was as old now as Zoranne had been on that Midwinter's Day.

As if the thought of Zoranne were enough to conjure her up, he found himself kissing her next. Their embrace was awkward; he had to lean over her belly, now big with child, to reach her lips.

Close by the two of them, a woman shouted, "Where's my Hermon?"

"It's all right, Ormisda," Krispos told her. "He's one of the archers we left behind to trap the wild man we couldn't catch. Anyone you don't see here is waiting in that ambush."

"Oh, Phos be praised!" Ormisda said. She kissed Krispos, too, though she was close to three times his age. More people kissed him—and one another—over the next hour than he'd seen during half a dozen Midwinter's Days rolled into one.

Then, in the middle of the celebration, the archers returned to the village. Though everyone fell on them with happy shouts—Ormisda almost smothered Hermon against her ample bosom—they hung back from fully joining the rest of the villagers. Krispos knew what that had to mean. "He got away," he said.

He knew it sounded like an accusation. So did the archers. They hung their heads. "We must have shot twenty arrows at him and his horse," one of them said defensively. "Some hit, too—the yells he let out had to be curses."

"He got away," Krispos repeated. It was the worst thing he could think of to say. No, not so; a moment later he found something worse yet: "He'll bring the rest of the Kubratoi down on us."

The celebration died very quickly after that.

THE NEXT FIVE DAYS PASSED IN A BLUR OF APPREHENSION FOR Krispos. That was true of most of the villagers, but Krispos' dread had two causes. Like everyone else, he was sure the Kubratoi would exact a terrible revenge for the slaughter of their raiding party. But that, for him, was only secondary, for his father's wounded shoulder had gone bad.

Phostis, as was his way, tried to make light of the injury. But he could barely use his left arm and quickly came down with a fever. None of the poultices the village women applied to the wound did any good. Phostis had always been burly, but now, with shocking suddenness, the flesh seemed to melt from his bones.

Thus Krispos was almost relieved when, late that fifth afternoon, a lookout posted in a tall tree shouted, "Horsemen!" Like the rest of the men, he dashed for his weapons—against Kubratoi, at least, he could hit back. And in the heat of fighting, he would have no time to worry about his father.

The lookout shouted again. "Hundreds of horsemen!" His voice wobbled with fear. Women and children were already streaming into the forest, to hide as best they could. "Hundreds and hundreds!" the lookout cried.

Some of the farmers threw down spears and bows and bolted with the women. Krispos grabbed at one who ran in front of him, but Idalkos shook his head. "What's the use?" the veteran said. "If they outnumber us that bad, a few more on our side won't matter much. We can't win; all we can do is hurt the bastards as bad as we're able."

Krispos clutched his spear shaft so tight his knuckles whitened on it. Now he did not need the lookout to know the wild men were coming. He could hear the hooves of their horses, quiet now but growing louder with dreadful speed.

He set himself. *Take one out with the spear,* he thought, *then drag another one off his horse and stab him.* After that—if he still lived after that—he'd see what other damage he could do.

"Won't be long now, lads," Idalkos said, calm as if the villagers were drawn up for parade. "We'll yell 'Phos!' again, just like we did the first time, and pray for the good god to watch over us."

"Phos!" That was not one of the farmers standing in ragged line in front of their houses. It was the lookout. He sounded so wild and shrill that Krispos wondered if he had lost his mind. Then the man said, "They're not Kubratoi, they're Videssian troopers!"

For a moment, the villagers stared at one another, as if the lookout had shouted in a foreign tongue. Then they cheered louder than they had after they first beat the Kubratoi. Idalkos' voice rose above the rest. "Stankos!" he said. "Stankos brought us our soldiers back!"

"Stankos!" everyone shouted. "Hurrah for Stankos!" "Good old Stankos!"

Stankos, Krispos thought, was getting more praise jammed into a few minutes than he'd had in the past five years. Krispos shouted the farmer's name, too, over and over, till his throat turned raw. He had stared death in the face since the lookout called. Nothing could ever frighten him worse. Now he, also, knew what reprieve felt like.

Before long, the Videssian cavalrymen pounded into the village. Stankos was with them, riding a borrowed horse. Half a dozen farmers pulled him off the beast, as if he were a Kubrati. The pounding he got was almost as hard as if he had been.

Krispos quickly counted the troopers. As best he could tell, there were seventy-one of them. So much for the lookout's frightened *hundreds and hundreds,* he thought.

The horsemen's captain bemusedly watched the villagers caper about. "You don't seem to have much need for us," he remarked.

"No, sir." Idalkos stiffened to attention. "We thought we did, when we didn't know for sure how many Kubratoi were about. You gave us a bad turn there—our lookout mistook you for a band of the wild men."

"By the bodies, I saw you'd dealt with the ones you found," the captain said. "Far as we know, that's the lot of them. I'd say they were just out for a little thievery. There's no general invasion, or anything like that."

A small band operating on its own, Krispos thought. The day he first picked up a sword, that was what Varades had told him the peasants might be able to handle. The veteran had known what he was talking about.

The Videssian captain turned to a priest beside him. "Looks like we won't need you today, Gelasios, except maybe for a prayer of thanksgiving."

"Nor am I sorry," Gelasios answered. "I can heal wounded men, aye, but I also think on the suffering they endure before I come to them, so I am just as well pleased not to ply my trade."

"Sir!" Krispos said. He had to repeat himself before the priest looked his way. "You're a healer, holy sir?"

"What of it, young man?" Gelasios said. "Phos be praised, you seem hale enough."

"Not me," Krispos said impatiently. "My father. This way."

Without looking to see whether Gelasios followed, he hurried toward his house. When he threw open the door, a new smell came out with the usual odors of stale smoke and food, a sweetish, sickly smell that made his stomach want to turn over.

"Yes, I see," Gelasios murmured at Krispos' elbow. The priest's nostrils flared wide, as if to gauge from the scent of corruption how great a challenge he faced. He went inside, stooping a little to get through the doorway. Now it was Krispos' turn to follow him.

Gelasios stooped beside Phostis, who lay near the edge of the straw bedding. Bright with fever, Phostis' eyes stared through the priest. Krispos bit his lip. In those sunken eyes, in the way his father's skin clung tight to bones beneath it, he saw the outline of coming death.

If Gelasios saw it, too, he gave no sign. He pulled Phostis' tunic aside, peeled off the latest worthless poultice to examine the wound. With the poultice came a thick wave of that rotting smell. Krispos took an involuntary step backward, then checked, hating himself—what was he doing, retreating from his father?

"It's all right, lad," Gelasios said absently, the first sign since he'd come into the house that he remembered Krispos was with him. He forgot him again, an instant later, and seemed to forget Phostis, too. His eyes went upward, as if to see the sun through the thatched roof of the cottage. "We bless thee, Phos, Lord with the great and good mind," he intoned, "by thy grace our protector, watchful beforehand that the great test of life may be decided in our favor."

Krispos echoed his prayer. It was the only one he knew all the way through; everyone in the whole Empire, he supposed, had Phos' creed by heart.

Gelasios said the prayer again, and again, and again. The priest's breathing grew slow and deep and steady. His eyes slid shut, but Krispos was somehow sure he remained very much aware of self and surroundings. Then, without warning, Gelasios reached out and seized Phostis' wounded shoulder.

The priest's hands were not gentle. Krispos expected his father to shriek at that rough treatment, but Phostis lay still, locked in his fever dream. Though Gelasios no longer prayed aloud, his breathing kept the same rhythm he had established.

Krispos looked from the priest's set face to his hands, and to the wound beneath them. The hair on his arms and at the nape of his neck suddenly prickled with awe—as he watched, that gaping, pus-filled gash began to close.

When only a thin, pale scar remained, Gelasios lifted his hands away from Phostis' shoulder. The flow of healing that had passed from him to Krispos' father stopped with almost audible abruptness. Gelasios tried to rise; he staggered, as if he felt the force of that separation.

"Wine," he muttered hoarsely. "I am fordone."

Only then did Krispos realize how much energy the healing had drained from Gelasios. He knew he should rush to fulfill the priest's request, but he could not, not at once. He was looking at his father. Phostis' eyes met his, and there was reason in them. "Get him his wine, son," Phostis said, "and while you're at it, you might bring some for me."

"Yes, Father, of course. And I pray your pardon, holy sir." Krispos was glad for an excuse to rummage for clean cups and the best skin of wine in the house: it meant no one would have to see the tears on his face.

"Phos' blessings on you, lad," Gelasios said. Though the wine put some color back in his face, he still moved stiffly, as if he had aged twenty years in the few minutes he'd needed to heal Phostis. Seeing the concern on Krispos' face, he managed a wry chuckle. "I'm not quite so feeble as I appear—a meal and good night's sleep, and I'll be well enough. Even without, at need I could heal another man now, likely two, and take no lasting harm."

Too abashed to speak, Krispos only nodded. His father said, "I just praise Phos you were here to heal me, holy sir. I do thank you for it." He twisted his head so he could peer down at his shoulder and at the wound there that, by the look of it, could have been five years old. "Isn't that fine?" he said to no one in particular.

He stood, more smoothly than Gelasios had. They walked out into the sunlight together. The men of the village raised a cheer to see Phostis returned to health. Somebody called, "And Tatze would have been such a tempting widow, too!" They all laughed, Phostis louder than anyone.

Krispos came out behind the two older men. While most of the villagers were still making much of his father, Idalkos beckoned to him. The veteran had been talking with the commander of the Videssian cavalry force. "I've told this gentleman—his name is Manganes—something about you," he said to Krispos. "He says—"

"Let me put it to him myself," Manganes said crisply. "From what your fellow villager here says, Krispos—do I have your name right?—you sound like a soldier the imperial army could use. I'd even offer you, hmm, a five goldpiece enlistment bonus if you rode back to Imbros with us now."

Without hesitating, Krispos shook his head. "Here I stay, sir, all the more so since, by your kindness and Gelasios' healing magic, my father has been restored to me."

"As you wish, young man," Manganes said. He and Idalkos both sighed.

Chapter III

KRISPOS CAME BACK FROM THE FIELDS ONE HOT, STICKY summer afternoon to find his mother, his sisters, and most of the other village women gathered round a peddler who was showing off a fine collection of copper pots. "Aye, these'll last you a lifetime, ladies, may the ice take me if I lie," the fellow said. He whacked one with his walking stick. Several women jumped at the clatter. The peddler held up the pot. "See? Not a dent in it! Made to last, like I said. None of this cheap tinker's work you see too often these days. And they're not too dear, either. I ask only three in silver, the eighth part of a goldpiece—"

Krispos waved to Evdokia, but she did not notice him. She was as caught up as any of the others by the peddler's mesmerizing pitch. Krispos walked on, a trifle miffed. He still wasn't used to her being out of the house, though she'd married Domokos nearly a year ago. She was eighteen now, but unless he made a conscious effort not to, he still thought of her as a little girl.

Of course, he was twenty-one himself, and the older men in the village still called him "lad" a lot of the time. No one paid any attention to change until it hit him in the head, he thought, chuckling wryly.

"Dear ladies, these pots—" The peddler broke off with a squeak that was no part of his regular sales pitch. Beneath his tan, blood mounted to his cheeks. "Do excuse me, ladies, I pray." His walk toward the woods quickly turned into an undignified dash. The women clucked sympathetically. Krispos had all he could do not to guffaw.

The peddler emerged a few minutes later. He paused at the well to draw up the bucket and take a long drink. "Your pardon," he said as he came back to his pots. "I seem to have picked up a touch of the flux. Where was I, now?"

He went back to his spiel with almost as much verve as he'd shown before. Krispos stood around and listened. He didn't intend to sell pots, but he had some piglets he was fattening up to take to market at Imbros soon, and the peddler's technique was worth studying.

Not much later, though, the man had to interrupt himself again. This time he went for the woods at a dead run. He did not look happy when he returned; his face was nearer gray than red.

"Ladies, much as I enjoy telling you about my wares, I think the time has come to get down to selling, before I embarrass myself further," he said.

He looked unhappy again through the bargaining that followed. The breaks in his talk had weakened his hold on the village women, and they dickered harder than he would have liked. He was shaking his head as he loaded pots back onto his mule.

"Here, stay for supper with us," one of the women called. "You shouldn't set out on the road so downcast."

The peddler managed a smile and a low bow. "You're too kind to a traveling man. Thank you." Before he got his bowl of stew, though, he needed to rush off to relieve himself twice more.

"I do hope he's well," Tatze said that evening to Phostis and Krispos.

A scream jerked the village awake the next morning. Krispos came running out of his house spear in hand, wondering who'd set upon whom. The woman who had invited the trader to stay over stood by his bedroll, horror on her face. Along with several other men, Krispos ran toward her. Had the wretch repaid her kindness by trying to rape her?

She screamed again. Krispos noticed she was fully clothed. Then, as she had, he looked down at the bedroll. "Phos," he whispered. His stomach churned. He was glad it was empty; had he had breakfast, he would have lost it.

The peddler was dead. He looked shrunken in on himself, and bruised; great violet blotches discolored his skin. From the way the blankets of the bedroll were drenched and stinking, he seemed to have voided all the moisture from his body in a dreadful fit of diarrhea.

"Magic," Tzykalas the cobbler said. "Evil magic." His hand made the sun-sign on his breast. Krispos nodded, and he was not the only one. He could imagine nothing natural that would result in such gruesome dissolution of a man.

"No, not magic," Varades said. The veteran's beard had been white for years, but Krispos had never thought of him as old till this moment. Now he not only looked his years, he sounded them, as well; his voice quivered as he went on, "This is worse than magic."

"What could be worse than magic?" three men asked at once.

"Cholera."

To Krispos it was only a word. By the way other villagers shook their heads, it meant little more to them. Varades filled them in. "I only saw it once, the good god be thanked, when we were campaigning against the Makurani in the west maybe thirty years ago, but that once was enough to last me a lifetime. It went through our army harder than any three battles—through the enemy the same way, I suppose, or they would've just walked over us."

Krispos looked from the veteran to the peddler's twisted, ruined corpse. He did not want to ask the next question: "It's . . . catching, then?"

"Aye." Varades seemed to pull himself together. "We burned the bodies of those that died of it. That slowed the spread, or we thought it did. I suppose we ought to do it for this poor bugger here. Something else we ought to do, too."

"What's that?" Krispos said.

"Fast as we can, ride to Imbros and fetch back a priest who knows healing. I think we're going to need one."

Smoke from the peddler's pyre rose to the sky. The villagers' prayers to Phos rose with it. As he had four years earlier when the Kubratoi came, Stankos set off for Imbros. This time, instead of a mule, he rode one of the horses captured from the wild men.

But for his being gone, and for the black, burned place on the village green, life went on as before. If other people worried every time they felt a call of nature, as Krispos did, they did not talk about it.

Five days, Krispos thought. Maybe a little less, because Stankos was on a horse now and could get to Imbros faster. Maybe a little more, because a priest might not ride back with the same grim urgency the Videssian troopers had shown—but Phos knew that urgency was real.

The healer-priest arrived on the morning of the sixth day after Stankos rode out of the village. He was three days behind the cholera. By the time he got there, the villagers had burned three more bodies, one the unfortunate woman who had asked the peddler to stay. More people were sick, diarrhea pouring out of them, their lips blue, their skin dry and cold. Some suffered from pain and cramps in their arms and legs, others did not. Out of all of them, though, flowed that endless stream of watery stool.

When he saw the victims who still lived, the priest made the sun-circle over his heart. "I had prayed your man here was wrong," he said, "but I see my prayer was not answered. In truth, this is cholera."

"Can you heal it?" Zoranne cried, fear and desperation in her voice—Yphantes lay in his own muck outside their cottage. "Oh, Phos, can you heal it?"

"For as long as the lord with the great and good mind gives me strength," the priest declared. Without stopping even to give his name, he hurried after her. The healthy villagers followed.

"He's called Mokios," Stankos said as he trooped along with the rest of them. "*Aii,* my arse is sore!" he added, rubbing the afflicted portion of his anatomy.

Mokios knelt beside Yphantes, who feebly tried to make the sun-sign when he recognized a priest. "Never mind that now," the priest said gently. He pushed aside the villager's befouled tunic, set hands on his belly. Then, as Gelasios had when healing Krispos' father, he recited Phos' creed over and over, focusing all his will and energy on the suffering man under his fingers.

Yphantes showed no external wound, as Phostis had. Thus the marvel of watching him grow well again was not there this time. Whether or not it was visible, though, Krispos could feel the current of healing pass from Mokios to the villager.

At last the priest took away his hands. He slumped back, weariness etching lines deep into his face. Yphantes sat up. His eyes were sunken but clear. "Water," he said hoarsely. "By the good god, I've never been so dry in my life."

"Aye, water." Mokios gasped. He sounded more worn than the man he had just healed.

Half a dozen villagers raced to be first to the well. Zoranne did not win the race, but the others gave way when she said, "Let me serve them. It is my right." With the pride of a queen, she drew up the dripping bucket, untied it, and carried it to her husband and Mokios. Between them, they all but drank it dry.

The priest was still wiping water from his mustache and beard with the sleeve of his blue robe when another woman tried to tug him to his feet. "Please, holy sir, come to my daughter," she got out through tears. "She barely breathes!"

Mokios heaved himself upright, grunting at the effort it took. He followed the woman. Again, the rest of the villagers followed him. Phostis touched Krispos on the shoulder. "Now we pray he can heal faster than we fall sick," he said softly.

Mokios succeeded again, though the second healing took longer than the first. When he was done, he lay full length on the ground, panting. "Look at the poor fellow," Krispos whispered to his father. "He needs someone to heal him now."

"Aye, but we need him worse," Phostis answered. He knelt and shook Mokios. "Please come, holy sir. We have others who will not see tomorrow without you."

"You are right," the priest said. Even so, he stayed down several more minutes and, when he did rise, he walked with the shambling gait of a man either drunk or in the last stages of exhaustion.

Krispos thought Mokios' next healing, of a small boy, would fail. How much, he wondered, could a man take out of himself before he had nothing left? Yet in the end Mokios somehow summoned up the strength to vanquish the child's disease. While the boy, with the resilience of the very young, got up and began to play, the healer-priest looked as if he had died in his place.

But others in the village were still sick. "We'll carry him if we have to," Phostis said, and carry him they did, on to Varades.

Again Mokios recited Phos' creed, though now in a voice as dry as the skins of the cholera victims he treated. The villagers prayed with him, both to lend him strength and to try to ease their own fears. He sank into the healing trance, placed his hands on the veteran's belly. They were filthy now, from the stools of the folk he had already cured.

Once more Krispos felt healing flow out of Mokios. This time, however, the priest slumped over in a faint before his task was done. He breathed, but the villagers could not bring him back to himself. Varades moaned and muttered and befouled himself yet again.

When they saw they could not rouse Mokios, the villagers put a blanket over him and let him rest. "In the morning, the good god willing, he'll be able to heal again," Phostis said.

By morning, though, Varades was dead.

Mokios finally roused when the sun was halfway up the sky. Videssian priests were enjoined to be frugal of food and drink, but he broke his fast with enough for three men. "Healers have dispensation," he mumbled round a chunk of honeycomb.

"Holy sir, so long as it gives you back the power to use your gift, no one would say a word if you ate five times as much," Krispos told him. Everyone who heard agreed loudly.

The priest healed two more, a man and a woman, that day. Toward sunset, he gamely tried again. As he had with Varades, though, he swooned away before the cure was complete. This time Krispos wondered if he'd killed himself until Idalkos found his pulse.

"Just what my father worried about," Krispos said. "So many of us are deathly ill that we're dragging Mokios down with us."

He'd hoped Idalkos might contradict him, but the veteran only nodded, saying, "Why don't you go on home and get away from the sickness for a while? You're lucky; none of your family seems to have come down with it."

Krispos made the sun-sign over his heart. A few minutes later, after seeing that Mokios was as comfortable on the ground as he could be, he took Idalkos' advice.

He frowned as he came up to his house. Being near the edge of the village, it was always fairly quiet. But he should have heard his father and mother talking inside, or perhaps Tatze teaching Kosta some trick of baking. Now he heard nothing. Nor was cooksmoke rising from the hole in the center of the roof.

All at once, his belly felt as if it had been pitched into a snowdrift. He ran for the door. As he jerked it open, out came the latrine stench with which he and the whole village had grown too horribly familiar over the last few days.

His father, his mother, his sister—they all lay on the floor. Phostis was most nearly conscious; he tried to wave his son away. Krispos paid him no heed. He dragged his father to the grass outside, then Tatze and Kosta. As he did, he wondered why he alone had been spared.

His legs ached fiercely when he bent to lift his mother, and when he went back for Kosta he found his arms so clenched with cramps that he could hardly hold her. But he thought nothing of it until suddenly, without willing it, he felt an overpowering urge to empty his bowels. He started for the bushes not far away, but fouled himself before he got to them. Then he realized he had not been spared after all.

He began to shout for help, stopped with the cry unuttered. Only the healer-priest could help him now, and he'd just left Mokios somewhere between sleep and death. If any of the villagers who were still healthy came, they would only further risk the disease. A moment later he vomited, then suffered another fit of diarrhea. With his guts knotted from end to end, he crawled back to his family. Perhaps their cases would be mild. Perhaps . . .

His fever was already climbing, so thought soon became impossible. He felt a raging thirst and managed to find a jar of wine in the house. It did nothing to ease him; before long, he threw it up.

He crawled outside again, shivering and stinking. The full moon shone down on him, as serene and beautiful as if no such thing as cholera existed. It was the last thing Krispos remembered seeing that night.

"OH, PHOS BE PRAISED," SOMEONE SAID, AS IF FROM VERY FAR away.

Krispos opened his eyes. He saw Mokios' anxious face peering down at him and, behind the priest, the rising sun. "No," he said. "It's still dark." Then the memory came crashing back. He tried to sit. Mokios' hands, still on him, held him down. "My family!" he gasped. "My father, my mother—"

The healer-priest's haggard face was somber. "Phos has called your mother to himself," he said. "Your father and sister live yet. May the good god grant them strength to endure until I recover enough to be of aid to them."

Then he did let Krispos sit. Krispos tried to weep for Tatze, but found the cholera had so drained his body that he could make no tears. Yphantes, now up and about, handed him a cup of water. He drank it while the priest drained another.

He had to force himself to look at Phostis and Kosta. Their eyes and cheeks were sunken, the skin on their hands and feet and faces tight and withered. Only their harsh breathing and the muck that kept flowing from them said they were not dead.

"Hurry, holy sir, I beg you," Krispos said to Mokios.

"I shall try, young man, truly I shall. But first, I pray"—he looked round for Yphantes—"some food. Never have I drained myself so."

Yphantes fetched him bread and salt pork. He gobbled them down, asked for more. He had eaten like that since he'd entered the village, but was thinner now than when he'd come. His cheeks, Krispos thought dully, were almost as hollow as Phostis'.

Mokios wiped at his brow. "Warm today," he said.

To Krispos, the morning still felt cool. He only shrugged by way of answer; as, not long before, he had been in fever's arms, he did not trust his judgment. He looked from his father to his sister. How long could they keep life in them? "Please, holy sir, will it be soon?" he asked, his nails digging into his palms.

"As soon as I may," the healer-priest replied. "Would I were younger, and recovered more quickly. Gladly would I—"

Mokios paused to belch. Considering how much he had eaten, and how quickly, Krispos saw nothing out of the ordinary in that. Then the healer-priest broke wind, loudly—as poor Varades never would again, Krispos thought; mourning the veteran with the small part of him not in anguish for his family.

And then utter horror filled Mokios' thin, tired face. For a moment, Krispos did not understand; the stench of incontinence by his house— indeed, throughout the village—was so thick a new addition did not easily make itself known. But when the healer-priest's eyes went fearfully to the wet stain spreading on his robe, Krispos' followed.

"No," Mokios whispered.

"No," Krispos agreed, as if their denial were stronger than truth. But the priest had tended many victims of the cholera, had smeared himself with their muck, had worked himself almost to death healing them. So what was more likely than a yes, or than that *almost* being no almost at all?

Krispos saw one tiny chance. He seized Mokios by both shoulders; weak as he was, he was stronger than the healer-priest. "Holy sir," he said urgently, "holy sir, can you heal yourself?"

"Rarely, rarely does Phos grant such a gift," Mokios said, "and in any case, I have not yet the strength—"

"You must try!" Krispos said. "If you sicken and die, the village dies with you!"

"I will make the attempt." But Mokios' voice held no hope, and Krispos knew only his own fierce will pushed the priest on.

Mokios shut his eyes, the better to muster the concentration he needed to heal. His lips moved soundlessly; Krispos recited Phos' creed with him. His heart leaped when, even through fever, even through sickness, Mokios' features relaxed toward the healing trance.

The priest's hands moved toward his own traitorous belly. Just as he was about to begin, his head twisted. Pain replaced calm confidence on his face, and he puked up everything Yphantes had brought him. The spasms of vomiting went on and on, into the dry heaves. He also fouled himself again.

When at last he could speak, Mokios said, "Pray for me, young man, and for your family, also. It may well be that Phos will accomplish what I cannot; not all who take cholera perish of it." He made the sun-sign over his heart.

Krispos prayed as he had never prayed before. His sister died that afternoon, his father toward evening. By then, Mokios was unconscious. Some time that night, he died, too.

AFTER WHAT SEEMED FOREVER BUT WAS LESS THAN A MONTH, cholera at last left the village alone. Counting poor brave Mokios, thirty-nine people died, close to one inhabitant in six. Many of those who lived were too feeble to work for weeks thereafter. But the work did not go away because fewer hands were there to do it; harvest was coming.

Krispos worked in the fields, in the gardens, with the animals, every moment he could. Making his body stay busy helped keep his mind from his losses. He was not alone in his sudden devotion to toil, either; few families had not seen at least one death, and everyone had lost people counted dear.

But for Krispos, going home each night was a special torment. Too many memories lived in that empty house with him. He kept thinking he heard Phostis' voice, or Tatze's, or Kosta's. Whenever he looked up, ready to answer, he found himself alone. That was very bad.

He took to eating most of his meals with Evdokia and her husband, Domokos. Evdokia had stayed well; Domokos, though he'd taken cholera, had suffered only a relatively mild case—his survival proved it. When, soon after the end of the epidemic, Evdokia found she was pregnant, Krispos was doubly glad of that.

Some villagers chose wine as their anodyne instead of work; Krispos could not remember a time so full of drunken fights. "I can't really blame 'em," he said to Yphantes one day as they both swung hoes against the weeds that had flourished when the cholera made people neglect the fields, "but I do get tired of breaking up brawls."

"We should all be grateful you're here to break them up," Yphantes said. "With your size and the way you wrestle, nobody wants to argue with you when you tell 'em to stop. I'm just glad you're not one of the ones who like to throw their weight around to show how tough they are. You've got your father's head on your shoulders, Krispos, and that's good in a man so young."

Krispos stared down as he hacked at a stinging nettle. He did not want Yphantes to see the tears that came to him whenever he thought of his family, the tears he'd been too weak and too dry inside to shed the day they died.

When he could speak again, he changed the subject. "I wonder how good a crop we'll end up bringing in?"

No farmer could take that question less than seriously. Yphantes rubbed his chin, then straightened to look out across the fields that were now beginning to go from green to gold. "Not very good," he said reluctantly. "We didn't do all the cultivating we should have, and we won't have as many people to help in the harvest."

"Of course, we won't have as many people eating this winter, either," Krispos said.

"With the harvest I fear we'll have, that may be just as well," Yphantes answered.

Not since he was a boy in Kubrat had Krispos faced the prospect of hunger so far in advance. What with the rapacity of the Kubratoi, every winter then had been hungry. Now, he thought, he would face starvation cheerfully if only he could starve along with his family.

He sighed. He did not have that choice. He lifted his hoe and attacked another weed.

"UH-OH," DOMOKOS WHISPERED AS THE TAX COLLECTOR AND his retinue came down the road toward the village. "He's a new one."

"Aye," Krispos whispered back, "and along with his clerks and his pack-horses, he has soldiers with him, too."

He could not imagine two worse signs. The usual tax collector, one Zabdas, had been coming to the village for years; he could sometimes be reasoned with, which made him a prince among tax men. And soldiers generally meant the imperial government was going to ask for something more than the ordinary. This year, the village had less than the ordinary to give.

The closer the new tax collector got, the less Krispos liked his looks. He was thin and pinch-featured and wore a great many heavy rings. The way he studied the village and its fields reminded Krispos of a fence lizard studying a fly. Lizards, however, did not commonly bring archers to help them hunt.

There was no help for it. The tax collector set up shop in the middle of the village square. He sat in a folding chair beneath a canopy of scarlet cloth. Behind him, his soldiers set up the imperial icons: a portrait of the Avtokrator Anthimos and, to its left, a smaller image of his uncle Petronas.

It was a new picture of Anthimos this year, too, Krispos saw, showing the Emperor with a full man's beard and wearing the scarlet boots reserved for his high rank. Even so, his image looked no match for that of Petronas.

The older man's face was hard, tough, able, with something about his eyes that seemed to say he could see behind him without turning his head. Petronas was no longer regent—Anthimos had come into his majority on his eighteenth birthday—but the continued presence of his image said he still ruled Videssos in all but name.

Along with the other villagers, Krispos bowed first to the icon of Anthimos, then to that of Petronas, and last to the fleshly representative of imperial might. The tax collector dipped his head a couple of inches in return. He drew a scroll from the small wooden case he had set beside his left foot, unrolled it, and began to read:

"Whereas, declares the Phos-guarded Avtokrator Anthimos, from the beginning of our reign we have taken a great deal of care and concern for the common good of affairs, we have been equally concerned to protect well the state which Phos the lord of the great and good mind has granted us. We have discovered that the public treasury suffers under many debts which weaken our might and make difficult the successful prosecution of our affairs. Even matters military have been damaged by our being at a loss for supplies, with the result that the state has been harmed by the boundless onslaughts of barbarians. According to our ability, we deem the situation worthy of needed correction . . ."

He went on in that vein for some time. Looking around, Krispos watched his neighbors' eyes glaze. The last time he'd heard rhetoric so turgid was when Iakovitzes ransomed the captive peasants from Kubrat. That speech, at least, had presaged a happy outcome. He doubted the same would be true of this one.

From the way the soldiers shifted their weight, as if to ready themselves for action, he knew when the tax man was about to come to the unpalatable meat of the business. It arrived a moment later: "Accordingly, all assessments for the present year and until the conclusion of the aforementioned emergency are hereby increased by one part in three, payment to be collected in gold or in kind at the times and locations sanctioned by long-established custom. So decrees the Phos-guarded Avtokrator Anthimos."

The tax collector tied a scarlet ribbon round his proclamation and stowed it away in its case. *One part in three,* Krispos thought. *No wonder he has soldiers with him.* He waited for the rest of the villagers to join him in protest, but nobody spoke. Perhaps he was the only one who'd managed to follow the speech all the way through.

"Excellent sir," he said, and waited till the tax man's eyes swung his way. "Excellent . . ." He waited again.

"My name is Malalas," the tax collector said grudgingly.

"Excellent Malalas, we can pay no extra tax this year," Krispos said. Once he found the boldness to speak, others nodded with him. He went on, "We would have trouble paying the usual tax. This has been a hard year for us, excellent sir."

"Oh? What's your excuse?" Malalas asked.

"We had sickness in the village, excellent sir—cholera. Many died, and others were left too weak to work for a long time. Our crop is small this year."

At the mention of the dread word *cholera,* some clerks and a few soldiers stirred nervously. Malalas, however, amazed Krispos by bursting into laughter. "Nice try, bumpkin! Name a disease to excuse your own laziness, make it a nasty one so we'll be sure not to linger. You'd fool some with that, maybe, but not me. I've heard it before."

"But it's the truth!" Krispos said, appalled. "Excellent sir, you've not seen us till now. Our old tax collector, Zabdas, would recognize how many faces he knew aren't here today, truly he would."

Malalas yawned. "A likely tale."

"But it's the truth!" Krispos repeated. The villagers backed him up: "Aye, sir, it is!" "By Phos, we had many dead, a healer-priest among 'em—" "My wife—" "My father—" "My son—" "I could hardly walk for a month, let alone farm."

The tax collector raised a hand. "This matters not at all."

Krispos grew angry. "What do you mean, it doesn't matter?" He ducked under Malalas' canopy, stabbed a finger down at the register on the tax man's knees. "Varades is dead. Phostis—that's *my* father—is dead, and so are my mother and sister. Tzykalas' son of the same name is dead . . ." He went through the whole melancholy list.

None of it moved Malalas a hairsbreadth. "As you say, young man, I am new here. For all I know—in fact, I think it likely—the people you name may be hiding in the woods, laughing up their sleeves. I've seen that happen before, believe you me."

Krispos did believe him. Had he not ferreted out such cheats, he would not have been so arrogantly certain of what was happening here. Krispos wished those cheats down to Skotos' ice, for they'd made the tax man blind to any real problems a village might have.

"The full proportion named is due and shall be collected," Malalas went on. "Even if every word you say is true, taxes are assessed by village, not by individual. The fisc has need of what you produce, and what the fisc needs, it takes." He nodded back toward the waiting soldiers. "Pay peaceably, or it will be the worse for you."

"Pay peaceably, *and* it will be the worse for us," Krispos said bitterly. Taxes were assessed collectively, he knew, to make sure villagers tolerated no shirkers among them and so they would have to make good the labor of anyone who left. To use the law to force them to make up for disaster was savagely unjust.

That did not stop Malalas. He announced the amount due from the village: so many goldpieces, or their equivalent in the crops just harvested, all of which were carefully and accurately listed in the register.

The villagers brought what they had set aside for the annual assessment. With much sweat and scraping, they had amassed an amount just short of what they'd paid the year before. Zabdas surely would have been satisfied. Malalas was not. "We'll have the rest of it now," he said.

Guarded by his soldiers, the clerks he'd brought along swarmed over the village like ants raiding a pot of lard. They opened storage pit after storage pit and shoveled the grain and beans and peas into leather sacks.

Krispos watched the systematic plundering. "You're worse thieves than the Kubratoi!" he shouted to Malalas.

The tax man spoiled it by taking it for a compliment. "My dear fellow, I should hope so. The barbarians have rapacity, aye, but no system. Do please note, however, that we are not arbitrary. We take no more than the Avtokrator Anthimos' law ordains."

"You please note, excellent sir"—Krispos made the title into a curse—"that what the Avtokrator's law ordains will leave some of us to starve."

Malalas only shrugged. For a moment, red fury so filled Krispos that he almost shouted for the villagers to seize weapons and fall on the tax collector and his party. Even if they massacred them, though, what good would it do? It would only bring more imperial soldiers down on their heads, and those troops would be ready to kill, not merely to steal.

"Enough, there!" Malalas called at length, after one of his clerks came up to whisper in his ear. "No, we don't need that barley—fill in the pit again. Now let us be off. We have another of these miserable little hamlets to visit tomorrow."

He remounted. So did his clerks and the cavalrymen who had protected them. Their harness jingled as they rode out of the village. The inhabitants stared after them, then to the emptied storage pits.

For a long time, no one spoke. Then Domokos tried to put the best light he could on things: "Maybe if we're all very watchful, we can . . ." His voice trailed away. Not even he believed what he was saying.

Krispos trudged back to his house. He picked up a trowel, went around to the side of the house away from the square, bent down, and started digging. Finding what he was looking for took longer than he'd expected; after a dozen years, he'd forgotten exactly where he'd buried that lucky goldpiece. At last, though, it lay gleaming on his muddy palm.

He almost threw the coin away; at that moment, anything with an Avtokrator's face on it was hateful to him. Common sense, however, soon prevailed. "Might be a good while before I see another one of these," he muttered. He struck the goldpiece in the pouch he wore on his belt.

He went into his house again. From their places on the wall he took down spear and sword. The sword he belted on next to his pouch. The spear would also do for a staff. He went outside. Clouds were building in the north. The fall rains had not yet started, but they would soon. When the roads turned to mud, a staff would be handy.

He looked around. "Anything else I need?" he asked out loud. He ducked inside one last time, came out with half a loaf of bread. Then he walked back to the village square. Domokos and Evdokia were still standing there, along with several other people. They were talking about Malalas' visit, in the soft, stunned tones they would have used after a flood or other natural disaster.

Domokos raised an eyebrow when he saw the gear Krispos carried. "Going hunting?" he asked his brother-in-law.

"You might say so," Krispos answered. "Hunting something better than this, anyhow. If the Empire can rob us worse than the wild men ever did, what's the use of farming? A long time ago, I wondered what else I could do. I'm off for Videssos the city, to try to find out."

Evdokia took his arm. "Don't go!"

"Sister, I think I have to. You and Domokos have each other. Me—" He bit his lip. "I tear myself up inside every time I go home. You know why." He waited until Evdokia nodded. Her face was twisted, too. He went on, "Besides, I'll be one less mouth to feed here. That's bound to help—a little, anyhow."

"Will you soldier, then?" Domokos asked.

"Maybe." Krispos still did not like the idea. "If I can't find anything else, I guess I will."

Evdokia embraced him. "Phos guard you on the road and in the city." Krispos saw by how quickly she stopped arguing that she realized he was doing what he needed to do.

He hugged her, too, felt the swell of her growing belly against him. He clasped Domokos' hand. Then he walked away from them, away from everything he'd ever known, west toward the highway that led south to the city.

FROM THE VILLAGE TO THE IMPERIAL CAPITAL WAS A JOURNEY of about ten days for a man in good condition and serious about his walking. Krispos was both, but took three weeks to get there. He stopped to help gather beans for a day here, to cut timber for an afternoon there, for whatever other odd jobs he could find. He got to Videssos the city with food in his belly and some money in his pouch besides his goldpiece.

He had already seen marvels on his way south, for as the road neared the city it came down by the sea. He'd stopped and stared for long minutes at the sight of water that went on and on forever. But that was a natural wonder, and now he was come to one worked by man: the walls of Videssos.

He'd seen city walls before, at Imbros and at several towns he'd passed on his journey. They'd seemed splendid things then, huge and strong. Next to the walls he approached now, they were as toys, and toddlers' toys at that.

Before Videssos' outer wall was a broad, deep ditch. That outwall loomed, five or six times as tall as a man. Every fifty to a hundred yards stood square or hexagonal towers that were taller still. Krispos would have thought those works could hold out Skotos himself, let alone any mortal foe the city might face.

But behind that outer wall stood another, mightier yet. Its towers were sited between those of the outwall, so some tower bore directly on every inch of ground in front of the wall.

"Don't stand there gawking, you miserable bumpkin," someone called from behind Krispos. He turned and saw a gentleman with a fine hooded cloak to keep him dry. The rain had started the night before; long since soaked, Krispos had stopped caring about it.

His cheeks hot, he hurried toward the gate. That proved a marvel in itself, with valves of iron and bronze and wood thick as a man's body. Peering up as he walked under the outwall, he saw troopers looking down at him through iron gates. "What are they doing up there?" he asked a guardsman who was keeping traffic moving smoothly through the gate.

The guard smiled. "Suppose you were an enemy and somehow you'd managed to batter down the outer door. How would you like to have boiling water or red-hot sand poured down on your head?"

"Not very much, thanks." Krispos shuddered.

The gate guard laughed. "Neither would I." He pointed to Krispos' spear. "Have you come to join up? You'll get better gear than that, I promise you."

"I might, depending on what kind of other luck I find here," Krispos said.

By the way the gate guard nodded, Krispos was sure he'd heard those words or ones much like them many times. The fellow said, "They use the meadow south of here, down by the sea, for a practice field. If you do need to look for an officer, you can find one there."

"Thanks. I'll remember," Krispos said. Everyone seemed to want to push him toward a soldier's life. He shook his head. He still did not want to be a soldier. Surely in a city as great as Videssos was said to be, a city as great as her walls proclaimed her to be, he would be able to find something, anything, else to do with his life. He walked on.

The valves of the inner wall's gates were even stouter than those of the outwall. As Krispos passed under the inner wall, he looked up and saw another set of murder-holes. Feeling quite the city sophisticate, he gave the soldiers over his head a friendly nod and kept going. A few more steps and he was truly inside Videssos the city.

Just as he had in front of the walls, he stopped in his tracks to stare. The only thing with which he could think to compare the view was the sea. Now, though, he gazed on a sea of buildings. He had never imagined houses and shops and golden-domed temples to Phos stretching as far as the eye could reach.

Again someone behind him shouted for him to get moving. He took a few steps, then a few more, and soon found himself walking through the streets of the city. He had no idea where he was going; for the moment, one place seemed as good as another. It was all equally strange, and all equally marvelous.

He flattened himself against the front of a shop to let a mule-drawn cart squeeze past. In his village, the driver would have been someone he knew. Even in Imbros, the fellow probably would have raised a finger to his forehead in thanks. Here, he paid Krispos no mind at all, though the squeaking wheels of his cart almost brushed the newcomer's tunic. By the set look on his face, he had someplace important to go and not enough time to get there.

That seemed to be a characteristic of the people on the streets. Living in the most splendid city in the world, they gave it even less notice than Krispos had the familiar houses of his village. They did not notice him, either, except when his slow walk exasperated them. Then they sidestepped and scooted past him with the adroitness, almost, of so many dancers.

Their talk, the snatches of it that he picked up over the squeal of axles, the banging of coppersmiths' hammers, and the patter of the rain, had the same quick, elusive quality to it as their walk. Sometimes he had to think to understand it, and some of what he heard eluded him altogether. It was Videssian, aye, but not the Videssian he had learned from his parents.

He wandered for a couple of hours. Once he found himself in a large square that he thought was called the Forum of the Ox. He did not see any oxen in it, though everything else in the world seemed to be for sale there.

"Fried squid!" a vendor shouted.

A twist of breeze brought the savory scent of hot olive oil, breading, and seafood to Krispos' nose. His stomach growled. Sightseeing, he realized suddenly, was hungry work. He wasn't sure what a squid was, but asked, "How much?"

"Three coppers apiece," the man answered.

Krispos still had some small change in his pouch from the last job he'd done before he got to the city. "Give me two."

The vendor plucked them from his brazier with a pair of tongs. "Mind your fingers, now, pal—they're hot," he said as he exchanged them for Krispos' coins.

Krispos almost dropped them, but not because they were hot. He shifted his spear to the crook of his elbow so he could point. "Can I eat these—these—" He did not even know the right word.

"The tentacles? Sure—a lot of people say they're the best part." The local gave him a knowing smile. "Not from around these parts, are you?"

"Er, no." Krispos lost himself in the crowd; he did not want the squid-seller watching while he nerved himself to eat what he'd bought. The meat inside the breadcrumbs proved white and chewy, without any pronounced flavor; the tentacles weren't much different, so far as he could tell, from the rest. He licked his fingers, flicked at his beard to dislodge stray crumbs, and walked on.

Darkness began to fall. Krispos knew just enough of cities to try to find an inn. At last he did. "How much for a meal and a room?" he asked the tall thin man who stood behind a row of wine and beer barrels that served as a bar.

"Five pieces of silver," the innkeeper said flatly.

Krispos flinched. Not counting his goldpiece, he did not have that much. No matter how he haggled, he could not bring the fellow down below three. "Can I sleep in the stables if I tend your animals or stand guard for you?" he asked.

The innkeeper shook his head. "Got a horseboy, got a bouncer."

"Why are you so dear?" Krispos said. "When I bought squid cheap this afternoon, I figured everything else'd be—how would you say it?—in pro-portion."

"Aye, squid and fish and clams are cheap enough," the innkeeper said. "If you just want a good fish stew, I'll give you a big bowl for five coppers. We have lots of fish here. How not? Videssos is the biggest port in the world. But we have lots of people, too, so space, now, space'll cost you."

"Oh." Krispos scratched his head. What the innkeeper said made a strange kind of sense, even if he was not used to thinking in those terms. "I'll take that bowl of stew, and thank you. But where am I supposed to sleep tonight? Even if it wasn't raining, I wouldn't want to do it on the streets."

"Don't blame you." The innkeeper nodded. "Likely you'd get robbed the first night—doesn't matter how sharp your spear is if you're not awake to use it. Armed that way, though, you could try the barracks."

"Not till I've tried everything else," Krispos said stubbornly. "If I sleep in the barracks once, I'll end up sleeping there for years. I just want a place to set my head till I find steady work."

"I see what you're saying." The innkeeper walked over to the fireplace, stirred the pot that hung over it with a wooden spoon. "Your best bet'd likely be a monastery. If you help with the chores, they'll house you for a while, and feed you, too. Not a nice stew like this"—he ladled out a large, steaming bowlful—"but bread and cheese and beer, plenty to keep you from starving. Now let's see those coppers, if you please."

Krispos paid him. The stew was good. The innkeeper gave him a heel of bread to sop up the last of it. He wiped his mouth on his damp sleeve, waited until the innkeeper was done serving another customer. Then he said, "A monastery sounds like a good idea. Where would I find one?"

"There must be a dozen of 'em in the city." The innkeeper stopped to think. "The one dedicated to the holy Pelagios is closest, but it's small and hasn't the room to take in many off the street. Better you should try the monastery of the holy Skirios. They always have space for travelers."

"Thanks. I'll do that. How do I get there?" Krispos made the innkeeper repeat the directions several times; he wanted to be sure he had them straight. Once he was, he stood in front of the fire to soak up as much warmth as he could, then plunged into the night.

He soon regretted it. The directions might have served well enough by daylight. In the dark, with half the firepots that should have lit the streets doused by rain, he got hopelessly lost. The innkeeper's fire quickly became only a wistful memory.

Few people were out and about so late. Some traveled in large bands and carried torches to light their way. Others walked alone, in darkness. One of those followed Krispos for blocks and sank back into deeper shadow whenever Krispos turned to look his way. Farm boy or not, he could figure out what that meant. He lowered his spear and took a couple of steps toward the skulker. The next time he looked around, the fellow was gone.

The longer Krispos walked, the more he marveled at how many streets, and how many miles of streets, Videssos the city had. From the way his feet felt, he had tramped all of them—and none twice, for nothing looked familiar. Had he stumbled on another inn, he would have spent his lucky goldpiece without a second thought.

Instead, far more by luck than design, he came upon a large low structure with several gates. All but one were barred and silent. Torches burned there, though, and a stout man in a blue robe stood in the gateway. He was armed with an even stouter cudgel, which he hefted when Krispos walked into the flickering circle of light the torches cast.

"What building is this?" he asked as he approached. He trailed his spear, to look as harmless as he could.

"This is the monastery that serves the memory of the holy Skirios, may Phos hallow his soul for all eternity," the watchman replied.

"May he indeed!" Krispos said fervently. "And may I beg shelter of you for the night? I've wandered the streets searching for this monastery for—for—well, it seems like forever."

The monk at the gate smiled. "Not that long, I hope, though it is the sixth hour of the night. Aye, come in, stranger, and be welcome, so long as you come in peace." He eyed Krispos' spear and sword.

"By Phos, I do."

"Well enough," the watchman said. "Enter then, and rest. When morning comes, you can present yourself to our holy abbot Pyrrhos with the others who came in out of the rain this evening. He, or someone under him, will assign you some task for tomorrow—or perhaps for some time, if you need a longer time of shelter with us."

"Agreed," Krispos said at once. He started to walk past the monk, then paused. "Pyrrhos, you say? I knew a man by that name once." He frowned, trying to remember where or when, but gave it up with a shrug after a moment.

The monk also shrugged. "I've known two or three myself; it's a fairly common name."

"Aye, so it is." Krispos yawned. The monk pointed the way to the common room.

THE ABBOT PYRRHOS WAS DREAMING. IT WAS ONE OF THOSE dreams where he knew he was dreaming but did not particularly want to break the mood by exerting his will. He was in a line of people coming before some judge, whether imperial or divine he could not say.

He could not hear the judgments the enthroned figure was passing on those in front of him, but he was not greatly concerned, either. He knew he had led a pious life, and his worldly sins were also small. Surely no harsh sentence could fall on him.

The line moved forward with dreamlike quickness. Only one woman stood between him and the judge. Then she, too, was gone. Had she walked away? Disappeared? Pyrrhos had not noticed, but that, too, was the way of dreams. The abbot bowed to the man—if it was a man—on the throne.

Eyes stern as those of Phos transfixed Pyrrhos. He bowed again and stayed bent at the waist. Almost he went to hands and knees and then to his belly, as if he stood before the Avtokrator. "Illustrious lord—" his dream-voice quavered.

"Silence, worm!" Now he could hear the judge's voice. It reverberated like a thunderclap in his head. "Do as I say and all will be well for Videssos; fail and all fails with you. Do you understand?"

"Aye, lord," dream-Pyrrhos said. "Speak, and I obey."

"Go then to the monastery common room. Go at once; do not wait for dawn. Call out the name Krispos, once, twice, three times. Give the man who answers every favor; treat him as if he were your own son. Get hence now, and do as I have ordained."

Pyrrhos woke to find himself safe in his own bed. A guttering lamp illuminated his chamber. Save for being larger and packed with books, it was like the cells in which his monks slept—unlike many abbots, he disdained personal comfort as a weakness.

"What a strange dream," he whispered. All the same, he did not get up. He yawned instead. Within minutes, he was asleep again.

He found himself before the enthroned judge once more. This time, he was at the head of the line. If he had thought those eyes stern before, they fairly blazed now. "Insolent wretch!" the judge cried. "Obey, or all totters around you. Summon the man Krispos from the common room, once, twice, three times. Give him the favor you would your own son. Waste no time in sottish slumber. This must be done! Now go!"

Pyrrhos woke with a violent start. Sweat beaded his forehead and his shaven crown. He still seemed to hear the last word of the judge's angry shout dinning in his ears. He started to get out of bed, then stopped. Anger of his own filled him. What business did a dream have, telling him what to do?

Deliberately he lay back down and composed himself for sleep. It came more slowly this time than before, but his disciplined mind enforced rest on him as if it were a program of exercise. His eyes sagged shut, his breathing grew soft and regular.

He felt a cold caress of terror—the judge was coming down from the throne, straight for him. He tried to run and could not. The judge seized him, lifting him as if he were light as a mouse. "Summon the man Krispos, fool!" he roared, and cast Pyrrhos from him. The abbot fell and fell and fell forever . . .

He woke up on the cold stone floor.

Trembling, Pyrrhos got to his feet. He was a bold man; even now, he started to return to his bed. But when he thought of the enthroned judge and those terrible eyes—and how they would look should he disobey yet again—boldness failed. He opened the door to his chamber and stepped out into the hallway.

Two monks returning to their cells from a late-night prayer vigil glanced up in surprise to see someone approaching them. As was his right, Pyrrhos stared through them as if they did not exist. They bowed their heads and, without a word, stood aside to let the abbot pass.

The door to the common room was barred on the side away from the men the monastery took in. Pyrrhos had second thoughts as he lifted the bar—but he had not fallen out of bed since he was a boy. He could not make himself believe he had fallen out of bed tonight. Shaking his head, he went into the common room.

As always, the smell hit him first, the smell of the poor, the hungry, the desperate, and the derelict of Videssos: unwashed humanity, stale wine, from somewhere the sharp tang of vomit. Tonight the rain added damp straw's mustiness and the oily lanolin reek of wet wool to the mix.

A man said something to himself as he turned over in his sleep. Others snored. One fellow sat against a wall, coughing the consumptive's endless racking bark. *I'm to pick one of these men to treat as my son?* the abbot thought. *One of* these?

It was either that or go back to bed. Pyrrhos got as far as putting his fingers on the door handle. He found he did not dare to work it. Sighing, he turned back. "Krispos?" he called softly.

A couple of men stirred. The consumptive's eyes, huge in his thin face, met the abbot's. He could not read the expression in them. No one answered him.

"Krispos?" he called again.

This time he spoke louder. Someone grumbled. Someone else sat up. Again, no one replied. Pyrrhos felt the heat of embarrassment rise to the top of his tonsured head. If nothing came of this night's folly, he would have some explaining to do, perhaps even—he shuddered at the thought—to the patriarch himself. He hated the idea of making himself vulnerable to Gnatios' mockery; the ecumenical patriarch of Videssos was far too secular to suit him. But Gnatios was Petronas' cousin, and so long as Petronas was the most powerful man in the Empire, his cousin would remain at the head of the ecclesiastical hierarchy.

One more fruitless call, the abbot thought, and his ordeal would be over. If Gnatios wanted to mock him for it, well, he had endured worse things in his service to Phos. That reflection steadied him, so his voice rang out loud and clear: "Krispos?"

Several men sat up now. A couple of them glared at Pyrrhos for interrupting their rest. He had already begun to turn to go back to his chamber when someone said, "Aye, holy sir, I'm Krispos. What do you want of me?"

It was a good question. The abbot would have been happier with a good answer for it.

KRISPOS SAT IN THE MONASTERY STUDY WHILE PYRRHOS BUS-tled about lighting lamps. When that small, homely task was done, the abbot took a chair opposite him. The lamplight failed to fill his eyesockets or the hollows of his cheeks, leaving his face strange and not quite human as he studied Krispos.

"What am I to do with you, young man?" he said at last.

Krispos shook his head in bewilderment. "I couldn't begin to tell you, holy sir. You called, so I answered; that's all I know about it." He fought down a yawn. He would sooner have been back in the common room, asleep.

"Is it? Is it indeed?" The abbot leaned forward, voice tight with suppressed eagerness. It was as if he were trying to find out something from Krispos without letting on that he was trying to.

By that sign, Krispos knew him. He had been just so a dozen years before, asking questions about the goldpiece Omurtag had given Krispos— the same goldpiece, he realized, that he had in his pouch. Save for the passage of time, which sat lightly on it, Pyrrhos' gaunt, intent face was also the same.

"You were up on the platform with Iakovitzes and me," Krispos said.

The abbot frowned. "I crave pardon? What was that?"

"In Kubrat, when he ransomed us from the wild men," Krispos explained.

"I was?" Pyrrhos' gaze suddenly sharpened; Krispos saw that he remembered, too. "By the lord with the great and good mind, I *was*," the abbot said slowly. He drew the circular sun-sign on his breast. "You were but a boy then."

It sounded like an accusation. As if to remind himself it was true no more, Krispos touched the hilt of his sword. Thus reassured, he nodded.

"But boy no more," Pyrrhos said, agreeing with him. "Yet here we are, drawn back together once more." He made the sun-sign again, then said something completely obscure to Krispos: "No, Gnatios will not laugh."

"Holy sir?"

"Never mind." The abbot's attention might have wandered for a moment. Now it focused on Krispos again. "Tell me how you came from whatever village you lived in to Videssos the city."

Krispos did. Speaking of his parents' and sister's deaths brought back the pain, nearly as strong as if he felt it for the first time. He had to wait before he could go on. "And then, with the village still all in disarray, our taxes went up a third, I suppose to pay for some war at the other end of the Empire."

"More likely to pay for another—or another dozen—of Anthimos' extravagant follies." Pyrrhos' mouth set in a thin, hard line of disapproval. "Petronas lets him have his way in them, the better to keep the true reins of ruling in his own hands. Neither of them cares how they gain the gold to pay for such sport, so long as they do."

"As may be," Krispos said. "It's not why we were broken, but that we were broken that put me on my way here. Farmers have hard enough times worrying about nature. If the tax man wrecks us, too, we've got no hope at all. That's what it looked like to me, and that's why I left."

Pyrrhos nodded. "I've heard like tales before. Now, though, the question arises of what to do with you. Did you come to the city planning to use the weapons you carry?"

"Not if I can find anything else to do," Krispos said at once.

"Hmm." The abbot stroked his bushy beard. "You lived all your life till now on a farm, yes? How are you with horses?"

"I can manage, I expect," Krispos answered, "though I'm better with mules; I've had more to do with them, if you know what I mean. Mules I'm good with. Any other livestock, too, and I'm your man. Why do you want to know, holy sir?"

"Because I think that, as the flows of your life and mine have come together after so many years, it seems fitting for Iakovitzes' to be mingled
with the stream once more, as well. And because I happen to know that
Iakovitzes is constantly looking for new grooms to serve in his stables."

"Would he take me on, holy sir? Someone he's never—well, just about
never—seen before? If he would . . ." Krispos' eyes lit up. "If he would, I'd
leap at the chance."

"He would, on my urging," Pyrrhos said. "We're cousins of sorts: his
great-grandfather and my grandmother were brother and sister. He also
owes me a few more favors than I owe him at the moment."

"If he would, if you would, I couldn't think of anything better." Krispos
meant it; if he was going to work with animals, it would be almost as if he
had the best of farm and city both. He hesitated, then asked a question he
knew was dangerous: "But why do you want to do this for me, holy sir?"

Pyrrhos sketched the sun-sign. After a moment, Krispos realized that
was all the answer he'd get. When the abbot spoke, it was of his cousin.
"Understand, young man, you are altogether free to refuse this if you wish.
Many would, without a second thought. I don't know if you recall, but
Iakovitzes is a man of—how shall I say it?—uncertain temperament, per-
haps."

Krispos smiled. He did remember.

The abbot smiled, too, but thinly. "That is one reason, of course, why
he constantly seeks new grooms. Truly, I may be doing you no favor,
though I pray to Phos that I am."

"Sounds to me like you are," Krispos said.

"I hope so." Pyrrhos made the sun-sign again, which puzzled Krispos.
Pyrrhos hesitated, then went on, "In justice, there is one other thing of
which I should warn you: Iakovitzes is said sometimes to seek, ah, services
from his grooms other than caring for his beasts."

"Oh." That made Krispos hesitate, too. His memory of the way
Iakovitzes had touched him was inextricably joined to the mortification
he'd known on that Midwinter's Day when the villagers poked fun at him
and Idalkos. "I don't have any leanings that way myself," he said carefully.
"But if he pushes too hard, I suppose I can always quit—I'd be no worse
off then than if I hadn't met you."

"What you say has a measure of truth in it," Pyrrhos said. "Very well,
then, if it is your wish, I will take you to meet Iakovitzes."

"Let's go!" Krispos leaped to his feet.

The abbot stayed seated. "Not quite at this instant," he said, his voice
dry. "Iakovitzes may occasionally go to bed in the ninth hour of the night,

but I assure you he is not in the habit of rising at this time. If we went to his home now, we *would* be turned away from his door, most likely with dogs."

"I forgot what time it was," Krispos said sheepishly.

"Go back to the common room. Sleep the rest of the night there. When morning comes, we will visit my cousin, I promise you." Pyrrhos yawned. "I may even try for a little more sleep myself, assuming I don't get thrown out of bed again."

"Holy sir?" Krispos asked, but the abbot did not explain.

Chapter IV

IAKOVITZES' HOUSE WAS LARGE BUT, FROM THE OUTSIDE, NOT otherwise impressive. Only a few windows interrupted the long white-washed front that faced the street. They were too narrow to let in any thief, no matter how young or skinny.

A second story stood above the first, and overhung it by three or four feet. In summer, that would have created shade; now, with the rain coming down again, it kept Krispos and Pyrrhos from getting any wetter as the abbot seized the horseshoe that served for a knocker and pounded it against Iakovitzes' stout front door.

A servant opened a little grillwork in the center of the door and peered through it. "Abbot Pyrrhos!" he said. Krispos heard him lift the bar. The door opened outward a moment later. "Come in, holy sir, and your friend as well."

Just inside the doorway lay a mat of woven straw. Pyrrhos stopped to wipe his muddy sandals on it before he walked down the hall. Admiring the wit of whoever had come up with such a useful device, Krispos imitated the abbot.

"Have you breakfasted, holy sir?" the servant asked.

"On monastery fare," Pyrrhos said. "That suits me well enough, but I daresay Krispos here would be grateful for a bit more. In any case, it is on his behalf that I have come to visit your master."

"I see. Krispos, you say his name is? Very well. Wait here, if you please. I'll have something sent him from the kitchen and will inform Iakovitzes directly."

"Thank you," Pyrrhos said. Krispos said nothing. He was too busy staring. "Here"—Iakovitzes' waiting room—was the most magnificent place he had ever seen. The floor was a mosaic, a hunting scene with men spearing boars from horseback. Krispos had seen mosaic work once before, in the dome of Phos' temple at Imbros. Never in his wildest dreams had he imagined anyone save perhaps the Avtokrator possessing a mosaic of his own.

The waiting room opened onto a courtyard that seemed about the size of the village square Krispos had so recently left. In the center stood a horse, frozen in mid-rear. Krispos needed a moment to realize it was a statue. Around it were patterned rows of hedges and flowers, though most of the blooms had already fallen because the season was so late. A marble fountain plashed just outside the waiting room, as happily as if rain had never been invented.

"Here you are, sir." The view so enthralled Krispos that the young man at his elbow might have spoken two or three times before he noticed. When he turned with a stammered apology, the servant handed him a covered silver tray. "Lobster tail in cream sauce, with parsnips and squash. I hope that suits you, sir."

"What? Oh. Yes. Of course. Thank you." Noticing he was babbling, Krispos shut up. So far as he could remember, no one had ever called him "sir" before. Now this fellow had done it twice in about as many sentences.

When he lifted the lid, the delicious aroma that floated up from the tray drove such maunderings out of his mind. The lobster tasted even better than it smelled, which amazed him all over again. It was sweeter than pork and more delicate than veal, and he could only regret that it disappeared so fast. Iakovitzes' cook knew more about what to do with squash and parsnips than any of the village women had, too.

He had just set down the tray and was licking cream sauce off his mustache when Iakovitzes came into the waiting room. "Hello, Pyrrhos." He held out his hand for the abbot's clasp. "What brings you here so early, and who's this stalwart young chap you have with you?" His eyes walked up and down Krispos.

"You've met him before, cousin," Pyrrhos said.

"Have I? Then I'd best arrange a guardian to oversee my affairs, for my memory is plainly not what it was." Iakovitzes clapped a hand to his forehead in melodramatic despair. He waved Pyrrhos and Krispos to a couch and sat down himself in a chair close to Krispos. He pulled it closer yet. "Explain to me, then, if you would, my evident decline into senility."

Pyrrhos was either long used to Iakovitzes' histrionics or, perhaps more likely, without enough sense of humor to react much to them. "Krispos here was a great deal younger then," the abbot explained. "He was the boy who stood on the platform with you to seal one of your ransoming bargains with Omurtag."

"The more I forget about those beastly trips to Kubrat, the happier I'll be." Iakovitzes paused, stroking his carefully trimmed beard while he studied Krispos again. "By Phos, I do recall!" he said. "You were a pretty boy then, and you're quite the handsome youth now. By that proud nose of yours, I'd almost guess you were a Vaspurakaner, though if you're from the northern border I don't suppose that's likely."

"My father always said his side of the family had Vaspurakaner blood," Krispos said.

Iakovitzes nodded. "It could be so; 'princes' resettled there after some old war—or some old treachery. Whether or not, the look becomes you."

Krispos did not know how to answer that, so he kept quiet. Some of the village girls had praised his looks, but never a man before.

To his relief, Iakovitzes turned back to Pyrrhos. "You were about to tell me, I expect, how and why dear Krispos here comes to be in the city instead of back at his rustic village, and also how and why that pertains to me."

Krispos saw how his sharp eyes bored into the abbot's. He also noted that Iakovitzes was not going to say anything of consequence until he heard Pyrrhos' story. He thought better of him for it; whatever Iakovitzes' taste in pleasures, the man was no fool.

The abbot told the tale as Krispos had given it to him, then carried it forward. His explanation of how he had come to call for Krispos in the monastery was vague. Krispos had thought so the night before. Iakovitzes, however, was in a position to call Pyrrhos on it. "I don't follow you there," he said. "Back up and tell me just how that happened."

Pyrrhos looked harassed. "Only if I have your vow by the lord with the great and good mind to let the story go no further—and yours as well, Krispos." Krispos swore the oath; after a moment, Iakovitzes did, too. "Very well, then," the abbot said heavily. He told of his three dreams of the night before, and of ending up on the floor after the last one.

Silence filled the waiting room when he was done. Iakovitzes broke it, asking, "And you think this means—what?"

"I wish I knew," Pyrrhos burst out. He sounded as exasperated as he looked. "That it is a sending, I think no one could deny. But whether it is for good or evil, from Phos or Skotos or neither, I would not begin to guess. I can only say that in some way quite unapparent to me, Krispos here is more remarkable than he seems."

"He seems remarkable enough, though perhaps not in the way you mean," Iakovitzes said with a smile. "So you brought him to me, eh, cousin, to fulfill your dream's commandment to treat him like a son? I suppose I should be flattered—unless you think your dream does bode ill and are not letting on."

"No. No priest of Phos could do such a thing without yielding his soul to the certainty of Skotos' ice," Pyrrhos said.

Iakovitzes steepled his fingertips. "I suppose not." He turned his smile, charming and cynical at the same time, on Krispos. "So, young man, now that you are here—for good or ill—what would you?"

"I came to Videssos the city for work," Krispos said slowly. "The abbot tells me you're hiring grooms. I've lived on a farm all my life but for the last couple of weeks. You won't find many city-raised folk better with beasts than I am."

"There is probably a good deal of truth in that." Iakovitzes raised an eyebrow. "Did my cousin the most holy abbot"—he spoke with such fulsome sincerity that the praise sounded like sarcasm—"also, ah, warn you that I sometimes seek more from my grooms than skill with animals alone?"

"Yes," Krispos said flatly, then kept still.

Finally, Iakovitzes prompted him: "And so?"

"Sir, if that's what you want from me, I expect you'll be able to find it elsewhere with less trouble. I do thank you for the breakfast, and for your time. Thank you as well, holy sir," Krispos added for Pyrrhos' benefit as he stood to go.

"Don't be hasty." Iakovitzes jumped to his feet, too. "I *do* need grooms, as a matter of fact. Suppose I take you on with no requirement past caring for the beasts, with room and board and—hmm—a goldpiece a week."

"You pay the others two," Pyrrhos said.

"Dear cousin, I thought you priests reckoned silence a virtue," Iakovitzes said. It was the sweetest snarl Krispos had heard. Iakovitzes turned back to him. "Very well, then, two goldpieces a week, though you lacked the wit to ask for them yourself."

"Just the beasts?" Krispos said.

"Just the beasts"—Iakovitzes sighed—"though you must not hold it against me if from time to time I try to find out whether you've changed your mind."

"Will *you* hold it against *me* if I keep saying no?"

Iakovitzes sighed again. "I suppose not."

"Then we've got ourselves a bargain." Krispos stuck out his hand. It almost swallowed Iakovitzes', though the smaller man's grip was surprisingly strong.

"Gomaris!" Iakovitzes shouted. The man who had let in Krispos and Pyrrhos appeared a moment later, panting a little. "Gomaris, Krispos will be one of the grooms from now on. Why don't you find him some clothes better than those rags he has on and then get him settled in with the rest of the lads?"

"Of course. Come along, Krispos, and welcome to the household." Gomaris waited till he was halfway down the hall, then added softly, "Whatever else it is around here, it's rarely dull."

"That," said Krispos, "I believe."

"HERE COMES THE FARM BOY."

Krispos heard the whisper as he came into the stable. By the way Barses and Meletios sniggered at each other, he had been meant to hear. He scowled. They were both younger than he, but they were also from the city, and from families of more than a little wealth. So were most of Iakovitzes' grooms. They seemed to enjoy making Krispos' life miserable.

Barses took a shovel off the wall and thrust it at Krispos. "Here you are, farm boy. Since you've lived with manure all your life, you can clean out the stalls today. You're used to smelling like the hind end of a horse." His handsome face split in a wide, mocking grin.

"It's not my turn to shovel out today," Krispos said shortly.

"Oh, but we think you should do it anyway," Barses said. "Don't we, Meletios?" The other groom nodded. He was even handsomer than Barses; almost pretty, in fact.

"No," Krispos said.

Barses' eyes went wide in feigned surprise. "The farm boy grows insolent. I think we'll have to teach him a lesson."

"So we will," Meletios said. Smiling in anticipation, he stepped toward Krispos. "I wonder how fast farm boys learn. I've heard they're not too bright."

Krispos' frown deepened. He'd known for a week that the hazing he'd been sweating out would turn physical sooner or later. He'd thought he was ready—but two against one wasn't how he'd wanted it to happen. He held up a hand. "Wait!" he said in a high, alarmed voice. "I'll clean 'em. Give me the shovel."

Barses held it out. His face showed an interesting mix of amusement, triumph, and contempt. "You'd best do a good job, too, farm boy, or we'll make you lick up whatever you—"

Krispos snatched the shovel from his hands, whirled, and rammed the handle into the pit of Meletios' stomach. The groom closed up on himself like a bellows, gasping uselessly for air.

Krispos threw the shovel aside. "Come on!" he snarled at Barses. "Or aren't you as good with your hands as you are with your mouth?"

"You'll see, farm boy!" Barses sprang at him. He was strong and fearless and knew something of what he was doing, but he'd never been through anything like the course in nasty fighting Krispos had taken from Idalkos. In less than two minutes he was down in the straw beside Meletios, groaning and trying to hold his knee, his groin, his ribs, and a couple of dislocated fingers, all at the same time.

Krispos stood over the other two grooms, breathing hard. One of his eyes was half closed and a collarbone had gotten a fearful whack, but he'd dished out a lot more than he'd taken. He picked up the shovel and tossed it between Meletios and Barses. "You can shovel out for yourselves."

Meletios grabbed the shovel and started to swing it at Krispos' ankles. Krispos stamped on his hand. Meletios shrieked and let go. Krispos kicked him in the ribs with force nicely calculated to yield maximum hurt and minimum permanent damage. "Come to think of it, Meletios, you do the shoveling today. You just earned it."

Even through his pain, Meletios let out an indignant squawk and cast a look of appeal toward Barses.

The other groom was just sitting up. He shook his head, then grimaced as he regretted the motion. "I'm not going to argue with him, Meletios, and if you have any sense, you won't, either." He managed a lopsided grin. "Nobody with any sense is going to argue with Krispos, not after today."

THE HARASSMENT DID NOT DISAPPEAR. WITH A DOZEN GROOMS ranging from their mid-teens up to Krispos' age, and all living in one another's pockets, that would hardly have been possible. But after Krispos dealt with Barses and Meletios, he was accepted as one of the group and got to hand it out as well as take it.

Not only that, he got himself listened to, where before the other grooms had paid no attention to what he thought. Thus when they were hashing over the best way to treat a horse with a mild but stubborn fever, one of them turned to Krispos and asked, "What would you have done about this in that backwoods place you came from?"

"The green forage is all very well," he said after a little thought, "and the wet, sloppy food and gruel, but we always said there was nothing like beer to speed things along."

"Beer?" The grooms whooped.

Barses asked, "For us or the animal?"

Krispos laughed, too, but said, "For the animal. A bucket or three ought to do the job."

"He means it," Meletios said in surprise. He turned thoughtful. He was all business where horses were concerned. Iakovitzes tolerated no groom who was not, whatever other charms he might have. In a musing tone, Meletios went on, "What say we try it? I don't see how it could do any harm."

So a couple of buckets of beer went into the horse's trough every morning, and if the grooms bought a bit more than the sick animal really needed, why, only they knew about that. And after a few days, the horse's condition did improve: his breathing slowed, his eyes brightened, and his skin and mouth lost the dry look and feel they'd had while he was ill.

"Well done," Barses said when the horse was clearly on the mend. "Next time I take a fever, you know what to do with me, though I'd sooner have wine, I think." Krispos threw a clod of dirt at him.

Iakovitzes had watched the treatment with as much interest as any of the grooms. When it succeeded, he handed Krispos a goldpiece. "And come sup with me this evening, if you care to," he said, his sharp voice as smooth as he could make it.

"Thank you very much, sir," Krispos said.

Meletios sulked for the rest of the day. Krispos finally asked him what was wrong. He glared. "If I told you I was jealous, you'd probably beat on me again."

"Jealous?" Krispos needed a few seconds to catch on. "Oh! Don't worry about that. I only fancy girls."

"So you say," Meletios answered darkly. "But Iakovitzes fancies you."

Krispos snorted and went back to work. Around sunset, he walked over to Iakovitzes' main house. This was the first meal he'd eaten there since his breakfast of lobster tail; the grooms had their own dining hall. Like as not, he thought, Meletios was fretting over nothing; if some big banquet was planned, Krispos might not even be at the same table as his master.

As soon as Gomaris led him to a chamber large enough only for two, Krispos knew Meletios had been right and he himself wrong. A small lamp on the table left most of the room in twilight. "Hello, Krispos," Iakovitzes said, rising to greet him. "Here, have some wine."

He poured with his own hand. Krispos was used to the rough vintages the villagers had made for themselves. What Iakovitzes gave him slid down his throat like a smooth whisper. He would have thought it mere grape juice but for the warmth it left in his middle.

"Another cup?" Iakovitzes asked solicitously. "I'd like the chance to toast you for your cleverness in dosing Stormbreeze. The beast seems in fine fettle again, thanks to you."

Iakovitzes raised his cup in salute. Krispos knew drinking too much with his master was not a good idea, but had no polite way to do anything else. The wine was so good, he scarcely felt guilty about soaking it up.

Gomaris fetched in supper, a platter of halibut grilled with garlic and leeks. The herbs' sharp flavors reminded Krispos of his home, but the only fish he'd had there was an occasional trout or carp taken from a stream, hardly worth mentioning beside a delicacy like this. "Delicious," he mumbled in one of the few moments when his mouth was not full.

"Glad you enjoy it," Iakovitzes said. "We have a proverb hereabouts: 'If you come to Videssos the city, eat fish.' At least this fish is to your liking."

After the fish came smoked partridges, one little bird apiece, and, after the partridges, plums and figs candied in honey. The grooms ate well enough, but not fare like this. Krispos knew he was stuffing himself. He found he did not care; after all, Iakovitzes had invited him here to eat.

His master rose to fill his cup again, then sent him a reproachful look when he saw its contents hardly touched. "Dear boy, you're not drinking. Does the vintage fail to suit you?"

"No, it's very good," Krispos said. "It's just that"—he groped for an excuse—"I don't want to get all sozzled and act the fool."

"A commendable attitude, but you needn't worry. I recognize that part of the pleasure of wine is not worrying so much over what one does. And pleasures, Krispos, do not come to us so often in this life that they are to be lightly despised." Remembering the troubles that had made him leave his village, Krispos found some truth in Iakovitzes' words. Iakovitzes went on, "For instance, I am sure, though you do not complain of it, that you must be worn from your toil with the horses. Let me soothe you if I can."

Before Krispos could reply, Iakovitzes hurried round behind his chair and began to massage his shoulders. He knew what he was about; Krispos felt the tension flowing out of him.

He also felt, though, the quivering eagerness Iakovitzes could not keep from his hands. He knew what that meant; he had known when he was nine years old. Not without some reluctance, he twisted in his seat so he faced Iakovitzes. "I said when you took me on that I didn't care for these games."

Iakovitzes kept his aplomb. "And I told you that wouldn't stop me from being interested. Were you like some I've known, I could offer you gold. Somehow, though, with you I don't think that would do much good. Or am I wrong?" he finished hopefully.

"You're not wrong," Krispos said at once.

"Too bad, too bad." The dim lamplight caught a spark of malice in Iakovitzes' eye. "Shall I turn you out on the street, then, for your obstinacy?"

"Whatever you like, of course." Krispos kept his voice as steady as he could. He refused to give his master such a hold on him.

Iakovitzes sighed. "That would be ungrateful of me, wouldn't it, after what you did for Stormbreeze? Have it as you wish, Krispos. But it's not as if I were offering you anything vile. Many enjoy it."

"I'm sure that's true, sir." Krispos thought of Meletios. "I just don't happen to be one of those folk."

"Too bad," Iakovitzes said. "Here, have some more wine anyhow. We might as well finish the jar."

"Why not?" Krispos drank another cup; it was too good to decline. Then he yawned and said, "It must be late. I'd best get back to my own chamber if I'm going to be worth anything in the morning."

"I suppose so," Iakovitzes said indifferently—one hour was as good as another to him. When he tried to kiss Krispos good night, Krispos thought he made his sidestep seem completely natural until he saw his master raise an ironic eyebrow.

After that, Krispos retreated in some haste. To his surprise, he found Barses and a couple of the other grooms waiting up for him. "Well?" Barses said.

"Well, what?" Krispos set himself. If Barses wanted revenge for their fight, he might get it. Three against one, in fact, just about guaranteed he would.

But that was not what Barses had in mind. "Well, you and Iakovitzes, of course. Did you? No shame to you if you did—the only reason I want to know is that I have a bet."

"Which way?"

"I won't tell you that. If you say it's none of my business, the bet waits until Iakovitzes makes things clear one way or the other. He will, you know."

Krispos was sure of that. The wine he'd drunk weakened whatever urge he had to keep the evening a secret. "No, we didn't," he said. "I like girls too well to be interested in the sports he enjoys."

Barses grinned and clapped him on the back, then turned to one of the other grooms with his palm up. "Pay me that goldpiece, Agrabast. I told you he wouldn't." Agrabast gave him the coin. "Next question," Barses said. "Did he toss you out for turning him down?"

"No. He thought about it, but he didn't."

"Good thing I didn't let you double the bet for that, Barses," Agrabast said. "Iakovitzes loves his beasts about as well as he loves his prick. He wouldn't throw away anybody who'd shown he knew something about horseleeching."

"I figured that out," Barses said. "I was hoping you hadn't."

"Well, to the ice with you," Agrabast retorted.

"To the ice with all of you, if you don't get out of my way and let me have some sleep." Krispos started to push past the other grooms, then stopped and added, "Meletios can stop worrying now."

Everyone laughed. When the chuckles died down, though, Barses said, "You *are* from the country, Krispos; maybe we look at things a little different from you. I meant what I said before—there'd be no shame in saying yes to Iakovitzes, and Meletios isn't the only one of us who has."

"I never said he was," Krispos answered. "But as far as I can see, he's the only one who's put some worry into it. So now he can stop."

"That's fair enough, I suppose," Barses said judiciously.

"Whether it is or whether it's not, out of my way before I fall asleep where I'm standing." Krispos made as if to advance on the other grooms. Laughing again, they moved aside to let him by.

ALL WINTER LONG, IAKOVITZES CAST LONGING LOOKS KRIS-pos' way. All winter long, Krispos pretended he did not see them. He tended his master's horses. Iakovitzes usually took along a groom when he went to a feast, Krispos as often as anyone else. And when he feasted other nobles in turn, all the grooms attended so he could show them off.

At first, Krispos viewed the Empire's nobility with the same awe he had given Videssos the city when he was just arrived. His awe for the nobles soon wore off. He found they were men like any others, some clever, some plain, some downright stupid. As Barses said of one, "It's a good thing for him he inherited his money, because he'd never figure out how to make any on his own."

By contrast, the more Krispos explored the city, the more marvelous he found it. Every alleyway had something new: an apothecary's stall, perhaps, or a temple to Phos so small only a double handful of worshipers could use it.

Even streets he knew well gave him new people to see: swarthy Makuraners in caftans and felt pillbox hats, big blond Halogai gaping at Videssos just as he had, stocky Kubratoi in furs. Krispos kept his distance from them; he could not help wondering if any had been among the riders who'd kidnapped him and his family or plundered the village north of the mountains.

And there were the Videssians themselves, the people of the city: brash, bumptious, loud, cynical, nothing like the farm folk among whom he'd grown up.

"To the ice with you, you blithering, bungling booby!" a shopkeeper shouted at an artisan one afternoon. "This pane of glass I ordered is half a foot too short!"

"Up yours, too, friend." The glassblower pulled out a scrap of parchment. "That's what I thought: seventeen by twenty-two. That's what you ordered, that's what I made. You can't measure, don't blame me." He was yelling, too. A crowd began to gather. People poked their heads out of windows to see what was going on.

The shopkeeper snatched the parchment out of his hand. "I didn't write this!"

"It didn't write itself, friend."

The glassblower tried to snatch it back. The shopkeeper jerked it away. They stood nose to nose, screaming at each other and waving their fists. "Shouldn't we get between them before they pull knives?" Krispos said to the man beside him.

"And wreck the show? Are you crazy?" By the fellow's tone, he thought Krispos was. After a moment, he grudgingly went on, "They won't go at it. They'll just yell till it's out of their systems, then go on about their business. You wait and see."

The local proved right. Krispos would have admitted it, but the man hadn't stayed to see the results of his prediction. After things calmed down, Krispos left, too, shaking his head. His home village hadn't been like this at all.

He was almost to Iakovitzes' house when he saw a pretty girl. She smiled when he caught her eye, strode up to him bold as brass. His home village hadn't been like that, either.

Then she said, "A piece of silver and I'm yours for the afternoon; three and I'm yours for the whole night, too." She ran her hand along his arm. Her nails and lips were painted the same shade of red.

"Sorry," Krispos answered. "I don't feel like paying for it."

She looked him up and down, then gave a regretful shrug. "No, I don't expect you'd need to very often. Too bad. I would've enjoyed it more with someone who didn't *have* to buy." But when she saw he meant his no, she walked on down the street, swinging her hips. Like most people in the city, she didn't waste time where she had no hope of profit.

Krispos turned his head and watched her till she rounded a corner. He decided not to go back to Iakovitzes' right away after all. It was too late for lunch, too early for supper or serious drinking. That meant a certain pert little barmaid he knew ought to be able to slip away for—for just long enough, he thought, grinning.

Snow gave way to sleet, which in turn yielded to rain. By the standards Krispos used to judge, Videssos the city had a mild winter. Even so, he was glad to see spring return. Iakovitzes' horses were, too. They cropped the tender new grass till their dung came thin and green. Shoveling it made Krispos less delighted with the season.

One fine morning when such shoveling was someone else's concern, he started out on an errand of his own—not the little barmaid, with whom he had broken up, but a more than reasonable substitute. He opened Iakovitzes' front door, then drew back in surprise. What looked like a parade was coming up to the house.

The city folk loved parades, so this one, not surprisingly, had a fair-sized crowd around it. Krispos needed a moment to see that at its heart were bearers with—he counted quickly—eleven silk parasols. The Avtokrator of Videssos rated only one more.

As Krispos realized who Iakovitzes' visitor had to be, a gorgeously robed servitor detached himself from the head of the procession. He declared, "Forth comes his illustrious Highness the Sevastokrator Petronas to call upon your master Iakovitzes. Be so good, fellow, as to announce him."

Properly, that was Gomaris' job. Krispos fled without worrying about such niceties. If the Emperor's uncle wanted something done, niceties did not matter.

By luck, Iakovitzes was up and about and had even finished breakfast. He frowned when Krispos burst into the waiting room where he was having a second cup of wine. When Krispos gasped out the news, he frowned again, in a very different way.

"Oh, plague! This place looks like a sty. Well, it can't be helped, not if Petronas wants to show up before anyone's awake." Iakovitzes gulped his wine and fixed Krispos with a glare. "What are you doing just standing around? Go tell his illustrious Highness I'm delighted to receive him—and any other sweet lies you can think up on the way."

Krispos dashed back to the door, expecting to relay the polite message to the Sevastokrator's man. Instead, he almost ran head-on into Petronas himself. Petronas' robe, of crimson shot with gold and silver thread, made his servant's shabby by comparison.

"Careful, there; don't hurt yourself," the Sevastokrator said, chuckling, as Krispos almost fell over himself trying to stop, bow, and go to his right knee all at once.

"H-highness," Krispos stammered. "My master is d-delighted to receive you."

"Not this early, he isn't." Petronas' voice was dry.

From his perch on one knee, Krispos glanced up at the most powerful man in the Empire of Videssos. The images he'd seen back in his village hadn't suggested that the Sevastokrator owned a sense of humor. They also made him out to be a few years younger than he was; Krispos guessed he was past fifty rather than nearing it. But his true features conveyed the same sense of confident competence as had his portraits.

Now he reached out to tap Krispos on the shoulder. "Come on, young fellow, take me to him. What's your name, anyhow?"

"Krispos, Highness," Krispos said as he got to his feet. "This way, if you please."

Petronas fell into step with him. "Krispos, while I'm engaged with your master, can you see to it that my retinue gets some wine, and maybe cheese or bread, as well? Just standing there and waiting for me to finish is boring duty for them."

"I'll take care of it," Krispos promised.

Iakovitzes, he saw as he led the Sevastokrator into the waiting room, had slipped into a new robe himself. It was also crimson, but not so deep and rich a shade as Petronas'. Moreover, while Iakovitzes still wore sandals, Petronas had on a pair of black boots with red trim. Only Anthimos was entitled to boots scarlet from top to toe.

When Krispos stuck his head into the kitchen with word of what Petronas wanted, the cook who had fixed Iakovitzes' breakfast yelped in dismay. Then he started slicing onion rolls and hard cheese like a man possessed. He shouted for someone to give him a hand.

Krispos filled wine cups—cheap earthenware cups, not the crystal and silver and gold from which Iakovitzes' fancy guests drank—and set them on trays. Other servants whisked them away to Petronas' men. Having done his duty, Krispos slipped out a side door to go meet his girl.

"You're late," she said crossly.

"I'm sorry, Sirikia." He kissed her, to show how sorry he was. "Just as I was leaving to see you, Petronas the Sevastokrator came to visit my master, and they needed my help for a little while." He hoped she would imagine more intimate help than standing in the kitchen pouring wine.

Evidently she did, for her annoyance vanished. "I met the Sevastokrator once," she told Krispos. She was just a seamstress. Though he would not have said so out loud, he doubted her until she proudly explained: "On Midwinter's Day a couple of years ago, he pinched my bottom."

"Anything can happen on Midwinter's Day," he agreed soberly. He smiled at her. "I thought Petronas was a man of good taste."

She thought that over for a moment, blinked, and threw her arms around his neck. "Oh, Krispos, you say the sweetest things!" The rest of the morning passed most enjoyably.

Gomaris spotted Krispos on his way back to the grooms' quarters that afternoon. "Not so fast," the steward said. "Iakovitzes wants to see you."

"Why? He knows this was my morning off."

"He didn't tell me why. He just told me to look out for you. Now I've found you. He's in the small waiting room—you know, the one next to his bedchamber."

Wondering what sort of trouble he was in, and hoping his master *did* remember he'd had the morning free, Krispos hurried to the waiting room. Iakovitzes was sitting behind a small table with several thick scrolls of parchment, looking for all the world like a tax collector. At the moment, his scowl made him look like a tax collector visiting a village badly in arrears.

"Oh, it's you," he said as Krispos walked in. "About time. Go pack."

Krispos gulped. "Sir?" Of all the things he'd expected, being so baldly ordered to hit the streets was the last. "What did I do, sir? Can I make amends for it?"

"What *are* you talking about?" Iakovitzes said peevishly. After a few seconds, his face cleared. "No, you don't know what I'm talking about. It seems there's some sort of squabble going on between our people and the Khatrishers over who owns a stretch of land between two little streams north of the town of Opsikion. The local eparch can't make the Khatrishers see sense—but then, trying to dicker with Khatrishers'd drive Skotos mad. Petronas doesn't want this mess blowing up into a border war. He's sending me to Opsikion to try to make sense of it."

The explanation left Krispos as confused as before. "What does that have to do with me packing?"

"You're coming with me."

Krispos opened his mouth, then closed it again when he discovered he had nothing worthwhile to say. This would be travel on far more comfortable terms than the slog from his village to Videssos the city. Once he got to Opsikion, he could also hope to learn a good deal about what Iakovitzes was doing and how he did it. The more he learned, he was discovering, the more possibilities opened up in his life.

On the other hand, Iakovitzes would surely use the trip as one long chance to try to get him into bed. He had trouble gauging just how big a nuisance that would be, or how annoyed Iakovitzes might get when he kept saying no.

An opportunity, a likelihood of trouble. As far as he could tell, they balanced. He certainly had no other good options, so he said, "Very well, excellent sir. I'll pack at once."

T HE ROAD DIPPED ONE LAST TIME. SUDDENLY, INSTEAD OF MOUNtains and trees all around, Krispos saw ahead of him hills dipping swiftly toward the blue sea. Where land and water met stood Opsikion, its red tile roofs glowing in the sun. He reined in his horse to admire the view.

Iakovitzes came up beside him. He also stopped. "Well, that's very pretty, isn't it?" he said. He let go of the reins with his right hand. As if by accident, it fell on Krispos' thigh.

"Yes, it is," Krispos said, sighing. He dug his heels into his horse's flanks. It started forward, almost at a trot.

Also sighing, Iakovitzes followed. "You are the most stubborn man I've ever wanted," he said, his voice tight with irritation.

Krispos did not answer. If Iakovitzes wanted to see stubbornness, he thought, all he needed to do was peer at his reflection in a stream. In the month they'd taken to ride east from Videssos the city to Opsikion, he'd tried seducing Krispos every night and most afternoons. That he'd got nowhere did not stop him; neither did the several times he'd bedded other, more complacent, partners.

Iakovitzes pulled alongside again. "If I didn't find you so lovely, curse it, I'd break you for your obstinacy," he snapped. "Don't push me too far. I might anyhow."

Krispos had no doubt Iakovitzes meant what he said. As he had before, he laughed. "I was a peasant taxed off my farm. How could you break me any lower than that?" As long as Iakovitzes knew he was not afraid of such threats, Krispos thought, the peppery little man would hesitate before he acted on them.

So it proved now. Iakovitzes fumed but subsided. They rode together toward Opsikion.

As they were in none-too-clean travelers' clothes, the gate guards paid no more attention to them than to anyone else. They waited while the guards poked swords into bales of wool a fuzzy-bearded Khatrisher merchant was bringing to town, making sure he wasn't smuggling anything inside them. The merchant's face was so perfectly innocent that Krispos suspected him on general principles.

Iakovitzes did not take kindly to waiting. "Here, you?" he called to one of the guards in peremptory tones. "Stop messing about with that fellow and see to us."

The guard set hands on hips and looked Iakovitzes over. "And why should I, small stuff?" Without waiting for a reply, he started to turn back to what he'd been doing.

"Because, you insolent, ill-smelling, pock-faced lout, I am the direct representative of his illustrious Highness the Sevastokrator Petronas and of his Imperial Majesty the Avtokrator Anthimos III, come to this miserable latrine trench of a town to settle matters your eparch has botched, bungled, and generally mishandled."

Iakovitzes bit off each word with savage relish. As he spoke, he unrolled and displayed the large parchment that proved he was what he claimed. It was daubed with seals in several colors of wax and bore the Avtokrator's signature in appallingly official scarlet ink.

The gate guard went from furious red to terrified white in the space of three heartbeats. "Sorry, Brison," he muttered to the wool merchant. "You've just got to hang on for a bit."

"Now there's a fine kettle of crabs," Brison said in a lisping accent. "Maybe I'll pass the time mixing my horses around so you won't be sure which ones you've checked." He grinned to see how the gate guard liked that idea.

"Oh, go to the ice," the harassed guard said. Brison laughed out loud. Ignoring him, the guard turned to Iakovitzes. "I—I crave pardon for my rough tongue, excellent sir. How may I help you?"

"Better." Iakovitzes nodded. "I won't ask for your name after all. Tell me how to reach the eparch's residence. Then you can go back to your petty games with this chap here. I suggest that while you're at it, you sword his beard as well as his wool."

Brison laughed again, quite merrily. The gate guard stuttered out directions. Iakovitzes rode past them. He kept his eyes straight ahead, not deigning to acknowledge either man any further. Krispos followed.

"I put that arrogant bastard in chain mail in his place nicely enough," Iakovitzes said once he and Krispos got into town, "but Khatrishers are too light-minded to notice when they've been insulted. Cheeky buggers, the lot of them." Failing to get under someone's skin always annoyed him. He swore softly as he rode down Opsikion's main street.

Krispos paid his master little attention; he was resigned to his bad temper. Opsikion interested him more. It was a little larger than Imbros; a year ago, he thought, it would have seemed enormous to him. After Videssos, it reminded him of a toy city, small but perfect. Even Phos' temple in the central square was modeled after the great High Temple of the capital.

The eparch's hall was across the square from the temple. Iakovitzes took out his frustration over leaving Brison in good spirits by baiting a clerk as mercilessly as he had the gate guard. His tactics were cruel, but also effective. Moments later, the clerk ushered him and Krispos into the eparch's office.

The local governor was a thin, sour-looking man named Sisinnios. "So you've come to dicker with the Khatrishers, have you?" he said when Iakovitzes presented his impressive scroll. "May you get more joy from it than I have. These days, my belly starts paining me the day before I talk with 'em and doesn't let up for three days afterward."

"What's the trouble, exactly?" Iakovitzes asked. "I presume we have documents to prove the land in question is ours by right?" Though he phrased it as a question, he spoke with the same certainty he would have used in reciting Phos' creed. Krispos sometimes thought nothing really existed in Videssos without a document to show it was there.

When Sisinnios rolled his eyes, the dark bags under them made him look like a mournful hound. "Oh, we have documents," he agreed morosely. "Getting the Khatrishers to pay 'em any mind is something else again."

"*I'll* fix *that*," Iakovitzes promised. "Does this place boast a decent inn?"

"Bolkanes' is probably the best," Sisinnios said. "It's not far." He gave directions.

"Good. Krispos, go set us up with rooms there. Now, sir"—this he directed to Sisinnios—"let's see these documents. And set me up a meeting with this Khatrisher who ignores them."

Bolkanes' inn proved good enough, and by the standards of Videssos the city absurdly cheap. Taking Iakovitzes literally, Krispos rented separate rooms for his master and himself. He knew Iakovitzes would be irked, but did not feel like guarding himself every minute of every night.

Indeed, Iakovitzes did grumble when he came to the inn a couple of hours later and discovered the arrangements Krispos had made. The grumble, though, was an abstracted one; most of his mind remained on the fat folder of documents he carried under one arm. He took negotiations seriously.

"You'll have to amuse yourself as best you can for a while, Krispos," he said as they sat down to a dinner of steamed prawns in mustard sauce. "Phos alone knows how long I'm liable to be closeted with this Lexo from Khatrish. If he's as bad as Sisinnios makes him out to be, maybe forever."

"If you please sir," Krispos said hesitantly, "may I join you at your talks?"

Iakovitzes paused with a prawn in midair. "Why on earth would you want to do that?" His eyes narrowed. No Videssian noble trusted what he did not understand.

"To learn what I can," Krispos answered. "Please remember, sir, I'm but a couple of seasons away from my village. Most of your other grooms know much more than I do, just because they've lived in Videssos the city all their lives. I ought to take whatever chances I have to pick up useful things to know."

"Hmm." That watchful expression did not leave Iakovitzes' face. "You're apt to be bored."

"If I am, I'll leave."

"Hmm," Iakovitzes said again, and then, "Well, why not? I'd thought you content with the horses, but if you think you're fit for more, no harm in your trying. Who can say? It may turn out to my advantage as well as yours." Now Iakovitzes looked calculating, a look Krispos knew well. One of the noble's eyebrows quirked upward as he went on, "I didn't bring you here with that in mind, however."

"I know." Krispos was beginning to learn to keep his own maneuvers hidden. Now his thoughts were that, if he made himself useful enough to Iakovitzes in other ways, the noble might give up on coaxing him into bed.

"We'll see how it goes," Iakovitzes said. "Sisinnios is setting up the meeting with the Khatrisher for around the third hour of the day tomorrow—halfway between sunrise and noon." He smiled a smile Krispos had seen even more often than his calculating look. "Reading by lamplight gives me a headache. I can think of a better way to spend the night . . ."

Krispos sighed. Iakovitzes hadn't given up yet.

SISINNIOS SAID, "EXCELLENCY, I PRESENT TO YOU LEXO, WHO represents Gumush the khagan of Khatrish. Lexo, here is the most eminent Iakovitzes from Videssos the city, and his spatharios Krispos."

The title the eparch gave Krispos was the vaguest one in the Videssian hierarchy; it literally meant "sword bearer," and by extension "aide." An Avtokrator's spatharios might be a very important man. A noble's spatharios was not. Krispos was grateful to hear it all the same. Sisinnios could have introduced him as a groom and let it go at that.

"And now, noble sirs, if you will excuse me, I have other business to which I must attend," the eparch said. He left a little more quickly than was polite, but with every sign of relief.

Lexo the Khatrisher was dressed in what would have been a stylish linen tunic but for the leaping stags and panthers embroidered over every inch of it. "I've heard of you, eminent sir," he told Iakovitzes, bowing in his seat. His beard and mustaches were so full and bushy that Krispos could hardly see his lips move. Among Videssians, such unkempt whiskers were only for priests.

"You have the advantage of me, sir." Iakovitzes would not let a foreigner outdo him in courtesy. "I am willing to assume, however, that any emissary of your khagan is sure to be a most able man."

"You are too gracious to someone you do not know," Lexo purred. His gaze swung to Krispos. "So, young fellow, you're Iakovitzes' spatharios, are you? Tell me, just where do you bear that sword of his?"

The Khatrisher's smile was bland. Even so, Krispos jerked as if stung. For a moment, all he could think of was wiping the floor with Lexo, who was more than twice his age and weighed more than he did though several inches shorter. But months of living with Iakovitzes had taught him the game was not always played with fists. Doing his best to pull his face straight, he answered, "Against his foes, and the Avtokrator's." He looked Lexo in the eye.

"Your sentiments do you credit, I'm sure," Lexo murmured. He turned back to Iakovitzes. "Well, eminent sir, how do you propose to settle what his excellency the good Sisinnios and I have been haggling over for months?"

"By looking at the facts instead of haggling." Iakovitzes leaned forward, discarding formal ways like a cast-off cloak. He touched the folder the eparch had given him. "The facts are here, you will agree. I have here copies of all documents pertaining to the border between Videssos and

Khatrish for as long as your state has been such, rather than merely nomad bandits too ignorant to sign a treaty and too treacherous to honor one. The latter trait, I notice, you still display."

Krispos waited for Lexo to explode, but the envoy's smile did not waver. "I'd heard you were charming," he said evenly.

Just as he was armored against insult, so was Iakovitzes against irony. "I don't care what you've heard, sir. I've heard—these documents say, loud and clear—that the proper frontier between our lands is the Akkilaion River, not the Mnizou as you have claimed. How dare you contradict them?"

"Because the memories of my people are long," Lexo said. Iakovitzes snorted. Lexo took no notice, but went on, "Memories are like leaves, you know. They pile up in the forests of our minds, and we go scuffing through them."

Iakovitzes snorted again, louder. "Very pretty. I hadn't heard Gumush was sending out poets to speak for him these days. I'd have thought their disregard for the truth disqualified them."

"You flatter me for my poor words," Lexo said. "Should you desire true poetry, I will give you the tribal lays of my folk."

He began to declaim, partly in his lisping Videssian, more often in a speech that reminded Krispos of the one the Kubratoi used among themselves. He nodded, remembering that the ancestors of both Khatrishers and Kubratoi had come off the Pardrayan steppe long ago.

"I could go on for some while," Lexo said after going on for some while, "but I hope you get the gist: that the great raid of Balbad Badbal's son reached the Mnizou and drove all Videssians over it. Thus it is only just for Khatrish to claim the Mnizou as its southern boundary."

"Gumush's grandfather didn't, nor his father either," Iakovitzes replied, unmoved by his opponent's oratory. "If you stack the treaties they signed against your tribal lays, the treaties weigh heavier."

"How can any man presume to know where the balance between them lies, any more than a man can know the Balance between Phos and Skotos in the world?" Lexo said. "They both have weight; that is what Sisinnios would not see nor admit."

"Believe in the Balance and go to the ice, they teach us in Videssos," Iakovitzes said, "so I'll thank you not to drag your eastern heresy into a serious argument. Just as Phos *will* vanquish Skotos in the end, so *shall* our border be restored to its proper place, which is to say, the Akkilaion."

"Just as my doctrine is your heresy, the reverse also applies." Where his faith was questioned, Lexo lost his air of detached amusement. In a sharper voice than he'd used before, he went on, "I might also point out that the land between the Mnizou and the Akkilaion has quite as many Khatrishers herding as it does Videssians farming. The concept of the Balance seems relevant."

"Throw precedent into your cursed Balance," Iakovitzes suggested. "It will weigh down on the side of truth—the side of Videssos."

"The lay of Balbad Badbal's son, as I have *suggested*"—irony again, this time laid on heavily enough to make Iakovitzes scowl—"is precedent older than any in that stack of moldering parchments in which you set your stock."

"That lay is a lie," Iakovitzes growled.

"Sir, it is not." Lexo met Iakovitzes' glare with his own. Had they been wearing swords, they might have used those, too.

In their duel, they'd so completely forgotten about Krispos that they both stared at him when he asked, "Is age the most important thing that goes into a precedent?"

"Yes," Lexo said in the same breath Iakovitzes used to say, "No."

"If it is," Krispos went on, "shouldn't Videssos claim all of Khatrish? The Empire ruled it long before the Khatrishers' forefathers arrived there."

"Not the same thing at all—" Lexo began, while Iakovitzes burst out, "By the good god, so we—" He, too, stopped before his sentence was done. Sheepishness did not suit his sharp-featured face, but it was there. "I think we've just been whirled round on ourselves," he said, much more quietly than he had been speaking.

"Perhaps we have," Lexo admitted. "Shall we thank your spatharios for the treatment?" He nodded to Krispos. "I must also crave your pardon, young sir. I see you do have some use beyond the ornamental."

"Why, so he does." Krispos would have been happier with Iakovitzes' agreement had his master sounded less surprised.

Lexo sighed. "If you set aside your folder there, eminent sir, I will sing you no more lays."

"Oh, very well." Iakovitzes seldom yielded anything with good grace. "Now, though, I have to find some other way to make you see that those herders you spoke of will have to fare north of the Akkilaion where they belong."

"I like that." Lexo's tone said he did not like it at all. "Why shouldn't your farmers be the ones to move?"

"Because nomads are nomads, of course. It's much harder to pack up good farmland and ride away with it."

The bargaining began again, in earnest this time, now that each man had seen he could not presume too far on the other. That first session yielded no agreement, nor did the second, nor the sixth. "We'll get our answer, though," Iakovitzes said one evening back at Bolkanes' inn. "I can feel it."

"I hope so." Krispos picked at the mutton in front of him—he was tired of fish.

Iakovitzes eyed him shrewdly. "So now you *are* bored, eh? Didn't I warn you would be?"

"Maybe I am, a little," Krispos said. "I didn't expect we would be here for weeks. I thought the Sevastokrator sent you here just because Sisinnios wasn't making any progress with Lexo."

"Petronas did, Sisinnios wasn't, and I am," Iakovitzes said. "These disputes take years to develop; they don't go away overnight. What, did you expect Lexo all of a sudden to break down and concede everything on account of the brilliance of my rhetoric?"

Krispos had to smile. "Put that way, no."

"Hrmmp. You might have said yes, to salve my self-respect. But schedules for how the Khatrishers withdraw, how much we pay them to go, and whether we pay the khagan or give the money direct to the herders who will be leaving—all such things have plenty of room in them for horse trading. That's what Lexo and I are doing now, seeing who ends up with a swaybacked old nag."

"I guess so," Krispos said. "I'm afraid it's not very interesting to listen to, though."

"Go ahead and do something else for a while, then," Iakovitzes said. "I expected you to give up long before this. And you've even been useful in the dickering a couple of times, too, which I didn't expect at all. You've earned some time off."

So KRISPOS, INSTEAD OF CLOSETING HIMSELF WITH THE DIPLO-mats, went wandering through Opsikion. After those of Videssos the city, its markets seemed small and for the most part dull. The only real bargains Krispos saw were fine furs from Agder, which lay in the far northeast, near the Haloga country. He had more money now than ever before, and less to spend it on, but he could not come close to affording a snow-leopard jacket. He came back to the furriers' stall several times, to peer and to wish.

He bought a coral pendant to take back to his seamstress friend. He almost paid for it with his lucky goldpiece. Since it had stopped being his only goldpiece, he'd kept it wrapped in a bit of cloth at the bottom of his pouch. Somehow it got loose. He noticed just in time to substitute another coin.

The jeweler weighed that one to make sure it was good. When he saw it was, he shrugged. "Gold is gold," he said as he gave Krispos his change.

"Sorry," Krispos said. "I just didn't want to part with that one."

"I've had other customers tell me the same thing," the jeweler said. "If you want to make sure you don't spend it by mistake, why not wear it on a chain around your neck? Wouldn't take me long to bore through it, and here's a very nice chain. Or if you'd rather have this one . . ."

Krispos came out of the shop with the lucky goldpiece bumping against his chest under his tunic. It felt odd there for the first few days. After that, he stopped noticing he was wearing it. He even slept with it on.

By that time, Iakovitzes had lost some of his earlier optimism. "That pox-brained Khatrisher is a serpent," he complained. "Just when I think I have something settled, he throws a coil around it and drags it back into confusion."

"Do you want me to join you again?" Krispos asked.

"Eh? No, that's all right. Good of you to ask, though; you show more loyalty than most your age. You'd probably be more help if you spent the time praying for me. Phos may listen to you; that stubborn donkey of a Lexo surely won't."

Krispos knew his master was just grumbling. He went to the temple across from Sisinnios' residence just the same. Phos was the lord of the good; Videssos' case here, he was convinced, was good; how, then, could his god fail to heed him?

The crowd round the temple was thicker than he'd seen it before. When he asked a man why, the fellow chuckled and said, "Guess you're not from these parts. This is the festal day of the holy Abdaas, Opsikion's patron. We're all come to give thanks for his protection for another year."

"Oh." Along with everyone else—everyone in the whole town, he thought, as three people stepped on his toes, one after the other—Krispos filed into the temple.

He had worshiped at the High Temple in the capital several times. The sternly beautiful gaze of the mosaic image of Phos in the dome there never failed to fill him with awe. Opsikion was only a provincial town. As he was depicted here, the lord with the great and good mind looked more cross than majestic. Krispos did not much care. Phos was Phos, no matter what his image looked like.

Krispos feared, though, that he would have to pay homage to the good god standing up. The benches had all but filled by the time he got to them. The last few rows had some empty places, but the press of people swept him past them before he could claim one. He was still a villager at heart, he thought wryly; a born city man would have been quicker.

Too late—by now he was most of the way down toward the altar. With sinking hope, he peered around for some place, any place, to sit. The woman sitting by the aisle was also looking around, perhaps for a friend who was late. Their eyes met.

"Excuse me, my lady." Krispos looked away. He knew a noblewoman when he saw one, and knew better than to bother her by staring.

Thus he did not see her pupils swell till, like a cat's, each filled for a moment its whole iris, did not see her features go slack and far away in that same instant, took no notice of the word she whispered. Then she said something he could not ignore: "Would you care to sit here, eminent sir?"

"My lady?" he said foolishly.

"There's room by me, eminent sir, I think." The woman pushed at the youth next to her, a lad five or six years younger than Krispos: a nephew, maybe, he thought, for the boy resembled her. The push went down the row. By the time it reached the end, there was indeed room.

Krispos sat, gratefully. "Thank you very much, ah—" He stopped. She might—she probably would—think him forward if he asked her name.

But she did not. "I am Tanilis, eminent sir," she said, and modestly cast down her eyes. Before she did, though, he saw how large and dark they were. With them still lowered, she went on, "This is my son Mavros."

The youth and Krispos exchanged nods. Tanilis was older than he'd thought; at first glance, he'd guessed her age to be within a few years of his.

He was still not used to being called *sir*. *Eminent sir* was for the likes of Iakovitzes, not him: how could he become a noble? Why, then, had Tanilis used it? He started to tell her, as politely as he could, that she'd made a mistake, but the service began and robbed him of the chance.

Phos' creed, of course, he could have recited asleep or awake; it was engrained in him. The rest of the prayers and hymns were hardly less familiar. He went through them, rising and taking his seat at the proper times, most of his mind elsewhere. He barely remembered to ask Phos to help Iakovitzes in his talks with Lexo, which was why he had come to the temple in the first place.

Out of the corner of his eye, he kept watching Tanilis. Her profile was sculptured, elegant; no loose flesh hung under her chin. But, though artfully applied powder almost hid them, the beginnings of lines bracketed her mouth and met at the corners of her eyes. Here and there a white thread ran through her piled-up curls of jet. He supposed she might be old enough to have a son close to his age. She was beautiful, even so.

She seemed to take no notice of his inspection, giving herself wholly to the celebration of Phos' liturgy. Eventually Krispos had to do the same, for the hymns of praise for the holy Abdaas were Opsikion's own; he had not met them before. But even as he stumbled through them, he was aware of her beside him.

The worshipers spoke Phos' creed one last time. From his place at the altar, the local prelate lifted up his hands in blessing. "Go now, in peace and goodness," he declared. The service was over.

Krispos rose and stretched. Tanilis and her son also stood up. "Thanks again for making room for me," he told them, as he turned to go.

"The privilege was mine, eminent sir," Tanilis said. Her ornate gold earrings tinkled softly as she looked down to the floor.

"Why do you keep calling me that?" he snapped, irritation getting the better of his manners. "I'm just a groom, and glad to be one—otherwise I expect I'd be starving somewhere. Come to think of it, I've done that, too, once or twice. It doesn't make you eminent, believe me."

Before he was halfway through, he knew he ought to keep quiet. If he offended a powerful local noblewoman like Tanilis, even Iakovitzes' connections at the capital might not save him. The capital was too far away for them to do him much good here. Even as that thought ran through his mind, though, he kept on till he was done.

Tanilis raised her head to look at him again. He started to stutter out an apology, then stopped. The last time he had seen that almost blind stare of perfect concentration was on the face of the healer-priest Mokios.

This time he watched her eyes go huge and black, saw her expression turn fixed. Her lips parted. This time ice ran through him as he heard the word she whispered: "Majesty."

She slumped forward in a faint.

Chapter V

K RISPOS CAUGHT HER BEFORE SHE HIT HER HEAD ON THE
bench in front of her. "Oh, Phos!" her son Mavros said. He rushed
up to help take her weight. "Thanks for saving her there, uh, Krispos.
Come on, let's get her out of the temple. She should be better soon."

He sounded so matter-of-fact that Krispos asked, "This has happened
before?"

"Yes." Mavros raised his voice to speak to the townsfolk who came hurrying up after Tanilis fell. "My mother just got out of her seat too quickly.
Let us by, please, so we can get her to fresh air. Let us by, please."

He had to repeat himself several times before people moved aside. Even
then, several women and a couple of men stayed with him. Krispos wondered why he did not shoo them away too, then realized they had to be
part of Tanilis' retinue. They helped clear a path so Krispos and Mavros
could carry the noblewoman up the aisle.

Tanilis muttered and stirred when the sun hit her face, but did not
wake at once. Krispos and Mavros eased her to the ground. The women
stood over her, exclaiming.

One of the servants said to Mavros, "I wish we'd come from the house
in town today, young master. Then she could go in the sedan chair."

"That would make fetching her home again easier, wouldn't it? How-ever . . ." Mavros shrugged whimsically. He turned to Krispos. "My mother sometimes . . . sees things, and sees them so strong she can't with-stand the force of the vision. I've grown used to it, watching it happen over the years, but I do wish she wouldn't always pick such awkward times and places. Of course, what I wish has very little to do with anything." He gave that shrug again.

"That's the way things often work." Krispos decided he thought well of Mavros. The youngster had not only kept his head coping with an awk-ward situation, but was even able to make light of it. From everything Krispos had ever seen, that was harder.

Mavros said, "Genzon, Naues, fetch the horses here from round the corner. The crowd's thinning out; you shouldn't have much trouble now."

"I'll go with them, if you like," Krispos said. "That way each man won't have to lead so many."

"Thanks, that's generous of you. Please, a moment first, though." Mavros took a couple of steps away from his retinue and motioned for Krispos to follow. In a low voice, he asked, "What did my mother say to you, there in the temple? Her back was to me; I didn't hear."

"Oh, that." Krispos scratched his head, looking embarrassed. "Do you know, in all the hubbub since, it's gone clean out of my mind."

He hurried after Genzon and Naues. He was unhappy about lying to Mavros, but he'd lied without hesitation. He needed to think much more about the unbelievably fascinating, unbelievably dangerous word Tanilis had spoken before he admitted to himself—let alone to anyone else—that he'd heard it.

Most of the horses the servants loosed from the hitching rail were ponies for Tanilis' female attendants. The four that were not were animals fine enough to have belonged in Iakovitzes' stables. Four—that meant Tanilis was no mean rider, then. Krispos found himself unsurprised. She was plainly a woman of many accomplishments.

She had managed to sit up by the time Krispos, Genzon, and Naues brought the horses back to the temple, but still did not seem fully aware of herself or her surroundings. Mavros clasped Krispos' hand. "Thank you again. I'm grateful for all your help."

"My pleasure." Krispos heard the dismissal in Mavros' voice. He dipped his head and went back to Bolkanes' inn.

Iakovitzes was not there; he was closeted with Lexo again. Krispos hoped his absentminded prayer had done his master some good. He went down to the taproom for some wine and for a chance to pick Bolkanes' brain.

Both came slower than he wanted. The inn was crowded with people celebrating the holy Abdaas' festal day less piously than those who had gone to
the temple. The tables were all filled. Working his way up to the bar took
patience, but patience Krispos had. "Red wine, please," he told Bolkanes.

The innkeeper dipped out a measure and filled an earthenware mug.
Only when he slid it across the counter did he look up to see whom he was
serving. "Oh, hello, Krispos," he said and then, to the next man who'd
wormed his way forward, "What'll it be for you today, Rekilas?"

Having gained his spot at the bar, Krispos did not give it up. He waited
while Bolkanes served two more men, then said, "I saw a truly striking noblewoman at the temple today. A man told me her name was—"

He broke off; someone had asked Bolkanes for a cup of something finer
than he kept in the barrels at the bar, and the innkeeper had to hurry away
to get what the fellow wanted. When he returned—and after he dealt with
another customer—Krispos started to repeat himself, but Bolkanes had
been listening, even if he was too busy to talk. He broke in: "That'd be
Tanilis, I expect."

"Yes, that was the name," Krispos said. "Sounds like she's well known
hereabouts."

"I should say so," Bolkanes agreed. "She has—hello, Zernes, more of
the white for you? Coming right up." Zernes not only wanted more white
wine but needed change from a goldpiece, and counted it three times once
he got it. Half a dozen men were waiting by the time he got done. Eventually Bolkanes resumed. "Tanilis? Aye, she has huge tracts of land hereabouts. A good many said she'd lose everything, trying to run 'em herself
after her husband—what was her husband's name, Apsyrtos?"

"Vledas, wasn't it?" Apsyrtos answered. "Let me have a cup of mead this
time, will you?"

"You head'll hurt come morning, mixing 'em that way," Bolkanes
warned, but he plied the dipper. When he was done, he turned back to
Krispos. "Vledas, that was it. He died ten, twelve years ago now, it must
be, and she's prospered since. Done well in good years and bad, they say,
though naturally I couldn't testify to that. But her estates do keep growing. It's almost uncanny—just a woman, you know."

"Mm-hmm," Krispos said, though he had the feeling Tanilis was just a
woman in the same way that Videssos was just a city.

Iakovitzes came in a little later. His good nature, always unreliable, had
vanished altogether by the time he worked his way to the bar through the
press of holiday drinkers. "Just because a holy man once cured a horse of
fleas is no reason to turn a town on its ear," he growled.

"Is that what the holy Abdaas did?" Krispos asked.

"How should I know? In a backwoods bastion like this, I doubt one would need do much more to be reckoned a miracle-worker." Iakovitzes gulped his wine, then slammed the mug down on the bar for a refill.

Krispos thought of Tanilis again. He'd seen more than horse-doctoring. He wondered how he could find out more about her. If she was as grand a noblewoman as Bolkanes made her out to be—and nothing Krispos had seen left him doubting it—he could not just go and seek a meeting with her. She'd slap him down for such presumption. Approaching through her son seemed a better bet. Mavros, on brief acquaintance, had the feel of being someone Krispos could like. Bolkanes might know the amusements the youth favored when he came into town. . . .

Iakovitzes had said something that Krispos missed in his musing. "I crave pardon."

His master frowned. "For all the attention you paid me there, I thought for a moment I was back talking with Lexo. He started in on his stinking tribal lays again today, the blackguard, until I asked him if he was willing to listen while I read to him from the histories of the reign of Stavrakios the Great. After that he came rather closer to reason, though not close enough. By Phos, I'll poison the bastard if his delays make me spend the winter in this miserable place."

A day before, Krispos would have agreed. After Videssos the city, Opsikion was small and backward and not very interesting—in a word, provincial. Now, with Tanilis' mystery before him, he hoped Iakovitzes would stay a while longer. "Drive him wild, Lexo," he whispered, too low for his master to hear.

BOLKANES WAS ROLLING A FRESH BARREL OF WINE FROM THE top of the cellar stairs to the taproom when Krispos walked into the inn a couple of afternoons later. "Want some help with that?" Krispos asked. Without waiting for an answer, he hurried forward.

"You would come in after I've done the hard part myself." Bolkanes wiped sweat from his forehead. "I can manage from here. Anyhow, a fellow's waiting for you at the bar. Been here an hour, maybe a bit longer."

"For me?" Krispos hadn't thought anyone in Opsikion knew him well enough to find him worth waiting for. He walked into the taproom. The tall, lanky man standing at the bar turned at the sound of his footsteps. "Naues!" Krispos said, then added with sudden doubt, "Or are you Genzon?"

Tanilis' servitor smiled. "I'm Genzon. I don't blame you for having to ask. Things were hurried and confused at the temple the other day."

"So they were." Krispos hesitated. "I hope your mistress is improved?"

"Yes, thank you." Genzon's prominent larynx bobbed as he swallowed the last of the wine in his cup. "She thanks you, also, for the care and concern you showed. To show her gratitude further, she bids you dine with her this evening, if you care to."

"She does?" Krispos blurted. Try as he would, he was still new to the notion of keeping thoughts to himself. He needed a moment to let urbanity return. "I'd be delighted. Can you give me a little while to change?"

"Certainly. What are a few more minutes, save a chance for another cup of wine?" Genzon nodded to Bolkanes, who, along with his tapman, was wrestling the new barrel into place under the bar.

Krispos told the innkeeper, "Please let Iakovitzes know I've been asked away for the evening." As soon as he was sure Bolkanes had heard, he walked over to the stairway. He would not run, not where Genzon could see him, but he bounded up the steps two at a time.

For once, he wished he could borrow Iakovitzes' clothes. He usually thought them gaudy, but now he wanted to put on something that would impress Tanilis. Since Iakovitzes was more than half a foot shorter than he was, and correspondingly narrower as well, borrowing a tunic was impractical. He threw on his own best one, of a sober dark blue, and a pair of breeches that matched it. He went downstairs so fast he had to grab at the railing to keep from landing on his head.

"Let me saddle my horse and I'll meet you out front," he called to Genzon. Tanilis' man nodded. Krispos went out to the stables behind the inn. He quickly put the saddle on his horse, made sure the cinch was tight—he'd learned about that back at the village, fortunately, or Iakovitzes' grooms never would have let him live it down—mounted, and walked the horse up to the street.

Genzon came out a couple of minutes later. "Good-looking animal," he said as he swung himself aboard his own mount.

"My master knows horses," Krispos said.

"Yes, I can see that. Nice smooth gait, too." Genzon started to say something more, visibly decided not to. Krispos thought he could guess the question Genzon swallowed: Why was the groom being invited to dine with his mistress, and not the visiting noble from the capital? As he had only hopes and wild speculations himself, he did not want to try to answer that.

Genzon led him out of Opsikion by the south gate. The road soon twisted away from the sea and ran up into the hills. Krispos' horse did not falter at the steep stretches. Indeed, the beast seemed to relish the challenge. Have to give him more exercise, Krispos thought.

Some of the hillsides were terraced. Up on the slopes, Krispos saw peasants weeding crops and pruning vines. They were too wrapped up in their tasks to look down at him. Watching them sent a remembered ache through his shoulders. Farming was the longest, hardest work there was. Having lived the peasant's life for so many years, he knew how lucky he was to have escaped it.

He wondered how his sister and brother-in-law were doing. He supposed he was an uncle by now, and hoped Evdokia had come through childbirth safely.

"All this is Tanilis' land," Genzon remarked.

"Is it?" Krispos said politely. He wondered what the scores, what the hundreds of people who worked it thought of that. Did she protect her peasants from the state's demands, or impose her own alongside them?

He hoped she looked after the people under her control. But, as he could not have a year before, he also wondered whether nobles who too effectively shielded their peasants from the state were good for Videssos. If nobles turned into petty kings on their own domains, how could the central government hope to function? He shook his head, thankful the problem was Anthimos'—or perhaps Petronas'—and not his.

He and Genzon rode on for some time. The sun was falling toward the jagged western horizon when Genzon pointed, saying, "There is Tanilis' villa."

The building ahead was so large Krispos had taken it for a fortress. It was well sited for one, on top of a rise that commanded the surrounding countryside. But as Krispos drew near, he saw it was too lightly made, with too many windows and too many doors, to serve as a stronghold.

He wondered how many peasants had gone hungry because they were busy building it instead of working their fields, then wondered again if such a thought had ever crossed one of the owners' minds. He doubted it. No one who owned a home like this—it made Iakovitzes' house look like Krispos' old cottage by comparison—had ever been a peasant.

Someone came out of the villa. As Krispos got closer, he saw it was Mavros. Tanilis' son recognized him—or more likely Genzon—a moment later. He waved. Genzon and Krispos waved back. They urged their horses into a trot.

Mavros came down to meet them. "About time you turned up," he said, grinning. "Mother's starting to fret and the cook's getting nervous. Never mind. You're here now, and that's what counts."

Boys hurried up to take the newcomers' horses and lead them back to the stables. Krispos expected his mount would get better care here than at Bolkanes'. Not that he had anything against the innkeeper, but Tanilis did not have to worry about how every copper was spent.

"You can have the rest of the day off, Genzon," Mavros said. The retainer dipped his head in thanks. Mavros turned to Krispos as Genzon hurried off. "Now you on the other hand, sirrah, you are in my mother's clutches."

"Oh? Why?" Krispos had—and ruthlessly stifled—a sudden, hungry vision of Tanilis clutching him, and him clutching back.

"The ice take me if I can tell you." Mavros shrugged in cheerful incomprehension. Krispos wished he could stay so jolly in the face of the unknown. In the life he'd led, unknown and dangerous were the same word. To Mavros, raised lacking for nothing, the world seemed a sunnier place. He went on, "She'll explain in her own good time, I'm sure. Me, I expect it has to do with whatever she said at the temple the other day. What was that, anyhow?"

"Hasn't she told you?" Krispos asked, surprised.

"She doesn't remember, not exactly. Her—visions are like that sometimes." Mavros shrugged again. "Whatever it was, it was something strong. Some of the old servants say the place hasn't been turned upside down like this since the Avtokrator Sermeios dined here in my grandfather's time."

"Since an Avtokrator—" Krispos echoed weakly. He tried to laugh, but only managed a ghastly chuckle. "I'm no Avtokrator, believe me."

"I believe you," Mavros said at once, but not so it sounded like an insult. "You seem a good fellow, though. I think so myself, and my mother wouldn't have invited you here if she'd seen anything wicked, now would she?"

"No," Krispos said. That he was going to eat where an Avtokrator had dined was stirring enough—but after all, Petronas had broken bread at Iakovitzes' house, and he was Emperor in all but name. But that an imperial-size fuss was being made over *him*—he wanted another try at laughing over that. He was sure he could do a proper job the second time around.

Mavros said, "Come in, come in. The longer I leave you standing around here, the longer everyone inside stands around fussing. The cook'll stop palpitating every time anything gets near done, which will be a great relief to everyone."

Krispos made the sun-sign over his heart as he walked beneath the image of Phos that hung above the door. The floor of the entrance hall was gleaming marble. "Is that you, son?" Tanilis' voice floated down it as Mavros slammed the door. "Where can Krispos be?"

"With me, as a matter of fact," Mavros said. Krispos heard Tanilis exclaim. Mavros told him, "Come on, she's out in the garden."

Krispos got a brief glimpse into each room that opened on the hallway as he hurried after Mavros. What he saw reminded him of Iakovitzes' splendid furnishings, but showed better taste and more money. That enormous round table inlaid with gold and ivory . . . not even an Avtokrator would have felt ashamed to eat a meal from a table like that.

The garden was also larger and finer than Iakovitzes', although, to be just, Krispos had never seen his master's garden in full bloom. Tanilis extended a slim hand. Krispos bowed over it. Rings glinted on her fingers. "Thank you, my lady, for inviting me here," he said. "This is— marvelous."

"It pleases me that you so say so, eminent sir. Surely, though, you must have seen homes far finer in Videssos the city."

He noted the title by which she addressed him. *She might not remember everything,* he thought, *but she hasn't forgotten everything, either.* Then his attention came back to what she'd said. "In truth, no," he said slowly. "The wonder of Videssos the city isn't any one home in it, but that there are so many homes, so many people, all in the same place."

"A thoughtful answer," Tanilis said. "I've never seen the city."

"Nor I." Mavros' face lit. "I'd love to go there one day, though it's hard for me to imagine a city bigger than Opsikion."

Krispos smiled. No matter how rich and easy Mavros' life was, he knew some things Tanilis' son did not. "If Videssos the city were a wolf, it could swallow a mouse like Opsikion without even chewing," he said.

Mavros whistled, soft and low, and shook his head. "Hard to believe."

"From everything your father said, it's true," Tanilis said. "Vledas went to the city once, when he was not much older than you are now, and never stopped talking about it to the day he died."

"I don't remember," Mavros said wistfully. He would have been a small boy when Vledas died, Krispos realized. He was surprised to think himself luckier in any way than this rich youth, but he'd known his father until he was a man grown.

Had Phostis died while he was young, say in Kubrat, who would have been there to keep him from doing all sorts of stupid things later? Most likely he would have ended up marrying Zoranne and staying a farmer all his life. A good part of a year away from the ceaseless labor that was farming, he no longer thought it the only right and proper way to live.

"You will see Videssos one day, too, son." Tanilis' voice was hollow; her eyes did not quite focus on Mavros. Krispos felt the hair on his arms trying to prickle upright. The oracular tone faded as she went on, "But for now, a shorter journey. Shall we go inside and eat?"

The cook, a nervous little man named Evtykhes, stopped fidgeting and sighed with relief as he saw his charges sit down around a small table topped with mother-of-pearl—it shimmered and almost seemed to shift in the glow of the lamps other servants set out.

"Soup?" Evtykhes asked. At Tanilis' nod, he dashed back to the kitchen. A boy appeared with the steaming bowls so quickly that Krispos suspected the cook was trying to make sure everyone kept sitting.

Back in his village, Krispos would have lifted the soup bowl straight to his lips. In taverns and eateries in the city, he still did. But he had learned to use a spoon at Iakovitzes'. Since Tanilis and Mavros ate with theirs, he imitated them. By the time he got to the bottom of the bowl, the soup was cold. Maybe the nobles didn't mind that, but he did. His breath went out in a silent sigh.

He was more used to his fork and was reaching for it when he saw Tanilis and Mavros pick up asparagus with their fingers. He imitated them again. Manners were confusing things.

The food kept coming: broiled duck in a glaze of candied berries, mushrooms stuffed with turtle meat, pureed chestnuts, a salad of oranges and apples, and at last a roast kid with a sweet-and-sour sauce and chopped onions. Mavros and Krispos ate ravenously, the one because he was still growing, the other because he'd learned to do so whenever he got the chance as a hedge against the hunger that was sure to follow. Tanilis sampled a little of every course and sent warm praise back to the cook after each one.

"By the good god," she said, watching her son and Krispos devastate the plate of cheese and strawberries that appeared after the kid, "I could get fat just from being in the same room with the two of you."

"You'd have to blame Krispos, then," Mavros said—rather blurrily, as his mouth was full. "If it came from being in the same room with me, it would've happened long ago."

Krispos eyed Tanilis, who was so perfectly and elegantly shaped that she might have been turned on a lathe. The phrase fit in more ways than one, he thought, for she plainly maintained her figure with a craftsman's disciplined artifice. He told her, "I don't think Phos—or you—would allow such a mishap."

She looked down at her wine cup. "A compliment and a truth together—indeed, the good god aids a man who helps himself."

"Then he aids me now." Mavros popped the last strawberry into his mouth.

"Son, you are incorrigible," Tanilis said fondly.

"It does seem that way," Mavros agreed.

Krispos sipped his own wine: something thick and sweet now, to complement the sharp taste of the cheese. He said, "Phos is the only one who knows why he does as he does. My lady, I hope you will be kind enough to tell me why you've been so good to me. I told you at the temple, I'm only a groom, and lucky to be that. I feel I'm taking advantage of you." *And if one day you feel the same way,* he did not add, *you could cause me untold grief.*

Tanilis waited until a servant left with the last plates. She got up and closed the door to the small dining chamber after the man departed. Only then did she answer, her voice low, "Tell me truly, Krispos, have you never wondered if you might one day be more than what you are now? Truly?"

Despite that double admonition, "No" was the first answer that rose to his lips. But before he spoke it aloud, he thought of Pyrrhos calling his name that rainy night in the monastery. A moment later, he remembered how both Pyrrhos and the Kubrati *enaree* had looked at him during the ceremony when Iakovitzes ransomed the stolen peasants. The word Tanilis had spoken in the temple also echoed in his head.

"I've . . . wondered," he said at last.

"And that you *should* wonder is plain to anyone who can . . . see as I do." Tanilis used the same sort of hesitation he had.

Mavros looked ready to burst from curiosity. "What *did* you say to him back in the temple?" he asked her. "I think you know again."

Instead of answering, she glanced toward Krispos. He hesitated, then gave his head a tiny shake. New-come from the farm though he might be, he knew that word was dangerous. Tanilis' nod of understanding was equally small. "I do, and you will, too, son," she said. "But not yet."

"Thank you so much," Mavros said. The words were sarcastic; the tone was not. Krispos decided Mavros was too good-natured ever to grow skilled at using the stinging wit Iakovitzes relished.

"Since you did see . . . what you saw, what do you want from me?" Krispos asked Tanilis.

"To profit from your rise, of course," she answered. He blinked; he had not expected her to be so direct. She went on, "For me, for my family, what we have now is as much as we ever will have. That, too, I have seen— unless we tie ourselves to one with higher hopes. That one, I think, is you."

Krispos looked around the room. He thought of the house of which that rich room was a part, of the vast estates surrounding that house. *Why,* he wondered, *would anyone want more than this?* He still wanted more than he had, but he did not have much, and that at the whim of his bad-tempered master. If Tanilis would help him get more, he'd play along. If she thought him a hand-puppet to move only at her bidding, she might get a surprise one day.

He knew better than to say that aloud. "What do you want from me?" he repeated. "And how will you help in this . . . rise . . . you saw?"

"The first thing I want is that you not grow too confident in your rise," she warned. "Nothing seen ahead of time is definite. If you think a thing will come to pass without your working toward it, that is the surest way I know to make certain it will never be."

The night the Kubratoi swept down on his village had taught Krispos once and for all that nothing in life was definite. He nodded. "What else?"

"That you take Mavros back to Videssos the city with you and reckon him your younger brother henceforth," Tanilis said. "The connections he makes there will serve him and you for the rest of his life."

"Me? The city? Really?" Mavros threw back his head and yowled with delight.

"He's welcome to go to Videssos by me," Krispos said, "but I'm not the one who'd have to choose to take him along. Iakovitzes would." He glanced over at Tanilis' son and tried to see him through Iakovitzes' eyes. "It might not be hard to get my master to ask him to go back with us, but—" He stopped. He would not speak ill of Iakovitzes, not before these people he hardly knew.

"I know of his habits," Tanilis said. "To his credit, he does not pretend to be other than what he is. Mavros, I think, will be able to take care of himself, and he's as good with horses—your master's other passion, are they not?—as anyone his age near Opsikion."

"That will help," Krispos agreed. He chuckled—one more handsome youth for Meletios and some of the other grooms to worry about. Growing serious again, he went on, "Besides Mavros, how will you aid me?" He felt he was horse trading with Tanilis, the only trouble being that she promised delivery of most of the horse some years from now. He wanted to make as sure as possible of the part he could see now.

"Gold, counsel, loyalty until your death or mine," Tanilis said. "If you like, I will take oath by the lord with the great and good mind."

Krispos thought that over. "If your word is bad, will your oath make it better?"

Tanilis lowered her eyes. Her hair hid her face. Even so, Krispos felt he had passed a test.

Mavros said plaintively, "Will the two of you please quit making deep plans without me? If I'm suddenly to leave for Videssos the city, shouldn't I know why?"

"You might be safer if you didn't," Tanilis said. But she must have seen the justice of her son's protest, for she pointed at Krispos and whispered the word she had spoken to him inside the temple.

Mavros' eyes widened. "Him?" he squeaked. Krispos did not blame him for sounding amazed. He did not believe the prediction either, not down deep.

But Tanilis answered, "It may be so." If all she'd said tonight was true, she would try to help it be so. Was she, then, simply following the path she had seen or trying to force it into existence? Krispos went round that dizzy loop of thought two or three times before he gave it up. Tanilis went on, "None of us should say that word again, not until the proper time comes, if it ever does."

"You're right." Mavros shook his head in wonder and grinned at Krispos. "I always figured I'd need a miracle to get me to Videssos the city, but I didn't know what one looked like till now."

Krispos snorted. "I'm no miracle." But he found himself grinning back. Mavros would make him a lively brother. He turned to Tanilis. "My lady, may I beg an escort from you? Otherwise, in the dark, I'd need a miracle to get back to Opsikion, let alone the city."

"Stay the night," she said. "I expected you would; the servants have readied a chamber for you." She rose and walked over to the dining room's doors. The small noise of their opening summoned two men. She nodded to one. "Xystos, please lead the eminent sir to his bedchamber."

"Certainly." Xystos bowed, first to Tanilis, then to Krispos. "Come with me, eminent sir."

As Krispos started to follow the servant away, Tanilis said, "Since we are become partners in this enterprise, Krispos, take a partner's privilege and use my name."

"Thank you, uh, Tanilis," Krispos said. Her encouraging smile seemed to stay with him after he turned a corner behind Xystos.

The bedroom was larger than the one Krispos had at Bolkanes' inn. Xystos bowed again and shut the door behind him. Krispos used the chamber pot. He took off his clothes, blew out the lamp Xystos had left, and lay down on the bed. It was softer than any he'd known before—and this, he thought, was only a guest room.

Even in darkness, he did not fall asleep at once. With his mind's eye, he kept seeing the smile Tanilis had given him as he left the dining room. Maybe she would slip in here tonight, to seal with her body the strange bargain they had made. Or maybe she would send in a serving girl, just as a kindness to him. Or maybe . . .

Maybe I'm a fool, he told himself when he woke the next morning, still very much alone in bed. He used the chamber pot again, dressed, and ran fingers through his hair.

He was going to the door when someone tapped on it. "Oh, good, you're awake," Mavros said when he opened it a moment later. "If you don't mind breakfasting on hard rolls and smoked mutton, we can eat while we ride back to town."

"Good enough." Krispos thought of how often he'd gone out to work in the fields after breakfasting on nothing. He knew Mavros had never missed a meal. He kept quiet, not just for politeness' sake but also because he'd long since decided hunger held no inherent virtue—life was better with a full belly.

They washed down the rolls and mutton with a skin of wine. "That's a very nice animal you're riding," Krispos said after a while.

"Isn't he?" Mavros beamed. "I'm not small, but my weight doesn't faze him a bit, not even when I'm in mail shirt and helmet." He took the reins in his left hand so he could draw a knife and make cut-and-thrust motions as if it were a sword. "Maybe one of these days I'll ride him to war against Makuran or Kubrat—or even Khatrish, if your master's mission fails. Take that, vile barbarian!" He stabbed a bush by the side of the road.

Krispos smiled at his enthusiasm. "Real fighting's not as . . . neat as you make it out to be."

"You've fought, then?" At Krispos' nod, Mavros' eyes went big and round. "Tell me about it!"

Krispos tried to beg off, but Mavros kept urging him until he baldly recounted the villagers' massacre of the Kubrati raiders. "Just our good luck there was only the one little band," he finished. "If the riders a couple of days later had been wild men instead of Videssian cavalry, I wouldn't be here now to give you the tale."

"I've heard true warriors don't speak much of glory," Mavros said in a rather subdued voice.

"What they call glory, I think, is mostly the relief you feel after you've fought and lived through it without getting maimed. If you have."

"Hmm." Mavros rode on in silence for some time after that. Before he and Krispos got to Opsikion, though, he was slaying bushes again. Krispos did not try to dissuade him. He suspected Mavros would make a better soldier than he did himself—the young noble seemed inclined to plunge straight ahead without worrying about consequences, a martial trait if ever there was one.

They got to Opsikion a little before midmorning. Being with Mavros got Krispos through the south gate with respectful salutes from the guards. When they came to Bolkanes' inn, they found Iakovitzes just sitting down to breakfast—unlike most folk, he did not customarily rise at dawn.

He fixed Krispos with a glare. "Nice of you to recall who your master is." His eyes flicked to Mavros. Krispos watched his expression change. "Or have you been cavorting with this magnificent creature?"

"No," Krispos said resignedly. "Excellent sir, let me present Mavros to you. He is the son of the noblewoman Tanilis, and is interested in returning to Videssos with us when your mission is done. He'd make a fine groom, excellent sir; he knows horses."

"Tanilis' son, eh?" Iakovitzes rose to return Mavros' bow; he'd evidently learned who Tanilis was. But he went on, "When it comes to grooms for my stables, I don't care if he's the Avtokrator's son, not that Anthimos has one."

He shot several searching questions at Mavros, who answered them without undue trouble. Then he went outside to look over the youth's mount. When he came back, he was nodding. "You'll do, if you're the one who's been tending that animal."

"I am," Mavros said.

"Good, good. You'll definitely do. We may even get to leave before fall comes; Lexo may see reason after all. At least I'm beginning to hope so again." Iakovitzes looked almost cheerful for a moment as he sat down. Then he found something new to complain about. "Oh, a plague! My sausage is cold. Bolkanes!"

As the innkeeper hurried up, Mavros whispered to Krispos, "Is your master always like that?"

"Now that you mention it, yes," Krispos whispered back.

"I wonder if I want to see Videssos the city enough to work for him." But Mavros was joking. He raised his voice to a normal level. "I'm going to ride home now, but I'll be in town a lot. If I'm not, just send a messenger for me and I'll come ready to travel." Bowing again to Iakovitzes, he left the taproom.

Around a mouthful of fresh, steaming sausage, Iakovitzes said, "So now you're hobnobbing with young nobles, are you, Krispos? You're coming up a bit in your choice of friends."

"If I hadn't spent these last months with you, excellent sir, I wouldn't have had any idea how to act around him," Krispos said. Flattery that was also true, he'd found, worked best.

It worked now. Iakovitzes' gaze lost the piercing quality it had when he was suspicious about something. "Hrmp," he said, and went back to his breakfast.

THREE DAYS LATER, MAVROS BROUGHT KRISPOS ANOTHER DINner invitation. Krispos went out and bought a new tunic, a saffron-yellow one that went well with his olive skin. After he paid for it, he felt odd. It was the first time he'd got a shirt just for the sake of having something new.

Tanilis' admiring glance that evening made the purchase seem worthwhile. She was worth admiring herself, in a thin dress of white linen that emphasized how small her waist was. More gold shone on her wrists and around her neck.

"You are welcome, as always," she said, holding out her hand.

Krispos took it. "Thank you, my . . . Tanilis." His tongue slipped by accident, but he watched her eyes fall as she heard the last two words together. Maybe his hope of the previous visit had not been so foolish after all.

But if that was so, she gave no hint of it during dinner. Indeed, she said very little. Mavros did most of the talking; he bubbled with excitement at the prospect of heading west for the city. "When will we leave?" he asked. "Do you know? How fare Iakovitzes' talks with the Khatrisher?"

"Better, I think," Krispos said. "He's hardly swearing at all when he gets back from the eparch's residence these days. With him, that's a very good sign."

"I'll start packing, then."

"Go ahead, but don't pack anything you might want before you go. He was like this once before, weeks ago, and then things fell apart again." Krispos took a last luscious bite of blackberry tart and turned to Tanilis. "I wish your cook could come with me along with your son. I don't think I've ever eaten so well."

"I'll tell Evtykhes you said so," she said, smiling. "Your praise will please him more than what he gets from us—you're not obliged to say kind things to him for politeness' sake."

Krispos had not thought about that. The servants at Iakovitzes' home were the only ones he'd known, and he was one among them. For that matter, Iakovitzes did not say kind things to anyone for politeness' sake. He used the rough edge of his tongue, not the smooth, to keep his people in line.

Tanilis said, "Though I must keep Evtykhes, Krispos, you will need more than you have if what we hope is to be accomplished. When you and Mavros do at last depart for the imperial city, I will send gold with you."

"My lady"—this time Krispos deliberately used her title rather than her name— "even with Mavros with me in Videssos, what's to keep me from spending the gold just on women and wine?"

"You are." Tanilis looked him full in the face. Those huge dark eyes held his; he had the uneasy feeling she could peer deeper into him than he could himself. Now he was the first to lower his gaze.

Mavros rose. "I'm off. If I'm to be leaving soon, I have some farewells to make."

Tanilis watched him go. "What was it you said about wine and women?" she asked Krispos. "Most of his farewells will be of that sort, I expect."

"He's coming into a man's years and a man's pleasures," Krispos replied from the peak of maturity that was twenty-two.

"So he is," Tanilis' voice was musing. Her eyes met Krispos again, but she looked through him rather than into him, back toward the past. "A man. How strange. I must have been about the age he is now when I bore him."

"Surely younger," Krispos said.

She laughed, without mirth but also without bitterness. "You are gallant, but I know the count of years. They are part of me; why should I deny them?"

Instead of answering, Krispos took a thoughtful sip from his wine cup. He'd made a mistake by breaking the rule of flattery he'd used on Iakovitzes. With someone like Tanilis, it did not do to make mistakes.

Before long, Krispos got up to go, saying, "Thank you again for inviting me here, and for the aid you promise, and for this second wonderful feast."

"Truly, if it does not unduly anger your master, you would be well advised to stay till morning," Tanilis said. "The ride back to Opsikion will be twice as long in the darkness, and there are brigands in the hills, try as we will to keep them down."

"Iakovitzes is angry most of the time, it seems. Unduly?" Krispos shrugged. "I expect I can talk him round. Thank you once more."

Tanilis called for Xystos. The servant took Krispos to the same guest chamber he had used before. That soft bed beckoned. He stripped off his clothes, slid under the single light blanket that was all he needed on a warm summer night, and fell asleep at once.

He was a sound sleeper, a legacy of the many years he had gone to bed every night too tired to wake to anything less than an earthquake. The first he knew of anyone else's being in the room was the bed shifting as the weight of another body settled onto it.

He jerked upright. "Wha—" he said muzzily.

Even the small, flickering flame of the lamp Tanilis held was enough to dazzle his sleep-dulled eyes. A secret smile tugged at the corners of her mouth. "I'm sorry," she said. "I didn't mean to startle you."

"It's—all right," he answered after a moment, when he had full control of himself. Still not altogether sure why she had come—and not daring to be wrong here, where his head might answer for it—he pulled the blanket up to cover more of himself.

That secret smile came out in the open. "Wise to be cautious. But never mind." Then her expression changed. "What is that coin you wear round your neck?" she asked, her voice suddenly sharp and interested.

"This?" Krispos' hand closed over the goldpiece. "It's just for luck."

"For more than luck, I think," Tanilis said. "Please, if you would, tell me how you came by it."

He told her how Omurtag had given him the coin at the ransoming ceremony back when he was a boy. Her eyes glittered in the lamplight as she followed his account. When he thought he was done, she questioned him about the incident as closely as Iakovitzes had grilled Mavros on horses.

Prodded so, he recalled more than he'd imagined he could, even to things like the expression on the Kubrati *enaree*'s face. The more he answered, though, the more glumly certain he became that she'd forgotten why she'd come to his bedroom in the first place. *Too bad,* he thought. The lamp's warm light made her especially lovely.

But she certainly seemed indifferent to their both being on the same bed. When she could pick no more memories from him, she said, "No wonder I saw as I did. The seeds of what you may be were sown long ago; at last they have grown toward the light of day."

He shrugged. At the moment, he cared little for the nebulous future. He was too busy thinking about what he wished he was doing in the very immediate present.

"You're rather a young man still, though, and not much worried about such things," Tanilis said. He gulped, wondering if she could read his mind. Then he saw she was looking down at the thin blanket, which revealed his thoughts clearly enough. He felt himself flush, but the smile was back on her face. "I suppose that's as it should be," she said, and blew out the lamp.

For a whole series of reasons, the rest of the evening proved among the most educational of Krispos' life. Every woman he'd been with before Tanilis suddenly seemed a girl by comparison. They *were* girls, he realized: his age or younger, chosen for attractiveness, kept for enthusiasm. Now for the first time he learned what polished art could add.

Looking back the exhausted morning after, he supposed Tanilis had taken him through his paces like Iakovitzes steering a jumper around a course. Had she taught him anything else that way, he was sure he would have resented her. He still did, a little, but resentment had to fight hard against languor.

He'd wondered for some little while if art was all she brought to the game. She moved, she stroked, she lay back to receive his caresses in silence, a silence that persisted no matter what he did. And though all her ploys were far more than just enjoyable, he also thought they were rehearsed.

Then at last some of his own urgency reached her. Kindled, she was less perfectly skilled than she had been before. Feeling her quiver beneath him, hearing her breath catch, made him want to forget all that perfect skill had wrought.

He wondered if the quivers, if the gasps, were also products of her art. He shrugged as he fastened the bone catches of his tunic. Art that fine was indistinguishable from reality; it was as if an icon of Petronas could move and speak with the Sevastokrator's voice.

Later, as he walked down the hall behind a servant toward the small dining chamber for breakfast, he decided he was wrong. If he'd altogether failed to please her, he doubted she'd give herself to him again.

She waited for him in the dining room, her self-possession absolute as usual. "I trust you slept well," she said in a tone any polite hostess might have used. Before he could answer, she went on, "Do try some of the honey on your bread. It's clover and orange together, and very fine."

He dipped it from the pot and tried it. It was good. He tried—as best he could with men and women of her household bustling in and out—to learn how she felt about the night before. She was impervious. That seemed ominous.

Then Mavros came in, looking rather the worse for wear, and Krispos had to give up. Tanilis showed more interest in her son's boasting than she'd given to Krispos' discreet questions.

Only as Krispos was saying his farewells did she give him even the smallest reason for hope. "Feel free to invite yourself here next time; you need not wait upon a formal invitation."

"Thank you, Tanilis, I'll do that," he said, and watched her face closely. Had she shown any trace of disappointment, he would never have gone back to the villa again. She nodded and smiled instead.

He made himself wait four days before he rode back again. Evtykhes the cook hadn't had anything special planned but, like Iakovitzes' chef, he could make the ordinary interesting.

What happened later that night was even more interesting, and not even slightly ordinary. "Don't delay so long the next time," Tanilis said as she slid out of the guest room bed to return to her own chamber. "Or did you think I was seeking to entrap you with my charms?"

Krispos shook his head. Tanilis slipped away without asking anything further of him. He was not nearly sure he had truthfully answered her last question; indeed, he hadn't trusted his voice not to give him away.

Even so, he knew he would come to the villa again, and in less than four days. Did that mean he was entrapped? Maybe it did, he thought wryly. He was sure he'd never found such tempting bait.

IAKOVITZES LOOKED UP FROM HIS BREAKFAST PORRIDGE AS Krispos walked toward his table in Bolkanes' taproom. The noble's eyebrows rose. "Good of you to join me," he said. "Such rare signs give me hope you do still remember you work for me."

Krispos felt his ears grow hot. He grunted—the safest response he could think of—and sat down.

Nothing was guaranteed safe with Iakovitzes. "Much as I hate to disrupt the lecherous tenor of your ways," he went on, "I fear your little arrangement with that laundress or whatever she is at Mavros' place will have to end."

Krispos had found no way to keep people from knowing how often he rode out to Tanilis' villa. Those visits—and the overnight stays that went with them—had to set tongues wagging. To make sure they did not wag in the wrong—or rather, the right—direction, he'd let on that he was having an affair with one of the servant girls. Now he said, still cautiously, "Oh? Why is that, excellent sir?"

"Because I've finally settled with that puff-adder of a Lexo, that's why."

"Have you really?" Krispos said in genuine surprise.

"Yes, I have really, and on more than decent terms. If you'd been around here as you were supposed to be instead of exercising your private parts, this might not have come as such a startling development to you."

Krispos hung his head at the rebuke. The acid in Iakovitzes' voice made it sting more than it might have otherwise, but he knew it was deserved. He also knew a certain amount of relief. If Iakovitzes was heading back to Videssos the city, he would have to accompany the noble. Not even Tanilis could think differently. A more convenient end to their liaison was hard to imagine.

Iakovitzes went on, "Since you do get out to Mavros' villa, however, be so good as to let him know I shall be departing shortly. Why I don't leave you here and head back just with him I couldn't say, let me tell you."

At first, the scolding washed over Krispos. If Iakovitzes meant to fire him, he would have done it long since. And even if the noble did give him the boot, Tanilis would still back him—or would she? Krispos grew more sober as he pondered that. If his fortunes changed, her vision might, too.

He decided he ought to stay in Iakovitzes' good graces after all, or as many of them as he could keep without letting the noble seduce him. "What were the terms you finally agreed to with Lexo, excellent sir?" he asked.

"As if you care," Iakovitzes jeered, but he was too full of himself to resist bragging about what he'd done. "The Khatrishers will all pull back of the Akkilaion by the end of next year, and three parts in four of the indemnity we pay for their leaving will go straight to the herders who get displaced, not to Gumush the khagan. I had to pay Lexo a little extra on the side to get him to go along with that, but it's money well spent."

"I see what you're saying." Krispos nodded. "If the indemnity stays with the local Khatrishers, they'll end up spending most of it here in Opsikion, so in the long run it'll come back to the Empire."

"Maybe that's why I keep you around in spite of the all-too-numerous faults you insist on flaunting," Iakovitzes said, "for your peasant shrewdness. Even Lexo didn't pick up the full import of that clause, and he's been in the business of cheating Videssos a good many years now. Aye, I snuck it past him, I did, I did." Nothing put Iakovitzes in a better mood than gloating over how he'd outsmarted an opponent.

"When do you sign the pact?" Krispos asked.

"Already did it—signed and sealed. I have one copy up in my room, and Lexo's got the other one wherever he keeps it." Iakovitzes knocked back a large cup of wine. Only when he swayed as he got to his feet did Krispos realize it was not his first, or even his third; his speech was perfectly clear. As the noble headed for the door, he said over his shoulder, "Come to think of it, I'm going across the square to the eparch's residence and rub the Khatrisher's nose in the break he gave me. Want to tag along?"

"Are you sure that's wise, excellent sir?" Krispos said, in lieu of publicly asking his master whether he'd lost his mind. If Iakovitzes angered Lexo enough—and he could do it if anyone could—what was to keep the Khatrisher from tearing up his signed and sealed copy and either starting the war Petronas did not want or at least forcing negotiations open again?

But Iakovitzes said, "Let him wallow in his own stupidity." He went out the door almost at a run.

Krispos heard the rumble and jingle of an approaching heavy wagon without listening to it; it was just one of the noises that went with staying in a city. Then he heard someone shout, "Watch out, you bloody drunken twit! Look over this—" That was harder to ignore; it came from right in front of the inn. At the cry of agony that followed hard on its heels, Krispos and everyone else in the taproom dashed out to see what had happened.

The wagon was full of blocks of gray limestone from one of the quarries in the hills back of Opsikion, and drawn by a team of six draft horses. Iakovitzes lay thrashing on the ground between the near wheeler and the wagon's right front wheel. Another yard forward and it would have rolled over his body.

Krispos ran forward and dragged his master away from the wagon. Iakovitzes shrieked again as he was moved. "My leg!" He clutched at it. "My leg!"

The white-faced driver gabbled, "Fool walked right in front of me. Right in front of me like I wasn't there, and this maybe the biggest, noisiest rig in town. Right in front of me! One of the horses must have stepped on him, or maybe more than one. Lucky I was fast on the brake, or all you could do with him is clean him off the cobbles. Right in front of me!"

A couple of passers-by confirmed that Iakovitzes had not noticed the wagon at all. "Way he was going," one said, "he wouldn't have noticed Phos coming down from heaven for him." A couple of more pious souls made the sun-sign over their hearts at the mention of the good god's name.

Krispos tugged up Iakovitzes' robe so he could see how badly the noble was hurt. The unnatural bend between knee and ankle of his master's left leg and the enormous black bruise that spread over the leg as he watched told him everything he needed to know. "It's broken," he said.

"Of course it's broken, you wide-arsed imbecile!" Iakovitzes screamed, pain and fury making him even louder and shriller than usual. "You think I need you to tell me that?" The inventive curses that spewed from him in the next couple of minutes proved his wits were intact, even if he did have cuts over both eyes and a bruise on one cheek. He finally slowed down enough to snarl, "Why are all you incest-loving cretins just standing around gaping? Someone fetch me a healer-priest!"

One of the locals trotted away. Iakovitzes kept swearing; Krispos did not think he repeated himself once in the quarter of an hour till the priest arrived. Some of the onlookers who might normally have gone about their business stayed to listen instead.

"What happened here?" the healer-priest asked when he finally arrived.

Several people in the crowd started to explain as they stood aside to let the priest—Sabellios, his name was—pass. From the ground, Iakovitzes yelled, "I broke my miserable leg, that's what. Why don't you stop gabbing there and start healing?"

"He's like that, holy sir," Krispos whispered to Sabellios as the healer-priest crouched beside him.

"It's not easy to be happy with a broken leg," Sabellios observed. "Easy, sir, easy," he went on to Iakovitzes, for the noble gasped and swore anew as the healer-priest set his hands on either side of the fracture.

Like the other healers Krispos had seen, Sabellios spoke Phos' creed again and again as he sank into his trance. Then the words trailed away, leaving nothing between Sabellios' will and the injury he faced. Krispos muttered with awe as he watched the swelling around the broken bone recede and the purple-black bruise fade.

The healer-priest released his hold. He wiped sweat from his forehead with the sleeve of his blue robe. "I have done what I can," he said in the worn voice every healer used just after his work was done. Krispos noted the effort he needed to raise his head to look up at the spectators who still ringed him and Iakovitzes. "One of you should go and bring Ordanes the physician here. He has a gentler touch for setting bones than I do."

"Setting bones?" Iakovitzes hissed from between clenched teeth. "Aren't you going to heal the break?"

Sebellios stared at him. "Heal—a fracture?"

"Why not?" Iakovitzes said. "I had it done for me once in Videssos the city, after I took a fall when my cursed mount couldn't leap a stream during a hunt. Some blue-robe from the Sorcerers' Collegium did it for me—Heraklonas, I think his name was."

"You were most fortunate to be treated by such a master of the art, excellent sir," the healer-priest said. "As with most of my brethren, my power is over flesh, not bone, which I have neither the strength nor the knowledge to heal. Bone, you see, is partly dead, so it lacks the vitality upon which the healing gift draws. No one in Opsikion—perhaps no one in any city save Videssos—can heal a broken bone. I am sorry to have to be the one to tell you that."

"Then what am I supposed to do?" Iakovitzes howled, anger now overcoming pain.

"Fear not, sir," Sebellios said. "Ordanes is a skilled bone-setter, and I can abate any fever you might contract during the healing process. Surely in two or three months you will be walking again and, if you exercise your leg once the splints come off, you may not even limp."

"Two or three months?" Iakovitzes rolled his eyes like a trapped animal. "How long before I can ride?"

Sebellios pursed his lips. "Somewhere near the same length of time, I should say. Controlling one's horse puts considerable strain on the lower leg, as you must know."

"Two or three months?" Iakovitzes repeated it unbelievingly. "You're saying it'll be winter by the time I'm up and about?"

"Well, yes, probably," Sebellios said. "What of it?"

"No ships in winter—too many storms. No good going overland, either, or not much—snowdrifts piled twice as high as a man." Iakovitzes had been speaking softly, almost to himself. Now, suddenly, he screamed. *You mean to tell me I'm stuck in this backwoods Phos-forsaken shitpot pesthole of an excuse for a town until spring?*"

"Hello, hello." A fat bald man pushed through the crowd and grinned down at Iakovitzes. "My, you sound cheerful today. Nothing like breaking a leg to do that to a man, is there?"

"I'd sooner break your neck," Iakovitzes snarled. "Which icepit did Skotos let you out of?"

"Name's Ordanes," the fat man answered calmly—he was, Krispos saw, one of the rare men Iakovitzes could not infuriate with a few ill-chosen words. "I'll set that leg for you, if you like—I expect you'll need it whole so as you can get back to cramming both feet into your face." As Iakovitzes gaped and spluttered, the physician went on, "I'll need a couple of stout souls here to help hold him down. He'll like this even less than he likes anything else."

"I'm one," Krispos said. "He's my master."

"Lucky you." Ordanes lowered his voice so Iakovitzes would not hear. "Hate to tell you this, young fellow, but you and your master are going to be stuck here a goodish while. That's what I heard him yelling about before, isn't it?"

Krispos nodded.

"If you're his man, you'll have to wait on him like he was a baby for a while, because for the first month or so he shouldn't even be out of bed, not if he expects those bones to heal straight. Think you're up to it? I don't envy you, and that's a fact."

The idea of waiting on Iakovitzes hand and foot for a solid month was more nearly appalling than appealing. All the same, Krispos said, "I'm up to it. He took me into his service from the streets of Videssos the city when I had nothing to my name but what I was wearing. I owe him more than a little for that; wouldn't do to repay him by running off when he really needs me."

"Hmm." Ordanes' eyes were tracked with red, half hidden in folds of fat, and very knowing. "Seems to me he's better served by his man than you are by your master, but that's none of my affair." The physician looked up at the crowd of spectators. "Come on, people, don't just stand there. Lend a hand, will you? Wouldn't you want somebody to help if it were *your* leg? You, there, and you there in the blue tunic."

As the men bent to hold Iakovitzes, Krispos realized one of his questions had just been answered for him. If he was not leaving Opsikion any time soon, he would see Tanilis again. . . . And again and again, he thought.

Iakovitzes hissed and then groaned as Ordanes set to work. Despite the noble's anguish, Krispos had all he could do to keep from giggling. Tanilis was a much more alluring prospect in bed than his master.

Chapter VI

THAT MONTH OF CONSTANT ATTENDANCE ON IAKOVITZES PROVED even more wearing than Ordanes had predicted. The physician had compared it to tending a baby. Babies only cried. Iakovitzes used his searing tongue to inform Krispos of all his whims and all Krispos' shortcomings.

By the noble's reckoning, Krispos had plenty of them. Iakovitzes blamed him when the water for sponge baths was too hot or too cold, when Bolkanes' kitchen came up with a meal Iakovitzes found inadequate, when the bedpan was not perfectly placed, and even when his healing leg itched, which it seemed to do most of the time.

As for that bedpan, sometimes Krispos felt like braining Iakovitzes with it. It was, however, his master's one significant advantage over a baby: Iakovitzes, at least, did not foul the bed. In a time that held few large advantages, Krispos cherished the small one.

One afternoon about three weeks after the noble got hurt, someone knocked on the door of his room. Krispos jumped. Few people had come to see Iakovitzes. Krispos opened the door with one hand on his knife. A good-looking youth stared at him with equal suspicion.

"It's all right, Krispos, Graptos," Iakovitzes called from his bed. "In fact, Krispos, it's better than all right. You can take the rest of the day off. I'll see you in the morning."

"Excellent sir?" Krispos said doubtfully.

"Bolkanes arranged this for me," Iakovitzes assured him. "After all, if I'm bedridden, I might as well *be* bed-ridden, if you see what I mean. And since you're so tiresomely obstinate on the subject—"

Krispos waited to hear no more. He closed the door behind him and hurried down to the stables. If Iakovitzes was going to sport, so would he. The sun was still an hour away from setting when he got to Tanilis' villa.

He had to wait some little time before he saw her; she was settling a dispute between two peasants who dwelt on her land. Neither seemed displeased as they walked past Krispos. He was unsurprised; Tanilis had more than enough sense to dispense justice.

She smiled as Naues led Krispos into her study. "I wondered if I would see you again, after your master's accident," she said. In front of her steward, her voice was perfectly controlled.

"I wondered, too." Krispos also kept his tone casual. He was sure Tanilis would be able to find all the double meanings he put into his words and perhaps some he left out. He went on, "The excellent Iakovitzes seems to be in better spirits these days." He explained who was taking care of the noble, and in what ways.

Naues snorted; the tiny curl of Tanilis' lip looked like less but spoke more. Aloud, she said, "You are welcome here regardless of the circumstances. Mavros may be back for the evening meal, but then again he may not. Now that he is sure he won't be leaving for the city till spring, he gives all his time to one girl, knowing, I suppose, that afterward time and distance will fade the attachment."

Such cool, calculated good sense sounded more like Tanilis than young Mavros; for a moment Krispos was reminded of listening to his own father back in the days when Zoranne was all he'd thought of. He hoped Mavros was clever enough to recognize that his mother was cleverer still.

"Naues, are there any more out there who need me?" Tanilis asked. When her man shook his head, she told him, "Go and warn Evtykhes, then, that Krispos certainly will stay for supper, and that I do have some hope my son will appear, as well."

Mavros did come back to the villa. When he found Krispos there, he condescended to stay for dinner. "How'd you get loose?" he asked. "I thought Iakovitzes wanted you there every minute?" Krispos explained again. Mavros burst out laughing. "Good for the old bugger! He's feeling better, then?"

"Aye, but he's not up and about yet. And with the fall rains due any day now, it's just as he feared. He won't be riding back to the city till spring; he can't even hobble yet, let alone sit a horse."

"Too bad," Mavros said dolefully. "Here I've been champing at the bit for weeks, and now I'll have to wait for months. Such a long time." With a moody sigh, he raised his wine cup to his lips.

Tanilis said, "Be thankful you're young enough that a few months seem a long time to you. To me, next spring feels like the day after tomorrow."

"Well, not to me," Mavros said.

For the most part, Krispos agreed with Mavros; at twenty-two, he thought the world passed too slowly to suit him. Still, even slowness could have its advantages. He said, "From what I've heard, you've got a girl now, so just think of it as having a longer-seeming time to spend with her."

"I wish it were that easy," Mavros said, "but somehow when I'm with her the time flies by, so it never seems like enough no matter how long it is. Which reminds me." He finished his wine, rose, and sketched bows to Tanilis and Krispos. "I promised I'd meet her before the moon came up." Not quite trotting, he left the dining room.

"My poor, bereft son," Tanilis said dryly. "He hasn't set eyes on his beloved for, oh, several hours now. In a way, I suppose, I should be jealous, but he just makes me smile instead."

Krispos thoughtfully ate one of Evtykhes' lemon tarts. Tanilis hadn't told him anything he didn't already know; her practiced sensuality was worlds apart from Mavros' enthusiastic infatuation. Nevertheless, Krispos wished his lover had not made it so plain he was not her beloved.

But no matter what she did, she came to him that night. If she found what they did together distasteful, she hid it marvelously well. Afterward, Krispos leaned up on one elbow. "Why me?" he asked. Tanilis made a questioning noise. "Why me?" Krispos repeated. "Who you are and what you are, you could pick any man within a hundred miles of Opsikion, and he'd come running. So why did you pick me?"

"Because of your looks, your youth, your vigor. Because, having seen you, I could not help picking you."

The words were all Krispos could have hoped to hear. But he also heard the faintest questioning tone in Tanilis' voice, as if she were offering him an explanation to see whether he'd accept it. Though he wanted to, he found he could not. He said, "You could find a dozen who outdo me on any of those at a glance— a hundred or a thousand with a little looking. I gather you haven't, which means you haven't answered me, either."

Now she sat up in bed. Krispos thought it was the first time she took him seriously for his own sake rather than as a cog in what she'd foreseen. After a short pause, she said slowly, "Because you don't take the easy way, but look to see what may lie behind it. That is rare at any age, doubly so at yours."

This time he felt she'd touched truth, but not given him the whole of it. "Why else?" he persisted.

He wondered if his drive to know would anger her, but soon saw it did not. If anything, it raised him in her estimation; when she replied, her voice had the no-nonsense tone of someone conducting serious business. "I'll not deny that the power implied by this"—she reached out to touch the goldpiece on its chain—"has its own attraction. In and around Opsikion, I have done everything, become everything I could hope to do and become. To set up my own son in Videssos the city, to have a connection to one who may be . . . what he may be: that could tempt me almost to anything. But only almost. Reckon me hard if you like, and calculating, and cunning, but you reckon me a whore at your peril." She did not sound businesslike then; she sounded dangerous.

Krispos nodded soberly. As with Iakovitzes, his chief shield against her was stubborn refusal to acknowledge that she could daunt him. "And so?" he asked.

The light from the single lamp in the bedchamber shifted shadows on her face to underscore her every change of expression. With that aid, Krispos saw he'd gained another point. "And so," she said, "I have no interest in men who seek to bed not me but my estates; nor in those who would reckon me only a prize possession, as if I were a hound; nor again in those who care just for my body and would not mind if Skotos dwelt behind my eyes. Do you see yourself in any of those groups?"

"No," Krispos said. "But in a way don't you fall into the first one, I mean with respect to me?"

Tanilis stared at him. "You dare—" He admired her for the speed with which she checked herself. After a few seconds, she even laughed. "You have me, Krispos; by my own words I stand convicted. But here I am on the other end of the bargain; and I must say it looks different from how it seemed before."

To you, maybe, Krispos thought.

Tanilis went on, "A final reason I chose you, Krispos, at least after the first time, is that you learn quickly. One of the things you still need to know, though, is that sometimes you can ask too many questions."

She reached up and drew his face down to hers. But even as he responded to her teaching, he remained sure there was no such thing as asking too many questions. Finding the right way and time to ask them might be something else again, he admitted to himself. And this, he thought before all thought left him, was probably not it.

H E WOKE THE NEXT MORNING TO RAIN DRUMMING ON THE roof. He knew that sound, though he was more used to the softer plashing of raindrops against thatch than the racket they made on tile. He hoped Tanilis' peasants were done with their harvest, then laughed at himself: they *were* done now, whether they wanted to be or not.

Tanilis, as was her way, had slipped off during the night. Sometimes he woke when she slid out of bed; more often, as last night, he did not. He wondered, not for the first time, if her servants knew they were lovers. If so, the cooks and stewards and serving maids gave no sign of it. He had learned from Iakovitzes' establishment, though, that being discreet was part of being a well-trained servant. And Tanilis tolerated no servant who was not.

He also wondered if Mavros knew. That, he doubted. Mavros was a good many things and would likely grow to become a good many more, but Krispos had trouble seeing him as discreet.

Her hair as perfectly in place as if he had never run his hands through it, Tanilis sat waiting for him in the small dining room. "You'll have a wet ride back to Opsikion, I fear," she said, waving him to the chair opposite her.

He shrugged. "I've been wet before."

"A good plate of boiled bacon should help keep you warm on the journey, if not dry."

"My lady is generous in all things," Krispos said. Tanilis' eyes lit as he dug in.

The road north had already begun to turn to glue. Krispos did not try to push his horse. If Iakovitzes could not figure out why he was late coming back to town, too bad for Iakovitzes.

Krispos wrung out his cloak in Bolkanes' front hall, then squelched up the stairs in wet boots to see how his master was doing. What he found in Iakovitzes' room startled him: the noble was on his feet, trying to stump around with two sticks. The only sign of Graptos was a lingering trace of perfume in the air.

"Hello, look what I can do!" Iakovitzes said, for once too pleased with himself to be snide.

"I've looked," Krispos said shortly. "Now will you please get back in bed where you belong? If you were a horse, excellent sir"—he'd learned the art of turning title to reproach—"they'd have cut your throat for a broken leg and let it go at that. If you go and break it again from falling because you're on it too soon, do you think you deserve any better? Ordanes told you to stay flat at least another fortnight."

"Oh, bugger Ordanes," Iakovitzes said.

"Go ahead, but make him get on top."

The noble snorted. "No thank you."

Krispos went on more earnestly, "I can't give you orders, excellent sir, but I can ask if you'd treat one of your animals the way you're treating yourself. There's no point to it, the more so since with the fall rains starting you're not going anyplace anyhow."

"Mrmm," Iakovitzes said—a noise a long way from any sort of agreement, but one that, when the noble changed the subject, showed Krispos he had got through.

Iakovitzes continued to mend. Eventually, as Ordanes had predicted, he was able to move about with his sticks, lifting and planting them and his splinted leg so heavily that once people in the taproom directly below his chamber complained to Bolkanes about the racket he made. Since the innkeeper was getting, if not rich, then at least highly prosperous from his noble guest's protracted stay, he turned a deaf ear to the complaints.

By the time Iakovitzes could stump about the inn, the rains made sure he did not travel much farther. Outside large towns, Videssos had few paved roads; dirt was kinder to horses' hooves. The price of that kindness was several weeks of impassable soup each fall and spring. Iakovitzes cursed every day that dawned gray and wet, which meant he did a lot of cursing.

Krispos tried to rebuke him. "The rain's a blessing to farmers, excellent sir, and without farmers we'd all starve." The words were several seconds out of his mouth before he realized they were his father's.

"If you like farmers so bloody well, why did you ever leave that pissant village you sprang from?" Iakovitzes retorted. Krispos gave up on changing his master's attitude; trying to get Iakovitzes to stop cursing was like trying to fit the moon in a satchel. The noble's bad temper seemed as constant as the ever-shifting phases of the moon.

And soon enough, Krispos came to curse the fall rains, too. As Iakovitzes grew more able to care for himself, Krispos found himself with more free time. He wanted to spend as much time as he could with Tanilis, both for the sake of his body's pleasure and, increasingly, to explore the boundaries of their odd relationship. Riding even as far as her villa, though, was not to be undertaken lightly, not in the fall.

Thus he was overjoyed, one cold blustery day when the rain threatened to turn to sleet, to hear her say, "I think I will go into Opsikion soon, to spend the winter there. I have a house, you know, not far from Phos' temple."

"I'd forgotten," Krispos admitted. That night, in the privacy of the guest chamber, he said, "I hope I'll be able to see you more often if you come to town. This miserable weather—"

Tanilis nodded. "I expect you will."

"Did you—" Krispos paused, then plunged: "Did you decide to go into Opsikion partly on account of me?"

Her laugh was warm enough that, though he flushed, he did not flinch. "Don't flatter yourself too much, my—well, if I call you my dear, you *will* flatter yourself, won't you? In any case, I go into Opsikion every year about this time. Should anything important happen, I might not learn of it for weeks were I to stay here in the villa."

"Oh." Krispos thought for a moment. "Couldn't you stay here and foresee what you need to know?"

"The gift comes as it will, not as I will," Tanilis said. "Besides, I like to see new faces every so often. If I'd prayed at the chapel here, after all, instead of coming into Opsikion for the holy Abdaas' day, I'd not have met you. You might have stayed a groom forever."

Reminded of Iakovitzes' jibe, Krispos said, "It's an easier life than the one I had before I came to the city." He also thought, a little angrily, that he would have risen further even if Tanilis hadn't met him. That he kept to himself. Instead, he said, "If you come to Opsikion, you might want to bring that pretty little laundress of yours—Phronia's her name, isn't it?—along with you."

"Oh? And why is that?" Tanilis' voice held no expression whatever.

Krispos answered quickly, knowing he was on tricky ground. "Because I've spread the word around that she's the reason I come here so often. If she's in Opsikion, I'll have a better excuse to visit you there."

"Hmm. Put that way, yes." Tanilis' measuring gaze reminded Krispos of a hawk eyeing a rabbit from on high. "I would not advise you to use this story to deceive me while you carry on with Phronia. I would not advise that at all."

A chill ran down Krispos' spine, though he had no interest in Phronia past any young man's regard for a pretty girl. Since that was true, the chill soon faded. What remained was insight into how Tanilis thought. Krispos' imagination had not reached to concealing one falsehood within another, but Tanilis took the possibility for granted. That had to mean she'd seen it before, which in turn meant other people used such complex ploys. *Something else to look out for,* Krispos thought with a silent sigh.

"What was that for?" Tanilis asked.

Wishing she weren't so alert, he said, "Only that you've taught me many things."

"I've certainly intended to. If you would be more than a groom, you need to know more than a groom."

Krispos nodded before the full import of what she'd said sank in. Then he found himself wondering whether she'd warned him about Phronia just to show him how a double bluff worked. He thought about asking her but decided not to. She might not have meant that at all. He smiled ruefully. Whatever else she was doing, she was teaching him to distrust first impressions . . . and second . . . and third. . . . After a while, he supposed, reality might disappear altogether, and no one would notice it was gone.

He thought of how Iakovitzes and Lexo had gone back and forth, quarreling over what was thought to be true at least as much as over what was true. To prosper in Videssos the city, he might need every bit of what Tanilis taught.

SINCE OPSIKION LAY BY THE SAILORS' SEA, KRISPOS THOUGHT winter would be gentler there. The winter wind, though, was not off the sea, but from the north and west; a breeze from his old home, but hardly a welcome one.

Eventually the sea froze, thick enough for a man to walk on, out to a distance of several miles from shore. Even the folk of Opsikion called that a hard winter. To Krispos it was appalling; he'd seen frozen rivers and ponds aplenty, but the notion that the sea could turn to ice made him wonder if the Balancer heretics from Khatrish might not have a point. The broad, frigid expanse seemed a chunk of Skotos' hell brought up to earth.

Yet the locals took the weather in stride. They told stories of the year an iceberg, perhaps storm-driven from Agder or the Haloga country, smashed half the docks before shattering against the town's seawall. And the eparch Sisinnios sent armed patrols onto the ice north of the city.

"What are you looking for, demons?" Krispos asked when he saw the guardsmen set out one morning. He laughed nervously. If the frozen sea was as much Skotos' country as it appeared, demons might indeed dwell there.

The patrol leader laughed, too. He thought Krispos had been joking.

"Worse than demons," he said, and gave Krispos a moment to stew before he finished: "Khatrishers."

"In this weather?" Krispos wore a squirrelskin cap with earflaps. It was pulled down low on his forehead. A thick wool scarf covered his mouth and nose. The few square inches of skin between the one and the other had long since turned numb.

The patrol leader was similarly muffled. His breath made a steaming cloud around him. "Grab a spear and come see for yourself," he urged. "You're with the chap from the city, right? Well, you can tell him some of what we see around here."

"Why not?" A quick trip back to the armory gave Krispos a spear and a white-painted shield. Soon he was stumbling along the icy surface of the sea with the troopers. It was rougher, more irregular ice than he'd expected, almost as if the waves had frozen instead of breaking.

"Always keep two men in sight," said the patrol leader, whose name, Krispos learned, was Saborios. "You get lost out here by yourself—well, you're already on the ice, so where will your soul end up?" Krispos blew out a smoky sigh of relief to discover he was not the only one who had heretical thoughts.

The guardsmen paid attention to what they were doing, but it was a routine attention, making sure they did nothing they knew to be foolish. It left plenty of room for banter and horseplay. Krispos trudged on grimly in the middle of the line. With neither terrain nor risks familiar to him, he had all he could do just to keep pace.

"Good thing it's not snowing," one of the troopers said. "If it was snowing, the Khatrishers could sneak an army past us and we'd never know the difference."

"We would when we got back," another answered. The first guard chuckled.

Everything looked the same to Krispos; sky and frozen sea and distant land all were shades of white and gray. Anything colorful, he thought, should have been visible for miles. What had not occurred to him was how uncolorful a smuggler could become.

Had the trooper to Krispos' left not almost literally stumbled over the man, they never would have spied him. Even then, had he stayed still, he might have escaped notice: he wore white foxskins and, when still, was invisible past twenty paces. But he lost his head and tried to run. He was no better at it on the slippery ice than his pursuers, who soon ran him down.

Saborios held out a hand to the Khatrisher, who had gone so far as to daub white greasepaint on his beard and face. "You don't by any chance have your import license along, do you?" the patrol leader asked pleasantly. The Khatrisher stood in glum silence. "No, eh?" Saborios said, almost as if really surprised. "Then let's have your goods."

The smuggler reached under his jacket, drew out a leather pouch.

The patrol leader opened it. "Amber, is it? Very fine, too. Did you give me all of it? Complete confiscation, you know, is the penalty for unlicensed import."

"That's everything, curse you," the Khatrisher said sullenly.

"Good." Saborios nodded his understanding. "Then you won't mind Domentzios and Bonosos stripping you. If they find you've told the truth, they'll even give you back your clothes."

Krispos was shivering in his furs. He wondered how long a naked man would last on the ice. Not long enough to get off it again, he was sure. He watched the smuggler make the same unhappy calculation. The fellow took a pouch from each boot. The patrol leader pocketed them, then motioned forward the two troopers he had named. They were tugging off the Khatrisher's coat when he exclaimed, "Wait!"

The imperials looked to the patrol leader, who nodded. The smuggler shed his white fox cap. "I need my knife, all right?" he said. Saborios nodded again. The smuggler cut into the lining, extracted yet another pouch. He threw down the dagger. "Now you can search me."

The troopers did. They found nothing. Shivering and swearing, the Khatrisher dove back into his clothes. "You might have got that last one by us," Saborios remarked.

"That's what I thought," the smuggler said through chattering teeth. "Then I thought I might not have, too."

"Sensible," Saborios said. "Well, let's take you in. We've earned our pay for today, I think."

"What will you do with him?" Krispos asked as the patrol turned back toward Opsikion.

"Hold him for ransom," Saborios answered. "Nothing else we can do, now that I've seen he's smuggling amber. Gumush will pay to have him back, never fear." Krispos made a questioning noise. Saborios explained, "Amber's a royal monopoly in Khatrish. The khagan likes to see if he can avoid paying our tariffs every so often, that's all. This time he didn't, so we get some for free."

"Does he sneak in enough to make it worth his while?"

"That's a sharp question—I thought you were Iakovitzes' groom, not his bookkeeper. The only answer I know is, he must think so or he wouldn't keep doing it. But not this run, though." The patrol leader's eyes, almost the only part of his face visible, narrowed in satisfaction.

Iakovitzes howled with glee when Krispos told him the story that evening. They were sitting much closer than usual to Bolkanes' big fire; Krispos had a mug of hot spiced wine close at hand. He smiled gratefully when one of the barmaids refilled it. Iakovitzes said, "It'll serve Gumush right. Nothing I enjoy more than a thief having to pay for his own thievery."

"Won't he just raise the price later on to make up for it?" Krispos asked. "The legitimate price, I mean."

"Probably, probably," Iakovitzes admitted. "But what do I care? I don't much fancy amber. And no matter how hard he squeezes, the world doesn't hold enough gold for him to buy his way out of embarrassment." Contemplating someone else's discomfiture would put Iakovitzes in a good mood if anything would.

A couple of nights later, Tanilis proved coldly furious that the amber had been seized. "I made the arrangements for it myself with Gumush," she said. "Four parts in ten off the going rate here, which still allowed him a profit, seeing as the tariff is five parts in ten. He already has half the money, too. Do you suppose he'll send it back when he ransoms his courier?" Her bitter laugh told how likely that was.

"But . . ." Krispos scratched his head. "The Avtokrator needs the money from the tariffs, to pay for soldiers and furs and roads and—"

"And courtesans and fine wines and fripperies," Tanilis finished for him; she sounded as scornful of Anthimos III as Pyrrhos had. "But even if it were only as you say, I need money, too, for the good of my own estates. Why should I pay twice as much for amber as I need to for the sake of a handful of rich men in Videssos the city who do nothing for me?"

"Don't they?" Krispos asked. "Seems to me I wouldn't have come here with my master if the men in the city weren't worried about the border with Khatrish. Or are you such a queen here that your peasants would have fought off the nomad horsemen on their own?" He recalled the Kubratoi descending on his vanished boyhood village as if it had happened only the day before.

Tanilis frowned. "No, I am no queen, so what you say has some truth. But the Avtokrator and Sevastokrator chose peace with Khatrish for their own reasons, not mine."

Remembering Petronas' ambitions against Makuran, Krispos knew she was right. But he said, "It works out the same for you either way, doesn't it? If it does, you ought to be willing to pay for it." He and his fellow villagers had been willing to pay anything within reason to prevent another invasion from Kubrat. Only the Empire's demands reaching beyond reason had detached him from the land, and the rest of the villagers were there still.

"You speak well, and to the point," Tanilis said. "I must confess, my loyalty is to my lands first, and to the Empire of Videssos only after that. What I say is true of most nobles, I think, almost all those away from Videssos the city. To us, the Empire seems more often to check our strength than to protect it, and so we evade demands from the capital as best we can."

The more Krispos talked with Tanilis, the more complex his picture of the world grew. Back in his village, he'd thought of nobles as agents of the Empire and thanked Phos that the freeholders among whom he'd lived owed service to no lord. Yet Tanilis seemed no ally to the will of Videssos the city, but rather a rival. But she was no great friend of the peasants, either; she simply wanted to control them herself in place of the central government. Krispos tried to imagine how things looked from Petronas' perspective. Maybe one day he'd ask the Sevastokrator—after all, he'd met him. He laughed a little, amused at his own presumption.

"What do you find funny?" Tanilis asked.

Krispos' cheeks grew warm. Sometimes when he was with Tanilis, he felt he was a scroll she could unroll and read as she wished. Annoyed at himself for being so open, and sure he could not lie successfully, he explained.

She took him seriously. She always did; he had to give her that. Though he was certain he often seemed very young and raw to her, she went out of her way not to mock his enthusiasms, even if she let him see she did not share many of them. Even more than the sweet lure of her body, the respect she gave him made him want to spend time with her, in bed and out of it. He wondered if this was how love began.

The thought so startled him that he missed her reply. She saw that, too, and repeated herself: "If Petronas would tell you, I daresay you'd learn a great deal. A regent who can keep the reins of power even after his ward comes of age—and in such a way that the ward does not hate him—is a man to be reckoned with."

"I suppose so." Krispos knew he sounded abstracted and hoped Tanilis would not figure out why. Loving her could only complicate his life, the more so as he knew she did not love him.

Slow as the flow of syrup on ice, news dripped into Opsikion through the winter. Krispos heard of the death of khagan Omurtag weeks after it happened; a son named Malomir ascended to the rule of Kubrat. In Thatagush, north and east of Khatrish, a band of Haloga raiders under a chief called Harvas Black-Robe sacked a whole string of towns and smashed the army that tried to drive them away. Some nobles promptly joined forces with the Halogai against their khagan. The King of Kings of Makuran sent a peace embassy to Videssos the city. Petronas sent it back.

"By the lord with the great and good mind, I gave Petronas what he wanted here," Iakovitzes said when that report reached him. "Now let's see what he does with it." His chuckle had a gloating tone to it. "Not as much as he wants, I'll wager."

"No?" Krispos helped his master out of a chair. The noble could walk with a stick these days, but he still limped badly; his left calf was only half as big around as his right. Krispos went on carefully, "The Sevastokrator strikes me as a man who generally gets what he wants."

"Oh, aye, he is. Here, I'm all right now. Thanks." Iakovitzes hissed as he put weight on his healing leg. Ordanes had given him a set of exercises to strengthen it. He swore through clenched teeth every time he began them, but never missed a day.

Now he took a couple of steps toward the stairway that led up to his room before he continued. "But what Petronas wants is to overthrow Makuran, and that won't happen. Stavrakios the Great couldn't do it, not when the Empire of Videssos ran all the way up to the border of the Haloga country. I suppose the Makurani King of Kings dreams of worshiping their Four Prophets in the High Temple in Videssos the city, and that won't happen, either. If Petronas can bite off a chunk of Vaspurakan, he'll have done something worthwhile, at any rate. We can use the metals there and the men, even if they are heretics."

A guardsman coming off duty threw open the door to Bolkanes' taproom. Though he slammed it again right away, Krispos and Iakovitzes both shivered at the icy blast he let in. He stood in the front hall brushing snow off his clothes and out of his beard.

"Beastly weather," Iakovitzes said. "I could ride now, but what's the point? The odds are too good I'd end up a block of ice somewhere halfway between here and the city, and that would be a piteous waste. Come to think of it, you'd freeze, too."

"Thank you for thinking of me," Krispos said mildly.

Iakovitzes cocked an eyebrow. "You're getting better at that innocent-sounding comeback, aren't you? Do you practice in front of a mirror?"

"Er—no." Krispos knew his fencing with Tanilis helped sharpen both his wits and his wit. He hadn't realized anyone else would notice.

"Maybe it's the time you spend knocking around with Mavros," Iakovitzes said. Krispos blinked; his master's guess was good enough to startle him. Iakovitzes went on, "He has a noble's air to him, even if he is young."

"I hadn't really noticed," Krispos said. "I suppose he gets it from his mother."

"Maybe." As he did whenever a woman was mentioned, Iakovitzes sounded indifferent. He reached the stairway. "Give me your hand, will you, for the way up?" Krispos complied. Chill or no, Iakovitzes was sweating by the time he got to the top of the stairs; his leg still did not take kindly to such work.

Krispos went through the usual small wrestling match he needed to get the noble to let go. "After a year with me, excellent sir, don't you believe I'm not interested?" he asked.

"Oh, I believe it," Iakovitzes said. "I just don't take it seriously." Having had, if not Krispos, then at least the last word, he hobbled down the hall toward his room.

RAIN PATTERED ON THE SHUTTERS OF THE BEDROOM WINDOW. "The second storm in a row with no snow in it," Tanilis said. "No sleet in this one either, or none to speak of. Winter is finally losing its grip."

"So it is." Krispos kept his voice noncommittal. The imminent return of good weather meant too many different things now for him to be sure how he felt about it.

Tanilis sat up in bed and ran a hand through her hair. The gesture, artfully artless, made her bare breasts rise for Krispos' admiration. At the same time, though, she said, "When the rain finally stops, I will be going back to my villa. I don't think you would be wise to visit me there."

Krispos had known she would tell him that, sooner or later. He'd thought he was ready. Actually hearing the words, though, was like taking a blow in the belly—no matter how braced he was, they still hurt. "So it's over," he said dully.

"This part of it," Tanilis agreed.

Again, he'd thought he could accept that, thought he could depart with Iakovitzes for Videssos the city without a backward glance. Had his master not broken his leg, that might well have been true. But wintering in Opsikion, passing so much more time with Tanilis, made it harder than he'd expected. All his carefully cultivated sangfroid deserted him. He clutched her to him. "I don't want to leave you!" He groaned.

She yielded to his embrace, but her voice stayed detached, logical. "What then? Would you turn aside from what I and others have seen for you, would you abandon this"—she touched the goldpiece Omurtag had given him—"to stay in Opsikion? And if you would, would I look on you with anything but scorn because of it?"

"But I love you!" Krispos said.

Down deep, he'd always been sure telling her that would be a mistake. His instinct proved sound. She answered, "If you stayed here because of that, I surely could never love you. I am already fully myself, while you are still discovering what you can be. Nor in the long run would you be happy in Opsikion, for what would you be here? My plaything, maybe, granted a small respect reflected from the larger one I have earned, but laughed at behind people's hands. Is that the most you want for yourself, Krispos?"

"Your plaything?" That made him angry enough not to listen to the rest of what she said. He ran a rough hand along the supple curves of her body, ending at the edge of the neatly trimmed hair that covered her secret place. "Is that all this has meant? Is that all I've been to you?"

"You know better, or you should," Tanilis said calmly. "How could I deny you've pleased me? I would not want to deny it. But it is not enough. You deserve to be more than a bedwarmer, however fine a bedwarmer you are. And if you stayed with me, you would not find it easy to be anything else. Not only do I have far more experience and vastly greater wealth than you, I do not care to yield to anyone the power I've earned by my own efforts over the years. So what would that leave you?"

"I don't care," Krispos said. Though he sounded full of fierce conviction, even he knew that was not true.

So, obviously, did Tanilis. "Do you not? Very well, then, let us suppose you stay here and that you and I are wed, perhaps on the next feast day of the holy Abdaas. Come the morning after, what do you propose to say to your new stepson, Mavros?"

"My—" Krispos gulped. He had no trouble imagining Mavros his brother. But his stepson? He could not even make himself say the word. He started to laugh, instead, and poked Tanilis in the ribs. She was not usually ticklish, but he caught her by surprise. She yipped and wiggled away.

"Mavros my—" He tried again, but only ended up laughing harder. "Oh, a pestilence, Tanilis, you've made your point."

"Good. There's always hope for anyone who can see plain sense, even if I did have to bludgeon you to open your eyes." She turned her head.

"What is it?" Krispos asked.

"I was just listening. I don't think the rain will let up for a while yet." Now her hand wandered, came to rest. She smiled a catlike smile. "By the feel of things, neither will you. Shall we make the most of the time we have left?"

He did not answer, not with words, but he did not disagree.

"LET ME GIVE YOU A HAND, EXCELLENT SIR," KRISPOS SAID AS A pair of stable boys led out his master's horse, his own, and their pack animals.

"Nonsense," Iakovitzes told him. "If I can't mount for myself, I surely won't be able to ride back to the city. And if I can't do that, I'm faced with two equally unpalatable alternatives: take up residence here, or throw myself off a promontory into the sea. On the whole, I believe I'd prefer throwing myself into the sea. That way I'd never have to find out what's become of my house while I've been gone." The noble gave a shudder of exquisite dread.

"When you wrote you'd been hurt, the Sevastokrator pledged to look after your affairs."

"So he did," Iakovitzes said with a skeptical grunt. "The only affairs Petronas cares anything about, though, are his own." He scowled at the boy who held his horse. "Back away, there. If I can't manage, high time I found out."

The stable boy retreated. Iakovitzes set his left foot in the stirrup, swung up and onto the horse's back. He winced as the newly healed leg took all his weight for a moment, but then he was mounted and grinning in triumph. He'd boarded the horse before, every day for the past week, but each time seemed a new adventure, both to him and to everyone watching.

"Now where's that Mavros?" he said. "I'm still not what you'd call comfortable up here. Anyone who thinks I'll waste time waiting that I could use riding will end up disappointed, I promise you that."

Krispos did not think Iakovitzes was speaking to him in particular; he sounded more as if he were warning the world at large. Krispos checked one last time to make sure all their gear was properly stowed on the pack-horses' backs, then climbed onto his own beast.

Bolkanes came to bid his longtime guests farewell. He bowed to Iakovitzes. "A pleasure to serve you, eminent sir."

"I should hope so. I've made your fortune," Iakovitzes answered, gracious to the end.

As the innkeeper beat a hasty retreat, Mavros rode up on a big bay gelding. He looked very young and jaunty, with two pheasant plumes sticking up from his broad-brimmed hat and his right hand on the hilt of his sword. He waved to Krispos and dipped his head in Iakovitzes' direction. "You look like you were all set to take off without me."

"I was," Iakovitzes snapped.

If he thought to intimidate the youth, he failed. "Well, no need for that now, seeing as I'm here," Mavros said easily. He turned to Krispos. "My mother said to be sure to tell you good-bye from her. Now I've done it." *One more chore finished*, his attitude seemed to say.

"Ah. That's kind of her," Krispos said. Although he hadn't seen or heard from Tanilis in more than a month, she was in his thoughts every day, the memory of her as liable to sudden twinges as was Iakovitzes' leg. A limp in the heart, though, did not show on the outside.

"If you two are done nattering like washerwomen, shall we be off?" Iakovitzes said. Without waiting for an answer, he used knees and reins to urge his horse forward. Krispos and Mavros rode after him.

Opsikion's gate guards still had not learned to take any special notice of Iakovitzes, who, after all, had not come near the edge of the city since the summer before. But the feisty noble had no cause for complaint about the treatment he was afforded. Being with Mavros drew him such a flurry of salutes and guardsmen springing to attention that he said, not altogether in jest, "Anthimos should come here, to see what respect is."

"Oh, I expect he gets treated about as well in his hometown," Mavros said. Iakovitzes had to look at him sharply to catch the twinkle in his eye. The noble allowed himself a wintry chuckle, the most he usually gave wit not his own.

That chuckle, Krispos thought, was the only thing wintry about the day. It was mild and fair. New bright green covered the ground to either side of the road. Bees buzzed among fresh-sprouted flowers. The sweet, moist air was full of the songs of birds just returned from their winter stay in warmer climes.

Though the road climbed swiftly into the mountains, this near Opsikion it remained wide and easy to travel, if not always straight. Krispos was startled when, with the sun still nearer noon than its setting, Iakovitzes reined in and said, "That's enough. We'll camp here till morning." But when he watched his master dismount, he hardly needed to hear the noble go on, "My thighs are as raw as a dockside whore's the night after the imperial fleet rows into port."

"No wonder, excellent sir," Krispos said. "Flat on your back as you were for so long, you've lost your hardening."

"I don't know about that," Mavros said. "I've had some lovely hardenings flat on my back."

Again, Iakovitzes' basilisk glare failed to wilt him. The noble finally grunted and hobbled off into the bushes, unbuttoning his fly as he went. Watching that slow, spraddling gait, Krispos whistled softly. "He is saddle-sore, isn't he? I guess he thought it couldn't happen to him."

"Aye, looks like he'll have to get used to it all over again. He won't be back from watering the grass right away, either." Mavros lowered his voice as he reached into a saddlebag. "Which means now is as good a time as any to pass this on to you from my mother. A parting gift, you might say. She told me not to give it to you when anyone else could see."

Krispos reached out to take the small wooden box Mavros held. He wondered what sort of last present Tanilis had for him and wondered even more, briefly alarmed, how much she'd told Mavros about what had passed between the two of them. Mavros as stepson, indeed, Krispos thought—she'd known how to cool him down, sure enough. *Maybe, though,* he said to himself, *it's like one of the romances minstrels sing, and she does love me but can't admit it except by giving me this token once I'm safely gone.*

The second the box was in his hand, its weight told him Tanilis' gift was the more pragmatic one she'd promised. "Gold?" he said.

"A pound and a half," Mavros agreed. "If you're going to be—what you're going to be—this will help. Money begets money, my mother says. And this will grow all the better since no one knows you have it."

A pound and a half of gold—the box fit easily in the palm of Krispos' hand. For Tanilis, it was not enough money to be missed. Krispos knew that if he were to desert his master and Mavros and make his way back to his village, he would be far and away the richest man there. He could go home as something close to a hero: the lad who'd made good in the big city.

But his village, he realized after a moment, was not home anymore, not really. He could no more go back now than he could have stayed in Opsikion. For better or worse, he was caught up in the faster life of Videssos the city. After a taste of it, nothing less could satisfy him.

Rustlings from the bushes announced Iakovitzes' return. Krispos hastily stowed away the box of coins. With a hundred and eight goldpieces in his hands, he thought, he did not need to keep working for Iakovitzes anymore, either. But if he stayed on, he wouldn't have to start spending them. He didn't need to decide anything about that right away, not when he was only a short day's journey out of Opsikion.

"I may live," Iakovitzes said. He grimaced as he sat down on the ground and started pulling off his boots. "Eventually, I may even want to. What have we for supper?"

"About what you'd expect," Krispos answered. "Twice-baked bread, sausage, hard cheese, and onions. We have a couple of wineskins, but it's a ways to the next town, so we ought to go easy if we want to make it last. I hear a stream off that way—we'll have plenty of water to wash things down."

"Water. Twice-baked bread." The petulant set of Iakovitzes' mouth showed what he thought of that. "The next time Petronas wants me to go traveling for him, I'll ask if I can bring a chef along. He does, when he's out on campaign."

"There ought to be crawfish in the stream, and trout, too," Mavros said. "I have a couple of hooks. Shall I go see what I can come up with?"

"I'll start a fire," Krispos said. "Roast fish, crawfish baked in clay . . ." He glanced over to see how Iakovitzes liked the idea.

"Could be worse, I suppose," the noble said grudgingly. "See if you can find some early marjoram, too, why don't you, Mavros? It would add to the flavor."

"I'll do my best." Mavros rummaged through his gear till he found the hooks and some light line. "A chunk of sausage should be bait enough for the fish, but what do you suppose I should use to lure out the marjoram?"

Iakovitzes threw a boot at him.

ONE DAY WHEN HE WAS CLOSE TO HALFWAY BACK TO THE CITY, Krispos came across the coral pendant he'd brought for Sirikia. He stared at it; the seamstress hadn't crossed his mind in months. He hoped she'd found someone new. After Tanilis, going back to her would be like leaving Videssos for his farming village: possible, but not worth thinking about.

He was no monk on the journey westward; abstinence was not in his nature. But he had finally learned not to imagine himself in love each time his lust needed slaking. Mavros still sighed whenever he left behind another barmaid or dyeshop girl.

The travelers lay over in a town called Develtos to rest their horses. Iakovitzes surveyed the place with a jaundiced eye. His one-sentence verdict summed it up perfectly. "By the good god, it makes Opsikion look like a metropolis."

Mavros spluttered at that, but Krispos knew what his master meant. Develtos boasted a stout wall and had little else about which to boast. Seeing how small and gloomy a town the works protected, Krispos wondered why anyone had bothered to build them in the first place.

"The road does need strongpoints every so often," Iakovitzes told him when he said that aloud. The noble took another long look, sighed in despair. "But we'll have to make our own fun, that's for certain. Speaking of which . . ." His gaze traveled back to Krispos.

It was the groom's turn to sigh. Iakovitzes had not bothered him much since Mavros joined them. So far as Krispos knew, he hadn't made advances at Mavros, either. Had Krispos not seen a good-looking young stablehand a couple of towns back wearing one of the noble's rings the morning they set out, he would have wondered if Iakovitzes was fully healed. He'd enjoyed the peace while it lasted.

The inn Iakovitzes picked proved livelier than the rest of Develtos, whose people seemed as dour as the grim gray stone from which their wall and buildings were made. That was not the innkeeper's fault; he was as somber as any of his townsfolk. But a group of close to a dozen mother-of-pearl merchants from the eastern island of Kalavria made the place jolly in spite of its proprietor. Krispos had even met one or two of them back at Opsikion; they'd landed there before heading inland.

"Why didn't you just sail straight on to Videssos the city?" he asked one of the traders over a mug of wine.

"Bring mother-of-pearl to the city?" exclaimed the Kalavrian, a hook-nosed fellow named Stasios. "I might as well fetch milk to a cow. Videssos has more than it needs already. Here away from the sea, though, the stuff is rare and wonderful, and we get good prices."

"You know your business best," Krispos said. From the way the merchants were spending money, they'd done well so far.

The taproom grew gloomy as evening came on. The innkeeper waited longer than Krispos liked before lighting candles; likely he'd hoped his guests would go to bed when it got dark and save him the expense. But the Kalavrians were in no mood for sleep. They sang and drank and swapped stories with Krispos and his companions.

After a while, one of the traders took out a pair of dice. The tiny rattle they gave as he rolled them on the table to test his luck made Iakovitzes scramble to his feet. "I'm going upstairs," he told Krispos and Mavros, "and if the two of you have any sense you'll come with me. You start gambling with Kalavrians and you'll still be at it when the sun comes up again."

The merchants laughed. "So they know our reputation even in the city?" Stasios said. "I'd have bet they did."

"I know you would," Iakovitzes said. "You'd bloody well bet on anything. That's why I'm heading off to bed, to keep from having to stay up with you."

Mavros hesitated, then went upstairs with him. Krispos decided to stay and play. The stakes, he saw with some relief, were pieces of silver, not gold. "We're all friends," one of the traders said, noticing his glance at the money they'd got out. "There'd be no joy in breaking a man, especially since he'd have to stay with us till fall even so."

"Good enough," Krispos answered. Before long, the man to his left threw double sixes and lost the dice. They came to him. He rattled them in his hand, then sent them spinning across the tabletop. Twin ones stared up at the gamblers. "Phos' little suns!" Krispos said happily. He collected all the bets.

"Your first throw!" a Kalavrian said. "With luck like that, no wonder you wanted to stay down here. You knew you'd clean us out."

"They're your dice," Krispos retorted. "For all I knew, you'd loaded them."

"No, that'd be Rhangavve," Stasios said. "He's not with us this year— somebody back home on the island caught him at it and broke his arm for him. He's richer than any of us, though, the cheating bastard."

Krispos won a little, lost a little, won a little more. Eventually he found himself yawning and not being able to stop. He got up from the table. "That's enough for me," he said. "I want to be able to ride tomorrow without falling off my horse."

A couple of Kalavrians waved as he headed for the stairs. More had eyes only for the spinning bone cubes. Behind the bar, the innkeeper sat dozing. He jerked awake every so often. "Aren't you gents tired, too?" he asked plaintively, seeing Krispos leave. The traders laughed at him.

Krispos had just got to the head of the stairs when he saw someone quietly emerging from Iakovitzes' room. His hand dropped to the hilt of his sword. Then he relaxed. Though only a couple of tiny lamps lit the hall, he recognized Mavros. The youth leaned back into the doorway for a moment, murmured something Krispos could not hear, and went to his own room. It was farther down the hall than Iakovitzes', so he turned his back on Krispos and did not notice him.

Krispos frowned as he opened his door, then barred it behind him. He tried to tell himself what he'd seen didn't mean what he thought it did. He could not make himself believe it. He knew what a good-night kiss looked like, no matter who was giving it.

He asked himself what difference it made. Living in Iakovitzes' household had taught him that the grooms who let the noble take them to bed were not much different from the ones who declined, save in their choice of pleasures. If Mavros enjoyed what Iakovitzes offered, it was his business and none of Krispos'. It did not make him any less cheerful, clever, or enthusiastic.

That thought consoled Krispos long enough to let him undress and get into bed. Then he realized it was his business after all. Tanilis had charged him to treat Mavros as a younger brother. No matter how his perspective had changed, he knew it would not be easy if his younger brother acted as Mavros had.

He sighed. Here was something new and unwelcome to worry about. He had no idea what to say to Mavros or what to do if, as seemed likely, Mavros answered, "So what?" But he found he could not sleep until he promised himself he would say something.

Even getting the chance did not prove easy. Some of the Kalavrians were still gambling when he and Mavros came down for breakfast the next morning, and this was one conversation he did not want overheard.

For that matter, some of the Kalavrians were still gambling when Iakovitzes came down for breakfast quite a bit later. He rolled his eyes. "You'd bet on whether Phos or Skotos will triumph at the end of time," he said in disgust.

Stasios and a couple of others looked up from the dice. "You know, we just might," he said. Soon the bleary-eyed merchants started arguing theology as they played.

"Congratulations," Mavros told Iakovitzes.

"By the ice, what for?" Iakovitzes was listening to the Kalavrians as if he could not believe his ears.

With a sly grin, Mavros answered, "How many people can boast they've invented a new heresy before their morning porridge?"

Krispos swallowed wrong. Mavros pounded him on the back. Iakovitzes just scowled. Through the rest of the day, he remained as sour toward Mavros as he was with anyone else. Krispos began to wonder if he'd made a mistake. But no, he knew what he'd seen.

As the last of the all-night gamblers among the Kalavrians went upstairs, the traders who had gone to bed began drifting down once more. The game never stopped. Krispos fretted. Having to wait only made him more nervous about what he'd say to Mavros.

After checking the horses the next morning, Iakovitzes decided to ride on. "Another day wouldn't hurt the beasts, I suppose, but another day stuck in Develtos with those gambling maniacs would do me in," he said.

He was too good a horseman to push the pace with tired animals and rested them frequently. When he went off to answer nature's call at one of those stops, Krispos found himself with the opportunity he'd dreaded. "Mavros," he said quietly.

"What is it?" Mavros turned toward him. When he saw the expression on Krispos' face, his own grew more serious. "What is it?" he repeated in a different tone of voice.

Now that he was at the point, Krispos' carefully crafted speeches deserted him. "Did you end up in bed with Iakovitzes the other night?" he blurted.

"What if I did? Are you jealous?" Mavros looked at Krispos again. "No, you're not. What then? Why should you care?"

"Because I was bid to be your brother, remember? I never had a brother before, only sisters, so I don't quite know how to do that. But I do know I wouldn't want any kin of mine sleeping with someone just to get in his good graces."

If Mavros knew about him and Tanilis, Krispos realized as soon as the words were out of his mouth, he'd throw that right back at him, no matter how unfairly. But Mavros must not have. He said, "Why do I need to get in Iakovitzes' good graces? Aye, he lives at the capital, but I could buy and sell him. If he gives me too bad a time, I'd do it, too, and he knows it."

Krispos started to answer, abruptly stopped. He'd judged Mavros' situation by his own, and only now did he see the two were not the same. Unlike him, Mavros had a perfectly satisfactory life to return to if the city did not suit him. With such independent means, though, why had he yielded to Iakovitzes? That was a question Krispos could ask, and did.

"To find out what it was like, why else?" Mavros said. "I've had plenty of girls, but I'd never tried it the other way round. From the way Iakovitzes talked it up, I thought I was missing something special."

"Oh." The straightforward hedonism in the reply reminded Krispos of Tanilis. He needed a moment to get up the nerve to ask, "And what did you think?"

Mavros shrugged. "It was interesting to do once, but I wouldn't want to make a habit of it. As far as I'm concerned, girls are more fun."

"Oh," Krispos said again. He felt foolish. "I guess I should have kept my big mouth shut."

"Probably you should have." But Mavros seemed to reconsider. "No, I take that back. If we are to be brothers, then you have the right to speak to me when something troubles you—and the other way round, too, I suppose."

"That's only fair," Krispos agreed. "This whole business takes some getting used to."

"Things my mother arranges usually do," Mavros said cheerfully, "but they have a way of working out right in the end. And if this particular arrangement works out right in the end—" He broke off. They were altogether alone except for Iakovitzes off somewhere in the bushes, but he was still wary of speaking about what Tanilis had seen. Krispos thought the better of him for it. He was a good deal more than wary himself.

"What were you two gossiping about?" Iakovitzes asked when he came back a couple of minutes later.

"You, of course," Krispos said in his best innocent voice.

"A worthy topic indeed." Iakovitzes was noticeably smoother mounting than he had been back at Opsikion. He used his legs and the reins to get his horse moving once more. Krispos and Mavros followed him toward the city.

Chapter VII

"Hurry up, Krispos! aren't you ready yet?" Iakovitzes said. "We don't want to be late, not to this affair."

"No, excellent sir," Krispos said. He had been ready for the best part of an hour. His master was the one who kept taking off one robe and putting on another, agonizing over how big a hoop to wear in his left ear and whether it should be gold or silver, bedeviling his servants about which scent to douse himself with. This once, Krispos did not blame Iakovitzes for fussiness. The Sevastokrator Petronas was giving the evening's feast.

"Come on, then," Iakovitzes said now. A moment later, almost as an afterthought, he added, "You look quite well tonight. I don't think I've seen that robe before."

"Thank you, excellent sir. No, I don't think you've seen it, either. I just bought it a couple of weeks ago."

The garment in question was dark blue, and of fine soft wool. Its sober hue and plain cut were suited to a man older and of higher station than Krispos. He'd used a few of Tanilis' goldpieces on clothes of that sort. One of these days, he might need to be taken seriously. Not looking like a groom could only help.

He rode half a pace behind Iakovitzes and to his master's left. Iakovitzes swore whenever cross traffic made them slow and grew livid to see how crowded the plaza of Palamas was. "Out of the way there, you blundering oaf!" he screamed when he got stuck behind a small man leading a large mule. "I have an appointment with the Sevastokrator."

Cheeky as most of the folk who called Videssos the city home, the fellow retorted, "I don't care if you've got an appointment with Phos, pal. I'm in front of you and that's how I like it."

After more curses, Iakovitzes and Krispos managed to swing around the muleteer. By then they were near the western edge of the plaza of Palamas, past the great amphitheater, past the red granite obelisk of the Milestone from which all distances in the Empire were reckoned.

"Here, you see, excellent sir, we're all right," Krispos said soothingly as traffic thinned out.

"I suppose so." Iakovitzes did not sound convinced, but Krispos knew he was grumbling only because he always grumbled. The western edge of the plaza bordered on the imperial palaces, and no one entered the palace district without business there. Soon Iakovitzes urged his horse up into a trot, and then into a canter.

"Where are we going?" Krispos asked, keeping pace.

"The Hall of the Nineteen Couches."

"The nineteen what?" Krispos wasn't sure he'd heard correctly.

"Couches," Iakovitzes repeated.

"Why do they call it that?"

"Because up until maybe a hundred years ago, people at fancy feasts ate while they reclined instead of sitting in chairs as we do now. Don't ask me why they did that, because I couldn't tell you—to make it easier for them to spill things on their robes, I suppose. Anyway, there haven't been any couches in there for a long time, but names have a way of sticking."

They swung round a decorative stand of willows. Krispos saw scores of torches blazing in front of a large square building, and people bustling around and going inside. "Is that it?"

"That's it." Iakovitzes gauged the number of horses and sedan chairs off to one side of the hall. "We're all right—not too early, but not late, either."

Grooms in matched silken finery led away his mount and Krispos'. Krispos followed his master up the low, broad stairs to the Hall of the Nineteen Couches. "Pretty stone," Krispos remarked as he got close enough to make out detail in the torchlight.

"Do you really think so?" Iakovitzes said. "The green veining in the white marble always reminds me of one of those crumbly cheeses that smell bad."

"I hadn't thought of that," Krispos said, truthfully enough. He had to admit the comparison was apt. Even so, he would not have made it himself. Iakovitzes' jaundiced outlook made him take some strange views of the world.

A servitor in raiment even more splendid than the grooms' bowed low as Iakovitzes came to the entrance, then turned and loudly announced, "The excellent Iakovitzes!"

Thus introduced, Iakovitzes swaggered into the reception hall, as well as he could swagger with a limp that was still pronounced. Krispos, who was not nearly important enough to be worth introducing, followed his master inside.

"Iakovitzes!" Petronas hurried up to clasp the noble's hand. "That was a fine piece of work you did for me in Opsikion. You have my gratitude." The Sevastokrator made no effort to keep his voice down. Heads turned to see whom he singled out for such public praise.

"Thank you, your Highness," Iakovitzes said, visibly preening.

"As I said, you're the one who has earned my thanks. Well done." Petronas started to walk away, stopped. "Krispos, isn't it?"

"Yes, your Imperial Highness," Krispos said, surprised and impressed the Sevastokrator remembered his name after one brief meeting almost a year before.

"Thought so." Petronas also seemed pleased with himself. He turned back to Iakovitzes. "Didn't you bring another lad with you from Opsikion, too? Mavros, was that the name? Tanilis' son, I mean."

Iakovitzes nodded. "As a matter of fact, I did."

"Thought so," Petronas repeated. "Bring him along one of these times when we're at a function together, if you could. I'd like to meet him. Besides which"—the Sevastokrator's smile was cynical—"his mother's rich enough that I don't want to get her annoyed with me, and chatting him up can only help me with her."

Petronas went off to greet other guests. Iakovitzes' gaze followed him. "He doesn't miss much," the noble mused, more to himself than to Krispos. "I wonder which of my people told him about Mavros." Whoever it was, Krispos did not envy him if his master found him out.

Still muttering to himself, Iakovitzes headed for the wine. He plucked a silver goblet from the bed of hoarded snow in which it rested, drained it and reached for another. Krispos took a goblet, too. He sipped from it as he walked over to a table piled high with appetizers. A couple of slices of boiled eggplant and some pickled anchovies took the edge off his appetite. He was careful not to eat too much; he wanted to be able to do justice to the supper that lay ahead.

"Your moderation does you credit, young man," someone said from behind him when he left the hors d'oeuvres after only a brief stay.

"Your pardon?" Krispos turned, swiftly added, "Holy sir. Most holy sir," he amended; the priest—or rather prelate—who'd spoken to him wore shimmering cloth-of-gold with Phos' sun picked out in blue silk on his left breast.

"Nothing, really," the ecclesiastic said. His sharp, foxy features reminded Krispos of Petronas', though they were less stern and heavy than the Sevastokrator's. He went on, "It's just that at an event like this, where gluttony is the rule, seeing anyone eschew it is a cause for wonderment and celebration."

Hoping he'd guessed right about what "eschew" meant, Krispos answered, "All I planned was to be a glutton a little later." He explained why he'd gone easy on the appetizers.

"Oh, dear." The prelate threw back his head and laughed. "Well, young sir, I appreciate your candor. That, believe me, is even rarer at these events than moderation. I don't believe I've seen you before?" He paused expectantly.

"My name is Krispos, most holy sir. I'm one of Iakovitzes' grooms."

"Pleased to meet you, Krispos. Since I see my blue boots haven't given me away, let me introduce myself, as well: I'm called Gnatios."

Just as only the Avtokrator wore all-red boots, only one priest had the privilege of wearing all-blue ones. Krispos realized with a start that he'd been making small talk with the ecumenical patriarch of the Empire of Videssos. "M-most holy sir," he stammered, bowing. Even as he bent his head, though, he felt a rush of pride—if only the villagers could see him now!

"No formality needed, not when I'm here to enjoy the good food, too," Gnatios said with an easy smile. Then those foxy features suddenly grew very sharp indeed. "Krispos? I've heard your name before after all, I think. Something to do with the abbot Pyrrhos, wasn't it?"

"The abbot was kind enough to find me my place with Iakovitzes, yes, most holy sir," Krispos said.

"That's all?" Gnatios persisted.

"What else could there be?" Krispos knew perfectly well what else; if Gnatios didn't, he was not about to reveal it for him.

"Who knows what else?" The patriarch's chuckle was thin. "Where Pyrrhos is involved, any sort of superstitious excess becomes not only possible but credible. Well, never mind, young man. Just because something is credible, that doesn't necessarily make it true. Not necessarily. A pleasant evening to you."

Gnatios' shaven skull gleamed in the torchlight like one of the gilded domes atop Phos' temple as he went on his way. Krispos took the rest of the wine in his cup at a gulp, then went over to the great basin of snow for another one. He was sweating in spite of the wine's chill. The patriarch, by the nature of his office, was the Avtokrator's man. Had he boasted to Gnatios instead of sensibly keeping his mouth shut . . . He wondered if he would even have got back to Iakovitzes' house safe and sound.

Little by little, the wine helped calm Krispos. Gnatios didn't seem to have taken seriously whatever tales he'd heard. Then a servant appeared at Krispos' elbow. "Are you Iakovitzes' groom?" he asked.

Krispos' heart jumped into his mouth. "Yes," he answered, readying himself to knock the man down and flee.

"Could you join your master, please?" the fellow said. "We'll be seating folk for dinner soon, and the two of you will be together."

"Oh. Of course." Krispos felt like giggling with relief as he scanned the Hall of the Nineteen Couches for Iakovitzes. He wished the noble were taller; he was hard to spot. Even though he had trouble seeing Iakovitzes, he soon heard him arguing with someone or other. He made his way over to him.

Servants carried away the tables of appetizers. Others brought out dining tables and chairs. Despite guests getting in their way, they moved with practiced efficiency. Faster than Krispos would have thought possible, the hall was ready and the servants began guiding diners to their seats.

"This way, excellent sir, if you please," a servitor murmured to Iakovitzes. He had to repeat himself several times; Iakovitzes was driving home a rhetorical point by jabbing a forefinger into the chest of a man who had been rash enough to disagree with him. The noble finally let himself listen. He and Krispos followed the servant, who said, "You have the honor of sitting at the Sevastokrator's table."

To Krispos, that said how much Petronas thought of the job Iakovitzes had done at Opsikion. Iakovitzes merely grunted, "I've had it before." His eyebrows rose as he neared the head table. "And up till now, I've never had to share it with barbarians, either."

Four Kubratoi, looking outlandish indeed in their shaggy furs, were already at the table. They'd quickly emptied one pitcher of wine and were shouting for another. The servant said, "They are an embassy from the new khagan Malomir and have ambassadors' privileges."

"Bah," was Iakovitzes' reply to that. "The one in the middle there, the big bruiser, you mean to tell me he's an ambassador? He looks more like a hired killer." Krispos had already noticed the man Iakovitzes meant. With his scarred, sullen face, wide shoulders, and enormous hands, he certainly resembled no diplomat Krispos had seen or imagined.

The servant answered, "As a properly accredited member of the party from Kubrat, he cannot be excluded from functions to which his comrades are invited." He lowered his voice. "I will say, however, that his principal area of prowess does appear to be wrestling, not reason."

Iakovitzes' expression was eloquent, but a second glance at the enormous Kubrati made him keep to himself whatever remarks he thought of making.

The servant seated him and Krispos well away from the Kubratoi, only a couple of places from Petronas. Krispos hoped the arrival of food would help quiet Malomir's envoys. It did help, but not much—it made them talk with their mouths full. Trays came and went, bearing soup, prawns, partridges, and lamb. After a while Krispos lost track of the number of courses he'd eaten. He only knew he was replete.

When the last candied apricots were gone, Petronas rose and lifted his goblet. "To the health and long life of his Imperial Majesty the Avtokrator of the Videssians, Anthimos III!" he declared. Everyone drank the toast. Petronas stayed on his feet. "And to the efforts of that clever and accomplished diplomat, the excellent noble Iakovitzes." Everyone drank again, this time with a spattering of polite applause.

Flushed with pleasure at being toasted next after the Emperor, Iakovitzes stood up. "To his Imperial Highness the Sevastokrator Petronas!"

Petronas bowed as the toast was drunk. He caught the eye of one of the Kubrati envoys. "To the long and peaceful reign of the great khagan Malomir, and to your own continued success, Gleb."

Gleb stood. He raised his goblet. "I drink also to the health of your Avtokrator," he said, his Videssian slow but clear, even polished.

"Didn't think he had manners enough for that," Iakovitzes said to Krispos. From the murmurs of pleasure that filled the hall, a good many other people were similarly surprised.

Gleb did not sit down. "Since his Imperial Highness the Sevastokrator Petronas has only now deigned to notice my lord the khagan Malomir and me"—suddenly the Hall of the Nineteen Couches grew still; Krispos wondered whether Iakovitzes' joy was worth the slight the Kubrati plainly felt—"I now propose a toast to remind him of the might of Kubrat. Thus I drink to the strength of my comrade here, the famous and ferocious Beshev, who has beaten every Videssian he has faced."

Gleb drank. So did the other Kubratoi. Most of the imperials in the hall kept their goblets in front of them.

"He goes too far!" Iakovitzes did not bother to speak softly. "I know Kubratoi are conceited and boastful, but this surpasses all due measure. He—"

Krispos made hushing motions. The famous and ferocious Beshev was climbing to his feet. As he rose, Krispos took his measure. He was surely very strong, but how much quickness did he have? By the way he moved, not a great deal. Indeed, if he was as slow as he seemed, Krispos wondered how he had won all his matches.

Beshev held his goblet high. His Videssian was much more strongly accented than Gleb's, but still understandable. "I drink to the spirit of the brave Stylianos, whose neck I broke in our fight, and to the spirits of the other Videssians I will slay in wrestlings yet to come."

He drained the goblet. With a satisfied smirk, Gleb drank, too. Petronas stared at the men from Kubrat, stony-faced. Angry shouts rang through the hall. None of them, though, Krispos noted, came from anywhere close to Beshev. Not even Iakovitzes felt like affronting the Kubrati to his face.

Krispos turned to his master. "Let me take him on!"

"Eh? What?" Iakovitzes frowned. As comprehension dawned, he looked to Beshev, back to Krispos, and slowly shook his head. "No, Krispos. Bravely offered, but no. That barbarian may be a muscle-bound hulk, but he knows what he's about. I don't care to lose you for no good purpose." He put his hand on Krispos' arm.

Krispos shook it off. "You wouldn't lose me to no good purpose," he said, angry now at Iakovitzes as well as the arrogant Kubrati. "And I know what I'm about, too. If you doubt it, remember how I handled Barses and Meletios a year and a half ago. I learned wrestling back in my village, from a veteran of the imperial army."

Iakovitzes looked at Beshev again. "That barbarian is as big as Barses and Meletios put together," he said, but now his tone was doubtful. "Are you really sure you can beat him?"

"Of course I'm not sure, but I think I have a chance. Do you want this banquet remembered for your sake, or just as the time when the Kubratoi bragged and got away with it?"

"Hmm." Iakovitzes plucked at the waxed ends of his mustache as he thought. With abrupt decision, he got to his feet. "All right, you'll get your chance. Come on—let's talk to Petronas."

The Sevastokrator turned around in his chair as Iakovitzes and Krispos came up behind him. "What is it?" he growled; Gleb and Beshev had taken the joy out of the evening for him.

"I have here, lord, a man who, if you call on him, would wrestle with this famous"—Iakovitzes loaded the word with scorn—"Kubrati. For his boasting is a great disgrace to us Videssians; it would grow even worse if he returned to Kubrat unbeaten."

"That is true enough. The Kubratoi are quite full of false pretensions as it is," Petronas said. He studied Krispos with an officer's experienced eye. "Maybe, just maybe," he said to himself, and slowly rose. He waited for silence, then lifted his goblet above his head. "I drink to the courage of the bold Krispos, who will show Beshev the folly of his insolence."

The silence held a moment longer, then suddenly the Hall of the Nineteen Couches was full of shouts: "Krispos!" "Krispos!" "Hurrah for Krispos!" "Kill the barbarian!" "Flatten him!" "Stomp him!" "Beat him to a pulp!" "Krispos!"

The sound of his name loud in a hundred throats tingled through Krispos' veins like wine. He felt strong enough to beat a dozen Kubratoi at the same time, let alone the one he was about to face. He sent a challenging stare toward Beshev.

The look the wrestler gave back was so cold and empty that it froze Krispos' excitement. To Beshev, he was just another body to break. Without a word, the Kubrati got to his feet and began taking off his clothes.

Krispos pulled his robe over his head and tossed it aside. He took off his thin undertunic, leaving himself in linen drawers and sandals. He heard a woman sigh. That made him smile as he unbuckled the sandals.

The smile faded when he glanced over at Beshev. He was taller than the Kubrati, but he saw his foe outweighed him. And none of Beshev's bulk was fat; by the look of his huge, hard muscles, he might have been carved from stone.

Petronas had been shouting orders while Krispos and Beshev stripped. Servants scurried to shove tables aside and clear an open space in the center of the Hall of the Nineteen Couches. The two wrestlers walked toward it. Krispos studied the way Beshev moved. He still did not seem quick. *He'd better not be,* Krispos thought, *or he'll break my neck just like Stylianos'.*

He went through his own private wrestling match to put that thought down. Fear could cost him the fight, sure as his foe's strength. He took several deep breaths and concentrated on the feel of the cool, slick marble under his feet.

Slick . . . He turned back to Petronas. "Highness, could you have them strew some sand out there? I wouldn't want this affair decided on a slip." *Especially not if I make it,* he thought.

The Sevastokrator looked a question at Beshev, who nodded. At

Petronas' command, four servants hurried away. Both wrestlers stood around and waited until the men returned, lugging two large tubs of sand. They dumped it out and spread it about with brooms.

When they were done, Krispos and Beshev took their places at opposite ends of the cleared space. Beshev's great hands opened and closed as he stared. Krispos folded his arms across his chest and stared back, doing his best to look contemptuous.

"Are you both ready?" Petronas asked loudly. He swung down his arm. "Wrestle!"

The two men slid toward one another, each crouched low with arms outstretched. Krispos feinted at Beshev's leg. The Kubrati knocked his hand aside. That first touch warned Krispos Beshev was as strong as he looked.

They circled, eyes flicking to feet, to hands, and back to eyes again. Beshev sprang forward. He knew what he was about; nothing gave away the move before he made it. All the same, Krispos ducked under his grasping hands and spun behind him. He grabbed Beshev by the waist and tried to throw him down.

Beshev, though, was too squat and heavy to be thrown. He seized Krispos' forearms, then flung himself backward. Krispos twisted so they landed side by side instead of with Beshev on top. They grappled, broke away from each other, scrambled to their feet, and grappled again.

Beshev had an uncanny ability to slip holds. Every time Krispos thought he was about to throw his foe, the Kubrati managed to break free. It was almost as if his skin were oiled, though it did not feel slick to Krispos. He shook his head, baffled and frustrated. Beshev seemed to have tricks old Idalkos had never heard of.

Fortunately, the hulking Kubrati also found Krispos difficult. They stood panting and glaring at each other after a passage where Beshev somehow escaped from a wristlock Krispos knew he'd set well and truly, and where a moment later only a desperate jerk of his head kept Beshev from gouging out an eye.

The brief rest let Krispos notice the din that filled the Hall of the Nineteen Couches. While he fought, the crowd's yells had simply washed over him. Now he heard Iakovitzes screaming for him to maim Beshev; heard Petronas' calls of encouragement; heard dozens of people he did not know, all crying out for him. The shouts helped restore his spirits and made him eager once more.

No one shouted for Beshev. Gleb and the other Kubratoi stood at the edge of the cleared space and watched their man wrestle, but they did not cheer him on. Gleb's face was a mask of concentration; his hands, which he held in front of his chest, twitched and wiggled as if with a life of their own.

Somewhere long ago Krispos had seen hands jerk like that. He had no time to grope for the memory—Beshev thundered down on him like an avalanche. The Kubrati needed no cheers to spur him on. Krispos dove to one side; Beshev snagged him by an ankle and hauled him back.

Beshev was slow. But once he got a grip, that mattered less. Krispos kicked him in the ribs with his free leg. Beshev only grunted. He did not let go. And when Krispos tried to lay hold of the Kubrati's arm, his hands slid off it.

Since Krispos could not tear free, he went with Beshev's hold and let his foe pull him close. He butted the Kubrati under the chin. Beshev's head snapped back. His grip slackened, only for an instant, but long enough to let Krispos escape.

Panting, he scrambled to his feet. Beshev also rose. He must have bitten his tongue; blood ran into his beard from the corner of his mouth. He scowled at Krispos. From just behind him, so did Gleb. Gleb's hands were still twitching.

Whose hands had writhed so? Krispos shifted his weight, and remembered how it shifted at every step up on the hide platform during the ransom ceremony that had set him on the path to this moment. On the platform with him had been Iakovitzes, Pyrrhos, Omurtag—and Omurtag's *enaree.*

When the shaman checked the quality of Iakovitzes' gold, his hands had moved as Gleb's moved now. So Gleb was working some minor magic, was he? Krispos' lips skinned back from his teeth in a fierce grin. He would have bet all the gold Tanilis had given him that he knew just what kind. No wonder he hadn't been able to get a decent hold on Beshev all night long!

Krispos stopped, picking up a handful of the sand the servants had strewn about. With a shout, he rushed at Beshev. The Kubrati sprang forward, too. But Krispos was quicker. He twisted past Beshev and threw the sand full in Gleb's face.

Gleb screeched and whirled away, frantically knuckling his eyes. "Sorry. An accident," Krispos said, grinning still. He spun back toward Beshev.

The brief look of surprise and dismay on his foe's face told Krispos his guess had been good. Then Beshev's eyes grew cold once more. Even without sorcerous aid, he remained large, skilled, and immensely strong. The match still had a long way to go.

They grappled again. Krispos let out a whoop of glee. Now Beshev's skin was just skin—slick with sweat, yes, but not preternaturally so. When Krispos grabbed him, he stayed grabbed. And when he hooked his leg behind Beshev's and pushed, Beshev went over it and down.

The Kubrati was a wrestler, though. He tried to twist while falling, as Krispos had before. Krispos sprang onto his back. Beshev levered himself up on his great arms. Krispos jerked them out from under him. Beshev went down flat on the sandy floor.

He tried to get up again. Krispos seized a great hank of greasy hair and slammed Beshev's face into the marble under the sand. Beshev groaned, then made one more effort to rise. Krispos smashed him down again. "For Stylianos!" he shouted. Beshev lay still.

Krispos climbed wearily to his feet. He felt the cheers of the crowd more than he heard them. Iakovitzes rushed up and kissed him, half on the cheek, half on the mouth. He did not even mind.

Something hit him in the heel. He whirled in shock—could Beshev want more? He was sure he'd battered the Kubrati into unconsciousness. But no, Beshev still had not moved. Instead, a goldpiece lay by Krispos' foot. A moment later, another one kicked up sand close by.

"Pick 'em up, fool!" Iakovitzes hissed. "They're throwing 'em for you."

Krispos started to bend down, then stopped. Was this how he wanted these nobles to remember him, scrambling for their coins like a dog chasing a thrown stick? He shook his head and straightened. "I fought for Videssos, not for gold," he said.

The cheers got louder. No one in the Hall of the Nineteen Couches knew why Krispos smiled so widely. Without the stake from Tanilis, he could never have afforded such a grand gesture.

He brushed at himself, knocking off as much sand as he could. "I'm going to put my robe back on," he said and walked out through the crowd. Men and women clasped his hands, touched him on the arm, and patted his back as he went by. Then they turned to jeer the Kubrati envoys who came into the open space to drag away their fallen champion.

The world briefly disappeared as Krispos pulled the robe on over his head. When he could see again, he found Petronas standing in front of him. He started to bow. The Sevastokrator raised a hand. "No formality needed, not after so handsome a victory," he said. "I hope you will not object if *I* choose to reward you, Krispos, so long as"—he let amusement touch his eyes—"it is not in gold."

"How could I refuse?" Krispos said. "Wouldn't that be—what do they call it?—lèse-majesté?"

"No, for I am not the Avtokrator, only his servant," Petronas said with a perfectly straight face. "But tell me, how were you able to overthrow the savage Kubrati who had beaten all our best?"

"He likely had some help from that Gleb." Krispos explained how he knew, or thought he knew, what Gleb had been up to. He went on, "So I figured I would see how well Beshev fought without him making those tiny little Kubrati-style passes, and the big fellow was a lot easier to handle after that."

Petronas scowled. "Gleb always fidgets that way when we're dickering, as well. Do you suppose he's trying to ensorcel *me*?"

"You'd be able to guess that better than I could," Krispos said. "Could it hurt, though, to have a wizard of your own there the next time you talk with him?"

"It could not hurt at all, and I will do it," Petronas declared. "By the lord with the great and good mind, I wondered why I said yes to some of those proposals the Kubrati set before me. Now perhaps I know, and now I have two reasons to reward you, for you have done me two services this night."

"I thank you." Krispos did bow this time, and deeply. As he straightened, his face bore a sly grin. "And I thank you."

Petronas started to answer, then checked himself. He gave Krispos a long, considering look. "So you have a working wit, do you, to go along with your strength? That's worth knowing." Before Krispos could reply, the Sevastokrator turned away from him and called to the servants. "Wine! Wine for everyone, and let no one's cup be empty the rest of the night! We have a victory to celebrate, and a victor. To Krispos!"

The Videssian lords and ladies rased goblets high. "To Krispos!"

Krispos PLIED THE CURRYCOMB WITH A RHYTHM THAT MATCHED the dull pounding in his head. The warm, smelly stuffiness of the stables did nothing to help his hangover, but for once he did not mind headache or sour stomach. They reminded him that, though he was back to the down-to-earth routine of his job, the night before had really happened.

Not far away, Mavros whistled while he plied the shovel. Krispos laughed softly. Anything more down-to-earth than shoveling horse manure was hard to image. "Mavros?" he said.

The shovel paused. "What is it?"

"How come a fancy young noble like you doesn't mind mucking out the stables? I've shoveled plenty, here and back in my village with the goats and cows and sheep and pigs, but I never enjoyed it."

"To the ice with goats and cows and sheep and pigs. These are horses," Mavros said, as if that explained everything.

Maybe it even did, Krispos thought. Iakovitzes didn't mind working up a sweat in the stables, but Krispos could not picture him having anything to do with a pigsty. He shook his head. To anyone farm-bred like him, livestock was livestock. Getting sentimental about it was a luxury he hadn't been able to afford.

Such mostly pointless musing helped him get through the quarter of an hour he needed to finish bringing the coat of the mare he was working on to an even glow. Satisfied at last, he patted her on the muzzle and went on to the next stall.

He'd just started in when he head someone come into the stable. "Krispos! Mavros!" Gomaris called.

"What?" Krispos said, curious. Iakovitzes' steward hardly ever came back where the grooms labored.

"The master wants the two of you, right now," Gomaris said.

Krispos looked at Mavros. They both shrugged. "Beats working," Mavros said. "But I hope he'll give me a few minutes to wash and change clothes." He held his nose. "I'm not what you call presentable."

"Right now," Gomaris repeated.

"Well, all right," Mavros said, shrugging again. "On his floors be it."

As Krispos followed Gomaris up to the house, he wondered what was going on. Something out of the ordinary, obviously. He didn't think he was in trouble, not if Iakovitzes wanted to see Mavros, too. Unless—had Iakovitzes learned more of his connection with Tanilis, or of what she'd seen? But how could he have, here in the city when he hadn't in Opsikion?

A gray-haired man Krispos had not met was waiting with Iakovitzes. "Here they are, Eroulos, in all their"—Iakovitzes paused for an ostentatious sniff—"splendor." He turned to his grooms. "Eroulos is steward of the household of his Imperial Highness the Sevastokrator Petronas."

Krispos bowed low. "Excellent sir," he murmured.

Mavros bowed even lower. "How may we serve you, eminent sir?"

"You will not serve me, but rather the Sevastokrator," Eroulos answered at once. He was still straight and alert, with the competent air Krispos would have expected from one of Petronas' aides. He went on, "His Imperial Highness promised you a reward for your courage last night, Krispos. He has chosen to appoint you chief groom of his stables. You, Mavros, are bidden to come to the palaces, as well, out of the respect the Sevastokrator bears for your mother."

While Krispos and Mavros gaped, Iakovitzes said gruffly, "You should both know I wouldn't permit such a raid on my staff from anyone less than Petronas. Even from him, I resent it. That's a waste of time, though; what the Sevastokrator wants, he gets. So go on, and show him and his folk what kind of people come from this house." That was Iakovitzes to the core, Krispos thought: as kind a farewell as the noble had in him, mixed with bragging and self-promotion.

Then Krispos stopped worrying about what suddenly seemed the past. Going to the household of the Sevastokrator! He felt like shouting. He made himself stay calm. "Could we have a little time to pack our belongings?"

"And bathe?" Mavros added plaintively.

Eroulos unbent enough to smile. "I expect so. If I send a man for you tomorrow morning, will that be all right?"

"Yes, eminent sir."

"That would be fine, excellent sir."

"Until tomorrow, then." Eroulos rose, bowed to Iakovitzes. "Always a pleasure to see you, excellent sir." He nodded to Gomaris. "If you will be so kind as to show me out?"

When Eroulos had gone, Iakovitzes said, "I trust neither of you young gentlemen, now having risen higher, will forget whose house was his first in the city."

"Of course not," Krispos answered, while Mavros shook his head. Krispos heard something new in Iakovitzes' voice. All at once, his master— or rather, he thought dizzily, his former master—spoke to him as to a person of consequence instead of taking his obedience for granted. Iakovitzes never wasted respect where it was not needed. That he gave it now was Krispos' surest sign of what Eroulos' visit meant.

The news of that visit had reached the grooms' quarters by the time Krispos and Mavros got back there. The other grooms waylaid them with a great jar of wine. Krispos did not start packing until late that night. He finished quickly—he did not have a lot to pack—and fell sideways across his bed.

"YOU CAN THROW THAT SACK ONTO ONE OF MY HORSES, IF YOU like," Mavros said the next morning.

"They're loaded enough already, thanks. I can manage." But for the spear he'd brought to the city from his village, everything Krispos owned fit into a large knapsack. He paced back and forth with the sack slung over his shoulder. "So where is this man of Petronas'?"

"Probably in a tavern, drinking his breakfast. When you're the Sevastokrator's man, who this side of the Emperor is going to complain that you're late?"

"No one, I suppose." Krispos kept pacing.

The promised servant did show up a little later. "May I carry that for you?" he asked, pointing to Krispos' knapsack. He seemed surprised when Krispos turned him down. With a shrug, he said, "Follow me, then."

He led Krispos and Mavros through the plaza of Palamas and into the palace quarter. The palaces, Krispos discovered, were a secret city unto themselves, with rows of carefully planted trees screening buildings from one another. He soon found himself in a part of the quarter he had never seen before. "What's that building over there, the one by the cherry trees?" he asked.

"Nothing for the likes of you to worry about—or me, either, come to that," the fellow answered, grinning. "That's the Avtokrator's private residence, that is, and his Imperial Majesty has his own imperial servants, believe you me. They think they're better'n anyone else, too. Of course," he went on after a brief pause, "most of 'em are eunuchs, so I suppose they have to have something to be proud of."

"Eunuchs." Krispos wet his lips. He'd seen eunuchs a few times here in the city, plodding plumply about their errands. They made him shiver; more than once, unbuttoning his fly or pulling up his robe to relieve himself, he'd thanked Phos he was a whole man. "Why eunuchs?"

The Sevastokrator's man chuckled to hear such naïveté. "For one thing, they can't go plotting to make themselves Avtokrator—having no stones disbars 'em. For another, who better to trust to serve the Emperor's wife?"

"Nobody, I suppose." What the servant said made sense. All the same, Krispos fingered his thick, dark, curly beard, gladder than glad he could grow it.

The servitor led Mavros to a building not far from the Emperor's private chambers. "You'll be quartered here, with Petronas' other spatharioi. Find an empty suite and get yourself comfortable there."

"So I'm to be a spatharios, am I?" Mavros said. "Well, there are spatharioi and then there are spatharioi, if you know what I mean. Which sort does Petronas have in mind for me to be, useful or just decorative?"

"Whichever sort you make yourself into, I expect," the servant answered. "I'll tell you this, though, for whatever you think it's worth: Petronas isn't ashamed to get his own hands dirty when he needs to."

"Good. Neither am I." When Mavros grinned, he looked even younger than he really was. "And if you doubt me, ask your Eroulos how I smelled when he came to Iakovitzes' yesterday."

"Will I stay here, too?" Krispos asked.

"Eh? No. You come on with me," Petronas' man said.

With a quick wave to Mavros, Krispos obeyed. The servant took him to one of the larger and more splendid buildings in the palace complex. It made three sides of a square, closely enclosing a yard full of close-trimmed shrubberies.

"The Grand Courtroom," the servant explained. "His Imperial Highness the Sevastokrator lives here in the wing we're going toward so he can be right at hand if anything comes up that he needs to deal with."

"I see," Krispos said slowly. Anthimos' residence, on the other hand, was well away from the courtroom. Petronas, Krispos decided, missed very little. Then something else struck him. He stopped. "Wait. Are you saying the Sevastokrator wants me to live here, too?"

"Them's the orders I have." The servant gave an it's-not-my-problem shrug.

"This is finer than I expected," Krispos said as Petronas' man led him to the Grand Courtroom. He stopped the fellow again. "Where are the stables? If I'm going to be chief groom, don't you think I should know how to get to my work?"

"Maybe, and then maybe not." The servant looked him up and down. "Hope you don't mind my saying it, but you strike me as a trifle . . . raw . . . to be chief groom when some of the men in the stables have been there likely since before your father was born."

"No doubt you're right, but that doesn't mean I can't put my hand to it. Or would Petronas want me to be a drone, any more than he would Mavros?"

Now the Sevastokrator's man stopped of his own accord. He looked at Krispos again, this time thoughtfully. "Mmm, maybe not, not if you don't care to be." He told Krispos how to get to the stables. "But first let's get you settled in here."

Krispos could not argue with that. The servant led him up a stairway. A couple of armed guards in mail shirts leaned against the first doorway they passed. "This whole floor belongs to his Imperial Highness," the servitor explained. "You want the next one up."

The story above the Sevastokrator's quarters was broken up into apartments. By the spacing of the doors, the one assigned to Krispos was among the smallest. All the same, it had both a living room and a bedroom. Though he did not say so, that enormously impressed Krispos. He'd never had more than one room to himself before.

The apartment also boasted both a large bureau and a closet. The storage space swallowed Krispos' knapsack-worth of belongings. He tossed his spear on the bed, locked the door behind him, and went down the stairs. The bright sun outside made him blink. He looked this way and that, trying to get his bearings. That long, low brick building behind the stand of willows should have been the stables, if he'd understood Petronas' man.

He walked toward the building. Soon both sound and smell told him he was right. The willows, though, had helped conceal the size of the stables. They dwarfed Iakovitzes' and Tanilis' put together. Someone saw Krispos coming and dashed into the building. He nodded to himself. He might have known that would happen.

By the time his feet crunched on the straw-strewn stable floor, the grooms and farriers and boys were gathered and waiting for him. He scanned their faces and saw resentment, fear, curiosity. "Believe me," he said, "my being here surprises me as much as it does you."

That won him a couple of smiles, but most of the stable hands still stood quietly, arms folded across their chests, wanting to learn how he would go on. He thought for a moment. "I didn't ask for this job. It got handed to me, so I'm going to do it the best way I can. A good many of you know more about horses than I do. I wouldn't think of saying you don't. You all know more about the Sevastokrator's horses than I do. I hope you'll help me."

"What if we don't care to?" growled one of the men, a tough-looking fellow a few years older than Krispos.

"If you go on doing what you're supposed to do, I don't mind," Krispos said. "That helps me, too. But if you try to make things hard for me on purpose, I won't like it—and neither will you." He pointed to a bruise under one eye. "You must have heard why Petronas took me into his service. After Beshev, I think I can handle myself with just about anybody. But I didn't come here to fight. I will if I have to, but I don't want to. I'd sooner work."

Now he waited to see how the stable hands would respond. They muttered among themselves. The tough-looking groom took a step toward him. He set himself. A smaller, gray-bearded man put a hand on the groom's arm. "No, hold on, Onorios," he said. "He sounds fair enough. Let's find out if he means what he says."

Onorios grunted. "All right, Stotzas, since it's you who's asking." He scowled at Krispos. "But what do you want to bet that inside a month's time he doesn't bother setting foot in here? He'll collect the pay you deserve more and he'll stay in the Grand Courtroom soaking up wine with the rest of that lot there."

"I'll take that bet, Onorios," Krispos said sharply. "At the end of a month—or two, or three, if you'd rather—loser buys the winner all he can drink. What do you say?"

"By the good god, you're on." Onorios stuck out his hand. Krispos took it. They squeezed until they both winced. When they let go, each of them opened and closed his fist several times to work the blood back in.

Krispos said, "Stotzas, will you show me around, please?" If the senior groom was willing not to despise him on sight, he would do his best to stay on Stotzas' good side.

Stotzas showed him the Sevastokrator's parade horse. "Pretty, isn't he? Too bad he couldn't catch a tortoise with a ten-yard start." Then his war horse. "Stay away from his hooves—he's trained to lash out. Maybe you should start giving him apples, so he gets to know you." Then the beasts Petronas took hunting, mares, a couple of retired stallions and geldings, up-and-coming colts—so many animals in all that Krispos knew he would not be able to remember every one.

By the time the tour was nearly done, Stotzas and Krispos were at the far end of the stables, well away from the other hands. The graybeard gave Krispos a sidelong look. "Think you can handle it?" he asked, his voice sly.

"I'll try. What more can I say right now? I only wish you could tell me about the people the same way you did about the horses."

Stotzas' shoulders shook. After a moment, Krispos realized the groom was laughing. "Ah, so you're not just a young fool with more muscles than he needs. I hoped you weren't. Aye, the people'll drive you madder than the beasts any day, but if you keep 'em happy and keep 'em tending to their jobs, things'll run smooth enough. If you have that trick, sonny, you'll do right well for yourself."

"I hope I do." Krispos met Stotzas' eyes. "I hope you'll help me, too."

"Won't stand in your road, anyhow," Stotzas said after a brief, thoughtful pause. "Any youngster who admits he don't know everything there is to know is worth taking a chance on, you ask me. And you handled Onorios pretty well. Reckon he'll be buying you wine a month from now instead of the other way round."

"That he will," Krispos promised.

"Well, let's head back," Stotzas said. As they walked down the center aisle of the stable toward the knot of expectantly waiting hands, the senior groom raised his voice a little to ask, "So what do you think we ought to do about that hunter with the sore shins?"

"You've been resting him, you said, and putting cold compresses on his legs?" Krispos waited for Stotzas' nod, then went on, "He doesn't look too bad. If you keep up with what you're doing for a few more days, then start exercising him on soft ground, he should do all right."

Neither of them let on that they'd quietly talked about the horse's problem in front of its stall. Stotzas rubbed his chin, nodded sagely. "Good advice, sir. We'll take it, I expect." He turned to the crowd of stable hands. "He'll do."

Allies made life easier, Krispos thought.

For the next several weeks, Krispos spent most of his waking hours in the stables. He learned more about horsemanship than he'd ever known, and more about the sometimes related art of guiding men, as well. When he collected his bet from Onorios, he made a point of also buying wine for the burly groom. After they drank together, Onorios hurried to do whatever Krispos needed and did it gladly. Stotzas said nothing, but a glint of amusement showed in his eyes once in a while.

Because he was working so hard, Krispos needed a while to notice how his life had changed since he moved to his apartment in the Grand Courtroom. At Iakovitzes', he'd been a servant. Here he had servants of his own. His bed linen was always clean; his clothes seemed to wash themselves as if by magic and reappear, spotless, in his closet.

He also learned that any small valuables he left out might disappear, as if by magic. He was glad he'd hidden Tanilis' gift behind a piece of molding he'd loosened. Every so often, he would move the small cabinet he'd put in front of the loose place and add more money to his store. He lived frugally. He was too busy to do anything else.

He was about to go to sleep one warm summer night when someone tapped on his door. He scratched his head. His acquaintance with the officials and courtiers who lived in the other apartments down this hall was nodding at best; he'd been at the stables too much to get to know them well. "Who is it?" he called.

"Eroulos."

"Oh!" Krispos had not seen Petronas' steward since the day he came to Iakovitzes' house for him. After hastily throwing his tunic back on, he unbarred the door. "Come in!"

"No, you come out with me," Eroulos said. "I am bidden to bring you downstairs to the Sevastokrator. His Imperial Highness is entertaining . . . a guest. He would like to have him meet you."

"A guest?"

"You'll see for yourself soon enough. Come along, if you please."

Krispos followed Eroulos down the hall and down the stairs. Petronas' guards gave the steward and him a thorough patting down at the doorway to the Sevastokrator's suite. Krispos let himself be searched without complaint; after all, he had never passed through this entrance before. But he was surprised Eroulos got the same treatment. If Petronas did not trust his own steward, whom did he trust? *Maybe no one,* Krispos thought.

Finally, nodding, the guards stood aside. One of them opened the door. Eroulos waved Krispos in ahead of him. Krispos had wondered how the Sevastokrator lived. What he saw reminded him of Tanilis' villa: a mix of great wealth and quiet good taste.

An icon of Phos arrested his eye. Respect for both the good god and the artist made him sketch the sun-sign over his heart; he'd never seen Phos portrayed with such perfectly mingled sternness and kindness. Eroulos followed his gaze. "That is the image, they say, after which the Phos in the dome of the High Temple is modeled," the steward remarked.

"I can well believe it," Krispos said. Even after he'd walked by, he had the uneasy feeling the god in the icon was still looking at him.

"Here we are," Eroulos said at length, halting before a door inlaid with lacy vines of gold and ivory. He tapped at it. For a moment, the two voices coming through it did not pause. One was Petronas. The other sounded lighter, younger. Eroulos tapped again. "All right, all right," Petronas growled.

The steward swung the door open. It moved silently, on well-greased hinges. "Here is Krispos, your Highness."

"Good." The Sevastokrator turned to the man sitting across a small table from him. "Well, nephew, I suppose the argument can wait a few minutes before we pick it up again. You wanted to see the fellow who overthrew the famous Beshev and sent Gleb back to Kubrat less high and mighty than he came here. This is Krispos."

Petronas' nephew! Krispos bowed low before the younger man, then went to his knees and down flat on his belly. "Your Majesty," he whispered.

"Up, up! How can I shake your hand when you're lying there?" Anthimos III, Avtokrator of the Videssians, waited impatiently while Krispos scrambled to his feet. Then he did as he'd said, giving Krispos' hand several enthusiastic pumps. "Nothing could be more boring than listening to the Kubratoi going on about how wonderful they are. Thanks to you, we don't have to for a while. I am in your debt, which means, of course, that all Videssos is in your debt." He cocked his head and grinned at Krispos.

Krispos found himself grinning back; Anthimos' slightly lopsided smile was infectious. "Thank you, Your Majesty," he said. For the moment, he was an awestruck peasant again. No matter what Tanilis might have foreseen, a big part of him had never really imagined he would feel the Emperor's flesh pressing his own, be close enough to smell wine on the Emperor's breath.

"Nephew, you might want to present Krispos with some tangible token of your gratitude," Petronas said smoothly.

"What? Oh. Yes, so I might. Here you are, Krispos." He chuckled as he pulled a golden chain from around his neck and put it over Krispos' head. "I do apologize. Having the imperial treasury to play with, I'm apt to forget that other people don't."

"You're very generous, Your Majesty," Krispos said, feeling the weight of the metal on his shoulders. "A poor man could feed himself and his family for a long time with so much gold."

"Could he? Well, I hope you're not a poor man, Krispos, and that my uncle is doing a satisfactory job of feeding you."

"Krispos is making a valued place for himself here as chief groom," Petronas said. "He might have treated the post as a sinecure, and the same gratitude you feel toward him, nephew, would have compelled me to let him retain it all the same. But he has plunged in, instead; indeed, his working with such diligence is the chief reason I have not been able to present him to you before—I seldom find him away from the stables."

"Good for him," Anthimos said. "A spot of work never hurt anyone."

Krispos wondered what Anthimos knew about work—by the look of him, not much. Though his features proclaimed him Petronas' close kin, they lacked the hard purpose that informed the Sevastokrator's face. That was not just youth, either; had Anthimos been Petronas' age rather than Krispos', he still would have looked indolent. Krispos could not decide what to make of him. He'd never known anyone who could afford the luxury of indolence except Tanilis and Petronas, and they did not indulge it.

Petronas said, "Wine, Krispos?"

"Yes, thank you."

The Sevastokrator poured for him. "For me once more, as well, please," Anthimos said. Petronas handed him a cup, as well. He tossed the wine down and held out the cup for a refill. Petronas poured again, and then again a moment later. He took occasional sips from his own cup, as did Krispos. They did not come close to emptying theirs.

The next time the Avtokrator held out his cup to his uncle, wine slopped over the rim and down onto his fingers when he pulled it back. He licked them off. "Sorry," he said with a slightly unfocused smile.

"No matter, Your Majesty," his uncle answered. "Now, if we may pick up the discussion in which we were engaged when Krispos came in, I still respectfully urge you to set your signature to the order I sent you last week for the construction of two new fortresses in the far southwest."

"I don't know that I want to sign it." Anthimos stuck out his lower lip. "Skombros says they probably won't ever be needed, because the southwest is a very quiet frontier."

"Skombros!" Petronas lost some of the air of urbanity Krispos had always seen from him before. He did not try to hide his contempt as he went on, "Frankly, I can't imagine why you even think of listening to your vestiarios on these matters. What a eunuch chamberlain knows of the proper placement of fortresses would fit into the ballocks he does not have. By the good god, nephew, you'd be better advised asking Krispos here what he thinks of the whole business. At least he's seen more of the world than the inside of the palaces."

"All right, I will," Anthimos said. "What *do* you think of the whole business, Krispos?"

"Me?" Krispos almost spilled his own wine. Drinking with the Sevastokrator and Avtokrator made him feel proud and important. Getting into the middle of their argument was something else again, something terrifying. He was all too conscious of Petronas' gaze on him as he picked his words with the greatest of care. "In matters of war, I think I would sooner rely on a warrior's judgment."

"Do you recognize plain truth when you hear it, Anthimos?" Petronas demanded.

The Avtokrator rubbed his chin. The tip of his beard was waxed to a point. Sounding faintly surprised, he said, "Yes, that is sensible, isn't it? Very well, Uncle, I'll sign your precious order."

"You will? Excellent!" Petronas sprang to his feet and slapped Krispos on the back hard enough to stagger him. "There's another present you'll have from me, Krispos, and another one you've earned, too."

"Your Highness is very kind," Krispos said.

"I reward good service," Petronas said. "Don't forget that. I also reward the other kind, as it deserves. Don't forget that, either. Now run along, why don't you? You'll just be bored if you hang about longer."

"Good to meet you, Krispos," Anthimos said as Krispos bowed his way out. Even half sozzled, the Avtokrator had a charming smile.

Petronas' voice came clearly through the door Krispos closed behind him: "There, you see, Anthimos? That groom has a better notion of what needs doing than your precious vestiarios." The Sevastokrator paused. His voice turned musing. "By Phos, so he does—"

"Here, I'll show you out," Eroulos said. Krispos jumped. He hadn't heard the steward come up behind him.

"The Emperor. You didn't tell me you were taking me to see the Emperor," Krispos said accusingly as Eroulos took him past the guards.

"I was told not to. The Sevastokrator wanted to see how you would react." Eroulos started up the stairs with Krispos. "Truly, though, you should not have been surprised. Petronas once ruled for the Avtokrator, and still rules—with him."

Krispos caught the tiny pause. *Through him,* Eroulos had started to say. But a man discreet enough to be the Sevastokrator's steward was too discreet to say such things aloud.

Something else turned Krispos' thoughts aside. "*Why* did he want to see how I'd react?"

"I do not presume to speak for his Imperial Highness," Eroulos answered discreetly. "Would you not think it wise, though, to learn what you can of the quality of men who serve you, not least those you appoint to responsible posts on brief acquaintance?"

That means me, Krispos realized. By then, he and Eroulos were at his door. He nodded thoughtfully as he went inside. Tanilis would have done the same sort of thing. And if Petronas thought like Tanilis—Krispos could find no higher compliment to pay the Sevastokrator's wits.

T ANILIS WOULD NEVER HAVE FORGOTTEN A PROMISED REWARD. Nor did Petronas. More, he gave it to Krispos publicly, coming to the stables to present him with a dagger whose hilt was lavishly chased with rubies. "For your quick thinking the other night," he said in a voice that carried.

Krispos bowed low. "You honor me, Highness." Out of the corner of his eye, he saw Onorios suddenly become very busy with his scissors as he trimmed a horse's mane. Krispos smiled to himself.

"You deserve it," Petronas said. "You're doing well here, from all I've heard, and from what I've seen of the condition of my animals."

"It's not all my doing. You had fine horses and fine hands long before you ever noticed me—not that I'm not grateful you did, Highness," Krispos added quickly.

"I'm glad you noticed, and also that you have the sense to share the credit. I know I am not in the habit of employing fools, and I'm increasingly pleased to discover I have not broken my rule with you." Petronas glanced into a stall, smiled a little at what he saw, and took a few paces to the next one. "Come, Krispos, walk with me."

"Of course, Highness."

As Stotzas had a few weeks before, the Sevastokrator waited until he and Krispos were out of earshot of most of the stable hands. Then he said, "Tell me what you know of a body servant's tasks."

"Highness?" The question caught Krispos by surprise. He answered slowly, "Not much, though, come to think of it, I guess you'd say I was Iakovitzes' body servant for a while there in Opsikion when he was laid up with a broken leg. I sort of had to be."

"So you did," Petronas agreed. "That may suffice. Indeed, I think it would. As here, in the post I have in mind you would be involved in overseeing others as much as with actually serving."

"What post is that?" Krispos asked. "Not your steward, surely. Or are you angry at Eroulos for something I don't know about?" If the Sevastokrator was displeased with Eroulos, the gossip of his household had not heard of it. That was possible, Krispos supposed, but unlikely.

And Petronas shook his head. "No, Eroulos suits me right well. I was thinking of rather a grander place for you. How would you like to be Anthimos' vestiarios one day?"

Krispos said the first thing that popped into his head: "Doesn't the vestiarios have to be a eunuch?" He felt his testicles creep up toward his belly as he spoke the word; he had all he could do to keep from shaping his hands into a protective cup over his crotch.

"It's usual, but by no means mandatory. I daresay we can manage to keep you entire." Petronas laughed, then went on, "I'm sorry; I'd not seen you look frightened before. I want you to think on this, though, even if I cannot promise you the office soon—or at all."

"*You* can't promise, Highness?" Krispos said, startled at the admission. "How could you lack the power? Aren't you both Sevastokrator and the Avtokrator's uncle? Wouldn't he heed you?"

"In this, perhaps not. His chamberlain also has his ear, you see, and so may not be easily displaced." Petronas took a slow, deep, angry breath. "That cursed Skombros is sly as a fox, too. He plots to weaken me and aggrandize his own worthless relations. I would not be surprised to learn he dreams of putting one of them on the throne, the more so as the Avtokrator's lady, the empress Dara, has yet to conceive."

"And so you want Anthimos to have a vestiarios loyal to you and without schemes of his own," Krispos said. "Now I understand."

"Yes, exactly so," Petronas said.

"Thank you for your trust in me."

"I place no great trust in any man," the Sevastokrator answered, "but in this I do trust: that having raised you, I can cast you down at need. Do you understand that, as well, Krispos?" His voice, though still quiet, had gone hard as stone.

"Very well, Highness."

"Good. I think the best way to do this—if, as I say, it can be done at all—is to place you in Anthimos' eye from time to time. You seem to think clearly, and to be able to put your thoughts into words that, although they lack polish, carry the ring of conviction. Living as he does among eunuchs, the Avtokrator is unused to plain ideas plainly stated, save perhaps from me. They may prove an exotic novelty, and Anthimos is ever one to be drawn to the new and exotic. Should he wish to see more of you, and then more again—well, that is as the good god wills." Petronas set a large, heavy hand on Krispos' shoulder. "Shall we try? Is it a bargain?"

"Aye, Highness, it is," Krispos said.

"Good," Petronas repeated. "We shall see what we shall see." He turned and tramped back toward the stable entrance without a backward glance.

More slowly, Krispos came after him. So the Sevastokrator expected him to remain a pliant creature, did he, even after becoming vestiarios? Krispos had said he understood that. He'd said nothing about agreeing with it.

Chapter VIII

THE HUNTERS AMBLED ALONG ON THEIR HORSES, LAUGHING and chatting and passing wineskins back and forth. They sighed with relief as they rode under a stand of trees that shielded them from the pounding summer sun. "Who'll give us a song?" Anthimos called out.

Krispos thought of a tune he'd known back in his village. "There was a young pig who got caught in a fence," he began. "A silly young pig without any sense . . ." If the pig had no sense, neither did the men who tried various unlikely ways of getting it loose.

When he was through, the young nobles who filled the hunting party gave him a cheer. The song was new to them; they'd never had to worry about pigs themselves. Krispos knew he was no great minstrel, but he could carry a tune. Past that, no one much cared. The wineskins had gone back and forth a good many times.

One of the nobles cast a glance at the sun, which was well past noon. "Let's head back to the city, Majesty. We've not caught much today, and we've not much time to catch more."

"No, we haven't," Anthimos agreed petulantly. "I'll have to speak to my uncle about that. This park was supposed to have been restocked with game. Krispos, mention it to him when we return."

"I will, Majesty." But Krispos was willing to believe it had been re-stocked. The way the Avtokrator and his companions rode thundering through woods and meadow, no animals in their right minds would have come within miles of them.

Grumbling still, Anthimos swung his horse's head toward the west. The rest of the hunters followed. They grumbled, too, and loudly, when they rode back out into the sunshine.

All at once, the grumbles turned to shouts of delight—a stag sprang out of the brush almost in front of the hunters' faces and darted across the grass.

"After him!" Anthimos yelled. He dug spurs into his horse's flank. Someone loosed an arrow that flew nowhere near the fleeing stag.

None of the hunters—not even Krispos, who should have paused to wonder—bothered to ask himself why the stag had burst from cover so close to them. They were young enough, and maybe drunk enough, to think of it as the perfect ending the day deserved. They were altogether off guard, then, when the pack of wolves that had been chasing the stag ran onto the meadow right under their horses' hooves.

The horses screamed. Some of the men screamed, too, as their mounts leaped and reared and bucked and did their best to throw them off. The wolves yelped and snarled; they'd been intent on their quarry and were at least as taken aback as the hunters by the sudden encounter. The stag bounded into the woods and vanished.

Maybe only Krispos saw the stag go. His mount was a sturdy gelding, fast enough and strong enough, but with no pretense to fine breeding. Thus he was in the rear of the hunters' pack when they encountered the wolves, and on a beast that did not have to be coaxed out of hysteria if a leaf blew past its nose.

No one, of course, rode a higher-bred horse than Anthimos'. Iakovitzes could not have thrown a finer fit than that animal did. Anthimos was a fine rider, but fine riders fall, too. He landed heavily and lay on the ground, stunned. Some of the other hunters cried out in alarm, but most were too busy trying to control their own mounts and fight off the wolves that snapped at their horses' legs and bellies and hindquarters to come to the Emperor's aid.

A big wolf padded toward him. It drew back for a moment when he groaned and stirred, then came forward again. Its tongue lolled from its mouth, red as blood. *Ah, crippled prey,* that lupine smile seemed to say. *Easy meat.*

Krispos shouted at the wolf. In the din, the shout was one among many.

He had a bow, but did not trust it; he was no horse-archer. He drew out an arrow and shot anyway. In a romance, his need would have made the shaft fly straight and true.

He missed. He came closer to hitting Anthimos than the wolf. Cursing, he grabbed the mace that swung from his belt for finishing off large game—in the unlikely event he ever killed any, he thought, disgusted with himself for his poor shooting.

He hurled the mace with all his strength. It spun through the air. The throw was not what he'd hoped, either—in his mind, he'd seen the spiky knob smashing in the wolf's skull. Instead, the wooden handle struck it a stinging blow on the nose.

That sufficed. The wolf yelped in startled pain and sat back on its haunches. Before it worked up the nerve to advance on the Avtokrator again, another hunter managed to get his horse between it and Anthimos. Iron-shod hooves flashed near its face. It snarled and ran off.

Someone who was a better archer than Krispos drove an arrow into another wolf's belly. The wounded animal's howls of pain made more of the pack take to their heels. A couple of wolves got all the way round the hunters and picked up the stag's scent again. They loped after it. As far as Krispos was concerned, they were welcome to it.

The hunters leaped off their horses and crowded round the fallen Emperor. They all yelled when, after a minute or two, he managed to sit. Rubbing his shoulder, he said, "I take it back. This preserve has quite enough game already."

Even the Avtokrator's feeblest jokes won laughter. "Are you all right, Your Majesty?" Krispos asked along with everyone else.

"Let me find out." Anthimos climbed to his feet. His grin was shaky. "All in one piece. I didn't think I would be, not unless that cursed wolf was big enough to swallow me whole. It looked to have the mouth for the job."

He tried to bend down, grunted, and clutched his ribs. "Have to be careful there." A second, more cautious, try succeeded. When he straightened again, he was holding the mace. "Whose is this?"

Krispos had to give his fellow hunters credit. He'd thought some ready-for-aught would speak up at once and claim he'd saved the Avtokrator. Instead, they all looked at one another and waited. "Er, it's mine," Krispos said after a moment.

"Here, let me give it back to you, then," Anthimos said. "Believe me, I won't forget where it came from."

Krispos nodded. That was an answer Petronas might have given. If the

Avtokrator had some of the same stuff in him as the Sevastokrator, Videssos might fare well even if something befell Anthimos' capable uncle.

"Let's head back toward the city," Anthimos said. "This time I really mean it." One of the young nobles had recaptured the Emperor's horse. He grimaced as he got into the saddle, but rode well enough.

All the same, the hunting party remained unusually subdued, even when they were back inside the palace quarter. They all knew they'd had a brush with disaster.

Krispos tried to imagine what Petronas would have done if they'd come back with the news that Anthimos had got himself killed in some fribbling hunting accident. Of course, the accident would have made the Sevastokrator Emperor of Videssos. But it would also have raised suspicions that it was no accident, that Petronas had somehow arranged it. Under such circumstances, would the Sevastokrator be better off rewarding the witnesses who established his own innocence or punishing them to show they should have protected Anthimos better?

Krispos found himself unsure of the answer and glad he did not have to find out.

As the hunting band broke up, a noble leaned over to Krispos and said quietly, "I think I'd give a couple of inches off my prong to have saved the Avtokrator the way you did."

Krispos looked the fellow over. He was scarcely out of his teens, yet he rode a fine horse that he surely owned, unlike Krispos' borrowed gelding. His shirt was silk, his riding breeches fine leather, and his spurs silver. His round, plump face said he'd never known a day's hunger. Even if he hadn't saved Anthimos, he was assured a more than comfortable life.

"I mean no disrespect, excellent sir, but I'm not sure the price you name is high enough," Krispos answered after a moment's pause. "I need the luck more than you do, you see, having started with so much less of it. Now if you'll excuse me, I have to get back to my master's stables."

The noble stared after him as he rode away. He suspected—no, he was certain—he should have held his tongue. He was already far better at that than most men his age. Now he saw he would have to grow better still.

"SO WHEN DOES THE MOST HOLY GNATIOS SET THE CROWN ON your head?" Mavros asked when he saw Krispos coming out of Petronas' stables a couple of days after the hunt.

"Oh, shut up," Krispos told his adopted brother. He was not worried about Mavros' betraying him; he just wanted him off his back. Mavros' teasing was the most natural thing in the world. Though Krispos hadn't bragged about what he'd done, the story was all over the palaces.

"Shut up? This humble spatharios hears and obeys, glad only that your magnificence has deigned to grant him the boon of words." Mavros swept off his hat and folded himself like a clasp knife in an extravagant bow.

Krispos wanted to hit him. He found himself laughing instead. "Humble, my left one." He snorted. Mavros had trouble taking anything seriously; after a while, so did anyone who came near him.

"Your left one would look very fine in a dish of umbles," Mavros said.

"Someone ought to run a currycomb over your tongue," Krispos told him.

"Is this another of your innovations in equestrian care?" Mavros stuck out the organ in question and crossed his eyes to look down at it. "Yes, it does seem in need of grooming. Go ahead; see if you can put a nice sheen on its coat."

Krispos did hit him then, not too hard. They scuffled good-naturedly for a couple of minutes. Krispos finally got a hammerlock on Mavros. Mavros was whimpering, without much conviction, when Eroulos came up to the two of them. "If you're quite finished . . ." the steward said pointedly.

"What is it?" Krispos let go of Mavros, who somehow contrived to look innocent and rub his wrist at the same time.

The theatrics were wasted; Eroulos took no notice of him. He spoke to Krispos instead, "Go back to the Grand Courtroom at once. One of his Imperial Majesty's servants is waiting for you there."

"For me?" Krispos squeaked.

"I am not in the habit of repeating myself," Eroulos said. Krispos waited no longer. He dashed for the Grand Courtroom. Mavros might have waved good-bye. Krispos did not turn his head to see.

The guards outside Petronas' wing of the Grand Courtroom swung down their spears when they saw someone running toward them. Recognizing Krispos, they relaxed. One of them pointed to a man leaning against the side of the building. "Here's the fellow been waiting for you."

"You are Krispos?" Anthimos' servitor was tall, thin, and erect, but his hairless cheeks and sexless voice proclaimed him a eunuch. "I was given to understand that you were the Sevastokrator's chief groom, not that you would stink of horses yourself." His own scent was of attar of roses.

"I work," Krispos said shortly.

The eunuch's sniff told what he thought of that. "In any event, I am commanded to bid you come to a festivity his Imperial Majesty will hold tomorrow evening. I shall return then to guide you. I most respectfully suggest that, no matter how virtuous you deem your labors, the odor of the stables would be out of place."

Krispos felt his cheeks heat. Biting back an angry retort, he nodded. The eunuch's bow was fluid perfection, or would have been had he not made it so deep as to suggest scorn rather than courtesy.

"You don't want to get into a meaner-than-thou contest with a eunuch," one of the guards remarked after the Avtokrator's servant was too far away to hear. "You'll regret it every time."

"You'd be mean, too, if you'd had that done to you," another guard said. All the troopers chuckled. Krispos also smiled, but he thought the guard was right. Having lost so much, eunuchs could hardly be blamed for getting their own back in whatever petty ways they could devise.

He knocked off a little early the next afternoon to go from the stables to a bathhouse; he would not give that supercilious eunuch another chance to sneer at him. He oiled himself, scraped his skin with a curved strigil, and paid a boy a copper to get the places he could not reach. The cold plunge and hot soak that followed left him clean and helped loosen tired, tight muscles. He was all but purring as he walked back to the Grand Courtroom.

This time he waited for the Avtokrator's eunuch to arrive. The eunuch gave a disapproving sniff; perhaps, Krispos thought, he was seeking the lingering aroma of horse. "Come along," he said, sounding no happier for failing to find it.

Krispos had never been to—had never even seen—the small building to which his guide led him. He was not surprised; the palace quarter held dozens of buildings, large and small, he'd never been to. Some of the large ones were barracks for the regiments of imperial guards. Some of the small ones held soldierly supplies. Others were buildings former Emperors had used, but that now stood empty, awaiting the pleasure of an Avtokrator yet to come. This one, secluded among willows and pear trees, looked to be where Anthimos himself awaited pleasure.

Krispos heard the music when he was still walking the winding path under the trees. Whoever was playing, he thought, had more enthusiasm than skill. Raucous voices accompanied the musicians. He needed a moment to recognize the tavern song they were roaring out. Only when they came to the refrain—"The wine gets drunk but you get drunker!"—was he sure. Loud applause followed.

"They seem to have started already," he remarked.

The eunuch shrugged. "It's early yet. They'll still have their clothes on, most of them."

"Oh." Krispos wondered whether he meant most of the revelers or most of their clothes. He supposed it was about the same either way.

By then they were at the door. A squad of guardsmen stood just outside, big blond Haloga mercenaries with axes. An amphora of wine almost as tall as they were stood beside them, its pointed end rammed into the ground. One of them saw Krispos looking at it. The northerner's wide, foolish grin said he'd already made use of the dipper that stuck out of the jug, and his drawling Haloga accent was not the only thing that thickened his speech. "A good duty here, yes it is."

Krispos wondered what Petronas would do if he caught one of his own guards drunk on duty. Nothing pleasant, he was certain. Then the eunuch took him inside, and all such musings were swept away.

"It's Krispos!" Anthimos exclaimed. He set down the flute he'd been playing—no wonder the music sounded ragged, Krispos thought—and rushed up to embrace the newcomer. "Let's have a cheer for Krispos!"

Everyone obediently cheered. Krispos recognized some of the young nobles with whom he'd hunted, and a few people who had been at some of the wilder feasts he'd gone to with Iakovitzes. Most of the folk here, though, were strange to him, and by the look of some of them, he would have been as glad to have them stay so.

Torches of spicy-smelling sandalwood lit the chamber. It was strewn with lilies and violets, roses and hyacinths, which added their sweet scents to the air. Many of the Emperor's guests were also drenched in perfume. Krispos admitted to himself that his eunuch guide had been right—the odor of horse did not belong here.

"Help yourself to anything," Anthimos said. "Later you can help yourself to anybody." Krispos laughed nervously, though he did not think the Avtokrator was joking.

He took a cup of wine and a puffy pastry that proved to be stuffed with forcemeat of lobster. As Petronas had in the Hall of the Nineteen Couches, a noble rose to give a toast. He had to wait a good deal longer for quiet than the Sevastokrator had. Getting some at last, he called, "Here's to Krispos, who saved his Majesty and saved our fun with him!"

This time the cheers were louder. No one here, Krispos thought, would be able to revel like this without Anthimos' largess. Had the wolf killed Anthimos, Petronas would surely have taken the throne for himself. After that, most of the people here tonight would have counted themselves lucky not to be whipped out of the city.

Anthimos set down his golden cup. "What goes in must come out," he declared. He picked up a chamber pot and turned his back on his guests. The chamber pot was also gold, decorated with fancy enamelwork.

Krispos wondered how many like it the Avtokrator had. For golden chamber pots, he thought, he'd been taxed off his land.

The notion should have made him furious. It did anger him, but less
than he would have thought possible. He tried to figure out why. At last
he decided that Anthimos just was not the sort of young man who inspired fury. All he wanted to do was enjoy himself.

A very pretty girl put her hand on Krispos' chest. "Do you want to?"
she asked, and waved to a mountain of pillows piled against one wall.

He stared at her. She was worth staring at. Her green silk gown was
modestly cut, but thinned to transparency in startling places. But that was
not why he gaped. His rustic standards had taken a beating since he came
to Videssos. Several times he'd gone off with female entertainers after a
feast, and once with the bored wife of one of the other guests. But "In
front of everyone?" he blurted.

She laughed at him. "You're a new one here, aren't you?" She left without even giving him a chance to answer. He took another cup of wine and
drank it quickly to calm his shaken nerves.

Before long, a couple did avail themselves of the pillows. Krispos found
himself watching without having intended to. He tore his gaze away. A
moment later, he found his eyes sliding that way again. Annoyed at himself, he turned his back on the whole wall.

Most of the revelers took no special notice of the entwined pair, by the
way they went on about their business, they'd seen such displays often
enough not to find them out of the ordinary. A few offered suggestions.
One made the man pause in what he was doing long enough to say, "Try
that yourself if you're so keen on it. I did once, and I hurt my back." Then
he fell to once more, matter-of-fact as if he were laying bricks.

Not far from Anthimos sat one who did nothing but watch the sportive
couple. The robes he wore were as rich as the Avtokrator's and probably
cost a good deal more, for they needed to be larger to cover his bulk. His
smooth, beardless face let Krispos count his chins. Another eunuch, he
thought, and then, Well, let him watch—it's probably as close as he can
come to the real thing.

Some of the entertainment was more nearly conventional. Real musicians took up the instruments Anthimos and his cronies had set down.
Acrobats bounced among the guests and sometimes sprang over them.
The only thing remarkable about the jugglers, aside from their skill, was
that they were all women, all lovely, and all bare or nearly so.

Krispos admired the aplomb one of them showed when a man came up
behind her and fondled her breast. The stream of fruit she kept in the air
never wavered—until a very ripe peach landed *splat!* on the fellow's head.

He swore and raised a fist to her, but the storm of laughter in the room made him lower it again, his dripping face like thunder.

"Zotikos draws the first chance of the evening!" Anthimos said loudly. More laughter came. Krispos joined in, though he wasn't quite sure what the Avtokrator meant. Anthimos went on, "Here, Skombros, go ahead and give him a real one."

The eunuch who had stared so avidly at the couple making love now rose from his seat. So this was Petronas' rival, Krispos thought. Skombros walked over to a table and picked up a crystal bowl full of little golden balls. With great dignity, he carried it over to Zotikos, who was trying to comb peach fragments out of his hair and beard.

Krispos watched curiously. Zotikos took one of the balls from the bowl. He twisted it between his hands. It came open. He snatched out the little strip of parchment inside. When he scanned it, his face fell.

Skombros delicately plucked the parchment from his fingers. The eunuch's voice was loud, clear, and musical as a middle-range horn's as he read what was written there: "Ten dead dogs."

More howls of laughter, and some out-and-out howls. Servants brought Zotikos the dead animals and dropped them at his feet. He stared at them, at Skombros, and at the bare-breasted juggler who had started his humiliation for the evening. Then, cursing, he stormed out of the hall. A chorus of yips pursued him and sped him on his way. By the time he got to the door, he was running.

"He didn't seem to want his chance. What a pity," Anthimos said. The Emperor's smile was not altogether pleasant. "Let's let someone else have a go. I know! How about Krispos?"

Anger filled Krispos as Skombros approached. Was this his reward for rescuing Anthimos—a chance to be one of the butts for the Avtokrator's jokes? He wanted to kick the crystal bowl out of Skombros' hands. Instead, grim-faced, he drew out a ball and opened it. The parchment inside was folded.

Skombros watched, cool and contemptuous, as Krispos fumbled with it. "Do you read, groom?" he asked, not bothering to keep his voice down.

"I read, eunuch," Krispos snapped. Nothing whatever changed in Skombros' face, but Krispos knew he had made an enemy. He finally got the parchment open. "Ten"—his voice suddenly broke, as if he were a boy—"ten pounds of silver."

"How fortunate of you," Skombros said tonelessly.

Anthimos rushed up and planted a wine-soaked kiss on Krispos' cheek. "Good for you!" he exclaimed. "I was hoping you'd get a good one!"

Krispos hadn't known there were any good ones. He stood, still dazed, as a servant brought him a fat, jingling sack. Only when he felt the weight of it in his hands did he believe the money was for him. Ten pounds of silver was close to half a pound of gold: thirty goldpieces, he worked out after a little thought.

To Tanilis, a pound and a half of gold—108 goldpieces—had been enough to set up Krispos as a man with some small wealth of his own. To Anthimos, thirty goldpieces—and belike three hundred, or three thousand—was a party favor. For the first time, Krispos understood the difference between the riches Tanilis' broad estates yielded and those available to a man with the whole Empire as his estates. No wonder Anthimos thought nothing of a chamber pot made of gold.

A couple of more chances were given out. One man found himself the proud possessor of ten pounds of feathers—a much larger sack than Krispos'. Another got ten free sessions at a fancy brothel. "You mean I have to pay if I want to go back a second night?" the braggart asked, whereupon the fellow who had won the feathers poured them over his head.

Ten pounds of feathers let loose seemed plenty to fill up the room. People flung them about as if they were snow. Servants did their best to get rid of the blizzard of fluff, but even their best took a while to do any good. While most of the servitors plied brooms and pillowcases, a few brought in the next courses of food.

Anthimos pulled a last bit of down from his beard and let it float away. He looked over toward the new trays. "Ah, beef ribs in fish sauce and garlic," he said. "My chef does them wonderfully well. They're far from a neat dish, but oh so tasty."

The ribs would be anything but neat, Krispos thought as he walked toward them—they were fairly swimming in the pungent fermented fish sauce—but they did smell good. One of the men with whom he'd hunted got to them first. The fellow picked up a rib and took a big bite.

The rib vanished. The young noble's teeth came together with a loud click. He'd drunk enough wine that he stared foolishly at his dripping but otherwise empty hand. Then his gaze swung to Krispos. "I did have one, didn't I?" He sounded anything but sure.

"I certainly thought you did," Krispos said. "Here, let me try." He took a rib off the tray. It felt solid and meaty in his hand. He lifted it to his mouth. As soon as he tried to bite it, it disappeared.

Some of the people watching made Phos' sun-sign. Others, wiser in the ways of Anthimos' feasts, looked to the Avtokrator. A small-boy grin was on his face. "I told the cooks to make them rare, but not so rare as that," he said.

"I suppose you're going to say you told them to get the plaster goose livers you served last time well done," someone called out.

"Half a dozen of my friends broke teeth on those livers," the Emperor said. "This is a safer joke. Skombros thought of it."

The eunuch looked smug and also pleased that Krispos had been one of the people his trick had deceived. Krispos stuck his fingers in his mouth to clean them of fish sauce and juice from the ribs. What he was able to taste was delicious. He thought how unfair it was for some sneaky bit of sorcery to deprive him of the tender meat.

He picked up another rib. "Some people," Skombros announced to no one in particular, "have more stubbornness than sense." The vestiarios settled back in his chair, perfectly content to let Krispos make as thorough a fool of himself as he wanted.

This time, though, Krispos did not try to take a bite off the rib. He'd already seen that doing that did not work—bringing his jaws together seemed to activate the spell. Instead, he picked up a knife from the serving table and sliced a long strip of meat off each side of the bone.

He raised one of the strips to his mouth. If the meat vanished despite his preparations, he knew he was going to look foolish. He bit into it, then grinned as he started to chew. He'd hoped cutting it off the bone would sever the spell that made it disappear.

Slowly and deliberately, he ate all the meat he'd sliced away. Then he dealt with another rib, put the meat he'd carved from it on a small plate, and carried the plate to Anthimos. "Would you like some, Your Majesty? You were right; they are very tasty."

"Thank you, Krispos; don't mind if I do." Anthimos ate, then wiped his fingers. "So they are."

Krispos asked, "Do you think your esteemed"—eunuchs had a special set of honorifics that applied to them alone—"vestiarios would care for some?"

The Avtokrator glanced over to Skombros, who stared back stonily. Anthimos laughed. "No, he's a good fellow, but he has plenty of meat on his bones already." Krispos shrugged, bowed, and walked away, as if the matter were of no importance. He could not think of a better way to twist the knife in Skombros' huge belly.

After Krispos showed how to eat the ribs, they vanished into the revelers rather than into thin air. Servants took away the trays. A new set of minstrels circulated through the crowd. Another erotic troupe followed them, then a group of dancers replaced the horizontal cavorters. All the acts did what they did very well. Krispos smiled to himself. Anthimos could afford the best.

Skombros strode through the hall every so often with his crystal bowl of chances. He came nowhere near Krispos. A noble who won ten pounds of gold took his stroke of luck with enough equanimity to make Krispos sure he was already rich. Anthimos confirmed that, saying "More money for slow horses and fast women, eh, Sphrantzes?"

"Fast horses, I hope, Majesty," Sphrantzes said amid general laughter.

"Why should you change now?" the Avtokrator asked. Sphrantzes spread his hands, as if to admit defeat.

Someone else chose ten peacocks for himself. Krispos wondered what peacock tasted like. But the birds the servants chivvied out were very much alive. They honked and squawked and spread their gorgeous tails and generally made nuisances of themselves. "What do I *do* with them?" wailed the winner, who had one bird under each arm and was chasing a third.

"I haven't the foggiest notion," Anthimos replied with a blithe wave of his hand. "That's why I put that chance in there—to find out."

The man ended up departing with his two birds in the hand and forgetting about the rest. After some commotion, revelers, entertainers, and servants joined in shooing the other eight peacocks out the door. "Let the Halogai worry about them," somebody said, which struck Krispos as a good enough idea.

Once the peacocks departed—shouts from outside said the imperial guards were having their own troubles with the bad-tempered birds—the feast grew almost calm for a little while, as if everyone needed some time to catch his breath. "Well, how is he going to top that?" Krispos said to the man next to him. They were standing by a bowl of sweetened gelatin and candied fruit, but neither felt like eating; the gelatin had peacock tracks.

"I don't know," the fellow answered, "but I expect he'll manage."

Krispos shook his head. Then Skombros went round with his bowl again. He stopped in front of the young man whose beef rib had vanished. "Would you care for a chance, excellent Pagras?"

"Huh?" By now, Pagras needed a moment to come out of his wine-soaked haze. He fumbled while he was getting the ball out of the bowl, and fumbled more in getting it open. He read the parchment; Krispos saw his lips move. But, instead of announcing what chance he'd chosen, he turned to Anthimos and said, "I don't believe it."

"Don't believe what, Pagras?" the Emperor asked.

"Ten thousand fleas," Pagras said, looking at the parchment again. "Not even you'd be crazy enough to get together ten thousand fleas."

At any other time, the noble might have lost his tongue for using it so freely. Anthimos, though, was drunk, too, and, as usual, a friendly drunk. "So you doubt me, eh?" was all he said. He pointed to the doorway from which a servant emerged with a large alabaster jar. "Behold: ten thousand fleas."

"Don't see any fleas. All I see is a damn *jar.*" Pagras lurched over to the servant and snatched it out of his hands. He yanked off the lid and stared down into the jar for several horrified seconds.

"If you plan on counting them, Pagras, you'd better do it faster," Anthimos said.

Pagras did not count fleas. He tried to clap the lid back on, but the jar slipped through his clumsy fingers and smashed on the marble floor. Krispos thought of a good-sized pile of ground black pepper. But this pile moved and spread without any breeze to stir it. A man yelled; a woman squealed and clapped a hand to the back of her leg.

The revel broke up very quickly after that.

K RISPOS SPENT THE NEXT MORNING SCRATCHING. WORKING AS he did in the stables, he got fleabites fairly often, but never so many all at once as after Anthimos' feast. And he'd been one of the lucky ones, not too close to the broken jar and not too far from the door. He wondered what poor Pagras looked like—raw meat, probably.

Petronas surprised him by dropping by not long before noon. A glance from the Sevastokrator sent stable hands scurrying out of earshot. "I understand my nephew had things hopping last night," Petronas said.

"That's one way to put it, yes, Highness," Krispos said.

Petronas allowed himself a brief snort of laughter before turning serious once more. "What did you think of the evening's festivities?" he asked.

"I've never seen anything like them," Krispos said truthfully. Petronas waited without saying anything. Seeing something more was expected of him, Krispos went on, "His Imperial Majesty knows how to have a good time. I enjoyed myself, up till the fleas."

"Good. Something's wrong with a man who can't enjoy himself. Still, I see you're here at work in the morning, too." Petronas' smile was twisted. "Aye, Anthimos knows how to have a good time. I sometimes think it's all he does know. But never mind that for now. I hear you also put a spike in Skombros' wheel."

"It wasn't so much." Krispos explained how he'd got round the spell on the disappearing ribs.

"I'd like to set a spell on Skombros that would make him disappear," the Sevastokrator said. "But making the fat maggot look foolish is even better than showing that he's wrong the way you did a few weeks ago. The worse he seems to my nephew, the sooner he won't be vestiarios anymore. And when he's not—Anthimos heeds whichever ear is spoken into last. Things would go smoother if he heard the same thing with both of them."

"Your voice, in other words," Krispos said. Petronas nodded. Krispos considered before he went on, "I don't see any large troubles there, Highness. From everything I've seen, you're a man of good sense. If I thought you were wrong—"

"Yes, tell me what you would do if you thought I was wrong," Petronas interrupted. "Tell me what you would do if you, a peasant from the back of beyond jumped to head groom here only by my kindness, would do if you thought that I, a noble who has been general and statesman longer than you've been alive, was wrong. Tell me that most precisely, Krispos."

Refusing to show he was daunted had taken Krispos a long way with Iakovitzes and Tanilis. Holding that bold front against Petronas was harder. The weight of the Sevastokrator's office and the force of his own person fell on Krispos' shoulders like heavy stones. Almost, he bent beneath them. But at the last moment he found an answer that kept his pride and might not bring Petronas' wrath down upon him. "If I thought you were wrong, Highness, I would tell you first, in private if I could. You once told me Anthimos never hears any plain speaking. Do you?"

"Truth to tell, I wonder." Petronas gave that snort again. "Very well, there is something to what you say. Any officer who does not point out what he sees as error to his commander is derelict in duty. But one who disobeys after his commander makes up his mind . . ."

"I understand," Krispos said quickly.

"See that you do, lad. See that you do, and one day before too long maybe you'll stop smelling of horse manure and take on the scents of perfumes and powders instead. What do you say to that?"

"It's the best reason I've heard yet for wanting to stay in the stables."

This time Petronas' laughter came loud and booming. "You *were* born a peasant, weren't you? We'll see if we can't make a vestiarios of you all the same."

KRISPOS HUNTED WITH THE AVTOKRATOR, WENT TO CHARIOT races at the Amphitheater in the boxes reserved for Anthimos' close comrades, and attended the feasts to which he was invited. As summer moved toward fall, the invitations came more often. He always found himself among the earliest to leave the nightlong revels, but he was one of the few at them who took their day work seriously.

Anthimos certainly did not. In all the time Krispos saw him, he gave scant heed to affairs of state. Depending on who had been at him last, he would say "Go see my uncle" or "Ask Skombros about that—can't you see I'm busy?" whenever a finance minister or diplomat did gain access to him and tried to get him to attend to business. Once, when a customs agent waylaid him outside the Amphitheater with a technical problem, he turned to Krispos and asked, "How would you deal with that?"

"Let me hear the whole thing over again," Krispos said. The customs man, glad for any audience, poured out his tale of woe. When he was done, Krispos said, "If I follow you rightly, you're saying that duties and road tolls at some border stations away from the sea or river transport should be lowered to increase trade through them."

"That's exactly right, excellent—Krispos, was it?" the customs agent said excitedly. "Because moving goods by land is so much more expensive than by water, many times they never go far from the sea. Lowering duties and road tolls would help counteract that."

Krispos thought of the Kalavrian merchants at Develtos and of the mother-of-pearl for which they had charged outrageous prices. He also thought of how seldom traders with even the most ordinary goods had visited his village, of how many things he'd never seen till he came to Videssos the city. "Sounds good to me," he said.

"So ordered!" Anthimos declared. He took the parchment from which the customs agent had been citing figures and scrawled his signature at the bottom of it. The bureaucrat departed with a glad cry. Anthimos rubbed his hands together, pleased with himself. "There! That's taken care of."

His cronies applauded. Along with the rest of them, Krispos accompanied the Avtokrator to the next feast he'd laid on. He was troubled all through it. Problems like the one he'd handled today should have been studied, considered, not attacked on the spur of the moment—if they were attacked at all. More often than not, Anthimos did not care to bother.

He disapproved of the Emperor for his offhandedness about such concerns, but had trouble disliking him. Anthimos would have made a fine innkeeper, he thought—the young man had a gift for keeping everyone around him happy. Unfortunately, being Avtokrator of the Videssians required rather more than that.

Which did not stop Krispos from enjoying himself immensely whenever he was in Anthimos' company—the Emperor kept coming up with new ways to make his revels interesting. He had a whole series of feasts built around colors: one day everything was red, the next yellow, and the next blue. At that last feast, even the fish were cooked in blue sauce, so they looked as if they'd come straight from the sea.

The Avtokrator's chances were never the same twice, either. Remembering what had happened to Pagras, the poor fellow who picked for himself "seventeen wasps" did not dare open the jar that held them. Finally Anthimos, sounding for once most imperial, had to order him to break the seal. The wasps proved to be exquisite re-creations in gold, with emeralds for eyes and delicate filigree wings.

Krispos rarely drew a chance. Skombros kept the crystal bowl and its hollow golden balls away from him. That did not bother him. He was just glad the vestiarios did not try slipping poison into his soup. Perhaps Skombros feared Petronas' revenge. In any case, he made do with black looks from afar. Sometimes Krispos returned them. More often he pretended not to see, which seemed to irk Skombros more.

Such byplay went straight by Anthimos. After a while, though, he did notice that Krispos had not had his hand in the bowl for weeks. "Go on over to him, Skombros," he said one night. "Let's see how his luck is doing."

"His luck is good, in that he enjoys Your Majesty's favor," Skombros said. Nevertheless, he took Krispos the crystal bowl, thrusting it almost into his face. "Here, groom."

"Thank you, esteemed sir." Anyone who had not seen Krispos and Skombros before would have reckoned his tone perfectly respectful. Almost hidden by fat, a muscle twitched near the eunuch's ear as he set his jaw.

Krispos twisted open a gold ball. This was Anthimos' day for the number forty-three. The chances had already allotted forty-three goldpieces to one man, forty-three yards of silk to another, forty-three parsnips to a third. "Forty-three pounds of lead," Krispos read.

Laughter erupted around him. "What a pity," Skombros said, just as if he meant it. A puffing servant brought out the worthless prize. The vestiarios went on, "I trust you will know what to do with it."

"As a matter of fact, I was thinking of giving it to you," Krispos said.

"A token of esteem? A crude joke, but then I would have expected no more from you." At last the eunuch let his scorn show.

"No, not at all, esteemed sir," Krispos answered smoothly. "I just thought you would be used to carrying around the extra weight."

Several people who heard Krispos took a step or two away from him, as if they'd just realized he carried a disease they might catch. He frowned, remembering his family and the all too real disease they'd taken. Skombros' anger, though, might be as dangerous as cholera. The vestiarios' face was red but otherwise impassive as he deliberately turned his broad back on Krispos.

Anthimos had been too far away to hear Skombros and Krispos sniping at each other, but the chamberlain's gesture of contempt was unmistakable. "Enough, the two of you," the Avtokrator said. "Enough, I say. I don't care to have two of my favorite people at odds, and I will not tolerate it. Do you understand me?"

"Yes, Your Majesty," Krispos said.

"Majesty," Skombros said, "I promise I shall always give Krispos all the credit he deserves."

"Excellent." Anthimos beamed. Krispos knew the eunuch's words had been no apology. Skombros would never think he deserved any credit. But even Skombros' hatred did not trouble Krispos, not for the moment. The Emperor had called him and the vestiarios "two of my favorite people." While he loathed Skombros, for Anthimos to mention him in the same breath with the longtime chamberlain was progress indeed.

Slow and ponderous as a merchant ship under not enough sail, Skombros returned to his seat. He sank into it with a sigh of relief. His small, heavily lidded eyes sought Krispos. Krispos gave back a sunny smile and lifted his wine cup in salute. Without Skombros' rudeness, he might have needed much longer to be sure how Anthimos felt about him.

The eunuch's suspicious frown deepened. Krispos' smile got wider.

Mavros stamped snow from his boots. "Warmer in here," he said gratefully. "All these horses are almost as good as a fireplace. Better, if you intend to go anyplace; you can't ride a fireplace."

"No, and I can't fling you into a horse for your foolish jokes, either, however much I wish I could," Krispos answered. "Was making that one the only reason you came? If it was, you've done your damage, so good-bye."

"Harumph." Mavros drew himself up, a caricature of offended dignity. "Just for that, I will go, and keep my news to myself." He made as if to leave.

Krispos and several stable hands quickly called him back. "What news?" Krispos said. Even here in Videssos the city, at the Empire of Videssos' heart, news came slowly in winter and was always welcome. Everyone who'd heard Mavros hurried over to find out what he'd dug up.

"For one thing," he said, pleased at the size of his audience, "that band of Haloga mercenaries under Harvas Black-Robe—remember, Krispos, we heard about them last winter back in Opsikion?—has plundered its way straight across Thatagush and out onto the Pardrayan steppe."

"It'll plunder its way right on back, then," Stotzas predicted. "The steppe nomads don't have much worth stealing."

"Who cares what happens in Thatagush, anyway?" someone else said. "It's too far away to matter to anybody." Several other people spoke up in agreement. Though he did not argue out loud, Krispos shook his head. Having known only his own village for so long, he found he wanted to learn everything he could about the wider world.

"My other bit of gossip you already know, Krispos, if you were at his Majesty's feast the night before last," Mavros said.

Krispos shook his head again, this time more emphatically. "No, I missed that one. Every so often, I feel the need to sleep."

"You'll never succeed till you learn to rise above such weaknesses," Mavros said with an airy wave of his hand. "Well, this also has to do with a Haloga, or rather with a Halogaina."

"A Haloga woman?" Two or three stable hands said it together, sudden keen interest in their voices. The big blond northerners often came to Videssos to trade or to hire on as mercenaries, but they left their wives and daughters behind.

Krispos tried to imagine what a Halogaina would look like. "Tell me more," he said. Again, his was not the only voice.

"Eyes the color of a summer sky, I heard, and the palest pink tips, and her hair gilded above and below," Mavros said. *It would be, wouldn't it?* Krispos thought; that hadn't occurred to him. The stable hands murmured, each painting his own picture in his mind. Mavros went on, "You could hardly blame Anthimos for trying her on then and there."

The murmurs got louder. "I wouldn't blame him for keeping her for a week or a month or a year or—" Onorios was all but panting. He must have liked the picture his mind painted.

But Krispos and Mavros said "No" at the same time. They glanced at each other. Krispos dipped his head to Mavros, who, he knew, was better with words. "His Majesty," Mavros explained, "only sleeps with a pleasure girl once. Anything more, he reckons, would constitute infidelity to the Empress."

That got the yowls and whoops Krispos had known it would. "Give me fidelity like that, any day," Onorios said. "Give it to me twice a day," someone else said. "Three times!" another groom added.

"The lot of you remind me of the rich old man who married a young wife and promised to kill her with passion," Krispos said. "He had her once, then fell asleep and snored all night long. When he finally woke up, she looked over at him and said, 'Good morning, killer.' "

The stable hands hissed at him. Grinning, he added, "Besides, if we spent all our time in bed, we'd never get anything done, and Phos knows there's plenty to do here." The men hissed again, but started drifting off toward their tasks.

"Not getting anything done doesn't seem to worry his Majesty," Onorios said.

"Ah, but he has people to do things for him. Unless you hired a servant while I wasn't looking, you don't," Krispos said.

"Afraid not, worse luck." Onorios sadly clicked his tongue and went back to work.

"LOOK AT THIS—THIS BLOODSUCKING!" PETRONAS SLAMMED A fist down on the pile of parchments in front of him. They were upside down to Krispos, but that did not matter because the Sevastokrator was in full cry. "Thirty-six hundred goldpieces—fifty *pounds* of gold!—that cursed leech of a Skombros has siphoned off for his worthless slug of a nephew Askyltos. And another twenty pounds for the worthless slug's stinking father Evmolpos. When I show these accounts to my nephew—"

"What do you think will happen?" Krispos asked eagerly. "Will he give Skombros the sack?"

But Petronas' rage collapsed into moroseness. "No, he'll just laugh, curse it. He already knows Skombros is a thief. He doesn't care. What he won't see is that the Skotos-loving wretch is setting up his own relations as great men. Dynasties have died that way."

"If his Majesty doesn't care whether Skombros steals, why do you keep shoving accounts in his face?" Krispos asked.

"To *make* him care, by Phos, before the fox he insists on thinking a lapdog sinks its teeth into him." The Sevastokrator heaved a sigh. "Making Anthimos care about anything save his own amusement is like pushing water uphill with a rake."

Petronas' loathing for his rival, Krispos thought, blinded him to any way of dealing with Skombros but the one that had already shown it did not work. "What would happen if Skombros didn't amuse him, or amused him in the wrong sort of way?" Krispos asked.

"What *are* you talking about?" Petronas demanded crossly.

For a moment, Krispos had no idea himself. One of the lessons he should have learned from Tanilis was keeping his mouth shut when he had nothing to say. He bent his head in humiliation. Humiliation . . . he remembered how he'd felt when he was just a youth, when a couple of village wits lampooned his wrestling in a Midwinter's Day skit. "How would Anthimos like the whole city laughing at his vestiarios? It's only a couple of weeks to Midwinter's Day, after all."

"What does that have to do with—" Petronas suddenly caught up with Krispos. "By the good god, so it is. So you want to make him look ridiculous, do you? Why not? He is." The Sevastokrator's eyes lit up. As soon as he saw his objective, he planned how to reach it with a soldier's directness. "Anthimos has charge of the Amphitheater skits. They entertain him, so he pays attention to them. All the same, I expect I can slide a new one into the list without his noticing. Have to give it an innocuous title so that even if he does spot it, he won't think anything of it. Have to find mimes who aren't already engaged. And costumes—curse it, can we get costumes made in time?"

"We have to figure out what the mimes are going to do, too," Krispos pointed out.

"Aye, that's true, though Phos knows there's plenty to say about the eunuch."

"Let me get Mavros," Krispos said. "He has an ear for scandal."

"Does he?" Petronas all but purred. "Yes, go fetch him—at once."

"Now this," Mavros said, "is what I call an amphitheater." He craned his neck to peer around and up.

"Only trouble is, I feel like I'm at the bottom of a soup bowl full of people," Krispos answered. Fifty thousand, seventy, ninety—he was not sure how many people the enormous oval held. However many it was, they were all here today. No one wanted to miss the Midwinter's Day festivity.

"I'd sooner be at the bottom than the top," Mavros said. "Who has better seats than we do?" They were in the very first row, right by what was a racecourse most of the time but would serve as an open-air stage today.

"There's always the people on the spine." Krispos pointed to the raised area in the center of the track.

Mavros snorted. "You're never satisfied, are you?" The spine was reserved for the Avtokrator, the Sevastokrator, the patriarch, and the chief ministers of the Empire. Krispos saw Skombros there, not far from Anthimos; the vestiarios was conspicuous for his bulk and his beardless cheeks. The only men on the spine who were not high lords or prelates were the axe-toting Halogai of the imperial guard. Mavros nodded toward them. "See? They don't even get to sit down. Me, I'd rather be comfortable here."

"I suppose I would, too," Krispos said. "Even so——"

"Hush! They're starting."

Anthimos rose from his throne and strode over to a podium set in the very center of the spine. He silently stood there, waiting. Quiet spread through the Amphitheater as more and more people saw him. When all was still, he spoke:

"People of Videssos, today the sun turns in the sky again." A trick of acoustics carried his voice clearly to the uppermost rows of the Amphitheater, from which he seemed hardly more than a bright-colored speck in his imperial robes. He went on, "Once more Skotos has failed to drag us down into his eternal darkness. Let us thank Phos the Lord of the great and good mind for delivering us for another year, and let us celebrate that deliverance the whole day long. Let joy pour forth unconfined!"

The Amphitheater erupted in cheers. Anthimos staggered as he walked back to his high seat. Krispos wondered if the acoustical trick worked in reverse, if all the noise in the huge building focused where the Emperor had stood. That would be enough to stagger anyone. On the other hand, maybe Anthimos had just started drinking at dawn.

"Here we go," Mavros breathed. The first troupe of mimes, a group of men dressed as monks, emerged from the gate that normally let horses onto the track. From the way one of them made a point of holding his nose, the horses were still much in evidence.

The "monks" proceeded to do a number of most unmonastic things. The audience howled. On Midwinter's Day, nothing was sacred. Krispos peered across the track to the spine to see how Gnatios enjoyed watching his clerics lampooned. The patriarch was paying the skit no attention at all; he was leaning over to one side of his chair so he could talk with his cousin Petronas. He and the Sevastokrator smiled at some private joke.

When the first mime troupe left, another took its place. This one tried to exaggerate the excesses at one of Anthimos' revels. The people who filled the stands alternately gasped and whooped. Unlike his uncle and Gnatios, the Emperor watched attentively and howled laughter. Krispos chuckled, too, not least because much of what the mimes thought wild enough to put in their act was milder than things he'd really seen at Anthimos' feasts.

The next troupe came out in striped caftans and felt hats that looked like upside-down buckets. The make-believe Makuraners capered about. The people in the stands jeered and hissed. In his high seat on the spine, Petronas looked pleased with himself.

"Make the men from the west look like idiots and weaklings and every-one will be more willing to go to war with them," Mavros said. He guf-fawed as one of the mimes pretended to relieve himself into his hat.

"I suppose so," Krispos said. "But there are a fair number of people from Makuran here in the city, rug-dealers and ivory merchants and such. They're just . . . people. Half the folk in the Amphitheater must have dealt with them at one time or another. They know Makuraners aren't like this."

"I daresay they do, when they stop to think about it. How many peo-ple do you know who always take the time to stop and think, though?"

"Not many," Krispos admitted, a little sadly.

The pseudo-Makuraners fled in mock terror as the next troupe, whose members were dressed as Videssian soldiers, came out. That won a last laugh and a cheer at the same time. The "soldiers" quickly proved no more heroic than the Makuraners they replaced, which to Krispos' way of think-ing weakened the message Petronas was trying to put across.

Act followed act, all competent, some very funny indeed. The city folk leaned back in their seats to enjoy the spectacle. Krispos enjoyed it, too, even while he wished the troupes were a little less polished. Back in his vil-lage, a big part of the fun had lain in taking part in the skits and poking fun at the ones that went wrong. Here no one save professionals took part and nothing went wrong.

When he grumbled about that, Mavros said, "For hundreds of years, Emperors have been putting on spectacles and entertaining people in the capital, to keep them from thinking up ways to get into mischief for them-selves. Save for riots, I don't think they know how to make their own en-tertainment anymore." He leaned forward. "See these dancers? They come on just before that troupe the Sevastokrator hired."

The dancers came on, went off. Krispos paid scant attention to them. He found he was pounding his fist on his thigh as he waited for the next company. He made himself stop.

The mimes came onto the track a few at a time. Some were dressed as ordinary townsfolk, others, once more, as imperial troops. The townsfolk acted out chatting among themselves. The troops marched back and forth. Out came a tall fellow wearing the imperial raiment. The soldiers sprang to attention; the civilians flopped down in comically overdone prostrations.

A dozen parasol-bearers, the proper imperial number, followed the mime playing the Avtokrator. But it soon became obvious they were not attached to him, but rather to the figure who emerged after him. That man was in a fancy robe, too, but one padded out so that he looked even wider than he was tall. A low murmur of laughter ran through the Amphitheater as the audience recognized who he was supposed to be.

"How much did we have to pay that mime to get him to shave his beard?" Krispos asked. "He looks a lot more like Skombros without it."

"He held out for two goldpieces," Mavros answered. "I finally ended up paying him. You're right; it's worth it."

"Aye, it is. You might also want to think about paying him for a holiday away from the city till his beard grows back again, at least if he wants to live to work next Midwinter's Day," Krispos said. After a moment's surprise, Mavros nodded.

Up on the spine, Petronas sat at ease, watching the mimes but still not seeming to pay any great attention to them. Krispos admired his coolness; no one would have guessed by looking at him that he'd had anything to do with this skit. Anthimos leaned forward to see better, curiosity on his face—whatever he'd been told about this troupe's performance, it was something different from this. And Skombros—Skombros' fleshy features were so still and hard, they might have been carved from granite.

The mock-Anthimos on the track walked around receiving the plaudits of his subjects. The parasol-bearers stayed with the pseudo-Skombros, who was also accompanied by a couple of disgusting hangers-on, one with gray hair, the other with black.

The actors playing citizens lined up to pay their taxes to the Emperor. He collected a sack of coins from each one, headed over to pay the soldiers. At last the mime-Skombros bestirred himself. He intercepted Anthimos, patted him on the back, put an arm around him, and distracted him enough to whisk the sacks away. The Avtokrator's befuddlement on discovering he had no money to give his troops won loud guffaws from the stands.

Meanwhile, the mime playing the vestiarios shared the sacks with his two slimy colleagues. They fondled the money with lascivious abandonment.

Almost as an afterthought, the pseudo-Skombros went back to the Emperor. After another round of the hail-fellow-well-met routine he had used before, he charmed the crown off Anthimos' head. The actor playing the Emperor did not seem to notice it was gone. Skombros took the crown over to his black-haired henchman, tried it on him. It was much too big; it hid half the fellow's face. With a shrug, as if to say "not yet," the vestiarios restored it to Anthimos.

The Amphitheater grew still during that last bit of business. Then, far up in the stands, someone shouted, "To the ice with Skombros!" That one thin cry unleashed a torrent of abuse against the eunuch.

Krispos and Mavros looked at each other and grinned. Over on the spine, Petronas kept up his pose of indifference. The real Skombros sat very still, refusing to notice any of the gibes hurled at him. He had nerve, Krispos thought grudgingly. Then Krispos' eyes slid to the man for whom the skit had been put on, the Avtokrator of the Videssians.

Anthimos rubbed his chin and stared thoughtfully from the departing troupe of mimes to Skombros and back again. "I hope he got it," Mavros said.

"He got it," Krispos said. "He may be foolish, but he's a long way from stupid. I just hope he takes notice of—hey!"

An apple flung by someone farther back in the crowd had caught Krispos in the shoulder. A cabbage whizzed by his head. Another apple, thrown by someone with a mighty arm, splashed not far from Skombros' seat. "Dig up the vestiarios' bones!" a woman screeched—the Videssian call to riot. In a moment, the whole Amphitheater was screaming it.

Petronas stood and spoke to the commander of the Haloga guards. Pale winter sun glittered on the northerners' axeblades as they swung them up over their shoulders. The Halogai yelled together, a deep, wordless shout that cut through the cries from the stands like one of their axes cleaving flesh.

"Now for the interesting question," Mavros said. "Will that hold them, or will we have ourselves an uprising right now?"

Krispos gulped. When he put his plan to Petronas, he hadn't thought of that. Getting rid of Skombros was one thing; pulling Videssos the city down with the eunuch was something else again. Given the capital's volatile populace, the chance was real.

The Halogai shouted again, the threat in their voices plain as the snarl of a wolf. Another troop of northerners, axes at the ready, tramped out onto the track from under the Amphitheater.

"There are enough people here to swamp them," Krispos said nervously.

"I know." Mavros seemed to be enjoying himself. "But are there enough people here willing to get maimed doing it?"

There weren't. Insults continued to rain down on Skombros, but the missiles more tangible than insults stopped. Finally someone yelled, "Get the soldiers off the track! We want the mimes!" Soon everyone took up the cry: "We want the mimes! We want the mimes!"

This time Anthimos spoke to the Haloga commander. The warrior bowed. At his command, the northerners lowered their weapons. The newly emerged band of imperial guards marched back through the gate from which they had come. A moment later, a fresh troupe of mimes replaced them. Cheers filled the Amphitheater.

"Fickle buggers," Mavros said with a contemptuous jerk of his head. "Half an hour from now, half of them won't remember what they were screaming about."

"Maybe not," Krispos said, "but Skombros will, and so will Anthimos."

"That is the point, isn't it?" Mavros leaned back in his chair. "Let's see what antics this new bunch has in 'em, shall we?"

THE THRONE IN THE GRAND COURTROOM BELONGED TO AN-thimos. Sitting in a raised chair in his own suite, dressed in his full Sevastokrator's regalia, Petronas looked quite imperial enough, Krispos thought from his place at his master's left.

He looked around. "This room is different somehow," he said.

"I've screened off that part of it." Petronas pointed. Sure enough, a wooden screen like the one that gave privacy to the imperial niche at the High Temple was in place.

The openings in the woodwork were so small that Krispos could not see what, if anything, lay behind it. He asked, "Why did you put the screen up?"

"Let's just say you're not the only one who ever comes up with bright ideas," the Sevastokrator said. Krispos shrugged. If Petronas didn't feel like explaining, he could hardly force him to.

Eroulos came in and bowed to Petronas. "His Majesty and the vestiarios are here, Highness."

"Show them in, by all means," the Sevastokrator said.

Petronas' efficient steward had already supplied Anthimos and Skombros with goblets. The Emperor lowered his to grin at Krispos as he and Petronas rose in greeting. Skombros' face was somber. Had he been less practiced at schooling his features, Krispos judged, he would have looked nervously from one of his foes to the other. As it was, his eyes flicked back and forth between them.

Petronas welcomed him affably enough, waved him to a seat beside Anthimos', which was even more splendid than the one in which Petronas sat—the Sevastokrator did not believe in giving unintentional offense. After Eroulos refilled Anthimos' wine cup, Petronas said, "And what can I do for you today, nephew and Majesty?"

Anthimos sipped, glanced from Petronas to Skombros, licked his lips, and took a hefty swig of wine. Thus fortified, he said, "My vestiarios here would like to, ah, try to repair any ill-feeling that may exist between the two of you. May he speak?"

"You are my Avtokrator," Petronas declared. "If it be your will that he speak to me, of course I shall hear him with all the attention he merits." He turned his head toward Skombros and waited expectantly.

"I thank you, your Imperial Highness. You are gracious to me," Skombros said, his sexless voice soft and persuasive. "As I seem somehow to have offended your Imperial Highness—and that was never my intent, for my concern, as yours, is solely for the comfort and especially for the glory of his Imperial Majesty whom we both serve—I thought it best at this time to offer my deepest and most sincere apologies for whatever I have done to disturb your Imperial Highness' tranquility and to tender my assurances that any such disturbance was purely inadvertent on my part and shall not be repeated."

He paused to take a deep breath. Krispos did not blame him; he could not have brought out such a long sentence to save his life. He doubted whether he could have written one so complex.

Petronas was more used to the grandiloquence of formal Videssian speech. Nodding to the vestiarios, he began, "Esteemed sir—"

From behind that newly installed screen, a soft chorus of female voices chanted, "You have five chins, and a lard belly below them." Krispos happened to be taking a sip of wine; he all but choked on it. But for the content of what that hidden chorus sang, its response was much like that of a temple choir to the prayers of a priest.

Skombros sat perfectly still, but could not help the flush that rose from his neck to the roots of his hair. Anthimos looked about in surprise, as if unsure where the chorus was or whether he'd truly heard it. And Petronas seemed to shake himself. "I'm sorry," he told Skombros. "I must have been woolgathering. What was it you wanted?"

The vestiarios tried again. "Your Imperial Highness, I ah, wanted to apologize for, ah, anything I may have done to, ah, offend you, and I certainly want to assure you I, ah, meant no harm." This time, Krispos noted, his delivery was less polished than before.

Petronas nodded. "Esteemed sir—"

"You have five chins, and a lard belly below them." The voices of the chorus rang out once more.

This time Krispos was ready for them and kept his face straight. Anthimos stared again, then giggled. Hearing that, Skombros seemed to wilt. Petronas prompted him, "You were saying?"

"Does it matter?" Skombros asked bleakly.

"Why, esteemed sir—"

The chorus took up where the Sevastokrator left off: "You have five chins, and a lard belly below them."

Anthimos giggled again, louder. Ignoring all courtly etiquette, Skombros heaved his bulk out of his chair and stalked toward the door. "Dear me," Petronas exclaimed as the eunuch slammed it behind him. "Do you think I said something wrong?"

Chapter IX

MAVROS, AS WAS HIS WAY, HEARD THE NEWS FIRST. "SKOM-bros resigned his position last night."

"What, the esteemed sir?" Krispos whistled the choral response.

"Aye, the very same." Mavros laughed—that story had spread through the palace complex like wildfire. "Not only that, he's had himself tonsured and fled into a monastery. So, they tell me, have his nephew Askyltos and his brother-in-law Evmolpos."

"If I were wearing their robes, I'd flee to a monastery, too," Krispos said. "Petronas respects the good god's followers, so he might leave them there and not take their heads now that their protector's fallen."

"So he might." Mavros sound regretful. Then he brightened. "Now that their protector's fallen, who's to be the new vestiarios?" Grinning, he pointed at Krispos.

"We'll see. It's the Avtokrator's choice, of course." For all his own good times with Anthimos, for all Petronas' urging, he knew the Emperor might just choose another eunuch as his new chamberlain. That would be easiest, and Anthimos liked doing things the easiest way.

But a couple of hours later, while Krispos was making sure the new

horseshoes on Petronas' favorite hunter were firmly nailed in place, Onorios came up to him and said, "There's a eunuch outside who wants to talk
with you."

"Thanks. I'll see him in a minute." Krispos had one more hoof to
check. As he'd expected, the blacksmith had done a good job. Knowing
was better than expecting, though. When he was through, he walked out
to see the Emperor's servant.

It was the tall, thin eunuch who had taken Krispos to his first revel with
Anthimos the summer before. Now the fellow made no snide remarks
about the smell of the stables. Instead, he bowed low. "Krispos, his Imperial Majesty bids you join his household as vestiarios, head of his domestic staff."

"He honors me. Tell me your name, please, esteemed sir. If we are both
of His Majesty's household, I should know you."

The eunuch straighted. "I am called Barsymes," he said with the first
approval Krispos had heard from him. "Now if you will follow me, ah—"
He stopped, frowning. "Should I call you 'esteemed sir' or 'eminent sir'?
You are vestiarios, a post traditionally held by an esteemed sir, and yet
you"—he hesitated again—"you have a beard. The proper protocol is a
puzzlement."

Krispos started to laugh, then realized he would be worrying about just
such concerns himself in his new post. "Either way is all right with me,
Barsymes," he said.

"I have it!" The eunuch looked as pleased as his doleful features would
allow. "Now if you will come with me, esteemed and eminent sir . . ."

Krispos obediently followed. If Barsymes had found a formula that satisfied him, well and good. They scuffed through snow together for a while
before Krispos said, "I hope you and your comrades will not be troubled,
serving with . . . serving with someone who has a beard."

"It is the Avtokrator's will," Barsymes said, which was no answer at all.
He walked on, not looking at Krispos. After a while, he decided to continue. "We do remember that you mocked Skombros for being a eunuch."

"Only when he mocked me first for being a groom," Krispos said.

"Yes, there is some truth in that," Barsymes said judiciously, "though by
now you will have noted, esteemed and eminent sir, that your condition is
rather easier to change than Skombros'." Being without any better reply,
Krispos could only nod. He felt a little easier when Barsymes went on, half
to himself, "Still, you may indeed be entitled to the benefit of the doubt."

They passed through a grove of cherry trees, bare-branched and skeletal with winter. Armed Halogai stood outside the entrance to the elegant

little building in the center of the grove. Krispos had seen some of them before, guarding Anthimos' revels. Most of them had been drunk then. Now they looked sober and reliable. He knew little of soldiers' ways, but the difference seemed remarkable.

As if reading his mind, Barsymes said, "Any guard who fails of alertness while protecting their Majesty's residence is forthwith banished back to Halogaland, forfeiting all pay and benefactions earned here."

"A good plan." Krispos wondered why it didn't hold wherever the Emperor was. Knowing Anthimos, probably because when he was having a good time, he wanted everyone else to have one, too.

The Halogai nodded to Barsymes and gave Krispos curious looks as he walked up the stairs with the eunuch. One of the guards said something in his own language. The others laughed. Krispos had no trouble imagining several rough jokes, most of them at his expense. He sighed. However much it meant to him, this business of taking over a eunuch's post brought complications.

His eyes needed a moment to adjust to the dimmer light inside the imperial residence, and a moment more to notice that what light there was came neither from torches nor, for the most part, from windows. Instead, panes of alabaster scraped to translucent thinness were set into the ceiling.

The pale, clear light that filtered through them displayed to best advantage the treasures set along both sides of the central hallway. Barsymes pointed to some of them as he led Krispos past. "Here is the battle helmet of a Makuraner King of Kings, taken centuries ago after a tremendous victory not far from Mashiz. . . . This is the chalice from which the assembled prelates of Phos drank together in ritual renunciation of Skotos at the great synod not long after the High Temple was built. . . . Here is a portrait of the Emperor Stavrakios, most often called the Conqueror. . . ."

The portrait drew Krispos' eye. Stavrakios wore the red boots, the imperial crown, and a gilded mail shirt, but he did not look like an Emperor to Krispos. He looked like a veteran underofficer about to give his troops a hard time for a sloppy piece of drill.

"Come along," Barsymes said when Krispos paused to study that tough face. He followed the eunuch down the hall, thinking that Anthimos did not look like his idea of an Emperor, either. He laughed at himself. Maybe he just didn't know what an Emperor was supposed to look like.

Another eunuch heard Barsymes and Krispos coming and stuck his head out a doorway. "You have him, eh?" he said. "Very well. His Majesty will be glad to see him." If the eunuch himself was glad to see Krispos, he concealed it magnificently.

The fellow's head disappeared again. Krispos heard his voice, too low to make out words, then Anthimos', louder: "What's that, Tyrovitzes? He's here? Well, bring him in." Barsymes heard, also, and led Krispos forward.

Anthimos sat at a small table eating cakes. Krispos went down on his belly in a full proskynesis. "Your Imperial Majesty," he murmured.

"Get up, get up," the Emperor said impatiently. "The bowing and scraping can stop when you're in here. You're part of my household now. You didn't bow and scrape when you were in your parents' household, did you?"

"No, Your Majesty," Krispos said. He wondered what his father would have made of having his household compared to the Avtokrator's. Most likely, Phostis would have laughed himself silly. That Anthimos could make the comparison only showed how little he realized what a special life he led.

The Emperor said, "Anything special you think you'll need, Krispos?"

"Having you remember I'm more used to tending horses than people would help a lot, Your Majesty," Krispos answered. Anthimos stared at him, then let out a startled laugh. Krispos went on, "I'm sure your other servants will help me learn what I need to know as fast as I can."

Anthimos glanced toward Barsymes. "Of course, Your Majesty," the eunuch said in his neutral voice.

"Good. That's settled, then," the Emperor said. Krispos hoped it was. Anthimos went on, "Take Krispos to his room, Barsymes. He can have the rest of today and tomorrow to move in; I expect the rest of you will be able to care for me and Dara till morning after next."

"We shall manage, Your Majesty," Barsymes agreed. "Now if you will excuse us? This way, Krispos." As he led Krispos down the hall, he explained, "The vestiarios' bedchamber is next to that of the Avtokrator, so that he may most conveniently attend his master at any hour of the day or night." The eunuch opened a door. "You will stay here."

Krispos gasped. He'd never seen such a profusion of gold and fine silks. Petronas surely had more, but did not flaunt it so. And the feather bed in the center of the room looked thick enough to smother in.

"You will understand, I hope," Barsymes said, seeing his expression, "that Skombros, having no hope of progeny, saw no point in stinting his personal comfort. The failing is not unique to us eunuchs, but is perhaps more common among us."

"I suppose so," Krispos said, still stunned by the room's opulence. Near that fabulous feather bed, a little silver bell hung from a red cord that ran up into the ceiling and disappeared. He pointed to it. "What's that for?"

"The cord runs to the imperial bedchamber next door. When that bell rings, you must attend."

"All right." Krispos hesitated, then went on, "Thanks, Barsymes. You've helped." He held out his hand.

The eunuch took it. His palms were smooth, but his grip showed surprising strength. "Not all of us were enamored of Skombros," he remarked. "If you do not despise us for what we are, we may be able to work together well enough."

"I hope so." Krispos was not making idle chitchat; as at Petronas' stables, he knew he would fail if the people he was supposed to oversee turned against him. And eunuchs, unlike the straightforward stable hands, moved with proverbial guile; he was not sure he was ready to counter their machinations. With luck, he wouldn't have to.

He was relieved to escape the room that had been Skombros' and was now his, though he wondered how the ex-vestiarios enjoyed a bare monastery cell, so different from this splendor. The image of Stavrakios caught his eye again as he walked down the hall. Imagining what that warrior-Emperor would have said about Skombros' luxuries—or Anthimos'—gave him something to smile about while he went back to say good-bye to his friends and collect his belongings.

At the stables, after the inevitable round of congratulations and back-slapping, he managed to get Stotzas off to one side for a few minutes. "Do you want my job now that I'm leaving?" he asked the senior groom. "The good god knows you're the best man with horses here, and I'd be pleased to speak with Petronas for you."

"You're a gentleman, lad, and I'm pleased you asked, but no thanks," Stotzas said. "You're right, it's the horses I fancy, and I'd have less time for 'em if I had to worry about bossing the men around instead."

Krispos nodded. He'd thought Stotzas would say that, but he hadn't been sure; if the graybeard wanted the job, he deserved it. Since he didn't, Krispos had someone else in mind to recommend to the Sevastokrator.

When he got back to his apartment in the Grand Courtroom, he discovered he needed more than one duffel bag for what he had inside. He smiled to himself as he went back to the stables to borrow Petronas' brown gelding one last time. The horse snorted reproachfully as he loaded it with his worldly goods.

"Oh, hush," he told it. "Better your back than mine." The horse did not seem convinced, but let him lead it over to the imperial residence.

THE BELL BESIDE KRISPOS' BED RANG. AT FIRST, HE TRIED TO
fit the sound into his dream. The bell kept ringing. He woke with a start.
Anthimos was calling him!

He sprang out of bed naked, threw on a robe, shoved his feet into sandals, and dashed for the imperial bedchamber. "Your Majesty," he said,
puffing. "How may I serve you?"

Wearing no more than Krispos had, Anthimos was sitting up in bed—
a bed that looked comfortable enough, but not nearly so magnificent as
the one Krispos had appropriated from Skombros. The Avtokrator
grinned at his new vestiarios. "I'll have to get used to your appearing so
quickly," he said, which eased Krispos' mind—he hadn't taken too long to
wake, then. Anthimos went on, "Time to face the day."

"Certainly, Your Majesty." The eunuchs had spent the previous afternoon talking themselves hoarse about the Emperor's routine. Krispos
hoped he remembered it. Beside the bed stood a chamber pot; first things
first, for Emperor as for peasant. Bowing, Krispos lifted it and handed it
to Anthimos.

While the Avtokrator stood up and used it, Krispos got him clean
drawers and a fresh robe. He helped Anthimos dress, then ceremoniously
escorted him to a mirror of polished silver. Anthimos made a face at his reflection while Krispos combed his hair and beard. "Looks like me," the
Emperor said when he was done. "Eyes aren't even too bloodshot—but
then, I got to sleep early last night." He turned back to the bed. "Didn't I,
Dara?"

"What's that?" Buried in blankets to the crown of her head, Anthimos'
Empress sounded more than half asleep herself.

"Didn't I get to bed early last night?" the Avtokrator repeated. "I've
even found an advantage to it—my eyes look much clearer than usual this
morning."

Dara rolled over and sat up. Krispos did his best not to stare—like Anthimos, she slept nude. Then she noticed him, squeaked, and yanked the
blankets up to her chin.

Anthimos laughed. "No need for such worries, my dear. This is
Krispos, the new vestiarios."

Keeping his eyes on his own toes, Krispos said in his most formal voice,
"I did not mean to startle you, Your Majesty."

"It's—all right," Dara said after a moment. "Seeing the beard caught
me by surprise, that's all. His Majesty said you were a whole man, but it
must have slipped my mind. Go ahead with what you were doing; I'll

summon a maidservant." She had a bellpull on her side of the bed, too, with a green cord. She held the blankets in place with one hand, reached out with the other.

Krispos fetched the Emperor's red boots from the closet and helped Anthimos into them. They were tight, and pulling them onto the imperial feet took some work. The maidservant came in while he was still fighting to get them on. She paid no attention to Krispos' beard. Indeed, with him bent down in front of the Emperor, she could hardly have noticed whether he had one—or whether he had horns and fangs, for that matter. She chose a gown from Dara's closet and whisked away the bedclothes so she could dress the empress.

Dara again glanced nervously toward Krispos, but relaxed when she saw him intent on his own duties. He did his best to take no special notice of her. If she had been easy in the presence of the former vestiarios, he did not want to rob her of that ease.

At the same time, even the brief, self-conscious glimpses he'd had of her showed she was a dazzling young woman. She was small and dark, with lustrous, almost blue-black hair that crackled as her maidservant brushed it. She had an aquiline profile, with high, sculptured cheekbones and a strong, rather pointed chin. Her body was as lovely as her face.

Krispos wondered why Anthimos, having such an Empress, also bedded any girl who caught his eye. Maybe Dara lacked passion, he thought. Or maybe Anthimos was like some of Petronas' stable hands, unable to pass up any opportunity he found. And unlike them, he found plenty— few would say no to the Avtokrator of the Videssians.

Such wherefores were not his concern, though. Getting the Emperor's boots on was. Grunting with effort, he finally succeeded. "Good job," Anthimos said, laughing and patting him on the head. "From all I've heard, you had a tougher time wrestling with my boots than you did with that giant Kubrati."

"Different sort of wrestling, Majesty." Krispos had to remind himself what came next in the routine. "And now, with what would you and your lady care to break your fast?"

"A bloater for me," Anthimos said. "A bloater and wine. How about you, my dear?"

"Just porridge, I think," Dara said. Krispos' sympathies lay with her. Smoked and salted mackerel was all very well, but not his idea of breakfast food.

He carried the imperial couple's requests back to the kitchens and had a bowl of porridge himself while the cook fixed a tray. "The good god be thanked his Majesty's in a simple mood today," the fellow said as he poured wine from an amphora into a silver carafe. "Have you ever tried fixing shrimp and octopus stew while he's waiting? Or, worse, had to go running out to try to buy oranges out of season because it crossed his mind he wanted some?"

"Did you find any?" Krispos asked, intrigued.

"Aye, there's a shop or two that sells 'em preserved by magic, for those who have the urge and the money at the same time. Didn't cost me above twenty times what they usually run, and what sort of thanks did I get? Precious little, I'll tell you."

Carrying the tray to a dining hall not far from the imperial bedchamber, Krispos wondered if Anthimos had even known the fruit was out of season. When would he have occasion to learn? All he needed to do was ask for something to have it appear before him.

The Emperor devoured his bloater with lip-smacking gusto. "Now, my dear," he said to Dara, "why don't you go and tend to your embroidery for a while? Krispos and I have some serious business to discuss."

Krispos would have resented such a cavalier dismissal. Whatever Dara felt, she did not let it show. She rose, nodded to Anthimos, and left without a word. She took as much notice of Krispos as of the chair on which he sat.

"What business is there, Your Majesty?" Krispos asked, curious and a little worried; none of the Emperor's eunuchs had warned him anything special was in the wind.

But Anthimos answered, "Why, we have to decide what the chances will be for tonight's festivities."

"Oh," Krispos said. Following the Emperor's pointing finger, he saw the ball-filled crystal bowl sitting on a shelf. He got it down, took apart the balls, and set their halves on the table between himself and Anthimos. "Where can I find pen and parchment, Your Majesty?"

"Somewhere around here," Anthimos said vaguely. While Krispos poked through drawers in a sideboard, Anthimos continued, "I think the number tonight will be eleven, after the paired single pips on the dice when someone throws Phos' little suns. What goes well with eleven?"

Krispos found writing materials at last. "Eleven dice, Your Majesty, since the number is taken from gambling?"

"Excellent! I knew you were clever. What else?"

"How about—hmm—eleven mice?"

"So you want to rhyme tonight, do you? Well, why not? I expect the servants can find eleven mice by evening. What else?"

They came up with eleven pounds of ice, eleven grains of rice, eleven lice— "I *know* the servants can find those," Anthimos said.—eleven drams of spice, eleven things nice, and eleven kinds of vice. "Both of those will send the winner to the stews," the Avtokrator declared.

"How about eleven gold*pice*?" Krispos suggested when their inspiration began to flag. "It's not a perfect rhyme—"

"It is if you write it that way," Anthimos said, so Krispos did.

"Your Majesty, could I get you to think on something else about these chances for a moment?" Krispos asked. At the Emperor's nod, he went on, "You might want to give them out to the entertainers along with your guests. They're not rich; think how overjoyed they'd be to pick one of the good chances."

Anthimos' answering smile was not altogether pleasant. "Yes, and think how downcast they'd be if they didn't. That could be amusing, too. We'll give it a try."

Krispos knew he hadn't got his way for the reason he wanted, but he'd got it. Some of the jugglers and musicians and courtesans would end up better off, and even the ones who came away from the chances disappointed would actually be in no worse state than before, he told himself.

"What's next?" the Avtokrator asked.

"I am given to understand a new Makuraner embassy has come to the city," Krispos said carefully. "If you cared to, I suppose you could meet the high ambassador."

Anthimos yawned. "Another time, perhaps. Petronas will tend to them. That's his proper function, seeing to such tiresome details."

"As you wish, Your Majesty." Krispos did not press the issue. He'd done his best to make the meeting sound dull. He knew Petronas wanted to keep his own hands firmly on the Empire's relations with its neighbors.

Instead of meeting with the Makuraner high ambassador, Anthimos went to the Amphitheater. He ate the coarse, greasy food the vendors sold there; he drank rough wine from a cracked clay cup; he awarded five hundred goldpieces to a driver who'd brought his chariot from the back of the pack to first in the last couple of laps. The crowd cheered his generosity. It all worked well enough, Krispos thought; they had a symbol, Anthimos had fun, and Petronas had the government.

And what do I have? Krispos wondered. Part of the answer was plain enough: good food, good lodging, even the ear of the Avtokrator of the Videssians—for such matters as chances at revels, anyhow. All that was marvelously better than the nothing with which he'd arrived at Videssos the city a few years before.

He was discovering, though, that the more he had, the more he wanted. He'd read two or three chronicles of the Empire's past. None of them recorded the name of a single vestiarios.

A FEW DAYS LATER, ANTHIMOS WENT HUNTING. KRISPOS STAYED behind. Running the imperial residence, even with the Emperor absent, was a full-time job. He was not unduly surprised when Eroulos came by a little before noon. This time Petronas' steward bowed to him. "His Imperial Highness the Sevastokrator would be pleased to take lunch with you, esteemed and eminent sir, your duties permitting."

"Of course." Krispos gave Eroulos a quizzical look. "So you've heard my new title?"

Eroulos sounded surprised that Krispos need ask. "It's my business to hear such things."

Petronas had heard it, too. "Ah, the esteemed and eminent vestiarios," he said, bowing back when Krispos went on one knee before him. "Here, have some wine. How fares my nephew?"

"Well enough, Highness," Krispos said. "He showed no great interest in making the acquaintance of the new envoy from Makuran."

"Just as well," Petronas said, scowling. "There will be war soon—if not this year, then the next. Probably next year. I'll have to take the field in person, and to do that, I need you solidly in place with Anthimos so he won't listen to too much nonsense while I'm away from the city in the westlands."

There lay the weakness in Petronas' position, Krispos thought: while he ruled, he was not Videssos' ruler. If Anthimos ever decided to take up the reins of power for himself, or if someone else steered him, the prestige that went with the imperial title might well make officials follow him rather than his uncle.

Krispos said, "I'm glad you place such confidence in me, Highness."

"We've discussed why I do." Petronas suavely changed the subject. "Anthimos' gain is my loss, I'm finding. The stable hands still do their individual work well enough, but there's less overall direction to things without you. I asked Stotzas if he wanted your job, but he turned me down flat."

"He did the same with me when I asked him if he wanted me to mention him to you." Krispos hesitated. "May I suggest someone else?"

"Why not? Whom do you have in mind?"

"How about Mavros? I know he's even younger than I am, but everyone likes him. And he wouldn't be slack; he takes horses seriously. He's more a real horseman than I, as a matter of fact. I got to the point where I knew what I was doing, but he comes by it naturally."

"Hmm." Petronas stroked his beard. At last he said, "You may have something there. He's likelier than anyone I'd thought of, at any rate. I'll see what Eroulos has to say; he's not Mavros' personal friend, as you are. If he thinks the youngster will answer, I may well give him a try. My thanks."

"I'm pleased to help, even if I'm not part of your household anymore." Krispos doubted Eroulos would have anything bad to say about Mavros. All the same, he took note of Petronas' caution. Knowing Krispos' advice was not disinterested, the Sevastokrator would not move until he heard some that was.

Another bit of business worth remembering, Krispos thought. He wondered if he'd ever have a chance to use it.

THE CHANCE CAME SOONER THAN HE'D EXPECTED. A FEW DAYS later, he received a letter from a certain Ypatios, asking if the two of them could meet to "discuss matters of mutual interest." Krispos had never heard of Ypatios. Some discreet inquiry among the eunuchs let him find out that the fellow headed a large trading house. Krispos arranged a meeting at the imperial residence on an afternoon when Anthimos was watching the chariots.

Barsymes ushered Ypatios into the antechamber where Krispos sat waiting. The man bowed. "A pleasure to make your acquaintance, esteemed sir," he began, and then stopped, seeming to notice Krispos' beard for the first time. "I meant no offense by that title, I want you to know. You are vestiarios, after all, but I see—"

"I'm usually styled 'esteemed and eminent.' " This routine, Krispos realized, was one he'd need to get used to.

Ypatios quickly recovered his poise. " 'Esteemed and eminent' it is. Very good." The merchant was about fifty, well fed and shrewd-looking. "As I said in my letter, esteemed and eminent sir, I believe we have interests in common."

"You said so," Krispos agreed. "You didn't say what they were, though."

"One can never tell who all reads a letter," Ypatios said. "Let me explain: my sons and I specialize in importing fine furs from the kingdom of Agder. For some time his Imperial Majesty, may his years be many, has had under consideration a law to lower the import duties upon such furs. His favorable action upon this law would, I'll not deny, work to our advantage."

"Would it?" Krispos steepled his fingertips. He began to see in which quarter the wind lay.

Ypatios nodded solemnly. "It would indeed. And my sons and I are prepared to be generous in our appreciation. As you are in such intimate contact with his Imperial Majesty, surely you might find occasion to suggest a course of action to him. Our own humble requests, expressed in written form, perhaps have not had the good fortune to come under his eyes."

"Maybe not," Krispos said. It occurred to him that even had Anthimos been the most conscientious ruler Videssos ever knew, he would have had trouble staying up with all the minutiae of the Empire. Since Anthimos was anything but, he undoubtedly had never seen the law he was supposed to be considering. Krispos went on, "Why are the duties against the furs so high now?"

Ypatios' lip curled in a fine round sneer. "Who can say why stupid laws remain in force? To make beggars of me and my family, I suspect." He did not look as if he'd be whining for crusts on a street corner any time soon. His next words confirmed that. "Still, I might see my way clear to investing twenty pieces of gold to repair the injustice presently on the books."

"I will be in touch with you" was all Krispos said. Ypatios' florid face fell. He bowed his way out. Krispos tugged at his beard and thought for a while. The gesture reminded him of Petronas. He decided to call on the Sevastokrator.

"And how may I help the esteemed and eminent sir this day?" Petronas asked. Krispos explained. Petronas said, "He only offered you twenty? Stick him for at least a pound of gold if you decide to do it. He may squeal a bit, but he can afford to pay you."

"Should I do it, though?" Krispos persisted.

"For things like that, make up your own mind, lad. I don't care one way or the other—too small to worry about. If you're not just out for the cash, maybe you *should* find out why the law is the way it is. That will give you a clue as to whether it needs changing."

Krispos did some digging, or tried to. Navigating the maze of Videssian bureaucracy proved anything but easy. The clerk of the courts referred him to the master of the archives. The master of the archives sent him to the office of the eparch of the city. The eparch of the city's adjutant tried to send him back to the clerk of the courts, at which point Krispos threw a tantrum. The adjutant had second thoughts and suggested he visit the customs commissioner.

The customs commissioner was not in his office and would not be back for a week; his wife had just had a baby. As Krispos grumpily turned to go, someone called, "Excellent sir! May I help you, excellent sir?"

Turning, Krispos found himself face-to-face with the customs agent whose scheme he'd urged on Anthimos outside the Amphitheater. "Maybe you can," he said, not bothering to correct the fellow's use of his title. "Here's what I need . . ."

"Yes, I can find that," the customs agent said when he was done. "A pleasure to be able to repay your kindness in some small way. Wait here if you would, excellent sir." He vanished into a room filled with boxes of scrolls. At last he reemerged, wiping dust from his hands and robe. "Sorry to be so long; things are in a frightful muddle back there. The law you mention turns out to have been promulgated to protect the livelihood of trappers and hunters who lived by the Astris River from competition from Agderian furs."

"By the Astris?" Krispos said. "But the Kubratoi have ruled the lands around there for hundreds of years."

"You know that, and I know that, but the law doesn't seem to have heard the news."

"It will," Krispos promised. "Thanks for your help."

"After what you did for me, excellent sir, it was my privilege."

Krispos went back to the imperial residence and scribbled a note to Ypatios. "Though your case has weight, it does not yet have enough weight to go forward." He was sure the merchant would be able to figure out that he was talking about the weight of coins.

Sure enough, when Ypatios met him again, the first thing he asked was, "Just how heavy does our case have to be?"

"A pound would do nicely," Krispos said, remembering Petronas' guess. He kept his voice bland, but waited nervously for Ypatios to scream at him.

The fur seller only sighed. "A pound it is, esteemed and eminent sir. You're still cheaper to do business with than Skombros was."

"Am I?" When Skombros became a priest, all his worldly possessions were forfeited to the imperial fisc. They would likely keep Anthimos in revels a good long time, Krispos thought, wondering just how many bribes the former vestiarios had taken.

After the gold changed hands, Krispos put the proposed change to Anthimos. "Why not?" the Avtokrator said. "Huzzah for cheaper furs!" Krispos produced the necessary document. Anthimos signed it with ink of imperial scarlet.

Krispos sent Petronas a dozen goldpieces. The Sevastokrator returned them with a note saying, "You need these more than I do, but I'll remember the thought." Since that was true, Krispos was glad to have them back. And since Petronas understood why he'd sent them, he got all the benefits of generosity without actually having to pay for it.

THE SINGER OPENED THE GOLDEN BALL, READ "FOURTEEN PIECES of gold," screamed—right on key—and kissed Krispos on the mouth. He would have enjoyed the kiss more had the singer been a woman. Other than that, the performer's reaction left nothing to be desired. The fellow ran through the hall, musically shrieking at the top of his lungs.

Fourteen goldpieces was nothing worth shrieking about for most of Anthimos' guests. As Krispos had expected, seeing someone get so excited about what they thought of as so little amused them mightily. Moreover, what the singer now had wasn't so little for him at all.

Laughing at himself—he hadn't had to worry about kisses from men since he left Iakovitzes' service—Krispos took a long pull at his wine. He'd learned to nurse his cups at Anthimos' affairs. Tonight, though, he hadn't done as good a job as usual; he could feel his head starting to spin.

He picked his way through the crowd back to the Emperor. "May I be excused, Your Majesty?"

Anthimos pouted. "So early?" It was somewhere near midnight.

"You have a midmorning meeting with Gnatios, if you'll remember, Majesty." Krispos grinned a wry grin. "And while *you* may be able to sleep until just before the time, or even to keep the most holy sir waiting, *I* have to be up early to make sure everything is as it should be."

"Oh, very well," Anthimos said grouchily. Then his eyes lit up. "Here, give me the bowl. I'll hand out chances myself for the rest of the evening." That was entertainment far less ribald than most of what he favored, but it was something new and therefore intriguing.

Krispos gladly surrendered the crystal bowl. The cool, sweet air of the spring night helped clear his head. The racket from the revel faded behind him as he walked to the imperial residence. The Haloga guards outside the entrance nodded as he went by them; they were long since used to him now.

He had just climbed into bed when the bell on the scarlet cord rang. He scowled as he scrambled into his robe in the dark; what was Anthimos doing back in his bedchamber already? The only thing he could think of was that the Emperor had sneaked after him to twit him for going to sleep so soon. That was the sort of thing Anthimos might do, but not when he'd been so excited about dealing out little gold balls.

Several lamps glowed in the imperial bedroom, but Anthimos was not there. The Empress sat up in bed. "I can't seem to get to sleep tonight, Krispos," Dara said. "Could you please fetch me a cup of wine? My serving maids are all asleep, and I heard you just coming in. Do you mind?"

"Of course not, Majesty," Krispos said. He told the truth—a vestiarios had better not mind doing what the Empress of Videssos asked of him. "I'll be back directly."

He found a jar of wine in the dining room and poured a cup from it. "My thanks," Dara said when he brought it to her. She tossed it down almost as quickly as Anthimos might have. She was as bare as she'd been the morning Krispos first came into the imperial bedchamber, but did not bother to pull up the sheet; to her, he might as well have been a eunuch. Holding out the cup, she told him, "Fetch me another, please."

"Of course," he repeated.

She drained the cup a second time as fast as she had the first, set it down empty on the night table by the bed. "Tell me," she said, "do you expect his Imperial Majesty to return any time soon?"

"I don't know when his Majesty will come back," Krispos answered. "When I left the feast, he still seemed to be enjoying himself."

"Oh," Dara said tonelessly. "He usually returns not long after you do, I've noticed. Why not tonight?"

"Because I have to be up early tomorrow morning, to make sure everything is ready for his Majesty's meeting with the patriarch. His Majesty was kind enough to let me leave before him."

"Oh," Dara said again. Without warning, tears started streaming from her eyes. They ran down her cheeks and splashed on her uncovered breasts. That Krispos should see her upset bothered her more than him seeing her nude; she choked out, "Go away!"

He all but fled. One foot was already out in the hall when the Empress said, "No, wait. Come back, please."

Reluctantly he turned. He would sooner have faced a wolf alone and unarmed than the distraught Empress. But he did not dare disobey her, either. "What's wrong, Your Majesty?" he asked in the same soft, calm tone he would have used to try to talk the wolf out of ripping his throat open.

Now she raised the sheet to her neck; if not as a man, she was aware of him as a person rather than a faceless servant. "What's wrong?" she echoed bitterly. "What could possibly be wrong, with me trapped here in the imperial residence and my husband at hunts or the horse races by day and his cursed revels by night?"

"But—he is the Avtokrator," Krispos said.

"And so he can do just as he pleases. I know," Dara said. "Sometimes I think he is the only free man in all the Empire of Videssos. And I am his Empress. Am I free? Ha! A tradesman's wife has more freedom than I do, far more."

Krispos knew she was right. Except for rare ceremonial appearances in the Grand Courtroom, the Empress lived a sheltered, indeed a sequestered life, always screened away from the wider world by her maidservants and the palace eunuchs. As gently as he could, he said, "But surely you knew this would be so when you consented to be his Majesty's bride?"

"There wasn't much consent to it," Dara said. "Do you know what a bride show is, Krispos? I was one of a long line of pretty girls, and Anthimos happened to pick me. I was so surprised, I couldn't even talk. My father owns estates in the westlands, not far from the border with Makuran. He was thrilled—he'd have an Avtokrator for a grandson. But I—haven't even managed—to do that as I—should have." She started to cry again.

"You still have time," Krispos said. "You're younger than I am."

That distracted her, as he'd hoped it would. She gave him a sharp look, gauging his years. "Maybe a little," she said at last, not fully convinced.

"I'm certain you are. And surely his Majesty still"—he paused to make sure he used the right words—"cares for you."

Dara understood. "Oh, aye, when he's here and not drunk asleep, or when he hasn't futtered himself out with one of his doxies—or with six of them." Fire flashed through her tears; Krispos saw she had a temper when she let it loose. Then her shoulders sagged and she bent her head. "But what's the use? I haven't given him a child, and if I don't he'll cast me out one of these days."

Again, Krispos knew she was right. Even Emperors like Anthimos, who worried about nothing, sooner or later worried about an heir. But Dara already felt far too hurt for him simply to agree with her. Instead, he said, "For all you know, you may be carrying the Avtokrator's son right now. I hope you are."

"I may be, but I don't think I am," Dara said. She studied him, curiosity on her face. "You sound as if you mean it. Skombros said the same thing, but I was always sure he was lying."

"Skombros was ambitious for his own nephew," Krispos said. With that, he thought of his niece—no, nieces now, he'd heard—back in his own village. He sent gold every year to his sister Evdokia and Domokos. Now that he had more, he resolved to send more.

"Yes, he was," Dara said distantly. "I'm glad he's gone." After a little while, she went on, "If you fetched me one more cup of wine, I think I could sleep now, Krispos."

He brought the jar into the bedchamber. "If you find you need a bit more, Your Majesty, here it is."

"Thank you, Krispos." She gave him the cup to fill. When he handed it back, her fingers closed over his for a moment. "Thank you, also, for listening to me. I think you're kind."

"I hope you do sleep, Majesty, and sleep well. Shall I blow out the lamps?"

"If you would. Leave the one on my night table burning, though, please. I'll tend to it when I'm ready." As Krispos bowed his way out of the bedchamber, Dara added, "I hope you sleep well, too."

Krispos bowed again. "Thank you for thinking of me, Majesty." He went back to his own room. Despite the wine he'd drunk at the Emperor's feast, he lay awake for a long time.

A NTHIMOS ROSE FROM HIS CHAIR. "CARE TO COME FOR A STROLL with me, Gnatios?"

Krispos felt like pounding his head against a wall. If the Avtokrator and the ecumenical patriarch were going out walking, then three parts in four of his preparations for this meeting had been wasted effort. More to the point, he could have slept an extra hour or two. A dull headache and scratchy eyes told him he should have.

Gnatios also rose. "Whatever Your Majesty wishes."

Maybe, Krispos thought hopefully, he could doze for a bit while his master and the patriarch talked. Then Anthimos said, "You come along too, Krispos."

Thinking resentful thoughts, Krispos came. A couple of imperial guards attached themselves to the party as the Emperor and his companions walked outside.

Anthimos made cheerful small talk as he led his little party through the palace complex. Gnatios' replies were polite enough, but also increasingly curious, as if he were unsure where the Emperor was going, either in the stroll or the conversation. Krispos quietly fumed. If Anthimos was only going to burble on about the weather, why did he need to see the patriarch at all?

The Avtokrator finally stopped in front of a tumbledown building set apart from its nearest neighbors—not that any were very near—by a thick grove of dark-green cypresses. "I've decided to study sorcery," he declared. "After you left last night, Krispos, a mage worked such marvelous feats that I decided then and there to learn how they were done."

"I see," Krispos said. He did, too; it was just like Anthimos to seize on a momentary enthusiasm and ride it till he got bored.

Gnatios said, "Forgive me, Your Majesty, but may I ask what your sudden interest in sorcery has to do with this elderly temple here?"

"You see what it is, then, or was? Good." Anthimos beamed. "Not all sorcery is easy or safe—you know that as well as I. What I propose to do, Gnatios, is knock the building down and replace it with a proper magical study. The site is ideal, you will agree, being isolated from the rest of the palaces."

"You want to tear the temple down?" the patriarch echoed.

"That's right. No one's used it for what must be decades. You should see the spiderwebs inside. Some of them could catch birds, I expect. It wouldn't be sacrilege or anything, really it wouldn't." The Emperor smiled his most engaging smile at Gnatios.

The ecumenical patriarch was more than twice his sovereign's age, and a good deal more than twice as serious as Anthimos. Nevertheless, the Emperor charmed him almost as if he were already using magic. Gnatios was shaking his head, but he answered, "Pyrrhos and his narrow-minded followers will rail at me, but technically, Your Majesty, I suppose you are correct. Very well, I agree; you may demolish this unused temple to employ the area for your own purposes."

"Perhaps, Your Majesty, you could have another temple built somewhere else in the city to make up for tearing down this one," Krispos put in.

"An excellent notion," Gnatios said. "Will you pledge to do that, Your Majesty?"

"Oh, certainly," Anthimos said. "Krispos, see to it that the logothetes at the treasury know to set aside funds for a new temple. We'll knock down this old ruin one day next week, then. Gnatios, I want you to be here."

Gnatios ran a hand over his shaven head. "As you wish, Your Majesty, but why am I required?"

"Why, to say a prayer while the temple gets demolished, of course." Anthimos flashed his charming smile again.

This time, it did not work. Gnatios slowly shook his head. "Your Majesty, I fear I cannot. There is in the liturgy a prayer for the construction of a temple, but we have not inherited from our forefathers a prayer over the demolition of a temple."

"Then invent one," Anthimos said. "You are a great scholar, Gnatios. Surely you can find words that will please the good god."

"How can he be pleased that one of his temples is destroyed?" the patriarch said. "Because the temple is old and has long stood vacant, he may tolerate it, but I dare not ask him to do more than that."

"Because this one is being torn down, he'll soon have a new one that won't be empty," Krispos said.

Gnatios gave him an unfriendly look. "I will joyfully pray at the erection of the new. I would do so in any event. But at the loss of a temple— no, I cannot pray over that."

"Maybe Pyrrhos would," Krispos said.

"No. Here we would agree . . . or would we?" Gnatios was as much politician as prelate. That undid him now. More to himself than to Krispos or Anthimos, he went on, "Who knows what Pyrrhos might do to gain imperial favor for his fanaticism?" After another pause, he said sourly, "Oh, very well, Your Majesty, you shall have your prayer from me."

"Splendid," Anthimos said. "I knew I could rely on you, Gnatios."

The patriarch set his jaw and nodded. Happily clapping him on the shoulder, Anthimos started back to the imperial residence. Gnatios and Krispos trailed along behind the Emperor. Gnatios said softly, "I wish you would have kept your mouth shut, vestiarios."

"I serve my master," Krispos said. "If I can help him get what he wants, I will."

"He and I will both look like fools because of this ceremony he's asked for," Gnatios said. "Is that your idea of good service?"

Krispos thought Gnatios worried more about Gnatios than about Anthimos, but all he said was, "His Majesty doesn't seem worried." Gnatios sniffed and stamped on ahead of him, blue boots scuffing flagstones.

A week later, a small crowd of priests and officials gathered for the function the Emperor had demanded. Petronas was not there; he was closeted with the Makuraner envoys. He had real work to do, Krispos thought.

Anthimos walked up and said, "Krispos, this chap with me is Trokoundos, the mage who will be instructing me. Trokoundos, this is my vestiarios, Krispos. If Trokoundos needs funds to secure apparatus or mystical goods, Krispos, make sure he has what he asks for."

"Very well, Your Majesty." Krispos eyed Trokoundos with suspicion. *Someone else who wants a grip on the Emperor,* he thought indignantly. The anger that surged through him brought him up short; all at once, he understood how Petronas felt about his nephew.

Trokoundos looked straight back at Krispos, his eyes heavy-lidded and clever. "I will see you often, for I have much to teach his Majesty," he said. His voice was deep and rich. It did not suit his frame—he was only of medium height and on the thin side. He shaved his head like a priest, but wore a robe of a most unpriestly orange.

"A pleasure to meet you, mage." Krispos' cool voice gave his words the lie.

"And you, eu—" Trokoundos stopped short. He'd started the same rude rejoinder Krispos had used against Skombros, only to notice, too late, that it did not apply. "And you, vestiarios," he amended lamely.

Krispos smiled. He was glad to find the mage human enough to miss things. "My title is esteemed and eminent sir," he said, rubbing Trokoundos' nose in the mistake.

"Ah, here comes Gnatios," Anthimos said happily. Krispos and Trokoundos both turned to watch the patriarch approach.

Gnatios stopped in front of the Avtokrator and prostrated himself with grim dignity. "I have composed the prayer you required of me, Your Majesty," he said as he rose.

"By all means say it, then, so the workmen may begin," the Emperor said.

Gnatios faced the temple to be torn down. He spat on the ground in rejection of Skotos, then raised his hands to the sky. "Glory to Phos the long-suffering at all times," he declared, "now, forever, and through eons upon eons. So may it be."

"So may it be," the assembled dignitaries echoed. Their voices were less hearty than they might have been; Krispos was not the only one who glanced over to see how the Emperor would respond to a prayer that as much as said Phos had to be patient to put up with his whims.

The implied criticism sailed past him. He bowed to Gnatios. "Thank you, most holy sir. Just what the occasion demanded." Then he called, "Go to it, lads," to the band of workmen standing by the temple.

The workers attacked the dilapidated old building with picks and crowbars. The ceremony over, court officers and prelates began drifting away. Krispos started to follow Anthimos back to the imperial residence when Trokoundos put a hand on his arm. He pulled free. "What do you want?" he asked roughly.

"I need enough money to purchase several hundred sheets of parchment," the mage answered.

"What do you need with several hundred sheets of parchment?"

"I have no need of them," Trokoundos said. "His Majesty does. If he would be a mage, he first must need copy out in his own hand the spells he will thereafter employ." He set hands on hips, plainly expecting Krispos to say no—and ready to go to Anthimos with the tale.

But Krispos said, "Of course. I'll have the money sent to you straightaway."

"You will?" Trokoundos blinked. His belligerent air vanished.

"In fact," Krispos went on, "if you want to come to the residence with me, I'll give you the gold right now; I'll take it from the household chest."

"You will?" Trokoundos said again. Those heavy-lidded eyes widened. "Thank you very much. That's most gracious of you."

"I serve his Majesty," Krispos said, as he had to Gnatios. "How much do you think you'll need?" However much it was, he would cheerfully pay it. If Trokoundos was going to set Anthimos to transcribing several hundred pages' worth of magical spells, he thought, the Avtokrator would not stay interested in sorcery for long. And that suited Krispos just fine.

"GNATIOS IS NOT HAPPY WITH YOU," PETRONAS SAID A COUPLE of days later, when Krispos found a chance to tell him how the ceremony had gone.

"Why, Highness?" Krispos asked. "I didn't think it was a matter of any importance, especially since Anthimos is going to build another temple to take the place of the one that got knocked down."

"Put that way, you're right." Despite reassuring words, Petronas still studied Krispos through narrowed eyes. "My cousin the patriarch, though, is, shall we say, unused to being faced down in front of the Emperor and having to do something he did not care to do in consequence."

"I wasn't trying to embarrass him," Krispos protested.

"You succeeded nevertheless," Petronas said. "Well, let it go. I'll soothe Gnatios' ruffled feathers for him. I didn't think you were quite so good at getting folk—especially a strong-willed fellow like my cousin—to go along with you."

"Oh," Krispos said. "You wanted me to be vestiarios because you thought I'd be able to help get Anthimos to do what you wanted. Why are you angry if I can do the same thing with someone else for his Majesty?"

"I'm not angry. Merely . . . thoughtful," the Sevastokrator said.

Krispos sighed, but consoled himself by remembering that Petronas never had trusted him much. He didn't think this latest brush would hurt his standing with Anthimos' uncle.

Petronas went on, "What's this I hear about some wizard sucking up to the Emperor?"

"Oh, that. I think I took care of that." Krispos explained how he'd given Trokoundos exactly what he wanted.

The Sevastokrator laughed out loud. "You'd kill a cat by drowning it in cream. That's better than I would have done; I'd have just sent the beggar packing, which would have made Anthimos sulk. And I don't need him sulking right now."

"The talks with the Makuraners aren't going well?" Krispos asked.

"They're not the problem," Petronas said. "The Makuraners like talk as much as we Videssians, and that's saying something. I just need to keep them talking a while longer, till I'm ready to fight. But I don't like the rumbles I hear out of Kubrat. Malomir's stayed quiet ever since old Omurtag died. If he decided to start raiding us now, then the war with Makuran might have to wait, and I don't want it to wait. I've waited too long already." He pounded a fist down on the padded arm of his chair.

Krispos nodded. Thinking of nomad horsemen sweeping down from the north could make him shiver even now. And if Videssos' armies were fully engaged in the far west, raids from Kubrat could reach all the way down to the walls of Videssos the city. The capital had stood Kubrati siege a couple of times. He wondered if the frontier with Kubrat wasn't more important than the one with Makuran, which would stay peaceful for a while if Petronas didn't stir it up.

Was he right? He wasn't sure himself; as the Sevastokrator had warned him, he'd had no practice making that kind of judgment. Maybe it wouldn't matter either way; maybe the Kubratoi would let themselves be bought off, as they sometimes did. He hoped so. Things would be simpler that way.

The higher he'd risen, though, and the closer he'd come to real power, the more complicated things looked.

ANTHIMOS KEPT AT HIS MAGICAL STUDIES WITH A PERSISTENCE that startled Krispos. While his new sanctum rose from the ruins of the temple, he transcribed texts at the imperial residence. Krispos had to go over to the clerks who scribbled by the Grand Courtroom to find out how they got ink off their fingers. When he fetched back some small pumice stones, Anthimos praised him to the skies.

"That's plenty for today," the Emperor said one hot, muggy summer afternoon, coming out of his study wringing his writing hand. "All work makes a man dull. What do we have laid on for tonight?"

"The feast features a troupe that performs with large dogs and tiny ponies," Krispos answered.

"Does it? Well, that should give the servants something new to clean up." Anthimos started down the hall. "Which robe have you chosen for me?"

"The blue silk. It should be coolest in this weather. Excuse me, Your Majesty," Krispos called to the Emperor's retreating back, "but I believe you've forgotten something."

Anthimos stopped. "What's that?"

"Your fingers are still stained. You forgot to pumice them. Do you want people to say the Avtokrator of the Videssians is his own secretary? Here, let me fetch you a stone."

Anthimos looked down at his right hand. "I did forget to clean off, didn't I?" Now it was his turn to make Krispos pause. "You needn't bring me the pumice stone. I can take care of this myself, I think."

Intense concentration on his face, the Emperor spread the ink-stained fingers of his writing hand. He waved his left hand above it and raised his voice in a rhythmic chant. Suddenly he cried out and clenched both hands into fists. When he opened them, they were both clean.

Krispos made the sun-sign over his heart. "You did it!" he exclaimed, then hoped he didn't sound as surprised as he felt.

"I certainly did," Anthimos said smugly. "A small application of the law of contagion, which states that objects once in contact may continue to influence one another. As that pumice had so often scoured my fingers, I simply re-created the cleansing action by magical means."

"I didn't realize you could start working magic before you had all your spells copied out," Krispos said. "Do you want me to take the pumice stones back to the clerks I got them from?"

"No, not yet. For one thing"—the Emperor grinned a small-boy grin— "Trokoundos doesn't know I *am* working magic. I don't think I'm supposed to be. For another, cleaning my hands that way was a lot harder than simply scraping off the ink. I wanted to show off for you, but it wore me out. And I don't want to be worn out, not when there will be so many interesting women at the revels tonight. There will be, won't there, Krispos?"

"Of course, Your Majesty. I always try to please you that way." Once more, Krispos wondered why Anthimos couldn't give, if not all, at least most of his attention to Dara. If nothing else, he'd have a better chance of begetting a legitimate heir if he spent some time with his own wife. It was not as if she were undesirable, Krispos thought—quite the opposite, in fact.

Whatever Anthimos' newfound sorcerous talents, he could not read minds. At the moment, perhaps, that was just as well. The Avtokrator went on, "I can hardly wait to show off my magecraft at a feast. For that, though, I'll need something rather more impressive than cleaning my hands without pumice. I tried something once, and it didn't work."

"You did?" Now Krispos didn't care if he sounded appalled. A mage who botched a spell was apt to be in even more immediate need of an heir than an Avtokrator. "What did you do?"

Anthimos looked sheepish. "I tried giving wings to one of the little tortoises that crawl through the gardens. I thought it would be amusing, flying around inside the hall where I usually have my feasts. But I must have done something wrong, because I ended up with a pigeon with a shell. Promise me you won't tell Trokoundos?"

"You're lucky you didn't end up shifting the shell to your own foolish face," Krispos said sternly. Anthimos shifted from foot to foot like a schoolboy taking a scolding he knew he deserved. As had happened so often before, Krispos found he could not stay angry at him. Shaking his head, he went on, "All right, I won't tell Trokoundos if you promise me you'll stop mucking about with things you don't understand."

"I won't," Anthimos said. He had gone off to look at the robe he would wear to the evening's festivities before Krispos noticed he hadn't quite made a promise. Even if he had, Krispos doubted he would have taken it seriously enough to keep. Anthimos just did not believe anything bad could ever happen to him.

Krispos knew better. If growing up on a farm had done nothing else for him, it had done that.

Chapter X

T HE BELL BESIDE KRISPOS' BED TINKLED SOFTLY. HE WOKE UP
muttering to himself. When Anthimos held a feast, he was expected
to roister along with the Emperor—and the Emperor was better than he
at doing without sleep. When Anthimos spent a night with Dara in the
imperial residence, Krispos expected to have the chance to catch up on his
rest.

Even as he slipped a robe over his head, he knew he was not being fair.
Though he'd got into the habit of keeping a lamp burning all night long
to help him dress quickly in case the Avtokrator needed him, Anthimos
seldom called him after he'd gone to bed. But tonight, he thought grouchily, only went to show that seldom didn't mean never.

He walked out his door and four or five steps down the hall to the imperial bedchamber. That door was closed, but a light showed under it. He
opened the door. Anthimos and Dara turned their heads toward him.

He stopped in his tracks and felt his face go flame-hot. "Y-your pardon,
I pray," he stammered. "I thought the bell summoned me."

"Don't go away, at least not yet. I did call you," the Emperor said, calm
as if he'd been interrupted playing draughts—or at one of his revels. After

that first startled glance toward the door, Dara looked down at Anthimos. Her long dark hair, undone now, spilled over her shoulders and veiled her so that Krispos could not see her face. Anthimos brushed some of that shining hair away from his nose and went on, "Fetch me a little olive oil, if you please, Krispos; that's a good fellow."

"Yes, Your Majesty," Krispos said woodenly. He hurried out of the bed-chamber. Behind him, he heard Anthimos say, "Why did you slow down, my dear? That was nice, what you were doing."

He found a jar of oil faster than he really wanted to. In truth, he did not want to go back to the bedchamber at all. Seeming a eunuch around Dara had been simple at first, but less easy after that night when she first let him see her as a person rather than an Empress. Now . . . now he would have trouble not imagining his body in place of Anthimos' under hers.

As he went back down the hall, he wondered what she thought. Maybe she was used to this, as Anthimos was. In that case, she would also be used to taking no notice of what servants imagined. Probably just as well, he thought.

He paused in the doorway. "Took you long enough," Anthimos said. "Don't just stand there, bring the oil over to me. How do you expect me to get it when you're half a mile away?"

Krispos reluctantly approached. Dara's head was lowered; her hair hid her face from him again. He did not want to speak or force her to notice his presence any more than she had to. Without a word, he held out the jar to the Avtokrator.

Anthimos dipped his fingers into it. "You can set it on the night table now, Krispos, in case we want more later on." Krispos nodded, did as he was told, and got out, but not before he heard the tiny smooth sound of Anthimos' slickened fingers sliding over Dara's skin.

He threw himself back into bed with what he knew was altogether un-necessary violence, and lay awake for a long time, staring at the ceiling. The flickering shadows the lamp cast there all looked lewd. Eventually it began to rain. The soft patter of raindrops on roof tiles lulled him to sleep at last.

He jerked in dismay when the bell woke him the next morning; return-ing to the Emperor's chamber was the last thing he felt like doing. What he felt like doing, however, mattered not in the least to Anthimos. The bell rang again, louder and more insistently. Krispos pulled on a clean robe and went to do his master's bidding.

But for the jar of olive oil on the table by the bed, the previous night might not have happened. As far as Anthimos was concerned, it plainly hadn't. "Good day," he said. "Rain, I see. Do you think it's just a shower, or is the fall wet season coming early this year?"

"It'll hurt the harvest if it is," Krispos answered, relieved to be able to talk dispassionately. "Do you prefer the purple robe today, Your Majesty, or the leek green?"

"The green, I think." Anthimos got out of bed and gave an exaggerated shiver. "Brr! Fall certainly seems to be in the air. Good thing for the heating ducts this building boasts, or I'd have to start thinking about sleeping in clothes." He glanced over at Dara, who was still under the covers. "That would be no fun at all, would it, my dear?"

"Whatever you say." The Empress reached out a slim arm and tugged on the bellpull for a maidservant.

Anthimos sniffed. He let Krispos dress him and help him on with his boots. "I'm for breakfast," he announced. He looked over at Dara again and frowned. "Aren't you coming, slugabed?"

"Presently." The Empress' serving girl had come in, but she showed no sign of being ready to get up. "Why don't you start without me?"

"Oh, very well. Krispos, ask the cook if he has any squab in the larder. If he does, I'll have a couple, roasted, with a jar of that sweet golden Vaspurakaner wine that goes so well with them."

"I'll inquire, Your Majesty."

The cook had squab. He grinned at Krispos. "With all the statues and towers in the city to draw pigeons, not likely I wouldn't. Roasted, you said his Majesty wants 'em? Roasted they'll be."

Krispos fetched Anthimos the little birds, along with bread, honey, and the wine he'd asked for. The Avtokrator ate with good appetite, then rose and said, "I'm off to be sorcerous." Dara and her maidservant came into the dining room just as he was going out. His voice echoed through the central hallway: "Tyrovitzes! Longinos! Fetch umbrellas, and smartly. I don't propose to swim to my little workshop."

The eunuchs' sandals slapped on the marble floor as they hurried to obey. Krispos asked Dara, "What would you care for this morning, Your Majesty?"

"I'm not very hungry," she answered. "Some of this bread and honey should do well enough for me."

She only picked at it. "Can I get you anything else, Your Majesty?" the serving maid asked. "You're not a bird, to stay alive on crumbs."

Dara looked at the crust she was holding, then set it down. "Maybe a muskmelon would suit me better, Verina—stewed, I think, not raw."

"I'll get one for you, Majesty." Verina stood up, impudently wrinkled her nose. "I'll spend the time it's stewing gossiping with the cook. Phestos knows everything that goes on here three days before it happens."

"Nice to think someone does." Dara listened to Verina's steps fading down the hall, then said quietly, "Krispos, I want you to know I did not expect An—his Majesty to summon you last night. If you were embarrassed, I can only say I'm sorry. I was, too."

"Oh." Krispos thought about that for a while, thought about how much he might safely say to even a contrite Empress. Finally he continued, "It was a little awkward, being treated as if I were only a—a convenience."

"That's well said." Dara's voice stayed low, but her eyes blazed. She clenched her hands together. "That's just how Anthimos treats everyone around him—as a convenience, a toy for his amusement, to be put back on the shelf to sit until he feels like playing with it again. And by the lord with the great and good mind, Krispos, I am no toy and I am sick to death of being used as one."

"Oh," Krispos said again, in a different tone. When angry, Dara was indeed no toy; she reminded him of Tanilis, but a Tanilis young and unskilled. Nor did the memory of her anger sustain her once it was gone, as Tanilis' did. Tanilis never would have let the Emperor keep her in the background like this.

"It was bad enough with Skombros, those tiny eyes staring and staring from that fat face," Dara said, "but after a while I got used to him and even pitied him, for what could he do but stare?"

Krispos nodded; he remembered having the same thought, watching the former vestiarios at that first revel he'd been to.

Dara went on, "But better he should have done without the oil, Krispos, or gotten it himself, than to have you bring it, you who have no need of such spectacles, who are whole and in every way as a man should be—" She broke off abruptly and stared down at her hands.

"I knew before last night that Your Majesty was beautiful," Krispos said softly. "Nothing I saw then makes me want to change my mind." He heard footfalls in the hall and raised his voice. "Here comes that melon. I hope you like it better than the bread and honey."

The Empress shot him a grateful look. "I think I will, thank you." Verina came in, uncovering the bowl in which the stewed muskmelon lay. "And thank you, Verina. That smells lovely."

"I hope it pleases you." The maidservant beamed as she watched her mistress eat the whole melon. "All a matter of finding out what you want, isn't it, Your Majesty?"

"So it is, Verina. So it is," Dara said. She did not look at Krispos; she knew how tiny and fragile a bubble privacy was in the palaces. For his part, Krispos understood for a new reason why vestiarioi were traditionally eunuchs.

"STAND ASIDE THERE, YOU LUMBERING BLOND BARBARIANS, OR I'll turn the lot of you into yellow eels!"

Krispos watched with amusement as the Halogai scrambled out of Trokoundos' way. Despite the mage's big, booming voice, the northerners were far more imposing men than he, all at least a head taller and twice as thick through the shoulders. But they did not care to find out whether he meant his words literally.

Trokoundos stamped up the broad steps. Water flew from puddles on them at every step. "You move, too," he snarled at Krispos.

"Wipe your boots on this rug here first," Krispos said. Glowering, Trokoundos obeyed. He trod so hard that Krispos suspected he wished he weren't stepping on mere carpet. "What's the trouble?" Krispos asked. "Shouldn't you be closeted with the Emperor?"

"He's given me the sack, that's what the trouble is," the mage said. "I just spent seventeen goldpieces on new gear, too, and I expect to get paid back. That's why I'm here."

"Of course, if you can show me receipts for what you bought," Krispos said.

Trokoundos rolled his eyes. "It would take a stronger wizard than I even dreamed of being to get money from anyone in the government without receipts—think I don't know that? Here you are." He pulled several folded pieces of parchment from the leather wallet he wore at his belt.

Krispos felt his lips move as he added up the sums. He checked himself, then said, "Seventeen it is. Come along with me; I'll pay you right now."

"Good," Trokoundos growled. "Then I'll never have to come back here again, so I won't run the risk of bumping into his damnfoolness of a Majesty and telling him just exactly what I think of him."

Hearing a loud, unfamiliar voice coming down the hall, Barsymes peered out of a dining room to see who it was. Hearing what the loud, unfamiliar voice had to say about his lord and master, the eunuch squeaked and pulled his head back in.

Krispos opened a strongbox and counted out coins. Trokoundos snatched them from his hand. "Now I'm not out anything but my patience and my digestion," he said, putting them into his wallet one by one.

"May I ask what went wrong?" Krispos said. "From what his Majesty's been saying, he's felt he's made good progress."

"Oh, he has. He's a promising beginner, maybe even better than promising. He can be very quick when he wants to be, and he has a good head for remembering what he learns. But he wants everything at once."

That sounded like Anthimos, Krispos thought. He asked, "How so?"

"Now that he has some of the basics down, he wants to leap straight into major conjurations—blasting fires, demons, who knows what will cross his mind next? Whatever it is, it's sure to be something big enough and difficult enough to be dangerous if anything goes wrong. I told him as much. That's when he sacked me."

"Couldn't you have guided him through some of the things he wanted to do, repaired any mistakes he might have made?"

"No, for two reasons. For one, I wouldn't let any other apprentice ask that of me, and his Imperial Majesty Anthimos III is no Avtokrator of magic, just another 'prentice." Krispos dipped his head to Trokoundos, respecting him very much for that. The mage went on, "For another, I'm not sure I *could* repair some of the things he wants to try if he botches them as badly as a 'prentice can. To be frank with you, esteemed and eminent sir, I don't really care to find out, either."

"What happens if he goes on without you?" Krispos asked in some alarm. "Is he likely to kill himself and everyone for half a mile around?" If he was, then this would be one time for Petronas to clamp down hard on his nephew.

But Trokoundos shook his head. "I don't think there's much danger of that. You see, as soon as he leaves his little laboratory today, all his books of spells will go blank. He's not the first rich dilettante I've tried to teach. There is magic to reconstitute them, but it has to be performed by the owner of the books, and it's not easy to work. I don't think his Majesty's quite up to it, and I doubt he'd have the patience to retranscribe the texts by hand."

"I didn't think he'd do it the first time," Krispos agreed. "So you've left him without magic? Won't he just find himself another mage?"

"Even if he does, he'll still have to start over from the beginning. But no, he's not altogether bereft—he'll still be able to use whatever he has memorized. Phos willing, that'll be enough to keep him happy."

Krispos considered, then slowly nodded. "I suspect it may. Most of what he wanted with it was to impress people at his feasts."

"I thought as much," Trokoundos said scornfully. "He doesn't have a bad head for it, or wouldn't, but there's no discipline to him. You can't succeed at anything unless you're willing to put in the hard work you need to learn your craft." He glanced at Krispos. "You know what I'm talking about, I think."

"I've done some wrestling," Krispos said.

"Then you know, all right." Trokoundos' gaze sharpened. "I remember—you're the one who beat that Kubrati, aren't you? You weren't vestiarios then. I might have connected the name with the story sooner if I hadn't seen you in your fancy robes all the time."

"No, I wasn't vestiarios, just a groom," Krispos said. He smiled, both at Trokoundos and at the way his fortunes had changed. "I didn't think I was *just* a groom then, if you know what I mean. I grew up on a farm, so anything else looked good by comparison."

"I've heard that said, yes." The mage studied Krispos; as he had sometimes with Tanilis, he got the odd feeling he was transparent to the man. "I'd teach you sorcery if you wanted me to. You'd do what was needed, I think, and not complain. But that isn't the craft you're learning, is it?"

"What do you mean?" Krispos asked. Trokoundos was already on his way out the door and did not answer. "Cursed wizards always want the last word," Krispos muttered to himself.

Anthimos was wild with fury when he discovered all his hard-won spells had disappeared. "I'll have that bastard's balls," he shouted, "and his ears and nose, too!"

Normally not a bloodthirsty soul, he went on about pincers and knives and red-hot needles until Krispos, worried that he might really mean it, tried to calm him by saying, "You're probably just as well rid of the mage. I don't think your uncle would like you studying anything as dangerous as sorcery."

"To the ice with my uncle, too!" Anthimos said. "He's not the Avtokrator, and I bloody well am!" But when he sent a squad of Halogai to arrest Trokoundos, sending a priest with them in case he resisted with magic, they found his house empty. "Knave must have fled to the hinterland," the Emperor declared with some satisfaction when they brought him the news. By then his usual good humor had returned. "I daresay that's worse punishment than any I could inflict."

"Aye, good riddance to bad rubbish," said Krispos, who had quietly sent word to Trokoundos to get out of the city for a while.

To Krispos' surprise and dismay, Anthimos did start recopying his tome of spells. He never quite quit transcribing, either, but before long the pace of his work slowed to a crawl. He turned one of his revels inside out with a spell that made cabbage intoxicating for a night and left wine mild as milk. "You see?" he triumphantly told Krispos the next morning. "I am a mage, even if that stinking Trokoundos tried to keep me from being one. Did you hear how they cheered me last night when the wizardry worked just as I said it would?"

"Yes, Your Majesty," Krispos said. His stomach rumbled like distant thunder. He'd eaten too much cabbage the night before. Given a choice, he would far soon have got drunk on wine.

Had he got drunk on wine, he might have chewed cabbage leaves to ease his morning-after pains. He wondered if a cup of wine would cure a cabbage hangover. Laughing, he decided to find out.

Midwinter's day came and went. one whole section of the Amphitheater was full of soldiers. As soon as the roads froze after the fall rains, Petronas had begun calling in levies from the eastern provinces for his war on Makuran. They made a raucous audience, drinking hard, then cheering and booing each skit as the fancy—or the wine—seized them.

The hangover that bedeviled Krispos the morning after Midwinter's Day had nothing to do with cabbage—and did not want to yield to it, either. The wines he drank now were smoother and sweeter than the ones he'd quaffed on holidays past, but that did not mean they were exempt from giving retribution.

Nor did it mean he wanted to go back to the rougher vintages he'd formerly known. Ypatios was far from the only prominent man willing, and eager, to pay for influence with the Emperor. Some he could not help; some he did not want to help. He refused their gold. What he took in from the rest made him well-to-do, even by the standards of Videssos the city.

He bought a horse. He took Mavros along when he went to the market not far from the Forum of the Ox. "Nice to know you have confidence in me," Mavros said. "Let's see what kind of horrible screw I can stick you with."

"I like that," Krispos said. "Is that your way of showing thanks for getting named chief groom?"

"Now that you mention it, yes. The job's too much like work; I liked lying around on my arse as a spatharios a lot better. If I weren't working with horses, I really would resent you."

"What would your mother say if she heard you talking so fondly of shirking?"

"What she usually says, I expect—stop complaining and get to it."

The first dealer they tried was a plump little man named Ibas whose eyes were so round and moist and trustworthy that Krispos grew wary at once. The horse trader bowed low, but not before he had checked the cut and fabric of their robes. "If you are seeking a riding animal, my masters, I can show you a magnificent gelding not above seven years old," he said.

"Yes, show us," Mavros said.

On seeing the animal, Krispos was encouraged. Magnificent was too fine a word for it, but he'd expected as much; sellers of horseflesh sucked in hyperbole with their mother's milk. But the horse's limbs were sound, its dark roan coat well tended and shining.

Mavros only grunted, "Let's see the teeth."

Nodding, Ibas walked with him up to the animal's head. "You see," he said while Mavros made his examination, "the four middle teeth in each jaw are nicely oval, and the mark—or cavity, as some call it—in the center of each tooth is quite as deep and dark as it should be."

"I see a horse with a mouth full of spit," Mavros complained. He looked thoughtfully at the small gap between the horse's upper and lower incisors. "Perhaps we'll be back another day, master Ibas. Thank you for showing him to us." Politely but firmly, he steered Krispos toward another dealer.

"What was wrong with him?" Krispos asked. "I rather fancied his looks."

"Seven, Ibas claimed? That horse is twelve if he's a day. Good old master Ibas is what they call a prelate—he takes away his horse's sins, usually with a file. He has a nice touch; with the animal's mouth so wet, I couldn't quite be sure of the rasp marks. But if you file down a horse's front teeth to give them the proper shape for a young animal, they won't quite meet, because you haven't done anything to the teeth in the back of the horse's mouth. And if Ibas has one like that, he'll have half a dozen, so we don't want to do business with him."

"I'm glad you're with me," Krispos said. "I might have bought the beast, for I did like him."

"So would I, were he sold for what he was. But to try to knock five years off him—no. Don't look so glum, my friend. There's more horses to suit you than just that one. All we have to do is keep looking."

Look they did, all that day and part of the next. At length, with Mavros' approval this time, Krispos bought a bay gelding of about the same age as Ibas had claimed for the roan. "By the teeth, this one really is seven or eight," Mavros said. "Not a bad animal at all. He wouldn't be the worst-looking horse in Petronas' stable—a long way from the best, but not the worst either."

"The best-looking animal in that stable is Petronas' show horse, and I wouldn't race him against a donkey," Krispos said.

"Something to that, too." Mavros patted the bay's neck. "I hope he serves you well."

"So do I." Even if the gelding spent most of the time in the stable, as it might very well, Krispos was pleased just to have it. Owning a horse was another sign of how far he'd come. No one in his village had owned a horse till they beat the Kubratoi; afterward, the animals had been owned in common. In the city, he'd cared for other people's horses and borrowed them when he needed to ride.

Now he had one of his own, and the hands in the imperial stables could see to its day-to-day care. That wasn't the proper attitude for a noble, but he didn't care. Nobles tended animals because they wanted to, not because they had to. Having had to, he didn't want to, not anymore.

"What will you call him?" Mavros asked.

"I hadn't thought." Krispos did. After a little while, he smiled. "I have it! The perfect name." Mavros waited expectantly. Krispos said, "I'll call him Progress."

ANTHIMOS ESSAYED A SPELL TO KEEP SNOW OFF THE PATH THAT led to the hall where he held his feasts. He only succeeded in turning the snow on the path bright blue. The miscarried magic left him undismayed. "I've always wanted to revel till everything turned blue," he said, "and here's my chance."

"As you say, Your Majesty." Krispos sent men with shovels to clear the tinted snow from the path so the Emperor and his guests could get to their revel. He wondered if Anthimos had learned a spell to heat the hall; fireplaces only reached so far. He doubted it—a magic so practical was not one likely to have appealed to the Emperor, or to have stuck in his memory if he'd ever learned it.

The revel itself Krispos enjoyed, at least for a time. But a steady diet of such carouses had begun to pall for him. He looked round for Anthimos. The Emperor was enjoying the attentions of an astonishingly limber girl—one of the evening's acrobats, Krispos saw when she assumed a new position. There were times, Krispos had found out, when Anthimos did not mind being interrupted in such pursuits, but he did not think asking permission to leave was important enough to bother him over. He just handed the bowl of chances to another servitor, found his coat, and departed.

The moon shone through patchy clouds. In its pale light, the snow the Emperor had colored looked almost black, making a strange border to the path. When Krispos got back to the imperial residence, he found that the Haloga guards had another word for it. "Isn't that the stupidest-looking thing you ever saw?" one of them said, pointing.

Krispos looked back toward the feast-hall, at the long blackish ribbon against the proper white snow that had come drifting down from Phos' sky. "Now that you mention it, yes."

The Halogai laughed. One of them, a veteran who'd served the Emperor for years, thumped him on the back. "You all right, Krispos," he said in his northern accent. "We make jokes like that with Skombros, he tell Anthimos, maybe we all shipped back to Halogaland." The rest of the guardsmen nodded.

"Thank you, Vagn," Krispos said; praise from the big blond warriors always pleased him. "You'll go home one day, I suppose, but better it's when you want to."

Vagn thumped him again, this time almost hard enough to pitch him down the steps into the snow. "Aye, you understand honor," the Haloga boomed in delight. He swung up his axe in salute, then held the door wide, as he might have for Anthimos. "Go in, warm yourself."

Krispos was glad to take Vagn's advice. The heating ducts under the floor gave some relief from the chill outside, but when he got to his room he lit a brazier all the same. He warmed his hands over it, stayed close by the welcome heat until his ears and nose began to thaw. Just as he started to take off his coat, the bell by his bed rang.

This time he knew Anthimos had not followed him home. But by now he was used to late-night summonses from the Empress; every so often, she liked to talk with him. "Your Majesty," he said as he came into the imperial bedchamber.

Dara waved him to a chair by the side of the bed. She was sitting up, but on this cold night she'd drawn blankets and furs over her shoulders. Krispos left the door open. Sometimes maidservants or eunuchs up raiding the larder peered in at them. Once Anthimos had come in while he and Dara were talking about horses. That was a nervous moment for Krispos, but the Avtokrator, far from being angry, had flopped down on the other side of the bed and argued with them till dawn.

Before Krispos sat down, he asked, "May I bring you anything, Majesty?"

"No, I thank you, but not tonight. Is his Majesty on his way, too?"

Remembering how Anthimos had been engaged when he left, Krispos answered, "I don't think so."

Something in his voice must have told more than he'd intended. "Why? What was he doing?" Dara asked sharply. When he could not come up with a plausible lie on the spur of the moment, she said, "Never mind. I suspect I can figure it out for myself." She turned her head away from him for a moment. "I find I've changed my mind. I might like some wine after all. Bring the jar, not just a cup."

"Yes, Your Majesty." Krispos hurried away.

When he came back, Dara said, "You may get another cup for yourself, if you care to."

"No, thank you. I had enough at—" Reminding Dara of the revel did not seem a good idea. "I've had enough," Krispos said, and let it go at that.

"Have you? How lucky you are." The Empress drank, wordlessly held out the cup to Krispos. He refilled it. She drank about half, then slammed the cup down so hard that wine splashed onto the night table. "What's the use? Sober or drunk, I still know."

Krispos found a rag and walked up to the night table to wipe away the spilled wine. "Know what, Your Majesty?"

"What do you think, Krispos?" Dara said bitterly. "Shall I spell it out in words a child can understand? All right, if you want me to: know that my husband—the Avtokrator, his Majesty, whatever you want to call him—is out enjoying himself with . . . no, let's mince no words at all, shall we? . . . is out fornicating with some new harlot. Again. For, let me see, the third night this week, or is it the fourth? I do lose track sometimes. Or am I wrong, Krispos?" She looked up at him, her eyes brimming but her face tensed with the effort to hold back the tears. "Can you tell me I'm wrong?"

Now Krispos could not meet her gaze, nor answer in words. Facing the wall, he shook his head.

"So that is what I know," Dara said. "I've known it for years. By the lord with the great and good mind, I've known it since a couple of days after they put the flower crowns of marriage on us in the High Temple. Most of the time, I manage not to think of it, but when I can't help it—" She stopped for most of a minute. "When I can't help it, it's very bad. And I don't know why."

"Your Majesty?" Krispos said.

"Why?" Dara repeated. "Why does he do it? He doesn't hate me. He's even kind to me, when he's here and when he remembers to be. So why, then, Krispos? Can you tell me?"

Krispos turned back toward her. "Your Majesty, if you'll forgive my speaking up so bold, I've wondered over that since the first morning I saw you."

She might not have heard him. "Can it be that he doesn't want me? Could I repel him so?" Suddenly she swept the coverings from the bed. Beneath them, as usual, she wore nothing. "Would I—do I—repel you, Krispos?"

"No, Your Majesty." His throat was dry. He'd seen the Empress nude countless times. Now she was naked. He watched her nipples stiffen from the chill in the room—or for another reason. He spoke her name for the first time. "Oh, no, Dara," he breathed.

"Lies come easy, with words," she said softly. "Shut the doors; then we'll see."

He almost went through the doorway instead of merely to it. He knew she wanted him more for revenge on Anthimos than for himself. And if he was caught in her bed, he might stay on as vestiarios, but likely after he was made like the others who had held that office.

But he wanted her. He'd been uneasily aware of that for months, however hard he tried to suppress it even from himself. Anthimos, he thought, would be occupied for some time yet. A eunuch or maidservant coming by would think the Empress here alone—he hoped. He closed the doors.

Dara felt the danger, too. "Hurry!" She held out her arms to him.

Slipping out of his robe was the work of a moment. He got down on the bed beside her. She clutched him as if she were drowning at sea and he a floating spar. "Hurry," she said again, this time into his ear. He did his best to oblige.

He thought of the sea once more as he separated from her some time later—the stormy sea. His lips were bruised; he began to feel the scratches she'd clawed in his back. And he'd wondered if she was without passion! "His Majesty," he said sincerely, "is a fool."

"Why?" Dara asked.

"Why do you think?" He stroked her midnight hair. She purred and snuggled against him. But, reluctantly, he left the bed. "I'd better dress." He got into his robe as fast as he'd taken it off. Dara slid back under the covers. He opened the doors again, then loosed a great sigh of relief out into the empty hallway. "We got away with it."

"So we did." Dara's eyes shone. She gestured him back to the chair that was his correct place in this room. "I'm glad we did."

"Glad we got away with it?" Krispos' shudder was not altogether exaggerated. "If we hadn't . . ." He'd already thought once about the consequences of not getting away with it. Once was plenty.

Dara shook her head. "I'm glad we did . . . what we did." She cocked her head and studied him. "You're different from Anthimos." Her voice was low; no one coming down the hall could have made out her words.

"Am I?" Krispos said, as neutral a response as he could find. Silence stretched between them. Finally, because she seemed to want him to, he asked, "How?"

"Everything he does, everything he has me do, is for his pleasure first, mine only afterward, if at all," Dara said.

That sounded like Anthimos, Krispos thought. What had he said to Dara, that night when he called Krispos while he was making love with her? *"Why did you slow down? That was nice, what you were doing."*

The Empress went on, "You, I think, were out to please . . . me." She hesitated, as if she had trouble believing it.

"Well, of course." Pity filled Krispos. "The better for you, the better for me, too."

"Anthimos doesn't think that way," Dara said. "I didn't know anyone did. How could I? He's the only man I've ever been in bed with till now. Till now," she repeated, half gloating over doing once to the Emperor what he'd done so often to her, half marveling at her own daring.

"I ought to go back to my chamber," Krispos said. Dara nodded. He got up from the chair, went over to the bed, and gave her a quick kiss. She smiled up at him, a lazy, happy smile.

"I may summon you again," she said when he was almost at the door.

"Your Majesty, I hope you do," Krispos answered. They both laughed.

The next thing I have to worry about, Krispos thought as he climbed into his own bed, *is not giving myself away when I go in there tomorrow morning.* He'd had practice in that kind of discretion with Tanilis. He expected he could manage it again. He hoped Dara could, too.

Anthimos noticed nothing out of the ordinary, so they must have done well enough. Krispos looked forward to the next time the little silver bell rang late at night.

K RISPOS BOWED LOW. "EXCELLENT SIR, I HOPE YOU'RE WELL."

"Well enough, esteemed and eminent sir." Iakovitzes' answering bow was as deep as Krispos'. Afterward, the little noble sank gratefully into a chair. "Well enough, though this cursed leg will never be quite the same. But that's not what I came here to talk with you about."

"I wouldn't have thought it was," Krispos agreed. He served Iakovitzes wine and prawns in a sauce of mustard and ginger. "What did you come to talk about, then?"

Before he answered, Iakovitzes made short work of the prawns. He wiped his lips and mustache on a square of linen. "I hear the war with Makuran will begin as soon as the spring rains stop." He waved a hand at the drops splashing against the windowpane.

"Excellent sir, that's hardly a secret," Krispos said. "The Sevastokrator's been mustering soldiers and supplies since last fall."

"I'm quite aware of it, thank you," Iakovitzes said, tart as usual. "What I'm also aware of, and what Petronas seems to be blithely ignoring, is that all the signs point to Malomir coming down out of Kubrat this spring, too. I've been in the Phos-forsaken place enough times over the years to hear what goes on there."

"Petronas does worry about Kubrat," Krispos said slowly. "Truly he does. But he's been set on this war against Makuran for years, you know, and now that he's finally ready to get on with it, he doesn't want to listen to anything that might set it back again. Have you told him what you just told me?"

"Every word and more. It's just as you said—he doesn't want to listen. He thinks the screen on the frontier will hold the wild men, 'if they do attack,' he says." Iakovitzes raised an eyebrow. "They will."

"He raised the tribute we pay Kubrat last year, didn't he?" Krispos said, trying to find a hopeful sign. "That might keep Malomir quiet."

"His illustrious Highness may think so. But Malomir's no idiot. If you give him money, he'll take it. And when he decides to fight, he'll bloody well fight. Kubratoi like to fight, you know. You of all people should, eh?" Iakovitzes said. Troubled, Krispos nodded. Iakovitzes went on, "What we have in the north isn't enough to stop the wild men if they do come down in force. Everything I know makes me think they're going to. That could be most unpleasant."

"Yes." Krispos thought of his nieces carried off into captivity as he had been—if they were lucky. He thought of what could happen to them if they were unlucky . . . and to his sister, and to everyone in his old village, and to countless people he'd never heard of. "How can we get Petronas to hold up again and reinforce the north?"

"*I* can't. The good god knows I've tried. But you, esteemed and eminent sir, you have the ear of his Majesty. And if the Avtokrator gives an order, not even the Sevastokrator may disobey." Iakovitzes grinned craftily. "And since, by an accident of fate and former status about which I would not presume to bore you by reminding you of it, I enjoy the good fortune of your acquaintance . . ."

Krispos grinned back. "You thought you'd take advantage of it."

"Of course I did. That's what having friends in high places is for, after all."

"I'll see what I can do," Krispos promised.

"Good," Iakovitzes said. "I'd kiss you to show how pleased I am, but you'd probably go and use that notorious influence of yours to get me sent to the mines if I tried, so I'll just take my leave instead."

"You're incorrigible."

"By the good god, Krispos, I certainly hope so."

Krispos was laughing as he escorted his one-time master from the imperial residence. The laughter faded when Iakovitzes was no longer there to see. Apprehension replaced it. If he tried to stop the war with Makuran, Petronas would not be pleased with him. And no matter how much influence he had with the Emperor, the Sevastokrator was far more powerful than he, and he knew it.

"YOUR IMPERIAL HIGHNESS," KRISPOS MURMURED, EYES ON THE ground as he went to one knee before Petronas.

The Sevastokrator frowned. "What's all this in aid of, Krispos? You haven't needed to be so formal with me for a long time, and you know it. That's all a waste of time, anyhow, and I have no time to waste right now, not if I'm going west once the rains ease up. So say what you have to say and have done."

"Yes, illustrious Highness," Krispos said. Petronas' frown deepened. Krispos took a deep breath before he went on, "Illustrious Highness, when you were gracious enough to help me become vestiarios, I promised I'd speak to you first over any doubts I had about what you were doing. I'm here today to keep that promise."

"Are you indeed?" Had Petronas been a lion, his tail would have lashed back and forth. "Very well, esteemed and eminent sir, you have my attention. Continue, by all means." Now he, too, was formal; dangerously so.

"Illustrious Highness, is it truly wise to use all the Empire's forces in your war against Makuran? Are you sure you've left behind enough to keep the northern frontier safe?" He explained Iakovitzes' concerns about what Malomir was going to do.

"I've heard this myself," Petronas said, when he was done. "It does not concern me."

"I think it should, though, your Imperial Highness," Krispos said when he was done. "Iakovitzes has had dealings with the Kubratoi for twenty years or so now. If anyone can divine what they plan, he's the man. And if he says they're likely to attack—would you risk the north for the sake of the west?"

"Given the choice, yes," Petronas said. "The westlands are richer and broader in extent than the country between here and the Kubrati border. But I say to you what I said to Iakovitzes—the choice does not arise. Malomir is being paid well to leave us at peace, and the border is not altogether denuded, as you seem to believe."

Krispos thought of the thousands of soldiers who funneled through Videssos the city on their way west. Those were the men whose presence made the Kubratoi stay in their own domain. Surely Malomir could not fail to notice they were gone.

When he said as much, Petronas answered, "You let that be my worry. I say to you that the Kubratoi will not attack. And if I am wrong and they do harass us, their bands will not be able to penetrate far past the frontier."

"I am reassured to hear you say it, illustrious Highness, but suppose you are mistaken?" Krispos persisted. "Could you stop fighting Makuran and send soldiers back to the north? That might not be easy."

"No, it might not," the Sevastokrator said. "But since it is not likely to become necessary, either, I do not intend to worry overmuch about it. And even if everything you describe should come to pass, ways remain of bringing the Kubratoi to heel, I assure you of that."

Krispos raised a skeptical eyebrow. "Would your Imperial Highness please explain them to me?"

"No, by the lord with the great and good mind, I will not. Listen to me, esteemed and eminent sir"—though never a servant, Petronas had learned the art of using titles to cut rather than praise—"and listen well: I need explain myself to no man in Videssos save only the Avtokrator himself. And I do not expect to have to do that in this case. Do I make myself quite clear, Krispos?"

"Aye, illustrious Highness." Petronas did not want him to raise the issue with Anthimos, Krispos thought. "I will have to think on what to do, though."

"Think carefully, Krispos." Now Petronas spoke in unmistakable warning. "Think very carefully indeed, before you seek to measure your influence with his Majesty against mine. Think also on the fate of Skombros, and on whether you care to spend the rest of your days in the bare cell of a celibate monk. You would find that harder to endure than a eunuch does, I assure you, and yet it is the best fate to which you might aspire. Anger me sufficiently and you may know far worse. Remember it always."

"Believe me, I will, illustrious Highness." Krispos rose to go. He did his best not to show how his heart pounded. "But I will also remember what I think best for the Empire." He bowed his way out. If nothing else, he thought, this marked the first time he'd ever had the last word with Petronas.

Leaves glowed green under the spring sun's cheerful rays. The chatty trills of newly returned wagtails and chiffchaffs came through the open windows of the imperial residence along with the sunbeams and the sweet scent of the cherry blossoms now in riotous pink bloom all around the building.

Krispos fetched a tray of wine and sweet pastries in to Anthimos and Petronas, then contrived to hang about in the hallway outside the chamber where they were talking. He had a dust rag and every so often made a swipe at one of the antiquities there, but no one would have thought he was doing anything but eavesdropping.

The Avtokrator and Sevastokrator exchanged pleasantries before they got down to business. Krispos' dusting hand jerked when Petronas asked after Dara. "She's quite well, thanks," Anthimos answered. "She seems happy these days."

"That's good," his uncle said. "May she give you a son soon."

As he cleaned the helmet of the long-ago King of Kings of Makuran, Krispos thought with a small smile that the odds of Dara's conceiving had improved these days. She had called him back to her bed after that first time, again and again. They still had to be cautious, they took all the chances they could.

After more inconsequential talk, Anthimos said, "Uncle, may the good god grant you victory in your wars on Makuran, but are you certain you have left behind enough forces to hold back the Kubratoi if they attack?" Krispos stopped dusting altogether and craned his neck to make sure he heard Petronas' reply.

It took a while to come. At last the Sevastokrator said, "I do not think the Kubratoi will launch any serious assaults this year."

"But they've already begun, it seems to me." Anthimos rustled parchments. "See, here I have two reports that have just arrived, one from near Imbros, the other some distance farther east, of raids by the wild men, cattle and sheep stolen. I don't like such reports. They concern me." Under most circumstances, the young Emperor did not hear news of things that went wrong. Krispos, though, had made sure these reports came to his attention.

"Let me see them." Another pause, presumably while Petronas skimmed through the documents. The Sevastokrator snorted. "These are pinpricks, as you must see, Anthimos. The frontier guards drove off both bands without difficulty."

"But what if they grow worse?" Anthimos persisted. "The guards you've left behind would not be able to drive them off then." Krispos nodded to himself. He'd managed to get his own urgency through to the Emperor, sure enough.

"I consider that most unlikely, Your Majesty," Petronas said.

"Uncle, I'm afraid I don't," Anthimos said. "If these attacks have begun already, they will only get larger. I really must insist that you strengthen the northern frontier with some of the troops you've shifted toward the westlands."

This time, Petronas was silent a long while. "Insist?" he said, as if he did not believe his ears. He repeated the word. "Insist, nephew?" Now he sounded as if he had caught Anthimos in an obvious error and was waiting for the Emperor to fix it.

But Anthimos, though his voice wobbled—Krispos knew his own would have wobbled, too, confronting Petronas' formidable presence—said, "Yes, I really must."

"Even if that means gutting the campaign against Makuran?" Petronas asked softly.

"Even then," Anthimos said, more firmly now. "After all, I am the Avtokrator."

"Certainly you are," Petronas said. "It's only that I'm surprised to find you taking so sudden an interest in the conduct of matters military. I'd thought I enjoyed your trust in such things." His voice was a finely tuned instrument, projecting now nothing but patience and reason.

"You do hold my trust. You know you do, Uncle," Anthimos said. Krispos feared he was weakening. But he went on, "In this particular case, though, I think your own eagerness for the fight makes you less cautious than you have been in the past."

"This is your final word, Your Majesty?"

"It is." Anthimos could sound most imperial when he cared to, Krispos thought. He wondered if that would be enough for him to impose his will on the Sevastokrator.

It was, and then again it was not. After yet another long, thoughtful pause, Petronas said, "Your Majesty, you know your word is my command." Krispos knew what a lie that was; he wondered if Anthimos did. He got no chance to find out, for the Sevastokrator continued, "Perhaps, though, you will be gracious enough to let me propose a solution that permits me to keep the entire army, yet will confound the Kubratoi."

"Go ahead," Anthimos said cautiously, as if, like Krispos, he was wondering how Petronas proposed to accomplish the two goals that seemed incompatible.

"Thank you, Anthimos; I will. Perhaps you remember hearing of a Haloga mercenary band led by a northerner called Harvas Black-Robe."

"Well, yes, now that you mention it. They've been making mischief for a while in Khatrish, haven't they?"

"Thatagush actually, Your Majesty. I've taken the liberty of inquiring of this Harvas what he would require to fall upon Kubrat instead. If his northerners do that, Malomir will be far too occupied with them to give us any trouble for some time to come, all without the use of a single good Videssian soldier. What say you to that?"

It was the Avtokrator's turn to hesitate. Out in the hall, Krispos kicked at the polished marble floor. Petronas had indeed had a scheme in reserve, and a good scheme to boot. Krispos learned what being outmaneuvered felt like.

"Uncle, I'll have to give that some thought," Anthimos said at last.

"Go ahead, but I hope you'll think quickly, for now that the weather is fine once more, every campaigning day lost counts against me," Petronas said.

"You'll know my decision tomorrow," the Avtokrator promised.

"Good enough," Petronas said jovially.

Krispos heard him set down his cup, then heard the chair shift under him as he got to his feet. He started to duck into another room—he did not want to face the Sevastokrator right now. But he was either too slow or too noisy, for Petronas came in after him. As protocol required, he went to one knee before the man with the second highest rank in the Empire of Videssos. "Your imperial Highness," he said, eyes on the ground.

"Look at me, esteemed and eminent sir," Petronas said. Unwillingly, Krispos obeyed. The Sevastokrator's face was hard and cold, his voice flat. "I did not intend throwing a fox out of the vestiarios' chamber only to replace him with a lion. I've warned you, not once but many times, that you would pay for disobeying me. All that remains is deciding how to punish you for your disobedience."

"I thought you were wrong to bare the border with Kubrat," Krispos said stubbornly. "I told you as much, and I still think so. I don't like your new plan much better. How much harm can a mercenary company do to a big country like Kubrat? Probably not enough to keep the wild men from going on with their raids against us."

"Thatagush is twice the size of Kubrat, and Harvas' raiders have kept it in chaos for years." Petronas nodded to Krispos. "That you don't grovel before me speaks well of you. Given age and experience, you could grow to be truly dangerous. I doubt you'll have the chance to gain them, though."

Krispos started to say that Anthimos would protect him against the Sevastokrator. He stopped—he knew better. The Sevastokrator's will was far stronger than his nephew's. One way or another, even if Anthimos ordered him not to, he would strike at Krispos. Anthimos might be sorry Krispos was gone, at least until he got used to the quiet, safe eunuch who would undoubtedly replace him. Dara would miss him more. But neither of them could keep Petronas from doing as he liked in the city.

Flight? If anyone in the Empire could track him down, Petronas could. Besides, he thought, what good was it to run away from the friends and allies he had? Getting rid of him might be harder here than on some lonely country road. Better to stay and do what he could. Now, still on that one knee, he met Petronas' eyes. "May I rise, your Highness?"

"Go ahead," Petronas said. "You'll fall again, soon enough."

K̲RISPOS DID HIS BEST TO TALK ANTHIMOS OUT OF LETTING Petronas use Harvas Black-Robe's Halogai instead of Videssian troops against the Kubratoi. Anthimos listened and shook his head. "But why, Your Majesty?" Krispos protested. "Even if the mercenaries do turn Kubrat topsy-turvy, Kubrati raiders will still wound your northern provinces."

Even being reminded by that "you" that the Empire was his personally did not change Anthimos' mind. "Maybe they will, but not that badly. Why should a little trouble on the frontier concern me? It can be set to rights later."

What was to Anthimos "a little trouble on the frontier" seemed a disaster in the making to Krispos. He wondered how the Avtokrator would have felt if he had a sister, nieces, a brother-in-law only too close to the wild men. But nothing that did not directly affect Anthimos was real to him.

With as much control as he could muster, Krispos said, "Your Majesty, truly the invasion you admit will happen could be stopped if we put our soldiers back where they belong. You know it's so."

"Maybe it is," Anthimos said. "But if I let Petronas go ahead, he'll be out of my hair for months. Think of the revels I could enjoy while he's not around." The Avtokrator leered in anticipation. Krispos tried to hide his disgust—was this the way an Emperor chose war or peace? Then Anthimos' face changed. All at once, he was as serious as Krispos had ever seen him. He went on quietly, "Besides, when it comes right down to it, I don't dare tell my uncle not to use the soldiers he's spent all this time mustering."

"Why not?" Krispos said. "Are you the Avtokrator or aren't you?"

"I am *now*," Anthimos answered, "and I'd like to keep being the Avtokrator a while longer, too, if you know what I mean. Suppose I order my uncle not to take his army to Makuran. Don't you think the first thing he'd use it for after that would be to throw me down? Then he'd march on Makuran anyway, and I'd miss all those lovely revels I saw you sneering about a moment ago."

Abashed, Krispos hung his head. After a little thought, he realized Anthimos was right. He was surprised the Emperor could see so clearly. When Anthimos wanted to be, he was able enough. Trouble was, most of the time he didn't bother. Krispos mumbled, "Thank you for backing me as far as you did then, Your Majesty."

"When I thought taking so many men west would pose a bad risk in the north, I was willing to argue with Petronas. But since he's managed to find a way to enjoy himself and have a good chance of checking the Kubratoi at the same time, why not let him have his fun? He doesn't begrudge me mine."

Krispos bowed. He knew he'd lost this duel with Petronas. "As Your Majesty wishes, of course," he said, yielding as graciously as he could.

"That's a good fellow. I don't want to see you glooming about." Anthimos grinned at Krispos. "Especially since there's no need for gloom. A good carouse tonight to wash the taste of all this boring business we've had to do out of our mouths, and we'll both feel like new men." The grin got wider. "Or, if you feel like a woman instead, I expect that can be arranged."

Krispos did feel like a woman that evening, but not one of the complacent girls who enlivened the Avtokrator's feasts. He wished he could talk with Tanilis, to find out how badly she thought being bested by Petronas would hurt him. Since Tanilis was far away, Dara would do. Though he still thought her chief loyalty lay with Anthimos rather than with him— Anthimos was Avtokrator, and he was not—he was sure she preferred him to Anthimos' uncle.

But when, as he had a good many times before, he tried to leave the revel early, the Emperor would not let him. "I told you I didn't want you glooming about. I expect you to have a good time tonight." He pointed to a statuesque brunette. "She looks like she'd be a good time."

The woman Krispos wanted was back at the imperial residence. Telling the Emperor so seemed impractical. Krispos had taken a couple of girls at the revels, just so Anthimos would not notice anything out of the ordinary. But now he said, "I'm not in the mood for it this evening. I think I'll go over to the wine and drink for a while." Without a doubt, drinking fell within the Emperor's definition of a good time.

"*I* know what you need!" Anthimos exclaimed. He snatched the clear crystal bowl out of Krispos' hands. "Here, take a chance. You've been dealing them out for so long, you haven't been able to be on the grabbing end."

Obediently Krispos reached into the bowl and drew out a golden ball. He undid it, then unfolded the parchment inside. "Twenty-four pounds of horse manure," he read. Anthimos laughed so hard, he almost dropped the bowl. Grinning servants presented Krispos with his prize. He looked at the stinking brown mound and shook his head. "Well, it's been that kind of day."

THE NEXT DAY WAS NO BETTER. HE HAD TO GREET PETRONAS when the Sevastokrator came to hear what Anthimos had decided. Then he had to endure Petronas' smirk of triumph after the Emperor's uncle emerged from being closeted with his nephew. "His Majesty is delighted that I set out for the westlands within the week," Petronas said.

Of course he is—this way you won't kill him and stick his head on the Milestone in the plaza of Palamas for the crowds to gape at, Krispos thought. Aloud he said, "May you triumph, your illustrious Highness."

"Oh, I shall," Petronas said. "First into Vaspurakan; the 'princes,' good soldiers all, will surely flock to me, for they follow Phos even if they are heretics, and will be glad to escape from the rule of those who worship the Four—false—Prophets. And then—on toward Mashiz!"

Krispos remembered what Iakovitzes had said about the centuries of inconclusive warfare between Videssos and Makuran. Petronas' planned trip to Mashiz would be quick and easy if his foes cooperated. If not, it was liable to take longer than the Sevastokrator expected. "May you triumph," he said again.

"What a smooth liar you've turned into, when you'd sooner see me ravens' meat. That's not likely, though, I'm afraid. No indeed. And in any event, as I told you before, your punishment awaits you. I don't think it will wait long enough for you to see me at all anymore, let alone in my victorious return. A very good afternoon to you, esteemed and eminent sir." Petronas swaggered away.

Krispos stared at his retreating back. He sounded very sure of himself. What was he going to do, hire a band of bravoes to storm the imperial residence? Bravoes who tangled with the Emperor's Halogai would end up catmeat. And whatever Krispos ate, Anthimos ate, too. Unless Petronas wanted to be rid of his nephew along with Krispos, poison was unlikely, and he showed no sign of wanting to be rid of his nephew, not so long as he got his way.

What did that leave? Not much, Krispos thought, if I lie low until Petronas heads west. The Sevastokrator could hire assassins from afar, but Krispos did not greatly fear a lone assassin; he was a good enough man of his hands to hope to survive such an attack. Maybe Petronas was only trying to make him afraid and subservient once more—or maybe his anger would cool, away in the westlands. No, Krispos feared that was wishful thinking. Petronas was not the sort to forget an affront.

A few days later, troops under the Sevastokrator's command marched and rode down to the docks. Anthimos came to the docks, too, and made a fiercely martial speech. The soldiers cheered. Gnatios the patriarch prayed for the army's success. The soldiers cheered again. Then they lined up to be loaded onto ferries for the short journey over the Cattle-Crossing, the narrow strait that separated Videssos the city from the Empire's western provinces.

Krispos watched the tubby ferryboats waddle across the water to the westlands; watched them go aground; watched as, tiny in the distance, the warriors began to clamber down onto the beaches across from the city; saw the bright spring sunlight sparkling off someone's armor. That would be a general, he thought, maybe even Petronas himself. No matter how the Sevastokrator threatened, he was far less frightening on the other side of the Cattle-Crossing.

Anthimos must have been thinking the same thing. "Well," he said, turning at last to go back to the palaces, "the city is mine for a while, by Phos, with no one to tell me what I must or must not do."

"There's still me, Your Majesty," Krispos said.

"Ah, but you do it in a pleasant tone of voice, and so I can ignore you if I care to," the Emperor said. "My uncle, now, I never could ignore, no matter how hard I tried." Krispos nodded, but wondered if Petronas would agree—the Sevastokrator seemed convinced his nephew ignored him all the time.

But having the wolf away from his door prompted Krispos to carouse with the best of them at the revel Anthimos put on that night "to celebrate the army's victory in advance," as the Avtokrator said. He was drinking wine from a large golden fruit bowl decorated with erotic reliefs when a Haloga guardsman came in and tapped him on the shoulder. "Somebody out there wants to see you," the northerner said.

Krispos stared at him. "Somebody out where?" he asked owlishly.

The Haloga stared back. "Out there," he said after a long pause. Krispos realized the guardsman was even drunker than he was.

"I'll come," Krispos said. He had almost got to the door when his sodden brain realized he was in no condition to fight off a toddler, let alone an assassin. He was about to turn around when the Haloga grabbed him by the arm and propelled him down the stairs—not, apparently, with malicious intent, but because the northerner needed help standing up himself.

"Krispos!" someone called from the darkness.

"Mavros!" He got free of the Haloga and stumbled toward his foster brother. "What are you doing here? I thought you were on the other side of the Cattle-Crossing with Petronas and the ret of his restinue—rest of his retinue," he corrected himself carefully.

"I was, and I will be again soon—I can't afford to be missed. I've got a little rowboat tied up at a quay not far from here. I had to come back across to warn you: Petronas has hired a mage. I came into his tent to ask him which horse he'd want tomorrow, and he and the wizard were talking about quietly getting rid of someone. They named no names while I was there, but I think it's you!"

Chapter XI

CERTAINTY WASHED THROUGH KRISPOS LIKE THE TIDE. "YOU'RE right. You have to be." Even drunk—perhaps more clearly because he was drunk—he could see that this was just how Petronas would deal with someone who had become inconvenient to him. It was neat and clean, with the Sevastokrator far away from any embarrassing questions, assuming they were ever asked.

"What are you going to do?" Mavros said.

The question snapped Krispos out of his rapt admiration for Petronas' cleverness. He tried to flog his slow wits forward. "Find a wizard of my own, I suppose," he said at last.

"That sounds well enough," Mavros agreed. "Whatever you do, do it quickly—I don't think Petronas will wait long, and the mage he was talking with seemed a proper ready-for-aught. Now I have to get back before I'm missed. The Lord with the great and good mind be with you." He stepped up, embraced Krispos, then hurried away.

Krispos watched him disappear into darkness and listened to his footfalls fade till they were gone. He thought how fortunate he was to have such a reliable friend in the Sevastokrator's household. Then he remembered what he had to do. "Wizard," he said aloud, as if to remind himself. Staggering slightly, he started out of the palace quarter.

He was almost to the plaza of Palamas before he consciously wondered where he was going. He only knew one sorcerer at all well, though. He was glad he hadn't been the one who'd antagonized Trokoundos. Otherwise, he thought, Anthimos' former tutor in magecraft would have been more likely to join Petronas' wizard than to help fend him off.

Trokoundos lived on a fashionable street not far from the palace quarter. Krispos pounded on his door, not caring that it was well past midnight. He kept pounding until Trokoundos opened it a crack. The mage held a lamp in one hand and a most unmystical short sword in the other. He lowered it when he recognized Krispos. "By Phos, esteemed and eminent sir, have you gone mad?"

"No," Krispos said. Trokoundos drew back from the wine fumes he exuded. He went on, "I'm in peril of my life. I need a wizard. I thought of you."

Trokoundos laughed. "Are you in such peril that it won't wait till morning?"

"Yes," Krispos said.

Trokoundos held the lamp high and peered at him. "You'd better come in," he said. As Krispos walked inside, the wizard turned his head and called, "I'm sorry, Phostina, but I'm afraid I have business." A woman's voice said something querulous. "Yes, I'll be as quiet as I can," Trokoundus promised. To Krispos, he explained, "My wife. Sit here, if you care to, and tell me of this peril of yours."

Krispos did. By the time he finished, Trokoundos was nodding and rubbing his chin in calculation. "You've made a powerful enemy, esteemed and eminent sir. Presumably he will have in his employment a powerful and dangerous mage. You know no more than you are to be assailed?"

"No," Krispos said, "and I'm lucky to know that."

"So you are, so you are, but it will make my task more difficult, for I will be unable to ward against any specific spells, but will have to try to protect you from all magics. Such a stretching will naturally weaken my own efforts, but I will do what I may. Honor will not let me do less, not after your gracious warning of his Majesty's wrath. Come along to my study, if you please."

The chamber where Trokoundos worked his magics was one part library, one part jeweler's stall, one part herbarium, and one part zoo. It smelled close and moist and rather fetid; Krispos' stomach flipflopped. Holding down his gorge with grim determination, he sat across from Trokoundos while the wizard consulted his books.

Trokoundos slammed a codex shut, rolled up a scroll, tied it with a ribbon, and put it back in its pigeonhole. "Since I do not know what form the attack upon you will take, I will use all three kingdoms—animal, vegetable, and mineral—in your defense." He went over to a large covered bowl and lifted the lid. "Here is a snail fed on oregano, a sovereign against poisonings and other noxiousnesses of all sorts. Eat it, if you would."

Krispos gulped. "I'd sooner have it broiled, with butter and garlic."

"No doubt, but prepared thus its virtue aims only at the tongue. Do as I say now: crack the shell and peel it, as if it were a hard-cooked egg, then swallow the creature down."

Trying not to think about what he was doing, Krispos obeyed. The snail was cold and wet on his tongue. He gulped convulsively before he could notice what it tasted like. Gagging, he wondered whether it would still protect him if he threw it up again.

"Very good," Trokoundos said, ignoring his distress. "Now then, the juice of the narcissus or asphodel will also aid you. Here is some, mixed with honey to make it palatable." Krispos got it down. After the snail, it was palatable. Trokoundos went on, "I will also wrap a dried asphodel in clean linen and give it to you. Carry it next to your skin; it will repel demons and other evil spirits."

"May the good god grant it be so," Krispos said. When Trokoundos gave him the plant, he tucked it under his tunic.

"Mineral, mineral, mineral," Trokoundos muttered. He snapped his fingers. "The very thing!" He rummaged among the stones on a table by his desk, held up a dark-brown one. "Here I have chalcedony, which, if pierced by an emery stone and hung round the neck, is proof against all fantastical illusions and protects the body against one's adversaries and their evil machinations. This is known as the counsel of chalcedony. Now where did that emery go?" He rummaged some more, until he finally found the hard stone he sought.

He clamped the chalcedony to the table and began to bore through it with the pointed end of the emery stone. As he worked, he chanted a wordless little song. "The power we seek lies within the chalcedony itself," the mage explained. "My chant is but to hasten the process that would otherwise be boring in two senses of the word. Ahh, here we are!" He worked a bit longer to enlarge the hole he had made, then held out the chalcedony to Krispos. "Have you a chain on which to wear it?"

"Yes." Krispos drew the chain on which he kept the goldpiece Omurtag had given him up over his head.

Trokoundos stared at the coin as it gleamed in the lamplight. "My, my," he said slowly. "What company my little stone will keep." He seemed about to ask Krispos about the goldpiece, then shook his head. "No time for my curiosity now. May the stone, the plant, and the snail keep you safe, that's all."

"Thank you." Krispos put the stone onto the chain, closed the catch, and slid the chain back onto his neck. "Now then, what do I owe you for your services?"

"Not a copper, seeing as I'd likely not be here to render those services had you not warned me the city would be unhealthy for a few weeks. No, I insist—this won't bankrupt me, I assure you."

"Thank you," Krispos repeated, bowing. "I had better get back to the imperial residence." He turned to go, then had another thought. "Not that I fail to trust your charms, but can I do anything to make them work even better?" He hoped the question would not offend Trokoundos.

Evidently it didn't, for the mage answered promptly. "Pray. The Lord with the great and good mind opposes all wicked efforts, and may well hear your sincere words and grant you his protection. Having a priest pray for you may also do some good; as Phos' holy men are sworn against evil, the good god naturally holds them in high regard."

"I'll do both those things," Krispos promised. As soon as he could he thought with wine-fueled intensity, he'd see Gnatios and ask for his prayers; who could be holier than the ecumenical patriarch?

"Good. I will pray for you as well," Trokoundos said. He yawned enormously. Whether that was a real yawn or a hint, Krispos knew it was time to go. He thanked the wizard one last time and took his leave. Dawn had already begun to pink the eastern sky. Krispos murmured two prayers to Phos, one for his own safety and the other that Anthimos would sleep late.

"YOU WERE A BUSY LAD LAST NIGHT," ANTHIMOS SAID ROGU-ishly as Krispos held up a robe for his approval. The Emperor had slept late, but not late enough. Krispos' head ached. Anthimos went on, "You weren't in your chamber when I got back. Did you go off with one of the wenches? Was she good?"

Without looking her way, Krispos sensed Dara listening closely for his reply. "Not a wench, Your Majesty," he said. "An old friend came to pay me a bet he owed, and afterward he and I went off and did a little more drinking."

"You should have told me before you left," the Emperor said. "Come to that, you could have brought your friend in. Who knows? He might have livened things up."

"Yes, Your Majesty. Sorry, Your Majesty." Krispos robed Anthimos, then went to the closet to get his master's red boots.

As he turned, he got a brief glimpse of Dara. He hoped that "he and I" had eased her mind. It had the advantage of being at least partly true; if she checked, she was sure to find someone who had seen him with Mavros. He hoped she would. If she thought he was betraying her, she had only to speak to Anthimos to destroy him. He did not like being so vulnerable to her. Maybe he should have worried more about that *before* he got into bed with her, he thought. Now was far too late.

Anthimos went off to the Amphitheater as soon as he had finished breakfast. Krispos stayed behind at the imperial residence for a little while, then headed for the patriarch's mansion. Gnatios was domiciled in the northern part of Videssos the city, in the shadow of the High Temple.

"You are . . . ?" a lesser priest haughtily asked at the door, looking down his nose at Krispos.

"I am the vestiarios to his Imperial Majesty Anthimos III, Avtokrator of the Videssians. I would have speech with the ecumenical patriarch, at once." He folded his arms and waited. He hoped he sounded arrogant rather than anxious; only Petronas and his mage knew when they would unleash their assault. He might need Gnatios' prayers right away.

He must have hit the proper tone—the priest deflated. "Yes, uh, esteemed, uh, eminent sir—"

"Esteemed *and* eminent," Krispos snapped.

"Yes, yes, of course; my apologies. The most holy sir is in his study. Come this way, please." Chattering nervously and bowing every few steps, the priest led him through the mansion. The artworks on the walls and set into niches were as fine as those in the imperial residence, but Krispos hardly noticed them. He followed close on his guide's heels, wishing the fellow would move faster.

Gnatios looked up frowning from the codex on his desk. "Curse it, Badourios, I told you I did not wish to be disturbed this morning." Then he saw who was behind the lesser priest and rose smoothly from his chair. "Of course I am always glad to make an exception for you, Krispos. Sit here, if you care to. Will you take wine?"

"No thank you, most holy sir," Krispos said, having mercy on his hangover. "May I ask for privacy, though?"

"You have only to reach behind you and close that stout door there," Gnatios said. Krispos did as he suggested. The patriarch leaned forward over the desk between them. "You've roused my curiosity, esteemed and eminent sir. Now, privately, what do you require?"

"Your prayers, most holy sir, for I have discovered that I am in danger of magical attack." As he started to explain to Gnatios, he realized that coming here was a mistake, a large mistake. His stomach knotted from something other than his hangover. Not only did the patriarch belong to Petronas' faction, he was the Sevastokrator's cousin. Krispos could not even tell him who had brought news of his danger for that might put Mavros at risk. Thus he knew his story limped as it came out.

Gnatios gave no sign of noticing. "Of course I shall pray for you, esteemed and eminent sir," he said fulsomely. "If you will give me the name of the man who so bravely brought word of this plot against you, I will pray for him as well. His courage should not go unrewarded."

The words were right. The tone was sincere—a little too sincere. Suddenly Krispos was certain that if he let Mavros' name slip out, the patriarch would get it to Petronas as fast as he could.

And so he answered, "Most holy sir, I fear I don't know her—uh, his—name. He came to me because, he said, he could not bear to see his master treat me unjustly. I don't even know who her—*his*—master is." With luck, those pretended slips would keep Gnatios from guessing how much Krispos knew and how he knew it.

"You will be in my thoughts and prayers for some time to come," the patriarch said.

Yes, but how? Krispos wondered. "Thank you, holy sir. You're very kind," he said. He bowed his way out, pondering what to do next. Ducking into a wineshop a few doors down the street from the patriarchal mansion let him ponder sitting down. He suspected Gnatios' prayers would not be for his continued good health. Who, then, could intercede with Phos for him?

While he sat and thought about that, a priest rushed past the wineshop. So close to the High Temple, blue robes were as common as fleas, but the fellow looked familiar. After a moment, Krispos recognized him: Badourios, Gnatios' doorkeeper. Where was he going in such a hurry? After tossing a couple of coppers on the table for the rather stale cake he'd eaten, Krispos slipped after him to find out.

Badourios was easy to follow; he did not seem to imagine he could be pursued. His destination soon became obvious: the harbor. Which meant, Krispos was sure, that as soon as he got over the Cattle-Crossing, Petronas would know his plans were no longer hidden from their intended victim.

And that, in turn, meant Krispos surely had very little time. It also meant everything he'd suspected about Gnatios was true, and then some. But that, for now, was a side issue. Through his robe, Krispos touched the chalcedony amulet Trokoundos had given him. The mage had as much as said the amulet, the asphodel, and the raw snail were not enough by themselves to ward him fully.

He started back toward the High Temple, intending to ask the first priest he saw to beseech Phos to protect him. Most blue-robes were fine men; he was willing to gamble on one chosen at random. Then he had a better idea. The abbot Pyrrhos had touched his life twice already. And not only was Pyrrhos notably holy, he was also bound to treat Krispos like his own son. Krispos turned, angry at himself for not having thought of Pyrrhos sooner. The monastery dedicated to the memory of the holy Skirios was—*that* way. Krispos headed for it faster than Badourios had gone to the harbor.

The gatekeeper made him wait outside the monastery. "The brethren just began their noontime prayers. They may not be disturbed for any reason."

Krispos drummed his fingers on the wall until the monks began filing out of the temple on the monastery grounds. The gatekeeper stood aside to let him pass. Their shaven heads and identical robes gave the monks no small uniformity, but Pyrrhos' tall, lean, erect figure stood out among them.

"Holy sir! Abbot Pyrrhos!" Krispos called. All the while, he kept expecting the spell from Petronas' mage to smash him down in the dust. The delay forced while the monks prayed might have given the wizard enough time to smite.

Pyrrhos turned, taking in Krispos' fine robe, so different from the plain blue wool he wore. Scorn sparked in the abbot's eyes. Then he recognized Krispos. His face changed—a little. "I have not seen you in some while," he said. "I gathered the loose life in the palaces was more to your liking than that which we live here."

Krispos felt himself flush, the more so because what Pyrrhos said held much truth. He said, "Holy sir, I need your aid," and waited to see what the abbot would do. If Pyrrhos only wanted to rant at him, he would go find another priest, and quickly.

But the abbot checked himself. Krispos saw he had not forgotten that strange night when Krispos first came to the monastery of the holy Skirios. "Phos bids us aid all men, that they may come to know the good," Pyrrhos said slowly. "Come to my study; tell me of your need."

"Thank you, holy sir," Krispos breathed. He followed the abbot through the narrow, dimly lit corridors of the monastery. He'd walked this way once before, he realized, but he had been too bemused then to make special note of his surroundings.

The study he remembered. Like Pyrrhos, it was spare and hard and served its purpose without superfluity. The abbot waved Krispos to an un-padded stool, perched on another, and leaned forward like a bearded bird of prey. "What is this aid you say you require? I would have thought you likelier to go to Gnatios these days, as he reckons most sins but a small matter."

Pyrrhos was not a man to make things easy, Krispos thought. But when he answered, "Gnatios would not help me, for the person from whom I need aid is the Sevastokrator Petronas." He knew he'd captured the abbot's attention.

"How did you fall foul of Petronas?" Pyrrhos asked. "Did you presume to suggest to the Emperor that his time might be better spent in attending to the duties of the state than in the wantonness and depravity in which, with his uncle's connivance, he currently wallows?"

"Something like that," Krispos said; he had indeed tried to get Anthimos to do more toward running the Empire. "And because of it, holy sir, the Sevastokrator, though now out of the city on campaign, seeks to slay me with sorcery. I've been told the prayers of a priest might help blunt the magic's power. Will you pray for my protection, holy sir?"

"By the good god, I will!" Pyrrhos sprang to his feet and caught Krispos by the arm. "Come to the altar with me, Krispos, and offer up your prayers as well."

The altar of the monastery temple was not of silver and gold and ivory and gems like the one in the High Temple. It was plain wood, as befitted the simplicity of monastic life. Pyrrhos and Krispos spat on the floor in front of it in ritual rejection of the dark god Skotos, Phos' eternal rival. Then they raised their hands to the heavens and spoke the creed together: "We bless thee, Phos, lord with the great and good mind, by thy grace our protector, watchful beforehand that the great test of life may be decided in our favor."

Krispos prayed on in silence. Pyrrhos, more used to ordering his thoughts aloud, kept speaking after the creed was done: "Phos, I beseech you to protect this upright young man from the evil that approaches him. May he walk safe and righteous through it, as he has walked safe through the iniquity of the palaces. I pray for him as I would pray for my own son." His eyes met Krispos' for a moment. Yes, he remembered that first night Krispos had come to the monastery.

"Will your prayer save me, holy sir?" Krispos asked when the abbot lowered his arms.

"That is as Phos wills," Pyrrhos answered, "and depends on what your future is meant to be—also, I'll not deny, on the power of the sorcery sent against you. Though Phos will vanquish Skotos in the end, the dark god still ranges free in the world. I have prayed. Within me, I pray yet. May that suffice, that and whatever other wardings you have."

Pyrrhos was narrow, but he was also straight: he would not promise what he could not deliver. At any other time, Krispos would have had only approbation for that. Now, he thought, a reassuring lie might have felt very good. He thanked the abbot, dropped a goldpiece into the monastery poorbox, and started back to the palaces.

H E SPENT THE REST OF THE DAY IN ANNOYED SUSPENSE. IF THE wizard was going to strike, he wished the fellow would *strike* and have done. Wondering whether he could withstand the attack seemed harder than waiting for it to come.

As he was carrying dinner in for Anthimos and Dara that evening, he got his wish. And, as is often the way of such things, he regretted ever making it. He was just lowering a wide silver tray from his shoulder to the table at which the Emperor and Empress sat when the strength suddenly flowed from his body like wine pouring from a jug. All at once, the tray seemed to weigh tons. Despite his desperate grip, it crashed to the floor.

Anthimos and Dara both jumped; the Empress let out a squeak. "That wasn't very good, Krispos," Anthimos said, laying a finger by the side of his nose. "Even if you think the meal is bad, you should give us the chance to fling it about."

Krispos tried to answer, but only a croak came from his mouth; he was not strong enough to force his tongue to shape words. As Dara began to ask, "Are you all right?" his legs gave out from under him and he slid bonelessly down into the messy ruins of the dinner he had brought.

By luck, he landed with his head to one side. That let him keep breathing. Had he fallen face down in spilled soup or gravy, he surely would have drowned, for he could not have shifted to clear the muck from his mouth and nose.

He heard Dara scream. He could not see her; his eyes pointed in the wrong direction and he could not move them. Each breath was a separate struggle for air. His heart stuttered, uncertain in his chest.

Anthimos stooped beside him and rolled him onto his back. Breathing grew a precious trifle easier. "What's wrong, Krispos?" the Emperor demanded, staring down at him. Fetched by the racket of the dropped tray and by Dara's scream, servants rushed into the dining room. "He's had some sort of fit, poor beggar," Anthimos told them.

Barsymes said, "Let's get him to his bed. Here, Tyrovitzes, help me move him out of this muck." Grunting, the two eunuchs pulled Krispos away from the spilled food. Barsymes clicked tongue between teeth. "On second thought, we'd better clean him up before we put him into bed. We'll just take him out to the hallway first." As if he were a sack of lentils, they dragged him away from the table and out of the dining room.

"Put him down a moment," Tyrovitzes said. Barsymes helped ease Krispos to the marble flooring. Tyrovitzes went back into the dining room. "Your Majesties, I am sorry for the disturbance. Someone will be along directly, I assure you, to clean up what was unfortunately spilled and to serve you a fresh meal."

Had he been able to, Krispos would have snickered. *So sorry the vestiarios turned to a puddle of mush right before your eyes, your Majesties. A fresh meal will be along directly, so don't worry about it.* But had someone else been stricken in the same way, he knew he also would have tried to keep things running smoothly. That was how life worked in the palaces.

"Krispos, can you hear me? Can you understand me?" Barsymes asked. Though the answer to both was yes, Krispos could not give it. He could only stare up at Barsymes. The eunuch's smooth face lengthened in thought. "If you do understand, can you blink your eyes?"

The effort was like lifting a boulder as big as he was, but Krispos managed to close his eyelids. The world went frighteningly dark. Sweat burst out on his face as he fought to open his eyes again. At last he succeeded. He felt as worn as if a hundred harvests had all been pressed into one day.

"He has his wits, then," Tyrovitzes said.

"Yes." Barsymes laid a cool hand on Krispos' forehead. "No fever, I'd say. The good god willing, we don't have to fear catching—whatever this is." The chamberlain undid Krispos' robe and eased his arms out of it as if he were a doll. "Fetch water and towels, if you would, Tyrovitzes. We'll wash him and put him to bed and see if he gets better."

"Aye, what else can we do?" Tyrovitzes' sandals flapped down the hall.

Barsymes squatted on his heels, studying Krispos. Watching him in return, Krispos realized how helpless he was. Any small remembered slight, any resentment the eunuch still felt at being passed over for a whole man, and Petronas' magic would prevail even if it had not—quite—killed him outright.

Tyrovitzes came back, setting a bucket next to Krispos' head. Without a word, the two eunuchs set to work. The water was chilly. Krispos found himself shivering. Movements not under his conscious control seemed to function, after a fashion. But that blink had been plenty to exhaust him; he could not have raised a finger to save his soul from Skotos' ice.

The eunuchs hauled him down the corridor to the chamber that had once been Skombros'. "One, two—" Barsymes said. At "three," he and Tyrovitzes lifted Krispos and put him on the bed.

Krispos stared up at the ceiling; he had no other choice. If this was what the Sevastokrator's magic had done to him while he was warded, he wondered what would have become of him without protection. About the same thing, he supposed, that happened to a bull when the fellow at the slaughterhouse hit it between the eyes with his hammer. He would have dropped down dead, and that would have been that.

Barsymes came back a little later with a wide, flat pan. As gently as he could, he worked it under Krispos' buttocks. "You won't want to soil the sheets," he observed. Krispos did his best to put a thank-you look on his blank face. That hadn't occurred to him. A lot about being completely unable to care for himself hadn't occurred to him. Over the dreadfully long, dreadfully slow course of that summer and fall, he found out about all of them.

The palace eunuchs kept him alive. They cared for members of the imperial family at all phases of life. Sometimes they treated Krispos like an infant, sometimes like a senile old man. Longinos held him upright while Barsymes massaged his throat to get him to swallow broth, a spoonful at a time. He watched himself grow thinner day by day.

Physicians poked and prodded him and went away shaking their heads. Anthimos ordered a healer-priest to come see him. The priest fell into a trance, but woke from it baffled and defeated. "I am sorry, Your Majesty, but the illness has no cause upon which my talent can light," he told the Avtokrator.

That was only a few days after Krispos was stricken. For those first few days, and for a while afterward, Anthimos was constantly in his chamber, constantly making suggestions to the eunuchs about his care. Some of the suggestions were good ones; he urged the eunuchs to roll Krispos from side to side periodically to slow the start of bedsores. But when Krispos showed no signs of leaping to his feet and getting on with his duties as if nothing had happened, the Emperor began to lose interest not so much in him but in his case, and came to see him less and less often.

Although he did not leap to his feet, ever so slowly Krispos did begin to mend. Had he stayed as weak and limp as he was when the magic laid him low, he likely would have died, of slow starvation or from fluid puddling in his flaccid lungs. The milestones he reached were small ones, at first so small he scarcely noticed them himself, for who pays attention to being able to blink, or to cough? From blinking and coughing, though, he progressed to swallowing on his own, and then, later still, to chewing soft food.

He still could not speak. That required control more delicate than his muscles could yet achieve. Being able to smile again, and to frown, seemed as valuable to him. Babies used no more to let people know how they felt.

Krispos especially valued the return of expressiveness to his face when Dara visited him. She did not go into his chamber often, certainly not as often as Anthimos had after he was laid low. But where Anthimos lost interest in him because his condition changed so slowly, Dara kept coming back.

Once in a while she would take a bowl and spoon from one of the eunuchs, prop Krispos up with pillows, and feed him a meal. Barsymes, Tyrovitzes, Longinos, and the rest of the chamberlains were gentler and neater than she was. Krispos did not care. He was part of their duty; she helped him only because she wanted to. Being able to smile back at her let her know he understood that.

Though he could not answer, she talked at him while she visited. He picked up palace gossip, and snatches of what went on in the wider world, as well. Petronas, he learned, was advancing in Makuraner-held Vaspurakan, but slowly. The breakthrough, the advance on Mashiz of which the Sevastokrator dreamed, was nowhere in sight. Some of his generals had started to grumble. He'd even sent one packing—a certain Mammianos now found himself commanding the western coastal lowlands, a rich province but one peaceful for so long as to be a graveyard for a fighting soldier.

If Petronas himself never came back from his western campaign, Krispos would not have shed a tear—had his condition allowed it, he might have danced around the room. He did hope Mavros was all right.

Krispos was less delighted to learn that Petronas' plan for handling Kubrat looked to be working exactly as the Sevastokrator had predicted. Harvas Black-Robe's Haloga mercenaries, falling on the Kubratoi from the north, left them too distracted to launch any large raids against the Empire.

"They say Malomir may even lose his throne," Dara told Krispos one warm summer evening. Wanting to hear more, he widened his eyes and did his best to look attentive. But instead of going on about the affairs of the Kubratoi, Dara looked out toward the hallway. "Quiet tonight," she said. Mixed anger and hurt showed in her eyes, a blend Krispos had seen there before. "Why shouldn't it be quiet? Anthimos has been out carousing since a little past noon, and the good god alone knows when he'll decide to honor us by coming back. So a great many folk, I have no doubt, have gone off to pursue their own pleasures."

The Empress' laugh was full of self-mockery. "And with you in this state, Krispos, I can't even do that, can I? I find I've missed you, more than I thought I would. Don't you wish we could . . ." Dara's voice sank to a throaty whisper as she described what she wished they could do. Either her imagination was very fertile, or she'd been thinking for a long time.

Krispos felt heat rise in him that had nothing to do with the weather. Something else also rose; those parts of him not under full conscious control had always been less subject to Petronas' magic than the rest.

Dara saw what her words had done. After another quick glance to the door, she reached out and stroked him through the bedclothes. "What a shame to waste it," she said. She stood up, hurried out of the room.

When she came back, she blew out the lamps. She went outside again, looked in, and nodded. "Dark enough," Krispos heard her say. She walked over to the bed and drew back the covers. "The door to my bedchamber is closed," she murmured to Krispos. "Anyone will think I'm there. And no one can see in here from the hallway. So, if we're quiet . . ."

She slipped off her drawers. She did not get out of her gown, but hiked it up so she could lower herself onto Krispos. She moved slowly, to keep the bed from creaking. Even so, he knew he would explode too soon to please her. Nothing he could do about that, though, he thought through building ecstasy.

Suddenly Dara froze, stifling a gasp that had nothing to do with passion. Krispos heard sandals in the hallway. Tyrovitzes walked past the door. Dara started to slide away, but the movement made the bed frame start to groan. She froze again. Krispos could not move at all, but felt himself shrinking inside her as fear overpowered lust.

The eunuch did not even glance in, but kept walking. Dara and Krispos stayed motionless until he came back, crunching on an apple. Once more, he paid no attention to the dark doorway. The sound of his footsteps and his chewing faded.

When everything was quiet again, Dara did get off the bed. She covered Krispos once more. Linen rustled against her skin as she slid her drawers up her legs. "I'm sorry," she whispered. "That was a bad idea." She slipped away. This time, she did not return.

Too late, Krispos was aroused again, with nothing whatever he could do about it. A bad idea indeed, he thought, more than a little annoyed. It had left everyone unsatisfied.

SUMMER WORE ON. ONE MORNING, KRISPOS WOKE UP ON HIS stomach. For a moment, he thought nothing of it. Then he realized he had rolled over in his sleep. He tried to roll back again and succeeded after an effort that left him panting.

Not long after that, his speech returned, first as a hoarse whisper, then, little by little, tones that sounded more as he remembered he should. As control slowly returned to his arms and legs, he sat up in bed and then, wobbly as any toddler, stood on his own two feet.

That made Anthimos notice him again. "Splendid," the Avtokrator said. "Good to see you on the mend. I look forward to having you serve me again."

"I look forward to it, too, Your Majesty," Krispos said, and found himself meaning it. After months of forced inactivity, he would have looked forward to a long, hot stint in the fields. *No,* he thought; *maybe to a* short *stint.* He did look forward to returning to the imperial bedchamber, both when Anthimos was occupying it and even more when he wasn't.

He found himself weak and clumsy as a pup. He began to exercise. At first, the least labor was plenty to wear him out. His strength slowly returned. A few weeks before the fall rains came, he went back to work. He bought handsome presents for the chamberlains who had cared for him so well and so long.

"This was not necessary," Barsymes said as he unwrapped a heavy gold chain. "The relief of having you on duty once more and no longer needing to try to keep up with his Majesty at those feasts of his . . ." The eunuch shook his head. But his long face, usually sour, wore a small, grudging smile. Krispos decided he had spent his money wisely.

He soon reconnected himself to the tendrils of the grapevine. He hardly needed to, for the first piece of news that came in was on everyone's lips: not only had Harvas Black-Robe's Halogai smashed the Kubratoi again, they had seized Pliskavos, the capital and the only real city Kubrat boasted. "By sorcery, I hear they took it," Longinos said, lowering his voice at the word and sketching the sun-sign over his heart.

The bare mention of magic was enough to make Krispos shudder. All the same, he shook his head. "Sorcery doesn't work well in battle," he said. "Everyone is too keyed up for it to stick, or so I've been told."

"And I," Longinos agreed. "But I also know that my sources in the north do not lie."

The palace eunuchs heard everything, and usually knew truth from rumor. Krispos scratched his head and worried a little. He sent a note to Iakovitzes. If anyone really knew what was happening north of the Paristrian mountains, the little noble was the man.

The next day, one of Iakovitzes' retainers brought an answering note: "Everything's gone to the ice up there. Harvas is a worse murderer than any of the khagans ever dreamed of being. Maybe he is a wizard, too. I can't think of any other way for him to have won so quickly and easily."

Krispos worried a little more, but only for a couple of days. Then he found something more important to worry about. A messenger sailed into Videssos the city from the westlands with word that Petronas was on his way home.

That news dismayed Anthimos, too. "He'll be impossible," the Emperor said, pacing back and forth the next morning while Krispos tried to dress him. "Impossible, I tell you. He's fought Makuran all summer long and he hasn't gained two towns worth having. He'll be humiliated and he'll take it out on me."

On you? Krispos thought. But he held his tongue. Since he recovered enough to talk, he'd told no one the Sevastokrator was to blame for his collapse. He had no proof save Mavros' word, and Mavros was with Petronas in the west. But he exercised harder than ever and began working with his sword again.

Petronas' imminent return made Anthimos start an incessant round of revels, as if he feared he would never get another chance once his uncle was back. Krispos' lingering weakness gave him the perfect excuse not to accompany his master to his carousings. As he'd hoped, the silver bell in his chamber sometimes rang even when the Avtokrator was away from the imperial residence.

After that dangerous fiasco while he'd been recovering, Dara took fewer chances. Her summonses most often came well after midnight, when the rest of the household could be counted on to be asleep. Sometimes, though, she called him openly in the early evening, just for the sake of talk. He did not mind; on the contrary. He'd learned from Tanilis that talk was intercourse, too.

"What do you think it will be like, having Petronas back again?" Dara said on one of those early visits, a few days before the Sevastokrator was due.

"Perhaps I'm not the one to ask," Krispos answered cautiously. "You know he and I didn't agree about his campaign. I will say that the Empire doesn't seem to have fallen apart while he was gone." That was as far as he was willing to go. He did not know how the Empress felt about Petronas.

He found out. "I wish the Makurani had slain him," she said. "He's done everything he could to keep Anthimos first a boy and then a voluptuary, so he can go on holding all the power in the Empire in his own fists."

Since that was inarguably true, and since Petronas had got Krispos the post of vestiarios the better to control the Emperor, he kept quiet.

Sighing, Dara went on, "I hoped that with Petronas away from the city, Anthimos might come into his own and act as an Avtokrator should. But he hasn't, has he?" She sadly shook her head. "I suppose I shouldn't have expected it. By now he is as his uncle made him." ·

"He's afraid of the Sevastokrator, too," Krispos said. "That's one of the reasons he let Petronas go fight in the westlands, for fear he'd have used his army here in the city if he were thwarted."

"I knew that," Dara said. "I didn't know anyone else did. I think he was right to be afraid. If Petronas seized the throne, what would become of Anthimos, or me—or you, come to that?"

"Nothing good," Krispos answered. Dara was not made for convent life—the best she could hope for—and Anthimos even less for the monastery. Krispos knew he himself would not be lucky enough to have a monastic cell saved for him. He continued, "But Anthimos has the power to override anything the Sevastokrator does, if only he can find the will to use it."

"If only." A world of cynical doubt lay behind Dara's words.

"But he almost did, this past spring," Krispos said, not thinking until later how odd it was for him to be defending his lover's husband to her. "Then Petronas came up with using Harvas' brigands against Kubrat, and that gave Anthimos an excuse for backing down, so he did. But I don't think he would have, otherwise."

"What do you think would have happened then?"

"Ask the lord with the great and good mind, not me. Anthimos is Avtokrator, aye, but Petronas had brought all those troops into the city. They might have obeyed Anthimos and, then again, they might not. The only soldiers I'm sure are loyal to him are the Halogai in the guards regiment, and they wouldn't have been enough by themselves. Maybe it's just as well he changed his mind."

"Yielding once makes yielding the next time easier." Dara turned her head to make an automatic scan of the doorway. Mischief sparked in her eyes; her voice dropped. "As I should know, and you, as well."

Krispos was glad enough to change the subject. Smiling with her, he said, "Aye, Your Majesty, and I'm glad that's so." But he knew that was not what Dara had meant at first, and knew she'd been right.

He wondered what Anthimos would require to stiffen his back so he would not yield to Petronas in a pinch. The threat of something worse happening if he yielded than if he didn't, Krispos supposed, or else a feeling that he could get away with defying his uncle. Unfortunately, Krispos had no idea where Anthimos could come up with either of those.

If PETRONAS WAS NOT RETURNING FROM MAKURAN IN TRIUMPH, he did his best to make sure the people of Videssos did not know it. He paraded two regiments of tough-looking troops from the Silver Gate up Middle Street to the palace quarter, with carts carrying booty and a few dejected Makuraner prisoners stumbling along in chains between mounted companies of his men. He himself headed to procession on his splendid but otherwise useless show horse.

As the soldiers tramped through the city, a herald cried out, "Glory to his illustrious Highness the Sevastokrator Petronas, the pale death of the Makurani! Phos' sun shines through him, the conqueror of Artaz and Hanzith, of Fis and Bardaa and Thelaw!"

"Glory!" shouted the soldiers. By the way they yelled and the herald proclaimed the names of the places Petronas had captured, anyone who did not know better would have taken them for great cities rather than Vaspurakaner hamlets that, all added together, might have produced a town not much smaller than, say, Imbros or Opsikion.

And, while Phos' sun may have shone through Petronas, it could not penetrate the thick gray clouds that overhung Videssos the city. Rain drenched the Sevastokrator's parade. Some Videssians stood under umbrellas and awnings and colonnades to cheer Petronas' troopers. More stayed indoors.

Krispos wore a wide-brimmed hat of woven straw to keep off the worst of the rain as he watched Petronas dismiss his soldiers to their barracks once they had traversed the plaza of Palamas and gotten out of the public eye. Then the Sevastokrator, cold water dripping from his beard, booted his horse into a slow trot—the only kind the animal possessed—and rode for his lodging in the building that housed the Grand Courtroom.

Anthimos received Petronas the next day. At Krispos' suggestion, he did so in the Grand Courtroom. Seated on the throne, decked in the full gorgeous imperial regalia, with chamberlains and courtiers and Haloga guardsmen formed up on all sides, the Avtokrator stared, still-faced, as Petronas walked up the long aisle toward him.

As custom required, Petronas halted about ten feet from the base of the throne. He went to his knees and then to his belly in full proskynesis before his nephew. As he started to go down, he spied Krispos, who was standing to the Emperor's right. His eyes widened, very slightly. Krispos' lips curved open in a show of teeth that was not a smile.

Petronas kept control of his voice. "Majesty," he said, face to the marble floor.

"Arise," Anthimos answered, a beat later than he might have: a subtle hint that Petronas did not enjoy his full favor, but one no courtier would fail to notice.

Petronas could not have failed to notice either, but gave no sign as he got to his feet. Nor did he give any sign that he had failed to accomplish all he'd hoped in the west. "Your Majesty, a promising start has been achieved against the vain followers of the Four Prophets," he declared. "When weather permits us to resume the campaign next spring, even grander triumphs will surely follow."

Standing close by Anthimos, Krispos stiffened. He had not thought the Sevastokrator would so boldly try to brazen out his failure and go on as if nothing had happened. The whispers that ran through the Grand Courtroom, soft as summer breeze through leaves, said the same. But while Anthimos sat on the imperial throne, Petronas had in truth controlled the Empire for well over a decade. How would the Avtokrator respond now?

Not even Krispos knew. The ancient formality of the court kept his head still, but his eyes slid toward Anthimos. Again the Emperor hesitated, this time, Krispos was sure, not to make a point but because he was uncertain what to say. At last he replied, "Next year's campaigning season is still a long way away. Between now and then, we shall decide the proper course to take."

Petronas bowed. "As Your Majesty wishes, of course." Krispos felt like cheering. For all his encouragement, and for all that he knew Dara had given, even getting Anthimos to temporize was a victory.

The rest of the court sensed that, too. Those soft whispers began again. Petronas withdrew from before the imperial throne, bowing every few paces until he had retreated far enough to turn and march away. But as he strode from the Grand Courtroom, he did not have the air of a defeated man.

KRISPOS SHOOK HIS HEAD. "PLEASE GIVE MY REGRETS TO HIS Imperial Highness, excellent Eroulos. I was ill almost all summer, and I fear I am too feeble to travel to the Sevastokrator's lodgings." That was the politest way he could find to say he did not trust Petronas enough to visit him.

"I will pass your words on to my master," Eroulos said gravely. Krispos wondered what part Petronas' steward had played in the sorcerous attempt on his life. He liked Eroulos, and thought Eroulos liked him. But Eroulos was Petronas' man, loyal to the Sevastokrator. Faction made friendship difficult.

Petronas did not deign to come to the imperial residence to visit Krispos. He was frequently there nonetheless, trying to talk his nephew round to letting him continue his war against Makuran. Whenever he saw Krispos, he stared through him as if he did not exist.

Despite all Krispos' urging, he could tell Anthimos was wavering. Anthimos was far more used to listening to Petronas than to Krispos . . . and Petronas commanded his armies. Glumly, Krispos braced himself for another defeat, and wondered if he would keep his post.

Then, much delayed on account of the vile winter weather, word reached Videssos the city from what had been the frontier with Kubrat. Bands of Harvas Black-Robe's Halogai had crossed the border in several places, looted villages on Videssian soil, massacred their inhabitants, and withdrawn.

Krispos made sure Anthimos read through the reports, which described the slaughter of the villagers in lurid detail. "This is dreadful!" the Emperor exclaimed, sounding more than a little sickened. He shoved the parchments aside.

"So it is, Your Majesty," Krispos said. "These northerners seem even more vicious than the Kubratoi."

"They certainly do." With a sort of horrid fascination, Anthimos picked up the reports and read them again. He shuddered and threw them down. "By the sound of things, they might have been doing Skotos' work."

Krispos nodded. "That's well put, Your Majesty. They do seem to be killing just for the sport of it, don't they? And remember, if you will, whose advice caused you to make those butchers the neighbors of the Empire. Also remember who wants you to go right on ignoring them so he can keep up his pointless war with Makuran."

"We'll have to find you a wife one day, Krispos," Anthimos said with a dry chuckle. "That was one of the smoothest 'I told you so's' I've ever heard." Krispos dutifully smiled, thinking it was not in the Avtokrator to stay serious about anything for long.

But Anthimos was serious. The next day, Petronas came to talk about the campaign he planned in the west. Anthimos wordlessly handed him the dispatches from the northern frontier. "Unfortunate, aye, but what of them?" Petronas said when he was done reading. "By the nature of things, we'll always have barbarians on that border, and barbarians, being barbarians, will probe at us from time to time."

"Exactly so," Anthimos said. "And when they probe, they should run up against soldiers, not find all of them away in the west. Uncle, I forbid you to attack Makuran until these new barbarians of yours learn we will respond to their raids and can keep them in check."

Out in the corridor, Krispos whistled a long, low, quiet note. That was stronger language than he'd ever expected Anthimos to use to Petronas. He plied his dust rag with new enthusiasm.

"You forbid me, Your Majesty?" Petronas' voice held a tone Krispos had heard there before, of grown man talking to beardless youth.

Usually Anthimos either did not catch it or paid it no mind. This time, it must have rankled. "Yes, by the good god, I forbid you, Uncle," he snapped back. "I am the Avtokrator, and I have spoken. Do you propose to disobey my express command?"

Krispos waited for Petronas to try to jolly him round, as he had so often. But the Sevastokrator only said, "I will always obey you, Majesty, for as long as you are Emperor." The feet of his chair scraped on polished marble as he rose. "Now if you will excuse me, I have other business to attend to."

Petronas walked past Krispos as if he were not there; had he stood in the middle of the corridor, he suspected the Sevastokrator would have walked over him rather than swerve aside. A couple of minutes later, Anthimos came out of the room where he'd met with Petronas. In a most unimperial gesture, he wiped his forehead with his sleeve.

"Whew!" he said. "Standing up to my uncle is bloody hard work, but by Phos, I did it! He said he'd obey." He sounded proud of himself. Krispos did not blame him.

Being who he was, Anthimos celebrated what he saw as his triumph over Petronas with a jar of wine, and then with another one. Thus fortified, he headed off for an evening of revels, dragging Krispos along.

Krispos did not want to revel. The more he listened to Petronas' words in his mind, the less they seemed a promise to obey. He had no trouble escaping the carouse; for one of the rare times since Krispos had known him, Anthimos drank himself insensible. Krispos ducked out of the feast and hurried back to the imperial residence.

Seeing a light under the closed door of the bedchamber the Emperor and Empress used, he softly tapped at the door. Dara opened it a moment later. She smiled. "You grow bold," she said. "Good." She pressed herself against him and tilted her face up for a kiss.

He gladly gave it, but then stepped away from her. "Tell me what you think of this," he said, and repeated Anthimos' conversation with Petronas as exactly as he could.

By the time he was done, Dara's expression had gone from lickerish to worried. "He'll obey as long as Anthimos is Emperor, he said? What happens if Anthimos isn't Emperor anymore?"

"That's just what I thought," Krispos said. "I wanted to be sure I wasn't imagining things. If Petronas wants to overthrow the Avtokrator, it shouldn't be hard for him. Most of the soldiers and almost all the high officers look to him, not to Anthimos. Till now, though, he hasn't wanted to."

"Why should he have bothered?" Dara said. "Anthimos was always pliant enough to suit him—till now, as you say. How are we going to stop him?" Her worry was fast becoming fear.

"We have to convince Anthimos that his uncle hasn't meekly backed down," Krispos said. "We ought to be able to manage that, the more so since I'm sure it's true. And if we do—" He paused, thinking hard. "How does this sound . . . ?"

Frowning, Dara listened to what he proposed. At one point, she raised a hand to stop him. "Not Gnatios," she said.

"No, by the good god, and I'm twice an idiot now for thinking of him," Krispos exclaimed, mentally kicking himself. Dara looked a question at him, but he did not explain. Instead, he went on, "I keep forgetting that even holy men have politics. The abbot Pyrrhos would serve as well, then, and he'd leap at the chance." He finished setting forth his scheme.

"Maybe," Dara said. "Maybe. And maybe, right now, looks better than any other chance we have. Let's try it."

"How may I serve you, your majesty?" Petronas asked offhandedly. His indifference, Krispos thought, was enough by itself to damn him and confirm all suspicions. If the Sevastokrator no longer cared what Anthimos did, that could only be because he was preparing to dispense with him.

"Uncle, I think I may have been hasty the other day," Anthimos said. Dara had suggested that he sound nervous; he was having no trouble following the suggestion.

"You certainly were," Petronas rumbled. No, no sign of give there, Krispos thought. The Sevastokrator went on, "That's what you get for heeding the rascal who keeps pretending to dust outside there." Krispos felt his ears blaze. So he hadn't gone unnoticed, then. Even so, he did not stop listening.

"Er, yes," Anthimos said—nervously. "Well, I hope I can make amends."

"It's rather late for that," Petronas said. Krispos shivered. He only hoped he and Dara were not too late to save Anthimos' crown.

"I know I have a lot to make amends for," the Emperor said. "Not just for ordering you to stand down the other day, but for all you've done for me and for the Empire as regent when my father died and also since I've come of age. I want to reward you as you deserve, so, if it please you, I'd like to proclaim you co-Avtokrator before the whole court three days from now. Having done so much of the work for so long, you deserve your full share of the title."

Petronas stayed quiet so long that Krispos felt his hands curl into tight fists, then his nails biting into his palms. The Sevastokrator could seize the full imperial power for himself—would he be content with the offer of part of it, legally given? He asked, "If I am to rule alongside you, Anthimos, does that mean you'll no longer try to meddle in the army and its business?"

"Uncle, you know more of such things than I do," Anthimos said.

"You'd best believe I do," Petronas growled. "High time you remembered it, too. Now the question is, do you mean all you say? I know how to find out, by the lord with the great and good mind. I'll say yes to you, lad—if you cast that treacherous scoundrel of a Krispos from the palaces."

"The moment I set the crown on your head, Uncle, Krispos will be cast not only from the palaces but from the city," Anthimos promised. Krispos and Dara had planned to have the Emperor tell Petronas just that. The risk remained that Anthimos would do exactly as he'd promised. If he feared Petronas more than he trusted his wife, his chamberlain, and his own abilities, he might pay the price for what he reckoned security.

"Hate to wait that long," Petronas said; then, at last, "Oh, very well, nephew, keep him another three days if it makes you happy. We have ourselves a bargain." The Sevastokrator got to his feet and triumphantly strode out of the chamber in which he had talked with Anthimos. Seeing Krispos outside, he spoke to him for the first time since he'd returned from the west: "Three days, wretch. Start packing."

His head lowered, Krispos dusted the gilded frame of an icon of Phos.

He did not reply. Petronas laughed at his dismay and strutted past him down the corridor.

Fine snow fell outside the grand courtroom as the grandees and high ministers of the Empire gathered to see Petronas exalted. Inside, heat ducts that ran under the floor from a roaring furnace kept the throne room warm.

When all the officials and nobles were in their places, Krispos nodded to the captain of Anthimos' Haloga bodyguards. The captain nodded to his men. Axes held at present-arms before them, they slow-marched out in double row to form an aisle down the center of the hall, through which the Avtokrator and his party would advance. Their gilded chain mail glittered in the torchlight.

Once that aisle was made, Anthimos, Dara, Pyrrhos, and Krispos walked along it toward the throne—no, thrones now, Krispos saw, for a second high seat had been placed beside the first; if there were to be co-Avtokrators, each required his own place of honor. A crown lay on that second seat.

Silks rustled as courtiers prostrated themselves when Anthimos passed them. As they rose, the nobles whispered among themselves. "Where's Gnatios?" Krispos heard one say to the fellow beside him. "Ought to have the patriarch here to crown a new Emperor."

"He's down with the flux, poor chap," the other grandee answered. "Pyrrhos is a very holy man in his own right. The good god won't mind."

Everyone at the patriarchal mansion was down with the flux, Krispos thought. Considering the number of goldpieces he'd spent to make sure a particular potion got into the mansion's kitchen, he was not surprised. Poor Gnatios and his clerical colleagues would be dashing to the outhouse for the next several days.

Anthimos climbed the three steps to the thrones and seated himself in the one that had always been his. Dara stood at his right hand on the highest step, Pyrrhos in the center of the lowest step. Krispos was also to the Emperor's right, but off the steps altogether. He had helped plan the spectacle that was to come, but it was Anthimos' to play out.

The Avtokrator sat unmoving, staring without expression back toward the entrance to the Grand Courtroom. Beside and in front of him, Dara and Pyrrhos might also have been statues. Krispos wanted to fidget. With an effort, he controlled himself.

Petronas came into the Grand Courtroom. His robe, of scarlet silk en-

crusted with gold and gems, was identical to Anthimos'. Only his bare
head declared that he was not yet Avtokrator. Marching with military pre-
cision, he approached the thrones. A tiny frown crossed his face when he
saw Krispos, but then his eyes went back to the crown waiting for him on
the throne that was to be his. He looked at Krispos again and smiled, unpleasantly.

Then, for the last time, he performed the proskynesis before his
nephew. He rose and bowed to Anthimos as to an equal. "Majesty," he
said. His voice was strong and proud.

"Majesty," Anthimos echoed. Some of the courtiers started whispering
again, thinking that the formal recognition of Petronas' elevation. But Anthimos went on in a musing tone, "Majesty is the word we use to denote
the sovereign of the state, the power that is his, a signpost of the imperial
office, if you will, rather like the red boots only the Avtokrator is privi-
leged to wear."

Petronas gravely nodded. Krispos watched him go from attention to at
ease. If Anthimos was going to make a speech before he got around to the
coronation, Petronas would endure it in dignified comfort.

And Anthimos was going to make a speech. He continued, "The Empire, of course, is indivisible. Ought not its sovereignty and the acknowledgment of that sovereignty to be the same? Many would say no, for
Videssos has known co-Avtokrators before; the creation of another would
be no innovation on the ancient customs of our state."

Petronas nodded once more, this time, Krispos thought, with a trace of
smugness. Anthimos was still speaking. "And yet, those former Avtokrators surely each had reasons they reckoned pressing when they invested
their colleagues with a share of the imperial dignity: perhaps to give a son
or other chosen successor a taste of responsibility before the passing of the
senior partner.

"My uncle Petronas, who stands before me now, is, as you all know, already familiar with the power inherent in the throne," Anthimos said.
Petronas nodded yet again. His nephew went on, "Indeed, for many years
the administration of the state and of its armies was entrusted to him. At
first this was because of my youth, later not least on account of his own
desire to continue what he had begun."

Petronas stood patiently, waiting for Anthimos to come to the point.
Now Anthimos did: "In his control of the armies, my uncle has fought
against our ancient foe Makuran. Having failed to win any victories to
speak of in his first year, he seeks a second year of campaigning; and this
at a time when other barbarians, brought near our northern frontier at his
urging, now threaten us."

The smile suddenly faded from Petronas' face. Anthimos took no notice, continuing, "When I urged him to consider this, he held it to be of scant import, and as much as told me he would use his influence over our soldiery to topple me from my throne if I failed to do as he wished." Anthimos raised his voice, called to the Halogai in the Grand Courtroom, "Soldiers of Videssos, who is your Avtokrator, Anthimos or Petronas?"

"Anthimos!" the northerners cried, so loud that echoes rang from the walls and high ceilings. "Anthimos!"

The Emperor rose from his throne. "Then seize this traitor here, who sought to terrify me into granting him a share of the imperial power to which he has no right!"

"Why, you—" Petronas sprang toward his nephew. Dara screamed, throwing herself in front of Anthimos. Before Petronas could reach the steps that led up to the throne, though, Krispos grappled with him, holding him in place until three Halogai, axes upraised, came clattering from their posts nearest the imperial seat.

"Yield or die!" one shouted to Petronas, who was still struggling against Krispos' greater strength. All the rest of the imperial guards also held their axes above their heads, ready to loose massacre in the Grand Courtroom if any of Petronas' backers among the Empire's assembled nobles and commanders sought to rescue the Sevastokrator. No one did.

Krispos thought Petronas' fury so great he would die before he gave up. But the Sevastokrator was a veteran soldier, long used to calculating the odds of success in battle. Although hatred burned in his eyes, he checked himself, stepped back from Krispos, and bent his head to the big blond axemen. "I yield," he choked out.

"You'd better, Uncle," Anthimos said, sitting once more. "By the good god, I'd sooner see Krispos here on the throne than you." From her place just below him, Dara nodded vigorously. He went on, "And since you have yielded, you must be placed in circumstances where you can no longer threaten us. Will you now willingly surrender up your hair and join the brotherhood of monks at a monastery of our choosing, there to spend the rest of your days in contemplation of the lord with the great and good mind?"

"Willingly?" By now Petronas had enough aplomb back to raise an ironic eyebrow. "Aye, considering the alternative, I'll abandon my hair willingly enough. Better to have my hair trimmed than my neck."

"Pyrrhos?" Anthimos said.

"With pleasure, Your Majesty." The abbot stepped down onto the floor of the Grand Courtroom. In the pouch on his belt he carried scissors and a glitteringly sharp razor. He bowed to Petronas and held up a copy of

Phos' scriptures. Formality kept from his voice any gloating he might have felt as he said, "Petronas, behold the law under which you shall live if you choose. If in your heart you feel you can observe it, enter the monastic life; if not, speak now."

Petronas took no offense at being addressed so simply—if he was to become a monk, the titles he had enjoyed were no longer his. He did permit himself one meaningful glance at the axemen around him, then replied, "I shall observe it."

"Shall you truly?"

"I shall truly."

"Truly?"

"Truly."

After Petronas affirmed his pledge for the third time, Pyrrhos bowed again and said, "Then lower your proud head, Petronas, and yield your hair in token of submission to Phos, the lord with the great and good mind." Petronas obeyed. Graying hair fell to the marble floor as the abbot plied his scissors. When he had it cropped short, he switched to the razor.

The crown Petronas had expected to wear lay on a large cushion of scarlet satin. After Pyrrhos was done shaving Petronas' head, he climbed the steps to that second throne and lifted the cushion. Beneath it, folded flat, was a robe of coarse blue wool. The abbot took it and returned to Petronas.

"The garment you now wear does not suit the station in life you will have henceforth," he said. "Strip it off, and those red boots as well, that you may don the robe of monastic purity."

Again Petronas did as he was told, unhooking the fastenings that held the imperial raiment closed. With a fine shrug of indifference, he let the magnificent robe fall to the floor, then yanked off the imperial boots. His undertunic and drawers were of smooth, glistening silk. He stood easily, waiting for Pyrrhos to proceed. Defeated or not, Krispos thought, he had style.

Pyrrhos frowned to see Petronas' rich undergarments. "Those will also be taken from you when we reach the monastery," he said. "They are far too fine for the simple life the brethren live."

"You may take them now, for all I care," Petronas said, shrugging again.

Krispos was sure he'd hoped to embarrass Pyrrhos. He succeeded, too; the abbot went red to the top of his shaven pate. Recovering, he answered, "As I said, that may wait until you join your fellow monks." He held out the blue robe to Petronas. "Put this on, if you please." While Petronas slipped on the monastic robe, Pyrrhos intoned, "As the garment of Phos' blue covers your body, so may his righteousness enfold your heart and preserve it from all evil."

"So may it be," Petronas said. He traced the circular sun-sign over his heart. So did everyone in the Grand Courtroom, save only the heathen Halogai. Krispos did not feel hypocritical as he silently prayed that the man who till moments before had been Sevastokrator would make a good monk. Like all his countrymen, he took his faith seriously—and better for Petronas, he thought, to end up in a monastic cell than to spill his blood on the polished marble in front of the throne.

"It is accomplished, Brother Petronas," Pyrrhos said. "Come with me now to the monastery of the holy Sirikios, that you may make the acquaintance of your comrades in Phos' service." He began to lead the new monk out of the Grand Courtroom.

"Holy sir, a moment, if you please," Anthimos said from his throne. Pyrrhos looked back at the Avtokrator with obedience but no great liking: he had worked with Anthimos to bring down Petronas, but felt even more scorn for the younger man's way of life than for the elder's. Nonetheless he waited as Anthimos went on, "You might be well advised to have Vagn, Hjalborn, and Narvikka there accompany you to the monastery, lest Brother Petronas, ah, suddenly repent of his decision to serve the good god."

Dara had been proudly watching Anthimos since the drama in the throne room began, as if she had trouble believing he could face down his uncle and was overjoyed to be proven wrong. Now, hearing her husband speak such plain good sense, the Empress brought her hands together in a small, involuntary clap of delight. Krispos wished she would look at him that way.

He fought down a stab of jealousy. Anthimos, this time, was right. That made jealousy unimportant. When Pyrrhos hesitated, Krispos put in, "Were things different, Petronas himself would tell you that was a good idea, holy sir."

"You've learned well, and may the ice take you," Petronas said. Then, surprisingly, he laughed. "I probably would, at that."

Pyrrhos nodded. "Very well. Such untimely repentance would be a great sin, and sin we must always struggle against. Let it be as you say, Your Majesty." Along with his new monk and the three broad, burly Haloga warriors, the abbot withdrew from the imperial presence.

"Anthimos, thou conquerest!" one of the courtiers shouted—the ancient Videssian cry of approval for an Avtokrator. In an instant, the Grand Courtroom was full of uproar, with everyone trying to outyell his neighbor to show his loyalty to the newly independent ruler: "Anthimos!" "Thou conquerest, Anthimos!" "Thou conquerest!" "Anthimos!"

Beaming, the Emperor drank in the praise. Krispos knew much of it was insincere, made by men still loyal to Petronas but too wise in the ways of survival at the imperial court to show it. He made a mental note to ask Anthimos to post Halogai around the monastery of the holy Sirikios to supplement Pyrrhos' club-wielding monks. But that could wait; for the moment, like Anthimos, Krispos was content to enjoy the triumph he'd helped create.

At last the Avtokrator raised a hand. Anthimos said, "As the first decree of this new phase of my reign, I command all of you here to go forth and live joyfully for the rest of your lives!"

Laughter and cheers rang through the Grand Courtroom. Krispos joined them. All the same, he was thinking Anthimos would need a more serious program than that if he intended to rule as well as reign. Krispos smiled a little. That program would have to come from someone. Why not him?

Chapter XII

"WHAT IS YOUR WILL, YOUR MAJESTY?" KRISPOS ASKED. "SHALL we continue your uncle's war against Makuran on the smaller scale we'll have to use because we've shifted men back to the north, or shall we make peace and withdraw from the few towns Petronas took?"

"Don't bother me right now, Krispos." Anthimos had his nose in a scroll. Had the scroll been too far away for Krispos to read, he would have been impressed with the Emperor's industry, for it was a listing of property that looked much like a tax document. But Krispos knew it listed the wines in Petronas' cellars, which had fallen to Anthimos along with the rest of his uncle's vast holdings.

Krispos persisted. "Your Majesty, spring is hard upon us." He gestured to the open window, which let in a mild, sweet-smelling breeze and showed brilliant sunshine outside. "If you don't want to meet the envoy the King of Kings has sent us, what shall I tell him?"

"Tell him to go to the ice," Anthimos snapped. "Tell him whatever you bloody well please. This catalogue says Petronas had five amphorae of golden Vaspurakaner wine, and my cellarers have only been able to find three. I wonder where he hid the other two." The Avtokrator brightened. "I know! I'll cast a spell of finding to sniff them out."

Krispos gave up. "Very well Your Majesty." He'd hoped to guide Anthimos. Like Petronas, he was discovering guiding was not enough most of
the time. If anything needed doing, he had to do it. And so, while the
Avtokrator busied himself with his spell of finding, Krispos bowed to
Chihor-Vshnasp, the Makuraner ambassador.

Chihor-Vshnasp bowed back, less deeply. That was not an insult. Like
most of his countrymen, Chihor-Vshnasp wore a bucket-shaped felt hat
that was liable to fall off if he bent too far. "I hope his Imperial Majesty re-
covers from his indisposition soon," he said in excellent Videssian.

"So do I," Krispos said, continuing the polite fiction he knew Chihor-
Vshnasp knew to be a polite fiction. "Meanwhile, maybe you and I can see
how close we get to settling things for his approval."

"Shall we try that, esteemed and eminent sir?" Chihor-Vshnasp's
knowledge of Videssian usages seemed flawless. Thoughtfully studying
Krispos, he went on, "Such was the custom of the former Sevastokrator
Petronas." It was as smooth a way as Krispos could imagine of asking him
whether he in effect filled Petronas' place.

"I think the Avtokrator will ratify whatever we do," he answered.

"So." Chihor-Vshnasp drew the first sound of the word out into a hiss.
"It is as I had been led to believe. Let us discuss these matters, then." He
looked Krispos full in the face. His large, dark eyes were limpid, innocent,
trusting as a child. They reminded Krispos of the eyes of Ibas, the horse
trader who doctored the teeth of the beasts he sold.

Chihor-Vshnasp dickered like a horse trader, too. That made life difficult for Krispos, who wanted to abandon Petronas' war on Makuran; because of what he'd known growing up on both sides of the northern
frontier and because of the unknown quantity Harvas Black-Robe's mercenaries represented, he thought the danger there more pressing than the
one in the west.

But Krispos also feared just walking away from Petronas' war. Some dis-
gruntled general would surely rise in rebellion if he tried. The high officers
in the Videssian army had all resworn their oaths to Anthimos after
Petronas fell, but if one rose, Krispos wondered whether the rest would resist him or join his revolt. He did not want to have to find out.

And so, remembering how Iakovitzes had gone round and round with
Lexo the Khatrisher, he sparred with Chihor-Vshnasp. At last they settled.
Videssos kept the small towns of Artaz and Hanzith, and the valley in
which they lay. Vaspurakaners from the regions round the other towns
Petronas had taken were to be allowed to move freely into Videssian terri-
tory, but Makuran would reoccupy those areas.

After Krispos swore by Phos and Chihor-Vshnasp by his people's Four Prophets to present to their sovereigns the terms on which they'd agreed, the Makuraner smiled a slightly triumphant smile and said, "Few from Fis and Thelaw and Bardaa will go over to you, you know. We saw that in the fighting last year—they loathe Videssos more for being heretic than Makuran for being heathen, and so did little to aid you."

"I know. I read the dispatches, too," Krispos said calmly.

Chihor-Vshnasp pursed his lips. "Interesting. You bargained long and hard for the sake of a concession you admit to be meaningless."

"It isn't meaningless," Krispos said, "not when I can present it to his Majesty and the court as a victory."

"So." Chihor-Vshnasp hissed again. "I have word, then, to take to his puissant Majesty Nakhorgan, King of Kings, pious, beneficent, to whom the God and his Prophets Four have granted many years and wide domains: that his brother in might Anthimos remains ably served by his advisors, even if the names change."

"You flatter me." Krispos tried not to show the pleasure he felt.

"Of course I do." Chihor-Vshnasp was in his mid-forties, not his late twenties. The look he gave Krispos was another act of flattery, for it seemed to imply that the two of them were equal in experience. Then he smiled. "That you notice says I have good reason to."

Krispos bowed in his chair toward the Makuraner envoy. He lifted his cup of wine. "Shall we drink to our success?"

Chihor-Vshnasp raised his cup, too. "By all means."

"BY THE GOOD GOD!" MAVROS EXCLAIMED, STARING WIDE-EYED at a troupe of young, comely acrobats who formed a pyramid with some most unconventional joinings. "I've never seen anything like *that* before!"

"His Majesty's revels are like no others," Krispos agreed. He'd invited his foster brother to the feast—Mavros was part of Anthimos' household these days. All of Petronas' men, all of Petronas' vast properties were forfeit to the Avtokrator when the Sevastokrator fell, just as Skombros' had been before. Anthimos had his own head groom, but Mavros' new post as that man's aide carried no small weight of responsbility.

And now, without warning, his eyes lit with a gleam Krispos had seen there before, but never so brightly. He turned and hurried off. "Where are you going?" Krispos called after him. He did not answer, but disappeared into the night. Krispos wondered if watching the acrobats had stirred him so much he had to go find some companionship. If that was what Mavros wanted, Krispos thought, he was foolish to leave. The women right here were more attractive than any he was likely to find elsewhere in the city—and Anthimos did not bid any likely to say no to come to his feasts. Krispos shrugged. He knew he didn't think things through all the time, however hard he tried. No reason Mavros should, either.

A man came out with a pandoura, struck a ringing chord, and began to sing a bawdy wedding song. Another fellow accompanied him with a set of pipes. The loud, cheerful music worked the same magic in the palace complex as in any peasant village throughout the Empire. It pulled people off couches and away from plates piled high with sea urchins and tuna, as-paragus and cakes. It made them want to dance. As at any village wedding throughout the Empire, they formed rings and capered round and round, drowning out the singer as they roared along with his song.

The Halogai might have shouted outside. If they did, no one ever heard them. The first Krispos knew of Mavros' return was when a woman facing the entrance screamed. Others, some men among them, screamed, too. Pan-doura and pipes played on for another few notes, then raggedly fell silent.

"Hello, Your Majesty," Mavros said, spotting Anthimos in one of the suddenly halted rings. "I thought it was a shame for your friend here to be missing all the fun." He clucked to the horse he was riding—one of An-thimos' favorites—and touched its flanks with his heels. Hooves clattering on the smooth stone floor, the horse advanced through the revelers toward the tables piled high with food.

"Don't just stand there, Krispos," Mavros called. "Feed this good fellow a strawberry or six."

Krispos felt like throwing something at Mavros for involving him in this mad jape. Reluctantly he stepped toward the tables. Refusing, he thought, would only look worse. He picked up the bowl of strawberries. Amid vast silence, the snuffling of the horse as it ate was the only sound.

Then Anthimos laughed. All at once, everyone else was laughing, too: whatever the Emperor thought funny could not be an outrage. "Why didn't you bring a mare in season?" Anthimos called. "Then he could share all the pleasures we do."

"Maybe next time, Your Majesty," Mavros said, his face perfectly straight.

"Yes, well, all right," Anthimos said. "Pity there's no entertainment that really could amuse him."

"Oh, I wouldn't say that, Your Majesty," Mavros answered blithely. "After all, he has us to watch—and if we aren't funny, what is?"

Anthimos laughed again. As far as he was concerned, Mavros' headlong style of wit was a great success. Thinking about it, though, Krispos wondered if his foster brother hadn't been telling the exact and literal truth.

The Emperor said, "One reward we can give him—if he's finished with those strawberries there, why don't you fill that bowl up with wine? Here, you can use this jar if you care to." Nodding, Mavros took the jar to which Anthimos had pointed. He brought it back to where the horse stood patiently waiting, upended over the bowl that still held a few mashed strawberries. The thick wine poured out, yellow as a Haloga's hair.

"Your Majesty!" Krispos exclaimed. "Is that jar from one of the missing amphorae from Petronas' cellars?"

"As a matter of fact, it is." Anthimos looked smug. "I was hoping you'd notice. The spell I employed worked rather well, wouldn't you say? It took my men right to the missing jars."

"Good for you." Krispos eyed the Avtokrator with more respect than he was used to giving him. Anthimos had stuck with his magic and worked to regain it with greater persistence than he devoted to anything else save the pleasures of the flesh. As far as Krispos could tell, he still botched conjurations every so often, but none—yet—in a way that had endangered him. If only he gave as much attention to the broader concerns of the Empire, Krispos thought. Whenever he wanted to be, he was plenty capable. Too often, he did not care to bother.

Krispos wondered how often he'd had that identical thought. Enough times, he was sure, that if he had a goldpiece for each one, the pen-pushers in the imperial treasury could lower the taxes on every farm in Videssos.

They wouldn't, of course; whenever new money came along, Anthimos always invented a new way to spend it. As now: the thought had hardly crossed Krispos' mind before the Avtokrator sidled up to him and said, "You know, I think I'm going to have a pool dug beside this hall, so I can stock it with minnows."

"Minnows, Your Majesty?" If Anthimos had conceived a passion for fishing, he'd done it without Krispos' noticing. "Trout would give you better sport, I'd think."

"Not that sort of minnows." Anthimos looked exasperated at Krispos' lack of imagination. He glanced toward a couple of the courtesans in the crowded room. "*That* sort of minnows. Don't you think they could be very amusing, nibbling around the way minnows do, in lovely cool water on a hot summer evening?"

"I suppose they might," Krispos said, "if you—and they—don't mind being mosquito food while you're sporting." Mosquitoes and gnats and biting insects of all sorts flourished in the humid heat of the city's summer.

The Emperor's face fell, but only for a moment. "I could hold the bugs at bay with magic."

"Your Majesty, if a bug-repelling spell were easy, everyone would use it instead of mosquito netting."

"Maybe I'll devise an easy one, then," Anthimos said.

Maybe he would, too, Krispos thought. Even if the Emperor no longer had a tutor, he was turning into a magician of sorts. Krispos had no interest whatever in becoming a wizard. He was, however, a solidly practical man. He said, "Even without sorcery, you could put a tent of mosquito netting over and around your pool."

"By the good god, so I could." Anthimos grinned and clapped Krispos on the back. He talked for the next half hour about the pool and the entertainments he envisioned there. Krispos listened, enthralled. Anthimos was a voluptuary's voluptuary; he took—and communicated—pleasure in talking about pleasure.

After a while, the thought of the pleasure he would enjoy later roused him to pursue some immediately. He beckoned to one of the tarts in the hall and took her over to an unoccupied portion of the pile of pillows. He'd hardly begun when he got a new idea. "Let's make a pyramid of our own," he called to the other couples and groups there. "Do you think we could?"

They tried. Shaking his head, Krispos watched. It wasn't nearly so fine as the acrobats' pyramid, but everybody in it seemed to be having a good time. That was Anthimos, through and through.

"MINNOWS," DARA HISSED.

Krispos had never heard the name of a small, nondescript fish used as a swear word before, and needed a moment to understand. Then he asked, "How did you hear about *that*?"

"Anthimos told me last night, of course," the Empress answered through clenched teeth. "He likes to tell me about his little schemes, and he was so excited over this one that he told me *all* about it." She glared at Krispos. "Why didn't you stop him?"

"Why didn't I what?" He stared at her. Anthimos was out carousing, but the hour was still early and the door from the imperial bedchamber to the hall wide open. Whatever got said had to be said in a tone of voice that would attract no notice from anyone walking down the corridor. Remembering that helped Krispos hold his temper. "How was I supposed to stop him? He's the Avtokrator; he can do what he likes. And don't you think he'd wonder why I tried to talk him out of it? What reason could I give him?"

"That that cursed pool—may Skotos' ice cover it all year around—is just another way, and a particularly vile one, for him to be unfaithful to me."

"How am I supposed to tell him that? If I sound like a priest, he's more likely to shave my head and put me in a blue robe than to listen to me. And besides . . ." He paused to make sure no one was outside to hear, then went on, "Besides, things being as they are, I'm hardly the one to tell him anything of the kind."

"But he listens to you," Dara said. "He listens to you more than to anyone else these days. If you can't get him to pay heed, no one can. I know it's not fair to ask you—"

"You don't begin to." Krispos had thought defending Anthimos to Dara was curious. Now she wanted him to get Anthimos to be more faithful to her so she would have less time and less desire to give to him because she would be giving more to her husband. He had not been trained in fancy logic at the Sorcerers' Collegium, but he knew a muddle when he stepped into one. He also knew that explaining it to her would be worse than a waste of time—it would make her furious.

Sighing, he tried another tack. "He listens to me when he feels like it. Even on the business of the Empire, that's not nearly all the time. When it comes to . . . things he really likes, he pays attention only to himself. You know that, Dara." He still spoke her name but seldom. When he did, it was a way to emphasize that what he said was important.

"Yes, I do know," she said in a low voice. "That's so even now that Petronas is locked up for good. All Anthimos cares about is doing just what he wants." Her eyes lifted and caught Krispos'. She had a way of doing that which made it next to impossible for him to tell her no. "At least try to get him to set his hand to the Empire. If he doesn't, who will?"

"I've tried before, but if you'll remember, I was the one who ended up hashing things out with Chihor-Vshnasp."

"Try again," Dara said, those eyes meltingly soft. "For me."

"All right, I'll try," Krispos said with no great optimism. Again he thought how strange it was for Dara to use her lover to improve her husband. He wondered just what that meant—probably that Anthimos was more important to her than he was. Whatever his flaws, the Avtokrator was handsome and affable—and without him, Dara would be only a westlands noble's daughter, not the Empress of Videssos. Having gained so much status through his connections to others, Krispos understood how she could fear losing hers if the person from whom it derived was cast down.

She smiled at him, differently from a moment before. "Thank you, Krispos. That will be all for now, I think." Now she spoke as Empress to vestiarios. He rose, bowed, and left her chamber, angry at her for changing moods so abruptly but unable to show it.

Having nothing better to do, he went to bed. Some time in the middle of the night, the small silver bell in his bedchamber rang. He wondered whether Anthimos was summoning him, or Dara. Either way, he thought grouchily as he dressed and tried to rub the sleep from his eyes, he would have to please and obey.

It was Dara; the Emperor was still out roistering. Even the comfort of her body, though, could not completely make up for the way she'd treated him earlier. As he had with Tanilis, he wanted to be more than a bed-warmer for her. That she sometimes remembered him as a person only made it worse when she forgot. One day, he thought, he'd have to talk with her about that—if only he could figure out how.

K RISPOS CARRIED THE LAST OF THE BREAKFAST DISHES TO THE kitchens on a tray, then went back to the dining room, where Anthimos was leaning back in his chair and working lazily on his first morning cup of wine. He'd learned the Avtokrator was more willing to conduct business now than at any other time of day. Whether "more willing" really meant "willing" varied from day to day. *I'll see,* Krispos thought.

"Your Majesty?" he said.

"Eh? What is it?" Anthimos sounded either peevish or a trifle the worse for wear. The latter, Krispos judged: the Emperor did not bounce back from his debauches quite as readily these days as he had when Krispos first became vestiarios. That was hardly surprising. Someone with a less resilient constitution might well have been dead by now if he abused himself as Anthimos did.

All that was beside the point—the Avtokrator in a bad mood was less likely to want to listen to anything that had to do with imperial administration. Nonetheless, Krispos had promised Dara he'd try—and if Anthimos was going to keep other people from becoming Emperor, he'd just have to handle the job himself. Krispos said, "Your Majesty, the grand logothete of the treasury has asked me to bring certain matters to your attention."

Sure enough, Anthimos' smile, lively enough a moment before, became fixed on his face. "I'm not really much interested right at the moment in what the grand logothete is worrying about."

"He thinks it important, Your Majesty. After listening to him, so do I," Krispos said.

Anthimos finished his cup of wine. His mobile features assumed a martyred expression. "Go on, then, if you must."

"Thank you, Your Majesty. The logothete's complaint is that nobles in some of the provinces more remote from Videssos the city are collecting taxes from the peasants on their lands but not turning the money over to the treasury. Some of the nobles are also buying up peasant holdings next to their lands, so that their estates grow and those of the free peasants who make up the backbone of the army suffer."

"That doesn't sound very good," the Emperor said. The trouble was, he didn't sound very interested.

"The grand logothete wants you to put out a law that would stop the nobles from getting away with it, with punishments harsh enough to make even the hardest thief think twice before he tries cheating the fisc. The logothete thinks it's urgent, Your Majesty, and it's costing you money you could be using to enjoy yourself. He's written a draft of the law, and he wants you to review it—"

"When I have the time," Anthimos said, which meant somewhere between *later* and *never*. He peered down into his empty cup, held it out to Krispos. "Fill this up again for me, will you? That's a good fellow."

Krispos filled the cup. "Your Majesty, the grand logothete gave me his draft. I have it here. I can show it to you—"

"When I have the time, I said."

"When will that be, Your Majesty? This afternoon? Tomorrow? Next month? Three years from now?" Krispos felt his temper slipping. He knew it was dangerous, but could not help it. Part of it was pent-up frustration over Anthimos' refusal to do anything that didn't gratify him right then and there. He'd been trying to change that ever since he became vestiarios. More irritation sprang from the anger he hadn't been able to let out at Dara the night before.

"You want to give me this stupid law your boring bureaucrat dreamed up?" Anthimos was angry, too, scowling at Krispos; not even Petronas had spoken to him like that. Breathing hard, he went on, "Bring it to me now, this instant. I'll show you what I think of it, by Phos."

In his relief, Krispos heard the Emperor's words without paying attention to the way he said them. "Thank you, Your Majesty. I'll fetch it right away." He hurried to his chamber and brought Anthimos the parchment. "Here you are, Your Majesty."

The Avtokrator unrolled the document and gave it one quick, disdainful glance. He ripped it in half, then in quarters, then in eighths. Then, with more methodical care than he ever gave to government, he tore each part into a multitude of tiny pieces and flung them about the room, until it looked as though a sudden interior blizzard had struck.

"*There's* what I think of this stupid law!" he shouted.

"Why, you—" Of itself, Krispos' fist clenched and drew back. Had Anthimos been any other man in all the Empire save who he was, that fist would have crashed into his nastily grinning face. A cold, clear sense of self-preservation made Krispos think twice. Very carefully, as if it belonged to someone else, he lowered his hand and made it open. Even more carefully, he said, "Your Majesty, that was foolish."

"And so? What are you going to do about it?" Before Krispos could answer, Anthimos went on, "I'll tell you what: quick now, get broom and dustpan and sweep up every one of these miserable little pieces and dump 'em in the privy. That's just where they belong."

Krispos stared at him. "Move, curse you," Anthimos said. "I command it." Even if he would not act like an Emperor, he sounded like one. Krispos had to obey. Hating himself and Anthimos both, he swept the floor clean. The Avtokrator stood over him, making sure he found every scrap of parchment. When he was finally satisfied, he said, "Now go get rid of them."

Normally Krispos took no notice of the privies' stench; stench and privies went together. This time, though, he was on business different from the usual, and the sharp reek bit into his nostrils. As the torn-up pieces of law fluttered downward to their end, he thought that Anthimos would have done the same thing to the whole Empire, were it small enough to take in his two hands and tear.

KRISPOS WAS STUBBORN. ALL THROUGH HIS LIFE, THAT HAD served him well. Now he brought his stubbornness to bear on Anthimos. Whenever laws were proposed or other matters came up that required a decision from the Emperor, he kept on presenting them to Anthimos, in the hope that he could wear him down and gradually accustom him to performing his duties.

But Anthimos proved just as mulish as he was. The Avtokrator quit paying day-to-day affairs even the smallest amount of attention he had once given them. He ripped no more edicts to shreds, but he did not sign them or affix the imperial seal to them, either.

Krispos took to saying, "Thank you, Your Majesty," at the end of each day's undone business.

Sarcasm rolled off Anthimos like water from a goose's feathers. "My pleasure," he'd answer day by day. The response made Krispos want to grind his teeth—it kept reminding him of all that Anthimos really cared about.

Yet Anthimos could work hard when he wanted to. That irked Krispos more than anything. He watched the Avtokrator patiently studying magic on his own because it interested him; he'd always known how much ingenuity Anthimos put into his revels. He could have been a capable Emperor. That, worse luck, did not interest him.

Krispos regretted trying to get him to handle routine matters when something came up that was not routine. Urgent dispatches from the northern frontier told of fresh raids of Harvas Black-Robe's Halogai. Though Anthimos had strengthened the border after forcing Petronas into the monastery, the raiding bands coming south were too large and too fierce for the frontier troops to handle.

Anthimos refused to commit more soldiers. "But Your Majesty," Krispos protested, "this is the border because of which you toppled your uncle when he would not protect it."

"That was part of the reason, aye." Anthimos gave Krispos a measuring stare. "Another part was that he wouldn't leave me alone. You seem to have forgotten that—you've grown almost as tiresome as he was."

The warning there was unmistakable. The troops did not go north. Krispos sent a message by imperial courier to the village where he'd grown up, urging his brother-in-law Domokos to bring Evdokia and their children down to Videssos the city.

A little more than a week later, a worn-looking courier brought his blowing horse up to the imperial residence and delivered Domokos' reply. " 'We'll stay here,' he told the rider who spoke with him, esteemed and eminent sir," the fellow said, consulting a scrap of parchment. " 'We're already too beholden to you,' he said, and, 'We don't care to depend on your charity when we can make a go of things where we are.' That's what he said, just as the other courier wrote it down."

"Thank you," Krispos said abstractedly, respecting his brother-in-law's pride and cursing him for being an obstinate fool at the same time. Meanwhile, the courier stood waiting. After a moment, Krispos realized why. He gave the man a goldpiece. The courier saluted in delight and hurried away.

Krispos decided that if he could not go through Anthimos to protect the farmers near the northern border, he would have to go around him. He spoke with Dara. She agreed. They asked to meet with Ouittios, one of the generals who had served under Petronas.

To their dismay, Ouittios refused to come. "He will not see you, except at the Avtokrator's express command," the general's adjutant reported. "If you will forgive his frankness, and me for relaying it, he fears being entrapped into what will later be called treason, as Petronas was."

Krispos scowled when he heard that, but had to admit it made sense from Ouittios' point of view. A couple of other attempted contacts proved similarly abortive. "This desperately needs doing, and I can't get it done," Krispos complained to Mavros after yet another high-ranking soldier refused to have anything to do with him.

"If you like, I think I can put you in touch with Agapetos," Mavros said. "He has lands around Opsikion. He used to know my father; my mother would speak of him from time to time. Do you want me to try?"

"Yes, by the good god, and quick as you can," Krispos said.

With Mavros as go-between, Agapetos agreed to come to the imperial residence and listen to Krispos and Dara. Even so, the general's hard, square face was full of suspicion as he eased himself down into a chair. Suspicion turned to surprise when he found out why he'd been summoned. "You want me to go up there and fight?" he said, scratching an old scar on his cheek. "I figured you were out to disband troops, not put them to proper use. So did everybody, after what happened with Petronas. Why this sneaking around behind his Majesty's back?"

"Because I put his back up, that's why. He just won't take care of things in the north, since I'm the one who argued too hard that he ought to," Krispos answered. "I'd sooner wait till he comes round on his own, but I don't think we have the time. Do you?"

"No," Agapetos answered at once. "I know we don't. I'm only surprised you do, too. After what befell the Sevastokrator, like I said before, if you'll excuse me for speaking out so plainly, I would've figured you to be out to weaken the army more, not give it useful work to do."

"Petronas did not fall because he was a soldier," Dara said. "He fell because he was a rebellious soldier, one who valued his own wishes above those of his overlord. Surely the same is not true of you, excellent sir?"

Agapetos' chuckle was more grim than amused. "If it were, Your Majesty, do you think I'd be dunce enough to admit it? All right, though, I take your point. But what happens to me when the Avtokrator finds out I've obeyed the two of you rather than him?"

"If you win, how can he blame you?" Krispos asked. "Even if he tries, we and your success will both shield you from him. And if you lose, you may well end up dead, in which case you'll worry about Phos' wrath, not Anthimos'."

"For all those fancy robes, you think like a soldier," Agapetos said. "All right, we'll try it your way. Anthimos said he wouldn't mind having you as Emperor, didn't he? I can see why. And I wouldn't mind having a go at the Halogai, truth to tell. Those axes the imperial guardsmen carry are fearsome enough, aye, but how would they fare against cavalry that knows something of discipline? It will be interesting to find out, yes it will."

Krispos could see him planning his new campaign, as if he were a carpenter picturing a new chair in his mind before he built it. "How many men will you take?" he asked.

"My whole army," Agapetos answered. "Say, seventy-five hundred troopers. That's plenty and then some to control raiding bands like the ones I expect we'll be seeing. The only time you need more is if you try to do something really enormous, the way Petronas did last year against Makuran. And look what that got him—no headway to speak of, and a blue robe and a cell at the end of it."

"His ambition earned him that, excellent Agapetos," Dara said. "I already asked you once if you had that kind of ambition, and you said no. You should be safe enough then, not so?"

The general said, "I expect you're right. Besides, from everything I've heard, this is something that needs taking care of, the sooner the better. If I set out inside the next ten days, will that suit you?"

Krispos and Dara looked at each other. Krispos had hoped for something more rousing, perhaps a cry of, *I'll ride for the frontier before the sun sets!* But he had seen enough since he came to the capital to understand that large organizations usually moved slower than small ones. "It will do," he said. Dara nodded.

"Well, with your leave, I'll be off, then," Agapetos said, rising from his chair. "I've a deal to make ready before we ride out." He dipped his head to Krispos, bowed deeply to Dara, and stamped away.

"I hope he'll serve," Krispos said when the general was gone. "From everything Harvas has done, he's a soldier who fights hard and moves fast. I just hope Agapetos understands that."

"The Halogai are foot soldiers," Dara said. "How can they move faster than our horsemen? More likely they'll flee at word of Agapetos' approach."

"You're probably right," Krispos said. He could not help thinking, though, that Harvas Black-Robe's Halogai had already beaten the Kubratoi, and the Kubratoi raised no mean cavalry, even if, as Agapetos had said, they lacked discipline.

He made himself shake off his worries. He'd done the best he could to protect the northern frontier. He'd certainly done more than Anthimos had. If Agapetos' army did not suffice, then Videssos would have a full-sized war on its hands. Not even Anthimos could ignore that—he hoped.

KRISPOS GOT MORE AND MORE USED TO WORKING AROUND Anthimos rather than through him. Petronas had managed for years. But Petronas had been Sevastokrator, of the imperial family and with prestige almost imperial—sometimes more imperial than Anthimos'. Because he was only vestiarios, Krispos had to work harder to convince people to see things his way.

Having Dara with him when he saw Agapetos had helped persuade the general to go along. Sometimes, though, Krispos needed to beard officials in their own lairs. Much as he wanted to, he could not bring the Empress along.

"You have my sincere apologies, esteemed and eminent sir, but without his Imperial Majesty's seal or signature I cannot implement this new law on codicils to bequests," declared a certain Iavdas, one of the aides to the logothete of the treasury.

Krispos stared. "But you're the one who asked for it. I have your memorandum here." He waved the parchment at Iavdas. "It's a good law, a fair law. It should go into effect."

"I quite agree, but for it to do so, seal or signature must be affixed. That, too, is the law, and I dare not disobey it."

"His Majesty isn't signing or sealing much these days," Krispos said slowly. The more he urged Anthimos to do, the less the Emperor did, a defense of principle that would have been admirable had the principle defended been more noble than Anthimos' right to absolute laziness. "I assure you, though, that I do have the authority to tell you to go ahead with this."

"Unfortunately, I must disagree." Like most treasury officials Krispos had met, Iavdas owned a relentlessly literal mind. He went on, "I must follow the letter of the law, not the spirit, for spirit, by its nature, is subject to diverse interpretations. Without formal imperial approval, I cannot proceed."

Krispos almost told him to go to the ice. He bit back his anger. How could he get Iavdas to do what even Iavdas admitted needed doing? "Suppose we don't call this a new law?" he said after some thought. "Suppose we just call it an amendment to a law that's already there. Would my say-so be enough then?"

Iavdas' eyes got a faraway look. "I suppose it would be technically accurate to term this a correction of an ambiguity in the existing law. It was not framed so, but it could be reworked to appear as a revised chapter of the present code on codicils. And for a mere revision, no, seal and signature are not required." He beamed at Krispos. "Thank you, esteemed and eminent sir. An ingenious solution to a complex problem, and one that evades not only the defects in current legislation but also those posed by the Avtokrator's obstinacy."

"Er—yes." Krispos beat a hasty retreat. Talking with high functionaries reminded him of the limits of his own education. He could read and write, add and subtract, but he still felt at sea when people larded their talk with big words for no better reason than to hear them roll off their lips. Why, he wondered, couldn't they say what they meant and have done? He did understand that Iavdas liked his plan. That would do.

But, as he complained to Dara when she called him to her bedchamber some time past midnight, "We shouldn't have to go through this rigmarole every time we need to get something done. I can't always come up with ways of getting around Anthimos, and because I can't, things don't happen. If only Anthimos would—" He broke off. Lying in Anthimos' bed with Anthimos' Empress, he did not want to talk about the Avtokrator. Sometimes, though, like tonight, he got too frustrated with Anthimos to stop himself.

Dara put the palm of her hand on his bare chest, felt his heartbeat slow toward normal after their coupling. Smiling, she said, "If he hadn't neglected me, we wouldn't have happened. Still, I know what you mean. Just as you did, I hoped he'd rule for himself once his uncle was gone. Now—

"Now he's so annoyed with me for trying to get him to rule that he won't even see to the little he did before." *You were the one who made me keep pushing at him, too,* he thought. He kept that to himself. Dara had been doing her best for her husband and the Empire. Had Anthimos responded, all would have been well.

"Never mind Anthimos now," Dara whispered, perhaps feeling some of the same awkwardness he had. She held him to her. "Do you think we can try again if we hurry?"

Krispos did his best to oblige. One did not say no, not to the Empress. Then he got out of bed and into his clothes. *Which turns me from lover back to vestiarios,* he thought with a touch of irritation. He slipped from the imperial bedchamber, shutting the doors behind him. He started to go back to his own room, then changed his mind and decided to have a snack first. He walked down the hall to the larder.

He was coming back, munching on a roll sticky with honey, when he saw a disembodied head floating toward him. His mouth dropped opened; a bit of roll fell out and landed on the floor with a wet smack. He needed a moment to gain enough control of himself to do anything more than stand, stare, and gurgle. In that moment of terror, before he could scream and flee, he recognized the head. It was Anthimos'.

The head recognized him, too. Winking, it spoke. Krispos frowned, tried to read its silent lips. "You'd eat better than that if you were with me," he thought it said.

"I s-suppose I would, Your Majesty," he got out. If Anthimos could work magic this potent while at a revel, he was turning into a very impressive sorcerer indeed, Krispos thought. Aloud, he added, "You almost scared me to death."

The Emperor's head grinned. As he looked at it, he realized it was not physically there; he could see through it. That made it a trifle easier to take—he did not have to imagine an acephalous Anthimos lying on a couch among his cronies. He tried to smile back.

Grinning still, the Avtokrator—or as much of him as was present—moved past Krispos. The head came to the door of the imperial bedchamber. Krispos expected it to drift through the wood. Had it come a few minutes earlier—he shivered. He knew what it would have seen.

But instead of sailing ghostlike through the closed doors, the Emperor's projected head fetched up against them with a bump that was immaterial but nonetheless seemed to hurt, judging by the expression the slightly misty face wore and the words it was mouthing.

Krispos fought to keep his own face straight; Anthimos might be turning into a powerful mage, but he was still a careless one. "Would you like me to open it for you, Your Majesty?" he asked politely.

"Piss off," Anthimos' head snarled. An instant later, it vanished.

Krispos leaned against the wall and let out a long, slow sigh. He suddenly realized his right hand was sticky—he'd squeezed that honeyed bun to pieces without even remembering he had it. He threw away what was left and went back to the larder for some water to wash his fingers. He did not take another bun. He'd lost his appetite.

ONE OF THE HALOGAI STANDING GUARD OUTSIDE THE IMPErial residence turned and spotted Krispos in the hallway. "Someone out here to see you," he called.

"Thanks, Narvikka. I'll be there in a minute." Krispos put away the

armful of newly washed robes he was carrying, then went out onto the
steps with the guardsmen. He blinked several times, trying to get his eyes
used to the bright afternoon sunshine outside.

He did not recognize the worn-looking man who sat waiting for him
on a worn-looking horse. "I'm Krispos," he said. "What can I do for you?"

The worn-looking man touched a finger to the brim of his straw traveler's hat. "My name's Bassos, esteemed and eminent sir. I'm an imperial
courier. I'm afraid I have bad news for you."

"Go ahead. Give it to me." Krispos held his voice steady, wondering
what had gone wrong now. His imagination painted plenty of possibilities: earthquake, pestilence, famine, rebellion, even invasion from Makuran in spite of the peace he thought he'd patched together.

But Bassos had meant bad news for *him,* not for the Empire. "Esteemed
and eminent sir, the gold you sent up to your sister and brother-in-law . . ."
The courier licked his lips, trying to figure out how to go on. At last he
did, baldly: "Well, sir, we couldn't deliver that gold, on account of there
wasn't much left of the village there after these new stinking barbarians
we're mixed up with went through it. I'm sorry, esteemed and eminent
sir."

Krispos heard himself say "Thank you" as if from very far away. Bassos
pressed a leather pouch into his hands and made him count the goldpieces
inside and sign a receipt. The Emperor's vestiarios was too prominent to
be cheated. The courier remounted and rode away. Krispos stood on the
steps looking after him. Evdokia, Domokos, two little girls he had never
seen . . . He never would see them now.

Narvikka walked over to him, setting a large hand on his shoulder.
"Their time came as it was fated to come, so grieve not for them," the
Haloga said. "If the gods willed it, they took foes with them to serve them
forever in the world to come. May it be so."

"May it be so," Krispos agreed. He had never had any use for the northerners' wild gods and fatalistic view of the world, but suddenly he very
much wanted his family to have servants in the afterlife, servants they had
slain with their own hands. That would be only just, and if justice was
hard to come by in this world, he could hope for it in the next.

But was their time fated? Had Domokos been less proud . . . had
Petronas not made his too-clever bargain with Harvas . . . had Anthimos
listened and sent troops north in good time—had Anthimos listened even
once, curse him . . .

Thinking of the Emperor's failing filled Krispos with pure and frightening rage. His fists clenched. Only then did he notice he was holding the

gold-filled leather pouch. He gave it to Narvikka, saying "Take it. I never want to see these coins again."

"I take it, I share them with the rest of the lads here." The Haloga nodded at the rest of his squad of guardsmen, who were watching him and Krispos. "Each of us, he takes a piece of your ill luck for himself."

"However you like," Krispos said mechanically. Much as he wanted not to, part of him responded to the Haloga's gesture. He found himself saying "My thanks. That's kind of you, to do such a thing for me."

Narvikka's massive shoulders moved up and down inside his mail shirt. "We would do it for each other, we will do it for a friend." As if Krispos were a child, the big northerner turned him round and gave him a light shove toward the imperial residence. "Is wine inside. You drink to remember them or to forget, whichever suits."

"My thanks," Krispos said again. Given a sense of purpose, his feet made for the larder without much conscious thought.

Before he got there, Barsymes came out of one of the other rooms that opened onto the corridor and saw him. The eunuch stared; later, remembering that look, Krispos wondered what expression his face had borne. Barsymes seemed to wrestle with courtesy, then spoke, "Your pardon, Krispos, but is something amiss?"

"You might say so," Krispos answered harshly. "Back at the village where I grew up, my sister, her husband, my nieces—Harvas Black-Robe's Halogai hit the place." He stopped, unable to go on.

To his amazement, he saw Barsymes' eyes fill with tears. "I grieve with you," the chamberlain said. "The loss of young kin is always hard. We eunuchs, perhaps, know that better than most; as we have no hope of progeny for ourselves, our siblings' children become doubly dear to us."

"I understand." As he never had before, Krispos wondered how eunuchs carried on through all the years after they were mutilated. A warrior should envy the courage that required, he thought, but most would only grow angry at being compared to a half-man.

Thinking of Barsymes' plight helped him grapple with his own. The eunuch said, "If you wish to leave off your duties the rest of the day, my colleagues and I will assume them. Under the circumstances, the Avtokrator cannot object—"

"Under the circumstances, I don't give a fart whether the Emperor objects," Krispos snapped. He watched Barsymes gape. "Never mind. I'm sorry. You don't know all the circumstances. Thank you for your offer. By your leave, I'll take advantage of it."

Barsymes bowed. "Of course," he said, but his face was still shocked and disapproving.

"I *am* sorry," Krispos repeated. "I shouldn't have lashed out at you. None of this is your fault."

"Very well," Barsymes said stiffly. Krispos kept apologizing until he saw the chamberlain truly relent. Barsymes awkwardly patted him on the shoulder and suggested, "Perhaps you should take a cup of wine, to help ease the shock to your spirit."

When Haloga and eunuch gave the same advice, Krispos thought, it had to be good. He drank one cup quickly, a second more slowly, then started to pour a third. He stopped. He had intended to drink to forget, but remembering suddenly seemed the better choice. He corked the jar and put it back on the shelf.

Outside, shadows were getting longer. The wine mounted from Krispos' stomach to his head. He yawned. *If I'm not going to attend their Majesties, I may as well sleep,* he thought. *Phos willing, all this will seem farther away when I wake up.*

He walked to his chamber. The wine and the muggy summer heat of Videssos the city left him covered with sweat. *Too warm to sleep in clothes,* he decided. He pulled his robe off over his head, though it did its best to stick to him.

He still wore the chain that held the chalcedony amulet Trokoundos had given him and his lucky goldpiece. He took off the chain, held the goldpiece in his hand, and looked at it a long time. The past couple of years, he'd thought little of what the coin might mean; in spite of being— perhaps because of being—so close to the imperial power, he hadn't contemplated taking it for himself.

Yet if Anthimos knew no rule save caprice, what then? Had the Emperor done his job as he should, Evdokia, Domokos, and their children would be fine today. Fury filled Krispos again—had Anthimos only paid attention to him, all would have been well. But the Avtokrator not only refused to rule, he refused to let anyone do it for him. That courted disaster, and had brought it to Krispos' family.

And so, the coin. Krispos wished he knew what message was locked inside it along with the gold. He did know he was no assassin. If the only way he could take the throne was by murdering Anthimos, he thought, Anthimos would stay Avtokrator till he died of old age. *To say nothing of the fact that the Halogai would chop to dogmeat anyone who assailed the Emperor,* the pragmatic side of his mind added.

Staring at the goldpiece told him nothing. He put the chain back around his neck and flopped heavily onto the soft bed that had once been Skombros'. After a while, he slept.

THE SILVER BELL WOKE HIM THE NEXT MORNING. HE DID NOT think much about it. It was part of his routine. He dressed, put on sandals, and went into the imperial bedchamber. Only when he saw Anthimos smiling from the bed he shared with Dara did memories of the day before come crashing back.

Krispos had to turn away for a moment, to make sure his features would be composed when he turned back to the Emperor. "Your Majesty," he said, voice expressionless.

Dara spoke before her husband. "I was saddened last night to hear of your loss, Krispos."

He could tell her sympathy was real, and warmed a little to it. Bowing, he said, "Thank you, Your Majesty. You're gracious to think of me." They had played the game of passing messages back and forth under Anthimos' nose before. She nodded very slightly, to show she understood.

The Emperor nodded, too. "I'm sorry, also, Krispos. Most unfortunate. A pity you didn't have your—brother-in-law, was it?—come south to the city before the raiders struck."

"I tried to get him to come, Your Majesty. He didn't wish to." After two polite, quiet sentences, Krispos found his voice rising toward a shout. "It's an even bigger pity you didn't see fit to guard the frontier properly. Then he could have lived his life as he wanted to, without having to fear raiders out of the north."

Anthimos' eyebrows shot up. "See here, sirrah, don't take that tone with me."

"By the good god, it's about time someone did!" Krispos yelled. He didn't remember losing his temper, but it was lost sure enough, lost past finding. "About time someone took a boot to your backside, too, for always putting your prick and your belly ahead of your empire."

"You be still this instant!" Anthimos shouted, loud as Krispos. Careless of his nakedness, the Avtokrator sprang out of bed and went nose to nose with his vestiarios. He shook a finger in Krispos' face. "Shut up, I tell you!"

"You're not man enough to make me," Krispos said, breathing heavily. "For a copper, I'd break you over my knee."

"Go ahead," Anthimos said. "Touch me, just once. Touch the Emperor. We'll see how long the torturers can keep you alive after you do. Weeks, I'd wager."

Krispos spat between Anthimos' feet, as if in rejection of Skotos. "You shield yourself behind your office whenever you choose to. Why don't you use it?"

Anthimos went white. "Remember Petronas," he said in a ghastly whisper. "By the good god, you may end up envying him if you don't curb your tongue."

"I remember Petronas well enough," Krispos shot back. "I daresay the Empire would have been better off if he'd managed to cast you down from your throne. He—"

The Avtokrator's hands writhed in furious passes. Suddenly Krispos found he could not speak; he had no voice, nor would his lips form words. "Are you quite through?" Anthimos asked. Krispos felt that he could nod. He refused to. Anthimos' smile was as vicious as any with which Petronas had ever favored Krispos. "I suggest you admit you are finished—or do you care to find out how you'd relish being without breath as well as speech?"

Krispos had no doubt the Emperor meant what he said, nor that he could do what he threatened. He nodded.

"Is that yes, you are through?" Anthimos asked. Krispos nodded again. The Emperor moved his left hand, muttering something under his breath. He said, "Your speech is restored. I suggest, however—no, I order—that you do not use it in my presence now. Get out."

Krispos turned to leave, shaking from a mixture of rage and fright he'd never felt before. He hadn't thought he could ever grow truly angry at Anthimos; the Emperor's good nature had always left him proof against full-blown fury. But even less had he imagined Anthimos as a figure of fear. A figure of fun, certainly, but never fear. Not till now. The Emperor had never shown he'd learned enough wizardry to be frightening till now.

At the door, Krispos almost bumped into a knot of eunuchs and maid-servants who had gathered to listen, wide-eyed, to his shouting match with Anthimos. They scattered before him as if he had something catching. So he did, he thought: the Avtokrator's disfavor was a disease that could kill.

He stamped back to his chamber and slammed the door behind him. He hit the wall a good solid whack, hard enough to send pain shooting up his arm. Then he used his restored voice to shout several very rude words. He was not sure whether he cursed the Emperor or his own foolish rashness. Either or both, he decided; he did no good either way.

That cold-blooded realization finally ended his fit of temper. He sat down at the edge of his bed and put his head in his hands. If he did not mean to strike at the Avtokrator, he should have kept his mouth shut. And he did not see how he could strike, not if he hoped to live afterward. "Stupid," he said. He meant it for a viler curse than any he'd used before.

Having been stupid, he had nothing left but to make the best of his stupidity. He came out of his room a few minutes later and went about his business—his business that did not directly concern Anthimos—as normally as he could. The rest of the servitors spoke to him in hushed voices, but they spoke to him. If he heard the whispers that followed him through the imperial residence, he could pretend he did not.

For all his outward show of calm, he jumped when, early that afternoon, Longinos said, "His Majesty wants to see you. He's in the bedchamber."

After a moment to gather himself, he nodded to the eunuch and walked slowly down the corridor. He could feel Longinos' eyes on his back. He wondered who waited in the imperial bedchamber. In his mind's eye he saw a masked, grinning torturer, dressed in crimson leather so as not to show the stains of his trade.

He had to will his finger first to touch and then to work the latch he'd gladly opened so many times late at night. Eyes on the floor, he went in. Going against the Kubratoi, spear in hand, had been easier—he'd thought that would be grand and glorious, till the fighting started.

Anthimos was alone; Krispos saw only the one pair of red boots. He took his courage in both hands and looked at the Avtokrator's face. Indignation ousted fright. Anthimos was smiling at him, as cheerfully as if nothing had happened in the morning.

"Your Majesty?" he said, much more than the simple question in his voice.

"Hello, Krispos," the Emperor said. "I was just wondering, have the silk weavers delivered the new robe they've been promising for so long? If it's here at last, I'd like to show it off at the revel tonight."

"As a matter of fact, Your Majesty, it got here a couple of hours ago," Krispos said, almost giddy with relief. He went to the closet, got out the robe, and held it in front of himself so the Emperor could see it.

"Oh, yes, that's very fine." Anthimos came up to run his fingers over the smooth, glistening fabric. He sighed. "All the poets claim women have skin soft as silk. If only they truly felt like this!" After a moment, he went on, "I will wear this tonight, Krispos. Make sure it's ready for me."

"Certainly, Your Majesty." Krispos hung up the robe. Nodding, Anthimos started to leave. "Your Majesty?" Krispos called after him.

The Avtokrator stopped. "What is it?"

"Is that *all*?" Krispos blurted.

Anthimos eyes widened, either from guilelessness or an all but perfect simulation of it. "Of course that's all, dear fellow. What else could there possible be?"

"Nothing. Nothing at all," Krispos said quickly. He'd known the Emperor's temper was mercurial, but he'd never expected it to cool so quickly. If it had, he was not about to risk rekindling it. Nodding again, Anthimos bustled out. Krispos followed, shaking his head. So much luck seemed too good to be true.

Chapter XIII

"Y OU'RE NOT MISSING A HEAD OR ANY OTHER VITAL APPENDAGE,
I see," Mavros said, waving to Krispos as he climbed the steps to the
imperial residence. "From all the gossip I've heard the last couple of days,
that's Phos' own special miracle. And miracles, my friend, deserve to be
celebrated." He held up a large jar of wine.

The Haloga guards at the top of the stairs laughed. So did Krispos.
"You couldn't have timed it better, Mavros. His Majesty just took off for a
carouse, which means we should have the rest of the night to ourselves."

"If you find a few cups, Krispos, we can share some of this with the
guardsmen here," Mavros said. "If his Majesty's not here to guard, surely
their bold captain can't object to their having a taste."

Krispos looked questioningly, the other Halogai longingly, toward the
officer, a middle-aged warrior named Thvari. He stroked his straw-yellow
beard as he considered. "Vun cup vill do no harm," he said at last, his
northern accent thick and slow. The guards cheered. Krispos hurried to
get cups while Mavros drew a dagger, sliced through the pitch that glued
the wine jar's cork in place, then stabbed the cork and drew it out.

Once in Krispos' chamber, Mavros poured hefty dollops for himself and Krispos. He lifted his silver goblet in salute. "To Krispos, for being in-tact!" he declared.

"That's a toast I'll gladly drink." Krispos sipped at the wine. Its vintage was as fine as any Anthimos owned; when Mavros bought, he did not stint. His robe was dark-green wool soft as duckdown, his neckcloth trans-parent silk dyed just the right shade of orange to complement the robe.

Now he raised a quizzical eyebrow. "And here's the really interesting question: *why* are you still intact, after calling Anthimos everything from a murderous cannibal to someone who commits unnatural acts with pigs?"

"I never called him *that*," Krispos said, blinking. He knew what rumor could do with words, but listening to it have its way with *his* words was doubly unnerving. He drank more wine.

"Never called him which?" Mavros asked with a wicked grin.

"Oh, keep still." Krispos emptied his cup and put it down on the arm of his chair. He stared at it for a few seconds, then said, "Truth is, may the ice take me if I know why Anthimos hasn't come down on me. I just thank Phos he hasn't. Maybe down deep he really is just a good-natured soul."

"Maybe." Mavros did not sound as though he believed it. "More likely, he was still so drunk in the morning that he'd forgotten by afternoon."

"I'd like to think so, but he wasn't," Krispos said. "He wasn't drunk at all. I can tell."

"Aye, you've seen him drunk often enough, haven't you?" Mavros said.

"Who, me?" Krispos laughed. "Yes, a time or twelve, now that you mention it. I remember the time he—" He stopped in surprise. The little silver bell by his bed was ringing. The scarlet cord on which it hung jerked up and down. Whoever was pulling it was pulling hard.

Mavros eyed the bell curiously. "I thought you said his Majesty was gone."

"He is." Krispos frowned. Had Anthimos come back for some reason? No. He would have heard the Emperor go by. He did not think Dara was summoning him; he'd let her know he had a friend coming by tonight. Surely she'd not be so indiscreet. But that left—no one. Krispos got up. "Excuse me. I think I'd better find out what's going on."

Mavros' smile was sly. "More of this good wine for me, then."

Snorting, Krispos hurried into the imperial bedchamber. It was Dara who waited for him there. Fright filled her face. "By the good god, what's wrong?" Krispos demanded. "Have we been discovered?"

"Worse," Dara said. He stared at her—he could not imagine anything worse. She started to explain, "When Anthimos left tonight, he didn't go carousing."

"How is that worse?" he broke in. "I'd think you'd be glad."

"Will you listen to me?" she said fiercely. "He didn't go carousing because he went to that little sanctum of his that used to be a shrine. He's going to work magic there, magic to kill you."

"That's crazy. If he wants me dead, all he has to do is tell one of the Halogai to swing his axe," Krispos said. But he realized it wasn't crazy, not to Anthimos. Where was the fun in a simple execution? The Emperor would enjoy putting Krispos to death by sorcery ever so much more. Something else struck him. "Why are you telling me this?"

"What do you mean, why? So you can stop him, of course." Dara needed a moment to see that the question went deeper. She took a deep breath, looked away from Krispos, let it out, and looked back. "Why? Because . . ." She stopped again, visibly willed herself to continue. "Because if I am to be Empress of Videssos, I would sooner be your Empress than his."

His eyes met hers. Those words, he knew, were irrevocable. She nodded, her resolve firming as she saw he understood.

"Strange," he said. "I always thought you preferred him."

"If you're that big a fool, maybe I've picked the wrong man after all." Dara slipped into his arms for a brief embrace. Drawing back, she said, "No time for more, not now. When you return . . ."

She let the words hang. It was his turn to nod. When he came back, they would need each other, she him to keep what she already had, he her to add legitimacy to what he'd gained. When he came back . . . "What will you do if Anthimos walks into this chamber instead of me?"

"Go on, as best I can," she said at once. He grimaced, nodding again. Tanilis would have said the same thing, for the same reason: ambition bound the two of them as much as affection. She went on, "But I will pray to Phos that it be you. Go now, and may the lord with the great and good mind go with you."

"I'll get my sword," Krispos said. Dara bit her lip—that brought home what she was setting in motion. But she did not say no. Too late for that, he thought. She made a little pushing gesture, urging him out of the room. He hurried away.

As he trotted the few steps back to his own chamber, he felt his lucky goldpiece bounce on its chain. Soon enough, he thought, he'd find out whether the coin held true prophecy or only delusion. He remembered the last time he'd really looked at the goldpiece, and remembered thinking he would never try to get rid of Anthimos. But if the Avtokrator was trying to get rid of him . . . Waiting quietly to be killed was for sheep, not men.

All that ran through his head before he got to his own doorway. Mavros raised his cup in salute when he came in, then stared when, instead of sitting down, he started buckling on his sword belt. "What in the world—" Mavros began.

"Treason," Krispos answered, which shut his foster brother's mouth with a snap. "Or it'll be treason if I fail. Anthimos is planning to kill me by sorcery tonight. I don't intend to let him. Are you with me, or will you denounce me to the Halogai?"

Mavros gaped at him. "I'm with you, of course. But by the good god, how did you find out? You told me he was going carousing tonight, not magicking."

"The Empress warned me just now," Krispos said in a flat voice.

"*Did* she?" Mavros looked at Krispos as if he'd never seen him before, then started to laugh. "You haven't told me everything you've been up to, have you?"

Krispos felt his cheeks grow hot. "No. I never told anyone. It's not the sort of secret to spread around, you know, not if—"

"Not if you want to live to go on keeping it," Mavros finished for him. "No, you're right."

"Come on then," Krispos said. "We've no time to lose."

The Halogai guarding the doorway to the imperial residence chuckled when Krispos came out wearing his sword. "You drink a little wine, you go into the city looking for somet'ing to fight, eh?" one of them said. "You should have been born a northern man."

Krispos chuckled, too, but his heart sank within him. As soon as he and Mavros were far enough away from the entrance for the guards not to hear, he said, "We have gone looking for something to fight. How many Halogai will the Emperor have with him?"

The night was dark. He could not see Mavros' expression change, but he heard his breath catch. "If it's more than one, we're in trouble. Armored, swinging those axes of theirs—"

"I know." Krispos shook his head, but continued, "I'm going on anyway. Maybe I can talk my way past 'em, however many there are. I'm his Majesty's vestiarios, after all. And if I can't, I'd sooner die fighting than whichever nasty way Anthimos has worked out for me. If you don't want to come along, the good god knows I can't blame you."

"I am your brother," Mavros said, stiffening with offended dignity.

Krispos clasped his shoulder. "You are indeed."

They hurried on, making and discarding plans. Before long, the gloomy grove of cypresses surrounding the Emperor's sanctum loomed before them. The path wound through it. The dark trees' spicy odor filled Krispos' nostrils.

As they were about to emerge from the cypresses, a red-orange flash of light, bright as lightning, burst from the windows and open doorways of the building ahead. Krispos staggered, sure his moment was here. His eyes, long used to blackness, filled with tears. How bitter, he thought, to have come just too late.

But nothing further happened, not right then. He heard Anthimos' voice begin a new chant. Whatever magic the Avtokrator was devising, he'd not yet finished it.

Beside Krispos, Mavros also rubbed his eyes. In that moment of fire, though, he'd seen something Krispos had missed. "Only the one guard," he murmured.

Squinting, wary against a new levinbolt, Krispos peered toward Anthimos' house of magics. Sure enough, lit by the glow of a couple of ordinary torches, a single Haloga stood in front of the door.

The northerner was rubbing at his eyes, too, but came to alertness when he heard footfalls on the path. "Who calls?" he said, swinging up his axe.

"Hello, Geirrod." Krispos did his best to sound casual in spite of the nervous sweat trickling down the small of his back. If Anthimos had told the guard why he was incanting here tonight . . .

But he had not. Geirrod lowered his bright-bladed weapon. "A good evening to you, Krispos, and to your friend." Then the Haloga frowned and half raised the axe again. "Why do you come here with brand belted to your body?" Even when he used Videssian, his speech carried the slow, strong rhythms of his cold and distant homeland.

"I've come to deliver a message to his Majesty," Krispos answered. "As for why I'm wearing my sword, well, only a fool goes out at night without one." He unbuckled the belt and held it out to Geirrod. "Here, keep it if you feel the need, and give it back when I come out."

The big blond guard smiled. "That is well done, friend Krispos. You know what duty means. I shall set your sword aside against your return." As he turned to lean the blade against the wall, Mavros sprang forward, sheathed dagger reversed in his hand. The round lead pommel thudded against the side of Geirrod's head, just in front of his ear. The Haloga groaned and toppled, his mail shirt clinking musically as he fell.

Krispos' fingers dug into the side of Geirrod's thick neck. "He has a pulse. Good," he said, grabbing the sword belt and drawing his blade. If he survived the night, the Halogai would be *his* guards. Slaying one of them would mean he could never trust his own protectors, not with the northern penchant for blood vengeance.

"Come on," Mavros said. He snatched up the Haloga's axe.

"No, wait. Tie and gag him first," Krispos said. Mavros dropped the axe, took off his scarf, and tore it in half. He quickly tied the guardsman's hands behind him, knotting the other piece of silk over his mouth and around his head. Krispos nodded. Together, he and Mavros stepped over Geirrod into the Avtokrator's sorcerous secretum.

The scuffle with the guard had been neither loud nor long. With luck, Anthimos would have been caught up in the intricacies of some elaborate spell and would never have noticed the small disturbance outside. With luck. As it was, he poked his head out into the hallway and called, "What was that, Geirrod?" When he saw Krispos, his eyes widened and his lips skinned back from his teeth. "You!"

"Aye, Your Majesty," Krispos said. "Me." He dashed toward the Emperor.

Fast as he was, he was not fast enough. Anthimos ducked back into his chamber and slammed the door. The bar crashed into place just as Krispos' shoulder smote the door. The bar was stout; he bounced away.

Laughing a wild, high-pitched laugh, Anthimos shouted, "Don't you know it's rude to come to the feast before you're invited?" Then he began to chant again, a chant that, even through thick wood, raised prickles of dread along Krispos' arms.

He kicked the door, hard as he could. It held. Mavros shoved him aside. "I have the tool for the job," he said. Geirrod's axe bit into the timbers. Mavros struck again and again. As he hewed at the door, the Avtokrator chanted on in a mad race to see who would finish first—and live.

Mavros weakened the door enough so he and Krispos could kick it open. At the same instant, Anthimos cried out in triumph. As his foes burst in on him, he extended his hands toward them. Fire flowed from his fingertips.

Had Anthimos controlled a true thunderbolt, he would have incinerated Krispos and Mavros. But while his fire flowed, it did not dart. They scrambled backward out of the chamber before the flames reached them. The fire splashed against the far wall and dripped to the floor. The wall was stone. It did not catch, but Krispos gagged on acrid smoke.

"Not so eager to come in and play anymore, my dears?" Anthimos said, laughing again. "I'll come out and play with you, then."

He stood in the doorway and shot fire at Krispos. Krispos threw himself flat on the floor. The flames passed over him, close enough that he smelled his hair scorch. He waited for Anthimos to lower his hands and burn him to a cinder.

Anthimos never got the chance. While his attention and his fire were aimed at Krispos, Mavros rushed him with the Haloga war axe. Anthimos whirled, casting flames close enough to Mavros to spoil his stroke. But the Emperor had to duck back into his chamber.

Some of his fire caught on the ruined door. It began to burn. Real, honest flames licked up toward the beams of the ceiling.

Krispos scrambled to his feet. "We have him!" he shouted. "He can't fight both of us at once out here, and trapped in there he'll burn." Already the smoke had grown thicker.

"You think you have me," Anthimos said. "All this fribbling fire is but a distraction. Now to get back to the conjuration I truly had in mind for you, Krispos, the one you so rudely interrupted. And when I finish, you'll wish you'd burned to death, you and your friend both."

The Avtokrator began to incant again. Krispos started through the burning doorway at him, hoping he could not use his flames while busy with this other, more fearful magic. But once summoned, the fire was at Anthimos' command. A blast of it forced Krispos back. Mavros tried too, and was similarly repulsed.

Anthimos chanted on. Krispos knew nothing of magic, but he could sense the magnitude of the forces Anthimos employed. The very air felt thin, and thrummed with power. Icy fear ran through Krispos' veins, for he knew that power would close on him. He could not attack the Emperor; flight, he was sure, would do no good. He stood and waited, coughing more and more as the smoke got worse.

Anthimos was coughing, too, and fairly gabbling his spell in his haste to get it all out before the fire sealed his escape as Krispos had said. Maybe that haste caused him to make his mistake; maybe, being at bottom a headstrong young man who took few pains, he would have made it anyhow.

He knew he'd erred—his chant abruptly broke off. Dread and horror in his voice, he shouted, "Him, not me! I didn't mean to say 'me'! I meant *him*!"

Too late. The power he had summoned did what he had told it to do, and to whom. He screamed, once. Peering through smoky, heat-hazed air, Krispos saw him writhe as if trapped in the grip of an invisible fist of monstrous size. The scream cut off. The sound of snapping bones went on and on. An uprush of flame blocked Krispos' view for a moment. When he could see again, Anthimos, or what was left of him, lay crumpled and unmoving on the floor.

Mavros pounded Krispos' shoulder. "Let's get out of here!" he yelled. "We're just as dead if we toast as if—that happens to us."

"Are we? I wonder." Anthimos was the most definitively dead man Krispos had ever seen. The last sight of the fallen Emperor stayed with him as, eyes streaming and lungs burning from the smoke, he stumbled with Mavros toward the doorway.

Cool, clean night air after that inferno was like cool water after an endless trek through the desert. Krispos sucked in breath after precious breath. Then he knelt beside Geirrod, who was just beginning to groan and stir. "Let's drag him away from here," he said, and listened to the roughness in his own voice. "We don't want him to burn, either."

"Something else first." Slowly and deliberately, Mavros went to his knees before Krispos, then flat on his belly. "Majesty," he declared. "Let me be the first to salute you. Thou conquerest, Krispos, Avtokrator of the Videssians."

Krispos gaped at him. In the desperate struggle with Anthimos, he'd forgotten the prize for which he'd been struggling. He spoke his first words as Emperor: "Get up, fool."

Geirrod's pale eyes were wide and staring, flicking back and forth from one man to the other. Mavros rose, but only to a crouch by the Haloga. "Do you understand what has happened this night, Geirrod? Anthimos sought to slay Krispos by sorcery, but blundered and destroyed himself instead. By the Lord with the great and good mind, I swear neither Krispos nor I wounded him. His death was Phos' own judgment on him."

"My friend—my brother—speaks truly," Krispos said. He drew the sun-circle over his heart. "By the good god I swear it. Believe me or not, Geirrod, as you see fit from what you know of me. But if you believe me, let me ask you in turn: will you serve me as bravely and loyally as you served Anthimos?"

Those eyes of northern blue might have been a hunting beast's rather than a man's, such was the intensity of the gaze Geirrod aimed up at Krispos. Then the guardsman nodded, once.

"Free him, Mavros," Krispos said. Mavros cut through the Haloga's bonds, then through the gag. Geirrod heaved himself upright and started to stagger away from the burning building behind him. "Wait," Krispos told him, then turned to Mavros. "Give him his axe."

"What? No!" Mavros exclaimed. "Even half out on his feet the way he is, with this thing he's more than a match for both of us."

"He's said he will serve me. Give him the axe." Part of that tone of command was borrowed from Petronas; more, Krispos realized, came from Anthimos.

Wherever it came from, it served its purpose. Mavros' eyes were eloquent, but he passed the axe to Geirrod. The Haloga took it, looking at it
as a father might look at a long-lost son who has come home. Krispos
tensed. If he was wrong and Mavros right, he would have the shortest
reign of any Avtokrator Videssos had ever known.

Geirrod raised the axe—in salute. "Lead me, Majesty," he said. "Where
now?"

Krispos watched Mavros' hand leave the hilt of his dagger. The little
blade would not have kept him or Krispos alive an extra moment against
an armed and armored Geirrod, but the protective gesture made Krispos
proud once more to have him for foster brother.

"Where now?" the guardsman repeated.

"To the imperial residence," Krispos answered after quick thought.
"You, Geirrod, tell your comrades what happened here. I will also speak to
them, and to the folk inside."

"What do you want to do about this place here?" Mavros asked, pointing back at Anthimos' sanctum. As he did, part of the roof fell in with a
crash.

"Let it burn," Krispos said. "If anyone sees it or gets close enough to
hear noise like that, I suppose he'll try and put it out, not that he'll have
much luck. But the grove is so thick that odds are no one will notice a
thing, and we certainly don't have time to mess about here. Or do you feel
otherwise?"

Mavros shook his head. "No indeed. We'll be plenty busy between now
and dawn."

"Aye." As he walked back toward the imperial residence, Krispos tried
to think of all the things he'd have to do before the sun came up again. If
he forgot anything of any importance, he knew, he would not keep the
throne he'd claimed.

The Halogai standing guard in front of the imperial residence grew
alert when they saw three men approaching. When Krispos and his companions got close enough for torchlight to reveal the state they were in,
one of the northerners shouted, "What happened to you?"

Krispos looked down at himself. His robe was torn and scorched and
stained with smoke. He glanced over at Mavros, whose face was streaked
from soot and sweat. His own, he was sure, could be no cleaner.

"The Avtokrator is dead," he said simply.

The Halogai cried out and came dashing down the stairs, their huge
axes at the ready. "Did you slay him?" one of them demanded, his voice
fierce.

"No, by Phos, I did not," Krispos said. As he had for Geirrod, he sketched the sun-sign over his breast. "You know he and I had a falling-out these past few days." He waited for the northerners to nod, then went on, "This evening I learned . . ." *Never mind where now,* he thought. "I learned he'd not forgiven me as he wanted me to believe, but was going to use the wizardry he'd studied to kill me."

He touched the sword that swung on his hip. "I went to defend myself, yes, but I did not kill him. Because I was there, he hurried his magic, and rather than striking me, it ate him up instead. In the name of the Lord with the great and good mind, I tell you I speak the truth."

Geirrod suddenly started talking to the northerners in their own language. They listened for a moment, then began asking questions and talking—sometimes shouting—among themselves. Geirrod turned to Krispos, shifting back to Videssian. "I tell them it be only justice now for you to be Emperor, since he who was Emperor try to slay you but end up killing self instead. I also tell them I fight for you if they say no."

While the Halogai argued, Mavros sidled close to Krispos and whispered, "Well, I admit you did that better than I would have."

Krispos nodded, watching the guards—and their captain. Sometimes, he had read, usurpers gained the imperial guards' backing with promises of gold. He did not think gold would sway Thvari, save only to make him feel contempt. He waited for the guard captain to speak. At last Thvari did. "Majesty." One by one, the Halogai echoed him.

Now Krispos could give rewards. "Half a pound of gold to each of you, a pound to Thvari, and two pounds to Geirrod for being first among you to acknowledge me." The northerners cheered and gathered round him to clasp his hand between their two.

"What do I get?" Mavros asked, mock-plaintively.

"You get to go to the stables, saddle up Progress and a horse for you, and get back here fast as you can," Krispos told him.

"Aye, that's right, give me all the work," Mavros said—but over his shoulder, for he was already heading for the stables at a fast trot.

Krispos climbed the steps to the imperial residence—*his* residence now and for as long as he could keep it, he realized suddenly. He could feel that he was running on nervous energy; if he slowed down even for a moment, he might not get moving again easily. He laughed at himself—when would he find the chance to slow down any time soon?

Barsymes and Tyrovitzes stood waiting a couple of paces inside the entrance. As with the Halogai before, Krispos' dishevelment made the eunuchs stare. Barsymes pointed out toward the guardsmen. "They called you Majesty," he said. Was that accusation in his voice? Krispos could not tell. The chamberlain had long practice in dissimulation.

"Yes, they called me Majesty—Anthimos is dead," Krispos answered bluntly, hoping to startle some more definite reaction from the eunuchs. But for making the sun-circle over their hearts, they gave him none. Their silence compelled him to go on to explain once more how the Emperor had perished.

When he was through, Barsymes nodded; he seemed far from startled. "I did not think Anthimos could destroy you so," he remarked.

Krispos started to take that as a simple compliment, then stopped, his eyes going wide. "You knew," he ground out. Barsymes nodded again. Krispos drew his sword. "You knew, and you did not warn me. How shall I pay you back for that?"

Barsymes did not flinch from the naked blade. "Perhaps while you consider, you should let the Empress Dara know you survived. I am certain she will be even more relieved to hear of it than we are."

Again Krispos started to miss something, again he caught himself. "You knew that, too?" he asked in a small voice. This time both eunuchs nodded back. He looked at his sword, then returned it to its sheath. "How long have you known?" Now he was whispering.

Barsymes and Tyrovitzes looked at each other. "No secret in the palaces is a secret long," Barsymes said with the slightest trace of smugness.

Dizzily, Krispos shook his head. "And you didn't tell Anthimos?"

"If we had, esteemed and—no, forgive me, I beg—Your Majesty, would you be holding this conversation with us now?" Barsymes asked.

Krispos shook his head again. "How shall I pay you back for *that*?" he said, then musingly answered himself: "If I'm to be Emperor, I'll need a vestiarios. The post is yours, Barsymes."

The eunuch's long, thin face was not made for showing pleasure, but his smile was less doleful than most Krispos had seen from him. "You honor me, Your Majesty. I am delighted to accept, and shall seek to give satisfaction."

"I'm sure you will," Krispos said. He hurried past the two eunuchs and down the hall. He passed the doorway that had been his and paused in front of the one he had entered so many times but that only now belonged to him. He raised a hand to knock softly, then stopped. He did not knock at his own door. He opened it.

He heard Dara's sharp intake of breath—she had to have been wondering who would come through that door. When she saw Krispos, she said, "Oh, Phos be praised, it's you!" and threw herself into his arms. Even as he held her, though, he thought that her words would have done for Anthimos' return just as well—no chance of making a mistake with them. He wondered how long she'd worked to come up with such a safe phrase.

"Tell me what happened," she demanded.

He explained Anthimos' downfall for the fourth time that night. He knew he would have to do it again before dawn. The more he explained it, the more the story got between him and the exertion and terror of the moment. If he told the tale enough times, he thought hopefully, perhaps he'd forget how frightened he'd been.

This was the first time Dara had heard it, which made it seem as real for her as if she'd been there. When he was through, she held him again. "I might have lost you," she said, her face buried against his shoulder. "I don't know what I would have done then."

She'd been sure enough earlier in the evening, he thought, but decided he could not blame her for forgetting that now. And her fear for him made him remember his own fear sharply once more. "You certainly might have," he said. "If he hadn't tripped over his own tongue—"

"You made him do it," she said.

He had to nod. At the end, Anthimos had been badly rattled, too, or likely he never would have made his fatal blunder. "Without you, I never would have known, I wouldn't have been there . . ." This time Krispos hugged Dara, acknowledging the debt he owed, the gratitude he felt.

She must have sensed some of that. She looked up at him; her eyes searched his face. "We need each other," she said slowly.

"Very much," he agreed, "especially now."

She might not have heard him. As if he hadn't spoken, she repeated, "We need each other," then went on, maybe as much to herself as to him, "We please each other, too. Taken together, isn't that a fair start toward . . . love?"

Krispos heard her hesitate before she risked the word. He would also have hesitated to speak it between them. Having been lovers did not guarantee love; that was another of Tanilis' lessons. Even so . . . "A fair start," he said, and did not feel he was lying. Then he added, "One thing more, anyhow."

"What's that?" Dara asked.

"I promise you won't have to worry about minnows with me."

She blinked, then started to laugh. But her voice had a grim edge to it as she warned, "I'd better not. Anthimos didn't have to care about what I thought, whereas you . . ."

She stopped. He thought about what she hadn't said: that he was a peasant-born usurper with no right to the throne whatever, save that his fundament was on it. He knew that was true. If he ruled well, he also knew it eventually would not matter. But eventually was not now. Now anything that linked him to the imperial house he had just toppled would help him hold power long enough for it to seem to belong to him. He could not afford to antagonize Dara.

"I said not a minute ago that you didn't need to worry about such things," he reminded her.

"So you did." She sounded as if she were reminding herself, too.

He kissed her, then said with mock formality so splendid Mavros might have envied it, "And now, Your Majesty, if you will forgive me, I have a few small trifles to attend to before the night is through."

"Yes, just a few," she said, smiling, her mood matching his. Almost as an afterthought, she added, "Your Majesty."

He kissed her again, then hurried away. The Halogai outside the imperial residence swung their axes to the ready in salute as he came out. A few minutes later, Mavros rode up, leading Krispos' horse Progress on a line. "Here's your mount, Kris—uh, Your Majesty. Now—" His voice sank to a conspiratorial whisper. "—what do you need the beast for?"

"To ride, of course," Krispos said. While his foster brother sputtered, he turned to Thvari and spoke for a couple of minutes. When he was done, he asked, "Do you have that? Can you do it?"

"I have it. If I can do it, I will. If I can't, I'll be dead. So will you, not much later," the northerner answered with the usual bloodthirsty directness of the Halogai.

"I trust you'll do your best, then, for both our sakes," Krispos said. He swung himself up onto Progress' back and loosed the lead line. "Now we ride," he told Mavros.

"I did suspect that, truly I did," Mavros said. "Do you have any place in particular in mind, or shall we just gallivant around the city?"

Krispos had already urged his bay gelding into a trot. "Iakovitzes' house," he said over his shoulder as he rode west toward the plaza of Palamas. "I just hope he's there; the only person I can think of who likes—liked—to carouse more than he does is Anthimos."

"Why are we going to Iakovitzes' house?"

"Because he's still in the habit of keeping lots of grooms," Krispos answered. "If I'm to be Avtokrator, people will have to know I'm Avtokrator. They'll have to see me crowned. That will have to happen as fast as it can, before anyone else gets the idea there's a throne loose for the taking. The grooms can spread word through the city tonight."

"And wake everyone up?" Mavros said. "The people won't love you for that."

"The people of this town love spectacle more than anything else," Krispos said. "They wouldn't forgive me if I didn't wake them up for it. Look at Anthimos—you can be anything in Videssos the city, so long as you're not dull."

"Well, maybe so," Mavros said. "I hope so, by the Lord with the great and good mind."

They reined in in front of Iakovitzes' house, tied their horses to the rail, and went up to the front door. Krispos pounded on it. He kept pounding until Iakovitzes' steward Gomaris opened the little grate in the middle of the door and peered through it. Whatever curses the steward had in mind got left unsaid when he recognized Krispos; he contented himself with growling, "By the good god, Krispos, have you gone mad?"

"No," Krispos said. "I must see Iakovitzes right now. Tell him that, Gomaris, and tell him I won't take no for an answer." He waited tensely—if Gomaris said his master was out, everything was up for grabs again. But the steward just slammed the grate shut and went away.

He returned in a couple of minutes. "He says he doesn't care if it's the Emperor himself who wants to see him."

"It is," Krispos said. "It is the Emperor, Gomaris." The little grate did not show much of Gomaris' face, but he saw the steward's right eye go wide. A moment later, he heard the bar lift. The door swung open.

"What's happened in the palaces?" Gomaris asked eagerly. No, he was more than eager, he was all but panting to hear juicy news before anyone else did. That, to an inhabitant of the city, was treasure more precious than gold.

"You'll know when Iakovitzes does," Krispos promised. "And now, hadn't you better run ahead and tell him you let Mavros and me in after all?"

"Aye, you're right, worse luck," the steward said, his voice suddenly glum. He hurried off toward his master's bedchamber. Krispos and Mavros, who still knew their way around the house where they had once served, followed more slowly.

Iakovitzes met them before they got to his bedroom. The fiery little noble was just knotting the sash of his dressing gown when he came up to his former protégés. He stabbed out a finger at Krispos. "What's this nonsense about the Emperor wanting to see me? I don't see any Emperor. All I see is you, and I wish I didn't."

"Excellent sir, you do see the Emperor," Krispos answered. He touched his own chest.

Iakovitzes snorted. "What *have* you been drinking? Go on home now, and if Phos is merciful I'll fall back to sleep, forget all about this, and never have to tell Anthimos."

"It doesn't matter," Krispos said. "Anthimos is dead, Iakovitzes."

As Gomaris' had just before, Iakovitzes' eyes went wide. "Hold that torch closer to him, Gomaris," he told his steward. Gomaris obeyed. In the better light, Iakovitzes examined Krispos closely. "You're not joking," he said at last.

"No, I'm not." Almost by rote, Krispos told the story he had already told four times that night. He finished, "That's why I've come to you, excellent sir, to have your grooms and servants spread word through the city that something extraordinary has happened and that people should gather at the High Temple to learn what."

To his surprise and indignation, Iakovitzes started to laugh. The noble said, "Your pardon, Your Majesty, but when you first came here, I never thought I had a future Avtokrator shoveling out my horseshit. Not many can say that, by Phos. Oh, no indeed!" He laughed again, louder than before.

"You'll help, then?" Krispos said.

Iakovitzes slowly sobered. "Aye, Krispos, I'll help you. Better you with the crown than some dunderheaded general, which is the other choice we'd likely have."

"Thanks, I suppose," Krispos said—Iakovitzes never gave praise without splashing vinegar on it.

"You're welcome, I'm sure," the noble said. He sighed. "And to think that with a little luck I could have had an Avtokrator in my bed as well as in my stables." Iakovitzes turned a look that was half glower, half leer on Mavros. "Why didn't you overthrow the Emperor?"

"Me? No, thank you," Mavros said. "I wouldn't take the job on a bet. I want to go through life without food tasters—and without using up a few of them along the way."

"Hrmmp." Iakovitzes gave his attention back to Krispos. "You'll have plenty to keep you occupied tonight, won't you? I suppose you'll want me to go and wake up everyone in the household. I may as well. Now that you've ruined my hope for a decent night's sleep, why should I let anyone else have one?"

"You're as generous and considerate as I remember you," Krispos said, just to see him glare. "By the good god, I promise you won't be sorry for this."

"If both our heads go up on the Milestone, I'll make sure mine reminds yours of that," Iakovitzes said. "Now get moving, will you? The faster this is done, the better the chance we all have of avoiding the chap with the cleaver."

Since Krispos had come to the same conclusion, he nodded, clasped Iakovitzes' hand, and hurried away. He and Mavros were just climbing onto their horses when Iakovitzes started making a horrible racket inside the house. Mavros grinned. "He doesn't do things by halves, does he?"

"He never did," Krispos said. "I'm only glad he's with us and not against us. Gnatios won't be so easy."

"You'll persuade him," Mavros said confidently.

"One way or another, I have to," Krispos said as they rode through the dark, quiet streets of the city. Only a few people shared the night with them. A couple of courtesans beckoned as they trotted by; a couple of footpads slunk out of their way; a couple of staggering drunks ignored them altogether. Once, off in the distance, Krispos saw for a moment the clump of torches that proclaimed respectable citizens traveling by night. He rounded a corner and they were gone.

More torches blazed in front of the patriarchal mansion. Krispos and Mavros tied their horses to a couple of the evergreens that grew there and walked up to the entrance. "I am heartily tired of rapping on doors," Krispos said, rapping on the door.

Mavros consoled him. "After this, you can have servants rap on them for you."

The rapping eventually had its result—the priest Badourios opened the door a crack and demanded, "Who dares disturb the ecumenical patriarch's rest?" Then he recognized Krispos and grew more civil. "I hope it is not a matter of urgency, esteemed and eminent sir."

"Would I be here if it weren't?" Krispos retorted. "I must see the patriarch at once, holy sir."

"May I tell him your business?" Badourios asked.

Mavros snapped, "Were it for you, be assured we would consult you. It is for your master, as Krispos told you. Now go and fetch him." Badourios glared sleepy murder at him, then abruptly turned on his heel and hurried away.

Gnatios appeared a few minutes later. Even fresh-roused from sleep, he looked clever and elegant, if none too happy. Krispos and Mavros bowed. As Gnatios responded with a bow of his own, Krispos saw him take in their dirty faces and torn robes. But his voice was smooth as ever as he asked, "What has so distressed his Majesty that he must have a response in the middle of the night?"

"Let us speak privately, not in this doorway," Krispos said.

The patriarch considered, then shrugged. "As you wish." He led them to a small chamber, lit a couple of lamps, then closed and barred the door. Folding his arms across his chest, he said, "Very well, let me ask you once more, if I may, esteemed and eminent sir: what theological concern has Anthimos so vexed he must needs rout me out of bed for his answer?"

"Most holy sir, you know as well as I that Anthimos never worried much about theology," Krispos said. "Now he doesn't worry about it at all. Or rather, he worries in the only way that truly matters—he's walking the narrow bridge between the light above and the ice below." He saw Gnatios' eyebrows shoot up. He nodded. "Yes, most holy sir, Anthimos is dead."

"And you, most holy sir, have been addressing the Avtokrator of the Videssians by a title far beneath his present dignity," Mavros added. His voice was hard, but one corner of his mouth could not help twitching upward with mischief.

Suave and urbane as he normally was, the patriarch goggled at that. "No," he whispered.

"Yes," Krispos said, and for the half-dozenth time that night told how Anthimos had perished. Listening to himself, he discovered he did have the story down pat; only a few words were different from the ones he'd used with Iakovitzes and Dara. He finished, "And that is why we've come to you now, most holy sir: to have you set the crown on my head at the High Temple in the morning."

Gnatios had regained his composure while Krispos spoke. Now he shook his head and repeated, "No," this time loudly and firmly. "No, I will not crown a jumped-up stableboy like you, no matter what has befallen his Majesty. If you speak the truth and he has died, others are far more deserving of imperial rank."

"By which you mean Petronas—your cousin Petronas," Krispos said. "Let me remind you, most holy sir, that Petronas now wears the blue robe."

"Vows coerced from a man have been set aside before," Gnatios said. "He would make a better Avtokrator than you, as you must admit."

"I admit nothing of the sort," Krispos growled, "and you're mad if you think I'd give over the throne to a man whose first act upon it would be to take my head."

"You're mad if you think I'll crown you," Gnatios retorted.

"If you don't, Pyrrhos will," Krispos said.

That ploy had worked before with Gnatios, but it failed now. The ecumenical patriarch drew himself up. "Pyrrhos is but an abbot. For a coronation to have validity, it must be at my hands, the patriarch's hands, and they shall not grant it to you."

Just then Badourios knocked urgently on the door. Without waiting for a reply, the priest tried the latch. When he found the door barred, he called through it: "Most holy sir, there's an unseemly disturbance building in the street outside."

"What's happening in the street outside does not concern me," Gnatios said angrily. "Now go away."

Krispos and Mavros looked at each other. "Maybe what's happening in the street *does* concern you, most holy sir," Krispos said, his voice silky. "Shall we go and see?"

The lines on Gnatios' forehead and those running down from beside his nose to the outer ends of his mouth deepened in suspicion. "As you wish," he said reluctantly.

Krispos heard the deep-voiced shouting as soon as he was out of the chamber. He looked at Mavros again. They both smiled. Gnatios scowled at each of them in turn.

When the three men got to the front entrance, the shouting abruptly stopped. Gnatios stared out in dismay at the whole regiment of imperial guards, hundreds of armed and armored Halogai drawn up in line of battle before the patriarchal mansion. He turned to Krispos, nervously wetting his lips. "You would not, ah, loose the barbarians here on, ah, holy ground?"

"How could you think such a thing, most holy sir?" Krispos sounded shocked. He made sure he sounded shocked. "We were just having a nice peaceable talk in there, weren't we?"

Before Gnatios could answer, one of the Halogai detached himself from their ranks and strode toward the mansion. As the warrior drew closer, Krispos saw it was Thvari. Gnatios stood his ground, but still seemed to shrink from the northerner, who along with his mail shirt and axe also bore a large, round bronze-faced shield.

Thvari swung up his axe in salute to Krispos. "Majesty," he said soberly. His gaze swung to Gnatios. He must not have liked what he saw on the patriarch's face, for his already wintry eyes grew colder yet. The axe twitched in his hands, as if with a life of its own.

Gnatios' voice went high. "Call him off me," he said to Krispos. The axe twitched again, a bigger movement this time. Krispos said nothing. Gnatios watched the axe blade with fearful fascination. He jumped when it moved again. "Please call him off me," he said shrilly; a moment later, perhaps realizing what was wrong, he added, "Your Majesty."

"That will be all, Thvari. Thank you," Krispos said. The Haloga nodded, turned, and stalked back to his countrymen.

"There," Gnatios said to Krispos, though his eyes stayed on Thvari till the northerner was back into the ranks of the guardsmen. "I've publicly acknowledged you. Are you satisfied?"

"You haven't yet honored his Majesty with a proskynesis," Mavros observed.

Gnatios looked daggers at him and opened his mouth to say something defiant. Then he glanced over to the Halogai massed in the street. Krispos watched the defiance drain out of him. Slowly he went to his knees, then to his belly. "Majesty," he said as his forehead touched the floor.

"Get up, most holy sir," Krispos said. "So you agree I am the rightful Avtokrator, then?" He waited for Gnatios to nod before he went on, "Then can you show that to the whole city by setting the crown on my head at the High Temple when morning comes?"

"I would seem to have little choice," Gnatios said bleakly.

"If I'm to be master of the Empire, I will be master of all of it," Krispos told him. "That includes the temples."

The ecumenical patriarch did not reply in words, but his expression was eloquent. Though emperors traditionally headed ecclesiastical as well as secular affairs, Anthimos had ignored both impartially, letting Gnatios run Videssos' religious life like an independent prince. The prospect of doing another man's bidding could not have appealed to him.

Mavros pointed down the street; at the same time, Haloga heads turned in the direction his finger showed. A man carrying a large, heavy bundle was coming toward the patriarchal mansion. No, not a man—as the person drew nearer, Krispos saw beardless cheeks and chin. But it was not a woman, either. . . . "Barsymes!" Krispos exclaimed. "What do you have there?"

Panting a little, the eunuch set down his burden. "If you are to be crowned, Your Majesty, you should appear before the people in the proper regalia. I heard your orders to the Halogai, and so I knew I could find you here. I've brought the coronation regalia, a crown, and a pair of red boots. I do hope the rude treatment I've given the silks hasn't wrinkled them too much," he finished anxiously.

"Never mind," Krispos said, touched. "That you thought to bring them to me is all that counts." He put a hand on Barsymes' shoulder. The eunuch, a formal soul if ever there was one, shrugged it off and bowed. Krispos went on, "It was bravely done, and perhaps foolishly done, as well. How would you have fought back if robbers fell upon you and stole this rich clothing?"

"Robbers?" Barsymes gave a contemptuous sniff. "A robber would have to be insane to dare assault one like me, who is so obviously a eunuch of the palace." For the first time, Krispos heard a sort of melancholy pride in Barsymes' description of himself. The eunuch continued, "Besides, even a madman would think three times before he stole the imperial raiment. Who could wear it but the Emperor, when even its possession by another is proof of treason and a capital crime?"

"I'm just glad you got here safely," Krispos said. If thinking himself immune from robbers had helped Barsymes come, he would not contradict the eunuch. Privately he suspected Barsymes had been more lucky than secure.

"Shall I vest you in the regalia now?" Barsymes asked.

Krispos thought for a moment, then shook his head. "No, let's do it at the High Temple, where the ecumenical patriarch will set the crown on my head." He glanced over at Gnatios, who nodded without speaking. Krispos looked eastward. Ever so slightly, the horizon was beginning to gray. He said, "We should go there now, to be ready when the new day comes."

He called to the Halogai. They formed up in a hollow rectangle that took the whole width of the street. Krispos, Mavros, Barsymes, and Gnatios took their places in the middle. Krispos thought Gnatios still wanted to bolt, but the patriarch got no chance. "Forward to the High Temple," Krispos said, and forward they went.

The Temple, as was only fitting, lay but a few steps from the patriarchal mansion. It bulked huge against the brightening sky; the thick piers that supported the weight of its great central dome gave it a squat, almost ungainly appearance from the outside. But within—Krispos knew the splendor that lay within.

The forecourt to the High Temple was as large as a couple of the smaller plazas in the city. The boots of the Halogai slammed down on slate flags; their measured tramp echoed from the building they approached.

Gnatios peered out between the marching guardsmen. "What are all these people doing, loitering in the forecourt so long before the dawn?" he said.

"A coronation must be witnessed," Krispos reminded him.

The patriarch gave him a look filled with grudging respect. "For an adventurer who has just seized the state, you've planned well. You will prove more difficult to dislodge than I would have guessed when you came pounding on my door."

"I don't intend to be dislodged," Krispos said.

"Neither did Anthimos, Your Majesty," Gnatios replied, putting a sardonic edge to the title Krispos was still far from used to.

The forecourt was not yet truly crowded; the Halogai had no trouble making their way toward the High Temple. Men and women scurried out of their path, chattering excitedly: "Look at 'em! Something big *must* be going on." "I wanted to kill the bloody sod who woke me, but now I'm glad I'm here." "Wouldn't want to miss anything. What do you think's happened?" One enterprising fellow had a tray with him. "Sausage and rolls!" he shouted, his eyes, like those of most who lived in Videssos the city, on the main chance. "Buy your sausage and rolls here!"

Priests prayed in the High Temple by night as well as by day. They stared from the top of the stairway at the imperial guards. Krispos heard them exclaim and call to one another; they sounded as curious as any of the onlookers gathering in front of the temple. But when the Halogai began to climb the low, broad stairs, the priests cried out in alarm and withdrew inside, slamming doors behind them.

Under their officers' direction, most of the northerners deployed on the stairway, facing out toward the forecourt. A band that included Thvari's warriors accompanied Krispos and his Videssian comrades up to the High Temple itself. Krispos looked from the closed doors before them to Gnatios. "I hope you'll be able to do something about this?"

Gnatios nodded. He knocked on the door and called sharply, "Open in there. Open, I say! Your patriarch commands it."

A grill slid open. "Phos preserve us," said the priest peering out. "It *is* the patriarch." A moment later, the doors were flung wide; Krispos had to step back smartly to keep from being hit. Ignoring him, the clerics hurled questions at Gnatios: "What's toward, most holy sir?" "What are all the Halogai doing here?" "Where's the Emperor, if all his guards have come?"

"What's toward? Change," Gnatios answered, raising an eyebrow at Krispos. "I would say that response covers the rest of your queries, as well."

Barsymes spoke up. "Holy sirs, will your kindness permit us to enter the narthex so his Majesty may assume the imperial vestments?"

"I shall also require a vial of the scented oil used in anointings," Gnatios added.

Krispos saw the priests' faces go momentarily slack with surprise, then heard their voices rise as they murmured among themselves. They were city men; they did not need to hear more to know what was in the wind. Without waiting for their leave, Krispos strode into the High Temple. He felt the clerics' eyes on him as they gave way before his confidence, but he did not look toward them. Instead, he told Barsymes, "Aye, this place will do well enough for robing. Help me, if you please."

"Of course, Your Majesty." The eunuch turned to the priests. "Could I trouble one of you, holy sirs, for a damp cloth wherewith to wipe clean his Majesty's face?" Not one but four clerics hurried away.

"I'll want to clean off after you do, Kris—Your Majesty," Mavros said. "The good god knows I must be as sooty as you are."

The cloth arrived in moments. With exquisite delicacy, Barsymes dabbed and rubbed at Krispos' cheeks, nose, and forehead. When at last he was satisfied, he handed the cloth—now grayish rather than white—to Mavros. While Mavros ran it over his own face, Barsymes began to clothe Krispos in the imperial regalia for the first time.

The garb for the coronation was of antique style, so antique that it was no longer worn at any other time. With Barsymes' help, Krispos donned blue leggings and a gold-belted blue kilt edged in white. His plain sword went into the bejeweled scabbard that hung from the belt. His tunic was scarlet, with gold threads worked through it. Barsymes set a white wool cape on his shoulders and fumbled to work the golden fibula that closed it at his throat.

"And now," the eunuch said, "the red boots."

They were a tight squeeze; Krispos' feet were larger than Anthimos'. They also had higher heels than Krispos was used to. He stumped around uncertainly inside the narthex.

Barsymes took from his bag a simple golden circlet, then a more formal crown: a golden dome set with rubies, sapphires, and glistening pearls. He set both of them aside; for the moment, Krispos remained bareheaded.

Mavros went to the doors to look out. "A lot of people there," he said. "Iakovitzes' lads did their job well." The noise of the crowd, which the closed doors had kept down to a sound like that of the distant sea, suddenly swelled in Krispos' ears.

"Is it sunrise?" he asked.

Mavros looked out again. "Near enough. It's certainly light."

Krispos glanced from him to Barsymes to Gnatios. "Then let's begin."

Mavros opened the doors once more, this time throwing them wide. The boom they made as they slammed back against the wall drew the eyes of the crowd to him. He stood in the doorway for a moment, then cried out as loud as he could, "People of Videssos, Phos himself has made this day! On this day, the good god has given our city and our Empire a new Avtokrator."

The hum from the crowd dropped as people quieted to hear what Mavros said, then redoubled when they took in the import of his words. He held up his hands and waited. Quiet slowly came. Into it, Mavros said,

"The Avtokrator Anthimos is dead, laid low by his own sorceries. People of Videssos, behold the Avtokrator Krispos."

Barsymes touched Krispos on the arm, but he was already moving forward to stand in the open doorway as Mavros stepped aside. Below him, on the steps, the Halogai raised their axes in salute—and in warning to any who would oppose him. "Krispos!" they shouted all together, their voices deep and fierce.

"Krispos!" yelled the crowd, save for the inevitable few who heard his name wrong and yelled "Priskos!" instead. "Thou conquerest, Krispos!"— the age-old Videssian shout of acclamation. "Many years to the Avtokrator Krispos!" "Thou conquerest!" "Krispos!"

Krispos remembered the heady feeling he'd had years before, when the nobles who filled the Hall of the Nineteen Couches all cried out his name after he vanquished Beshev, the thick-shouldered wrestler from Kubrat. Now he knew that feeling again, but magnified a hundredfold, for this was not a hallful of people, but rather a plazaful. Buoyed up on that great tide of acclamation, he forgot fatigue.

"The people proclaim you Emperor, Krispos!" Mavros cried.

The acclaim got louder. Shouts of "Thou conquerest, Krispos!" came thick and fast. One burden of worry gone, Krispos thought. Had the crowd not accepted him, he would never have lasted as Avtokrator; no matter what other backing he had, it would have evaporated in the face of popular contempt. The chronicles told of a would-be Emperor named Rhazates, whom the mob had laughed off the steps of the High Temple for no better reason than that he was grossly fat. A rival ousted him within days.

Thvari held up the bronze-faced shield, displaying it to the crowd. The people quieted; they knew what that shield was for. With Mavros behind him, Krispos walked down to where the Haloga waited.

Too quietly for the people in the forecourt to hear, Krispos told Thvari, "I want you, Geirrod, Narvikka, and Vagn."

"It shall be as you wish," the northerner agreed. Geirrod stood close by; neither of the other guardsmen Krispos had named was far away. Thvari would know which soldiers he favored, Krispos thought. At the officer's gesture, the two Halogai set down their axes and hurried over.

Barsymes approached, handing Mavros the golden circlet he'd brought. As Thvari had the bronze-faced shield, Mavros showed the circlet to the crowd. Those at the back of the courtyard could hardly have been able to see it, but they sighed all the same—like the shield, it had its place in the ritual of coronation.

The ritual went on. Mavros offered Krispos the circlet. He held out his hands, palms away from his body, in a gesture of refusal. Mavros offered the circlet again. Again Krispos rejected it. Mavros paused, then tried to present it to Krispos once more. This time Krispos bowed his head in acquiescence.

Mavros set the circle on his brow. The gold was cool against his forehead. "Krispos, with this circlet I join the people in conferring on you the title of Avtokrator!" Mavros said proudly.

As Mavros spoke, as the crowd erupted in fresh cheers, Thvari set the bronze-faced shield flat on the stair beside him. Krispos stepped up onto it. Thvari, Geirrod, Narvikka, and Vagn stooped and grasped the rim of the shield. At a grunted command from Thvari, they lifted together.

Up went the shield to the height of their shoulders, raising Krispos high above them and showing the people that he enjoyed the soldiers' support as well as theirs. "Krispos!" all the Halogai shouted once more. For a moment he felt more like one of their pirate chieftains about to set forth on a plundering expedition than a staid and civilized Avtokrator of the Videssians.

The guardsmen lowered him back to the stone steps. As he got off the shield, he wondered if it was the one upon which Anthimos had stood—and who would be exalted on it after he was gone. *My son, Phos willing, one day many years from now,* he thought, then shoved that concern far away.

He looked up to the top of the stone steps. Gnatios stood in the open doorway, holding a satin cushion on which lay the imperial crown and the vial of oil he would use to anoint Krispos' head. The patriarch nodded. Heart pounding, Krispos climbed the stairs toward him. Having been accepted by the people and the army, he needed only ecclesiastical recognition to complete his coronation.

Gnatios nodded again as Krispos took his place beside him. But instead of beginning the ceremony of anointing, the patriarch looked out to the expectantly waiting crowd in the forecourt below. Pitching his voice to carry to the people, the patriarch said, "Perhaps our new master will honor us with a few brief words before I set the crown on his head."

Krispos turned around to glare at Gnatios, who blandly looked back. He heard Mavros' angry hiss—this was no normal part of the coronation. Krispos knew what it was: it was Gnatios hoping he would play the fool in front of much of the city, and blight his reign before it properly began.

The expanding crowd in the forecourt grew still, waiting to hear what Krispos would say. He paused a moment to gather his thoughts, for he saw he could not keep from speaking. Before he began, though, he scowled at Gnatios again. He would never be able to trust the patriarch, not after this.

But when he looked out to the still-waiting throng, all thoughts of Gnatios vanished from his mind. "People of Videssos," he said, then once more, louder, "people of Videssos, Anthimos is dead. I do not want to speak ill of the dead, but you know as well as I that not everything in the city or in the empire ran as well as it might have while he was Emperor."

He hoped someone would shout out in agreement and bring a laugh from the crowd. No one did. People stood silent, listening, judging. He took a deep breath and reminded himself to try to keep his rustic accent under control; he was glad his years in the city had helped smooth it. He plunged ahead.

"I served Anthimos. I saw how he neglected the Empire for the sake of his own pleasure. Pleasure has its place, aye. But the Avtokrator has to look to Videssos first, then to himself. As far as I can, I will do that."

He paused to think again. "If I did everything I might possibly do, I think I'd need to pack three days into every one." His rueful tone was real; as he stood there, looking out at the people who were under his rule alone, picturing their fellows all the way to the borders of the Empire, he could not imagine why anyone would want the crushing weight of responsibility that went with being Avtokrator. No time to worry about that now, either. He had the responsibility. He would have to bear up under it. He went on, "With the good god's help, I'll be able to do enough to help Videssos. I pray I can. That's all."

As he turned back to Gnatios, he listened to the crowd. No thunderous outpouring of applause, but he hadn't expected one, not after the patriarch ambushed him into coming up with a speech on the spot. But no one jeered or booed or hissed. He'd got through it and hadn't hurt himself. That was plenty.

Gnatios realized it, too. He masked himself well, but could not quite hide his disappointment. "Carry on, most holy sir," Krispos said coldly.

"Yes, of course, Your Majesty." Gnatios nodded, bland still. He raised his voice to speak to the crowd rather than the Emperor. "Bow your head for the anointing."

Krispos obeyed. The patriarch drew the stopper from the vial of scented oil and poured its contents over Krispos' head. He spoke the ritual words: "As Phos' light shines down on us all, so may his blessings pour down on you with this anointing."

"So may it be," Krispos responded, though as he did, he wondered whether a prayer had to be sincerely meant to be effective. If so, Phos' ears were surely closed to Gnatios' words.

The patriarch rubbed the oil through Krispos' hair with his right hand. While he completed the anointing, he recited Phos' creed, intoning, "We bless thee, Phos, lord with the great and good mind, by thy grace our protector, watchful beforehand that the great test of life may be decided in our favor."

Krispos echoed the prayer, which, since it did not mention him, he supposed the patriarch truly meant. The city folk gathered in the forecourt below also recited the creed. Their voices rose and fell like surf, individual words lost but the prayer's rhythm unmistakable.

And then, at last, Gnatios took the imperial crown in both hands and set it on Krispos' lowered head. It was heavy, literally as well as for what it meant. A sigh ran through the crowd. A new Avtokrator ruled Videssos.

After a moment, the noise began to build again, to a crest of acclamation: "Thou conquerest!" "Krispos!" "Many years!" "Krispos!" "Hurrah for the Emperor!" "Krispos!" "Krispos!" "Krispos!"

He straightened. Suddenly the crown seemed to weigh nothing at all.

Book II

KRISPOS OF VIDESSOS

To Constantine VII
(who liked rice pudding)
and Leo the Deacon

Chapter I

THE GOLD FLAN WAS FLAT AND ROUND, ABOUT AS WIDE AS Krispos' thumb—a blank surface, about to become a coin. Krispos passed it to the mintmaster, who in turn carefully set it on the lower die of the press. "All ready, Your Majesty," he said. "Pull this lever here, hard as you can."

Your Majesty. Krispos hid a smile. He'd been Avtokrator of the Videssians for only eight days, and still was far from used to hearing his new title in everyone's mouth.

He pulled the lever. The upper die came down hard on the flan, whose soft gold was squeezed and reshaped between it and the one beneath.

The mintmaster said, "Now if you please, Your Majesty, just ease back there so the die lifts again." He waited until Krispos obeyed, then took out the newly struck goldpiece and examined it. "Excellent! Had you no other duties, Your Majesty, you would be welcome to work for me." After laughing at his own joke, he handed Krispos the coin. "Here, Your Majesty, the very first goldpiece of your reign."

Krispos held the coin in the palm of his hand. The obverse was uppermost: an image of Phos, stern in judgment. The good god had graced

Videssos' coinage for centuries. Krispos turned the goldpiece over. His own face looked back at him, neatly bearded, a bit longer than most, nose high and proud. Yes, his image, wearing the domed imperial crown. A legend ran around his portrait, in letters tiny but perfect: KRISPOS AVTOKRATOR.

He shook his head. Seeing the goldpiece brought home once more that he *was* Emperor. He said, "Thank your die-maker for me, excellent sir. To cut the die so fast, and to have the image look like me—he did splendidly."

"I'll tell him what you've said, Your Majesty. I'm sure he'll be pleased. We've had to work in a hurry here before, when one Avtokrator replaced another rather suddenly, so we, ah—"

The mintmaster found an abrupt, urgent reason to stare at the coin press. He knew he'd said too much, Krispos thought. Krispos' own ancestry was not remotely imperial; he'd grown to manhood on a peasant holding near Videssos' northern frontier—and spent several years north of that frontier, as a serf toiling for the nomads of Kubrat.

But after a cholera outbreak killed most of his family, he'd abandoned his village for Videssos the city, the great imperial capital. Here he'd risen by strength and guile to the post of vestiarios—chamberlain—to the Emperor Anthimos III. Anthimos had cared for pleasure more than for ruling; when Krispos sought to remind him of his duties, Anthimos tried to slay him by sorcery. He'd slain himself instead, with a bungled spell. . . . *And so,* Krispos thought, *my face goes on goldpieces now.*

"We're cutting more dies every day, both for this mint and those out in the provinces," the mintmaster said, changing the subject. "Soon everyone will have the chance to know you through your coins, Your Majesty."

Krispos nodded. "Good. That's as it should be." He'd been a youth, he remembered, when he first saw Anthimos' face on a goldpiece.

"I'm glad you're pleased, Your Majesty." The mintmaster bowed. "May your reign be long and happy, sir, and may our artisans design many more coins for you."

"My thanks." Krispos had to stop himself from bowing in return, as he would have before the crown came to him. A bow from the Avtokrator would not have delighted the mintmaster; it would have frightened him out of his wits. As Krispos left the mint, he had to hold up a hand to keep all the workers from stopping their jobs to prostrate themselves before him. He was just learning how stifling imperial ceremony could be for the Emperor.

A squad of Halogai stood outside the mint. The imperial guardsmen swung up their axes in salute as Krispos emerged. Their captain held his horse's head to help him mount. The big blond northerner was red-faced and sweating on what seemed to Krispos no more than a moderately warm day; few of the fierce mercenaries took Videssos' summer heat well.

"Where to now, Majesty?" the officer asked.

Krispos glanced down at a sheet of parchment on which he'd scrawled a list of the things he had to do this morning. He'd had to do so much so fast since becoming Avtokrator that he'd given up trying to keep it all in his head. "To the patriarchal mansion, Thvari," he said. "I have to consult with Gnatios—again."

The guardsmen formed up around Krispos' big bay gelding. He touched the horse's flanks with his heels, twitched the reins. "Come on, Progress," he said. The imperial stables held many finer animals; Anthimos had fancied good horseflesh. But Progress had belonged to Krispos before he became Emperor, and that made the beast special.

When the Halogai reached the edge of the palace quarter and came to the plaza of Palamas, they menacingly raised their axes and shouted, "Way! Way for the Avtokrator of the Videssians!" As if by magic, a lane through the crowded square opened for them. That was an imperial perquisite Krispos enjoyed. Without it, he might have spent most of an hour getting to the other side of the plaza—he had, often enough. Half the people in the world, he sometimes thought, used the plaza of Palamas to try to sell things to the other half.

Though the presence of the Emperor—and the cold-eyed Halogai—inhibited hucksters and hagglers, the din was still dreadful. He rubbed an ear in relief as it faded behind him.

The Halogai tramped east down Middle Street, Videssos the city's chief thoroughfare. The Videssians loved spectacle. They stopped and stared and pointed and made rude remarks, as if Krispos could not see or hear them. Of course, he realized wryly, he was so new an Avtokrator as to be interesting for novelty's sake, if nothing else.

He and his guards turned north toward the High Temple, the grandest shrine to Phos in all the Empire. The patriarch's home stood close by. When it came into view, Krispos braced himself for another encounter with Gnatios.

The meeting began smoothly. The ecumenical patriarch's aide, a lesser priest named Badourios, met Krispos at the mansion door and escorted him to Gnatios' study. The patriarch sprang from his chair, then went to his knees and then to his belly in full proskynesis—so full, indeed, that Krispos wondered, as he often did with Gnatios, if he was being subtly mocked.

Though his shaven pate and bushy beard marked him as a cleric, they did not rob the patriarch of his individuality, as often happened with priests. Krispos always thought of him as foxlike, for he was clever, elegant, and devious, all at the same time. Had he been an ally, he would have been a mighty one. He was not an ally; Anthimos had been a cousin of his.

Krispos waited for Gnatios to rise from his prostration, then settled into a chair across the desk from the patriarch. He motioned Gnatios to sit and plunged in without preamble. "I hope, most holy sir, you've seen fit to reverse yourself on the matter we discussed yesterday."

"Your Majesty, I am still engaged in a search of Phos' holy scriptures and of canon law." Gnatios waved to the scrolls and codices piled high in front of him. "But I regret to say that as yet I have failed to find justification for performing the ceremony of marriage to join together you and the Empress Dara. Not only is her widowhood from his late Majesty the Avtokrator Anthimos extremely recent, but there is also the matter of your involvement in Anthimos' death."

Krispos drew in a long, angry breath. "Now see here, most holy sir, I did not slay Anthimos. I have sworn that again and again by the lord of the great and good mind, and sworn it truthfully." To emphasize his words, his hand moved in a quick circle over his heart, the symbol of Phos' sun. "May Skotos drag me down to the eternal ice if I lie."

"I do not doubt you, Your Majesty," Gnatios said smoothly, also making the sun-sign. "Yet the fact remains, had you not been present when Anthimos died, he would still be among men today."

"Aye, so he would—and I would be dead. If he'd finished his spell at leisure, it would have closed on me instead of him. Where in Phos' holy scriptures does it say a man may not save his own life?"

"Nowhere," the patriarch answered at once. "I never claimed that. Yet a man may not hope to escape the ice if he takes to wife the widow of one he has slain, and by your own statements you were in some measure a cause of Anthimos' death. Thus my continued evaluation of your degree of responsibility for it, as measured against the strictures of canon law. When I have made my determination, I assure you I shall inform you immediately."

"Most holy sir, by *your* own statements there can be honest doubt about this—men can decide either way. If you find against me, I am sure I can discover another cleric to wear the patriarch's blue boots and decide for me. Do you understand?"

"Oh, indeed, painfully well," Gnatios said, putting a wry arch to one eyebrow.

"I'm sorry to be so blunt," Krispos said, "But it strikes me your delays have more to do with hindering me than with Phos' sacred words. I will not sit still for that. I told you the night you crowned me that I was going to be Emperor of all Videssos, including the temples. If you stand in my way, I will replace you."

"Your Majesty, I assure you this delay is unintentional," Gnatios said. He gestured once more to the stacks of volumes on his desk. "For all you say, your case is difficult and abstruse. By the good god, I promise to have a decision within two weeks' time. After you hear it, you may do with me as you will. Such is the privilege of Avtokrators." The patriarch bowed his head in resignation.

"Two weeks?" Krispos stroked his beard as he considered. "Very well, most holy sir. I trust you to use them wisely."

"TWO WEEKS?" DARA GAVE HER HEAD A DECISIVE SHAKE. "NO, that won't do. It gives Gnatios altogether too much time. Let him have three days to play with his scrolls if he must, but no more than that. Tomorrow would be better."

As he often had, Krispos wondered how Dara fit so much stubbornness into such a small frame. The crown of her head barely reached his shoulder, but once she made up her mind she was more immovable than the hugest Haloga. Now he placatingly spread his hands. "I was just pleased I got him to agree to decide within any set limit. And in the end I think he'll decide for us—he likes being patriarch and he knows I'll cast him from his throne if he tells us we may not wed. That amount of time we can afford."

"No," Dara said, even more firmly than before. "I grudge him every grain of sand in the glass. If he's going to find for us, he doesn't need weeks to do it."

"But why?" Krispos asked. "Since I've already agreed to this, I can't change my mind without good reason, not unless I want him preaching against me in the High Temple as soon as I leave him."

"I'll give you a good reason," Dara said: "I'm with child."

"You're—" Krispos stared at her, his mouth falling open. Then he asked the same foolish question almost every man asks his woman when she gives him that news: "Are you sure?"

Dara's lips quirked. "I'm sure enough. Not only have my courses failed to come, but when I went to the privy this morning, the stench made me lose my breakfast."

"You're with child, all right," Krispos agreed. "Wonderful!" He took her in his arms, running a hand through her thick black hair. Then he had another thought. It was not suited for the moment, but passed his lips before he could hold it back: "Is it mine?"

He felt her stiffen. The question, unfortunately, was neither idle nor, save in its timing, cruel. Dara had been his lover, aye, but she'd also been Anthimos' Empress. And Anthimos had not been immune to the pleasures of the flesh—far from it.

When at last she looked up at him, her dark eyes were troubled. "I think it's yours," she said slowly. "I wish I could say I was certain, but I can't, not really. You'd know I was lying."

Krispos thought back to the time before he'd seized the throne; as vestiarios, he'd had the bedchamber next to the one Dara and Anthimos had shared. The Emperor had gone carousing and reveling many nights, but not all. Krispos sighed, stepping back and wishing life did not give him ambiguity where he most wanted to be sure.

He watched Dara's eyes narrow and her mouth thin in calculation. "Can you afford to disown a child of mine, no matter who it looks like in the end?" she asked.

"I just asked myself the same question," he said, respect in his voice. Nothing was wrong with Dara's wits, and just as Gnatios liked being patriarch, she liked being Empress. She needed Krispos for that, but he knew he also needed her— because she was Anthimos' widow, she helped confer legitimacy on him by connecting him to the old imperial house. He sighed again. "No, I don't suppose I can."

"By the good god, Krispos, I hope it's yours, and I think it is," Dara said earnestly. "After all, I was Anthimos' Empress for years without quickening. I never knew him to get bastards on any of his tarts, either, and he had enough of them. I have to wonder at the strength of his seed."

"That's so," Krispos said. He felt relieved, but not completely. Phos he took on faith. His years in Videssos the city had taught him the danger of similar faith in anything merely human. Yet even if the child was not his by blood, he could set his mark on it. "If it's a boy, we'll name him Phostis, for my father."

Dara considered, nodded. "It's a good name." She touched Krispos' arm. "But you do see the need for haste, not so? The sooner we're wed, the better; others can count months as well as we can. A babe a few weeks early will set no tongues wagging. Much more, though, especially if the child is big and robust—"

"Aye, you're right," Krispos said. "I'll speak to Gnatios. If he doesn't like being hurried, too bad. It's just deserts for surprising me and making me speak unprepared when he was crowning me. By the good god, I know he was hoping I'd flub."

"Just deserts for that piece of effrontery would be some time in the prisons under the government office buildings on Middle Street," Dara said. "I've thought so ever since you first told me of it."

"It may come to that, if he says me nay here," Krispos answered. "I know he'd sooner see Petronas come out of the monastery and take the throne than have me on it. Being Anthimos' cousin means he's Anthimos' uncle's cousin, too."

"He's not your cousin, that's for certain," Dara said grimly. "You ought to have your own man as patriarch, Krispos. One who's against you can cause you endless grief."

"I know. If Gnatios does tell me no, it'll give me the excuse I need to get rid of him. Trouble is, if I do, I'd likely have to replace him with Pyrrhos the abbot."

"He'd be loyal," Dara said.

"So he would." Krispos spoke without enthusiasm. Pyrrhos was earnest and able. He was also pious, fanatically so. He was a far better friend to Krispos than Gnatios ever would be, and far less comfortable to live with.

Dara said, "Now I hope Gnatios does stand up on his hind legs against you, if you truly mean to slap him down for it."

All at once, Krispos was tired of worrying about Gnatios and what he might do. Instead he thought of the child Dara would have—*his* child, he told himself firmly. He stepped forward to take her in his arms again. She squeaked in surprise as he bent his head to kiss her, but her lips were eager against his. The kiss went on and on.

When at last they separated, Krispos said, "Shall we go to the bedchamber?"

"What, in the afternoon? We'd scandalize the servants."

"Oh, nonsense," Krispos said. After Anthimos' antic reign, nothing save perhaps celibacy could scandalize the palace servants, though he did not say so aloud. "Besides, I have my reasons."

"Name two," Dara said, mischief in her voice.

"All right. For one, if you are pregnant, you're apt to lose interest for a while, so I'd best get while the getting's good, as they say. And for another, I've always wanted to make love with you with the sun shining in on us. That's one thing we never dared do before."

She smiled. "A nice mix of the practical and the romantic. Well, why not?"

They walked down the hall hand in hand. If maidservants or eunuch chamberlains gave them odd looks, neither one noticed.

Barsymes bowed to krispos. "the patriarch is here, Your Majesty," the eunuch vestiarios announced in his not-quite-tenor, not-quite-alto voice. He did not sound impressed. Few things impressed Barsymes.

"Thank you, esteemed sir," Krispos answered; palace eunuchs had their own honorifics, different from those of the nobility. "Show him in."

Gnatios prostrated himself as he entered the chamber where Krispos had been wrestling with tax documents. "Your Majesty," he murmured.

"Rise, most holy sir, rise by all means," Krispos said expansively. "Please be seated; make yourself comfortable. Shall I send for wine and cakes?" He waited for Gnatios' nod, then waved to Barsymes to fetch the refreshments.

When the patriarch had eaten and drunk, Krispos proceeded to business. "Most holy sir, I regret summoning you so soon after I promised you would have your two weeks, but I must seek your ruling on whether Dara and I may lawfully wed."

He had expected Gnatios to splutter and protest, but the patriarch beamed at him. "What a pleasant coincidence, Your Majesty. I was going to send you a message later in the day, for I have indeed reached my decision."

"And?" Krispos said. If Gnatios thought this affable front would make a rejection more palatable, Krispos thought, he was going to get a rude awakening.

But the ecumenical patriarch's smile only grew broader. "I am delighted to be able to inform you, Your Majesty, that I find no canonical impediments to your proposed union with the Empress. You may perhaps hear gossip at the haste of the match, but that has nothing to do with its permissibility under ecclesiastical law."

"Really?" Krispos said in glad surprise. "Well, I'm delighted to hear you say so, most holy sir." He got up and poured more wine for the two of them with his own hands.

"I am pleased to be able to serve you with honor in this matter, Your Majesty," Gnatios answered. He lifted his cup. "Your very good health."

"And yours." Avtokrator and patriarch drank together. Then Krispos said, "From what you've just told me, I don't suppose you'd mind celebrating the wedding yourself." If Gnatios was just going along for the sake of going along, Krispos thought, he ought to balk or at least hesitate.

But he replied at once, "It would be my privilege, Your Majesty. Merely name the day. From your urgency, I suppose you will want it to come as soon as possible."

"Yes," Krispos said, still a bit taken aback at this wholehearted cooperation. "Will you be able to make everything ready in—hmm—ten days' time?"

The patriarch's lips moved. "A couple of days after the full moon? I am your servant." He inclined his head to the Emperor.

"Splendid," Krispos said. When he rose this time, it was a sign Gnatios' audience was done. The patriarch did not miss the signal. He bowed himself out. Barsymes took charge of him and escorted him from the imperial residence.

Krispos gave his attention back to the cadasters. He smiled a little as he took up his stylus to scrawl a note on a waxed tablet. That had been easier than he'd figured it would be, he thought with a twinge of contempt for Gnatios. The patriarch seemed willing to pay whatever price he had to in order to keep his position. A firm line with him would get Krispos anything he required.

Nice to have one worry settled, he thought, and went on to the next tax register.

"DON'T WORRY, YOUR MAJESTY. WE HAVE PLENTY OF TIME YET," Mavros said.

Krispos looked at his foster brother with mixed gratitude and exasperation. "Nice to hear someone say so, by the good god. All of Dara's seamstresses are having kittens, wailing that they'll never be able to have her dress ready on the day. And if they're having kittens, the mintmaster is having bears—big bears, with teeth. He says I can send him to Prista if I like, but that still won't get me enough goldpieces with my face on them to use for largess."

"Prista, he?" Amusement danced in Mavros' eyes. "Then he probably means it." The lonely outpost on the northern shore of the Videssian Sea housed the Empire's most incorrigible exiles. Few people went there willingly.

"I don't care if he means it," Krispos snapped. "I need to have that gold to pass out to the people. We grabbed power too quickly the night I was crowned. This is my next good chance. If I don't do it now, the city folk will think I'm mean, and I'll have no end of trouble from them."

"I daresay you're right," Mavros said, "but does it all have to be *your* gold? Aye, that would be nice, but you hold the treasury as well as the mint. So long as the coin is good, no one who gets it will care whose face it bears."

"Something to that," Krispos said after a moment's thought. "The mintmaster will be pleased. Tanilis would be, too, to hear you; you're your mother's son after all."

"I'll take that for a compliment," Mavros said.

"You'd better. I meant it for one." Krispos had nothing but admiration for Mavros' mother. Tanilis was one of the wealthiest nobles of the eastern town of Opsikion, and seer and mage, as well. She'd foretold Krispos' rise, helped him with money and good advice, and fostered Mavros to him. Though she was a decade older than Krispos, they'd also been lovers for half a year, until he had to return to Videssos the city—Mavros did not know about that. She was still the standard by which Krispos measured women, including Dara—Dara did not know about *that*.

Barsymes politely tapped at the open door of the chamber where Krispos and Mavros were talking. "Your Majesty, eminent sir, your presence is required for another rehearsal of assembling for the wedding procession." In matters of ceremony, the vestiarios ordered the Avtokrator about.

"We'll be with you shortly, Barsymes," Krispos promised. Barsymes withdrew, a couple of paces' length. He did not go away. Krispos turned back to Mavros. "I think I'll use the wedding to declare you Sevastos."

"You will? Me?" Mavros was in his mid-twenties, a few years younger than Krispos, and had a more openly excitable temperament. Now he could not keep his surprised delight from showing. "When did you decide to do that?"

"I've been thinking about it ever since this crown landed on my head. You act as my chief minister, so you should have the title that says what you do. And the wedding will be a good public occasion to give it to you."

Mavros bowed. "One of these days," he said slyly, "you ought to tell your face what you're thinking, so it'll know, too."

"Oh, go howl," Krispos said. "Naming you Sevastos will also make you rich, even apart from what you stand to inherit. It'll also set you up as my heir if I die without one." As he said that, he wondered again whether Dara's child was his. He suspected—he feared—he would keep on wondering until the baby came, and perhaps for years afterward as well.

"I see that, since you're Emperor, you don't have to listen to people anymore," Mavros said. Realizing he hadn't been listening and had missed something, Krispos felt himself flush. With the air of someone doing an unworthy subject a great favor, Mavros repeated himself. "I said that if you die without an heir, it will likely mean you've lost a civil war, in which case I'll be a head shorter myself and in no great position to assume the throne."

In his breezy way, Mavros had probably hit truth there, Krispos thought. He said, "If you don't want the honor, I could bestow it on Iakovitzes."

They both laughed. Mavros said, "I'll take it, then, just to save you from that. With his gift for getting people furious at him, you'd lose any civil war where he was on your side, because no one else would be." Then, as if afraid Krispos might take him seriously, he added, "He is in the wedding party, isn't he?"

"Of course he is," Krispos answered. "Do you think I want the rough side of his tongue for leaving him out? He gave it to me often enough in the days when I was one of his grooms—and to you, too, I'd bet."

"Who, me?" Mavros assumed a not altogether convincing expression of innocence.

Before Krispos could reply, Barsymes stepped back into view. Implacably courteous, he said, "Your Majesty, the rehearsal will commence at any moment. Your presence—and yours, eminent sir"—he turned to Mavros—"would be appreciated."

"Coming," Krispos said obediently. He and Mavros followed the vestiarios down the hall.

B ARSYMES BUSTLED UP AND DOWN THE LINE, CLUCKING LIKE a hen not sure all her chicks were where they belonged. His long face was set in doleful lines made more than commonly visible by his beardless cheeks. "Please, excellent sirs, eminent sirs, Your Majesty, try to remember all we've practiced," he pleaded.

"If the army had its drill down as well as we do, Videssos would rule the bloody world," Iakovitzes said, rolling his eyes. The noble stroked his graying beard. "Come on, let's get this nonsense done with, shall we?"

Barsymes took a deep breath and continued as if no one had spoken. "Smooth and steady and stately will most properly awe the people of Videssos the city."

"Phos coming down from behind the sun with Skotos all tied up in colored string wouldn't properly awe the people of Videssos the city," Mavros said, "so what hope have we?"

"Take no notice of any of my comrades," Krispos told Barsymes, who looked about ready to burst from nerves. "We are in your capable hands."

The vestiarios sniffed, but eased a little. Then he went from mother hen to drillmaster in one fell swoop. "We begin—now," he declared. "Forward to the plaza of Palamas." He marched east from the imperial residence, past lawns and gardens and groves, past the Grand Courtroom, past the Hall of the Nineteen Couches, past the other grand buildings of the palace quarter.

Dara and her companions, Krispos knew, were traversing the quarter by another route. If everything went as planned, his party and hers would meet at the edge of the plaza. It had happened in rehearsals. Barsymes acted convinced it would happen again. To Krispos, his confidence seemed based on sorcery, but so far as he knew, no one had used any.

Magic or not, when his party turned a last corner before the plaza of Palamas, he saw Dara and the noblewomen with her round an outbuilding and come straight toward him. Once they got a few steps closer, he also saw the relief on her face; evidently she'd worried, too, about whether their rendezvous would go as planned.

"You look lovely," he said as he took her right hand with his left. She smiled up at him. A light breeze played with her hair; like him, she wore no golden crown today. Her gown, though, was of dark gold silk that complemented her olive complexion. Fine lace decorated cuffs and bodice; the gown, cinched tight at the waist, displayed her fine figure.

"Forward!" Barsymes called again, and the newly united wedding party advanced into the plaza. The palace quarter had been empty. The plaza was packed with people. They cheered when they saw Krispos and his companions, and surged toward them. Only twin rows of streamers—and Halogai posted every ten feet or so along them—kept the way open.

Instead of his sword, Krispos wore a large leather sack on the right side of his belt. He reached into it, dug out a handful of goldpieces, and threw them into the crowd. The cheers got louder and more frantic. All his groomsmen were similarly equipped; they also flung largess far and wide. So did a dozen servants, who carried even larger bags of coins.

"Thou conquerest, Krispos!" people shouted. "Many years!" "The Avtokrator!" "Many sons!" "Hurrah for the Empress Dara!" "Happiness!" They also shouted other things: "More money!" "Throw it this way!" "Over here!" And someone yelled, "A joyous year to the Emperor and Empress for each goldpiece I get!"

"What an ingenious combination of flattery and greed," Iakovitzes said. "I wish I'd thought of it."

The fellow was close; Krispos saw him waving like a madman. He pulled on a servant's sleeve. "Give him a hundred goldpieces."

The man screamed with delight when the servant poured gold first into his hands, then into a pocket that looked hastily sewn onto his robe—he'd come ready for any good that might happen to him. "That was kindly done, Krispos," Dara said, "but however much we wish it, we won't have a hundred years."

"I'll bet that chap won't have a hundred goldpieces by the time he gets out of the plaza, either," Krispos answered. "But may he do well with those he manages to keep, and may we do well with so many years."

The wedding party pushed out of the plaza of Palamas onto Middle Street. Long colonnades shielded the throngs there from the sun. More servants—these accompanied by an escort of armored Halogai—brought up fresh bags of goldpieces. Krispos dug deep and threw coins as far as he could.

As he had when visiting Gnatios, he turned north off Middle Street with his companions. This time they bypassed the patriarchal mansion with its small dome of red brick for the High Temple close by. Mavros tapped Krispos on the shoulder. "Remember the last time we saw the forecourt here so packed with people?"

"I should hope so," Krispos said. That had been the day he'd taken the throne, the day Gnatios had set the crown on his head in the doorway to the High Temple.

Dara sighed. "I wish I could have been here to see you crowned."

"So do I," Krispos said. They both knew that would not have looked good, though, not when he was replacing the man to whom she'd been wed. Even this ceremony would stir gossip in every tavern and sewing circle in the city. But Dara was right—with a child in her belly, they could not afford to wait.

More Halogai stood on the steps of the High Temple, facing outward to protect Krispos and his comrades as they had when he'd been crowned. At the top of the steps, Gnatios stood waiting. The patriarch looked almost imperially splendid in his blue boots and pearl-encrusted robe of cloth-of-gold and blue. Mere priests in less magnificent raiment swung thuribles on either side of him; Krispos' nose twitched as he caught a whiff of the sweet smoke that wafted from them.

When he and Dara started to climb the low, broad stairs, he held her hand tightly. He wanted not the slightest risk of her falling, not when she was pregnant. The wedding party followed. Behind them, servants flung the last handsful of gold coins into the crowd.

Gnatios bowed when Krispos reached the top step but did not prostrate himself. The temple was, after all, his primary domain. Krispos returned the bow, but less deeply, to show he in fact held superior rank even here. Gnatios said, "Allow me to lead you within, Your Majesty." He and his acolytes turned to enter the narthex. The last time Krispos had gone in there, it was for Barsymes to robe him in the coronation regalia.

"A moment," he said now, holding up a hand.

Gnatios stopped and turned back, a small frown on his face. "Is something wrong?"

"No, not at all. I just want to speak to the people before we go on."

The ecumenical patriarch's frown grew deeper. "Your doing so is not a planned part of the ceremony, Your Majesty."

"No, eh? That didn't bother you when you asked me to speak before you would crown me." Krispos kept his tone light, but he was sure he was glaring at Gnatios. The patriarch had tried to ruin him then, to make him sound like a bumbler in front of the people of the city, the most critical and fickle audience in the world.

Now Gnatios could only bow in acquiescence. "What pleases the Avtokrator has the force of law," he murmured.

Krispos looked out to the packed forecourt and held up his hands. "People of Videssos," he called, then again, "People of Videssos!" Little by little they gave him quiet. He waited until it had grown still enough for everyone to hear. "People of Videssos, this is a happy day for two reasons. Not only am I to be wed today—"

Cheers and applause drowned him out. He smiled and let them run their course. When they were through, he resumed, "Not only that, but today before you all I can also name my new Sevastos."

The crowd remained quiet, but suddenly the quiet became alert, electric. A new high minister was serious business, the more with a new, as yet little-known, and childless Emperor on the throne. Into that expectant hush, Krispos said, "I give you as Sevastos my foster brother, the noble Mavros."

"May his Highness be merciful!" the people called, as if with one voice. Krispos blinked; he hadn't thought there would be a special cry for the proclamation of a Sevastos. He was beginning to suspect Videssian ceremonial had a special cry or ritual for everything.

Grinning enormously, Mavros waved to show himself to the crowd. Krispos nudged him. "Say something," he whispered.

"Who, me?" Mavros whispered back. At Krispos' nod, the new Sevastos waved again, this time for quiet. When he got it, or at least enough of it to speak through, he said, "The good god willing, I will do as well in my office as our new Avtokrator does in his. Thank you all." As the crowd cheered, Mavros lowered his voice and told Krispos, "Now it's on your shoulders, Your Majesty. If you start going astray, I have every excuse to do the same thing."

"Oh, to the ice with you," Krispos said. He dipped his head to Gnatios. "Shall we get on with it?"

"Certainly, Your Majesty. By all means." Gnatios' expression reminded Krispos the delay had not been his idea in the first place. Without another word, he strode into the High Temple.

As Krispos followed him into the narthex, his eyes needed a moment to adjust to the dimmer light. The antechamber was the least splendid portion of the High Temple; it was merely magnificent. On the far wall, a mosaic depicted Phos as a beardless youth, a shepherd guarding his flock against wolves that fled, tails between their legs, back to their dark-robed master Skotos. The evil god's face was full of chilling hate.

Other mosaics set into the ceiling showed those whom Skotos' blandishments had seduced. The souls of the lost stood frozen into eternal ice. Demons with outstretched black wings and mouths full of horrid fangs tormented the damned in ingenious ways.

Not an inch of the High Temple was without its ornament. Even the marble lintel of the doorway into the narthex was covered with reliefs. Phos' sun stood in the center, its rays nourishing a whole forest of broadtoothed pointed leaves that had been carved in intricate repeating interlaced patterns.

Krispos paused to glance over to a spot not far from the doors. There by torchlight Barsymes had invested him with the leggings and kilt, the tunic and cape, and the red boots that were all part of the imperial coronation regalia. The boots had been tight; Anthimos' feet turned out to be smaller than Krispos'. Krispos was still wearing tight boots, though the cordwainers promised him pairs cut to his measure any day now.

Gnatios took a couple of steps before he noticed Krispos had stopped. The patriarch turned back and asked, "Shall we get on with it?" He did such an exquisite job of keeping irony from his voice that it was all the more ironic for being less so.

Unable to take offense no matter how much he wanted to, Krispos followed Gnatios out of the narthex and into the main chamber of the High Temple. Seated within were the high secular lords and soldiers of Videssos and their ladies, as well as the leading prelates and abbots of the city. They all rose to salute the Avtokrator and patriarch.

The nobles' rich robes, brightly dyed, shot through with gold and silver thread, and encrusted with gems hardly less glittering than those that adorned the soft flesh and sparkled in the hair of their wives and consorts, would irresistibly have drawn the eye to them in any other setting in the world. Within the High Temple, they did not dominate. They had to struggle to be noticed.

Even the benches from which the lords and ladies rose were works of art in themselves. They were blond oak, waxed to shine almost as brightly as the sun, and inset with ebony and red, red sandalwood; with semiprecious stones; and with mother-of-pearl that caught and brightened every ray of light.

Indeed, the huge interior of the High Temple seemed awash with light, as was only fitting for a building dedicated to Phos. "Here," Krispos had read in a chronicle that dealt in part with the raising of the Temple, "the immaterial became material." Had he seen the phrase in some provincial town far from the capital, he never would have understood it. In Videssos the city, the example lay before him.

Silver foil and gold leaf worked together with the mother-of-pearl to reflect light softly into every corner of the High Temple, illuminating with an almost shadowless light the moss-agate–faced columns that supported the building's four wings. Looking down, Krispos could see himself reflected in the polished golden marble of the floor.

More marble, this white as snow, gleamed on the interior walls of the Temple. Together with sheets of turquoise and, low in the east and west, rose quartz and ruddy sardonyx, it reproduced indoors the brilliance and beauty of Phos' sky.

Viewing the sky led the eye imperceptibly upward, to the twin semidomes where mosaics commemorated holy men who had been great in the service of Phos. And from those semidomes, it was impossible not to look farther yet, up and up and up into the great central dome overhead, from which Phos himself surveyed his worshipers.

The base of the dome was pierced by dozens of windows. Sunlight streamed through them and coruscated off the walls below; the beams seemed to separate the dome from the rest of the Temple below. The first time Krispos saw it, he'd wondered if it really was linked to the building it surmounted or if, as felt more likely, it floated up there by itself, suspended, perhaps, from a chain that led straight up into the heavens.

Down from the heavens, then, through the shifting sunbeams, Phos gazed upon the mere mortals who had gathered in his temple. The Phos portrayed in the dome was no smiling youth. He was mature, bearded, his long face stern and somber, his eyes . . . The first time Krispos had gone into the High Temple to worship, not long after he came to Videssos the city, he had almost cringed from those eyes. Large and omniscient, they seemed to see straight through him.

That was proper, for the Phos in the dome was judge rather than shepherd. In the long, spidery fingers of his left hand, he held to his chest a bound volume wherein all of good and evil was inscribed. A man could but hope that good outweighed the other. If not, eternity in the ice awaited, for while this Phos was just, Krispos could not imagine him merciful.

The tesserae that surrounded the god's head and shoulders in the dome were glass filmed with gold, and set at slightly varying angles. Whenever the light shifted, or whenever an observer below moved, different tiny tiles gleamed forth, adding to the spiritual solemnity of the depiction.

As it always did, tearing his eyes away from Phos' face cost Krispos a distinct effort of will. Temples throughout the Empire of Videssos held in their central domes images modeled on the one in the High Temple. Krispos had seen several. None held a fraction of the brooding majesty, the severe nobility, of this archetype. Here the god had truly inspired those who portrayed him.

Even after Krispos looked to the great silver slab of the altar that stood below the center of the dome, he felt Phos' gaze pressing down on him with almost physical force. Not even sight of the patriarchal throne of carven ivory behind the altar, a breathtaking work of art in its own right, could bring Krispos fully back to himself, not while everyone stood in silent awe, waiting for the ceremony to proceed.

Then Gnatios raised his hands to the god in the dome and to the god beyond the dome and beyond the sky. "We bless thee, Phos, lord with the great and good mind," he intoned, "by thy grace our protector, watchful beforehand that the great test of life may be decided in our favor."

Krispos repeated Phos' creed along with the ecumenical patriarch. So did everyone else in the High Temple; beside him he heard Dara's clear soprano. His hand tightened on hers. She squeezed back. Out of the corner of his eye he saw her smile.

Gnatios lowered his hands. The assembled grandees seated themselves. Krispos felt their gaze on him, too, but in a way different from Phos'. They were still wondering what sort of Avtokrator he would make. The good god already knew, but left to Krispos the working out of his fate.

Gnatios waited for quiet, then said what had been in Krispos' thoughts: "The eyes of all the city are on us today. Today we see joined in marriage the Avtokrator Krispos and the Empress Dara. May Phos bless their union and make it long, happy, and fruitful."

The patriarch began to pray again, now and then pausing for responses from Krispos and Dara. Krispos had memorized some of his replies, for the long-set language of the liturgy was growing apart from the tongue spoken in the streets of the city.

Gnatios delivered a traditional wedding sermon, touching on the virtues that helped make a good marriage. Then the patriarch said, "Are the two of you prepared to cleave to these virtues, and to each other, so long as you both may live?"

"Yes," Krispos said, and then again, louder, so that people besides himself and Dara could hear, "Yes."

"Yes," Dara agreed, not loudly but firmly.

As they spoke the words that bound them together, Mavros set a wreath of roses and myrtle on Krispos' head. One of Dara's attendants did the same for her.

"Behold them decked in the crowns of marriage!" Gnatios shouted. "Before the eyes of the entire city, they are shown to be man and wife!"

The grandees and their ladies rose from their benches to applaud. Krispos hardly heard them. He cared only about Dara, who was looking back at him with that same intent expression. Although it was no part of the ceremony, he took her in his arms. He smelled the sweet fragrance of her marriage crown as she held him tightly.

The cheers got louder and more sincere. Someone shouted bawdy advice. "Thou conquerest, Krispos!" someone else yelled, in a tone of voice altogether different from the usual solemn acclamation.

"Many heirs, Krispos!" another wit bawled.

Iakovitzes came up to Krispos. The noble was short and had to stand on tiptoe to put his mouth near Krispos' ear. "The ring, you idiot," he hissed. Perhaps because he had no interest whatever in women, he was immune to the joy of the marriage ceremony and cared only that it be correctly accomplished.

Krispos had forgotten the ring and was so relieved to be reminded of this that he took no notice of how Iakovitzes spoke to him; for that matter, Iakovitzes relished playing the gadfly no matter whom he was talking to. Krispos had the ring in a tiny pouch he wore on the inside of his belt so it would not show. He freed the heavy gold band and slipped it onto Dara's left index finger. She hugged him with renewed strength.

"Before the eyes of the whole city, they are wed!" Gnatios proclaimed. "Now let the people of the city see the happy pair!"

With the patriarch at their side, Krispos and Dara walked down the aisle by which they had approached the altar, through the narthex, and out onto the top of the stairway. The crowd in the forecourt cheered as they came down the steps. It was a smaller crowd now, even though the wedding attendants had fresh, full bags in their hands. They would not fling gold, but figs and nuts, fertility symbols from time out of mind.

Even the often dour Halogai were grinning as they formed up around the wedding party. Geirrod, the first of the northerners to acknowledge Krispos as Emperor, told him, "Do not fail me, Majesty. I have big bet on how many times tonight."

Dara squawked in indignation. Krispos' own humor was earthier, but he said, "How do you hope to settle that? By the good god, it's something only the Empress and I will ever know."

"Majesty, you served in the palaces before you ruled them," Geirrod said, his gray eyes knowing. "Was there anything servants could not learn when they needed to?"

"Not that," Krispos said, then stopped, suddenly unsure he was right. "At least, I hope not that."

"Huh," was all Geirrod said.

Giving his guardsman the last word, Krispos paraded with his new bride and their companions back the way they had come. Even without expectations of more money, a fair crowd still lined the streets and filled the plaza of Palamas; the folk of the city loved spectacle almost as well as largess.

After the plaza, the calm of the palace quarter came as a relief. Most of the Halogai departed for their barracks; only the troops assigned to guard the imperial residence accompanied the wedding party there. Save for Krispos and Dara, everyone stopped at the bottom of the steps. They pelted the newlywed couple with leftover figs and gave Krispos more lewd advice.

He endured that with the good humor a new groom is supposed to show. When he didn't feel like waiting any longer, he slid his arm round Dara's waist. Led by Mavros, the groomsmen and bridesmaids whooped. Krispos stuck his nose in the air and turned away from them, drawing Dara with him. They whooped louder than ever.

The happy shouts of the wedding party followed Dara and him down the hall to the bedchamber. The doors were closed. He opened them and found that the servants had turned down the bedcovers and left a jar of wine and two cups on the night table by the bed. Smiling, he closed the doors and barred them.

Dara turned her back on him. "Would you unfasten me, please? The maidservant took half an hour getting me into his gown; it has enough hooks and eyelets and what-have-you for a jail, not something you'd wear."

"I hope I can get you out of it faster than half an hour," Krispos said. He did, but not as fast as he might have; the more hooks he undid, the more attention his hands paid to the soft skin he was revealing and the less to the fasteners that remained.

Finally the job was done. Dara turned to him. They kissed for a long time. When at last they broke apart, she ruefully looked down at herself. "Every pearl, every gem, every metal thread on that robe of yours has stamped itself into me," she complained.

"And what will you do about that?" he asked.

A corner of her mouth quirked upward. "Let's see if I can keep it from happening again." Her disrobing of him also proceeded more slowly than it might have, but he did not mind.

The two of them hung their crowns of marriage on the bedposts for luck, then lay down together. Krispos caressed Dara's breasts, lowered his mouth to one of them. She stirred, but not altogether in pleasure. "Be gentle, if you can," she said. "They're sore."

"Are they?" Under the fine skin, he could see a new tracery of blue veins. He touched her again, as carefully as he could. "Another sign you're carrying a child."

"I don't have much doubt, not anymore," she said.

"All those nuts and figs did a better job than they know," he said, straight-faced.

Dara started to nod, then snorted and poked him in the ribs. He grabbed her and held her close to keep her from doing it again. They did not separate, not until they were both spent. Then, his breath still coming quick, Krispos reached for the wine jar and said, "Shall we see what they gave us to keep us going?"

"Why not?" Dara answered. "Pour a cup for me, too, please."

Thick and golden, the wine gurgled out of the jar. Krispos recognized the sweet, heady bouquet. "This is that Vaspurakaner vintage from Petronas' cellars," he said. When Anthimos broke his ambitious uncle's power, he'd confiscated all of Petronas' lands, his money, his horses, and his wines. Krispos had drunk this one before. He raised the cup to his lips. "As good as I remember it."

Dara sipped, raised an eyebrow. "Yes, that's quite fine—sweet and tart at the same time." She drank again.

Krispos held his cup high. "To you, Your Majesty."

"And to you, Your Majesty," Dara answered, returning his salute with vigor—so much that a few drops flew over the rim and splashed on the bedclothes. As she looked at the spreading stain, she started to laugh.

"What's funny?" Krispos said.

"I was just thinking that this time no one will expect to find a spot of blood on the sheet. After my first night with Anthimos, Skombros marched in, peeled that sheet off the bed—he almost dumped me out to get it—then took it outside and waved it about. Everyone cheered, but it was a ritual I could have done without. As if I were a piece of raw meat, checked to make sure I hadn't spoiled."

"Ah, Skombros," Krispos said. The fat eunuch had been Anthimos' vestiarios before Petronas got Krispos the post. An Emperor's chamberlain was in a uniquely good position to influence him, and Petronas had wanted no one but himself influencing Anthimos. And so Skombros had gone from the imperial residence to a bare monastery cell; Krispos wondered if Petronas had ever thought the same fate could befall him.

"I liked you better than Skombros as vestiarios," Dara said with a sidelong look.

"I'm glad you did," Krispos answered mildly. All the same, he understood why imperial chamberlains were most of them eunuchs, and was not sorry his own vestiarios followed that rule. Since Dara had cheated for him, how could he be sure she would never cheat against him?

He glanced toward his Empress, wondering again whether the child she carried was his or Anthimos'. If even she could not say, how would he ever know?

He shook his head. Doubts at the very beginning of a marriage did not bode well for contentment to come. He tried to put them aside. If ever a husband had given his wife reason to be unfaithful, he told himself, Anthimos had provoked Dara with his orgies and his endless parade of paramours. As long as he treated her well himself, she should have no reason to stray.

He took her in his arms again. "So soon?" she said, startled but not displeased. "Here, let me set my wine down first." She giggled as his weight pressed her to the bed. "I hope your Haloga bet high."

"So do I," Krispos said. Then her lips silenced him.

K RISPOS WOKE, YAWNED, STRETCHED, AND ROLLED OVER ONTO his back. Dara was sitting up in bed beside him. By the look of her, she'd been awake for some time. Krispos sat up, too. He glanced at where sunbeams hit the far wall. "Phos!" he exclaimed. "What hour is it, anyway?"

"Somewhere in the fourth, I'd say—more than halfway to noon," Dara told him. The Videssians gave twelve hours to the day and another twelve to the night, reckoning them from sunrise and sunset respectively. Dara gave him a quizzical look. "What do you suppose you were doing last night that left you so tired?"

"I can't imagine," Krispos said, only partly in irony. He'd grown up a peasant, after all, and what labor was more exhausting than farming? Yet he'd risen with the sun every day. On the other hand, he'd gone to bed with the sun, too, and he'd been up considerably later than that the night before.

Yawning again, he got up, ambled over to the bureau to put on some drawers, then opened a tall wardrobe, picked out a robe, and pulled it on over his head. Dara watched him bemusedly. He was reaching for a pair of red boots when she asked, "Have you forgotten you have a vestiarios to help you with such things?"

He paused. "As a matter of fact, I did," he said sheepishly. "That was foolish of me, wasn't it? But it's also foolish for Barsymes to help me just because I'm Avtokrator. I didn't need his help before." As if to defy custom, he tugged on his own boots.

"It's also foolish not to let Barsymes do his job, which is to serve you," Dara said. "If you don't allow him to perform his proper function, then he has none. Is that what you want?"

"No," Krispos admitted. But having done entirely without service most of his life, and having given it first as groom in Iakovitzes' and Petronas' stables, then as Anthimos' vestiarios, he still felt odd about receiving it.

Dara, a western noble's daughter, had no such qualms. She reached for a green cord that hung by her side of the bed and pulled down on it. A couple of rooms away, a bell tinkled. Moments later, a maidservant tried to open the doors to the imperial bedchambers. "They're still locked, your Majesties," she said.

Krispos walked over and lifted the bar. "Come in, Verina," he said.

"Thank you, Your Majesty." The serving maid stared at him in surprise and no little indignation. "You're dressed!" she blurted. "What are you doing being dressed?"

He did not turn around to see the I-told-you-so look in Dara's eyes, but he was sure it was there. "I'm sorry, Verina," he said mildly. "I won't let it happen again." A scarlet bellpull dangled next to his side of the bed. He pulled it. This bell was easier to hear—the vestiarios' chamber, the chamber that had until recently been his, was next door to the bedchamber.

Barsymes' long pale face grew longer when he saw Krispos. "Your Majesty," he said, making the title into one of reproach.

"I'm sorry," Krispos said again; though he ruled the Empire of Videssos, he wondered if he was truly master of the palaces. "Even if I did dress myself, I'm sure I'm no cook. Will you be less angry at me after you escort me to breakfast?"

The vestiarios' mouth twitched. It could have been a smile. "Possibly a trifle, Your Majesty. If you'll come with me?"

Krispos followed Barsymes out of the bedchamber. "I'll join you soon," Dara said. She was standing nude in front of her wardrobe, chattering with Verina about which gown she should wear today. Barsymes' eyes never went her way. Not all eunuchs were immune from desire, even if they lacked the capacity to satisfy it. Krispos wondered whether the vestiarios felt no stirring or was just a discreetly excellent servant. He knew he could never ask.

Barsymes fussed over seating him in a small dining room. "And how would you care to break your fast this day, Your Majesty?"

"A big hot bowl of porridge, a chunk of bread and some honey, and a couple of rashers of bacon would do me very well," Krispos said. That was the sort of hearty breakfast he'd had back in his home village when times were good. Times hadn't been good often enough. Sometimes breakfast had been a small bowl of porridge, sometimes nothing at all.

"As you wish, Your Majesty," Barsymes said tonelessly, "though Phestos may be disappointed at having nothing more elaborate to prepare."

"Ah," Krispos said. Anthimos had gloried in the exotic; he'd thought his own more mundane tastes would be a relief to everyone. But if Phestos wanted a challenge . . . "Tell him to make the goat seethed in fermented fish sauce and leeks tonight, then."

Barsymes nodded. "A good choice."

Dara came in, asked for a stewed muskmelon. The vestiarios went to take her request and Krispos' to the cook. With a wry smile, she patted her belly. "I just hope it stays down. The past couple of days, I've hardly wanted to look at food."

"You have to eat," Krispos said.

"I know it full well. My stomach's the one that's not convinced."

Before long, Barsymes brought in the food. Krispos happily dug in and finished his own breakfast while Dara picked at her melon. When Barsymes saw Krispos was done, he whisked away his dishes and set in front of him a silver tray full of scrolls. "The morning's correspondence, Your Majesty."

"All right," Krispos said without enthusiasm. Anthimos, he knew, would have pitched a fit at the idea of handling business before noon—or after noon, for that matter. But Krispos had impressed on his servants that he intended to be a working Avtokrator. This was his reward for their taking him at his word.

He pawed through the proposals, petitions, and reports, hoping to begin with something moderately interesting. When he found a letter still sealed, his eyebrows rose. How had the secretaries who scribbled away in the wings that flanked the Grand Courtroom let it slip past them unopened? Then he exclaimed in pleasure.

Dara gave him a curious look. "You don't usually sound so gleeful when you go over those parchments."

"It's a letter from Tanilis," he said. Then he remembered that, for a variety of reasons, he'd told Dara little about Tanilis, so he added, "She's Mavros' mother, you know. She and Mavros were both kind to me when I went there with Iakovitzes a few years ago; I'm glad to hear from her."

"Oh. All right." Dara took another bite of muskmelon. Krispos supposed that hearing Tanilis described—truthfully—as Mavros' mother made her picture the noblewoman—most untruthfully—as plump, comfortable, and middle-aged. Though she had to be nearly forty now, Krispos was sure Tanilis retained all the elegant sculpted beauty she'd had when he knew her.

He began to read aloud. " 'The lady Tanilis to his Imperial Majesty Krispos, Avtokrator of the Videssians: My deepest congratulations on your accession to the throne and on your marriage to the Empress Dara. May your reign be long and prosperous.' " Then his glance happened to stray to the date above the salutation. "By the good god," he said softly, and sketched Phos' sun-circle above his heart.

"What is it?" Dara asked.

He passed her the letter. "See for yourself." He pointed to the date.

For a moment, it meant nothing to her. He watched her eyes widen. She made the sun-sign, too. "That's the day *before* you took the throne," she whispered.

"So it is," he said, nodding. "Tanilis—sees things. When I was in Opsikion, she foresaw that I might become Emperor. By then I was Iakovitzes' spatharios—his aide. A couple of years before, I'd been a farmer laboring in the field. I thought I'd already risen as high as I could." Some days he could still be surprised he was Avtokrator. This was one of them. He reached across the table and took Dara's hand. A brief squeeze reminded him this was no dream.

She gave the letter back to him. "Read it out loud, if you don't mind."

"Of course." He found his place and resumed. " 'May your reign be long and prosperous. My gratitude for your naming Mavros Sevastos—' " He broke off again.

"If she knew the rest, no reason she wouldn't know that," Dara pointed out.

"I suppose not. Here, I'll go on: '. . . for your naming Mavros Sevastos. I am sure he will serve you to the best of his ability. One favor I would beg of you in regard to my son. Should he ever desire to lead troops against the northern barbarians, I pray that you tell him no. While he may win glory and acclaim in that pursuit, I fear he will not have the enjoyment of them. Farewell, and may Phos bless you always.' "

Krispos set down the parchment. "I don't know that Mavros ever would want to go out on campaign, but if he does, telling him no won't be easy." He made a troubled sound with tongue and teeth.

"Not even after this?" Dara's finger found the relevant passage in the letter. "Surely he knows his mother's powers. Would he risk defying them?"

"I've known Mavros a good many years now," Krispos said. "All I can say is that he'll do as he pleases, no matter who or what gets defied in the doing. The lord with the great and good mind willing, the matter won't ever come up. Tanilis didn't say it was certain."

"That's true," Dara agreed.

But Krispos knew—and knew also Dara knew—the matter might very well arise. Having overthrown the khagan of Kubrat on Videssos' northern frontier, an adventurer called Harvas Black-Robe and his band of Haloga mercenaries had begun raiding the Empire, as well. The generals on the border had been having little luck with them; before too long, someone would have to drive them back where they belonged.

One of the palace eunuchs stuck his head into the dining chamber. "What is it, Tyrovitzes?" Krispos asked.

"The abbot Pyrrhos is outside the residence, Your Majesty," Tyrovitzes said, puffing a little—he was as fat as Barsymes was lean. "He wants to speak with you, at once, and will not speak with anyone else. For your ears alone, he insists."

"Does he?" Krispos frowned. He found Pyrrhos' narrow piety harsh and oppressive, but the abbot was no one's fool. "Very well, fetch him in. I'll hear him."

Tyrovitzes bowed as deeply as his rotund frame would permit, then hurried away. He soon returned with Pyrrhos. The abbot bowed low to Dara, then prostrated himself before Krispos. He did not seek to rise, but stayed on his belly. "I abase myself before you, Your Majesty. The fault is mine, and let my head answer for it if that be your will."

"What fault?" Krispos said testily. "Holy sir, will you please get up and talk sense?"

Pyrrhos rose. Though a graybeard, he was limber as a youth, a kinder reward of the asceticism that also thinned his face to almost skeletal leanness and left his eyes dark burning coals. "As I told Your Majesty, the fault is mine," he said. "Through some error, whether accidental or otherwise I am investigating, the count of the monks in the monastery dedicated to the memory of the holy Skirios may have been inaccurate last night. It was surely one too low this morning. We do indeed have a runaway monk."

"And who might this runaway be?" Krispos inquired, though he was sickly certain he knew the answer without having to ask. No trivial disappearance would make the abbot hotfoot it to the imperial residence with the news.

Pyrrhos saw his certainty and gave a grim nod. "Aye, Your Majesty, it is as you fear—Petronas has escaped."

Chapter II

Trying to meet bad news with equanimity, Krispos said, "I don't think he's going to be very pleased with me."

Only after the words were out of his mouth did he realize what an understatement that was. Petronas had virtually ruled the Empire for a decade and more while his nephew Anthimos reveled; he had raised Krispos to the post of vestiarios. Finally Anthimos, worried lest his uncle supplant him on the throne, a worry abetted by Krispos and Dara, clapped him into the monastery . . . for good, Krispos had thought.

Dara said bitterly, "While all the eyes of the city were on us yesterday, Petronas took the chance to get out."

Krispos knew she was just echoing Gnatios' words, but what she said raised echoes in his own mind, echoes of suspicion. He'd wondered why Gnatios had suddenly become so obliging about the wedding. Now maybe he knew. "The patriarch did keep harping on that, didn't he? He and Petronas are cousins, too, and if anyone could arrange to have a monk taken from his monastery without the abbot's knowledge, who better than Gnatios?"

"No one better, Your Majesty," Pyrrhos said, following Krispos' line of thought. His sharp-curved nose, fierce eyes, and shaven head made him resemble a bird of prey.

"Tyrovitzes!" Krispos shouted. When the fat eunuch reappeared, Krispos told him, "Take a squad of Halogai and fetch Gnatios here at once, no matter what he's doing."

"Your Majesty?" Tyrovitzes said. At Krispos' answering glare, he gulped and said, "Yes, Your Majesty."

Tyrovitzes had hardly left before Krispos shouted, "Longinos!" As soon as that eunuch responded, Krispos said, "Go to Captain Thvari. Take all the Halogai save enough to guard me here, take whatever other troops are in the city, and start a search. Maybe Petronas has gone to ground inside the walls."

"Petronas?" Longinos said, staring.

"Yes; he's escaped, curse him," Krispos answered impatiently. The chamberlain started to go. Then Krispos had an afterthought. "If Thvari does use our own troops along with the northerners, have him make sure he puts more Halogai than Videssians in each party. I know his men are loyal."

"As you say, Your Majesty." Longionos bowed deeply and departed.

He was scarcely gone when Krispos yelled, "Barsymes!" The vestiarios might have been waiting right outside; he came in almost at once. "Go to the house of Trokoundos the wizard and bring him here, if you please."

"Certainly, Your Majesty. I suppose you'll want him to interrogate Gnatios," Barsymes said calmly. At Krispos' expression of surprise, he went on, "You have not kept your voice down, you know, Your Majesty."

Krispos thought about that. "No, I suppose I haven't. Go get me Trokoundos now, if you please. If Gnatios did have a hand in Petronas' escape—" He pounded a clenched fist down on the tabletop. "If that's so, we'll have a new ecumenical patriarch before the day is out."

"Your pardon, Majesty, but perhaps not so quickly as that," Pyrrhos said. "You may of course remove a prelate as you wish, but the naming of his successor lies in the hands of a synod of clerics, to whom you submit a list of three candidates for their formal selection."

"You understand that all that rigmarole would just delay your own choice," Krispos said.

Pyrrhos bowed. "Your Majesty is gracious. All the same, however, observances must be fulfilled to ensure the validity of any patriarchal enthronement."

"If Gnatios helped Petronas get away, he deserves worse than being deposed," Dara said. "Some time with the torturers might be a fit answer for his treason."

"We'll worry about that later," Krispos said. With peasant patience, he settled down to see whether Gnatios or Trokoundos would be brought to the imperial residence first. When Pyrrhos began to look restive, he sent him back to his monastery. Sitting quietly, he kept on waiting.

"How can you be so easy about this?" demanded Dara, who was pacing back and forth.

"Nothing would change if I fussed," he said. Dara snorted and kept pacing.

Rather to Krispos' surprise, Tyrovitzes' party fetched back Gnatios before Barsymes arrived with Trokoundos. "Your Majesty, what is the meaning of this?" the patriarch said indignantly after the eunuch chamberlain escorted him into Krispos' presence. "I find it humiliating to be seized in the street like some low footpad and fetched here with no more consideration for my feelings than such a criminal would receive."

"Where's Petronas, Gnatios?" Krispos asked in a voice like iron.

"Why, in the monastery sacred to the holy Skirios." Gnatios' eyebrows rose. "Or are you telling me he is not? If you are, I have no idea where he is."

The patriarch sounded surprised and curious, just as he would if he were innocent. But Krispos knew he had no small rhetorical talents; sounding innocent was child's play for him. "While all the eyes of the city were on us yesterday, Gnatios, Petronas was spirited out of the monastery. To be blunt, I know you have scant love for me. Do you wonder that I have doubts about you?"

"Your Majesty, I can see that you might." Gnatios smiled his most engaging smile. "But after all, Your Majesty, you know where I was yesterday. I could hardly have helped Petronas escape at the same time as I was performing the wedding ceremony for you and your new Empress." He smiled again, this time at Dara. She stared stonily back. His smile faded.

"No, but you could have planned and arranged a rescue," Krispos said. "Will you take oath on your fear of Skotos' ice that you had no part of any sort in Petronas' getting out of the monastery?"

"Your Majesty, I will swear any oath you wish," Gnatios answered at once.

Just then, Krispos saw Barsymes standing in the hall with a short spare man who shaved his head like a priest but wore a red tunic and green trousers. He carried a bulging carpetbag.

"Your Majesty," Trokoundos said. The mage started a proskynesis, but Krispos waved for him not to bother. "How may I serve you, Your Majesty?" he asked, straightening. His voice was deep and rich, the voice to be expected of a man a head taller and twice as wide through the shoulders.

"Most holy sir, I will require no oath of you at all," Krispos said to Gnatios. "You might throw away your soul for the sake of advantage in this world, and that would be very sad. Instead, I will ask you the same questions you have already heard, but with this wizard standing by to make sure you speak the truth."

"I will need a little while to ready myself, Your Majesty," Trokoundos said. "I have here some of the things I may use, if your vestiarios spoke accurately about your requirements." He began taking mirrors, candles, and stoppered glass vials of various sizes and colors out of the carpetbag.

Gnatios watched him prepare with indignation but no visible fear. "Your Majesty, I will even submit to this outrage, but I must inform you that I protest it," he said. "Surely you cannot imagine that I would violate my oath."

"*I* can," Dara said.

Krispos took a different line. "I can imagine many things, most holy sir," he told the patriarch. "I can even imagine giving you over to the torturers to find out what I must know. A mage, I think, will hurt your body and your pride less, but I can go the other way if you'd rather."

"As you will, Your Majesty," Gnatios said, so boldly that Krispos wondered if he was indeed innocent. The patriarch added, "My thanks for showing consideration for me, at least to the extent you have."

"Just stay right there, if you would, most holy sir," Trokoundos said. Gnatios nodded regally as the mage set up a mirror on a jointed stand a few feet in front of him. Between mirror and patriarch, Trokoundos lit a candle. He opened a couple of his vials and shook powder from them onto the flame, which changed color and sent up a large cloud of surprisingly sweet-smelling smoke.

Muttering to himself, Trokoundos set up another mirror a few feet behind Gnatios and slightly to one side: this one faced the one he'd set up before. He fussily adjusted the two squares of polished silver until Gnatios' face, reflected from the first, was visible in the second. Then he lit another candle between the second mirror and Gnatios' back. He sprinkled different powders over this flame, whose smoke proved as noxious as the other's had been pleasant.

Coughing a little, the mage said, "Go ahead, Your Majesty; ask what you will."

"Thank you." Krispos turned to the patriarch. "Most holy sir, did you help Petronas escape from the monastery dedicated to the holy Skirios?"

He watched Gnatios' lips shape the word "No" but did not hear him speak it. At the same time, the patriarch's second reflection, the one in the mirror behind him, loudly and clearly said, "Yes."

Gnatios jerked as if stung. Krispos asked, "How did you do it?"

He thought the patriarch tried to say "I had nothing to do with it." The reflection answered for him: "I sent in a monk who rather resembled him to take his place while he was at solitary prayer and to stay into the evening. Then, last night, I sent a priest who asked for the substituted monk by his proper name and brought him out of the monastery once more."

"What is the name of this monk?" Krispos demanded.

This time Gnatios stood mute. His reflection answered for him nonetheless. "Harmosounos."

Krispos nodded to Trokoundos. "This is an excellent magic." The wizard's heavy-lidded eyes lit up.

Gnatios shifted from foot to foot, awaiting the next question. "Where did Petronas plan to go?" Krispos asked him.

"I do not know," he answered, out of his own mouth.

"A moment, Your Majesty," Trokoundos said sharply. He fiddled with the mirrors again. "He sought to move enough to shift his image from the second mirror."

"Don't play such games again, most holy sir. I promise you would regret it," Krispos told Gnatios. "Now I will ask once more, where did Petronas plan to go?"

"I do not know," Gnatios repeated. This time, strangely, Krispos heard the words both straight from him and from the mirror at his back. He glanced toward Trokoundos.

"He speaks the truth, Your Majesty," the wizard said.

"I was afraid that was what that meant," Krispos said. "Let's try something else, then. Answer me this, most holy sir: you being kinsman to Petronas, where would you go in his boots?"

Gnatios plainly tried to lie again; his lips moved, but no sound came out of his mouth. Instead, his doubly reflected image replied, "Petronas' greatest estates are in the westlands, between the towns of Garsavra and Resaina. There he would find the most support for any bid to take the crown."

"You expect him to do that, eh?" Krispos said.

The answer to that question was so obvious, Krispos did not expect Gnatios to bother giving it aloud. And, indeed, the patriarch stayed silent. But under Trokoundos' spell, his second image spoke for him. "Don't you expect it, Your Majesty?"

Krispos' chuckle was dry. "Well, yes, as a matter of fact." He turned to Trokoundos. "I'm in your debt once more, it seems."

Trokoundos waved that away. "I'm happy to do what I can for you, Your Majesty. Your warning saved me from Anthimos' wrath a couple of years ago."

"And your wizardry let me live through the enchantment with which Petronas would have killed me otherwise," Krispos said. "Don't be shy when you name your fee for today."

"Your Majesty, people have accused me of many things, but never of being shy about my fees," Trokoundos said.

Whether anxious over his fate or simply resentful at being forgotten for the moment, Gnatios burst out, "What will you do with me, Your Majesty?"

"A good question," Krispos said musingly. "If helping to set up a rival Emperor isn't treason, what is? Shall I put your head on the Milestone as a warning to others, Gnatios?"

"I'd rather you didn't," the patriarch answered, coolly enough to win Krispos' reluctant admiration.

"I think you should, Krispos," Dara said. Gnatios winced as she went on, "What does a traitor deserve but the axe? What would Petronas do to you, and to me, and to our child, if—Phos prevent it—he beat you?"

Gnatios missed very little. Though he could not have known of Dara's pregnancy before she mentioned it, he used it at once, saying, "Your Majesty, would you slay the man who performed your marriage ceremony and so made your heir legitimate?"

"Why not," Dara shot back, "when part of the reason you married us was to draw attention away from the holy Skirios' monastery so you could loose Petronas against us?" The patriarch winced again.

"I don't think I'll kill you now," Krispos said. Gnatios looked delighted, Dara disappointed. Krispos went on, "I do cast you down from the patri-archal throne. In your place I intend to propose the name of the abbot Pyrrhos."

Gnatios winced a third time. "I'd almost rather you killed me, if afterward you named in my place someone not a fanatic."

"I can trust the clerics of his faction. If I thought I could trust one from yours, I'd take you up on that."

"I did say 'almost,' Your Majesty," the patriarch reminded him quickly.

"So you did. Here's what I will do. Till the synod names Pyrrhos, I will send you to the monastery of the holy Skirios. There you will be under his hand as abbot. That should be enough to keep you out of mischief for the time being." Krispos watched Gnatios open his mouth to speak. "Think twice if you are about to say again that you'd rather be dead, most holy sir—no, holy sir, for you are but a monk now. I just may oblige you."

Gnatios glared at him but said nothing.

Krispos turned to Tyrovitzes. "You heard what I ordered?" The eunuch nodded. "Good. Take this monk to the monastery, then, and tell the abbot he is not to leave no matter what happens. Take the Halogai with you as you go, too, to make sure the man doesn't get stolen on the way."

"As you say, Your Majesty." Tyrovitzes nodded to Gnatios. "If you will come with me, holy sir?" Unlike Krispos, Tyrovitzes adjusted to changing honorifics without having to think twice. Still in his patriarch robe, Gnatios followed the chamberlain away.

"I wish you'd slain him," Dara said.

"He may still have some use alive," Krispos said. "Besides, I don't think he'll be going anywhere, not now. He and Pyrrhos have despised each other for years. Now that he's in Pyrrhos' clutches, he'll be locked up tighter and watched better than if he was in prison—and fed worse, too, I'd wager."

He sighed. "All this would be much easier if I really believed the soldiers would turn up Petronas still inside the city. If they don't—" Krispos stood thinking for a while, trying to work out what he would have to do to hunt down Petronas loose in the countryside.

"I fear they won't," Dara said.

"So do I," Krispos told her. Petronas was both clever and nervy. The only flaw Krispos had ever noted in him was a streak of vanity; because he could do so much, he thought he could do anything. Some time in the monastery might even have cured him of that, Krispos reflected gloomily.

"You should proclaim him outlaw," Dara said. "A price on his head will make folk more likely to betray him to you."

"Aye, I'll do that," Krispos said. "I'll also send a troop of cavalry out to the estates that used to be his. Though Anthimos took them over, I expect most of the men on them will still be people Petronas chose, and they may still be loyal to him."

"Be careful of the officer you choose to command that troop," Dara warned. "You won't want anyone who served under him."

"You're right," Krispos said. But Petronas had headed the imperial army while his nephew frittered away the days. That meant every Videssian officer had served under him, at least indirectly. The commanders in the city had sworn oaths of loyalty to Krispos. Those in the field were sending in written pledges; a couple arrived every day. How much would such pledges mean, when measured against years of allegiance to a longtime leader? Krispos was convinced oaths and pledges were only as reliable as the men who gave them. He wished he'd had time to learn more about his officers before facing a challenge like this.

As is the way of such things, wishing failed to furnish him the time he needed. He sighed again. "I'll pick as carefully as I can."

DAYS PASSED. THE SEARCH OF THE CITY FAILED TO YIELD ANY trace of Petronas. At Krispos' order, scribes calloused their fingers writing scores of copies of a proclamation that branded Petronas outlaw, rebel, and renegade monk. They posted them in the plaza of Palamas, in the lesser square called the forum of the Ox, in the forecourts to the High Temple, and at each of the gates in Videssos the city's walls. Before long, dozens of people claimed to have seen Petronas. So far as Krispos could tell, no one really had.

Imperial couriers galloped east and west from the city with more copies of the proclamation. A cavalry troop also galloped west. Other couriers took ship to carry word of Petronas' escape to coastal towns more quickly than horses could reach them.

Despite the worry that gnawed at him, Krispos carried on with the routine business of the Empire. Indeed, he threw himself into it; the busier he was, the less chance he had to notice Petronas was still free.

He also wasted no time in organizing the synod that would ratify his choice of Pyrrhos to succeed Gnatios as ecumenical patriarch. That was connected to Petronas' disappearance, but gave Krispos satisfaction nonetheless; on Gnatios, at least, he could take proper vengeance.

Yet even the synod proved more complicated than he'd expected. As custom required, he summoned to it abbots and high-ranking priests from the capital, as well as the prelates of the larger suburbs on both sides of the Cattle-Crossing, the strait that separated Videssos the city from its western provinces. Having summoned them, he assumed the rest of the process would be a formality. After all, as Avtokrator he headed the ecclesiastical hierarchy no less than he did the state.

But many of the prelates who gathered at his command in the chapel in the palace quarter owed their own appointments to Gnatios, were of his moderate theological bent, and did not take kindly to choosing the head of the more zealous faction to replace him.

"May it please Your Majesty," said Savianos, prelate of the western suburb known simply as Across because it lay directly opposite Videssos the city, "but the abbot Pyrrhos, holy though he is, is also a man of harsh and severe temper, perhaps not ideally suited to administering all aspects of ecclesiastical affairs." By the way Savianos' bushy eyebrows twitched, he would have said a good deal more than that had he dared. Talking to his fellow clerics, he probably had said a good deal more than that.

Krispos said politely, "I have, after all, submitted three names to this holy synod." He and all the clerics knew he'd done so only because the law required it of him. Moreover, he'd taken no chances with his other two candidates.

Savianos understood that, too. "Oh, aye, Your Majesty, Traianos and Rhepordenes are very pious," he said. Now his eyebrows leapt instead of twitching. The two clerics, one the prelate of the provincial town of Develtos, the other an abbot in the semidesert far southwest, were fanatical enough to make even Pyrrhos seem mild by comparison.

"Never having known discipline, the holy Savianos may fear it more than is warranted," observed a priest named Lournes, one of Pyrrhos' backers. "The experience, though novel, should prove salutary."

"To the ice with you," Savianos snapped.

"You are the one who will know the ice," Lournes retorted. The clerics on either side yelled and shook their fists at those on the other. Krispos had seen little of prelates till now, save in purely ceremonial roles. Away from such ceremony, he discovered, they seemed men like any others, if louder than most.

He listened for a little while, then slammed the flat of his hand down on the table in front of him. Into sudden quiet he said, "Holy sirs, I didn't think I'd need the Halogai to keep you from one another's throats." The hierarchs looked briefly shamefaced. He went on. "If you reckon the holy Pyrrhos a heretic or an enemy of the faith, do your duty, vote him down, and give the blue boots to one of the other men I've offered you. If not, make that plain with your vote, as well."

"May it please Your Majesty," Savianos said, "my questions about the holy Pyrrhos do not pertain to his orthodoxy; though I love him not, I will confess he is most perfectly orthodox. I only fear that he will not recognize as orthodox anyone who fails to share his beliefs to the last jot and tittle."

"That is as it should be," said Visandos, an abbot who supported Pyrrhos. "The truth being by definition unique, any deviation from it is unacceptable."

Savianos shot back, "The principle of theological economy grants latitude of opinion on issues not relating directly to the destination of one's soul, as you know perfectly well."

"*No* issue is unrelated to the destination of one's soul," Visandos said. The ecclesiastics started yelling louder than ever.

Krispos whacked the table again. Silence came more slowly this time, but he eventually won it. He said, "Holy sirs, you have more wisdom than I in these matters, but I did not summon you here to discuss them. Gnatios has shown himself a traitor to me. I need a patriarch I can rely on. Will you give him to me?"

Since even Savianos had admitted Pyrrhos was orthodox, the result of the synod was a foregone conclusion. And since no cleric cared to risk the Avtokrator's wrath, the vote for Pyrrhos was unanimous. The priests and abbots began arguing all over again, though, as they filed out of the chapel.

As Savianos rose to depart, he told Krispos, "Majesty, I pray that you always recall we did this only at your bidding."

"Why? Do you think I will regret it?" Krispos said.

Savianos did not reply, but his eyebrows were eloquent.

In spite of the prelate's forebodings, Krispos remained convinced he had done a good day's work. But his satisfaction lasted only until he finished the walk from the chapel to the imperial residence. There he found an imperial courier waiting for him. The man's face was drawn with fatigue and pain; a bloodstained bandage wrapped his left shoulder.

Looking at him, Krispos wondered where disaster had struck now. The last time a courier had waited for him like this, it was with word that Harvas Black-Robe's savage followers had destroyed the village where he'd grown up and that his sister, brother-in-law, and two nieces were gone forever. Did this man bring more bad news from the north, or had things gone wrong in the west?

"You'd best tell me," Krispos said quietly.

The courier saluted like a soldier, setting his clenched right fist over his heart. "Aye, Your Majesty. The troops you sent to Petronas' estates—well, sir, they found him there. And their captain and most of the men . . ." He paused, shook his head, and went on as he had to: "They went over to him, sir. A few fled that night. I heard what happened from one of those. We were being pursued; we separated to try to make sure one of us got to you with the news. I see I'm the first, sir. I'm sorry."

Krispos did his best to straighten his face; he hadn't realized he'd let his dismay show. "Thank you for staying loyal and bringing it to me . . ." He paused to let the courier give his name.

"I'm called Themistios, Your Majesty," the fellow said, saluting again.

"I'm in your debt, Themistios. First find yourself a healer-priest and have that shoulder seen to." Krispos pulled a three-leafed tablet from the pouch on his belt. He used a stylus to write an order. Then he drew out the imperial sunburst seal and pushed it into the wax below what he had written. He closed the tablet, handing it to Themistios. "Take this to the treasury. They'll give you a pound of gold. And if anyone tries to keep you from getting it, find out his name and give it to me. He won't try twice, I promise."

Themistios bowed. "I was afraid my head might answer for bringing you bad news, Your Majesty. I didn't expect to be rewarded for it."

"Why not?" Krispos said. "How soon good news comes makes no difference; good news takes care of itself. But the sooner I hear of anything bad, the longer I have to do something about it. Now go find a healer-priest, as I told you. You look as if you're about to fall over where you stand."

Themistios saluted once more and hurried away. One of the Halogai with Krispos asked, "Now that you know where Petronas is, Majesty, and now you have longer to do something about it, what will you do?"

Krispos had always admired the big, fair-haired barbarians' most un-Videssian way of coming straight to the point. He did his best to match it. "I aim to go out and fight him, Vagn."

Vagn and the rest of the guardsmen shouted approval, raising their axes high. Vagn said, "While you were still vestiarios, Majesty, I told you you thought like a Haloga. I am glad to see you do not change now that you are Avtokrator."

The other northerners loudly agreed. Forgetting Krispos' imperial dignity, they pounded him on the back and boasted of how they would hack their way through whatever puny forces Petronas managed to gather, and how they would chop the rebel himself into pieces small enough for dogs to eat. "Small enough for baby dogs," Vagn declared grandly. "For puppies straight from bitches' teats."

For as long as he listened to them, Krispos grinned and, buoyed by their ferocity, almost believed disposing of Petronas would be as easy as they thought. But his smile was gone by the time he got to the top of the stairs that led into the imperial residence.

BARSYMES STOOD BEHIND KRISPOS' BACK, FUMBLING WITH UN-familiar catches. "There," he said at last. "You look most martial, Your Majesty."

"I do, don't I?" Krispos sounded surprised, even to himself. His shoulders tightened to bear the weight of the mail shirt the vestiarios had just finished fastening. He suspected he'd ache by the time he took it off. He had fought before, against Kubrati raiders, but he'd never worn armor.

And such armor! His was no ordinary mail shirt. Even in the pale light that sifted through the alabaster ceiling panels of the imperial residence, its gilding made it gleam and sparkle. When the Avtokrator of the Videssians went on campaign with his troops, no one could doubt for an instant who was in command.

He set his conical helmet on his head, fiddled with it until it fit comfortably over his ears. The helmet was gilded, too, with a real gold circlet soldered around it at about the level of the top of his forehead. His scabbard and sword belt were also gilded, as was the hilt of the sword. About the only things he had that were not gilded were the sword's blade, his red boots, and the stout spear in his right hand. He'd carried that spear with him when he walked from his native village to Videssos the city. Along with a lucky goldpiece he wore on a chain round his neck, it was all he had left of the place where he'd grown up.

Dara threw her arms around him. Through the mail and the padding beneath it, he could not feel her body. He hugged her, too, gently, so as not to hurt her. "Come back soon and safe," she said—the same wish women always send with their men who ride to war.

"I'll come back soon enough," he answered. "I'll have to. With summer almost gone, the fighting season won't last much longer. I only hope I'll be able to beat Petronas before the rains come and turn the roads to glue."

"I wish you weren't going at all," Dara said.

"So do I." Krispos still had a peasant farmer's distaste for soldiering and the destruction it brought. "But the soldiers will perform better under my eye than they would otherwise." Better than they would under some general who might decide to turn his coat, Krispos meant. The officers of the regiment he would lead out were all of them young and ambitious, men who would rise faster under a young Emperor weeding rebels from the army than they could hope to if an old soldier with old cronies wore the crown. Krispos hoped that would keep them loyal. He avoided thinking about his likely fate if it didn't.

Dara understood that, too. "The good god keep you."

"May that prayer fly from your mouth to Phos' ear." Krispos walked down the hall toward the doorway. As he passed one of the many imperial portraits that hung on the walls, he paused for a moment. The long-dead Emperor Stavrakios was shown wearing much the same gear Krispos had on. Blade naked in his hand, Stavrakios looked like a soldier; in fact, he looked like one of the veterans who had taught Krispos what he knew of war. Measuring himself against that tough, ready countenance, he felt like a fraud.

Fraud or not, though, he had to do his best. He walked on, pausing in the doorway to let his eyes get used to the bright sunshine outside—and to take a handkerchief from his belt pouch to wipe sweat from his face. In Videssos the city's humid summer heat, chain mail was a good substitute for a bathhouse steam room.

A company of Halogai, two hundred men strong, saluted with their axes as Krispos appeared. They were fully armored, too, and sweating worse than he was. He wished he could have brought the whole regiment of northerners to the westlands with him; he knew they were loyal. But he had to leave a garrison he could trust in the city, or it might not be his when he returned.

A groom led Progress to the foot of the steps. The big bay gelding stood quietly as Krispos lifted his left foot into the stirrups and swung aboard. He waved to the Halogai. "To the harbor of Kontoskalion," he called, touching his heels to Progress' flanks. The horse moved forward at a walk. The imperial guards formed up around Krispos.

People cheered as the Emperor and his Halogai paraded through the plaza of Palamas and onto Middle Street. This time they turned south off the thoroughfare. The sound of the sea, never absent in Videssos the city, grew steadily louder in Krispos' ears. When he first came to the capital, he'd needed some little while to get used to the endless murmur of waves and their slap against stone. Now he wondered how he would adjust to true quiet once more.

Another crowd waited by the docks, gawking at the Videssian troops drawn up on foot there. Sailors were loading their horses onto big, beamy transports for the trip to the west side of the Cattle-Crossing; every so often, a sharp curse cut through the low-voiced muttering of the crowd. Off to one side, doing their best to look inconspicuous, were Trokoundos and a couple of other wizards.

Along with the waiting soldiers stood the new patriarch Pyrrhos. He raised his hands in benediction as he saw Krispos approach. The soldiers stiffened to attention and saluted. The noise from the crowd got louder. Because the horses did not care that the Emperor had come, the sailors coaxing them onto and along the gangplanks did not care, either.

The Halogai in front of Krispos moved aside to let him ride up to the ecumenical patriarch. Leaning down from the saddle, he told Pyrrhos, "I'm sorry we had to rush the ceremony of your investiture the other

day, most holy sir. What with trying to deal with Petronas and everything
else, I know I didn't have time to do it properly."

Pyrrhos waved aside the apology. "The synod that chose me was well
and truly made, Your Majesty," he said, "so in the eyes of Phos I have been
properly chosen. Next to that, the pomp of a ceremony matters not at all;
indeed, I am just as well pleased not to have endured it."

Only so thoroughgoing an ascetic as Pyrrhos could have expressed such
an un-Videssian sentiment, Krispos thought; to most imperials, ceremony
was as vital as breath. Krispos said, "Will you bless me and my warriors
now, most holy sir?"

"I shall bless you, and pray for your victory against the rebel," Pyrrhos
proclaimed, loud enough for the soldiers and city folk to hear. More softly,
for Krispos' ears alone, he went on, "I first blessed you twenty years ago,
on the platform in Kubrat. I shall not change my mind now."

"You and Iakovitzes," Krispos said, remembering. The noble had gone
north to ransom the farmers the Kubratoi had stolen; Pyrrhos and a
Kubrati shaman were there to make sure Phos and the nomads' false gods
heard the bargain.

"Aye." The patriarch touched the head of his staff, a gilded sphere as big
as a fist, to Krispos' shoulder. Raising his voice, he declared, "The Avtokrator of the Videssians is the good god's vice-regent on earth. Whoso
opposes him opposes the will of Phos. Thou conquerest, Krispos!"

"Thou conquerest!" people and soldiers shouted together. Krispos
waved in acknowledgment, glad Pyrrhos was unreservedly on his side. Of
course, if Petronas ended up beating him, that would only prove Phos' will
had been that he lose, and then Pyrrhos would serve a new master. Or if
he refused, it would be from distaste at Petronas' way of life, not because
Petronas had vanquished Krispos. Determining Phos' will could be a subtle art.

Krispos did not intend that Pyrrhos would have to weigh such subtleties. He aimed to beat Petronas, not to be beaten. He rode down the
dock to the *Suncircle,* the ship that would carry him across to the westlands. The captain, a short, thickset man named Nikoulitzas, and his
sailors came to attention and saluted as Krispos drew near. When he dismounted, a groom hurried forward to take charge of Progress and lead the
horse aboard.

Once on the *Suncircle,* Progress snorted and rolled his eyes, not much
caring for the gently shifting planks under his feet. Krispos did not much
care for them, either. He'd never been on a ship before. He told his stomach to behave itself; the imperial dignity would not survive hanging over

the rail and giving the fish his breakfast. After a few more internal mutterings, his stomach decided to obey.

Nikoulitzas was very tan, but years of sun and sea spray had bleached his hair almost as light as a Haloga's. Saluting again, he said, "We are ready to sail when you give the word, Your Majesty."

"Then sail," Krispos said. "Soonest begun, soonest done."

"Aye, Your Majesty." Nikoulitzas shouted orders. The *Suncircle*'s crew cast off lines. Along with its sail, the ship had half a dozen oars on each side for getting into and out of harbors. The sailors dug in at them. That changed the motion of the *Suncircle* and Progress snorted again and laid his ears back. Krispos spoke soothingly to the horse—and to his stomach. He fed Progress a couple of dried apricots. The horse ate them, then peered at his hands for more. Nothing was wrong with *his* digestion, at any rate.

The voyage over the Cattle-Crossing took less than half an hour. The *Suncircle* beached itself a little north of the western suburb called Across; none of Videssos the city's suburbs had docks of their own, lest they compete with the capital for trade. The sailors took out a section of rail and ran out the gangplank from the *Suncircle*'s gunwale to the sand. Leading Progress by the rein, Krispos walked down to the beach. His feet and the horse's hooves echoed on the planks.

The rest of the transports went aground to either side of the *Suncircle*. Some Halogai had sailed on Krispos' ship; those who had not hurried up to join their countrymen and form a protective ring around him. The Videssian troops, by contrast, paid more attention to recovering their horses. The afternoon was well along before the regimental commander rode up to Krispos and announced, "We are ready to advance, Your Majesty."

"Onward, then, Sarkis," Krispos said.

Sarkis saluted. "Aye, Your Majesty." He shouted orders to his men. His Videssian had a slight throaty accent; that, along with his wide face, thick beard, and imperious promontory of a nose, said he was from Vaspurakan. So were a good many of his troopers—the mountain land bred fine fighting men.

A small strain of Vaspurakaner blood also flowed in Krispos' veins, or so his father had always said. That was one of the reasons Krispos had chosen Sarkis' regiment. Another was that the "princes"—for so every Vaspurakaner reckoned himself—were heretics in Videssian eyes and found fault, themselves, with the imperial version of Phos' faith. As outsiders in Videssos, they, like the Halogai, had little reason to favor an old-line noble like Petronas—or so Krispos hoped.

Scouts trotted ahead of the main line of soldiers. Still surrounded by the Halogai, Krispos rode along near the middle of that line. Mule-drawn baggage wagons rattled along behind him, followed by the rearguard.

The Cattle-Crossing and its beach vanished as they moved west down a dirt road toward Petronas' lands. From the road, Krispos could see farms and farming villages as far as his eyes reached; the western coastal lowlands held perhaps the most fertile soil in all the Empire. After a while Krispos dismounted, stepped into a field, and dug his hand deep into the rich black earth. He felt of it, smelled it, tasted it, and shook his head.

"By the good god," he said, as much to himself as to any of his companions, "if I'd worked soil like this, nothing could have made me leave it." Had the soil of his native village been half this good, he and his fellows there could easily have grown enough to meet the tax bill that forced him to seek his fortune in the city. On the other hand, had the soil there been better, the tax bill undoubtedly would have been worse. Videssos' tax collectors let nothing slip through their fingers.

A few farmers and a fair number of small boys stayed in the fields to gape at the soldiers and Avtokrator as they went by. More did what Krispos would have done had he worn their sandals: they turned and fled. Soldiers did not always plunder, rape, and kill, but the danger of it was too great to be taken lightly.

As the crimson ball of the sun neared the western horizon, the army camped in a field of clover not far from a grove of fragrant orange trees. Cookfires drew moths, and the bats and nightjars that preyed on them.

Krispos had ordered that he be fed the same as any soldier. He stood in line for hard cheese, harder bread, a cup of rough red wine, and bowl of stew made from smoked pork, garlic, and onions. The cook who ladled out the stew looked nervous. "Begging your pardon, Your Majesty, but I'm afraid this isn't so fine as what you're used to."

Krispos laughed at him. "The gravy's thicker than what I grew up with, by the good god, and there's more in the kettle here, too." He spooned out a piece of pork and chewed thoughtfully. "My mother would have thrown in some thyme, I think, if she had it. Otherwise I can't complain."

"He's an army cook, Your Majesty," one of the Videssian cavalrymen said. "You expect him to know what he's doing?" Everyone who heard jeered at the cook. Krispos finished quickly and held out his bowl for a second helping. That seemed to make the luckless fellow sweating over his pots a little happier.

Three mornings later, as the army drew near a small town or large village called Patrodoton, one of the scouts came riding back at a gallop. He spoke briefly to Sarkis, who led him to Krispos. "You'd best hear this your-self, Your Majesty," the general said.

At Krispos' nod, the scout said, "A couple of the farmers up ahead warned me there's already soldiers in that town."

"Did they?" Krispos clicked his tongue between his teeth.

"Can't expect Petronas just to sit back and let us do as we like," Sarkis remarked.

"No, I suppose not. I wish we could." Krispos thought for a few sec-onds. He asked the scout, "Did these farmers say how many men were there?"

The scout shook his head. "Can't be too many, though, I figure, or we'd have some idea they were around before this."

"I think you're right." Krispos turned to Sarkis. "Excellent sir, what if we take a couple of companies of our horsemen here and . . ." He spent a couple of minutes explaining what he had in mind.

But for one broken tooth in front, Sarkis' smile was even and very white. His closed fist thumped against his mail shirt over his heart as he saluted Krispos. "Your Majesty, I think I just may enjoy serving under you."

At the general's command, the panpipers blew "Halt." Sarkis chose his two best company commanders and gave them their orders. They grinned, too; like Sarkis and Krispos, they were young enough to enjoy cleverness for its own sake. Before long, their two contingents trotted down the road toward Patrodoton. The men rode along in loose order, as if they had not a care in the world.

The rest of the army settled down to wait. After a bit, Sarkis ordered them into a defensive position, with the Halogai in the center blocking the road and the remaining Videssian cavalry on either wing. Glancing apologetically over at Krispos, the general said, "We ought to be ready in case it goes wrong."

Krispos nodded. "By all means." Both Tanilis and Petronas had taught him not to take success for granted. But he'd never led large numbers of troops before; he didn't automatically know the right way to ensure against mischance. That was why he had Sarkis along. He was glad the general had prudence to go with his dash.

Waiting stretched. The soldiers drank wine, gnawed bread, sang songs, and told each other lies. Krispos stroked his beard and worried. Then one of the Halogai pointed southwest, in the direction of Patrodoton. Krispos saw the dust rising over the roadway. A good many men were heading this way. The Halogai raised their axes to the ready. The Videssians were first and foremost archers. They quickly strung their bows, set arrows to them, and made sure sabers were loose in their scabbards.

But one of Sarkis' two picked company commanders, a small, lean fellow named Zeugmas, rode in front of the oncoming horsemen. His wave was full of exuberance. "We've got 'em!" he shouted. "Come see!"

Krispos touched his heels to Progress' flanks. The horse started forward. Thvari and several other Halogai stepped close together to keep Krispos from advancing. "Let me through!" he said angrily.

The northerner's captain shook his head. "No, Majesty, not by yourself, not when it could be a trap."

"I thought you were my guards, not my jailers," Krispos said. Thvari and the others stood implacable. Krispos sighed. In his younger days, he hadn't wanted to be a soldier, but if he had taken up sword and spear, no one would have kept him from risking his life. Now that he wanted to go into action, the Halogai would not let him. He sighed again, struck by the absurdity of it, but could only yield. "As you wish, gentlemen. Will you come with me?"

Thvari saluted. "Aye, Majesty. We come."

Accompanied by a squad of Halogai—*not that they'll do me much good if the bowmen shoot a volley at me,* he thought—Krispos went out to see what the companies he'd sent out had accomplished. The troopers didn't seem to find that cowardly. They yelled and grinned and waved—and laughed at the glum, disarmed riders in their midst.

"There, you see?" Krispos told Thvari. "It's safe enough."

Thvari's broad shoulders went up and down in a slow, deliberate shrug. "We did not know. Your duty is to rule, Majesty. Ours is to guard." Shamed by the reproach in the captain's voice, Krispos had to nod.

Then Zeugmas came up. "Couldn't have worked better, Your Majesty," he said happily. "We bagged the lot of 'em and didn't lose a man doing it. Just like you said, we rode on in cursing you for a bloody usurper and everything else we could think of, and their leader—that sour-faced bastard with the thick mustaches over there; his name's Physakis—figured we'd come to join the rebels, too. Seeing as we had twice his numbers, he was glad to see us. He posted us with his men and didn't take any precautions. We just passed the word along, made sure we got the drop on 'em all at the same time, and—well, here we are."

"Wonderful." Krispos found himself grinning, too. He was no professional soldier, but his stratagem had taken in a man who was. He pointed to Physakis. "Bring him here. Let's see what he knows."

At Zeugmas' orders, a couple of troopers made the rebel officer dismount and marched him over to Krispos. He peered up at Krispos from under lowered brows. "Your Majesty," he mumbled. As Zeugmas had said, his mustaches were luxuriant; Krispos could hardly see his lips move when he spoke.

"You didn't call me 'Majesty' before you got caught," Krispos said. "What shall I do with you now?"

"Whatever you want, of course," Physakis answered. He did indeed look sour, not, Krispos judged, from fear, but more as if his stomach pained him.

"If I decide your parole is good, I'll send you north to serve against Harvas Black-Robe and his cutthroats," Krispos said.

Physakis brightened; he must have expected to meet the axe traitors deserved. With the threat Harvas posed, though, Krispos could not afford to rid himself of every officer who chose Petronas. "You have mages with you, then?" Physakis asked.

"Aye." Krispos contented himself with the bare word. He'd almost gone west without sorcerous aid. Because of the passions that filled men in combat, battle magic was notoriously unreliable. But Petronas had tried before to slay him with sorcery; he wanted protection close at hand if Anthimos' uncle tried again. Wizards were also useful for such noncombat tasks as testing the sincerity of paroles and oaths.

The troopers took Physakis back to Trokoundos and his comrades. One by one, the rest of the captured officers and underofficers of the troop followed him. The common soldiers were another matter. Krispos did not merely want their pledge to fight him no more; he wanted them to take service with him.

When he put that to them, most agreed at once. So long as they had leadership and food, they cared little as to which side they were on. A few, stubbornly loyal to Petronas, refused. As Physakis had before them, they waited nervously for Krispos to decree their fate.

"Take their horses, their mail shirts, and all their weapons but one dagger each," he told his own men. "Then let them go. I don't think they'll be able to do us much harm after that."

"Leave us our money, too, Majesty?" one of them called.

Krispos shook his head. "You earned it by opposing me. But you've shown yourselves to be honest men. You'll find the chance to make more."

While his soldiers disarmed those of Krispos' men who refused to go over to him, the wizards listened to the rest of the troopers from Patrodoton give their oaths of allegiance. When that ceremony was done, Trokoundos approached Krispos. A squad of Halogai followed, along with three increasingly unhappy-looking Videssians.

Trokoundos pointed to them, each in turn. "These three, Majesty, swore falsely, I am sorry to say. While they granted you their pledges, in their hearts they still intended to betray you."

"I might have guessed that would happen," Krispos said. He turned to the Halogai. "Strip them, give them a dozen lashes well laid on, and send them on their way naked. Such traitors are worse than honest foes."

"Aye, Majesty," said Narvikka, the leader of the squad. One of the Videssians tried to bolt. The Halogai grabbed him before he could even break out of their circle. They drove tent pegs into the ground, tied the three captives to them facedown, and swung the whip. The troopers' shrieks punctuated its harsh, flat cracks. When the strokes were done, the Halogai cut the men loose and let them stagger away.

That night the wind began to blow from the northwest. It swept away the hot, humid air that had hung over the coastal lowlands and had made travel in armor an even worse torment than usual. When Krispos came out of his tent the next morning, he saw dirty gray clouds stacked along the northern horizon.

He frowned. Back in his village, fall was on the way when those clouds started piling up over the Paristrian Mountains. And with fall came the fall rains that turned dirt roads to quagmires. "They'd be early if they started so soon."

He didn't realize he'd spoken aloud until Sarkis, who was emerging from the tent next to his, nodded and answered, "Aye, so they would, Majesty. And wouldn't we have a jolly time trying to run Petronas down when we're all squelching through mush?"

Krispos spat, rejecting Sarkis' words as if the officer had invoked Skotos. Sarkis laughed, but they both knew it was no joke. Krispos said, "We'll have to push harder, that's all. The lord with the great and good mind willing, I want to bring Petronas to bay now, while he's still on the run. I don't want him to have the winter to get in touch with all his old cronies and build up his strength."

"Sensible." Sarkis nodded. "Aye, sensible, Majesty. Come next year, you'll have Harvas Black-Robe to worry about; you won't want to split time between Petronas and him."

"Exactly." Krispos' estimation of Sarkis went up a notch. Not many soldiers worried about Harvas, or about the northern frontier in general, as much as he did. Then he wondered if Sarkis was agreeing with his concern just to curry favor. Being Avtokrator meant making an unending string of such judgments. He hadn't expected that. He didn't care for it, either.

He lined up for breakfast, taking a thick slice of bread and a handful of salted olives. He spat out the last olive pit from atop Progress. His soldiers drove toward Petronas' estates as fast as they could. The suddenly milder weather helped keep men and horses fresh, but every time Krispos looked northward over his shoulder he saw more clouds building up. He could not even urge the troops to better speed, not unless he wanted to leave the Halogai in the cavalry's dust. He could grumble, and he did.

Nor were his spirits lifted when an imperial courier caught up with the army from behind; that only reminded him he could have been going faster. The rolled-up parchment the rider delivered was sealed with sky-blue wax. "From the patriarch, eh?" Krispos said to the courier. "Did he give you the gist of it?" People who sent messages sometimes did, to make sure that what they had to say got through even if their written words were lost.

But the courier shook his head. "No, Your Majesty."

"All right, I'll see for myself." Krispos broke the seal. Florid salutations and greetings from Pyrrhos took up half the sheet. Krispos skipped over them, looking for meat. At last he found it, two chunks: Gnatios was still immured in the monastery, where he had begun to compile a chronicle to help pass the time, and Pyrrhos had seen fit to depose an abbot and two prelates for false doctrines and another abbot for refusing to acknowledge his authority.

Krispos rubbed the side of his head with his hand. He'd expected Pyrrhos to be contentious; why should he be surprised now to have the man prove him right?

"Is there a reply, Majesty?" the courier asked. He took out a waxed tablet and stylus.

"Yes." Krispos paused to order his thoughts, then said, " 'Avtokrator Krispos to the patriarch Pyrrhos: Greetings. I hope you will keep peace among the priests and monks, prelates and abbots of the temples. With a rebel in the field and an enemy on our border, we have no need for more strife.' That's all. Let me hear it, if you would."

The courier read the message back. At Krispos' nod, he closed the tablet. He carried a stick of sealing wax. Someone not far away had a torch going; easier to bring fire along than to start it fresh every night. The soldier fetched the torch; in a moment, melted wax dripped down onto the closed tablet. While the wax was still soft, Krispos sealed it with the imperial sunburst. The courier saluted and rode away.

Because of his complete success at Patrodoton, Krispos gained another day and a half to advance unopposed. He knew he was nearing Petronas' estates. He also knew that was fortunate. Rain began to fall toward evening of the first day out of Patrodoton and showed no sign of letting up during the night.

At first the rain was welcome, for it kept down the choking clouds of dust the horses would otherwise have raised. But as the next day wore on and the rain kept coming, Krispos felt Progress begin to work to pick up his feet and heard the horse's hooves pull loose from the thickening mud with wet, sucking sounds.

In the fields, farmers worked like men possessed as they battled to get in their crops before the rains ruined them. They were even too frantic to be afraid of Krispos' army. Remembering the desperation the folk of his village had felt once or twice because of early fall rains, he knew what they were going through and wished them well.

Just after noon on the second day of the rains, Krispos and his soldiers came to the Eriza River, a fair-sized stream that ran south into the Arandos. A wooden bridge should have spanned the Eriza. In spite of the rain, the bridge was burned. Peering across to the western bank, Krispos made out patrolling riders.

In spite of the rain, they saw him and his men, too. They shook their fists and shouted insults Krispos could barely hear through the rain and across a hundred years of water. One cry, though, he made out clearly: "Petronas Avtokrator!"

Rage ripped through him. "Give them a volley," he barked to Sarkis.

The general's bushy eyebrows came together above his nose as he frowned. "With the bows we have, the range isn't short, and we'll get our bowstrings wet when we shoot," he said. "If they have men on this side of the river, too, that could leave us in a nasty spot."

Reluctantly, Krispos nodded. "A company, then," he said. "Just something to shut their mouths."

"Aye, why not?" Sarkis rode down the line to the troopers Zeugmas led. Krispos watched Zeugmas object as the regimental commander had, watched Sarkis talk him round. The horsemen in Zeugmas' company quickly strung their bows, plucked arrows from quivers, and let fly. Some tried second shots, a few third. Then, fast as they'd taken them out, they put away their bowstrings to protect them from the rain.

On the far side of the Eriza, the jeers abruptly turned to cries of alarm and pain. Krispos saw one man slide from the saddle. The rest set spur to their horses and drew away from the riverbank. A couple of Petronas' troopers shot back. An arrow buried itself in the mud not far from Krispos. Another clattered off a Haloga's axe. No one on this side of the river seemed hurt.

"We can't cross here," Krispos said.

"Not unless we want to swim," Sarkis agreed, watching the brown waters of the Eriza foam creamily against the pilings of the burned bridge.

The regimental commander was not downhearted. "The farmers here-abouts will know where the fords are, I expect."

"So they will," Krispos said; he'd known all the best places to cross the streams near his old village. "But we'd best not waste time finding one. This river's going to start rising, and it's big enough that if it does, we won't be able to cross anywhere."

The peasants hereabouts were stolid, serious people, altogether unlike the clever magpie men who called Videssos the city home. The sight of gold in Krispos' palm quickly turned them voluble, though. "Aye, lord, there's a good place to ford half a league north of here, there is, by the dead elm tree," a farmer said. "And there's another, not so good, rather more than that southward, where the Eriza takes a little jog, if you know what I mean."

"My thanks." Krispos gave the peasant two goldpieces. To his embar-rassment, the fellow clumsily prostrated himself in the mud. "Get up, you fool! Ten years ago I was just a farmer myself, working a field not near so fine as this one."

The peasant scrambled to his feet, filthy and dripping, his eyes puzzled. "You—were a farmer, lord? How could you be a farmer? You are Avtokra-tor!"

Krispos gave it up. He would only be sure of staying Avtokrator if he got across the Eriza. He turned Progress away from the farmer. His cap-tains, who had gathered round to hear his exchange with the man, were al-ready shouting orders. "North half a league to a dead elm tree!"

They squelched along by the river, moving more slowly than they would have when the weather was good. Normally, a local landmark like a dead elm would have been easy to find. In the rain, they almost rode past it. Krispos urged Progress into the river. The water rose to the horse's belly before he was a quarter of the way across. "This isn't as easy as that peas-ant made it out to be," he said.

"So it isn't." Sarkis pointed across to the western bank of the river. Horsemen with bows and lances waited there. More came trotting up while he and Krispos watched.

"We outnumber them," Krispos said without conviction.

"So we do." Sarkis sounded unhappy, too. He pointed out what Krispos had also seen. "We can't bring our numbers to bear, though, not by way of a narrow ford. Where numbers count, they have more than we do."

"They knew where this ford was," Krispos said, thinking aloud. "As soon as we came to the bridge, they started gathering here."

Sarkis nodded mournfully. "They're probably at the other one, as well, the one where the Eriza jogs."

"Curse these early rains!" Krispos snarled.

"Just have to hunt up some more farmers," Sarkis said. "Sooner or later we'll find a ford that's unguarded. Once we're across, we may be able to roll up the rebels all along the river." The regimental commander was not one to stay downcast long.

Krispos' spirits lifted more slowly. The rain that splashed against his face and trickled through his beard did nothing to improve his mood. "If the river keeps rising, there won't be any fords, no matter what we learn from the farmers."

"True enough," Sarkis said, "but if we can't get at them for a while, they can't get at us, either."

Though Krispos nodded, that thought consoled him less than it did Sarkis. As was fitting and proper, the regimental commander thought like a soldier. As Avtokrator, Krispos had to achieve a wider vision. All the Empire of Videssos was his by right; any part that did not obey his will diminished his rule, in an odd way diminished him personally.

"We'll find a ford," Sarkis said.

Finding one that Petronas' men were not covering took two days and wore Krispos' patience to rags. At last, though, squad by squad, his troopers began making their way across the Eriza. Though the peasant who'd told of the ford swore it was an easy one, the horses had to fight to move forward against the rain-swollen stream.

The Halogai waited with Krispos. When they crossed, they would hang onto the tails of the last cavalry company's horses; the Eriza might well have swept away a man who tried that ford afoot. They found the fall rains funny. "In our country, Majesty, rain is for the end of spring and for summer," Vagn said. The rest of the northerners around Krispos chorused agreement.

"No wonder so many of you come south," he said.

"Aye, that's the way of it, Majesty," Vagn said. "To a Haloga, even the weather in Kubrat would seem good."

Having spent several years in Kubrat, Krispos found that prospect appalling. It gave him a measure of how harsh life in Halogaland had to be—and a new worry. He asked, "With Harvas Black-Robe and his mercenaries holding Kubrat, does that mean more Halogai might come south to settle there?"

"It could, Majesty," Vagn said after a thoughtful pause. "That would bear hard on Videssos, were it so."

"Yes," was all Krispos answered. He already knew he could not rely on all his Videssian soldiers against Petronas. When he took the field against Harvas, would he be able to trust his own Haloga guards?

One thing at a time, he told himself. After he dealt with Petronas, almost all the rank-and-file troopers in Videssian service would rally to him, especially if he campaigned against a foreign foe.

"Your Majesty?" someone called. "Your Majesty?"

"Here," Krispos answered. The Halogai who had been about to cross the Eriza turned back and formed up around him, weapons ready. That unthinking protective move told him more plainly than any oaths that these were loyal troops.

The man who asked for Krispos proved to be an imperial courier who sat soaked and bedraggled atop a blowing horse. "I have a dispatch from the Sevastos Mavros, Your Majesty," he said, holding out a tube of waxed and oiled leather. "If you like, I can give you the news it bears. I must tell you, it is not good."

"Let me hear it, and I will judge," Krispos said, wondering how bad it would be. It was bad enough, he saw, to make the courier nervous. "Speak! By the good god, I know you only bring news; you don't cause it."

"Thank you, Your Majesty." Even in the rain, the courier licked his lips before he went on. And when he did, the word he gave was worse than any Krispos had imagined. "Majesty, Harvas and his raiders have sacked the town of Develtos."

Chapter III

KRISPOS NOTICED HE WAS GRINDING HIS TEETH. HE MADE himself stop. All the same, he felt pulled apart. How was he supposed to deal with Petronas if Harvas Black-Robe invaded the Empire? And how could he deal with Harvas if Petronas clung to his revolt?

"Majesty?" the courier said when he was some time silent. "What is your will, Majesty?"

A good question, Krispos thought. He laughed harshly. "My will is that Harvas go to Skotos' ice, and Petronas with him. Neither of them seems as interested in my will as you do, though, worse luck for me."

Taking the liberty the courier dared not, Sarkis asked, "What will you do, Majesty?"

Krispos pondered that while the rain muttered down all around. Not the least part of his pondering was Sarkis himself. If he left the regimental commander here by the Eriza alone, would he stay loyal or desert to Petronas? If he did go over, all the westlands save perhaps the suburbs across from Videssos the city would be lost. But if Krispos gave his attention solely to overthrowing Petronas, how much of the Empire would Harvas ravage while he was doing it?

He realized that was but a different phrasing for the unpalatable questions he'd asked himself before. As if he had no doubt Sarkis would remain true—as if the notion that Sarkis could do otherwise had never crossed his mind—he said, "I'll go back to the city. I can best deal with Harvas from there. Now that we've pushed over the Eriza, I want you to go after Petronas with everything you have. If you can seize him this winter, few rewards would be big enough."

The regimental commander's eyes were dark and fathomless as twin pools reflecting the midnight sky. Nevertheless, Krispos thought he saw a faint light in them, as if a star were shining on those midnight pools. Saluting, Sarkis said, "You may rely on me, Your Majesty."

"I do," Krispos said simply. He wished he did not have to. He hoped Sarkis did not know that, but suspected—half feared—the Vaspurakaner soldier was clever enough to grasp it.

Thvari said, "My men will escort you back to the city, Majesty."

"A squad will do," Krispos said. "I want the rest of you to stay with Sarkis and help him run Petronas to earth."

But Thvari shook his head. "We are your guardsmen, Majesty. We took oath by our gods to ward your body. Ward it we shall; our duty is to you, not to Videssos."

"The eunuchs in the palace think they have the right to tell the Avtokrator what to do," Krispos said, his voice somewhere between amusement and chagrin. "Do you claim it, too, Thvari?"

The Haloga captain folded his arms across his broad chest. "In this, Majesty, aye. Think you—you travel a land in revolt. A squad, even a troop, is not enough to assure your safety."

Krispos saw Thvari would not yield. "As you wish," he said, reflecting that the longer he held the throne, the less absolute his power looked.

As it happened, he and the Halogai met not a single foeman on their long, muddy slog back to Videssos the city. They did see one fellow, though, who plainly took them for enemies: a monk going west on muleback, the hood of his blue robe drawn up over his shaven pate to protect him from the rain. He kicked his mount into a stiff-legged trot and rode far around the oncoming soldiers before he dared return to the highway.

The Halogai snickered at the monk's fear. With delicate irony, Krispos asked, "Bold Captain Thvari, do you think a squad of your heroes would have been enough to save me from that desperado?"

Thvari refused to be baited. "By the look of him, Majesty, belike he would have set on a mere squad." Krispos had to laugh. The northerner went on more seriously. "Besides, who's to say that if you had only the squad, you mightn't have come across a whole horde of Petronas' rogues? The gods delight in sending woe to folk who scant their safety. No man outwits his fate, but it may entrap him before his time."

"I know why that monk turned aside from us," Krispos said: "for fear of having to argue theology with you."

"Few Halogai turn to Phos, but not for the priests' lack of trying," Thvari said. "Your god suits you of the Empire, and our gods suit us." Krispos remained convinced the northerners' gods were false, but could not deny the quality of the men who followed them.

He and his guards reached the suburbs across from the imperial city two days later. The courier had preceded them; boats were waiting to take them over the Cattle-Crossing. The short trip left Krispos green-faced and gulping, for the northerly winds that brought the fall rains had also turned the strait choppy. He sketched the sun-circle over his heart when he was back on dry land. Through the thick, gray rain clouds, though, Phos' sun could not be seen.

Long faces greeted him when he entered the imperial residence. "Cheer up," he said. "The world hasn't ended." He tapped the message tube the courier had brought him. "I know losing Develtos is a hard blow, but I think I have a way around it, or at least a way to keep Harvas quiet until I've settled Petronas."

"Very good, Your Majesty. I am pleased to hear it." But Barsymes did not seem pleased, nor did his features lighten. *Well,* Krispos told himself, *that's just his way—he never looks happy.* Then the vestiarios said, "Majesty, I fear the evil news does not stop at Develtos."

Krispos stiffened. Just when he could hope he'd solved one problem, another came along to throw him back again. "You'd better tell me," he said heavily.

"I hear and obey, Majesty. No doubt you can comprehend that the most holy Pyrrhos' elevation to the patriarchate entailed some confusion for the monastery dedicated to the memory of the holy Skirios. So forceful an abbot as Pyrrhos, I daresay, would not have suffered others there to gain or exercise much authority. Thus no one, it appears, paid close enough attention to the comings and goings of the monks. In fine, Your Majesty, the former patriarch Gnatios is nowhere to be found."

Krispos grunted as if he'd taken a blow in the belly. All at once he remembered the westbound monk who'd been so skittish on seeing him and the Halogai. He had no way of knowing whether that was Gnatios, but the fellow had been going where Gnatios, if free, was likeliest to go— toward land Petronas controlled. He said that aloud, adding, "So now

Petronas will have a patriarch of his own, to crown him properly and to call Pyrrhos' appointment illegal."

"That does seem probable," Barsymes agreed. He dipped his head to Krispos. "For one new to the throne—indeed, to the city and its intrigues—you show a distinct gift for such maneuvers."

"It's what I'd do, were I in Petronas' boots," Krispos said, shrugging.

"Indeed. Well, Petronas is no mean schemer, so you have not contradicted me."

"I know that only too well. From whom do you think I learned?" Krispos thought for a while, then went on. "When you go, Barsymes, send in a secretary. I'll draft a proclamation of outlawry against Gnatios and offer a reward for his capture or death. I suppose I should also have Pyrrhos condemn him on behalf of the temples."

"The ecumenical patriarch has already seen to that, Your Majesty," Barsymes said. "Yesterday he issued an anathema against Gnatios and read it publicly at the High Temple. It was quite a vituperative document, I must say, even for one of that sort. Some of the phrases that stick in the mind are 'perverter of the patriarchate,' 'spiritual leper,' and 'viper vilely hissing at the altar.' "

"They never were fond of each other," Krispos observed. Barsymes let one eyebrow rise in understated appreciation for the understatement. Sighing, Krispos continued, "Trouble is, Gnatios will just fling his own anathemas right back at Pyrrhos, so neither set will end up accomplishing anything."

"Pyrrhos' will appear first, and he does control the ecclesiastical hierarchy and preach from the High Temple. His words should carry the greater weight," Barsymes said.

"That's true," Krispos said. The thought consoled him a little. As it was the only consolation he'd had for the last several days, he cherished it as long as he could.

THE GENERAL AGAPETOS RUBBED A RAW NEW PINK SCAR THAT puckered his right cheek. In size and placement, it almost matched an old pale one on the other side of his face. He looked relieved to be reporting his failure in a chamber off the Grand Courtroom rather than from a prison cell to an unsympathetic jailer. "By the good god, Majesty, I still don't know how the bugger got past me to Develtos with so many men," he said, his deep voice querulous. "I don't know how he took the place so quick, either."

"That puzzles me, too," Krispos said. He'd been through Develtos, a cheerless gray fortress town that helped ward the road between the capital and the eastern port of Opsikion. Its walls had seemed forbiddingly tall and solid.

"I hear magic toppled one of the towers and let the savages in," Iakovitzes said.

Agapetos snorted. "That's always the excuse of those who run first and fastest. They lie as fast as they run, too. If battle magic worked even a quarter of the time, wizards would fight wars and soldiers could go home and tend their gardens."

"As far as I know, the only ones who got out of Develtos alive were the ones who ran first and fastest," Mavros put in. "All the rest are dead."

"Aye, that's so," Agapetos said. "The Halogai are bloodthirsty devils, and this Harvas strikes me as downright vicious. Still and all, my lads were keeping the raiders to their side of the frontier. Then somehow he slid a whole army past us. Maybe it *was* magic, Your Majesty. I don't see how else he could have done it. May the ice take me if I lie."

"I've heard that claimed of Harvas before," Krispos said. "I never really believed it; whenever a man has great good fortune, people naturally think he's a mage. But now I do begin to wonder."

"The Halogai slew all the priests in the city, it's said," Mavros observed. "If Harvas is a wizard, he is not one who works by the power of Phos."

"Of course a heathen Haloga doesn't work magic by the power of Phos," Iakovitzes said. "And if the savages were killing everyone in the city, I doubt they'd have bothered to spare anyone just because he was wearing a blue robe. Would you?" He lifted an elegantly arched eyebrow.

Mavros knew better than to take him seriously. "I'm sorry, excellent sir, but I must confess that, never having sacked a town, I really couldn't say."

A little of Iakovitzes' sarcasm was bracing. More than a little had a way of disrupting things. Not wanting that to happen now, Krispos said, "The real question is, what to do next? If I fight Petronas and Harvas at the same time, I split my forces and can't concentrate on either one. But if I neglect one and just fight the other, the one I ignore has free rein."

"Are you wondering why you ever wanted to be Avtokrator in the first place?" Iakovitzes asked with malicious relish.

"I didn't particularly want to be Avtokrator," Krispos retorted, "but letting Anthimos go ahead and kill me didn't look all that good, either."

"You're going to have to buy time with one of your foes so you can crush the other one, Krispos," Mavros said. "If you hadn't already been at war with Petronas, I could have led a fresh force out from the city and joined Agapetos against Harvas. As it was, I didn't dare, in case you were defeated in the westlands and needed aid."

"I'm glad you stayed here," Krispos said quickly, remembering Tanilis' letter. He went on, "It galls me, but I fear you're right. And it galls me worse that the one I'll have to buy off is Harvas. Petronas paid him to invade Kubrat, so I know he takes gold. And once I've beaten Petronas—why, then, the good god willing, master Harvas may just have to give that gold back, among other things. If he thinks I'll ever forget Develtos, or forgive, he's mistaken."

"Still, you're making the right choice," Iakovitzes said, nodding vigorously. "You can't afford to treat with Petronas; that would be as much as recognizing him as your equal. A reigning Avtokrator has no equals inside Videssos. But paying off a foreign prince who's made a nuisance of himself—why, it happens all the time."

Krispos glanced to Mavros, who also nodded. Agapetos said, "Aye, Majesty, settle the civil war first. Once the whole Empire is behind you, then you can have another go at Harvas when the time is ripe."

"How much did Petronas pay Harvas to bring his murderers south into Kubrat?" Krispos asked.

"Fifty pounds of gold—thirty-six hundred goldpieces," Iakovitzes answered at once.

"Then you can offer him up to twice that much if you have to, and buy me a year's peace with him," Krispos said. "I trust you'll be able to get him to settle for less, though, being the able dickerer you are."

Iakovitzes glared at him. "I was afraid you were leading up to that."

"You're the best envoy I have," Krispos said. "How many embassies to the folk of the north have you headed? We first met in Kubrat, remember? I still wear that goldpiece you gave the old khagan Omurtag when you were ransoming the lot of kidnapped peasants I was part of. So you know what you need to do, and I know I can rely on you."

"If it were a mission to the Kubrat that was, or to Khatrish, or even Thatagush, I'd say aye without thinking twice, though all those lands are bloody barbarous," Iakovtizes said slowly. "Harvas, now . . . Harvas is something else. I tell you frankly, Krispos—Your Majesty—he alarms me. He wants more than just plunder. He wants slaughter, and maybe more than that."

"Harvas alarms me, too," Krispos admitted. "If you think you're going into danger, Iakovtizes, I won't send you."

"No, I'll go." Iakovtizes ran a hand through his graying hair. "After all, what could he do? For one thing, he may have to send an embassy here one fine day, and I know—and he'd know—you'd avenge any harm that came to me. And for another, I'm coming to pay him tribute, lots of tribute. How could I making him angry doing that?"

Mavros leered at the short, feisty noble. "If anyone could manage, Iakovitzes, you're the man."

"Ah, Your Highness," Iakovitzes said in a tone of sweet regret, "were you not suddenly become second lord in all the land, be assured I would tell you precisely what sort of cocky, impertinent, jumped-up little snipsnap bastard son of a snake and a cuckoo you really are." By the time he finished, he was shouting, red-faced, his eyes bulging.

"Kind and gracious as always," Krispos told him, doing his best not to laugh.

"You, too, eh?" Iakovitzes growled. "Well, you'd just better watch out, Your Majesty. As best I can tell, I can call *you* anything I bloody well please for a while and not worry a bit about lèse-majesté, because if you send me to the chap with the axe, you can't send me to Harvas."

"That depends on where I tell him to cut," Krispos said.

Iakovitzes grabbed his crotch in mock horror. Just then Barsymes brought in a fresh jar of wine and a plate of smoked octopus tentacles. The eunuch looked down his long nose at Iakovitzes. "There are not many men to whom I would say this, excellent sir, but I suspect you would be as much a scandal without your stones as with them."

"Why, thank you," Iakovitzes said, which made even the imperturbable vestiarios blink. Krispos raised his cup in salute. So long as Iakovitzes had his tongue, he was armed and dangerous.

IAKOVITZES SET OUT ON HIS MISSION TO HARVAS A FEW DAYS later. Krispos promptly put him in a back corner of his mind; what with the state of the roads during the fall rains and the blizzards that would follow them, he did not expect the noble to be back before spring.

Of more immediate concern was Sarkis' continuing campaign against Petronas. By his dispatches, the regimental commander was making progress, but at a snail's pace thanks to the weather. The rains were still falling when he reached the first of Petronas' estates. "Drove off to westward the cavalry who sought to oppose us," he wrote, "then attempted to fire the villa and outbuildings we had taken. Too wet for a truly satisfactory job, but no one will be able to use them for a good long while yet."

When Krispos was a youth, the world in winter had seemed to contract to no more than his village and the fields around it. Even as Avtokrator, something similar happened. Though news came in from all over the Empire, everything beyond Videssos the city seemed dim and distant, as if seen through thick fog. Not least because of that, he paid more attention to the people closest to him.

By Midwinter's Day, Dara was visibly pregnant, though not in the thick robes she wore to the Amphitheater to watch the skits that celebrated the sun's swing back toward the north. Midwinter's Day was a time of license; a couple of the pantomime shows lewdly speculated on what Dara's relationship with Krispos had been before Anthimos died. Krispos laughed even when the jokes on him weren't funny. After looking angry at first, Dara went along, though she said, "Some of those so-called clowns should be horsewhipped through the plaza of Palamas."

"It's Midwinter's Day," Krispos said, as if that explained everything. To him, it did.

Some of the servants had started a bonfire in front of the steps that led into the imperial residence. It still blazed brightly when the imperial party returned from the Amphitheater. Krispos dismounted from Progress. He tossed the reins to a groom. Then, holding the crown on his head with one hand, he dashed toward the fire, sprang into the air. "Burn, ill luck!" he shouted as he flew over the flames.

A moment later he heard more running feet. "Burn, ill luck!" Dara called. Her jump barely carried her across the fire. She staggered when she landed. She might have fallen, had Krispos not reached out a quick hand to steady her.

"That was foolish," he said, angry now himself. "Why have you been traveling in a litter the past month, but to keep you from wearing yourself out or hurting yourself? Then you go and risk it all—and for what? Holiday hijinks!"

She pulled away from him. "I'm not made of pottery, you know. I won't shatter if you look at me sideways. And besides"—she lowered her voice—"what with Petronas, Gnatios, and Harvas Black-Robe, don't you think more ill luck is out there than one alone can easily burn away?"

His anger melted, as the snow had around the campfire. "Aye, that's so." He put an arm round her shoulder. "But I wish you'd be more careful."

She shook him off. He saw he'd somehow annoyed her again. Then she said, "Is that for my sake, or just on account of the child in my belly?"

"For both," he answered honestly. Her eyes stayed narrowed as she studied him. He said, "Come on, now. Have you seen me building any minnow ponds?"

She blinked, then found herself laughing. "No, I suppose not." Minnows had been a euphemism Anthimos used for one of the last of his debauched schemes—one of the few times Anthimos bothered with euphemism, Krispos thought. Dara went on, "After living with such worries so long, do you wonder that I have trouble trusting?"

By way of answer, he put his arm around her again. This time she let it stay. They walked up the steps and down the hallway together. When they got to their bedchamber, she closed and barred the doors behind them. At his quizzical look, she said, "You were the one who was talking about it being Midwinter's Day."

They wasted no time undressing and sliding under the blankets. Though brick-lined ducts under the floor brought warm air from a central furnace, the bedchamber was still chilly. Krispos' hand traced the small bulge rising around Dara's navel. Her mouth twisted into a peculiar expression, half pride, half pout. "I liked myself better flat-bellied," she said.

"I like you fine the way you are." To prove what he said, Krispos let his hand linger.

She scowled ferociously. "Did you like me throwing up every morning and every other afternoon? I'm not doing that as often now, the good god be praised."

"I'm glad you're not," Krispos said. "I—" He stopped. Under his palm, something—fluttered? rolled? twisted? He could not find the right word. Wonder in his voice, he asked, "Was that the baby?"

Dara nodded. "I've felt him"—she always called the child to come *him*—"moving for a week or ten days now. That's the hardest wiggle yet, though. I'm not surprised you noticed it."

"What does it feel like to you?" he asked, all at once more curious than aroused. He pressed lightly on her belly, hoping the baby inside would stir again.

"It's rather like—" Dara frowned, shook her head. "I started to say it felt like gas, like what would happen if I ate too much cucumber and octopus salad. It did, when he first started moving. But these bigger squirmings don't feel *like* anything, if you know what I mean. You'd understand, if you were a woman."

"Yes, I suppose I would. But since I'm not, I have to ask foolish questions." As if on cue, the baby moved again. Krispos hugged Dara close. "*We* did that!" he exclaimed, before he recalled he might not have had anything to do with it at all.

If Dara remembered that, too, she gave no sign. "*We* may have started it," she said tartly, "but *I'm* the one who has to do the rest of the work."

"Oh, hush." The feel of Dara's warm, smooth body pressed against his own reminded Krispos why they were in bed together. He rolled her onto her back. As they joined, he looked down at her and said, "Since you're complaining, I'll do the work tonight."

"Fair enough," she said, her eyes glowing in the lamplight. "We won't be able to do it this way too much longer anyhow—someone coming between us, you might say. So let's"—she paused, her breath going short for a moment—"enjoy it while we can."

"Oh, yes," he said, "Oh, yes."

T HE MESSAGE IAKOVITZES HAD SENT OUT WELL BEFORE MID-winter's Day arrived several weeks after the festival was over. All the same, Krispos was glad to have it. "Harvas wants to take the tribute. We've been haggling over how much. His is not simple Haloga greed; he fights for every copper like a prawn-seller in the city (not a prawn to be had here, worse luck—nothing but bloody mutton and bloody beef). By the lord with the great and good mind, Majesty, he nearly frightens me: he is very fierce and very clever. But I give as good as I get, I think. Yours in frigid resignation from the blizzards of Pliskavos—"

Krispos smiled as he rolled up the parchment. He could easily summon a picture of Iakovitzes' sharp tongue carving strips off a barbarous warlord too slow-witted to realize he'd been insulted. Then Krispos read the letter again. If Harvas Black-Robe was clever—and everything Krispos knew of him pointed that way—Iakovitzes' acid barbs might sink deep.

He closed the letter once more and tied a ribbon around it. Iakovitzes had been treating with barbarians for close to thirty years—for as long as Krispos had been alive. He'd know not to go too far.

What had been a quiet winter in matters ecclesiastical heated up when Pyrrhos abruptly expelled four priests from their temples. Seeing the blunt announcement in with the rest of the paperwork, Krispos summoned the patriarch. "What's all this in aid of?" he asked, tapping the parchment. "I thought I told you I wanted quiet in the temples."

"So you did, Majesty, but without true doctrine and fidelity, what value has mere quiet?" Pyrrhos, as Krispos had long known, was not one to compromise. The patriarch went on, "As you will note in my memorandum there, I had reason in each case. Bryones of the temple of the holy Nestorios was heard to preach that you were a false Avtokrator and I a false patriarch."

"Can't have that," Krispos agreed. He wished Gnatios had never gotten out of his monastic cell. Not only did he confer legitimacy on Petronas' revolt, but as patriarch-in-exile he also provided a focus for clerics who found Pyrrhos' strict interpretation of ecclesiastical law and custom unbearable.

"To continue," the patriarch said, ticking off the errant priests' transgressions on his fingers, "Norikos of the temple of the holy Thelalaios flagrantly cohabited with a woman, an abuse apparently long tolerated thanks to the laxness that prevailed under Gnatios. The priest Loutzoulos had the habit of wearing robes with silk in the weave, vestments entirely too luxurious for one of his station. And Savianos . . ." Pyrrhos' voice sank in horror to a hoarse whisper. "Savianos has espoused the Balancer heresy."

"Has he?" Krispos remembered Savianos speaking out against Pyrrhos' nomination as patriarch. He was sure Pyrrhos had not forgotten, either. "How do you know?" he asked, wondering how vindictive Pyrrhos was: more than a little, he suspected.

"By his own words I shall convict him, Majesty," Pyrrhos said. "In his sermons he has declared that Skotos darkens Phos' radiant glory. How could this be so unless the good god and the master of evil"—he spat in renunciation of Skotos—"stand equally matched in the Eternal Balance?"

Imperial orthodoxy preached that in the end Phos was sure to vanquish Skotos. The eastern lands of Khatrish and Thatagush also worshiped Phos, but their priests maintained no man could know whether good or evil would triumph in the end—thus their concept of the Balance.

Krispos knew the Balance had its attractions even for some Videssian theologians. But he asked, "Are you sure that's the only meaning you can put on what Savianos said?"

Pyrrhos' eyes glittered dangerously. "Name another."

Not for the first time, Krispos wished his formal education went further than reading and writing, adding and subtracting. "Maybe it was just a fancy way of saying there is still evil in the world. Phos hasn't won yet, you know."

"Given the sad state of sinfulness I see all around me, I am but too aware of that." Pyrrhos shook his head. "No, Majesty, I fear Savianos' speech cannot be interpreted so innocently. When a man of that stripe admires Skotos' strength, his remarks must have a sinister import."

"Suppose a priest who had always supported you spoke in the same way," Krispos said. "What would you do then?"

"Upbraid him, chastise him, and expel him," Pyrrhos said at once. "Evil is evil, no matter from whose lips it comes. May the lord with the great and good mind guard against it." He drew the sun-circle over his heart.

Krispos also signed himself. He studied the ecumenical patriarch he had created. At last, reluctantly, he decided he had to believe Pyrrhos. The patriarch was narrow, aye, but within his limits just. Sighing, Krispos said, "Very well, then, most holy sir, act as you think best."

"I shall, Your Majesty, I assure you. These four are but the snow-covered tip of a mountain of corruption. They are the ones who shine most brightly when Phos' sun lights their misdeeds, but their glitter shall not blind me to the rest of the mountain, either."

"Now wait one moment, if you please," Krispos said hastily, holding up his hand. "I did not name you to your office to have you spread chaos through the temples."

"What is the function of the patriarch but to root out sin where he finds it?" Pyrrhos said. "If you think some other duty comes before it, then cast me down now." He bowed his head to show his acceptance of that imperial prerogative.

Krispos realized that in Pyrrhos he had at last found someone more stubborn than he was. Seeing that, he also realized he had been naive to hope the greater responsibilities of the patriarchate would temper Pyrrhos' pious obstinacy. And finally, he understood that since he could not afford to oust Pyrrhos from the blue-boots—no other man, hastily set in place, could serve as much of a counterweight to Gnatios—he was stuck with him for the time being.

"As I told you, most holy sir, you must act as you think best," he said. "But, I pray you, remember also the"—what had Savianos called it?—"the principle of theological economy."

"Where the principle applies, Majesty, rest assured that I shall," Pyrrhos said. "I must warn you, though, its application is less sweeping than some would claim."

No, Krispos thought, Pyrrhos was not a man to yield much ground. He gave a sharp, short nod to show the audience was over. Pyrrhos prostrated himself—whatever his flaws, disrespect for the imperial office was not one of them—and departed. As soon as he was gone, Krispos shouted for a jar of wine.

LOOKING AT A MAP OF THE EMPIRE, KRISPOS OBSERVED, "I'M just glad Harvas' murderers decided to withdraw after they took Develtos. If they'd pressed on, they could have reached the Sailors' Sea and cut the eastern provinces in half."

"Yes, that would have spilled the chamber pot into the soup, wouldn't it?" Mavros said. "As is, though, you're still going to have to restore the town, you know."

"I've already begun to take care of it," Krispos said. "I've sent word out through the city guilds that the fisc will pay double the usual daily rate for potters and plasterers and tilemakers and carpenters and stonecutters and what have you willing to go to Develtos for the summer. From what the guildmasters say, we'll have enough volunteers to make the place a going concern again by fall."

"The guilds are the best way to get the people you'll need," Mavros agreed. Labor in Videssos the city was as minutely regulated as everything else; the guildmasters reported to the eparch of the city, as if they were government functionaries themselves. Mavros pursed his lips, then went on. "Stonecutters, aye; they'll need more than a few of those, considering what happened to Develtos' wall."

"Yes," Krispos said somberly. The reports from survivors of the attack and later witnesses told how one whole side of the fortifications had been blasted down, most likely by magic. Afterward Harvas' northern mercenaries swarmed into the stunned town and began their massacre. "Till now, I thought battle magic was supposed to be a waste of time, that it didn't work well with folk all keyed up to fight."

"I thought the same thing," Mavros said. "I talked with your friend Trokoundos and a couple of other mages. From what they say, the spell that knocked over the wall wasn't battle magic, strictly speaking. Harvas or whoever did it must have spirited his soldiers past the frontier and got them to Develtos with no one the wiser. That made the sorcery a lot easier, because the garrison wasn't expecting attack and didn't get into that excited state until the stones came crashing down onto them."

"Which was too late," Krispos said. Mavros nodded. Krispos added, "The next question is, how did Harvas get his army over the border like that?"

Mavros had no answer. Neither did anyone else. Krispos knew Trokoundos had interrogated Agapetos with the same double mirror arrangement he'd used on Gnatios. Even sorcerously prodded, the general had no idea how Harvas' men eluded his. Maybe magic had played a part there, too, but nobody could be sure.

Krispos said, "By the good god, I hope Harvas and his murderers can't spring out of nowhere in front of Videssos the city and smash through the walls here." The imperial capital's walls were far stronger than those of a provincial town like Develtos, so much so that no foreign foe had ever taken the city. Nor had any Videssians, save by treachery. Harvas Black-Robe, though, was looking like a foe of an uncommon sort.

"Now we'll have wizards ever on the alert here," Mavros said. "Taking us by surprise won't be as easy as it was in Develtos. And surprise, the mages say, was the main reason he succeeded there."

"Yes, yes." Krispos still fretted. Maybe that was because he was so new on the throne, he thought; with more experience, he might have a better sense of just how dangerous Harvas truly was. All the same, like any sensible man, he preferred to be ready for a threat that wasn't there than to ignore one that was. He said, "I wish Petronas wouldn't have picked now to rebel. If he gave up, I'd be happy to let him keep his head. Harvas worries me more."

"Even after you're buying Harvas off?"

"Especially after I'm buying Harvas off." Krispos plucked at his thick, curly beard, then snapped his fingers in sudden decision. "I'll even tell Petronas as much, in writing. If he and Gnatios will come back to the monastery, I won't take any measures against them." He raised his voice to call for a secretary.

Before the scribe arrived, Mavros asked, "And if he says no?"

"Then he says no. How am I worse off?"

Mavros considered, then judiciously pursed his lips. "Put that way, I don't suppose you are."

When the secretary came in, he set down his tablet and stylus so he could prostrate himself before Krispos. Krispos waited impatiently till the man had got to his feet and taken up his writing tools once more. He had given up on telling underlings not to bother with the proskynesis. All it did was make them uneasy. He was the Avtokrator, and the proskynesis was the way they were accustomed to showing the Avtokrator their respect.

After he was done dictating, Krispos said, "Let me hear that once more, please." The secretary read him his words. He glanced over at Mavros. The Sevastor nodded. Krispos said, "Good enough. Give me a fair copy of that, on parchment. I'll want it today." The scribe bowed and hurried away.

Krispos rose, stretched. "All that talking has made me thirsty. What do you say to a cup of wine?"

"I generally say yes, and any excuse will do nicely," Mavros answered, grinning. "Are you telling me your poor voice is too worn and threadbare to call Barsymes? I'll do it for you, then."

"No, wait," Krispos said. "Let's scandalize him and get it ourselves." He knew it was a tiny rebellion against the stifling ceremony that hedged him round, but even a tiny rebellion was better than none.

Mavros rolled his eyes. "The foundations of the state may crumble."

Not least because he had trouble taking things seriously himself, he sympathized with his foster brother's efforts to keep some of his humanity intact.

Chuckling like a couple of small boys sneaking out to play at night, Avtokrator and the Sevastos tiptoed down the hall toward the larder. They even stopped chuckling as they sneaked past the chamber where Barsymes was directing a cleaning crew. The vestiarios' back was to them; he did not notice them go by. The cleaners needed his direction, for thick dust lay over the furnishings inside the chamber and the red-glazed tile that covered its floor and walls. The Red Room was only used—indeed, was only opened—when the Empress was with child. The baby—Krispos' heir, if it was a boy—would be born there.

I wonder if it's mine, he thought for the thousandth time. For the thousandth time, he told himself it did not matter—and tried to make himself believe it.

The wine, successfully gained and successfully drunk, helped him shove the unanswerable question to the back of his mind once more. He picked up the jar. "Another cup?" he asked Mavros.

"Thank you. That would be lovely."

Barsymes stalked into the larder while Krispos was still pouring. The eunuch's long smooth disapproving face got longer and more disapproving. "Your Majesty, you have servants precisely for the purpose of serving you."

Had he sounded angry, Krispos would have gotten angry in return. But he only sounded sad. Absurdly, Krispos felt guilty. Then he *was* angry, angry at his own feeling of guilt. "You'd like to wipe my arse for me, too, wouldn't you?" he snarled.

The vestiarios said nothing, did not even change his expression. Krispos felt his own face go hot with shame. Barsymes and the other chamberlains *had* wiped his arse for him, and tended all his other needs, no matter how ignoble, a couple of summers before when he lay paralyzed from Petronas' wizardry. He hung his head. "I'm sorry," he mumbled.

"Many men would not have remembered," Barsymes said evenly. "I see you do. Can we bargain, Your Majesty? If your need to be free of us grows so pressing from time to time, will you tolerate us more readily the rest of the time on account of these occasional escapes?"

"I think so," Krispos said.

"Then I will essay not to be aggrieved when I see you occasionally serving yourself, and I hope you will remain sanguine when I and the rest of your servants perform our office." Bowing, Barsymes withdrew.

Once the vestiarios was gone, Mavros said, "Who rules here, you or him?"

"I notice you lowered your voice before you asked me that," Krispos said, laughing. "Is it for fear he'll hear?"

Mavros laughed, too, but soon sobered. "There have been vestiarioi who controlled affairs far beyond the palaces—Skombros, for one."

"Me for another," Krispos reminded him. "I haven't seen any of that from Barsymes, the lord with the great and good mind be praised. As long as he runs the palace, he's content to let me have the rest of the Empire."

"Generous of him." Mavros emptied his cup and picked up the jar of wine. "I'm going to pour myself another. Can I do the same for you? That way he'll have nothing with which to be offended."

Krispos held out his own cup. "Go right ahead."

THE IMPERIAL COURIER SAT GRATEFULLY IN FRONT OF A ROAR-ing fire. Outside, mixed sleet and rain poured down. Krispos knew that meant spring was getting closer. Given a choice between snow and this horrible stuff, he would have preferred snow. Instead, he would get weeks of slush and glare ice and mud.

The courier undid his waterproof message pouch and handed Krispos a rolled parchment. "Here you are, Your Majesty."

Even had the fellow's face not warned Krispos that Petronas was not about to come back to his monastery, the parchment would have done the job by itself. It was bound with a scarlet ribbon and sealed with scarlet wax, into which had been pressed a sunburst signet. It was not *the* imperial seal—Krispos wore that on the middle finger of his right hand—but it was an imperial seal.

"He says no, does he?" Krispos asked.

The courier set down the goblet of hot wine laced with cinnamon from which he'd been drinking. "Aye, Majesty, that much I can tell you. I haven't seen the actual message, though."

"Let's see how he says no, then." Krispos cracked the sealing wax, slid the ribbon off the parchment, and unrolled it. He recognized Petronas' firm, bold script at once—his rival had responded to him in person.

The response sounded like Petronas, too, Petronas in an overbearing mood: " 'Avtokrator of the Videssians Petronas, son of Agarenos Avtokra-tor, brother of Rhaptes Avtokrator, uncle to Anthimos Avtokrator, crowned without duress by the true most holy ecumenical patriarch of the Videssians Gnatios, to the baseborn rebel, tyrant, and usurper Krispos: Greetings.' "

Krispos found reading easier if he did it aloud in a low voice. He didn't realize the courier was listening until the man remarked, "I guess he wouldn't say you aye after a start like that, would he?"

"Doesn't seem likely." Krispos read on: " 'I know that advice is a good and goodly thing: I have, after all, read the books of the learned ancients and Phos' holy scriptures. But at the same time, I reckon that this condition obtains when matters may be remedied. But when the times themselves are dangerous and drive one into the worst and most terrible circumstances, then, I think, advice is no longer so useful. This is most true of advice from you, impious and murderous wretch, for not only did you conspire to confine me unjustly in a monastery, but you also pitilessly slew my nephew the Avtokrator.'

"That, by the way, is not so," Krispos put in for the courier's benefit. He resumed. " 'So, accursed enemy, do not urge me to deliver my life into your hands once more. You will not persuade me. I, too, am a man with a sword at my belt, and I will struggle against one who has sought to lay my family low. For either I shall regain the imperial glory and furnish you, murderer, a full requital, or I shall perish and gain freedom from a disgusting and unholy tyranny.' "

The courier's eyes were wide by the time Krispos rolled up the parchment once more. "That's the fanciest, nastiest 'no' I ever heard, Your Majesty."

"Me, too." Krispos shook his head. "I didn't really think he'd say yes. A pity you and your comrades got drenched carrying the letters there and back again, but it was worth a try."

"Oh, aye, Majesty," the courier said, "I've done my soldiering time, fighting against Makuran on the Vaspurakaner frontier. Anything you can try to keep from having a war is worth doing."

"Yes." But Krispos had begun to wonder just how true that was. He'd certainly believed it back in his days at the farming village. Now, though, he was sure he would have to fight Petronas. Just as Petronas could not trust him, he knew a victory by his former patron would only bring him to a quick end, or more likely a slow one.

And he would have to fight a war against Harvas Black-Robe. Though he paid Harvas tribute for the moment, that was only buying time, not solving the problem. If he let a wild wolf like Harvas run loose on his border, more peasants who wanted nothing but peace would be slaughtered or ruined than if he fought to keep them safe. He also knew the ones who were ruined and the loved ones of those slaughtered in his war would never understand that. He wouldn't have himself, back in the days before he wore a crown.

"That's why the Empire needs an Emperor," he said to himself: "to see farther and wider than the peasants can."

"Aye, Majesty. Phos grant that you do," the courier said. Krispos sketched the sun-circle over his heart, hoping the good god would hear the fellow's words.

THE RAINS DRAGGED ON. IN SPITE OF THEM, KRISPOS SENT OUT couriers ordering his forces to assemble at Videssos the city and in the westlands. Spies reported that Petronas was also mustering troops. Krispos was glumly certain Petronas had spies of his own. He did his best to confuse them, shuttling companies back and forth and using regimental standards for companies and the other way round.

Thanks to the civil war, his strength in the north and east were less than it should have been. Thus he breathed a long sigh of relief when Iakovitzes wrote: "Harvas has agreed to a year's truce, at the highest price you would suffer me to pay him. By the lord with the great and good mind, Majesty, I would sooner gallop a ten-mile steeplechase with a galloping case of the piles than chaffer again with that black-robed bandit. I told him as much, in so many words. He laughed. His laugh, Majesty, is not a pleasant thing. Skotos might laugh so, to greet a damned soul new-come to the ice. Never shall I be so glad as the day I leave his court to return to the city. Phos be praised, that day will come soon."

When Krispos showed Mavros the letter, the Sevastos whistled softly. "We've both seen Iakovitzes furious often enough, but I don't think I ever heard him sound frightened before."

"Harvas has done it to him," Krispos said. "It's been building all winter. Just one more sign we should be fighting Harvas now. May the ice take Petronas for keeping me from what truly needs doing."

"We settle him this year," Mavros said. "After that, Harvas will have his turn."

"So he will." Krispos glanced outside. The sky was still cloudy, but held patches of blue. "Before long we can move on Petronas. One thing at a time, I learned on the farm. If you try to do a lot of things at once, you end up botching all of them."

Mavros glanced at him, mobile features sly. "Perhaps Videssos should draw its Emperors from the peasantry more often. Where would a man like Anthimos have learned such a simple lesson?"

"A man like Anthimos wouldn't have learned it on the farm, either.

He'd have been one of the kind—and there are plenty of them, the good god knows—who go hungry at the end of winter because they haven't raised enough to carry them through till spring, or because they were careless with their storage pits and let half their grain spoil."

"You're probably right," Mavros said. "I've always thought—"

Krispos never found out what his foster brother had always thought. Barsymes came into the chamber and said, "Forgive me, Your Majesty, but her Majesty the Empress must see you at once."

"I'll come as soon as I'm done with Mavros here," Krispos said.

"This is not a matter that will wait on your convenience, Your Majesty," Barsymes said. "I've sent for the midwife."

"The—" Krispos found his mouth hanging open. He made himself shut it, then tried again to speak. "The midwife? The baby's not due for another month."

"So her Majesty said." Barsymes' smile was always wintry, but now, like the weather, it held a promise of spring. "The baby, I fear, is not listening."

Mavros clapped Krispos on the shoulder. "May Phos grant you a son."

"Yes," Krispos said absently. How was he supposed to stick to his one-thing-at-a-time dictum if events kept getting ahead of him? With some effort, he figured out the one thing he was supposed to do next. He turned to Barsymes. "Take me to Dara."

"Come with me," the vestiarios said.

They walked down the hall together. As they neared the imperial bedchamber, Krispos saw a serving maid mopping up a puddle. "The roof stayed sound all winter," he said, puzzled, "and it's not even raining now."

"Nor is that rain," Barsymes answered. "Her Majesty's bag of waters broke there."

Krispos remembered births back in his old village. "No wonder you called the midwife."

"Exactly so, Your Majesty. Fear not—Thekla has been at her trade more than twenty years. She is the finest midwife in the city; were it otherwise, I should have sent for someone else, I assure you." Barsymes stopped outside the bedchamber door. "I will leave you here until I come to take her Majesty to the Red Room."

Krispos went in. He expected to find Dara lying in bed, but instead she was pacing up and down. "I thought I would wait longer," she said. "I'd felt my womb tightening more often than usual the last couple of days, but I didn't think anything of it. Then—" She laughed. "It was very strange—it was as if I was making water and couldn't stop myself. And after I was done dripping . . . now I know why they call them labor pains."

No sooner had she finished speaking than another one took her. Her face grew closed, secret, and intent. Her hands found Krispos' arms and squeezed hard. When the pain passed, she said, "I can tolerate that, but my labor's just begun. I'm afraid, Krispos. How much worse will they get?"

Krispos helplessly spread his hands, feeling foolish and useless and male. He had no idea how bad labor pains got—how could he? He remembered village women shrieking as they gave birth, but that did not seem likely to reassure Dara. He said, "Women are meant to bear children. It won't be worse than you can take."

"What do you know?" she snapped. "You're a man." Since he had just told himself the same thing, he shut up. Nothing he said was apt to be right, so he leaned over her swollen belly to hug her. That was a better idea.

They waited together. After a while, a pain gripped Dara. She clenched her teeth and rode it out. Once it had passed, though, she lay down. She twisted back and forth, trying to find a comfortable position. With her abdomen enormous and labor upon her, there were no comfortable positions to find. Another pain washed over her, and another, and another. Krispos wished he could do something more useful than hold her hand and make reassuring noises, but he had no idea what that something might be.

Some time later—he had no idea how long—someone tapped on the bedchamber door. Krispos got up from the bed to open it. Barsymes stood there with a handsome middle-aged woman whose short hair was so black, Krispos was sure it was dyed. She wore a plain, cheap linen dress. The vestiarios said, "Your Majesty, the midwife Thekla."

Thekla had a no-nonsense air about her that Krispos liked. She did not waste time with a proskynesis, but pushed past Krispos to Dara. "And how are we today, dearie?" she asked.

"I don't know about you, but I'm bloody awful," Dara said.

Unoffended, Thekla laughed. "Your waters broke, right? Are the pangs coming closer together?"

"Yes, and they're getting harder, too."

"They're supposed to, dearie. That's how the baby comes out, after all," Thekla said. Just then Dara's face twisted as another pain began. Thekla reached under Dara's robes to feel how tight her belly grew. Nodding in satisfaction, she told Dara, "You're doing fine." Then she turned to Barsymes. "I don't want her walking to the Red Room. She's too far along for that. Go fetch the litter."

"Aye, mistress." Barsymes hurried away. Krispos judged Thekla's skill by the unquestioning obedience she won from the vestiarios.

Barsymes and a couple of the other chamberlains soon returned. "Put the edge of the litter right next to the side of the bed," Thekla directed. "Now, dearie, you just slide over. Go easy, go easy—there! That's fine. All right, lads, off we go with her." The eunuchs, faces red but step steady, carried the Empress out the door, down the hall, and to the Red Room.

Krispos followed. When he got to the entrance of the Red Room, Thekla said firmly, "You wait outside, if you please, Your Majesty."

"I want to be with her," Krispos said.

"You wait outside, Your Majesty," Thelka repeated.

This time the midwife's words carried the snap of command. Krispos said, "I am the Avtokrator. I give orders here. Why should I stay out?"

Thekla set hands on hips. "Because, your most imperial Majesty, sir, you are a pest-taken man, that's why." Krispos stared at her; no one had spoken to him like that since he wore the crown, and not for a while before then, either. In slightly more reasonable tones, Thekla went on, "And because it's woman's work, Your Majesty. Look, before this is done, your wife is liable to shit and piss and puke, maybe all three at once. She's sure to scream, likely a lot. And I'll have my hands deeper inside her than you ever dreamed of being. Do you really want to watch?"

"It is not customary, Your Majesty," Barsymes said. For him, that settled the matter.

Krispos yielded. "Phos be with you," he called to Dara, who was carefully wiggling from the litter to the bed in the Red Room. She started to smile at him, but a pain caught her and turned the expression to a grimace.

"Here, Your Majesty, come with me," Barsymes said soothingly. "Come sit down and wait. I'll bring you some wine; it will help ease your worry."

Krispos let himself be led away. As he'd told Mavros, he ruled the Empire but his servants ruled the palaces. He drank the wine Barsymes set before him without noticing if it was white or red, tart or sweet. Then he simply sat.

Barsymes brought in a game board and pieces. "Would Your Majesty care to play?" he asked. "It might help pass the time."

"No, not now, thank you." Krispos' laugh was ragged. "Besides, Barsymes, you'd have a hard time losing gracefully today, for my mind wouldn't be on the board."

"If you notice how I lose, Majesty, then I don't do so gracefully enough," the vestiarios said. He seemed chagrined, Krispos noted, as if he thought he had failed in the quest for perfect service.

"Esteemed sir, just let me be, if you would," Krispos said. Barsymes bowed and withdrew.

Time crawled by. Krispos watched a sunbeam slide across the floor and start to climb the far wall. A servant came in to light lamps. Krispos only noticed him after he was gone.

He was not close to the Red Room. Barsymes, clever as usual, had made sure of that. Moreover, the door to the birthing chamber was closed. Whatever cries and groans Dara made, for a long time he did not hear them. But as the lamps' flickering light grew brighter than the failing day, she shrieked with such anguish that he sprang from his chair and dashed down the hall.

Thekla was indeed a veteran of her trade. She knew who pounded on that door, and why. "Nothing to worry about, Your Majesty," she called. "I was just turning the baby's head a little so it'll pass through more easily. The babe has dark hair, a lot of it. Won't be too much longer now."

He stood outside the door, clenching and unclenching his fists. Against Petronas or Harvas, he could have charged home at the head of his troops. Here he could do nothing—as Thekla had said, this was woman's work. Waiting seemed harder to bear than battle.

Dara made a noise he had never heard before, part grunt, part squeal, a sound of ultimate effort. "Again!" he heard Thekla say. "Hold your breath as long as you can, dearie—it helps the push." That sound burst from Dara once more. "Again!" Thekla urged. "Yes, that's the way."

Krispos heard Dara gasp, strain—and then exclaim in excitement. "Your Majesty, you have a son," Thekla said loudly. A moment later, the high, thin, furious cry of a newborn baby filled Krispos' ears.

He tried the door. It was locked. "We're not ready for you yet, Your Majesty," Thekla said, annoyance and amusement mixed in her voice. "She still has the afterbirth to pass. You'll see the lad soon enough, I promise. What will you call him?"

"Phostis," Krispos answered. He heard Dara say the name inside the Red Room, too. Sudden tears stung his eyes. He wished his father had lived to see a grandson named for him.

A few minutes later Thekla opened the door. The lamplight showed her dress splashed with blood—no wonder she hadn't worn anything fancy, Krispos realized. Then Thekla held out to him his newborn son, and all such thoughts vanished from his mind.

The baby was swaddled in a blanket of soft lamb's wool. "Five fingers on each hand, five toes on each foot," Thekla said. "A little on the scrawny side, maybe, but that's to be expected when a child comes early." The midwife fell silent when she saw Krispos wasn't listening.

He peered down at Phostis' red, wrinkled little face. Part of that was the awe any new father feels on holding his firstborn for the first time. Part, though, was something else, something colder. He searched those tiny, new-formed features, trying to see in them either Anthimos' smooth, smiling good looks or his own rather craggier appearance. So far as he could tell, the baby looked like neither of its possible fathers. Phostis' eyes seemed shaped like Dara's, with the inner corner of each lid folding down very slightly.

When he said that out loud, Thekla laughed. "No law says a boy child can't favor his mother, Your Majesty," she said. "Speaking of which, she'll want another look at the baby, too, I expect, and maybe a first try at nursing him." She stepped aside to let Krispos go into the Red Room.

The chamber stank; Thekla had meant her warning. Krispos did not care. "How are you?" he asked Dara, who was still lying on the bed on which she had given birth. She looked pale and utterly exhausted; her hair, soaked with sweat, hung limply. But she managed a worn smile and held out her hands for Phostis. Krispos gave her the baby.

"He doesn't weigh anything," Dara exclaimed.

Krispos nodded; his arms hardly noticed Phostis was gone. He saw Dara giving Phostis the same careful scrutiny he had, no doubt for the same reason. He said, "I think he looks like you."

Dara's eyes went wary as she glanced at him. He smiled back, though he wondered if he would ever be sure who Phostis' father really was. As he had so often before, he told himself it did not matter. As he had so often before, he almost made himself believe it.

"Hold him again, will you?" Dara said. Phostis squalled at being passed back and forth. Krispos clumsily rocked him in his arms. Dara unfastened her dress and tugged it off one shoulder to bare a breast. "I'll take him now. Let's see if this will make him happy."

Phostis rooted, found the nipple, and began to suck. "He likes them," Krispos said. "I don't blame him—I like them, too."

Dara snorted. Then she said, "Ask the kitchen to send me supper, would you, Krispos? I'm hungry now, though I wouldn't have believed it if you'd told me I would be."

"You haven't eaten for quite a while," Krispos said. As he hurried off to do what Dara had asked, he paused and thanked Thekla.

"My pleasure, Your Majesty," the midwife said. "Phos grant that the

Empress and your son do well. No reason she shouldn't, and he's not too small to thrive, I'd say."

Chamberlains and maidservants congratulated Krispos on having a son as he walked to the kitchens. He wondered how they knew; a baby girl's cry would have sounded the same as Phostis'. But palace servants had their own kind of magic. The moment Krispos walked through the door, a grinning cook pressed into his hands a tray with a jar of wine, some bread, and a covered silver dish on it. "For your lady," the fellow said.

Krispos carried the tray to Dara himself. Barsymes saw him and said not a word. When he got back to the Red Room, he helped her sit up and poured wine for her. He poured for himself, as well; the cook had thoughtfully set two goblets on the tray. He raised his. "To Phostis," he said.

"To our son," Dara agreed. That was not quite what Krispos had said, but he drank her toast.

Dara attacked her meal—it proved to be roast kid in fermented fish sauce and garlic—as if she'd had nothing for days. Krispos watched her eat and watched Phostis, who was dozing on the bed next to her, turn his head from side to side. Thekla had been right; for a baby, Phostis did have a lot of hair. Krispos stood up and reached out a gentle hand to touch it. It was soft and fine as goose down. Phostis squirmed. Krispos took his hand away.

Dara sopped up the last of the sauce with the heel of her bread. She finished her wine and set the goblet down with a sigh. "That helped," she said. "A bath and about a month of sleep and I'll be—not good as new, but close enough." She sighed again. "Thekla says it's better for a baby to nurse with his own mother the first few days, so I won't get that sleep right away. Afterward, though, a wet nurse can get up with him when he howls."

"I've been thinking," Krispos said in an abstracted tone that showed he'd hardly heard what she said.

"What about?" she asked cautiously. Without seeming to notice what she did, she moved closer to Phostis, as if to protect him.

"I think we ought to declare the baby co-Avtokrator even before I go out on campaign against Petronas," he answered. "It will let the whole Empire know I intend my family to hold this throne for a long time."

Dara's face lit up. "Yes, let's do that," she said at once. Even more gently than Krispos had, she touched Phostis' head, murmuring, "Sleep well, my tiny Emperor." Then, after a little while, she added, "I was afraid you were thinking something else."

Krispos shook his head. Even since he'd known Dara was pregnant, he'd also known he'd have to act as if her child was surely his. Now that the boy was born, he would not stint. If anything, he would make a show of favoring him, to make sure no one else had any doubts—or at least any public doubts—about Phostis' paternity.

What he did was everyone's affair. What he thought was his own.

Chapter IV

BARSYMES CARRIED A MEDIUM-SIZED SILVER BOX AND A FOLDED sheet of parchment in to Krispos. The vestiarios looked puzzled and a bit worried. "The Halogai just found this on the steps, Your Majesty. As they do not read, they asked me what the parchment said. I saw it had your name on the outside, so I brought it here."

"Thank you," Krispos said. Then he frowned. "What do you mean, the Halogai found it on the steps? Who brought it there?"

"I don't know, Your Majesty. Neither do the guardsmen. From what they say, it wasn't there one moment and was the next."

"Magic," Krispos said. He stared suspiciously at the box. After almost killing him once by sorcery, did Petronas think he would fall into the trap again? If so, he would be disappointed. "Send someone for Trokoundos, Barsymes. Until he tells me it's all right, that box will stay closed."

"No doubt you are wise, Your Majesty. I shall send someone directly."

Krispos even wondered if unfolding the parchment was safe. He grew impatient waiting for Trokoundos to come, though, and opened it up. Nothing lethal or sorcerous—nothing at all—happened when he did. The note inscribed within was written in a crabbed, antique hand. Though it was not signed, it could only have come from Harvas Black-Robe; it read: "I accept your purchase of a year's peace with gold. Your envoy has left my court and wends his way homeward. I believe you will find him much improved on account of that which is enclosed herewith."

When Trokoundos arrived, Krispos showed him the parchment and explained his own suspicions. The mage nodded. "Quite right, Your Majesty. If that box hides sorcery, be sure I shall bring it to light."

He set to work with powders and jars of bright-colored liquids. After a few minutes one of the liquids suddenly went from blue to red. Trokoundos grunted. "Ha! There *is* magic here, Your Majesty." He made quick passes, all the while chanting under his breath.

Krispos watched the red liquid turn blue again. He asked, "Does that mean the spell is gone?"

"It should, Your Majesty." But Trokoundos did not sound sure. He explained. "The only spell I detected was one of preservation, such as some fancy fruiterers use to let rich clients have their wares fresh but out of season. Forgive me, but I cannot imagine how such a spell could be harmful in any way. Whether it was or not, though, I have dispersed it."

"Then nothing should happen if I open the box?" Krispos persisted.

"Nothing *should*." Trokoundos took out more sorcerous apparatus. "If anything does, I am prepared to meet it."

"Good." Krispos flipped the catch that held the box shut. As he did so, Trokoundos stepped up to protect him from whatever was inside. He opened the lid. Inside the box was a curiously curved piece of meat, bloody at the thick end.

Trokoundos' brows came together at the anticlimax. "What is that?" he demanded.

Krispos needed a minute to recognize it, too. But he had butchered a good many cows and sheep and goats in his farming days. This was too small to have come from a cow, but a sheep had one much like it . . . "It's a tongue," he said. Then horror ran through him as he remembered the note that had accompanied this gift. "It's—Iakovitzes' tongue," he choked out. He slammed the lid shut, turned his head, and vomited on the fine mosaic floor.

NEAR THE SOUTH END OF VIDESSOS THE CITY'S WALL WAS A broad field where soldiers often exercised. Several regiments of horsemen, lancers and archers both, were drawn up in formation there. Their banners rippled in the spring breeze. They saluted as Krispos and Agapetos rode past in review.

Krispos was saying "Draw out whatever garrison troops you think the towns can spare, if they're men who'd be any good in the field. The Kubrati nomads always liked to play the raid-and-run game. Now it'll be our turn. If Harvas thinks he can sell us peace at the price of maiming an ambassador, we'll teach him different. The way I see it, he's stolen a hundred pounds of gold. We'll take it back from his land."

"Aye, Majesty," Agapetos said. "But what happens if one of my raiding bands comes up against too many men for them to handle?"

"Then pull back," Krispos told him. "Your job is to keep Harvas and his cutthroats too busy in their own country to come down into the Empire. I won't be able to send you much support, not until Petronas is beaten. After that, the whole army will move to the northern frontier, but until then, you're on your own."

"Aye, Majesty. I shall do as you require." Agapetos saluted, then raised his right arm high. Trumpets brayed brassily, pipes skirled, and drums thuttered. The cavalry regiments rolled forward. Krispos knew they were good troops. Agapetos was a good soldier, too; Videssian generals made a study of the art of war and learned scores of tricks for gaining the most with the smallest expenditure of manpower.

Then why am I worried? Krispos asked himself. Maybe it was because the competent, serious Videssian soldiers had not faced warriors like Harvas' Halogai before. Maybe it was because competent, serious Agapetos had already let Harvas trick him once. *And maybe,* Krispos thought, *it's for no reason at all. No matter how well he acts the part, Harvas isn't Skotos come again. He can be beaten. In the end, even Skotos will be beaten.*

Then why am I worried? he asked again. Angry at himself, he yanked Progress' head around sharply enough to draw a reproachful snort from the horse. He rode back to the city at a fast trot. He knew he should already have been in the westlands, moving against Petronas. But for Harvas' latest outrage, that campaign would have begun a fortnight before.

Krispos rode not to the palaces, but to the Sorcerers' Collegium north of the palace quarter. Iakovitzes had reached the capital the night before, more dead than alive. The Empire's most skillful healer-priests taught at the Collegium, passing on their art to each new generation in turn. The desperately ill came there, too, in hope of cures no one less skilled could give. Iakovitzes fell into the latter group.

"How is he?" Krispos demanded of Damasos, the head of the healing faculty.

The skin under Damasos' eyes was smudged with fatigue, part of the price a healer-priest paid for his gift. "Majesty," he began, and then paused to yawn. "Your pardon, Majesty. I think he may yet recover, Majesty. We are at last to the point where we may attempt the healing of the wound it-self."

"He's been here most of a day now," Krispos said. "Why haven't you done anything before this?"

"We have done a great deal, Majesty," Damasos said stiffly. He was of middle height and middle years, his pate tan, his untrimmed beard going gray. He continued, "We've had to do a great deal, much of it in conjunc-tion with sorcerers who are not healers, for added to this mutilation was something I have never before encountered and pray to the good god I never see again: a spell specifically intended to thwart healing. First discov-ering and then defeating that spell has occupied us up to this time."

"A spell *against* healing?" Krispos felt queasy; the very idea was an abomination worse than the torture Harvas had inflicted on Iakovitzes. "Who could conceive such a wicked thing?"

"For too long, we did not, Majesty," Damasos said. "Even after we re-alized what we faced, we needed no small space of time to overcome the wizardry. Whoever set it on the wound bound it with the power of the vic-tim's blood, making it doubly hard to banish. It was, in effect, a deliberate perversion of my own ritual." Tired though he was, Damasos set his jaw in outrage.

Krispos asked, "You are ready to heal now, you say?" At the healer-priest's nod, he went on. "Take me to Iakovitzes. I would see him healed, as best he may be." He also wanted Iakovitzes to see him, to know how guilty he felt for sending him on an embassy about which he'd had misgiv-ings.

He gasped when Damasos ushered him into Iakovitzes' chamber. The little noble, usually so plump and dapper, was thin, ragged, and filthy. Krispos coughed at the foul odor that rose from him: not just that of a body long unwashed, but worse, a ripe stench like rotting meat. Yellow pus dribbled from the corner of his mouth. His eyes were wide and blank with fever.

Those blank eyes slid past Krispos without recognizing him. A healer-priest sat beside the bed where Iakovitzes thrashed. Four beefy attendants stood close by. Damasos spoke to the priest. "Are you ready, Nazares?"

"Aye, holy sir." Nazares' glance rested on Krispos for a moment. When Krispos showed no sign of leaving, the healer-priest shrugged and nodded to the attendants. "Commence, lads."

Two of the men seized Iakovitzes' arms. A third grabbed his head to pull down his lower jaw, then wedged a stout stick padded with cloth between his teeth. Iakovitzes had not seemed aware of his surroundings till then.

But the instant the stick touched his lips, he began to struggle like a man possessed, letting out bloodcurdling shrieks and a string of gurgles that tried to be words.

"Poor fellow," Damasos whispered to Krispos. "In his delirium, he must think we're about to cut him again." Krispos' nails bit into his palms.

In spite of the battle Iakovitzes put up, the fourth attendant forced a metal gag into his mouth, of the sort horse doctors used to hold an animal's jaws apart so they could trim its teeth. When the gag was in place, Nazares reached into Iakovitzes' forcibly opened mouth. Seeing Krispos still watching, the healer-priest explained, "For proper healing, I must touch the wound itself."

Krispos started to answer, then saw Nazares was dropping into a healer's trance. "We bless thee, Phos, lord with the great and good mind, watchful beforehand that the great test of life may be decided in our favor." The priest repeated the creed again and again, using it to distract his conscious mind and to concentrate his will solely on the task of healing before him.

As always, Krispos felt awed to watch a healer-priest at work. He could tell just when Nazares began to heal by the way the man suddenly went rigid. Iakovitzes continued to moan and kick, but he could have burst into flames without turning Nazares from his purpose. Almost as if lightning were in the air, Krispos felt the current of healing as it passed from Nazares to Iakovitzes.

Then, all at once, Iakovitzes quit struggling. Krispos took a step forward in alarm, afraid his onetime patron's heart had given out. But Iakovitzes continued to breathe and Nazares continued to heal; had something been wrong, the healer-priest surely would have sensed it.

At last Nazares withdrew his hand. He wiped pus-smeared fingers on his robe. The attendant removed the gag from Iakovitzes' mouth. Krispos saw the noble was in full possession of his senses again. Now when he moved in the grip of the two men who held him, they let him go.

He bowed low to the healer-priest, then made a series of yammering noises. After a moment, he realized no one could understand him. He signed for something to write with. One of the attendants brought him a waxed wooden tablet and stylus. He scribbled and handed the tablet to Nazares.

" 'What are you all standing around for?' " Nazares read, his voice slow and dragging from the crushing fatigue that followed healing. " 'Take me to the baths—I stink like a latrine. I could use some food, too, about a year's worth.' "

Krispos could not help smiling—Iakovitzes might never speak an intelligible word again, but he still sounded like himself. Then Iakovitzes wrote some more and handed the tablet to him. "Next time, send someone else."

Sobered, he nodded, saying "I know gold and honor will never give you back what you have lost, Iakovitzes, but what they can give, you will have."

"I'd better. I earned them," Iakovitzes wrote.

He felt inside his mouth with his fingers, poking and prodding, then let out a soft grunt of wonder and bowed again to Nazares. He scrawled again, then handed the healer-priest the tablet. " 'Holy sir, the wound feels as if it happened years ago. Only the memory is yet green,' " Nazares read. Behind the brassy front Iakovitzes habitually assumed, Krispos saw the terror that still lived in his eyes

An attendant touched Iakovitzes on the arm. He flinched, then scowled at himself and dipped his head in apology to the man. "Excellent sir, I just wanted to tell you I would take you to a bathhouse now, if you like," the attendant said. "There's one close by the Sorcerers' Collegium here."

Iakovitzes tried to speak, scowled again, and nodded. Before he left with the attendant, though, Krispos said, "A moment, Iakovitzes, please. I want to ask you something." Iakovitzes paused. Krispos went on. "By the messages you sent me, you and Harvas traded barbs all winter long. What did you finally say that made him do—that—to you?"

The noble flinched again, this time from his own thoughts. But he bent over the tablet and wrote out his reply. He gave it to Krispos when he was done. "I didn't even intend to insult him, worse luck. We'd settled on a price for the year's truce and were swearing oaths to secure it. Harvas would not swear by the spirits, Kubrati-style, nor would he take oath by the Haloga gods of his followers. 'Swear by Phos, then,' I told him—a truce is no truce without oaths, as any child knows. Better I had told him to go swive his mother, I think. In a voice like thunder, he cried out, 'That name shall never be in my mouth again, nor in yours either.' And then—" The writing stopped there, but Krispos knew what had happened then.

He sketched the sun-sign over his heart. Iakovitzes did the same. Krispos promised, "We'll avenge you, avenge this. I've just sent out a force under Agapetos to harry Harvas' land. When I'm done with Petronas, Harvas will face the whole army."

Again Iakovitzes tried to reply with spoken words, again he had to stop in frustration. He nodded instead, held up one finger while he pointed to the west, then two while he pointed northeastward. He nodded again, to show he approved of Krispos' course. Krispos was glad of that; while Iakovitzes had helped him form his priorities the winter before, he could hardly have blamed the noble for changing his mind after what had befallen him. That he hadn't helped convince Krispos he was on the right course.

Iakovitzes turned to the attendant and mimed scrubbing himself. The man led him out of the chamber.

"I am in your debt," Krispos said to Nazares.

"Nonsense." The healer-priest waved his words away. "I praise the good god that I was able to end Iakovitzes' agony. I only regret his injury is such that it will continue to trouble him greatly despite being healed. And the charm set on the wound to keep from healing it . . . that was most wicked, Your Majesty."

"I know." Krispos opened the waxed tablet and read again the words that had cost Iakovitzes his tongue. No man unwilling to say Phos' name, or even to hear it, was likely to be good. *If only Harvas were as inept as he was evil,* Krispos thought, *and if only Petronas would disappear, and if only Pyrrhos would grow mild, and if only I could be certain I'm Phostis' father, and if only I could rule by thinking "if only" . . .*

EVEN IN EARLY SPRING, THE COASTAL LOWLANDS WERE HOT AND sticky. The roads were still moist enough, though, that armies on the march kicked up only a little dust—as good a reason as any for campaigning in the spring, Krispos thought as he trotted along on Progress toward the Eriza River.

The army in whose midst he traveled was the biggest he had ever seen, more than ten thousand men. Had Sarkis captured or killed Petronas over the winter, this new round of civil war would not have been needed. By keeping Anthimos' uncle from gaining ground, though, the Vaspurakaner soldier had managed the next best thing: he'd convinced the generals of the local provinces that Krispos was the better bet. Those generals and their troopers rode with the force from Videssos the city now.

Krispos saw the inevitable host of farmers busy in their fields on either side of the road. Though the force with which he traveled was far larger than the one that had fought Petronas the previous fall, fewer farmers fled. He took that for a good sign. "They know we'll keep good order," he remarked to Trokoundos, who rode nearby. "Peasants shouldn't fear soldiers."

"This far before harvest, they have little to steal anyhow," Trokoundos said. "They know that, too, and take courage from it."

"You've been drinking sour wine this morning," Krispos said, a trifle startled; such cynicism was worthy of Iakovitzes.

"Maybe so," Trokoundos said. "We also have supplies for the army well arranged, this being territory that stayed loyal to you. We'll see how the men behave when we enter country that had been under Petronas' hand."

"Oh, aye, we'll do a bit of plundering if our supply train has trouble," said Mammianos, one of the provincial generals who had at last cast his lot with Krispos. He was in his mid-fifties and quite round, but a fine horseman for all that. "But we'll do a bit of fighting, too, which makes up for a lot."

Krispos started to say nothing could make plundering his own people right. He kept the words to himself. If folk farther westward worked for his rival and against him, they and their fields became fair targets for his soldiers—Petronas' men, he was sure, would not hold back if they reached territory he controlled. Either way, the Empire and the fisc would suffer.

When he did speak aloud, he said, "Civil war," as if it were a curse.

"Aye, the times are hard," Mammianos agreed. "There's but one thing worse than fighting a civil war, and that's losing it." Krispos nodded.

Two days later he and his army forded the Eriza—the ruined bridges were yet to be rebuilt. This time the crossing was unopposed, though Krispos found himself looking back over his shoulder lest some imperial courier come riding up with word of a new disaster. But no couriers appeared. That in itself buoyed Krispos' spirits.

He began seeing traces of the fighting Sarkis had done the previous winter: wrecked villages, fields standing idle and unplanted, the shells of burned-out buildings. Peasants on this side of the Eriza, those who were left, fled his soldiers as if they were so many demons.

The land began to rise toward the westlands' rugged central plateau. The rich, deep black earth of the lowlands grew thinner, dustier, grayer. Because of the early season, the countryside was still bright green, but Krispos knew the sun would bake it dry long before summer was done. In the lowlands, they sometimes raised two crops a year. On the central plateau, they were lucky to get one; broad stretches of land were better suited to grazing cattle than growing crops.

Krispos' advance stopped being a walkover about halfway between the Eriza and the town of Resaina. He had started to wonder if Petronas would ever stand and fight. Then, all at once, the scouts who rode ahead of his army came pelting back toward the main body of men. He watched them turn to shoot arrows back over their shoulders, then saw other horsemen pursuing them.

"Those must be Petronas' men!" he exclaimed, pointing. Only by the way they attacked his own cavalry could he be sure: Their gear was identical to what his own forces used. One more hazard of civil war that hadn't occurred to him, he thought uneasily.

"Aye, by the good god, those are the rebels," Mammianos said. "A whole bloody great lot of them, too." He turned his head to shout orders to the musicians whose calls set the army in motion. As martial music blared out and units hurried from column to line of battle, Mammianos sped them into place with bellowed commands. "Faster there, the ice take you! Here's the fight we've been waiting for, the chance to smash the stinking traitor once for all. Come on, deploy, deploy, deploy!"

The fat general showed more energy in a couple of minutes than he had used all through the campaign thus far, so much more that Krispos stared at him in surprise. The curses he kept calling down on Petronas' head, and the spleen with which he hurled them forth, were also something new. When Mammianos paused to draw breath, Krispos said, "General, forgive me for ever having doubted your loyalty."

Mammianos' eyes were shrewd. "In your boots, Majesty, I'd doubt my own shadow if it wasn't in front of me. May I speak frankly?"

"I hope you will."

"Aye, you seem to," Mammianos said judiciously. "I know I didn't lend you much aid last fall."

"No, but you didn't aid Petronas, either, for which I'm grateful."

"As well you might be. Truth to tell, I was sitting tight. I won't apologize for it, either. If you'd stolen the throne without deserving it, Petronas would've made quick hash of you. Likely I would have joined him afterward, too; the Empire doesn't need a weakling Avtokrator now. But since you did well enough against him, and since most of the decrees you've issued have made sense"—Mammianos clapped his hands together in savage glee—"I'll help you nail the whoreson's hide to the wall instead. Put me on the shelf, will he?"

"On the shelf?" Krispos echoed, perplexed. "But you're the general of—"

"—a province that usually needs a general about as much as a lizard needs a bathtub," Mammianos interrupted. "I was with Petronas when he invaded Vaspurakan a couple of years ago. I told him to his face he didn't have the wherewithal to push the Makuraners out."

"I told him the same, back at the palaces," Krispos said.

"What'd he do to you?" Mammianos asked.

"He tried to kill me." Krispos shivered, remembering Petronas' sorcerous assault. "He almost did, too."

Mammianos grunted. "He told me that if I didn't want to fight, he'd send me someplace where I wouldn't have to, which is how I got stuck in the lowlands where nothing ever happens. Except now it has, and I get a chance to pay the bastard back." He shook his fist at Petronas' horsemen. "You'll get yours, you lice!"

Krispos watched the oncoming soldiers, too. His military eye was still unpracticed, but he thought his rival's army was about the size of his own. His lips skinned back from his teeth. That was only likely to make the battle more expensive but less decisive.

A blue banner with gold sunburst flew above the center of Petronas' force, a twin to the one a standardbearer carried not far from Krispos. He shook his head. This sort of fight was worse than confusing. It was as if he battled himself in a mirror.

A great shout rose from his men: "Krispos! Krispos Avtokrator!" Petronas' men shouted back, crying out the name of their commander.

Krispos drew his sword. He was no skilled soldier, but had learned that did not always matter in the confusion of the battlefield. A company of Halogai, the sharpened edges of their axe blades glittering in the spring sunshine, formed up in front of him to try to make sure he did no fighting in any case. He'd given up arguing with them. He knew he might see action in spite of them; not even a captain of guardsmen could always outguess combat.

Arrows flew in beautiful, deadly arcs. Men fell from their saddles. Some thrashed and tried to rise; others lay still. Horses fell, too, crushing riders beneath them. Animals and men screamed together. More horses, wounded but not felled, ran wild, carrying the soldiers on them out of the fight and injecting chaos into their comrades' neat ranks.

The two lines closed with each other. Now, here and there, men thrust with light lances and slashed with sabers rather than shooting arrows at one another. The din of shouts and shrieks, drumming hooves, and clashing metal was deafening. Peering this way and that, Krispos could see no great advantage for either side.

He looked across the line, toward that other imperial banner. With a small shock, he recognized Petronas, partly by the gilded armor and red boots his rival also wore, more by the arrogant ease with which Anthimos' uncle sat his horse. Petronas saw him, too; though they were a couple of hundred yards apart, Krispos felt their eyes lock. Petronas swung his sword down, straight at Krispos. He and the men around him spurred their mounts forward.

Krispos dug his roweled heels into Progress' flanks. The big bay gelding squealed in pain and fury and bounded ahead. The Halogai, though, were waiting for Krispos. One big man after another grabbed at Progress' reins, at his bridle, at the rest of his trappings. "Let me through, curse you!" Krispos raged.

"No, Majesty, no," the northerners yelled back. "We will settle the rebel for you."

Petronas and his companions were very close now. He had no Haloga guards, but the men who rode with him had to be his closest retainers, the bravest and most loyal of his host. Sabers upraised and gleaming, lances poised and ready, they crashed into the ranks of the imperial bodyguards.

For all the tales he had heard, Krispos had never actually seen the Halogai fight before. Their first couple of ranks simply went down, bowled over by their foes' horses or speared before they were close enough to swing their axes. But Petronas' men fell, too; their chain mail might have been linen for all it did to keep those great axes from their flesh. Their horses, which wore no armor, suffered worse. The axes abattoir workers used to slaughter beeves were shorter, lighter, and less keen than the ones in the northerners' strong hands. One well-placed blow dropped any horse in its tracks; another usually sufficed for its rider.

A barricade of flesh, some dead, some writhing, quickly formed between Krispos' men and Petronas'. The Halogai hacked over it. Petronas' mounted men kept trying to bull their way through. The ranks of the guardsmen thinned. Krispos found himself ever closer to the fighting front. Now the Halogai, battling for survival themselves, could not keep him away.

And there was Petronas! Red smeared his saber; no one had told him he was too precious to risk. Krispos spurred Progress toward him. With warrior's instinct, Petronas' head whipped round. He snarled at Krispos, blocked his cut, and returned one that clattered off Krispos' helmet.

They cursed each other, the same words in both their mouths. "Thief! Bandit! Bastard! Robber! Whoreson!"

More Halogai still stood than Petronas' companions. Shouting Krispos' name, they surged toward the rebel. Petronas was too old a soldier to stay and be slaughtered. Along with those of his guards who yet lived, he pulled back, pausing only to shake his fist one last time at Krispos. Krispos answered with a two-fingered gesture he'd learned on the streets of Videssos the city.

The center had held. Krispos looked round to see how the rest of the battle was doing. It still hung in the balance. His own line sagged a little on the left, Petronas' on the right. Neither commander had enough troops to pull some out of line and exploit his small advantage without the risk of giving his foe a bigger one. And so men hacked and thrust and hit and swore and bled, all to keep matters exactly as they had been before the battle started.

That tore at Krispos. To his way of thinking, if war had any purpose whatsoever, it was to make change quick and decisive. Such suffering with nothing to show for it seemed a cruel waste.

But when he said as much to Mammianos, the general shook his head. "Petronas has to go through you before he can move on the capital. A drawn fight gains him nothing. This is the first real test of fighting skill and loyalty for your men. A draw for you is near as good as a win, because you show the Empire you match him in those things. Given that, and given that you hold Videssos the city, I like your chances pretty well."

Reluctantly Krispos nodded. Mammianos' cool good sense was something he tried to cultivate in himself. Applying it to this wholesale production of human agony before him, though, took more self-possession than he could easily find.

He started to tell that to Mammianos, but Mammianos was not listening. Like a farmer who scents a change in the wind at harvesttime and fears for his crop, the general peered to the left. "Something's happened there," he said, certainty in his voice.

Krispos also stared leftward. He needed longer than Mammianos to recognize a new clumping of men at the wing, to hear the new shouts of alarm and fury and, a moment later, triumph. The sweat that dripped from the end of his nose suddenly went cold. "Someone's turned traitor."

"Aye." Mammianos packed a world of meaning into a single word. He bellowed for a courier and started a series of frantic orders to plug the gap. Then he broke off and looked again. As if against his will, a grin of disbelief stretched itself over his fat face. "By the good god," he said softly. "It's one of theirs, going over to us."

Since he felt it himself, Krispos understood Mammianos' surprise. He'd feared the reliability of his own troops, not Petronas'. But sure enough, a sizable section—more than a company, perhaps as much as a regiment—of Petronas' army was now shouting "Krispos!"

And the defectors did more than shout. They turned on the men to their immediate right, the men who held the rightmost position in Petronas' line. Beset by them as well as by Krispos' own supporters, the flank guards broke and fled in wild confusion.

Mammianos' amazement did not paralyze him for long. Though he'd done nothing to force the break in Petronas' line, he knew how to exploit it once it was there. He sent the left wing of Krispos' army around Petronas' shattered right, seeking to roll up the whole rebel army.

But Petronas also knew his business. He did not try to salvage a battle already lost. Instead, he dropped a thin line back from the stump of his army's broken right wing, preventing Krispos' men from surrounding too many more of his own. His forces gave ground all along their line now, but nowhere except on the far right did they yield to panic. They were beaten, but remained an army. Breaking off combat a little at a time, they retreated west toward Resaina.

Krispos wanted to press the pursuit hard, but still did not feel sure enough of himself as battlefield commander to override Mammianos, who kept the army under tight control. The bulk of Petronas' troops escaped to the camp they had occupied before they came out to fight, leaving Krispos' men in possession of the field.

Healer-priests went from man to wounded man, first at a run, then at a walk, and finally at a drunken shamble as the exhaustion of their trade took its toll on them. More mundane leeches, men who worked without the aid of magic, saw to soldiers with minor wounds, here sewing up a cut, there splashing an astringent lotion onto flesh lacerated when chain mail was driven through padding and leather undertunic alike.

And Krispos, surrounded not only by the surviving Halogai of the imperial guard but also by most of Sarkis' cavalry regiment, approached the troopers whose defection had cost Petronas the fight. He and all his men stayed ready for anything; Petronas was devious enough to throw away a battle to set up an assassination.

The leader of the units that had changed sides saw Krispos coming. He rode toward him. Krispos had the odd feeling he'd seen the fellow before, though he was sure he had not. The middle-aged officer, plainly a noble, was short and slim, with a narrow face, a thin arched nose, and a neat beard the color of his iron helmet. He set his right fist over his heart in salute to Krispos. "Your Majesty," he said. His voice was a resonant tenor.

"My thanks for your aid there, excellent sir," Krispos said. He wondered how big a reward the officer would want for it. "I fear I don't know your name."

"I am Rhisoulphos," the fellow said, as if Krispos ought to know who Rhisoulphos was.

After a moment, he did. "You're Dara's father," he blurted. No wonder the man looked familiar! "Your daughter takes after you, excellent sir."

"So I've been told." Rhisoulphos let out a short bark of laughter. "I daresay she wears the face better than I do, though."

Mammianos studied Dara's father, then said, "What was the Avtokrator's kinsman by marriage doing in the ranks of the Avtokrator's foes?" Suspicion made his tone harsh. Krispos leaned forward in his saddle to hear how Rhisoulphos would reply.

The noble dipped his head first to Mammianos, then to Krispos. "Please recall that, until Anthimos walked the bridge between light and ice, I was also Petronas' kinsman by marriage. And after Anthimos did die"—Rhisoulphos looked Krispos full in the face—"I was not sure what sort of arrangement you had with my daughter, Your Majesty."

Sometimes Krispos also wondered what sort of arrangement he had with Dara. He said, "You have a grandson who will be Emperor, excellent sir." That remained true no matter who Phostis' father was, he thought. He felt like giving his head a wry shake, but was too well schooled to reveal himself so in front of Rhisoulphos.

He saw he had said the right thing. Rhisoulphos' eyes, so like Dara's with their slightly folded inner lids, softened. His father-in-law said, "So I heard, and it set me thinking: what would that boy be if Petronas won the throne? The only answer I saw was an obstacle and a danger to him. I showed Petronas none of my thoughts, of course. I pledged him my loyalty again and again, loudly and rather stupidly."

"A nice touch," Mammianos said. His eyes slid toward Krispos. Krispos read them without difficulty: if Rhisoulphos could befool Petronas, he was a man who needed watching.

Krispos had already worked that out for himself. Now, though, he could only acknowledge Rhisoulphos' aid. "Our first meeting was well timed, excellent sir," he said. "After Petronas is beaten, I will show you all the honor the Avtokrator's father-in-law deserves."

Rhisoulphos bowed in the saddle. "I will do my best to earn that honor on the field, Your Majesty. I know my soldiers will support me—and you."

"I'm sure they will," Krispos said, resolving to use Rhisoulphos' men but not to trust them with any truly vital task until Petronas was no longer a threat. "Now perhaps you will join my other advisors as we plan how to take advantage of what we've won with your help."

"I am at your service, Your Majesty." Rhisoulphos slid down from his horse and walked over to the imperial tent. Seeing that Krispos did not object, the Halogai in front of the entrance bowed and let him pass. Krispos also dismounted. Grunting and wheezing with effort, so did Mammianos.

Along with Rhisoulphos, Sarkis and Trokoundos the mage waited inside the tent for Krispos. They rose and bowed when he came in. "A fine fight, Your Majesty," Sarkis said enthusiastically. "One more like it and we'll smash this rebellion to bloody bits." The rest of the soldiers loudly agreed. Even Trokoundos nodded.

"I don't want another battle, not if I can help it," Krispos said. The other men in the tent stared at him. He continued, "If I can, I want to make Petronas give up without more fighting. Everyone who falls in the civil war, on my side or his, could have fought for me against Harvas. The fewer who fall, then, the better."

"Admirable, Your Majesty," Mammianos rumbled. "How do you propose to bring it off?" His expression said he did not think Krispos could.

Krispos spoke for several minutes. By the time he was done, he saw Rhisoulphos and Sarkis running absentminded fingers through their beards as they thought. Finally Rhisoulphos said, "It might work, at that."

"So it might," Sarkis said. He grinned at Krispos. "I wasn't wrong, Your Majesty—you are a lively man to serve under. We have a saying in Vaspurakan about your kind—'sneaky as a prince out to sleep with another man's princess.' "

Everyone in the tent laughed. "I have a princess of my own, thank you," Krispos said, which won him an approving glance from Rhisoulphos. His own mirth soon faded, though; he remembered the days when Dara had not been his, and how the two of them had both done some sneaking to be able to sleep with each other. Sarkis' Vaspurakaner saying held teeth the officer did not know about.

Mammianos' yawn almost split his head in two. "Let's get on with it," he said. "The Emperor's scheme has to move tonight if it moves at all, and afterward I aim to sleep. If the scheme doesn't come off—maybe even if it does—we'll have more fighting in the morning, and I for one am not so young as I used to be. I need rests between rounds, in battle as in other things."

"Sad but true," said Rhisoulphos, who was within a few years of the fat general's age. He yawned, too, less cavernously.

"Go get some of your scouts, Sarkis," Krispos said. "They're the proper men for the plan." Sarkis saluted and hurried away. Along with the rest of his companions, Krispos stepped outside the tent to await his return. A couple of Halogai stayed almost within arm's length of him, their axes at the ready, their eyes never leaving Rhisoulphos. He must have known they were watching him, and why, but gave no sign. Krispos admired his sangfroid.

A few minutes later Sarkis returned with fifteen or twenty soldiers. "All young and unmarried, as you asked," he told Krispos. "They don't care if they live or die."

The scouts thought that was very funny. Their teeth gleamed whitely in their dirty faces as they chuckled. Krispos realized that what Sarkis had said was literally true for most of them; they did not believe in the possibility of their own deaths, not down deep. Had he been so foolish himself, ten or twelve years before? He probably had.

"Here's what I want you to do," he said, and the scouts drew closer to listen. "I want you to get into Petronas' camp tonight, when everything there is still in disorder. I don't care whether you pretend to be his soldiers or you take off your armor and make as if you're farmers from around here. Whatever you do, you need to get among his men. I don't order this of you. Anyone who doesn't care to risk it may leave now."

No one left. "What do we do once we're in there, Majesty?" one of the scouts asked. The light from the campfires played up the glitter of excitement in his eyes. To him it was all a game, Krispos thought. He breathed a prayer to Phos that the youngster would come through safe.

"Here's what," he answered. "Remind Petronas' soldiers that I offered him amnesty, and tell them they can have it, too, for the asking . . . if they don't wait too long. Tell them I'll give them three days. After that, we'll attack again, and we'll treat any we capture as enemies."

The young men looked at one another. "Sneaky as a prince out to sleep with another man's princess," one of them said with a strong Vaspurakaner accent. As Sarkis had, he sounded admiring.

When they saw Krispos was done, the scouts scattered. Krispos watched them slip out of camp, heading west. Some rode out, armed and armored; others left on foot, wearing knee-length linen tunics and sandals.

Mammianos watched them go, too. After the last one was gone, he turned to Krispos and asked, "Now what?"

"Now," Krispos said, picking a phrase more likely in Barsymes' mouth than his own, "we await developments."

THE FLOOD OF DESERTERS HE'D HOPED FOR DID NOT MATERIalize. A few riders came over from the rebel camp, but Petronas' cavalry pickets stayed alert and aggressive. If they'd given up on the chief they followed, they showed no sign of it.

To Krispos' relief, all his own scouts managed to return safely. He would have felt dreadful, sacrificing them without gaining the advantage he'd expected. On the third day after he'd sent them out, he began readying his forces for an attack on the morrow. "Since I warned Petronas' men, I can't make myself out a liar now," he told Mammianos.

"No, Your Majesty," Mammianos agreed mournfully. "I might wish, though, that you hadn't been so exact. Since Petronas must know we're coming, who can guess what sort of mischief he'll have waiting for us?" Without words, his round face said, *You wouldn't be in this mess if you'd listened to me.*

Krispos did not need to be reminded of that. Thinking to save lives, he'd probably cost Videssos—and his own side in particular—a good many men instead. As he sought his tent that evening, he told himself that he had generals along for a reason, and kicked himself for ignoring Mammianos' sage advice to pursue his own scheme.

Thanks to his worry, he took awhile to fall asleep. Once slumber took him, he slept soundly; he had long since learned to ignore the usual run of camp noises. The commotion that woke him was nothing usual. He grabbed sword and shield and clapped a helmet on his head before he peered out through the tent flap to see what was going on.

His first thought was that Petronas had decided to beat him to the punch with a night attack. But while the noise outside was tremendous, it was not the din of battle. "It sounds like a festival," he said, more than a little indignant.

Geirrod and Vagn stood guard in front of his tent. They turned to look at him. "Good, you're up, Majesty," Geirrod said. "We'd have roused you any time now, had the clamor not done it for us. Two of Petronas' best generals just came into camp."

"*Did* they?" Krispos said softly. "Well, by the good god." Just then Mammianos came out of his tent, which was next to Krispos'. Krispos felt like putting his thumbs in his ears, twiddling his fingers, and sticking out his tongue at the fat general. Instead, he simply waited for Mammianos to notice him.

The general's own guards must have given him the news. He glanced over toward the imperial tent and saw Krispos there. Slowly and deliberately, he came to attention and saluted. A moment later, as if deciding that was not enough, he doffed his helm as well.

Krispos waved back, then asked the guards, "Who are these generals, anyway?"

"Vlases and Dardaparos, their names are, Majesty," Geirrod said.

To Krispos they were only names. He said, "Have them fetched here. What they can tell me of Petronas and his army will be beyond price." As the Haloga walked off to do his bidding, Krispos waved Mammianos over. He was sure his general would know everything worth knowing about them.

Guards brought up the pair of deserters within a couple of minutes. One officer was tall and thickset, though muscular rather than fat like Mammianos. He proved to be Vlases. Dardaparos, on the other hand, was small, skinny, and bowlegged from a lifetime spent in the saddle; by looks, he might have been father to some of Sarkis' scouts. He and his comrade both went down in proskynesis before Krispos, touching their foreheads to the ground. "Majesty," they said together.

Krispos let them stay prostrate a beat longer than he would have with men he fully trusted. After he told them to rise, he asked, "How long ago did you last give Petronas imperial honors?"

Dardaparos spoke for both of them. "Earlier this evening. But we came here trusting your amnesty, Your Majesty. We'll serve you as loyally as ever we served him."

"There's a fine promise," Mammianos growled. "Does it mean you'll desert the Avtokrator just when he needs you most?"

"Surely not, Mammianos," Krispos said smoothly, seeing Dardaparos and Vlases stiffen. To them he added, "And my promise is good—you'll not be harmed. Tell me, though, what made you decide to come over to me now?"

"Majesty, we decided you'd likely win with us or without us," Vlases answered. His voice made Krispos blink. It was a high, sweet tenor, as surprising from such a big man as Trokoundos' bass from a small one. He went on. "Petronas said you were nothing but a jumped-up stable boy, begging your pardon, Your Majesty. The campaign you've run against him showed us different, though."

Dardaparos nodded. "Aye, that's how it was, Your Majesty. Any time an able man holds Videssos the city, a rebel's in deep from the get-go. You're abler than we thought when we first picked Petronas. We were wrong, and own it now."

Krispos drew Mammianos to one side. "What do you think?" he asked quietly.

"I'm inclined to believe them." Mammianos sounded as if he regretted his inclination. "If they'd told you they couldn't stand the idea of being traitors anymore, or some such high-sounding tripe, I'd keep 'em under guard—in irons, too, most likely. But I've known both of 'em for years, and they have a keen-honed sense of where their interest lies."

"That's about as I saw it." Krispos walked back over to the generals.

"Very well, excellent sirs, I welcome you to my cause. Now tell me how you think Petronas will dispose his forces to meet the attack I intend to make tomorrow."

"He won't dispose them so well, with us gone," Dardaperos said at once. Krispos had no idea how good a general he was, but he certainly had a high officer's sense of self-worth.

"Likely he won't," Krispos said. He found himself yawning enormously. "Excellent sirs, on second thought I'm going to leave the rest of your questioning to Mammianos here. And I hope you will forgive me, but I intend to keep you under guard until after the fighting is done tomorrow. I don't know what harm you could do me there, but I'd sooner not find out."

"Spoken like a sensible man, Your Majesty," Vlases said. "You may welcome us, but you have no reason to trust us. By the lord with the great and good mind, we'll give you reason soon enough."

He stooped, found a twig, and started drawing in the dirt. Grunting with the effort it cost him, Mammianos also stooped. Krispos watched for a few minutes as Vlases laid out Petronas' plans, then yawned again, even more widely than before. By the time he sought his cot, though, he'd learned enough to decide that the movements he and Mammianos had already devised would still serve his aims.

They would, that is, if Vlases and Dardaperos spoke the truth. He suddenly realized he could find out if they did. He sprang from bed once more, shouting for Trokoundos. The mage appeared shortly, dapper as ever. Krispos explained what he wanted.

"Aye, the two-mirror trick will tell whether they lie," Trokoundos said, "but it may not tell you everything you need to know. It won't tell you what changes Petronas has made in his plans because they deserted. And it won't tell whether he encouraged them to go over to you, maybe so subtly they don't even grasp it themselves, just for the sake of putting you in confusion and doubt like this."

"I can't believe that. They're two of his best men." But Krispos sounded unsure, even to himself. Petronas was a master of the game of glove within glove within glove. He'd twisted Anthimos round his finger for years. If he wanted to manipulate a couple of his generals, Krispos was convinced he could.

Angrily Krispos shook his head. A fine state of affairs, when even learning the truth could not tell him whether to change his plans or keep them. "Find out what you can," he told Trokoundos.

Once Trokoundos had gone, Krispos lay down again. Now, though, sleep was slower coming. And after Krispos' eyes closed and his breathing grew deep and regular, he dreamed he followed Petronas down a path that twisted back on itself until Petronas was following him. . . .

AFTER A NIGHT OF SUCH DREAMS, WAKING TO THE CERTAINTY of morning was a relief. Krispos found himself looking forward to battle in a way he never had before. For good or ill, battle would yield but one outcome, not the endlessly entrapping webs of possibility through which he had struggled in the darkness.

As Krispos gnawed a hard roll and drank sour wine from a leather jack, Trokoundos came up to report: "So far as Dardaparos and Vlases know, they're honest traitors, at any rate."

"Good," Krispos said. Trokoundos, duty done, departed, leaving Krispos to chew on his phrasing. Honest traitors? The words could have come straight from his near nightmare.

Scrambling up into Progress' saddle gave him the same feeling of release he'd known on waking, the feeling that something definite was about to happen. The Haloga guardsmen had to stay tight around him to keep him from spurring ahead of the army to the scouts who led its advance.

Before the day was very old, those scouts began trading arrows with the ones Petronas had sent out. Petronas' men drew back; they were far in advance of their own army, while Krispos' main body of troops trotted on, close behind his scouting parties. Had he not already known where Petronas' force lay, the retreating scouts would have led him to it.

Petronas' camp was in the middle of a broad, scrubby pasture, placed so no one could take it unawares. The rebel's forces stood in line of battle half a mile in front of their tents and pavilions. Petronas' imperial banner flapped defiantly at the center of their line.

Mammianos glanced at Krispos. "As we set it up?"

"Aye," Krispos said. "I think we'll keep him too busy to cut us in half." He showed his teeth in what was almost a smile. "We'd better."

"That's true enough." Mammianos half grunted, half chuckled. He yelled to the army musicians. Horns, drums, and pipes sent companies of horsemen galloping from the second rank to either wing as they bore down on Petronas' force.

The rebels were also moving forward; the momentum of horse and rider played a vital part in mounted warfare. Petronas had musicians of his own. Their martial blare shifted his deployments to match Krispos'.

"Good," Krispos said. "He's dancing to our tune for a change." He'd most feared Petronas trying to smash through his army's deliberately weakened center. Now—he hoped—the fight would be on his terms.

Arrows flew. So did war cries. The rebels still acclaimed Petronas. Along with Krispos' name, his men had others to hurl at their foes—those of Rhisoulphos, Vlases, and Dardaperos. They also shouted one thing more. "Amnesty! We spare those who yield!"

The armies collided first at the wings. Saber and lance took over for the bow. Despite defections, Petronas' men fought fiercely. Krispos bit his lip as he watched his own troops held in place. The treachery he'd looked for simply was not there.

When he complained of that, Mammianos said, "Can't be helped, Your Majesty. But aren't you glad to be worrying over the loyalty of the other fellow's army and not your own?"

"Yes, as a matter of fact," Krispos said. Only last fall he'd wondered if any Videssian soldiers at all would cleave to him. Only days before he'd wondered if his army would hold together through combat. Now Petronas' bowels were the ones that griped at each collision of men. Amazing what a victory could do, Krispos thought.

The fight ground on. Thanks to Rhisoulphos' defection, Krispos had more men in it than Petronas. Rhisoulphos' men were not in a hotly engaged part of the line—they held the middle of the right wing. But their presence freed up other warriors for the attack. The men on the extreme right of Petronas' line found themselves first outnumbered, then outflanked.

They bent back. That was not enough to save them; Krispos' horsemen, scenting victory, folded round them like a wolf's jaws closing on a tasty gobbet of meat. Petronas' men were brave and loyal. For half an hour and more, they fought desperately, selling themselves dear for their comrades' sake. But flesh and blood will only bear so much. Soldiers began casting swords and lances to the ground and raising their hands in token of surrender.

Once the yielding started—and once Petronas' men saw that, as promised, those who yielded were not butchered—it ran from the end of Petronas' line toward the middle. The line shook, like a man with an ague. Shouting, Krispos' warriors pressed hard.

All at once Petronas' army broke into fragments. Some men fled the field, singly and in small groups. More, sometimes whole companies at a time, threw down their weapons and surrendered. A hard core of perhaps three thousand men, Petronas' firmest followers, withdrew in a body toward hill country that corrugated the horizon toward the northwest.

"After them!" Krispos cried in high excitement, pounding his fist against Mammianos' armored shoulder. "Don't let a one of them get away!"

"Aye, Majesty." Mammianos shouted for couriers and stabbed his finger out toward Petronas' retreating soldiers. He roared orders that, properly carried out, would have bagged every fugitive.

Somehow, though, the pursuit did not quite come off. Some of Krispos' men rode after Petronas' hard core of strength. But others were still busy accepting surrenders, or relieving of their portable property soldiers who had surrendered. Still others made for Petronas' camp, which lay before them, tempting as a naked woman with an inviting smile. And so Petronas' followers, though in a running fight all the way, reached the hills and set up a rear guard to hold the gap through which they fled.

By the time the column that had given chase to Petronas returned empty-handed, night was falling. Krispos swore when he found out they had failed. "By the lord with the great and good mind, I'd like to send the fools who stopped to plunder straight to the ice," he raged.

"And if you did, you'd have hardly more men left than those who escaped with Petronas," Sarkis said.

"They should have chased Petronas first and plundered later," Krispos said.

Sarkis answered with a shrug, "Common soldiers don't grow rich on army pay, Your Majesty. They're lucky to hold their own. If they see the chance to steal something worth stealing, they're going to do it."

"And think, Your Majesty," Mammianos added soothingly, "had everyone gone after Petronas, who would have protected you if his men decided all at once to remember their allegiance?"

"I should have gone after Petronas myself," Krispos said, but then he let the matter drop. What was done was done; no matter how he complained, he could not bring back an opportunity lost. That did not mean he forgot. He filed the failure away in his mind, resolving not to let it happen again with any army of his.

"Any way you look at it, Majesty, we won quite a victory," Mammianos said. "Here's a great haul of prisoners, Petronas' camp taken—"

"I'll not deny it," Krispos said. He'd hoped to win the whole war today, not just a battle, but, as he'd just reminded himself, one took what one got. He was not so mean-spirited as to forget that. He undid his tin canteen from his belt, raised it, then swigged a big gulp of the rough wine the army drank. "To victory!" he shouted.

Everyone who heard him—which meant a good part of the army—turned at the sound of his voice. In a moment, bedlam filled the camp. "To victory!' soldiers roared. Some, like Krispos, toasted it. Others capered round campfires, filled with triumph or simple relief at being alive.

And others, the crueler few, taunted the prisoners they had taken. The former followers of Petronas, disarmed now, dared not reply. From taunts, some of the ruffians moved on to roughing up their captives. Krispos did not care to think about how far their ingenuity might take them if he gave them free rein.

Hand on sword hilt, he stalked toward the nastiest of the little games nearby. Without his asking, Halogai formed up around him. Narvikka said, "Aye, Majesty, there's a deal of us in you, I t'ink. You look like a man about to go killing mad."

"That's how I feel." Krispos grabbed the shoulder of a trooper who had been amusing himself by stomping on a prisoner's toes. The man whirled round angrily when his sport was interrupted. The curse in his mouth died unspoken. Quickly, shaking with fear, he prostrated himself.

Krispos waited till he was flat on his belly, then kicked him in the ribs. Pain shot up his leg—the fellow wore chain mail. By the way he twisted and grabbed at himself, he felt the kick, too, through links, leather, and padding. Krispos said, "Is that how you give amnesty: tormenting a man who can't fight back?"

"N-no, Majesty," the fellow got out. "Just—having a little fun, is all."

"Maybe you were. I don't think he was." Krispos kicked the trooper again, not quite so hard this time. The man grunted, but otherwise bore it without flinching. Krispos drew back his foot and asked, "Or do you enjoy it when I do this? Answer me!"

"No, Majesty." Overbearing while on top, the soldier shrank in on himself when confronted with power greater than his petty share.

"All right, then. If you ever want to get mercy, or deserve it, you'd best give it when you can. Now get out of here." The soldier scrambled to his feet and fled. Krispos glared around. "Hurting a man who's yielded, especially one who's promised amnesty, is Skotos' work. The next trooper who's caught at it gets stripes and dismissal without pay. Does everyone understand?"

If anybody had doubts, he kept them to himself. In the face of Krispos' anger, the camp went from boisterous to solemn and quiet in moments. Into that sudden silence, the fellow he'd rescued said, "Phos bless you, Your Majesty. That was done like an Avtokrator."

"Aye." Several Halogai rumbled agreement.

"If I have the job, I should live up to it." Krispos glanced over at the prisoner. "Why did you fight against me in the first place?"

"I come from Petronas' estates. He is my master. He was always good to me; I figured he'd be good for the Empire." He studied Krispos, his head cocked to one side. "I still reckon that might be so, but looks to me now like he's not the only one."

"I hope not." Krispos wondered how many men throughout the Empire of Videssos could run it capably if they somehow found themselves on the throne. He'd never had that thought before. More than a few, he decided, a little bemused. But he was the one with the job, and he aimed to keep it.

"What is it, Majesty?" Narvikka asked. "By the furrow of your brow, I'd guess a weighty thought."

"Not really." Laughing, Krispos explained.

Narvikka said, "Bethink yourself on your good fortune, Majesty: of all those might-be Avtokrators, only Petronas wears the red boots in your despite."

"Even Petronas is one man too many in them." Krispos turned to go back to his tent, then stopped. A grin of pure mischief slowly spread over his face. "I know just how to get him out of them, too." His voice rose. "Trokoundos!"

The mage hurried over to him. "How may I serve Your Majesty?" he asked, bowing.

Krispos told Trokoundos what he needed, then said anxiously, "This isn't battle magic, is it?"

Trokoundos' heavy-lidded eyes half closed as he considered. At last he said, "It shouldn't be. And even if Petronas' person is warded, as it's sure to be, who would think of protecting his boots?" His smile was a slyer version of Krispos'. "The more so as we won't do them a bit of harm."

"So we won't," Krispos said. "But, the lord with the great and good mind willing, we'll do some to Petronas."

Chapter V

P ETRONAS, AS WAS HIS HABIT, WOKE SOON AFTER DAWN. HIS back and shoulders ached; too many years of sleeping soft in Videssos the city—aye, and even when he took the field—left him unused to making do with a single blanket for a bedroll. At that, he was luckier than most of the men who still clove to him, for he had a tent to shelter him from the nighttime chill. Theirs were lost, booty now for the army that followed Krispos.

"Krispos!" Petronas mouthed the name, making it into a curse. He cursed himself, too, for he had first taken Krispos into his own household, then introduced him into Anthimos'.

He'd never imagined Krispos' influence with his nephew could rival his own—till the day he found himself, his head shorn, cast into the monastery of the holy Skirios. He ran a hand through his hair. Only now, most of a year after he'd slipped out of the monastery, did he have a proper man's growth once more.

He'd never imagined Krispos would dare seize the throne, or that Krispos could govern once he had it—everyone, he'd been sure, would flock to his own banner. But it had not happened so. Petronas cursed himself again, for putting that fat fool of a Mammianos in a place that had proven so important.

And with that fat fool, Krispos had beaten him twice now—and by the good god, Petronas had never imagined *that*! Just how badly he'd underestimated Krispos, and Krispos' knack for getting other people to do what he needed, was only now sinking in, when it was on the very edge of being too late.

Petronas clenched a fist. "No, by Phos, not too late!" he said out loud. He pissed in a chamber pot—likely the last of those left to his army—then decked himself in the full imperial regalia. Seeing him in the raiment rightfully his could only hearten his men, he told himself.

He stooped to go out through the tent flap and walked over to his horse, which was tied nearby. He sprang onto the beast's back with a surge of pride—he might be nearing sixty, but he could still ride. He smiled maliciously to think of Gnatios, who quivered atop anything bigger than a mule.

But as Petronas rode through the camp, his smile faded. Years of gauging armies' tempers made him worry about this one. The men were restive and discouraged; he did not like the way they refused to meet his eye. When a soldier did look his way, he liked the fellow's stare even less. "By the ice, what are you gaping at?" he snarled.

The trooper looked apprehensive at being singled out. "B-begging your pardon, Your Majesty, but why did you don black boots to wear with your fine robe and crown?"

"Are you mad?" Petronas took his left foot from the stirrup and kicked his leg up and down. "This boot's as red as a man's arse after a week in the saddle."

"Begging your pardon again, Majesty, but it looks black to me. So does the right one, sir—uh, sire. May the ice take me if I lie."

"Are you telling me I don't know red when I see it?" Petronas asked dangerously. He looked down at his boots. They were both a most satisfactory crimson, the exact imperial shade. Petronas had seen it worn by his father, by his brother, and by his nephew; it was as familiar to him as the back of his hand—more familiar than his own face, for sometimes he did not see a mirror for weeks at a stretch.

Instead of answering him directly, the trooper turned to his mates. "Tell his Majesty, lads. Are those boots red or are they black?"

"They're black," the soldiers said in one voice. Now it was Petronas' turn to stare at them; he could not doubt they meant what they said. One man added, "Seems an unchancy thing to me, wearing a private citizen's boots with all that fancy imperial gear."

Another said, "Aye, there's no good omen in that." Several troopers drew Phos' sun-circle over their hearts.

Petronas glanced at his boots again. They still looked red to him. If his men did not see them so—he shivered. That omen seemed bad to him, too, as if he had no right to the imperial throne. He clenched his teeth against the idea that Phos had turned away from him and toward that accursed upstart Krispos . . .

The moment his rival's name entered his mind, he knew Phos was not the one who had arranged the omen. He shouted for his wizard. "Skeparnas!" When the mage did not appear at once, he shouted again, louder this time. *"Skeparnas!"*

Skeparnas picked his way through the soldiers. He was a tall, thin man with a long, lean face, a beard waxed to a point, and the longest fingers Petronas had ever seen. "How may I serve you, Your Majesty?"

"What color are my boots?" Petronas demanded.

He'd seldom seen Skeparnas taken aback, but now the wizard blinked and drew back half a step. "To me, Your Majesty, they look red," he said cautiously.

"To me, too," Petronas said. But before the words were out of his mouth, the soldiers all around set up a clamor, insisting they were black. "Shut up!" he roared at them. To Skeparnas he went on, more quietly, "I think Krispos magicked them, the stinking son of a spotted snake."

"Ahh." Skeparnas leaned forward, like a tower tilting after an earthquake. "Yes, that would be a clever ploy, wouldn't it?" His hands writhed in quick passes; those spidery fingers seemed almost to knot themselves together.

Suddenly Petronas' soldiers called out: "They're red now, Your Majesty!"

"There, you see?" Petronas said triumphantly.

"A lovely spell, most marvelously subtle," Skeparnas said with a connoisseur's appreciation. "Not only did it have no hold on you, it was also made to be invisible to anyone who perceived it with a mage's eye, thus perhaps delaying its discovery and allowing it to work the maximum amount of confusion."

"Very fornicating lovely," Petronas snapped. He raised his voice to address his men. "You see, my heroes, there's no omen here. This was just more of Krispos' vile work, aiming to make you think something's wrong when it's not. Just a cheap, miserable trick, not worth fretting over."

He waited, hoping for an answering cheer. It did not come. Determinedly, though, he rode through the army as if it had. He waved to the men, making his horse rear and caracole.

"How do we know those boots weren't really black till the mage spelled 'em red again?" one soldier asked another as he came by. He rode on, but keeping his face still after that was as hard as if he'd taken a lance in the guts.

Trokoundos staggered, then steadied himself. "they've broken the spell," he gasped. "By the good god, I could do with a cup of wine." Greasy sweat covered his fine-drawn features.

Krispos poured with his own hand. "How much good do you think it's done?"

"No way to guess," Trokoundos said, gasping again after he'd drained the cup at a single long draft. "You know how it is, Majesty: If the soldiers are truly strong for Petronas, they'll stay with him come what may. If they're wavering, the least little thing could seem a bad omen to 'em."

"Aye." More and more, Krispos was coming to believe the art of leading men was a kind of magic, though not one sorcerers studied. What folk thought of a ruler, oftentimes, seemed more important than what he really was.

"Shall I try the spell again this afternoon, Majesty, or maybe tomorrow morning?" Trokoundos asked.

After some thought, Krispos shook his head. "That would make them sure it was our sorcery, I think. If it only happens the once, they can't be certain quite what it is."

"As you wish, of course," Trokoundos said. "What then?"

"I'm going to let Petronas stew in his own juice for a couple of days," Krispos answered. "When I do hit him again, I'll hit hard. People who know this country have already told me of other passes through the hills, and he doesn't have enough men to cover them all. If he stays where he is, I can leave enough men here to keep him from bursting out onto the plain again, while I take the rest around to hit him from behind."

"What if he flees?"

"If he flees now, after losing to me twice, he's mine," Krispos said. "Then it's just a matter of running him to earth."

While Petronas—he hoped—stewed, Krispos spent the next few days catching up on the dispatches that never stopped coming from the capital. He approved a commercial treaty with Khatrish, scribbled minor changes on an inheritance law before he affixed his seal to it, commuted one death sentence where the evidence looked flimsy, and let another stand.

He wrote to Mavros of his second victory, then read through his foster brother's gossipy reports of doings in Videssos the city. From them, and from Dara's occasional shorter notes, he gathered that Phostis, while still small, was doing well. That filled him with sober satisfaction; whether a baby lived to grow up was always a roll of the dice.

Mavros also forwarded dispatches from the war against Harvas Black-Robe. Krispos read and reread those. Agapetos' preemptive attack had bogged down, but he still stood on enemy soil. Maybe, Krispos thought, the peasants near the northern border would be able to get in a crop in peace.

Other documents also came from the city. Krispos began to dread opening the ones sealed with sky-blue wax. Every time he did, he read that Pyrrhos had deposed another priest or abbot for infractions that seemed ever more trivial. Casting a man from his temple for trimming his beard too close, for instance, left Krispos shaking his head. He wrote a series of increasingly blunt notes to the patriarch, urging Pyrrhos to show restraint.

But restraint did not seem to be part of Pyrrhos' vocabulary. Letters of protest also came to Krispos from ousted clerics, from clerics afraid they would be ousted, and from delegations of prominent citizens from several towns seeking protection for their local priests.

More and more, Krispos wished he could have retained Gnatios as ecumenical patriarch. He'd never imagined that one of his strongest allies could become one of his greatest embarrassments. And yet Pyrrhos remained zealous in his behalf. With Petronas and Gnatios still to worry about, Krispos put off a decision on his rigorist patriarch.

He sent a holding force under Sarkis against the pass through which Petronas had fled, then led the rest of the army north and west through another gap to get behind his rival. His part of the army was just entering that second pass when a courier from Sarkis galloped up on a blowing, foam-spattered horse. The man was panting as hard as if he'd done all that running himself. "Majesty!" he called. "Rejoice, Majesty! We're through!"

"You're through?" Krispos stared at him. "Sarkis forced the pass, you mean?" That was good luck past all expectation. Petronas knew how to find defensive positions. A handful of determined men could have held the pass for days, so long as they were not outflanked.

But the courier said, "Looks like Petronas' army's gone belly-up, the lord Sarkis told me to tell you. Some have fled, more are yielding themselves up. The fight isn't in 'em anymore, Majesty."

"By the good god," Krispos said softly. He wondered what part—if any—the magic he'd suggested had played. *Have to ask some prisoners,* he told himself before more urgent concerns drove the matter from his mind. "What's become of Petronas, then? Has he surrendered?"

"No, Majesty, no sign of him, nor of Gnatios, either. The lord Sarkis urges speed on you, to help round up as many flying soldiers as we may."

"Yes." Krispos turned to Thvari, the captain of his Haloga guards. "Will you and your men ride pack horses, brave sir, to help us move the faster?"

Thvari spoke to the guardsmen in their own slow, rolling speech. They shouted back, grinning and waving their axes. "Aye," Thvari said unnecessarily. He added, "We would not miss being in at the kill."

"Good." Krispos called orders to the army musicians. The long column briefly halted. The baggage-train handlers shifted burdens on their animals, freeing up enough to accommodate the Halogai. They waved away soldiers who wanted to help; men without their long-practiced skill at lashing and unlashing bundles would only have slowed them down.

The musicians blew *At the trot*. The army started forward again. The Halogai were no horsemen, but most managed to stay on their mounts and keep them headed in the right direction. That was plenty, Krispos thought. If they needed to fight, they would dismount.

"Where do you think Petronas will go if his army has broken up?" Krispos asked Mammianos.

The fat general tugged at his beard as he thought. "Some failed rebels might flee to Makuran, but I can't see Petronas as cat's-paw for the King of Kings. He'd sooner leap off a cliff, I think. He might do that anyway, Your Majesty, to keep you from gloating over him."

"I wouldn't gloat," Krispos said.

Mammianos studied him. "Mmm, maybe not. But he would if *he* caught *you*, and we always reckon others from ourselves. Likeliest, though, Petronas'll try and hole himself up somewhere, do what he can against you. Let me think . . . There's an old fortress not too far from here, place called—what in the name of the ice *is* the place called? Antigonos, that's what it is. That's as good a guess as any, and better than most."

"We'll head there, then," Krispos said. "Do you know the way?"

"I expect I could find it, but you'll have men who could do it quicker, I'll tell you that."

A few questions called to the soldiers showed Krispos that Mammianos was right. With a couple of locally raised men in the lead, the army pounded toward Antigonos. Krispos spent a while worrying what to do if Petronas was not in the fortress. Then he stopped worrying. His column was heading in the right direction to cut off fugitives anyhow.

The riders ran into several bands from Petronas' disintegrating army.

None included the rival Emperor; none of his men admitted knowing where he had gone. From what they said, he and some of his closest followers had simply disappeared the morning before, leaving the rest of the men to fend for themselves. One trooper said bitterly, "If I'd known the bugger'd run like that, I never would have followed him."

"Petronas thinks of his own neck first," Mammianos said. Remembering his own dealings with Anthimos' uncle, Krispos nodded.

He and his men reached the fortress of Antigonos a little before sunset. The fortress perched atop a tall hill and surveyed the surrounding countryside like a vulture peering out from a branch on top of a high tree. The iron-faced wooden gate was slammed shut; a thin column of cooksmoke rose into the sky from the citadel.

"Somebody's home," Krispos said. "I wonder who." Beside him, Mammianos barked laughter. Krispos turned to the musicians. "Blow *Parley*."

The call rang out several times before anyone appeared on the wall to answer it. "Will you yield?" Krispos called, a minor magic of Trokoundos' projecting his voice beyond bowshot. "I still offer amnesty to soldiers and safe passage back to the monastery for Petronas and Gnatios."

"I'll never trust myself to you, wretch," shouted the man on the wall.

Krispos started slightly to recognize Petronas' voice. It, too, carried; *Well,* Krispos thought, *I've known he had a mage along since he broke the spell on his boots.* He touched the amulet he wore with his lucky goldpiece. Petronas used wizards for purposes darker than extending the range of his voice. Without Trokoundos by him, Krispos would have feared to confront his foe so closely.

"I could have ordered you killed the moment I took the throne." Krispos wondered if he should have done just that. Shrugging to himself, he went on, "I have no special yen for your blood. Only pledge you'll live quietly among the monks and let me get on with running the Empire."

"*My* Empire," Petronas roared.

"Your empire is that fortress you're huddling in," Krispos said. "The rest of Videssos acknowledges me—and my patriarch." If he was stuck with Pyrrhos, he thought, he ought to get some use out of him, even if only to make Petronas writhe in his cage.

"To the ice with your patriarch, the Phos-drunk fanatic!"

Krispos smiled. For once, he and Petronas agreed on something. He had no intention of letting his rival know it. He said, "You're walled up as tightly here as you would be in the monastery of the holy Skirios. How do you propose to get away? You might as well give up and go back to the monastery."

"Never!" Petronas stamped down off the wall. His curses remained audible. He must have noticed that and signaled to his magician, for they cut off in the middle of a foul word.

Krispos nodded to Trokoundos, who chanted a brief spell. When Krispos spoke again, a moment later, his voice had only its usual power once more. "He won't be easy to pry out of there."

"Not without a siege train, which we don't have with us," Mammianos agreed. "Not unless we can starve him out, anyway."

Rhisoulphos stood close by, looking up at the spot on the wall that Petronas had just vacated. He shook his head at Mammianos' words. "He has supplies for months in there. He spent the winter strengthening the place against the chance that the war would turn against him."

"Smart of him." Mammianos also glanced toward the fortress of Antigonos. "Aye, he's near as clever as he thinks he is."

"We'll send for a siege train, by the good god, and sit round the fortress till it gets here," Krispos said. "If Petronas wants to play at being Avtokrator inside till the rams start pounding on the walls, that's all right with me."

"Your sitting here may be just what he wants," Trokoundos said. "Remember that he tried once to slay you by sorcery. Such an effort would be all the easier to repeat with you close by. We've just seen his mage is still with him."

"I can't very well leave before he's taken, not if I intend to leave men of mine behind here," Krispos said.

Mammianos and Rhisoulphos both saluted him, then looked at each other as if taken by surprise. Mammianos said, "Majesty, you may not be trained to command, but you have a gift for it."

"As may be." Krispos did not show how pleased he was. He turned to Trokoundos. "I trust you have me better warded than I was that night."

"Oh, indeed. The protections I gave you then were the hasty sort one uses in an emergency. I thank the lord with the great and good mind that they sufficed. But since you gained the throne, I and my colleagues have hedged you round with far more apotropaic incantations."

"With what?" Krispos wanted to see if the wizard could repeat himself without tripping over his tongue.

But Trokoundos chose to explain instead: "Protective spells. I believe they will serve. With magecraft, one is seldom as sure as one would like."

"Come to that, we aren't sure Petronas and his wizard will attack me," Krispos said.

"He will, Your Majesty," Rhisoulphos said positively. "What other chance in all the world has he now to become Avtokrator?"

"Put that way—" Krispos clicked his tongue between his teeth. "Aye, likely he will. Here I stay, even so. Trokoundos will keep me safe." What he did not mention was his fear that, if he returned to Videssos the city, Petronas might suborn some soldiers and get free once more.

"Maybe," Mammianos said hopefully, "he hasn't had the chance to fill the cisterns in there too full. Summers hereabouts are hot and dry. With luck, his men will get thirsty soon and make him yield."

"Maybe." But Krispos doubted it. He'd seen that Petronas could be matched as a combat soldier. For keeping an army in supplies, though, he had few peers. If he'd taken refuge in the fortress of Antigonos, he was ready to stand siege there.

Krispos ringed his own army round the base of the fortress' hill. He staged mock attacks by night and day, seeking to wear down the defenders. Trokoundos wore himself into exhaustion casting one protective spell after another over Krispos and over the army as a whole. That Petronas' mage bided his time only made Trokoundos certain the stroke would be deadly when it came.

The siege dragged on. The healer-priests were much busier with cases of dysentery than with wounds. A letter let Krispos know that a train of rams and catapults had set out from Videssos the city for Antigonos. Behind a white-painted shield of truce, a captain approached the fortress and read the letter in a loud voice, finishing "Beware, rebels! Your hour of justice approaches!" Petronas' men jeered him from the walls.

Trokoundos redoubled his precautions, festooning Krispos with charms and amulets until his chains seemed heavier than chain mail. "How am I supposed to sleep, wearing all this?" Krispos complained. "The ones that don't gouge my back gouge my chest."

With a look of martyred patience, Trokoundos said, "Your Majesty, Petronas must know he cannot hope to last long once the siege engines arrive. Therefore he will surely try to strike you down before that time. We must be ready."

"Not only will I be ready, I'll be stoop-shouldered, as well," Krispos said. Trokoundos' martyred look did not change. Krispos threw his hands in the air and walked off, clanking as he went.

But that night, alone at last in his tent, he tossed and turned until a sharp-pointed amethyst crystal on one of his new amulets stabbed him just above his right shoulder blade. He swore and clapped his other hand to the injury. When he took it away, his palm was wet with blood.

"That fornicating does it!" he snarled. He threw aside the light silk coverlet and jumped to his feet. He took off the offending chain and flung it on the floor. It knocked over one of the other charms that ringed the bed like a fortress' wall. Finally, breathing hard, Krispos lay down again. "Maybe Petronas' wizard will pick tonight to try to kill me," he muttered, "but one piece more or less shouldn't matter much. And if he does get me, at least I'll die sound asleep."

What with his fury, naturally, he had trouble drifting off even after the chain was gone. He tossed and turned, dozed and half woke. His shoulder still hurt, too.

Some time toward morning, a tiny crunch made him open his eyes yet again. He was frowning even as he came fully awake—the crunch had sounded very close, as if it was inside the tent. A servant who disturbed him in the middle of the night—especially the middle of this miserable night—would regret the day he was born.

But the man crouching not three paces away was no servant of his. He was all in black—even his face was blacked, likely with charcoal. His right hand held a long knife. And under one of his black boots lay the crushed remains of one of Trokoundos' charms. Had he not trod on it, Krispos would never have known he was there until that knife slid between his ribs or across his throat.

The knifeman's dark face twisted in dismay as he saw Krispos wake. Krispos' face twisted, too. The assassin sprang toward him. Krispos flung his coverlet in the fellow's face and shouted as loud as he could. Outside the tent, his Haloga guard also cried out.

While the assassin was clawing free of the coverlet, Krispos seized his knife arm with both hands. His foe kicked him in the shin, hard enough to make his teeth click together in anguish. He tried to knee the knifeman in the crotch. The fellow twisted to one side and took the blow on the point of his hip.

With a sudden wrench, he tried to break Krispos' grip on his wrist. But Krispos had wrestled since before his beard came in. He hung on grimly. The assassin could do what he pleased, so long as he did not get that dagger free.

Thunnk! The abrupt sound of blade biting into flesh filled Krispos' ears and seemed to fill the whole tent. Hot blood sprayed his belly. The assassin convulsed in his arms. A latrine stench said the man's bowels had let go. The knife dropped from his hands. He crumpled to the ground.

"Majesty!" Vagn cried, horror on his face as he saw Krispos spattered with blood. "Are you hale, Majesty?"

"If my leg's not broken, yes," Krispos said, giving it a gingerly try. The pain did not get worse, so he supposed he'd taken no real damage. He looked down at the knifeman and at the spreading pool of blood. He whistled softly. "By the good god, Vagn, you almost cut him in two."

Instead of warming to the praise, the Haloga hung his head. He thrust his dripping axe into Krispos' hands. "Kill me now, Majesty, I beg you, for I failed to ward you from this, this—" His Videssian failed him; to show what he meant, he bent down and spat in the dead assassin's face. "Kill me, I beg you."

Krispos saw he meant it. "I'll do no such thing," he said.

"Then I have no honor." Vagn drew himself up, absolute determination on his face. "Since you do not grant me this boon, I shall slay myself."

"No, you—" Krispos stopped before he called Vagn an idiot. Filled with shame as he was, the northerner would only bear up under insults like a man bearing up under archery and would think he deserved each wound he took. Krispos tried to get the shock of battling the assassin out of his mind, tried to think clearly. The harsh Haloga notion of honor served him well most of the time; now he had to find a way around it. He said, "If you didn't ward me, who did? The knifeman lies dead at your feet. I didn't kill him."

Vagn shook his head. "It means nothing. Never should he have come into this tent."

"You were at the front. He must have got in at the back, under the canvas." Krispos looked at the assassin's contorted body. He thought about what it must have taken, even dressed in clothes that left him part of the night, to come down from the fortress and sneak through the enemy camp to its very heart. "In his own way, he was a brave man."

Vagn spat again. "He was a skulking murderer and should have had worse and slower than I gave him. Please, Majesty, I beg once more, slay me, that I may die clean."

"No, curse it!" Krispos said. Vagn turned and walked to the tent flap. If he left, Krispos was sure he would never return alive. He said quickly, "Here, wait. I know what I'll do—I'll give you a chance to redeem yourself in your own eyes."

"In no way can I do that," Vagn declared.

"Hear me out," Krispos said. When Vagn took another step toward the flap, he snapped, "I order you to listen." Reluctantly the Haloga stopped. Krispos went on, "Here's what I'd have you do: first, take this man's head. Then, unarmored if you like, carry it up to the gates of Antigonos and leave it there to show Petronas the fate his assassin earned. Will that give you back your honor?"

Vagn was some time silent, which only made the growing hubbub outside the imperial tent seem louder. Then, with a grunt, the Haloga chopped at the knifeman's neck. The roof of the tent was too low to let him take big, full swings with his axe, so the beheading required several strokes.

Krispos turned away from the gory job. He threw on a robe and went out to show the army he was still alive. The men whom his outcry had aroused shouted furiously when he told how the assassin had crept into his tent. He was just finishing the tale when Vagn emerged, holding the man's head by the hair. The soldiers let out such a lusty cheer that the guardsman blinked in surprise. Their approval seemed to reach him where Krispos' had not; as the cheering went on and on, he stood taller and straighter. Without a word, he began to tramp toward the fortress of Antigonos.

"Wait," Krispos called. "Do it by daylight, so Petronas can see just what gift you bring him."

"Aye," Vagn said after a moment's thought. "I will wait." He set down the assassin's head, lightly prodding it with his foot. "So will he." The joke struck Krispos as being in poor taste, but he was glad to hear the Haloga make it.

Trokoundos plucked at Krispos' sleeve. "We were right in guessing Petronas aimed to treacherously slay you," he said, "wrong only in his choice of stealth over sorcery. But had we relied on his using stealth, he surely would have tried with magic."

"I suppose so," Krispos said. "And as for that, you can cheer up. Without your magecraft, I'd be a dead man right now."

"What do you mean?" Trokoundos scratched his shaven head. "After all, Petronas did but send a simple knifeman against you."

"I know, but if the fellow hadn't stepped on one of those charms you insisted on scattering everywhere, I never would have woke up in time to yell."

"Happy to be of service, Your Majesty," Trokoundos said in a strangled voice. Then he saw how hard Krispos' face was set against laughter. He allowed himself a dry chuckle or two, but still maintained his dignity.

Too bad for him, Krispos thought. He laughed out loud.

WHEN THE SIEGE TRAIN REACHED THE FORTRESS OF ANTIGONOS, Krispos watched the soldiers on the walls watching his artisans assemble the frames for stone-throwing engines, the sheds that would protect the men who swung rams against stones or boiling oil from above.

The assassin's head still lay outside the gate. Petronas' men had let Vagn come and go. By now even the flies had tired of it.

As soon as the first catapult was done, the craftsmen who had built it recruited a squad of common soldiers to drag up a large stone and set it in the leathern sling at the end of the machine's throwing arm. Winches creaked as the crew tightened the ropes that gave the catapult its hurling power.

The throwing arm jerked forward. The catapult bucked. The stone flew through the air. It crashed against the wall of the fortress with a noise like thunder. The soldiers began to haul another rock into place.

Krispos sent a runner to the engines' crew with a single word: "Wait." Then one of his men advanced toward the fortress with a white-painted shield of truce. After some shouting back and forth, Petronas came up to the battlements.

"What do you want of me?" he called to Krispos, or rather toward Krispos' banner. As at the last parley, his wizard amplified his voice to carry so far.

Trokoundos stood by Krispos to perform the same service for him. "I want you to take a good look around, Petronas. Look carefully—I give you this last chance to yield and save your life. See the engines all around. The rams and stone-throwers will pound down your walls while the dart-shooters pick off your men from farther than they can shoot back."

Petronas shook his fist. "I told you I would never yield to you!"

"Look around," Krispos said again. "You're a soldier, Petronas. Look around and see what chance you have of holding out. I tell you this: once we breach your walls—and we will—we'll show no mercy to you or any-one else." Maybe, he thought, Petronas' men would force him to give up even if he did not want to.

But Petronas led his tiny empire still. He made a slow circuit of the wall, then returned at last to the spot from which he had set out. "I see the engines," he said. By his tone, he might have been discussing the heat of the day.

"What will you do, Petronas?" Krispos asked.

Petronas did not answer, not with words. He scrambled up from the walkway to the wall itself and stood there for most of a minute looking out at the broad expanse of land that, so unaccountably, he did not rule. Then, slowly and deliberately, with the same care he gave to everything he did, he dove off.

Inside and outside the fortress of Antigonos, men cried out in dismay. But when some of Krispos' soldiers rushed toward the crumpled shape at the base of the wall, Petronas' men shot at them. "The truce is still good," Krispos shouted. "We won't hurt him further, by the good god—we'll save him if we can."

"There's a foolish promise," Mammianos observed. "Better to put him out of his misery and have done. I daresay that's what he'd want."

Krispos realized he was right. The pledge, though, was enough to give the rebels an excuse to hold their fire. When his own men did nothing but crowd round Petronas, Krispos thought they were only showing their share of Mammianos' rough wisdom. Then a sweating, panting trooper ran up to him and gasped out, "Majesty, he landed on his head, poor sod."

Of itself, Krispos' hand shaped the sun-circle over his heart. "The war is over," he said. He did not know what to feel. Relief, yes, that so dangerous a foe was gone. But Petronas had also raised him high, in his own household and then in Anthimos'. That had been in Petronas' interest, too, but Krispos could not help remembering it, could not help remembering the years in which he and Petronas had worked together to manage Anthimos. He sketched the sun-sign again. "I would have let him live," he murmured, as much to himself as to the men around him.

"He gave you his answer to that," Mammianos said. Krispos had to nod.

Without their leader, Petronas' men felt the urge to save their lives. The strong gate to the fortress of Antigonos opened. A soldier came out with a shield of truce. The rest of the garrison filed slowly after him. Krispos sent in troopers to make Antigonos his own once more.

The gleam of a shaven pate caught his eye. He smiled, not altogether kindly. To his bodyguards, he said, "Fetch me Gnatios."

Now in sandals and a simple blue monk's robe rather than the patriarchal regalia Krispos would have bet he'd had inside the fortress, Gnatios looked small, frail, and frightened between the two burly Halogai who marched him away from his fellows. He cast himself down on the ground in front of Krispos. "May Your Majesty's will be done with me," he said, not lifting his face from the dust.

"Get up, holy sir," Krispos said. As Gnatios rose, he went on, "You would have done better to keep faith with me. You would still wear the blue boots now, not Pyrrhos."

A spark of malicious amusement flared in Gnatios' eyes. "From all I've heard, Majesty, your patriarch has not succeeded in delighting you."

"He's not betrayed me, either," Krispos said coldly.

Gnatios wilted again. "What will you do with me, Your Majesty?" His voice was tiny.

"Taking your head here and now would likely cause me more scandal than you're worth. I think I'll bring you back to the city. Recant—say, in the Amphitheater, with enough people watching so you can't go back on your word again—and publicly recognize Pyrrhos as patriarch, and for all of me you can live out the rest of your days in the monastery of the holy Skirios."

Gnatios bowed in submission. Krispos had been sure he would. Pyrrhos now, Pyrrhos would have gone to the headsman singing hymns before he changed his views by the breadth of a fingernail paring. That made him stronger than Gnatios; Krispos was less ready to say it made him better. It certainly made him harder to work with.

"If ever you're outside the monastery without written leave from me and Pyrrhos both, Gnatios, you'll meet the man with the axe then and there," Krispos warned.

"That walls me up for life," Gnatios said, a last, faint protest.

"Likely it does." Krispos folded his arms. He was ready to summon an executioner at another word from Gnatios. Gnatios saw that. He bit his lip till a bead of blood showed at the corner of his mouth, but he nodded.

"Take him away," Krispos told the Halogai. "While you're about it, put him in irons." Gnatios made an indignant noise. Krispos ignored it, continuing, "He's already escaped once, so I'd sooner not give him another chance." Then he turned to Gnatios. "Holy sir, I pledged I would not harm you. I said nothing of your dignity."

"I can see why," Gnatios said resentfully.

"A chopped dignity grows back better than a chopped neck," Krispos said. "Remember that. Soon enough you'll be back at your chronicle."

"There is that." Krispos was amused to see Gnatios brighten at the thought. Political priest and born intriguer though he was, he was also a true scholar. He went off with the Halogai without another word of complaint.

Krispos scanned the men still emerging from the fortress of Antigonos. When at last they stopped coming, he frowned. He walked toward them. Halogai fell in around him. "Where's Petronas' wizard?" he demanded.

The men looked around among themselves, then back toward the fortress. "Skeparnas?" one said with a shrug. "I thought he was with us, but he doesn't seem to be." Others spoke up in agreement.

"I want him," Krispos said. He wondered if he looked as savagely eager as he felt. Petronas' wizard had cost him a season of lying in bed limp as a dead fish; only Trokoundos' countermagic kept the fellow from taking his life. Sorcery that aimed at causing death was a capital offense.

When Krispos summoned him, Trokoundos studied with narrowed eyes the group of ragged, none too clean men who had come out of the fortress. "He might be hiding in plain sight," he explained to Krispos, "using another man's semblance to keep from being seen."

The mage took out two coins. "The one in my left hand is gilded lead. When I touch it against the true goldpiece in my right hand while reciting the proper spell, by the law of similarity other counterfeits will also be exposed."

He began to chant, then touched the two coins, false and true, together. A couple of men's hair suddenly went from black to gray, which made the Halogai round Krispos guffaw. But other than that, no one's features changed. "He is not here," Trokoundos said. He frowned, his eyes suddenly doubtful. "I do not think he is here—"

He touched the coins of gold and lead against each other once more and held them in his closed fist. Now he used a new chant, harsh and sonorous, insisting, demanding.

"By the good god," Krispos whispered. In the crowd of soldiers and others who had come out of the fortress, one man's features were running like wax over a fire. Before his eyes, the fellow grew taller, leaner. Trokoundos let out a hoarse shout of triumph.

The disguised wizard's face worked horribly as he realized he was discovered. His talonlike fingers stabbed at Trokoundos. The smaller mage groaned and staggered; goldpiece and lead counterfeit fell to the ground. But Trokoundos, too, was a master mage: had he been less, Anthimos would never have chosen him as instructor in the sorcerous arts. He braced himself against empty air and fought back. A moment later Skeparnas bent as if under a heavy weight.

The sorcerers' duel caught up both men—they were so perfectly matched that neither could work great harm unless the other blundered. Neither had any thought for his surroundings; each, of necessity, focused solely on his foe.

Krispos shoved his Halogai toward Skeparnas. "Capture or slay that man!" The imperial guardsmen obeyed without question or hesitation.

They were almost upon the wizard before he knew they were there. He started to send a spell their way, but in tearing his attention from Trokoundos, he left himself vulnerable to the other mage's sorcery. He was screaming as he turned and tried to run. The axes of the Halogai rose and fell. The scream abruptly died.

Trokoundos lurched like a drunken man. "Wine, someone, I beg," he croaked. Krispos undid his own canteen and passed it to the mage. Trokoundos drained it dry. He sank to his knees, then to his haunches. Worried, Krispos sat beside him. He had to lean close to hear Trokoundos whisper, "Now I understand what getting caught in an avalanche must be like."

"Are you all right?" Krispos asked. "What do you need?"

"A new carcass, for starters." With visible effort, Trokoundos drew up the corners of his mouth. "He was strong as a plow mule, was Skeparnas. Had the northerners not distracted him . . . well, Your Majesty, let me just say I'm glad they did."

"So am I." Krispos glanced over to Skeparnas' body. The rest of the men from the fortress had pulled back as if the wizard were dead of plague. "I think we can guess his conscience was troubling him."

"He didn't seem anxious to meet you, did he?" Trokoundos' smile, though still strained, seemed more firmly attached to his face now. He got to his feet, waving off Krispos' effort to help. Trokoundos' gaze also went to Skeparnas' sprawled corpse. He wearily shook his head. "Aye, Your Majesty, I'm very glad the Halogai distracted him."

KRISPOS LOOKED OVER THE CATTLE-CROSSING EAST TO VIDESSOS the city. Behind its seawalls, nearly as massive as the great double rampart that shielded its landward side, the city reared on seven hills. Gilded spheres atop the spires of innumerable temples to Phos shone under the warm summer sun, as if they were so many tiny suns themselves.

As he climbed down into the imperial barge that would carry him across the strait to the capital, Krispos thought, *I'm going home.* The notion still felt strange to him. He'd needed many years in Videssos the city before it, rather than the village from which he sprang, seemed his right and proper place in the world. But his dwelling was there, his wife, his child. Probably his child, at any rate—certainly his heir. Sure as sure, that all made home.

The rowers dug in. The barge glided through the light chop of the Cattle-Crossing toward the city. Krispos was so happy to see it draw near that he ignored his stomach's misgivings over being at sea.

The barge drew to a halt in front of the westernmost gate in the seawall, the gate closest to the palaces. The two valves swung open just as the barge arrived. By now Krispos had come to expect imperial ceremonial to operate so smoothly. The barge captain waved to his sailors. They tied up the barge, set a gangplank in place, then turned and nodded to Krispos. He strode up the plank and into the city.

Along with some of his palace servitors, a delegation of nobles awaited Krispos within the gate. They prostrated themselves before him, shouting, "Thou conquerest, Krispos Avtokrator!" For once, he thought, bemused, the ancient acclamation was literally true. "Thou conquerest!" his greeters cried again as they rose.

Among them he saw Iakovitzes. Clad in bright silks, impeccably groomed, the noble looked himself again, though he was no longer plump. But he perforce stood mute while his companions cried out praise for the Emperor. The unfairness of that tore at Krispos. He beckoned to Iakovitzes, giving him favor in the eyes of his fellows. Iakovitzes' chest puffed out with pride as he came up to Krispos and bowed before him.

"Now the small war, the needful war, is done," Krispos said. "Now we can start the greater fight and give you the vengeance you deserve. By the lord with the great and good mind, I pledge again that you will have it."

He'd thought that would give the nobles and servants another chance to cheer. Instead they stood silently, as if bereft of their tongues as Iakovitzes. Iakovitzes himself unhooked from his belt a tablet ornamented with enamelwork and precious stones; his stylus looked to be made of gold. When the noble opened the tablet, Krispos' nose told him the wax was perfumed. Maimed Iakovitzes might be, but he'd adapted to his injury with panache.

He wrote quickly. "Then you haven't heard, Your Majesty? How could you not have?"

"Heard what?" Krispos said when he'd read the words.

Several people guessed what he meant and started to answer, but Iakovitzes waved them to silence. His stylus raced over the wax with tiny slithery sounds. When he was done, he handed the tablet to Krispos. "About ten days ago, Agapetos was heavily defeated north of Imbros. Mavros gathered what force he could and set out to avenge the loss."

Krispos stared at the tablet as if the words on it had betrayed him. "The good god knows, enough couriers brought me dispatches from the city while I was in the westlands. Set against this news, every word they carried was so much gossip and fiddle-faddle. *So why was I not told?*" His gaze fastened on Barsymes.

The vestiarios' face went pale as milk. "But Majesty," he quavered, "the Sevastos assured me he was keeping you fully informed before he departed for the frontier and promised to continue doing so while on campaign."

"I don't believe you," Krispos said. "Why would he do anything so"—he groped for a word—"so foolhardy?" But that was hardly out of his mouth before he saw an answer. His foster brother had known Krispos did not want him to go out of the city to fight, but not why. If Mavros thought Krispos doubted his courage or ability, he might well have wanted to win a victory just to prove him wrong. And he would have to do it secretly, to keep Krispos from stopping him.

But Krispos knew Mavros was able and brave—would he have named him Sevastos otherwise? What he feared was for his foster brother's safety. Tanilis was not the sort to send idle warnings.

The taste of triumph turned bitter in his mouth. He turned and dashed back through the seawall gate, ignoring the startled cries that rose behind him. The captain and crew of the imperial barge gaped to see him reappear. He ignored their surprise, too. "Row back across the Cattle-Crossing fast as you can," he told the captain. "Order Mammianos to ready the whole army to cross to this side as fast as boats can bring it here. Tell him I intend to move north against Harvas the instant the whole force is here. Do you have all that?"

"I—think so, Your Majesty." Stammering a little, the barge captain repeated his orders. Krispos nodded curtly. The captain bawled orders to his men. They cast off the ropes that held the barge next to the wall, then backed oars. As if it were a fighting galley, the imperial barge pivoted almost in its own length, then streaked toward the westlands.

Krispos stood back. Barsymes stood in the gateway. "What of the celebratory procession down Middle Street tomorrow, Your Majesty?" he said. "What of the festival of thanksgiving at the High Temple? What of the distribution of largess to the people?"

"Cancel everything," Krispos snapped. After a moment he reconsidered. "No, go on and pay out the largess—that'll keep the city folk happy enough for a while. But with the northern frontier coming to pieces, I don't think we have much to celebrate."

"As you wish, Your Majesty," Barsymes said with a sorrowful bow: he lived for ceremonial. "What will you do with your brief time in the city, then?"

"Talk with my generals," Krispos said—the first thing that entered his mind. He went on, "See Dara for a bit." Not only did he miss her, he knew he had to stay on good terms with her, the more so now that her father was with him. As something close to an afterthought, he added, "I'll see Phostis, too."

"Very well, Your Majesty." Now Barsymes sounded as if all was very well; with no chance for a child of his own, the eunuch doted on Phostis. "As your generals are still on the far side of the Cattle-Crossing, shall I conduct you to the imperial residence in the meantime?"

"Good enough." Krispos smiled at the vestiarios' unflagging efficiency. Barsymes waved. A dozen parasol-bearers—the imperial number—lined up in front of Krispos. He followed the colorful silk canopies toward the grove of cherry trees that surrounded his private chambers—not, he thought, that anything having to do with the Emperor's person was what would be reckoned private for anyone else.

The Halogai outside the residence sprang to attention when they saw the parasol-bearers. "Majesty!" they shouted.

"Your brothers fought bravely, battling the rebel," Krispos said.

Grins split the northerners' faces. "Hear how he speaks in our style," one said. Krispos grinned, too, glad they'd noticed. He climbed the steps and strode into the imperial residence.

Barsymes bustled past him. "Let me fetch the nurse, Your Majesty, with your son." He hurried down the hall, calling for the woman. She came out of a doorway. Phostis was in her arms.

She squeaked when she saw Krispos. "Your Majesty! We hadn't looked for you so soon. But come see what a fine lad your son's gotten to be." She held out the baby invitingly. Krispos took him. The bit of practice he'd had holding Phostis before he went on campaign came back to him. He had a good deal more to hold now.

He lifted the baby up close to his face. As he always did, he tried to decide whom Phostis resembled. As if deliberately to keep him in the dark, Phostis still looked like his mother—and like himself. His features seemed far more distinctly his own than they had when he was newborn. He did have his mother's eyes, though—and his grandfather's.

Phostis was looking at Krispos, too, without recognition but with interest. When his eyes met Krispos', he smiled. Delighted, Krispos smiled back.

"See how he takes to you?" the nurse crooned. "Isn't that sweet?"

The baby's face scrunched up in fierce concentration. Krispos felt the arm he had under Phostis' bottom grow warm and damp. He handed him back to the nurse. "I think he's made a mess." A moment later any possible doubt left him.

"They have a habit of doing that," the nurse said. Krispos nodded; with a farm upbringing, he was intimately familiar with messes of every variety. The nurse went on, "I'll clean him up. I expect you want to see your lady, anyhow."

"Yes," Krispos said. "I don't think I'll be in the city very long." That did not surprise the nurse, but then, she'd known about the disaster near Imbros longer than he had.

Barsymes said, "Her Majesty will be at the needle this time of day." He led Krispos past the portrait of Stavrakios. Krispos wondered how the tough old Avtokrator would have judged his first war.

The sewing room had a fine north-facing window. Dara sat by it, bent close to her work. The tapestry on which she labored might not be finished in her lifetime; when one day it was, it would hang in the Grand Courtroom. She knew sober pride that the finest embroiderers in the city judged her skill great enough to merit inclusion in such a project.

She did not notice the door open behind her. Only when Krispos stepped between her and the window and made the light change did she look up; even after that, she needed a moment to return from the peacock whose shining feathers spread wider with each stitch she took.

"It's beautiful work," Krispos said.

She heard the praise in his voice, nodded without false modesty. "It was going well today, I thought." She jabbed needle into linen, set the tapestry aside, and got to her feet. "Which doesn't mean I can't put it down to hail a conqueror." Smiling now, she squeezed him hard enough to make the air whoosh from his lungs, then tilted her face up for a kiss.

"Aye, one victory won," he said after a bit. His hands lingered, not wanting to draw away from her. He saw that pleased her, but saw also by the way her eyebrows lowered slightly and pinched together that she was not altogether content. He thought he knew why. His tone roughened. "But, also, I learn just now, a loss in the north to balance it."

That further sobered her. "Yes," she said. Then, after a pause, she asked, "How do you mean, you just now learn? Surely Mavros sent word on to you of what had happened to Agapetos."

"Not a whisper of it," Krispos said angrily, "nor that he aimed to take the field himself. I think he hid it from me on purpose because he knew I'd forbid him on account of his mother's letter."

"I'd forgotten that." Dara's eyes went wide. "What will you do, then?"

"Go after him and—I hope—rescue him from his folly." Krispos scowled, irritated as much with himself as with Mavros. "I wish I'd flat-out told him what Tanilis wrote. But I was afraid he'd sally forth then just to prove he wouldn't let her run his life. And so I didn't spell things out— and he's sallied forth anyhow."

He misliked that; it had the air of the working out of some malign fate. He drew the sun-circle over his heart to turn aside the evil omen.

Dara also signed herself. She said, "Not all foretelling is truth, for which the lord with the great and good mind be praised. Who could bear to live, knowing that someone less than the good god knew what was to come? Maybe Tanilis felt a mother's fear and made too much of it. Now that I have Phostis, I know how that can be."

"Maybe." But Krispos did not believe it. Tanilis had called him "Majesty" when only a madman could have imagined he would ever dwell in the imperial residence, wearing imperial robes. Only a madman—or one who saw true.

"Have you further need for my services, Majesties?" Barsymes asked. Krispos and Dara, their eyes on each other, shook their heads at the same time. "Then if you will excuse me—" The vestiarios bowed his way out.

No sooner had he gone than Dara demanded, "And how many willing, pretty country girls kept your bed warm while you were away in the west-lands?"

It might have been a joke; she kept her tone light. But Krispos did not think it was. After being married to Anthimos, Dara could hardly be blamed for doubting his fidelity when he was not under her eye—maybe even when he was. After a little thought he answered, "Do you think I'd be stupid enough to do anything like that when your father was in camp with me for most of the campaign?"

"No, I suppose not," she said judiciously. She set hands on hips and looked up as she had to do to meet his eyes. "You slept alone, then, all the time you were away from the city?"

"I said so."

"Prove it."

Krispos let a long, exasperated breath hiss out. "How am I supposed to—?" In the middle of his sentence, he saw a way. Four quick steps took him to the door. He slammed and barred it. As quickly, he returned to her side and took her in his arms. His lips came down on hers.

Some while later she said, "Get off me, will you? Not only is the floor hard, it's cold, and I expect I have the marks of mosaic tiles on my back-side, too."

Krispos sat back on his haunches. Dara drew one leg up past him and rolled away. He said, "Yes, as a matter of fact, you do."

"I thought as much," she said darkly. But in spite of herself, she could not contrive to sound annoyed. "I hadn't looked for your proof to be so—vehement."

"That?" Krispos raised an eyebrow. "After going without for so long, that was just the beginning of my proof."

"Braggart," she said before her eyes left his face. Then her brows also lifted. "What have we here?" Smiling, she reached out a hand to discover what they had there. That, too, rose to the occasion. Before they began again, she said, "Can the second part of your proof wait till we go to the bedchamber? It would be more comfortable there."

"So it would," Krispos said. "Why not?" An advantage of the imperial robes was that they slid off—and now on—quickly and easily. Their prin-cipal disadvantage became obvious when the weather got cold. Peasants sensibly labored in tunics and trousers. Krispos shivered when he thought of rounding up sheep in winter with an icy wind whistling up a robe and howling around his private parts.

That was not a worry at the moment. Serving maids grinned as Krispos and Dara headed for the bedchamber hand in hand. Krispos carefully took no notice of the grins. He had begun to resign himself to the prospect of a life led with scant privacy. That had been easy for Anthimos, who'd owned no inhibitions of any sort. It could still sometimes unnerve Krispos. He wondered if the servants kept count.

When he was behind a closed door again, such trivial concerns vanished. He doffed his robe a second time, then helped Dara off with hers. They lay down together. This time they made slower, less driven love, kissing, caressing, joining together, and then separating once more to spin it out and make it last. As the afterglow faded, Krispos said, "I think I'll bring your father along with me when I take the army north."

Beside him, Dara laughed. "You needn't do it for my sake. I couldn't hope for more or better proof than you've given me. Or could I?" Her hand lazily toyed with him. "Shall we see what comes up?"

"I think you'll have to get your comeuppance another time," he said.

She snorted, gave him an almost painful squeeze, then sat up. Abruptly she was serious. "As I think on it, having my father with you might be a good idea. If he stayed here in the city while you were away, he could forget on whose head the crown properly belongs."

"I can see that," Krispos said. "He's an able man, and able, too, to keep his own counsel. Maybe that comes of his living by the western frontier; from all I've seen, it's rare among folk here in the city. People here show off what they know, to make themselves seem important."

"You've always been able to keep secret what needs keeping," Dara said. Krispos nodded; the very bed in which they lay testified to that. Dara went on, "Why are you surprised others can do the same?"

"I didn't say that." Krispos paused to put what he felt into words. "It was easier for me because people looked down at me for so long. They didn't take me seriously for a long time—I don't think Petronas took me seriously until the siege train came up to Antigonos. But he'd known your father for years, and your father managed to keep his trust till the instant he came over to me."

"He's always held things to himself," Dara said. "He can be . . . surprising."

"I believe you." Krispos did not want Rhisoulphos to surprise him. The more he thought about it, the more keeping his father-in-law under his eye seemed a good idea. He let out a long sigh.

"What's the matter?" Dara asked in some concern. "You're not usually one to be sad afterward."

"I'm not—not about that. I just wish I could have more than moments stolen now and again when I didn't have to fret about every single thing that went on in the palaces and in the city and in the Empire and in all the lands that touch on the Empire—and in all the lands that touch on those lands, too, by the good god," Krispos added, remembering that the first he'd heard of Harvas Black-Robe was when his raiders ravaged Thatagush, far to the northeast of Videssian territory.

Dara said, "You could do as Anthimos did, and simply not fret about things."

"Look where that got Anthimos—aye, and the Empire, too," Krispos said. "No, I'm made so I have to fret over anything I know of that needs fretting over."

"And over things you don't know but wish you could find out," Dara said.

Krispos' wry chuckle acknowledged the hit. "Think how much grief I could have saved everyone if I'd known Gnatios was going to help Petronas escape from his monastery. As it worked out in the end, I'd even have saved Petronas grief."

Dara shook her head. "No. He lived for power, not for the trappings but for the thing itself. You saw that. You would have let him live on as a monk, but he'd sooner have died—and he did."

Krispos thought about it and decided she was right. "If he'd given me the same choice, I'd have yielded up my hair and forgotten the world."

"Even though that means giving up women, as well?" Dara asked slyly. She slid her thigh over till it brushed against his.

He blinked at her. "Which of us missed the other more?"

"I don't know. That we missed each other at all strikes me as a good sign. We have to live with each other; more pleasant if we're able to enjoy it."

"Something to that," Krispos admitted. He took stock of himself. "If you wait just a bit longer, I might manage another round of proof."

"Might you indeed?" Dara got up on hands and knees, bent her head over him. "Maybe I can help speed that wait along."

"Maybe you can . . . Oh, yes." He reached out to stroke her. Her curls twisted round his fingers like black snakes.

Later, he lay back and watched the bedchamber grow shadowy as afternoon slid toward evening. Hunger eventually overcame his lassitude. He started to reach up to the scarlet bellpull, then stopped and got into his robe first. He was not Anthimos, after all.

Moving just as slowly, Dara also dressed. "What will you do after supper?" she asked once he'd told Barsymes what he wanted.

"Spend the night staring at maps with my generals," Krispos said. To please her, he tried to sound glum. But he looked forward, not to the campaign that lay ahead, but to the planning that went into it. He'd never seen a map before he came to Videssos the city. That there could be pictures of the world fascinated him; establishing on one of those pictures where he would be day by day gave him a truly imperial feeling of power.

"Think what you could be doing instead," Dara said.

"If you think so, you flatter me," he told her. "I'm surprised I can walk." She stuck out her tongue at him. He laughed. Despite the hard news that began it, this had not been a bad day.

Chapter VI

KRISPOS SHADED HIS EYES WITH A HAND AS HE LOOKED NORTH-
ward. The horizon ahead was still smooth. He sighed and shook his
head. "When I start seeing the mountains, I'll know I'm close to the country where I grew up," he said.

"Close also to where the trouble is," Sarkis observed.

"Aye." Krispos' brief nostalgia deepened to true pain and anger. The
summer before, Harvas' raiders had gone through the village where he'd
grown up. His sister, her husband, and their two girls had still lived in the
village. No one lived there now.

Ungreased wheels squeaked—sometimes screamed—as supply wagons
rattled along. Horses, mules, and men afoot kicked up choking clouds of
dust. Soldiers sang and joked. *Why not?* Krispos thought. *They're still in
their own country.* If they sang as they came home again, he would have
done something worth remembering.

Sarkis said, "The riders we sent ahead toward Mavros' army should get
back to us in the next couple of days. Then we'll know how things stand."

"They'll get back to us in a couple of days if all's gone well and Mavros
has pressed forward," Mammianos said. "If he's taken a reverse, they

won't have had so far to travel to meet up with him, so they'll be back sooner."

But none of them—Mammianos, Sarkis, or Krispos—expected the riders to begin coming back that afternoon, the third of their march out from Videssos the city. Yet come back they did, with horses driven to bloody-mouthed exhaustion and with faces grim and drawn. And behind them, first by ones and twos, then in larger groups, came the shattered remains of Mavros' army.

Krispos ordered an early halt for his troops as evening neared. Advancing farther would have been like trying to make headway against a strong-flowing stream. A stream, though, did not infect with fear the men who moved against it. Seeing what had befallen their fellows, Krispos' soldiers warily eyed every lengthening shadow, as if screaming northern warriors might erupt from it at any moment.

While the army's healer-priests did what they could for the wounded, Krispos and his generals questioned haler survivors, trying to sift fragments of order from catastrophe. Not much was to be found. A young lieutenant named Zernes told the tale as well as anyone. "Majesty, they caught us by surprise. They waited in the brush along either side of the road south of Imbros and hit us as we passed them by."

"By the good god!" Mammianos exploded. "Didn't you have scouts out?" He muttered something into his beard about puppies who imagined they were generals.

"The scouts *were* out," Zernes insisted. "They *were,* by the lord with the great and good mind. The Sevastos knew he was not fully trained to command and left all such details to his officers. They might not have been so many Stavrakioi come again, but they knew their craft. The scouts found nothing."

Mammianos wheezed laughter at the lieutenant's youthful indiscretion. Krispos had ears only for the long string of past tenses the man used. "The Sevastos knew? He left these details? Where is Mavros now?"

"Majesty, on that I cannot take oath," Zernes said carefully. "But I do not think he was one of the people lucky enough to break free from the trap. And from what we saw, the Halogai wasted time with few prisoners."

"May he bask in Phos' light forevermore," Mammianos said. He sketched the sun-sign over his breast.

Mechanically Krispos did the same. The young officer's words seemed to reach him from far away. Even with the foreboding he'd had since he learned Mavros was on campaign, he could not believe his foster brother dead. Mavros had been always at his side for years, had fought Anthimos with him, had been first to acknowledge him as Avtokrator. How could he be gone?

Then he found another question, a worse one because it dealt with the living. How was he to tell Tanilis?

While he grappled with that, Mammianos asked Zernes, "Were you pursued? Or don't you know, having fled so fast no foes afoot could keep up with you?"

The lieutenant bristled as he set a hand to the hilt of his saber. He forced himself to ease. "There was no pursuit, excellent sir," he said icily. "Aye, we were mauled, but we hurt the northerners, too. When they broke off with us, they headed back toward the mountains, not south on our tails."

"Something," Mammianos grunted. "What of Imbros, then?"

"Excellent sir, that I could not say, for we never reached Imbros," Zernes answered. "But since Agapetos was beaten north of the town and we to the south, I fear the worst."

"Thank you, Lieutenant. You may go," Krispos said, trying to make himself function in the face of disaster. First Mavros throwing his life away, now Imbros almost surely lost . . . Imbros, the only city he'd ever known till he left his village and came south to the capital. He'd sometimes sold pigs there, and thought it a very grand place, though the whole town was not much larger than the plaza of Palamas in Videssos the city.

"What do we do now, Your Majesty?" Mammianos asked.

"We go on," Krispos said. "What other choice have we?"

As the army advanced, scouts not only examined stands of brush and other places that might hold an ambush—they also shot arrows into them. Some of the lesser mages who served under Trokoundos rode with the scouting parties to sniff out sorcerous concealments. They found none. As Zernes said, Harvas' army had headed back to its northern home after crushing Mavros.

Flocks of ravens and vultures and crows, disturbed from their feasting, rose into the air like black clouds when Krispos' men came to that dolorous field. The birds circled overhead, screeching and cawing resentfully. "Burial parties," Krispos ordered.

"It will cost us the rest of the day," Mammianos said.

"Let it. I don't think we'll catch them on this side of the frontier anyhow," Krispos said. Mammianos nodded and passed the command along. As the soldiers began their grim task, a twist of breeze brought Krispos the battlefield stench, worse than he had ever smelled it before. He coughed and shook his head.

He walked the field despite the stench, to see if he could find Mavros' body. He could not tell it by robes or fine armor; Harvas' men had stayed long enough to loot. After several days of hot sun and carrion birds, no corpse was easy to identify. He saw several that might have been his foster brother, but was sure of none.

The soldiers were quiet in camp that night, so quiet that Krispos wondered if pausing to bury Mavros' dead had been wise. A sudden attack might well have broken them. But the night passed peacefully. When morning came, priests led the men in prayers of greeting to Phos' new-risen sun. Perhaps heartened by that, they seemed in better spirits than they had before.

Before the morning was very old, a pair of scouts came galloping back to the main body of men. They rode straight to Krispos. Saluting, one said, "Majesty, ahead is something you must see."

"What is it?" Krispos asked.

The scout spat in the dust of the roadway, as if to show his rejection of Skotos. "I won't dirty my tongue with the words to tell you, Your Majesty. My eyes have been soiled; let my mouth stay clean." His comrade nodded vigorously. Neither would say more.

Krispos traded glances with his officers. After a moment he nodded and urged Progress forward. The Halogai of the imperial guard came with him. So did Trokoundos. The wizard muttered to himself, choosing charms and readying them in advance against need.

"How far is it?" Krispos asked the scouts.

"Round this bend in the road here, Your Majesty," answered the horseman who had spoken before. "Just past these oaks."

While the fellow was not watching, Krispos made sure his saber was loose in its scabbard. A troop of guardsmen pushed ahead of him as the party swung past the trees. Even so, from atop his horse he could see well enough.

First he noticed only the bodies, a hundred or so, and that their gear proclaimed them to be Videssian soldiers. Then he saw that each man's hands had been tied behind his back. The dead soldiers' feet were toward him, so he needed a few seconds more than he might have otherwise for his eyes to travel beyond the bodies to the neat pyramid of heads that lay beyond them.

"You see, Your Majesty," said the scout who liked to talk.

"I see," Krispos answered. "I see helpless prisoners butchered for the sport of it." He clutched Progress' reins so hard, his knuckles whitened.

"Butchered, aye. That is well said, Majesty." Krispos had never heard a Haloga recoil from war and its consequences. Now Geirrod did. Without prompting, the guardsman explained why: "Where is the honor, where even is the rightness, in using captives so? This is the work of one more used to slaying cattle than men."

"It's of a piece with what we've seen from Harvas and those who follow him." Krispos hesitated before he went on, but what he had to say needed saying sooner or later. "Most of those who follow Harvas come out of Halogaland. Will you have qualms about fighting them?"

The guardsmen shouted angrily. Geirrod said, "Majesty, we knew this. We talked among ourselves, aye we did, on how such a fight might be, swapping axe strokes with our own kind. But no man who could slaughter so, or stand by to see others slaying, is kin of mine." The other northerners shouted again, this time in loud agreement.

"Shall we start burying this lot, Majesty?" the scout asked.

Krispos slowly shook his head. "No. Let the whole army see them, and with them the sort of foe we fight." He knew he was running a risk. The massacred prisoners had been set in the road to terrify, and his men were none too steady after listening to the survivors from Mavros' force. But he thought—he hoped—this cold-blooded killing would raise in all his soldiers the same fury he and the Halogai felt.

A few minutes later the head of the long column rounded that bend in the road. Krispos gave the guards quick orders. They formed up in the roadway and directed the leading horsemen off the track and onto the grass and shrubs that grew alongside. Some of the troopers began to argue until they saw Krispos with the Halogai, also waving them off.

He watch closely as his men came upon the grisly warning Harvas had left behind. They all stared. Horror filled their faces, as was only natural, but on most outrage soon ousted it. Some soldiers swore, others sketched the sun-sign; not a few did both at once.

Their eyes swung from the bodies—and from that ghastly pyramid beyond them—to Krispos. He raised his voice. "This is the enemy we have loose in our land. Shall we run back to Videssos the city now, with our tails between our legs, and let him do as he likes in the northlands?"

"No." The word came, deep and determined, from many throats at once, like the growl of some enormous wolf. Krispos wished Harvas could have heard it. Soon enough, in effect, he would. Krispos set clenched right fist over his heart to salute his soldiers.

He stayed by the slain Videssians until the last wagon jounced past. The troops from the middle and back of the column had an idea of what lay ahead of them; if armies traveled at the speed of whispers, they could cross the Empire in a day and a night. But knowing and seeing were not the same. Company by company, men stared at the sorry spectacle—first, even knowing, in disbelief, then with ever-growing anger.

"Now we may bury them," Krispos said when everyone had seen. "They've given us their last service by showing what our enemy is like." He saluted the dead men before he rode on to retake his place in the advance.

The mood in camp that night was savage. No speech Krispos made could have inspired his troops like the fate of their fellows. Hoping against hope, he asked his generals, "Is there any chance we'll catch up with Harvas' men on our side of the mountains?"

Mammianos plucked at his beard as he examined the map. "Hard to say. They're foot soldiers, so we move faster than they do. But they have some days' start on us, too."

"Much depends on what's happened at Imbros," Sarkis added. "If the garrison there still holds firm, that might help delay the raiders' retreat."

"I think Imbros still stands," Krispos said. "If it had fallen, wouldn't we be seeing fugitives from the sack, the way we did from Mavros' army?" Even now, a day after he knew the worst, he found himself forgetting his foster brother was dead, only to be brought up short every so often when he was reminded of it: As if he had taken a wound, he thought, and the injured part pained him every time he tried to use it.

Rhisoulphos said, "My best guess is that you're right, Your Majesty. There are always refugees from a city that falls: the lucky; the old; sometimes the young, if an enemy has more mercy than Harvas looks to own." His mouth tightened as he went on, "That we've seen no one from Imbros at all tells me its people are still safe behind their wall." He waved to a plan of the town. "It seems well enough fortified."

"It's like your holding, Rhisoulphos," Mammianos said. "On the border, we still need our walls. Some of the towns in the lowlands in the west, though, where they haven't seen war for a couple of hundred years, they've knocked most of 'em down and used the stone for houses."

"Fools," Rhisoulphos said succinctly.

Krispos turned the talk back to the issue at hand. "Suppose we find Harvas' men, or some of them, still besieging Imbros? What's the best way to hurt them then?"

"Pray to Phos the Lord who made the princes first that we catch them so, Your Majesty," Sarkis said; the strange epithet he used for the good god made Krispos recall his Vaspurakaner blood. He went on, "If we do, they'll be smashed between our hammer and an anvil of the garrison."

"May it be so," Krispos said. All the generals murmured in agreement.

Pragmatic as usual, Rhisoulphos had the last word. "One way or the other, we'll know for certain in a couple of days."

Half a day south of Imbros, the land began to look familiar to Krispos. That was as far as he'd ever traveled, back in the days before he set out for Videssos the city. He took it as a signal to order the army to full battle alert. That brought less change than it might have under other circumstances, for the men had kept themselves ready to fight since they'd seen the slaughtered prisoners.

Scouts darted ahead to sniff out the enemy. When they returned, their news brought a sober smile to Krispos' face, for they'd spied hundreds, perhaps thousands of people outside Imbros. "What could that be, save Harvas' besieging force?" he exulted. "We have them!"

Trumpets shouted. Krispos' army knew what that meant, knew what it had to mean. The Videssian soldiers, thoroughgoing professionals the lot of them, waved their lances and yowled like so many horse nomads off the steppes of Pardraya. Against a foe like Harvas, even professionals grew eager to fight.

Smooth with long practice, the troops swung themselves from column to line of battle. *Forward!* cried horns and drums. The army surged ahead, wild and irresistible as the sea. Officers shouted, warning men to keep horses fresh for combat.

"We have them!" Krispos said again. He drew his saber and brandished it over his head.

Mammianos stared, a trifle goggle-eyed at the ferocity the soldiers displayed. "Aye, Majesty, if Harvas truly did sit down in front of Imbros, we just may. I'd not reckoned him so foolish."

The general's words set off a warning bell in Krispos' mind. Harvas had shown himself cruel and vicious. Never yet, so far as Krispos could see, had he been foolish. Counting on his stupidity now struck Krispos as dangerous.

He said as much to Mammianos. The fat general looked thoughtful. "I see what you mean, Majesty. Maybe he wants us to come haring along so he can serve us as he did Mavros. If we miss an ambush—"

"Just what I'm thinking," Krispos said. He called to the musicians. Soldiers cursed and shouted when *At a walk* rang out. Krispos yelled for Trokoundos. When the mage rode up, he told him, "I want you out in front of the army. If you can't sense sorcerous screening for an ambush, no one can."

"As may be so, Your Majesty," Trokoundos answered soberly. "Harvas has uncommon—and unpleasant—magical skill. Nevertheless, I shall do what I can for you." He clucked to his horse, using reins and his boot heels to urge the animal into a trot. With the rest of the army walking, he was soon up among the scouts. The advance continued, though more slowly than before.

No cunningly hidden sorcerous pit yawned in the roadway. No hordes of Halogai charged roaring from the shelter of brush or trees. The only damage was to the fields the army trampled as it moved ahead in line of battle. Looking off to left and right, Krispos saw ruined villages and suspected few farmers were left to work those fields in any case.

A gray smudge on the northern horizon, light against the green woods and purple mountains behind it: Imbros' wall. Now it was Krispos' turn to yowl. He turned to Mammianos and showed his teeth like a wolf. "We're here, excellent sir, in spite of all our worries."

"By the good god, so we are." Mammianos glanced first to Krispos, then to the musicians. Krispos nodded. "*At the trot,* gentlemen," Mammianos said. The musicians passed along the command. The soldiers cheered.

Imbros drew nearer. Krispos saw in the distance the people outside the walls that his scouts had reported. His wolf's grin grew wider . . . but then slipped from his face. Why did Harvas' men simply hold their position? If he saw them, surely they had seen him. But no one around the walls moved, nor did anyone seem to be *on* those walls.

Up ahead with the scouts, Trokoundos suddenly wheeled his horse and galloped back toward Krispos. He was shouting something. Over the noise any moving army makes, Krispos needed a few seconds to hear what it was. "Dead! They're all dead!"

"Who? Who's dead?" troopers yelled at the wizard. Krispos echoed them. For a heady moment, he imagined disease had struck down Harvas' host where they stood. They deserved nothing better, he thought with somber glee.

But Trokoundos answered, "The folk of Imbros, all piteously slain." He reined in, leaned down onto his horse's neck, and wept without shame or restraint.

Krispos spurred his horse forward. After Trokoundos' warning, after the way the wizard, usually so self-controlled, had broken down, he thought he was braced for the worst. He needed only moments to discover how little he had imagined what the worst might be. The people of Imbros were not merely slain. They had been impaled, thousands of them—men, women, and children—each on his own separate stake. The stakes were uniformly black all the way to the ground with old dried blood.

The soldiers who advanced with Krispos stared in disbelieving horror at the spectacle Harvas had left behind for them. They were no strangers to dealing out death; some of them, perhaps, were no strangers to massacre, on the sordid but human scale of the butchered prisoners farther south. But at Imbros the size of the massacre was enough to daunt even a monster of a man.

Sarkis swatted at the flies that rose in buzzing clouds from the swollen, stinking corpses. "Well, Your Majesty, now we know why no fugitives came south from Imbros to warn us of its fall," he said. "No one was able to flee."

"This can't be everyone who lived in Imbros," Krispos protested. He knew his heart was speaking, not his mind; he could see how many people squatted on their stakes in a ghastly parody of alertness.

In a way, though, he was proven right. As the army made its way through the neat concentric rows of bodies to Imbros' wall, the men soon discovered how Harvas' warriors had entered the city: the northern quadrant of those walls was cast down in ruins, down to the very ground.

"Like Develtos," Trokoundos said. His eyes were red; tears still tracked his cheeks. He held his voice steady by force of will, like a man controlling a restive horse. "Like Develtos, save that they must have been hurried there. Here they had the time to do their proper job."

When Krispos entered Imbros, he found what had befallen the rest of the folk who had dwelt there. They lay dead in the streets; the town had been burned over their heads after they fell.

"Mostly men in here, I'd say," Mammianos observed. "And look—here's a mail shirt that missed getting stolen. These must have been the ones who tried to fight back. Once they were gone, looks like Harvas had his filthy fun with everyone else."

"Aye," Krispos said. Calmly discussing the hows and whys of wholesale slaughter as he went through its aftermath struck him as grotesque. But if he was to understand—as well as an ordinary man could ever grasp such destruction—what else were he and his followers to do?

He walked the dead streets of the murdered city, Trokoundos at his side and a troop of Halogai all around him to protect against anything that might lurk there yet. The northerners peered every which way, their pale eyes wide. They muttered to themselves in their own tongue.

At last Narvikka asked, "Majesty, why all this—this making into nothing? To sack a town, to despoil a town, is all very well, but for what purpose did our cousins slay this town and then cast the corpse onto the fire?"

"I'd hoped you could tell me," Krispos said. The guardsman, as was the Haloga way, had stripped the problem to its core. War for loot, war for be-

lief, war for territory made sense to Krispos. But what reason could lie behind war for the sake of utter devastation?

Narvikka made a sign with his fingers—had he been a Videssian,
Krispos guessed he would have drawn the sun-circle over his heart. That
guard said, "Majesty, I cannot fathom the minds of the men who fought
here. That they are of my folk raises only shame in me. Renegades and
outlawed men would not act so, much less warriors from honest holdings." Other northerners nodded.

"But they did act so," Krispos said. Every time he breathed, he took in
the miasma of dead flesh and old smoke. He let his feet lead him through
Imbros; even after so many years away, they seemed to remember how the
bigger streets ran. Before long, he found himself in the central market
square, looking across it toward the temple.

Once he'd thought that temple the grandest building he'd ever seen.
Now he knew it was but a provincial imitation of Phos' High Temple in
Videssos the city, and not a particularly impressive one, either. But even
fire-ravaged as it was now, it still raised memories in him, memories of awe
and faith and belief.

Those memories clashed terribly with the row of impaled bodies in
front of the temple, the first he'd seen inside Imbros who had received that
treatment rather than the quicker, cleaner death of axe or sword or fire.
What with the stains of blood and smoke, he needed a moment to realize
those victims all wore the blue robe. He sketched the sun-sign.

So did Trokoundos beside him. "Did I not hear they were savage to
priests in Develtos, as well?" the wizard asked quietly.

"Aye, so they were." Krispos' boots clicked on flagstones as he walked
across the square toward the temple. He stepped around a couple of
corpses of the ordinary, crumpled sort. By now, numb with the scale of the
butchery here, he found them hardly more than obstacles in his path.

But what the priests had suffered penetrated even that numbness.
Though some days dead, their bodies still gave mute testimony to those
special torments. As if impalement were insufficient anguish, some had
had their manhood cut away, other their guts stretched along the ground
for the carrion birds, still others their beards—and their faces—burned
away.

Krispos turned his back on them, then made himself look their way
once more. "May Phos take their souls into the light."

"So may it be," Trokoundos said. "But Skotos seems to have had his
way with their bodies." Together, he and Krispos spat.

Krispos said, "All this ground will have to be blessed before we can rebuild. Who would want to live here otherwise, after this?" He nodded to himself. "I'll suspend taxes for the new folk I move in, and keep them off for a while, to try another way to make people want to stay once they've come."

"Spoken like an Emperor," Trokoundos said.

"Spoken like a man who wants Imbros to be a living city again soon," Krispos said impatiently. "It's a bulwark against whoever raids down from Kubrat, and in peacetime it's the main market town for the land near the mountains."

"And now, Majesty?" Trokoudnos said. "Will you pause to bury the dead here?"

"No," Krispos said, impatient still. "I want to come to grips with Harvas as soon as I can." He glanced toward the sun, which stood low in the west—days were shorter now than they had been while he laid siege to Petronas. Again he cursed the time he'd had to spend in civil war. "There's not a lot of summer left to waste."

"No denying that, Your Majesty," Trokoundos said. "But—" He let the word hang.

Krispos had no trouble finishing for him. "But Harvas knows that, too. Aye, I'm all too sure he does. I'm all too sure he has some deviltry brewing, too, just waiting for us. I trust my soldiers to match his. As for magic—how strong can Harvas be?"

Trokoundos' lips twisted in a grin that seemed gayer than it was. "I expect, Your Majesty, that before too long I shall find out."

MORE EAGER FOR FIGHTING THAN ANY ARMY KRISPOS HAD known, his force stormed north up the highway after Harvas' raiders. "Imbros!" was their cry; the name of the murdered city was never far from their lips.

The Paristrian Mountains towered against the northern horizon now, the highest peaks still snow-covered even in later summer. Some of the men from the western lowlands exclaimed at them. To Krispos they were—not old friends, for he remembered the kind of weather that blew over them through half the year, but a presence to which he was accustomed all the same.

Everything hereabouts seemed familiar, from the quality of the light, paler and grayer than it was in Videssos the city, to the fields of ripening wheat and barley and oats—worked now only by the few farmers lucky enough to have escaped Harvas' men—to the way little tracks ran off the highway, now to the east, now to the west.

Krispos pulled Progress out of the line of march when he came to one of those roads. He stared west along it for a long time, his mind ranging farther than his eyes could reach.

"What is it, Majesty?" Geirrod asked at last. He had to speak twice before Krispos heard him.

"My village lies down this road," Krispos answered. "Or rather it did; Harvas' bandits went through here last year." He shook his head. "When I left, I hoped I'd come back with money in my belt pouch. I never dreamed it would be as Avtokrator—or that the people I grew up with wouldn't be here to greet me."

"The world is as it is, Majesty, not always as we dream it will be."

"Too true. Well, enough time wasted here." Krispos tapped Progress' flanks with his heels. The big bay gelding walked, then went into a trot that soon brought Krispos back to his proper place in the column.

The road ran straight up toward the gap in the mountains, past empty fields, past stands of oak and maple and pine, past a small chuckling stream, and, as the ground grew higher, past more and more outcroppings of cold gray stone. Though Krispos had not seen it since he was perhaps nine years old, the gray landscape seemed eerily familiar. He and his parents and sisters had come down this road after Iakovitzes ransomed them and hundreds of other Videssian peasants from captivity in Kubrat. He must have been keyed up almost to fever pitch then, for fear the Kubratoi would change their minds and swoop down again, for everything on that journey remained as vivid in his mind as if he'd lived it yesterday. The way water splashed from that clump of rocks in the stream had not changed at all in the two decades since, save that frogs had perched on them then.

The mountains themselves . . . *I've always been happier to see them getting smaller,* Krispos thought. They were not getting smaller now, worse luck. Krispos peered up and ahead. Now he could see the opening of the pass that led to Kubrat. *Agapetos got through with less force than I have,* he thought. *I will, too.*

When he said that aloud, Mammianos grunted. "Aye, Agapatos got through, but he couldn't maintain himself north of the mountains. And Harvas beat him again on this side, then came down first on Imbros and then onto Mavros' army. Strikes me he's been able to defeat us in detail, if you know what I mean."

"Are you telling me I shouldn't attack?" Krispos asked, scowling. "After all he's done to us, how can I halt now?"

The image of thousands of bodies, each gruesomely buggered by its own stake, shoved itself forward in his mind. With it came a new vision, that of hundreds of men matter-of-factly cutting and sharpening those stakes. How could they have kept to their work, knowing what the stakes would be used for? Even Kubratoi would have gagged on such cruelty, he thought. And Halogai, judging by long experience with the imperial guards, were harsh but rarely vicious. What made Harvas' men so different?

Mammianos' reply brought him back to the here and now. "All I'm saying, Your Majesty, is that Harvas strikes me as dangerous enough to need hitting with everything the Empire has. The more I see, the more I think that. What we have with us is strong, aye, but is it strong enough?"

"By the good god, Mammianos, I aim to find out," Krispos said. Mammianos bowed his head in submission. He could suggest, but when the Avtokrator decided, his lot was to obey. *Or to mutiny,* Krispos thought. But Mammianos had seen plenty of better chances than this for mutiny. His disagreement with Krispos lay in how best to hurt Harvas, not whether to.

The army camped just out of bowshot of the foothills that night. Peering north in the darkness, Krispos saw the slopes of the mountains ahead dimly illuminated by orange, flickering light. He summoned Mammianos and pointed. "Does that mean what I think?"

"Bide a moment, Majesty, while the campfire glare leaves my eyes." Like Krispos, Mammianos stood with his back to the imperial camp. At last he said, "Aye, it does. They're encamped there, waiting for us."

"Forcing the pass won't be easy," Krispos said.

"No, it won't," the general agreed. "All kinds of things can go wrong when you try to barge through a defended pass. A holding force at the narrowest part will plug it up while they roll rocks down from either side, or maybe come charging down from ambush—that'd be easy for Harvas' buggers, because they're foot soldiers."

"Perhaps I should have listened to you before," Krispos said.

"Aye, Majesty, perhaps you should," Mammianos said—as close to criticism of the Emperor as he would let himself come.

Krispos plucked at his beard. He could not pull back, not having come so far, not having seen Imbros, not unless he wanted to forfeit the army's faith in him forevermore. Going blindly forward, though, was a recipe for disaster. If he had some idea of what lay ahead . . . He whistled to one of his guardsmen. "Fetch me Trokoundos," he said.

The wizard was yawning when he arrived, but cast off sleepiness like an old tunic when Krispos explained what he wanted. He nodded thoughtfully. "I know a scrying spell that should serve, Your Majesty, one subtle enough that no barbarian mage, no mage not formally trained, should even be able to detect it, let alone counteract it. Against Petronas it would not have sufficed, for Skeparnas was my match, near enough. But against Harvas it should do very well; however strong in magic he may be, he is bound to be unschooled. If you will excuse me—"

When Trokoundos returned, he held in his hand a bronze bracelet. "Haloga workmanship," he explained as he showed it to Krispos. "I found it outside of Imbros; I think we may take it as proven that one of Harvas' raiders lost it. By the law of contagion, it is still bonded to its onetime owner, a bond we may now use to our advantage."

"Spare the lecture, sir mage," Mammianos said. "So long as you learn what we need to know, I care not how you do it."

"Very well," Trokoundos said stiffly. He held the bracelet out at arm's length toward the north, then started a slow, soft chant. The chant went on and on. Krispos was beginning to get both worried and annoyed when Trokoundos finally lowered the bracelet. As he turned, the campfire shadowed the lines of puzzlement on his face. "Let me try again, with a variant of the spell. Perhaps the owner of the bracelet was slain; nonetheless, it remains affiliated, albeit more loosely, with the army as a whole."

He began to chant once more. Krispos could not tell any difference between this version of the spell and the other, but was willing to believe it was there. But he found no difference in the result: after some time, Trokoundos halted in baffled frustration.

"Majesty," he said, "so far as I can tell by my sorcery, there's no one at all up ahead."

"What? That's absurd," Krispos said. "We can see the fires—"

"They could be a bluff, Your Majesty," Mammianos put in.

"You don't believe that," Krispos said.

"No, Your Majesty, I don't, but it could be so. I tell you what, though: I'll send out a couple of scouts. They'll come back with what we need to know."

"Good. Do it," Krispos said.

"Aye, do it," Trokoundos agreed. "By the good god, excellent sir, I hope it is a bluff ahead, as you say. The alternative is believing that Harvas has a renegade Videssian mage in his service, and after Imbros I would sooner not believe that." The wizard made a sour face, decisively shook his head. "No, it can't be. I'd have sensed that my spell was being masked. I didn't have that feeling, only the emptiness I'd get if there truly were no men ahead."

The scouts slipped out of camp. They looked to be ideal soldiers for their task; had Krispos met them on the streets of Videssos the city, he would have unhesitatingly guessed they were thieves. Small, lithe, and wary, they carried only daggers and vanished into the night without a sound.

Yawning, Krispos said, "Wake me as soon as they get back." Worn though he was, he did not sleep well. Thoughts of Imbros would not leave his mind or, worse, his dreams. He was relieved when a guardsman came in to rouse him and tell him the scouts had returned.

A thin crescent moon had risen in the east; dawn was not far away. The scouts—there were three of them—prostrated themselves before him. "Get up, get up," he said impatiently. "What did you see?"

"A whole great lot of Halogai, Your Majesty," one of them answered in a flat, up-country accent like the one Krispos had had before he came to Videssos the city. The other two scouts nodded to confirm his words. He went on, "And you know how the pass jogs westward so you can't see all the way up it from here? Just past the jog, they've gone and built themselves a breastwork. Be nasty getting past there, Your Majesty."

"Their army's real, then," Krispos said, more than a little surprised. Trokoundos would not be pleased to learn his sorcery had gone astray.

"Majesty, we sneaked close enough to smell the shit in their slit trenches," the scout answered. "You don't get a whole lot realer than that."

Krispos laughed. "True enough. Two goldpieces to each of you for your courage. Now go get what rest you can."

The scouts saluted and hurried off toward their tents. Krispos thought about going back to bed, too, decided not to bother. Better to watch the sun come up than to toss and turn and think about stakes . . .

The eastern rim of the sky grew gray, then the pale bluish-white that seems to stretch the eye to some infinite distance, then pink. When the sun crawled above the horizon, Krispos bowed to it as if to Phos himself, recited the creed, and spat between his feet to show he rejected Skotos. Most of the time, he hardly thought about that part of the ritual. Not now. Imbros reminded him of what he was rejecting.

The camp stirred with the sun, at first slowly, blindly, like a plant's silent striving toward light, but then with greater purpose as horns rang out to rout sleepers from tents and prod them into the routine of another day. They lined up with bowls in front of cookpots where barley porridge bubbled; gnawed at hard bread, cheese, and onions; gulped wine under the watchful eyes of underofficers who made sure they did not gulp too much; and tended to their horses so the animals would also be ready for the day's work ahead.

Krispos went back to his tent and armed himself. He swung himself up onto Progress and rode over to the musicians. At his command, they played *Assemble*. The troopers gathered before them. Krispos raised a hand for silence and waited until he had it.

"Soldiers of Videssos," he said, hoping everyone could hear him, "the enemy waits for us ahead. You've seen the kind of foe he is, how he loves to slay those who can't fight back." A low growl ran through the army. Krispos went on, "Now we can pay Harvas back for everything, for the slaughters in Develtos last year and Imbros now, and for Agapetos' men, and Mavros', too. Will we turn aside?"

"No!" the men roared. "Never!"

"Then forward, and fight bravely!" Krispos drew his saber and held it high overhead. The soldiers whooped and cheered. They were eager to fight; Krispos needed no fancy turns of phrase to inspire them today. That was as well—he knew Anthimos, for instance, had been a far better speaker than he would ever be. He owned neither the gift nor the inclination for wrapping around his ideas of the flights of fancy that Videssian rhetoric demanded. His only gift, such as it was, was for plain thoughts plainly spoken.

As the army left camp, Krispos told Sarkis, "We'll want plenty of scouts out in front of us, and farther ahead than usual."

"It's taken care of, Your Majesty," the Vaspurakaner officer said with a small, tight smile. "The country ahead reminds me all too much of the land where I grew up. You soon learn to check out a pass before you send everyone through, or you die young." He chuckled. "I suppose, over the generations, it improves the breed."

"Dismount some of those scouts, too," Krispos said as a new worry struck him. "We'll want to spy out the sides of the pass, not just the bottom, and they can't do that from horseback." He stopped, flustered. So much for plain thoughts plainly spoken. "You know what I mean."

"Aye, Your Majesty. It's taken care of," Sarkis repeated. He sketched a salute. "For one who came so late to soldiering, you've learned a good deal. Have I told you of the saying of my people, 'Sneaky as a prince—?' "

Krispos cut him off. "Yes, you have." He knew he was rude, but he was also nervous. The scouts had just followed the western jog of the pass and disappeared from sight. He clucked to Progress, leaned forward in the saddle, and urged the gelding up to a fast trot with the pressure of knees and heels.

Then he rounded that jog himself. The breastwork, of turf and stones and brush and whatever else had been handy, stood a few hundred yards ahead, blocking the narrowest part of the pass. Behind it, Krispos saw at last the warriors who had ravaged the Empire so savagely.

The big, fierce, fair-haired men saw him, too, or the imperial banner that floated near him. They jeered and brandished—weapons? No, Krispos saw; Harvas' men were holding up stout stakes carved to a point at both ends—impaling stakes.

Fury filled him, rage more perfect and absolute than any he had ever known. He wanted to slay with his own sword every marauder in front of him. Only a wild charge by all his men seemed a bearable second best. He filled his lungs to cry out the order.

But something cold and calculating dwelt within him, too, something that would not let him give way to impulse, no matter how tempting. He thought again and shouted, "Arrows!"

Bowstrings thrummed as the Videssian archers went to work from horseback. Instead of their stakes, the Halogai lifted yardwide shields of wood to turn aside the shafts. They were not bowmen; they could not reply.

Here and there, all along the enemy line, men crumpled or lurched backward, clutching at their wounds and shrieking. But the raiders wore mail shirts and helms; even shafts that slipped between shields and over the rampart were no sure kills. And however steeped in wickedness they might have been, Harvas' followers were not cowards. The archery stung them. It could do no more.

By the time he saw that, Krispos had full control of himself once more. "Can we flank them out?" he demanded of Mammianos.

"It's steep, broken ground to either side of that breastwork," the general answered. "Better going for foot than for horse. Still, worth a try, I suppose, and the cheapest way to go about it. If we can get in their rear, they're done for."

Despite his doubts, the general yelled orders. Couriers dashed off to relay them to the soldiers on both wings. Several companies peeled off to try the rough terrain on the flanks. Harvas' Halogai rushed men up the slopes of the pass to head them off.

The northerners had known what they were about when they built their barricade; they had walled off all the ground worth fighting on. The horses of their Videssian foes had to pick their way forward step by step. Afoot, Harvas' men were rather more agile, but they, too, scrambled, stumbled, and often fell.

Some did not get up again; now that the foe was away from cover and concerned more with his footing than his shield, he grew more vulnerable to archery. But the Videssians could not simply shoot their way to victory. They had to force the northerners from their ground. And at close quarters, the foot soldiers gave as good as they got, or better.

Saber and light lance against axe and slashing sword— Krispos watched his men battle the Halogai who followed Harvas. Sudden pain made him wonder if he was wounded until he realized he had his lip tight between his teeth. With a distinct effort of will, he made himself relax. A moment later the pain returned. This time he ignored it.

For all the encouragement he shouted, for all the courage the Videssian cavalry displayed, the terrain proved too rugged for them to advance against determined foes. Krispos wished Harvas' northerners were less brave than his own guardsmen. They did not seem so. He watched a Haloga with a lance driven deep into his side hack from the saddle the man who had skewered him before he, too, toppled.

"No help for it," Mammianos bawled in his ear. "If we want 'em, we'll have to go through 'em, not around."

"We want 'em," Krispos said. Mammianos nodded and turned to the musicians. They raised horns and pipes to their lips, poised sticks over drums. The wild notes of the charge echoed brassily from the boulders that studded both slopes of the pass. The Videssians in the front rank raised a cheer and spurred toward the breastwork that barred their way north.

The front was too narrow for more than a fraction of the imperial army to engage the enemy at once. Rhisoulphos, who led the regiments just behind the van, shouted for his troops to hold up. A gap opened between them and the men ahead.

When Krispos looked back and saw that gap, his own suspicions about his father-in-law and Dara's warning came together in a hard certainty of treason. He slapped a courier on the shoulder. "Fetch me Rhisoulphos, at once. If he won't come, either drag him here or kill him." The rider stared, then set spurs to his horse. With an angry squeal, the beast bounded away.

Krispos' fist gripped the hilt of his saber as tightly as if that were Rhisoulphos' neck. Leave the head of the army to face Harvas' howling killers by itself, would he? Krispos was so sure Rhisoulphos would not willingly accompany his courier that, when his father-in-law did ride up to him, the best he could do was splutter, "By the good god, what are you playing at?"

"Giving our troops room to retreat in, of course, Your Majesty," Rhisoulphos answered. If he was a traitor, he did it marvelously well. *So what? I already know he's good at that,* Krispos thought. But Rhisoulphos went on, "It's a standard ploy when fighting Halogai, Your Majesty. Feigning a withdrawal will often lure them out of their position so we can wheel about and take them while they're in disorder."

Krispos glanced over at Mammianos. The fat general nodded. "Oh," Krispos said. "Good enough." His ears were hot, but his helmet covered them so no one could see the flame.

The Videssians at the barriers slashed and thrust at Harvas' men, who chopped at them and their horses both. The shrieks and oaths dinned through the pass. Then above them rose a long, mournful call. The horsemen wheeled their mounts and broke off combat.

The northerners screamed abuse in their own language, in the speech of the Kubratoi, and in broken Videssian. A couple of men started to scramble over the breastwork to pursue the retreating imperials. Their own comrades dragged them back by main force.

"Oh, a plague on them!" Mammianos said when he saw that. "Why can't they make it easy for us?"

"That's better discipline than they usually show," Rhisoulphos said. "The military manuals claim that tactic hardly ever fails against the northerners."

"I don't think Harvas shows up in the military manuals," Krispos said.

One corner of Rhisoulphos' mouth twitched upward. "I suspect you're right, Your Majesty." He pointed. "But there he stands, whether he's in the manuals or not."

Krispos' eyes followed Rhisoulphos' finger. Of course that tall figure behind the enemy line had to be Harvas Black-Robe; none of his followers was garbed in similar style. Despite the chieftain's sobriquet, Krispos had looked for someone gaudily clad—a ruler needed to stand out from his subjects. So Harvas did, but by virtue of plainness rather than splendor. Had his hooded robe been blue rather than black, he could have passed for a Videssian priest.

Regardless of how he dressed, no doubt he led. Halogai heavily ran here and there at his bidding, doing their best to ignore the weight of mail on their shoulders. And when Harvas raised his arms—those wide black sleeves flapped like vultures' wings—the northerners held their places. For Halogai, that was the more remarkable.

Mammianos glowered at the northerners as if their good order personally affronted him. With a wheezy sigh, he said, "If they won't come out after us, we'll have to get in there nose to nose with them and drive them away." The words plainly tasted bad in his mouth; getting in there nose to nose was not a style of fighting upon which the subtle imperials looked kindly.

But when subtlety failed, brute force remained. As captains dressed their lines and troopers reached over their shoulders to see how many arrows their quivers held, the fierce notes of the charge rang out once more. The Videssians thundered toward the breastwork ahead. "Krispos!" they shouted, and "Imbros!"

Harvas raised his arms. This time he pointed not toward his soldiers or their rampart, but up the slope of the pass. Not far from Krispos, Trokoundos reeled in the saddle. "Call the men back, Majesty!" he cried, clinging to his seat more by determination than anything else. "Call them back!"

Krispos and his generals stared at the mage. "By the good god, why should I?" Krispos demanded angrily.

"Battle magic," Trokoundos croaked. The roar of boulders bounding downslope drowned him out.

Because he was looking at Trokoundos, Krispos did not see the first great stones leap free of the ground on which they had placidly rested for years, perhaps for centuries. That night one of the soldiers who had seen them said, "You ever watch a rabbit that's all of a sudden spooked by a hound? That's what those rocks were doing, except they didn't jump every which way. They came down on us."

The noise the boulders made as they crashed into the Videssian cavalrymen was the noise that might have come from a smithy in the instant a giant stepped on it. Horses went down as if scythed, pitching riders off their backs. The beasts behind them could not stop fast enough and crashed into them and into the stones. That only made the chaos worse.

The men and horses of the very foremost ranks were almost upon the breastwork when the avalanche began. Soldiers turned their heads to gape at what had happened to their comrades. Some drew rein in consternation; other pressed on toward the barricade. Now the Halogai, howling with ferocious glee, swarmed over it to meet them. The imperials at the head of the charge fought back desperately. No one could come to their aid through the writhing tangle behind them.

Krispos watched and cursed and slammed a fist against his thigh as Harvas' northerners overwhelmed his men one by one. Harvas raised his arms and pointed again. More boulders sprang from their proper places and crashed down on the Videssian army's van.

"Make them stop!" Krispos screamed to Trokoundos.

"I wish I could." The wizard's face was haggard, his eyes wild. "He shouldn't be able to do this. The stress, the excitement of combat weaken magic's grip, even if the sorceries are readied in advance. I've tried counterspells—they go awry, as they should."

"What can we do, then?"

"Majesty, I have not the power to stand against Harvas, not even with my colleagues here." Trokoundos sounded as if admitting that cost him physical pain. "Perhaps with more mages, masters from the Sorcerers' Collegium, he may yet be defeated."

"But not now," Krispos said.

"No, Majesty, not now. He screened his encamped army so I could not detect it, he works battle magic so strong and unexpected that it almost broke me when he unleashed it . . . Majesty, a good many years have passed since I owned myself daunted by any sorcerer, but today Harvas daunts me."

Ahead at the barricade, almost all the Videssians were down. They and the crushed soldiers behind them blocked the army's way forward. Krispos' glance slid to the slopes of the pass. Who could guess how many more boulders needed only Harvas' sorcerous command to smash into the imperials, or what other magics Harvas had waiting?

"We retreat," Krispos said, tasting gall.

"Good for you, Your Majesty," Mammianos said. Startled, Krispos turned in the saddle to stare at him. "Good for you," the fat general repeated. "Knowing when to cut your losses is a big part of this business. I feared you'd order us to press on regardless, and turn a defeat into a disaster."

"It's already a disaster," Krispos said.

Even as the call to retreat rang mournfully through the pass, Mammianos shook his head. "No, Majesty. We're still in decent order, there's no panic, and the men will be ready to fight another day—well, maybe another season. But if that he-witch ahead does much more to us, they'll turn tail every time they see his ruffians, whether he's with 'em or not."

Cold comfort, but better—a bit better—than none. Krispos' own Halogai closed around him as rear guard while the army withdrew from the pass. If the northerners wanted to slay him and go over to their countrymen, they would never have a better chance. The imperial guardsmen looked back only to shake fists at Videssos' foes.

And yet, in a way, the guards were the least of Krispos' worries. His eyes, like those of so many others with him, kept sliding up the sides of the pass while he wondered whether more great stones would smash men and horses to jelly. If Harvas had time to ready stones through the whole length of the pass, disaster great enough to satisfy even Mammianos' criteria might yet befall the army.

Somehow, retreat did not become rout. The boulders on the slopes held their places. At last those slopes grew lower and farther apart as the pass opened out into the country below the mountains. "Back to our old campsite?" Mammianos asked.

"Why not?" Krispos said bitterly. "That way we can pretend today never happened—those of us who are still alive, at any rate."

Mammianos tried to console him. "We can't do these little tricks without losses."

"Seems we can't even do them *with* losses," Krispos said, to which the general only grunted by way of reply.

Any camp is joyless after a defeat. Wounded men scream round winners' tents, too, but they and their comrades who come through whole know they have accomplished what they set out to do. Losers enjoy no such consolation. Not only have they suffered, they have suffered and failed.

Failure, Krispos remembered, made Petronas' army break up. He ordered stronger sentry detachments posted south of the camp than to the north. The officers to whom he gave the command did not remark on it, but nodded knowingly as they saw to carrying it out.

Krispos walked to the outskirts of the camp, where badly wounded men lay waiting for healer-priests to attend to them. The soldiers not too far gone in their own anguish saluted him and tried to smile, which made him feel worse than he had before. But he made sure he saw all of them and spoke to as many as he could before he went back to his own tent.

Darkness had fallen by then. Krispos wanted nothing more than to sleep, to forget about the day's misfortunes, if only for a few hours. But a duty harder even than visiting the wounded lay ahead of him. He'd kept putting off writing to Tanilis of Mavros' death; he'd hoped to be able to say he had avenged it. Now that hope had vanished—and how much, in any case, would it have mattered to her? Her only son was gone. Krispos inked his pen and sat staring at the blank parchment in front of him. How to begin?

"Krispos Avtokrator of the Videssians to the excellent and noble lady Tanilis: Greetings." Thus far formula took him, but no further. He needed the smooth phrases that came naturally to anyone who had the rhetorical training that went with a proper education. He did not have them, and would not entrust this letter to a secretary.

"Majesty?" Geirrod's deep voice came from outside the tent.

"What is it?" Krispos put down the pen with a strange mixture of relief and guilt.

The guardsman's reply warned him he had known relief too soon. "A matter of honor, Majesty."

The last Haloga to speak of honor in that tone of voice had been Vagn, talking about killing himself. Krispos ducked out through the tent flap in a hurry. "What's touched your honor, Geirrod?" he asked.

"Not my honor alone, Your Majesty, but the honor of all my folk who take your gold," Geirrod said. Krispos was tall for a Videssian. He still had to look up at Geirrod as the stern northerner went on, "I am chosen to stand for all of us, since I was first to bow before you as lord."

"So you were," Krispos agreed, "and I honor you for that. Do you doubt it?" Geirrod shook his massive head. Exasperated, Krispos snapped, "Then how have I failed you—aye, and all the other Halogai, too?"

"By not sending us forth in combat this day against those who follow Harvas, and holding us back despite what we told you on the road south of Imbros," Geirrod said. "It struck many among us as a slur, as a token you lack trust in us. Better we fare home to Halogaland than carry our axes where we may not blood them. Videssians delight in having troops for show. We took oath to fight for you, Majesty, not to look grand in your processions."

"If you truly think I held you back for fear you would betray me, blood your axe now, Geirrod." Not without second thoughts—the Halogai could be grimly literal—Krispos bent his head and waited. When no blow came, he straightened up and looked at Geirrod again. "Since you do not think so, how can you have lost any honor on account of me?"

The guardsman stiffened to attention. "Majesty, you speak sooth. I see this cannot be so. I shall say as much to my countrymen. Any who doubt me may measure their doubt against this." He hefted his axe.

"Good enough," Krispos said. "Tell them also that I didn't send them forward because I hoped I could clear the Halogai—Harvas' Halogai, I mean—away from the barricade with archery. If it had worked, we would have won the fight without costing ourselves too dear."

Geirrod let out a loud snort. "You may think partway as we Halogai do, Majesty, but I see that at bottom you're a Videssian after all. As it should be, I guess; can't be helped, come what may. But a fight has worth for its own sweet sake. The time for reckoning up the cost is afterward, not before."

"As you say, Geirrod." To Krispos, the northerner's words were insanely reckless. He knew the Halogai knew most Videssians thought as he did, and also knew the Halogai reckoned imperials overcautious at best in war, at worst simply dull. The Halogai fought for the red joy of it, not to gain advantage. That, he supposed, was why no Videssians served a northern chieftain as bodyguards, nor likely ever would.

As he went back into the tent, Geirrod resumed his post outside, evidently satisfied with their exchange. Krispos allowed himself the luxury of a long, quiet sigh. He hadn't lied to Geirrod, not quite, but he had entertained doubts about the Halogai. But by asking Geirrod if *he* believed his countrymen were held back from fear of treachery, Krispos had taken the onus off himself. The next time he faced Harvas' men, though, he did not think he would have to hold back his guardsmen.

He sat down at the little folding table that served him for a desk in the field. Parchment and pen were where he'd left them when Geirrod called. But for the salutation, the parchment remained blank. Krispos sighed again. He wished Trokoundos knew a spell to make unpleasant letters write themselves, but that probably went beyond sorcery into out-and-out miracle-working.

After one more sigh, Krispos inked the pen again. As was his habit, he plunged straight ahead with what he had to say. "My lady, while I was fighting Petronas in the westlands, Mavros heard Agapetos had been beaten and took an army north from Videssos the city to stop Harvas Black-Robe from moving farther forward. I grieve to have to tell you that, as you foresaw, your son was also beaten and was killed."

Setting down the words brought back to him afresh the loss of his foster brother. He studied what he'd written. Was it too bald? He decided it was not. Tanilis approved of straightforward truth . . . and in any case, he thought, she might well already know Mavros was dead, being who and what she was.

He thought for a while before he wrote more. "I loved Mavros as if he were my brother by birth. I would have kept him from attacking Harvas if I'd known that was in his mind, but he hid it from me till too late. You will know better than I do that going ahead no matter what was always his way."

He spread fine sand over the letter to dry the ink. Then he turned over the parchment and wrote on the reverse, "The excellent and noble lady Tanilis, on her estate outside Opsikion." He sanded those words dry, too, then rolled the letter up into a small tube with them on the outside. After tying it shut, he let several large drops of sealing wax fall across the ribbon that closed it. While the wax was still soft, he pressed his signet into it. He stared at the imperial sunburst for a long time. It remained as perfect as if his armies had won three great victories instead of being thrashed three times running and seeing a city sacked and its populace destroyed.

He stuck his head out of the tent to call for a courier. As the fellow stuffed the letter into a waterproof tube, Krispos promised himself that before the war with Harvas was done, the Empire would again become as whole and complete as its seal. He was glad he'd made the vow, but would have felt easier about it had he been surer he could bring it to pass.

Chapter VII

V IDESSOS THE CITY MOURNED. ALONG WITH THE MOURNING
came no little fear. Not since the wild days three centuries before,
when the Khamorth tribes swarmed off the steppes of Pardraya to carve
Kubrat, Khatrish, and Thatagush from the Empire of Videssos, had the
folk of the capital felt threatened from the north.

"People act as if we're going to be besieged tomorrow," Krispos complained to Iakovitzes a few days after he'd returned to the city. "Harvas'
killers are on their own side of the Paristrian Mountains; they'll likely stay
there till spring."

Iakovitzes scribbled in his tablet and passed it to Krispos. "Not even
Harvas is wizard enough to stop the fall rains." He pointed upward, cocking a hand behind his ear.

Krispos nodded; raindrops were drumming on the roof. "Last year I
cursed the rains when they came early, because they kept me from going
after Petronas. Now I bless them, because they keep Harvas out of the Empire."

Iakovitzes took back the tablet and wrote some more. "Phos closes his
ears to curses and blessing both, as far as weather goes. He hears too many
of each."

"No doubt you're right," Krispos said. "It doesn't stop people from sending them up, though. And Harvas' being a couple of hundred miles from here doesn't stop people from looking north over their shoulders every time they hear a loud noise in the next street."

"It won't last," Iakovitzes wrote with confident cynicism. "Remember, city folk are fickle. Pyrrhos will give them something new to think about soon enough."

Krispos winced. "Don't remind me." More than ever, he wished Gnatios had stayed loyal to him. Gnatios was politician as well as priest, which made him pliable. Pyrrhos chose a course and pursued it with all the power he had—and as ecumenical patriarch he had more power, perhaps, than anyone save Krispos. He also cared not a copper whether the course he chose raised the hackles of every other ecclesiastic in the Empire. Sometimes Krispos thought he aimed at just that. Whether he did or not, he was accomplishing it.

"I've known him longer than you have, if you'll remember," Iakovitzes wrote. "After all, he's my cousin. He doesn't approve of me, either. Of course, he doesn't approve of anything much, as you'll have noticed." He made the throaty noise he used for laughter.

"No wonder he doesn't approve of you!" Krispos laughed, too. Iakovitzes' sybaritic habits and unending pursuit of handsome youths did not endear him to his stern, ascetic cousin. Krispos went on, "I notice you haven't slowed down, either. If anything, you're squiring more lads around than ever." Krispos wondered if, after his mutilation, Iakovitzes had plunged so deeply back into the world of the senses to remind himself he was still alive.

The noble made that throaty noise again. "Backward, Your Majesty," he wrote. "These days they squire me."

Krispos started to laugh once more, too, but stopped when he saw Iakovitzes' face. "By the good god, you mean it," he said slowly. "But how—why? You know I mean you no disrespect, excellent sir, but you've baffled me."

Iakovitzes wrote one word, in big letters: "UNIQUE." Grinning, he pointed to himself, then wrote again. "Where else would they find the like? And like it they do." He leered at Krispos.

Krispos did not quite know whether to laugh some more or to be revolted. Barsymes came in and saved him from his dilemma. "I have here a petition for Your Majesty," the vestiarios said, holding out a folded piece of parchment. "It is from the monk Gnatios." Nothing in his voice showed that Gnatios had ever held high rank.

"Speak of him and he pops up," Krispos observed. He took the parchment from Barsymes. The eunuch bowed his way out. Krispos glanced toward Iakovitzes as he opened the petition. "Do you want to hear this?"

At Iakovitzes' nod, Krispos read aloud: " 'The humble, sinful, and repentant monk Gnatios to his radiant and imperial Majesty Krispos, Avtokrator of the Videssians: Greetings.' " He snorted. "Likes to lay it on thick, doesn't he?"

"He's a courtier," Iakovitzes wrote, which seemed to say everything he thought necessary.

Krispos resumed. " 'I beg leave to request the inestimable privilege of a brief interruption in my sojourn in the monastery dedicated to the memory of the holy Skirios so that I might enjoy the boon of your presence and acquaint you with the results of certain of my historical researches, these having been resumed at your behest, as the said results, reflections of antiquity though they be, also appear of significance in the Empire's current condition.' " He put down the parchment. "Whew! If I have trouble understanding his request, why should I expect his historical researches, whatever those are, to make any better sense?"

"Gnatios is no one's fool," Iakovitzes wrote.

"I know that," Krispos said. "So why does he take me for one? This must be some sort of scheme to have him escape again. He'd pop up all over the countryside till we caught him again; he'd preach against Pyrrhos and do his best to raise a schism among the priests. With Harvas to worry about, trouble in the temples is the last thing I need. That can lead to civil war."

"You won't hear him?" Iakovitzes wrote.

"No, by the lord with the great and good mind." Krispos raised his voice: "Barsymes, fetch me pen and ink, please." When he had the writing tools, he scrawled "I FORBID IT—K." at the bottom of Gnatios' petition, using letters even bolder than the ones Iakovitzes had employed to call himself unique. Then he folded the parchment and handed it to Barsymes. "See that this is delivered back to the monk Gnatios." He made Gnatios' title deliberately dismissive.

"It shall be done, Your Majesty," the vestiarios said.

"Thank you, Barsymes." As the eunuch chamberlain started to leave, Krispos added, "When you're done with that, could you bring me something from the kitchen? I don't much care what, but I feel like a snack. You, too, excellent sir?"

Iakovitzes nodded. "And some wine, if you would, esteemed sir," he wrote, holding up his tablet so Barsymes could read it.

Before long, the vestiarios carried in a silver tray with a jar of wine, two cups, and a covered serving dish. When he lifted the cover, savory steam rose. "Quails cooked in a sauce of cheese, garlic, and oregano, Your Majesty. I hope they will do?"

"Fine," Krispos assured him. He attacked his little bird with gusto and finished it in a few bites.

Iakovitzes made slower going of his quail. He had to cut the meat into very small pieces, and he washed down each little mouthful by tilting back his head and taking a swallow of wine: without a tongue, he could not push food around inside his mouth or move it toward his throat. Here, though, as in other things, he evidently managed, for he'd regained most of the weight his ordeal had taken from him.

As the noble sucked the last scrap of meat from a leg bone, Krispos raised his cup in salute. "I'm glad to see you doing so well," he said.

"I'm glad to see myself doing so well, too," Iakovitzes wrote. Krispos snorted. They drank together.

DARA STRAIGHTENED, HER FACE PALE. A MAIDSERVANT WIPED the Empress' mouth and chin with a damp cloth, then stooped to pick up the basin at her feet and carry it away. "I wish I just had *morning* sickness," Dara said wearily, "but I seem to be vomiting any time of the day or night."

Krispos handed her a cup of wine. "Here, get the taste out of your mouth."

Dara took a small, cautious sip. She cocked her head and waited, gauging the wine's effect on her stomach. When the first swallow sat well, she drank more. She said, "Maybe I should have nursed Phostis myself after all. The midwives say it's harder for a nursing mother to conceive."

"I've heard that," Krispos said. "I don't know whether it's so. Whether or not, I hope you're better soon."

"So do I." Dara rolled her eyes. "But if I do with this baby as I did with Phostis, I'll keep on puking for the next two months."

"Oh, I hope not." But Krispos knew he would keep a close eye on the date Dara's morning sickness stopped and on the day the baby was born. He did not doubt her, not really. Though he'd been in Videssos the city only a couple of days between the campaigns against Petronas and Harvas, he and she'd been anything but idle during that little while, and her sickness had begun about the right length of time after it—no use reckoning by her courses, which were still disrupted after Phostis' birth.

But he'd watched the days, all the same. Dara had cheated with him, which meant she might cheat against him. He thought that unlikely, but Avtokrators who ignored the unlikely did not reign long.

Dara said, "Phostis sat up by himself yesterday."

"So his nurse told me." Krispos did his best to sound pleased. Try as he would, he had trouble warming to Phostis. He could not help wondering if he was raising a cuckoo's chick. *If this next child is a boy* . . . he said to himself, and in thinking how much he would enjoy raising it, he discovered he was sure it was his.

Dara changed the subject. "How are the tax revenues looking?"

"From the westlands, pretty well. From the island of Kalavria, from the peninsula of Opsikion, from the lands right around the city, pretty well. From the north—" Krispos did not need to go on. Only carrion birds found anything worth picking over anywhere near the Paristrian Mountains.

"Will we have enough to fight Harvas next spring?" Dara asked. She was a general's daughter; she knew armies needed money and everything it bought as much as they needed men.

"The logothetes in the treasury say we should," Krispos answered. "And with Petronas gone at last, we'll be able to bring all our soldiers to bear against him." He shook his head. "How I wish we could have done that this year. We might have saved Imbros. Phos be praised that the Empire is united now."

That might have been a mime show cue. The eunuch Longinos came bustling into the room, moving so fast that sweat beaded his fat, beardless face. "Majesty," he gasped. "There's word of rioting around the High Temple, Majesty."

Krispos got up and glared at him so fiercely that the eunuch flinched back in alarm. With an effort, he took hold of his temper. "Tell me about it," he said.

"Save the news itself, Your Majesty, I know no more," Longinos quavered. "A soldier carried the report here; I've brought it to you fast as I could."

"You did right, Longinos; thank you," Krispos said, in control of himself again. "Take me to this soldier. I'll hear what he has to say for myself."

The eunuch turned and left. As Krispos followed him out the door, Dara spoke one word. "Pyrrhos."

"That thought had crossed my mind, yes," Krispos said over his shoulder. He trotted down the hall after Longinos.

When Krispos came out of the imperial residence, the soldier prostrated himself, then quickly got to his feet. He looked like a man who had been caught in a riot; his tunic was torn, the crown of his wide-brimmed hat had been caved in, his nose was bloody, and a bruise purpled his right cheekbone. "By the good god, man, what happened?" Krispos said.

The man shook his head and ran a sleeve under his nose. "The ice take me if I know, Your Majesty. I was goin' along mindin' my own business when this crowd boiled out of the forecourt to the High Temple. They was all screamin' and whalin' each other with whatever they had handy. Then they lit into me. I still don't have no notion of what it's all about, but I figured you got to hear of it straightaway, so I came here." He wiped his nose again.

"I'm grateful," Krispos said. "Give me your name, if you would."

"I'm Tzouroulos, Your Majesty, file closer in Mammianos' command—Selymbrios is captain of my company."

"You're file leader now, Tzouroulos, and you'll have a reward you can spend, too." Krispos turned to the Halogai, who had listened to the exchange with interest. "Vagn, go to, hmm, Rhisoulphos' regiment in the barracks. Get them over to the High Temple as fast as they can march. Tell them it's riot duty, not combat—if they start slaying people out of hand, the whole city's liable to go up in smoke."

"Aye, Majesty. Rhisoulphos' regiment it is." Vagn saluted and jogged away. His long fair braid flapped against his back at every step he took.

Krispos said to Longinos, "After we get order back—by the good god's mercy, we will—I'll also want to speak with the most holy ecumenical patriarch Pyrrhos, to see if he can shed some light on what might have touched off this fighting. Be so good, esteemed sir, as to draft for my signature a formal summons for him to come to the Grand Courtroom and explain himself."

"Of course, Your Majesty. Directly. To the Grand Courtroom, you say? Not here?"

"No. Riots round the temples are a serious business. I want to remind Pyrrhos just how dim a view I take of them. Making my inquiries in the Courtroom should help him understand that."

"Very well, Your Majesty." Lips moving as he tasted phrases, Longinos went back into the imperial residence.

Krispos stared east and north, toward the High Temple. The residence and the other buildings of the palace quarter hid its great dome and the gilded spheres that topped its spires, but arson often went with riot. He did not see the black column of smoke he feared. It was the rainy season, after all, he thought hopefully. Even if it was only drizzling today, walls and fences would still be damp.

He went inside. Longinos approached him with the summons. He read it over, nodded, and signed and sealed it. The chamberlain took the parchment away. Krispos waited and worried. He knew he'd given the proper orders. But even the imperial power had limits. He needed others to turn those orders into reality.

The sun was low in the west when a messenger came from Rhisoulphos with word that the disturbances had been quelled. "Aye," the fellow said cheerfully, "we broke some heads. The city folk don't have the gear to stand against us and, besides, they keep on fighting each other. Civilians," he finished with a sneer.

"I'll want to see some prisoners, so I can find out what got these civilians started," Krispos said.

"We have some," the messenger agreed. "They're sending them back to the jail in the government office building on Middle Street."

"I'll go there, then," Krispos said, glad of something he could do. But he could not simply walk over to the big red granite building, as any private citizen might. Before he set out from the imperial residence, he required a squad of Halogai and the dozen parasol-bearers. Gathering the retinue took awhile, so that by the time he set out, he needed torchbearers, too.

One of the palace eunuchs must have sent word ahead of his procession, for the warders and soldiers at the government offices were ready when he arrived. They escorted him to a chamber on the ground level, one floor above the cells. As soon as he was settled, two warders hauled in a captive whose hands were chained in front of him. "On your belly before his Majesty," they growled. He went to his knees, then awkwardly finished the prostration. One of the warders said, "Majesty, this here is a certain Koprisianos. He tried to smash in a trooper's skull, he did."

"Would've done it, too, Your Majesty, 'cept the bastard was wearing a helmet," Koprisianos said thickly. He had an engagingly ugly face, though now his lip was swollen and split and a couple of teeth looked to be freshly gone.

"Never mind that," Krispos said. "I want to know what started the fighting in the first place."

"So do I," Koprisianos said. "All I know is, somebody hit me. I turned around and hit him back—at least I think it was him; lots of people were running by just then, all of 'em screaming about heretics and Skotoslovers and Phos knows what all else. I was giving as good as I got till some stupid soldier broke a spearshaft over my head. After that, next thing I know is, I wake up here."

"Oh." Krispos turned to the warders. "Take him away. He just looks to have found himself in the middle of a brawl and enjoyed it. Bring me people who saw the riot start, or who made it start, if you can find any who'll admit to that. I want to get to the bottom of how it began."

"Yes, Your Majesty," the warders said together. One of them added, "Come on, you," as they led away Koprisianos. They were gone for some time before they returned with an older man who wore the tattered remnants of what had been a fine robe. "This here is a certain Mindes. He was captured inside the forecourt to the High Temple. On your belly, you!"

Mindes performed the proskynesis with the smoothness of a man who had done it before. "May it please Your Majesty, I have the privilege of serving as senior secretary to the ypologothete Gripas," he said as he rose.

A mid-level treasury official, Krispos thought. He said, "Having men sworn to uphold the state captured rioting pleases me not at all, Mindes. How did you come to disgrace yourself that way?"

"Only because I wanted to hear the most holy patriarch Pyrrhos preach, Your Majesty," Mindes said. "His words always inspire me, and he was particularly vigorous today. He spoke of the need for holy zeal in routing out the influence of Skotos from every part of our lives and from our city as a whole. Even some priests, he said, had tolerated evil too long."

"Did he?" Krispos said with a sinking feeling.

"Aye, Your Majesty, he did, and a great deal of truth in what he said, too." Mindes drew the sun-sign as well as he could with his hands chained. He went on, "People talked about the sermon afterward, as they often do while leaving the High Temple. Several priests notorious for their laxness were named. Then someone claimed Skotos could also profit from too much rigor in the holy hierarchy. Someone else took that as a deliberate insult against Pyrrhos, and—" Mindes' chains clanked as he shrugged.

"And your own part in this was purely innocent?" Krispos asked.

"Purely, Your Majesty," Mindes said, the picture of candor.

One of the warders coughed dryly. "When captured, Your Majesty, he was carrying five belt pouches, not counting the one on his own belt."

"A treasury official indeed," Krispos said. The warders laughed. Mindes looked innocent—with the smoothness of a man who has done it before, Krispos thought. He said, "All right, take him back to his cell and bring me someone else who was there at the start of things."

The next man told essentially the same story. Just to be sure, Krispos had one more summoned and heard the tale over again. Then he went back to the imperial residence and spent the night pondering what to do with Pyrrhos. Ordering the patriarch to wear a muzzle at all times struck him as a good idea, but he suspected Pyrrhos would find some theological justification for disobeying.

"He might not, you know," Dara said when he mentioned his conceit out loud. "He might take it for some wonderful new style of asceticism and try to enforce it on the whole clergy." She chuckled.

So did Krispos, but only for a moment. Knowing Pyrrhos, there was always the chance Dara was right.

THE GRAND COURTROOM WAS HEATED BY THE SAME KIND OF system of ducts under the floor that the imperial residence used. It was far larger than any room in the residence, though; the ducts kept one's feet warm, but not much more.

Krispos' throne stood on a platform a man's height above the floor; not even his feet were warm. Some of the courtiers who flanked the double row of columns that led up to the throne shivered in their robes. The Haloga guards were warm—they wore trousers. Back in his old village, Krispos would have been wearing trousers, too. He cursed fashion, then smiled as he imagined Barsymes' face if he'd proposed coming to the Grand Courtroom in anything but the scarlet robe custom decreed.

The smile went away when Pyrrhos appeared at the far end of the hall. The patriarch advanced toward the throne with the steady stride of a much younger man. He was entitled to vestments of blue silk and cloth-of-gold, vestments almost as rich as the imperial raiment. All he wore, though, was a monk's simple blue robe, now soaked and dark. As he drew near, Krispos heard his feet squelching in his blue boots; he refused to acknowledge the rain by covering himself against it.

He prostrated himself before Krispos, waiting with his forehead on the ground till given leave to rise. "How may I serve Your Majesty?" he asked. He did not hesitate to meet Krispos' eye. If his conscience troubled him, he concealed it perfectly. Krispos did not think it did; unlike most Videssians, Pyrrhos had no use for dissembling.

"Most holy sir, we are not pleased with you," Krispos said in the formal tone he'd practiced for occasions such as this. He stifled a grin of pleasure at remembering to use the first-person plural.

"How so, Your Majesty?" Pyrrhos said. "In my simple way, I have striven only to speak the truth, and how can the truth displease any man who has no reason to fear it?"

Krispos clamped his teeth together. He might have known this would not be easy. Pyrrhos wore righteousness like chain mail. Krispos answered, "Stirring up quarrels within the temples serves neither them nor the Empire as a whole, the more so as Harvas Black-Robe alone will profit if we fight among ourselves."

"Your Majesty, I have no intention of stirring up dissent," Pyrrhos said.

"I merely aim to purify the temples of the unacceptable practices that have entered over years of lax discipline."

What Krispos wanted to do was scream, *"Not now, you cursed idiot!"* Instead he said, "Since these practices you don't approve of have been a long time growing, maybe you'd be wiser to ease them out of the ground instead of jerking them up by the roots."

"No, Your Majesty," Pyrrhos said firmly. "These are the webs Skotos spins, the tiny errors that grow larger, more flagrant month by month, year by year, until at last utter wickedness and depravity become acceptable. I tell you, Your Majesty, thanks to Gnatios and his ilk, Videssos the city is a place where the dark god roams free!" He spat on the polished marble floor and traced the sun-circle over the sodden wool above his heart.

Several courtiers imitated the pious gesture. Some looked fearfully toward Krispos, wondering how he dared ask the patriarch to restrain his attack on evil.

But Krispos said, "You are wrong, most holy sir." His voice was hard and certain. That certainty made Pyrrhos' eyes widen slightly; he was more used to hearing it in his own voice than from another. Krispos said, "No doubt Skotos sneaks about in Videssos the city, as he does all through the world. But I have seen a city where he roamed free; I see Imbros still in my dreams."

"Exactly so, Your Majesty. It is to prevent Videssos the city from suffering the fate of Imbros that I strive. The evil within us, given time, will devour us unless, to use your phrase, we root it out now."

"The evil Harvas Black-Robe loves will devour us right now unless we root it out," Krispos said. "How do you propose to minister to the soul of an impaled corpse? Most holy sir, think which victory is more urgent at the moment."

Pyrrhos thought; Krispos gave him credit for it. At length the patriarch said, "You have your concerns, Majesty, but I have mine, as well." He sounded troubled, as if he had not expected Krispos to make him admit even so much. "If I see evil and do nothing to rid the world of it, I myself have done that evil. I cannot pass it by in silence, not without consigning my soul to the eternal ice."

"Not even if other men, men of good standing in the temples, fail to see anything evil in it?" Krispos persisted. "Do you say that anyone who disagrees with you in any way will spend eternity in the ice?"

"I would not go so far as that, Your Majesty," Pyrrhos said, though by the look in his eyes, he wanted to. Reluctantly he continued, "The principle of theological economy does apply to certain beliefs that cannot be proven actively pernicious."

"Then while we are at war with Harvas, stretch it as wide as you can. If you did not go out of your way to make enemies in the temples, most holy sir, you would find many who might be your friends. But think again now and answer me truly: can you see stretching economy to fit Harvas or his deeds?"

Again Pyrrhos paused for honest thought. "No," he admitted, the word expressionless. As much as he wanted to keep his face straight, he looked like a man who suspected, too late, he'd been cheated at dice. He bowed stiffly. "Let it be as you say, Your Majesty. I shall essay to practice economy where I can, for so long as this Harvas remains in arms against us."

One or two courtiers burst into applause, amazed and impressed that Krispos had wrung any concession from Pyrrhos. Krispos was amazed and impressed, too, but did not let on; he also noted the qualifying phrases the patriarch used to keep those concessions as small as possible. He said, "Excellent, most holy sir. I knew I could rely on you."

The patriarch bowed again, even more like an automaton than before. He started to prostrate himself once more so he could leave the imperial presence.

Krispos held up a hand. "Before you go, most holy sir, a question. Did the monk Gnatios ask leave of you to come out of his monastery not long ago?"

"Why, so he did, Your Majesty—and in proper form, too," Pyrrhos added grudgingly. "I rejected the petition even so, of course: no matter what reasons he gives for wishing to come forth, no doubt he mainly seeks to work mischief."

"As you say, most holy sir. I thought the same."

Pyrrhos' face twisted. For a moment he seemed about to smile. In the end, as befit his abstemious temperament, he contented himself with a sharp, short nod. He performed the proskynesis, rose, and backed away from the throne until he was far enough from it to turn his back on Krispos without giving offense. No sooner had he gone than a servitor with a rag scurried out to wipe up the rainwater that had dripped from his robe.

Krispos surveyed the Grand Courtroom with a broad, benign smile. The courtiers were not shouting, "Thou conquerest, Krispos!" at him, but he knew he'd won a victory, just the same.

Phostis rolled from belly to back, from back to belly. The baby started to roll over one more time. Krispos grabbed him before he went off the edge of the bed. "Don't do that," he said. "You're too smart to be a farmer, aren't you?"

" 'Too smart to be a farmer'?" Dara echoed, puzzled.

"The only way a farmer ever learns anything is to hit himself in the head," Krispos explained. He held Phostis close to his face. The baby reached out, grabbed a double handful of beard, and yanked. "Ow!" Krispos said. He carefully worked Phostis' left hand free, then the right— by which time, the left was tangled in his beard again.

After another try, he was able to put down the baby. Phostis promptly tried to roll off the bed. Krispos caught him again. "I told you not to do that," he said. "Why don't babies listen?"

"You're very gentle with him," Dara said. "I think that's good, especially considering—" She let her voice trail away.

"Not much point to whacking him till he's big enough to understand what he's being whacked for," Krispos said, deliberately choosing to misunderstand. *Considering he might be another man's son,* Dara had started to say. She wondered, too, then. Phostis refused to give either of them much in the way of clues.

The baby tried to roll off the bed once more. This time he almost made it. Krispos snagged him by an ankle and dragged him back. "You're not supposed to do that," he said. Phostis laughed at him. He thought being rescued was a fine game.

"I'm glad you'll be here the winter long," Dara said. "He'll get a chance to know you now. When you were out on campaign the whole summer, he'd forgotten you by the time you came back again."

"I know." Part of Krispos wanted to keep Phostis by him every hour of the day and night, to leave the child, if not Krispos himself, no doubt they were father and son. Another part of him wanted nothing to do with the boy. The result was an uneasy blend of feelings that grew only more complicated as day followed day.

The baby started to fuss, jamming fingers into his mouth. "He's cutting a tooth, poor dear little one," Dara said. "He's probably getting hungry, too. I'll ring for the wet nurse." She tugged the green bell cord that rang back in the maidservants' quarters.

A minute later someone tapped politely on the bedchamber door. When Krispos opened it, he found not the wet nurse but Barsymes standing there. The vestiarios bowed. "I have a letter for you."

"Thank you, esteemed sir." Krispos took the sealed parchment from him. Just then the wet nurse came bustling down the hall. She smiled at Krispos as she brushed past him and hurried over to the baby, who was still crying.

"Who sent the letter?" Dara asked as the wet nurse took Phostis from her.

Krispos did not need to open it to answer. He had recognized the seal, recognized the elegantly precise script that named him the addressee. "Tanilis," he said. "You remember—Mavros' mother."

"Yes, of course." Dara turned to the wet nurse. "Iliana, could you carry him someplace else for a bit, please?" Anthimos had been good at acting as if servants did not exist when that suited him. Dara had more trouble doing so, and Krispos more still—he'd had no servants till he was an adult. Iliana left; Barsymes, perfect servitor that he was, had already disappeared. Dara said, "Read it to me, will you?"

"Certainly." Krispos broke the seal, slid off the ribbon around the letter, unrolled the parchment. " 'Tanilis to his imperial Majesty Krispos, Avtokrator of the Videssians: Greetings. I thank you for your sympathy. As you say, my son died as he lived, going straight ahead without hesitating to look to either side of the road.' "

The closeness of the image to the way Mavros' army had actually been caught made Krispos pause and reminded him how Tanilis saw more than met the ordinary man's eye. He collected himself and read on: " 'I have no doubt you did all you could to keep him from his folly, but no one, in the end, can be saved from himself and his will. Therein lies the deadly danger of Harvas Black-Robe, for, having known the good, he has forsaken it for evil. Would I were a man, to face him in the field, though I know he is mightier than I. But perhaps I shall meet him even so; Phos grant it may be. And may the good god bless you, your Empress, and your sons. Farewell.' "

Dara seized on one word of the letter. "Sons?"

Krispos checked. "So she wrote."

Dara sketched the sun-circle over her heart. "She does see true, you say?"

"She always has." Krispos reached out to set a hand on Dara's belly. The child did not show yet, not even when she was naked, certainly not when she wore the warm robes approaching winter required. "What shall we name him?"

"You're too practical for me—I hadn't looked so far ahead." As Dara frowned in thought, the faintest of lines came out on her forehead and at the corners of her mouth. They hadn't been there when Krispos first came to the imperial residence as vestiarios. She was the same age as he, near enough; her aging, minor though it was, reminded him he also grew no younger. She said, "You named Phostis. If this truly is a son, shall we call him Evripos, after my father's father?"

"Evripos." Krispos plucked at his beard as he considered. "Good enough."

"That's settled, then. Another son." Dara drew the sun-sign again. "A pity Mavros had none of his mother's gift." Her eyes went to the letter Krispos was still holding.

"Aye. He never showed a sign of it that I saw. If he'd had it, he wouldn't have gone out from the city. I know he didn't fear for himself; he was wild to be a soldier when I met him." Krispos smiled, remembering Mavros hacking at bushes as they rode from Tanilis' villa into Opsikion. "But he never would have taken a whole army into danger."

"No doubt you're right." Dara hesitated, then asked, "Have you thought about appointing a new Sevastos?"

"I expect I'll get around to it one of these days." The matter seemed less urgent to Krispos than it had when he'd named Mavros to the post. Now that no rebel was moving against him, he had less need to act in two places at the same time, and thus less need for so powerful a minister. Thinking out loud, he went on, "Most likely I'd pick Iakovitzes. He's served me well and he knows both the city and the wider world."

"Oh." Dara nodded. "Yes, he would make a good choice."

The words were commonplace. Something in the way she said them made him glance sharply at her. "Did you have someone else in mind?"

She was swarthy enough to make her flush hard to spot, but he saw it. Her voice became elaborately casual. "Not that so much, but my father was curious to learn if you were thinking of someone in particular."

"Was he? He was curious to learn if I was thinking of him in particular, you mean."

"Yes, I suppose I do." That flush grew deeper. "I'm sure he meant nothing out of ordinary by asking."

"No doubt. Tell him this for me, Dara: tell him I think he might make a good Sevastos, if only I could trust him with my back turned. As things are now, I don't know that I can, and his sneaking questions through you doesn't make me think any better of him. Or am I wrong to be on my guard?" Dara bit her lip. Krispos said, "Never mind. You don't have to answer. That question puts you in an impossible spot."

"You already know my father is an ambitious man," Dara said. "I will pass on to him what you've told me."

"I'd be grateful if you would." Krispos let it go at that. Pushing Dara too hard was more likely to force her away than to bind her to him.

To give himself something impersonal to do, he read through Tanilis' letter again. He wished she could face Harvas in the field. If anyone could best him, she might be that person. Not only would her gifts of foreknowledge warn her of his ploys, but the loss he'd inflicted on her would focus her sorcerous skill against him as a burning glass focused the rays of the sun.

Then Krispos put the letter aside. From what he'd seen thus far, unhappily, no Videssian wizard could face Harvas Black-Robe in the field. That left Krispos a cruel dilemma: how was he to overcome Harvas' Halogai if the evil mage's magic worked and his own did not?

Posing the question was easy. Finding an answer anywhere this side of catastrophe, up till now, had been impossible.

TROKOUNDOS LOOKED HARASSED. EVERY TIME KRISPOS HAD seen him this fall and winter, he'd looked harassed. Krispos understood that. As much as he could afford to, he even sympathized with Trokoundos. He kept summoning the wizard to ask him about Harvas, and Trokoundos had no miracles to report.

"Your Majesty, ever since I returned from the campaign, the Sorcerers' Collegium has hummed like a hive of bees, trying to unravel the secrets behind Harvas' spells," Trokoundos said. "I've had myself examined under sorcery and drugs to make sure my recall of what I witnessed was perfectly exact, in the hope that some other mage, given access to my observations, might find the answer that has eluded me. But—" He spread his hands.

"All your bees have made no honey," Krispos finished for him.

"No, Your Majesty, we have not. We are used to reckoning ourselves the finest wizards in the world. Oh, maybe in Mashiz the King of Kings of Makuran has a stable to match us, but that a solitary barbarian mage should have the power to baffle us—" Trokoundos' heavy-lidded eyes flashed angrily. Being beaten so ate at his pride.

"You have no idea, then, how he does what he does?" Krispos asked.

"I did not quite say that. What makes his magic effective is easy enough to divine. He is very strong. Strength may accrue to any man of any nation—even, perhaps, such strength as his. But he also possesses technique refined beyond any we can match here in Videssos the city. How he acquired that, and how we may meet it . . . well, an answer there will go far toward piecing the puzzle together. But we have none."

Krispos said, "Not too long ago I got a note from our dear friend Gnatios. He claims he has your answers all tied up with a scarlet ribbon. Of course, he would claim dung was cherries if he thought he saw a copper's worth of advantage in it."

"He's a trimmer, aye, but he's no fool," Trokoundos said seriously, echoing Iakovitzes. "What answer did he give? By the lord with the great and good mind, I'll seize whatever I can find now."

"He *gave* none," Krispos said. "He just claimed he had one. As best I could tell, his main aim was escaping the monastery. He thinks I forget the trouble he's caused me. If he hadn't got Petronas loose, I could have turned on Harvas close to half a year sooner."

"Would you have won on account of that?" Trokoundos asked.

"Up till this instant I'd thought so," Krispos answered. "If I couldn't beat him then with the full power of Videssos behind me, how may I hope to next spring? Or are you telling me I shouldn't go forth at all? Should I wait here in the city and stand siege?"

"No. Better to meet Harvas as far from Videssos the city as you may. How much good did walls do either Develtos or Imbros?"

"None at all." Krispos started to say something more, then stopped, appalled, and stared at Trokoundos. Videssos the city's walls were incomparably greater than those of the two provincial towns. Imagining them breached was almost more than Krispos could do. That was not quite the mental image that dismayed him. Winter was the quiet time of year on the farm, the time when people would do minor repairs and get ready for the busyness that would return with spring. In his mind's eye he saw Harvas' Halogai sitting round their hearths, some with skins of ale, others with their feet up, and every last one of them sharpening stakes, sharpening stakes, sharpening stakes . . . Of itself, his anus tightened.

"What is it, Your Majesty?" Trokoundos asked. "For a moment there you looked—frightened and frightening at the same time."

"I believe it." Krispos was glad he'd had no mirror in which to watch his features change. "This I vow, Trokoundos: we'll meet Harvas as far from Videssos the city as we can."

PᴿOGRESS PACED DOWN MIDDLE STREET AT A SLOW WALK. BESIDE the big bay gelding, eight servants tramped along with the imperial litter. Their breath, the horse's, and Krispos' rose in white, steaming clouds at every exhalation.

The city was white, too, white with new-fallen snow. Over his imperial robes, Krispos wore a coat of soft, supple otter furs. He still shivered; he'd lost track of his nose a while before. Dara had a brazier inside the litter. Krispos hoped it did her some good.

Only the Haloga guardsmen who marched ahead of and behind Krispos and his lady literally took winter in their stride. Marched, indeed, was not the right word: they strutted, their heads thrown back, chests thrust forward, backs as resolutely straight as the columns that supported the colonnades running along either side of Middle Street. Their breath fairly burst from their nostrils; they took in great gulps of the air Krispos reluctantly sipped. This was the climate they were made for.

Narvikka turned his head back. "W'at a fine morning!" he boomed. The rest of the northerners nodded. Some of them wore braids like Vagn's, tied tight with crimson cords; these bobbed like horses' tails to emphasize their agreement. Krispos shivered again. Inside the litter, Dara sneezed. He didn't like that. With her pregnant, he wanted nothing out of the ordinary.

The small procession turned north off Middle Street toward the High Temple. When they arrived, one of the Halogai held Progress' head while Krispos dismounted. The litter-bearers and all but two of the guardsmen stayed outside with the horse. The pair who accompanied Krispos and Dara into the temple had diced for the privilege—and lost. Halogai cared nothing for hymns and prayers to Phos.

A priest bowed low when he saw Krispos. "Will you sit close by the altar as usual, Your Majesty?" he asked.

"No," Krispos answered. "Today I think I'll hear the service from the imperial niche."

"As you will, of course, Your Majesty." The priest could not keep a note of surprise from his voice, but recovered quickly. Bowing again, he said, "The stairway is at the far end of the narthex there."

"Yes, I know. Thank you, holy sir." One Haloga fell in in front of Krispos and Dara, the other behind them. Both guards held axes at the ready, though the service was still an hour away and the narthex deserted but for themselves, the Avtokrator and Empress, and a few priests.

As she went up the stairs, Dara complained, "I'd much rather stay down on the main level. Inside the niche, you have trouble seeing out through the grillwork, you're too far away anyhow, and half the time you can't hear what the patriarch is saying."

"I know." Krispos climbed the last stair and walked forward into the imperial niche. The blond oak benches there were bedecked with even more precious stones than those on which less exalted worshipers sat. Mother-of-pearl and gleaming silver ornamented the floral-patterned grillwork. Krispos stood by it for a moment. He said, "I can see well enough, and Pyrrhos is loud enough so I won't have trouble hearing him. I want to find out what goes on when I'm not at the temple, the kind of things Pyrrhos says when I'm not here to listen."

"Spies would do that just as well," Dara said reasonably.

"It's not the same if I don't hear it myself." Krispos didn't know why it wasn't the same—probably because he'd been Emperor for less than a year and a half and still wanted to do as much as he could for himself. Come to that, Pyrrhos was not the sort to change his words because Krispos was in the audience.

"You just want to play spy," Dara said.

His grin was sheepish. "Maybe you're right. But I'd feel even more foolish going down now than I would staying." Dara's eyes rolled heavenward, but she stopped arguing.

Down below, worshipers filed into their places. When they all rose, Krispos and Dara stood, too: the patriarch was approaching the altar. "We bless thee, Phos, lord with the great and good mind, by thy grace our protector, watchful beforehand that the great test of life may be decided in our favor," Pyrrhos declaimed. Everyone recited with him, everyone save the two Halogai in the niche, who stood as silent and unmoving—and probably as bored—as if they were statuary.

More prayers followed Phos' creed. Then came a series of hymns, sung by the congregation and by a chorus of monks who stood against one wall. "May Phos hear our entreaties and the music of our hearts," Pyrrhos said as the last echoes died away in the dome far above his head.

"May it be so," the worshipers responded. Then, at the patriarch's gesture, they sank back onto their benches. Dara let out a small sigh of relief as she sat.

Pyrrhos paused to gather his thoughts before he began to preach. "I shall begin today by considering the thirtieth chapter of Phos' holy scriptures," he said. " 'If you understand the commands the good god has given, all hereafter will be for the best: well-being and suffering, the one for the just, the other for the wicked. Then in the end shall Skotos cease to flourish, while those of good life shall reap the promised reward and bask forevermore in the blessed light of the lord with the great and good mind.'

"Again, in the forty-sixth chapter we read, 'But he who rejects Phos, he is a creature of Skotos, who in the sight of the evil one is best.' And yet again, in the fifty-first: 'He who seeks to destroy for whatever cause, he is a son of the creator of evil, and an evildoer to mankind. Righteousness do I call to me to bring good reward.'

"How do we apply these teachings? That the vicious foe who prowls our borders is wicked is plain to all. Yet note how perfectly the holy scriptures set forth his sin: he is a destroyer, an evildoer to mankind, a son of the creator of evil, and one who gives no thought to the commands of the good god. And indeed, one day the eternal ice shall be his home. May it be soon."

"May it be soon," Krispos said. Beside him, Dara nodded. A low mutter also rose from the congregation below.

Pyrrhos went on, "Aye, with Harvas Black-Robe and the savage barbarians who follow him, the recognition of what is good and what evil comes easily enough. Would that Skotos knew no guises more seductive. But the dark god is a trickster and a liar, constantly seeking to ensnare and deceive men into thinking they do good when in fact their acts lead only toward the ice.

"What shall we say, for example"—the patriarch loaded his voice with scorn—"of priests and prelates who make false statements for their own advantage, or who condone the sins of others, or who remain in concord with those who condone the sins of others?"

"He's whipping Gnatios again," Dara said.

"So he is," Krispos said. "Trouble is, he's using Gnatios to whip all the priests in the whole hierarchy who don't spend every free moment mortifying their flesh, and I told him not to do that." Now he wished he was down by the altar. He could rise up in righteous wrath and denounce the patriarch on the spot—and wouldn't that make a scandal to resound all through the Empire! He laughed a little, enjoying the idea.

The laughter left his lips as Pyrrhos repeated, "What shall we say of these men who have blinded themselves to Phos' sacred words? By the lord with the great and good mind, here is my answer: a man of such nature no longer deserves the appellation of priest. He is rather a wild animal, an evil scoundrel, a sinful heretic, a whore, one who does not deserve and is not worthy to wear a blue robe. He will spend all eternity in the ice with his true master Skotos. His tears of lamentation shall freeze to his cheeks— and who would deny this is his just desert?"

The patriarch sounded grimly pleased at the prospect. He went on, "This is why we root out misbelievers when and where we find them. For a priest who errs in his faith condemns not only himself to Skotos' clutches, but gives over his flock as well. Thus a misbelieving priest is doubly damned and doubly damnable, and must not be suffered to survive, much less to preach."

Krispos did not like the buzz of approval that rose to the imperial niche. Religious strife was meat and drink to the folk of Videssos the city.

Pyrrhos might have promised to exercise economy, but the promise went too much against his nature for him to keep it: he was a controversialist born.

"I'll have to get rid of him," Krispos said, though saying it aloud made him wince. Pyrrhos had given him his start in the city. Driven by some mystic vision, the then-abbot had taken him to Iakovitzes, thus starting the train of events that led to the throne. But now that Krispos was on the throne, how could he afford a patriarch who kept doing his best to turn Videssos upside down?

"With whom would you replace him?" Dara asked. Krispos shook his head. He had no idea.

Pyrrhos was finishing his sermon. "As you prepare to leave the temple and return to the world, offer up a prayer to the Avtokrator of the Videssians, that he may lead us to victory against all who threaten the Empire."

That only made Krispos feel worse. Pyrrhos remained solidly behind him. But the patriarch threatened the Empire, too. Krispos had tried to tell him so, every way he knew how. Pyrrhos had not listened—more accurately, had refused to hear. As soon as Krispos could decide on a suitable replacement, it would be back to the monastery for the zealous cleric.

The congregation recited Phos' creed a last time to mark the end of the service. "This liturgy is accomplished," Pyrrhos declared. "Go now, and may each of you walk in Phos' light forevermore."

"May it be so," the worshipers said. They rose from their benches and began filing out to the narthex.

Krispos and Dara also rose. The Halogai behind them unfroze from immobility. One of the northerners muttered something in his own tongue to the other. The second guardsman started to grin until he saw Krispos watching him. His face congealed into soldierly immobility. *Laughing at the ceremony,* Krispos guessed. He wished the Halogai would see the truth of Phos. On the other hand, an Avtokrator who proselytized too vigorously was liable to see the size of his bodyguard shrink.

The Halogai preceded the imperial couple down the stairs. The men and women in the narthex bowed low as Krispos emerged. No proskynesis was required, not here: this was Phos' precinct first. Flanked by watchful guardsmen fore and aft, Krispos and Dara went out to the forecourt.

With a flourish, the chief litter-bearer opened the door to the conveyance so Dara could slip in. Narvikka came over to hold Progress' head. Krispos had his left foot in the stirrup when somebody not far away shouted, "You'll go to the ice with the lax priest you follow!"

"Too much pickiness will send *you* to the ice, Blemmyas, for condemning those who don't deserve it," someone else shouted back.

"Liar!" Blemmyas shouted.

"Who's a liar?" Fist smacked flesh with a meaty *thwock.* In an instant, people all over the forecourt were screaming and cursing and pounding and kicking at one another. Wan sunlight sparkled off the sharpened edge of a knife. "Dig up Pyrrhos' bones!" someone yelled. The ice that walked Krispos' spine had nothing to do with chilly weather—digging up somebody's bones was the call to riot in the city.

A stone whizzed past his head. Another clattered off the side of Dara's litter. She let out a muffled shriek. Krispos sprang into the saddle. "Give me your axe!" he shouted to Narvikka. The Haloga stared, then handed him the weapon. "Good!" Krispos said. "You, you, you, and you"—he pointed to guardsmen—"stay here and help the bearers keep the Empress' litter safe. The rest of you, follow me! Try not to kill, but don't let yourselves get hurt, either."

He spurred Progress toward the center of the forecourt. The Halogai gaped, then cheered and plunged after him.

The axe was an impossible weapon to swing from horseback—too long, too heavy, balanced altogether wrong. Had Progress not been an extraordinarily steady mount, Krispos' first wild swipe would have pitched him out of the saddle. As it was, he missed the man at whom he'd aimed. The flat of the axehead crashed into the side of a nearby man's head. The fellow staggered as if drunk, then went down.

"Go back to your homes. Stop fighting," Krispos yelled, again and again. Behind him, the armored Halogai were happily felling anyone rash enough to come near them or too slow to get out of the way. From the cries of anguish that rose into the sky, Krispos suspected they weren't paying much heed to his urge of caution.

The riot, though, was murdered before it had truly been born. People in the forecourt broke and ran. They were too afraid of the fearsome northerners to remember why they had been battling one another. That suited Krispos well enough. He held the axe across his knees as he brought Progress to a halt.

When he looked back, he saw about what he'd expected: several men and a woman down and unmoving. The Halogai were busy slitting belt pouches. Krispos looked the other way. Things could have got very sticky had they not waded into the crowd in his wake.

From the top of the steps, priests peered down in dismay at the blood that splashed the snow in the forecourt. Under that snow, old blood still stained the flagstones from the last riot Pyrrhos had inspired. Enough was enough, Krispos thought.

He leaned down from the saddle and returned Narvikka's axe to him. "Maybe one day I show you what to do with it," the Haloga said with a sly smile.

Krispos' ears heated; that stroke had looked as awkward as it felt, then. He pointed to a couple of corpses. "Take their heads," he said. "We'll set them at the foot of the Milestone with a big placard that says 'rioters.' The good god willing, people will see them and think twice."

"Aye, Majesty." Narvikka went about his grisly task with no more concern than if he'd been slaughtering swine. He glanced over to Krispos when he was done. "You go at them like a northern man."

"It needed doing. Besides, if I hadn't, the fighting just would have spread and gotten worse." That was a most un-Halogalike notion. To the northerners, fighting that spread was better, not worse.

Krispos rode the few steps to the litter. The bearers saluted. One of them had a cut on his forehead and a blackened eye. He grinned at Krispos. "Thanks to you, Majesty, we were only at the edge of things. They plumb stopped noticing us when you charged into the middle of 'em."

"Good. That's what I had in mind." Krispos leaned down and spoke into the small window set into the litter door. "Are you all right?"

"I'm fine," Dara answered at once. "I was in the safest place in the whole forecourt, after all." *The safest place as long as the bearers didn't run away,* Krispos thought. *Well, they didn't.* Dara went on, "I'm just glad you came through safe."

He could hear that she meant it. He'd worried about her, too. This was not the fiery sort of love about which lute players sang in wineshops, this marriage of convenience between them. All the same, bit by bit he was coming to see it was a kind of love, too.

"Let's get back to the palaces," he said. The litter-bearers stooped, grunted, and lifted. The Halogai fell into place. Narvikka swaggered along, holding by their beards the two heads he'd taken. City folk either stared at the gruesome trophies or turned away in horror.

Narvikka had fought to defend the Emperor whose gold he'd taken, and had enjoyed every moment of it. How, Krispos wondered uncomfortably, did that make him different from the Halogai who followed Harvas? The only answer he found was that Narvikka's violence was under the control of the state and was used to protect it, not to destroy.

That satisfied him, but not altogether. Harvas could trumpet the same claim for his conquests, no matter how vicious they were. The difference was, Harvas lied.

"A PETITION FOR YOU, YOUR MAJESTY," BARSYMES SAID.

"I'll read it," Krispos said resignedly. Petitions to the Avtokrator poured in from all over the Empire. Most of them he did not need to see; he had a logothete in aid of requests who dealt with those. But even the winter slowdown did not keep them from coming into the city, and the logothete could not handle everything.

He unrolled the parchment. His nostrils twitched, as if at the smell of bad fish. "Why didn't you tell me it was from Gnatios?"

"Shall I discard it, then?"

Krispos was tempted to say yes, but had second thoughts. "As long as it's in my hands, I may as well read it through." Not the smallest part in his decision was Gnatios' beautifully legible script.

" 'The humble monk Gnatios to his imperial Majesty Krispos, Avtokrator of the Videssians: Greetings.' " Krispos nodded to himself—gone were the fawning phrases of Gnatios' first letter. Having seen they did no good, the former patriarch was wise enough to discard them. They were not his proper style anyhow. Krispos read on:

" 'Again, Your Majesty, I beg the boon of an audience with you. I am painfully aware that you have no reason to trust me and, indeed, every reason to mistrust me, but I write nonetheless not so much for my own sake as for the sake of the Empire of Videssos, whose interest I have at heart regardless of who holds the throne.' "

That might even be true, Krispos thought. He imagined Gnatios scribbling in the scriptorium or in his own monastic cell, pausing to seek out the telling phrase that would make Krispos relent, or at least read further. He'd succeeded in the latter, if not in the former; Krispos' eyes kept moving down the parchment.

" 'Let me speak plainly, Your Majesty,' " Gnatios wrote. " 'The cause of Videssos' present crisis is rooted three hundred years in the past, in the theological controversies that followed the invasions off the Pardrayan steppe, the invasions that raped away the lands now known as Thatagush, Khatrish, and Kubrat. As a result, you will need to consider those controversies and their consequences in contemplating combat against Harvas Black-Robe.' "

The jingling alliteration, though very much the vogue in sophisticated Videssian circles, only irritated Krispos. So did Gnatios' confident "as a result . . ." Of course the past shaped the present. Krispos enjoyed histories and chronicles for exactly that reason. But if Gnatios claimed the Empire's current problems were in fact three hundred years old, he also needed to say why he thought so.

And he did not. Krispos tried to find his reasons for holding back. Two quickly came to mind. One was that the deposed patriarch was lying. The other was that he thought he had the truth, but feared to set it down on parchment lest Krispos use it and keep him mewed up in the monastery all the same.

If that was what troubled him, he was naïve—Krispos could send him back to the monastery of the holy Skirios after hearing what he had to say as easily as he could after reading his words. Gnatios was many things, Krispos thought, but hardly naïve. Most likely, that meant he was lying.

"Bring me pen and ink, please, Barsymes," Krispos said. When the eunuch returned, he took them and wrote, "I still forbid your release. Krispos Avtokrator." He gave the parchment to Barsymes. "Arrange to have this returned to the holy sir, if you would."

"Certainly, Your Majesty. Shall I reject out of hand any further petitions from him?"

"No," Krispos said after thinking it over. "I'll read them. I don't have to do anything about them, after all." Barsymes dipped his head and carried the petition away.

Krispos whistled between his teeth. Gnatios was everything Pyrrhos was not: he was smooth, suave, rational, and tolerant. He was also pliable and devious. Krispos had taken great and malicious glee in confining him to the monastery of the holy Skirios for a second time after Petronas' rebellion failed. Now he wondered whether Gnatios had learned enough humility in the monastery to serve as patriarch once more.

When that occurred to him, he also wondered whether he'd lost his own mind. The monastery had changed Petronas not at all, save only to fill him with a brooding desire for vengeance. If Pyrrhos was intolerable on the patriarch throne, what would Gnatios be but intolerable in some different way? Surely it would be better to replace Pyrrhos with an amiable nonentity, the priestly equivalent of barley porridge.

Yet somehow the idea of restoring Gnatios, once planted, would not go away. Krispos got up, still whistling, and went to the sewing room to ask Dara what she thought of it. She jabbed her needle into the linen fabric on her lap and stared up at him. "I can see why you want Pyrrhos out," she said, "but Gnatios has kept trying to wreck you ever since you took the crown."

"I know," Krispos said. "But Petronas is dead, so Gnatios has no reason—well, less reason—for treachery now. He made Anthimos a good patriarch."

"You should have struck off his head when he surrendered at Antigonos. Then your own wouldn't be filled with this moonshine now."

Krispos sighed. "No doubt you're right. His petitions are probably moonshine, too."

"What petitions?" Dara asked. After Krispos explained, her lip curled in a noblewoman's sneer. "If he knows so much about these vast secrets he's keeping, let him tell them. They'd have to be vast indeed to earn him his way out of his cell."

"By the good god, so they would." Krispos bent down to kiss Dara. "I'll summon him and hear him out. If he has nothing, I can send him back to the monastery for good."

"Even that's better than he deserves." Dara did not sound quite happy at having her sarcasm taken literally. "Remember where you'd be, remember where we'd all be"—she patted her belly—"if he'd had his way."

"I'll never forget it," Krispos promised. He made a wry face. "But I also remember what Iakovitzes told me, and Trokoundos, too: that Gnatios is no one's fool. I don't have to like him, I don't have to trust him, but I have the bad feeling that I may need him."

Dara stabbed her needle into the cloth again. "I don't like it."

"I don't, either." Krispos raised his voice to call for Barsymes. When the eunuch came into the sewing room, he said, "Esteemed sir, I'm sorry, but I've changed my mind. I think I'd best talk, or rather listen, to Gnatios after all."

"Very well, Your Majesty. I shall see to it at once." Barsymes could make his voice toneless as well as sexless, but Krispos had now had years to learn to read it. He found no disapproval there. More than anything else, that convinced him he was doing the right thing.

Chapter VIII

FREEZING RAIN PELTED DOWN. GNATIOS SHIVERED IN HIS BLUE robe as he walked up to the imperial residence. The troop of Halogai who surrounded him—Krispos was taking no chances on any schemes the ex-patriarch might have hatched—bore the nasty weather with the resigned air of men who had been through worse.

Krispos met Gnatios just inside the entranceway to the residence. Wet and dripping, Gnatios prostrated himself on the chilly marble floor. "Your Majesty is most gracious to receive me," he said through chattering teeth.

"Rise, holy sir, rise." Gnatios looked bedraggled enough to make Krispos feel guilty. "Let's get you dry and warm; then I'll hear what you have to say." At his nod, a chamberlain brought towels and furs to swaddle Gnatios.

Krispos led Gnatios down the hall and into a chamber fitted out for audiences. Gnatios' step was sure, but then, Krispos remembered, he'd been here many times before. Iakovitzes waited inside the chamber. He rose and bowed as Krispos led in the former patriarch. Krispos said, "Since I intend to name Iakovitzes as Sevastos to succeed Mavros, I thought he should hear you along with me."

Gnatios bowed to Iakovitzes. "Congratulations, your Highness, if I may anticipate your coming into your new office," he murmured.

Iakovitzes' stylus raced over wax. He held up what he'd written so Krispos and Gnatios both could read it. "Never mind the fancy talk. If you know how to hurt Harvas, tell us. If you don't, go back to your bleeding cell."

"That's how it is, holy sir," Krispos agreed.

"I am aware of it, I assure you," Gnatios said. For once his clever, rather foxy features were altogether serious. "In truth, I do not know how to hurt him, but I think I know who—'what' may be the better word—he is. I rely on Your Majesty's honor to judge the value of that."

"I'm glad you do, since you have no other choice save silence," Krispos said. "Now sit, holy sir, and tell me your tale."

"Thank you, Your Majesty." Gnatios perched on a chair. Krispos sat down beside Iakovitzes on the couch that faced it. Gnatios said, "As I have written, this tale begins three hundred years ago."

"Go on," Krispos said. He was glad he had Iakovitzes with him. He'd enjoyed the histories and chronicles he'd read, but the noble was a truly educated man. He'd know if Gnatios tried to sneak something past.

Gnatios said, "Surely you know, Your Majesty, of the Empire's time of troubles, when the barbarians poured in all along our northern and eastern frontiers and stole so many lands from us."

"I should," Krispos said. "The Kubratoi kidnapped me when I was a boy, and I aided Iakovitzes in his diplomatic dealings with Khatrish some years ago. I know less of Thatagush, and worry about it less, too, since its borders don't touch ours."

"Aye, we deal with them as nations now, like Videssos if neither so old nor so mighty," Gnatios said. "But it was not always so. We had ruled for hundreds of years the provinces they invaded. We—the Empire of Videssos—had a comfortable world then. Save for Makuran, we knew no other nations, only tribes on the Pardrayan steppe and in frigid Halogaland. We were sure Phos favored us, for how could mere tribes do us harm?"

Iakovitzes scribbled, then held up his tablet. "We found out."

"We did indeed," Gnatios said soberly. "Within ten years of the borders being breached, a third of Videssos' territory was gone. The barbarians rode where they would, for once past the frontier they found no forces to resist them. Videssos the city was besieged. Skopentzana fell."

"Skopentzana?" Krispos frowned. "That's no city I ever heard of." Wondering if Gnatios had invented the place, he glanced toward Iakovitzes.

But Iakovitzes wrote, "It's ruins now. It lies in what's Thatagush these days, and the folk there still have but scant use for towns. In its day, though, it was a great city, maybe next greatest in the Empire after Videssos; in no way were more than two towns ahead of it."

"Shall I go on?" Gnatios asked when he saw Krispos had finished reading. At Krispos' nod, he did: "As I said, Skopentzana fell. From what the few survivors wrote afterward, the sack was fearsome, with all the usual pillage and slaughter and rape magnified by the size of the city and because no one had imagined such a fate could befall him till the day. Among the men who got free was the prelate of the city, one Rhavas."

Krispos sketched the sun-circle over his heart. "The good god must have kept him safe."

"Under other circumstances, Your Majesty, I might agree with you. As is—well, may I digress briefly?"

"The whole business so far has seemed pretty pointless," Krispos said, "so how am I to know when you wander off the track?" The story Gnatios spun was interesting enough—the man had a gift for words—but seemed altogether unconnected to Harvas Black-Robe. If he could do no better, Krispos thought, he'd stay in his monastery till he was ninety.

"I hope to weave my threads together into a whole garment, Majesty," Gnatios said.

"Whole cloth, you mean," Iakovitzes wrote, but Krispos waved for Gnatios to go on.

"Thank you, Your Majesty. I know you have no special training in theology, but you must be able to see that a catastrophe like the invasion off the steppes brought crisis to the ecclesiastical hierarchy. We had believed—comfortably, again—that just as we went from triumph to triumph in the world, so Phos could not help but triumph in the universe as a whole. That remains our orthodoxy to this day—" Gnatios sketched the sun-sign. "—but it was sorely tested in those times.

"For, you see, now so many folk made the acquaintance of misfortune and outright evil that they began to doubt Phos' power. Out of this eventually arose the Balancer heresy, which still holds sway in Khatrish and Thatagush—aye, and even in Agder by Halogaland, which though still Videssian by blood has its own king. But worse than that heresy arose, as well. As I said, Rhavas escaped the sack of Skopentzana."

Krispos' eyebrows rose. "Worse came from the man who was prelate of an important city?"

"It did, Your Majesty. Rhavas, I gather, was connected not too distantly to the imperial house of the time, but earned his position by ability, not through his blood. He might have been ecumenical patriarch had Skopentzana not fallen, and he might have been a great one. But when he made his way to Videssos the city, he was . . . changed. He had seen too much of evil when the Khamorth took Skopentzana; he concluded Skotos was mightier than Phos."

Even Iakovitzes, whose piety ran thin, drew the sun-sign when he heard that. Krispos said, "How did the priests of the time take to that?"

"With poor grace, as you might expect." Pyrrhos' reply would have been fierce and full of horror. Gnatios let understatement do the same job. Krispos found he preferred Gnatios' way. The scholarly monk went on, "Rhavas, though, was become as great a zealot for the dark god as he had been for Phos. He preached his new doctrine to all who would listen, first in the temples and then in the streets after the patriarch of the day banned him from the pulpit."

Now Krispos was interested in spite of himself. "They didn't let that go on, did they?" The thought of Videssos the city filled with worshipers of evil filled him with dread.

"No, they didn't," Gnatios said. "But because Rhavas was well connected, they had to try him publicly in an ecclesiastical court, which meant he had the privilege of defending himself against the charges they lodged. And because he was able—well, no, he was more than able; he was brilliant. I've read his defense, Your Majesty. It frightens me. It must have frightened the prelates of the day, too, for they sentenced him to death."

"I ask you again, holy sir—how does this apply to the trouble we're in now? If this Rhavas is three centuries dead, then evil as he may have become—"

"Your Majesty, I am not at all sure Rhavas is three centuries dead," Gnatios said heavily. "I am not sure he is dead at all. He laughed when the court sentenced him, and told them they had not the power to be his death. He was left in his cell for the night, to brood on his misbelief and on the crimes he had committed in the belief they furthered his god's ends. Guards came the next morning to take him to the headsman and found the cell empty. The lock had not been tampered with, there were no tunnels. But Rhavas was gone."

"Magic," Krispos said. The small hairs on his forearms and the back of his neck prickled erect.

"No doubt you are right, Your Majesty, but because of the nature of Rhavas' offense the cell was warded by the finest sorcerers of the day. Afterward they all took oath their wards were undisturbed. Yet Rhavas was gone."

Iakovitzes bent over his tablet. He held it up to show what he had written. "You're saying this Rhavas is Harvas, aren't you?" He screwed up his face to show what he thought of that. But then he lowered the tablet so he could see it himself. When he raised it again, he pointed with his stylus to each name in turn.

For a moment, Krispos had no idea what he was driving at. *Harvas* was an ordinary Haloga name, *Rhavas* an ordinary Videssian one. But was it coincidence that both of them were formed from the same letters? The renewed prickle of alarm he felt told him no.

Gnatios stared at the two names as if he'd never seen them before. His eyes flicked from one to the other, then back again. "I didn't notice—" he breathed.

Iakovitzes set the tablet in his lap so he could write. He passed it to Krispos, who read it aloud: " 'No wonder he wouldn't swear by Phos.' " Iakovitzes believed, too, then.

"But if we're battling a . . . a three-hundred-year-old wizard," Krispos faltered, "how do we, how can we hope to beat him?"

"Your Majesty, I do not know. I was hoping you could tell me," Gnatios said. His voice held no irony. Krispos was the Avtokrator. Defeating foreign foes came with the job.

Iakovitzes wrote again. "If we do face an undying wizard who worships Skotos and hates everything Phos stands for, why hasn't he troubled Videssos long before now?"

That made Krispos doubt again. But Gnatios answered, "How do we know he has not? By the lord with the great and good mind, your Highness, the Empire has suffered its full share of disasters over the years. How many of them might Rhavas have caused or made worse? Our ignorance of the force behind the misfortune fails to prove the force did not exist."

"Holy sir, I think—I fear—you are right," Krispos said. Only a man— or whatever this Rhavas or Harvas was, after so long—who loved Skotos could have inflicted such brutal savagery on Imbros. And only a man who had studied sorcery for three centuries could have so baffled a clever, well-trained mage like Trokoundos. The pieces fit as neatly as those of a wooden puzzle, but Krispos cringed from the shape they made.

Gnatios said, "Now do with me as you will, Your Majesty. I know you have no reason to love me, nor, truth to tell, have I any to love you. But this tale needed telling for the Empire's sake, not for yours or mine."

"How peculiar," Iakovitzes wrote. "I thought him a man completely without integrity. Shows you can't rely on adverbs, I suppose."

"Er, yes." Krispos handed the tablet back to Iakovitzes. When Gnatios saw he would not be invited to read Iakovitzes' comment, one eyebrow arched. Krispos ignored it. He was thinking hard. At last he said, "Holy sir, this deserves a reward, as you well know."

"Being out of the monastery, even if but for a brief while, is reward in itself." Gnatios raised that eyebrow again. "How ever did you arrange for the most holy ecumenical patriarch of the Videssians"—Gnatios put irony in his voice with a scalpel, not a shovel—"to acquiesce in my release?"

"That's right, we both had to agree to it, didn't we?" Krispos grinned sheepishly. "As a matter of fact, holy sir, I forgot to ask him, and I gather an imperial summons for you was enough to overawe your abbot."

"Evidently so." Gnatios paused before continuing. "The most holy patriarch will not be pleased with you for having enlarged me so."

"That's all right. I haven't been pleased with him for some time." Only after the words were out of his mouth did Krispos wonder how impolitic it was for him to run down the incumbent patriarch to a former holder of the office.

Not even Gnatios' eyebrow stirred; Krispos admired that. Gnatios chose his words with evident care: "Exactly how great a reward did Your Majesty contemplate?"

Iakovitzes gobbled. Gnatios turned his way in surprise; Krispos, by now, was used to the noble's strange laugh. He felt like laughing himself. "So you want your old post back, do you, holy sir?"

"I suppose I should feel chagrin at being so obvious, but yes, Your Majesty, I do. To be frank"—Krispos wondered if Gnatios was ever frank—"the idea of that narrow zealot's possessing the patriarchal throne makes my blood boil."

"He loves you just as well," Krispos remarked.

"I'm aware of that. I respect his honesty and sincerity. Have you not found, though, Your Majesty, that an honest fanatic poses certain problems of his own?"

Krispos wondered how much Gnatios knew of Pyrrhos' summons to the Grand Courtroom, of the riots outside the High Temple. *Quite a lot,* he suspected. Gnatios might be confined to his monastic cell, but Krispos was willing to bet he heard every whisper in the city.

"Holy sir, there is some truth in what you say," he admitted. He leaned forward, as if he were in the marketplace of Imbros—back in the days when Imbros' marketplace held life—haggling over the price of a shoat. "How can I hope to trust you, though, after you've betrayed me not once but twice?"

"Always an interesting question." Gnatios sighed, spreading his hands in front of him. "Your Majesty, I have no good answer for it. I will say that I would be a better patriarch than the one you have now."

"For as long as you take to decide someone else would make a better Emperor than the one you have now."

Gnatios bowed his head. "An argument I cannot counter."

"Here is what I will do, holy sir: from now on, you may come and go as you will, subject to the wishes of your abbot. I daresay you'll need something in writing." Krispos called for pen and parchment, wrote rapidly, signed and sealed the document, and handed it to Gnatios. "I hope you'll overlook faults of style and grammar."

"Your Majesty, for this document I would overlook a great deal," Gnatios said. In one sentence, that summed up the difference between him and Pyrrhos. Pyrrhos never overlooked anything for any reason.

"If you find anything more in your histories, be sure to let me know at once," Krispos said.

Gnatios understood the audience was over. He prostrated himself, rose, and started for the door. Barsymes met him there. The vestiarios asked, "Shall the Halogai accompany the holy sir back to his monastery?"

"No, let him go back by himself," Krispos said. He succeeded in surprising his chamberlain, no easy feat. With a bow of acquiescence and an expression that spoke volumes, Barsymes led Gnatios toward the door of the imperial residence.

Krispos listened to the two sets of footsteps fading down the hall. He turned to Iakovitzes. "Well, what now?"

"Do you mean, what now as in giving Gnatios the High Temple back, or what now as in Harvas?" Iakovitzes wrote.

"I don't know," Krispos said, "and by the good god, I never expected the two questions to be wrapped up with each other." He sighed. "Let's talk about the patriarch first. Pyrrhos must go." In the two weeks since Krispos went up into the imperial niche at the High Temple, two more fights had broken out there—both of them, fortunately, small.

Iakovitzes scribbled. "Aye, my dear cousin's not the most yielding sort, is he? If you do want Gnatios back, maybe you can keep him in line by threatening to feed him to the Halogai the first time the word *treason* so much as tiptoes across the back of his twisty little mind."

"Something to that." Krispos remembered how Gnatios had cringed from a guardsman's axe the night he seized the Empire. He looked down at the tablet in his lap, then admiringly over to Iakovitzes. "Do you know, I hear your voice whenever I read what you write. Your words on wax or parchment capture the very tone of your speech. Whenever I try to set thoughts down, they always seem so stiff and formal. How do you do it?"

"Genius," Iakovitzes wrote. Krispos made as if to break the tablet over his head. The noble reclaimed it, then wrote a good deal more. He handed it to Krispos. "If you must have a long answer, for one thing, I came to writing earlier in life than you and have used it a good deal longer. For another, this *is* my voice now. Shall I be silent merely because I can no longer utter the more or less articulate croaks that most men use for speech?"

"I see the answer is no," Krispos said, thinking that Iakovitzes was about as unyielding as his cousin Pyrrhos. Refusing to yield to adversity struck him as more admirable than refusing to yield to common sense. The thought of Iakovitzes' adversity led to the one who had caused it. "Now, what of Harvas?"

Bright fear widened Iakovitzes' eyes, then left them as he visibly took a grip on himself. He bent over the tablet, used the blunt end of his stylus to smooth down the wax and give himself room to write. At last he passed Krispos his words. "Fight him as best we can. What else is there? Now that we have some notion of what he is, perhaps the wizards will better be able to arm themselves against him."

Krispos thumped himself on the forehead with the heel of his hand. "By the lord with the great and good mind, I haven't any mind at all. Gnatios has to tell his tale to Trokoundos before the day is through." He shouted for Barsymes again. The vestiarios transcribed his note and took it to a courier for delivery to Trokoundos.

That accomplished, Krispos leaned back on the couch. He had the battered feeling of a man to whom too much had happened too fast. If Harvas or Rhavas or whatever his proper name was had been perfecting his dark sorcery over half a dozen men's lives, no wonder he'd overcome a mere mortal like Trokoundos.

"To the ice with Harvas or Rhavas or whatever his proper name is," he muttered.

"What about Pyrrhos?" Iakovitzes wrote.

"You like to poke people with pointy sticks, just to see them jump," Krispos said. Iakovitzes' look of shocked indignation might have convinced someone who hadn't met him more than half a minute before. Krispos went on, "I don't wish the ice for Pyrrhos. I just wish he'd go back to his monastery and keep quiet. I'm not even likely to get that, worse luck. He won't bend, the stiff-necked old—"

Krispos stopped. His mouth hung open. His eyes went wide. "What are you gawping at?" Iakovitzes wrote. "It had better be Phos' holy light, to account for that idiotic expression you're wearing."

"It's the next best thing," Krispos assured him. He raised his voice: "Barsymes! Are you still there? Ah, good. I want you to draft me a note to the most holy patriarch Pyrrhos. Here's what you need to say—"

Barsymes stuck his head into the audience chamber. "The most holy patriarch Pyrrhos is here to see you, Your Majesty."

"Good. He should be done to a turn by now." Krispos had put off four days of increasingly urgent requests from the patriarch for an audience. He turned to Iakovitzes, Mammianos, and Rhisoulphos. "Excellent and eminent sirs, I ask you to bear careful witness to what takes place here today, so that you may take oath on it at need."

The three nobles nodded, formally and solemnly. Mammianos said, "This had better work."

"The beauty of it is, I'm no worse off if it doesn't," Krispos answered. "Now to business. I hear Pyrrhos coming."

The patriarch prostrated himself with his usual punctiliousness. He glanced at the three high-ranking men who sat to Krispos' left, but only for a moment. His eyes sparked as he swung them back to Krispos. "Your Majesty, I must vehemently protest this recent decision of yours." He drew out the note Krispos had sent him.

"Oh? Why is that, most holy sir?"

Pyrrhos' jaw set. He knew when he was being toyed with. With luck, he did not know why. He ground out, "Because, Your Majesty, you have restored to the monk Gnatios—the treacherous, wicked monk Gnatios—as much liberty as is enjoyed by the other brethren of the monastery dedicated to the sacred memory of the holy Skirios. Moreover, you have done so without consulting me." Plainer than words, his face said what he would have answered had Krispos consulted him.

"The monk Gnatios did a great service for me and for the Empire," Krispos said. "Because of that, I've decided to overlook his past failings."

"I haven't," Pyrrhos said. "This interference in the internal affairs of the temples is unwarranted and intolerable."

"In this special case, I judged not. And let me remind you that the Avtokrator is Avtokrator over all the Empire, cities and farms and temples alike. Most holy sir, I have the right if I choose to use it, and I choose to use it here."

"Intolerable," Pyrrhos repeated. He drew himself up. "Your Majesty, if you persist in you pernicious course, I have no choice but to submit to you my resignation in protest thereof."

Off to Krispos' left, someone sighed softly. He thought it was Rhisoulphos. It was all the applause he would ever get, but it was more than enough. "I'm sorry to hear that from you, most holy sir," he said to Pyrrhos. Just by a hair's breath, the patriarch began to relax. But Krispos was not finished. "I accept your resignation. These gentlemen will attest you offered it of your own free will, with no coercion whatsoever."

Iakovitzes, Mammianos, and Rhisoulphos nodded, formally and solemnly.

"You—planned this," Pyrrhos said in a ghastly voice. He saw everything, too late.

"I did not urge you to resign," Krispos pointed out. "You did it yourself. Now that you have done it, Barsymes will prepare a document for you to sign."

"And if I refuse to set my signature upon it?"

"Then you have resigned even so. As I said, holy sir"—Pyrrhos scowled at the abrupt devaluation of his title—"you resigned of your own accord, in front of witnesses. That may be smoothest all around. I would have removed you if you insisted on staying on—you promised to practice theological economy and tolerate what you could, but none of your sermons has shown even one drop of tolerance."

Pyrrhos said, "I see everything now. You will replace me with that panderer to evil, Gnatios. Without your knowing it, the dark god has taken hold of your heart."

Krispos leaned forward and spat on the floor. "That to the dark god! Look at your cousin here, holy sir. Remember what Harvas Black-Robe did to him. Would he fall into any trap Skotos might lay?"

"Were it baited with a pretty boy, he might," Pyrrhos said.

Iakovitzes used a two-fingered gesture common on the streets of Videssos the city. Pyrrhos gasped. Krispos wondered when that gesture had last been aimed at a patriarch—no, an ex-patriarch, he amended. Iakovitzes wrote furiously and passed his tablet to Rhisoulphos. Rhisoulphos read it: " 'Cousin, the only bait you need is the hope of tormenting everyone who disagrees with you. Are you sure you have not swallowed it?' "

"I know I believe the truth; thus anyone who holds otherwise embraces falsehood," Pyrrhos said, "I see now that that includes those here. Majesty, you may ban me from preaching in the High Temple, but I shall take my message to the streets of the city—"

Now Krispos knew Pyrrhos was no intriguer. A man wiser in the ways of stirring up strife would never have warned what he planned to do. Krispos said, "If what you believe is the truth, holy sir, and if I have fallen into evil, how do you explain the vision that bade you help me like a son?"

Pyrrhos opened his mouth, then closed it again. Rhisoulphos leaned over to whisper to Krispos, "If nothing else, Your Majesty, you've confused him."

Grateful even for so much, Krispos nodded. He told Pyrrhos, "Holy sir, I'm going to give you an honor guard of Halogai to escort you to the monastery of the holy Skirios. If you do decide to yell something foolish to the people in the street, they'll do what they have to, to keep you quiet." Pyrrhos could not terrify the heathen northerners with threats of Skotos' ice.

He could not be intimidated, either. "Let them do as they will."

"The monastery of the holy Skirios, eh?" Mammianos said. One eyelid rose, then fell. "I'm sure the holy sir and Gnatios will have a good deal to say to each other."

Having planted his barb, the fat general leaned back to enjoy it. Pyrrhos did not disappoint him. The cleric's glare was as cold and withering as the fiercest of ice storms. Mammianos affected not to notice it. He went on, "Of course, Gnatios will have the blue boots back soon enough."

"The good god shall judge between us in the world to come," Pyrrhos said. "I rest content with that." He turned to Krispos. "Phos shall judge you, as well, Your Majesty."

"I know," Krispos answered. "Unlike you, holy sir, I'm far from sure of my answers. I do the best I can, even so."

Pyrrhos surprised him by bowing. "So the good god would expect of you. May your judgment be better in other instances than it is with me. Now summon your northerners, if you feel you must. Wherever you send me, I shall continue to praise Phos' holy name." He sketched the sun-circle over his heart.

In an abstract way, Krispos respected Pyrrhos' sincere piety. He did not let that respect blind him. When Pyrrhos departed from the imperial residence, he did so under guard. Iakovitzes nodded approval. "Just because someone sounds humble is no sure reason to trust him," he wrote.

"From what I've seen at the throne, there's no sure reason to trust anyone."

To his secret dismay, both Rhisoulphos and Mammianos nodded at that. Iakovitzes wrote, "You're learning." Krispos supposed he was, but did not care for the lessons his office taught him.

For the first time since Harvas' magic turned back the imperial army on the borders of Kubrat, Trokoundos seemed something more than gloomy. "I hope you intend to reward Gnatios for what he ferreted out," he told Krispos. "Without it, we'd still be stumbling around like so many blind men."

"I have a reward in mind, yes," Krispos said; at that moment, a synod of prelates and abbots was contemplating Gnatios' name for the patriarchate once more, along with those of two other men whom the assembled clerics knew they had better ignore. "Now that you know more of Harvas, will he be easier to defeat?"

"Knowing a bear has teeth, Your Majesty, doesn't take those teeth away," Trokoundos said. At Krispos' disappointed look, he went on, "Still, since we know where he grew them, perhaps we can do something more about them. Perhaps."

"Such as?" Krispos asked eagerly.

"It's a fair guess, Majesty, that if he follows Skotos and draws his power from the dark god, his spells will invert the usages with which we're familiar. That may make them easier to meet than if he, say, truly clove to the Haloga gods or the demons and spirits the steppe nomads revere. Magic from the nomads or the northerners can come at you from any direction, if you know what I mean."

"I think so," Krispos said. "But if their mages or shamans or what have you can invoke their gods and demons and have magic work, does that make those gods and demons as true as Phos and Skotos?"

Trokoundos tugged thoughtfully at his ear. "Majesty, I think that's a question better suited to the patriarch's wisdom, or that of an ecumenical synod, than to one who aspires to nothing more than competent wizardry."

"As you wish. In any case, it takes us off the track. You know the direction from which Harvas' spells will come, you say?"

"So I believe, Your Majesty. This aids us to a point, but only to a point. Harvas' strength and skill must still be overcome. The one, I have already seen, is formidable. As for the other, three centuries ago it sufficed to free him from a warded cell. He can only have refined it in all the years since. That he remains alive to torment us proves he has refined it."

"What shall we do, then?" Krispos asked. He'd hoped having a handle on Harvas would give the mages of Videssos the means to defeat him with minimal risk to themselves or to the Empire. But he'd long since found that things in the real world had a way of being less simple and less easy than in storytellers' tales. This looked like another lesson from that school.

Trokoundos' words confirmed his own thoughts. "The best we can, Your Majesty, and pray to the lord with the great and good mind that it be enough."

BAD WEATHER SETTLED IN NOT LONG BEFORE MIDWINTER'S DAY. Blizzard after blizzard roared into Videssos the city from the northwest, off the Videssian Sea. On Midwinter's Day itself, the snow blew so hard and quick that even Krispos, with the best seat in the Amphitheater, made out little of the skits performed on the track before him. The people in the upper reaches of the huge oval stadium could have discerned only drifting white.

The final troupe of mimes changed its act at the last minute. They came out carrying canes and tapped their way through their routine, as if they'd all suddenly been stricken blind. On the spine of the Amphitheater, Krispos laughed loudly. So did many in his entourage, and in the first few rows of seats around the track. Everyone else must have wondered what was funny—which was just the point the mimes were making. Krispos laughed even more when he worked that out.

On the way back to the palaces after the show in the Amphitheater was done, he leaped over a bonfire to burn away misfortune for the coming year. That fire was but one of many that blazed each Midwinter's Day. This year, though, the good-luck bonfires brought misfortune with them. Whipped by winter gales, two got out of control and ignited nearby buildings.

Now Krispos saw through swirling snow the smudges of smoke he'd feared during the religious riots Pyrrhos had caused. The snow did little to slow the flames. Firefighting teams dashed through the city with hand pumps to shoot water from fountains and ponds, with axes and sledgehammers to knock down homes and shops to build firebreaks. Krispos had no great hope for them. When fire got loose, it usually pleased itself, not any man.

The teams amazed him. They succeeded in stopping one of the fires before it had eaten more than a block of buildings. The other blaze, by luck, had started near the city wall. It burned what it could, then came to the open space inside the barrier and died for lack of fuel.

Krispos presented a pound of gold to the head of the team that beat the first fire, a middle-aged fellow with a fine head of silver hair and a matter-of-fact competence that suggested years as a soldier. Nobles and logothetes in the Grand Courtroom applauded the man, whose name was Thokyodes.

"Along with this reward from the grateful state," Krispos said, "I also give you ten goldpieces from my private purse."

More applause rose. Thokyodes clenched his right fist over his heart in salute—he *was* a veteran, then. "Thank you, Your Majesty," he said, pleased but far from obsequious.

"Maybe you'll use one of those ten on a potion to make your eyebrows grow back faster," Krispos said, soft enough that only he and the team leader heard.

Not a bit put out, Thokyodes laughed and ran the palm of his hand across his forehead. "Aye, I do look strange without 'em, don't I? They got singed right off me." He made no effort to keep his voice down. "Fighting fires is just like fighting any other foe. The closer you get, the better you do."

"You did the city a great service," Krispos said.

"Couldn't've done it without my crew. By your leave, Your Majesty, I'll share this with all of them." Thokyodes held up the sack of goldpieces.

"It's your money now, to do with as you please," Krispos said. The applause that rang out this time was unrehearsed, sincere, and startled. Few of the courtiers, men who had far more than this fireman, would have been as generous, and they knew it. Krispos wondered if he would have matched the man had fate led him to an ordinary job instead of the throne. He hoped so, but admitted to himself that he was not sure.

"I think you would have," Dara said when he wondered again later in the day, this time aloud. "This I'll tell you—Harvas wouldn't."

"Harvas? Harvas would have stood next to the fire with his cheeks puffed out, to blow it along." Krispos smiled at his conceit. A moment later the smile blew out. He sketched Phos' sun-circle. "By the good god, how do I know his magic didn't help the blazes spread?"

"You don't, but if you start seeing him under our bed whenever anything goes wrong, you'll have your head down there all the time, because we don't need Harvas to know misfortune."

"That's true," Krispos said. "You have good sense." His smile came back, this time full of gratitude. Harvas was quite bad enough without a fearful imagination making him worse.

Dara said, "I do try. It's nice that you notice. I remember when—" She stopped without telling Krispos what she remembered when. It had to do with Anthimos, then. Krispos did not blame her for steering away from that time; it had not been happy for her. But that meant several years of her life, the ones before Krispos became vestiarios, were almost blank to him, which occasionally led to awkward pauses like this one.

He wondered if every second husband and second wife endured them. *Probably,* he thought. It would have been more awkward yet had her marriage to Anthimos been a good one. A lot more awkward, he realized with an inward chuckle, because then she would not have told him Anthimos intended to kill him. "Can't get much more awkward than that," he muttered under his breath.

"Than what?" Dara asked.

"Never mind."

WHENEVER FAT LONGINOS BURST IN ON HIM ON THE DEAD RUN, Krispos braced for trouble. The chamberlain, to his disappointment, did not disappoint him. "Majesty," Longinos gasped, wiping his brow with a silken kerchief—only a fat eunuch could have been sweaty after so trivial an exertion; it was freezing outside and not a great deal warmer inside the imperial residence. "Majesty, the most holy patriarch Pyrrhos—I'm sorry, Your Majesty, I mean the monk Pyrrhos—is preaching against you in the street."

"*Is* he, by the good god?" Krispos sprang up from his desk so quickly that a couple of tax registers fluttered to the floor. He let them lie there. So Pyrrhos' indignation at being removed from the patriarchal throne really had overcome his longtime loyalty, had it? "What's he saying?"

"He's spewing forth a great vomit of scandal, Your Majesty, over, ah, over your, ah, your relationship with her Majesty the Empress Dara before you, ah, rose to the imperial dignity." Longinos sounded indignant for his master's sake, though he had known Krispos and Dara were lovers long before they were man and wife.

"*Is* he?" Krispos said again. "He'll spew forth his life's blood before I'm through with him."

Longinos' eyes went large with dismay. "Oh, no, Your Majesty. To cut down one but lately so high in the temples, one still with many backers who—begging your pardon, Your Majesty—deem him more holy than the present wearer of the blue boots . . . Your Majesty, it would mean more blood than Pyrrhos' alone. It would mean riots."

He'd found the word he needed to stop Krispos in his tracks. Dividing the city—dividing the Empire—against itself was the one thing Krispos could not afford. "But," he said, as if arguing with himself, "I can't afford to let Pyrrhos defame me, either. If that nonsense goes on for long, it'll bring some would-be usurper out of the woodwork, sure as sure."

"Indeed, Your Majesty," Longinos said. "Were you ten years on the throne rather than two—not even two—you might let him rant, confident he would be ignored. As it is—"

"Aye. As it is, people will listen to him. They'll take him seriously, too, thanks to his piety." Krispos snorted. "As if anyone could take Pyrrhos any way but seriously. I've hardly seen him smile in all the years I've known him, the somber old—" He stopped, laughing out loud. When he could speak again, he asked, "Where is Pyrrhos giving this harangue of his?"

"In the Forum of the Ox, Your Majesty," Longinos said.

"All right; he should be easy enough to find there. Now, esteemed sir, this is what I want you to do—" He spoke for several minutes, finishing. "Do you think you should have something in writing from me, to make sure my orders get carried out?"

"Yes, that would be best." Longinos looked half amused, half scandalized. Krispos wrote quickly and handed him the scrap of parchment. The eunuch read it over, shook his head, then visibly pulled himself together. "I shall have this delivered immediately, Your Majesty."

"See that you do," Krispos said. Longinos hurried away, calling for a courier. Krispos prided himself on not wasting time, so he reviewed another tax document before he ambled out to the entrance to the imperial residence. The Halogai there stood to stiff attention. "As you were, lads," he told them. "We're going for a walk."

"Where are your parasol-bearers, then, Majesty?" Geirrod asked.

"They'd just get in the way today," Krispos said. The Halogai stirred at that. A couple of them ran fingers down the edges of their axeblades to make sure the weapons were sharp. One must have found a tiny nick, for he took out a whetstone and went to work with it. When he checked again, the axe passed his test. He put away the stone.

"Where to, Majesty?" Geirrod said.

"The Forum of the Ox," Krispos answered lightly. "Seems the holy Pyrrhos isn't taking kindly to not being patriarch anymore. He's saying some rather rude things about me there."

The Halogai stirred again, this time in anticipation. "You want us to curb his tongue for him, eh?" said the one who had sharpened his axe. He examined his edge anew, as if to make certain it could bite through a holy man's neck.

But Krispos said, "No, no. I don't aim to harm the holy sir, just to shut him up."

"Better you should kill him," Geirrod said. "Then he'll not trouble you ever again." The rest of the guardsmen nodded.

Krispos wished he could view the world with the ferocious simplicity the Halogai used. In Videssos, though, few things were as simple as they seemed. Without answering Geirrod, Krispos strode down the stairs. The northerners came after him, surrounding him to hold potential assassins at bay.

The Forum of the Ox was a mile and half, perhaps two miles east down Middle Street from the palace quarter. Krispos walked briskly to keep warm. He was glad of his escort as he passed through the plaza of Palamas; as usual, the Halogai marched in a way that said they would trample anyone who did not get clear. Crowds melted before them, as if by magic.

He hurried down Middle Street. He wanted to catch Pyrrhos in the act of preaching against him; whatever punishment he might mete out after the fact, no matter how savage, would not have the effect he wanted. Making a martyr out of the prelate was the last thing he had in mind.

A few hundred yards past the government office building, Middle Street jogged to the south. The Forum of the Ox lay not far ahead. Krispos sped up till he was almost trotting. To have Pyrrhos get away from him now would be unbearably frustrating. He hoped again that his orders had gone through on time.

In ancient days, the Forum of the Ox had been Videssos the city's chief cattle market. It was still an important trading center for goods bulkier, more mundane, and less expensive than those sold in the plaza of Palamas: livestock, grain, cheap pottery, and olive oil. People here stared at Krispos' escort before they got out of the way. In the plaza of Palamas, close by the palaces, they were used to seeing the Avtokrator. He was a much less frequent visitor in this poorer part of the city.

A quick glance around the square showed him what he sought: a knot of men and women gathered around a man in a blue monk's robe. The monk—even across the square, Krispos recognized Pyrrhos' tall, thin frame and lean face—stood on a barrel or box or stone that raised him head and shoulders above his audience. Krispos pointed. "Over there." The Halogai nodded. They moved on Pyrrhos with the directness of a pack of wolves advancing on a wisent.

Pyrrhos was a trained orator. Long before he reached the rear edge of the crowd that listened to the cleric, Krispos could hear what he was saying. So could half the people in the Forum of the Ox. "He must have learned his corruption from the master he formerly served, for surely depravity was the name by which Anthimos was better known. Yet in his own way, Krispos outdid Anthimos in vice, first seducing the previous Avtokrator's wife, then using her against her husband to climb over his dead body to the throne. How will—how can—Phos bless our efforts with such a man inhabiting the palaces?"

Pyrrhos must have seen Krispos and his bodyguards approach, but he did not pause in his address. Krispos already knew he had courage. Pyrrhos also did not suddenly break off his speech to point out to his audience that the adulterous monster he had been denouncing was here. That, in his sandals, Krispos might have tried, if he truly aimed to overthrow someone. But Pyrrhos did not deviate from what he had decided to say: his mind was made up, which left no room in it for change.

Krispos folded his arms to listen. Pyrrhos continued his harangue as if the Avtokrator were not there. He paid even less attention to the squad of firemen who dashed into the Forum of the Ox. Others round the square glanced up in some alarm at the sight of the men armed with Haloga-style axes and with a hand pump carried by two men who were sweating even in the chill of winter. Especially after the close escape on Midwinter's Day, fire was a constant fear in the city.

But the fire team made straight for the crowd round the gesticulating monk. "Make way!" the fire captain shouted.

People tumbled away from the crew. "Where's the fire?" somebody yelled.

"Right here!" Thokyodes yelled back. "Leastways, I got orders to put out this incendiary here." He waved to his crew. One of them swung the pump handle up and down. The other turned his hose toward Pyrrhos.

Cold water from the hand pump's wooden tub gushed forth. The people nearest Pyrrhos stampeded away from him, cursing and spluttering as they went. Pyrrhos himself tried to speak on through his drenching, but started to sneeze whether he wanted to or not. The fire team kept hosing him down until the tub was empty. Then Thokyodes looked over to Krispos. "Shall we fill 'er up again, Your Majesty?"

Pyrrhos looked as if a little more would drown him. "No, that's fine, Thokyodes, thank you," Krispos said. "I think he's been cooled down very nicely."

"Cooled down—*ahhchoo!*—am I?" Pyrrhos shouted. Water dripped from his beard and from the end of his nose. "Nay, I've just—*ahhchoo!*—begun to speak the truth about our imperial adulterer. Now hear me, people of Videssos—"

"Go home and dry off, holy sir," someone called, not unkindly. "You'll take a flux on the lungs if you go on like this."

"Aye, your tale's as soggy as your robe anyhow," someone else said.

A woman added, "Save the fire in your belly to warm yourself."

"No, the crew just doused that fire," a man said. He chuckled at his own wit.

Pyrrhos had lived all his adult life in monasteries or attached to one temple or another. He was used to respect from the laity, not gibes—not even gibes kindly meant. But worse than those gibes was the laughter that sprang from so many throats at the spectacle of a furious, drenched, shivering holy man standing on his perch—it was an overturned box, Krispos saw—trying to keep on with his denunciation through teeth that chattered loud as the wooden finger cymbals Vaspurakaner dancers used to clack out their rhythm.

He might have stood up against being ignored: because they preached the virtues of a way of life more austere than most folk would willingly embrace, monks were often ignored. But laughter he could not endure. Glaring at the crowd in general and Krispos in particular, he awkwardly scrambled down from his box and stalked away. A fresh sneezing spasm robbed even his departure of dignity.

"Phos with you, drippy Pyrrhos!" a man with a loud voice yelled after him. New laughter rang out. Pyrrhos' back, already stiff, jerked as if someone had stuck a knife into him. "Drippy Pyrrhos, good old drippy Pyrrhos," the crowd sang. His departure turned to headlong retreat; by the time he reached the edge of the Forum of the Ox, he was all but running.

Geirrod turned to Krispos. "He'll love you no better for this, Majesty," the guardsman said. "Make a man out a fool and he'll reckon himself at feud with you no less than if you'd slashed him with sword."

"He's already at feud with me, and with everyone else who won't think and do just as he does," Krispos answered. "Now, though, the good god willing, people won't take him so seriously. The holy Pyrrhos—until lately, the most holy Pyrrhos—was someone whose notions you'd respect. But how much attention would you pay to good old drippy Pyrrhos?"

"Ahh, now I see it," Geirrod said slowly. "You've poisoned his word." He spoke in his own language to his fellow northerners. Their deep voices rose and fell; their eyes swung toward Krispos. Geirrod said, "Who but a Videssian would think to slay a man with laughter?" The other Halogai nodded solemnly.

A few feet away, Thokyodes gestured to his crew. The two men who had hauled the pump around now set it down with grunts of relief. The rest leaned on their fire axes, save for one who strolled off toward a fellow selling roasted chickpeas.

Thokyodes caught Krispos' eye. When Krispos did not look away, the fire captain came over to him. "Well, Your Majesty, I hope we put out some trouble for you there," he said. Thokyodes was Videssian and, by his accent, a city man. He required no explanations to understand what Krispos had planned.

"I think you did," Krispos said. "You'll be rewarded for it, too."

"I thank you," Thokyodes said briskly. He did not try to protest his own unworthiness. Business was business.

Krispos raised his voice and called out, "All right, folks, the show is over for today." The crowd that had been listening to Pyrrhos rapidly melted away. A few people averted their faces as they went by Krispos, as if they did not want him to know they had been anywhere near someone who preached against him. More, though, went off chattering happily; as far as they were concerned, Pyrrhos' harangue and Krispos' response to it might have been arranged only for their amusement. City folk were like that, Krispos thought with a touch of exasperation.

By the time he and the Halogai got back to the palaces, winter's short day was almost done. Longinos looked ready to burst from curiosity when Krispos came into the imperial residence. "Your Majesty, surely you didn't—"

"—treat Pyrrhos as if he were a fire that needed putting out?" Krispos broke in. "Oh, but I did, esteemed sir." He explained how Thokyodes and his crew had hosed down the cleric, finishing, "Most of the people who saw it got a good laugh out of it."

Like the fire captain, Longinos caught on in a hurry. "Hard to take a laughingstock seriously, eh, Your Majesty?"

"Just so, esteemed sir. I remembered how much trouble Petronas had, trying to get rid of Skombros when he was vestiarios. No matter how plainly he showed Anthimos that Skombros was a scoundrel, Anthimos stood by him. But when he arranged to have Skombros laughed at, he was out of the palaces within a week."

"Ah, yes, Skombros," Longinos murmured. By his voice, he might have forgotten that the eunuch who was once Petronas' rival as the chief power behind Anthimos' throne had ever existed. Krispos was undeceived. Longinos went on, "The good god willing, Your Majesty, Pyrrhos will have been dealt with as, ah, thoroughly as Skombros was."

Krispos sketched the sun-sign. "May it be so."

IRON-SHOD HOOVES CLATTERED ON COBBLESTONES. CHAIN MAIL jingled. "Eyes to the right!" an officer bawled. As the regiment rode past the reviewing stand, the lead troopers looked over to Krispos and saluted.

He put his fist over his heart in return. The crowd that lined both sides of Middle Street cheered. The soldiers, most of them in Videssos the city for the first time, grinned at the cheers and went back to gaping at the wonders of the imperial capital. Awed expressions aside, the young men from the westlands' central plateau looked like solid troops, well mounted and in good spirits despite the long, grueling slog that had at last brought them here to the city.

A raindrop splashed off Krispos' cheek, then another and another. The soldiers riding by reached up to tug the hoods of their surcoats lower on their foreheads. Some spectators opened umbrellas; other retreated under the colonnades that flanked the thoroughfare.

When the last horse had trotted past, Krispos stepped down from the reviewing stand with a sigh of relief. By then he was just about as wet as Pyrrhos had been after Thokyodes turned the pump on him. He was glad to mount Progress and head back to the imperial residence. A brisk toweling, a bowl of hot mutton stew, and a fresh robe worked wonders for his attitude. After all, he thought, it had been rain, not snow. Winter's grip would ease soon. When the roads dried, the army he was assembling here would move north against Harvas. He hoped to have seventy thousand men under arms. Surely the Empire's full weight, backed by the cleverest mages of the Sorcerers' Collegium, could overcome one wicked wizard who somehow refused to die.

Barsymes carried away the silver bowl that had held stew. He paused in the doorway. "Majesty, do I need to remind you that the envoy of the King of Kings of Makuran has arranged for an audience with you this afternoon?"

"I remember," Krispos said, not altogether happily. He wished he could forget about Videssos' great western neighbor, the more so as he was concentrating so much of his army against the Empire's northern foe. He had already discovered that wishes availed little in statecraft.

Chihor-Vshnasp, the Makuraner envoy, was an elegant man of middle years, with a long rectangular face, deep hollows under his cheekbones, and large, soulful brown eyes that looked perfectly candid. Looks, Krispos knew, were not to be trusted. When Chihor-Vshnasp performed the proskynesis before him, the ambassador's headgear, a brimless gray felt hat that looked like nothing so much as a bucket, fell from his head and rolled a few feet away. "That happens every time you come to see me," Krispos observed.

"So it does, Your Majesty. A small indignity of no import between friends." Chihor-Vshnasp retrieved the errant hat and replaced it on his head. His Videssian was excellent; only a trace of his native hiss said he was not an educated native of Videssos the city. He went on, "I bring you the greetings of his puissant Majesty Nakhorgan, King of Kings, pious, beneficent, to whom the God and his Prophets Four have granted many years and wide domains."

"I am always glad to have the greetings of his puissant Majesty," Krispos said. "In your next dispatch to Mashiz, please send him mine."

Chihor-Vshnasp bowed in his seat. "He will be honored to receive them. He also wishes me to convey to you his hope for your success against the vicious barbarians who assail your northern frontier. Makuran has suffered inroads from such savages; his puissant Majesty knows what Videssos is enduring now and sympathizes with your pain."

"His puissant Majesty is very kind." Krispos thought he had caught the drift of the conversation. He hoped he was wrong.

Unfortunately, he was right. Chihor-Vshnasp continued, "I add my hopes to his: may your war be successful. Since you have invested so much of Videssos' strength in it, no doubt you will vanquish your foes. Without peace with Makuran, there can be no doubt that some of your armies would have remained in the westlands. Indeed, your decision to commit them speaks well of your confidence in the enduring amity between our two great empires."

Now Krispos knew what was coming. The only question was how expensive it would prove. "Should I think otherwise?" he asked.

"Not all leaders of Videssos have felt as you do," Chihor-Vshnasp reminded him. "Only yesterday, it seems, the Sevastokrator Petronas launched an unprovoked assault against Makuran."

"I opposed that war," Krispos said.

"I remember, and I honor you for it. Nonetheless, you must be aware of what would happen if his puissant Majesty Nakhorgan, King of Kings, chose this summer to avenge himself for the insult offered to Makuran. With your forces directed away from your western border, our brave horsemen would charge ahead, sweeping all before them."

Krispos wanted to bite his lip. He held his face still instead. "You're right, of course," he said. Chihor-Vshnasp's iron-gray eyebrows arched. That was not how the game was played. Krispos went on, "If his puissant Majesty really intended to invade Videssos, you wouldn't come here to warn me. How much does he want for being talked out of it?"

Those eyebrows rose again; the envoy was an artist with them. He said, "It is an intolerable affront to the God and his Prophets Four that Makuran should remain bereft of the valley that contains the great cities of Hanzith and Artaz."

Between them, the two little Vaspurakaner town might have held half as many people as, say, Opsikion. "Makuran may have them back." Krispos said, abandoning with a sentence the valley that was the sole fruit of Petronas' war of three years before, the war Petronas had thought would take him all the way to Mashiz.

"Your Majesty is gracious and generous," Chihor-Vshnasp said with a small smile. "With such goodwill, all difficulties between nations may yet fall by the wayside, and peace and harmony prevail. Yet his puissant Majesty the King of Kings Nakhorgan remains aggrieved that you love other sovereigns more than him."

"How can you say such a thing?" Krispos cried, the picture of shock and dismay. "No ruler could be dearer to my heart than your master."

Chihor-Vshnasp sadly shook his head. "Would that his puissant Majesty could believe you! Yet he has seen you fling great sums of gold to this wretch known as Harvas Black-Robe, who rewarded you with nothing but treachery. And his puissant Majesty, the good and true friend of Videssos, has not known so much as a copper of your great bounty."

"How many coppers would satisfy him?" Krispos asked dryly.

"You paid Harvas a hundred pounds of gold, not so? Surely a good and true friend is worth three times as much as a lying barbarian who takes· your money and then does as he would have had you never paid him. Indeed, Your Majesty, I reckon that a bargain."

"A bargain?" Krispos clapped a dramatic hand to his forehead. "I reckon that an outrage. His puissant Majesty is looking to suck Videssos' blood and asks us to give him a solid gold straw with which to drink."

The dickering went on for several days. Krispos knew he would have to pay Nakhorgan more than he had given Harvas; the King of Kings' honor demanded it. But paying Nakhorgan a lot more than he had given Harvas went against Krispos' grain. For his part, Chihor-Vshnasp haggled more like a rug merchant than a Makuraner grandee.

At last they settled on a hundred fifty pounds of gold: 10,800 gold-pieces. "Excellent, Your Majesty," Chihor-Vshnasp said when they reached agreement.

Krispos did not think it was excellent; he'd hoped to get away with something closer to a hundred twenty-five pounds. But Chihor-Vshnasp knew too well how badly he needed peace with Makuran. He said, "His puissant Majesty has an able servant in you."

"You give me credit beyond my worth," Chihor-Vshnasp said, but his voice had a purr in it, like a stroked cat's.

"No indeed," Krispos said. "I will order the gold sent out today."

"And I shall inform his puissant Majesty that it has begun its journey to him." Looking as pleased with himself as if the hundred fifty pounds of gold were going to him instead of his master, Chihor-Vshnasp made his elaborate farewells and departed.

"Barsymes!" Krispos called.

The vestiarios appeared in the doorway, prompt and punctual as usual. "How may I help you, Your Majesty?"

"What in Skotos' cursed name does puissant mean?"

P HOSTIS TODDLED OUT OF THE IMPERIAL RESIDENCE ON UN-certain legs. He blinked at the bright spring sunshine, then decided he liked it and smiled. One of the Halogai grinned and pointed. "The little Avtokrator, he has teeth!"

"Half a dozen of them," Krispos agreed. "Another one's on the way, too, so he'll chew your greaves off if you let him get near you."

The guardsmen drew back in mock fright, laughing all the while. Phostis charged toward the stairs. He'd only been able to walk without holding on to something for about a week, but he had the hang of it. Going down stairs was something else again. Phostis' plan was to walk blithely off the first one he came to, just to see what would happen. Krispos caught him before he found out.

Far from feeling rescued, Phostis squirmed and kicked and squawked in Krispos' arms. "Aren't you the ungrateful one?" Krispos said as he carried the toddler to the bottom of the stairway. "Would you rather I'd let you smash your silly head?"

By all indications, Phostis would have preferred exactly that. When Krispos put him down at the base of the stairs, he refused to stay there. Instead, he started to climb back toward the top. He had to crawl to do it; the risers were too tall for him to raise his little legs from one to the next. Krispos followed close behind, in case ascent turned to sudden and unplanned descent. Phostis reached the top unscathed—then spun around and tried to jump down. Krispos caught him again.

In the entranceway to the residence, someone clapped. Krispos looked up and saw Dara. "Bravely done, Krispos," she called, mischief in her voice. "You've saved the heir to the state." The Halogai bowed as she came out into the sunshine. Now no robe, no matter how flowing, could conceal her swelling abdomen.

Krispos looked down at Phostis. "The heir to the state won't live to inherit it unless somebody keeps an eye on him every minute of the day and night." As soon as the words were out of his mouth, he wondered if Dara would take them the wrong way; he'd lived in Videssos the city too long to be unaware that plotting, even ahead of the races in the Amphitheater, was its favorite sport.

She only smiled and said, "Babies are like that." She turned toward the sun and closed her eyes. "During the winter, you think it will never get warm and dry again. I'd like to be a lizard and just stand here and bask." But after she'd basked for a minute or two, her smile faded. "I always used to wish winter would end as soon as it could. Now I half want it to last longer—the good weather means you'll be going out on campaign, doesn't it?"

"You know it does," Krispos said. "Unless we get another rainstorm, the roads should be dry enough to travel by the end of the week."

Dara nodded. "I know. Will you be angry if I tell you I'm worried?"

"No," he answered after some thought. "I'm worried, too." He looked north and east. He couldn't see much, not with the cherry trees that surrounded the imperial residence in such riotous pink bloom, but he knew Harvas was there waiting for him. The knowledge was anything but reassuring.

"I wish you could stay here behind the safety of the city's walls," Dara said.

He remembered his awe on the day he first came to Videssos the city and saw its massive double ring of fortifications. Surely even Harvas could find no way to overthrow them. Then he remembered other things as well: Develtos, Imbros, and Trokoundos' warning that he should meet Harvas as far from the city as he could. Trokoundos had a way of knowing what he was talking about.

"I don't think there's safety anywhere, not while Harvas is on the loose," he said slowly. After a moment, Dara nodded again. He saw how much it cost her.

Phostis wiggled in his arms. He set the boy down. A Haloga took out his dagger, undid the sheath from his belt, and tossed it near Phostis. Gold inlays ornamented the sheath. Their glitter drew Phostis, who picked it up and started chewing on it.

"It's brass and leather," Krispos told him. "You won't like it." A moment later Phostis made a ghastly face and took the sheath out of his mouth. A moment after that, he started gnawing on it again.

From behind Dara, Barsymes said, "Here are some proper toys." He rolled a little wooden wagon to Phostis. Inside it were two cleverly carved horses. Phostis picked them up, then threw them aside. He raised the wagon to his mouth and began to chew on a wheel.

"Stick him by a river, he'll cut down trees like a beaver," a Haloga said. Everyone laughed except Barsymes, who let out an indignant sniff.

Krispos watched Phostis playing in the sunshine. He suddenly bent down to run a hand through the little boy's thick black hair. He saw Dara's eyes widen with surprise; he seldom showed Phostis physical affection. But he knew beyond any possible doubt that, even if Phostis happened to be Anthimos' son rather than his own, he would far, far sooner, see him ruling the Empire of Videssos than Harvas Black-Robe.

Chapter IX

THE IMPERIAL ARMY WAS LIKE A CITY ON THE MARCH. AS FAR as Krispos could see in any direction were horses and helmets and spearpoints and wagons. They overflowed the road and moved northward on either side. Yet even in the midst of so many armed men, Krispos did not feel altogether secure. He had gone north with an army before and come back defeated.

"What are our chances, Trokoundos?" he asked, anxious to be reassured.

The wizard's lips twitched; Krispos had asked the same question less than an hour before. As he had before, Trokoundos answered: "Were no magic to be used by either side, Majesty. I could hope to ascertain that for you. As it is, spells yet to be cast befog any magic I might use. I assure you, though, Harvas enters this campaign as blind as we do."

Krispos wondered how true that was. Harvas might have no sorcerous foretelling, but he'd lived as long as five or six ordinary men. On how much of that vast experience could he draw, to scent what his foes would do next?

"Will we have enough mages to hold him in check?"

"There, Your Majesty, I can be less certain," Trokoundos said. "By the lord with the great and good mind, though, we now have a better notion of how to try to cope with him, thanks to the researches of Gnatios."

"Thanks to Gnatios," Krispos repeated, not altogether happily. Now instead of a patriarch who backed him absolutely but thought nothing of setting the whole Empire ablaze for the sake of perfect orthodoxy, he had once more a patriarch who was theologically moderate but not to be trusted out of sight—or in it, for that matter. He hoped the trade would prove worthwhile.

Trokoundos continued, "When I faced Harvas last year, I took him for a barbarian wizard, puissant but—why are you laughing, Your Majesty?"

"Never mind," Krispos said, laughing still. "Go on, please."

"Ahem. Well, as I say, I reckoned Harvas Black-Robe to be powerful but unschooled. Now I know this is not the case—just the reverse obtains, in fact. Having now, thanks to Gnatios, a better notion of the sort of magic he employs, and having also with me more—and more potent—colleagues, I do possess some hope that we shall be able to defend against his onslaughts."

All the finest mages of the Sorcerers' Collegium rode with the army. If Trokoundos could but hope to withstand Harvas by their combined efforts, that in itself spoke volumes about the evil wizard's strength. They were not volumes Krispos cared to read. He said, "Can we sorcerously strike back at the northerners who follow Harvas?"

"Your Majesty, we will try," Trokoundos said. "The good god willing, we will distract Harvas from the magics he might otherwise hurl at us. Past that, I have no great hope. Because battle so inflames men's passions, magic more readily slips aside from them then and is more easily countered. That is why battle magic succeeds so seldom . . . save Harvas'." Krispos wished the wizard had not tacked on that codicil.

Rhisoulphos rode by at a fast trot. "Why aren't you with your regiment?" Krispos called.

His father-in-law reined in and looked around, as if wondering who presumed to address him with such familiarity. His face cleared when he saw Krispos. "Greetings, Your Majesty," he said, saluting. "I just gave a courier a note to a friend in the city, and now I am indeed returning to my men. By your leave . . ." He waited for Krispos' nod, then dug his heels into his horse's flanks and urged the animal on again.

Krispos followed him with his eyes. Rhisoulphos did not look back. He rode as if in a competition of horsemanship, without a single wasted motion. "He's so smooth," Krispos said, as much to himself as to Trokoundos. "He rides smoothly, he talks smoothly, he has smooth good looks and smooth good sense."

"But you don't like him," Trokoundos said. It was not a question.

"No, I don't. I want to. I ought to. He's Dara's father, after all. But with so much smoothness on the top of him, who can be sure what's underneath? Petronas guessed wrong and paid for it, too."

"Set next to Harvas—"

"Every other worry is a small one. I know. But I have to keep an eye on the small things, too, for fear they'll grow while my back was turned. I wonder who he was writing to. You know, Trokoundos, what I really need is a spell that would give me eyes all around my head and let me stay awake day and night both. Then I'd sleep better—except I wouldn't sleep, would I?" Krispos stopped. "I've confused myself."

Trokoundos smiled. "Never mind, Your Majesty. No wizard can give you what you asked for, so there's no point in fretting over it."

"I suppose not. Fretting over Rhisoulphos, though, is something else again." Krispos looked ahead once more, but the general had vanished—smoothly—among the swarms of riders heading north.

The army did not cover much more ground in a day than a walking man might have. When the troopers moved, they set a decent pace. But getting them moving each morning and getting them into camp every night ate away at the time they were able to spend on the road. That had also been true of the forces Krispos led against Petronas and against Harvas the summer before, but to a lesser degree. One of the things a huge army meant was huge inefficiency.

"That's just the way it goes," Mammianos said when Krispos complained. "We can't move out in the morning till the slowest soldiers are ready to go. If we let quicker regiments just rush on ahead, after a few days we'd have men strung out over fifty miles. The whole point of a big army is to be able to use all the troops you've brought along."

"Supplies—" Krispos said, as if it were a complete sentence.

Mammianos clapped him on the shoulder. "Majesty, unless we crawl north on our hands and knees, we'll manage. The quartermasters know how fast—how slow, if you like—we travel. They've had practice keeping armies this size in bread, I promise you."

Krispos let himself be reassured. The Videssian bureaucracy had kept the Empire running throughout Anthimos' antic reign and through worse reigns than his in the past. Avtokrators came, ruled, and were gone; the gray, efficient stewards, secretaries, and logothetes went on forever. The army quartermasters belonged to the same breed.

He wondered what would happen if one day an Emperor died and no one succeeded him. He suspected the bureaucrats would go on ruling competently if unspectacularly . . . at least until some important paper needed signing. Then, for want of a signature, the whole state would come crashing down. He chuckled softly, pleased at his foolish conceit.

The next day the army rode past the field when Harvas' raiders had beaten and killed Mavros. The mass graves Krispos' men had dug afterward still scarred the earth. Now new grass, green and hopeful, was spreading over the squares of raw dirt. Krispos pointed to it. "Like the grass, may our victory spring from their defeat."

"From your lips to the ear of Phos," Trokoundos said, sketching the sun-sign with his right hand. He sent Krispos a sly look. "I hadn't thought Your Majesty had so much of a poet in him."

"Poet?" Krispos snorted. "I'm no poet, just a farmer—well, a man who used to be a farmer. The grass will grow tall over those graves, with the bodies of so many brave men manuring the fields."

The mage nodded soberly. "That's a less pleasing image, but I daresay a truer one."

They camped three or four miles past the battlefield, far enough, Krispos hoped, to keep the troopers from brooding on it. As was his habit each evening, Krispos wrote a brief note to Iakovitzes detailing the day's progress. When he was done, he called for a courier.

A rider came trotting up to the imperial tent hardly a minute later. He saluted Krispos and said, "All right, Your Majesty, let's have yours, too, and I'll be off for the city."

He sat his horse with a let's-get-on-with-it, don't-waste-my-time attitude that made Krispos smile. That attitude and the blithe cheek of his words left Krispos certain he was a city man himself. "Mine, too, is it, eh? Well, sir, with whose letter is mine lucky enough to travel?"

"It's all in the family, you might say, Your Majesty: yours and your father-in-law's will go together, both in the same pouch."

"Will they?" Krispos raised an eyebrow. He knew his use of the gesture did not have the flair that Chihor-Vshnasp, say, put into it, but it got the job done. "And to whom is the eminent Rhisoulphos writing?"

"Just let me look and I'll tell you." Like any man from Videssos the city, the courier took it for granted that he knew things lesser mortals didn't. He opened his leather dispatch pouch and drew out a roll of parchment sealed with enough wax to keep a poor family in candles for a month. He had to turn it between his fingers to find out where the address was. "Here we go, Your Majesty. It's to the most holy patriarch Gnatios, it is. Leastways, I think he's most holy patriarch this week, unless you made him into a monk again while I wasn't looking, or maybe into a prawn salad."

"A prawn salad? He'll end up wishing he was a prawn salad when I get through with him." Maybe Rhisoulphos was writing to Gnatios for enlightenment on an abstruse theological point or for some other innocuous reason. Krispos didn't believe it, not for a minute. The two of them were both intriguers, and he the logical person against whom they would intrigue. He plucked at his beard as he thought, then turned to one of the Halogai who stood guard in front of his tent. "Vagn, fetch me Trokoundos, right away."

"The mage, Majesty? Aye, I bring him."

Trokoundos was picking at his teeth with a fingernail as he followed Vagn to the imperial tent. "What's toward, Your Majesty?"

"This fellow"—Krispos pointed to the courier—"is carrying a letter from the excellent Rhisoulphos to the most holy patriarch Gnatios."

"Is he indeed?" No one had to draw pictures for Trokoundos. "Are you curious about what's in that letter?"

"You might say so, yes." Krispos held out a hand. The courier was not a man to be caught napping. With a flourish, he gave Krispos Rhisoulphos' letter. Krispos passed it to Trokoundos. "As you see, it's sealed tighter than a winter grain pit. Can you get it open and then shut again without breaking the seals?"

"Hmm. An interesting question. Do you know, sometimes these small conjurations are harder than the more grandiose ones? I'm certain I can get the wax off and on again, but the first method that springs to mind would surely ruin the writing it shelters—not what you have in mind, unless I miss my guess. Let me think . . ."

He proceeded to do just that, quite intensely, for the next couple of minutes. Once he brightened, then shook his head and sank back into his study. At last he nodded.

"You can do it, then?" Krispos said.

"I believe so, Your Majesty. Not a major magic, but one that will draw upon the laws of similarity and contagion both, and nearly at the same time. I presume privacy would be a valuable adjunct to this undertaking?"

"What? Oh, yes; of course." Krispos held the tent flap open with his own hands, then followed Trokoundos inside.

The wizard said, "You must have some parchment in here, yes?" Laughing, Krispos pointed to the portable desk where he'd just finished his note to Iakovitzes. Several other sheets still curled over one another. Trokoundos nodded. "Excellent." He took one, rolling it into a cylinder of about

the same diameter as the sealed letter from Rhisoulphos to Gnatios. Then
he touched the two of them together and squinted at the place where their
ends joined. "I'll use the law of similarity in two aspects," he explained.
"First in that parchment is similar to parchment, and second in that these
are two similar cylinders. Now just a dab of paste to let this one hold its
shape—can't use ribbon, don't you know, for it wouldn't be in precisely
the right place."

Krispos didn't know, but he'd already seen that Trokoundos liked to lecture as he worked. The mage set his new parchment cylinder upright on
the desk. "By the law of contagion, things once in contact continue to influence each other after that contact ends. Thus—" He held the letter upright in one hand and made slow passes over it with the other, chanting all
the while.

Sudden as a blink, the sealing wax disappeared. Trokoundos pointed to
the parchment cylinder he'd made. "You did it!" Krispos exclaimed—that
new cylinder wore a wax coat now. Every daub and spatter that had been
on the letter was there.

"So I did," Trokoundos said with a touch of smugness. "I had to make
certain my cylinder was no wider than the one Rhisoulphos made of his
letter. That was most important, for otherwise the wax would have
cracked as it tried to form itself around my piece of parchment."

He went on explaining, but Krispos had stopped listening. He held out
his hand for the letter. Trokoundos gave it to him. He slid off the ribbon,
unrolled the document, and read: " 'Rhisoulphos to the most holy ecumenical patriarch Gnatios: Greetings. As I said in my last letter, I think it
self-evident that Videssos would best be ruled by a man whose blood is
of the best, not by a parvenu, no matter how energetic.' " He paused.
"What's a parvenu?"

"Somebody able who just came off a farm himself, instead of having a
great-great-grandfather who did it for him," Trokoundos said.

"Oh." Krispos resumed: " 'As you are scion of a noble house yourself,
most holy sir, I am confident you will agree with me and will seize the opportunity to expound this position to the people when the proper circumstances arise. What with the uncertainty and danger of the campaign upon
which Krispos has embarked, that moment may come at any time.' " He
stopped again.

Trokoundos said, "Nothing treasonous so far—quite. He could as well
be worrying about what happens if you die in battle as over anything else."

"So he could. But he sends himself to the ice with his next five words.
Listen: " 'It might even be hastened.' "

"Aye, that's treason," Trokoundos said flatly. "What will you do about it?"

Krispos had been thinking about that from the instant he'd learned Rhisoulphos was corresponding with Gnatios. Now he answered, "First, I want you to seal the letter up again." He handed it to Trokoundos.

"Of course, Your Majesty." Trokoundos rerolled the letter and put the ribbon around it once more. His left hand shaped a quick pass; he spoke a low-voiced word of command. The ribbon changed place on the parchment. "I've returned it to its exact previous position, Your Majesty, so the restored wax will fit over it perfectly."

Without waiting for Krispos' nod, the mage held the letter upright. The ribbon did not stir; evidently the minor magic held it where it belonged. Trokoundos began the chant he had used before to remove the sealing wax. This time, though, his fingers fluttered downward in his passes rather than up toward the ceiling of the imperial tent.

Again Krispos missed the transfer of wax from one parchment to the other. One instant it was on the roll that stood on his desk; the next, back on Rhisoulphos' letter. With a bow Trokoundos returned the letter to Krispos.

"Thanks." Krispos went back outside. The courier was waiting with no sign of impatience; the sorcery could not have taken long. Krispos gave him the letter. "Everything's fine," he said, smiling. "Go on and deliver this to the patriarch; he'll be glad to have it."

The courier saluted. "Just as you say, Your Majesty." He clucked to his horse and dug in his heels. With a small snort, the animal trotted away.

Krispos turned to Vagn. "Can you find me, hmm, half a dozen of your countrymen? I need quiet men, men who can not only keep their mouths shut but also move quietly."

"I bring them, Majesty," Vagn said at once.

Trokoundos sent Krispos a curious look. He ignored it. A few minutes later Vagn returned with six more burly blond northerners. For all their bulk, they moved like hunting cats. Krispos held the tent flap open. "Brave sirs, come in. I have a task for you—"

KRISPOS WOKE AT SUNRISE EVERY DAY. *MAYBE I'D BE ABLE TO sleep late if my great-great-grandfather were the one who'd come off the farm,* he thought as he put his feet on the ground. He listened to the camp stirring to life.

He was just buckling on his sword belt when shouts of alarm cut through the usual morning drone of chattering men, clanking mail, and bubbling cookpots. He stuck his head outside, savoring a long breath of cool, fresh air; soon enough the day would turn hot and sticky. "What's going on?" he asked Narvikka, who was standing morning guard duty.

"Majesty, the noble Rhisoulphos seems to have disappeared," the Haloga answered.

"Disappeared? What do you mean, disappeared?"

"He is not in his tent, Majesty, not anywhere about the camp," Narvikka said stolidly.

"That's terrible news. What could have happened to him?" Since Narvikka only shrugged a musical chain mail shrug, Krispos hurried over to Rhisoulphos' tent, which lay not far away. The tent was surrounded by men and officers, all of them agitated. Krispos strode up to Rhisoulphos' second-in-command. "What's happened, excellent Bagradas?"

"Your Majesty!" Bagradas saluted. He was a short, pudgy man of about forty who looked and often acted more like a dressmaker than a soldier. Krispos knew he was one of the two or three best swordsmen in the imperial army. That did not keep him from wringing his hands now. "Your wife the lady Empress' father has been stolen away from us, whether by wicked men or dark sorcery I cannot say."

"Can Harvas' magic have reached into our camp? May Phos prevent it!" Krispos drew the sun-circle over his heart.

So did Bagradas. "Truly I hope not, Your Majesty. I am inclined to say not, for the sentry who guarded Rhisoulphos' tent was found unconscious this morning by his relief. Magic might have dealt with the general, but would it have needed to lay low his guard as well? That seems more like the work of ordinary men."

"You reason like a priest explaining Phos' holy scriptures," Krispos said. A broad, pleased grin spread across Bagradas' face. Krispos went on, "Take me to this sentry."

Bagradas led him through the crowd. The officer's rank and shouts were not enough to clear a path. But when Krispos raised his voice, men stumbled backward out of the way. Bagradas said, "Your Majesty, this is the file closer Nogeto, who had the late-night duty outside the eminent Rhisoulphos' tent."

Nogeto drew himself to stiff, indeed trembling, attention. "Tell me what happened to you last night, soldier," Krispos said.

"Majesty, begging your pardon, but everybody's been asking me that, and may the ice take me if I *know* what happened to me. One minute I was standing here not thinking real hard, the way you do when it's late and you know nothing's going to go wrong. Only it did. Next thing I knew I was lying on the ground with my relief shaking me awake. And his eminence the general was gone."

"Did somebody sap you?"

"No, Majesty." Nogeto emphatically shook his head. "I've been sapped before, and I know what it's like. I don't feel like I'm fixing to die now, the way I would be. I just feel like I went to sleep and then got woke up. Only I couldn't have. By the good god, I didn't." The guard's eyes widened with fear. Sentries who fell asleep at their posts earned the sword and the chopping block.

"He's always been a good soldier, Your Majesty," Bagradas put in. "He'd not have been chosen to guard the general's tent if he weren't."

"Is there any reason to think you didn't just fall asleep when you were, ah, not thinking real hard, soldier?" Krispos asked sternly.

Nogeto said, "Majesty, for whatever you think it's worth, just before I—" He changed tack. "Just before whatever happened happened, I mean, I thought I felt—oh, I don't know; I thought I felt a cobweb blow across my face. I thought I'd picked up my hand to brush it away, but—oh, I don't know."

Krispos glanced at Bagradas. "He's not making it up as he stands here, Your Majesty," the officer said. "He said as much before you came."

"Will you let a wizard examine you to learn if you speak truly?" Krispos asked Nogeto. The sentry nodded without hesitation. Krispos told Bagradas, "Take him to Trokoundos. If he's not lying"—Krispos pursed his lips, made a wry face—"well, we'll just have to look in some other direction, that's all."

"Aye, Your Majesty. Who could have done such a vicious, evil deed?"

"Maybe Nogeto will be able to give us a clue once Trokoundos works on him," Krispos said. "Meanwhile, we have to go on as best we can. Excellent Bagradas, do you feel you can lead this regiment until Rhisoulphos turns up again, whenever that may be?"

"Me, Your Majesty? Oh, you're far too generous." Bagradas realized he might have affected too much humility, for he quickly added, "If you feel I can handle the command, I am honored to accept."

"I'm sure you'll lead bravely, excellent Bagradas. Good; I'm glad that much is settled, then." Krispos turned to go, then stopped, as with an afterthought. "Bagradas, you know my father-in-law and I worked closely together. He was helping to manage some rather delicate business for me in the city. Now that he's disappeared, I'll have to deal with it myself. Can you make sure any letters he gets are sent straight on to me before they're unsealed?"

"I'll see to it, Your Majesty," Bagradas promised. He spun on his heel and set hands on hips as he glared at the gaggle of men still milling around Rhisoulphos' tent. "Come on, come on, you lugs!" he shouted. "We still have to ride today, whether the eminent sir is here or not. *Get* cracking, *if* you please!"

The men moved smartly to obey. Krispos nodded to himself; Rhisoulphos had been a canny soldier, but the regiment would not suffer under its new leader.

The army moved out a few minutes later than it might have, but not enough to upset even the veteran underofficers who were responsible for keeping their units in good order. Krispos rode Progress up and down the long line of march. Wherever he went, the troopers were buzzing about Rhisoulphos' disappearance. Some thought Bagradas had got rid of his commander; others blamed sorcery; others, not surprisingly, were lewd. "He'll be back in a couple of days, all sleepy and with his breeches unbuttoned," one fellow guessed.

"Oh, go on, Dertallos, you've just saying what you'd do in his sandals," a mate replied.

"If I were in his sandals right now, I wouldn't be wearing sandals, if you know what I mean," Dertallos said. Half a dozen voices barked deep male laughter.

One slow mile followed another. Halfway through the day, Krispos reported that Nogeto had been telling the truth. "He was drugged somehow, poor sod," the wizard said.

"How very strange," Krispos answered. "All right, then; let him return to duty."

Scouts rode well in advance of the main imperial army. With them rode wizards, not the journeymen who had accompanied Krispos' last northern foray but masters for the Sorcerers' Collegium. If they could not sniff out a trap, no one could. If no one could, Krispos was uneasily aware, that trap would close on his army. And who then would defend Videssos the city, his wife, his heir, and his son to be? No one. He knew that all too well.

The farther north the army traveled, the fewer the farms Krispos saw being worked. That tore at him. Next to harvesttime, spring should have been the busiest season of the year, with men and oxen in the fields plowing, planting, and watering. But what was the point, when raiders might sweep down at any moment? Many little farming villages stood deserted, their former inhabitants fled to ground they hoped safer. If somehow he beat Harvas, Krispos knew he would have to import peasants to replace the ones who had run away or been slain. Otherwise the whole land would start to go back to wilderness.

As the Paristrian Mountains climbed higher into the northern sky, men began to peer suspiciously at every clump of brush, every stand of elms they passed. Krispos had known that same feeling the summer before as he approached Imbros: wondering how and where Harvas would strike. Now that he neared Imbros again, he knew it again, doubly strong.

About two days south of the murdered city, a scout came galloping back to Krispos. The fellow saluted and said, "Majesty, one of the wizards thinks he senses something up ahead. He can't tell what, he's not even sure it's there, but—maybe something." The scout looked irked at having to report what likely was just a mage's vagary.

The most Krispos hoped for, though, was detecting Harvas' snares at all. Expecting them to announce themselves with bells and whistles was too much to ask. He turned to the army musicians. "Play *Form line of battle,* then *Hold in place.* We'll see what's gong on up ahead." As the music rang out and the soldiers began to move, Krispos reflected that he'd be wasting a good part of a day's travel if the wizard had discovered nothing more than his overactive imagination. But better that than ignoring a true warning and throwing away his army.

He touched Progress' flanks with his heels, urging the horse forward. Soon he had pressed ahead of the main body of soldiery. A few other riders advanced with him—wizards all. They knew what a halt had to mean. Trokoundos waved from atop a gray that trotted with a dancer's grace. Krispos waved back.

He reined Progress in close behind a knot of scouts and sorcerers. To his untrained senses, the country ahead looked no different from that through which the army had been traveling: fields—too many of them untended—punctuated by stands of oak, maple, elm, and fir. Shadows raced over them, keeping time with the fluffy clouds that drifted across the sky. It all seemed too lovely, too peaceful, to have anything to do with Harvas.

"What's wrong?" Krispos asked.

One of the sorcerers, a young, gangly man whose thin beard imperfectly covered his acne scars, bowed and said, "Your Majesty, I'm called Zaidas. I feel—not a wrongness ahead, nor even a lack of rightness, but rather—oh, how best to say it?—an absence of both rightness and wrongness, which could be unusual." He cracked his knuckles and peered nervously at the innocent-appearing countryside.

"If you don't sense anything, who knows what's hiding there? Is that what you're saying?" Krispos asked. Zaidas nodded. Krispos turned to the other mages. "Do you also feel this, ah, absence?"

"No, Majesty," one of them said. "That does not mean it is not there, though. Despite his youth, Zaidas has great and unusual sensitivity, which is the reason we bade him accompany us. What he perceives, or fails to perceive, may well be genuine." Zaidas' larynx bobbed up and down as he shot his colleague a grateful glance.

Krispos made a sour face. " 'May well be' cuts no ice, sorcerous sirs. I could starve, hunting a grouse that may well be there. How do we find out?"

Trokoundos strolled up just then to join the discussion. "We find out by testing. Is it not so, brothers?" The other wizards nodded. Trokoundos went on, "The lord with the great and good mind willing, we may even surprise Harvas, who should be confident we've noticed nothing."

Trokoundos was an able mage, but no general. "If he's there, he'll know we've noticed," Krispos said. "We don't form line of battle every time a rabbit hops across the road. What we have to find out is, what is our line of battle moving toward?"

"You're right, of course, Your Majesty." Trokoundos shook his head in chagrin, then began a technical discussion with the rest of the wizards that lost Krispos by the fourth sentence. He was beginning to wonder if they would spend the whole morning chattering at one another when Trokoundos seemed to remember he was there. The mage said, "Your Majesty, a number of spells could create the illusion of normality ahead. We think one is more likely, given that Harvas could both pervert and amplify its power through blood sacrifice. We will try to break through it now, assuming it to be the one we guess."

"Do it," Krispos said at once. Acting against Harvas instead of reacting to him felt like a victory in itself.

The wizards went to work with the practiced efficiency of a squad of soldiers who had fought side by side for years. Krispos watched Trokoundos, who smeared his eyelids with an ointment another mage ceremoniously handed him. "The gall of a cat mixed with the fat of an all-white hen," Trokoundos explained. "It gives the power to see that which others may not."

He held up a pale-green stone and a goldpiece, touched the two of them together. "Chrysolite and gold drive away foolishness and expel fantasies, the good god willing." Behind him, the voice of the rest of the wizards rose and fell as some invoked Phos while others chanted to bring their building spell to sharper focus.

A wizard threw a gray-green leaf on a brazier; the puff of smoke that arose smelled sweet. Trokoundos set a small, sparkling stone in a copper bowl, smashed it to fragments with a silver hammer. "Opal and laurel, when used with the proper spell, may render a man—or, with sufficient strength, maybe, an army—invisible. Thus we destroy both, and thus we destroy with spell." With the last words Trokoundos' voice rose to a shout. His right finger stabbed out toward the peaceful-looking landscape ahead.

For a long moment, for more than a moment, nothing happened. Krispos glared at Zaidas, who was watching the unchanged terrain with the same dejected expression his colleagues bore. Aye, he was very sensitive, Krispos thought—he could even detect traps that weren't there.

Then the air rippled, as if it were the surface of a rough-running stream. Krispos blinked and rubbed at his eyes. Trokoundos raised a fist and shouted in triumph. Zaidas looked like a man reprieved when the sword was already on its way up. And while the landscape to the north did not change, when the ripples cleared they revealed a great army of foot soldiers drawn up in battle array across the road, across the fields, one end of their line anchored by a pond, the other by a grove of apple trees. They could not have been more than a mile away.

Horns cried out behind Krispos. Drums thumped. Pipes squealed. His men shouted. They saw the enemy, too, then. He gave the wizards a formal military salute. "Thank you, magical sirs. Without you, we would have blundered straight into them."

Just then Harvas' men must have realized they were discovered. They shouted, too, not with the disciplined hurrah of Videssian troops but loud and long and fierce, like so many bloodthirsty wild beasts. The sun sparked cheerfully off axe blades, helms, and mail coats as they surged toward the imperial army.

Krispos turned to the wizards once more. "Magical sirs, if it's to be battle, I suggest you get clear before you're caught in the middle." That possibility did not seem to have occurred to some of the sorcerers. They scrambled onto horses and mules and rode off with remarkable celerity. Krispos rode away, too, back to where the imperial standard snapped in the breeze at the center of the imperial line.

Mammianos greeted him with a salute and a wry grin. "Worried for a minute there that I'd have to run this battle without you," the fat general grunted.

"Nice to know you think I'm of some use," Krispos answered.

Mammianos grunted again. His grin got wider. He said, "Aye, you're of some use, Your Majesty. Fair gave me a turn, it did, when those buggers appeared out of thin air. If we'd just walked on into them, well, it could have ruined our whole day."

"That's one way to put it, yes." Krispos grinned, too, at Mammianos' sangfroid. He ran an eye up and down the Videssian line. It was as he and his marshals had planned, with lancers—some mounted on horses wearing mail of their own—in the front ranks on either wing and archers behind them, ready to shoot over their heads into the ranks of the enemy. In the center stood the Halogai of the imperial guard.

The guardsmen did not know it, but native units on either side had orders to turn on them if they went over to Harvas. That might suffice to keep the imperial army alive. Krispos knew it would not save him. He drew his saber and scowled at the advancing enemy.

Mammianos spoke to the musicians. New calls rang through the air. The horsemen on either wing slid forward, seeking to envelop Harvas' front. Krispos scowled again, this time when he noticed how broad that front was. "He has more men than we'd reckoned," he said to Mammianos.

"Aye, so he does," the general agreed glumly. "The northerners must have been streaming south from Halogaland ever since Harvas seized Kubrat. To them the land and climate look good."

"True, true." Krispos had entertained the same thought himself. He'd spent several years north of the Paristrian Mountains after Kubrati raiders kidnapped everyone in his village. He remembered Kubrat as bleak and cold. If Halogai found it attractive, he shivered to think what that said of their homeland.

Then he stopped worrying about Halogaland and started worrying about the Halogai in front of him. Harvas' men fought with the same disregard for life and limb—their own or their foes'—as did the northerners who served Videssos. They shouted their evil chieftain's name as they swung their axes in sweeping arcs of death.

The imperials shouted, too. The cry Krispos heard most often was a cry for revenge: "Imbros!" The lines crashed together in bloody collision. After moments of that fight, even men previously uninitiated into the red brotherhood of war could honestly call themselves veterans. A little fighting against the northerners went a long way.

Here a lancer spitted a Haloga, as if to roast him over some huge fire. There another Haloga crashed to the ground, his armor clattering about him, as a cleverly aimed arrow found the gap between shield top and helm. But Harvas' men dealt out deadly wounds as well as suffering them. Here an axeman hewed down first horse and then rider, splashing friend and foe alike with gore. There yet another northerner, already bleeding from a dozen wounds, pulled a Videssian from the saddle and stabbed him before falling in death.

In front of Krispos, the combat was foot soldier against foot soldier, Haloga against Haloga, as the warriors who followed Harvas met those who had given their allegiance to the Avtokrator of the Videssians. As in any battle where brother met brother, that was the fiercest fight of all, a war within the greater war. The Halogai swung and struck and swung again, all the while cursing one another for having chosen the wrong side. Once hatred was too hot even for weapons, as two Halogai who had been screaming abuse as they fought threw aside axes and shields to batter each other with fists.

The northerners who had taken Videssos' gold never wavered; Krispos knew shame for having doubted them. All because they'd sworn they would, they battled and bled and died for a land that was not theirs, with a courage few of its native sons could match.

"How do we fare?" Krispos shouted to Mammianos.

"We're holding them," the general shouted back. "From all I can tell, that's better than Agapetos or Mavros—Phos keep them in his light—ever managed to do. If the wizards can keep Harvas from buggering us while we're looking the other way, we may end up celebrating the day instead of cursing it."

Most of the wizards, by now, clustered behind the imperial line, not far from where Krispos sat atop Progress. They gathered in a tight knot around Zaidas; if any of their number could sense Harvas Black-Robe's next move, the young mage was probably the one. Krispos hoped his skinny shoulders could carry that weight of responsibility.

Even as the thought crossed Krispos' mind, Zaidas jerked where he stood. He spoke rapidly to his comrades, who burst into action. Krispos noted what they did less closely than he might have, for at that same moment he was afflicted by a deep and venomous itch. Put any man in armor and he will itch—sweat will dry on his skin, and he cannot scratch. Rather than go mad, he learns to ignore it. Krispos could not ignore this itch; it was as if cockroaches scrambled over the very core of him. Of themselves, his fingertips scraped against his gilded shirt of mail.

And he was not alone. Up and down the Videssian line, men clawed at themselves, forgetting the foes before them. Harvas' warriors were not afflicted. In the twinkling of any eye, a score of imperial soldiers went down, too distracted by their torment even to protect themselves. The Videssian line wavered.

Ice ran through Krispos, chilling even his itch for an instant. If this went on for long, the army would fall apart. Even as first blood welled from beneath torn nails, his head turned toward the wizards. Led by Trokoundos, they were incanting frantically. Those not actually involved in shaping the spell scratched as hard as anyone else. The ones who were casting it needed their hands for passes; the discipline they required to carry on would have made Pyrrhos jealous.

All at once, as if a portcullis had fallen, the itching stopped. The imperials looked to their weapons again and cut down the Halogai who, confident they would not be able to resist, had thrust forward into their line.

"A cheer for the mages of the Sorcerers' Collegium!" Krispos yelled. His soldiers took up the cry and made it ring out over the field. From behind the enemy line, an answering scream rose, a scream of such hatred, rage, and frustration that for a moment all other war cries, Videssian and Haloga alike, tremblingly fell silent. That, Krispos thought, was the voice of the man—if man he still was—who wanted to rule Videssos. He shuddered.

Harvas' northerners seemed for a moment dismayed at the failure of their dark chieftain's magic. But with or without Harvas, they were warriors fierce and bold, men who had grown used to winning glory by always crushing their foes in combat; they would have been ashamed to be deprived of it now through defeat at the hands of Videssians. So they fought on, giving no quarter and seeking none.

The Videssians had been more hesitant at the start of the fight. Some had experienced Harvas' sorcery in the campaigns of the summer before. All had heard of it, nor had the tales shrunk in the telling. Only now were they beginning to see, beginning to believe their wizards could counter Harvas, leaving the outcome of the battle to them alone. Battle against merely mortal foes held only terrors they already knew. They pressed against the Halogai with renewed spirit.

Krispos realized Gnatios had done the Empire a great service by discovering Harvas' nature. He hoped for the patriarch's sake that his response to Rhisoulphos would prove benign. If it was not, Gnatios would answer for it, no matter what aid he had rendered in the fight against Harvas.

A fresh charge from Harvas' men yanked his mind back to the immediate. The Halogai seemed to have inhuman endurance, to be as strong and uncomplaining as the horses the Videssians rode. They were roaring again, their blue eyes wide and staring, their faces blood-crimson. By their set expressions, many of them were drunk.

The imperial guards met their cousins breast to breast, defied them to advance a foot. As one guard fell, another deliberately stepped forward to take his place. Fewer ranks stood between Krispos and the enemy than had been in place when the fight began.

The shrieks of the wounded began to drown out war cries on both sides. Some hurt men staggered away from the line, clutching at themselves and biting their lips to hold back screams. Comrades dragged aside others, not least so they could reach over them to fight some more. Healer-priests, gray-faced with fatigue, did what they could for the most desperately hurt. No one helped the horses, whose screams were more piteous than those of the soldiers.

Krispos saw, surprised, how long his shadow had grown. He glanced toward the sun. It had sunk far down in the west. The battle went on, still perfectly balanced. Though night was near, neither side showed any sign of giving way. Krispos had an uneasy vision of the fight coming down to a duel between the last living Videssian and his Haloga counterpart.

Suddenly the wizards stirred again. Krispos ground his teeth. Harvas Black-Robe had his own notions of how the battle should end, and the strength and will to bring those notions to reality. For just an instant, Krispos' sight grew dim, as if night had already fallen. He rubbed at his eyes, nor was he the only Videssian to do so. But then his vision cleared. Once more Harvas screamed in rage and hate.

Trokoundos walked over to Krispos. The mage looked as worn as any healer-priest, but sober triumph lit his eyes. "Your Majesty, he tried to draw the night and the darkness that is Skotos' down upon us. We foiled him more easily this time than before; that spell is potent, but can come from only one direction. Our strength together sufficed to wall it away."

The assembled might of the finest wizards of the Sorcerers' Collegium, then, was more or less a match for Harvas Black-Robe alone. In a way, that was encouraging; Krispos had feared nothing and no one could match Harvas. But it was also frightening in and of itself, for it gave some notion of the might the sorcerer had acquired in the long years since he turned away from Phos toward Skotos.

Harvas cried out again, this time in a tone of command. What his dark sorcery had failed to do, the axes of his followers might yet accomplish. The Halogai rushed forward in an all-out effort to break the ranks of their foes. "Steady, men, steady!" officers shouted from one end of the line to the other. It would do, Krispos thought, as a watchword for the Empire of Videssos. The northerners could rage like the sea; like Videssos the city's sea walls, the imperial army would hold them at bay.

Hold them the army did, if barely. As the Haloga surge began to ebb, Mammianos nudged Krispos. "Now's our time to hit back."

Krispos glanced west again. The sun was down now; the sky where it had set was red as the blood that splashed the battlefield. In the gathering gloom above, the evening star blazed bright and clear. "Aye," Krispos said.

"Everything we have." He turned to the military musicians. "Sound the charge."

High and sweet and urgent, the notes rang through the battle din. Krispos held his saber high over his head. "Come on!" he cried. "Will you let yourselves be beaten by a bunch of barbarians who fight on foot and don't know the first thing about horsemanship?"

"No!" yelled every Videssian trooper who heard him.

"Then show them what we can do!"

The imperials raised a great, wordless shout and spurred against Harvas' men. For several minutes the Halogai resisted as desperately and as successfully as their foes had not long before. Then, on the imperial left, a band of lancers at last broke through their line and got into their rear. More followed, their voices high and excited in triumph. Beset from front and rear at once, the Halogai could not withstand the Videssian onslaught. They broke and fled northward.

Krispos set spurs to Progress. The big bay gelding snorted and bounded forward through the thinned ranks of the imperial bodyguards. Krispos was far from an enthusiastic warrior; he'd seen war young, and from a peasant's perspective. But now he wanted to strike a blow at the marauders who had done Videssos such grievous harm.

His guardsmen shouted and grabbed for Progress' bridle, trying to hold him back. Krispos spurred the horse again, harder this time. All at once, quite abruptly, no one stood between him and the foe. Progress pounded toward Harvas' Halogai. The Videssian horsemen, seeing Krispos heading toward the fight, cheered even harder than they had before.

A northerner turned to face him. The fellow wore a mail shirt that reached down to his knees, carried a hacked and battered round wooden shield. He was bareheaded; if he'd ever had a helmet, he'd lost it in the fighting. He still had his axe. It was streaked with the brown of drying blood and with fresh red. He chopped at Progress' forelegs.

The stroke was too quick, and missed. Krispos slashed at the Haloga. He missed, too. Then Progress was past the man. Krispos never knew whether the northerner escaped or was finished by other Videssians. Battle, he had discovered, was often like that.

Soon Progress caught up with another foe. This one did not turn. He kept trotting heavily toward the north, intent only on escape. Krispos aimed for the hand-wide gap between the base of his helmet and the collar of his coat of mail. He swung with all his strength. His saber clattered off iron. The blow jolted him in the saddle. The Haloga staggered but did not fall. His dogged trot went on.

Krispos reined in. Even a slight taste of battle burned out the desire for more. As well that as a youth he had ignored others' urgings and refused to become a soldier, he thought. If this was the best he could do, he would have been ravens' meat all too quickly.

Up ahead, a band of Halogai turned at bay, buying time for their countrymen to get free. Now more stars than the evening star shone in the sky; black night was near. In the darkness and confusion, victory could unravel . . . and Krispos would sooner have stepped on a scorpion in the dark than encounter Harvas there. He looked round for a courier, but found none. *This is what I get for running ahead of the people I need,* he thought, feeling absurdly guilty.

Just then a call he knew sang out, loud and insistent: *Hold in place.* His shoulders sagged with relief. Mammianos was thinking along with him. Videssians began pulling up, taking off their helmets to wipe their brows. Those who had come through unhurt started chattering about what a splendid fight it had been.

A Haloga came up beside Krispos. He gasped and started to raise his saber before he realized the fellow wore the raiment of the imperial guard. Geirrod looked at him with doubly reproachful eyes. "Majesty, you should not leave us. We serve to keep you safe."

"I know, Geirrod. Will you forgive me if I admit I made a mistake?"

Geirrod blinked, taken off guard by such quick and abject surrender. "Aye, well," he said, "I suppose the man in you threw down the Emperor. That is not bad." He saluted and walked off. But Krispos knew he had made a mistake. He had to be Avtokrator first and man second. If he threw his life away on a foolish whim, far more than he alone would suffer. The lesson was hard. He hoped one day to learn it thoroughly.

Jubilation ran high in camp that night, despite the continuing groans and cries of the wounded. From the excitement the men showed, they were as excited and overjoyed at their victory as was Krispos himself, likely for the same reason: Down deep, they must have doubted they could beat Harvas. Now that they had done it once, the next time might come easier.

"Tonight we feast!" Krispos shouted, which only made the camp more joyful. Cattle were slaughtered as quickly as they could be led up, adding further to the blood that drenched the area. Soon every trooper seemed to have a big gobbet of beef roasting over a fire. Krispos' nostrils twitched at the savory scent, which reminded him he'd eaten nothing since morning. He stood in line to get some meat of his own.

After he'd eaten, he met with his generals. Several of them had men they wanted promoted for bravery on the battlefield. "We'll do it right now," Krispos said. "That way everyone will be able to applaud them."

The musicians played *Assembly.* The troops packed themselves around the imperial tent. One by one Krispos called names. As the soldiers came forward to be rewarded, their commanders shouted out what they had done. Their comrades cheered lustily.

"Who's next?" Krispos whispered.

"A file leader named Inkitatos," Mammianos whispered back.

"File leader Inkitatos!" Krispos yelled as loud as he could, then again. "File leader Inkitatos!"

Inkitatos elbowed his way through the crush to stand on the podium between Krispos and Mammianos. Mammianos called to the listening soldiers, "File leader Inkitatos' brave and well-trained war horse dashed out the brains of four northerners with blows from its hooves."

"Hurrah!" the men shouted.

"File leader Inkitatos, I am proud to promote you to troop leader," Krispos declared. The soldiers cheered again. Grinning, Krispos added, "And I promote your horse, too." The troops whooped and waved and yelled louder than ever.

"If he's promoted, do I get his new pay?" Inkitatos asked with the accent and ready opportunism of a man born in Videssos the city.

Krispos laughed out loud. "By the good god, you've earned it." He turned to the military scribe who was recording the night's promotions. "Note that Inkitatos here will draw troop leader's pay once for himself and once for his horse." The scribe's indulgent chuckle broke off when he saw that Krispos meant it. He was shaking his head as he made the notation.

It must have been close to midnight by the time the last promotion was awarded. By then the crowd round the imperial tent had thinned out. Krispos envied the troopers who could go off to their bedrolls any time they felt like it. He had to stay up on the podium until the whole ceremony was done. When he did finally get to bed, he remembered nothing after he lay down.

Sunrise came far too soon. Krispos' eyes felt gritty and his head ached. He knew he should have been eager to press on after Harvas, but found exhausting the prospect of anything more vigorous than an enormous yawn. Yawning over and over, he went outside for breakfast.

When the army moved out, archers were in the van, ready to harass Harvas' men as they retreated. With them rode the wizards, Zaidas in front of them all. Harvas could have left any number of sorcerous ambushes behind to delay or destroy the Videssians. Krispos worried even more that the raiders would choose to stand siege in Imbros. With the leisure that would bring Harvas, who could guess what wickedness he might invent?

Delays the army found. Haloga rear guards twice stood and fought. They sold their lives as bravely as Videssians might have if they were protecting their countrymen. The imperial army rode over them and pressed on.

Imbros was almost in sight when a wall of darkness, twice the height of a man, suddenly rose up before the soldiers. Zaidas waved for everyone to halt. The soldiers were more than willing. They had no idea whether the wall was dangerous and did not care to learn the hard way.

The wizards went into a huddle. Trokoundos cast a spell toward that blank blackness. The sorcerous wall drank up the spell and remained unchanged. Trokoundos swore. The wizards tried a different spell. The black wall drank up that one, too. Trokoundos swore louder. A third try yielded results no better. What Trokoundos said should have been hot enough to melt the wall by itself.

"What now?" Krispos asked. "Are we blocked forever?" The wall stretched east and west, far as the eye could see.

"No, by the lord with the great and good mind!" Trokoundos' scowl was as dark as the barrier Harvas had placed in the imperial army's path. "Were such facile creations as potent as this one appears, the sorcerous art would be altogether different from what in fact it is." He paused, as if listening to his own words. Then, right hand outstretched, he walked up to the black wall and tapped it with a fingertip.

The other mages and Krispos, not believing he would dare do that, cried out in dismay. Zaidas reached out to pull Trokoundos back—too late. Lightning crackled, surrounding Trokoundos in a dreadful nimbus. But when it faded, the wall faded, too. The wizard was left unharmed.

"I thought as much," he said, his voice silky with self-satisfaction. "Just a bluff, designed to keep us dithering here as long as we would."

"You were very brave and very foolish," Krispos said. "Please don't do that again—I expected to see you die there."

"I didn't, and now the way lies open," Trokoundos answered. With that Krispos could not argue. He signaled to the musicians. The call *Advance,* all eager horns and pounding drums, rang forth. The army moved ahead.

What with rear guards and sorcerous ploys, Harvas had succeeded in putting space between himself and his pursuers. When Imbros came into sight late that afternoon, Krispos approached the town with more than a little trepidation, fearing Harvas had used the time he'd gained to establish himself inside.

But Imbros stood empty, surrounded by its forest of stakes. Over the winter, most of the impaled corpses had fallen from them; bone gleamed whitely on the ground. Here and there, though, a mummified body still stood, as if in macabre welcome.

Krispos' soldiers' muttered to themselves as they made camp not far away. They had heard of Harvas' atrocity, but only a relative handful had seen it till now. Stories heard, no matter how vile, could be discounted in the mind. What came before the eye was something else again.

An imperial guardsman stuck his head into Krispos' tent. "The general Bagradas would see you, Majesty."

"Send him in." Krispos stuffed a last large bite of bread and cheese into his mouth, then washed it down with a swig of wine. He waved Bagradas to a folding canvas chair. "What can I do for you, excellent sir? You led your—or rather Rhisoulphos'—regiment bravely against the Halogai."

"Thank you, Your Majesty. I did my best. I find myself embarrassed, though. When the fight was over, I found a pair of letters had come for Rhisoulphos, and it slipped my mind till now that you wanted to see all such."

"So I did," Krispos said. "Well, no harm done, excellent sir. Let me have them, if you please."

"Here you are, Your Majesty." Bagradas sadly shook his head. "I wish he could have seen how his men fought yesterday. They did him proud, and many used his name as a battle cry, reckoning that Harvas had feared him enough to make away with him. Most mysterious and distressing, his disappearance."

"Yes, so it was." Krispos' voice was abstracted. One of the letters to Rhisoulphos was from the patriarch Gnatios. That one he had been waiting for. The other came as a complete and unpleasant surprise. It was from Dara.

He waited until Bagradas had saluted and bowed his way out, then sat and waited a little longer, weighing the two letters in his hand without opening either of them. He had repeatedly warned the ecumenical patriarch not to betray him again, and he knew all his warnings might well have been wasted. But Dara . . . Ever since he'd taken the throne, he'd relied on her, and she'd never given him any reason to doubt his trust. Yet how did a relatively short connection with him weigh against a lifetime's devotion to her father?

He found he did not want to know, not right away. He set down the letter from Dara and broke the seals on the one from Gnatios. It was daubed with as much wax as if it had come from the imperial chancery. When at last he could unroll it, he held it close to a lamp to read:

"Gnatios, ecumenical patriarch of the Videssians, to the eminent and noble sir Rhisoulphos: Greetings. As you know, I have suffered many indignities at the hands of the peasant whose fundament currently defiles

the imperial throne. I have long believed that those of noble birth, confident in their own excellence, can best rule the state without feeling the
constant and pressing need to interfere in the affairs of the temples. Thus,
eminent sir, should any accident, genuine or contrived, befall Krispos, rest
assured that I shall be delighted to proclaim your name from the altar at
the High Temple."

Krispos tossed the letter aside. Sure enough, Gnatios could no more
turn away from treachery than a fat man could turn away from sweetness.
A fat man's taste just made him heavier. Gnatios, though, would soon be
lighter—by a head, Krispos promised himself, not without regret. But he
had forgiven his patriarch too many times already.

What of his wife? What was he to do if he found her plotting against
him? He put his hands over his face—he had no idea. At last he made
himself unseal the letter. He recognized Dara's smooth-flowing script at
once:

"Dara to her father: Greetings. May Phos keep you safe through all the
fighting that is to come and may he give Krispos the victory. I am well,
though enormous. The midwife says second births are easier than first.
The good god grant that she be right. Phostis has another tooth, and says
mama plain as day. I wish you and Krispos could see him. Give Krispos
my love and tell him I will write to him tomorrow. Love to you as well,
from your affectionate daughter."

Ashamed of his worries, Krispos rolled up the letter. To be Avtokrator
was to be schooled in suspicion. Had he not been suspicious, he might not
have found Rhisoulphos' plot till it found him. But to suspect his wife
flayed his conscience, all the more so since she had but written her father
an innocent, friendly letter.

Fool, Krispos said to himself, *would you rather have discovered she was
guilty?*

He stepped out into the night. His Haloga guard stiffened to attention.
"I'm going over to Mammianos' tent," Krispos said. The guardsman nodded and saluted.

Mammianos' guards were Videssians. They, too, saluted as Krispos
came up. "I'd like to see your master," he said. One of the guards went into
the tent. He emerged a moment later and held the flap wide.

Mammianos had a roasted chicken leg in one hand and a cup of wine
in the other. He gestured to a platter on the ground in front of him.
"Plenty more where this came from, Your Majesty. Help yourself."

"Later, maybe," Krispos said. "First I want to known the latest word on
Harvas' movements."

"I talked with some scouts not a quarter of an hour ago." Mammianos paused for another bite. "They've pushed into the woods that start north of Imbros. By all the signs, Harvas' raiders are in full retreat. The men had that Zaidas with them, so I don't think Harvas could have cozened them the way he did poor Mavros."

"If they aren't making a stand in the woods, that means they have to go all the way back to the mountain pass, doesn't it?"

"I think so, yes." Mammianos paused again, this time thoughtfully. "Once past the woods, there's no place between here and the mountains where I'd care to fight with foot soldiers against horse, at any rate."

"Good enough," Krispos said. "I'm going to leave the army in your hands for a while, then—maybe a week, maybe a little longer. I have to get back to Videssos the city as fast as I can; I've had word of a plot against me."

Too late, he wondered if Mammianos was part of the conspiracy. If so, the army might not be his when he came back to it. But the fat general had certainly had countless chances to overthrow him and had used none of them. Now he only nodded gravely and said, "Gnatios has decided he'd sooner be Emperor-maker than patriarch after all, has he? Or is it someone new this time?"

"No, it's Gnatios," Krispos said. He doubted Mammianos once more, but only for a moment. The general needed no guilty knowledge to make that guess, just the keen political sense he'd shown as long as Krispos had known him.

Mammianos sighed. "He's just like Petronas, Gnatios is: thinks he's cleverer than anyone else. Will you finally go and settle him for good?"

"Yes," Krispos said. "He's wriggled out of what he deserves too often, and then gone and deserved it again. I'll ride the courier relays down to the city and drop on him before he realizes I've come. Meanwhile, I want you to press ahead. If Harvas has fallen back to the pass, don't try to force your way through into Kubrat. We came to grief with that last year. But don't let him back into Videssos, either. With the men and mages you have, that should be no problem."

"No indeed, Majesty," Mammianos agreed. "But it's an expensive way to keep him out, if you'll forgive my being so bold as to say so."

"I know," Krispos said. "I'm beginning to have an idea about that, but it's not ripe yet. I'll talk more about it with you after I get back."

"As you say, Majesty." Mammianos tossed aside a bare bone. "Now, would you care for a chunk of this bird? The white wine I have here goes nicely with it, too. You wouldn't want to set out riding on an empty stomach, would you?"

"No, I suppose not." Krispos ate and drank with Mammianos.

Through a mouthful of meat, he said, "I'll even sleep here through the night. Can't go far in the darkness, anyhow."

"True, true. If you don't want anything more there, I'll finish that off for you. Ah, thanks very much." With a little help from Krispos, Mammianos had completely devoured the chicken. He sighed. "I'm still hungry."

"I envy you your appetite," Krispos said.

Mammianos chuckled hoarsely. "I'm getting old, Your Majesty. Nice that one of my appetites works as it did when I was young, or maybe even better. It's not the one I would have chosen, but then, the choice wasn't up to me."

Krispos went back to his own tent a few minutes later. "I want to be roused at first light," he told the guard. "Tell your relief to have Progress saddled and ready for me."

"It shall be done, Majesty," the guardsman promised.

Done it was, but when Krispos went to climb aboard Progress, he found the scout commander Sarkis and a squad of his men waiting, each of them already mounted. "Best we ride back to the city with you, Your Majesty, to keep you safe."

Krispos glared. "By the good god, excellent sir, can I do nothing secret?"

"Not if it puts you in danger," Sarkis answered firmly. His men nodded. Krispos glared again. It did no good. He spurred Progress, moving quickly into a trot and then a gallop. The scouts' horses were nothing special to look at, but had no trouble keeping pace.

Every couple of hours, he and his unwanted companions changed mounts at a courier relay station. His backside and inner thighs grew chafed and sore long before the end of the first day in the saddle—riding hard from dawn to dusk was far different from ambling along at the slow pace of the imperial army. But the miles melted away.

That night Krispos slept like a dead man. The attendants at the relay station had to shake him awake when morning came. He rose grumpily from his bedroll, but managed to say, "Thanks for not worrying about my imperial dignity there."

One of the attendants grinned. "Majesty, right now you smell more like a horse than an Avtokrator, if you know what I mean."

"I hadn't even noticed," Krispos said; after so long in close contact with horses, his nose no longer reported their presence. "It's not a bad smell." He'd spent years in the stables, first for Iakovitzes, then for Petronas.

Sarkis and the scouts were ready to go when Krispos mounted his latest horse. He scowled at them for being so fresh. His own rear end gave a painful protest as he settled himself in the saddle. He did his best to ignore it. His best was not good enough.

His eyes blurred with tears from the wind of his passage. He rode on. One of the horses he took had a gait hard enough to shake his teeth and his kidneys loose. He rode on. A scout's horse went lame. The fellow rode double to the next station. He got a fresh animal and they all rode on.

When Krispos stopped at last on that second day, he dismounted with the slow, brittle caution of a man twice his age. Even the iron-arsed scouts were less limber than when they'd set out. But Sarkis said, "One day more and we're in the city."

"A good thing, too," Krispos said feelingly, "for I'd never make two days more." None of the scouts laughed at him. That was the best sign he'd done enough to win their respect.

Everyone grumbled the next morning, but everyone wearily scrambled onto a horse and rode south. The horses were fresh. They went hard to the next station, but then got to rest. There was no rest for Krispos and the scouts.

Just when he was convinced he'd been on horseback forever and would stay on horseback forevermore, the walls of Videssos appeared on the southwestern horizon ahead. It was late afternoon. "Under three days," Sarkis said. "Your Majesty, were I the head of the imperial courier service, I'd hire you."

"Oh, no you wouldn't, for it's not work I'd ever seek," Krispos retorted. The scouts laughed. Krispos spurred his horse on toward the capital.

Chapter X

GNATIOS STOOD AT THE ALTAR IN THE CENTER OF THE HIGH
Temple, chanting the sunset prayers that thanked Phos for the day's
light and bid the sun to return safely on the morrow. The benches were
mostly empty; only a few pious souls joined him in the day's last liturgy.

Still wearing the trousers and tunic in which he'd ridden, Krispos strode
up the temple aisle toward the ecumenical patriarch. He felt bowlegged
and wondered if it showed. Behind him, sabers drawn, came Sarkis and
the squad of scouts. Behind them tramped a squad of Halogai, part of the
company that had been left behind to protect Dara and Phostis.

Krispos waited in grim silence until Gnatios finished the prayer that
was last as well as first: "We bless thee, Phos, lord with the great and good
mind, watchful beforehand that the great test of our life may be decided
in our favor. This liturgy now is ended. May Phos be with us all." One or
two worshipers got up to go. The rest stayed in their seats, curious to see
what would happen next. Gnatios bowed to Krispos. "I thought you with
the army, Your Majesty. How may I serve you?"

"You may not," Krispos said curtly. He turned to the Halogai. "Arrest
him. The charge is treason." The guardsmen swarmed forward. Gnatios

turned as if to run, then considered their upraised axes and thought better of it. They seized him; their big hands wrapped round his forearms in an unbreakable grip. "Take him to the Grand Courtroom."

The priests and worshipers in the High Temple cried out in dismay as the imperial guards dragged Gnatios away, but the weapons the Halogai and Sarkis' scouts carried kept them from doing anything more than cry out. Krispos had counted on that.

The streets of the city were never empty, but they were less crowded after the sun went down. The party of soldiers marched back to the palace quarter unimpeded. Surrounded by tall Halogai, Gnatios was almost invisible in their midst. Krispos had counted on that, too.

A bonfire blazed in front of the Grand Courtroom. By its light, nobles, courtiers, and high-ranking bureaucrats filed into the building. "Well done, Barsymes," Krispos said. "You look to have gotten just about everyone here."

"I did my best on short notice, Your Majesty," the vestiarios said.

"You did fine. Take charge of the guards and Gnatios here, would you? You'll know when to send them out where people can see them."

"Oh, indeed, Your Majesty." Barsymes gestured to the Halogai. "Wait here in this alcove for the time being, gentlemen. I shall tell you when to proceed."

Krispos walked down the long central aisle toward the throne. The officials who had been chattering among themselves, wondering why they'd been so abruptly summoned, fell silent when they saw him. They resumed once he was past, this time in whispers.

Closest to the throne stood Iakovitzes. He knew what was toward. "Everything all right at your end?" Krispos asked. At the Sevastos' nod, he went on, "We'll settle that later tonight, with more privacy. Meanwhile"— He climbed the steps to the throne, turned, sat, and looked out at the assembled grandees. They looked back at him.

"Noble sirs," he said, "I apologize for ordering you together so quickly this evening, but what has arisen will not wait. I must get back to the army as soon as I can; we've won a victory against Harvas and hope to win more."

"Thou conquerest, Krispos! Thou conquerest!" the courtiers shouted in union. Echoes reverberated from the high ceiling of the Grand Courtroom. The acclamation sounded more fulsome than usual. News of the victory could only have beaten Krispos to the city by a day, and it was the first victory ever over Harvas.

The outcry ceased at Krispos' upraised hand. He said, "In spite of that victory, I had to leave the army to come here to deal with a dangerous case of treason. That is why you are gathered together now." Somehow, without moving a muscle, on hearing the word *treason* the assembled nobles all contrived to look perfectly innocent. Saddened and amused at the same time, Krispos went on, "Here is the prisoner."

At a slow march, the Halogai led Gnatios, still in his patriarchal robes, down the long aisle to the imperial throne. Gusts of whispers trailed him. No one, though, exclaimed in horror or amazement. That, too, saddened Krispos, but did not surprise him. Everybody knew what Gnatios was like. The guardsmen shoved him forward. He prostrated himself before Krispos.

"I will read a letter Gnatios sent to an officer in the imperial army." Krispos drew Gnatios' letter to Rhisoulphos from his belt pouch and read it without naming Rhisoulphos. Then he cast the letter in front of Gnatios. He also threw down the fragments of the patriarch's seal of sky-blue wax. "Can you deny these are your words, written in your hand, sealed with your seal?"

Gnatios stayed on his belly and did not dare even to raise his head. "Majesty, I—" he began. Then he stopped, as if realizing nothing could save him now.

"Gnatios, you are guilty of treason," Krispos declared. "I have forgiven you before, twice over. I cannot, I do not, I will not forgive you again. Tomorrow morning you will meet the headsman, and your head will go up on the Milestone as a warning to others."

A voiceless sigh rose throughout the Grand Courtroom. Again, though, none of the courtiers seemed surprised or dismayed. Softly, Gnatios began to weep.

"Take him away," Krispos said. The guardsmen lifted Gnatios. They had to bear most of his weight as they marched him back along the central aisle, for his legs could hardly carry him. "Thank you for witnessing the sentence," Krispos told the grandees. "You may go, and may Phos bless you all."

The nobles filed out of the Grand Courtroom, talking quietly among themselves. Krispos picked up the damning letter, then caught Iakovitzes' eye. Iakovitzes nodded.

Krispos went back to the imperial residence. Dara stood in the entranceway, waiting for him. She looked uncomfortable, not least because she also looked as if she could have her baby at any moment. "What did you do with Gnatios?" she asked as he came up the steps.

"He loses his head tomorrow," Krispos said. He walked down the hall.

"Good. He should have lost it a long time ago," Dara said with a vigorous nod of approval. Then she let worry enter her voice. "Now, what didn't you tell me this afternoon, when you rode in with such a rush?"

Krispos sighed. He'd always been glad Dara was clever. Now he wished, just a little, that she wasn't. He took out Gnatios' letter to Rhisoulphos and showed it to her. She carefully read it through. When she was done, she sagged against him. "No," she whispered. "Not Father."

"I'm afraid so." He drew out the other letter his pouch contained, the one from Rhisoulphos to Gnatios. He handed it to her. "Dara, I'm sorry."

She shook her head back and forth, back and forth, like a wild creature thrashing in a trap. "What will you do?" she asked at last. "Not—" Her voice broke. She could not say the word, but Krispos knew what she meant.

"Not if he doesn't force me to it," he promised. "I have something else in mind." He was glad word of Rhisoulphos' disappearance hadn't yet got back to the imperial city.

A few minutes later the eunuch Tyrovitzes came in and said, "Your Majesty, the Sevastos Iakovitzes is outside the entrance, along with several of his, ah, retainers." The chamberlain sniffed; he had a low opinion of the handsome youths with whom Iakovitzes surrounded himself.

"I'll come out." Krispos turned to Dara. "Wait here, if you would. This has to do with you and with your father. I'll be back in just a moment." He left before she could argue.

Iakovitzes' grooms, all of them stalwart and muscular young men, bent themselves double in deep bows to Krispos. Iakovitzes also bowed, less deeply. That left one man standing straight in the middle of the crowd. Bowing would have been hard for him in any case, for his hands were tied behind his back. He did nod, politely. "Your Majesty," he said.

"Hello, Rhisoulphos," Krispos said. "I daresay you're glad to be anyplace outside of Iakovitzes' basement."

"Yes and no. Given a choice between the basement and the chopping block, I prefer the basement. In fact, I also like the basement rather better than the rolled-up carpet in which I was brought to it."

"You don't need to worry about the carpet anymore. The chopping block is something else again," Krispos said. "Come along with me—you and I and your daughter have a few things to discuss. You come, too, Iakovitzes, if you please."

Iakovitzes nodded. He pulled out his tablet and wrote, "That's all, lads," and showed it to the grooms. They nodded and started away from the imperial residence and out of the palace quarter. Iakovitzes wrote something else and passed the tablet to Krispos. "Such a pity—these days I can only pick from among lads who know how to read." Krispos screwed up his face and gave the tablet back.

When Rhisoulphos came into the chamber where Dara was sitting, she looked up at him and said, "Why, Father? Why?" Her voice trembled; tears stood in her eyes, ready to fall.

"I thought I could," he answered with a shrug. "It appears I was wrong. I would have made your son my heir, for whatever that's worth."

"Nothing," Krispos said flatly. "Gnatios goes to the block tomorrow. Give me one good reason you shouldn't follow him."

"Because I am Dara's father," Rhisoulphos said at once. "How would you dare to fall asleep beside her after you put me to death?"

Krispos wanted to kick him—he was still smooth and still right. "As you say. But if you want to live, it will cost you your hair. You'll go into a monastery for the rest of your days."

"I agree," Rhisoulphos said, again without hesitation.

Iakovitzes scowled furiously and held up his tablet so Krispos could read it. "Are you mad, Your Majesty? How many people have you clapped into monasteries, only to see them pop right out again?"

"I wasn't finished yet." Krispos turned back to Rhisoulphos. "It won't be the monastery of the holy Skirios for you. No matter what Iakovitzes thinks, I have learned better than that. If you want to live, you'll serve the good god at a monastery in Prista."

For an instant, Rhisoulphos' smooth façade cracked and revealed raw red rage. The town of Prista lay far to the north and west of Videssos the city, across the Videssian Sea. It sat on the southern tip of a peninsula that dangled down from the steppes of Pardraya and served as the Empire's listening post for the plains. It was also the most Phos-forsaken spot in the Empire to which to exile a man.

"Well, Rhisoulphos?" Krispos said.

"Let it be as you say," Rhisoulphos answered at last, his self-control restored. He nodded again to Krispos. "I appear to have underestimated you, Your Majesty. My only consolation is that I'm not the first to make that mistake."

Krispos paid hardly any attention to him after he said yes. He was looking at Dara instead, hoping she could accept the choice he'd made. After some endless time that was less than a minute, she, too, nodded. The gesture was eerily like her father's. Krispos did not care. Now once more he blessed her good sense. She saw what had to be done.

Krispos called Tyrovitzes. When the chamberlain came in, he told him, "We need a priest here, esteemed sir. Tell him to bring along scissors, razor,

Phos' holy scriptures, and a new blue robe: the eminent Rhisoulphos has decided to enter a monastery."

"Indeed, Your Majesty" was all Tyrovitzes said. He bowed and left the room.

The eunuch chamberlain returned within an hour, a priest at his side. After praying, the priest told Rhisoulphos, "Bend your head." Rhisoulphos obeyed. The priest used scissors first, then the razor. Lock by lock, Rhisoulphos' iron-gray hair fell to the floor. When all his scalp was bare, the priest held out the scriptures to him and said, "Behold the law under which you shall live if you choose. If in your heart you feel you can observe it, enter the monastic life; if not, speak now."

"I will observe it," Rhisoulphos declared. Twice more the priest asked him; twice more he affirmed his will. If he did so with irony in his voice, the priest took no notice of it.

After the third affirmation, the priest said, "Doff your garment." Rhisoulphos obeyed. The priest gave him the monastic robe to put on. "As the garment of Phos' blue covers your naked body, so may his righteousness enfold your heart and preserve it from all evil."

"So may it be," Rhisoulphos said; he formally became a monk with those words.

"Thank you, holy sir," Krispos said to the priest. "Your temple will learn that I'm grateful. Tyrovitzes, escort him back, if you would be so kind, and settle those arrangements. You needn't haggle overmuch."

"As you say, Your Majesty," Tyrovitzes murmured. Krispos knew he would haggle anyhow, on general principles. Perhaps this way he would not skin the priest too badly.

When the chamberlain had led the priest away, Krispos turned to Rhisoulphos. "Come with me, holy sir."

Rhisoulphos rose, but said, "A moment, if you please." He put a hand on Dara's shoulder. "Daughter, I wish it had turned out better. It could have."

She would not look at him. "I wish you would have left well enough alone," she said in a voice filled with tears.

"So do I, child, so do I." Rhisoulphos straightened, then dipped his head to Krispos. "Now I will accompany you."

More Halogai than the usual squad of guards stood outside the imperial residence. The extra men converged on Rhisoulphos. Krispos said, "Take the holy sir here to the *Sea Lion,* which is tied up at the Neorhesian harbor. Put him aboard; in fact, stay aboard with him until the *Sea Lion* sails for Prista in the morning."

The guardsmen saluted. "We obey, Majesty," one of them said.

"You have everything ready for me," Rhisoulphos observed. "Nicely done."

"I try," Krispos said shortly. He nodded to the Halogai. They took charge of the new-made monk. Krispos watched them march him down the path till it rounded a corner and took them out of his sight. He sighed and drank in a long lungful of sweet night air. Then he went back inside.

When he walked into the audience chamber, Iakovitzes' eyes flickered from him to Dara and back again. The Sevastos quickly got to his feet. "I'd best be going," he wrote in large letters. He held up the tablet to show it to both Krispos and Dara, then bowed and left with what would have been unforgivable abruptness in most circumstances. As it was, Krispos did not blame Iakovitzes for being so precipitate. He just wished the Sevastos would have stayed longer.

No help for it: he was alone with Dara after sending her father into exile. "I'm sorry," he said, and meant it. "I didn't see what else to do."

She nodded. "If you want to keep the throne, if you want to stay alive, you did what you had to do. I know that. But"—she turned her head away from him; her voice broke—"it's hard."

"Aye, it is." He came over to her and stroked her lustrous black hair. He was afraid she would shy from him, but she sat steady. He went on, "When I was a peasant, I used to think how easy the Avtokrator must have it. All he needs to do is give an order, and people do things for him." He laughed briefly. "I wish it were that simple."

"I wish it were, too. But it's not." Dara looked up at him. "You seldom speak of your days on the farm."

"Most of them aren't worth talking about. Believe me, this is better," Krispos said. Dara did not pursue it, which suited him fine. The chief reason he rarely mentioned his early days to her was that he did not want to remind her how lowly his origins were. Since explaining would also have brought that to the fore, he was pleased to get away without having to.

"Let's go to bed," Dara said. "The lord with the great and good mind knows I won't sleep much with the baby kicking me and getting me up to make water half a dozen times a night, but I ought to try to get what I can."

"All right," Krispos said. Before long, the last lamp was blown out and he lay in the darkness beside Dara. He remembered Rhisoulphos' gibe. Was he safe next to her now, with Rhisoulphos on a ship bound for Prista? He must have decided he was, for he fell asleep while he was still mulling over the question, and did not wake the rest of the night.

At THE NORTHERN EDGE OF THE PALACE QUARTER, NOT FAR from the Sorcerers' Collegium, was a small park known to city wits as the hunting ground. It was not stocked with boar or antlered stag. In the center of that hedge-surrounded patch of greensward stood a much-hacked oak stump whose height was convenient for a kneeling man's neck.

His back to the early-morning sun, Krispos waited not far from that stump. A couple of Haloga guards stood by, chatting with each other in their own language. They kept sneaking glances at the headsman, who was leaning his chin on the pommel of his sword. He was a tall man, almost as tall as a Haloga. Finally one of the northerners could hold out no more. He walked over to the headsman and said, "Please, sir, may I try the heft of that great blade?"

"Be my guest."

The headsman watched the guard get the feel of the two-handed grip, smiling at his whistle over the sword's weight. The Haloga backed off and swung it a couple of times, first across at waist level, then up and down. He whistled again, gave it back. "A brave brand indeed, but too heavy for me."

"You handle it better than most," the headsman said. "Must be that you're used to the axe, which isn't light, either. I've seen big strong men, but ones who're used to these cavalry sabers that don't weigh nothin', almost fall over when they try my sword."

They went on talking for a few minutes, two professionals in related fields passing the time until one of them had to do his job. Then more Halogai brought Gnatios into the little park. He wore a plain linen robe, not even blue. His hands were tied behind him.

He stopped when he saw Krispos. "Please, Your Majesty, I beseech you—" He fell to his knees. "Have mercy, in the name of Phos, in the name of the service I gave you in the matter of Harvas—"

Krispos bit his lip. He'd come to witness the execution because he thought he owed Gnatios that much. But did he owe him mercy—again? He shook his head. "May Phos judge you more kindly than I must, Gnatios, in the name of the service you gave me in the matter of Petronas, and in the matter of Rhisoulphos. Who would be next?" He turned to the guardsmen. "Take him to the stump."

They dragged Gnatios the last few feet, not kindly but not cruelly either, just going about their business. One told him, "Hold still and it will be over soonest."

"Aye, he's right," the headsman said. "You'd not want to twist and maybe make me have to strike twice."

Still not roughly, the guards forced Gnatios' head down to the stump. His eyes were wide and bright and staring, with white all around the iris. He sucked in great noisy gulps of air; his chest rose and fell against the thin fabric of his robe in an extremity of fear. "Please," he mouthed over and over again. "Oh, please."

The headsman stepped up beside the oak stump. He swung the two-handed sword over his head. Gnatios screamed. The sword came down. The scream cut off abruptly as the heavy blade bit through flesh and bone. Gnatios' head rolled away, cleanly severed at the first stroke. Krispos was appalled to see its eyes blink twice as it fell from the stump.

Every muscle in Gnatios' body convulsed at the instant of beheading. It jerked free of the Halogai. Blood fountained from the stump of his neck as his heart gave a couple of last beats before it realized he was dead. His bowels and bladder emptied, befouling his robe and adding their stenches to the hot iron smell of blood.

Krispos turned away, more than a little sickened. He'd read of blood-thirsty tyrants who liked nothing better than seeing the heads of their enemies—real or imagined—roll. All he wondered was whether the chunk of bread he'd had on the way over would stay down. Watching a helpless man die was worse than anything the battlefield had shown him. How Harvas could have struck down a whole city grew only more mysterious, and more dreadful.

Krispos turned to the headsman, who stood proudly, expecting praise, conscious of a job well done. "He didn't suffer," Krispos said—the best he could do. The headsman beamed, so it must have been enough. Krispos went on, "Take the head"—he would not look at it—"to the Milestone. I'm going back to the imperial residence."

"As you say, Your Majesty." The headsman bowed. "Your presence here honored me this morning."

Not long after Krispos returned to the residence, Barsymes asked him what he wanted for lunch. "Nothing, thanks," he said. The vestiarios did not change expression, but still conveyed that his answer was not an acceptable response. Krispos felt he had to explain. "You needn't fear I'll make a bloodthirsty tyrant, esteemed sir. I find I don't have the stomach for it."

"Ah." Now Barsymes' voice showed he understood. "Will you return to the army later today, then?"

"I have a couple of things to do before I go. Do I remember rightly that Pyrrhos, while he was patriarch, condemned the hierarch Savianos for some tiny lapse or other?"

"Yes, Your Majesty, that's so." Barsymes' eyes narrowed. "Am I to infer, then, that you will name Savianos ecumenical patriarch rather than restoring Pyrrhos to his old throne?"

"That's just what I intend to do, if he wants the job. I've had a bellyful of quarrelsome clerics. Will you arrange to have Savianos brought here as quickly as you can?"

"I shall have to find out in which monastery he's been confined, but yes, I will deal with that at once."

Toward evening that day Savianos prostrated himself before Krispos. "How may I serve Your Majesty?" he asked as he rose. His face was craggy and intelligent; beyond that, Krispos had learned better than to guess character from features.

He came straight to the point: "Gnatios' head went up on the Milestone this morning. I want you to succeed him as ecumenical patriarch."

Savianos' shaggy gray eyebrows leaped like startled gray caterpillars. "Me, Your Majesty? Why me? For one thing, I'm more nearly of Gnatios' theological bent than Pyrrhos', and I even spoke against Pyrrhos when you named *him* patriarch. For another, why would I want the patriarchal throne if you just killed the man who was on it? I have no interest in making the headsman's acquaintance just because I somehow offended you."

"Gnatios didn't meet the headsman for offending me. He met him for plotting against me. If you plan on meddling in politics after you put on the blue boots, you'd best stay where you are."

"If I'd wanted to meddle in politics, I'd have become a bureaucrat, not a priest," Savianos said.

"Good enough. As for the other, I remember your speaking up for Gnatios. That took courage. It's one of the reasons I want you to be patriarch. And my own beliefs aren't as, as"—Krispos groped for a word—"rigid as Pyrrhos'. I didn't object to Gnatios' doctrines, only to his treason. So, holy sir, shall I submit your name to the synod?"

"You really mean it," Savianos said in a wondering tone. He studied Krispos, giving him a more thorough and critical scrutiny than he was used to getting since he'd become Avtokrator. At last, with a nod, the priest said, "No, you're not one to butcher for the sport of it, are you?"

"No," Krispos answered at once, queasily remembering how Gnatios' head had blinked as it bounced from the stump onto the grass.

"No," Savianos agreed. "All right, Your Majesty, if you want to give it to me, I'll take it on. Shall we aim to work without biting each other's tails?"

"By the good god, that's just what we need to do." Krispos felt like cheering. He'd said that to Pyrrhos and Gnatios both, time and again;

each in his own way had chosen to ignore it. Now an ecclesiastic was saying it for himself! "Holy sir—most holy sir to be—I already feel I've picked the right man."

Savianos' chuckle had a wry edge to it. "Don't praise the horse till you've ridden him. If you tell me as much three years from now, we'll both have reason to be pleased."

"I'm pleased right now. Let me come up with a couple of truly ghastly names to go along with the rules of the synod and I'll be able to get back to the army knowing the temples are in good hands."

After Savianos left the imperial residence, Krispos summoned the grand drungarios of the fleet, a solidly built veteran sailor named Kanaris. That meeting was much shorter than the one with Savianos. But then, unlike Savianos, Kanaris did not need to be persuaded—when he heard what Krispos wanted, he rushed away as fast as he could go, all eager to start at once. Krispos wished he could look forward to the ride back to the army with equal anticipation.

THE RIDE NORTH WAS AS FAST AS THE RIDE SOUTH HAD BEEN, but even harder to endure. Krispos had hoped he would be inured to the endless rolling, jouncing hours in the saddle, but it was not so. By the time he returned to camp, his best walk was a spraddle-legged shamble. Sarkis and the squad of scouts were in hardly better shape. The worst of it was, Krispos knew more long days of riding lay ahead.

The soldiers cheered as he rode up to the imperial tent. He waved back to them and put all the exuberance he had left into that wave. They would have been less flattered to know why he was so pleased, but he kept that to himself. He'd most dreaded coming upon their broken remnants as he hurried north.

"Things have been quiet while you were gone," Mammianos reported that evening, when Krispos met with his officers. "A few skirmishes here, a few there, but nothing major. Oh, the wizards have had a bit to do, too, so they have."

Krispos glanced at Trokoundos. "Aye, a bit to do," the mage said. Krispos concealed a start at the sound of his voice—he sounded more than tired, he sounded old. Battling Harvas had taken its toll on him. But he continued with sober pride, "Everything the Skotos-lover has hurled at us, we have withstood. I'll not deny he's cost us a handful of men, but only a handful. Without us, the army would be in ruins."

"I believe you, magical sir," Krispos said. "All Videssos owes you and your fellows a great debt of thanks. With everything safe here, I can give you my own news from the capital." Everyone leaned toward him. "First, Gnatios is patriarch no more. He plotted against me once too often, and I took his head."

Only nods greeted that announcement, not exclamations of surprise. Krispos nodded, too. Trokoundos and Mammianos had both known why he'd returned to the city in such a hurry, and he hadn't ordered either one of them to keep quiet about it. For that matter, he often thought ordering a Videssian to keep quiet about anything was a waste of breath.

He went on, "Next, I bring word of the eminent Rhisoulphos. He turns out to have given up the soldier's life for that of a monk, and is spending his days in Phos' service at a monastery in Prista."

That produced all the reaction he could have wanted. "Prista?" Bagradas burst out. "By the good god, what's he doing in Prista? How'd he get there?" Several other officers loudly wondered the same thing. Krispos did not answer. One by one the soldiers and mages noticed he was not an-swering. They started to use their brains instead of their mouths. No Videssian of reasonable rank ignored politics; ignoring politics was unsafe. Before long they reached the proper conclusion. "I'm to keep my regi-ment, then?" Bagradas asked.

"I'd say it's very likely," Krispos agreed with a straight face.

"A nice bit of work, that, Your Majesty," Mammianos said. Almost everyone echoed him. Nobles and courtiers had an artist's appreciation for underhandedness brought off with panache.

"I did one more brief bit of business while I was in the capital," Krispos said. "I ordered Kanaris to send a fleet of dromons up the Astris River. If the Halogai want to cross into Kubrat to fight for Harvas, why should we let them have an easy time of it?"

Fierce growls of approval rose from the officers. "Aye, let's see 'em take on our dromons with the canoes they hollow out of logs," Mammianos said.

"All this may hurt Harvas indirectly, but how do we do more than that?" Sarkis asked. "We can't go through him; we tried that last summer." He pointed to a map that a couple of stones held down and unrolled on Krispos' portable desk. "The next pass north into Kubrat is easily eighty miles east of here. That's too far to coordinate with a flying column, and if we set the whole army moving, what's to keep Harvas from shifting, too, on his side of the mountains?"

"We could double back—" Mammianos began. Then he shook his head. "No, it's too complicated, too likely to go wrong. Besides, if we march away from here, what's to keep Harvas from just jumping right back down into Videssos?"

"There is a pass closer than eighty miles from here," Krispos said.

Wizards and officers crowded close around the portable desk, peered down. Sarkis pointed out the obvious. "It's not on the map, Your Majesty."

"I know it's not," Krispos said. "I've been through it all the same, when I was maybe six years old and the Kubratoi herded my whole village up into their country. The outlet at the southern end is hard to find; a forest and a spur of hillside hide it away unless you come at it from the right angle. The pass is narrow and winding; a squad of troops could hold back an army inside it. But if you gentlemen don't know of it, the odds are decent that Harvas doesn't, either."

"The Kubratoi won't have told him, that's certain," Mammianos said. Everybody nodded at that; by all accounts, Harvas and his Halogai had been no gentler in Kubrat than they were in the Empire of Videssos.

Sarkis said, "I mean no offense, Your Majesty, but even if all is as you say, you have not been six years old for some time. How can you lead us to this hidden pass now?"

Krispos looked to Trokoundos. "The good god willing, between them the talented mages here should be able to pull the way from my mind. I traveled it, after all."

"The memory is there," Trokoundos affirmed. "As for bringing it into the open once more . . . We can try, Your Majesty. I would not presume to say more than that."

"Then tomorrow you will try," Krispos said. "I'd say tonight, but I'm so tired right now that I don't think I have any mind left to look into." The officers chuckled, all but Sarkis, who had ridden with Krispos. Sarkis was too busy yawning.

TROKOUNDOS CEREMONIOUSLY HANDED KRISPOS A CUP. "DRINK this, if you please, Your Majesty."

Before he drank, Krispos held the cup under his nose. Beneath the sweet, fruity odor of red wine, he caught others smells, more pungent and musty. "What's in it?" he asked, half curious, half suspicious.

"It's a decoction to help loosen your wits from the here and now," the mage answered. "There are roasted henbane seeds in it, ground hemp leaves and seeds, a distillate from the poppy, and several other things as well. You'll likely feel rather drunk all through the day; past that, the brew is harmless."

"Let's be about it." With an abrupt motion, Krispos knocked back the cup. His lips twisted; it tasted nastier than it smelled.

Trokoundos eased him down into a folding chair. "Are you comfortable, Your Majesty?"

"Comfortable? Yes, I—think so." Krispos listened to himself answer, as if from far away. He felt his mind float, detach itself from his body. Despite what Trokoundos had said, it was not like being drunk. It was not like anything he had ever known. It was pleasant, though. He wondered vaguely if Anthimos had ever tried it. Probably. If anything yielded pleasure, Anthimos would have tried it. Then Anthimos, too, slid away from Krispos' mind. He smiled, content to float.

"Majesty? Hear me, Your Majesty." Trokoundos' voice echoed and re-echoed inside Krispos' head. He found he could not ignore it, found he did not want to ignore it. The mage went on, "Your Majesty, cast your mind back to journeying through the passes between Videssos and Kurat. I conjure you, remember, remember, remember."

Obediently—he did not seem to have much will of his own—Krispos let his mind spin back through time. All at once he gasped; his distant body stiffened and began to sweat. Halogai chopped down his horsemen at the barricade. A black-robed figure gestured, and boulders sprang from the hillsides to smash his army. "Harvas!" he said harshly.

"Further, reach further," Trokoundos said. "Remember, remember, remember."

The lost battle of the summer before misted over and vanished from Krispos' thoughts. He rolled back and back and back, one gray year after another passing away. Then all at once he was in the pass again, the pass he had tried and failed to force—somehow he both knew and did not know that at the same time. A short, plump man in the robes of a Videssian noble rode by. He looked cocky and full of spit. Krispos knew his name, and knew—and did not know—much more than that. "Iakovitzes!" he exclaimed. He exclaimed again, wordlessly, for the voice that came from his lips was not his own but a boy's high treble.

"How old are you?" Trokoundos demanded.

He thought about it. "Nine," the boy's voice answered for him.

"Further, reach further. Remember, remember, remember."

Again he whirled through time. Now he emerged from a forest track toward what seemed at first only a spur of hillock in front of the mountains. But shouting men on ponies urged him and his companions on with curses and threats. Beyond that spur was a narrow opening. A man in a tunic of homespun wool steadied him with a hand on his shoulder.

He looked up in thanks. Amazement ran through him—he thought he was looking at himself. Then the amazement doubled. "Father," he whispered in a child's voice, a younger child's voice now.

Trokoundos broke into his—vision? "How old are you?"

"I—think I'm six."

"Do you see before you the pass of which your adult self spoke? See it now with adult eyes as well as those of a child. Mark well everything about it, so that you may find it once more. Can you do this and remember afterward?"

"Yes," Krispos said. His voice was an odd blend of two, of boy's and man's, both of them his own. He did not simply look at the opening to the pass anymore, he studied it, considered the forest from which he'd emerged, contemplated the streak of pinkish stone that ran through the spur, examined the mountains and fixed their precise configuration in his mind. At last he said, "I will remember."

Trokoundos put another cup in his hand. "Drink this, then."

It was a hot, meaty broth, rich with the taste of fat. With every swallow, Krispos felt his mind and body rejoin each other. But even when he was himself again, he remembered everything about the pass—and the feel of his father's strong hand on his shoulder, guiding him along. "Thank you," he said to Trokoundos. "You gave me a great gift. Not many men can say their father touched them long years after he was dead."

Trokoundos bowed. "Your Majesty, I'm pleased to help in any way I can, even that one which I did not expect."

"Any way you can," Krispos mused. He nodded, more than half to himself. "Ride with me, then, Trokoundos. If need be, you can use your magic again to help me find the pass. We'll need a sorcerer along anyhow, to keep Harvas from noticing us as we slip around his flank. If he catches us in that narrow place, we're done for."

"I will ride with you," Trokoundos said. "Let me go back to my tent now, to gather the tools and supplies I'll need." He bowed again and walked away, rubbing his chin as he thought about just what he ought to take.

Krispos thought about that, too, but in terms of manpower rather than sorcerous paraphernalia. Sarkis and his scouts, of course . . . Krispos smiled. No matter how sore Sarkis' backside was, he couldn't complain his Emperor had ordered him to do anything Krispos wasn't also doing. But he'd need more than scouts on this mission. . . .

The column rode south out of camp the next day before noon. The imperial standard still fluttered over Krispos' tent; imperial guards still tramped back and forth before it. But some dozens of horsemen concealed blond hair beneath helms and surcoat hoods. They stayed clustered around one man in nondescript gear who rode a nondescript horse—Progress was also still back at camp.

Once well out of view of their own camp and that of the foe, the soldiers paused. Trokoundos went to work. At last he nodded to Krispos. "If Harvas tries to track us by magic, Your Majesty, he will, Phos willing, perceive us as continuing southward, perhaps on our way to the imperial capital. Whereas in reality—"

"Aye." Krispos pointed to the east. The riders swung off the north–south thoroughfare and onto one of the narrow dirt tracks that led away from it. The forest pressed close along either side of the track; the column lengthened, simply because the troopers lacked the room to ride more than four or five abreast.

Every so often, even smaller paths branched off from the track and wound their way back toward the mountains. Scouts galloped down each one of them to see if it seemed to dead-end against a spur of hillock with a streak of pink stone running through it. Krispos thought his flanking column was still too far west, but took no chances.

The soldiers camped that night in the first clearing large enough to hold them all that they found. Krispos asked Trokoundos, "Any sign Harvas knows what we're up to?"

He wanted the mage to grin and shake his head. Instead, Trokoundos frowned. "Your Majesty, I've had the feeling—and it is but a feeling—that we are being sorcerously sought. Whether it's by Harvas or not I cannot say, for the seeking is at the very edge of my ability to perceive it."

"Who else would it be?" Krispos said with a scoffing laugh. Trokoundos laughed, too. He was not scoffing. Magicians did not scoff about Harvas. Monster he surely was, but they took him most seriously.

Krispos sent double sentry parties out on picket duty and ordered them to set up farther than usual from the camp. He had doubts about how much good that would do. If Harvas found him out, the first he was likely to know of it would be a magical onslaught that wrecked the flying column. The sentries went out even so, on the off chance he was wrong.

As usual, he got up at sunrise. He gnawed hard bread, drank rough wine, mounted, and rode. As he headed east, he kept peering at the mountains through breaks in the trees. By noon he knew he and his men were getting close. The granite shapes that turned the horizon jagged looked ever more familiar. He began to worry about overrunning the pass.

Hardly had the thought crossed his mind when a sloppily dressed scout came pounding up to him. "Majesty, I found it, Majesty!" the fellow said. "A pink vein of rock on the spur, and when I rode in back of it, sure enough, it opens out. I'll take us there!"

"Lead us," Krispos said, slapping the scout on the back. The order to halt ran quickly through the column—horns and drums were silent, for fear Harvas might somehow detect their rhythmic calls at a range beyond that of merely human ears.

The scout led the troopers back to a forest path no different from half a dozen others they'd passed earlier in the day. As soon as Krispos plunged into the woods, he knew he'd traveled this way before. Almost as if it came from the leaves and branches around him, he picked up a sense of the fear and urgency he'd had the last time he used this track. He thought for a moment he could hear guttural Kubrati voices shouting for him to hurry, hurry, but it was only the wind and a cawing crow. All the same, sweat prickled under his armpits and ran down his flanks like drops of molten lead.

Then the path seemed to come to a dead end against a spur of rock with a pink streak through it. The scout pointed and asked excitedly, "Is this it, Your Majesty? It looks just like what you were talking about. Is it?"

"By the lord with the great and good mind, it is," Krispos whispered. Awe on his face, he turned and bowed in the saddle to Trokoundos. The place looked as familiar as if he'd last seen it day before yesterday—and so, thanks to the mage's skill, he had. Before he ordered the army into the pass, he asked Trokoundos, "Are we detected?"

"Let me check." After a few minutes of work the wizard answered, "Not so far as I can tell. I still think we may be sought, but Harvas has not found us. I do not say this lightly, Your Majesty: I stake my life on the truth of it no less than yours."

"So you do." Krispos took a deep breath and brought up his arm to point. "Forward!"

The pass was as narrow and winding as he remembered. If the sides did not seem quite so overwhelmingly high, he was now a full-grown man on horseback rather than a boy stumbling along afoot. He was as afraid now as then, though. A squad of Harvas' Halogai could plug the pass; if men waited up above with boulders, the evil wizard would need no wizardry to rid himself of this entire column.

The troopers felt the danger as starkly as he did. They leaned forward over their horses' necks, gently urging the animals to more and more speed. And the horses responded; they liked being in that narrow, echoing, gloomy place—it was so steep, the sun could not reach down to the bottom—no better than did their riders.

"How long till we're through?" Sarkis asked Krispos as the gloom began to deepen toward evening. "By the good god, Majesty, I don't want to have to spend the night in this miserable cleft."

"Neither do I," Krispos said. "I think we're close to the end of it."

Sure enough, less than an hour later the advance guard of the column burst out of the pass and into the foothill country on the northern side of the mountains. Looking north, Krispos saw nothing but those hills leading down to a flatter country of plains and patches of forest. He turned round to the granite mass of the mountains. To have them behind him instead of before seemed strange and unnatural, as if sky and land had changed places on the horizon.

Full darkness was close at hand. The evening star dominated the western sky, though a thin fingernail-paring of moon also hung there. More and more stars came out as crimson and then gray faded into black.

The soldiers buzzed with excitement as they set up camp. They'd flanked Harvas and he didn't know it. Day after tomorrow they would crash into his unguarded rear; he and his men would be caught between their hammer and the anvil of the main imperial army. One trooper told his tentmate, "They say the bastard's a good wizard. He'll need to be better than good to get away from us now."

"He is better than good," the second soldier answered.

Krispos sketched Phos' sun-circle over his heart to avert any possible omen. Then he went to check with Trokoundos. The mage said, "No, we are not found. I still feel we are sought, but I would also have that feeling because of Harvas' sorcerous scrutiny of the supposed southward journey of this army."

"How much longer can that trick hold up?" Krispos asked.

"Long enough, I hope. The farther Harvas' magic has to reach, the less omniscient it becomes. There are no guidelines, I admit, the more so for a unique sorcerer like Harvas. But as I say, what we have done should suffice."

That was as much reassurance as Krispos could reasonably expect. He arranged himself in his bedroll confident that Harvas would not turn him into a spider while he slept. And sleep he did; despite aches in every riding muscle, he went out like a blown lamp while he was still trying to get a blanket up to his chin.

Camp broke quickly the next morning. Everyone knew the column had stolen a march on Harvas, and everyone wanted to take advantage of it. Underofficers had to warn men not to wear out their horses by riding too hard too soon.

Off in the distance Krispos saw other small mounted parties. They saw his men, too, and promptly fled. He did not know what to feel as he watched them gallop away. So these were the fierce Kubratoi who had scourged Videssos' northern provinces all through his childhood! Now they only wanted to escape.

His pride at that was punctured when Trokoundos remarked, "I wonder whether they think we're really who we are or some of Harvas' men."

Near noon a band of about a dozen nomads approached the column instead of running away. "You horsemen, you imperials?" one of them called in broken Videssian.

"Aye," the soldiers answered, ready to kill them if they turned to take that news to Harvas Black-Robe.

But the Kubrati went on, "You come to fight Harvas?"

"Aye," the soldiers repeated, with a yell this time.

"We fight with you, we fight for you." The nomad held his bow over his head "Harvas and his axemen, they worst in world. You Videssians, you gots to be better. Better you rule over us than Harvas any day, any day better." He spoke to his companions in their own language. They shouted what had to be agreement.

Krispos lifted his helmet so he could scratch his head. *Kubratoi* had meant *enemies* to him since he was six years old. Even imagining them as comrades came hard. But the nomad had spoken the truth in a way he probably did not suspect. The land of Kubrat had been Videssian once. If the imperial army beat Harvas, it would become Videssian again— Krispos did not intend to turn it over to some Kubrati chieftain who would stay grateful until the day he thought he could safely raid south of the mountains, and not a moment longer. Gnatios had taught him some hard lessons about how long loyalty was apt to last.

Still, if he did succeed in annexing—reannexing, he reminded himself— Kubrat, the goodwill of the locals would be worth something. "Aye, join us," he told the nomads. "Help drive the invaders out of Kubrat." He did not say *out of your land*. None of the Kubratoi noticed the fine distinction.

Most of the nomads who saw the flying column continued to avoid it. But several more groups came in, so that by the end of the day close to a hundred Kubratoi camped with the Videssians. Their furs and boiled-leather cuirasses contrasted oddly with the linen surcoats and iron shirts the imperials wore. Their ponies also looked like nothing much next to the bigger, handsomer horses that came from south of the mountains. But those ponies hadn't breathed hard while they kept up with the column, and Krispos knew the Kubratoi could fight. He was glad to have them.

"We can't be more than three or four hours away from Harvas," Krispos said to Sarkis, "but we haven't seen a single Haloga. He doesn't know we're here."

"So it seems, Your Majesty." Sarkis' white teeth flashed in the firelight, very bright against his thick black beard and mustaches. "I said a couple of years ago, when I first served under you, that things wouldn't be dull. Who else would have found a way to sneak up on the nastiest wizard the world's ever seen?"

"I hope we *are* sneaking up on him," Trokoundos said. "My feeling of being sought grows ever stronger. It worries me, and yet surely Harvas would assail us if he knew we were here. I wish Zaidas were along, to tell me all my fears are so much moonshine. The good god grant that I hold Harvas befooled yet a little longer."

"So may it be," Krispos and Sarkis said in the same breath. They both sketched the sun-sign.

Sarkis added, "This also shows the risk of depending too much on magic. If Harvas had his scouts properly posted, he'd already know we were loose in his country."

"It's not his country," Krispos said. "It's ours." He explained the thoughts he'd had when the first Kubrati party attached itself to the column, finishing, "We'll never have another chance like this to bring Kubrat back under our rule."

Sarkis let out a soft, approving grunt. Trokoundos cocked his head to one side and studied Krispos. "You've grown, Your Majesty," he said. "You've come into the long view of things you need to make a proper Avtokrator. Who but a man with that long view would say that taking Kubrat, which has been a thorn in our flesh for three centuries now, is bringing it *back* under our rule?"

Both pleased and amused, Krispos said, "The good god willing, I've learned a bit from that long past of ours." He yawned. "Right now, this whole day seems a very long past all by itself. It's hard to remember when I've been out of the saddle except to squat by the side of the road or to sleep, which is what I'm going to do now."

"This is a sound strategy," Sarkis said, his voice filled with such military seriousness that Krispos came to attention and saluted. Then, laughing, he went off to spread out his blankets.

The next morning the troopers checked their swords' edges and made sure their arrows were straight and well fletched, as they did when they were certain they would be going into battle before long. They leaped onto their horses and stormed westward. Krispos knew the only thing that made veterans hurry toward a fight was confidence they would win.

All that kept his own confidence from soaring equally was Trokoundos' attitude. The mage kept looking back over his shoulder, as if he expected to see Harvas on the horse right behind him. "We are sought," he said over and over again, his voice haunted.

But despite his forebodings, neither Krispos nor any of the soldiers in the flying column had any sense that Harvas knew they were there. He'd posted no guards, not in land he thought his own. And there, ahead in the distance, lay the northern mouth of the pass through the mountains in which the wizard and his Halogai were about to be bottled.

"Unfurl our banner," Krispos said. The imperial standard, gold sunburst on blue, fluttered free at the head of the column.

But before the men could even begin to raise a cheer, Trokoundos went white as milk. "We are found," he whispered. His eyes were huge and frightened.

"Too late," Krispos said fiercely, trying to restore his spirit. "We have Harvas now, not the other way round." The words were hardly out of his mouth before a wall of blackness sprang up in front of the column. It stretched north and south, far as the eye could see. The troopers in the lead quickly reined in to keep from running into it headlong.

It did not dishearten Krispos. "There, you see?" he said to Trokoundos. "It's the same paltry trick he used to slow down the army south of the mountains. One touch from you then and the whole silly wall just disappeared. Does he think to fool us the same way twice?"

Trokoundos visibly revived. "Aye, you're right, Your Majesty. He must indeed be panicked, to forget he already used this illusion against us. And a panicked sorcerer is a weakened sorcerer. Let me get rid of this phantasm, and then on to the attack."

The soldiers in earshot yelled and clapped. They swatted Trokoundos on the shoulder as his smooth-gaited gray approached the barrier with mincing steps. The mage dismounted a few feet away, walked straight up to it. He stretched out a hand, leaned forward, shouted, "Begone!"

Far, far off in the distance, Krispos thought he heard a woman's voice crying, "No! Wait!" He shook his head, annoyed at his ears' playing tricks on him. In any case, the cry came too late. Trokoundos' forefinger had met the wall of blackness.

As they had before, lightnings crackled round the mage. Men who had not been close by when he pierced the barrier south of the mountains cried out in alarm and dismay. Krispos sat smiling on his horse, waiting for the barrier to dissolve.

Trokoundos screamed, a raw, wordless sound of terror and agony. His spine spasmed and arched backward, as if it were a bow being bent. He screamed again, this time intelligibly, "Trap!" He flung his arms out wide. His back bent still farther, impossibly far. He cried out one last time, again without words.

His hands writhed. The motions reminded Krispos of sorcerous passes. If they were, they did no good. With a sound like that of a cracking knuckle but magnified a thousand times, Trokoundos' backbone broke. He fell to the ground, limp and dead.

The black wall—Harvas Black-Robe's black wall—remained.

Along with his soldiers, Krispos stared in consternation at Trokoundos' crumpled corpse. What would happen to him now, with his own chief wizard slain and Harvas all too aware of exactly where he was? *You'll die in whatever dreadful way Harvas wants you to die* was the first answer that sprang to mind. He cast about for a better one, but did not find any.

Shouts came from the right flank of the column. The Kubratoi who had briefly attached themselves to Krispos' force were galloping off as fast as their little ponies would take them. "Shall we pursue?" Sarkis asked.

"No, let them go," Krispos answered wearily. "You can't blame them for changing their minds about our chances, can you?"

"No, Majesty, not when I've just changed my own." Sarkis managed a grin, but not of the cheery sort—it looked more like the snarl of a hunting beast brought to bay. "What do we do now?"

To his relief, Krispos did not have to answer that at once. A trooper from the rear guard rode up, saluted, and said, "Your Majesty, there's a party of maybe fifteen or twenty horsemen coming up on us from behind."

"More Kubratoi?" Krispos asked. "They'll turn tail when they see the mess we're in." His eyes flicked to Trokoundos' body again. Soon, he knew, he would feel the loss of a friend as well as that of a mage. He had no time for that, not now, not yet.

The trooper said, "Your Majesty, they don't look like Kubratoi, or ride like 'em, either. They look like Videssians, is what they look like."

"Videssians?" Krispos' rather heavy eyebrows drew together over his nose. Had Mammianos sent men after him for some reason? If he had, would Harvas have spotted the party because it was not warded? And could the evil wizard have been led from that party to the flying column Krispos led? The chain of logic made all too much sense. Cold anger in his voice, Krispos went on, "Bring them here to me, this instant."

"Aye, Your Majesty." The trooper wheeled his horse and set spurs to it. The animal squealed a loud protest but quickly went into a gallop. Clods of dirt flew up from its hooves as it bounded away.

Krispos fought down the urge to ride after the fellow, making himself wait. Before long the trooper returned with the band of which he'd spoken. By their horses, by their gear, they were Videssians, as he'd said. As they drew closer, Krispos' frown deepened. He recognized none of them that he could see, though some were hidden behind others. Surely Mammianos would have sent out someone he knew.

"Who are you people?" he said. "What are you doing here?"

The answer came from the back of the group. "Majesty, we are come to give you aid, as we may."

Krispos stared. So did every man who heard that light, clear voice or saw the beardless, sculptured profile beneath that conical cavalry helm. Tanilis might don chain mail, but no one anywhere would ever mistake her for a man.

With an effort, Krispos found his own voice. "My lady, the good god knows you're welcome and more than welcome. But how did you track us here? Trokoundos was sure he'd screened off the column from sorcerers' senses. Of course, Trokoundos proved not to know everything there was to know." His mouth twisted; he jerked his chin toward the mage's corpse.

Tanilis' eyes moved with his gesture. A slim finger sketched the sun-circle above her left breast. She said, "Honor to his skill, for had I depended on finding your soldiers, I should not have been aware of their true path till far too late. But I sought *you* with my magic, Your Majesty; our old ties of friendship made that possible where the other would have failed."

"Aye, friendship," Krispos said slowly. Their ties had been more intimate than that, back a decade before when he'd wintered in Opsikion, helping Iakovitzes recover from a badly broken leg. He studied her. She was ten years older than he, or a bit more; her son Mavros had been only five years younger. Some of her years showed, but not many. Most of them had only added character to a beauty that had once been almost beyond needing it.

She sat her horse quietly, waiting under his scrutiny. She did not wait long; that had never been her way. "However skilled your mage was, in Harvas Black-Robe he found one stronger than himself. Do you think Harvas sits idly on the other side of that wall he made, that wall black as his robes, black as his heart?"

"I very much fear he doesn't," Krispos said, "but with Trokoundos slain, how can I answer him? Unless . . ." His voice trailed away.

"Just so," Tanilis said. "I tried to warn your wizard, there at the end, but he was too full of himself to hear or heed me."

"*I* heard you," Krispos exclaimed.

"I thought you might have. Harvas is also stronger than I am. This I know. I will stand against him all the same, for my Emperor and for my son." She slid down from her horse and approached the barrier Harvas had set in front of the flying column. After some minutes' study, she turned back to Krispos. "Considering what you may find on the other side, your warriors would be well advised to form line of battle."

"Aye." Krispos waved. The command ran down the column. The troopers moved smoothly into place. They still sent wary glances toward the black wall, but the routine of having orders to follow soaked up some of their fear.

Instead of stabbing at the barrier with a peremptory index finger, Tanilis gently touched it with the palm of her hand. Krispos held his breath; his heard pounded as he wondered if the livid lightnings would consume her as they had Trokoundos. The lightnings flashed. Some of the soldiers groaned—they had no great hope for her.

"Is she mad?" one man said.

"No, she knows what she's about," another answered, his eastern accent hinting that he came from somewhere not far from Opsikion. "That's the lady Tanilis, that is, mother to Mavros the dead Sevastos and a sorceress in her own right, if the tales be true." His words went up and down the line, faster than Krispos' command had: rumors were more interesting than orders.

Tanilis' back stiffened, arched . . . but only a little. "No, Harvas, not now," she said, so softly Krispos barely heard. "You have already hurt me worse than this." It was as if she did not fight against whatever torment the black barrier dealt out, but rather accepted it, and in accepting defeated it.

The wall seemed to sense that. The lightnings blazed ever brighter around Tanilis as it sought to lay her low. But she refused to topple. "No," she said again, very clearly. Again the lightnings increased, this time to a peak of such brilliance that Krispos had to turn his head away, his eyes watering. "No," Tanilis said for a third time from the heart of that firestorm.

Through slitted eyelids, Krispos looked back toward her. She still stood defiant—and all at once the black wall's force yielded to her stronger will. The lightning ceased; the barrier melted into the thin air from which it had sprung.

The imperial soldiers cried out in triumph at that. Then, a moment later, they cried out again. The black wall's vanishing revealed the Halogai who had been advancing on the flying column under its cover. Harvas, too, would have let the barrier disappear, no doubt, but at a time of his own choosing.

"Forward!" Krispos shouted. "The cry is 'Mavros'!"

"Mavros!" the Videssians thundered. They rolled toward Harvas' Halogai, then rolled over them. The northerners were caught in loose order, confident they would find foes ripe for the slaughter. Some of them turned tail when the downfall of the barrier showed that Krispos' men were more ready for battle than they. More stood and fought. They followed a wicked leader, but kept their own fierce pride. It availed them nothing. The imperials rode them down, then rode on toward the northern mouth of the pass. "Mavros!" they shouted again and again, and another cry: "Tanilis!"

"We may yet bottle Harvas up in there," Sarkis yelled to Krispos, his black eyes snapping with excitement.

"Aye." When Krispos' horse even thought of slowing, he roweled it with his spurs. Normally he was gentle to his mounts, but now he would not willingly lose so much as an instant. A solid line across the outlet to the pass and Harvas' army was done for.

The exultation in the thought almost made Krispos drunk. Almost. That army would be done for unless Harvas magicked it free. Despite Tanilis, despite all the mages from the Sorcerers' Collegium, the possibility remained real. Any time Krispos was tempted to forget it, he had only to think of Trokoundos' twisted body, now more than a mile behind him.

He saw the mouth of the pass ahead. Get his men across it and— "Rein in!" he shouted, and followed that with a volley of curses. Harvas' Halogai were already streaming north out of the trap. Some carried axes at the ready, others bore them over their shoulders. The long files of fighting men were ready for action, unlike the now-shattered band that had been on the way to deal with Krispos' column.

"Too many for us to head," Sarkis said, gauging the enemy's numbers with a practiced eye.

"I fear you're right, worse luck for us," Krispos answered. "He's pulled them out just in time. Maybe he could tell when his wall went down, or some such. Even if we can't keep him there, though, let's see how much we can hurt his soldiers. They're giving us their flank for a target."

Sarkis nodded and brought up his hand in salute. "Mammianos said you were learning the trade of war. I see he's right." The scout commander raised his voice. "Archers!"

Shouting enthusiastically, the bowmen began to ply their trade. Shooting from horseback did not make for accurate archery, but with a massed target like the one they had, they did not need to be accurate. Halogai screamed; Halogai stumbled; Halogai fell.

Some of the northerners awkwardly shifted their shields to their right sides to help ward themselves from the arrows that rained down on them. Others, singly and then by troops and companies, rushed toward their tormentors. The archers could not come close to shooting all of them before they closed the gap and began to swing axe and sword. Imperial lancers spurred forward to protect the bowmen. Half a dozen melees developed all along the imperial line. As more and more Halogai poured out of the pass, Krispos' men found themselves outnumbered.

"Pull back!" he shouted. "We didn't come here to take on Harvas' whole bloody army by ourselves. He's out of the pass, and that's what counts. Do you think he can hold all the rest of our own troops out of Kubrat with just a rear guard? Not likely!"

An army of Halogai would either have ignored Krispos' order or taken it as a signal to panic. They fought as much for the joy of fighting as to gain advantage. The Videssians were less ferocious and more flexible. They drew back, stinging Harvas' foot soldiers with more arrows as they did so. The lancers nipped in to cut off and destroy bands of Halogai who pursued with too much spirit. Again and again the Halogai paid in blood to learn that lesson.

"I don't think Harvas is leaving much of a rear guard in there," Sarkis said late that afternoon. By then the running fight had moved close to ten miles into Kubrat; Krispos was hard-pressed to stretch the limited manpower of his column to cover all of Harvas' army.

Like wildfire, a cheer ran up the Videssian line from the south. At last it—and the news that caused it—reached Krispos, who was near the northern end of his force as it skirmished with Harvas' scouts and vanguard. "Our own men are coming up out of the pass!" someone bawled in his ear.

"That's good," Krispos said automatically. Then the full meaning of what he'd heard sank in. He let loose with a yell that made his horse sidestep and switch its ears in reproach. "We have him!"

But as Harvas had shown south of Imbros, he was general as well as wizard. Rear guards had to be beaten down; sorcerous screens had to be cautiously probed and even more cautiously eliminated. By the time night fell, he had succeeded in breaking off contact between his army and most of his Videssian pursuers, though the flying column still hung just off his right flank.

Krispos made his way back to where the main imperial army was setting up camp. He smiled to find his own tent erect and waiting for him. He invited Mammianos over. When the fat general arrived, he clapped him on the back. "You couldn't have done a better job of timing your attack on Harvas' barricade," he said.

"I thank you kindly, Your Majesty." But Mammianos did not sound as proud as he might have. In fact, he shuffled from foot to foot like an embarrassed schoolboy. "It, uh, wasn't exactly my idea, though."

"Oh?" Krispos raised an eyebrow. "What then?"

"Might as well hear it from me instead of somebody else, I suppose," Mammianos said. He shifted his weight again before he went on. "That Zaidas—you know, the young wizard—he came up and told me he didn't think things were going any too well for you this morning."

"He was right," Krispos said, remembering the sound Trokoundos' spine had made as it snapped and his own fear when the wizard died. Trokoundos had a wife—a widow, now—in Videssos the city. Krispos reminded himself to provide for her, not that gold could make up for the loss of her man.

"I figured he might be, seeing as he was the one who sniffed out Harvas' army down south of Imbros," Mammianos said. "So I asked him if we could help you by having a go at the barricade, and he said yes. So we had a go, and maybe Harvas was distracted on account of trying to deal with your lot, because we broke through. The rest I guess you know."

"I'm just glad you listened to Zaidas," Krispos said.

Mammianos rumbled laughter. "Now that you mention it, Your Majesty, so am I."

Chapter XI

KRISPOS AND TANILIS RODE SIDE BY SIDE. THEY'D RIDDEN side by side ever since the imperial army entered Kubrat. By now, more than a week later and half the way to the Astris River, no one even gave them a sidelong glance. No one had ever had the temerity to say anything to Krispos about it.

Perhaps someone might have, had Tanilis not proven her worth so solidly. The mages from the Sorcerers' Collegium—all, Krispos noted, save Zaidas—had muttered when she included herself in their labors against Harvas, but the mutters died away soon enough. Inside of a day she became as much their spearhead as Trokoundos had ever been. Again and again Harvas' sorcerous assaults failed. Again and again his army, out-flanked by the more mobile Videssians, had to retreat.

"I think he's falling back on Pliskavos," Krispos said. "In all of Kubrat, it's the only place where he could hope to stand siege." The prospect of Harvas under siege still worried him. A siege would give the evil wizard the leisure he needed to exercise his ingenuity to the fullest. Krispos grimaced at the prospect of facing whatever that exercised ingenuity came up with.

Tanilis' gaze became slightly unfocused. "Yes," she said, a few seconds too late for a proper reply. "He is falling back on Pliskavos." She sounded as certain as if she'd said the sun would rise the next morning. A moment later she came back to herself, a small frown on her face. "I have a headache," she remarked.

Krispos passed her his canteen. "Here's some wine," he said. As she drank, he ran his hands over his arms, trying to smooth down the goose-flesh that had prickled up at her foretelling. He'd seen the mantic fit take her far more strongly than that, not least on the day when he'd first met her, the day she'd terrified him by calling him *Majesty*.

Then he'd wondered if she saw true. Now he knew she did. Knowing that, he thought to take advantage of her gift. He called for a courier. "Get Sarkis over here," he said. The courier saluted and rode away.

He soon returned with the scout commander. "What can I do for you, Your Majesty?" Sarkis asked.

"Time to send out another column," Krispos said, and watched Sarkis grin. "Harvas *is* on his way back to Pliskavos." Sarkis caught his certainty and glanced over to Tanilis. Krispos nodded. He went on, "If we can put a few thousand men into the place before he gets there, say, or burn down a good part of it—"

Sarkis' grin got wider. "Aye, Your Majesty, we can try that. We can swing wide and get around behind his men, the good god willing. Horses go faster than shank's mare. It should work. I'll get right on it."

"Good." Krispos grinned, too, savagely. Let Harvas find out for a change what being hunted was like, feel what it meant to move to some-one else's will, to move in fear lest the tiniest error bring the fabric of all his designs down in ruin. He'd inflicted misery on Videssos for too long—perhaps for the whole span of his unnatural life. Only fitting and proper to mete misery out to him at last.

The column clattered away from the main Videssian army late that af-ternoon, heading off to the west to circle round Harvas' Halogai. The troopers who stayed on the primary line of march whooped as their com-rades departed. One outflanking move had forced Harvas out of his strong position in the pass. Another might ruin him altogether. The soldiers were cheerful as they encamped for the night.

As was his habit, Krispos picked a line at random and patiently ad-vanced toward the cookpot at the end of it. Anthimos, with his love of rare delicacies, would have turned up his toes at army fare. Used to worse for much of his life, Krispos minded it not at all. Peas, beans, onions, and cheese made a savory stew, enlivened, as it had seldom been in his peasant days, with small chunks of salty sausage and beef. He slapped his stomach and raised a belch. The men around him laughed. They knew they ate better because he shared their food.

After he had eaten, Krispos walked along the lines of tethered horses, stopping to chat now and then with a trooper grooming his mount or prying a pebble out from under a horseshoe. His years as a groom after he came to Videssos the city made him easy with horsy talk, though he was not one of the fairly common breed who cared for nothing else by day or night. For the most part, the men treated their animals well; their lives might depend on keeping the beasts in good condition.

The short, full darkness of summer night had fallen by the time Krispos made his way back to his own tent, which stood, as always, in the center of the camp. The Haloga guardsmen in front of it came to attention as he approached. "As you were," he said, and ducked through the flap. Unlike the heavy canvas under which most of the troopers sweltered, his summer tent was of silk. He got whatever breeze there was. Tonight there was no breeze.

He was not ready to sleep yet, not quite. He sat down in a folding chair of wood and wicker, set his chin in his hand, and thought about what the coming days would bring. He no longer believed Harvas would be able to enspell his army this side of Pliskavos. He'd had to summon most of the sorcerous talent in the Empire to match the undying renegade, but he'd done it. He thought Harvas was beginning to understand that, too. If his magic would not serve him, that left his soldiers. Some time soon he might try battle. If he found a piece of ground that suited him—

Outside the tent, the sentries shifted their weight. Their boots scuffed the dirt; their mail shirts rang softly. The small sounds so close by made Krispos glance up toward the entrance. His right hand stole toward the hilt of his saber. Then one of the sentries said, "How do we serve you, my lady?"

In all the sprawling imperial camp, there was only one "my lady." Tanilis said, "I would speak with his Majesty, if he will see me."

One of the guardsmen stuck his head into the tent. Before he could speak Krispos said, "Of course I will see the lady." He felt his heartbeat shift from walk to trot. However they rode during the day, Tanilis had not come to his tent at night before.

The guard held the flap wide for her. Silk rustled as it fell after she came in. Krispos got to his feet, taking a step toward a second chair so he could unfold it for her. Before he reached it, Tanilis went smoothly to her knees and then to her belly. Her forehead touched the ground in the most graceful act of proskynesis he had ever seen.

He felt his face grow hot. "Get up," he said, his voice so soft the guards could not listen but rough with emotions he was still sorting through. "It's not right—not fitting—for you to prostrate yourself before me."

"And wherefore not, Your Majesty?" she asked as she rose with the same liquid elegance she had used in the proskynesis. "You are my Avtokrator; should I not grant you the full honor your station deserves?"

He opened the other chair. She sat in it. He went back to the one in which he had been sitting. His thoughts refused to muster themselves into any kind of order. At last he said, "It's not the same. You knew me before I was Emperor. By the lord with the great and good mind, my lady, you knew me before I was much of anything."

"I gave you leave long ago, as a friend, to call me by my name. I could scarcely deny my Emperor the same privilege." A tiny smile tugged up the corners of Tanilis' mouth. "And you seem to have become quite a lot of something, if I may take a friend's privilege and point it out."

"Thank you." Krispos spoke carefully, to ensure that he did not stammer. Being with Tanilis took him back to the days when he had been more nearly boy than man. He did not want to show that, not to her of all people. Now he made himself think clearly and said, "And thank you also for making sure I left Opsikion—and you—that spring, whether I wanted to or not."

She inclined her head to him. "Now you have come into a man's wisdom, to see why I did as I did. I could tell that Opsikion was too small for you—and I, at the time I was rather too large. You were not yet what you would become."

Her words so paralleled his own thoughts that he nodded in turn. As he did, he gazed at her. She had held her beauty well enough to remain more than striking even in harshest daylight. Lamps were kinder; now she seemed hardly to have aged a day.

Seeing her, hearing her, also reminded him of how they had spent a good part of their time together. He'd gone on campaign before without seriously wanting to bring a woman into his tent to keep his cot warm. Part of that, he admitted to himself with a wry grin, was nervousness about Dara. But another part, a bigger part, came from fondness for his wife.

Now he found he wanted Tanilis. None of what he felt for Dara had gone away. It just did not seem relevant anymore. He'd known Tanilis, known her body, long before he'd ever imagined he would meet Dara. Wanting to take her to bed again did not feel like being unfaithful; it felt much more like picking up an old friendship.

He did not stop to wonder what his taking Tanilis to bed would feel like to Dara. He got up, stretched, and walked over to the map table in one corner of the tent. Videssos had not ruled in Kubrat for three hundred years; the imperial archives nevertheless held detailed if archaic maps of the land, stored against the day when it might become a province of the Empire once more.

But he only glanced at the ragged parchment with its ink going brown and pale from age. He stretched again, then walked about as if at random. It was no accident, though, that he ended up behind Tanilis' chair. He rested a hand on her shoulder.

She twisted her head up and back to look at him. Her small smile grew. She made a pleased noise, almost a purr, deep in her throat. Her hand covered his. Her skin was smooth, her flesh soft. A ruby ring on her index finger caught the dim lamplight and glowed like warm blood.

Krispos bent down and lightly kissed her. "Like old times," he said.

"Aye, like old times." Her pleased purr got louder. Her eyes were almost all pupil. Then, suddenly, those huge eyes seemed to be looking past Krispos, or through him. "For a little while," she said in a voice altogether different from the one she'd used a moment before. That distant expression faded before Krispos was quite sure he'd seen it. Her voice returned to normal, too, or better than normal. "Kiss me again," she told him.

He did, gladly. When the kiss ended, she got to her feet. Afterward he was never sure which of them took the first step toward the cot. She pulled her robe over her head, slid out of her drawers, and lay down to wait while he undressed. She did not wait long. "Do you want to blow out the lamps?" she whispered.

"No," he answered as softly. "For one thing, it would tell the guardsmen just what we're doing. For another, you're beautiful and I want to see you." Even more than her face, her body had retained its youthful tautness.

Her eyes lit. "No wonder I recall you so happily." She held up her arms to him. He got down beside her.

The cot was narrow for two; the cot, in truth, was narrow for one. They managed all the same. Tanilis was as Krispos remembered her, or even more so, an all but overwhelming blend of passion and technique. Soon his own excitement drove memory away, leaving only the moment.

Even after they were spent, they lay entangled—otherwise one of them would have fallen off the cot. Tanilis' hand stole down his side and stroked him with practiced art. "Another round?" she murmured, her breath warm in his ear.

"In a bit, maybe," he answered after taking stock of himself. "I'm older than I was when I visited Opsikion, you know. I wasn't spending long days in the saddle then, either." One of his eyebrows quirked upward against the velvety skin of her throat. "At least, not on horseback."

She bit him in the shoulder, hard enough to hurt. He started to yelp, but checked himself in time. The small pain seemed to spur him, though; sooner than he had expected, he found himself rising to the occasion once more. Tanilis let out a voiceless sigh as they began again.

From outside the tent one of the guardsmen called, "Majesty, a courier is here with a dispatch from the city."

Krispos did his best not to hear the Haloga. "Don't be foolish," Tanilis said; she retained as much self-control as Krispos remembered. She made a small pushing motion against his chest. "Go on; see what news the rider brings. I'll be here when you get back."

Knowing she was right helped only so much. More than a little grumpily, he separated from her, climbed off the cot, dressed, and went out into the night. "Here you are, Your Majesty," the courier said, handing him a sealed roll of parchment. After a salute, the fellow twitched his mount's reins and headed out toward the long lines of tethered horses.

Krispos ducked back into the tent. As he did so, his cheeks started to flame. The Halogai had never been shy about sticking their heads inside when they needed him to come out. If they called now, it had to be because they knew what he was doing in there. "Oh, to the ice with it," he muttered. The longer he ruled, the more resigned he became to having no privacy.

The sight of Tanilis waiting for him drove such minor annoyances clean out of his mind. He yanked off his robe and let it fall to the ground. Tanilis frowned. "The dispatch—"

"Whatever it is, it will keep long enough."

She lowered her eyes in acquiescence. "Then hurry here, Your Majesty." Krispos hurried.

Afterward, languid, he wanted to forget about the roll of parchment, but he knew Tanilis would think less of him for that—and he would think less of himself when morning came. He got into his robe again and broke the seal on the message. Tanilis projected an air of silent approval as she, also, put her clothes back on.

His impatient thoughts full of her, he hadn't bothered to hold the dispatch up to a lamp to find out who'd sent it. Now, as he read the note inside, he learned: "The Empress Dara to her husband Krispos, Avtokrator of the Videssians: Greetings. Yesterday I gave birth to our second son, as

Mavros' mother Tanilis foretold. As we agreed, I've named him Evripos.
He is large and seems healthy, and squalls at all hours of the day and night.
The birth was hard, but all births are hard. The midwife acts pleased with
him and me both. The good god grant that you are soon here in the city
once more to see him and me."

Krispos had felt no guilt before. Now it all crashed down on him at
once. When he said nothing for some time, Tanilis asked, "Is the news so
very bad, then?" Wordlessly he passed the letter to her. She read quickly
and without moving her lips, something Krispos still found far from easy.
"Oh," was all she said when she was done.

"Yes," Krispos said: only two words between them, but words charged
with a great weight of meaning.

"Shall I come here to your tent no more then, Your Majesty?" Tanilis
asked, her voice all at once cool and formal.

"That might be best," Krispos answered miserably.

"As you wish, Your Majesty. Do recall, though, that you knew of the
Empress'—your wife's—condition before this dispatch arrived. I grant
that knowing and being reminded are not the same, but you had the
knowledge. And now, by your leave—" She tossed Dara's letter onto the
cot, strode briskly to the tent flap, ducked through it, and walked away.

Krispos stared after her. Minutes before they had been gasping in each
other's arms. He picked up the letter to read it again. He had another son,
and Dara was well. Good news, every bit of it. Even so, he crumpled the
parchment into a ball and flung it to the ground.

Scouts pushed ahead before dawn the next morning,
probing to make sure no ambushes lay ahead of the imperial army. The
main force soon followed, a long column with its supply wagons, protected by a sizable knot of mounted men, rattling along in the middle.

The unwieldy arrangement never failed to make Krispos nervous. "If
Harvas had even a few Kubrati horse-archers on his side, he could give us
no end of grief," he remarked to Bagradas, who led the force guarding the
baggage train. Concentrating on the army's affairs helped Krispos keep his
mind off his own, and off the fact that today Tanilis had chosen not to ride
beside him, but rather with the rest of the magicians.

Bagradas did not notice that—or if he did, had sense enough not to let
on. He said, "Whatever Kubratoi still have fight in them want to come in
on our side, Your Majesty, not against us. We picked up another few dozen
yesterday. Of course, when it comes to real fighting, they may do us as lit-

tle good as that group that stayed with you out of the pass all the way up until things looked dangerous and then took off." The regimental commander lifted a cynical eyebrow.

"As long as they aren't raiding us, they can do as they please," Krispos said. "We brought along enough of our own folk to do our fighting for us." He lifted a hand from Progress' neck to pluck at his beard. "I wonder how that column I sent out is faring."

"My guess would be that they are still out swinging wide, Your Majesty," Bagradas said. "If they turn north too close to us, Harvas might be able to position men in front of them."

"They were warned about that," Krispos said. One more thing to worry about—

He urged Progress ahead toward the group of sorcerers. They were, he saw without surprise, gathered around Tanilis. Zaidas, who had been animatedly chattering with her, looked over with almost comic startlement as Krispos rode up beside him.

"A good thing I'm not Harvas," Krispos remarked dryly. He bowed in the saddle to Tanilis. "My lady, may I speak with you?"

"Of course, Your Majesty. You know you have only to command." She spoke without apparent irony and flicked the reins to get her horse into a trot and away from the wizards. Krispos did the same. Zaidas and the other wizards stared after them in disappointment. When enough clear space had opened up to give them some privacy, Tanilis inclined her head to Krispos. "Your Majesty?"

"I just wanted to say I feel bad about the way things ended between us last night."

"You needn't trouble yourself about it," she replied. "After all, you are the Avtokrator of the Videssians. You may do just as you wish."

"Anthimos did just as he wished," Krispos said angrily. "Look what it got him. I want to try to do what's right, so far as I can see what that is."

"You've chosen a harder road than he did." After a small pause, Tanilis went on in a dispassionate tone of voice, "Few would say that bedding a woman not your wife falls into that category."

"I know, I know, I know." He made a fist and slammed it down on his thigh just below the bottom edge of his coat of mail. "I don't make a habit of it, you know."

"I would have guessed that, yes." Now she sounded amused, perhaps not in an altogether pleasant way.

"It isn't funny, curse it." Doggedly, clumsily, he went ahead: "I'd known you—loved you for a while, though I know you didn't love me—for such a long time, and now I'd seen you again, when I never expected to, well, I never worried about what I was doing till I'd done it. Then that note came, and I got brought up short—"

"Aye, you did." Tanilis studied him. "I might have guessed your marriage was one of convenience only, but two sons born close together argues against that, the more so as you've spent a good part of your reign in the field."

"Oh, there's something of convenience in it, for me and for her both," Krispos admitted, "but there turns out to be more to it than that, too." He laughed without mirth. "You noticed that, didn't you? But all the same, when we'd made love and the courier brought the letter, I had no business treating you the way I did. That's not right, either, and I'm sorry for it."

Tanilis rode on for a little while in silence. Then she remarked, "I think riding into battle might be easier for you than saying what you just said."

Krispos shrugged. "One thing I'm sure of is that putting a crown on my head doesn't make me right all the time. The lord with the great and good mind knows I didn't learn much from Anthimos about how to rule, but I learned that. And if I was wrong, what's the point in being ashamed to say so?"

"Wherever you learned to rule, Krispos"—he warmed to hear her use his name again, rather than his title—"you appear to have learned a good deal. Shall we return to being friends, then?"

"Yes," he answered with relief. "How could I be your enemy?"

Mischief sparkled in Tanilis' eyes. "Suppose I came to your tent again tonight. Would you take up saber and shield to drive me away?"

In spite of all his good intentions, his manhood stirred at the thought of her coming to his tent again. He ignored it. *I'm too old to let my prick do my thinking for me,* he told himself firmly. A moment later he added, *I hope.* Aloud, he said, "If you're trying to tempt me, you're doing a good job." He managed a smile.

"I would not seek to tempt you into something you find improper," Tanilis answered seriously. "If that is how it is, let it be so. I said back in Opsikion, all those years ago, that we would not suit each other over the long haul. It still seems true."

"Yes," Krispos said again, with no small regret. He still wondered if he and Dara suited each other over the long haul. Ever since he became Emperor, he'd been away on campaign so much that they'd had scant chance to find out. He went on, "I'm glad we can be friends."

"So am I." Tanilis looked around at the Kubrati countryside through which they were riding. Her voice sank to a whisper. "Being friendless in such a land would be a dreadful fate."

"It's not that bad," Krispos said, remembering his childhood years north of the mountains. "It's just different from Videssos." The sky was a paler, damper blue than inside the Empire. The land was a different shade of green, too, deeper and more like moss; the gray-green olive trees that gave Videssos so much of its distinctive tint would not grow here. The winters, Krispos knew, had a ferocity worse than any Videssos suffered.

But perhaps Tanilis was not seeing the material landscape that was all Krispos could perceive. "This land hates me," she said, shivering though the day was warm. Her sepulchral tone made Krispos want to shiver, too. Then Tanilis brightened, or rather grew intent on her prey. "If we can pull Harvas down, let it hate me as much as it will."

With that Krispos could not argue. He gazed out at Kubrat again. Far off in the northwest, he spied a rising smudge of dirty gray smoke against the horizon. He pointed to it. "Maybe that's the work of the column I sent out," he said hopefully.

Tanilis' gaze swung that way. "Aye, it is your column," she said, but she did not sound hopeful. Krispos tried to make himself believe she was still fretting over the way the land affected her.

But the next morning, as the main body of the army was getting ready to break camp, riders began straggling in from the west. Krispos did not want to talk with the first few of them; as he'd learned, men who got away first often had no idea what had really gone wrong—if anything had.

Sarkis came in about midmorning. A fresh cut seamed one cheek; his right forearm was bandaged. "I'm sorry, Majesty," he said. "I was the one who made the mistake."

"You own up to it, anyhow," Krispos said. "Tell me what happened."

"We came across a village—a town, almost—that isn't on our old maps," the scout commander answered. "I'm not surprised—it looked as if the Halogai were still building it: longhouses are their style, anyhow. Not a lot of men were in it, but those who were came boiling out, and their women with them, armed and fighting as fierce as they were."

Sarkis picked at a flake of dried blood on his face. "Majesty, beating them wasn't the problem. We had plenty of men for that. But I knew our true goal was Pliskavos and I wanted to get there as quick as I could. So instead of doing much more than skirmishing and setting the village ablaze—"

"We saw the smoke," Krispos broke in.

"I shouldn't wonder. Anyhow, I didn't want to lose time by riding around the place, either. So I swung us in on this side instead, and we rode straight north—right into a detachment from Harvas' army. They had more troopers than we did and they beat us, curse 'em."

"Oh, a plague," Krispos said, as much to himself as to Sarkis. He thought for a few seconds. "Any sign of magic in the fight?"

"Not a bit of it," Sarkis answered at once. "The northerners looked to be heading west themselves, to try to cut us off from riding around their army. Thanks to that miserable, stinking flea-farm of a village, they got the chance and they took it. Let me have another go at them, Your Majesty, or some new man if you've lost faith in me. The plan was good, and we still have enough room to maneuver to make it work."

Krispos thought some more and shook his head. "No. A trick may work once against Harvas if it catches him by surprise. I can't imagine him letting us try one twice. Something ghastly would be waiting for us; I feel it in my bones."

"You're likely right." Sarkis hung his head. "Do what you will with me for having failed you."

"Nothing to be done about it now," Krispos answered. "You tried to pick the fastest way to carry out my orders, and it happened not to work. May you be luckier next time."

"May the good god grant it be so!" Sarkis said fervently. "I'll make you glad you've trusted me—I promise I will."

"Good," Krispos said. Sarkis saluted and rode away to see the men who were still coming in from the column. Krispos sighed as he watched him go. It would have to be the hard way, then, with the butcher's bill that accompanied the hard way.

He'd already thought about putting peasants back into the border regions south of the mountains. He would also have to find soldiers to replace those who fell in this campaign. Where, he wondered, would all the men come from? He laughed at himself, though it wasn't really funny. Back in his days on the farm, he'd never imagined the Emperor could have any reason to worry, let alone a reason so mundane as finding the people to do what needed doing. He laughed again. Back in his days on the farm, he'd never imagined a lot of things.

HARVAS SKIRMISHED, SCREENED, AVOIDED PITCHED BATTLE. HE seemed content to let the war turn on what happened after he got to Pliskavos. That worried Krispos. Even the Kubratoi and the Videssian-speaking peasants who flocked to his army and acclaimed him as a liberator failed to cheer him. Kubrat would return to imperial rule if he beat Harvas, aye. If he lost, the nomads and peasants both would only suffer more for acclaiming him.

As his force neared Pliskavos, he began sending out striking columns again, not to cut Harvas off from the capital of Kubrat but rather to ensure that he and his army went nowhere else. One of the columns sent men galloping back in high excitement. "The Astris! The Astris!" they shouted as they returned to the main force from the northwest. They were the first imperial soldiers to reach the river in three hundred years.

Another column came to the Astris east of Pliskavos a day later. Instead of sending back proud troopers to boast of what they'd done, they shouted for reinforcements. "A whole raft of Halogai are crossing the river on boats," a rider gasped as he rode in, mixing his metaphors but getting the message across.

Krispos dispatched reinforcements on the double. He also sent a company of soldiers from the first column that had reached the Astris to ride west along its bank toward the Videssian Sea. "Find Kanaris and bring him here," he ordered. "This is why we have ships on the Astris. Let's see the northerners put more men across it once he sails up."

He saw the Astris himself the next day. The wide gray river flowed past Pliskavos, which lay by its southern bank. The stream was wide enough to make the steppes and forests on the far bank seem distant and unreal. Unfortunately quite real, however, were the little boats that scurried across it. Each one brought a new band of Halogai to help Harvas hold the land he'd seized. Krispos raged, but could do little more until the grand drungarios of the fleet arrived. While he waited, the army began to built a palisade around Pliskavos.

"Something occurs to me," Mammianos said that evening. "I don't know as much as I'd like about fighting on water or much of anything about magic, but what's to keep Harvas from hurting our dromons when they do come up the Astris?"

Kristos gnawed on his lower lip. "We'd better talk with the magicians."

By the time the talk was done, Krispos found himself missing Trokoundos not just because the mage had been a friend. Trokoundos had been able to make sorcerous matters clear to people who were not wizards. His colleagues left Krispos feeling as confused as he was enlightened. He gathered, though, that sorcery aimed at targets on running water tended to be weakened or to go astray altogether.

He didn't care for the sound of that *tended to.* "I hope Harvas has read the same magical books you have," he told the wizards.

"Your Majesty, I see no sorcerous threat looming over Kanaris' fleet," Zaidas said.

"Nor do I," Tanilis agreed. Zaidas blinked, then beamed. He sent Tanilis a worshipful look. She nodded to him, a regal gesture Krispos knew well. The force of it seemed to daze Zaidas, who was younger and more susceptible than Krispos ever had been when he knew her. Krispos shook his head; noticing how young other people were was a sign he wasn't so young himself. But he had as much assurance from his wizards as he could hope for. That was worth a slight feeling of antiquity.

THE PALISADE AROUND PLISKAVOS GREW STRONGER OVER THE next couple of days. The troopers dug a ditch and used the dirt from it to build a rampart behind it. They mounted shields on top of the rampart to make it even higher. All the same, the gray stone wall of Pliskavos stood taller still.

The Halogai sallied several times, seeking to disrupt the men who were busy strengthening the palisade. They fought with their folk's usual reckless courage and paid heavily for it. Each day, though, dugouts brought fresh bands of northerners across the Astris and into Pliskavos.

"Halogaland must be grim indeed, if so many of the northerners brave the trip across Pardraya in hopes of settling here," Krispos observed at an evening meeting with his officers.

"Aye, true enough, for the lands hereabouts are nothing to brag of," Mammianos said. Krispos did not entirely trust the fat general's sense of proportion; the coastal lowlands where Mammianos had been stationed were the richest farming country in the whole Empire.

Sarkis put in, "I wonder how many villages like the one that gave me trouble have been planted on Kubrati soil. We'll have to finish the job of uprooting them once we're done here." A gleam came into his dark eyes. "I wouldn't mind uprooting one or two of those gold-haired northern women myself."

Several of the men in Krispos' tent nodded. Fair hair was rare—and exotically interesting—in Videssos. "Have a care now, Sarkis," Mammianos rumbled. "From what you've told us, the Haloga wenches fight back."

Everyone laughed. "You should have tried sweet talk, Sarkis," Bagradas said. The laughter got louder.

"I hadn't gone there to woo them then," Sarkis answered tartly.

"Back to business," Krispos said, trying without much success to sound stern. "How soon can we be ready to storm Pliskavos?"

His officers exchanged worried looks. "Starving the place into submission would be a lot cheaper, Your Majesty," Mammianos said. "Harvas can't have supplies for all the men he's jammed in there, no matter how full his warehouses are. His troops'll start taking sick before long, too, crowded together the way they must be."

"So will ours, in spite of everything the healer-priests can do," Krispos answered. Mammianos nodded; camp fevers could cost an army more men than combat. Krispos went on, "Even so, I'd say you were right most of the time. But not against Harvas Black-Robe. The more time he has to ready himself in there, the more I fear him."

Mammianos sighed. "Aye, some truth in what you say. He is a proper bugger, isn't he?" He glanced around to the other officers, as if hoping one of them would speak out for delay. No one did. Mammianos sighed again. "Well, Majesty, we have ladders and such in the baggage train, and all the metal parts and cordage for siege engines. We'll need some time to knock down trees for their frames and cut the wood to fit, but as soon as that's done we can take a crack at it."

"How long?" Krispos insisted.

"A week, maybe a day or two less," Mammianos said, obviously reluctant to be pinned down. "Other thing is, though, that Harvas'd have to be blind not to see what we're up to as we prepare. He's a lot of nasty things, but blind isn't any of them."

"I know," Krispos said. "Still, he knows what we're here for anyhow. We didn't fight our way across Kubrat to offer to harvest his turnips. Let's get those engines started." Mammianos and the rest of the officers saluted. With orders given, they would obey.

The next morning, armed parties rode out to chop timber. By midday horses and mules began hauling back roughly trimmed logs. Under the watchful eyes of the engineers who would assemble and direct the use of the catapults and rams, soldiers cut the wood to proper lengths. The noise of carpentry filled the camp.

Mammianos had been right: the Halogai on Pliskavos' walls had no doubt what the imperials were doing. They jeered and waved their axes and swords in defiance. The ones with a few words of Videssian yelled out what sort of welcome the attackers were likely to receive. Some of Krispos' soldiers yelled back. Most just kept working.

A tall, thin pillar of smoke rose into the sky from somewhere near the center of Pliskavos. When Zaidas saw it, he turned pale and drew the sun-circle over his heart. All the wizards with the imperial army redoubled their apotropaic spells.

"What exactly is Harvas up to?" Krispos asked Zaidas, reasoning he would be most likely to know because of his sensitive sorcerous vision.

But the young mage only shook his head. "Nothing good," was the sole answer he would give. "That smoke—" He shuddered and sketched the sun-sign again. This time Krispos did the same.

The wizards' concern made Krispos more and more edgy. Nor was his temper improved when a dozen more dugouts full of Halogai landed at Pliskavos' quays before the sun reached its zenith. In the late afternoon, Videssian watchers on the shore of the Astris spied another small flotilla getting ready to set out from the northern bank.

The news went straight to Krispos. He slammed his fist down onto his portable desk and scowled at the messenger. "By the good god, I wish we could do something about these bastards," he growled. "Every one of them who gets into town means another one who'll be able to kill our men."

Seldom in a man's life are prayers answered promptly; all too seldom in a man's life are prayers answered at all. But Krispos was still fuming when another messenger burst into his tent, this one fairly hopping with excitement. "Majesty," he cried, "we've spotted Kanaris' ships rowing their way upstream against the current!"

"Have you?" Krispos said softly. He rolled up the message he'd been reading. It could wait. "This I want to see for myself." He hurried out of the tent, shouting for Progress. He booted the gelding into a gallop. In a few minutes, the horse stood blowing by the riverbank.

Krispos peered west, using a hand to shield his eyes from the sun. Sure enough, up the river stormed the lean shark-shapes of the imperial dromons. Their twin banks of oars rose and fell in swift unison. Spray flew from the polished bronze rams the ships bore at their bows. Sailors and marines hurried about on the decks, readying the dromons for combat.

The Halogai had paddled their dugout canoes scarcely a quarter of the way across the Astris. They might have turned around and got back safe to the northern shore, but they did not even try: retreat was a word few northerners knew. They only bent their backs and paddled harder. A few of the dugouts sported small masts. Sails sprouted from those now.

For a moment Krispos thought the Halogai might win their race into Pliskavos, but the Videssian warships caught them a couple of hundred yards from the quays. Darts flew from the catapults at the dromons' bows. So did covered clay pots, which trailed smoke as they arced through the air. One burst in the middle of a dugout. In an instant the canoe was ablaze from one end to the other. So were the men inside. Thinned by long travel over water, their screams came to Krispos' ears. The Halogai who could plunged into the Astris. Their mail shirts dragged them to the bottom, an easier end than one filled with flame.

A dromon's ram broke a dugout in half. More Halogai, these unburned, thrashed in the water, but not for long. Videssian marines shot those who did not sink at once from the weight of their armor.

Another canoe broke free from the midriver melee and sprinted for the protection of Pliskavos' docks. Halogai on the walls of the town cheered their countrymen on. But a dromon quickly closed on the canoe. Instead of ramming, the captain chose a different form of fire. A sailor aimed a wooden tube faced inside with bronze at the fleeing dugout. Two more men worked a hand pump similar to the ones the fire brigades used in Videssos the city. But they did not pump water—out spurted the same incendiary brew that had incinerated the first Haloga canoe. This one suffered a like fate, for the sheet of fire that covered it was nearly as long as it was. The northerners writhed and wilted in the fire like moths in a torch-flame.

Krispos' head swiveled back and forth as he looked around for more dugout canoes. He saw none. In the space of a couple of minutes, the imperial dromons had swept the river clear. Only a couple of chunks of flaming debris that drifted downstream and were gone said any folk but the Videssians had ever been on the Astris.

The soldiers by the water who had watched the fight yelled themselves hoarse as the dromons came in to beach themselves on the riverbank. Inside Pliskavos, the Halogai were as silent as if the town were uninhabited.

The grand drungarios' barred pennant snapped at the stern of a galley not far from Krispos. He rode Progress over to the dromon and got there just as Kanaris was coming down the gangplank to the ground. "Well done!" Krispos called.

Kanaris waved to him, then saluted more formally. "Well done yourself, Majesty," he answered, his deep, gruff voice pitched to carry over wind and wave. "Sorry we were west of here, but who thought you'd push all the way to Pliskavos? Well done indeed."

Praise from a longtime warrior always made Krispos proud, for he knew what an amateur he was in matters military. He called for a messenger. When one came up, he told the fellow, "Fetch some of the wizards here. The fleet will need them."

As the messenger rode away, Kanaris said, "We have our own wizards aboard, Majesty."

"No doubt," Krispos said. "But I've brought the finest mages from the

Sorcerers' Collegium up with the army. Harvas Black-Robe is no ordinary enemy, and you've given him special reason to hate you and your ships right now."

"Have it your way, then, Majesty," the grand drungarios said. "By the look of things, you've been right so far."

"Aye, so far." Krispos sketched the sun-sign to turn aside any evil omen. He also reminded himself never to take anything for granted against a foe like Harvas.

K RISPOS RAISED HIS CUP. "TO TOMORROW," HE SAID.

"To tomorrow," the officers in the imperial tent echoed. They, too, held their wine cups high, then emptied them and filed out. Twilight still tinged the western sky, but they all had many things to see to before they sought their bedrolls. Tomorrow the imperial army would attack Pliskavos.

Krispos paced back and forth, trying again to find holes in the plan he and his generals had hammered out. For all their planning, there would be holes and the attack would reveal them. War, he had learned, was like that. If he could find one or two of them before the trumpets blew, he would save lives.

But he could not. He kept pacing for a while anyhow, to work off nervous energy. Then he blew out all the lamps save one, undressed, and lay down on his cot. Sleep would be slow coming. Best to start seeking it early.

He was warm and relaxed and just drifting off when Geirrod poked his head into the tent. "Majesty, the lady Tanilis would see you," the imperial guardsman said.

"*Must* see you," Tanilis corrected from outside.

"Wait a minute," he said muzzily. Cursing under his breath at having rest jerked out from under him, he pulled a robe on over his head and relit a couple of the lamps he'd put out not long before. As he went about that homely labor, his bad temper eased and his wits began to clear. He nodded to Geirrod. "Let her come in."

"Aye, Majesty." The Haloga managed to bow and hold the tent flap open at the same time. "Go in, my lady," he said, his voice as respectful as if Tanilis were of imperial rank.

Any thought that she was seeking to seduce him for her own advantage disappeared when Krispos got a good look at her face. For the first time he saw her haggard, her hair awry, her eyes hollow and dark-circled, lines harshly carved on her forehead and at the corners of her mouth. "By the good god!" he exclaimed. "What's wrong?"

Without asking leave—again most unlike her—Tanilis sank into a folding chair. The motion held none of her usual grace, only exhaustion. "You will assail Harvas in his lair tomorrow," she said.

It was flat statement, not question. She had not been at the officers' conclave, but the signs of a building attack were hard to hide. Krispos nodded. "Aye, we will. What of it?"

"You must not." Again Tanilis' voice held no room for doubt; only Pyrrhos, perhaps, pronouncing on some point of dogma, could have sounded as certain. "If you do, much the greater part of the army will surely be destroyed."

"You've—seen—this?" Even as the words passed his lips, Krispos knew how foolish they were. Tanilis would not trouble him with ordinary worries.

She did not twit him for stupidity, either, as she might have were the matter less urgent and she less worn. She simply answered, "I have seen this." She rested for a moment, slumped down with her chin in her hands. Then, drawing on some reserve of resolution, she straightened. "Yes, I have seen. When I wrote you after Mavros was slain, I said I know Harvas' power was greater than mine, but I hoped to face him nonetheless. Now I have faced him. His power—" She shivered, though the night was warm and muggy. When she slumped again, the heels of her hands covered her eyes.

Krispos went to her and put his hand on her shoulder. He'd done the same just before they made love, but this touch had nothing of the erotic to it. It was support and care, as he might have given any friend brought low by killing labor. He said, "What did you do, Tanilis?"

The words dragged from her, one by one. "Since Harvas was willing to stand siege, I sought to spy, to seek—aye, to sneak— from his mind how he aimed to answer us when the time came. I did not plan to confront him directly; had I done so, I would now be lying dead in my tent. I came near enough to that as it was."

She paused to rest again. Krispos poured her a cup of wine. She seemed a little restored after she drank it. Her voice was stronger as she went on, "Even entering the corners of that mind is like tiptoeing through a maze of death. He has shields and spike-filled snares in his head, snares beyond counting. Be thankful you are mindblind, dear Krispos, that you never need to touch such evil. I made myself very small, hoping he would not notice me . . ." Tears ran down her cheeks. She did not seem to know they were there.

"What did you do?" Krispos asked again.

"I found what I sought. Were Harvas less arrogant, less sure of himself, he would have caught me no matter what I did. But down deep, he will not believe any mere mortal truly able to challenge him. And so, beneath his notice, I found what he intended—and I fled."

Of themselves, Krispos' hands curled into fists. "And what is waiting for us?" he demanded.

"Fire." Tanilis answered. "I know not how—nor did I stay to try to learn—but Harvas has made the city wall of Pliskavos a great reservoir of flame. At his will or signal, the wall can be ignited. Most likely he would wait until our men are on it everywhere, perhaps beginning to drop down into Pliskavos. Then he could burn those on the wall and climbing up it, and also trap the intrepid souls who aimed to take the fight farther."

"But he'd burn the defenders on the wall, too," Krispos said.

"Would he care?" Tanilis asked brutally.

"No," Krispos admitted, "not if they served his purpose. It would, too—he wouldn't have to have many Halogai up there, just enough to slow us, to make us think we were overpowering them because of our might. And then—" He did not want to think about "and then," not so soon after watching what the dromons' invincible fire did to dugout canoes and men.

"Exactly so," Tanilis said. "You see you must delay the attack, then, until our mages devise some suitable countermeasure to abate the menace of this—"

"Hold on," Krispos said. Tanilis tried to continue. He shook his head at her. "Hold on," he repeated, more sharply this time. A couple of ideas rattled around in his head. If he could bring them together . . . He did, with almost an audible click. His eyes widened. "Suppose we lit the wall first," he whispered. "What then?"

Fatigue fell from Tanilis like a discarded cloak as she surged to her feet. "Yes, by the lord with the great and good mind!" She and Krispos hugged, not so much like lovers as like conspirators who realized they'd hatched the perfect plot.

Krispos stuck his head out of the tent. Geirrod came to smart attention. "Never mind that," Krispos said. "Get me Mammianos and then get me Kanaris."

D RAWN UP IN FULL BATTLE ARRAY, THE IMPERIAL ARMY RINGED the entire landward perimeter of Pliskavos. Horns and drums and pipes

whipped the soldiers toward full martial fury. The men shouted Krispos'
name and bellowed abuse and threats at the Halogai on the walls.

The Halogai roared back, crying defiance to the sky. "Come on, little
men, try us!" one shouted. "We make you littler still!" He threw his axe
high in the air and caught it with a flourish.

Siege engines bucked and snapped. Stones and great darts flew toward
Pliskavos. Engineers returned the machines' throwing arms to their proper
positions, checked ropes, reloaded, then hauled on windlasses to tighten
the cordage to the point where the engines could cast again. Meanwhile
archers skipped forward to add their missiles to those of the catapults.

Not many Halogai were bowmen; the fighting they reveled in was hand
to hand. Those who had bows shot back. A couple of Videssians fell; more
northerners tumbled from the wall. The main body of imperial troops
shouted and made as if to surge toward the wall. The Halogai roared back.

Krispos watched all that from the riverbank west of Pliskavos. It was a
fine warlike display, with banners flying and polished armor gleaming
under the morning sun. He hoped Harvas found it as riveting as he did
himself. If all the wizard's attention focused there, he would pay no heed
to the pair of dromons now gliding up the Astris toward his town.

With their twin banks of oars, thirty oars to a bank, the war galleys reminded Krispos of centipedes striding over the water. Such smooth motion seemed impossible. As with anything else, it came by dint of endless
practice.

Closer and closer to the quays at the bottom of the wall came the two
dromons. Krispos watched the marines who were busy at their bows. A
few Halogai watched, too, watched and jeered. A whole fleet of dromons
might have carried enough warriors to attack Pliskavos from the river. Two
were no threat.

Aboard each vessel, an officer raised his hand, then let it fall. The
marines at the hand pumps swing their handles up and down, up and
down. Twin sheets of flame belched from the wood-and-bronze siphon
tubes. The quays caught at once. Black smoke shot skyward. Then the
flames splashed against the wall.

For most of a minute, as the marines aboard the dromons kept pump-
ing out their incendiary mixture, Krispos could not tell whether Tanilis
had stolen the truth from Harvas' mind, whether his own scheme could
disrupt the wizard's plan. Then the tubs of firemix went dry. The fiery
streams stopped pouring from the siphons. The wall still burned.

Slowly at first, then quicker and quicker, the flames spread. The
dromons backed oars to get away from a conflagration greater than any

they were intended to confront. The Halogai atop the river wall poured buckets of water down onto the fire. It kept burning, kept spreading. The Halogai poured again, with no better luck. Krispos saw them stare down, the images of their bodies wavering through heat-haze. Then they gave up and ran away.

The flames were already running as fast as a man could. They burned a brilliant yellow, brighter and hotter than the orange-red fire that had spawned them. They reached the top of the wall and threw themselves high into the air, as if in play.

"By the good god," Krispos whispered. He sketched Phos' sun-sign. At the same time, he narrowed his eyes against the growing glare from Pliskavos. His face heated, as if he were standing in front of a fireplace. So he was, but several hundred yards away.

Halogai ran all along the wall now, even where the flames had not yet reached. Their terrified shouts rose above the crackle and hiss of the fire. Then the flames that had gone one way around Pliskavos met those that had gone the other, and there was nowhere to run anymore. Harvas' city was a perfect ring of fire.

The wall itself burned with a clean, almost smokeless flame. Before long, though, smoke did start rising up from inside Pliskavos—and no wonder, Krispos thought. By then he had already moved back from the fire twice. Houses and other buildings could not move back. So close to so much heat, they had to ignite, too.

Kanaris came up to Krispos. The grand drungarios of the fleet pursed his lips in a soundless whistle as he watched Pliskavos burn. "There's a grim sight," he said. As a lifelong sailing man, he feared fire worse than any foe.

Krispos remembered the fright fire had given him the winter before, when wind whipped Midwinter's Day blazes out of control. All the same he said, "It's winning our war for us. Would you sooner have watched our soldiers burn as they tried to storm those walls? Harvas intended the flames for us, you know."

"Oh, aye, he and his deserve them," Kanaris answered at once, "and the ice they'll meet in the world to come, as well. But there are easier ways of dying." He pointed toward the base of the wall.

Some Halogai had chosen to leap to their deaths rather than burn. As is the way of such things, not all had killed themselves cleanly. They burned anyway, most of them, and had the added torment of splintered bones and crushed organs to accompany the anguish of the fire that ate their flesh. The strongest and luckiest tried to crawl away from the flames toward the Videssian line. Forgetting for a moment that they were deadly enemies, imperial troopers darted out to drag two or three of them to safety. Healer-priests hurried up to do what they could for the Halogai.

The fire burned on and on. Krispos ordered his men out of their battle line. Until the flames subsided, they screened Pliskavos better than the wall from which they sprang. The soldiers watched the fire with something approaching awe. They cheered Krispos almost frantically, whether for having raised the fire or for having saved them from it he could not tell.

He wondered what Harvas was doing, was thinking, there inside his burning wall. After three hundred years of unnatural life, did the evil wizard have teeth left to gnash? Whether or no, his hopes were burning with the wall. A sudden savage grin twisted Krispos' mouth. Maybe Harvas had even been on the wall when it went up. That would be be justice indeed!

Afternoon came, and evening. Pliskavos kept burning. The sky grew dark; the evening star appeared. It might still have been noon in the Videssian camp, so brilliant was the firelight. Only its occasional flicker said that light was born of flames rather than the sun.

Krispos made himself go into his tent. Sooner or later the flames would die. When they did, the army would need orders. He wanted to be fresh, to be sure he gave the right ones. But how was he to sleep when the glow that came through the silk fabric of his tent testified to the fearful marvel outside?

And outside one of the guards said, "Aye, my lady, he's within." The Haloga looked into the tent. "The lady Tanilis would see you, Majesty. Ah, good, you're up and about." Krispos hadn't been, but hearing *my lady* had bounced him from his cot faster than anything short of a sally out of Pliskavos.

When Tanilis came in, Krispos pointed to the bright light that played on the silk. "That victory is yours, Tanilis," he said. Then he gave her the salute properly reserved for the Emperor alone: "Thou conquerest!" He took her in his arms and kissed her.

He'd intended nothing more than that, but she returned the kiss with a desperate intensity unlike anything he'd known from her before. She clung to him so tightly that he could feel her heartbeat through her robe and his. She would not let him go. Before long, all his continent intentions, all his promises to control himself and his body, were swept away in a tide of furious excitement that seemed as hot and fiery as Pliskavos' flaming wall. Still clutching each other, he and Tanilis tumbled to the cot, careless of whether it broke beneath them, as it nearly did.

"Quickly, oh, quickly," she urged him, not that he needed much urging. The cool, practiced competence she usually brought to bed was gone now, leaving only desire. When she arched her back beneath him and quivered at the final instant, she cried out his name again and again. He scarcely heard her. A moment later, he, too, cried out, wordlessly, as he spent himself.

The world apart from their still-joined bodies returned to him little by little. He leaned up on his elbows, or began to, but Tanilis' arms tightened round his back. "Don't leave me," she said. "Don't go. Don't ever go."

Her eyes, scant inches from his own, were huge and staring. He wondered if she was truly looking at him. The last time—the only time—he'd seen eyes so wide was when Gnatios met the executioner. He shook his head; the comparison disturbed him. "What's wrong?" He stroked her cheek.

She did not respond directly. "I wish we could do it again, right now, one last time," she said.

"Again?" Krispos had to laugh. "After that, Tanilis, I'm not sure I could do it again in a week, let alone right now." Then he frowned as he listened again in his own mind to all of what she'd said. "What do you mean, one last time?"

Now she shoved him away from her. "Too late," she whispered. "Oh, too late for everything."

Once more Krispos hardly heard her. This time, though, it was not because of passion but rather pain. Agony such as he had never known filled every crevice of his body. Again he thought of the burning walls of Pliskavos. Now that fire seemed to blaze within his bones, to be consuming him from the inside out. He tried to scream, but his throat was on fire, too, and no sound came forth.

A new voice echoed in the tiny corner of his mind not given over to torment: "Little man, thinkest thou to thwart me? Thinkest thou thy fribbling futile mages suffice to save what I would slay? Aye, they cost me effort, but with effort cometh reward. Learn of my might as thou diest, and despair."

Tanilis must have heard that cold, hateful voice, too, for she said, "No, Harvas, you may not have him." Her tone now was as calm and matter-of-fact as if the wizard were in the tent with them.

Krispos felt a tiny fragment of his anguish ease as Harvas shifted his regard to Tanilis. "Be silent, naked slut, lest I deal with thee next."

"Deal with me if you can, Harvas." Tanilis' chin went up in defiance. "I say you may not have this man. This I have foreseen."

"Damnation to thy foreseeing, and to thee," Harvas returned. "Since thou'dst know the wretch's body, know what it suffereth now, as well."

Tanilis gasped. With a great effort of will, Krispos turned his eyes toward her. She was biting her lip to keep from crying out. Blood trickled from the corner of her mouth. But she would not yield. "Do your worst to me," she told Harvas. "It cannot be a tithe of the harm Krispos and I worked against your wicked scheme this day."

Harvas screamed then, so loudly that for a moment Krispos wondered why no guardsmen burst in to see who was slaying whom. But the scream sounded only in his mind, and in Tanilis'. More torment lifted from him. Tanilis said, "Here, Harvas. As you give, so shall you get. Let me be a mirror, to reflect your gifts. This is what I feel from you now."

Harvas screamed again, but in an altogether different way. He was used to inflicting pain, not to receiving it. Krispos' anguish went away. He thought Tanilis had forced the wizard to yield, simply by making him experience what he was used to handing out. But when Krispos glanced over at her, he saw her fine features were still death-pale and twisted in torment. Her struggle with Harvas was not yet done.

Krispos drew in a long, miraculously pain-free breath. He opened his mouth to shout for more wizards to come to Tanilis' rescue. No sound emerged. Despite everything Tanilis was doing to him—everything he was doing to himself—Harvas still had the strength to enjoin silence on Krispos. And Tanilis agreed. "This is between the two of us now, Krispos." She returned her attention to her foe. "Here, Harvas: This is what I felt when I learned you had slain my son. You should know all your gifts in full."

Harvas howled like a wolf with its leg crushed in the jaws of a trap. But he was trapper as well as victim. He had endured a great deal in his sorcerously prolonged span of days. Though Tanilis wounded him as he had never been wounded before, he did not release her from agony he, too, felt. If he could bear it longer than she, victory would in the end be his. Krispos caught an echo of what he whispered, longingly, again and again to Tanilis: "Die. Oh, die."

"When I do, may you go with me," she answered. "I will rise to Phos' light while you spend eternity in the ice of your master Skotos."

"I usher in my master's dominion to the world. Thy Phos hath failed; only fools feel it not. And thou hast not the power to drag me into death with thee. See now!"

Tanilis whimpered on the cot beside Krispos. Her hand reached out and clutched his forearm. Her nails bit into his flesh, deep enough to draw blood. Then all at once that desperate grip went slack. Her eyes rolled up; her chest no longer rose and fell with breath. Krispos knew she was dead.

While the link with Harvas held, he heard in his mind the beginning of a frightened wail. But the link was abruptly cut, clean as a cord sword-severed. Had Tanilis succeeded in taking the evil wizard down to death with her? If not, she had to have left him hurt and weakened. But the price she'd paid—

Krispos bent down to brush his lips against those that had so recently bruised his. Now they did not respond. "May you be avenged," he said softly.

A new and bitter thought crossed his mind: he wondered if she'd foreseen her own doom when she set out from Opsikion to join the imperial army. Being who and what she was, she must have. Her behavior argued for it—she'd acted like someone who knew she had very little time. But she'd come all the same, heedless of her safety. Krispos shook his head in wonder and renewed grief.

He heard rapid footsteps outside, footsteps that came to a sudden stop in front of the imperial tent. "What do you want, wizard?" a Haloga guardsman demanded.

"I must see his Majesty," Zaidas answered. His young, light voice cracked in the middle of the sentence.

"You must, eh?" The guardsman did not sound impressed. "What you must do, young sir, is wait."

"But—"

"Wait," the guard said implacably. He raised his voice, pitching it so Krispos would notice it inside the tent. "Majesty, a wizard out here would have speech with you." The guard did not poke his head right into the tent now, not after Tanilis had gone in. Yes, he had his own ideas about what was going on in there. Krispos wished he was right.

Wishing did as much good as usual, no more and no less. Krispos slowly got to his feet. "I'll be with you soon," he called to the guard and Zaidas. He put on his robe, then covered Tanilis' body with hers. He straightened. No help for it now. "Let the wizard come in."

Zaidas started to fall to his knees to prostrate himself before Krispos but broke off the ritual gesture when he saw Tanilis lying dead on the cot. Her eyes were still open, staring up at nothing.

"Oh, no," Zaidas whispered. He sketched the sun-sign over his heart. Then he looked at Tanilis again, this time not in shocked surprise but with the trained eye of a mage. He turned to Krispos. "Harvas' work," he said without hesitation or doubt.

"Yes." Krispos' voice was flat and empty.

Lines of grief etched Zaidas' face; in that moment, Krispos saw what the young man would look like when he was fifty. "I sensed the danger," Zaidas said, "but only the edges of it, and not soon enough, I see. Would I had been the one to lay down life for you, Majesty, not the lady."

"Would that no one ever needed to lay down life for me," Krispos said as flatly as before.

"Oh, aye, Your Majesty, aye," Zaidas stammered. "But the lady Tanilis, she was—she was—something, someone special." He scowled in frustration at the inadequacy of his words. Krispos remembered how Zaidas had hung on everything Tanilis said when the wizards gathered together, remembered the worshipful look in the younger man's eye. He'd loved her, or been infatuated with her—at his age, the difference was hard to know. Krispos remembered that, too, from Opsikion.

Love or infatuation, Zaidas had spoken only the truth. "Someone special? She was indeed," Krispos said. Harvas had cost him so many who were dear to him: his sister Evdokia, his brother-in-law, his nieces, Mavros, Trokoundos, now Tanilis. But Tanilis had hit back, hit back harder than Harvas could have expected. How hard? Now Krispos' voice held urgency. "Zaidas, see what you can sense of Harvas for me."

"Of his plans, do you mean, Your Majesty?" the young mage asked in some alarm. "I could not probe deeply without his detecting me; probing at all is no small risk—"

"Not his plans," Krispos said quickly. "Just see if he's there and active inside Pliskavos."

"Very well, Your Majesty; I can do that safely enough, I think," Zaidas said. "As you've seen, even the subtlest screening techniques leave signs of their presence, the more so if they screen a presence as powerful as Harvas'. Let me think. We bless thee, Phos, lord with the—"

Zaidas' voice grew dreamy and far away as he repeated Phos' creed to focus his concentration and slide into a trance, much as a healer-priest might have done. But instead of laying hands on a wounded man, Zaidas turned toward Pliskavos. His eyes were wide and unblinking and seemed sightless, but Krispos knew they sensed more than any normal man's.

After a couple of minutes of turning ever so slightly this way and that, as if he were a hunting dog unsure of a scent, Zaidas slowly came back to himself. He still looked like a puzzled hound, though, as he said, "Your Majesty, I can't find him. I feel he ought to be there, but it's as if he's not. It's no screen I've ever met before. I don't know what it is." He did not enjoy confessing ignorance.

"By the good god, magical sir, I think *I* know what it is. It's Tanilis." Krispos told Zaidas the whole story of her struggle against Harvas Black-Robe.

"I think you're right, Your Majesty," Zaidas said when he was through. The young mage bowed to the cot on which Tanilis lay as if she were a living queen. "Either she slew Harvas as she herself was slain, or at the very least hurt him so badly that his torch of power is reduced to a guttering ember too small for me even to discern."

"Which means all we face in Pliskavos is an army of ferocious Halogai," Krispos said. He and Zaidas beamed at each other. Next to the prospect of battling Harvas Black-Robe again, any number of berserk, fearless axe-swinging northerners seemed a stroll in the meadow by comparison.

Chapter XII

THE WALLS OF PLISKAVOS BURNED ALL THROUGH THE NIGHT. Only when morning came again did the flames begin to subside. Smoke still rose here and there inside the town from the fires the blazing wall had started.

Two heralds, one a Videssian, the other from Krispos' force of Haloga guards, approached the wall as closely at its heat would allow. In the imperial speech and the tongue of Halogaland, they called on the northerners inside Pliskavos to yield, ". . . the more so," as the Videssian-speaker put it, "since the evil wizard who brought you to this pass can no longer aid you."

Krispos held his breath at that, afraid in spite of everything that Harvas had been lying low for reasons of his own and would now reappear with redoubled malice and might. But of Harvas there was no sign. The Halogai did not yield, either. The heralds called out their message again and again, then withdrew to the imperial lines. Pliskavos remained silent, smoky, and enigmatic the whole day long.

At the officers' meeting just after sunset, Krispos said, "If the walls have cooled enough by morning, we'll send men up onto them to see what's going on in there."

"Aye," Mammianos said. "It's not like the cursed northerners to keep so quiet so long. They're up to something we'll likely regret—unless they've all been roasted, but that's too much to ask for, worse luck."

The rest of the generals loudly and profanely agreed with him. Then Bagradas raised his wine cup and said, "Let's drink to the brave lady Tanilis, who made sure they were the ones who roasted rather than us, and who made Harvas choke on his own bile."

"Tanilis!" The officers shouted out her name. Krispos spoke it with the rest of them and drank with them as well. The meeting broke up soon afterward. The soldiers filed out of the imperial tent, leaving him alone.

He sat down on the edge of the cot. He shook his head. The night before, Tanilis and he had shared the cot first in triumph, then in terror. Now she was dead, and Bagradas' well-meaning toast did not, could not, begin to do justice to what she'd accomplished. Zaidas understood far more. Krispos wondered how much he understood himself.

Too much had happened too fast—his emotions were still several jumps behind events. Instead of victorious or full of grief, he mostly felt battered, as if he'd gone through rapids without a boat.

He drained his cup, then poured another and drained that. Then he set down the jar of wine. Tanilis would have wanted him to stop, he thought: he'd need a clear head come morning. He undressed and lay down where he had lain with Tanilis; the scent of her still clung to the blanket. Tears filled his eyes. He angrily brushed them aside. Tears were no fit monument for Tanilis. Finishing what she'd made possible was. He did his best to sleep.

"MAJESTY!" A HALOGA GUARD BOOMED. "THERE'S STIRRING INside Pliskavos, Majesty."

Krispos woke with a grunt. A guttering lamp gave the tent all the light it had; the sun was not yet up. "I'll be out soon," he called. He got out of bed, used the chamber pot, and put on his gilded coat of mail.

He saw the eastern sky had turned gray. "What's toward?" he asked the guardsman.

"That we don't yet know, Majesty. But through the grates of the portcullises some scouts have spied the warriors within Pliskavos milling about. Come the dawn, we'll have a better notion of why."

"True enough," Krispos said. "We'd best be ready for the worst, though." Night or day, a detachment of military musicians remained on duty. Krispos went over to them. "Call the men from their tents and to assembly." As the martial music rang out, he hurried up to the palisade to see what was going on for himself.

As the guard had said, no one could tell just what was going on in Pliskavos, but something definitely was. The wooden gates had been burned to ashes when the wall caught fire, but the portcullises' iron grills survived. Through the grillwork Krispos saw shadowy motion. He could not make out more than that, even as twilight brightened toward dawn.

Behind him, noise quickly built as the imperial army readied itself for whatever might come. Men called back and forth; underofficers shouted; swords and quivers and armor rattled; horses snorted and complained as troopers tightened girths. Through it all, the musicians kept playing. Their music got louder, too, as more of them came on duty.

The sun rose. Krispos sketched Phos' circle over his heart as he murmured the creed. It was also on other men's lips as they caught the day's first sight of the chiefest symbol of the good god.

Mammianos came up to Krispos. He said, "If they are going to try to break out, Your Majesty, do you want to meet them behind the palisade or before it?"

"If everything goes well, meeting them behind the palisade would be cheapest," Krispos mused. "But we'd be stretched all along the line around Pliskavos, and they might well rush their men at one point and smash their way through us." He rubbed his chin. "I hate to say it, but I think we have to meet them face-to-face. What do you say, Mammianos? I halfway hope you can talk me out of it."

The fat general grunted, far from happily. "No, I fear you have the right of it, Your Majesty. I was hoping you could talk me round to the other way, but you see the same dangers I do." He grunted again. "I'll pass on the word, then."

"Thank you, eminent sir."

The musicians' calls changed from *Assembly* to *Battle Stations*. Officers' orders amplified the music. "No, not behind the rampart, lads. Today we're going to let them see what they'll be tangling with if they have the stones for it."

Krispos made his own way back through the crowd to the imperial tent. As he'd expected, Progress was saddled and waiting for him. He checked the straps under the saddle for tightness, then swung his left foot into the stirrup. Climbing onto Progress reminded him how Mavros had helped him choose the big bay gelding, and helped haggle the price down, too.

"One more win, foster brother of mine—one more win and you and your mother are both avenged," he said softly.

He rode out through a gap in the palisade and took his place at the center of the imperial army that was rapidly forming up in front of Pliskavos.

He thought about sending his heralds up to the town to call once more for the Halogai to surrender, but decided not to. Soon enough the northerners would show what they intended to do.

The thought had hardly crossed his mind when the portcullises began to rise. They did not move smoothly; one, indeed, warped by the heat of the burning wall, stuck in its track with its spiked lower edge about four feet off the ground. That did not keep hundreds of armed Halogai from ducking under it as they filed out of Pliskavos. More of the big blond warriors came through other gates.

"They don't look like men about to yield," Mammianos said.

"No, they don't," Krispos agreed glumly. The leading ranks of Halogai carried big shields that protected them almost from head to foot. Behind that shield wall—almost a palisade in itself—the rest of the northerners began to deploy. Krispos swore. "If we had all our men in place, we could break them before they got set up themselves." He scowled at the Halogai. "By the good god, let's hit them anyway. With us mounted, we can choose when and where the attack goes in."

"Aye, Majesty." Mammianos opened his mouth to shout orders, then stopped, staring in amazement at one of the gates where the portcullis had gone all the way up.

Krispos followed his gaze. He started, too. A company of Halogai on horseback was coming out. "I didn't think any of them were riders," he said.

"I didn't, either." Mammianos made a noise half cough, half chuckle. "By the look of them, they aren't too sure themselves."

The Halogai were on Kubrati ponies, the only sort of horses they could have found inside Pliskavos. Some of the blond warriors so outmatched their mounts in size that their feet almost brushed the ground. They brandished swords and axes as they formed a ragged line. From his own experience in the courtyard of the High Temple, Krispos knew a foot soldier's axe was no proper weapon for a cavalryman.

"They do try to learn new things, don't they?" Mammianos said in a thoughtful tone. "That makes them more dangerous, or rather dangerous in a different sort of way, than, say, the Makuraners, who do what they do very well, but always in the same old way."

"If they want to learn, let's see that they pay for their first lesson." Krispos turned to a courier. "Order Bagradas to send one of his companies out into the ground between our army and the barbarians. We'll find out what sort of riders they are." The courier grinned nastily as he hurried away.

Bagradas' troopers, a band of archers and lancers about equal in numbers to the mounted Halogai, rode into the no-man's-land. There they stopped and waited. After a moment the Halogai understood the challenge. They yelled and spurred their horses toward the imperials.

The Videssians also raised a shout. They urged their horses forward, too. The archers used their knees to control their mounts as they let fly again and again. A couple of Halogai fell from the saddle. More ponies were wounded and went bounding out of the fight, beyond the ability of their inexperienced riders to control.

But the archers could account for only so many of their foes before the two companies came together. Then it was the lancers' turn. Their long spears gave them far greater reach than the northerners. They spitted Halogai out of the saddle without getting close enough for their foes to strike back. The imperials had also mastered the art of fighting as a unit rather than man by man. The Halogai fought that way afoot, but had never practiced it on horseback. As Krispos had been sure they would, they paid dearly for instruction.

Finally, however brave they were, the Halogai could bear no more. They wheeled their horses and fled for the protection of their comrades on foot. The imperials pursued. The archers accounted for several more men before they and their comrades turned about and rode back to their own lines. The Videssians cheered thunderously. The Halogai, with nothing to cheer about, advanced on the imperial army in grim silence.

"They must be getting desperate, to challenge us mounted when they can barely stay on their horses," Mammianos observed.

"Our cavalry's beaten them again and again, first south of the mountains and now up here," Krispos answered. "If they are desperate, we've made them that way. And now, remember, they don't have Harvas to help them anymore." *I hope they don't,* he added to himself.

"Aye, that's so." Mammianos cocked his head to one side. "From what I hear, we have the lady Tanilis and you to thank for it, Your Majesty."

"Give the lady the credit," Krispos said firmly. "If it had just been me, you'd be looking for a new Emperor right now, or more likely in too much trouble to worry about finding one."

Companies of horse archers cantered forward to pour arrows into the oncoming Halogai. They could not miss such a bunched target, but did less damage than Krispos had hoped. The first ranks of northerners had those head-to-foot shields; the men behind them raised their round wooden bucklers high to turn aside the shafts. Some got through, but not enough. Inexorable as the tide, the Halogai tramped forward.

The Videssian archers withdrew into the protection of their line. The musicians sounded the charge. Lancers couched spears, dug spurs into horses' flanks. Slowly at first, then faster and faster, they rumbled toward the Halogai.

"This isn't going to be pretty," Mammianos shouted over the thunder of hoofbeats.

"So long as it works," Krispos shouted back. The two lines collided then. Videssian horsemen spitted northerners, using their mounts to bowl over and ride down others. Unlike the cavalry fight, they did not have it all their own way, not for a moment. At close quarters, the axes of the Halogai hewed down men and horses alike; those big, swift strokes bit through mail shirts to hack flesh and split bones.

The battle line did not move twenty yards forward or back for some time. Halogai pressed forward as their comrades were killed. They blunted charge after charge by fresh troops of lancers. Each side dragged its wounded to safety as best it could. Dead horses and soldiers hindered the living from reaching one another to slay some more.

Shouts of alarm rose from the far right as the northerners, borrowing from the Videssian book, tried to slide round the imperial army's flank. After a few tense minutes, a messenger reported to Krispos. "We've held 'em, Majesty, looks like. A good many bowmen had to pull out their sabers before we managed it, though."

"That's why they carry them," Krispos answered.

The imperials shouted his name over and over. They also had another cry, one calculated to unnerve the Halogai. "Where's Harvas Black-Robe?" The northerners were not using the wizard's name as their war cry. When they shouted, they most often called the name Svenkel.

Krispos learned soon enough who Svenkel was. An enormous Haloga, tall even for that big breed, swung an axe that would have impressed the imperial headsman. No one came within its length of him and lived. After he felled a Videssian with a stroke that caved in the luckless fellow's chest, all the northerners who saw cried out his name. He had presence as well as strength and warrior's skill: before he went back to battle, he waved to show he heard the cheers.

"Shall we send one of our champions against him?" Mammianos asked.

"Why risk a champion?" Krispos said. "Enough arrows will take care of him. Give the archers word to shoot at him till he goes down."

"That's not sporting," Mammianos said with a laugh, "but it's the right way to go about war. Let's just see how long Svenkel the hero lasts."

But along with being a warrior bold even by Haloga standards, Svenkel the hero was far from a fool. When three or four arrows in quick succession pincushioned his shield and another glanced off his helm, he knew he was a marked man. Instead of drawing back among his comrades, as most might have done, he led a wedge of northerners into the center of the imperial line against his countrymen who warded Krispos. They were axemen like himself; when they tried to slay him, he could strike back.

The imperial guards had seen hard fighting in all the clashes since the campaign began south of Imbros. The Halogai who were hale still fought as fiercely as ever, but their ranks had been thinned. Svenkel's wedge punched deep. If it broke through, it would cut the imperial army in half.

Krispos drew his saber. He looked at Mammianos. The fat general also had his sword out. He shrugged. "Ah, well, Your Majesty, sometimes we have to be sporting, whether we want to or not."

"So we do." Krispos raised his voice and cried, "Videssos!" He spurred Progress toward the sagging line of guardsmen. Mammianos rode with him. So did the couriers who had congregated around them.

By then, only a handful of Halogai in imperial service stood in Svenkel's way. He must have seen victory just ahead. His mouth flew open in a great snarl when horsemen rode up to aid the guards. Then he realized who led the makeshift band. In Videssian, he shouted to Krispos: "Leader to leader, then!"

It didn't quite work that way; war was too chaotic a business to conform to anyone's expectations, even a hero's. Krispos got into the battle a few feet to Svenkel's right, against a Haloga almost as big as the northern chieftain. The fellow swung up his axe to chop at Progress. Before he could, Krispos slashed at his face. He missed, but made the Haloga shift his weight backward so his own stroke fell short. Krispos slashed again. This time he felt his blade bite. The Haloga howled and reeled away, clutching a forearm gashed to the bone.

Seeing Krispos in the fight made his surviving guardsmen redouble their efforts. Svenkel's men still battled for all they were worth, but could push forward no farther. The guards threw themselves at Svenkel, one after another. One after another he beat them back. His strokes never faltered; he might have been a siege engine himself, powered by twisted cords rather than flesh and sinew.

As the guardsmen sought to cut down Svenkel, so his warriors went for Krispos. Krispos fought desperately, trying for nothing more than staying alive. He knew he was no great master of the soldier's art and was very glad when Geirrod came up to stand by Progress' right flank and help him beat back the foe.

Step by step, some of Svenkel's men began to give ground. Others, stubborn with the peculiar Haloga stubbornness, preferred dying where they stood to falling back. Die they did, one after another, along with the imperial guardsmen and Videssian troopers they slew before they went down.

There at the forefront of the fighting, what scholarly chroniclers would later call a line hardly deserved such a dignified name. It was more like knots of grunting, cursing, sweating, bleeding men all entangled with one another. Krispos struck and struck and struck—and knew most of his strokes were useless, either because they clove only air or because they rebounded from mail. He did not much mind; no one in that crush could have hoped to do better.

Then he saw a Haloga close by swing up an axe to chop at one of the guardsmen. He lashed out with his saber. It cut deep into the northerner's wrist. The axe flew from his hand. The Haloga bellowed in pain and whirled around.

Krispos was startled to see it was Svenkel. Svenkel looked startled, too, but was neither too startled nor too badly hurt to raise his shield before Krispos could cut at him again. But that did not save him for long. Geirrod's axe bit into the shield, once, twice . . . on the third blow, the round slab of wood split in two. Geirrod struck once more. Blood sprayed. Svenkel's armor clattered as he fell.

The imperials raised a great cheer. The Halogai still fought ferociously, but something at last went out of them with their chieftain's death. Now the fighters in the wedge that had been his drew back more quickly. As they did so, Geirrod turned to Krispos and said, "Out of the line for you now, Majesty. You did what was needful; we'll go on from here."

Krispos was not sorry to obey. He'd never been an eager warrior. He'd also learned that the Emperor, like any other high-ranking officer, usually was more useful directing the fighting than caught in the thick of it.

He looked round for Mammianos and was relieved to see the general had also got out of the press. But Mammianos had not come through unscathed; he bared his teeth in a grimace of pain as he awkwardly tried to tie a strip of cloth around his right forearm. The cloth was soaked with red.

"Here, let me help you," Krispos said, sheathing his saber. "I have two free hands."

"Thank you, Your Majesty. Aye, get it good and tight. There, that should do it." The fat general shook his head. "I'm lucky it's not a bloody stump, I suppose. Been too long since I last tried trading handstrokes."

"What was it you said? Sometimes we have to be sporting? But trooper's not your proper trade anymore."

"Too right it isn't. And a good thing, else I'd long since be dead." Mammianos grimaced. "As is, this arm's the only thing that's killing me."

Shouts rang out, far off at the end of the imperial army's left wing. Krispos and Mammianos both stared in that direction. For the moment, that was all they could do—their couriers were still battling to drive back Svenkel's men. Some of the shouts were full of excitement, others of dismay. From several hundred yards off, Krispos could not tell which came from the Halogai, which from the imperials.

He kept his neck craned leftward, fearing above all else to see the Videssians driven back in rout. He saw no soldiers fleeing on horseback, which he took as a good sign. All the same, he fidgeted atop Progress for the next several minutes, until at last a rider came galloping his way from the left.

The horseman's grin told him most of what he needed to know before the fellow began to speak. "Majesty, we've flanked them! Sarkis got his scouts round their right and now we're rolling 'em up."

"The good god be praised," Krispos said. "That's what I most wanted to hear. Go back there and tell all the officers on that wing to pour as many men after Sarkis as they can spare without thinning their line too much."

"Majesty, they're already doing it," the messenger said.

"They're good soldiers, most of them," Mammianos put in. The rider's news banished pain from his face. "A good soldier doesn't wait for orders when he sees a chance like that. He just ups and grabs it."

"It's all right with me," Krispos said. His grin stretched wider than the one the messenger was wearing. "In fact, it's better than all right."

Faster even than he'd dared hope, the Haloga right came to pieces. The northerners faced a cruel dilemma. If they turned at bay and formed an embattled circle, nothing would keep the Videssians from simply riding into Pliskavos. But if they fell back toward the gates, they risked fresh breakthroughs as the imperials probed flimsy, makeshift lines.

Some turned at bay, some fell back. The Videssians did break through, repeatedly, forcing more and more Halogai to make the unpalatable choice. Sarkis could easily have seized Pliskavos. Instead, with even deadlier instinct, he urged his men—and the other imperials in their wake—all around the rear of the Haloga army. Krispos traced their progress by the panic-filled yells that rose first from the northerners' shattered right, then the center, and then their left—the imperial right. A few minutes later, the imperials on the right yelled, too, in triumph.

"By the lord with the great and good mind, they're in the sack," Mammianos said. "Now we slaughter them." He did not sound as if he took any great joy in the prospect, merely as if it was a job that needed doing. The imperial headsman plied his trade in that matter-of-fact, deadly fashion.

The Videssian army went about its business the same way, methodically using bows, lances, and sabers against the northerners. As Mammianos had said, it was a slaughter. Then all the Halogai suddenly turned round and rushed against the Videssians who stood between them and Pliskavos. That part of the imperial line remained thinner than the rest. Shouting wildly, the northerners hacked their way through.

"After them!" Krispos yelled. Quite without orders, the musicians played *Charge*. They were soldiers, too, and out to grab the chance.

The Videssians surged forward in pursuit of their fleeing foes. Here and there a Haloga stood and fought. Those who did were beset by several men at once and quickly fell. Many more were cut down or speared from behind. And more than one, rather than dying at the imperials' hands or doffing his helm in token of surrender, plunged a sword into his own belly or a knife between his ribs. The way the northerners so deliberately killed themselves chilled Krispos.

"Why do they do that?" he asked Geirrod.

"We Halogai, we think that if a man be slain by an enemy, he serves him in the world to come," the guardsman answered. "Some of us, we would liefer live free after we die, if you take my meaning, Majesty."

"I suppose I do." Krispos sketched the sun-sign over his heart. He wished the Halogai could be persuaded to follow Phos. Every so often zealous priests went to preach the good god's doctrines in Halogaland. If they were fearless men, the northerners generally let them live. But they won few converts; the Halogai stubbornly clung to their false gods.

Such reflections ran through his mind and then were gone, lost in the chase. Now he wished Sarkis had sent men to secure Pliskavos' gates. A few Videssians made for them, but the rush of Halogai overwhelmed the riders. The big blond men streamed into the town. More turned at bay, to give their comrades the chance to save themselves.

Krispos swore. "If we had ladders ready, we could storm the place. It would fall at the first rush."

"Aye, likely so, Your Majesty," Mammianos said, "but ladders aren't of much use in a pitched battle, which is what we were set to fight. This isn't one of those minstrels' romances, where the bold hero always thinks of everything ahead of time. If it were, I wouldn't have this." He held up his bandaged arm.

The imperials charged again and again at the Haloga rear guards. Then some of the northerners gained the walls of Pliskavos and began shooting at their foes and pelting them with stones. Under the cover of that barrage, most of the Halogai managed to withdraw into the city. Portcullises slammed down in the Videssians' faces.

Only when the fighting finally died away did Krispos notice how far toward the east his shadow stretched. The sun was nearly set. He looked over the battlefield and shook his head in wonder. Softly he said, "How many Halogai are down!"

"That's the way of it when one side breaks," Mammianos said. "Remember, Agapetos and Mavros paid in this coin for us."

"I remember," Krispos said. "Oh, yes, I remember."

The Videssians ranged over the field. They dragged and carried their wounded countrymen back to their healer-priests. Most of the Halogai not yet dead got shorter shrift. Some—those who had been seen to fight with special bravery and those who looked rich enough to be worth ransoming—were spared.

Horse leeches went here and there, doing what they could for injured animals. Other soldiers went here and there, too, plundering the dead. Piles of Haloga shields, too big and bulky to be of use to horsemen, grew and grew. Krispos saw so many that he ordered a count made, to give him some idea of how many northerners had fallen. He also wondered what his horsemen would do with the war axes and heavy swords they were happily taking away.

"Some will be inlaid with gold, and so worth something," Geirrod said when he spoke that thought aloud. "As for the others, well, Majesty, even you southrons deem it worth recalling that you overcame brave men." Krispos had to nod.

Burial parties began their work—a pit that would make a mass grave for the fallen Halogai, individual resting places for the far smaller number of Videssians who had died. Krispos told the soldiers to dig a special grave for Tanilis, apart from all the others. "Set a wooden marker over it for now," he said. "When this land is ours and peaceful once more, the finest marble will be none too good for her."

The men counting northern shields came to him with their total: over twelve thousand. He knew fewer Halogai than that had died; some would have discarded their shields to flee the faster. It was still a great total, especially when set against imperial losses, which were under two thousand.

That evening, as the army rested in camp, Krispos went to see some of the Haloga prisoners. Archers stood guard over them as they dejectedly sat around in their linen drawers and undertunics—their armor was already booty. They stirred with interest as he approached. Some of them glowered at their countrymen who guarded him.

He ignored that, announcing "I need a man who understands Videssian to listen to my words and take them to your comrades in Pliskavos. Who will do this for me?" Several northerners raised their hands. He chose a solid-looking fellow with gray mixed in his golden hair and beard. He asked the man, "What is your name?"

"I am Soribulf, Videssian emperor," the Haloga said, politely but without the elaborate respect imperials used.

"Well, Soribulf, tell this to your chiefs in Pliskavos: if they yield the city and set free any Videssian prisoners they are holding, I will let them cross to the north shore of the Astris without ordering my fleet to burn their boats."

"We are the Halogai," Soribulf said, drawing himself up proudly. "We do not yield."

"If we weren't already burying them, you could see all the Haloga corpses on today's field," Krispos said. "If you don't yield, every one of you inside Pliskavos will die, too. Do you think we can't take the town with our siege engines and our ships that shoot fire?"

Soribulf's mouth puckered, as if he were chewing on something sour. "How do we trust you not to burn us even so, when we are on the water and cannot ward ourselves?"

"My word is good," Krispos said. "Better than that of the evil mage you followed."

"Aye, you speak truth there, Videssian emperor. He told us you would burn with the wall, but our warriors were the ones the bright blaze bit. And then after, he helped us no more; some say he fled. I know not the truth of that, but we saw none of him today when swords struck."

"Pass on what I say, then, and my warning," Krispos urged.

Soribulf swayed back and forth. "He mourns," a guardsman whispered to Krispos. Soribulf spoke in his own language. The guard translated: "The glory of Haloga arms is dead. Will we now yield ingloriously to Videssos and travel back to our homeland in defeat? Never have we done so—braver to conquer or die."

"Die you will, if you fight on," Krispos said. "Shall I choose someone else as my messenger?"

"No." Soribulf returned to the imperial speech. "I will bear your words to my people. Whether they choose to hear, I could not guess."

Krispos nodded to a couple of the archers who guarded the Haloga prisoners. "You men take him to the rampart and let him go to Pliskavos." He turned back to Soribulf. "If your chiefs are willing to speak of yielding, tell them to show a white-painted shield above the central gate first thing tomorrow morning."

"I shall tell them," Soribulf said. The guards led him away.

Krispos sent an order to Kanaris the grand drungarios of the fleet: to have his dromons sailing back and forth on the Astris by dawn, as a warning that the trapped northerners had no way out unless the imperials granted it to them. Then, while the rest of the army celebrated the great victory they had won, Krispos went to bed.

When he woke the next morning, he looked to the walls of Pliskavos. Halogai marched along them, but he saw no truce shield. Glowering, he ordered the engineers to ready their dart-shooters and stone-throwers. "Don't make any secret of what you're doing, either," he told them.

The Halogai watched from the walls as the artisans ostentatiously checked the ropes and timbers of their engines, made sure they had plenty of stones and sheaves of outsized arrows close at hand, and squinted toward Pliskavos as if checking range and aim for the catapults. Dew was still damp on the grass when a shield went up over the gate.

"Well, well." Krispos let out a long sigh of relief. Even without magic used against his men, storming the town would have been desperately expensive. "Have Progress saddled up for me," he said to his guardsmen. "I'll parley with their chief."

"Not alone!" the guards said in one voice. "If the foe sallies—"

"I hadn't intended to go out there alone," Krispos answered mildly, "not for fear of treachery and not for my dignity's sake, either."

He approached Pliskavos in the midst of a full company of Haloga guards. Another company, this one of Videssian horse-archers, flanked the guards on either side. The horsemen had arrows nocked and ready in their bows.

He reined in about a hundred feet from the wall. "Who will speak with me?" he called.

A Haloga stood atop one of the low stretches of battlement. "I am Ikmor," he called back. "Those inside will obey me." His Videssian was good; a moment later he explained why: "Years ago, in my youth, I served in the city as guard to the Avtokrator Rhaptes. I learned your speech then."

"You served Anthimos' father, eh? Good enough," Krispos said. "Soribulf brought you my terms. Will you take them, or will you go on with a fight you cannot win?"

"You are a hard man, Videssian Emperor, harder than Rhaptes who was," Ikmor answered. "I grieved the whole night long at the ruin of our grand army, struggling with my spirit over whether to yield or battle on. But I saw in the end that I must give over, though it is bitter as wormwood to me. Yet a war leader must not surrender to sorrow, but try in every way to save the lives of the warriors under him."

"Spoken like a wise man," Krispos said. *Spoken like a man who indeed spent time in Videssos,* he thought. A Haloga fresh from his native land would have been unlikely to take such a long view.

"Spoken like a man who finds himself without choice," Ikmor answered bleakly. "To show I am in earnest, I will send out the captives from your people whom we hold."

The Haloga chieftain turned, shouting in his own language. The portcullis beneath him creaked up. One by one dark-haired men came through the gateway, most of them in rags, many pale and thin as only longtime prisoners become. Some rubbed at their eyes, as if unused to sunlight. When they saw the imperial banner that floated above Krispos' head, they cheered and pelted toward him.

His own eyes filled with tears. He called to the officer who led the cavalry company. "Take them back to our camp. Feed them, get clothes for them. Have the healer-priests check them, too, those who aren't too worn from work with our wounded." The captain saluted and told off a squad to take charge of the newly released Videssians.

No sooner was the last imperial out of Pliskavos than the portcullis slammed down again. Ikmor said, "Videssian Emperor, if we come out ourselves, how do we know you will not treat us as . . . as—" He hesitated, but had to say it: "—as we treated Imbros?"

"Do you not trust my pledge?" Krispos said.

"Not in this," Ikmor answered at once. After a moment's anger, Krispos reluctantly saw his point: having done deeds that deserved retribution, no wonder the Halogai feared it. Ikmor went on, "Let us come forth in arms and armor, to ward ourselves at need."

"No," Krispos said. "You could start the battle over then, looking to take us by surprise." He stroked his beard as he thought. "How's this, Haloga chief? Wear your swords and axes, if you will. But leave shields behind and carry your mail shirts as part of your baggage, rolled up on your backs."

It was Ikmor's turn to ponder. At last he said. "Let it be as you will. We shall need our weapons against the Khamorth nomads as we trek north over the plains to Halogaland."

With luck, Krispos thought, the nomads would take a good bite out of the Halogai before they made it back to their own cold country. That might them think twice about moving south against Videssos again. Come to that, he might help luck along. Aloud, he said, "One other thing, brave Ikmor."

"What would you, Videssian Emperor?"

"When you northerners come out of Pliskavos, you will all come through this same gate through which you let out your Videssian prisoners. I want to post wizards there, to make sure Harvas Black-Robe doesn't sneak out among you."

Ikmor's laugh was unkind. "Then you should have checked the captives, too, eh?" Krispos ground his teeth—the Haloga chieftain was right. Ikmor continued, "But we will do as you say once more, though for our own sake rather than yours. If you do find Harvas, let our axes drink his blood, for he betrayed us." He spoke in his own tongue to the men on the wall with him. They growled and hefted their weapons in a way that left no doubt of what they thought of Harvas.

Krispos said, "If you love him so well, why didn't you turn on him before?"

"Before, Videssian Emperor, he led us to victory and helped us settle this fine new land. Even a war leader with the soul of a carrion crow will hold his followers thus," Ikmor said. "But when his fires turned against his own folk, when after that he vanished from our ken instead of staying to battle on as a true man would, he showed us he had not even a carrion crow inside himself, only the splattered white turd one leaves behind after it has fed and flown on."

Some of the Halogai on the wall—the ones who followed Videssian, Krispos supposed—nodded vigorously. So did some of the soldiers with Krispos, impressed by Ikmor's ability to revile without actually cursing.

"If you agree, Ikmor, we will bring the wizards into place tomorrow," Krispos said.

"No, give us four days' time," Ikmor answered. "We will use timber from the town to knock together rafts and go out through the river gates to put them at the quays."

"If you try to escape on them before the day we agreed to, the dromons will burn you," Krispos warned.

"We have seen the fire they fling, the fire they spit. We will hold to these terms, Videssian Emperor."

"Good enough." Krispos gave Ikmor a Videssian salute, clenched fist over his heart. He was not surprised to see the Haloga return it. As quickly as ceremony permitted, or maybe a little quicker, he withdrew to the camp. The first thing he did there was to summon Zaidas.

By the time he was done talking, the young mage's face mirrored the concern he knew his own showed. "Aye, Your Majesty, I'll attend to it directly," Zaidas said. "It would be a dreadful blow if Harvas the accursed profited thus from the misery of our own people. But if he is among them, I shall sniff him out." The picture of determination, he started away from the imperial tent.

"Take a squad of soldiers, in case you need to do more than sniff," Krispos called after him. Zaidas did not turn around but waved to show he had heard.

Krispos spent the rest of the day worrying, half afraid he would hear of trouble from where the liberated Videssians sat and ate and talked and marveled at being free, half afraid he wouldn't because Harvas had managed to outfox Zaidas. But toward sunset Zaidas reported, "He is not among those who are there, Your Majesty. On that I would take oath by the lord with the great and good mind. If no other captives came from Pliskavos, we may rest easy. The officers and men who have dealt with them believe them to be all the ones the Halogai released."

"The good god be praised," Krispos said. He could not be perfectly sure Harvas hadn't been among the freed captives, but the older he got, the less he was perfectly sure of anything. With a nod toward Zaidas, he said, "Ready yourself and your comrades to study the Haloga when they leave Pliskavos."

"We shall be fully prepared," Zaidas promised. "Harvas hale could hope to stand against us. Harvas as he is after the lady Tanilis smote him"—his voice softened as he spoke her name, but his eyes flashed—"is small beer, as the saying goes. If he is there, we will smoke him out."

"Good." Krispos was not usually vindictive, but he wanted to lay hands on Harvas, to make him suffer for all the suffering he had inflicted on Videssos. Then he remembered a saying himself: "To make rabbit stew, first catch a rabbit."

The Halogai inside Pliskavos gave no sign of breaking the terms to which Ikmor had agreed. Kanaris brought word that the northerners really were building rafts. All the same Krispos held off sending word of his victory south to the city. Once he'd caught his rabbit—or, in this case, seen it across the Astris—would be time enough.

On the fourth morning, he ordered his army to advance on Pliskavos. The soldiers came fully armed and ready for battle. He had strong forces covering each gate, not merely the one through which Ikmor had promised the Halogai would march. Mammianos nodded at that. "If we show 'em we're set for everything, they're less likely to try anything."

Zaidas and the rest of the wizards took their place outside the central gate. They waved to Krispos to show they were ready. He peered into the town through the grid of the portcullis. A lot of men looked to be lined up there. Then the portcullis rose, screeching in its track every inch of the way.

One man came through alone. He tramped past the Videssian mages without sparing them a glance and made straight for the imperial banner. He saluted Krispos. "I am Ikmor. For my folk I stand before you. Do as you will with me if we play you false."

"Go with your people," Krispos said. "I did not ask this of you."

"I know that. I give it to you, for my honor's sake. I shall stay."

Krispos had learned better than to argue about a Haloga's prickly sense of honor. "As you will, northern sir." He undid his canteen, swigged, and passed it to Ikmor. "Share wine with me."

"Aye." Ikmor drank. A couple of drops splashed on his white tunic, which was already none too clean. The Haloga was a well-made man of middle height, snub-nosed and gray-eyed. He was bald on top of his head, but let the hair above his ears grow long. His mustaches were also long, though the rest of his beard was rather thin. In each ear he wore a thick gold ring set with pearls—Iakovitzes would have wanted a pair of them, Krispos thought irrelevantly. When he handed the canteen back to Krispos, it was empty.

The Halogai filed out of Pliskavos a few at a time, walking between Zaidas and the other wizards. Most of the northerners made Ikmor seem immaculate by comparison. More than a few showed the marks of burns from when the wall caught fire, wounds from the latest battle, or both. They glared at the imperials who had overcome them, as if they still could not believe the campaign had gone against them.

Looking at them, Krispos also wondered how he'd won. The Halogai were big, fierce men who might have been specially made for war. Fighting came less naturally to Videssians. In the end, though, trained skill had overcome ferocity.

Mammianos was thinking along similar lines. He remarked, "They want another chance at us. You can see it in their eyes."

"They won't have such an easy time trying again," Krispos answered. "Now that we rule all the way up to the Astris again, I expect we'll keep a flotilla of dromons patrolling the river. I wouldn't want to try crossing it in the face of them."

He spoke as much to Ikmor as to Mammianos. Out of the corner of his eye, he saw the Haloga chief's mouth turn down. The message had got through, then.

A few minutes later a warrior broke ranks and strode toward Krispos. He touched his sword. His guardsmen tensed, readying themselves to cut the fellow down. But he paused at a safe distance and spoke loudly in his own language. Krispos glanced at Ikmor. "What does he say?"

Ikmor looked even less happy. "He wants to take service with you, Videssian Emperor."

"What? Why?"

Ikmor spoke to the Haloga, then listened to his reply. "He says his name is Odd the son of Aki, and that he will only fight among the best soldiers in the world. Till now he thought those were his own people, but you have beaten us, so he must have been wrong."

"For that I'll find him a place," Krispos said, grinning. Ikmor translated. Odd the son of Aki dipped his head to Krispos, then stepped aside. A Videssian officer took charge of him.

As the day went on, more Halogai broke ranks and asked leave to join the imperial army. Most of them gave the same reason Odd had. By the time the last northerner filed out of Pliskavos, Krispos found he had recruited a good-sized company. Ikmor turned his back on the men who had gone over.

The Halogai marched around Pliskavos toward the quays. More evidence of imperial might awaited them there: Kanaris' warships, holding their place against the current of the Astris like so many sparrowhawks hovering above a mousehole.

Krispos rode Progress up toward the riverbank so he could watch the northerners embark on their rafts. Ikmor paced alongside him, though two guardsmen made sure they were between the chieftain and the Avtokrator at all times.

The Halogai paddled the first raft out onto the Astris a little past noon. A dromon shadowed it all the way across the river, the fearsome siphon tube pointing straight at it. The wallowing raft was completely at the dromon's mercy. No one, Haloga or imperial, could doubt it. More than anything else, that first river crossing brought home who had won and who had lost.

More and more rafts set out. Not all of them enjoyed the attentions of a dromon all the way across the Astris, but the warships stayed close enough to leave no question of what they could do at need. Destroying the northerners' dugout canoes had been an unequal struggle. Attacking the rafts would have been a massacre.

Zaidas made his way through the crowd to Krispos. "All the Halogai passed before me, Your Majesty. I found no sign of Harvas' presence."

"Go rest, then," Krispos told him. The young mage had always been reedy. Now he was a thin reed indeed.

Even so, he tried to protest. "I ought to go into the town, to see whether the evil wizard still lurks within." He weakened his own words with an enormous yawn.

"The shape you're in, you're likelier to fall asleep than find him," Krispos said. "I'll keep wizards posted at each gate. If he's in there, he won't get out." He did his best to look stern and imperial. It probably wasn't a very good best; Zaidas winked at him. But the mage went back toward the camp, which was what Krispos had in mind.

The rafts the Halogai had built carried only a fraction of them over the Astris that first day. The northerners who were left behind spread their bedrolls outside of Pliskavos. The countrymen's campfires blazed from the far shore. Between the two groups, up and down, up and down along the river, the dromons of the imperial fleet prowled all night long.

Videssian archers stood guard through the night on the southern bank of the Astris, alert in case the Halogai proved treacherous. But most of the imperial army returned to the camp on the other side of the palisade. At the officers' meeting that evening, Sarkis gave Krispos a sly look. "May I read your mind, Majesty?"

"Go ahead," Krispos told him.

"You're wishing a nice big band of Khamorth would pitch into the Halogai on their way north and finish the job we started."

"Who, me?" As he tried to look imperial to Zaidas, now Krispos tried to look innocent. "That would be a terrible fate to wish on a foe we've just made peace with."

"Aye, so it would, Majesty." Sarkis' eyes twinkled. "But didn't I see you send a couple of men with horses to the north shore of the Astris? Unless they're going to keep the northerners company on their way back to Halogaland, they're probably up there to talk with one of the local Khamorth khagans."

"With more than one," Krispos admitted. "One of the local clan leaders by himself wouldn't have enough men to risk tangling with such a big Haloga army. Three or four together might, in hopes of getting gold from us for the favor. I'd sooner spend gold than soldiers; we've spent enough soldiers against the Halogai."

A low mutter of approval ran through the officers. Bagradas turned to Krispos and said, "Your Majesty, you are truly what an Avtokrator of the

Videssians should be." The rest of the commanders solemnly nodded. Krispos felt himself swell with pride.

Sarkis asked, "What would you have done had Ikmor made you pledge not to send envoys to the Khamorth?"

"I would have kept my word," Krispos answered. "But since he didn't think of it, I saw no reason to bring it up myself."

"Aye, a Videssian indeed," Sarkis murmured, reminding Krispos that the scout commander sprang from Vaspurakan. A moment later Sarkis softened his words. "No blame to you, though, Majesty, not after what the northerners have done to Videssos. They've earned whatever they catch."

Again the officers nodded and called out, many with fierce eagerness. But Krispos asked, "Whatever they catch? What of Imbros?"

Abrupt silence fell inside the imperial tent. Krispos was relieved to hear it. No one who preferred Phos to Skotos could feel easy about imagining Imbros' fate for any group, no matter what its crimes, and he was glad none of his officers thirsted so much for revenge as to forget it.

ZAIDAS SEEMED MUCH MORE HIS OLD SELF WHEN MORNING came. Along with several other wizards, he entered Pliskavos to continue the search for Harvas Black-Robe. A substantial armed band went along to guard them: the Halogai were out of Pliskavos and in the process of crossing the Astris, but some of the folk who had lived there before Harvas, before the Halogai, still remained.

The guard party would have been smaller had Krispos not decided to go into Pliskavos with the mages. Not only did he want to be in at the kill if Harvas was captured, he also wanted to see what would be needed to restore the town to a provincial capital after its occupation first by the Kubratoi for centuries and then by the evil wizard and the northerners.

His first horrified thought was that everything inside the fortifications should be torched, to cleanse the place and start again. The fires that had spread from the burning wall had done some of that, but not enough. Half-burned wooden buildings were everywhere, along with the stenches of stale smoke and of burned and rotting flesh. Once or twice heads peeked out of ruins to eye the newcomers. Krispos saw more than one glint of weapons in the shadows and was glad for his armed escort.

"This was once a Videssian town of note?" he said, shaking his head. "I can't believe it."

"It's true, Your Majesty." Zaidas pointed. "See that stone building, and that one, and what's left of that one over there? You'll find the same sort of work in Videssos the city. And the streets, or some of them, still keep to the square grid pattern we usually use."

"You know town planning as well as wizardry?" Krispos asked.

Zaidas flushed. "My older brother is a builder."

"If he serves his craft as well as you do yours, he'll be one of the best," Krispos said, which made the young mage turn pink all over again.

As they rode on toward the center of town, they came across more and more stretches of unburned buildings. Now people did emerge to stare. Some were of Kubrati blood, stocky, the men heavily bearded. Others, slimmer, their features more sharply sculpted, could have been poor Videssians by the look of them. They all watched soldiers, wizards, and Emperor as if wondering what fresh misfortunes these newcomers would bring down on them.

"How will you sniff out Harvas from among them and from among others who may be hiding?" Krispos asked Zaidas.

"I will have to ride through the whole of Pliskavos, I think," the wizard answered. "I know the reek of his magic, and I know the blankness with which he seeks to disguise it. To detect either, I will have to be close to it, for thanks to the lady Tanilis his power is less than a shadow of what it once was."

"If he is here at all," Krispos added.

"Aye, Your Majesty, if he is here at all."

In a park in the heart of Pliskavos stood an ornately carved wooden palace, the former residence of the khagans of Kubrat. A new carving was set above the doorway: twin three-pronged lightning flashes. Zaidas' finger stabbed toward them. "That is Skotos' mark!" He sketched Phos' suncircle.

So did Krispos. "Harvas laired here, then?" he asked.

"Harvas once laired here," Zaidas agreed. "Be thankful you cannot feel the effluvium of his past power." He grew thoughtful. "I wonder if now he seeks to hide there, hoping no one will notice his present small bad odor in the great stench of the past. We must closely examine that building."

One of the other Videssian mages, a stout, middle-aged man named Gepas, stirred in the saddle and said, "Do pray remember we're not your servants, Zaidas."

"Are you the Empire's servants, Gepas?" Krispos asked sharply. The wizard stared, startled. His eyes fell. He nodded. "Good," Krispos said. "For a moment there, I wondered. Do you deny that Zaidas speaks good sense, or do you just wish you'd spoken before he did? Does Harvas' palace need looking at, or not?"

"It does, Your Majesty," Gepas admitted.

"Then let's look at it." Krispos urged Progress forward and tied the horse at the rail in front of the palace.

Neither his guards nor the mages would hear of his going in first. He'd wondered if the doors would be locked, but they opened at the guards' touch. Zaidas turned to Gepas. With unaffected politeness, the young wizard asked, "Sir, would it please you to stand guard here at the doorway, to ensure that Harvas cannot sneak past you?"

"Better, youngling." Gepas puffed out his chest and pulled in his belly. His voice got deeper. "Aye, I'll do that. He shan't escape by this road."

"Good." Zaidas' face was perfectly straight. Krispos had to work to keep his the same way. He wondered whether Zaidas was a natural innocent or a schemer subtle beyond his years. Either way, he got results.

Wizards fanned out through the wooden palace. Krispos stayed with Zaidas. The guards, naturally, stayed with him. Together they made their way into the hall that was, Krispos supposed, the equivalent of the Grand Courtroom back at the capital. He pointed to the white throne that stood out against the gloom at the far end. "Is that ivory, like the patriarch's throne?"

Zaidas studied it, murmuring briefly to himself. His large larynx worked. "It's—bone," he said at last. Just then Krispos saw Skotos' symbol on the wall above the high seat. He decided not to ask what sort of bone.

The hall held a sour, metallic smell. Without much enthusiasm, Krispos walked down the hard dirt aisleway toward the throne. A few feet in front of it, his boot heels sank into a soggy spot. The smell got worse. "That's blood," he said, hoping Zaidas would contradict him.

Zaidas didn't. He said, "We already knew Harvas practiced abominations. We also know now that he is not in this hall, which was our purpose in coming here. Let's go on to see where he may be."

"Yes, let's," Krispos said in a small voice, admiring the young mage's ability to stay calm in the face of horror.

To the left of the bone throne was a door. In the twilight that filled the hall with all torches dark, its outline was invisible until one came right up to it. Again, Krispos' guards would not let him go in first. One of them tugged at the latch. The door did not open. The guardsman used his axe with a will.

Moments later he tried the door again. This time he easily pulled it open. When he did, he and everyone else in the hall drew back a pace, or more than a pace, for darkness seemed to well out toward them. Krispos' hand shaped the sun-circle. Loudly and clearly Zaidas declared, "We bless thee, Phos, lord with the great and good mind, watchful beforehand that the great test of life may be decided in our favor."

The spreading darkness faded. Krispos wondered if it had really been there. Even after it was gone, the open doorway remained black and forbidding. He glanced toward Zaidas. The young wizard licked his lips and seemed to gather his courage. Then he strode into the room. Remembering Trokoundos, Krispos started to shout for him to come back.

But Zaidas said, "Ah, as I thought," with such scholarly satisfaction that Krispos knew he'd come to no harm. The mage went on, "It is a shrine dedicated to Skotos. They speak of them at the Sorcerers' Collegium, but I'd never seen one before."

Krispos had never seen one, either, or wanted to see one. But his pride would not let him stay back while Zaidas was inside. He was glad to have his guardsmen form up around him. They went into the small room together.

The hall of the throne had been dark. Even so, his eyes needed a minute or so to adapt to the deeper shadow inside. As the eye went to the altar in one of Phos' temples, so it did here. Indeed, this altar at first glance resembled one from a temple—not surprising, Krispos supposed, since Harvas the evil mage, the apostate, had in his earlier days been Rhavas the prelate of Skopentzana. But no altar dedicated to Phos would have had knives lying on it.

One of Phos' temples would have been full of icons, holy images of the good god and his work in the world. As Krispos' vision adapted to the gloom, he saw icons on the wall above the altar here, too. He saw the dark god, wreathed in blackness, fighting Phos, driving him, and slaying him. He saw other things, as well, things he thought no man could have dreamed of taking brush to panel to portray. He saw things that made the forest of stakes outside Imbros seem a mercy. One of his guardsmen, a warrior who delighted in battle like most Halogai, lurched out into the great hall and was noisily sick there.

"This is what he would have brought to Videssos the city," Zaidas said quietly.

"I know," Krispos said. But knowing and seeing were not the same. He'd found that out in a different context when he'd got word of Evripos' birth while Tanilis was in his bed. He looked at the icons again, and at the altar. He saw small bones among the knives. His little sister Kosta would have had bones about that size, a couple of years before cholera killed her. For a moment he thought he would be sick himself.

"A pity the flames from the wall didn't reach here," he said. "We'll just have to fire this building ourselves." More than anything else, he wanted Phos' icons to burn.

One of the guardsmen clapped him on the back, hard enough to stagger him. Zaidas said, "Excellent, Your Majesty. Fire and its light are gifts from Phos, and will cleanse the evil that has put its roots down here. May something better arise from the ashes. And," he added, his voice suddenly hopeful, "if Harvas has managed to elude us here, fire will cleanse the world of him as well."

"So may it be," Krispos said. After that, he was not ashamed to leave the dark chapel. Zaidas followed close on his heels. The young mage carefully closed the splintered door behind him, as if to make sure what dwelt inside stayed there.

All the wizards gathered by the entrance that Gepas still guarded. They'd not found Harvas, nor had any of the rest of them stumbled onto anything as black as Skotos' altar. Not one, however, offered a word of protest at what Krispos proposed to do to the palace.

He unhitched Progress and led the gelding well away from the wooden building. The mages still kept a close watch on it, as if they could sense even at a distance the evil Harvas had brought into it. Very likely they could, Krispos thought. Most of his guardsmen stayed by him, but one hurried back to the imperial camp.

The guard returned fairly soon. He was carrying a jar of lamp oil and a smoking torch. He handed Krispos the torch, unstoppered the jar, and splashed oil on the palace wall. "Light it, Majesty," he urged.

As Krispos touched the torch to the oil, he reflected that the dromons' incendiary mix would have served even better. But the lamp oil did the job. Flames walked across the weathered surface of the wooden wall, crept into cracks, climbed over carvings. Before long the wood caught, too. No hearth logs could have been better seasoned than the old timbers of the palace. They burned quick and hard and hot. A pillar of smoke rose to the sky.

Imperials ran and rode up in alarm, fearing the blaze had broken out on its own. Krispos kept some of them close by, to help fight the fire in case it spread. But the palace was set apart from Pliskavos' other buildings, as if to give the khagans of Kubrat the sense of space they might have enjoyed on the steppe. It had plenty of room in which to burn safely.

Krispos watched the fire for a while. He wished he could know whether Harvas was burning with those flames. Whether or not, though, the power he had forged to strike at Videssos was broken; those of his raiders who lived were boarding rafts under the eyes and arrows of imperial troops. And Harvas' own power was broken, as well, thanks to Tanilis. Krispos shook his head, wishing for the thousandth time the price of the latter breaking had not been so high.

But he knew that Tanilis had willingly paid the price, and that she would not have wanted him to grieve in victory. The knowledge helped— some. He swung himself up onto Progress and twitched the reins. The horse turned till Krispos felt the warmth of the burning palace on his back. He touched Progress' flanks with his heels and rode away.

With a hand shading his eyes to ease the glare, krispos peered across the Astris. Tiny in the distance, the last of Harvas' Halogai trudged away from the northern back of the river. "This land is ours now," Krispos said, slightly embarrassed to hear slight surprise in his voice. "Ours again," he amended.

Mammianos was also watching the Halogai go. "A very neat campaign, Your Majesty," he said. "The provincial levies will be back on their farms in time to help with the harvest. Very neat indeed."

"So they will." Krispos turned to the fat general. "And what of you, Mammianos? Shall I send you back to your province, too, to govern the coastal lowlands for me?"

"This for the coastal lowlands." Mammianos yawned a slow, deliberate, scornful yawn. "The only reason I was there is that Petronas sent me to the most insignificant place he could think of." The yawn gave way to a smug expression. "Turned out not to be so insignificant after all, the way things worked out, eh, Your Majesty?"

"You're right about that," Krispos said. Mammianos had given him the opening he'd hoped for. "If you're bored with the lowlands, eminent sir, will you serve as my governor here, as the first governor of the new province of Kubrat?"

"Ah. That job wouldn't soon grow dull, now would it?" Mammianos didn't sound surprised, but then Mammianos was no one's fool. His voice turned musing. "Let's see, what all would I be doing? Keeping the nomads on their side of the Astris, and the Halogai, too, if they think about getting frisky again—"

"Cleaning up the Haloga settlements that got started here, like the one that gave Sarkis so much trouble," Krispos put in.

"Aye, and the Kubratoi might decide to rise up again, once they get over being grateful to us for ridding them of dear Harvas, which is to say any time starting about day after tomorrow."

"Oh, we ought to be good until next week," Krispos said. Both men chuckled, although Krispos knew he wasn't really joking. He went on, "We'll start resettling farmers, too, to start giving you enough men to use as a balance against the Kubratoi. People will want to come if we forgive, say, their first five years' taxes after they get here. It's not the worst farming country, not if the Kubratoi don't come by every fall to steal half your crop."

"You'd know about that, wouldn't you, Your Majesty?"

"Oh, yes." Even across more than two decades and the vast gulf that separated the man he was from the boy he had been, Krispos could still call up the helpless fury he'd felt as the nomads plundered the peasants they'd kidnapped.

Mammianos glanced over to the walls of Pliskavos not far away. "I'll need artisans to help set the town right, and merchants to come live in it, aye, and priests, as well, for the good god"—he sketched Phos' sun-circle—"seems mostly forgotten here." He hardly seemed to notice he'd agreed to take the job.

"The artisans will come," Krispos promised, "though Imbros needs them, too." Mammianos nodded. Krispos continued, "I'll see that priests come, too. They'll be happier if we have a temple ready for them." He snapped his fingers in happy inspiration. "And I know just where—on the spot where the old wooden palace stood."

"That's very fine, Your Majesty. The traders'll come, too, I expect. They'll be eager for the chance to do direct business with the nomads north of the Astris instead of going through Kubrati middlemen. Come to that, there'll be trade down the Astris, too, in the days ahead, from Pliskavos to Videssos the city direct by water. Aye, the merchants will come."

"I think you're right," Krispos said. "You'll be busy, making all of that happen."

"I'd sooner be busy than bored, unlike half the useless drones back in the city," Mammianos said. His eyes narrowed as he studied Krispos. "You think you'll stay busy yourself, Your Majesty, without a civil war and a foreign one to juggle?"

"By the good god, eminent sir, I hope not!" Krispos exclaimed. Mammianos stared at him, then started to laugh. Krispos said, "Trouble is, though, something always comes along. By the time I'm back to the capital, I'll have something new to worry about. One thing I can think of right away: before too long, I have to decide whether to keep paying tribute to Makuran or take the chance on another war by cutting it off."

"We're not ready for another war," Mammianos said seriously.

"Don't I know it! But we can't let the King of Kings go on sucking our blood forever, either." Krispos sighed. "This Avtokrator business is hard work, if you try to do it the way you should. I understand Anthimos better than I used to, and why he forgot about everything save women and wine. Sometimes I think he had the right idea after all."

"No, you don't," Mammianos said.

Krispos sighed again. "No, I suppose I don't. But there are times when packing it in can look awfully good."

"A farmer can't afford to pack it in, and he only has to deal with one plot of land," Mammianos said. "You have the whole Empire to look out for. On the other hand, you get rewards that poor farmer will never see, starting with the parade down Middle Street when you do get back to the city."

"Anthimos arranged for people to cheer him, too."

"Ah, but there's a difference. You'll have earned these cheers—and you know it." Mammianos thumped Krispos lightly on the back. Krispos thought it over. At last, he nodded.

Chapter XIII

THE GREAT VALVES OF THE SILVER GATE SWUNG OPEN. TRUMpeters on the wall above blared out a fanfare. Krispos flicked Progress' reins. Along with his victorious army, he rode into Videssos the city.

As he passed through the covered way between the outer and inner walls, his mind went back to the day, now more than a decade behind him, when he'd first walked into the great imperial capital. Then no one had known—or cared—he was arriving. Now the whole city waited for him.

He came out of the shadow of the covered way and into the city. Another fanfare blew. Ahead of him in the procession, a marching chorus began to chant. "Behold, Krispos comes in triumph, who subjected Kubrat! Once he served the folk north of the mountains, but now they serve him!"

People packed both sides of Middle Street. They jeered the chained Haloga prisoners who dejectedly clanked along in front of Krispos. When they saw him, the jeers turned to cheers. "Thou conquerest, Krispos!" they shouted. "Thou conquerest!"

In his two years as Avtokrator, he'd heard that acclamation many times.

As often as not, it was as much for form's sake as a cobbler's giving his neighbor good morning. Every once in a while, though, people sounded as if they truly meant it. This was one of those times.

He smiled and waved as he rode up the city's main thoroughfare. Protocol demanded that an Emperor stare straight ahead, looking neither to the left nor to the right, to emphasize how far above the people he was. Barsymes would probably scold him when he got back back to the palaces, but he didn't care. He wanted to feel the moment, not to pretend it wasn't happening.

On either side of Progress marched more Halogai, members of the imperial guards. Some wore crimson surcoats that matched Krispos' boots, others blue ones that went along with the banner of Videssos. The guardsmen seemed to ignore the people they strode past, but the axes they carried were not just for show.

Behind Krispos clattered the iron-shod hooves of Sarkis' unit of scouts. The scouts were looking into the crowd, all right, and didn't pretend otherwise. They knew what they were looking for, too. "Hey, pretty lass, I hope I find you tonight!" one of them called.

Hearing that, Krispos made a note to himself to make sure extra watchmen were on the street after the procession was done. Wine shops and joyhouses would both be jumping, and he wanted no trouble to mar the day. His smile turned ironic for a moment. Automatically thinking of such things was part of what it meant to be Avtokrator.

Then he thought of Dara and how good it was not to be just one more man prowling the city for whatever he could find for a night. When he came to the palaces, he was coming home. He wondered what Evripos looked like. Soon enough he'd find out. He even wondered how Phostis was doing. About time his heir got to know him.

"Kubrat is ours again!" the people shouted. Some of them, he was certain, had no idea in which direction Kubrat lay or how long it had been out of Videssian hands. They shouted anyway. If he'd got himself killed in the campaign, they would have shouted just as hard for whichever general seized the throne. Some of them would have shouted just as loud for Harvas Black-Robe, were he riding down Middle Street in triumph.

Krispos' smile disappeared altogether. Ruling over the Empire was making him expect the worst in men, because the consequences of misfortune were so often what he saw and had to try to repair. Folk who led good and quiet lives seldom came to his notice. But he needed to remember the good still existed; if he forgot that, he began to walk the path Harvas had followed. And if he needed to remember the good, he had only to think of Tanilis.

The procession moved on along Middle Street, past the dogleg where it bent more nearly due west, through the Forum of the Ox, and on toward the plaza of Palamas. After a while Krispos grew bored. Even adulation staled, when it was the same adulation again and again. He did his best to keep smiling and waving anyhow. While he heard the same praise, the same chorus over and over, the parade was fresh and new to each person he passed. He tried to make it as fine as he could for all of them.

The sun was a good deal higher in the sky by the time he finally reached the plaza of Palamas. Much of the big square was packed as tight with people as the sidewalks of Middle Street had been. A thin line of watchmen and soldiers held the crowd back from its center, to give all the units in the parade room to assemble.

A temporary wooden platform stood close to the Milestone. Atop it paced a shaven-headed, gray-bearded man in a robe of blue and cloth-of-gold. Krispos guided Progress toward the platform. He caught the eye of the man on it and nodded slightly. Savianos nodded back. He looked most patriarchal. Of course, so had Pyrrhos and Gnatios. As Savianos himself had said, how well he would wear remained to be learned. All the same, seeing his new patriarch in full regalia for the first time sent hope through Krispos.

He rode up to the stairs on the side of the platform nearest the red granite obelisk that was the center of distance measure throughout the Empire. Geirrod stepped forward with him and held Progress' head while he dismounted.

"Thanks," he said to the Haloga guard. He started for the stairway, then stopped. Gnatios' severed head was still displayed on the base of the Milestone, along with a placard that detailed his treacheries. After some weeks exposed to the elements, the head was unrecognizable without the placard. *Your own fault,* Krispos said to himself. He went up the steps with firm, untroubled stride.

"Thou conquerest, Majesty!" Savianos said loudly as Krispos reached the top of the platform.

"Thou conquerest!" the crowd echoed.

Savianos prostrated himself before Krispos, his forehead pressed against rough boards.

"Rise, most holy sir," Krispos said.

Savianos got to his feet. He turned half away from Krispos to face the crowd. His hands rose in benediction. He recited Phos' creed: "We bless thee, Phos, lord with the great and good mind, watchful beforehand that the great test of life may be decided in our favor."

Krispos spoke the creed with him. So did the great throng who watched them both. Their voices fell like rolling surf with the rhythms of the prayer. Krispos thought that if he listened to that oceanic creed a few times, he might discover for himself how healer-priests and mages used the holy words to sink into a trance.

But instead of repeating the creed, Savianos addressed the people who packed the plaza of Palamas. "We call our Avtokrator the vice-regent of Phos on earth. Most often this strikes us as but a pleasant conceit, a compliment, even a flattery, to the man who sits on the high throne in the Grand Courtroom. For we know that, while he does rule us, he is but a man, with a man's failings.

"But sometimes, people of the city, sometimes we find the fulsome title enfolds far more than fulsomeness. I submit to you, people of the city, that we have just passed through such a time. For great evil threatened from the north, and only through the good god's grace could his champion have overcome it."

"Thou conquerest, Krispos!" The shout filled the square. Savianos kept facing the crowd, but his eyes slid to Krispos. Krispos waved to the people. The shouts redoubled. Krispos waved again, this time for quiet. Slowly, slowly, the noise faded.

The patriarch resumed his speech. Krispos listened with half an ear; the opening had been enough to tell him Savianos was indeed the man he wanted wearing the blue boots: intelligent, pious, yet mindful that only the Emperor was the chief power of Videssos.

Instead of listening, Krispos watched the people who were watching him. He also finally got to watch his parade, as unit after unit entered the plaza. After the imperial guards and the scouts came the northerners who had chosen to serve Videssos rather than returning to Halogaland. After them rode Bagradas' company, which had routed the Halogai who tried to fight on horseback. A contingent of Kanaris' marines marched behind them; without the grand drungarios' dromons, the northerners could have crossed the Astris in safety and lingered near Kubrat, ready to swoop down again at any moment. A unit of military musicians had played all the way up Middle Street. The men fell silent as they came into the plaza of Palamas, so as not to drown out Savianos.

The patriarch finished just as the last troop of horsemen entered the square. He waved his hand toward Krispos and said, "Now let the Avtokrator himself tell you of his dangers, and of his triumphs." With a deep bow, he urged Krispos to the forward edge of the platform.

Krispos' attitude toward speeches was the same as his attitude toward combat: they were a part of being Avtokrator he wished he could do without. Along with the people, polished courtiers would be weighing his words, smiling at his unsophisticated phrases. *Too bad for them,* he thought. He attacked speeches as if they were armored foes and went straight at them. The approach was less than elegant, but it worked.

"People of the city, brave soldiers of Videssos, we have won a great victory," he began. "The Halogai are bold warriors. No one would say otherwise, or we would not want them as the Emperor's guards. We should applaud the Halogai who fought for me and for the Empire. They served as loyally as any of our men, though they fought their own countrymen. Without their courage, I would not be talking to you today."

He pointed down at his guardsmen and clapped his hands together. The assembled units of the army were the first to join him in paying tribute to the Halogai; they'd seen the northerners in action. More slowly, cheers filled the rest of the plaza of Palamas. Some of the imperial guards grinned. Others, not used to such plaudits, looked at their boots and shuffled half a step this way and that.

Krispos went on, "We should also cheer our own brave soldiers, who made the fierce men from the north yield for the first time in history. Some of the Halogai you see now are their captives. Some joined Videssos' army of their own free will after their chief Ikmor surrendered Pliskavos to us—we'd shown them we were the better soldiers."

The soldiers cheered first again. Many of them cried, "Hurrah for us!" The rest of the crowd joined in more quickly this time; cheering their fellow Videssians made the people of the city happier than applauding foreigners, even foreigners in imperial service.

"We did not face danger from the Halogai alone," Krispos said when something not far from quiet returned once more. "We also faced a wizard who worshiped Skotos." As always in Videssos, the dark god's name brought forth first shocked gasps, then complete, attentive, almost fearful silence. Into that silence, Krispos continued, "Truth to tell, the accursed one did us more harm than the Halogai. But in the end, the mages of the Sorcerers' Collegium were able to stymie his wicked attacks, and one, the brave sorceress Tanilis of Opsikion, broke his power, though she herself died in that combat."

People sighed when they heard that. Krispos heard a few women weep. Some of the soldiers called out Tanilis' name. All of that was as it should be. None of it was close to what she deserved.

"What we've won is important," he said. "Kubrat is ours again; wild horsemen will raid south of the mountains no more. And the Astris is a broad, swift river. The nomads will not easily slip over it to steal away the land we've regained. With this victory, Videssos is truly stronger. It's no sham triumph, unlike some you may have seen in the past." He could not resist the dig at Petronas, who had celebrated his undistinguished campaign against Makuran as if he'd overthrown Mashiz.

"People of the city, you deserve more than a parade to mark what we have done," Krispos proclaimed. "That's why I declare the next three days holidays throughout the city. Enjoy them!"

This time the ordinary people in the plaza of Palamas cheered faster and louder than the soldiers. "May Phos be with us all!" Krispos shouted through the din.

"May Phos be with you, Your Majesty!" the people shouted back.

Savianos stepped close to Krispos. "You've made them like you, Your Majesty," he said, too quietly for anyone but Krispos to hear in the turmoil.

Krispos eyed him curiously. "Not 'love,' most holy sir? Most men would say that, if they aimed to pay a compliment."

"Let most men say what they will and curry favors as they will," Savianos answered. "Wouldn't you like to have at least one man around who tells you what he thinks to be the truth?"

"Now I have two," Krispos said. It was Savianos' turn to look curious. Krispos went on, "Or has Iakovitzes died in the last quarter of an hour?" He knew perfectly well that Iakovitzes hadn't died. Were the Sevastos still able to speak, he'd have been on the platform with Krispos and the patriarch.

Savianos dipped his head. "There you have me, Your Majesty." One of his bushy eyebrows lifted. "At least I won't envenom it before I give it to you."

"Ha! I ought to tell him you said that, just to see some venom come your way. But since the good god knows you're not altogether wrong, I'll let you get away with it."

"Your Majesty is merciful," Savianos said. His eyebrow went up again.

"Oh, hogwash," Krispos said with a snort. He and his patriarch smiled at each other. Then he turned to face the crowd once more. He raised his hands. A few at a time, people noticed him, pointed. The plaza of Palamas grew if not quiet, quieter. "People of the city, soldiers of the Empire, as far as I'm concerned, this gathering is done," he said. "Go on and celebrate!"

One last cheer, louder than the rest, filled the square and reverberated from the Milestone and the outer wall of the Amphitheater. Krispos waved to the crowd, then started for the stairs that led down from the platform. "And how will you celebrate, Your Majesty?" Savianos called after him.

"Not with revels like the ones Anthimos enjoyed," Krispos answered. "Me, I'm just another man with a family, coming back from the war. All I want to do right now is see my new baby and my wife."

THE PALM OF DARA'S HAND CRACKED AGAINST KRISPOS' CHEEK. He caught her wrist before she could hit him again. "Let me go, you bastard!" she screamed. "You think you can pull off your robe as soon as you go on campaign, do you? And with Mavros' mother, of all people? By the good god, she must be old enough to be your mother, too."

Hardly, Krispos thought, but he knew better than to say that out loud. What he did say was, "Will you listen to me, please?" He was more than a little appalled. He'd thought of so much on the campaign just past; he hadn't thought that rumors about Tanilis and him would get back to Videssos the city so fast.

"What's there to listen to, curse you?" Dara tried to kick him in the shins. "Did you take her to bed with you or not?"

"Yes, but—" She punctuated the sentence by trying to kick him again. This time she succeeded.

"Aii!" he said. The pain roused his own anger. When she started screaming at him again, he outyelled her. "If it weren't for Tanilis, I'd be dead now, and the whole army with me."

"Bugger the army, and bugger you, too."

"Why are you so furious at me?" he demanded. "Anthimos was unfaithful to you twice a day—three or four times, when he could manage that many—and you put up with him for years."

Dara opened her mouth to screech more abuse at him but hesitated. He enjoyed a moment of relief—the first moment he'd enjoyed since he walked into the imperial residence. In slightly softer tones than she'd used thus far, she said, "I expected it from Anthimos. I didn't expect it from you."

Krispos heard the hurt in her voice along with the outrage. "I didn't expect it from me, either, not exactly," he said. "It's just that, well, Tanilis and I knew each other a long time ago, before I ever came to the palaces."

"*Knew* each other?" Now it was all outrage again. "That makes it worse, not better. If you missed her so much, why didn't you just send for her when you got the urge?"

"It wasn't like that," Krispos protested. "And it wasn't as if I set out to seduce her for the first time. It was just—" The more he talked, the deeper in trouble he found himself. He gave up and spread his hands in defeat. "I made a mistake. What can I say? The only thing I can think of is that it's not the sort of mistake I'm likely to make again."

Dara twisted the knife. "There aren't another threescore women you *knew* in those long-lost and forgotten days out there pining for you now?" But then she hesitated again. "I don't think I ever heard Anthimos say he made a mistake."

One of the things Krispos had learned from repeated meetings with his officers was to change the subject when he didn't have all the answers. He said, "Dara, could I please see my new son?"

He'd hoped that would further soften her. It didn't work. Instead, she flared up again. "*Your* new son? And what were *you* doing while *I* was panting like a dog and screaming like a man on the rack to make *your* son come into the world? You don't need to tell me with whom you were doing it. I already know that."

"By the letter you sent, on the day Evripos was born, the army was fighting its way north from the mountains into Kubrat. And I wasn't doing anything more with Tanilis then than traveling in the same army." What he'd been doing when her letter arrived . . . but she hadn't asked him that.

"*Then,*" she said, a word that spoke volumes all by itself. She went on bitterly, "You even had the brass to acclaim her to the people today."

He wondered how she'd learned that. Nothing in Videssos the city flew faster than gossip. He said, "Whatever you think of me, whatever you think of her, she deserved to be acclaimed to them. I told you once, you'd be a widow now if not for her."

Dara gave him a long, cold, measuring stare. "That might be better. I warned you not to trifle with me."

Krispos remembered what Rhisoulphos had asked him—how would he dare fall asleep beside her? He said, "Careful, there. You'd have had no joy bargaining with Harvas Black-Robe over the fate of the Empire."

"I would have bargained with someone besides Harvas." She was angry enough to add one thing more: "I still may. I brought you the throne, after all."

"And you think you can take it away again, is that what you're saying? That the only reason I belong on it is because I married you?" He shook his head. "Maybe that was so two years ago. I don't think it is anymore. I beat Petronas, I beat Harvas. People are used to me with a crown on my head, and they see I can manage well enough." Now he glared coldly at her. "And so, if I wanted to, I expect I could send you to a convent, go on about my affairs here, and get away with it quite handily. Do you doubt me?"

"You wouldn't."

"To save myself, I would. But I don't want to. If we only had a marriage of convenience"—as he groped for the phrase, he remembered Tanilis using it. He shook his head, wishing he hadn't come up with the memory at exactly this moment—"I think I could put you aside now and not have much trouble over it. I just told you that. I could have arranged it as I was on the way home from Kubrat. I came back here, though, because I love you, curse it."

Dara was not ready to give in, or to let him down easy. "I suppose you'd say the same thing if Tanilis had come back with you."

He winced, as if from a low blow. For all his wishing that Tanilis had lived, he hadn't thought about how he would handle her and Dara both. *Badly* was the answer that sprang to mind; between the two of them, they'd have made mincemeat of him in short order. Dara was doing a good job by herself.

He answered as best he could: "Might-have-beens don't matter. They aren't real, so how can you tell what's true about them? That just makes for more arguments. We don't need more arguments right now."

"Don't we? I trusted you, Krispos. How am I ever supposed to trust you again, now that I know you've been unfaithful?"

"It comes in time, if you give it a chance," he said. "I grew to trust you, for instance."

"Me? What about me?" Dara's eyes flashed dangerously. "Don't go twisting things. I've never been unfaithful to you, by the good god, and you'd better know it, too."

"I'm not twisting things, and I do know that," Krispos said. "But you were unfaithful to Anthimos with me, so I've known all along that you could be unfaithful to me, too. It used to worry me. It used to worry me a lot. It took a long time for me to decide I didn't need to worry about it anymore."

"You never let on," Dara said slowly. She looked at him as if she were seeing him for the first time. "You never let on at all."

"What would have been the point? I always figured that showing I was worried would have made things worse, not better, so I just kept quiet."

"Yes, that's like you, isn't it? You would have just kept quiet about Tanilis, too, and gone about your business." But some of the heat finally left Dara's voice. She kept studying Krispos. In spite of her temper—and in spite of the good reason he'd given her for losing it—she was thoroughly practical down deep. Krispos waited. At last she said, "Well, you may as well have a look at Evripos."

"Thank you." The two words took in much more than her last sentence alone. He'd known her a long time. He counted on her to hear that.

Not a servant was in sight when Krispos and Dara emerged from the imperial bedchamber. His mouth twisted wryly. He said, "All the eunuchs and women must be afraid to get anywhere near us. What with the row we were having, I can't blame them."

"Neither can I," Dara said, with the first half smile she'd given him. "They're probably waiting to find out which one of us comes out of there alive—if either of us does."

The nursery was around a couple of corners from the bedchamber. Only when Krispos and Dara rounded the last corner did they encounter Barsymes in the hallway. The vestiarios bowed. "Your Majesties," he said. With the subtle shifts of tone of which he was a master, he managed to make the innocuous greeting mean something like, *Are your majesties done sticking knives in each other yet?*

"It's—" Krispos started to say it was all right, but it wasn't. Maybe in time it would be. "It's better, esteemed sir." He glanced toward Dara, wondering if she would make a liar of him.

"It's some better, esteemed sir," she said carefully. Krispos clicked his tongue between his teeth. That would have to do.

"I'm pleased to hear it, Your Majesties." Barsymes actually did sound pleased. He had to see the palm-sized patch of red on Krispos' cheek, but he made sure he did not notice it. He bowed again. "If you will excuse me—" He walked past Krispos and Dara. Palace servants had a magic all their own. Within minutes everyone in the imperial residence would know what the vestiarios knew.

Krispos opened the nursery door and let Dara precede him through it. The woman sitting inside quickly got up and started to prostrate herself. "Never mind, Iliana," Krispos said. The wet nurse smiled, pleased he remembered her name. He went on, "Everything's quiet, so Evripos must be asleep."

"So he is, Your Majesty," Iliana said. She smiled again, in a different way this time: the haggard smile of anyone who takes care of a baby. She pointed to the cradle against one wall.

Krispos walked over to it and peered in. Evripos lay on his stomach. His right thumb was in his mouth. His odor, the peculiar mix of inborn baby sweetness and stale milk, wafted up to Krispos. Krispos said the first thing that came into his mind. "He doesn't have as much hair as Phostis did."

"No, he doesn't," Dara agreed.

"I think he's going to look like you, Your Majesty," Iliana said to

Krispos. She seemed oblivious to the fight he and Dara had just had. If she'd been here by herself with Evripos all the while, maybe she was. If so, she had to be the only person in the imperial residence who was. She continued, "His face is longer than Phostis' was at the same age, and I think he'll have your nose."

Krispos examined Evripos again. He found himself shrugging. For one thing, he'd been in the field when Phostis was this age, so comparing the two little boys was hard for him. For another, he didn't think Evripos' button of a nose looked anything like his own formidable beak. He asked, "How old is he now?"

"Six weeks, a couple of days more," Dara answered. "He's a bigger baby than Phostis was."

"Second babes often are," Iliana put in.

"Maybe he does look like me," Krispos said. "We'll have to train him to be always at his brother's right hand when the time comes for Phostis to rule." That won him a genuinely grateful look from Dara: here with a son surely his, he said nothing of removing Phostis from the succession.

The nursery door opened. Phostis came in, accompanied by Longinos the eunuch. The little boy was much more confident on his feet than he had been when Krispos set out on campaign. He looked at Krispos, as much at his robes as at his face. "Dada?" he said, tentatively.

Maybe he's not sure, either, Krispos thought. He scowled at himself, then smiled his biggest smile at Phostis. "Dada," he said. Phostis ran to him and hugged him around the legs. He reached down to ruffle Phostis' hair. "How does he know who I am?" he asked Dara. "Do you suppose he remembers? I've been gone a long time, and he's not very big."

"Maybe he does. He's clever," Dara said. "But I've also shown him the pictures of old-time Avtokrators in their regalia and said 'Emperor' and 'dada.' If he didn't recognize you, I wanted to be sure he recognized the robes."

"Oh . . . That was thoughtful of you," Krispos said. Dara didn't answer. Just as well, Krispos thought. If she had answered, she'd have been only too likely to come back with something like, *Yes, and look what you were doing while I was busy reminding him who you were.*

"Up," Phostis said. Krispos picked him up and held him out at arm's length so he could look him over. Phostis kicked and giggled. Krispos had no idea whom Evripos looked like. Phostis looked like Dara: his coloring, the shape of his face, that unusual small fold of skin at the inner corner of each eyelid all recalled her.

Krispos tossed him a couple of feet into the air, caught him, then gently shook him. Phostis squealed with glee. Krispos wanted to shake him harder, to shake out of him once and for all who his father was.

"Dada," Phostis said again. He stretched out his own little arms to Krispos. When Krispos drew him close, he wrapped them around Krispos' neck. Krispos hugged him, too. From whosoever seed he sprang, he was a fine little boy.

"Thank you for helping him to keep me in mind," Krispos said to Dara. "He seems happy to see me."

"Yes, so he does." Dara's voice softened, most likely because she was talking about Phostis.

Longinos handed Krispos an apricot candied in honey. "The young Majesty is especially fond of these."

"Is he?" Krispos held the fruit where Phostis could see it. The toddler wiggled in delight and opened his mouth wide. Krispos popped in the apricot. Phostis made small *nyum-nyum-nyum* noises as he chewed. Krispos said, "I think he has more teeth than he did when I left the city."

"They do keep growing them," Dara said.

Phostis finished the candied apricot. "More?" he said hopefully. Laughing, Krispos held out his hand to Longinos. The chamberlain produced another apricot. Krispos gave it to Phostis. *"Nyum-nyum-nyum."*

"You'll spoil his supper," Iliana said. Then she remembered to whom she was speaking, and hastily added, "Your Majesty."

"One spoiled supper won't matter," Krispos said. He knew that was true, but also wondered how often it was wise to say such things. He suspected no one had ever said no to Anthimos about anything. He didn't want Phostis to grow up that way.

Barsymes stuck his head into the nursery. "As the afternoon is drawing on, Your Majesty, Phestos the cook wishes to know how you care to dine this evening."

"By the good god, one big, fine supper won't spoil me either, not after eating camp food ever since I left the city," Krispos said. "Tell Phestos to let himself go."

"He'll be pleased to hear that, Your Majesty," Barsymes said. "He told me that if you asked him to do up a pot of army stew, he'd leave the palaces."

"He'd better not," Krispos exclaimed, laughing. "I like good food all the time, and I've come to enjoy fancy meals now and again, too. This one will be the more welcome after eating plain for so long."

The vestiarios hurried away to carry his word back to the kitchens. Krispos tossed Phostis in the air again. "And what do you want to eat tonight, Your Majesty?"

Phostis pointed to the pocket where Longinos kept the candied apricots. With a frown of regret, Longinos turned the pocket inside out. "I'm dreadfully sorry, young Majesty," he said. "I have no more." Phostis started to cry. Krispos tried cuddling him. Against the tragedy of no more candied fruit, cuddling did no good. Krispos turned him upside down. He decided that was funny. Krispos did it again. Phostis chortled.

"I wish we could so easily forget the things that hurt us," Dara said.

Krispos thought that *we* was really an *I*. He said, "We can't forget. The best we can do is not let them rankle."

"I suppose so," Dara said, "though vindictiveness has a bittersweet savor in which so many Videssians delight. Many nobles would sooner forget their names than a slight." Krispos knew some small measure of relief that she did not include herself in that number.

Just then Evripos woke up with a whimper. Phostis pointed to the cradle. "Baby."

"That's your baby brother," Krispos said.

"Baby," Phostis repeated.

Evripos cried louder. Iliana picked him up. Krispos turned Phostis upside down again, lowered him to the floor, and set him down. "Let me hold Evripos," he said.

Iliana passed him the baby. He took a gingerly grip on his son. "Put one hand behind his head, Your Majesty," Iliana said. "His neck still wobbles."

Krispos obeyed. He examined Evripos anew. The cheek on which the baby had been sleeping was bright red. Evripos' eyes would be brown; already they were several shades darker than the blue-gray of a newborn's. He looked at Krispos. Krispos wondered if he'd ever seen anyone with a beard before. Then he wondered if the baby was old enough even to notice it.

Evripos' eyes opened wide, as if he was really waking up now. His face worked— "He smiled at me!" Krispos said.

"He's done it a few times," Dara said.

"Give him to me, if you please, Your Majesty," Iliana said. "He'll be hungry." Krispos returned the baby to her. He averted his eyes as she undid her smock. He did not want Dara to see him look at another woman's breasts, not now of all times. Evripos seized the wet nurse's nipple and started making sucking and gulping noises.

"Milk," Phostis said. "Baby." He stuck out his tongue.

"You were fond of it till not so long ago," Iliana told him, a smile in her voice. Phostis paid no attention to her. With such delicious things as candied apricots in the world, he cared for the breast no more.

"Well, what do you think of your son?" Dara asked.

"I think well of both my sons," Krispos said.

"Good." Dara sounded truly pleased. Maybe she knew the words were an offer of truce, but they were the right one to make. She went on, "Evripos should stay awake for a while. Do you want to play with him a bit longer when he's done nursing?"

"Yes, I'll do that," Krispos said.

Soon Iliana presented him with the baby. "See if you can get him to burp," she said. He patted Evripos on the back. At the same time as Iliana said, "Not so hard, Your Majesty," Evripos let out a surprisingly deep belch. Krispos grinned a vindicated grin.

He held the baby for a while. Evripos was still too small to give back very much. Every so often his eyes would focus intently on Krispos' face. Once, when Krispos smiled at him, he smiled back, but his attention drifted away again before long.

Phostis tugged at Krispos' robe. "Up," he demanded. Krispos passed Evripos back to Iliana and lifted Phostis. After the baby, the older boy seemed to weigh quite a lot. He threw himself backward to show he wanted to play the upside-down game again.

Krispos lowered him to the floor, then picked him up so they were nose to upside-down nose. "You trusted me there, didn't you?" he said.

"Why shouldn't he?" Dara said. "You never dropped him on his head." Krispos clicked tongue between teeth, hearing her unspoken *as you did me*.

Before long Phostis got bored with going upside down. Krispos returned him to solid ground. He ran over to a toy chest, where he drew out a carved and painted wooden horse, dog, and wagon. He neighed, barked, and did an alarmingly realistic impression of the squeak of a big wagon's ungreased wheels.

Krispos bent down. He barked and neighed, too. He made the dog chase the horse, then made the horse jump into the wagon. Phostis laughed. He laughed louder when Krispos made loud wheel-squeaks and had the toy dog run off in pretended terror.

He played with Phostis a bit longer, then held Evripos again until the baby started to fuss. Iliana took him back and gave him her breast. He fell asleep while he was nursing. She set him in the cradle. By then Krispos was playing with Phostis again.

Dara said, "This must be your most domestic afternoon in a long time."

"This is my most domestic afternoon ever," Krispos said. "It has to be. I never had two sons to play with before." He thought for a few seconds. "I like it."

"I see that," Dara said quietly.

Barsymes came into the nursery. "Your Majesty, Phestos is ready for you and your lady."

"Is it that time already?" Krispos said, startled. He looked at where the sunlight stood on the nursery wall, considered his stomach. "By the good god, so it is. All right, esteemed sir, we'll come with you." Dara nodded.

Phostis started to wail when Krispos and Dara walked to the door. "He's tired, Your Majesties," Longinos said apologetically. "He should have had a nap some time ago, but he was too excited playing with his father."

Dara's eyes flickered to Krispos. All he said was, "I enjoyed it, too." No matter who Phostis' father was, he was a delightful little boy. Krispos realized he should have noticed that long ago. In the end, it was what counted.

Barsymes took Krispos and Dara to the smallest of the several dining chambers in the imperial residence. Lamps already burned there against the coming of evening. A jar of wine stood in the center of the table, a silver goblet before each place. As he sat, Krispos glanced down into his. "White wine," he observed.

"Yes, Your Majesty," Barsymes said. "As you've been so long inland, Phestos thought all the courses tonight should come from the sea, to welcome you back to the fare of Videssos the city."

When the vestiarios had gone, Krispos raised his goblet to Dara. "To our sons," he said, and drank.

"To our sons." She also held the cup to her lips. She looked at Krispos over it. "Thank you for picking a toast I can drink to."

He nodded back. "I did try." He was glad to have any truce between them, no matter how fragile.

Barsymes brought in a crystal bowl. "A salad with small squid sliced into it," he announced. "Phestos bids me tell you it is dressed with olive oil, vinegar, garlic, oregano, and some of the squids' own ink: thus the dark color." He served a portion to Krispos, another to Dara, and bowed his way out.

Krispos picked up his fork and smiled, trying to remember the last time he'd used any utensil but spoon or belt knife. The last time he'd been in the city, he decided. He ate a forkful of salad. "That's very good."

Dara tasted hers, too. "So it is." As long as they talked about something safe like the food, they were all right together.

At precisely the proper moment, Barsymes reappeared to clear away the salad. He came back with soup bowls and a gold tureen and ladle. A wonderful odor rose from the tureen. "Prawns, leeks, and mushrooms," he said, ladling out the soup.

"If this tastes as good as it smells, tell Phestos I've just raised his pay," Krispos said. He dipped his spoon and brought it to his lips. "It does. I have. Tell him, Barsymes."

"I shall, Your Majesty," the vestiarios promised.

The sharp taste of leeks, though lessened by their being boiled, made a perfect contrast to the prawns' delicate flavor. The mushrooms added the earthy savor of the woods where they'd been picked. Krispos used the ladle himself, until the tureen was empty. When Barsymes returned to take it away, Krispos held out his bowl to him. "Take this back to the kitchens and fill it up again first, if you please, esteemed sir."

"Of course, Your Majesty. If I may make so bold, though, do not linger with it overlong. The other courses advance apace."

Sure enough, as soon as that last bowl was done, Barsymes brought in a covered tray. "What now, esteemed sir?" Krispos asked him.

"Roast lampreys stuffed with sea urchin paste, served on a bed of cracked wheat and pickled grape leaves."

"I expect I'll grow fins by the time I'm done," Krispos said with a laugh. "What's that old saying? 'When in Videssos the city, eat fish,' that's it. Well, no one could hope to eat better fish than I am tonight." He raised his cup to salute Phestos. When he set it down, it was empty. He reached for the jar. That was empty, too.

"I'll fetch more directly, Your Majesty," Barsymes said.

"Can't go through a feast like this without wine," Krispos said to Dara.

"Indeed not." She drained her own cup, put it down, then stared across the table at Krispos. "As well I hadn't had any to drink earlier this afternoon, though. I'd have tried to put a knife in you, I think." Her eyes fell to the one with which she'd been cutting her lamprey.

"You—didn't do badly as it was," he said cautiously. He looked at her knife, too. "You're not trying to carve me now. Does that mean—I hope that means—you forgive me?"

"No," she said at once, so sharply that he grimaced. She went on, "It does mean I don't want to kill you just this minute. Will that do?"

"It will have to. If we had some wine, I'd drink to it. Ah, Barsymes!" The vestiarios brought in a new jar and used a knife to slice through the pitch that held the stopper in place. He poured the wine. Krispos said, "Here's to letting knives cut up fish and not people."

He and Dara both drank. Barsymes said, "That, Your Majesty, is an excellent toast."

"Isn't it?" Krispos said expansively. He touched the end of his nose. It was getting numb. He smiled. "I can feel that wine." He took another sip.

Barsymes cleared the table. "I shall return shortly with the main course," he said. As usual, he was as good as his word. He set down the latest tray with a flourish. "Tuna, your majesties, poached in resinated wine with spices."

"I *will* grow fins," Krispos declared. "I'll enjoy every bit of it, too." He let Barsymes serve him a large piece of flaky, pinkish-white fish. He tasted it. "Phestos has outdone himself this time." Dara was busy chewing, but made a wordless noise of agreement.

"He will be pleased to know he has pleased you, Your Majesties," Barsymes said. "Now, would you care for some boiled chickpeas, or beets, or perhaps the parsnips in creamy onion sauce?"

After the tuna, Barsymes brought in a bowl of red and white mulberries. Krispos was normally fond of them. Now he rolled his eyes and looked over at Dara. She was looking at him with a similarly overwhelmed expression. They both started to laugh. In an act of conscious—and conscientious—bravery, Krispos reached for the bowl. "Have to eat a few, to keep from hurting Phestos' feelings."

"I suppose so. Here, let me have some, too." Dara washed them down with another swallow of wine. She set down her cup harder than she might. "Strange you worry about the cook's feelings more than mine."

Krispos grunted, looking down at the mulberries. "It wasn't something I made a habit of."

"Bad enough once," she said.

Being without a good answer to that, Krispos kept quiet. Barsymes came in and took away the bowl of fruit. He seemed willing not to see that it had hardly been touched. "Would you care for anything else, your Majesties?" he asked.

Dara shook her head. "No, thank you, esteemed sir," Krispos said. The vestiarios bowed to him and Dara, then strode silently out of the dining chamber. Krispos hefted the wine jar. "Would you like some more?" he asked Dara.

She pushed her cup toward him. He filled it, then poured what was left in the jar into his own. They drank together. Only the lamps lit the dining chamber; the sun was long down.

"What now?" Krispos asked when the wine was gone.

Now Dara would not look at him. "I don't know."

"Let's go to bed," he said. Seeing her scowl, he amended, "To sleep, I mean. I'm too full and too worn to think about anything else tonight anyway."

"All right." She pushed her chair back from the table and got up.

Krispos wondered if he ought to check the cutlery to make sure she hadn't secreted a knife up her sleeve. *You're being foolish,* he told himself as he, too, rose from the table. He hoped he was right.

In the bedchamber, he pulled off the imperial boots, then let out a long sigh of relief as he clenched and unclenched his toes. He took off his robe and noticed he hadn't spilled anything on it at dinner—Barsymes would be pleased. He lay down on the bed, sighing again as the mattress enfolded him in softness.

Dara was also undressing, a little more slowly; she'd always had the habit of sleeping without clothes. Krispos remembered the first time he'd been her, the first time he'd come into this chamber as Anthimos' vestiarios. Her body had been perfect then. It wasn't quite perfect anymore. After two births, her waist was thicker than it had been. And with the second one so recently past, the skin on her belly hung a little loose, while her breasts drooped softly.

Krispos shrugged. She was still Dara. He still found himself wanting her. As he'd told Tanilis, it was rather more than a marriage of convenience. If he wanted it to remain so, he suspected he ought to stop thinking about what he'd told Tanilis. That seemed dreadfully unfair, but he'd learned a good deal of life was unfair. He shrugged again. Unfair or not, you went on anyway.

"Get up, please," Dara said. When Krispos did, she pulled back the spread, leaving just the sheet and a light coverlet. "It's a warm night."

"All right." He slid under the sheet and blew out the lamp that stood on the night table. A moment later Dara got into bed with him. She blew out her lamp. The bedchamber plunged into darkness. "Good night," Krispos said.

"Good night," she answered coolly.

The bed was big enough to leave a good deal of space between them. *Here I am, returned in triumph, and I might as well be sleeping alone,* Krispos thought. He yawned enormously. His eyes slid shut. He slept.

H E WOKE AT SUNRISE THE NEXT MORNING WITH A BLADDER full to bursting. He glanced over at Dara. She'd kicked off the covers some time during the night, but was still peacefully asleep. Carefully, so as not to wake her, he got out of bed and used the chamber pot. He lay down again. Dara did not wake.

He slid toward her. Very, very gently, his tongue began to tease her right nipple. It crinkled erect. She smiled in her sleep. All at once her eyes opened. She stiffened, then twisted away from him. "What are you trying to do?" she snapped.

"I thought that would be plain enough," he said. "Your body answered mine, or started to, even if you're angry with me."

"Bodies are fools," Dara said scornfully.

"Aye, they are," Krispos said. "Mine was, too."

She'd opened her mouth to say something, and likely something harsh. That made her shut it. Even so, she shook her head. "You think that if I lie with you, we'll be fools together and I'll forget about what you did."

"I don't think you'll forget." Krispos sighed. "I wish you could, but I know better. Not even the mages have a magic to make things as if they'd never happened. But if we do lie together, I hope you will remember I love you." He nearly finished that sentence *I love you, too.* One hastily swallowed syllable stood between him and disaster, a nearer brush than in any fight against the Halogai.

"If we are to live as man and wife, I suppose we'll have to be man and wife," Dara said, as much to herself as to Krispos. Her lip curled. "Otherwise, you'd surely take your nets and go trolling for other women. Very well, Krispos; as you will." She lay back and stared up at the ceiling.

He did not go to her. Sucking in a deep, irritated breath, he said, "I don't want you just to be having you, curse it. That was Anthimos' sport. I don't care for it. If we can't meet halfway, better not to bother when we're angry at each other."

She lifted her head from the mattress to study him. "You mean that," she said slowly.

"Yes, by the good god, I do. Let's just ring for the servants and start the new day." He reached for the crimson bell pull by his side of the bed.

"Wait," Dara said. His hand stopped. He raised a questioning eyebrow. After a moment she went on, "Let it be a—a peace-offering between us, then. I can't promise to enjoy it, Krispos. I will do more than endure it."

"Are you sure?" he asked.

"I'm sure . . . Be gentle, if you can. I'm not that long out of childbed."

"I will," he promised. Now he reached out to clasp her breast. Her hand closed on his.

Their lovemaking was, perhaps, the strangest he'd known—certainly the most self-conscious. Both her physical frailty and knowing she remained just this side of furious at him constrained him until he was almost afraid to touch her. Despite her pledge, she lay still and unstirred under his caresses.

Her jaw was clamped with apprehension when he entered her. "Is it all right?" he asked. She hesitated, considering. Finally she nodded. He went on, as carefully as he could. At last he gasped and jerked, even then cautiously. He realized he was lying with all his weight on her. He slid out of her, then away from her. "I'm sorry," he said. "I'd hoped to please you better."

"Never mind—don't worry about it," she answered. He looked at her in some surprise, for she sounded serious. Then she nodded to show she was. She went on, "I told you I doubted I was happy enough with you to take full part in it now. But I noticed how you did what you did, how you were careful with me. Maybe I even noticed that more because I wasn't swept away. You wouldn't have been so . . . regardful if I were just so much convenient flesh to you."

"I've never thought of you like that," Krispos protested.

"A woman often wonders," Dara said bleakly, "especially a woman who has known Anthimos, and most especially a woman who, when her husband goes away while she must stay behind, learns he's found some other convenient flesh with which to dally for a while. Me, I mean."

Krispos started to say, "It wasn't like that." But knowing when to hold his tongue had served him well through the years. This was as good a time as any, and better than most. He knew he was right—what he and Tanilis had done together was far more than dallying with convenient flesh. At the moment, though, being right mattered little; if he pressed it, being right was indeed liable to be worse than being wrong. Peace with Dara was worth giving her the last word.

What he did say, not even a beat late, was, "I'm no Anthimos. I hope you've noticed."

"I have," she said. "I was quite sure of it till you went on campaign. Then—" She shook her head. "Then I doubted everything. But maybe, just maybe, we can go on after all."

"I want us to," Krispos said. "I've packed a lifetime's worth of upheavals into the last two years. I don't need any more."

Suddenly Dara made a wry face. She quickly sat, then looked down between her legs. Krispos took a few seconds to be sure the snort she let out was laughter. She said, "The maidservant who changes the bed linen will be sure we've reconciled. I suppose we may as well."

"Good," Krispos said. "I'm glad."

"I . . . think I am, too."

With that Krispos had to be content. Considering how Dara had greeted him the day before, it was as much as he could have hoped for. Now he did yank at the bellpull. Barsymes appeared as promptly and silently as if he'd been conjured up. "Good morning, Your Majesty. I trust you slept well?"

"Yes, thank you, esteemed sir."

The vestiarios brought him a pair of drawers and pointed to a robe in the closet. Krispos nodded at his choice. Barsymes drew out the robe. Krispos let the eunuch dress him. Dara must have used her bellpull, too, for a serving maid came in while Barsymes was fussing over Krispos. She helped Dara into her clothes and combed out her shining black hair.

"And how would you care to break your fast this morning, Your Majesty?" Barsymes asked.

Krispos slapped his belly with the flat of his hand. "Seeing that I ate enough for three starving men last night, I hope Phestos won't be put out if I just ask for a small bowl of porridge and half a stewed melon."

"I trust he will be able to restrain his chagrin, yes," the vestiarios agreed blandly. Krispos gave him a sharp look—Barsymes' wit was drought-dry. The chamberlain turned to Dara. "And you, Your Majesty?"

"The same as for Krispos, I think," she said.

"I shall so inform Phestos. No doubt he will be pleased to find the two of you in accord." With that oblique comment on yesterday's fight, Barsymes strode out of the imperial bedchamber.

When the vestiarios cleared away the few breakfast dishes, Krispos knew he ought to start in on all the scrolls and parchments that had piled up at the palaces while he was on campaign. The most pressing business had followed him even to Pliskavos, but much that was not pressing remained important—and would swiftly become urgent if he neglected it. But he could not make himself get up and attend to business, not on his first full day back in Videssos the city. Hadn't he earned at least one day of rest?

He was still arguing with himself when Longinos brought Phostis into the dining room. "Dada!" Phostis exclaimed, and ran to him. Krispos decided the parchments could wait. He scooped up Phostis and gave him a noisy kiss.

Phostis scrubbed at his cheek with the palm of his hand. After a moment, Krispos realized the boy was not used to being kissed by anyone who wore a beard. He kissed him again. Phostis rubbed again.

"You're doing that on purpose, just to confuse him with your whiskers," Dara said.

"If he gets to know me, he has to get to know my beard, too," Krispos answered. "The lord with the great and good mind willing, I'll be able to stay in the city long enough now to keep him from forgetting me."

Dara yielded. "May Phos hear that prayer." Phostis stood up on Krispos' lap. He wrapped his arms around Krispos' neck and made a loud kissing noise. Krispos found himself grinning. Dara smiled a mother's smile. She said, "He seems fond of you."

"He does, doesn't he? That's good." Krispos glanced to Longinos, then to the doorway. The eunuch, trained to the nuances of palace service, gave a half bow that turned his plump cheeks pink, then stepped into the hall. Krispos lowered his voice and said to Dara, "You know, at last I find I don't care who his father really was. He's a fine little boy, that's all."

"I've thought so all along," she answered. "I never wanted to say it very often, though, for fear of making you worry more about that than you would have otherwise." She studied him, nodding thoughtfully as if he'd passed a test.

He wondered if he had. Was he showing maturity about Phostis' lineage, or merely resignation? He didn't know himself. Whatever it was, it seemed to please Dara. That practical consideration carried more weight with him than any fine-spun point of philosophy.

He chuckled. "What?" Dara asked.

"Only that I'd never make a good sorcerer or theologian," he said.

"You're probably right," she replied. "On the other hand, precious few sorcerers or theologians would make a good Avtokrator, and you're shaping pretty well for that."

He dipped his head to her in silent thanks. Then, all unbidden, Harvas rose to the surface of his mind. Harvas had been theologian and sorcerer both, and wanted to rule the Empire of Videssos. What sort of Avtokrator would he have made? Krispos knew the answer to that and shuddered at the knowledge.

But Harvas was menace no more, thanks to Tanilis; even if he could not speak of her to Dara, Krispos reflected, how could he erase her from his memory? Maybe one day the sorcerer would arise and threaten Videssos again, but Krispos did not think it would be any year soon. If it did happen, he would deal with it as best he could, or Phostis would, or Phostis' son, or whoever wore the Avtokrator's crown in some distant time.

With the infallible instinct palace servants develop, Longinos knew he could come back into the dining room. "Shall I take charge of the young Majesty again?" he asked Krispos.

Krispos expected Phostis to go to the eunuch, with whom he was far more familiar. But Phostis stayed close by. "I'll keep him awhile, if it's all right with you, Longinos," Krispos said. "He's mine, after all."

"Indeed, Your Majesty. Phos has blessed you—blessed you twice now."

The chamberlain's voice, not quite tenor, not quite alto, was wistful. Phos would not bless him, not that way.

When Krispos got up from the table and went out into the hall, Phostis toddled after him. He slowed his steps to let the little boy keep up. Phostis walked over to a carved marble display stand and tried to climb up it. Krispos didn't think he was strong enough to knock it over, but took no chances. He lifted Phostis into his arms.

Displayed on the marble stand was a conical helm once worn by a Makuraner King of Kings, part of the spoil from a Videssian triumph of long ago. On the wall above the helmet hung a portrait of the fierce-looking Avtokrator Stavrakios, who had beaten the Halogai in their own country. Every time Krispos saw it, he wondered how he would measure up in Stavrakios' uncompromising eyes.

Phostis pointed to the portrait and frowned in intense concentration. "Emp'ror," he said at last.

"Yes, that's true," Krispos said. "He was Emperor, a long time ago."

Phostis wasn't finished. He pointed to Krispos, almost sticking a finger in his eye. "Emp'ror," he said again, adding a moment later, "Dada."

Krispos hugged the little boy. "That's true, too," he agreed gravely. "I am the Emperor, and your dada. Come to think of it, young Majesty, you're an emperor yourself." Now he pointed at Phostis. "Emperor."

"Emp'ror?" Phostis laughed, as if that were the funniest thing he'd ever heard. Krispos laughed, too. It was a preposterously unlikely notion, when you got right down to it. But it was also true.

Krispos hugged Phostis tighter, till the boy squirmed. Every year, so many, many peasants left their farms and came to Videssos the city to seek their fortunes. Unlike almost all of them, he'd found his.

"Emperor," he said wonderingly. He lowered Phostis to the floor. They walked down the hall together.

Book III

KRISPOS THE EMPEROR

Chapter I

Krispos sopped a heel of bread in the fermented fish sauce that had gone over his mutton. He ate the bread in two bites, washed it down with a final swallow of sweet, golden Vaspurakaner wine, set the silver goblet back on the table.

Before he could even let out a contented sigh, Barsymes came into the little dining chamber to clear away his dishes. Krispos cocked an eyebrow at the eunuch chamberlain. "How do you time that so perfectly, esteemed sir?" he asked. "It's not sorcery, I know, but it always strikes me as magical."

The vestiarios hardly paused as he answered, "Your Majesty, attention to your needs is the proper business of every palace servitor." His voice was a tone for which Videssian had no name, halfway between tenor and contralto. His long, pale fingers deftly scooped up plates and goblet, knife and fork and spoon, set them on a vermeil tray.

As Barsymes worked, Krispos studied his face. Like any eunuch gelded before puberty, the vestiarios had no beard. That was part of what made him look younger than he was, but not all. His skin was very fine, and had hardly wrinkled or sagged through the many years Krispos had known

him. Being a eunuch, he still had a boy's hairline, and his hair was still
black (though that, at least, might have come from a bottle).

Suddenly curious, Krispos said, "How old are you, Barsymes? Do you
mind my asking? When I became Avtokrator of the Videssians, I would
have sworn on Phos' holy name that you had more years than I. Now,
though, I'd take oath the other way round."

"I would not have Your Majesty forsworn either way," Barsymes answered seriously. "As a matter of fact, I do not know my exact age. If I were
forced to guess, I would say we were not far apart. And, if Your Majesty
would be so gracious as to forgive me, memories are apt to shift with time,
and you have sat on the imperial throne for—is it twenty-two years now?
Yes, of course; the twenty-year jubilee was summer before last."

"Twenty-two years," Krispos murmured. Sometimes the day when he
walked down to Videssos the city to seek his fortune after being taxed off
his farm seemed like last week. He'd had more muscle than brains back
then—what young man doesn't? The only trait he was sure he kept from
his peasant days was a hard stubbornness.

Sometimes, like tonight, that trek down from his village seemed so distant, it might have happened to someone else. He was past fifty now,
though like Barsymes he wasn't sure just how old he was. The imperial
robes concealed a comfortable potbelly. His hair had gone no worse than
iron gray, but white frosted his beard, his mustache, even his eyebrows.
Perverse vanity kept him from the dye pot—he knew he was no boy any
more, so why pretend to anyone else?

"Will Your Majesty forgive what might perhaps be perceived as an indiscretion?" Barsymes asked.

"Esteemed sir, these days I'd *welcome* an indiscretion," Krispos declared.
"One of the things I do miss about my early days is having people come
right out and tell me what they think instead of what they think will
please me or what's to their own advantage. Go on; say what you will."

"Nothing of any great moment," the vestiarios said. "It merely crossed
my mind that you might find it lonely, eating by yourself at so many
meals."

"Banquets can be dull, too," Krispos said. But that wasn't what
Barsymes meant, and he knew it. Here in the residence where the Avtokrator and his family had more privacy than anywhere else (not much, by
anyone else's standard—Barsymes, for instance, was in the habit of dressing Krispos every morning), meals should have been a time when everyone could just sit around and talk. Krispos remembered many such
meals—happy even if sometimes short on food—in the peasant huts
where he'd grown to manhood.

Maybe if Dara were still alive . . . His marriage to his predecessor's widow began as an alliance of convenience for both of them, but despite some quarrels and rocky times it had grown into more than that. And Dara had always got on well with their sons, too. But Dara had gone to Phos' light, or so Krispos sincerely hoped, almost ten years before. Since then . . .

"Evripos and Katakolon, I suppose, are out prowling for women," Krispos said. "That's what they usually do of nights, anyhow, being the ages they are."

"Yes," Barsymes said tonelessly. He had never prowled for women, nor would he. Sometimes he took a sort of melancholy pride in being above desire. Krispos often thought he must have wondered what he was missing, but he'd never have the nerve to ask. Only those far from the palace quarter imagined the Avtokrator as serene and undisputed master of his household.

Krispos sighed. "As for Phostis, well, I just don't know what Phostis is up to right now."

He sighed again. Phostis, his eldest, his heir—his cuckoo's egg? He'd never known for sure whether Dara had conceived by him or by Anthimos, whom he'd overthrown. The boy's—no, young man's now—looks were no help, for he looked like Dara. Krispos' doubts had always made it hard for him to warm up to the child he'd named for his own father.

And now . . . Now he wondered if he'd been so nearly intolerable as he was growing into manhood. He didn't think so, but who does, looking back on his own youth? Of course, his own younger years were full of poverty and hunger and fear and backbreaking work. He'd spared Phostis all that, but he wondered if his son was the better for it.

He probably was. There were those in Videssos the city who praised the hard, simple life the Empire's peasants led, who even put into verse the virtues that life imbued into those peasants. Krispos thought they were full of the manure they'd surely never touched with their own daintily manicured fingers.

Barsymes said, "The young Majesty will yet make you proud." Fondness touched his usually cool voice. Since he could have no children of his own, he doted on the ones he'd helped raise from infancy.

"I hope you're right," Krispos said. He worried still. Was Phostis as he was because of Anthimos' blood coming through? The man Krispos had supplanted in Dara's bed and then in the palaces had had a sort of hectic brilliance to him, but applied it chiefly in pursuit of pleasure. Whenever Phostis did something extravagantly foolish, Krispos worried about his paternity.

Was Phostis really spoiled from growing up soft? Or, asked the cold, suspicious part of Krispos that never quite slept and that had helped keep him on the throne for more than two decades, was he just getting tired of watching his father rule vigorously? Did he want to take the Empire of Videssos into his own young hands?

Krispos looked up at Barsymes. "If a man can't rely on his own son, esteemed sir, upon whom can he rely? Present company excepted, of course."

"Your Majesty is gracious." The vestiarios dipped his head. "As I said, however, I remain confident Phostis will satisfy your every expectation of him."

"Maybe," was all Krispos said.

Accepting his gloom, Barsymes picked up the tray and began to take it back to the kitchens. He paused at the doorway. "Will Your Majesty require anything more of me?"

"No, not for now. Just make sure the candles in the study are lit, if you'd be so kind. I have the usual pile of parchments there waiting for review, and I can't do them all by daylight."

"I shall see to it," Barsymes promised. "Er—anything besides that?"

"No, eminent sir, nothing else, thank you," Krispos said. He'd had a few women in the palaces since Dara died, but his most recent mistress had seemed convinced he would make her relatives rich and powerful regardless of their merits, which were slender. He'd sent her packing.

Now—now his desire burned cooler than it had in his younger days. Little by little, he thought, he was beginning to approach Barsymes' status. He had never said that out loud and never would, for fear both of wounding the chamberlain's feelings and of encountering his pungent sarcasm.

Krispos waited a couple of minutes, then walked down the hall to the study. The cheerful glow of candlelight greeted him from the doorway: As usual, Barsymes gave flawless service. The stack of documents on the desk was less gladsome. Sometimes Krispos likened that stack to an enemy city that had to be besieged and then taken. But a city had to be captured only once. The parchments were never vanquished for good.

He'd watched Anthimos ignore administration for the sake of pleasure. Perhaps in reaction, he ignored pleasure for administration. When the pile of parchments was very high, as tonight, he wondered if Anthimos hadn't known the better way after all. Without a doubt, Anthimos had enjoyed himself more than Krispos did now. But equally without a doubt, the Empire was better served now than it had been during Anthimos' antic reign.

Reed pens and the scarlet ink reserved for the Avtokrator of the Videssians alone, stylus and wax-covered wooden tablets, and sky-blue sealing wax waited in a neat row at the left edge of the desk, like regiments ready to be committed to battle against the implacable enemy. Feeling a moment's foolishness, Krispos saluted them, clenched right fist over his heart. Then he sat down and got to work.

Topping the pile was a tax report from the frontier province of Kubrat, between the Paristrian Mountains and the Istros River, north and east of Videssos the city. When Krispos' reign began, it had been the independent khaganate of Kubrat, a barbarous nation whose horsemen had raided the Empire for centuries. Now herds and farms and mines brought gold rather than terror south of the mountains. Solid progress there, he thought. He scrawled his signature to show he'd read the cadaster and approved its revenue total.

The second report was also from Kubrat. Even after most of a generation under Videssian rule, the prelate of Pliskavos reported, heresy and outright heathenism remained rife in the province. Many of the nomads would not turn aside from their ancestral spirits to worship Phos, the good god the Empire followed. And the folk of Videssian stock, subject for centuries to the invaders from the steppe, had fallen into strange usages and errors because they were so long cut off from the mainstream of doctrine in Videssos.

Krispos reinked the pen, reached into a pigeonhole for a blank parchment. *Krispos Avtokrator to the holy sir Balaneus: Greetings,* he wrote, and then paused for thought. The pen scratched across the sheet as he resumed: *By all means keep on with your efforts to bring Kubrat and its inhabitants back to the true faith. The example of our new, perfectly orthodox colonists should help you. Use compulsion only as a last resort, but in the end do not hesitate: as we have only one Empire, so we must have only one faith within it. May Phos shine his light on your work.*

He sanded the letter dry, lit a stick of sealing wax at one of the candles on the desk, let several drops fall on the letter, and pressed his ring into the blob of wax while it was still soft. A courier would take the letter north tomorrow; Balaneus ought to have it in less than a week. Krispos was pleased with the prelate and his work. He was also pleased with his own writing; he hadn't done much of it before he became Emperor, but had grown fluent with a pen since.

Another tax report followed, this one from a lowland province in the westlands, across the strait called the Cattle-Crossing from Videssos the city. The lowland province yielded four times as much revenue as Kubrat.

Krispos nodded, unsurprised. The lowlands had soil and climate good enough for two crops a year, and had been free of invasion for so long that many of the towns there had no walls. That would have been unimaginable—to say nothing of suicidal—in half-barbarous Kubrat.

The next report was sealed; it came from the latest Videssian embassy to Mashiz, the capital of Makuran. Krispos knew he had to handle that one with careful attention: the King of Kings of Makuran were the greatest rivals Videssian Avtokrators faced, and the only rulers they recognized as equals.

He smiled when he broke the seal and saw the elegant script within. It was almost as familiar as his own hand. "Iakovitzes to the Avtokrator Krispos: Greetings," he read, moving his lips slightly as he always did. "I trust you are cool and comfortable in the city by the sea. Were Skotos' hell to be charged with fire rather than the eternal ice, Mashiz would let the dark god get a good notion of what he required."

Krispos' smile broadened. He'd first met Iakovitzes when he was nine years old, when the Videssian noble ransomed his family and other peasants from captivity in Kubrat. In the more than forty years since, he'd seldom known the plump little man to have a kind word for anyone or anything.

Warming to his theme (if that was the proper phrase), Iakovitzes continued, "Rubyab King of Kings has gone and done something sneaky. I have not yet learned what it is, but the little waxed tips to his mustaches quiver whenever he deigns to grant me an audience, so I presume it is something not calculated to make you sleep better of nights, Your Majesty. I've spread about a few goldpieces—the Makuraners coin only silver, as you know, so they lust for gold as I do after pretty boys—but without success as yet. I keep trying."

The smile left Krispos' face. He'd sent Iakovitzes to Makuran precisely because he was so good at worming information out of unlikely places. He read on: "Other than his mustaches, Rubyab is being reasonably cooperative. I think I shall be able to talk him out of restoring that desert fortress his troops won in our last little skirmish for the donative you have in mind. He also seems willing to lower the tolls he charges caravans for permission to enter Videssos from his realm. That, in turn, may, should, but probably will not, enable those thieves to lower their prices to us."

"Good," Krispos said aloud. He'd been after Makuran to lower those tolls since the days of Rubyab's father Nakhorgan. If the King of Kings finally intended to yield there, and to restore the fortress of Sarmizegetusa, maybe Iakovitzes was reading too much into waggling waxed mustachios.

Another cadaster followed Iakovitzes' letter from Makuran. Krispos wondered if Barsymes deliberately arranged the parchments to keep him from being stupefied by one tax list after another. The vestiarios had served in the palaces a long time now; his definition of perfect service grew broader every year.

After scrawling *I have read it—Krispos* at the bottom of the tax document, Krispos went on to the parchment beneath it. Like Balaneus' missive, this one also came from an ecclesiastic, here a priest from Pityos, a town on the southern coast of the Videssian Sea, just across the Rhamnos River from Vaspurakan.

"The humble priest Taronites to Krispos Avtokrator: Greetings. May it please Your Majesty, I regret I must report the outbreak of a new and malignant heresy among the peasants and herders dwelling in the hinterlands of this Phos-forsaken municipality."

Krispos snorted. Why that sort of news was supposed to please him had always been beyond his comprehension. Formal written Videssian, he sometimes thought, was designed to obscure meaning rather than reveal it. His eyes went back to the page.

"This heresy strikes me as one particularly wicked and also as one calculated as if by the foul god Skotos to deceive both the light-minded and those of a certain type of what might in other circumstances be termed piety. As best I can gather, its tenets are—"

The more Krispos read, the less he liked. The heretics, if Taronites had things straight, believed the material world to have been created by Skotos, not Phos. Phos' light, then, inhabited only the soul, not the body in which it dwelt. Thus killing, for example, but liberated the soul from its trap of corrupting flesh. Arson was merely the destruction of that which was already dross. Even robbery had the salutary effect on its victim of lessening his ties to the material. If ever a theology had been made for brigands, this was it.

Taronites wrote, "This wickedness appears first to have been perpetrated and put forward by a certain Thanasios, wherefrom its adherents style themselves Thanasioi. I pray that Your Majesty may quickly send both many priests to instruct the populace hereabouts on proper doctrine and many troops to lay low the Thanasioi and protect the fearful orthodox from the depredations. May Phos be with you always in your struggle for the good."

On the petition, Krispos wrote, *Your requests shall be granted.* Then he picked up stylus and tablet and scribbled two notes to himself, for action in the morning: to see Oxeites the ecumenical patriarch on sending a priestly delegation to Pityos, and to write to the provincial governor to get him to shift troops to the environs of the border town.

He read through the note from Taronites again, put it down with a shake of his head. A naturally argumentative folk, the Videssians were never content simply to leave their faith as they had found it. Whenever two of them got together, they tinkered with it: theological argument was as enjoyable a sport as watching the horses run in the Amphitheater. This time, though, the tinkering had gone awry.

He used the third leaf of the waxed tablet for another self-reminder: to draft an imperial edict threatening outlawry for anyone professing the doctrines of Thanasios. *Patriarch, too,* he scribbled. Adding excommunication to outlawry would strengthen the edict nicely.

After that, he was relieved to get back to an ordinary, unthreatening tax register. This one, from the eastern province of Develtos, made him feel good. A band of invading Halogai from the far north had sacked the fortress of Develtos not long after he became Avtokrator. This year, for the first time, revenues from the province exceeded what they'd been before the fortress fell.

Well done, he wrote at the bottom of the register. The logothetes and clerks who handled cadasters for the treasury would know he was pleased. Without their patient, usually unloved work, Videssos would crash to the ground. As Emperor, Krispos understood that. When he'd been a peasant, he'd loved tax collectors no better than any other kind of locust.

He got up, stretched, rubbed his eyes. Working by candlelight was hard, and had grown harder the past few years as his sight began to lengthen. He didn't know what he would do if his eyes kept getting worse: would he have to have someone read each petition to him and hope he could remember enough to decide it sensibly? He didn't look forward to that, but had trouble coming up with any better answer.

He stretched again, yawned until his jaw creaked. "The best answer right now is some sleep," he said aloud. He lit a little lamp at one of the candles, then blew them out. The smell of hot wax filled his nostrils.

Most of the torches in the hallway had gone out. The guttering flames of those that still burned made Krispos' shadow writhe and swoop like something with a life of its own. The lamp he carried cast a small, wan pool of light around him.

He walked past Barsymes' chamber. He'd lived there once himself, when he'd been one of the rare vestiarioi who were not eunuchs. Now he occupied the room next door, the imperial bedchamber. He'd slept there longer than in any other quarters he'd ever had. Sometimes that just seemed a simple part of the way his world worked. Tonight, though, as often happened when he thought about it, he found it very strange.

He opened the double doors. Inside the bedchamber, someone stirred. Ice ran up his back. He stooped to pluck a dagger from his scarlet boot, filled his lungs to shout for help from the Haloga guards at the entranceway to the imperial residence. Avtokrators of the Videssians too often died in unpeaceful ways.

The shout died unuttered; Krispos quickly straightened. This was no assassin in his bed, only one of the palace serving maids. She smiled an invitation at him.

He shook his head. "Not tonight, Drina," he said. "I told the esteemed sir I intended to go straight to sleep."

"That's not what he said to me, Your Majesty," Drina answered, shrugging. Her bare shoulders gleamed in the lamplight as she sat up taller in bed. The lamp left most of the rest of her in shadow, making her an even greater mystery than woman ordinarily is. "He said to come make you happy, so here I am."

"He must have misheard." Krispos didn't believe that, not for a minute. Barsymes did not mishear his instructions. Every so often he simply decided not to listen to them. This seemed to be one of those nights. "It's all right, Drina. You may go."

In a small voice, the maid said, "May it please Your Majesty, I'd truly sooner not. The vestiarios would be most displeased if I left you."

Who rules here, Barsymes or I? But Krispos did not say that, not out loud. He ruled the Empire, but around the palaces what was pleasing to the vestiarios had the force of law. Some eunuch chamberlains used their intimacy with the Avtokrator for their own advantage or that of their relatives. Barsymes, to his credit, had never done that. In exchange, Krispos deferred to him on matters affecting only the palaces.

So now he yielded with such grace as he could: "Very well, stay if you care to. No one need know we'll sleep on opposite sides of the bed."

Drina still looked worried but, like any good servant, knew how far she could safely push her master. "As you say, Your Majesty." She scurried over to the far side of the bed. "Here, you rest where I've been lying. I'll have warmed it for you."

"It's not winter yet, by the good god, and I'm no invalid," Krispos said with a snort. But he pulled his robe off over his head and draped it on a bedpost. Then he stepped out of his sandals, blew out the lamp, and got into bed. The warm silk of the sheets was kind to his skin. As his head met the down-filled pillow, he smelled the faint sweetness that said Drina had rested there before him.

For a moment, he wanted her in spite of his own weariness. But when he opened his mouth to tell her so, what came out was an enormous yawn. He thought he excused himself, but fell asleep so fast he was never sure.

He woke up some time in the middle of the night. That happened more and more often as the years went by. He needed a few seconds to realize what the round smoothness pressed against his side was. Drina breathed smoothly, easily, carefree as a sleeping child. Krispos envied her lack of worry, then smiled when he thought he was partly responsible for it.

Now he did want her. When he reached over her shoulder to cup her breast in his hand, she muttered something drowsy and happy and rolled onto her back. She hardly woke up as he caressed her and then took her. He found that kind of trust strangely touching, and tried hard to be as gentle as he could.

Afterward, she quickly slipped back into deep sleep. Krispos got out of bed to use the chamber pot, then lay down beside her again. He, too, was almost asleep when he suddenly wondered, not for the first time, whether Barsymes knew him better than he knew himself.

THE TROUBLE WITH THE HALL OF THE NINETEEN COUCHES, Phostis thought, was that the windows were too big. The ceremonial hall, named back in the days when Videssian nobles actually ate reclining, was cooler in summer than most, thanks to those large windows. But the torches, lamps, and candles needed for nighttime feasts were lodestones for moths, mosquitoes, water bugs, even bats and birds. Watching a crisped moth land in the middle of a bowl of pickled octopus tentacles did not inflame the appetite. Watching a nightjar swoop down and snatch the moth out of the bowl made Phostis wish he'd never summoned his friends to the feast in the first place.

He thought about announcing it was over, but that wouldn't do, either. Inevitably, word would get back to his father. He could already hear Krispos' peasant-accented voice ringing in his ears: *The least you could do, son, is make up your mind.*

The imagined scolding seemed so real that he whipped his head around in alarm, wondering if Krispos had somehow snuck up behind him. But no—save for his own companions. he was alone here.

He felt very much alone. One thing his father had succeeded in doing was to make him wonder who cared for him because he was himself and who merely because he was junior Avtokrator and heir to the Videssian throne. Asking the question, though, often proved easier than answering it, so he had lingering suspicions about almost everyone he knew.

"You won't need to look over your shoulder like that forever, Your Majesty," said Vatatzes, who was sitting at Phostis' right hand. He trusted Vatatzes further than most of his friends; being only the son of a mid-level logothete, the youth was unlikely to have designs on the crown himself. Now he slapped Krispos on the shoulder and went on, "Surely one day before too long, you'll be able to hold your feasts when and as you like."

One more word and he would have spoken treason. Phostis' friends frequently walked that fine line. So far, to his relief, nobody had forced him to pretend not to hear something. He, too, wondered—how could he help but wonder?—how long his father would stay vigorous. It might be another day, it might be another twenty years. No way to tell without magic, and even that held risks greater than he cared to take. For one thing, as was but fitting, the finest sorcerous talent in the Empire shielded the Avtokrator's fate from those who would spy it out. For another, seeking to divine an Emperor's future was in and of itself a capital crime.

Phostis wondered what Krispos was doing now. Administering affairs, probably; that was what his father usually did. A couple of years before, Krispos had tried to get him to share some of the burden. He'd tried, too, but it hadn't been pleasant work, especially because Krispos stood behind him while he shuffled through parchments.

Again, he could almost hear his father: "Hurry up, boy! One way or another, you have to decide. If you don't do it, who will?"

And his own wail: "But what if I'm wrong?"

"You will be, sometimes." Krispos had spoken with such maddening certainty that he wanted to hit him. "You try to do a couple of things: You try not to make the same mistake twice, and you take the chance to set one right later if it comes along."

Put that way, it sounded so easy. But after a couple of days of case after complex case, Phostis concluded ease in anything—fishing, sword-swallowing, running an empire, anything—came only with having done the job for years and years. As most young men do, he suspected he was brighter than his father. He certainly had a better education: He was good at ciphering, he could quote secular poets and historians as well as Phos' holy scriptures, and he didn't talk as if he'd just stepped away from a plow.

But Krispos had one thing he lacked: experience. His father did what needed doing almost without thinking about it, then went on to the next thing and took care of that, too. Meanwhile Phostis himself floundered and bit his lip, wondering where proper action lay. By the time he made one choice, three more had grown up to stare him in the face.

He knew he'd disappointed his father when he asked to be excused from his share of imperial business. "How will you learn what you need to know, save by this work?" Krispos had asked.

"But I can't do it properly," he'd answered. To him, that explained everything—if something didn't come easy, why not work at something else instead?

Krispos had shaken his head. "Wouldn't you sooner find that out now, while I'm here to show you what you need, than after I'm gone and you find the whole sack of barley on your back at once?"

The rustic metaphor hadn't helped persuade Phostis. He wished his family's nobility ran back farther than his father, wished he wasn't named for a poor farmer dead of cholera.

Vatatzes snapped him out of his gloomy reverie. 'What say we go find us some girls, eh, Your Majesty?"

"Go on if you care to. You'll probably run into my brothers if you do." Phostis laughed without much mirth, as much at himself as at Evripos and Katakolon. He couldn't even enjoy the perquisites of imperial life as they did. Ever since he'd discovered how many women would lie down with him merely on account of the title he bore, much of the enjoyment had gone out of the game.

Some nobles kept little enclosures where they hand-raised deer and boar until the animals grew tame as pets. Then they'd shoot them. Phostis had never seen the sport in that, or in bedding girls who either didn't dare say no or else turned sleeping with him into as cold-blooded a calculation as any Krispos made in the agelong struggle between Videssos and Makuran.

He'd tried explaining that to his brothers once, not long after Katakolon, then fourteen, seduced—or was seduced by—one of the women who did the palace laundry. Exalted by his own youthful prowess, he'd paid no heed whatever to Phostis. As for Evripos, he'd said only, "Do you want to don the blue robe and live out your life as a monk? Suit yourself, big brother, but it's not the life for me."

Had he wanted a monastic life, it would have been easy to arrange. But the sole reason he'd ever considered it was to get away from his father. He lacked both a monkish vocation and a monkish temperament. It wasn't that he sought to mortify his flesh, but rather that he—usually—found loveless or mercenary coupling more mortifying than none.

He often wondered how he would do when Krispos decided to marry him off. He was just glad that day had not yet arrived. When it did, he was sure his father would pick him a bride with more of an eye toward advantage for the imperial house than toward his happiness. Sometimes marriages of that sort worked as well as any others. Sometimes—

He turned to Vatatzes. "My friend, you know not how fortunate you are, coming from a family of but middling rank. All too often, I feel my birth more as a cage or a curse than as something in which to rejoice."

"Ah, Your Majesty, you've drunk yourself sad, that's all it is." Vatatzes turned to the panpiper and pandoura player who made soft music as a background against which to talk. He snapped his fingers and raised his voice. "Here, you fellows, give us something lively now, to lift the young Majesty's spirits."

The musicians put their heads together for a moment. The man with the panpipes set them down and picked up a kettle-shaped drum. Heads came up all through the Hall of the Nineteen Couches as his hands evoked thunder from the drumhead. The pandoura player struck a ringing, fiery chord. Phostis recognized the Vaspurakaner dance they played, but it failed to gladden him.

Before long, almost all the feasters snaked along in a dance line, clapping their hands and shouting in time to the tune. Phostis sat in his place even when Vatatzes tugged at the sleeve of his robe. Finally, with a shrug, Vatatzes gave up and joined the dance. *He prescribed for me the medicine that works for him,* Phostis thought. He didn't want to be joyous, though. Discontent suited him.

When he got to his feet, the dancers cheered. But he did not join their line. He walked through the open bronze doors of the Hall of the Nineteen Couches, down the low, broad marble stairs. He looked up at the sky, gauging the time by how high the waning gibbous moon had risen. Somewhere in the fifth hour of the night, he judged—not far from midnight.

He lowered his eyes. The imperial residence was separated from the rest of the buildings of the palace compound and screened off by a grove of cherry trees, to give the Avtokrator and his family at least the illusion of privacy. Through the trees, Phostis saw one window brightly lit by candles or lamps. He nodded to himself. Yes, Krispos was at work there. With peasant persistence, his father kept on fighting against the immensity of the Empire he ruled.

As Phostis watched, the window went dark. Even Krispos occasionally yielded to sleep, though Phostis was sure he would have evaded it if he could.

Somebody stuck his head out through one of the Hall's many big windows. "Come on back, Your Majesty," he called, voice blurry with wine. "It's just starting to get bouncy in here."

"Go on without me," Phostis said. He wished he'd never gathered the feasters together. The ease with which they enjoyed themselves only made his own unhappiness seem worse by comparison.

He absently swatted at a mosquito; there weren't as many out here, away from the lights. With the last lamps extinguished in the imperial residence, it fell into invisibility behind the cherry grove. He started walking slowly in that direction; he didn't want to get there until he was sure his father had gone to bed.

Haloga guardsmen stood outside the doorway. The big blond northerners raised their axes in salute as they recognized Phostis. Had he been a miscreant, the axes would have gone up, too, but not as a gesture of respect.

As always, one of the palace eunuchs waited just inside the entrance. "Good evening, young Majesty," he said, bowing politely to Phostis.

"Good evening, Mystakon," Phostis answered. Of all the eunuch chamberlains, Mystakon was closest to his own age and hence the one he thought most likely to understand and sympathize with him. It hadn't occurred to him to wonder how Mystakon felt, going through what should have been ripe young manhood already withered on the vine, so to speak. "Is my father asleep?"

"He is in bed, yes," Mystakon answered with the peculiarly toneless voice eunuchs could affect to communicate subtle double meanings.

Phostis, however, noticed no subtleties tonight. All he felt was a surge of relief at having got through another day without having to confront his father—or having his father confront him. "I will go to bed, too, prominent sir," he said, using Mystakon's special title in the eunuch hierarchy.

"Everything is in readiness for you, young Majesty," Mystakon said, a tautology: Phostis would have been shocked were his chamber not ready whenever he needed it. "If you would be so kind as to accompany me—"

Phostis let the chamberlain guide him down the hallways he could have navigated blindfolded. In the torchlight, the souvenirs of long centuries of imperial triumph seemed somehow faded, indistinct. The conical helmet that had once belonged to a King of Kings of Makuran was just a lump of iron, the painting of Videssian troops pouring over the walls of Mashiz was a daub that could have depicted any squabble. Phostis shook his head. Was he merely tired, or was the light playing tricks on his eyes?

His bedchamber lay as far from Krispos' as it could, in a tucked-away corner of the imperial residence. It had stood empty for years, maybe centuries, until he chose it as a refuge from his father not long after his beard began to sprout.

The door to the chamber stood ajar. Butter-yellow light trickling through the opening said a lamp had been kindled. "Do you require anything further, young Majesty?" Mystakon asked. "Some wine, perhaps, or some bread and cheese? Or I could inquire if any mutton is left from that which was served to your father."

"No, don't bother," Phostis said, more sharply than he'd intended. He tried to soften his voice. "I'm content, thank you. I just want to get some rest."

"As you say, young Majesty." Mystakon glided away. Like many eunuchs, he was soft and plump. He walked in soft slippers, silently and with little mincing steps. With his robes swirling around him as he moved, he reminded Phostis of a beamy merchant ship under full sail.

Phostis closed and barred the door behind him. He took off his robe and got out of his sandals. They were all-red, like his father's—about the only imperial prerogative he shared with Krispos, he thought bitterly. He threw himself down on the bed and blew out the lamp. The bedchamber plunged into blackness, and Phostis into sleep.

He dreamed. He'd always been given to vivid dreams, and this one was more so than most. In it he found himself pacing, naked and fat, through a small enclosure. Food was everywhere—mutton, bread and cheese, jar upon jar of wine.

His father peered at him from over the top of a wooden fence. Phostis watched Krispos nod in sober satisfaction . . . and reach for a hunting bow.

Next thing he knew, he was awake, his heart pounding, his body bathed with cold sweat. For a moment, he thought the darkness that filled his sight meant death. Then full awareness returned. He sketched Phos' sun-circle above his chest in thanks as he realized his nightmare was not truth.

That helped calm him, until he thought of his place at court. He shivered. Maybe the dream held some reality after all.

ZAIDAS WENT DOWN ON HIS KNEES BEFORE KRISPOS, THEN TO his belly, letting his forehead knock against the bright tesserae of the mosaic floor in full proskynesis. "Up, up," Krispos said impatiently. "You know I have no great use for ceremonial."

The wizard rose as smoothly as he had prostrated himself. "Yes, Your Majesty, but *you* know the respect a mage will show to ritual. Without ritual, our art would fall to nothing."

"So you've said, many times these past many years," Krispos answered. "Now the ritual is over. Sit, relax; let us talk." He waved Zaidas to a chair in the chamber where he'd been working the night before.

Barsymes came in with a jar of wine and two crystal goblets. The vestiarios poured for Emperor and mage, then bowed himself out. Zaidas savored his wine's bouquet for a moment before he sipped. He smiled. "That's a fine vintage, Your Majesty."

Krispos drank, too. "Aye, it is pleasant. I fear I'll never make a proper connoisseur, though. It's all so much better than what I grew up drinking that I have trouble telling what's just good from the best."

Zaidas took another, longer, pull at his goblet. "What we have here, your Majesty, is among the best, let me assure you." The mage was a tall, slim man, about a dozen years younger than Krispos—the first white threads were appearing in the dark fabric of his beard. Krispos remembered him as a skinny, excitable youth, already full of talent. It had not shrunk with his maturity.

Barsymes returned, now with a tureen and two bowls. "Porridge with salted anchovies to break your fast, Your Majesty, excellent sir."

The porridge was of wheat, silky smooth, and rich with cream. The anchovies added piquancy. Krispos knew that if he asked his cook for plain, lumpy barley porridge, the man would quit in disgust. As with the wine, he knew this was better, but sometimes he craved the tastes with which he'd grown up.

When his bowl was about half empty, he said to Zaidas, "The reason I asked you here today was a report I've had from the westlands about a new heresy that seems to have arisen there. By this account, it's an unpleasant one." He passed the mage the letter from the priest Taronites.

Zaidas read it through, his brow furrowing in concentration. When he was done, he looked up at Krispos. "Yes, Your Majesty, if the holy sir's tale is to be fully credited, these Thanasioi seem most unpleasant heretics indeed. But while there is some considerable connection between religion and sorcery, I'd have thought you'd go first to the ecclesiastical authorities rather than to a layman like me."

"In most cases, I would have. In fact, I've already directed the ecumenical patriarch to send priests to Pityos. But these heretics sound so vile—if, as you say, Taronites is to be believed—that I wondered if they have any connection to our old friend Harvas."

Zaidas pursed his lips, then let air hiss out between. Harvas—or perhaps his proper name was Rhavas—had dealt the Empire fierce blows in the north and east in the first years of Krispos' reign. He was, or seemed to be, a renegade priest of Phos who had gone over to the dark god Skotos and thus prolonged his own wicked life more than two centuries beyond its natural terms. With help from Zaidas, among others, Videssian forces had vanquished the Halogai that Harvas led at Pliskavos in Kubrat; his own power was brought to nothing there. But he had not been taken, alive or dead.

"What precisely do you wish me to do, Your Majesty?" Zaidas asked.

"You head the Sorcerers' Collegium these days, my friend, and you were always sensitive to Harvas' style of magic. If anyone can tell through sorcery whether Harvas is the one behind these Thanasioi, I expect you're the man. Is such a thing possible, what with the little we have to go on here?" Krispos tapped Taronites' letter with a forefinger.

"An interesting question." Zaidas looked through rather than at Krispos as he considered. At last he said, "Perhaps it may be done, Your Majesty, though the sorcery required will be most delicate. A basic magical principle is the law of similarity, which is to say, like causes yield like effects. Most effective in this case, I believe, would be an inversion of the law in an effort to determine whether like effects—the disruption and devastation of the Empire now and from Harvas' past depredations— spring from like causes."

"You know your business best," Krispos said. He'd never tried to learn magical theory himself; what mattered to him were the results he might attain through sorcery.

Zaidas, however, kept right on explaining, perhaps to fix his ideas in his own mind. "The law of contagion might also prove relevant. If Harvas was in physical contact with any of these Thanasioi who then came into contact with the priest Taronites, directly or indirectly, such a trace might appear on the parchment here. Under normal circumstances, two or three intermediate contacts would blur the originator beyond hope of detection. Such was Harvas' power, however, and such was our comprehension of the nature of that power, that it ought to be detectable at several more removes."

"Just as you say," Krispos answered agreeably. Perhaps because of his lectures at the Sorcerers' Collegium, Zaidas had a knack for expounding magecraft so clearly that it made sense to the Avtokrator, even if he lacked both ability and interest in practicing it himself. He asked, "How long before you will be ready to try your sorcery?"

That faraway look returned to Zaidas' eyes. "I shall of course require the parchment here. Then the research required to frame the precise terms of the spell to be employed and the gathering of the necessary materials . . .

not that those can't proceed concurrently, of course. Your Majesty, were it war, I could try tomorrow, or perhaps even tonight. I would be more confident of the results obtained, though, if I had another couple of days to refine my original formulation."

"Take the time you need to be right," Krispos said. "If Harvas is at the bottom of this, we must know it. And if he appears not to be, we must be certain he's not concealing himself through his own magic."

"All true, Your Majesty." Zaidas tucked the letter from Taronites into the leather pouch he wore on his belt. He rose and began to prostrate himself again, as one did before leaving the Avtokrator's presence. Krispos waved a hand to tell him not to bother. Nodding, the wizard said, "I shall begin work at once."

"Thanks, Zaidas. If Harvas *is* on the loose—" Krispos let the sentence slide to an awkward halt. If Harvas was stirring up trouble again, he wouldn't sleep well until the wizard-prince was beaten . . . or until he was beaten himself. In the latter case, his sleep would be eternal.

Zaidas knew that as well as he did. "One way or the other, Your Majesty, we shall know," he promised. He bustled off to begin shaping the enchantments he would use to seek Harvas' presence.

Krispos listened to his footfalls fade down the corridor. He counted himself lucky to be served by men of the quality of Zaidas. In his less modest moments, he also thought their presence reflected well on his rule: would such good and able men have served a wicked, foolish master?

He got up from his seat, stretched, and went out into the corridor himself. Coming his way was Phostis. Both men, young and not so young, stopped in their tracks, Krispos in the doorway, his heir in the middle of the hall.

Among all the other things Phostis was, he served as a living reminder that Krispos' rule would not endure forever. Krispos remembered taking him from the midwife's arms and holding him in the crook of his elbow. Now they were almost of a height; Phostis still lacked an inch, maybe two, of Krispos' stature, but Dara had been short.

Phostis was also a living reminder of his mother. Take away his neatly trimmed dark beard—these days thick and wiry, youth's downiness almost gone—and he wore Dara's face: his features were not as craggy as Krispos', and his eyes had the same distinctive small fold of skin at the inner corner that Dara's had.

"Good morning, Father," he said.

"Good morning," Krispos answered, wondering as always if he *was* Phostis' father. The young man did not look like him, but he did not look like Anthimos, either. Phostis did not have Krispos' native obstinacy, that was certain; the one time he'd tried showing the lad how the Empire worked, Phostis quickly lost interest. Krispos' heart ached over that, but he'd seen enough with Anthimos to know a man could not be forced to govern against his will.

Good morning was as much as Krispos and Phostis usually had to say to each other. Krispos waited for his eldest son to walk by without another word, as was his habit. But Phostis surprised him by asking, "Why were you closeted with Zaidas so early, Father?"

"There's some trouble with heresy out in the westlands." Krispos spoke matter-of-factly to keep Phostis from knowing he was startled. If the youngster did want to learn, he would teach him. More likely, though, Krispos thought with a touch of sadness, Phostis asked just for Zaidas' sake; the wizard was like a favorite uncle to him.

"What sort of heresy?" Phostis asked.

Krispos explained the tenets of the Thanasioi as well as he could from Taronites' description of them. This question surprised him less than the previous one; theology was Videssos' favorite intellectual sport. Laymen who pored over Phos' holy scriptures were not afraid to try conclusions with the ecumenical patriarch himself.

Phostis rubbed his chin as he thought, a gesture he shared with Krispos. Then he said, "In the abstract, Father, the doctrines sound rigorous, yes, but not necessarily inspired by Skotos. Their followers may have misinterpreted how these doctrines are to be applied, but—"

"To the ice with the abstract," Krispos growled. "What matters is that these maniacs are laying the countryside to waste and murdering anyone who doesn't happen to agree with them. Save your precious abstract for the schoolroom, son."

"I simply started to say—" Phostis threw his hands in the air. "Oh, what's the use? You wouldn't listen anyhow." Muttering angrily under his breath, he marched down the corridor past Krispos.

The senior Avtokrator sighed as he watched his son's retreating back. Maybe it was better when they just mouthed platitudes at each other: then they didn't fight. But how Phostis could find anything good to say about heretics who were also bandits was beyond Krispos. Only when his heir had turned a corner and disappeared did Krispos remember that he'd interrupted the lad before he finished talking about the Thanasioi.

He sighed again. He'd have to apologize to Phostis the next time he saw him. All too likely, Phostis would take the apology the wrong way and that would start another fight. Well, if it did, it did. Krispos was willing to take

the chance. By the time he thought of going down the corridor and apologizing on the spot, though, it was too late. Phostis had already left the
imperial residence.

Krispos went about the business of governing with only about three-
fourths of his attention for the next couple of days. Every time a messenger or a chamberlain came in, the Avtokrator forgot what he was doing in
the hope the fellow would announce Zaidas' sorcery was ready. Every time
he was disappointed, he went back to work in an evil temper. No miscreants were pardoned while Zaidas prepared his magic.

When at last—within the promised two days, though Krispos tried not
to notice that—Zaidas was on the point of beginning, he came himself to
let the Emperor know. Krispos set aside with relief the cadaster he was
reading. "Lead on, excellent sir!" he exclaimed.

One difficulty with being Avtokrator was that going anywhere automatically became complicated. Krispos could not simply walk with Zaidas
over to the Sorcerers' Collegium. No, he had to be accompanied by a
squad of Haloga bodyguards, which made sense, and by the dozen parasol-
bearers whose bright silk canopies proclaimed his office—which, to his
way of thinking, didn't. Throughout his reign, he'd fought hard to do
away with as much useless ceremonial as he could. He knew he was losing
the fight; custom was a tougher foe than Harvas' blood-maddened barbarians had ever been.

At last, though, not too interminably much later, he stood inside
Zaidas' chamber on the second story of the Sorcerers' Collegium. One big
blond axeman went in there with him and the wizard; two more guarded
the doorway. The rest waited outside the building with the parasol-
bearers.

Zaidas drew forth the parchment on which Taronites had written his
accusations against the Thanasioi. He also produced another parchment,
this one yellowed with age. Seeing Krispos' raised eyebrow, he explained,
"I took the liberty of visiting the archives, Your Majesty, to secure a document indited personally by Harvas. My first spell will compare them
against each other to determine whether a common malice informs both."

"I see," Krispos said, more or less truthfully. "By all means carry on as
if I were not here."

"Oh, I shall, Your Majesty, for my own safety's sake above any other reason," Zaidas said. Krispos nodded. That he understood completely; he'd
seized the crown after Anthimos, intent on destroying him by sorcery,
botched an incantation and slew himself instead.

Zaidas intoned a low-voiced prayer to Phos, ending by sketching the sun-circle over his heart. Krispos imitated the gesture. The Haloga guard did not; like most of his fellows in Videssos the city, he still followed his own nation's fierce and gloomy gods.

The wizard took from a covered dish a couple of red-brown, shriveled objects. "The dried heart and tongue of a porpoise," he said. "They shall confer invincible effect on my charm." He cut strips off them with a knife, as if he were whittling soft wood, then tossed those strips into a squat bowl of bluish liquid. With each additional fragment, the blue deepened.

Stirring his mix left-handed with a silver rod, Zaidas chanted over the bowl and used his right hand to make passes above it. He frowned. "I can feel the wickedness we face here," he said, his voice tight and tense. "Now to learn whether it comes from one parchment or both."

He took the stirring rod and let a couple of drops of the mixture in the bowl fall on a corner of the letter from the archives, the one Harvas had written. The liquid flared bright red, just the color of fresh-spilled blood.

Zaidas drew back a pace. Though he was a layman, he drew the sun-circle again, even so. "By the good god," he murmured, now sounding shocked and shaken. "I never imagined a response as intense as that. Green, even perhaps yellow, but—" He broke off, staring at Harvas' letter as if it were displaying its fangs.

"I take it you expect the petition from Taronites to do the same if Harvas has a hand in turning the Thanasioi loose on us," Krispos said.

"I sincerely hope the solution does not turn crimson, Your Majesty," Zaidas said. "That would in effect mean Harvas lurked just outside the temple wherein Taronites was writing. But the change of color will indicate the degree of relationship between Harvas and these new heretics."

More cautiously than he had before, the wizard daubed some of the liquid onto Taronites' letter. Krispos leaned forward, waiting to see what color the stuff turned. He did not know whether it would go red, but he expected some change, and probably not a small one. By Zaidas' choice of words, so did he.

But the liquid stayed blue.

Both men stared at it; for that matter, so did the bodyguard. Krispos asked, "How long must we wait for the change to take place?"

"Your Majesty, if it was going to occur, it would have done so by now," Zaidas answered. Then he checked himself. "I must always bear in mind that Harvas is a master of concealment and obfuscation. Being such, he might be able to evade this test, porpoise heart or no. But there is a cross check I do not think he can escape, try as he might."

The wizard picked up the two parchments, touched the damp spots on them together. "Being directly present in the one letter, Harvas' essence cannot fail to draw forth from the other any lingering trace of him." He held the two parchments against each other long enough to let a man draw five or six breaths, then separated them.

The blue smear on Taronites' petition remained blue, not green, yellow, orange, red, or even pink. Zaidas looked astonished. Krispos was not only astonished but also profoundly suspicious. He said, "Are you saying this means Harvas has nothing whatever to do with the Thanasioi? I find that hard to believe."

"So do I, Your Majesty," Zaidas said. "If you ask what I say, I say the connection between the two is all too likely. My magic, however, seems to be saying something else again."

"But is your magic right, or have you just been deceived?" Krispos demanded. "Can you tell me for certain, one way or the other? I know you understand how important this is, not just to me but to Videssos now and in the future."

"Yes, Your Majesty. Having faced Harvas once, having seen the evils he worked and those to which he inspired his followers, I know you want to be as positive as possible as to whether you—and we—confront him yet again."

"That is well put," Krispos said. He doubted he could have been so judicious himself. Truth was, as soon as he'd seen Taronites' letter, the fear of Harvas rose up in his mind like a ghost in one of the romances that the booksellers hawked in the plaza of Palamas. No matter what Zaidas' magical tests said about the Thanasioi, his own terror spoke louder to him. So he went on, "Excellent sir, have you any other sorceries you might use to find out whether this one is mistaken?"

"Let me think," Zaidas said, and proceeded to do just that for the next several minutes, standing still as a statue in the center of his study. Suddenly he brightened. "I know something which may serve." He hurried over to a cabinet set against one wall and began opening its small drawers and rummaging through them.

The Haloga guardsman moved to place himself between Krispos and Zaidas, in case the wizard suddenly whipped out a dagger and tried to murder the Avtokrator. This he did though Zaidas was a longtime trusted friend, and though the chamber doubtless held weapons far more fell than mere knives. Krispos smiled but did not seek to dissuade the northerner, who was but doing his duty as he reckoned best.

Zaidas let out a happy grunt. "Here we are." He turned around, displaying not a dagger but rather a piece of highly polished, translucent white stone. "This is nicomar, Your Majesty, a variety of alabaster. When properly evoked, it has the virtue of generating both victory and amity. Thus we shall see if any amity, so to speak, lies between the two letters now in our possession. If so, we shall know Harvas indeed has a hand in the heresy of the Thanasioi."

"Alabaster, you say?" Krispos waited for Zaidas to nod, then continued: "Some of the ceiling panels in the imperial residence are also of alabaster, to let in more light. Why don't, ah, victory and amity always dwell under my roof?" He thought of his unending disagreements with Phostis.

"When properly evoked, I said, the stone brings forth those virtues," Zaidas answered, smiling. "The evocation is not easy, nor is the effect lasting."

"Oh." Krispos hoped he didn't sound too disappointed. "Well, go ahead and do what you need to do, then."

The wizard prayed over the gleaming slab of nicomar and anointed it with sweet-smelling oil, as if it were being made a prelate or an Emperor. Krispos wondered if he would be able to feel the change in the stone, as even a person of no sorcerous talent could feel the curative current that passed between a healer-priest and his patient. To him, though, the nicomar remained simply a stone. He had to trust that Zaidas knew what he was about.

With a final pass that seemed to require nearly jointless fingers, Zaidas said, "The good god willing, we are now ready to proceed. First I shall examine the letter known to have been written by Harvas."

He set the nicomar over the place where he had previously splashed his magical liquid. Fierce red light blazed through the stone. Krispos said, "This tells us what we already knew."

"So it does, Your Majesty," Zaidas answered. "It also tells me the nicomar is performing as it should." He lifted the thin slab of stone and held it over a brass brazier from which the pungent smoke of frankincense coiled slowly toward the ceiling. Before Krispos could ask what he was doing, he explained: "I fumigate the nicomar to remove from it the influence of the parchment it just touched. Thus on the crucial test to come, the workings of the law of contagion shall not be permitted to influence the result. Do you see?"

Without waiting for Krispos' reply, the wizard set the polished alabaster down on the letter from Taronites. Krispos waited for another flash of red. But only a steady blue light penetrated the nicomar. "What does that mean?" Krispos asked, half hoping, half dreading Zaidas would tell him something other than the obvious.

But the wizard did not. "Your Majesty, it means that, so far as my sorcery can determine, no relationship whatever exists between the Thanasioi and Harvas."

"I still find that hard to believe," Krispos said.

"As I told you before, so do I," Zaidas answered. "But if you have a choice between believing whatever you happen to feel at the moment and that which has evidence to support it, which course will you take? I trust I know you well enough to know what you would say were it a matter of law rather than one of magic."

"There you have me," Krispos admitted. "You are so confident in what these conjurations tell you, then?"

"I am, Your Majesty. Were it anyone but Harvas, the first test alone would have contented me. With the confirmation of its import by the nicomar, I would stake my life on the accuracy of what I have divined today."

"You may be doing just that, you know," Krispos said with a grim edge to his voice.

Zaidas looked startled for a moment, then nodded. "Yes, that's so, isn't it? Harvas on the loose once more would terrify the bravest." He spat on the floor between his feet to show his rejection of the evil god Skotos, the god Harvas had for a patron. "But by Phos, the lord with the great and good mind, I tell you again that Harvas is in no way connected to the Thanasioi. Misguided they may be; guided amiss by Harvas they are not."

He sounded so certain that Krispos had to believe him despite his own misgivings. As the sorcerer had said, evidence counted for more than vague feelings. And if Harvas' dread hand did not lie behind the Thanasioi, why, how dangerous could they possibly be? The Avtokrator smiled. Over the past couple of decades, he'd faced and overcome enough merely human foes to trust he had their measure.

"Thank you for relieving my mind, excellent sir. Your reward will not be small," he told Zaidas. Then, because the wizard had a habit of putting such rewards into the treasury of the Sorcerers' Collegium, he added, "Keep some for yourself this time, my friend. I command it."

"You needn't fear for that, Your Majesty," Zaidas said. "In fact, I have already received the same instruction from one I reckon higher in rank than you."

Normally, the only entity a Videssian would reckon higher in rank than his Avtokrator was Phos. Krispos, though, knew perfectly well about whom Zaidas was talking. Chuckling, he said, "Tell Aulissa I say she is a good, sensible woman and makes you an excellent wife. Be sure you listen to her, too."

"I will pass your words to her as you say them," Zaidas promised. "With some other women, I might not, for fear of inflaming their notions of how important they are in the scheme of things. But since my dear Aulissa is as sensible as you say, I know she'll accept the compliment for what it's worth and not a copper more."

"The two of you are a good deal alike that way," Krispos said. "You're lucky to have each other."

Even when Dara was still alive, he'd sometimes envied Zaidas and Aulissa their tranquil happiness. They seemed to know each other's needs and adjust to each other's foibles as if they were two halves of the same person. His own marriage had not been like that. He and Dara got along well enough on the whole, but they'd always had their fall storms and wintry blizzards along with the warmth of summer. Zaidas and his wife seemed to live in late spring the year round.

The wizard said, "Besides, Your Majesty, Aulissa has noted that Sotades is now twelve years old. The boy will soon begin his serious schooling, which, as she pointed out, requires serious quantities of gold."

"Ah, yes," Krispos said wisely, though as Avtokrator he had not had to worry about the expense of educating his sons: every scholar in the city was eager to have any or all of them as his pupils. Having taught the Emperor's child could only improve a savant's reputation . . . and one of those children would likely be Avtokrator himself one day. In Krispos' experience, scholars were no more immune to seeking influence than any other men.

"I am relieved for you, Your Majesty, and for the Empire of Videssos," Zaidas said, nodding toward the table where he'd carried out his magic.

"I'm relieved, too." Krispos picked up the letter from Harvas which the wizard had used and quickly read it. It was the one wherein Harvas declared he had cut out Iakovitzes' tongue because the diplomat's freedom with it displeased him. Krispos was not sorry to put down the parchment. That had been far from the worst of Harvas' atrocities. Being spared the worry of another round of them was worth a goodly sum of gold.

When the Avtokrator left the conjuration chamber, the Haloga guard fell in behind him. The two axemen who had stood watch at the doorway preceded him out of the Sorcerers' Collegium. The parasol-bearers had been sitting around outside the building and passing the time with the rest of the squad of imperial guards. Their canopies fluttered in agitation when the Avtokrator reappeared. After a moment, though, they formed themselves into the neat pairs that always accompanied Krispos in public.

On the trip back to the palace compound, their presence was pure ostentation, for almost the entire short journey was under covered colonnades. Not for the first time—not for the hundredth—Krispos wished he'd been able to get away with cutting the stifling ceremonial that surrounded him every hour of the day and night. But by the horror that thought evoked in the palace staff, in officials of the government, and even among his guards, he might have proposed offering sacrifice to Skotos on the altar of the High Temple. Fights against custom just were not winnable.

He turned around, glanced back north toward the Sorcerers' Collegium. He would reward Zaidas well indeed, not least for relieving his mind. If the Thanasioi had come up with their foolish heresy all on their own, he was sure he would have no trouble putting them down. In his two decades and more as Avtokrator, after all, he'd gone from one triumph to another. Why should this struggle be any different?

Chapter II

F ROM THE OUTSIDE, PHOS' HIGH TEMPLE SEEMED MORE MAS-
sive than beautiful. The heavy buttresses that carried the weight of
the great central dome to the ground reminded Phostis of the thick,
columnar legs of an elephant; one of the immense beasts had been imported to Videssos the city from the southern shore of the Sailors' Sea
when he was a boy. It hadn't lived long, save in his memory.

A poem he'd read likened the High Temple to a glowing pearl concealed
within an oyster. He didn't care as much for that comparison. The Temple's exterior was not rough and ugly, as oysters were, just plain. And its interior outshone any pearl.

Phostis climbed the stairway from the paved courtyard surrounding the
High Temple up to the narthex or outer hall. Being only a junior Avtokrator, he was less hemmed round with ceremony than his father; only a pair
of Haloga guardsmen flanked him on the stairs.

Many nobles hired bodyguards; none of the other people heading for
the service paid Phostis any special heed. The High Temple was not
crowded in any case, not for an early afternoon liturgy on a day of no particular ritual import. Instead of going up the narrow way to the screened-

off imperial niche, Phostis decided to worship with everyone else in the main hall surrounding the altar. The Halogai shrugged and marched in with him.

He'd been going into the High Temple for as long as his memory reached, and longer. He'd been just a baby when he was proclaimed Avtokrator here. For all that infinite familiarity, though, the Temple never failed to awe him.

The lavish use of gold and silver sheeting; the polished moss-agate columns with the acanthus capitals; the jewels and mother-of-pearl inserts set into the blond oak of the pews; the slabs of turquoise, pure white crystal, and rose quartz laid into the walls to simulate the sky at morning, noon, and eventide—for all these he had perspective; he had grown up among similar riches and lived with them still. But they served only to lead the eye up and up to the great dome that surmounted the altar and the mosaicwork image of Phos in its center.

The dome itself had the feel of a special miracle. Thanks to the sunbeams that penetrated the many small windows set into its base, it seemed to float above the rest of the Temple rather than being a part of it. The play of light off the gold-faced tesserae set at irregular angles made its surface sparkle and shift as one walked along far beneath it. Phostis could not imagine how the merely material might better represent the transcendence of Phos' heaven.

But even the glittering surround of the dome was secondary to Phos himself. The lord with the great and good mind stared down at his worshipers with eyes that not only never closed but also seemed to follow as they moved. If anyone concealed a sin, that Phos would see it. His long, bearded visage was stern in judgment. In his left hand, the good god held the book of life, wherein he recorded each man's every action. With death came the accounting: those whose evil deeds outweighed the good would fall to the eternal ice, while those who had worked more good than wickedness shared heaven with their god.

Phostis felt the weight of Phos' gaze each time he entered the High Temple. The lord with the great and good mind shown in the dome would surely grant justice, but mercy? Few men are arrogant enough to demand perfect justice, for fear they might get it.

The power of that image reached even the heathen Halogai. They looked up, trying to test their stares against the eternal eyes in the dome. As generations of men and women had learned before them, the test was more than any a mere man could successfully undertake. When they had to lower their gaze, they did so almost furtively, as if hoping no one had noticed them withdrawing from a struggle.

"It's all right, Bragi, Nokkvi," Phostis murmured as he sat between them. "No man can count himself worthy to confront the good god."

The big blond northerners scowled. Bragi's cheeks went red; with his fair, pale skin, the flush was easy to track. Nokkvi said, "We are Halogai, young Majesty. Our life is to fear nothing, to let nothing overawe us. In this picture dwells magic, to make us reckon ourselves less than what we are." His fingers writhed in an apotropaic sign.

"Measured against the good god, we are all less than we think ourselves to be," Phostis answered quietly. "That is what the image in the dome shows us."

Both his guards shook their heads. Before they could argue further, though, a pair of blue-robed priests, their pates shaven, their beards bushy and untrimmed, advanced down the aisle toward the altar. Each wore on his left breast a cloth-of-gold circlet, symbol of the sun, the greatest source of Phos' lights. The gem-encrusted thuribles they swung emitted great clouds of sweetly fragrant smoke.

As the priests passed each row of pews, the congregants sitting in it rose to their feet to salute Oxeites, ecumenical patriarch of the Videssians, who followed close behind them. His robe was of gold tissue, heavily overlain with pearls and precious stones. In all the Empire, only the Avtokrator himself possessed more splendid raiment. And, just as footgear all of red was reserved for the Emperor alone, so only the patriarch had the privilege of wearing sky-blue boots.

A choir of men and boys sang a hymn of praise to Phos as Oxeites took his place behind the altar. Their sweet notes echoed and reechoed from the dome, as if emanating straight from the good god's lips. The patriarch raised both hands over his head, looked up toward the image of Phos. Along with everyone in the High Temple save only his own two bodyguards, Phostis imitated him.

"We bless thee, Phos, lord with the great and good mind," Oxeites intoned, "by thy grace our protector, watchful beforehand that the great test of life may be decided in our favor."

All the worshipers repeated Phos' creed. It was the first prayer a Videssian heard, being commonly uttered over a newborn babe; it was the first prayer a child learned; it was the last utterance a believer gasped out before dying. To Phostis, it was as utterly familiar as the shape of his own hands.

More prayers and hymns followed. Phostis continued to make his responses without much conscious thought. The ritual was comforting; it lifted him out of himself and his petty cares of the moment, transformed him into part of something great and wise and for all practical purposes immortal. He cherished that feeling of belonging, perhaps because he found it here so much more easily than in the palaces.

Oxeites had the congregation repeat the creed with him one last time, then motioned for the worshipers to be seated. Phostis almost left the High Temple before the patriarch began his sermon. Sermons, being by their nature individual and specific, took him out of the sense of belonging he sought from worship. But since he had nowhere to go except back to the palaces, he decided to stay and listen. Not even his father could rebuke him for piety.

The ecumenical patriarch said, "I would like to have all of you gathered together with me today pause for a moment and contemplate the many and various ways in which the pursuit of wealth puts us in peril of the eternal ice. For in acquiring great stores of gold and gems and goods, we too easily come to consider their accumulation an end in itself rather than a means through which we may provide for our own bodily survival and prepare a path for our progeny."

Our progeny? Phostis thought, smiling. The Videssian clergy was celibate; if Oxeites was preparing a path for *his* progeny, he had more sins than greed with which to concern himself.

The patriarch continued, "Not only do we too readily value goldpieces for their own sake, those of us who do gain riches, whether honestly or no, often also endanger ourselves and our hope of joyous afterlife by grudging those who lack a share, however small, of our own good fortune."

He went on in that vein for some time, until Phostis felt ashamed to have a belly that was never empty, shoes on his feet, and thick robes and hypocausts to warm him through the winter. He raised his eyes to the Phos in the dome and prayed to the lord with the great and good mind to forgive him his prosperity.

But as his gaze descended from the good god to the ecumenical patriarch, he suddenly saw the High Temple in a new, disquieting light. Till this moment, he'd always taken for granted the flood of goldpieces that had been required to erect the Temple in the first place and the further flood that had gone into the precious stones and metals that made it the marvel it was. If those uncounted thousands of goldpieces had instead fed the hungry, shod the barefoot, clothed and warmed the shivering, how much better their lot would have been!

He knew the temples aided the poor; his own father told and retold the story of spending his first night in Videssos the city in the common room of a monastery. But for Oxeites, who wore cloth-of-gold, to urge his listeners to give up what they had to aid those who had not struck Phostis as nothing less than hypocrisy. And worse still, Oxeites himself seemed to have no sense of that hypocrisy.

Anger drove shame from Phostis. How did the ecumenical patriarch have the crust to propose that others give up their worldly goods when he said not a word about those goods the temples owned? Did he think they somehow acquired immunity from being put to good use—being put to the very use he himself advocated—because they were called holy?

By the tone of his sermon, he very likely did. Phostis tried to understand his way of thinking, tried and failed. The junior Avtokrator again glanced up toward the famous image of Phos. How did the lord with the great and good mind view calls to poverty from a man who undoubtedly possessed not just one but many sets of regalia, the value of any of which could have supported a poor family for years?

Phostis decided the good god would set down grim words for Oxeites in his book of judgment.

The patriarch kept preaching. That he did not realize the contradiction inherent in his own views irked Phostis more with every word he heard. He hadn't enjoyed the courses in logic Krispos ordained for him, but they'd left their mark. He wondered if next he would hear a raddled whore extolling the virtues of virginity. It would, he thought, be hardly less foolish than what he was listening to now.

"We bless thee, Phos, lord with the great and good mind, by thy grace our protector, watchful beforehand that the great test of life may be decided in our favor," Oxeites proclaimed for the last time. Even without his robes, he would have been tall and slim and distinguished, with a pure white beard and silky eyebrows he surely combed. When he wore the patriarchal vestments, he seemed to the eye the very image of holiness. But his words rang hollow in Phostis' heart.

Most of the worshipers filed out of the High Temple after the liturgy was over. A few, though, went up to the ecumenical patriarch to congratulate him on his sermon. Phostis shook his head, bemused. Were they deaf and blind, or merely out to curry favor? Either way, Phos would judge them in due course.

As he walked down the steps from the Temple to the surrounding courtyard, Phostis turned to one of his guardsmen and said, "Tell me, Nokkvi, do you Halogai house your gods so richly in your own country?"

Nokkvi's ice-blue eyes went wide. He threw back his head and boomed laughter; the long blond braid he wore bounced up and down as his shoulders shook. When he could speak again, he answered, "Young Majesty, in Halogaland we have not so much for ourselves that we can give our gods such spoils as you fashion for your Phos. In any case, our gods care more for blood than for gold. There we feed them well."

Phostis knew of the northern gods' thirst for gore. The holy Kveldulf, a Haloga who came to revere Phos, was reckoned a martyr in Videssos: his own countrymen had slaughtered him when he tried to convert them to worshiping the lord with the great and good mind. Indeed, the Halogai would have been far more dangerous foes to the Empire did they not incessantly shed one another's blood.

Nokkvi stepped down on the flat flagstones of the courtyard. When he turned to look back at the High Temple, his gaze went wolfish. He said, "I tell you this, too, young Majesty: let but a few shiploads full of my folk free to reive in Videssos the city, and your god, too, will know less of gold and more of blood. Maybe that savor will better satisfy him."

Phostis gestured to turn aside the northerner's words. The Empire was still rebuilding and repeopling towns that Harvas' Halogai had sacked around the time he was born. But even having such a store of riches here in the imperial capital was a temptation not just to the fierce barbarians from the north, but also to avaricious men within the Empire. Any store of riches was such, in fact.

He stopped, his mouth falling open. All at once, he began to understand how the Thanasioi came by their doctrines.

THE GREAT BRONZE VALVES OF THE DOORWAY TO THE GRAND Courtroom slowly swung open. Seated on the imperial throne, Krispos got a sudden small glimpse of the outside world. He smiled; the outside world seemed only most distantly connected to what went on here.

He sometimes wondered whether the Grand Courtroom wasn't even more splendid than the High Temple. Its ornaments were less florid, true, but to them was added the ever-changing spectacle of the rich robes worn by the nobles and bureaucrats who lined either side of the colonnade leading from the bronze doors to Krispos' throne. The way between the two columns was a hundred yards of emptiness that let any petitioner think on his own insignificance and the awesome might of the Avtokrator.

In front of the throne stood half a dozen Haloga guardsmen in full battle gear. Krispos had read in the histories of previous reigns that one Emperor had been assassinated on the throne and three others wounded. He did not aim to provide similarly edifying reading for any distant successor.

A herald, distinguished by a white-painted staff, had his place beside the northerners. He took one step forward. The courtiers left off their own chattering. Into the silence, the herald said, "Tribo, the envoy from Nobad, son of Gumush, the khagan of Khatrish, begs leave to approach the Avtokrator of the Videssians." His trained voice was easily audible from one end of the Grand Courtroom to the Other.

"Let Tribo of Khatrish approach," Krispos said.

"Let Tribo of Khatrish approach!" Sprung from the herald's thick chest, the words might have been a command straight from the mouth of Phos.

From a small silhouette in the bright but distant doorway, Tribo grew to man-size as he sauntered up the aisle toward the throne. He slowed every so often to exchange a smile or a couple of words with someone he knew, thereby largely defeating the intimidation built into that walk.

Krispos had expected nothing less; Khatrishers seemed born to subvert any existing order. Even their nation was less than three centuries old, born when Khamorth nomads from the plains of Pardraya overran what had been Videssian provinces. To some degree, they aped the Empire these days, but their ways remained looser than those that were in good form among Videssians.

Tribo paused the prescribed distance from the imperial throne, sinking down to his knees and then to his belly in full proskynesis: some Videssian rituals could not be scanted. As the envoy remained with his forehead pressed against the polished marble of the floor, Krispos tapped the left arm of the throne. With a squeal of gears, it rose several feet in the air. The marvel was calculated to overawe barbarians. From his new height, Krispos said, "You may rise, Tribo of Khatrish."

"Thank you, Your Majesty." Like most of his folk, the ambassador spoke Videssian with a slight lisping accent. In Videssian robes, he could have passed for an imperial but for his beard, which was longer and more unkempt than even a priest would wear. The khagans of Khatrish encouraged that style among their upper classes, to remind them of the nomad raiders from whom they had sprung. Tribo was also un-Videssian in his lack of concern for the imperial dignity. Cocking his head to one side, he remarked, "I think your chair needs oiling, Your Majesty."

"You may be right," Krispos admitted with a sigh. He tapped the arm of the throne again. With more metallic squeaks, servitors behind the courtroom wall returned him to his former place.

Tribo did not quite smirk, but the expression he assumed shouted that he would have, in any other company. He definitely was less than overawed. Krispos wondered if that meant he couldn't be reckoned a barbarian. Perhaps so: Khatrish's usages were not those of Videssos, but they had their own kind of understated sophistication.

All that was by the way—though Krispos did make a mental note that he need not put the crew of musclemen behind the wall next time he granted Tribo a formal audience. The Avtokrator said, "Shall we to business, then?"

"By all means, Your Majesty." Tribo was not rude, certainly not by his own people's standards and not really by the Empire's, either. He just had a hard time taking seriously the elaborate ceremonial in which Videssos delighted. The moment matters turned substantive, his half-lazy, half-insolent manner dropped away like a discarded cloak.

As Avtokrator, Krispos had the privilege of speaking first: "I am not pleased that your master the khagan Nobad son of Gumush has permitted herders from Khatrish to come with their flocks into territory rightfully Videssian, and to drive our farmers away from the lands near the border. I have written to him twice about this matter, with no improvement. Now I bring it to your attention."

"I shall convey your concern to his mighty Highness," Tribo promised. "He in turn complains that the recently announced Videssian tariff on amber is outrageously high and is being collected with overharsh rigor."

"The second point may perhaps concern him more than the first," Krispos said. Amber from Khatrish was a monopoly of the khagan's; his profits on its sale to Videssos helped fatten his treasury. The tariff let the Empire profit, too. Krispos had also beefed up customs patrols to discourage smuggling. In his younger days, he'd been to Opsikion near the border with Khatrish and seen amber smugglers in action. The firsthand knowledge helped combat them.

Tribo assumed an expression of outraged innocence. "The khagan Nobad son of Gumush wonders at the justice of a sovereign who seeks lower tolls from the King of Kings on his western border at the same time as he imposes higher ones to the detriment of Khatrish."

A low mutter ran through the courtiers; few Videssians would have spoken so freely to the Avtokrator. Krispos doubted whether Nobad knew about his discussions with Rubyab of Makuran over caravan tolls. Tribo, however, all too obviously did, and served his khagan well thereby.

"I might reply that any soverign's chief duty is to promote the advantage of his own realm," Krispos said slowly.

"So you might, were you not Phos' viceregent on earth," Tribo replied.

The mutter from the nobles got louder. Krispos said, "I do not find it just, eminent envoy, for you who are a heretic to use to your own ends my position in the faith as practiced within Videssos."

"I crave Your Majesty's pardon," Tribo said at once. Krispos stared suspiciously; he hadn't thought things would be that easy. They weren't. Tribo resumed, "Since you reminded me I am a heretic in your eyes, I will employ my own usages and ask you where in the Balance justice lies."

Videssian orthodoxy held that Phos would at the end of time surely vanquish Skotos. Theologians in the eastern lands of Khatrish and Thatagush, however, had needed to account for the eruption of the barbarous and ferocious Khamorth into their lands and the devastation resulting therefrom. They proclaimed that good and evil lay in perfect balance, and no man could be certain which would triumph in the end. Anathemas from Videssos the city failed to bring them back to what the Empire reckoned the true faith; abetted by the eastern khagans, they hurled anathemas of their own.

Krispos had no use for the Balancer heresy, but he had trouble denying that it was just for Khatrish to expect consistency from him. Concealing a sigh, he said, "Room for discussion about how we impose the tariffs may possibly exist."

"Your Majesty is gracious." Tribo sounded sincere; maybe he even was.

"As may be," Krispos said. "I also have complaints that ships from out of Khatrish have stopped and robbed several fishing boats off the coast of our dominions, and even taken a cargo of furs and wine off a merchantman. If such piracy goes on, Khatrish will face the Empire's displeasure. Is that clear?"

"Yes, Your Majesty," Tribo said, again sincerely. Videssos' navy was vastly stronger than Khatrish's. If the Avtokrator so desired, he could ruin the khaganate's sea commerce without much effort.

"Good," Krispos said. "Mind you, I'll expect to see a change in what your people do; fancy promises won't be enough." Anyone who didn't spell that out in large letters to a Khatrisher deserved the disappointment he would get. But Tribo nodded; Krispos had reason to hope the message was fully understood. He asked, "Have you any more matters to raise at this time, eminent envoy?"

"Yes, Your Majesty, may it please you, I do."

The reply caught Krispos by surprise; the agenda he'd agreed upon with the Khatrisher before the audience was complete. But he said, as he had to, "Speak, then."

"Thank you for your patience, Your Majesty. But for the theological, er, discussion we just had, I would not presume to mention this. However: I know you believe that we who follow the Balance are heretics. Still, I must question the justice of inflicting upon us your own different and, if I may say so, more pernicious heresies."

"Eminent sir, I hope you in turn will forgive me, but I haven't the faintest idea of what you're talking about," Krispos answered.

Tribo's look said he'd thought the Emperor above stooping to such tawdry denials. That only perplexed Krispos the more; as far as he knew, he was telling the truth. Then the ambassador said, as scornfully as he could to a sovereign stronger than his own, "Do you truly try to tell me you have never heard of the murderous wretches who call themselves Thanasioi? Ah, I see by your face that you have."

"Yes, I have; at my command, the most holy sir the ecumenical patriarch Oxeites is even now convening a synod to condemn them. But how do you know of their heresy? So far as I have learned, it's confined to the westlands, near our frontier with Makuraner-held Vaspurakan. Few places in the Empire of Videssos lie farther from Khatrish."

"That may be so, Your Majesty, but merchants learn the goods most worth shipping a long way are those with the least bulk," Tribo said. "Ideas, so far as I know, have no bulk at all. Perhaps some seamen picked up the taint in Pityos. Be that as it may, we have bands of Thanasioi in a couple of our coastal towns."

Krispos ground his teeth. If Khatrish held Thanasioi, their doctrines had undoubtedly spread to Videssian ports, as well. And that meant Videssos the city probably—no, certainly—had Thanasioi prowling its streets. "By the good god, eminent envoy, I swear we've not tried to spread this heresy to your land. Very much the opposite, in fact."

"Your Majesty has said it," Tribo said, by which Krispos knew that were he addressing anyone save the Avtokrator of the Videssians, he would have called him a liar. Perhaps realizing that even by Khatrisher standards he'd been overblunt, the envoy went on, "I pray your forgiveness, Your Majesty, but you must understand that, from the perspective of my master Nobad son of Gumush, stirring up religious strife within our bounds is a ploy Videssos might well attempt."

"Yes, I can see that it might be," Krispos admitted. "You may tell your master, though, that it's a ploy I don't care to use. Since Videssos should have only one faith, I'm not surprised to find other sovereigns holding the same view."

"Please note I intend it for a compliment when I say that, for an Avtokrator of the Videssians, you are a moderate man," Tribo said. "Most men who wear the red buskins would say there should be only one faith through all the world, and that the one which emanates from Videssos the city."

Krispos hesitated before he answered; Tribo's "compliment" had teeth

in it. Because Videssos had once ruled all the civilized world east of Makuran, universality was a cornerstone of its dealings with other states and of
its theology. To deny that universality would give Krispos' nobles an excuse to mutter among themselves. He wanted them to have no such ex-
cuses.

At last he said, "Of course there should be only one faith; how else may
a realm count on its folk remaining loyal to it? But since we have not met
that ideal in Videssos, we would be in a poor position to pursue it elsewhere. Besides, eminent envoy, if you accuse us of introducing a new
heresy into Khatrish, you can hardly at the same time accuse us of trying
to force your people into orthodoxy."

Tribo's mouth twisted into a smile that lifted only one corner of it.
"The first argument has some weight, Your Majesty. As for the second
one, I'd like it better in a school of logic than I do in the world. You could
well hope to throw us into such religious strife that your folk might enter
Khatrish and be acclaimed as rescuers."

"Your master Nobad son of Gumush is well served in you, eminent
envoy," Krispos said. "You see more facets in a matter than a jeweler could
carve."

"Thank you, Your Majesty!" Tribo actually beamed. "Coming from a
man with twenty-two years on the throne of Videssos, there's praise indeed.
I shall convey to his mighty Highness that Videssos is itself plagued by
these Thanasioi and not responsible for visiting them upon my country."

"I hope you do, for that is the truth."

"Your Majesty." Tribo prostrated himself once more, then rose and
backed away from the throne until he had gone far enough to turn around
without offending the Avtokrator of the Videssians. As far as Krispos was
concerned, the ambassador could simply have turned his back and walked
away, but the imperial dignity did not permit such ordinary behavior in
his presence. He sometimes thought of his office as having a personality of
its own, and a stuffy one at that.

Before he left the Grand Courtroom, he reminded himself to have the
gear train behind his throne oiled.

"GOOD MORNING, YOUR MAJESTY." WITH A MOCKING SMILE ON
his face, Evripos made as if to perform a proskynesis right in the middle of
the corridor.

"By the good god, little brother, let it be," Phostis said wearily. "You're
just as much—and just as little—Avtokrator as I am.

"That's true, for now. But I'll forever be just as little Avtokrator as you are, where after a while I won't be just as much. Do you expect me to be happy about that, just because you were born first? I'm sorry, Your Majesty"—the scorn Evripos put into the title was withering—"but you ask too much."

Phostis wished he could punch his brother in the face, as he had when they were boys. But Evripos was his little brother now only in age; he had most of a palm on Phostis in height and was thicker through the shoulders to boot. These days, he'd be the one to do most of the punching in a fight.

"I can't help being eldest, any more than you can help being born second," Phostis said. "Only one of us will be able to rule when the time comes; that's just the way things are. But who better than my brothers to—"

"—be your lapdogs," Evripos broke in, looking down his long nose at Phostis. Like Phostis, he had his mother's distinctive eyes, but the rest of his features were those of Krispos. Phostis also suspected Evripos had more of their father's driving ambition than he himself had . . . or perhaps it was simply that Evripos was in a position where ambition stood out more. If events continued in their expected course, Phostis would be *the* Avtokrator of the Videssians. Evripos wanted the job, but was unlikely to get it by any legitimate means.

Phostis said, "Little brother, you and Katakolon can be my mainstays on the throne. Better to have family aid a man than outsiders—safer, too." *If I can trust you,* he added to himself.

"So you say now," Evripos retorted. "But I've had to read the historians just as you have. Once one son becomes Emperor, what's left for the others? Nothing, maybe less. They only show up in the books because they've raised a rebellion or else because they get a name for debauchery."

"Who gets a name for debauchery?" Katakolon asked as he came down the corridor of the imperial residence. He grinned at his two grim-faced brothers. "Me, I hope."

"You're well on your way to it, that's certain," Phostis told him. The remark should have been cutting; instead, it came out with an unmistakable ring of envy. Katakolon's grin got wider.

Phostis felt like punching him, too, but he was Evripos' size or bigger. Like Evripos, he favored Krispos in looks. Of the three of them, though, he had the sunny disposition. Being the heir set heavy responsibilities on Phostis. Evripos saw only Phostis standing between him and what he wanted. Both older brothers had better claims to the throne than Katakolon, who didn't seem interested in sitting on it, anyhow. All he wanted was to enjoy himself, which he did.

Evripos said, "His imperial Majesty here is deigning to parcel out to us our subordinate duties once he becomes senior Avtokrator."

"Well, why not?" Katakolon said. "That's how it's going to be, unless Father ties him in a weighted sack and flings him into the Cattle-Crossing. Father might, too, the way they go at each other."

Had Evripos said that, Phostis probably would have hit him. From Katakolon, it was just so many words. Not only was the youngest brother slow to take offense, he had trouble giving it, too.

Katakolon went on, "I know one of the subordinate duties I'd like, come the day: supervising the treasury subbureau that collects taxes from within the city walls."

"By the good god, why?" Evripos said, beating Phostis to the punch. "Isn't that rather too much like work for your taste?"

"That subbureau of the treasury collects tax receipts from and generally has charge of the city's brothels." Katakolon licked his lips. "I'm certain any Avtokrator would appreciate the careful inspection I'd give them."

For once, Phostis and Evripos looked equally disgusted. It wasn't that Evripos failed to delight in venery; he was at least as bold a man of his lance as Katakolon. But Evripos did what he did without chortling about it to all and sundry afterward. Phostis suspected he was disgusted with Katakolon more for revealing a potential vulnerability than for his choice of supervisory position.

Phostis said, "If we don't stick together, brothers, there are plenty in the city who would turn us against one another, for their own benefit rather than ours."

"I'm too busy with my own tool to become anyone else's," Katakolon declared, at which Phostis threw up his hands and stalked away.

He thought about going to the High Temple to ask Phos to grant his brothers some common sense, but decided not to. After Oxeites' hypocritical sermon, the High Temple, an edifice in which he had taken pride like almost every other citizen of Videssos the city and indeed of the Videssian Empire, now seemed only a repository for mountains of gold that could have been better spent in countless other ways. He could hate the ecumenical patriarch for that alone, for destroying the beauty and grandeur of the Temple in his mind.

As he stamped out of the imperial residence, a pair of Halogai from the squadron at the entrance attached themselves to him. He didn't want them, but knew the futility of ordering them back to their post—they would just answer, in their slow, serious northern voices, that *he* was their post.

Instead, he tried to shake them off. They were, after all, encumbered with mail shirts, helms, and two-handed axes. For a little while, he thought he might succeed; sweat poured down their faces as they sped up to match his own quick walk, and their fair skins grew pink with exertion. But they were warriors, in fine fettle, and refused to wilt in heat worse than any for which their northern home had prepared them. They clung to him like limpets.

He slowed down as he reached the borders of the palace compound and started across the crowded plaza of Palamas. He thought of losing himself among the swarms of people there, but, before he could transform thought to deed, the Halogai moved up on either side of him and made a break impossible.

He was even glad of their presence as he traversed the square. Their broad, mailed shoulders and forbidding expressions helped clear a path through the hucksters, soldiers, housewives, scribes, whores, artists, priests, and folk of every other sort who used the plaza as a place wherein to sell, to buy, to gossip, to cheat, to proclaim, or simply to gawp.

Once Phostis got to the far side of the plaza of Palamas, he headed east along Middle Street without even thinking about it. He walked past the red granite pile of the government office building before he consciously realized what he'd done: a few more blocks, a left turn, and his feet would have taken him to the High Temple even though the rest of him didn't want to go there.

He glared down at his red boots, as if wondering if his brothers had somehow suborned them. With slow deliberation, he turned right rather than left at the next corner. He made a few more turns at random, leaving behind the familiar main street of Videssos the city for whatever its interior might bring him.

The Halogai muttered back and forth in their own language. Phostis could guess what they were saying: something to the effect that two guards might not be enough to keep him out of trouble in this part of town. He pushed ahead anyhow, reasoning that although bad things could happen, odds were they wouldn't.

Away from Middle Street and a few other thoroughfares, Videssos the city's streets—lanes might have been a better word, or even alleys—forgot whatever they might have known about the idea of a straight line. The narrow little ways were made to seem narrower still because the upper stories of buildings extended out over the cobblestones toward each other.

The city had laws regulating how close together they could come, but if any inspector had been through this section lately, he'd been bribed to look up with a blind eye toward the scrawny strip of blue that showed between balconies.

People on the streets gave Phostis curious looks as he walked along: it was not a district in which nobles in fine robes commonly appeared. No one bothered him, though; evidently two big Haloga guards *were* enough. A barmaid-pretty girl of about his own age stopped and smiled at him. She drew up one hand to toy with her hair and incidentally show off her breasts to the best advantage. When he didn't pause, she gave him the two-fingered street gesture that implied he was effeminate.

The shops in this part of town kept their doors closed. When a customer opened one, Phostis saw its timbers were thick enough to grace a citadel. But for their doors, probably just as thick, houses presented blank fronts of stucco or brick to the street. Though that was normal in Videssos the city, most dwellings being built around courtyards, here it seemed as if they were making a point of concealing whatever they had.

Phostis was on the point of trying to make his way back to Middle Street and his own part of town when he came upon men in ragged cloaks and worker's tunics and women in cheap, faded dresses filing into a building that at first looked no more prepossessing than any other hereabouts. But on its roof was a wooden tower topped with a globe whose gilding had seen better days: this, too, was a temple to Phos, though as different from the High Temple as could be imagined.

He smiled and made for the entrance. He'd wanted to pray when he left the palaces, but hadn't been able to stomach listening to Oxeites celebrate the liturgy again. Maybe the good god had guided his footsteps hither.

The ordinary people going in to pray didn't seem to think Phos had anything to do with it. The stares they gave Phostis weren't curious; they were downright hostile. A man wearing the bloodstained leather apron of a butcher said, "Here, friend, don't you think you'd be more content praying somewheres else?"

"Somewhere fancy, like you are?" a woman added. She didn't sound admiring; to her the word was one of reproach.

Some of the shabby band of worshipers carried knives on their belts. In a run-down part of the city like this, snatching up paving stones to hurl would be the work of a moment. The Halogai realized that before Phostis did, and moved to put themselves between him and what could become a mob.

"Wait," he said. Neither northerner even turned to look at him. Keep-

ing their eyes on the crowd in front of the little temple, they wordlessly
shook their heads. He was barely tall enough to peer at the people over
their armored shoulders. Pitching his voice to carry to the Videssians, he
declared, "I've had my fill of worshiping Phos at fancy temples. How can
we hope the good god will hear us if we talk about helping the poor in a
building richer than even the Avtokrator enjoys?"

No one had noticed his red boots. Behind the Halogai, they would be
all but invisible. Like the people in the streets, the congregants must have
taken him for merely a noble out slumming. His words made the city folk
pause and murmur among themselves.

After a small pause, the butcher said, "You really mean that, friend?"

"I do," Phostis answered loudly. "By the lord with the great and good
mind, I swear it."

Either his words or his tone must have carried conviction, for the band
of worshipers stopped scowling and began to beam. The butcher, who
seemed to be their spokesman, said, "Friend, if you do mean that, you can
hear what our priest, the good god bless him, has to say. We don't even ask
that you keep quiet about it afterward, for it's sound doctrine. Am I right,
my friends?"

Everyone around him nodded. Phostis wondered whether this congregation employed *friend* as a general term or if it was just the man's way of
speaking. He rather hoped the former was true. The usage might be unusual among Phos' followers, but he liked its spirit.

Still grumbling, the Halogai grudgingly let him go into the temple,
though one preceded him and the other followed close behind. A few
icons with images of Phos hung on the roughly plastered walls; otherwise,
the place was bare of ornament. The altar behind which the priest stood
was of carven pine. His blue robe, of the plainest wool, lacked even a
cloth-of-gold circle above his heart to symbolize Phos' sun.

The good god's creed and liturgy, though, remained the same regardless
of setting. Phostis followed this priest as easily as he had the ecumenical
patriarch. The only difference was that this ecclesiastic spoke with an up-
country accent even stronger than that of Krispos, who had worked hard
to shed his peasant intonation. The priest came from the west, Phostis
judged, not from the north like his father.

When the required prayers were over, the priest surveyed his congregants. "I rejoice that the lord with the great and good mind has brought
you back to me once more, friends," he said. His eyes fixed on Phostis and
the Haloga guards as he uttered that last word, as if he wondered whether
they deserved to come under it.

Giving them the benefit of the doubt, he continued: "Friends, we have not been cursed with much in the way of material abundance." Again he gave Phostis a measuring stare. "I praise the lord with the great and good mind for that, for we have not much to give away before we come to be judged in front of his holy throne."

Phostis blinked; this was not the sort of theological reasoning he was used to hearing. This priest took off from the point at which Oxeites had halted. But he, unlike the patriarch, lacked hypocrisy. He was plainly as poor as his temple and his congregation. That in and of itself inclined Phostis to take him seriously.

He went on, "How can we hope to rise to the heavens while weighted down with gold in our belt pouches? I will not say it cannot be, friends, but I say that few of the rich live lives sufficiently saintly to rise above the dross they value more than their souls."

"That's right, holy sir!" a woman exclaimed. Someone else, a man this time, added, "Tell the truth!"

The priest picked that up and set it into his sermon as neatly as a mason taking a brick from a new pile. "Tell the truth I shall, friends. The truth is that everything the foolish rich run after is but a snare from Skotos, a lure to drag them down to his eternal ice. If Phos is the patron of our souls, as we know him to be, then how can material things be his concern? The answer is simple, friends: they cannot. The material world is Skotos' plaything. Rejoice if you have but little share therein; would it were true for all of us. The greatest service we can render to one who knows not this truth is to deprive him of that which ties him to Skotos, thereby liberating his soul to contemplate the higher good."

"Yes," a woman cried, her voice high and breathy, as if in ecstasy. "Oh, yes!"

The butcher who had spoken to Phostis still sounded solid and matter-of-fact. "I pray that you guide us in our renunciation of the material, holy sir."

"Let your own knowledge of moving toward Phos' holy light be your guide, friend," the priest answered. "What you renounce is yours only in this world at best. Will you risk an eternity in Skotos' ice for its sake? Only a fool would act so."

"We're no fools," the butcher said. "We know——" He broke off to give Phostis yet another measuring stare; by this time, Phostis was sick of them. Whatever he had been about to say, he reconsidered, starting again after a barely noticeable pause: "We know what we know, by the good god."

The rest of the people in the shabby temple knew whatever it was the butcher knew. They called out in agreement, some loudly, some softly, all with more belief and piety in their voices than Phostis had ever heard from the prominent folk who most often prayed in the High Temple. His brief anger at being excluded from whatever they knew soon faded. He wished he could find something to believe in with as much force as these people gave to their faith.

The priest raised his hands to the heavens, then spat between his feet in ritual rejection of Skotos. He led the worshipers in Phos' creed one last time, then announced the end of the liturgy. As Phostis turned and left the temple, once more bracketed fore and aft by his bodyguards, he felt a sense of loss and regret on returning to the mundane world that he'd never known when departing from the superficially more awesome setting of the High Temple. An impious comparison crossed his mind: it was almost as if he were returning to himself after the piercing pleasure of the act of love.

He shook his head. As the priest had said, what were those thrashings and moanings, what were any earthly delights, if they imperiled his soul?

"Excuse me," someone said from behind him: the butcher. Phostis turned. So did the Halogai with him. The axes twitched in their hands, as if hungry for blood. The butcher ignored them; he spoke to Phostis as if they were not there: "Friend, you seem to have thought well of what you heard in the temple. That's just a hunch of mine, mind you—if I'm wrong, you tell me and I'll go my way."

"No, good sir, you're not wrong." Phostis wished he'd thought to say "friend," too. Well, too late now. He continued, "Your priest there preaches well, and has a fiery heart like few I've heard. What good is wealth if it hides in a hoard or is wantonly wasted when so many stand in need?"

"What good is wealth?" the butcher said, and let it go at that. If his eye flicked over the fine robe Phostis wore, they did so too fast for the younger man to notice. The butcher went on, "Maybe you would like to hear more of what the holy sir—his name's Digenis, by the way—has to say, and hear it in a more private setting?"

Phostis thought about that. "Maybe I would," he said at last, for he did want to hear the priest again.

Had the butcher smiled or shown triumph, his court-sharpened suspicions would have kindled. But the fellow only gave a sober nod. That convinced Phostis of his sincerity, if nothing more. He decided he would indeed try to have that more private audience with Digenis. He'd found this morning that shaking off his bodyguards was anything but easy. Still, there might be ways . . .

Katakolon stood in the doorway to the study, waiting until Krispos chanced to look up from the tax register he was examining. Eventually Krispos did. He put down his pen. "What is it, son? Come in if you have something on your mind."

By the nervous way in which Katakolon approached his desk, Krispos could make a pretty good guess as to what "it" might be. His youngest son confirmed that guess when he said, "May it please you, Father, I should like to request another advance on my allowance." His smile, usually so sunny, had the hangdog air it assumed whenever he had to beg money from his father.

Krispos rolled his eyes. "*Another* advance? What did you spend it on this time?"

"An amber-and-emerald bracelet for Nitria," Katakolon said sheepishly.

"Who's Nitria?" Krispos asked. "I thought you were sleeping with Varina these days."

"Oh, I still am, Father," Katakolon assured him. "The other one's new. That's why I got her something special."

"I see," Krispos said. He did, too, in a strange sort of way. Katakolon was a lad who generally liked to be liked. With a youth's enthusiasm and stamina, he also led a love life more complicated than any bureaucratic document. Krispos knew a small measure of relief that he'd managed to remember the name of his son's current—or, by the sound of things, soon to be current but one—favorite. He sighed. "How much of an allowance do you get every month?"

"Twenty goldpieces, Father."

"That's right, twenty goldpieces. Do you have any idea how old I was, son, before I had twenty goldpieces to my name, let alone twenty every month of the year? When I was your age, I—"

"—lived on a farm that grew only nettles, and you ate worms three meals a day," Katakolon finished for him. Krispos glared. His son said, "You make that same speech every time I ask you for money, Father."

"Maybe I do," Krispos said. Thinking about it, he was suddenly certain he did. That annoyed him; was he getting predictable as he got older? Being predictable could also be dangerous. But he added, "You'd be better off if you hadn't heard it so many times you've committed it to memory."

"Yes, Father," Katakolon said dutifully. "May I please have the advance?"

Sometimes Krispos gave in, sometimes he didn't. The cadaster he'd put down so he could talk with his son brought good news: the fisc had gained more revenue than expected from the province just south of the Paristrian Mountains, the province where he'd been born. Gruffly he said, "Very well. I suppose you haven't managed to bankrupt us yet, boy. But not another copper ahead of time till after Midwinter's Day, do you understand me?"

"Yes, Father. Thank you, Father." Little by little, Katakolon's merry expression turned apprehensive. "Midwinter's Day is still a long way off, Father." Like anyone who knew Krispos well, the Avtokrator's third son also knew he was not in the habit of making warnings just to hear himself talk. When he said something, he meant it.

"Try living within your means," Krispos suggested. "I didn't say I was cutting you off without a copper, only that I wouldn't give you any more money ahead of time till then. The good god willing, I won't have to do it afterward, either. But you notice I didn't demand that."

"Yes, Father." Katakolon's voice tolled like a mourning bell.

Krispos fought to keep his face straight; he remembered how much he'd hated to be laughed at when he was a youth. "Cheer up, son. By anyone's standards, twenty goldpieces a month is a lot of money for a young man to get his hands on. You'll be able to entertain your lady friends in fine style during that little while when you're not in bed with them." Katakolon looked so flabbergasted, Krispos had to smile. "I recall how many rounds I could manage back in my own younger days, boy. I can't match that now, but believe me, I've not forgotten."

"Whatever you say, Father. I do thank you for the advance, though I'd be even more grateful if you'd not tied that string round its leg." Katakolon dipped his head and went off to pursue his own affairs—very likely, Krispos thought, in the most literal sense of the word.

As soon as his son was out of earshot, Krispos did laugh. Young men could not imagine what being older was like; they lacked the experience. Perhaps because of that, they didn't believe older men retained the slightest notion of what being young meant. But Krispos knew that wasn't so; his younger self dwelt within him yet, covered over with years but still emphatically there.

He wasn't always proud of the young man he had been. He'd done a lot of foolish things, as young men will. It wasn't because he'd been stupid; he'd just been callow. If he'd known then what he knew now . . . He laughed again, this time at himself. Graybeards had been singing that song since the world began.

He went back to his desk and finished working through the tax register. He wrote *I have read and approved—Krispos* in scarlet ink at the bottom of the parchment. Then, without so much as looking at the report that lay beneath it, he got up from the desk, stretched, and walked out into the hallway.

When he got near the entrance to the imperial residence, he almost bumped into Barsymes, who was coming out of the small audience chamber there. The vestiarios' eyes widened slightly. "I'd expected you would still be hard at the morning's assemblage of documents, Your Majesty."

"To the ice with the morning's assemblage of documents, Barsymes," Krispos declared. "I'm going fishing."

"Very well, Your Majesty. I shall set the preparations in train directly."

"Thank you, esteemed sir," Krispos said. Even something as simple as a trip to the nearest pier was not free from ceremony for an Avtokrator of the Videssians. The requisite twelve parasol-bearers had to be rounded up; the Haloga captain had to be alerted so he could provide the even more requisite squadron of bodyguards.

Krispos endured the wait with the patience that years of waiting had taught him. He chose several flexible cane rods, each a little taller than he was, from a rack in a storage room, and a rather greater number of similar lengths of horsehair line. In the tackle box beside the rack of fishing poles were a good many barbed hooks of bronze. He preferred that metal to iron; though softer, it needed less care after being dunked in salt water.

Off in the kitchens, a servant would be catching him cockroaches for bait. He'd done it himself once, but only once; it scandalized people worse than any of Anthimos' ingenious perversions had ever managed to do.

"All is in readiness, Your Majesty," Barsymes announced after a delay shorter than Krispos had expected. He held out to the Emperor an elaborately chased brass box from Makuran. Krispos accepted it with a grave nod. Only tiny skittering noises revealed that inside the elegant artifact were frantic brown-black bugs about the size of the last joint of his thumb.

The palace compound boasted several piers at widely spaced points along the sea wall; Krispos sometimes wondered if they'd been built to give an overthrown Avtokrator the best chance for escape by sea. As he and his retinue paraded toward the one closest to the imperial residence, though, he stopped worrying about blows against the state or against his person. When he stepped down into the little rowboat tied there, he was as nearly free as an Emperor could be.

Oh, true, a couple of Halogai got into another rowboat and followed him as he rowed out into the lightly choppy waters of the Cattle-Crossing. Their strokes were strong and sure; scores of narrow inlets pierced the rocky soil of Halogaland, so its sons naturally took to the ocean.

And true, a light war galley would also put to sea, in case conspirators mounted an attack on the Avtokrator too deadly for a pair of northern men to withstand. But the galley stayed a good quarter mile from Krispos' rowboat, and even the houndlike Halogai let him separate himself from them by close to a furlong. He could imagine he sat alone on the waves.

In his younger days, he had never thought of fishing as a sport he might favor. It was something he occasionally did to help feed himself when he had the time. Now, though, it gave him the chance to escape not only from his duties but also from his servitors, something he simply could not do on land.

Being the man he was, he'd also become a skillful fisherman over the years; whatever he did, for whatever reasons, he tried to do well. He tied a cork float to his line to keep his hook at the depth he wanted it. To that hook he wired several little pieces of lead from the tackle box to help it have the semblance of natural motion in the water. Then he opened the bait box Barsymes had given him, seized a roach between thumb and fore-finger, and impaled it on the hook's barbed tip.

While he was catching the roach, a couple of others leapt out of box and scuttled around the bottom of the rowboat. For the moment, he ig-nored them. If he needed them later, he'd get them. They weren't going anywhere far.

He tossed the line over the side. The float bobbed in the green-blue water. Krispos sat holding the rod and let his thoughts drift freely. Sea mist softened the outline of the far shore of the Cattle-Crossing, but he could still make out the taller buildings of the suburb known simply as Across.

He turned his head. Behind him, Videssos the city bulked enormous. Past the Grand Courtroom and the Hall of the Nineteen Couches stood the great mass of the High Temple. It dominated the capital's skyline from every angle. Also leaping above the rooftops of other buildings was the red granite shaft of the Milestone at the edge of the plaza of Palamas, from which all distances in the Empire were reckoned.

Sunlight sparked from the gilded domes that topped the dozens—perhaps hundreds—of temples to Phos in the city. Krispos thought back to his own first glimpse of the imperial capital, and the globes flashing like suns themselves under the good god's sun.

The Cattle-Crossing was full of ships: lean war galleys like the one that watched him; trading ships full of grain or building stone or cargoes more diverse and expensive; little fishing boats whose crews scoured the sea not for sport but for survival. Watching them pull their nets up over the side, Krispos wondered whether they might not work harder even than farmers, a question that had never crossed his mind about any other trade.

His float suddenly jerked under the water. He yanked up the rod and pulled in the line. A shimmering blue flying fish twisted at the end of it. He smiled, grabbed it, and tossed it into the bottom of the boat. It wasn't very big, but it would be tasty. Maybe his cook could make it stretch in a stew—or maybe he'd catch another one.

He foraged in the bait box, grabbed another cockroach, and skewered it on the hook to replace the one that had been the luckless flying fish's last meal. The roach's little legs still flailed as it sank beneath the sea.

After that, Krispos spent a good stretch of time staring at the float and waiting for something to happen. Fishing was like that sometimes. He had sometimes thought about asking Zaidas if sorcery could help the business along, but always decided not to. Catching fish was only part of the reason he came out here in the little boat. The other part, the bigger part, was to get away from everyone around him. Making himself a more efficient fisherman might net him more fish, but it would cost him some of the precious time he had to himself.

Besides, if fishing magic were possible, the horny-handed, sun-browned sailors who made their living from their catch would surely employ it. No, maybe not: it might be feasible, but too expensive to make it worthwhile for anyone not already rich to afford it. Zaidas would know. Maybe he *would* ask him. And maybe he wouldn't. Now that he thought about it, he probably wouldn't.

His float disappeared again. When he tried to pull up the rod this time, it bent like a bow. He pulled once more, and once more the fish fought back. He walked his hands up to the tip of the rod, then pulled in the line hand over hand. "By the good god, here's a treat indeed!" he exclaimed when he saw the fat red mullet writhing on his hook.

He snatched up a net and slid it up over the fish from below. The mullet was as large as his forearm, and meaty enough to feed several. Had he fished for a living, he could have sold it in the plaza of Palamas for a fine price: Videssos the city's gourmets reckoned it their favorite, even to the point of nicknaming it the emperor of fishes.

Though called red, the mullet had been brownish with yellow stripes when he took it from the sea. It turned a crimson almost the color of his boots, however, as it struggled for its life, then slowly began to fade toward gray.

Mullets were famous for their spectacular color changes. Krispos remembered one of Anthimos' revels, where his predecessor had ordered several of them slowly boiled alive in a large glass vessel so the feasters could appreciate their shifting hues as they cooked. He'd watched with as much interest as anyone else; only looking back on it did it seem cruel.

Perhaps a sauce with garlic-flavored egg whites would do this one justice, he thought; even the head of a mullet pickled in brine was esteemed a delicacy. He'd have to talk with the cook when he went back to the imperial residence.

He gently set the prized catch in the bottom of the rowboat, treating it with far more care than he had the flying fish. If he'd used fishing as anything but an excuse to get away from the palaces, he would have rowed back to the pier with as much celerity as his arms could give him. Instead, he caught another cockroach, rebaited the hook, and dropped the line into the water again.

He quickly made another catch, but it was only an ugly, tasteless croaker. He pulled the barbed hook out of its mouth and tossed it back into the water, then opened the bait box for another bug.

After that, he sat and sat for a long time, waiting for something to happen and accepting with almost trancelike calm the nothing that fate was giving him. The boat shifted gently in the waves. His stomach had been a bit uncertain the first few times he went to sea. With greater familiarity, the motion had come to soothe him; it was as if he sat in a chair that not only rocked but also swiveled. Of course, he did not take the rowboat out on stormy days, either.

"Your Majesty!" The call across the water snapped Krispos out of his reverie. He looked back toward the dock from which he'd rowed out, expecting to see someone standing there with a megaphone. Instead, a rowboat was approaching his own as fast as the man in it could ply the blades. He wondered how long the fellow had been hailing him before he noticed.

The Halogai, who had been fishing, too, grabbed for their oars and moved to block the newcomer's path. He paused in his exertion long enough to snatch up a sealed roll of parchment and wave it in their direction. After that, Krispos' bodyguards let him come on, but rowed beside him to make sure he could try nothing untoward if his precious message proved a ruse.

Proskynesis in a rowboat was impractical; the fellow with the parchment contented himself with dipping his head to Krispos. Panting, he said, "May it please Your Majesty, I bring a dispatch just arrived from the environs of Pityos." He handed Krispos the parchment across the palm's breadth of water that separated their boats.

As often happened, Krispos had the bad feeling his Majesty was not going to be pleased. Scrawled on the outside of the parchment in a hasty hand was *For Krispos Avtokrator—vital that he read the instant received.* No wonder the messenger had leapt into a rowboat, then.

Krispos flicked off the wax seal with his thumbnail, then used a scaling knife from the tackle box to slice through the ribbon that held the parchment closed. When he unrolled it, he found the message inside written in the same hand as the warning of urgency on the outer surface. It was also to the point:

> Troop Leader Gainas to Krispos Avtokrator: Greetings. We were attacked by Thanasioi two days' march southeast of Pityos. I grieve to report to Your Majesty that most of the forces sent there not only yielded themselves up to the heretics and rebels but indeed took their cause against the rest. The leader of this action was the merarch Livanios, the chief aide to our commander Briso.
>
> Because of this, those loyal to you were utterly defeated; the priests we were escorting to Pityos were captured and most piteously massacred. May the good god redeem their souls. Forgive one of my lowly rank for writing to you directly, Your Majesty, but I fear I am the senior loyal officer left alive. The Thanasioi must now be reckoned to control the whole of this province. Skotos surely awaits them in the world to come.

Krispos read through the message twice to make sure he'd missed nothing. He started to toss it down with the fish he'd caught, but decided it was too likely to be ruined by seawater. He stowed it in the tackle box instead. Then he seized the rowboat's oars and headed back for the pier. The messenger and the Halogai followed in his wake.

As soon as he reached the dock, he tossed the tackle box up onto the tarred timbers, then scrambled up after it. He grabbed the box and headed for the imperial residence at a trot that left the parasol-bearers hurrying after him and complaining loudly as they did their futile best to catch up. Even the Halogai who hadn't gone to sea needed a hundred yards and more before they could assume their protective places around him.

He'd taken the Thanasioi too lightly before. That wouldn't happen now. He wrote and dictated orders far into the night; the only pauses he

made were to gulp smoked pork and hard cheese—campaigning food—
and pour down a couple of goblets of wine to keep his voice from going
raw.

Not until he'd got into bed, his thoughts whirling wildly as he tried
without much luck to sleep, did he remember that he'd left the mullet of
which he'd been so proud lying in the bottom of the boat.

Chapter III

CIVIL WAR. RELIGIOUS WAR. KRISPOS DIDN'T KNOW WHICH OF the two was worse. Now he had them both, wrapped around each other. Worse yet, fall was not far away. If he didn't move quickly, rain would turn the westlands' dirt roads to gluey mud that made travel difficult and campaigning impossible. That would give the heretics the winter to consolidate their hold on Pityos and the surrounding territory.

But if he did move quickly, with a scratch force, he risked another defeat. Defeat was more dangerous in civil war than against a foreign foe; it tempted troops to switch sides. Figuring out which course to take required calculations more exacting than he'd needed in years.

"I wish Iakovitzes were here," he told Barsymes and Zaidas as he weighed his choices. "Come to that, I wish Mammianos were still alive. When it came to civil war, he always had a feel for what to do when."

"He was not young even in the first days of Your Majesty's reign," Zaidas said, "and he was always fat as a tun. Such men are prime candidates for fits of apoplexy."

"So the healer-priests advised me when he died up in Pliskavos," Krispos said. "I understand that. I miss him all the same. Most of these young soldiers I deal with lack sense, it seems to me."

"This is a common complaint of the older against the young," Zaidas said. "Moreover, most of the younger officers in your army have spent more time at peace than was usual in the tenure of previous Avtokrators."

Barsymes said, "Perhaps Your Majesty might do more to involve the young Majesties in the preparations against the Thanasioi."

"I wish I knew how to do that," Krispos said. "If they were more like me at the same age, there'd be no problem. But—" His own first taste of combat had come at seventeen, against Kubrati raiders. He'd done well enough in the fighting, then puked up his guts afterward.

"But," he said again, shaking his head as if it were a complete sentence. He made himself amplify it. "Phostis has chosen now to get drunk on the lord with the great and good mind and on the words of this priest he's been seeing."

"Will you reprove piety?" Barsymes asked, his own voice reproving.

"Not at all, esteemed sir. Along with our common Videssian language, our common orthodox faith glues the Empire together. That, among other things, is what makes the Thanasioi so deadly dangerous: they seek to soak away the glue that keeps all Videssos' citizens loyal to her. But neither would I have my heir make himself into a monk, not when Emperors find themselves forced to do unmonkish things."

"Forbid him to see this priest, then," Zaidas suggested.

"How can I?" Krispos said. "Phostis is a man in years and a man in spirit, even if not exactly the man I might have wished him to be. He would defy me, and he would be in the right. One of the things you learn if you want to stay Avtokrator is not to fight wars you have no hope of winning."

"You have three sons, Your Majesty," Barsymes said. The vestiarios was subtle even by Videssian standards, but could be as stubborn in his deviousness as any blunt, straightforward, ironheaded barbarian.

"Aye, I have three sons." Krispos raised an eyebrow. "Katakolon would no doubt be willing enough to go on campaign for the sake of the camp followers, but how much use he'd be in the field is another question. Evripos, now, Evripos is a puzzle even to me. He doesn't want to be like his brother, but envies him his place as eldest."

Zaidas spoke in musing tones: "If you ordered him to accompany the army you send forth, and gave him, say, spatharios' rank and a place at your side, that might make Phostis—what's the word I want?—thoughtful, perhaps."

"Worried, you mean." Krispos found himself smiling. Spatharios was about the most general title in the imperial hierarchy; though it literally meant *sword bearer, aide* more accurately reflected its import. An Emperor's spatharios, even when not also the Emperor's son, was a very prominent personage indeed. Krispos' smile got wider. "Zaidas, perhaps I'll dispatch you instead of Iakovitzes on our next embassy to the King of Kings. You have the plotter's instinct."

"I'd not mind going, Your Majesty, if you think I could serve you properly," the wizard answered. "Mashiz is the home of many clever mages, of a school different from our own. I'd learn a great deal on such a journey, I'm certain." He sounded ready to leave on the instant.

"One of these years, then, I may send you," Krispos said. "You needn't go pack, though; as things stand, I need you too much by my side."

"It shall be as Your Majesty wishes, of course," Zaidas murmured.

"Shall it?" Krispos said. "On the whole, I'll not deny it has been as I wish, more often than not. But I have the feeling that if I ever start to take success for granted, it will run away from me and I'll never see it again."

"That feeling may be the reason you've held the throne so long, Your Majesty," Barsymes said. "An Avtokrator who takes anything for granted soon finds the high seat slipping out from under his fundament. I watched it happen with Anthimos."

Krispos glanced at the eunuch in some surprise; Barsymes seldom reminded him of having served his predecessor. He cast about for what Barsymes, in his usual oblique way, might be trying to tell him. At last he said, "Anthimos' example taught me a lot about how best not to be an Avtokrator."

"Then you have drawn the proper lesson from it," Barsymes said approvingly. "In that regard, his career had a textbook perfection whose like would be difficult to find."

"So it did." Krispos' voice was dry. Had Anthimos granted to ruling even a tithe of the attention he gave to wine, wenching, and revelry, Krispos might never have tried to supplant him—and if he had, he likely would have failed. But that was grist for the historians now, too. He said, "Esteemed sir, draft for me a letter of appointment for Evripos, naming him my spatharios for the upcoming campaign against the Thanasioi."

"Not one for Phostis as well, Your Majesty?" the vestiarios asked.

"Oh, yes, go ahead and draft that one, too. But don't give it to him until he finds out his brother was named to the post. Stewing him in his own juices is the point of the exercise, eh?"

"As you say," Barsymes answered. "Both documents will be ready for your signature this afternoon."

"Excellent. I rely on your discretion, Barsymes. I've never known that reliance to be misplaced." When he was new on the throne, Krispos would have added that it had better not be misplaced here, either. Now he let Barsymes add those last words for himself, as he knew the vestiarios would. Little by little, over the years, he'd picked up some deviousness himself.

PHOSTIS BOWED LOW BEFORE DIGENIS. GULPING A LITTLE, HE told the priest, "Holy sir, I regret I will not be able to hear your wisdom for some time to come. I depart soon with my father and the armament he has readied against the Thanasioi."

"If it suited you, lad, you could remain in the city and learn despite his wishes." Digenis studied him. The priest's thin shoulders moved in a silent sigh. "But I see the world and its things still hold you in their grip. Do as you feel you must, then; all shall surely result as the lord with the great and good mind desires."

Phostis accepted the priest's calling him merely *lad,* though by now Digenis of course knew who he was. He'd thought about telling Digenis to address him as *Your Majesty* or *young Majesty,* but one of the reasons he visited the priest again and again was to rid himself of the taint of sordid materialism and learn humility. Humility did not go hand in hand with ordering a priest about.

But even though he sought humility, he embraced it only so far. Trying to justify himself, he said earnestly, "Holy sir, if I let Evripos serve as my father's aide, it might give my father cause to have him succeed, rather than me."

"And so?" Digenis said. "Would the Empire crumble to pieces on account of that? Is your brother so wicked and depraved that he would cast it all into the fire to feed his own iniquity? Better even perhaps that he should, so the generations which come after us would have fewer material possessions with which to concern themselves."

"Evripos isn't wicked," Phostis said. "It's just that—"

"That you have become accustomed to the idea of one day setting your baser parts on the throne," the priest interrupted. "Not only accustomed to it, lad, but infatuated with it. Do I speak the truth or a lie?"

"The truth, but only after a fashion," Phostis said. Digenis' eyebrow was silent but nonetheless eloquent. Flustered, Phostis floundered for justification: "And remember, holy sir, if I succeed, you will already have imbued me with your doctrines, which I will be able to disseminate throughout the Empire. Evripos, though, remains attached to the sordid matter that Skotos set before our souls to entice them away from Phos' light."

"This is also a truth, however small," Digenis admitted, with the air of a man making a large concession. "Still, lad, you must bear in mind that any compromise with Skotos that you form in your mind will result in compromising your soul. Well, let it be; each man must determine for himself the proper path to renunciation, and that path is often—always— strait. If you do accompany your father on this expedition of his, what shall your duties be?"

"For a good part of it, probably nothing at all," Phostis answered, explaining, "We'll go by ship to Nakoleia, to reach the borders of the revolted province as quickly as we can. Then we march overland to Harasos, Rogmor, and Aptos; my father is arranging for supplies to be ingathered at each. From Aptos we'll strike toward Pityos. That's the leg of the journey where we'll most likely start real fighting."

In spite of his efforts to sound disapproving, he heard the excitement in his own voice. War, to a young man who has never seen it face-to-face, owns a certain glamour. Krispos never talked about fighting, save to condemn it. To Phostis, that was but another reason to look forward to it.

The priest just shook his head. "How your grand cavalcade of those who love too well their riches shall progress concerns me not at all. I fear for your soul, lad, the only piece of you truly deserving of our care. Without a doubt you will abandon my teachings and return to your old corrupt ways, just as a moth seeks a flame or a fly, a cow turd."

"I'll do no such thing," Phostis said indignantly. "I've discovered a great deal from you, holy sir, and would not think of turning aside from your golden words."

"Ha!" Digenis said. "Do you see? Even your promises of piety betray the greed that remains yet in your heart. Golden words? To the ice with gold! Yet still it holds you in its honeyed grip, sticking you down so Skotos may seize you."

"I'm sorry," Phostis said, humble now. "It was only a figure of speech. I meant no harm by it."

"Ha!" Digenis repeated. "There are tests to see whether you have truly embraced piety or are but dissembling, perhaps even to yourself."

"Give me one of those tests, then," Phostis said. "By the lord with the great and good mind, holy sir, I'll show you what I'm made of."

"You are less easy to test than many might be, you know, lad," the priest said. At Phostis' puzzled look, he explained: "Another young man I might send past a chamber wherein lay some rich store of gold or gems. For those who came to manhood in hunger and want, such would be plenty to let me look into their hearts. But you? Gold and jewels have been your baubles since you were still pissing on your father's floor. You might easily remain ensnared in spiritual error and yet pass them by."

"So I might," Phostis admitted. Almost in despair, he cried out, "But I would prove myself to you, holy sir, if only I knew how."

Digenis smiled. He pointed to a curtained doorway in the rear wall of the dingy temple over which he presided. "Go through there, then, and it may be you shall learn something of yourself."

"By the good god, I will!" But when Phostis pulled aside the curtain, only blank blackness awaited him. He hesitated. His guardsmen waited for him outside the temple, the greatest concession they would make. Assassins might await him in the darkness. He steadied himself: Digenis would not betray him so. Very conscious of the weight of the priest's gaze on his back, he plunged ahead.

The curtain fell back into place behind him. As soon as he turned a corner, the inside of the passage was so absolutely black that he whispered Phos' creed to hold away any supernatural evils that might dwell there. He took a step, then another. The passage sloped steeply down. To keep from breaking his neck, he put his arms out to either side and shifted this way and that until one outstretched finger brushed a wall.

That wall was rough brick. It scraped his fingertips, but he was glad to feel it, even so; without it, he would have groped around as helplessly as a blind man. In effect, he *was* a blind man here.

He walked slowly down the corridor. In the darkness, he could not be sure whether it was straight or followed a gently curving path. He was certain it ran under more buildings than just the temple to Phos. He wondered how old it was and why it had been built. He also wondered if even Digenis knew the answers to those questions.

His eyes imagined they saw shifting, swirling colored shapes, as if he had shut them and pressed knuckles hard against his eyelids. If any beings phantasmagorical did lurk down here, they could be upon him before he decided they were something more than figments of his imagination. He said the creed under his breath again.

He had gone—well, he didn't know how far he had gone, but it was a goodly way—when he saw a tiny bit of light that neither shifted nor swirled. It spilled out from under the bottom of a door and faintly illuminated the floor just in front of it. Had the tunnel been lit, he never would have noticed the glow. As things were, it shouted its presence like an imperial herald.

Phostis' fingers slid across planed boards. After so long scratching over brick, the smoothness was welcome. Whoever was on the other side of the door must have had unusually keen ears, for no sooner had his hand whispered over it than she called, "Enter in friendship, by the lord with the great and good mind."

He groped for a latch, found it, and lifted it. The door moved smoothly on its hinges. Though but a single lamp burned in the chamber, its glow seemed bright as the noonday sun to his light-starved eyes. What he saw, though, left him wondering if those eyes were playing tricks on him: a lovely young woman bare on a bed, her arms stretched his way in open invitation.

"Enter in friendship," she repeated, though he was already inside. Her voice was low and throaty. As he took an almost involuntary step toward her, the scent she wore reached him. Had it had a voice, that would have been low and throaty, too.

A second, longer look told him she was not quite bare after all: a thin gold chain girded her slim waist. Its glint in the lamplight made him take another step toward the bed. She smiled and moved a little to make room beside her.

His foot was already uplifted for a third step—which would have been the last one he needed—when he caught himself, almost literally, by the scruff of the neck. He swayed off balance for a moment, but in the end that third step went back rather than ahead.

"You are the test against which Digenis warned me," he said, and felt himself turn red at how hoarse and eager he sounded.

"Well, what if I am?" The girl's slow shrug was a marvel to behold. So was the long, slow stretch that followed it. "The holy sir promised me you would be comely, and he told the truth. Do as you will with me; he shall never know, one way or the other."

"How not?" he demanded, his suspicions aroused now along with his lust. "If I have you here, of course you'll bear the tale back to the holy sir."

"By the lord with the great and good mind, I swear I will not," she said. Her tone carried conviction. He knew he should not believe her, but he did. She smiled, seeing she'd got through to him. "We're all alone, only the two of us down here. Whatever happens, happens, and no one else will ever be the wiser."

He thought about that, decided he believed her again. "What's your name?" he asked. It was not quite a question out of the blue.

The girl seemed to understand that. "Olyvria," she answered. Her smile grew broader. As if by their own will rather than hers, her legs parted a little.

When Phostis raised his left foot, he did not know whether he would go toward her or away. He turned, took two quick strides out of the chamber, and closed the door behind him. He knew that if he looked on her for even another heartbeat, he would take her.

As he leaned against the bricks of the passageway and tried to find a scrap of his composure, her voice pursued him: "Why do you flee from pleasure?"

Not until she asked him did he fully comprehend the answer. Digenis' test was marvelous in its simplicity: only his own conscience stood between himself and an act that, however sweet, went square against everything the priest had been telling him. Digenis' teaching must have had its effect, too: regardless of whether the priest learned what he'd been up to, Phostis knew *he* would always know. Since he found that reason enough to abstain, he supposed he had met the challenge.

Even so, he made as much haste as he could away from that dangerous doorway, although Olyvria did not call to him again. When he looked back to find out whether he could still see the light trickling under the bottom of the door, he discovered he could not. The passage did have a curve to it, then.

A little while later, he came upon another door with a lighted lamp behind it. This time, he tiptoed past as quietly as he could. If anyone in the chamber heard him, she—or perhaps he—gave no sign. Not all tests, Phostis told himself as he pressed ahead, had to be met straight on.

Pitch darkness or no, he could see Olyvria's lovely body with his mind's eye. He was sure both his brothers would have enjoyed themselves immensely while failing Digenis' test. Had he not become dubious of the pleasures of the flesh exactly because they were so easy for him to gain, he might well have failed, too, in spite of all the priest's inspiring words.

Moving along without light made him realize how very much he depended on his eyes. He could not tell whether he was going uphill or down, left or right. Just when he began to wonder if the passage under the city ran on forever, he saw a faint gleam of light ahead. He hurried toward it. When he pulled aside the curtain that covered the entrance to the tunnel, he found himself back in the temple again.

He stood blinking for a few seconds as he got used to seeing once more. Digenis did not seem to have moved while he was gone. He wondered how long that had been; his sense of time seemed to have been cast into darkness down in the tunnel along with his vision.

Digenis studied him. The priest's eyes were so sharp and penetrating that Phostis suspected he might have been able to see even in the black night of the underground passage. After a moment, Digenis said, "The man who is truly holy turns aside from no test, but triumphantly surmounts it."

Quite against his conscious will, Phostis thought of himself triumphantly surmounting Olyvria. Turning his back on the distracting mental image, he answered, "Holy sir, I make no special claim to holiness of my own. I am merely as I am. If I fail to please you, drive me hence."

"Your father, or rather your acceptance of his will, has already sufficed in that regard. But while not a man destined to be renowned among Phos' holy elite, you have not done badly, I admit," Digenis said. That was as near to praise as he was in the habit of coming. Phostis grinned in involuntary relief. The priest added, "I know it is no simple matter for a young man to reject carnality and its delights."

"That's true, holy sir." Only after Phostis had replied did he notice that, this once, Digenis sounded remarkably like his father. His opinion of the priest went down a notch. Why couldn't old men leave off prating about what young men did or didn't do? What did they know about it, anyhow? They hadn't been young since before Videssos was a city, as the saying went.

Digenis said, "May the good god turn his countenance—and his continence—upon you during your wanderings, lad, and may you remember his truths and what you have learned from me in the hour when you will be tested all in earnest."

"May it be so, holy sir," Phostis answered, though he didn't understand just what the priest meant by his last comment. Weren't his lessons Phos' truth in and of themselves? He set that aside for later consideration, bowed deeply to Digenis, and walked out of the little temple.

His Haloga guards were down on one knee in the street, shooting dice. They paid off the last bet and got to their feet. "Back to the palaces, young Majesty?" one asked.

"That's right, Snorri," Phostis answered. "I have to ready myself to sail west." He let the northerners escort him out of the unsavory part of the capital. As they turned onto Middle Street, he said, "Tell me, Snorri, how are you better for having your mail shirt gilded?"

The Haloga turned back, puzzlement spread across his blunt features. "Better, young Majesty? I don't follow the track of your thought."

"Does the gilding make you fight better? Are you braver on account of it? Does it keep the iron links of the shirt from rusting better than some cheap paint might?"

"None of those, young Majesty." Snorri's massive head shook slowly back and forth as if he thought Phostis ought to be able to see that much for himself. In fact, he likely was thinking something of the sort.

Phostis didn't care. Buoyed by Digenis' inspiring word and by pride at turning down what Olyvria had so temptingly offered, he had at the moment no use for the material things of the world, for everything which had throughout his life stood between him and hunger, discomfort, and fear. As if fencing with a rapier of logic, he thrust home. "Why have the gilding, then?"

He didn't know what he'd expected—maybe for Snorri to rush out and buy a jug of turpentine so he could remove the offending pigment from his byrnie. But whether the gilding helped the Haloga or not, he was armored against reasoned argument. He answered, "Why, young Majesty? I like it; I think it's pretty. That's plenty for me."

The rest of the trip to the palaces passed in silence.

LINES CREAKED AS THEY RAN THROUGH PULLEYS. THE BIG SQUARE sail swung to catch the breeze from a new angle. Waves slapped against the bow of the *Triumphant* as the imperial flagship turned toward shore.

Krispos knew more than a little relief at the prospect of being on dry land to stay. The voyage west from Videssos the city had been smooth enough; he'd needed to use the lee rail only once. The galleys and transport ships never sailed out of sight of land, and beached themselves every evening. That wasn't why Krispos looked forward to putting in at Nakoleia.

The trouble was, he'd grown to feel isolated, cut off from the world around him, in his week at sea. No new reports stacked up on his desk. His cabin, in fact, had no desk, only a little folding table. He felt like a healer-priest forced to remove his fingers from a sick man's wrist in the middle of taking his pulse.

He knew that was foolish. A week was not a long time to be away from events; Anthimos, even while physically remaining in Videssos the city, had neglected his duties for months on end. The bureaucracy kept the Empire more or less on an even keel; that was what bureaucracy was for.

But Krispos would be glad to return to a location more definite than *somewhere on the Videssian Sea.* Once he landed, the lodestone that was the imperial dignity would attract to his person all the minutiae on which he depended for his understanding of what was going on in Videssos.

"You can't let go, even for a second," he murmured.

"What's that, Father?" Katakolon asked.

Embarrassed at getting caught talking to himself, Krispos just grunted by way of reply. Katakolon gave him a quizzical look and walked on by.

Katakolon had spent a lot of time pacing the deck of the *Triumphant;* the week at sea was no doubt his longest period of celibacy since his beard began to sprout. He'd likely do his best to make up for lost time in the joy-houses of Nakoleia.

The port was getting close now. Its gray stone wall was drab against the green-gold of ripening grain in the hinterland. Behind it, blue in the distance, hills rose up against the sky. The fertile strip was narrow along the northern coast of the westlands; the plateau country that made up the bulk of the big peninsula began to rise less than twenty miles from the sea.

Katakolon went by again. Krispos didn't want him, not right now. "Phostis!" he called.

Phostis came, not quite fast enough to suit Krispos, not quite slow enough for him to make an issue out of it. "How may I serve you, Father?" he asked. The question was properly deferential, the tone was not.

Again, Krispos decided to let it lie. He stuck to the purpose for which he'd called his son. "When we dock, I want you to visit all merarchs and officers of higher rank. Remind them they have to take extra care on this campaign because they may have Thanasioi in their ranks. We don't want to risk betrayal at a time when it could hurt us most."

"Yes, Father," Phostis said unenthusiastically. Then he asked, "Why couldn't you simply have your scribes write out as many copies of the order as you need and distribute them to the officers?"

"Because I just told you to do this, by the good god," Krispos snapped. Phostis' glare made him realize that was taking authority too far. He added, "Besides, I have good practical reasons for doing it this way. Officers get too many parchments as is; who but Phos can say which ones they'll read and which ones they'll toss into a pigeonhole or into a well without ever unsealing them? But a visit from the Avtokrator's son—that they'll remember, and what he says to them. And this is an important order. Do you see?"

"I suppose so," Phostis said, again without great spirit. But he did nod. "I'll do as you say, Father."

"Well, I thank your gracious Majesty for that," Krispos said. Phostis jerked as if a mosquito had just bitten him in a tender place. He spun round and stalked away. Krispos immediately regretted his sarcasm, but nothing could recall a word once spoken. He'd learned that a long time before, and should have had it down pat by now. He stamped his foot, angry at himself and Phostis both.

He peered out toward the docks. The fleet had come close enough to let him pick out individuals. The fat fellow with six parasol-bearers around him would be Strabonis, the provincial governor, the scrawny one with three, Asdrouvallos, the city eparch. He wondered how long they'd been standing there, waiting for the fleet to arrive. The longer it was, the more ceremony they'd insist on once he actually got his feet on dry land. He intended to endure as much as he could, but sometimes that wasn't much.

Along with the dignitaries stood a lean, wiry fellow in nondescript clothes and a broad-brimmed leather traveler's hat. Krispos was much more interested in seeing him than either Strabonis or Asdrouvallos: imperial scouts and couriers had an air about them that, once recognized, was unmistakable. The governor and the eparch would make speeches. From the courier, Krispos would get real news.

He called for Evripos. His second son was no quicker appearing than Phostis had been. Frowning, Krispos said, "If I'd wanted slowcoaches, I'd have made snails my spatharioi, not you two."

"Sorry, Father," Evripos said, though he didn't sound particularly sorry.

At the moment, Krispos wished Dara had borne girls. Sons-in-law might have been properly grateful to him for their elevation in life, where his own boys seemed to take status for granted. On the other hand, sons-in-law might also have wanted to elevate themselves further, regardless of whether Krispos was ready to depart this life.

He made himself remember why he'd summoned Evripos. "When we land, I want you to check the number and quality of remounts available here, and also to make sure the arsenal has enough arrows in it to let us go out and fight. Is that martial enough for you?"

"Yes, Father. I'll see to it," Evripos said.

"Good. I want you back with what I need to know before you sleep tonight. Make sure you take special notice of anything lacking, so we can get word ahead to our other supply dumps and have their people lay hold of it for us."

"Tonight?" Now Evripos didn't try to hide his dismay. "I was hoping to—"

"To find someone soft and cuddly?" Krispos shook his head. "I don't care what you do along those lines after you take care of what I ask of you. If you work fast, you'll have plenty of time for other things. But business first."

"You don't tell Katakolon that," Evripos said darkly.

"You complain because I don't treat you the same as Phostis, and now you complain because I don't treat you the same as Katakolon. You can't have it both ways, son. If you want the authority that comes with power, you have to take the responsibility that comes with it, too." When Evripos didn't answer, Krispos added, "Don't scant the job. Men's lives ride on it."

"Oh, I'll take care of it, Father. I said I would, after all. And besides, you'll probably have someone else taking care of it, too, so you can check his answers against mine. That's your style, isn't it?" Evripos departed without giving Krispos a chance to answer.

Krispos wondered whether he should have left his sons back in Videssos the city. They quarreled with one another, they quarreled with him, and they didn't do half as much as might some youngster from no particular family who hoped to be noticed. But no—they needed to learn what war was about, and they needed to let the army see them. An Avtokrator who could not control his soldiers would end up with soldiers controlling him.

The *Triumphant* eased into place alongside the dock. Strabonis peered down into the ship. Seen close up, he looked as if he'd yield gallons of oil if rendered down. Even his voice was greasy. "Welcome, welcome, thrice welcome, your imperial Majesty," he declared. "We honor you for coming to the defense of our province, and are confident you shall succeed in utterly crushing the impious heretics who scourge us."

"I'm glad of your confidence, and I hope I will deserve it," Krispos answered as sailors stretched a gangplank painted with imperial crimson from his vessel to the dock. He, too, remained confident he would beat the Thanasioi. He'd beaten every enemy he'd faced in a long reign save only Makuran—and no Avtokrator since the fierce Stavrakios had ever really beaten Makuran, while even Stavrakios' victory did not prove lasting. But Strabonis sounded as if defeating the heretics would be easy as a promenade down Middle Street. Krispos knew better than that.

He walked across the gangplank to the dock. Strabonis folded his fat form into a proskynesis. "Rise," Krispos said. After a week aboard the rolling ship, solid ground seemed to sway beneath his feet.

Asdrouvallos prostrated himself next. As he got back to his feet, he started to cough, and kept on coughing till his wizened face turned almost as gray as his beard. A tiny fleck of blood-streaked foam appeared at one corner of his mouth. A quick flick of his tongue swept it away. "Phos grant Your Majesty a pleasant stay in Nakoleia," he said, his voice gravelly. "Success against the foe as well."

"Thank you, excellent eparch," Krispos said. "I hope you've seen a healer-priest for that cough?"

"Oh, aye, Your Majesty; more than one, as a matter of fact." Asdrouvallos' bony shoulders moved up and down in a shrug. "They've done the best they can for me, but it's not enough. I'll go on as long as the good god wills, and afterward, well, afterward I hope to see him face-to-face."

"May that day be years away," Krispos said, though Asdrouvallos, who was not much above his own age, looked as if he might expire at any moment. Krispos added, "By all means consider your oration as given. I do not require you to tax your lungs. Videssos has quite enough taxes without that."

"Your Majesty is gracious," Asdrouvallos said. In truth, Krispos was concerned for the eparch's health. And in showing that concern, he'd also managed to take a formidable bite out of speeches yet to come.

He wished he could have found some equally effective and polite way to make Strabonis shut up. The provincial governor's speech was long and florid, modeled after the rhetoric-soaked orations that had been the style in Videssos the city before Krispos' time—and probably would be again, once his peasant-bred impatience for fancy talk was safely gone. He tried clearing his throat; Strabonis ignored him. At last he started shifting from foot to foot as if he urgently needed to visit the jakes. That got Strabonis' attention. As soon as he subsided, so did Krispos' wiggles. The governor sent the Avtokrator an injured look Krispos pretended not to see.

After that, he had to endure only an invocation from the hierarch of Nakoleia, who proved himself a man able to take a hint by making it mercifully brief. Then Krispos could at last talk with the courier, who had waited through the folderol with more apparent patience than the Avtokrator could muster.

The fellow started to prostrate himself. "Never mind that," Krispos said. "Any more nonsense and I'll die of old age before I get anything done. By the good god, just tell me what you have to say."

"Aye, Your Majesty." The courier's skin was brown and leathery from years in the sun, which only made his surprised smile seem brighter. That smile, however, quickly faded. "Your Majesty, the news isn't good. I have to tell you that the Thanasioi put your supply dumps at Harasos and Rogmor to the torch, the one three days ago, the other night before last. Damage—mm, there's a lot of it, I'm sorry to say."

Krispos' right hand clenched into a fist. "A pestilence," he ground out between his teeth. "That won't make the campaign against them any easier."

"No, Your Majesty," the courier said. "I'm sorry to be the one who gives you that word, but it's one you have to have."

"You're right. I know it's not your fault." Krispos had never made a habit of condemning messengers for bad news. "See to yourself, see to your horse. No—tell me your name first, so I can commend you to your chief for good service."

The courier's flashing smile returned. "I'm called Evlalios, Your Majesty."

"He'll hear from me, Evlalios," Krispos promised. As the courier turned away, Krispos started thinking about his own next step. If he hadn't already known the Thanasioi now had a real soldier at their head, the raids on his depots would have told him as much. Bandits might have attacked the dumps to steal what they needed for themselves, but only an experienced officer would have deliberately wrecked them to deny his foes what they held. Soldiers knew armies did more traveling, encamping, and eating than fighting. If they couldn't get where they needed to go, or if they arrived half starved, they wouldn't be able to fight.

He'd already sent Phostis and Evripos on errands. That left— "Katakolon!" he called. Ceremonial had trapped his youngest son, who'd been unable to sneak off and start sampling the fleshly pleasures Nakoleia had to offer.

"What is it, Father?" Katakolon sounded like a martyr about to be slain for the true faith.

"I'm afraid you'll have to keep your trousers on a bit longer, my boy," Krispos said, at which his son looked as if the fatal dart had just struck home. Ignoring the virtuoso mime performance, Krispos went on, "I need an accounting of the contents of all the storehouses in this town, and I need it tonight. See the excellent Asdrouvallos here; no doubt he'll have a map to send you on your way from one to the next as fast as you can go."

"Oh, yes, Your Majesty," Asdrouvallos said. Even the short sentence was enough to set him coughing again. By his expression, Katakolon hoped the eparch wouldn't stop. Unfortunately for him, Asdrouvallos drew in a couple of deep, sobbing breaths and managed to break the spasm. "If the young Majesty will just accompany me—"

Trapped, Katakolon accompanied him. Krispos watched him go with a certain amount of satisfaction—which, he thought, was more in the way of satisfaction than Katakolon would get tonight: now all three of his sons, however unwillingly, were doing something useful. If only the Thanasioi would yield so readily.

He feared they wouldn't. That they'd known just where he was storing his supplies forced him to relearn a lesson in civil war he hadn't had to worry about since he vanquished Anthimos' uncle Petronas at the start of his reign: the enemy, thanks to spies in his camp, would know everything he decided almost as soon as he decided it. He'd have to keep moves secret until just before he made them, and so would his officers. He'd have to re-mind them about that.

Forgetting his thought of a moment before that all his sons were use-fully engaged, he looked around for one to yell at. Then he remembered, and laughed at himself. He also remembered he'd sent Phostis out on pre-cisely that mission. His laugh turned sour. How was he supposed to beat the Thanasioi if he found himself turning senile before he ever met them in battle?

SARKIS REMINDED PHOSTIS OF A PLUMP BIRD OF PREY. THE Vaspurakaner cavalry commander was one of Krispos' longtime cronies, and close to Krispos in years—which, to Phostis' way of thinking, made him about ready for the boneyard. A great hooked beak of a nose pro-truded from his doughy face like a big rock sticking out of a mud flat. He was munching candied apricots when Phostis came into his quarters, too, which did not improve the young man's opinion of him.

As he already had a score of times that afternoon and evening, Phostis repeated the message with which Krispos had charged him; he'd give Krispos no chance to accuse him of shirking a task once accepted. Sarkis paused in his methodical chewing only long enough to shove the bowl of apricots toward him. He shook his head, not quite in disgust but not quite politely, either.

Sarkis' heavy-lidded eyes—piggy little eyes, Phostis thought distaste-fully—glinted in mirth. "Your first campaign, isn't it, young Majesty?" he said.

"Yes," Phostis said shortly. Half the officers he'd seen had asked the same question. Most of them seemed to want to score points off his inex-perience.

But Sarkis just smiled, showing orange bits of apricot between his heavy teeth. "I wasn't much older than you are now when I first served under your father. He was still learning how to command then; he'd never done it before, you know. And he had to start at the top and make soldiers who'd been leading armies for years obey him. It couldn't have been easy, but he managed. If he hadn't, you wouldn't be here listening to me flap-ping my gums."

"No, I suppose not," Phostis said. He knew Krispos had started with nothing and made his way upward largely on his own; his father went on about it often enough. But from his father, it had just seemed like boast-ing. Sarkis made it feel as if Krispos had accomplished something remark-

able, and that he deserved credit for it. Phostis, however, was not inclined
to give Krispos credit for anything.

The Vaspurakaner general went on, "Aye, he's a fine man, your father.
Take after him and you'll do well." He swigged from a goblet of wine at
his elbow, then breathed potent fumes into Phostis' face. The throaty accent of his native land grew thicker. "Phos made a mistake when he didn't
let Krispos be born a prince."

The folk of Vaspurakan followed Phos, but heretically; they believed
the good god had created them first among mankind, and thus they styled
themselves princes and princesses. The anathemas Videssian prelates flung
their way were one reason most of them were well enough content to see
their mountainous land controlled by Makuran, which judged all forms
of Phos worship equally false and did not single out Vaspurakaners for
persecution. Even so, many folk from Vaspurakan sought their fortune in
Videssos as merchants, musicians, and warriors.

Phostis said, "Sarkis, has my father ever asked you to conform to
Videssian usages when you worship?"

"What's that?" Sarkis dug a finger into his ear. "Conform, you say? No,
never once. If the world won't conform to us princes, why should we conform ourselves to it?"

"For the same reason he seeks to bring the Thanasioi to orthodoxy?" By
the doubt in his voice, Phostis knew he was asking the question as much
of himself as of Sarkis.

But Sarkis answered it: "He doesn't persecute princes because we give
no trouble outside of our faith. You ask me, the Thanasioi are using religion as an excuse for brigandage. That's evil on the face of it."

Not if the material world is itself the evil, Phostis thought. He kept that
to himself. Instead, he said, "I know some Vaspurakaners do take on orthodoxy to help further their careers. You call them Tzatoi in your language, don't you?"

"So we do," Sarkis said. "And do you know what that means?" He
waited for Phostis to shake his head, then grinned and boomed, "It means
'traitors,' that's what. We of Vaspurakan are a stubborn breed, and our
memories long."

"Videssians are much the same," Phostis said. "When my father set out
to reconquer Kubrat, didn't he take his maps from the imperial archives
where they'd lain unused for three hundred years?" He blinked when he
noticed he'd used Krispos as an example.

If Sarkis also noticed, he didn't remark on it. He said, "Young Majesty,
he did just that; I saw those maps with my own eyes when we were plan-

ning the campaign, and faded, rat-chewed things they were—though use-ful nonetheless. But three hundred years—young Majesty, three hundred years are but a fleabite on the arse of time. It's likely been three hundred eons since Phos shaped Vaspur the Firstborn from the fabric of his will."

He grinned impudently at Phostis, as if daring him to cry heresy. Phostis kept his mouth shut; Krispos had baited him too often to make it so easy to get a rise out of him. He did say, "Three hundred years seems a long enough time to me."

"Ah, that's because you're young," Sarkis exclaimed. "When I was your age, the years seemed to stretch like chewy candy, and I thought each one would never end. Now I haven't so much sand left in my glass, and I re-sent every grain that runs out."

"Yes," Phostis said, though he'd pretty much stopped listening when Sarkis started going on about his being young. He wondered why old men did that so much; it wasn't as if he could help being the age he was. But if he had a goldpiece for every time he'd heard *that's because you're young,* he was sure he could remit a year's worth of taxes to every peasant in the Em-pire.

Sarkis said, "Well, I've kept you here long enough, young Majesty. When you get bored with chatter, just press on. That's the advantage of rank, you know: you don't have to put up with people you find tedious."

Only my father, Phostis thought: a single exception that covered a lot of ground. But that was not the sort of thought he could share with Sarkis, or indeed with anyone save possibly Digenis. He was somehow sure the priest would understand, though to him any concern not directly related to Phos and the world to come was of secondary importance.

Having been given an excuse to depart, he took advantage of it.

Even with an army newly arrived and crowding its streets, Nakoleia seemed a tiny town to anyone used to Videssos the city. Tiny, backwater, provincial . . . the scornful adjectives came readily to Phostis' mind. Whether or not they were true, they would stick.

Nakoleia was sensibly laid out in a grid. He made his way back to Krispos through deepening dusk and streaming soldiers without undue difficulty. His father's quarters were at the eparch's residence, across the town square from the chief temple to Phos. Like many throughout the Empire, that building was modeled after the High Temple in the capital. Phostis' first reaction was that it was a poor, cheap copy. His second, con-trary one was to wish fewer goldpieces had been spent on the structure.

He stopped in his tracks halfway across the square. "By the good god," he exclaimed, careless of who might hear him, "I'm on my way to being a Thanasiot myself."

He wondered why that hadn't occurred to him sooner. Much of what Digenis preached was identical to the doctrines of the heretical sect, save that he made those doctrines seem virtuous, whereas to Krispos they were base and vicious. Given a choice between his father's opinions and those of anyone else, Phostis automatically inclined to the latter.

The irony of his position suddenly struck him. What business had he sallying forth to crush the vicious heretics when he agreed with most of what they taught? He imagined going to Krispos and telling him that. It was the quickest way he could think of to unburden himself of all his worldly goods.

It would also forfeit the succession if anything would. Suddenly that mattered a great deal. The Avtokrator was a great power in the ecclesiastical hierarchy. If *he* were Avtokrator, he could guide Videssos toward Digenis' teachings. If someone stodgy or orthodox—Evripos sprang to mind—began to wear the red boots, persecution would continue. It behooved him, then, not to give Krispos any reason to supplant him.

With that thought in mind, he hurried across the cobblestones toward the eparch's mansion. The Halogai newly posted outside it stared suspiciously until they recognized him, then swung up their axes in salute.

His father, as usual, was wading through documents when he came into the chamber. Krispos looked up with an irritated frown. "What are you doing back here already? I sent you out to—"

"I know what you sent me out to do," Phostis said. "I have done it. Here." He pulled a parchment from the pouch on his belt and threw it down on the desk in front of Krispos. "These are the signatures of the officers to whom I transmitted your order."

Krispos leaned back in his seat so he could more easily scan the names. When he looked up, the frown had disappeared. "You did well. Thank you, son. Take the rest of the evening as your own; I have no more tasks for you."

"As you say, Father." Phostis started to walk away.

The Avtokrator called him back. "Wait. Don't go off angry. How do you think I've slighted you now?"

The way Krispos put the question only annoyed Phostis more. Forgetting he intended to keep on his father's good side, he growled, "You might sound happier that I did what you wanted."

"Why should I?" Krispos answered. "You did your duty well; I said as much. But the task was not that demanding. Do you want special praise every time you piddle without getting your boots wet?"

They glowered at each other in mutual incomprehension. Phostis wished he'd just shown Krispos the parchment instead of giving it to him.

Then he could have torn it up and thrown it in his face. As it was, he had to content himself with slamming the door behind him as he stamped out.

Full darkness had fallen by the time he was out on the plaza again. The Haloga guards gave him curious looks, but his face did not encourage questions. Only when he'd put the eparch's residence well behind him did he realize he had no place to go. He paused, plucked at his beard—a gesture very like his father's—and tried to figure out what to do next.

Drinking himself insensible was one obvious answer. Torches blazed in front of all the taverns he could see, and doubtless on ones he couldn't, as well. He wondered if the innkeepers had imported extra wine from the countryside while the imperial army's quartermasters brought their supplies into Nakoleia. It wouldn't have surprised him; to sordid materialists, the arrival of so many thirsty soldiers had to look like a bonanza.

He didn't take long to decide against the taverns. He had nothing against wine in its place; it was healthier to drink than water, and less likely to give you the flux. But drunkenness tore the soul away from Phos and left it base and animalistic, easy meat for the temptations of Skotos. The state of his soul mattered a great deal to him at the moment The less he did to corrupt it, the surer his hope of heaven.

He glanced across the square to the temple. Its entrance was also lit, and men filed in to pray. Some, by the way they walked, had got drunk first. Phostis' lip curled in contempt. He didn't want to pray with drunks. He didn't want to pray in a building modeled after the High Temple, either, not when he discovered himself in sympathy with the Thanasioi.

A breeze from off the Videssian Sea had picked up with the coming of evening. It was not what sent a chill through him. So long as his father held the throne, he was in deadly danger—had placed himself there, in fact, the instant he understood what Digenis' preaching implied. The odds that Krispos would turn away from materialism were about as slim as those of oranges sprouting from stalks of barley. Having been born with nothing—as he never tired of repeating—Krispos put about as much faith in things as he did in Phos.

So what did that leave? Phostis didn't want to drink and he didn't want to pray. He didn't feel like fornicating, either, though the whores of Nakoleia were probably working even harder than the taverners—and probably cheating their customers less.

In the end, he went back aboard the *Triumphant* and curled up in the bunk inside his tiny cabin. After a few hours ashore, even the small motion of the ship as it rocked back and forth beside the dock felt strange. Before long, though, it lulled him to sleep.

Horns blared, pipes shrilled, and deep-toned drums thumped. Videssos' banner, gold sunburst on blue, flew tall and proud at the head of the army as it marched forth from Nakoleia's land gate. Many of the horsemen had tied blue and yellow strips of cloth to their mounts' manes. The sea breeze stirred them into a fine martial display.

People packed the walls of Nakoleia. They cheered as the army rode out of the city. Some of the cheers, Krispos thought, had to be sincere. Some were probably even regretful, from tavernkeepers and merchants whose business had soared thanks to the soldiers. And a few—Krispos hoped only a few—were lies from the throats of Thanasioi spying out his strength.

He turned to Phostis, whose horse stood beside his as they watched the troops ride past. "Go back to Noetos, who commands the rear guard. Tell him to have his men be especially alert to anyone sneaking out of Nakoleia. We don't want the heretics to know exactly what all we have along with us."

"Not everyone leaving the city is sneaking out," Phostis answered.

"I know," Krispos said sourly. Like every army, this one had its camp followers, women and occasional men of easy virtue. Also following the imperial force was a larger number of sutlers and traders than Krispos was happy about. He went on, "What can I do? With our bases at Harasos and Rogmor burned out, I'll need all the help I can get feeding the troops."

"Harasos *and* Rogmor?" Phostis said, raising an eyebrow. "I'd not heard that."

"Then you might be the only one in the whole army who hasn't." Krispos gave his eldest an exasperated glare. "Don't you take any notice of what's going on around you? They hit both caches while we were still asea; by the good god, they seemed to know what we were up to almost before we did."

"How do you suppose they managed to learn where we were storing supplies?" Phostis asked in a curiously neutral voice.

"As I've said over and over"—Krispos rubbed Phostis' nose in his inattention—"we have traitors among us, too. I wish I knew who they were, by Phos; I'd make them regret their treachery. But that's the great curse of civil war: the foe looks just like you, and so can hide in your midst. D'you see?"

"Hm? Oh, yes. Of course, Father."

Krispos sniffed. Phostis hadn't looked as if he was paying attention; his face had a withdrawn, preoccupied expression. If he wouldn't give heed to something that was liable to get him killed, what *would* hold his interest? Krispos said, "I really wish I knew how the heretics heard about my plans. They'd have needed some time to plan their attacks, so they must have known my route of march about as soon as I decided on it—maybe even before I decided on it."

He'd hoped the little joke would draw some kind of reaction from Phostis, but the youngster only nodded. He turned his horse toward the rear of the army. "I'll deliver your order to Noetos."

"Repeat it back to me first," Krispos said, wanting to make sure Phostis had done any listening to him at all.

His eldest reacted to that, with a scowl. He gave back the order in a precise, emotionless voice, then rode away. Krispos stared after him—something about the set of his back wasn't quite right. Krispos told himself he was imagining things. He'd pushed Phostis too far there, asking him to repeat a command as if he were a raw peasant recruit with manure on his boots.

Of course, raw peasant recruits had more incentive to remember accurately than did someone who could aspire to no higher station than the one he already held. It was, in fact, difficult to aspire to a lower station than raw peasant recruit: about the only thing lower than peasant recruit was peasant. Krispos knew about that. Sometimes he wished his sons did, too.

THE ARMY WAS RIDING FORWARD, PHOSTIS BACK. THAT BROUGHT him toward Noetos twice as fast as he would have gone otherwise and cut in half his time to think. He had a pretty good idea how the Thanasioi had learned where the imperial army would set up its supply dumps: he'd named them for Digenis. He hadn't intended to betray his father's campaign, but would Krispos believe that?

Phostis didn't for a moment imagine Krispos wouldn't find out. He did not see eye to eye with his father, but he did not underestimate him, either. Nobody incapable stayed on the throne of Videssos for more than twenty years. When Krispos set his mind to learning something, sooner or later he would. And when he did . . .

Phostis wasn't sure what the consequences of that would be, but he was sure they'd be unpleasant—for him. They wouldn't stop at scolding, either. Ruining a campaign was worse than a scolding matter. It was the sort of matter that would put his head on the block were he anyone but a junior Avtokrator. Given his father's penchant for evenhanded—at the moment, Phostis thought of it as heavyhanded—justice, it might put his head on the block anyway.

He wondered whether he ought to pass his father's order on to Noetos. If he truly adhered to the principles of the Thanasioi, how could he hinder the cause of his fellow believers? But if he had any thought for his own safety, how could he not transmit the order? Krispos would descend on him like an avalanche for that. And if his father's suspicions were aroused, his own role in the matter of the supply dumps grew more likely to emerge.

What to do? No more time for thought—there was the rearguard commander's banner, blue sunburst on gold. The reversed imperial colors marked the rear of the army, and out from under the banner, straight toward him, rode Noetos, a solid, middle-aged officer like so many who served under Krispos, unflappable rather than brilliant. He saluted and called out in a ringing voice, "How may I serve you, young Majesty?"

"Uh," Phostis said, and then "Uh" again; he still hadn't made up his mind. In the end, his mouth answered, not his brain. "My father bids you to be especially alert for anyone sneaking out of Nakoleia, lest the stranger prove a Thanasiot spy." He hated himself as soon as he had spoken, but that was too late—the words were gone.

They proved not to matter, though. Noetos saluted again, clenched fist over his heart, and said, "You may tell his imperial Majesty the matter is already being attended to." Then one of the officer's eyelids fell and rose in an unmistakable wink. "You can also tell Krispos not to go trying to teach an old fox how to rob henhouses."

"I'll—pass on both those messages," Phostis said faintly.

He must have looked a trifle wall-eyed, for Noetos threw back his head and let go with one of those deep, manly chortles that never failed to turn Phostis' stomach. "You do that, young Majesty," he boomed. "This'd be your first campaign, wouldn't it? Aye, of course it would. Good for you. You'll learn some things you'd never find out in the palaces."

"Yes, I'm discovering that," Phostis said. He started back toward the front of the army. That was a slower trip than the one from the front to the rear guard, for now he was moving with the stream and gaining more slowly on any point within it. He had the time to think he could have used before. He certainly was learning new things away from the palaces, not least among them how to be afraid much of the time. He doubted that was what Noetos had meant.

The baggage train traveled in the center of the strung-out army, the safest position against attack. Beeves shambled along, lowing. Wagons rattled and squeaked and jounced; ungreased axles squealed loud and shrill enough to set Phostis' teeth on edge. Some of the wagons carried hard-baked bread; others fodder for the horses; others arrows tied in neat sheaves of twenty, ready to be popped into empty quivers; still others carried the metal parts and tackle for siege engines whose timbers would be cut and trimmed on the spot under direction of the military engineers.

Noncombatants traveled with the baggage train. Healer-priests in robes of blue rode mules that alternated between walk and trot to keep up with the longer-legged horses. A few merchants with stocks of fancy goods for officers who could afford them preferred buggies to horseback. So did some of the loose women any army attracts, though others rode astride with as much aplomb as any man.

Some of the courtesans gave Phostis professionally interested smiles. He was used to that, and found it unsurprising: after all, he was young, reasonably well favored, rode a fine horse, and dressed richly. If a woman was mercenary or desperate enough to sell her body to live, he made a logical customer. As for buying such a woman, though—he left that to his brothers.

Then one of the women not only waved but smiled and called out to him. He intended to ignore her as he had all the others, but something about her—maybe the unusual combination of creamy skin and black, black hair that framed her face in ringlets—seemed familiar. He took a longer look . . . and almost steered his horse into a boulder by the side of the road. He'd seen Olyvria, naked and stretched out on a bed, somewhere under Videssos the city.

He felt himself turn crimson. What did she expect him to do, ride over and ask how she'd been since she put some clothes on? Maybe she did, because she kept on waving. He looked straight ahead and dug his knees into his horse's ribs, urging the beast up into a fast canter that hurried it away from the baggage train and the now-dressed wench.

He thought hard as he drew near Krispos. What *was* Olyvria doing here, anyhow? The only answer that occurred to him was spying for Digenis. He wondered if she'd somehow sailed with the imperial army. If not, she'd made better time overland than he'd have thought possible for anyone but a courier.

He wondered if he ought to tell his father about her—she certainly was the sort of person about whom Krispos worried. But his father had no reason to believe he knew anything about her, and she was likely a Thanasiot herself. He had no reason to give her away, not even his own advantage.

Krispos rode at the head of the army. Phostis came up and delivered both messages from Noetos. Krispos laughed when he heard the second one. "He is an old fox, by the good god," he said. Then he turned serious again. "I would have failed in my duty, though, if I'd failed to give him that order. There's a lesson you need to remember, son: an Avtokrator can't count on things happening without him. He has to make sure they happen."

"Yes, Father," Phostis said, he hoped dutifully. He knew Krispos lived by the principles he espoused. His father had given the Empire of Videssos two decades of stable government, but at the cost of turning fussy, driven, and suspicious.

He'd also developed an alarming facility for picking thoughts out of Phostis' head. "You no doubt have in mind that you'll do it all differently when your backside warms the throne. I tell you, lad, there are but two ways, mine and Anthimos'. Better you should shoulder the burden yourself than let it fall on the Empire."

"So you've said, more than once," Phostis agreed: more than a thousand times, he meant. Hearing the resignation in his voice. Krispos sighed and returned his attention to the road ahead.

Phostis started to carry the argument further, but forbore. He'd been about to put forward the wisdom and reliability of a small group of trusted advisors who might carry enough of the administrative burden to keep it from overwhelming an Avtokrator. Before he spoke, though, he remembered the false friends and sycophants he'd already had to dismiss, people who sought to use him for their own gain. Just because advisors were trusted did not mean they wouldn't be venal.

He jerked on the reins; his horse snorted indignantly as he pulled its head away from that of Krispos' mount. But conceding his father a point always annoyed him. By riding away from Krispos, he wouldn't have to concede anything, either to his father or to himself.

By the end of the day, the imperial army had moved far enough inland to make sunset a spectacle very different from what Phostis was used to. Having land all around seemed suddenly confining, as if he were closed off from the infinite possibilities for travel available at Videssos the city. Even the sounds were strange: night birds unknown in the imperial capital announced their presence with trills and strange drumming noises.

Krispos' tent, however, did its best to re-create the splendor of the imperial palaces, using canvas rather than stone. Torches and bonfires held night at bay; officers going in and out took the place of the usual run of petitioners. Some emerged glum, others pleased, again as it would have been back in the city.

As in the capital, Phostis had no choice but to establish his own lodging uncomfortably close to that of his father. Also as in Videssos the city, he did choose to stay as far from Krispos as he could. The servitors who raised his tent carefully did not raise their eyebrows when he ordered them to place it to the rear and off to one side of Krispos' larger, grander shelter.

Phostis ate from the cookpot the Halogai set up in front of Krispos' pavilion. He ran no risk of bumping into his father there; by all accounts, Krispos' habit on campaign was to share the rations of his common soldiers, so he was probably off somewhere standing in line with a bowl and a spoon like any cavalry trooper.

Had he sampled his own guards' stew that evening, he would not have been happy with it. It had a sharp, bitter undertaste that made Phostis' tongue want to shrivel up. The Halogai liked it no better than he, and were less restrained in suggesting appropriate redress.

"Maybe if so bad next time, we cut up cook and mingle his meat with the mush," one of them said. The rest of the northerners nodded so soberly that Phostis, who had at first smiled, began to wonder if the Haloga was joking.

He'd hardly finished supper when his guts knotted and cramped. He made for the latrines at a dead run and barely managed to hike up his robes and squat over a slit trench before he was noisomely ill. Wrinkling his nose at the stench, he got painfully to his feet. A Haloga crouched a few feet away. Another came hurrying up a moment later. Before he could tear down his breeches, he cried in deep disgust, "Oh, by the gods of the north, I've gone and shit myself!"

Phostis made several more trips out to the slit trenches as the night wore on. He began to count himself lucky that he hadn't had to echo the Haloga's melancholy wail. More often than not, several guardsmen were at the latrine with him.

Finally, some time past midnight, he found himself alone in the darkness out there. He'd gone a good ways away from his tent in the hope of finding untrodden, unbefouled ground. Just as he started to squat, someone called from beyond the slit trenches: "Young Majesty!"

His head went up in alarm—it was a woman's voice. But what he had to do was more urgent than any embarrassment. When he'd finished, he wiped sick sweat from his forehead and started slowly back toward his tent.

"Young Majesty!" The call came again.

This time he recognized the voice: it was Olyvria's. "What do you want with me?" he growled. "Haven't you seen me mortified enough, here and back in the city?"

"You misunderstand, young Majesty," she said in injured tones. She held up something; in the dark, he couldn't tell what it was. "I have here a decoction of the wild plum and black pepper that will help relieve your distress."

Had she offered him her body, he would have laughed at her. He'd already declined that when he was feeling perfectly fine. But at the moment, he would have crowned her Empress for something that stopped his insides from turning inside out.

He hurried over to her, skipping across slit trenches as he went. She held a small glass vial out to him; distant torchlight reflected faintly from it. He yanked off the stopper, raised the vial to his lips, and drank.

"Thank you," he said—or started to. For some reason, his mouth didn't want to work right. He stared at the vial he still held in his hand. All at once, it seemed very far away, and receding quickly. Agonizingly slow, a thought trickled across his brain: *I've been tricked.* He turned and tried to run, but felt himself falling instead. *I've been*— Unconsciousness seized him before he could find the word *stupid*.

Chapter IV

"LET'S GET MOVING," KRISPOS SAID IRRITABLY. "WHERE'S PHOSTIS taken himself off to, anyhow? If he thinks I'll hold up the whole army for his sake, he's wrong."

"Maybe he's fallen into the latrine," Evripos said. Bad food was a risk on campaign; plenty of Halogai had been running back and forth in the night. The gibe might have been funny had Evripos sounded less hopeful it was true.

Krispos said, "I haven't time for anyone's nonsense today, son—his or yours." He turned to one of his guardsmen. "Skalla, stick your head into his tent and rout him out."

"Aye, Majesty." Like a lot of his fellows, Skalla looked even fairer— paler was probably a better word—than usual this morning. He strode off to do Krispos' bidding, but returned to the imperial pavilion a moment later with a puzzled expression on his face. "Majesty, he is not there. The coverlet is thrown back as if he'd got out of his cot, but he is not there."

"Well, the ice take it, where is he, then?" Krispos snapped. What Evripos had said sparked a thought. He told Skalla, "Pick a squad of guards and go up and down the slit trenches in a hurry, to make sure he wasn't taken ill there."

"Aye, Majesty." Skalla's voice was doleful. For one thing, now that morning had come, the latrines were busy. Anyone who spotted Phostis there would have raised an uproar. For another . . .

"Pick men the flux missed," Krispos said. "I wouldn't want the stink to make them sick all over again."

"I thank you, Majesty." The Halogai were not what one would call a cheerful folk, but Skalla seemed more pleased with the world.

That did not mean he and the squad of guardsmen had any luck turning up Phostis. When he came back to report failure to Krispos, the Avtokrator said, "I'm not going to wait for him, by the good god. Let's get everyone moving. He'll turn up—where else is he going to go? And when he does, I shall have a word or two with him—a pungent word or two."

Skalla nodded; from everything Krispos had gleaned of how life worked in Halogaland, sons there knew better than to give already grizzled fathers more gray hair. He let out a mordant chuckle—it sounded too good to be true.

The imperial army did not get moving as fast as he would have wanted; it was newly mustered and still shaking down. He'd been sure Phostis would appear before the troops really started heading south and west. But his eldest did not appear. Evripos opened his mouth to say something that surely would have proved ill-advised. Krispos' glare made certain it never crossed the barrier of his son's lips.

By the time the army had been an hour on the road, Krispos' anger melted into worry. He sent couriers to each regiment to summon Phostis by name. The couriers returned to him. Phostis did not. Krispos turned to Evripos. "Fetch me Zaidas, at once." Evripos did not argue.

The wizard, not surprisingly, had a good notion of why he'd been summoned. He came straight to the point. "When was the young man last seen?"

"I've been trying to find out," Krispos answered. "He seems to have been taken with the same flux that seized a fair number of the Halogai last night. Several of them saw him once, or more than once, squatting over a latrine trench. No one, though, has any clear memory of spotting him there after about the seventh hour of the night."

"An hour or so past midnight, then? Hmm." Zaidas' eyes went far away, into a place Krispos could not follow. Despite that, though, he was a thoroughly practical man. "The first thing to determine, Your Majesty, is whether he be alive or dead."

"You're right, of course." Krispos bit his lip. For all his quarrels with his eldest, for all his doubts as to whether Phostis *was* his eldest, he discovered he feared for Phostis' life as might any father, true or adoptive. "Can you do that at once, eminent and sorcerous sir?"

"A hedge wizard could do as much, Your Majesty, with the abundance of Phostis' effects present here," the mage answered, smiling. "An elementary use of the law of contagion: these effects, once handled by the young Majesty, retain an affinity for him and will demonstrate it under sorcerous prodding . . . assuming, of course, that he yet remains among the living."

"Aye, assuming," Krispos said harshly. "Find out at once, then, if we can go on making that assumption."

"Of course, Your Majesty. Have you some artifact of your son's that I might use?"

Krispos pointed. "There's his bedding, slung over the back of the horse he should be riding. Will that do?"

"Excellently." Zaidas rode over to the animal at which Krispos had pointed and pulled a coverlet from the lump of cinched-down bedding. "This is a very basic spell, Your Majesty, one that requires no apparatus, merely a concentration of my will to increase the strength of the link between the blanket here and the young Majesty."

"Just get on with it," Krispos said.

"As you say." Zaidas laid the blanket across his knees, as he switched the reins to his left hand. He chanted briefly in the archaic dialect of Videssian most often used in the liturgy for Phos' Temple, at the same time moving his right hand in small, swift passes above the coverlet.

The square of soft wool rippled gently, like the surface of the sea when stirred by a soft breeze. "Phostis is alive," Zaidas declared in a voice that brooked no contradiction. "Had he left mankind, the coverlet would have lain quiescent, as it did before I completed the incantation."

"Thank you, eminent and sorcerous sir," Krispos said. Some of the great weight of worry he'd borne rolled off his shoulders—some, but far from all. The next question followed like one winter storm rolling into Videssos the city hard on the heels of another: "Having found that he is among the living, can you now learn among which living folk he is at the moment?"

Zaidas nodded, not in answer, Krispos thought, but to show he'd expected the Avtokrator would ask that. "Yes, Your Majesty, I can do so," he said. "It's not quite so simple a spell as the one I just used, but one like it springs from the workings of the law of contagion."

"I don't care if it springs from the ground when you pour pig manure around the place where you planted it," Krispos answered. "If you can work your magic while we move, so much the better. If not, I'll give you all the guards you need for as long as you need them."

"That shouldn't be necessary," Zaidas said. "I think I have with me all I shall require." He drew from a saddlebag a short, thin stick and a small silver cup. From his canteen, he poured wine into the cup until it was nearly full, then passed it to Krispos. "Hold this a moment, Your Majesty, if you would be so kind." As soon as he had both hands free, he teased a fuzzy length of wool loose from Phostis' blanket, then wrapped it around the stick.

He held out a hand for the silver cup, which Krispos returned to him. When he had it back, he dropped in the stick so it floated on the wine. "This spell may also be accomplished with water, Your Majesty, but I am of the opinion that the spirituous component of the wine improves its efficacy."

"However you think best," Krispos said. Listening to Zaidas cheerfully explain how he did what he did helped the Emperor not think about all the things that could have happened to Phostis.

The wizard said, "Once I have chanted, the little stick here, by virtue of its connection to the wool that was once connected to your son, will turn in the cup to reveal the direction in which he lies."

This spell, as Zaidas had said, was more intricate than the first one he'd used. He needed both hands for the passes, and he guided his horse by the pressure of his knees. At the climax of the incantation, he stabbed down at the floating stick with a rigid forefinger, crying out at the same time in a loud, commanding voice.

Krispos waited for the stick to quiver and point like a well-trained hunting dog. Instead, it spun wildly in the cup, splashing wine up over the edge and then sinking out of sight in the rich ruby liquid. Krispos stared. "What does *that* mean?"

"Your Majesty, if I knew, I would tell you." Zaidas sounded even more surprised than the Avtokrator had. He paused for a moment to think, then went on, "It might mean this blanket was in fact never in direct contact with Phostis. But no—" He shook his head. "That cannot be, either. Had the blanket no affinity for your son, it would not have responded to the spell that showed us he is alive."

"Yes, I follow your reasoning," Krispos said. "What other choices have we?"

"Next most likely, or so it seems to me, is that my sorcerous efforts are somehow being blocked, to keep me from learning where the young Majesty is," Zaidas said.

"But you are a master mage, one of the leaders of the Sorcerers' Collegium," Krispos protested. "How can anyone keep you from working what you wish?"

"Several ways, Your Majesty. I am not the only sorcerer of my grade within the Empire of Videssos. Another master, or perhaps even a team of lesser wizards, may be working to keep the truth from me. Notice the spell did not send us off in a direction that later proved false, but merely prevented us from learning the true one. That is an easier magic."

"I see," Krispos said slowly. "You named one way, or possibly even two, in which you could be deceived. Are there others?"

"Yes," Zaidas answered. "I am a master in wizardry based on our faith in Phos and rejection of his dark foe Skotos." The mage paused to spit. "This is, you might say, a two-poled system of magic. The Halogai with their many gods, or the Khamorth of the steppe with their belief in supernatural powers animating each rock or stream or sheep or blade of grass, view the world from such a different perspective that their sorcery is more difficult for a mage of my school to detect or counter. The same applies in lesser degree to the Makuraners, who filter the power of what they term the God through the intermediary of the Prophets Four."

"Assuming this blocking magic is from some school other than ours, can you fight through it?" Krispos asked.

"Your Majesty, there I am imperfectly certain. In theory, since ours is the only true faith, magic developed from it will in the end prove mightier than that based on any other system. In practice, man's creations being the makeshifts they are, a great deal depends on the strength and skill of the mages involved, regardless of the school to which they belong. I can try my utmost, but I cannot guarantee success."

"Do your utmost," Krispos said. "I suppose you will need to halt for your more complicated spells. I'll leave you a courier; send word the moment you have results of any sort."

"I shall, Your Majesty," Zaidas promised. He looked as if he wanted to say something more. Krispos waved for him to go on. He did: "I pray you forgive me, Your Majesty, but you might also be wise to send out riders to beat the countryside."

"I'll do that," Krispos said with a sinking feeling. Zaidas was warning him not to expect success in a hurry, if at all.

The squads of horsemen clattered forth, some ahead of the army, some back toward Nakoleia, others out to either side of the track. No encouraging word came from them by sundown. Krispos and the main body of his force rode on, leaving Zaidas behind to set up his search magic. A company stayed with him to protect him from Thanasioi or simple robbers. Krispos waited and waited for the courier to return. At last, just as weariness was about to drive him to his cot, the fellow rode into the encampment. Seeing the question in the Emperor's eyes, he just shook his head.

"No luck?" Krispos said, for the sake of being sure.

"No luck," the courier answered. "I'm sorry, Your Majesty. The wizard's magic failed again: more than once, from what he told me."

Grimacing, Krispos thanked the man and sent him to his own rest. He hadn't really believed Zaidas would stay baffled. He lay down on the cot as he'd intended, but found sleep a long time coming.

S TUPID. THE WORD SLID SLUGGISHLY THROUGH PHOSTIS' MIND. Because he saw only darkness, he thought for a confused moment that he was still back at the latrines. Then he realized a bandage covered his eyes. He reached up to pull it off, only to discover his hands had been efficiently tied behind his back, his legs at knees and ankles.

He groaned. The sound came out muffled—he was also gagged. He groaned again anyhow. His head felt like an anvil on which a smith about as tall as the top of the High Temple's dome was hammering out a complicated piece of ironwork. He was lying on something hard—boards, he found out when a splinter dug into the thin strip of flesh between blindfold and gag.

Adding to the pounding agony behind his eyes were squeaks and jolts. *I'm in a wagon, or maybe a cart,* he thought, amazed and impressed that his poor benighted brain functioned at all. He groaned one more time.

"He's coming around," said somebody—a man—above and in front of him. The fellow laughed, loudly and raucously. "It's took him long enough, it has, it has."

"Shall we let him see where he's going?" another voice, a woman's, asked. After a moment, Phostis recognized it: Olyvria's. He ground his teeth in helpless fury; he felt he'd already used up all the groans in him.

The man—the driver?—said, "Nah, our orders was to bring him the first stage of the way to Livanios without him knowin' nothin' about it. That's what your pa done said, and that's what we does. So don't go untyin' him, either, you hear me?"

"I hear you, Syagrios," Olyvria answered. "It's too bad. We'd all be happier if we could get him cleaned up a bit."

"I've smelled worse, out in the fields at manuring time," Syagrios said. "The stink won't kill him, and it won't kill you, neither."

Phostis had been aware of a foul smell since his wits returned. He hadn't realized he was the cause of it. He must have gone on fouling himself after Olyvria's potion—the one that was supposed to end his internal turmoil—forced him down into oblivion. *I'll have revenge for that, by the good god,* he thought. *I'll*—He gave up. No vengeance seemed savage enough to suit him.

Olyvria said, "I wish he would have come and talked with me when he saw me by the baggage train. He recognized me, I know he did. I think I could have persuaded him to come with us of his own will. I know he follows Thanasios' gleaming path, at least in large measure."

Syagrios gave a loud, skeptical grunt. "How d'you know that?"

"He wouldn't bed me when he had the chance," Olyvria answered.

Her companion grunted again, in a slightly different tone. "Well, maybe. It don't matter, though. Our orders was to snatch him fast as we could, and we done did it. Livanios will be happy with us."

"So he will," Olyvria said.

She and Syagrios went on talking, but Phostis stopped heeding them. He hadn't figured out for himself—though he supposed he should have—that his kidnappers were Thanasioi. As it did Olyvria, the irony of that struck him, though in his case the impact was far more forcible. Given any sort of choice in the matter, he would have picked a different way of coming into their number. But they had not given him any choice.

He closed his lips on the gag and tried to draw a tiny bit of the cloth into his mouth. He needed several tries before he nipped it between upper and lower front teeth. After working awhile on chewing through it, he decided that was easier said than done. He labored instead to get it down so his mouth would be free. Just when he thought he'd succeed about the time he got to wherever Livanios was, the top edge of the gag slid down over his upper lip. Not only could he talk now if he had to, he could also breathe much more easily.

Even though he could talk, he resolved not to, lest his captors gag him more securely. But his body tested his resolve in ways he hadn't anticipated. At last he said, "Could you people please stop long enough to let me make water?"

Syagrios' startled jerk shook the whole wagon. "By the ice, how'd he get his mouth loose?" He turned around, then growled, "Well, why should we bother? You already stink."

"We aren't just stealing him, Syagrios, we're bringing him to us," Olyvria said. "There's no one on the road; why shouldn't we just stand him up and let him do what needs doing? It won't take long."

"Why should we? You didn't lift him in there, and you won't have to lift him out." The man grumbled a little longer, then said, "All right, have it your way." He must have pulled on the reins; the jingle of harness ceased as the wagon stopped. Phostis felt himself lifted by arms as thick and powerful as any Haloga's. He leaned against the side of the wagon on legs that did not want to hold him up. Syagrios said, "Go ahead and piss. Be quick about it."

"It's not that simple for him, you know," Olyvria said. "Here, wait—I'll help." The wagon shifted behind Phostis as she got down. He listened to her come around and stand by him. She hiked up his robe so he wouldn't wet it. As if that weren't mortification enough, she took him in hand and said, "Go on; now you won't splash on your boots."

Syagrios laughed coarsely. "You hold him like that for very long and he'll be too stiff to piss at all."

Phostis hadn't even thought about that aspect of things; what rang through his mind was his father's voice back at Nakoleia, asking him if he wanted praise for piddling without getting his feet wet. At the moment, such praise would have been welcome. He relieved himself as fast as he could; never before had the phrase possessed such real and immediate meaning for him. His sigh when he was through was involuntary but heartfelt.

The robe fluttered down around his tied ankles. Syagrios picked him up and, grunting, lifted him back into the wagon. The fellow talked like a villain and, without Phostis' excuse for filth, was none too clean, but he had brute strength to spare. He set Phostis down flat in the wagon bed, then returned to his place and got his team moving once more.

"You want to gag him again?" he asked Olyvria.

"No," Phostis said—quietly, so they would see he did not have to be gagged. Then he used a word most often perfunctory for an Avtokrator's son: "Please." It was not perfunctory now.

"I think I'd better," Olyvria said after a brief pause. She must have swung round on the seat; her feet came down in the wagon close by Phostis' head. "I'm sorry," she told him as she slipped the gag over his mouth and tied it behind his neck, "but we just can't trust you yet."

Her fingers were smooth and warm and briskly capable; had she given him the chance, he would have bitten them to the bone. He didn't get the chance. He was already discovering she knew how to do much more than lie temptingly naked on a bed.

That discovery would have surprised his brothers even more than it did him. Evripos and Katakolon were convinced lying naked on a bed was all women were good for. Since he was less concerned about finding them there, he found it easier to envision them doing other things. But not even he had imagined finding one who made such an effective kidnapper.

Olyvria got back up beside Syagrios. She remarked, apparently to no one in particular, "If he gets that one off, he'll regret it."

"I'll *make* him regret it." Syagrios sounded as if he looked forward to doing just that. Phostis, who had already started working on the new gag, decided not to go on. He chose to believe Olyvria had given him a hint.

The day was the longest, driest, hungriest, and generally most miserable he'd ever endured. After some endless while, he began to see real black rather than gray through the blindfold. The air grew cooler, almost chilly. *Night,* he thought. He wondered if Syagrios would drive straight on till dawn. If Syagrios did, Phostis wondered if he would still be alive by the time his eyes saw gray once more.

But not long after dark, Syagrios stopped. He picked Phostis up, leaned him against the side of the wagon, then descended, picked him up again, and slung him over his shoulder like a sack of chickpeas. Behind him, Olyvria got the horses moving at a slow walk.

From ahead came a metallic squawk of rusty hinges, then the scrape of something moving against resistance from dirt and gravel: *a gate opening,* Phostis thought. "Hurry up," an unfamiliar male voice said.

"Here we go," Syagrios answered. He picked up his pace. By their hoofbeats, so did the horses behind him. As soon as they stopped, the gate went scrape-squeak. *Closing,* Phostis thought. The slam of a bar falling into place confirmed that. "Ah, good," Syagrios said. "Think we can untie him for now and take the rag off his eyes?"

"I don't see why not," the other man said. "If he gets away from this place, by the good god, he's earned it. And didn't I hear he's halfway set foot on the gleaming path himself?"

"Aye, I've heard that, too." Syagrios laughed. "Thing is, I didn't get to be as old as I am believing everything I hear."

"Set him down so I can cut the ropes easier," Olyvria said. Syagrios put Phostis onto the ground more carefully than if he'd been chickpeas, but not much. Somebody—presumably Olyvria—slit his bonds, then slid the blindfold from his face.

He blinked; his eyes filled with tears. After a day in enforced darkness, even torchlight seemed shockingly bright. When he tried to lever himself up, neither arms nor legs would obey him. He set his teeth against the pain of returning blood. Pins and needles was too mild a phrase for it; it felt more like nails and spikes. They got worse with every passing moment, until he wondered if the maltreated members would fall off.

"It will ease soon," Olyvria assured him.

He wondered how she could know—had she ever been trussed up like a suckling pig on its way to market? But she was right. After a little while, he tried again to stand. This time he made it, though he swayed like a tree in a windstorm.

"He don't look too good," said the fellow who went with this . . . farmhouse, Phostis supposed it was, though the man, lean, pale, and furtive, looked more like a sneak thief than a farmer.

"He'll be hungry," Syagrios said, "and tired." Syagrios seemed very much the stalwart bruiser Phostis had expected. He wasn't even of average height for a Videssian, but had shoulders as wide as any Haloga's and arms thick with corded muscle. At some time in the unknown past, his nose had intercepted a chair or other instrument of strong opinion.

A big gold hoop dangled piratically from his left ear. Phostis pointed at it. "I thought folk who followed the gleaming path didn't wear ornaments like that."

Syagrios' startled stare quickly slid into a scowl. "None of your cursed business what I wear or don't—" he began, folding one big hand into a fist.

"Wait," Olyvria said. "This is something he needs to know." She turned to Phostis. "You're right and yet you're wrong. When we go among men not of our kind, sometimes lack of ostentation can betray us. We have the right to disguise our appearance, just as we may deny our creed to save ourselves."

Phostis bit down hard on that one. A Videssian's faith was his proudest possession; many had been martyred for refusing to compromise the creed. Letting a man—or a woman—dissemble in time of danger went square against everything he'd ever been taught . . . but also made good sense from a practical standpoint.

Slowly he said, "My father will have a hard time sifting those who follow Thanasios' ways from the generality, then." Krispos wouldn't have looked for that. Most heresies, believing themselves orthodox, trumpeted their tenets and made themselves easy targets. But suppressing the Thanasioi would be like striking smoke, which gave way before blows yet was not destroyed.

"That's right," Olyvria said. "We'll give the imperial army more trouble than it can handle. Before long, we'll give the whole Empire more trouble than it can handle." Her eyes sparkled at the prospect.

Syagrios turned to the fellow who'd let them into the courtyard. "Where's the food?" he boomed, slapping his bulging belly with the palm of one hand. No matter what Olyvria said, Phostis had trouble picturing him as an ascetic.

"I'll get it," the skinny man said, and went into the house.

"Phostis needs it more than you," Olyvria said to Syagrios.

"So?" he answered. "I was the one with the wit to ask for it. Of course, our friend here wasn't likely to listen to the likes of him." Phostis thought he deliberately avoided naming the other man. That showed more wit than he'd credited Syagrios with having. If he ever escaped . . . but did he want to escape? He shook his head, bewildered. He didn't know what he wanted.

He didn't know what he wanted, that is, until the fellow who looked like a thief came out with a loaf of black bread, some runny yellow cheese, and a jar of the sort that commonly held cheap wine. Then his growling stomach and spit-filled mouth loudly made their wishes known.

He ate like a starving badger. The wine mounted from his belly to his head. He felt more nearly human that he had since he was drugged, but that wasn't saying much. He asked, "May I have a cloth or a sponge and some water to wash myself? And some clean clothes, if there are any?"

The skinny fellow looked at Syagrios. Syagrios, for all his bluster, looked at Olyvria. She nodded. The skinny fellow said to Phostis, "You're my size, near enough. You can wear one of my old tunics. I'll get it. There's a pitcher and a sponge on a stick in the privy."

Phostis waited until he had the rough, colorless homespun garment in his hands, then headed for the privy. The robe he wore was worth dozens of the one he put on, but he made the exchange with nothing but delight.

He looked down at himself as he came out of the privy. He was no peacock, like some of the young men who swaggered around Videssos the city displaying themselves and their finery on holidays. Even if he'd had such longings—as Katakolon did, to some degree—Krispos wouldn't have let him indulge them. Having been born on a farm, Krispos still kept the poor man's scorn for fancy clothes he couldn't afford himself. Nonetheless, Phostis was sure he'd never worn anything so plain in his whole life.

The thin man pointed at him. "See! Without the embroidered robes, he looks like anybody else. That's what Thanasios says, bless him—take away the riches that separate one man from another and we're all pretty much the same. What we have to do is make sure *nobody* has riches. The lord with the great and good mind will love us for that."

"Other way to make us all the same is let everybody have riches." Syagrios cast a covetous eye on the befouled robe Phostis had been so happy to remove. "Clean that up and it'd bring a pretty piece of change."

"No," Olyvria said. "Try to sell it and you shout 'Here I am!' to Krispos' spies. Livanios ordered us to destroy everything Phostis had when we took him, and that's what we'll do."

"All right, all right," Syagrios said, voice surly. "Still seems a waste, though."

The skinny man rounded on him. "Your theology's not all it should be. The goal is the destruction of riches, says Thanasios, not the equality, for Phos best loves those who give up all they have for the sake of his truth."

"Oh, I don't know about that," Syagrios said. "If all were alike, poor or rich, we wouldn't be jealous of each other, and if jealousy ain't a sin, what is, eh?" He set hands on hips and smiled triumphantly at the thin man.

"I'll tell you what," the other answered hotly, ready as any Videssian to do battle for the sake of his dogmas.

"No, you won't." Olyvria's tone reminded Phostis of the one Krispos used when delivering judgment from the imperial throne. "The forces of materialism are stronger than we are. If we quarrel among ourselves, we are lost . . . so we shall not quarrel."

Syagrios and the skinny fellow both glared at her, but neither one of them carried the argument any further. Phostis was impressed. He wondered what power Olyvria had over her henchmen. Whatever it was, it worked. Maybe she carried an amulet . . . or would a heretic's charm be efficacious? Then again, were the Thanasioi heretics or the most perfect of the orthodox?

Before Phostis could formulate an answer to either of those questions, the skinny man jerked a thumb in his direction and said, "What do we do with this one tonight?"

"Keep watch on him," Olyvria said. "Tomorrow we move on."

"I'm going to tie him up, too, just in case," the skinny fellow said. "If he gets loose, the imperial executioners have a lot of ways to keep you alive when you'd rather be dead."

"I don't think we need to do that," Olyvria said. This time, though, her tone was doubtful, and she looked to Syagrios for support. The short, muscular man shook his head; he sided with the thin fellow. Olyvria's mouth twisted, but she gave over arguing. With a shrug, she turned to Phostis and said, "I think you'd be safe unbound, but they don't trust you enough yet. Try not to hate us for it."

Phostis also shrugged. "I won't deny I've thought long and hard about becoming one of you Thanasioi, but I never thought I'd be . . . recruited . . . this way. If you expect me to be happy about it, I fear you're in for disappointment."

"You're honest, at any rate," Olyvria said.

Syagrios snorted. "He's but a babe, same as you, lass. He don't believe nothin' bad can happen to him, not in his guts, not in his balls. You're young, you say what you want and don't give a fart for what happens next on account of you think you're gonna live forever anyways."

That was the most words Phostis had heard from Syagrios at any one time. Try as he would, he couldn't keep his face straight. His laughter had a high, hysterical edge to it, but it was laughter.

"What's so funny?" Syagrios growled. "You laugh at me, you'll go to the ice. I've sent better and tougher men there than you, by the good god."

When Phostis tried to stop laughing, he found it wasn't easy. He had to take a deep breath, hold it, and let it out slowly before the fit would pass. At last, carefully, he said, "I will apologize, Syagrios. It's just that—that—I never expected you to talk like—like—my father." He held his breath again to stave off another wild attack of laughter.

"Huh." Syagrios' smile revealed several broken teeth and a couple of gaps. "Yeah, maybe that is funny. I guess if you've been around awhile, you start thinkin' one kind o' way."

Before Phostis could answer that or even think about it very much, the skinny man came up to him with a fresh length of rope. "Put your hands behind you," he said. "I won't tie 'em as tight as they was before. I—"

Phostis made his move. The romances he'd read insisted a man whose cause was just could overcome several villains. The writers of those romances had never run into the skinny fellow. Phostis' eyes must have given him away, for the thin man kicked him square in the crotch almost before he managed to raise an arm. He fell in a moaning heap and threw up most of the food he'd eaten. He knew he ought not to writhe and clutch at himself, but he could not help it. He'd never known such pain.

"You were right," Olyvria told the skinny man, her voice curiously neutral. "He needs to be tied tonight."

Skinny nodded. He waited for Phostis' thrashings to cease, then said, "Get up, you. Don't be stupid about it, either, or I'll give you another dose."

Swiping at his mouth with the sleeve of his homespun tunic, Phostis struggled to his feet. He had needed to get used to Digenis' addressing him as *lad* rather than *young Majesty;* now he hurt too much to bridle at being roughly called *you.* At the thin man's gesture, he put his hands behind his back and let himself be tied. Maybe the rope wasn't as tight as it had been before. It was none too loose, either.

His kidnappers brought out a blanket that smelled of horse and draped it over him once he'd lain down. The two men went inside the farmhouse, leaving Olyvria behind for the first watch. She had both a hunting bow and a knife that would have made a decent shortsword.

"You keep an eye on him," Syagrios called from the doorway. "If he tries to get loose, hurt him and holler for us. We can't let him get away."

"I know," Olyvria said. "He shan't."

By the way she handled the bow, Phostis could see she knew what to do with it. He had no doubt she'd shoot him to keep him from escaping. With the dull, sickening ache still in his stones, he wasn't going anywhere anyhow, not for a while. He said as much to Olyvria.

"You were stupid to try to break away there," she answered, again in that odd, dispassionate tone.

"So I found out." The inside of Phostis' mouth tasted like something that had just been scraped out of a sewer.

"Why did you do it?" she asked.

"I don't know. Because I thought I might succeed, I suppose." Phostis thought a little, then added, "Syagrios would probably say because I'm young and stupid." What he thought about both Syagrios and his opinions he would not repeat to a woman, not even one who'd shown him her nakedness, who'd drugged him and stolen him.

He could, at the moment, think of Olyvria's nakedness with absolute detachment. He knew he wasn't ruined for life, but he certainly was ruined for the evening. He wriggled around a little on the hard-packed ground, trying to find some position less uncomfortable than most of the others.

"I'm sorry," Olyvria said, as contritely as if they were friends. "Did you want to rest?"

"What I want to do and what I can do aren't the same," he answered.

"I'm afraid I can't help that," she said, sharply now. "If you'd not been so foolish, I might have managed something, but since you were—" She shook her head. "Syagrios and our other friend are right—we have to get you safe to Livanios. I know he'll be delighted to see you."

"To have me in his hands, you mean," Phostis retorted. "And what puts you so high in Livanios' council? How can you *know* what he will or won't be?"

"It's not hard," Olyvria answered. "He's my father."

ZAIDAS LOOKED WORN. HE'D RIDDEN HARD TO CATCH UP WITH the army. Still in the saddle, he bowed his head to Krispos. "I regret, Your Majesty, that I have had no success in locating your son by sorcerous means. I shall accept without complaint any penalty you see fit to exact for my failure."

"Very well, then," Krispos said. Zaidas stiffened, awaiting the Avtokrator's judgment. Krispos delivered it in his most imperial voice: "I order you henceforth to be forcibly prevented from mouthing such nonsense." He started talking normally again. "Don't you think I know you're doing everything you know how to do?"

"You're generous, Your Majesty," the wizard said, not hiding his relief. He took the reins in his left hand for a moment so he could pound his right fist down onto his thigh. "You can't imagine how this eats at me. I'm used to success, by the lord with the great and good mind. Knowing a mage out there can thwart me makes me furious. I want to find out who he is and where he is so I can thrash him with my bare hands."

His obvious anger made Krispos smile. "A man who believes he can't be beaten is most often proved right." But his grin soon slipped. "Unless, of course, he's up against something rather more than a man. If you were wrong back in the city and we do, in fact, face Harvas—"

"That thought crossed my mind," Zaidas said. "Being beaten by one of that sort would surely salve my self-respect, for who among mortal men could stand alone against him? Before I rejoined you, I ran the same sorcerous tests I'd used at the Sorcerers' Collegium, and others besides. Whoever he may be, my foe is not Harvas."

"Good," Krispos said. "That means Phostis does not lie under Harvas' hands—a fate I'd wish on no one, friend or foe."

"There we agree," Zaidas answered. "We will all be better off if Harvas Black-Robe is never again seen among living men. But knowing he is not the agency of your son's disappearance hardly puts us closer to learning who is responsible."

"Responsible? Who but the Thanasioi? That much I assume. What puzzles me—and you as well, obviously—is how they're able to hide him." Krispos paused, plucked at his beard, and listened over again in his mind to what Zaidas had just said. After a moment's thought, he slowly went on, "Knowing Harvas isn't responsible for stealing Phostis lifts a weight from my heart. Have you any way to learn by sorcery who is to blame?"

The mage bared his teeth in a frustrated grimace that had nothing to do with a smile save in the twist of his lips. "Majesty, my sorcery can't even find your son, let alone who's to blame for absconding with him."

"I understand that," Krispos said. "Not quite what I meant. Sometimes in ruling I find problems where, if I tried to solve them all at once with one big, sweeping law, a lot of people would rise up in revolt. But they still need solving, so I go about it a little at a time, with a small change here, another one there, still another two years later. Anyone who thinks he can solve a complicated mess in one fell swoop is a fool, if you ask me. Problems that grow up over years don't go away in a day."

"True enough, Your Majesty, and wise, too."

"Ha!" Krispos said. "If you're a farmer, it's something you'd better know."

"As may be," Zaidas answered. "I wasn't going to go on with flattery, believe me. I was just going to say I didn't see how your principle, though admirable, applies in this case."

"Someone's magic is keeping you from learning where Phostis is—am I right?" Krispos didn't wait for Zaidas' nod; he knew he was right. He continued, "Instead of looking for the lad for the moment, can you use your magic to learn what sort of sorcery shields him from you? If you can find out who's helping to conceal Phostis, that will tell us something we hadn't known and may help our physical search. Well? Can it be done?"

Zaidas hesitated thoughtfully. At last he said, "The art of magecraft lost a great one when you were born without the talent, Your Majesty. Your mind, if you will forgive a crude comparison, is as twisty as a couple of mating eels."

"That's what comes of sitting on the imperial throne," Krispos answered. "Either it twists you or it breaks you. Does the idea have merit, then?"

"It . . . may," Zaidas said. "It certainly is a procedure I had not considered. I would not promise results, not before trial and not out here away from the resources of the Sorcerers' Collegium. If it works, it will require sorcery of the most delicate sort, for I would not want to alert my quarry to his being scrutinized in this fashion."

"No, that wouldn't do." Krispos reached out and set a hand on Zaidas' arm for a moment. "If you think this worth pursuing, eminent and sorcerous sir, then do what you can. I have faith in your ability—"

"More than I do, right now," Zaidas said, but Krispos neither believed him nor thought he believed himself.

The Avtokrator said, "If the idea turns out not to work, we're no worse off: am I right?"

"I think so, Your Majesty," the wizard answered. "Let me explore what I have here and the techniques I might use. I'm sorry I can't give you a quick answer as to the practicability of your scheme, but it really does require more contemplation and research. I promise I'll inform you as soon as I either see a way to attempt it or discover I have not the skill, knowledge, or tools to undertake it."

"I couldn't ask for more." Halfway through the sentence, Krispos found himself talking to Zaidas' back. The mage had swung his horse away. When he got hold of an idea, he worried it between his teeth—and ceased to worry about protocol or even politeness. In Krispos' mind, his long record of success would have justified far worse lapses of behavior than that.

The Avtokrator soon forced magical schemes and even worry about Phostis to the back of his mind. Early that afternoon, the imperial army rode into Harasos, which let him see firsthand the devastation the Thanasioi had worked on the supply dumps there. In spite of himself, he was impressed. They'd done a job that would have warmed the heart of the most exacting military professional.

Of course, the local quartermasters had made matters easier for them, too. Probably because the warehouses inside the shabby little town's shabby little wall were inadequate, sacks of grain and stacks of cut firewood had been stored outside. Burned black smears on the ground and a lingering smell of smoke showed where they'd rested.

Next to the black smears was an enormous purple one. The broken crockery still in the middle of it said it had been the army's wine ration. Now the men would be reduced to drinking water before long, which would increase both grumbling and diarrhea.

Krispos clicked his tongue between his teeth, sorrowing at the waste. The country hereabouts was not rich; collecting this surplus had taken years of patient effort. It might have seen the district through a famine or, as here, kept the army going without its having to forage on the countryside.

Sarkis rode up and looked over the damage with Krispos. The cavalry general pointed to what had been a corral. "See? They had beeves waiting for us, too."

"So they did." Krispos sighed. "Now the Thanasioi will eat their share of them."

"I thought they had scruples against feasting on meat," Sarkis said.

"That's right, so they do. Well, they've slaughtered some"—the Avtokrator wrinkled his nose at the stench from the bloated carcasses inside the ruined fence—"and driven off the rest. We'll have no use from them, that's certain."

"Aye. Too bad." By his tone, Sarkis worried more about filling his own ample belly than the effect of the raid on the army as a whole.

"We'll be able to bring in a certain amount of food by sea at Nakoleia,"

Krispos said. "By the good god, though, that'll be a long supply line for us to maintain. Will your men be able to protect the wagons as they make their way toward us?"

"Some will get through, Your Majesty. Odds are most will get through. If they hit us, though, we'll lose some," Sarkis answered. "And we'll lose men guarding those wagons, too. They'll be gone from your fighting force as sure as if the rebels shot 'em all in the throat."

"Yes, that's true, too. Rude of you to remind me of it, though." Krispos knew how big a force he could bring to bear against the Thanasioi; he'd campaigned enough to make a good estimate of how many men Sarkis would have to pull from that force to protect the supply line against raiders. Less certain was how many warriors the rebels could array in line of battle. When he'd set out from Videssos the city, he'd thought he had enough men to win a quick victory. That looked a lot less likely now.

Sarkis said, "A pity the wars can't be easy all the time, eh, Your Majesty?"

"Maybe it's just as well," Krispos answered. Sarkis raised a bushy, gray-flecked eyebrow. Krispos explained, "If they were easy, I'd be tempted to fight more often. Who needs that?"

"Aye, something to what you say."

Krispos raised his eyes from the ruined supply dump to the sky. He gauged the weather with skill honed by years on a farm, when the difference between getting through a winter and facing hunger often rode on deciding just when to start bringing in the crops. He didn't like what his senses told him now. The wind had shifted so it was coming out of the northwest; clouds began piling up, thick and black, along the horizon there.

He pointed to them. "We don't have long to do what needs doing. My guess is, the fall rains start early this year." He scowled. "They would."

"Nothing's ever as simple as we wish, eh, Your Majesty?" Sarkis said. "We'll just have to push on as hard as we can. Smash them once and the big worry goes, even if they keep on being a nuisance for years."

"I suppose so." But Sarkis' solution, however practical, left Krispos dissatisfied. "I don't want to have to keep fighting and fighting a war. That will cause nothing but grief for me and for Phostis." He would not say out loud that his kidnapped eldest might not succeed him. "Give a religious quarrel half a chance and it'll fester forever."

"That's true enough, as who should know better than one of the princes?" Sarkis said. "If you imperials would just leave our theology in peace—"

"—the Makuraners would come in and try to convert you by force to the cult of the Four Prophets," Krispos interrupted. "They've done that a few times, down through the years."

"And they've had no better luck than Videssos. We of Vaspurakan are stubborn folk," Sarkis said with a grin that made Krispos remember the lithe young officer he'd once been. He remained solid and capable, but he'd never be lithe again. Well, Krispos wasn't young anymore, either, and if he'd put on less weight than his cavalry commander, his bones still ached after a day in the saddle.

He said, "If I had to rush back to Videssos the city from the borders of Kubrat now, I think I'd die before I got there."

Sarkis had been on that ride, too. "We managed it in our puppy days, though, didn't we?" He looked down at his own expanding frontage. "Me, I'd be more likely to kill horses than myself. I'm as fat as old Mammianos was, and I haven't as many years to give me an excuse."

"Time does go on." Krispos looked northwest again. Yes, the clouds were gathering. His face twisted; that thought had too ominous a ring to suit him. "It's moving on the army, same as it is on each of us. If we don't want to get bogged down in the mud, we have to move fast. You're right about that."

He wondered again whether he should have waited till spring to start campaigning against the Thanasioi. Losing a battle to the heretics would be bad enough, but not nearly so dangerous as having to withdraw in mud and humiliation.

With deliberate force of will, he made his mind turn aside from that path. Too late now to concern himself with what he might have done had he made a different choice. He had to live with the consequences of what he had chosen, and do his best to carve those consequences into the shape he desired.

He turned to Sarkis. "With the supply dump as ruined as it is, I see no point to encamping here. Spending a night by the wreckage wouldn't be good for the soldiers' spirit, either. Let's push ahead on the route we've planned."

"Aye, Your Majesty. We ought to get to Rogmor day after tomorrow, maybe even tomorrow evening if we drive hard." The cavalry commander hesitated. "Of course, Rogmor's burned out, too, if you remember."

"I know. But from all I've heard, Aptos isn't. If we move fast, we ought to be able to lay hold of the supplies there before we start running out of what we brought from Nakoleia."

"That would be good," Sarkis agreed. "If we don't, we're liable to face the lovely choice between going hungry and pillaging the countryside."

"If we start pillaging our own land one day, we put ten thousand men into the camp of the Thanasioi by the next sunrise," Krispos said, grimacing. "I'd sooner retreat; then I'd just seem cautious, not a villain."

"As you say, Your Majesty." Sarkis dipped his head. "Let's hope we have a swift, triumphant advance, so we needn't worry about any of these unpleasant choices."

"That hope is all very well," Krispos said, "but we also have to plan ahead so misfortune, if it comes, doesn't catch us by surprise and strike us in a heap because we were napping instead of thinking."

"Sensible." Sarkis chuckled. "Seems to me I've told you that a good many times over the years—but then, you generally *are* sensible."

"Am I? I've heard what was meant to be greater flattery that I liked less." Krispos tasted the word. " 'He was sensible.' I'd sooner see that than most of the lies stonecutters are apt to put on a memorial stele."

Sarkis made a two-fingered gesture to turn aside even the implied mention of death. "May you outlast another generation of stonecutters, Your Majesty."

"And stump around Videssos as a spry eighty-year-old, you mean? It could happen, I suppose, though the lord with the great and good mind knows most men aren't so lucky." Krispos looked around to make sure neither Evripos nor Katakolon was in earshot, then lowered his voice all the same. "If that does prove to be my fate, I doubt it will delight my sons."

"You'd find a way to handle them," Sarkis said confidently. "You've handled everything the good god has set in your path thus far."

"Which is no promise the prize will be mine next time out," Krispos answered. "As long as I remember that, I'm all right, I think. Enough jabbering for now; the sooner we get to Aptos, the happier I'll be."

After serving under Krispos for his whole reign, Sarkis had learned the trick of understanding when the Emperor meant more than he said. He set spurs to his horse—despite advancing years and belly, he still had a fine seat and enjoyed a spirited mount—and hurried away at a bounding canter. A moment later, the horns of the military musicians brayed out a new command. The whole army picked up the pace, as if fleeing the storm clouds piling up behind.

Harasos lay at the inland edge of the coastal plain. From it, the road toward Rogmor climbed onto the central plateau that took up the majority of the westlands: drier, hillier, poorer country than the lowlands. Along riverbanks and in places that drew more rain than most, farmers brought in one crop a year, as they did in the country where Krispos had grown up. Elsewhere on the plateau, grass and scrub grew better than grain, and herds of sheep and cattle ambled over the ground.

Krispos eyed the plateau country ahead with suspicion, not because it was poor but because it was hilly. He much preferred a horizon that stretched out for miles on every side. Attackers had to work to set an ambush in country like that. Here sites for ambuscades came up twice in every mile.

He ordered the vanguard strengthened, lest the Thanasioi delay the army on its push to Rogmor. When the whole strung-out force ascended to the plateau, he breathed a heartfelt sigh of relief and a prayer of thanks to Phos. Had he commanded the heretics, he would have hit the imperial army as early and as hard as he could: delaying it on its march now would be worth as much as a great battle later. Thinking thus, he made sure his own saber slid smoothly from its scabbard. Though no great champion, he fought well enough when combat came his way.

The leader of the Thanasioi thought with him strategically, but not in terms of tactics. Not long after the army from Videssos the city reached the plateau, some sort of disturbance broke out at the rear. Krispos' force stretched for more than a mile. He needed a while to find out what was happening: as if the army were a long, thin, rather stupid dragon, messages from the tail took too long to get up to the head.

When at last he was sure the disturbance really meant fighting, he ordered the musicians to halt his whole force. No sooner had their peremptory notes rung out than he wondered if he'd made a mistake. But what else could he do? Leaving the rear to fend for itself while the van kept moving forward was an invitation to getting destroyed.

He turned to Katakolon, who sat his horse a few yards away. "Get back there at the gallop, find out what's truly going on, and let me know. At the gallop, now!"

"Aye, Father!" Eyes snapping with excitement, Katakolon dug spurs into the horse's side. It squealed an indignant protest at such treatment, but bounded off with such celerity that Katakolon almost went over its tail.

The Avtokrator's youngest son returned faster than Krispos would have thought possible. His anger faded when he saw Katakolon had in tow a messenger he recognized as one of Noetos' men. "Well?" he barked.

The messenger saluted. "May it please Your Majesty, we were attacked by a band of perhaps forty. They came close enough to shoot arrows at us; when we rode out to drive them off, most fled but a few stayed behind and fought with the saber to help the others escape."

"Casualties?" Krispos asked.

"We lost one killed and four wounded, Your Majesty," the messenger answered. "We killed five of theirs, and several more were reeling in the saddle as they rode away."

"Did we capture any of them?" Krispos demanded.

"We were still in pursuit when I left to bring this word to you. I know of no prisoners, but my knowledge, as I say, is incomplete."

"I'll ride back and find out for myself." Krispos turned to Katakolon. "Tell the musicians to order the advance." As his son hurried off to obey, he told the messenger, "Take me to Noetos. I'll hear his report of the action directly."

Krispos fumed as he rode toward the rear of the army. Forty men had held him up for a solid hour. A few more such pinpricks and the army would go hungry before it got to Aptos. *Better cavalry screens,* he told himself. Raiders had to be beaten back before they reached the main body. Screening parties could fight and keep moving, or fall back on their comrades if hard-pressed.

He hoped the rear guard had managed to lay hold of some Thanasioi. One interrogation was worth a thousand guesses, especially when he knew so little about the enemy. He knew the methods his men would use to wring truth out of any captives. They did not please him, but any man taken in arms against the Avtokrator of the Videssians was on the face of it a traitor and rebel, not to be coddled if that meant danger to the Empire.

One of the wounded imperials lay on a wagon, a blue-robed healer-priest bent over him. The soldier thrashed feebly; an arrow protruded from his neck. Krispos reined in to watch the healer-priest at work. He wondered why the blue-robe hadn't drawn the arrow, then decided it was all that kept the wounded man from bleeding to death in moments. This would be anything but an easy healing.

The priest repeated the creed again and again. "We bless thee, Phos, lord with the great and good mind, by thy grace our protector, watchful beforehand that the great test of life may be decided in our favor." As he used the prayers to sink down toward the healing trance, he set one hand on the trooper's neck, the other on the arrow that bobbed back and forth as the fellow fought to breathe.

All at once, the blue-robe jerked the arrow free. The trooper let out a bubbling shriek. Bright blood spurted, splashing against the priest's face. So far as breaking his concentration went, it might have been water, or nothing at all.

As abruptly as if the blue-robe had turned a spigot, the spurting stopped. Awe prickled through Krispos, as it always did when he watched a healer-priest at work. He thought the air above the injured trooper should have shimmered, as if from the heat of a fire, so strong was the force of healing that passed between priest and soldier. But the eye, unlike other, less easily nameable senses, perceived nothing.

The healer-priest released his hold on the injured man and sat up. The blue-robe's face was white and drained, a token of what the healing had cost him. A moment later, the soldier sat, too. A pale scar marred the skin of his neck; by its seeming, he might have worn it for years. Wonder filled his face as he picked up the bloodstained arrow the priest had pulled from his neck.

"Thank you, holy sir," he said, his voice as unhurt as the rest of him. "I thought I was dead."

"As I think I am now," the healer croaked. "Water, I pray you, or wine." The trooper pulled free the flask that still dangled from his belt, handing it to the man who had saved him. The blue-robe's larynx worked as he threw back his head and gulped down great drafts.

Krispos urged his horse forward, glad the soldier was hale. Healer-priests were better suited to dealing with the consequences of skirmishes than battles, for they quickly exhausted their powers—and themselves. In large conflicts, they helped only the most desperately hurt, leaving the rest to those who fought wounds with sutures and bandages rather than magic.

Noetos rode toward Krispos. Saluting, he said, "We drove the bastards off with no trouble, Your Majesty. Sorry we had to slow you down to do it."

"Not half so sorry as I am," Krispos answered. "Well, the good god willing, that won't happen again." He explained his plan to extend the cavalry screen around the army. Noetos nodded with sober approval. Krispos went on, "Did your men capture any of the rebels?"

"Aye, we got one in the pursuit after I sent Barisbakourios to you," Noetos said. "Shall we squeeze the Thanasiot cheese till the whey runs out of him?" A couple of his lieutenants were close by; they chuckled grimly at the rearguard commander's truth in jest's clothing.

"Presently, at need," Krispos said. "Let's see what magic can do with him first. Bring him here. I want to see him."

Noetos called orders. Some of his troopers frogmarched a young man in peasant homespun into the Avtokrator's presence. The captive must have taken a fall from his horse. His tunic was out at both elbows and over one knee; he was bloody in all three of those places and a couple of others, as well. Serum oozed down into one eye from a scrape on his forehead.

But he remained defiant. When one of the guards growled, "Down on your belly before his Majesty, wretch," he bent his head, sure enough, but only to spit between his feet as if in rejection of Skotos. All the soldiers snarled then, and roughly forced him into a proskynesis in spite of his struggles.

"Haul him to his feet," Krispos said, thinking the cavalrymen were likely to have done worse to their prisoner had they not been under his eye. When the ragged, battered youth—he might have been Evripos' age, more likely Katakolon's—was on his feet, Krispos asked him, "What have I done to you, that you treat me like the dark god?"

The prisoner worked his jaw, perhaps preparing to spit once more. "You don't want to do that, sonny," one of the troopers said.

The young man spat anyhow. Krispos let his captors shake him a little, but then raised a hand. "Hold on. I want this question answered as freely as may be, given what's happened here. What have I done, to be hated so? We've been at peace most of the years since he was born; taxes are lower now than then. What does he have against me? What *do* you have against me, sirrah? You may as well speak your mind; the headsman's shadow already falls across your fate."

"You think I fear death?" the prisoner said. "By the good god, I laugh at death—it takes me out of this trap of Skotos, the world, and sends me on to Phos' eternal light. Do your worst to me; that's but for a moment. Then I shake free of the dung we call a body, like a butterfly bursting from its cocoon."

His eyes blazed, though he kept blinking the one beneath the scrape. The last set of eyes Krispos had seen burning with such fanaticism had belonged to the priest Pyrrhos, first his benefactor, then his ecumenical patriarch, and at last such a ferocious and inflexible champion of orthodoxy that he'd had to be deposed.

Krispos said, "Very well, young fellow"—he realized he was speaking as if to one of his sons who'd been foolish—"you despise the world. Why do you despise my place in it?"

"Because you're rich, and wallow in your gold like a hog in mud," the young Thanasiot answered. "Because you choose the material over the spiritual, and give over your soul to Skotos in the process."

"Here, you speak to his Majesty with respect, or it'll go the harder for you," one of the cavalrymen growled. The prisoner spat on the ground again. His captor backhanded him across the face. Blood started from the corner of his mouth.

"Enough of that," Krispos said. "He'll be one of many who feel that way. He's eaten up bad doctrine and sickened on it."

"Liar!" the young man shouted, careless of his own fate. "You're the one with false teachings poisoning your mind. Abandon the world and the things of the world for the true and lasting life, the one yet to come." He could not raise his arms, but lifted his eyes to the heavens. "We bless thee, Phos, lord with the great and good mind—"

Hearing the heretic pray to the good god with the identical words he himself used, Krispos wondered for a moment if the fellow could be right. Pyrrhos, in his day, might have come close to saying yes, but not even the rigorously ascetic Pyrrhos could have countenanced destroying all the things of this world for the sake of the afterlife. How were men and women to live and raise families if they wrecked their farms or shops, abandoned parents or children?

He put the question to the prisoner: "If you Thanasioi had your way, wouldn't you soonest let mankind die out in a single generation's time, so no one would be left alive to commit any sins?"

"Aye, that's so," the youth answered. "It won't be so simple; we know that—most folk are too cowardly, too much in love with materialism—"

"By which it sounds as if you mean a full belly and a roof over one's head," Krispos broke in.

"Anything that ties you to the world is evil, is from Skotos," the prisoner insisted. "The purest among us stop taking food and let themselves starve, the better to join Phos as soon as they may."

Krispos believed him. That streak of fanatic asceticism ran deep in many Videssians, whether orthodox or heretic. The Thanasioi, though, seemed to have found a way to channel that religious energy to their own ends, perhaps more effectively than the comfortable clergy who came from Videssos the city.

"Me, I aim to live in this world as long and as well as I can," the Avtokrator said. The Thanasiot laughed scornfully. Krispos did not care. Having known privation in his youth, he saw no point to embracing it when he did not have to. He turned to the men who had hold of the youngster. "Tie him onto a horse. Don't let him escape or harm himself. When we encamp tonight, I'll have Zaidas the wizard question him. And if magic doesn't get me what I need to know . . ."

The guards nodded. The young heretic just glared. Krispos wondered how long that defiance would last if confronted with fire and barbed iron. He hoped he wouldn't have to find out.

Late in the afternoon, the Thanasioi again tried to raid the imperial army. A courier carried a dripping head back to Krispos. His stomach lurched; the hacking was as crude as that of any farmer who slaughtered a pig, while the iron smell of fresh blood also brought back memories of butchering.

If the courier had any such memories, they didn't bother him. Grinning, he said, "We drove the whoresons off, Your Majesty—spreading us wider was a fine plan. Junior here, he didn't run fast enough."

"Good," Krispos said, trying not to meet Junior's sightless eyes. He dug in the pouch at his belt and tossed the courier a goldpiece. "This is for the good news."

"Phos bless you, majesty," the fellow exclaimed. "Shall we put this lad on a pike and carry him ahead of us for a standard?"

"No," Krispos said with a shudder. An army that seemed bent on wanton killing would be just what the countryside needed to throw it into the rebels' camp. Controlling his features as best he could, the Avtokrator went on, "Bury it or toss it in a ditch or do whatever you please, as long as you don't display it. We want the people to know we've come to root out the heretics, not to glory in gore."

"However you'd have it, Your Majesty," the courier said cheerfully. He rode off happy enough with his reward, even though the Emperor had turned down the suggestion he'd made. Krispos knew some Avtokrators—not the worst of rulers Videssos had ever had, either—would have taken him up on it, or had the idea for themselves. But he did not have the stomach for it.

After the army made camp, he went over to Zaidas' pavilion. He found the Thanasiot prisoner tied to a folding chair and the mage looking frustrated. Zaidas gestured to the apparatus he'd set up. "You are familiar with the two-mirror spell for determining truth, Your Majesty?"

"I've seen it used, yes," Krispos answered. "Why? Are you having trouble with it?"

"That would be putting it mildly. It yields me nothing—nothing, do you hear?" Normally among the gentlest of men, Zaidas looked ready to tear the answer to his failure out of the prisoner with red-hot pincers.

"Can it be shielded against?" Krispos asked.

"Obviously it can." Zaidas gave the Thanasiot another glare before continuing. "This I knew before. But I never thought to find such shielding on a fleabitten trooper like this. If all the rebels are warded in like fashion, interrogation will become less certain and more bloody."

"The good god's truth armors me," the young captive declared. He sounded proud, as if he failed to realize his immunity would only cause him to be given over to torment.

"Any chance he's telling the truth?" Krispos asked.

Zaidas made a scornful noise, then suddenly turned thoughtful. "Maybe his fanaticism does afford some protection," the mage said. "One of the reasons sorcery so often fails in battle is that men at a high pitch of excitement are less vulnerable to its effects. Fervent belief in the righteousness of his cause may raise this fellow to a similar, less vulnerable, plane."

"Can you learn whether this is so?"

"It would take some time." Zaidas pursed his lips and seemed on the point of retreating into one of his brown studies.

Krispos forestalled him. Whenever magic touched the Thanasioi, something went wrong. Zaidas hadn't been able to learn where the heretics had taken Phostis—whose absence, unexpectedly, was an ache that only the endless work of the campaign held at bay—he hadn't been able to learn *why* he couldn't learn that, and now he couldn't even squeeze truth from an ordinary prisoner. To him, that made the young Thanasiot an intriguing challenge. To Krispos, it made the rebel an obstacle to be crushed, since he would not yield to gentler methods.

Harshly the Avtokrator said, "Let the men in red leather have him." Interrogators who used no magic wore red to hide the stains of their trade.

In his youth, Krispos would have been slower to give that order. He knew his years on the throne—and his desire to remain there for more years—had hardened him; even corrupted might not have been too strong a word. But he was also introspective enough to recognize that hardening and resist it save in times of dire need. This, he judged, was one of those times.

The Thanasiot's shrieks kept him awake long into the night. He was a ruler who did what he thought he had to do; he was no monster. Some time past midnight, he downed a beaker of wine and let the grape put a blurry curtain between him and the screaming. At last he slept.

Chapter V

AFTER A LIFETIME SPENT WITHIN HEARING OF THE SEA, Phostis found the hill country he traveled through strange in more ways than he could count. The moaning wind sounded wrong. It even smelled wrong, carrying the odors of dirt and smoke and livestock, but not the salt tang he'd never noticed till he met it no more.

Instead of being able to look out from a tall window and see far across blue water, he now found his horizon limited to a few hundred yards of gray rock, gray-brown dirt, and gray-green brush. The wagon in which he rode bumped along over winding trails so narrow he wouldn't have thought a horse able to use them, let alone a vehicle with wheels.

And, of course, no one had ever used him as Syagtios and Olyvria did now. All through his life, people had jumped to obey, even to anticipate, his every whim. The only exceptions he'd known were his father, his mother when she was alive, and his brothers—and, being the eldest, he was pretty good at getting his way with Evripos and Katakolon. That a rebel officer's daughter and a ruffian could not only disobey him but give orders themselves had never crossed his mind, even in nightmare.

That they could do anything else had never crossed their minds. As the road took another of its innumerable twists, Syagrios said, "Down flat, you. Anybody who sees you is likely to be one of us, but ain't nobody gets old on 'likely.' "

Phostis scrambled down into the wagon bed. The first time Syagrios told him to do that, he'd balked—whereupon Syagrios clouted him. He couldn't jump out of the wagon and run; a stout rope bound his ankle to a post. He could stand up and yell for help, but as Syagrios had said, most of the people hereabouts were themselves Thanasioi.

Syagrios had said something else, too, when he tried to disobey: "Listen, boy, you may think you can pop up like a spring toy and get us killed. You may even be right. But you better think about this, too: I promise you won't be around to see our heads go up on the Milestone."

Was he bluffing? Phostis didn't think so. A couple of times, other wagons or horsemen had trotted past, but he'd lain quiet. Most of the times he was ordered into the wagon bed, as now, no one came round the blind corner. After a minute or two, Syagrios said, "All right, kid, you can come back up."

Phostis returned to his place between the burly driver and Olyvria. He said, "Where are you taking me, anyhow?"

He'd asked that question ever since he was kidnapped. As usual, Olyvria answered, "What you don't know, you can't tell if you're lucky enough to get away." She brushed back a curl that had slipped out to tickle her cheek. "If you decide you want to try to get away, that is."

"I might be less inclined to, if you'd trust me more," he said. In his theology he was not far from the Thanasioi. But he had a hard time loving people who'd drugged, kidnapped, beaten, and imprisoned him. He considered that from a theological point of view. Should he not approve of them for removing him from the obscenely comfortable world in which he'd dwelt?

No. Maybe he was imperfectly religious, but he still thought of those who tormented him as his enemies.

Olyvria said, "I'm not the one who can decide whether you're to be trusted. My father will do that when you come before him."

"When will that be?" Phostis asked for at least the dozenth time.

Syagrios answered before Olyvria could: "Whenever it is. You ask too bloody many questions, you know that?"

Phostis maintained what he hoped was a dignified silence. He feared hope outran reality. Dignity came easily when backed up with embroidered robes, unquestioned authority, and a fancy palace with scores of servants. It was harder to bring off for someone in a threadbare tunic with a rope round his ankle, and harder still when a few days before he'd fouled himself while in the power of the people he was trying to impress.

The wagon rattled around another bend, which meant Phostis spent more time hiding—or was the proper expression *being hidden*? Even his grammar tutor would have had trouble deciding that—in the back of the wagon. This time, though, Syagrios grunted in satisfaction when the corner was safely turned; Olyvria softly clapped her hands together.

"Come on up, you," Syagrios said. "We're just about there." Although he couldn't smell the sea, Phostis still thought *there* would be the port of Pityos. He'd never seen Pityos, but imagined it to be something on the order of Nakoleia, though likely even smaller and dingier.

The town ahead was smaller and dingier that Nakoleia, but there its resemblance to Phostis' imaginings ceased. It was no port at all, just a huddle of houses and shops in a valley a little wider than most. A stout fortress with walls of forbidding gray limestone dominated the skyline as thoroughly as did the High Temple in Videssos the city.

"What *is* this place?" Phostis asked. He regretted his tone at once; he'd plainly implied the town was unfit for human habitation. As a matter of fact, that was his opinion—how could anyone want to live out his life trapped in a single valley? And how could anyone trapped in a single valley have a life worth living? But letting his captors know what he thought seemed less than clever.

Syagrios and Olyvria looked at each other across him. When she spoke, it was to her comrade: "He'll find out anyhow." Only when Syagrios reluctantly nodded did she answer Phostis: "The name of this town is Etchmiadzin."

For a moment, he thought she'd sneezed. Then he said, "It sounds like a Vaspurakaner name."

"It is," Olyvria said. "We're hard by the border here, and a fair number of princes still call this town home. More to the point, though, Etchmiadzin is where the pious and holy Thanasios first preached, and the chief center of those who follow his way."

If Etchmiadzin was the chief center of the Thanasioi, Phostis was glad his kidnappers hadn't taken him to some outlying hamlet. Back at Videssos the city, he would have blurted out that thought, had it occurred to him. His friends and hangers-on—sometimes it was hard to tell the one group from the other—would have bawled laughter, probably drunken laughter, too. In his present circumstances, silence again seemed the smarter course.

The people of Etchmiadzin went stolidly about their business, taking no notice of the incognito arrival in their midst of a junior Avtokrator. As Olyvria had said, a good many of them seemed to be of Vaspurakaner blood, broader-shouldered and thicker-chested than their Videssian neighbors. An old Vaspurakaner priest, his robe of different cut and a darker blue than those orthodox clerics wore, stumped down an unpaved street, leaning on a stick.

The men on guard outside the fortress were about as far removed from the Halogai in the gilded mail shirts as was possible while still retaining the name of soldier. Not one fighter's kit matched his comrade's; the guards leaned and slouched at every angle save the perpendicular. But Phostis had seen the measuring stare in these wolves' eyes on the faces of the northern men in the capital as they sized up some new arrival at the palaces.

As soon as the guards recognized Syagrios and Olyvria, though, they came to excited life, whooping, cheering, and pounding one another on the back. "By the good god, you did nab the little bugger!" one of them yelled, pointing toward Phostis. As a form of address, that hit a new low.

"Inform my father that he's here, if you would, friends," Olyvria said; from her lips, as from Digenis', the greeting of the Thanasioi came fresh and sincere.

The rough men hurried to do her bidding. Syagrios reined in and alighted from the wagon. "Give me your foot," he told Phostis. "You ain't gonna run away from here." As if reading his captive's mind, he added, "If you try to kick me in the face, boy, I won't just beat you. I'll stomp you so hard you won't breathe without hurting for the next year. You believe me?"

Phostis did, as fully as he believed in the lord with the great and good mind, not least because Syagrios looked achingly eager to do as he'd threatened. So the heir to the imperial throne sat quietly while the driver cut through the rope. Perhaps he and Syagrios shared the Thanasiot theology. That would never make them friends. Phostis had made orthodox enemies when orthodox himself; he saw no reason why one Thanasiot should not despise another as a man, even if they held to the same dogmas.

The guards came straggling back, one a few paces behind the other. The fellow who got back to his post first waved to usher Olyvria, Syagrios, and even Phostis into the fortress. Syagrios shoved Phostis forward, none too gently. "Get moving, you."

He got moving. More soldiers—no, warriors was probably a better word for them, as they had ferocity but seemed without discipline— traded strokes or shot at propped-up bales of hay or simply sat around and chattered in the inner ward. They waved to Syagrios, nodded respectfully to Olyvria, and paid Phostis no attention whatever. In his plain, cheap tunic, he did not look as if he deserved attention.

The iron-fronted door to the keep was open. Propelled by another shove from Syagrios, Phostis plunged into gloom. He stumbled, not sure where he was going and even less sure of his footing. Olyvria murmured, "Turn left at the first opening."

He obeyed gratefully. Only when he was inside the chamber did he think to wonder if Syagrios was really as harsh and Olyvria as kindly as they appeared to be. Snapping him back and forth between them like a ball thrown in a bathhouse struck him as a good way to weaken whatever resolve he had left.

"Come in, young Majesty, come in!" exclaimed the slim little man sitting in a high-backed chair at the far end of the chamber. So this was Livanios, then. He sounded as cordial as if he and Phostis were old friends, not captor and captive. The smile on his face was warm and inviting— was, in fact, Olyvria's smile set in a face framed by a neat, graying beard and marred from a couple of sword cuts. It made Phostis want to trust him—and made him want to distrust himself on account of that.

The chamber itself had been set up to imitate, as closely as was possible in the keep of a fortress in the middle of the back of beyond, the Grand Courtroom in the palace compound back at Videssos the city. To someone who had never seen the real Grand Courtroom, it might have been impressive. Phostis, who'd grown up there, found it ludicrous. Where was the marble double colonnade that led the eye to the distant throne? Where were the elegant and richly clad courtiers who took their place along the way to the Emperor? The handful of rudely staring soldiers made a poor substitute. Nor were the ragged priest and the nondescript fellow in a striped caftan adequate replacements for the ecumenical patriarch and the lofty Sevastos who stood before the Avtokrator's high seat.

Phostis knew a weird mental shift as he reminded himself he'd come to despise the pomp and ostentation that surrounded his father. He also wondered why the leader of the radically egalitarian Thanasioi wanted to mimic that pomp.

He had, however, bigger worries. Livanios brought them into sudden sharp focus, saying, "So how much will your father give to have you back. I don't mean gold; we of the gleaming path despise gold. But surely he will yield land and influence to restore you to his side."

"Will he? I wonder." Phostis' bitterness was not altogether feigned. "We've always quarreled, my father and I. For all I know, he's glad to have

me gone. Why not? He has two other sons, both of them more to his liking."

"You undervalue yourself in his eyes," Livanios said. "He's turned the
countryside around the imperial army upside down searching for you."

"He searches sorcerously as well, and with the same determination," the
man in the caftan said. His Videssian held a vanishing trace of accent.

Phostis shrugged. Maybe what he heard was true, maybe not. Either
way, it mattered little. He said, "Besides, what makes you think I want to
go back to my father? By all I've heard of you Thanasioi, I'd sooner live out
my days with you than smother myself in things back at the palace."

He didn't know whether he was telling the truth, telling part of the
truth, or flat-out lying. The doctrines of the Thanasioi drew him power-
fully. Of so much he was sure. But would men who observed all those fine-
sounding principles stoop to something so sordid as kidnapping? Maybe
they would, if their faith let them pretend to be orthodox to preserve
themselves. If so, they were the best actors he'd ever run across. They even
fooled him.

Livanios said, "I've heard somewhat of this from my daughter and the
holy Digenis both. The possibilities are . . . interesting. You'd truly rather
live out your days in the want that is our lot than in the luxury you've always known?"

"I fear more for my soul than for my body," Phostis said. "My body is
but a garment that will wear out all too soon. When it's tossed on the midden, what difference if it once was stained with fancy dyes? My soul,
though—my soul goes on forever." He sketched Phos' sun-sign above his
breast.

Livanios, the priest, Olyvria, even Syagrios also traced quick circles.
The man in the caftan did not. Phostis wondered about that. An imperfectly pious Thanasiot struck him as a contradiction in terms. Or perhaps
not—that label fit him pretty well. Was he claiming more belief than he
really felt to get Livanios to treat him mildly? He had trouble reading his
own heart.

"What shall we do with you?" Livanios said musingly. By his tone,
Phostis would have bet the heretics' leader was wondering about the same
questions that had gone through his own mind. Livanios went on, "Are
you one of us, or do we treat you merely as a piece in the board game, to
be placed in the square of greatest advantage to us at the proper time?"

Phostis nodded at the analogy; whatever else could be said about him,
Livanios knew how to compare ideas. Pieces taken off the board in the
Videssian game of stylized combat were not gone for good, but could be

returned to action on the side of the player who had captured them. That made the board game harder to master, but also made it a better model for the involuted intricacies of Videssian politics and civil strife.

"Father, may I speak?" Olyvria said.

Livanios laughed. "When have I ever been able to tell you no? Aye, say what's in your mind."

"There is a middle way in this, then," she said. "No one of spirit, whether he followed the gleaming path or not, could be happy with us after we stole him away and brought him here against his will. But once here, how could one of goodwill not see how we truly live our lives in conformity to Phos' holy law?"

"Many might fail to see that," Livanios said dryly. "Among them I can name Krispos, his soldiers, and the priests he has in his retinue. But *I* see you're not yet finished. Say on, by all means."

"What I was going to suggest was not clapping Phostis straightaway into a cell. If and when we do return him to the board, we don't want him turning back against us the instant he finds the chance."

"Can't just let him run loose, neither," Syagrios put in. "He tried to get away once, likely thought about it a lot more'n that. You're just askin' to have him run back home to his papa if he gets on a horse without nobody around him."

Phostis kicked himself for a fool for trying to make a break at the farmhouse. The skinny fellow had kicked him, too, a lot harder.

Olyvria said, "I wasn't going to suggest we let him run loose. You're right, Syagrios; that's dangerous. But if we take him around Etchmiadzin and to other places where the gleaming path is strong, we can show him the life he was on the edge of embracing for himself before we lay hold of him. Once he sees it, as I said, once he accepts it, he may become fully one of us regardless of how he got here."

"That might have some hope of working," Livanios said, and Phostis' heart leaped. The heresiarch, however, was very Videssian in his ability to spot betrayal before it sprouted: "It might also give him an excuse for hypocrisy and let him pick his own time and place to flee us."

"Aye, that's so, by the good god," Syagrios growled.

Steepling his fingers, Livanios turned to Phostis. "How say you, young Majesty?" In his mouth the title was, if not mocking, at least imperfectly respectful. "This affects you, after all."

"So it does." Phostis tried to match dry with dry. If he'd thought fulsome promises would have kept him out of a small, dark, dank chamber, he would have used them. But he guessed Livanios would assume fulsome promises to be but fulsome lies. He shrugged and answered, "The choice is yours. If you don't trust me, you won't believe what I say in any case."

"You're clever enough, aren't you?" Sitting in his high-backed chair, Livanios reminded Phostis of a smug cat who'd appointed himself judge of mice. Phostis had never been a mouse before; he didn't care for the sensation. Livanios went on, "Well, we can see how it goes. All right, young Majesty, no manacles for you." *Not now,* Phostis heard between the words. "We'll let you see us—with suitable keepers, of course—and we'll see you. Later on we'll decide what's to be done with you in the end."

The priest who stood in front of Livanios smiled as widely as his pinched features would permit and made the sun-sign once more. The man in the caftan, who stood at Livanios' right, half turned and said, "Are you sure this is wise?"

"No," Livanios answered frankly; he did not seem annoyed to have his decision questioned. "But I think the reward we may reap repays the risk."

"They would never take such a chance back in—"

Livanios held up a hand. "Never mind what they would do there. You are here, and I hope you will remember it." He might listen to his advisor's opinion, but kept a grip on authority. The man in the caftan put both hands in front of him and bowed almost double, acknowledging that authority.

"If he is to be enlarged, even in part, where shall we house him?" Olyvria asked her father.

"Take him up to a chamber on the highest floor here," Livanios answered. "With a guard in the corridor, he'll not escape from there unless he grows wings. Syagrios, when he is out and about, you'll be his principal keeper. I charge you not to let him flee."

"Oh, he won't." Syagrios looked at Phostis as if he hoped the younger man would try to get away. Phostis had never seen anyone who actually looked forward to hurting him before. His testicles crawled up into his belly.

He said, "I don't want to go anywhere right now, except maybe to sleep."

"Spoken like a soldier," Livanios said with a laugh. Syagrios shook his head, denying Phostis deserved the name. Phostis didn't know if he did or not. He might have found out, had the Thanasioi not kidnapped him. But could he have fought against them? He didn't know that, either. He contented himself with ostentatiously ignoring Syagrios. That made Livanios laugh harder.

"If he wants to sleep, he may as well," Olyvria said. "By your leave, Father, I'll take him up to one of the rooms you suggested."

Livanios waved an airy hand as if he were the granting a boon. Having watched Krispos all his life, Phostis had seen the gesture better done. Olyvria led him toward the spiral stairway. Syagrios pulled an unpleasantly long, unpleasantly sharp knife from his belt and followed the two of them. The ruffian, Phostis thought, was not subtle in his messages.

Doing his best to keep on pretending Syagrios did not exist, Phostis turned to Olyvria and said, "Thank you for keeping me out of the dungeon, at any rate." He wondered why she'd taken his side; from a young man raised in the palaces, calculation of advantage came naturally as breathing.

"It's simple enough: I think that, given the chance, you will take your place on the gleaming path," Olyvria answered. "Once you forgive us for the unkind way we had to grab you, you'll see—I'm sure you'll see—how we live in accord with Phos' teachings, far more so than those who pride themselves on how fat their bellies are or how many horses or mistresses they own."

"How could anyone doubt surfeit is wrong?" Phostis said, and Olyvria beamed. But Phostis wondered if sufficiency was wrong, too: the glutton deserved the scorn he got, but was having a belly not growling with hunger every hour of the day also something to condemn? He knew what his father's answer would have been. Then again, he also remained sure his father did not have all the answers.

In normal circumstances, he might have enjoyed arguing the theology of it, especially with an attractive young woman. The knife Syagrios held a couple of feet from his kidneys reminded him how abnormal these circumstances were. Theological disputation would have to wait.

The way he wobbled by the time he got to the head of the stairs also reminded him he was not all he could have been. His own belly grumbled and cried out for more nourishment than he'd had lately.

The chamber to which Olyvria led him was severely simple. It held a straw pallet covered with linen ticking, a blanket that looked as if it had seen better years, a couple of three-legged stools, and a chamber pot with some torn rags beside it. The rest—floors, wall, ceiling—was blocks of bare gray stone. Livanios did not have to fret about his growing wings, either: even if he did sprout feathers, he couldn't have slipped through the slit window that gave the little room what light it had.

The door had no bar on the outside, but it had none on the inside, either. Syagrios said, "Someone will be in the hall watching you most of the time, boy. You'll never know when. Even if you do get lucky, someone will catch you in the stairs or in the hall or in the ward. You can't run. Get used to it."

Olyvria added, "Our hope is that you won't want to run, Phostis, that you'll find you've gained by coming here, no matter how little you care for the way you traveled. When you see Etchmiadzin, when you see the gleaming path as it leads toward Phos and his eternal life, we hope you'll become one of us."

She sounded very earnest. Phostis had trouble believing she was acting—but she'd fooled him before. He wondered if her father truly wanted him to take his place on the gleaming path. As things stood, Livanios led the Thanasioi, at least in battle. But an Avtokrator's son had a claim on leadership merely because of who he was. Maybe Livanios thought Phostis would be a pliant puppet. Phostis had his own opinion of that.

"We'll leave you to your rest now," Olyvria said. "Come tomorrow, you'll begin to see how the followers of the pious and holy Thanasios shape their lives."

She and Syagrios walked out. She closed the door after them. It wasn't much of a barrier, but it would have to do. Phostis looked around at his cell—that struck him as a better name for the place than room and in truth no monk would have complained its furnishings were too luxurious. It was, however, not a dungeon. He did indeed have that for which to be grateful to Olyvria.

He lay down on the pallet. Dry straw rustled under his weight. It smelled musty. Straws poked through the thin linen covering, and in a couple of places through his tunic as well. He wiggled till he was no longer being stabbed, then drew the blanket up to his neck. When he did that, his feet stuck out. He wiggled some more and managed to get all of himself covered. Competing fears and worries roared in his head so loudly he could clearly hear none of them. He fell asleep almost at once.

RAIN BLEW INTO KRISPOS' FACE. HE CAST AN UNHAPPY COUNTE-nance up to the heavens—and got an eyeful of raindrops for his presumption. "Well," he said in a hollow voice, "at least we won't be hungry."

Sarkis rode at his left hand. "That's true, Your Majesty. We got the flying column into Aptos just in time to drive off the Thanasiot raiders. It was a victory."

"Why don't I feel victorious?" Krispos said. Rain trickled between his hat and cloak and slithered down the back of his neck. He wondered how well the gilding and grease on his coat of mail repelled rust. He had the feeling he'd find out.

To his right, Evripos and Katakolon looked glum. They looked worse than glum, in fact—they looked like a couple of drowned cats. Katakolon tried to make the best of it. He caught Krispos' eye and said, "I usually like my baths warm, Father."

"If you go out in the field, you have to take that up with Phos, not with me," Krispos said.

"But you're his viceregent on earth. Don't you have his ear?"

"Aye, viceregent on earth—so they say. But nowhere, son, will you find that an Avtokrator has jurisdiction over what the heavens decide to do. Oh, I can tell the clouds not to drop rain on me, but will they listen? They haven't yet, not to me or any of the men who came before me."

Evripos muttered something sullen under his breath. Krispos looked at him. He shook his head, muttered again, and rode a little farther away so he wouldn't have to say anything out loud to his father. Krispos thought about pressing him, decided it wouldn't be worth the argument, and kept his own mouth shut.

Sarkis said, "If you could command the weather, Your Majesty, you'd have started doing it your first fall on the throne, when Petronas raised his revolt against you. The rains came early that year, too."

"That's true; they did. I wish you hadn't reminded me," Krispos said. The rains then had kept him from following up a victory and let Petronas regroup and continue the fight the next year. He hoped he'd manage a genuine victory against the Thanasioi before the downpour made warfare impossible.

Katakolon said, "I'd expected the heretics to come out and really fight against us by now." He sounded disappointed that they hadn't; he was only seventeen, with no true notion of what combat was about. Krispos had got his own first taste at about the same age, and sickened on it. He wondered if Katakolon would do the same.

But his son had raised a legitimate point. Krispos said, "I'd thought they would come out and fight, too. But this Livanios of theirs is a canny one, curse him to the ice. He knows he gains if I don't destroy him this campaigning season."

"He doesn't gain if we take back Pityos," Sarkis said.

Krispos' horse put a foot in a hole concealed by water and almost stumbled. When he'd saved his seat and brought the gelding back under control, he said, "I'm starting to think we'll need a break in the rain even to get to Pityos."

"Even if the Thanasioi attack us, it'll be a poor excuse for a battle," Sarkis said. "By the time a man's shot his bow twice, the string'll be too wet to use again. Not much chance for tactics after that—just out saber and slash."

"A soldiers' battle, eh?" Krispos said.

"Aye, that's what they call it," Sarkis said, "the ones who live to call it anything, that is."

"Yes," Krispos said. "What it really means is, some stupid general's fallen asleep on the job." Soldiers' battles were part of the Videssian military tradition, but not a highly esteemed part. Videssos honored cleverness in warfare as in everything else; the point was not simply to win, but to win with minimum damage to oneself. That could make unnecessary what would have been the next battle.

Sarkis said, "In this campaign, a soldiers' battle would favor us. But for the band of turncoats who went over with Livanios, most of the Thanasioi are odds and sods who oughtn't to have the discipline they need to stand up in a long fight."

"From your mouth to the good god's ear," Krispos said.

"Cowardly scum, the lot of them," Evripos growled; he'd been listening after all. By his tone, he hated the Thanasioi less for their doctrinal errors than for making him get cold and wet.

"They won't be cowards, young Majesty; that's not what I meant at all," Sarkis said earnestly. 'They'll have fire and dash aplenty, unless I miss my guess. What I doubt is their sticking power. If they don't break us at the first onset, they should be ours."

Evripos grunted once more, wordlessly this time. Krispos peered through the rain at the territory ahead. He didn't like it: too many hills to pass between on the way to Pityos. Maybe he would have done better to stick to the coastal plain. He hadn't expected the rains so soon. But he was too far in to withdraw; the best course now was to forge ahead strongly and hope things would come out right in the end.

That was, however, also the least subtle course. Against the odds and sods Sarkis had mentioned, he'd have been confident of success. But Livanios had shown himself to be rather better at the game of war than that. Krispos wondered what he had in mind to counter it, and how well the ploy would work.

"One more thing I'll have to find out the hard way," he murmured. Sarkis, Katakolon, and even Evripos looked curiously at him. He didn't explain. His sons wouldn't have understood, not fully, while the cavalry commander probably followed him only too well.

Camp that night was soaked and miserable. The cooks had trouble starting their fires, which meant the army was reduced to bread, cheese, and onions. Evripos scowled in distaste at the hard, dark little loaf a fellow handed him out of a greased leather sack. After one bite, he threw it down in the mud.

"No more for you this evening," Krispos ordered. "Maybe hunger'll give you a better appetite for breakfast."

Evripos started worse than the rain that beat down on him. Long used to ignoring importunate men pleading their cases at the top of their lungs, Krispos ignored him. The Avtokrator saw nothing particularly wrong with the army bread. Phos had granted him good teeth, so he had no trouble eating it. He didn't like it as well as the white bread he ate in the palaces, but he wasn't in the palaces now. In the field, you made the best of what you had. Evripos hadn't figured that out yet.

Whether from his own good sense or, more likely, fear of igniting his father, Katakolon ate up his ration without complaint. Young face unwontedly thoughtful, he said, "I wonder what Phostis is eating tonight."

"I wonder if he's eating anything tonight," Krispos said. With the evening's orders given, with the morrow's line of march planned, he had nothing to keep him from brooding over the fate of his eldest. He couldn't stand that sort of helplessness. Trying to hold it at bay, he went over to Zaidas' tent to see what the mage had learned.

When he stuck his head into the tent, he found Zaidas scraping mud off his boots. Chuckling to catch his friend at such untrammeled mundanity, he asked, "Couldn't you do that by magic instead?"

"Oh, hello, Your Majesty. Aye, belike I could," the wizard answered. "Likely it would take three times as long and leave me drained for two days afterward, but I could. One of the things you have to learn if you go into magic is when to leave well enough alone."

"That's a hard lesson for any man to learn, let alone a mage," Krispos said. Zaidas got up and unfolded a canvas chair for him; he sank into it. "Perhaps I've not learned it myself in fullness. If I had, I might not come here to tax you on what you've found out about Phostis."

"No one could think ill of you for that, Your Majesty." Zaidas spread his hands. "I only wish I had more news—or, indeed, any news—to give you. Your eldest son remains hidden from me."

Krispos wondered whether that showed Phostis was in fact a cuckoo's egg in his nest. But no: the magic Zaidas worked sought Phostis for himself, not on account of his relation—if any—to the Avtokrator. Krispos said, "Have you progressed toward learning what sort of sorcery conceals his whereabouts?"

Zaidas bit his lip; not even a friend casually tells his Avtokrator he has failed to accomplish something. The wizard said, "Your Majesty, I must confess I have continued to devote most of my efforts toward locating Phostis rather than on analyzing why I cannot locate him."

"And what sort of luck have you had in those efforts?" The question was rhetorical; had Zaidas had any luck other than bad, he would have proclaimed it with trumpet and drum. Krispos went on, "Eminent and sorcerous sir, I strongly urge you to give over your direct efforts, exactly because they've not succeeded. Learn what you can about the mage who opposes you. If you have any better fortune there, you can go back to seeking out Phostis."

"It shall of course be as Your Majesty suggests," Zaidas said, understanding that an imperial recommendation was tantamount to a command. The wizard hesitated, then continued, "You must be aware I would still have no guarantee of success, especially here in the field. For this delicate work, the tomes and substances accumulated within the Sorcerers' Collegium are priceless assets."

"So you've said," Krispos answered. "Do your best. I can ask no more of any man."

"I shall," Zaidas promised, and reached for a codex as if about to start incanting on the spot. Before he could demonstrate such diligence, Krispos left the tent and headed back to his own pavilion. He was disappointed in his chief mage, but not enough to say anything more to Zaidas than he'd already said: Zaidas had been doing the best he could, by his own judgment. An emperor who castigated the men he'd chosen for their expert judgment would not long retain such experts around him.

Rain drummed on the oiled silk; mud squelched underfoot. The tent was a joyless place. Krispos felt the weight of every one of his years. Even with the luxuries his rank afforded him—enough room to stand and walk around, a cot rather than just a bed roll—campaigning was hard on a man as old as him. The only trouble was, not campaigning would in the long run prove harder still.

So he told himself, at any rate. as he blew out the lamps, lay down, and tried to sleep. So men always told themselves when they went off to war. So, no doubt, Livanios was telling himself somewhere not far enough away. Only by looking backward through the years could anyone judge who had been right, who wrong.

Outside the entrance to the tent, the Haloga guards chatted back and forth in their own slow, sonorous speech. Krispos wondered if they ever had doubts when they lay down at night. They were less simple than many Videssians made them out to be. But they did actively like to fight, where Krispos avoided battle when he could.

He was still wishing life could be less complicated when at last he surrendered to exhaustion. When he woke up the next morning, his mind bit down on that as if he'd never slept. He dressed and went out to share a breakfast as dank and miserable as the supper the night before.

Getting the army moving helped kick him out of his own gloom, or at least left him too busy to dwell on it. By now the soldiers were more efficient than they had been when they set out from Nakoleia. Knocking down tents, then loading them onto horses and mules and into wagons, took only about half as long as it had earlier. But, as if to make sure no blessing went unmixed, the rain made travel slower and tougher than Krispos had counted on. He'd planned to reach Pityos six or seven days after he set out from Aptos. That would stretch now.

The army rode through a village. But for a couple of dogs splashing through the mud between houses, the place was deserted. The peasants and herders who called it home had fled into the hills. That was what peasants and herders did when a hostile army approached. Krispos bit his lip in frustrated anger and sorrow that his subjects should reckon forces he led hostile.

"They're most of them Thanasioi, is my guess," Evripos answered when he said that aloud. "They know what they have to look forward to when we stamp out this heresy of theirs."

"What would you do with them after we win?" Krispos asked, interested to learn how the youth would handle a problem whose solution he did not clearly see himself.

Evripos was confident, if nothing else: "Once we beat the rebel army in the field, we peel this land like a man stripping the rind off an orange. We find out who the worst of the traitors are and give them fates that will make the rest remember for always what opposing the Empire costs." He shook his fist at the empty houses, as if he blamed them for putting him here on horseback in the cold rain.

"It may come to that," Krispos said, nodding slowly. Evripos' answer was one a straightforward soldier might give—was, in fact, not very different from what Sarkis had proposed. The lad could have done worse, Krispos thought.

Confident in his youth that he'd hit on not just an answer but *the* answer, Evripos spoke out in challenge: "How could you do anything but that, Father?"

"If we can lure folk back to the true faith by persuasion rather than fear, we cut the risk of having to fight the war over again in a generation's time," Krispos answered. Evripos only snorted; he thought in terms of weeks and months, not generations.

Then Krispos had to stop thinking about generations, or even weeks: a scout from the vanguard came splattering back, calling, "The bastards aim to try and hold the pass up ahead against us!"

Open fighting at last, Krispos thought—*Phos be praised.* Already, at Sarkis' bawled orders, the musicians were ordering the imperial army to deploy. While it traveled as a strung-out snake, it could not fight that way. It began to stretch out into line of battle.

But, as Krispos saw when he rode forward to examine the ground for himself, the line of battle could not stretch wide. The Thanasioi had cunningly chosen the place for their stand: the sides of the pass were too steep for cavalry, especially in the rain, while at the narrowest point the enemy had erected a rough barricade of logs and rocks. It would not stop the attackers, but it would slow them down . . . and here and there, behind the barrier, cloth-covered awnings sprouted like drab toadstools.

Krispos pointed to those as Sarkis came up beside him. "They'll have archers under there, or I miss my guess. The barricade to hold us in place, the bowmen to hurt us while we're held."

"Likely you're right, Your Majesty," the cavalry commander agreed glumly. "Livanios, curse him, is a professional."

"We'll send some infantry around the barricade to either side to see if we can't push them back, then," Krispos decided. It was the only maneuver he could think of, but not one in which he had great confidence. The foot soldiers were the poorest troops in his force, both in fighting quality and literally: they were the men who could not afford to outfit themselves or be outfitted by their villages with horse and cavalry accouterments.

Being a horseman himself, Sarkis shared and more than shared the Avtokrator's distrust of infantry. But he nodded, not having any better plan to offer. A courier hurried off to the musicians. At their call, the infantry went forward to outflank the Thanasioi, who waved spears and yelled threats from behind their barricade.

"We'll send the horse forward at the same time, Your Majesty, if that's all right with you," Sarkis said, and Krispos nodded in turn. Keeping as many of the enemy as possible busy would go a long way toward winning the fight.

Shouting "Phos with us!" and "Krispos!" the imperials advanced. As the Emperor and Sarkis had thought they would, bowmen under cover from the rain shot at soldiers who had trouble answering back. Here and there along the line, a man crumpled or a wounded horse screamed and broke away from its rider's control.

Then the enemy's awnings shook, as if in a high breeze—but there was no breeze. Several of them fell over, draping Thanasiot archers in yards of soaked, clinging cloth. The stream of arrows slackened. Krispos' men raised a cheer and advanced. The Avtokrator looked round for Zaidas. He did not see the sorcerer, but had no doubt he'd caused the collapse. Battle magic might have trouble touching men, but things were another matter.

Yet the Thanasioi, even with their strategem spoiled, were far from beaten. Their men swarmed forward to fight the foot soldiers who sought to slide around their barrier. The heretics' war cry was new to Krispos: "The path! The gleaming path!"

Their ferocity was new, too. They fought as if they cared nothing whether they lived or died, so long as they hurt their foes. Their impetuous onslaught halted Krispos' infantry in its tracks. Some of his men kept fighting, but others scrambled out of harm's way, skidding and falling in the muck as they ran.

Krispos cursed. "The ice take them!" he shouted. "The good god knows I didn't expect much from them, but this—" Fury choked him.

"Maybe the rebels will make a mistake," Sarkis said, seeking such solace as he could find. "If they come out to chase our poor sorry lads, the cavalry'll nip in behind 'em and cut 'em off at the knees."

But the Thanasioi seemed content to hold off the imperial army. Again Krispos saw the hand of a well-trained soldier in their restraint: raw recruits, elated at success, might well have swarmed forward to take advantage of it and left themselves open to a counterblow like the one Sarkis had proposed. Not here, though. Not today.

The imperial cavalry tried to force its way through the barrier the rebels had thrown up. On a clear day, they could have plied their poorly armored foes with arrows and made them give ground. With the sky weeping overhead, that didn't work. They fought hand to hand, slashing with sabers and using light spears against similarly armed opponents who, while not mounted, used the barricade as if it were their coat of mail.

"They've got more stick in them than I looked for," Sarkis said with a grimace. "Either they put the real soldiers who defected in the middle or . . ." He let that hang. Krispos finished it mentally: *or else we're in more trouble than we thought.*

Unlike the infantry, the imperial horsemen stayed and fought. But they had no better luck at dislodging the stubborn heretics. Curses rose above the clash of iron on iron and the steady drumming of the rain. Wounded men and wounded horses shrieked. Healer-priests labored to succor those sorest hurt until they themselves dropped exhausted into the mud.

Time seemed stuck. The gray mat of clouds overhead was so thick,

Krispos had no better way to gauge the hour than by his stomach's growls. If his belly did not lie, afternoon was well advanced.

Then, not far away, shouts rang out, first in the squadron of Haloga guards and then from the Thanasioi. Through the confused uproar of battle came a new cry: "To me! For the Empire!"

"By the good god!" Krispos exclaimed. "That's Evripos!"

At the head of a couple of dozen horsemen, the Avtokrator's second son forced a breach in the heretic's barrier. In amongst them, he lay about him with his saber, making up in fury what he lacked in skill. Half the Halogai poured into that gap, as much to protect him as to take advantage of it in any proper military sense.

The result was satisfactory enough. At last driven back from their barricade, the heretics became more vulnerable to the onslaught of the better-disciplined imperial troops. Their confident yells turned suddenly frantic. "Push them hard!" Krispos shouted. "If we break them here, we have an easy road on to Pityos!" With its major city taken, he thought, how could the revolt go on?

But the Thanasioi kept fighting hard, even in obvious defeat. Krispos thought about the prisoner he'd ordered tortured, about the contempt the youth had shown for the material world. That, he saw, had not been so much cant. Rear guards sold themselves more dearly than he would have imagined, fighting to the death to help their comrades' retreat. Some men who had safety assured even abandoned it to hurl themselves at the imperials and their weapons, using those to remove themselves forever from a worldly existence they judged only a trap of Skotos'.

Because of that fanatical resistance, the imperial army gained ground more slowly than Krispos wanted. Not even more daredevil charges from Evripos could break the heretics' line.

Sarkis pointed ahead. "Look, Your Majesty—they're filing over that bridge there."

"I see," Krispos answered. Ten months out of the year, the stream spanned by that ramshackle wooden bridge would hardly have wet a man's shins as he forded it. But with the fall rains, it not only filled its banks but threatened to overflow them. If Krispos' men could not seize the bridge, they'd have to break off pursuit.

"They took a long chance here, provoking battle with their backs to the river," Sarkis said. "Let's make them pay for it."

More and more of the Thanasioi gained the safety of the far bank. Yet another valiant stand by a few kept the imperial soldiers away from the bridge. Just when they were about to gain it in spite of everything the heretics could do to stop them, the wooden structure exploded into flame in spite of the downpour.

"Magic?" Krispos said, staring in dismay at the heavy black smoke that poured from the bridge.

"It could be, Your Majesty," Sarkis answered judiciously. "More likely, though, they painted it with liquid fire and just now touched it off. That stuff doesn't care about water when it gets to burning."

"Aye, you're right, worse luck," Krispos said. Made from naphtha, sulfur, the foul-smelling oil that seeped up between rocks here and there in the Empire, and other ingredients—several of them secret—liquid fire was the most potent incendiary Videssos' arsenal boasted. A floating skin of it would even burn on top of water. No wonder it took no notice of the rain.

The last handful of Thanasioi still on the eastern side of the stream went down. "Come on!" Evripos shouted to the impromptu force he led. "To the ice with this fire! We'll go across anyhow."

Not all the men followed him, and not only men but also horses failed him. His own mount squealed and reared in fright when he forced it near the soddenly crackling flames. He fought the animal back under control, but did not try again to make it cross.

That proved as well, for the bridge collapsed on itself a couple of minutes later. Charred timbers splashed into the river and, some, still burning, were swept away downstream. The Thanasioi jeered from the far bank, then began vanishing behind the curtain of rain.

Krispos sat glumly on his horse, listening to the splash and tinkle of the storm and, through it, the cries of wounded men. He squared his shoulders and did his best to rally. Turning to Sarkis he said, "Send companies out at once to seize any nearby routes east that remain open."

"Aye, Your Majesty, I'll see to it at once." After a moment, Sarkis said, "We have a victory here, Your Majesty."

"So we do." Krispos' voice was hollow. As a matter of fact, Sarkis' voice was hollow, too. Each seemed to be doing his best to convince the other everything was really all right, but neither appeared to believe it. Krispos put worry into words: "If we don't find another route soon, we'll have a hard time going forward."

"That's true." Sarkis seemed to deflate like a pig's bladder poked with a pin. "A victory that gets us nothing is scarcely worth the having."

"My thought exactly," Krispos said. "Better we should have stayed in Videssos the city and started this campaign in the spring than be forced to cut it off in the middle like this." He forced himself away from recrimination. "Let's make camp, do what we can for our hurt, and decide what we try next."

"A lot of that will depend on what the scouting parties turn up," Sarkis said.

"I know." Krispos did his best to stay optimistic. "Maybe the Thanasioi won't have knocked down every bridge for miles around."

"Maybe." Sarkis sounded dubious. Krispos was dubious, too. Against a revolt made up simply of rebellious peasants, he would have had more hope. But Livanios had already proved himself a thoroughgoing professional. You couldn't count on him to miss an obvious maneuver.

Krispos put the future out of his mind. He couldn't even plan until the scouts came back and gave him the information he needed. He rode slowly through the army, praising his men for fighting well, and congratulating them on the victory. They were not stupid; they could see for themselves that they hadn't accomplished as much as they might have. But he put the best face he could on the fight. "We've driven the bastards back, showed them they can't stand against us. They won't come yapping round our heels again like little scavenger dogs any time soon."

"A cheer for his Majesty!" one of the captains called. The cheer rang out. It was not one to make the hillsides echo, but it was not dispirited or sardonic, either. All things considered, it satisfied Krispos.

He rode up close to the bridge. Some of its smoldering support timbers still stood. Evripos looked across the river toward the now-vanished Thanasioi. He turned his head to see who approached, then nodded, one soldier to another. "I'm sorry, Father. I did my best to get over, but my stupid horse wouldn't obey."

"Maybe it's for the best," Krispos answered. "You would have been trapped on the far side when the bridge went down. I can't afford to lose sons so prodigally." He hesitated, then reached out to whack Evripos on his mailed back. "You fought very well—better than I'd looked for you to do."

"It was—different from what I expected." A grin lightened Evripos' face. "And I wasn't afraid, the way I thought I'd be."

"That's good. I was, my first time in battle. I puked up my guts afterward, as a matter of fact, and I'm not ashamed to admit it." Krispos studied his son in some bemusement. "Have I gone and spawned a new Stavrakios? I've always expected good things from you, but not that you'd prove a fearsome warrior."

"Fearsome?" Evripos' grin got wider; all at once, in spite of his beard and the mud that streaked his face, he reminded Krispos of the little boy he'd been. "Fearsome, you say? By the good god, I like it."

"Don't like it too well," Krispos said. "A taste for blood is more expensive than even an emperor can afford." He realized he laid that on too thick and tried to take some of it off: "But I was glad to see you at the fore. And if you go through the encampments tonight, you'll find out I wasn't the only one who noticed."

"Really?" Krispos could see Evripos wasn't used to the idea of being a hero. By the way the young man straightened up, though, the notion sat well. "Maybe I'll do that."

"Try not to let them get you too drunk," Krispos warned. "You're an officer; you need to keep your head clear when you're in the field." Evripos nodded. Remembering himself at the same age, Krispos doubted his son would pay the admonition too much heed. But he'd planted it in Evripos' mind, which was as much as he could do.

He went off to see how Katakolon had fared in his first big fight. His youngest son had already disappeared among the tents of the camp followers, so Krispos silently shelved the lecture on the virtues of moderation. He did seek out a couple of officers who had seen Katakolon in action. By their accounts, he'd fought well enough, though without his brother's flair. Reassured by that, Krispos decided not to rout him from his pleasures. He'd earned them.

Krispos had urged Evripos to go through the camp to soak up adulation. He made his own second tour for a more pragmatic reason: to gauge the feel of the men after the indecisive fight. He knew a certain amount of relief that none of the regiments had tried to go over to the foe.

A fellow who had his back turned and so did not know the Avtokrator was close by said to his mates, "I tell you, boys, at this rate it's gonna take us about three days less'n forever to make it to Pityos. If the mud don't hold us back, mixing it with the cursed heretics will." His friends nodded in agreement.

Krispos walked away from them less happy than he might have been. He breathed a silent prayer up to Phos that the scouting parties could discover an undefended river crossing. If his men didn't think they could do what he wanted from them, they were all too likely to prove themselves right.

Even though he'd not fought, himself, the battle left him worn. He fell asleep as soon as he lay down on his cot and did not wake until the gray dawn of another wet day. When he came out of the tent, he wished he'd stayed in bed, for Sarkis greeted him with unwelcome news: "Latest count is, we've lost, ah, thirty-seven men, Your Majesty."

"What do you mean, lost?" Krispos' wits were not yet at full speed.

The cavalry commander spelled it out in terms he could not misunderstand: "That's how many slipped out of camp in the night, most likely to throw in with the Thanasioi. The number'll only grow, too, as all the officers finish morning roll for their companies." No sooner were the words out of his mouth than a soldier came up to say something to him. He nodded and sent the man away, then turned back to Krispos: "Sorry, Your Majesty. Make that forty-one missing."

Krispos scowled. "If we have to use half the army to guard the other half, it'll be only days before we can't fight with any of it."

"Aye, that's so," Sarkis said. "And how will you be able to tell beforehand which half to use to do the guarding?"

"You have a delightful way of looking at things this morning, don't you, Sarkis?" Krispos peered up at the sky from under the broad brim of his hat. "You're as cheery as the weather."

"As may be. I thought you wanted the men around you to tell you what was so, not what sounded sweet. And I tell you this: if we don't find a good road forward today—well, maybe tomorrow, but today would be better— this campaign is as dead and stinking as last week's fish stew."

"I think you're right," Krispos said unhappily. 'We've sent out the scouts; that's all we can do for now. But if they don't have any luck . . ." He left the sentence unfinished, not wanting to give rise to any evil omen.

He sent out more scouting parties after breakfast. They splashed forth, vanishing into rain and swirling mist. Along with Krispos, the rest of the soldiers passed a miserable day, staying under canvas as much as they could, doing their best to keep weapons and armor greased against the ravages of rust, and themselves as warm and dry as they could—which is to say, not very warm and not very dry.

The first scouting parties returned to camp late in the afternoon. One look at their faces gave Krispos the bad news. The captains filled in unpleasant details: streams running high, ground getting boggier by the hour, and Thanasioi out in force at any possible crossing points. "If it could have been done, Your Majesty, we'd have done it," one of the officers said. "Truth is, it can't be done, not here, not now."

Krispos grunted as if kicked in the belly. Agreeing with Sarkis that he wanted to hear from his subjects what was so was one thing. Listening to an unpalatable truth, one that flew in the face of all he wanted, was something else again. But he had not lasted two decades and more on the throne by substituting his desires for reality: another lesson learned from poor wild dead Anthimos.

"We can't go forward," he said, and the scout commanders chorused agreement. "The lord with the great and good mind knows we can't stay here." This time, if anything, the agreement was louder. Though the bitter words choked him, Krispos said what had to be said: "Then we've no choice but to go back to Videssos the city." The officers agreed once more. That did nothing to salve his feelings.

THE THANASIOI TRAMPING INTO THE KEEP OF ETCHMIADZIN DID not look like an army returning in triumph. Phostis had watched—had taken part in—triumphal processions down Middle Street in Videssos the city, testimonials to the might of his father's soldiers and to the guile of his father's generals.

Looking down from his bare little cell in the citadel, he saw none of the gleam and sparkle, none of the arrogance, that had marked the processions with which he was familiar. The fighting men below looked dirty and draggled and tired unto death; several had bandages, clean or not so clean, on arms or legs or heads. And, in fact, they'd not won a battle. In the end, Krispos' army had forced them back from the position they tried to hold.

But even defeat hadn't mattered. Instead of pressing forward, the imperial force was on its way back to the capital.

Phostis was still trying to grasp what that meant. He and Krispos had clashed almost every time they spoke to each other. But Phostis, however much he fought with his father, however much he disagreed with much of what he thought his father stood for, could not ignore Krispos' long record of success. Somewhere down deep, he'd thought Krispos would deal with the Thanasioi as he had with so many other enemies. But no.

The door behind him swung open. He turned away from the window. Syagrios' grin, always unpleasant, seemed especially so now. "Come on down, you," the ruffian said. "Livanios wants a word with you, he does."

Phostis did not particularly want a word with the Thanasiot leader. But Syagrios hadn't offered him a choice. His watchdog stepped aside to let him go first, not out of deference but to keep Phostis from doing anything behind his back. Being thought dangerous felt good; Phostis would have been even happier had reality supported that thought.

The spiral stair had no banister to grab. If he tripped, he'd roll till he hit bottom. Syagrios, he was sure, would laugh the louder for every bone he broke. He planted his feet with special care, resolved to give Syagrios nothing with which to amuse himself.

As he did every time he came safe to the bottom of the stairs, he breathed a prayer of thanks to Phos. As he also did every time, he made certain no one but he knew it. Through the years, Krispos had gained some important successes simply by not letting on that anything was wrong. Even if the tactic was his father's, Phostis had seen that it worked.

Livanios was still out in the inner ward, haranguing his troops about the fine showing they'd made. Phostis could wait on his pleasure. Unused to waiting on anyone's pleasure save his own—and Krispos'—Phostis quietly steamed.

Then Olyvria came out of one of the side halls whose twists Phostis was still learning. She smiled and said to him, "You see, the good god himself has blessed the gleaming path with victory. Isn't it exciting? By being with us as we sweep away the old, you have the chance to fully become the man you were meant to be."

"I'm not the man I would have been, true," Photsis said, temporizing. Had he still been back with the army, half his heart, maybe more than half, would have swayed toward the Thanasioi. Now that he was among them, he was surprised to find so much of his heart leaning back the other way. He put it down to the way in which he'd come to Etchmiadzin.

"Now that our brave soldiers have returned, you'll be able to get out more and see the gleaming path as it truly is," Olyvria went on. If she'd noticed his lukewarm reply, she ignored it.

Syagrios, worse luck, seemed to notice everything. Grinning his snag-toothed grin, he put in, "You'll have a tougher time running off, too."

"The weather's not suited to running," Phostis answered as mildly as he could. "Anyhow, Olyvria is right: I do want to watch life along the gleaming path."

"She's right about more than that," Syagrios said. "Your cursed father can't hurt us the way he thought he could. Come spring, all these lands'll be flowing smooth as a river under Livanios, you bet they will."

A river that didn't flow smooth had won more for the Thanasioi than their soldiers' might, or so Phostis had heard. He kept that thought to himself, too.

Olyvria said, "It shouldn't be a matter of running in any case. We won't speak of that again, for we want you to remain and be contented among us."

"I'd also like to be contented among you," Phostis answered. "I hope it proves possible."

"Oh, so do I!" Olyvria's face glowed. For about the first time since she'd helped kidnap him, Phostis longingly remembered how she'd looked naked in the lamplight, in the secret chamber under Videssos the city. If he'd gone forward instead of back . . .

Outside in the inner ward, Livanios finished his speech. The Thanasiot soldiers cheered. Syagrios set a strong hand on Phostis' arm. "Come on. Now he'll have time to deal with the likes of you."

Phostis wanted to jerk away, not just from the contempt in his keeper's voice but also from being handled as if he were only a slab of meat. Back at the palaces, anyone who touched him like that would be gone inside the hour, and with stripes on his back to reward his insolence. But Phostis wasn't back at the palaces; every day reminded him of that in a new way.

Olyvria trailed along as Syagrios led him out to Livanios. The Thanasioi who still filled the courtyard made room for the ruffian and for Livanios' daughter to pass. Phostis they eyed with curiosity: some perhaps wondering who he was; and others, who knew *that* much, wondering what he was doing here. He wondered what he was doing here himself.

Livanios' smile instantly changed him from stern soldier to trusted leader. He turned its full warmth on Phostis. "And here's the young Majesty!" he exclaimed, as if Phostis were sovereign rather than prisoner. "How fare you, young Majesty?"

"Well enough, eminent sir," Phostis answered. He'd seen courtiers who could match Livanios as chameleons, but few who could top him.

The Thanasiot leader said, "Save your fancy titles for the corrupt old court. I'm but another man making his way along the gleaming path that leads to Phos."

"Yes, sir," Phostis said. He noticed Livanios did not reject that title of respect.

"Father, I do think he'll choose to join you on the gleaming path," Olyvria said.

"I hope he does," Livanios said, and then to Phostis: "I hope you do. Our brave and bright warriors surely kept your father from making life difficult for us this year. We have a whole season now in which to build and grow. We'll use it well, I assure you."

"I don't doubt that," Phostis said. "Your little realm here already reminds me of the way the Empire is run."

"Does it?" Livanios sounded pleased. "Maybe you can help keep it running as it should, as a matter of fact. Knowing your father, he's doubtless made sure you have some of the same skills he uses, though now you'd turn them to the cause of righteousness."

"Well, yes, some," Phostis said, not caring to admit he'd disliked and scanted administering imperial affairs. He wanted Livanios to think of him as someone useful, not as foe or a potential rival to be disposed of.

"Good, good." Livanios beamed. "We'll yet scour greed and miserliness and false doctrine from the face of the earth, and usher in such a reign of virtue that Phos' triumph over Skotos will be soon and certain."

Olyvria clapped her hands in delight at the vision her father put forward. It excited Phostis, too; this was the way Digenis had spoken. Before, Livanios had seemed more an officer out for his own advantage than someone truly committed to Thanasios' preaching. If he meant to put it into effect, Phostis would have more reason to think hard about fully binding himself to the movement.

Syagrios said, "We'll hit the imperials some more licks, too. I want to be in on that, by the good god."

"There'll be slaughter aplenty for you, never fear," Livanios told him. Phostis' newly fired zeal chilled as suddenly as it had heated. How, he wondered, could you get rid of greed and at the same time maintain a red zest for slaughter? And how could the gleaming path simultaneously contain both righteousness and Syagrios?

One thing was clear: he'd have time to find out. Now that his father's push had failed, he'd stay among the Thanasioi indefinitely. Had he really wanted that as much as he'd thought before he got it? He'd find that out, too.

Chapter VI

KRISPOS PACED THE PALACE CORRIDORS LIKE A CAGED ANImal. The fall rains were done; now sleet and snow came down from the cold gray heavens. The occasional clear days or even, once or twice, clear weeks were salt in his wounds: If they but lasted, he could fare forth once more against the Thanasioi.

One long stretch of good weather sorely tempted him, but he restrained himself: he knew too well it would not hold. But each successive bright morning gave a fresh twist of the knife. That once, he welcomed the blizzard that blew in. Though it trapped him, it let him feel sagacious.

Now Midwinter's Day, the day of the winter solstice, drew near. Krispos ticked off the passing days on the calendar one by one, but somehow they raced too swiftly even so. He faced the coming solstice with more resignation than joy. Midwinter's Day was the greatest festival of the religious year, but he found himself in no mood to celebrate.

Not even previewing the mime troupes that would perform in the Amphitheater restored his good humor. Among other things, Midwinter's Day gave folk more license than any other festival, and a good many of the skits poked fun at him for failing to put down the Thanasioi. More than one teased him for losing Phostis, too.

Not only would he have to watch this foolishness from the imperial box on the spine of the Amphitheater, he'd have to be seen to laugh. An Avtokrator who couldn't take what the mimes dished out quickly forfeited the city mob's fickle favor.

He took advantage of the imperial dignity to complain loud and often. At last Mystakon, the eunuch chamberlain who had most often served Phostis, said, "May it please Your Majesty, I am of the opinion that the young Majesty, were he able, would gladly assume the duty you find onerous."

Krispos felt his cheeks flame. "Yes, no doubt you're right," he mumbled. After that, he bottled his forebodings up inside himself.

Perhaps in one of Barsymes' efforts to cheer him, the serving maid Drina showed up in his bed again after a particularly trying day. This time he actively wanted her, or at least his mind did. His body, however, failed to rise to the occasion despite her ingenuity.

When it became clear nothing was going to happen, she said, "Now don't you fret, Your Majesty. It happens to everyone now and again." She spoke so matter-of-factly, he got the idea she was talking from experience. She added, "I'll tell you something else, too: you foolish men make more of a much about it than women ever do. It's just one of those things."

"Just one of those things," Krispos echoed between clenched teeth. Drina wrapped a robe around her and slipped out of the imperial bedchamber, leaving him alone in the darkness. "Just one of those things," he repeated, staring up at the ceiling. "Just one more thing that doesn't work."

Maybe Drina knew better than to gossip, or maybe—and more likely, given the way news of any sort raced through the palaces—the servitors knew better than to show the Avtokrator they knew anything. Back in his own days as vestiarios, he'd chattered about Anthimos, though never where Anthimos could listen. At any rate, he heard no sniggers, which relieved him in a way altogether different from the one he'd sought with Drina.

Compared to failing in bed, the ordeal of facing public mockery on Midwinter's Day suddenly seemed much more bearable. When the day finally dawned, cold and clear, he let Barsymes pour him into his finest ceremonial robe as if it were chain mail to armor him against the taunts he expected.

The procession from the palaces to the Amphitheater took him past bonfires blazing in the plaza of Palamas. People dressed in their holiday best—women with lace at their throat and ankles, perhaps with a couple of bodice buttons undone or skirts slit to show off a pretty calf; men in robes with fur collars and cuffs—leapt over the fires, shouting "Burn, ill-luck!"

"Go on, Your Majesty, if you care to," Barsymes urged. "It will make you feel better."

But Krispos shook his head. "I've seen too much to believe ill-luck's so easy to get rid of, worse luck for me."

Preceded by the dozen parasol-bearers protocol required, flanked by bodyguards, the Avtokrator crossed the racetrack that circled the floor of the Amphitheater and took his place on the seat at the center of the spine. Looking up to the top of the great oval was like looking up from the bottom of a soup tureen, save that the Amphitheater was filled with people, not soup. To the folk in the top rows, Krispos could have been only a scarlet dot; to anyone shortsighted up there, he was surely invisible.

But everyone in the Amphitheater could hear him. He thought of that as magic of a sort, though in fact it was nothing more—or less—than cleverly crafted acoustics. When he spoke from the Emperor's seat, it was as if he spoke straight into the ear of all the tens of thousands of men, women, and children who packed the arena.

"People of Videssos," he said, and then again, after his first words won quiet, "people of Videssos, after today the sun, the symbol of the lord with the great and good mind, turns to the north once more. Try as Skotos will, he has not the power to pull it from the sky. May the solstice and the days that follow it give everyone a lesson: even when darkness seems deepest, longer, brighter days lie ahead. And when darkness seems deepest, we celebrate to show we know it cannot rule us. Now let the Midwinter's Day festivities begin!"

He knew the cheer that rose had more to do with his opening the festival than with what he'd said. Nonetheless, the noise avalanched down on him from all sides until his head rang with it; just as from the Emperor's seat his voice flew throughout the Amphitheater, so every sound within the stone bowl was focused and magnified there.

Though he'd known in advance his speech would be largely ignored, he spoke, as always, from the center of what most concerned him at the moment. The people would forget his words the moment they were gone; he tried to take them to heart. When things seemed blackest, carrying on was never easy. But if you didn't carry on, how could you make your way to better times?

Squeals of glee greeted the first mime troupe to appear. The crowd's laughter dinned around Krispos as the performers, some dressed as soldiers, others as horses, pretended to be stuck in the mud. Even if they did lampoon his ill-fated campaign in the westlands, he found himself amused at first. Their act was highly polished, as were most that appeared in the Amphitheater. Rotten fruit and sometimes stones greeted troupes that did not live up to what the city folk thought their due.

The next group of mimes put on a skit whose theme puzzled Krispos. One of their number wore a costume that turned him into a skeleton. The other three seemed to be servants. They brought him ever more elaborate meals, finally wheeling out a prop feast that looked sumptuous enough to feed half the people in the Amphitheater. But the fellow in the skeleton suit refused everything with comic vehemence, and finally lay stiff and still in the dirt of the racetrack. His underlings picked him up and hauled him away.

The audience didn't quite know what to make of that show, either. Most of them sat on their hands. A few roared laughter; a couple of shouts of "Blasphemy!" rang out.

Krispos got up and walked over to Oxeites the patriarch, who sat a few yards down the spine from his own place. "Blasphemy?" he asked. "Where is the blasphemy—for that matter, where is the point?—in refusing food, most holy sir? Or does the blasphemy lie in mocking that refusal?"

"Your Majesty, I do not know." The patriarch sounded worried to admit it. Well he might; if he could not untie a theological knot, who in Videssos the city could?

All the performers in the professional mime troupes were male. It wasn't that way in peasant villages like the one where Krispos had grown up; he smiled to remember the village women and girls doing wicked impressions of their husbands and brothers. But the fellow who played a woman in the next troupe seemed so feminine and so voluptuous that the Avtokrator, who knew perfectly well what he was, found lubricious thoughts prancing through his mind all the same.

The performer turned his—or her—wiles on another member of the troupe, one dressed in a robe of priestly blue. The cleric proved slaveringly eager to oblige.

The crowd howled laughter. No one yelled "Blasphemy!" Krispos turned to Oxeites again. He contented himself with raising a questioning eyebrow; if he spoke from the Emperor's seat, the whole Amphitheater would hear him.

Oxeites coughed in embarrassment. "There was, Your Majesty, an, ah, unfortunate incident concerning celibacy while you were, ah, on campaign."

Krispos walked over to the patriarch's chair so he could talk without being overheard. "I saw no written reports on this, most holy sir. Did you think it would escape my notice? If so, do not make such a mistake again. When a priest drags the reputation of the temples through the bathhouses, I *will* find out about it Have I made myself clear enough?"

"Y-yes, Your Majesty." The patriarch was as pale as the pearls that ran riot over his regalia. Keeping unsavory secrets secret was part of the game of Videssian bureaucracy, secular and ecclesiastical alike. Getting found out meant you'd lost a round in that game.

The Avtokrator began to hope the mimes, poke fun at him as they might, would largely forget Phostis' kidnapping. That hope lasted until the next troupe came on and lampooned him for misplacing his eldest son; by the way the actor in fancy robes portrayed Krispos, his heir might have been a gold coin that had fallen through a hole in his belt pouch. The fellow kept looking behind prop bushes and under stones, as if certain he'd turn up the vanished heir in a moment.

The audience thought it all very funny. Krispos looked over to see how his other two sons were taking the mimes. He'd seldom seen such rage on Katakolon's face; his youngest son seemed ready to grab a bow and do his best to slaughter the whole troupe. The pretty girl next to Katakolon had her face carefully blank, as if she wanted to laugh but didn't dare.

A few seats away, Evripos was laughing as hard as some tinker up near the top row of the Amphitheater. He happened to catch Krispos' eye. He choked and grew sober as abruptly as if he'd been caught in some unnatural act. Krispos nodded grimly, as if to say Evripos had better keep himself quiet He knew his second son hungered for the throne; in Evripos' shoes, he would have hungered for it, too. But displaying exultation because his brother had disappeared would not do.

By the time the last troupe made its bows and left the Amphitheater, the year's shortest day was almost done. By then, several troupes had satirized Phostis' kidnapping. Krispos endured it as best he could. Evripos sat so still, he might have been carved from stone.

To end the show, Krispos spoke to the crowd. "Tomorrow the sun will come sooner and leave the sky later. Once again Skotos"—he spat in rejection of the evil god—"has failed to steal the light. May Phos bless you all, and may your days also be long and filled with light."

The crowd cheered, almost universally forgetting they'd giggled at the Avtokrator's expense bare minutes before. That was the way of crowds, Krispos knew. He'd started learning how to manipulate the Videssian mob while still a groom in Petronas' service, to help push out Anthimos' then-vestiarios so he could take the eunuch's place. The decades that had passed since had done little to increase his respect for the people in a collective body.

He got up from the Emperor's seat and took a few steps away from the acoustical focus. Only then could he privately talk aloud, even to himself. "Well, it's over," he said. He'd got through it; his family had got through it, and he didn't think any of the skits had done him permanent harm. Given the way the preceding few months had gone, he could hardly have hoped for better.

Twilight deepened quickly as, in the company of parasol-bearers and Haloga bodyguards, he made his way out of the Amphitheater. He, of course, had his own special exit. Had he wanted to, he could have gone straight back to the palaces under a covered way. But walking through the plaza of Palamas, as he had on the way to the mime show in the Amphitheater, gave him a chance to finger the pulse of the city. Ceremonial separated him from his subjects too much as things were. When he got a chance like this, he took it, and so he headed back toward the imperial residence through the square.

More bonfires burned there now than had when he went into the Amphitheater. People coming out of the mime show queued up to jump over them and burn away the year's accumulated misfortune. A few turned their heads as the Emperor and his retinue went by. One or two even called out, "Joy on the day, Your Majesty!"

"And to you and yours," he called back. On impulse, he added, "May I beg to steal a place in line?"

Men and women scrambled out of the way to give him what he'd asked for. Some of the Halogai stayed close by him; others, knowing Videssian ways, hurried to the far side of the fire. Krispos took a running start. The scarlet imperial boots were less than perfect footgear for running, but he managed. Leaping with all his strength, he yelled, "Burn, ill-luck!" as he soared over and through the flames. Maybe, as he'd said earlier in the day, it would do no good. But how could it do harm?

He landed heavily, staggering. One of the guardsmen grabbed his arm and steadied him. "Thanks," he said. His heart pounded, his breath came quick. A run and a jump—was that exerting himself? When he first took the throne, he'd have laughed at the idea. Now it seemed less funny. He shrugged. The only alternative to getting older was *not* getting any older. This wasn't perfect, but it was better.

A couple of bonfires over, a young man stooped to ignite a torch. He waved it over his head. Sparks flew through the night. The young man weaved among slower-moving people in the square. Still waving his torch, he shouted, "The gleaming path! Phos bless the gleaming path!"

For a moment, the cry did not register with Krispos. Then he stopped in midstride, stared, and pointed toward the young man. "That is a Thanasiot. Arrest him!"

Thinking back afterward, he realized he could have handled things better. Some of his guards dashed after the Thanasiot. So did some people in the crowd. Others, mistaking Krispos' target, chased the wrong man—several wrong men—and got in the way of those pursuing the right one. Shouts and fistfights erupted.

The young heretic kept right on running and kept right on chanting the Thanasiot war cry. To Krispos' horror, he cast his torch into one of the wood-and-canvas market stalls that were closed for the Midwinter's Day celebration. Flames clung and began to grow.

All at once Krispos, a lump of ice in his belly, wished the holiday had seen a blizzard or, better yet, a driving rainstorm. *Rain in the westlands when I didn't want it,* he thought wildly, *but none now when I can really use it.* The weather was not playing fair.

Neither were the Thanasioi. That first arsonist, no longer obvious for what he was as soon as he'd thrown his torch, vanished into the crowd. But others of his kind dashed here and there, waving torches and yelling acclaim for the gleaming path. In fewer than half a dozen minutes, more than half a dozen fires began to burn.

The people in the plaza of Palamas surged like the sea in storm, some toward the blazes but many more away from them. Fire in Videssos the city—fire in any town—was a great terror, for the means of fighting it were so pitifully few. Great fires, with winds whipping walls of flame ahead of them, had slain thousands and burned out whole quarters of the city. Most of those—all of them, as far as Krispos knew—sprang from lightning or accident. To use fire in a city—in *the* city—as a weapon . . . Krispos shivered. The Thanasioi were not playing fair, either.

He tried to pull himself together. "Bucket and siphon men!" he yelled to one of the chamberlain. "Fetch them on the double!"

"Aye, Your Majesty." The eunuch pelted into the palace compound. A company of firemen was stationed there, attached to the imperial guards. Several other companies had bases in other parts of the city. They were brave, they were skilled, they were even useful if they could get to a fire before it went wild. But if the Thanasioi were throwing torches around in the Forum of the Ox as well as the plaza of Palamas, and in the coppersmiths' district, and over by the High Temple, some of those blazes would surely get loose.

Krispos shouted, "Twenty goldpieces for every arsonist slain, fifty for every one taken alive!" With luck, the price differential would keep cutthroats from murdering innocent bystanders and then claiming a reward.

"Will you retire to the palaces, Your Majesty?" Barsymes asked.

"No." Krispos saw he'd surprised the vestiarios. He explained, "I want to be seen fighting this madness. I'll do it from the plaza here."

"As you say, Your Majesty," Barsymes answered in the peculiarly toneless voice he used when he thought Krispos was making a mistake.

Before long, Krispos, too, wondered if he hadn't made a mistake. Messengers who ran to the palaces didn't find him there. Because of that, he learned later than he should have that not only arson but also full-scale rioting had broken out in some of the poorer districts of the city. The two went hand in hand in every Avtokrator's nightmares: arson might leave him without a capital to rule, while riots could keep him from ruling at all.

But setting up his headquarters out where the people could see him had advantages, too. Not only did he shout for men to form a bucket brigade from the nearest fountain, he pitched in and passed buckets himself. "This is my city as well as yours," he told anyone who would listen. "We all have to work together to save it if we can."

For a while, that looked anything but certain. A bucket brigade was hopelessly inadequate to put out a fire once it got going. Even if some excited citizens didn't know that much, Krispos did. At his direction, the fellows at the far end of the brigade concentrated on wetting down the buildings and market stalls around the growing blaze to try to keep it from spreading.

He was beginning to think even that would be beyond their power when someone yelled, "Here's the fire company!"

"Oh, Phos be praised," Krispos panted. Already his shoulders ached from unaccustomed exertion; tomorrow, he suspected, he would be stiff and sore all over. Well, he'd worry about that tomorrow. Tonight, fighting the fire counted for more. He silently thanked the good god that, while he'd put on weight since he came to the throne, he hadn't got so fat as to kill himself if he had to do physical labor.

Instead of a hand bucket, the fire crew carried a great wooden tub on poles like those of a sedan chair. They filled it at the fountain, then—with shouts of "Gangway!"—dashed to the fire. Instead of dumping the big bucket on the blaze, two of the men worked a hand pump mounted in the bucket, while a third directed the stream of water that issued from the nozzle of an oiled canvas hose.

The bucket brigade shifted its efforts to keeping the tub full. Even so, it emptied faster than they could pour water into it. The firemen snatched it up by its cradle, filled it at the fountain again, then lugged it back with much swearing and grunting. The pumpers worked like men possessed; the fellow at the hose, a gray-haired veteran named Thokyodes, played his stream right at the heart of the blaze.

That second tubful began to give the fire company the upper hand. The blaze had eaten two or three stalls and damaged a couple of others, but it would not turn into a conflagration. Thokyodes came over to Krispos and greeted him with a crisp military salute, clenched fist over heart. "You called us in good time, Your Majesty. We've managed to save this lot."

"Not the first service you've done the city—or me," Krispos answered; Thokyodes had served on the fire crews for longer than Krispos had been Emperor. "I wish I could tell you to stand easy the rest of the night, but I fear we'll have more fires set."

"Ah, well, Midwinter's Day is always a nervous time for us." Thokyodes stopped, staring at the Avtokrator. "Set, did you say? This wasn't just one of the bonfires' blowing embers that caught?"

"I wish it had been," Krispos said. "But no, no such luck. The Thanasioi are raising riot, and when they riot, they seem to like to burn, too. The less anyone has, the better they're pleased."

Thokyodes made a horrible face. "They're fornicating crazy, begging your pardon, Your Majesty. Those bastards ever see anybody who's burned to death? They ever smelled a burned corpse? They ever try rebuilding what's been burned down?"

"I don't think they care about any of that. All they want is to get out of the material world as fast as they can."

"Send 'em on to me, then," Thokyodes growled. He carried a hatchet at his belt, to break down a wall so he could use his siphon or break through a door if he needed to effect a rescue. Now he grabbed the oak handle as if he had something else in mind for the tool. "Aye, I'll send 'em on to the ice real soon, I will, by the good god. Start their own fires, will they?" Like any fireman, he had a fierce, roaring hatred for arsonists of any sort, religious or secular.

A messenger came up to Krispos. Blood ran down his face from a scalp wound. When Krispos exclaimed over it, the man shook off his concern. "I'll live, Your Majesty. The rock glanced off, and my father always told me I had a hard head. Glad the old man was right. But I'm here to tell you it's getting worse than just riots in the poor part of town south of Middle Street. It's regular war—they're fighting with everything they have. Not just rocks like what got me, but bows and shortswords and I don't know what all else."

"Do you know where the barracks are in the palace compound, and can you get there without falling over?" Krispos asked. When he got nods to both questions, he went on, "Rout out Noetos' regiment of regulars. If the Thanasioi want to pretend they're soldiers, let's see how well they do facing soldiers instead of the city watch."

"Aye, Your Majesty," the messenger said. "You ought to send some priests out, too, for the heretics have one at their head, leather-lunged blue-robe name of—I think—Digenis."

Krispos frowned; while he knew he'd heard the name before, he needed a little while to place it. When he did, he snarled something that made the messenger's eyes widen. "That's the blue-robe Phostis fell in love with before he got kidnapped," he ground out. "If he's a Thanasiot—"

He stopped. If Digenis was a Thanasiot, did that mean Phostis had joined the heresy, too? Thinking so appalled Krispos, but he also realized that just about everything he did appalled Phostis, if for no other reason than because he did it. And if his eldest had become a Thanasiot, had he really been kidnapped at all? Or had he run off to join the rebels of his own free will?

One way or another, Krispos had to have answers. He said, "Pass the word—a hundred goldpieces for this Digenis alive, and may the lord with the great and good mind have mercy on anyone who slays him, for I'll have none."

"I'll make your wishes—your commands—known, Your Majesty." The messenger took off at a dead run.

Krispos had no time to brood on the fellow's news; two men dashed into the plaza of Palamas from different directions, each screaming "Fire!" at the top of his lungs. "Thokyodes!" Krispos yelled. The veteran asked both panicky men a few sharp questions, decided whose plight was more urgent, and went off with that fellow. The other man stamped his feet and looked about ready to burst. Krispos hoped he wouldn't lose all that he owned by the time the fire company got back.

A bitterly cold wind began to blow out of the northwest, the direction from which the winter storms came. Krispos would have welcomed one of those storms, but bright stars glittered in a blue-black sky. No storm tonight; maybe, he thought, tasting the wind, no storm tomorrow, either. Of course not. He needed one.

Some of the palace servitors scurried about the plaza of Palamas, setting up awnings to protect him from whatever weather might come. Since he'd decided to make his headquarters here, the servants would see that he had such comforts as they could provide. Barsymes eyed him, daring him to make something of it. He kept quiet.

Along with the servitors, people of every sort swarmed through the plaza—soldiers, messengers, firemen, and revelers determined to celebrate Midwinter's Day as they pleased no matter what was going on around them. The skinny fellow in the dark tunic didn't look the least out of place as he worked his way up to Krispos. When he got to within a couple of paces of the Avtokrator, he pulled out a dagger and screamed, "Phos bless the gleaming path!"

He stabbed overhand, which was less than wise. Krispos threw up a hand and caught the fellow's wrist before the knife struck home. The would-be assassin twisted and tried to break free, screaming all the while about the gleaming path. But Krispos had learned to wrestle from an army veteran about the time his beard began to sprout, and he had gained his first fame in Videssos the city by outgrappling a Kubrati champion. Shouting and twisting were not nearly enough to break away from him.

He bore the knifeman to the cobbles, squeezing hard on the tendons inside his wrist. Involuntarily, the Thanasiot's hand opened. When the knife fell out, the fellow tried to roll and grab for it. Krispos brought up a knee, hard, between his legs. It was unsporting but extremely effective. The fellow stopped screaming about the gleaming path and started screaming in good earnest.

A Haloga's axe came down with a meaty *thunk*. The screams rose to a brief high note, then stopped. Krispos scrambled to his feet to keep his robes from soaking up the quickly spreading pool of blood.

"I'd like to have asked him some questions," he said mildly.

"Honh!" the bodyguard answered, a northern exclamation full of contempt. "He attacked you, Your Majesty; he did not deserve to live, even for a moment."

"All right, Trygve," Krispos said. If he criticized the northerner too harshly, Trygve was liable to decide the knifeman had managed to come so close to the Emperor because of his own failing, and slay himself to make up for it. The Halogai were wonderful guards, but they had to be handled very differently from Videssians. Krispos had spent twenty years groping toward an understanding of their gloomy pride; given another twenty, he thought he might come close.

Thokyodes and his fire company returned to the plaza of Palamas. The fellow whose earlier plea they'd rejected fell on them like a starving bear. Without so much as a chance to draw breath, they hurried away in his wake. Krispos wondered if they'd find anything left to save.

From out of the palace complex, their armor clashing about them, marched the troops who had served as Krispos' rear guard in the ill-fated western campaign. They looked angry, first at being confined to barracks on Midwinter's Day and then at getting called out not to celebrate but to fight. As they grimly tramped through the plaza of Palamas, Krispos reflected that he wouldn't have cared to get in their way this evening.

A few minutes later, the noise floating into the square from the rest of the city suddenly redoubled. It did not sound like happy noise. Happy was the grunt that came from Trygve's throat. "Your soldiers, they go breaking heads." To him, the prospect seemed blissful.

Krispos watched the stars wheel slowly across the sky. He caught himself yawning. Though he was far more likely than most Videssians to stay up well into the night—who, after all, could better afford candles than the Avtokrator?—he still went to bed early by choice. Well, tonight he had no choice.

A trooper came back to report on the fighting south of Middle Street. He didn't seem to notice his iron pot of a helmet had been knocked sideways on his head. Saluting, he confirmed the headgear's mute testimony: "Your Majesty, them whoresons is putting up a regular battle, they is. They's been ready for it awhile, too, or I miss my guess."

"Don't tell me they're beating the regiment," Krispos exclaimed. *You'd better not tell me that,* he thought, *or some of my officers won't be officers by this hour of the night tomorrow.*

But the trooper shook his head. "Oh, nothing like that. They has spunk, aye, and more stay to 'em than I'd have looked for from a mob, but they ain't got armor and they ain't got many shields. We can hurt them a lot more than they can hurt us."

"Tell Noetos to do what he has to do to put them down," Krispos said. "Remind him also to make every effort to seize the priest Digenis, who I've heard is leading the rioters."

"Aye, there's a blue-robe flouncing about, shouting all sorts of daft nonsense. I figures we'd just knock him over the head." Krispos winced; somehow rumor seemed to spread every word but the one he wanted spread. "But if you want him took alive, we'll try and manage that."

"There's a reward," Krispos said, which made the messenger hurry back toward the brawl.

Waiting was hard. Krispos would much rather have been with a fire company or the regiment of soldiers. They were actually doing something. But if he did it with them, he'd lose track of how all his forces in the city were doing, save only the one he was with. Sometimes standing back to look at the whole mosaic was better than walking right up to it and peering closely at one tile. Better, maybe, but not easier.

Without his noticing, the servitors had fetched cots from the imperial residence—or perhaps from a barracks—and set them under the awning they'd erected. Evripos dozed on one, Katakolon on another. The girl who'd come to the Amphitheater with him was gone. Krispos knew his son would sooner have been in her bed than the one he occupied, but he felt a certain amount of amused relief that Katakolon hadn't dared leave. The boy knew better than that, by the good god.

Glancing over at Evripos, Krispos was surprised at how badly he wanted to wake him and put him to work. The lad—no, Evripos had shown himself the fair beginnings of a man—could have given him another pair of eyes, another pair of hands. But Krispos let him sleep.

Even though the fires in the plaza of Palamas were long since extinguished, Krispos smelled smoke from time to time, wafted from blazes elsewhere in the city. The wind, fortunately, had died down. With luck, it would not spread flames and embers in one of those running fires that left whole quarters bare behind them; rebuilding after one like that took years.

Krispos sat down on his cot. *Just for a few minutes,* he told himself. He dimly remembered leaning over sideways, but didn't know he'd fallen asleep until someone yelled, "Your Majesty! Wake up, Your Majesty!"

"Wuzzat? I *am* awake," Krispos said indignantly. But the gluey taste in his mouth and the glue that kept trying to stick his eyelids together gave him the lie. "Well, I'm awake now," he amended. "What's toward?"

"We've nailed Digenis, Your Majesty," the messenger told him. "Had a couple of lads hurt in the doing, but he's in our hands."

"There's welcome news at last, by the lord with the great and good mind," Krispos breathed. With it, he really did come all the way awake. He must have been out for two hours or so; the buildings to the southeast were silhouetted against the first gray glow of morning twilight. When he got to his feet, twinges in the small of his back and one shoulder announced how awkwardly he'd rested. That wouldn't have happened in his younger days, but it happened now.

"We're bringing the bastard—begging your pardon for speaking so of a priest, Your Majesty, but he's a right bastard if ever there was one—anyhow, we're bringing him back here to the plaza," the messenger said. "Where will you want him after that?"

"In the freezingest icepit of Skotos' hell," Krispos said, which jerked a startled laugh from the soldier who'd carried him the news. The Avtokrator thought fast. "He shouldn't come here, anyway—too much chance of his getting loose. Head up Middle Street—he'll be coming that way, yes?—and tell the men to haul him to the government office building there and secure him in one of the underground gaol cells. I'll be there directly myself."

Pausing only long enough to return the messenger's salute, Krispos shook Katakolon awake and ordered him to fetch Zaidas to the government office building. "What? Why?" asked Katakolon, who'd slept through the messenger's arrival. His eyes went wide when his father explained.

Haloga officers booted their men back to consciousness to guard Krispos on the way down Middle Street. With his usual quiet efficiency, Barsymes—who probably had not slept at all—started spreading word of where the Avtokrator would be so any sudden urgent word could quickly reach him.

The government office building was a granite pile of no particular loveliness. It housed bureaucrats of station insufficiently exalted to labor in the palaces, records of antiquity great enough that they were not constantly consulted, and, belowground, prisoners who rated more than a fine but less than the headsman. It looked like a fortress; in seditions past, it had served as one.

Today's riot, though, did not lap around it. Some of the Halogai deployed at the doorway in case trouble should approach. Others accompanied Krispos into the entry hall, which was quiet and, but for their torches, dark. Krispos took the stairway down.

Noise and light and strong odors of torch smoke, stale food, and unwashed humanity greeted him on the first basement floor. The prison guards hailed him with salutes and welcoming shouts—his coming was enough out of the ordinary to make their labor seem worthwhile again.

A senior guard said, "The one you're after, Your Majesty, they're holding him in cell number twelve, down that hallway there." The wine on his breath added a new note to the symphony of smells. It being the morning after Midwinter's Day, Krispos gave no sign he noticed, but made a mental note to check whether the fellow drank on duty other days, as well.

Instead of the usual iron grillwork, cell number twelve had a stout door with a locked bar on the outside. The gaoler inserted a big brass key, twisted, and swung the bar out of the Avtokrator's way. Flanked by a pair of Halogai, Krispos went in.

A couple of soldiers from Noetos' regiment already stood guard over Digenis, who, wrists tied behind him and ankles bound, lay on a straw pallet that had seen better years. "Haul him to his feet," Krispos said roughly.

The guard obeyed. Blood ran down Digenis' face from a small scalp wound. Those always bled badly, and, being a priest, Digenis had no hair to shield his pate from a blow. He glared defiance at Krispos.

Krispos glared back. "Where's Phostis, wretch?"

"Phos willing, he walks the gleaming path," Digenis answered, "and I think Phos may well be willing. Your son knows truth when he hears it."

"More than I can say for you, if you follow the Thanasiot lies," Krispos snapped. "Now where is he?"

"I don't know," Digenis said. "And if I did, I'd not tell you, that's certain."

"What's certain is that your head will go up on the Milestone as belonging to a proved traitor," Krispos said. "Caught in open revolt, don't think you'll escape because you wear the blue robe."

"Wealth is worth revolting against, and I don't fear the headsman because I know the gleaming path will lead me straight to the lord with the great and good mind," Digenis said. "But I could be as innocent as any man the temples revere as holy and still die of your malice, for the patriarch, far from being the true leader of the ecclesiastical hierarchy, is but your puppet, mouthing your impious words."

Stripped of the venom with which he spoke them, Digenis' words held a certain amount of truth: if Oxeites turned against Krispos, he would soon find himself out of the ecumenical patriarch's blue boots. But none of that mattered, not here, not now. "You're captured for no ecclesiastical offense, sirrah, but for the purely secular crimes of rebellion and treason. You'll answer for them as any other rebel would."

"I'll sing hymns to Phos thanking you for freeing me from the stench-filled world that strives unceasingly to seduce and corrupt my soul," Digenis said. "But if you do not travel the gleaming path yourself, no hymns of mine will save you. You'll go to the ice and suffer for all eternity, lured to destruction by Skotos' honied wiles."

"Given a choice between sharing heaven with you and hell with Skotos, I believe I'd take Skotos," Krispos said. "He at least does not pretend to virtues he lacks."

Digenis hissed like a viper and spat at Krispos, whether to ward off the dark god's name or from simple hatred, the Avtokrator could not have said. Just then Zaidas came into the cell. "Hello," he said. "What's all this?" He set down the carpetbag in his left hand.

"This," Krispos said, "is the miserable excuse for a priest who sucked my son into the slimy arms of the Thanasioi. Wring what you can from the cesspit he calls a mind."

"I shall of course make every effort, Your Majesty, but . . ." Zaidas' voice trailed away. He looked doubtful, an expression Krispos was unused to seeing on his face. "I fear I've not had the best of luck, probing for the heretics' secrets."

"You gold-lovers are the heretics," Digenis said, "casting aside true piety for the sake of profit."

Emperor and wizard both ignored him. "Do your best," Krispos said. He hoped Zaidas would have better fortune with Digenis than he had with other Thanasiot prisoners or with learning what sort of magic screened him away from finding Phostis. Despite the rare sorcerous tools and rarer scrolls and codices in the Sorcerers' Collegium, the chief wizard had been unable to learn why he was unable to seek Phostis out by sorcery.

Zaidas started pulling sorcerous gear from the bag. "I'll try the two-mirror test, Your Majesty," he said.

Krispos wanted to hear confidence in his voice, wanted to hear him say he would have the truth out of Digenis no matter what the renegade priest did. What he heard, with ears honed by listening behind the words of thousands of petitioners, officers, and officials, was doubt. Doubt from Zaidas fed his own doubt: because magic drew so strongly from the power of belief, if Zaidas didn't truly believe he could make Digenis speak, he'd likely fail. He'd already failed on a Thanasiot with the two-mirror test.

"What other strings do you have to your bow?" the Emperor asked. "How else can we hope to pull answers from him?" He could hear his own delicacy of phrase. He wanted Zaidas to think about alternatives, but didn't want to demoralize the mage or suggest he'd lost faith in him . . . even if he had.

Zaidas said, "Should the two-mirror test fail, our strongest hope of learning truth goes with it. Oh, a decoction of henbane and other herbs, such as the healers use, might loosen this rascal's tongue, but with it he'd spew as much gibberish as fact."

"One way or another, he'll spew, by the good god," Krispos said grimly, "if not to you, then to the chap in the red leathers."

"Torment my flesh as you will," Digenis said. "It is but the excrement of my being; the sooner it slides down the sewer, the sooner my soul soars past the sun to be with the lord with the great and good mind."

"Go on," Krispos told Zaidas. Worry on his face, the wizard set up his mirrors, one in front of Digenis, the other behind him. He got a brazier going; clouds of fumigants rose in front of the mirrors, some sweet, some harsh.

But when the questioning began, not only did Digenis stand mute, so did his image in the mirror behind him. Had the spell been working as it should have, that second image would have given out truth in spite of his efforts to lie or remain silent.

Zaidas bit his lip in angry, mortified frustration. Krispos sucked in a long, furious breath. He'd had the bad feeling Digenis would remain impervious to interrogation of any sort. The vast majority of men broke under torture. Maybe the priest would, or maybe he'd spill his guts under the influence of one of Zaidas' potions. But Krispos wasn't willing to bet on either.

As if to rub in his determination, Digenis said, "I shall praise Phos' holy name for every pang you inflict on me." He began to sing a hymn at the top of his lungs.

"Oh, shut up," Krispos said. Digenis kept on singing. Someone scratched at the door to the cell. Axe ready to strike, a Haloga pulled it open. A priest started to walk in, then drew back in alarm at the upraised axe blade. "Come on, come on," Krispos told him. "Don't stand there dithering—just tell me what you want."

"May it please Your Majesty," the priest began nervously, and Krispos braced for trouble. The blue-robe tried again: "M-may it please Your Majesty, I am Soudas, an attendant at the High Temple. The most holy ecumenical patriarch Oxeites, who was commemorating the day by celebrating a special liturgy there, directed me to come to you on hearing that the holy priest Digenis had been captured, so to speak, in arms, and bade me remind Your Majesty that ecclesiastics are under all circumstances immune from suffering bodily torment."

"Oh, he did? Oh, they are?" Krispos glared at the priest, who looked as if he wished he could sink through the floor—though that would only have put him in a deeper level of the gaol. "Doesn't the most holy ecumenical patriarch recall that I took the head of one of his predecessors for treason no worse than this Digenis has committed?"

"If you mentioned the fate of the formerly most holy Gnatios—may Phos grant his soul mercy—I was instructed to point out that, while capital punishment remains your province, it is a matter altogether distinct from torture."

"Oh, it is?" Krispos made his glare fiercer still. It all but shriveled Soudas, but the priest managed a shaky nod. Krispos dropped his scowl to his red boots; could he have scowled at his own face, he would have done it. The part of him that weighed choices like a grocer weighing out lentils swung into action. Could he afford a row with the regular temple hierarchy while at the same time fighting the Thanasiot heretics? Reluctantly, he decided he could not. Growling like a dog that has reached the end of its chain and so cannot sink its teeth into a man it wants to bite, he said, "Very well, no torture. You may tell the patriarch as much. Generous of him to let me use my own executioners as I see fit."

Soudas bobbed his head in what might have been a nod, then wheeled about and fled. Digenis hadn't missed a note of his hymn. Krispos tried to console himself by doubting whether the renegade would have broken under torment. But he craved the chance to find out.

The Avtokrator swung toward Zaidas. The wizard had listened to his talk with the priest. Zaidas was anything but a fool; he could figure out for himself that the burden on him had just grown heavier. If he couldn't pry secrets from Digenis, those secrets would stay unknown for good. The wizard licked his lips. No, he was not long on confidence.

Digenis ended his hymn. "I care not if you go against the patriarch," he said. "His doctrine is false in any case, and I do not fear your torments."

Krispos knew a strong temptation to break Digenis on the rack, to tear at his flesh with red-hot pincers, not so much in the hope that he would tell where Phostis was—if in fact he knew—but to see if he so loudly despised torment after suffering a good deal of it. Krispos had enough control over himself to recognize the temptation as base and put it aside, but he felt it all the same.

Digenis not only remained defiant but actually seemed to seek out martyrdom. "Your refusal to liberate me from my polluting and polluted envelope of flesh is but another proof of your own foul materialism, your rejection of the spiritual for the sensual, the soul for the penis, the—"

"When you go to the ice, I hope you bore Skotos with your stupid maunderings," Krispos said, a sally that succeeded in making Digenis splutter in outrage and then, better still, shut up. The Emperor added, "I've wasted enough time on you." He turned to Zaidas. "Try anything and everything you think might work. Bring in whatever colleagues you need to give you aid. One way or another, I will have answers from this one before the dark god takes him forever."

"Aye, Your Majesty." Zaidas' voice was low and troubled. "The good god willing, others from the Sorcerers' Collegium will have more success than I at smashing through his protective shell of fanaticism."

Accompanied by his bodyguards, Krispos left the cell and the subterranean gaol. About halfway up the stairs to the entrance hall, one of the Halogai said, "Forgive me, Majesty, but may I ask if I heard the blue-robe aright? Did he not blame you there for failing to flay him?"

"Aye, that's just what he did, Frovin," Krispos answered.

The northerner's blue eyes mirrored his confusion. "Majesty, I do not understand. I do not fear hurt and gore; that were unmanly. But neither do I run forth and embrace them like man clasping maid."

"Nor do I," Krispos said. "A streak of martyrdom runs through some of the pious in Videssos, though. Me, I'd sooner live for the good god than die for him."

"Spoken like a man of sense," Frovin said. The other bodyguards rumbled approval, down deep in their chests.

When he went outside, the gray light of winter dawn was building. The air smelled of smoke, but with stoves, fireplaces, and braziers by the tens of thousands, the air of Videssos the city always had a smoky tang to it. No great curtains of black billowed up into the lightening sky. If the Thanasioi had thought to burn down the city, thus far they'd failed.

Back in the plaza of Palamas, Evripos still slept. To Krispos' surprise, he found Katakolon in earnest conversation with Thokyodes the fire captain. "If you're sure everything's out in that district, why don't you get some rest?" his youngest son was saying. "You won't do us or the city any good if you're too worn to answer the next summons."

"Aye, that's good advice, young Majesty," Thokyodes answered, saluting. "We'll kip right out here, if that suits—and if you can find us some blankets."

"Barsymes!" Katakolon called. Krispos nodded approvingly—Katakolon might not know where things were, but he knew who would. His son spotted him. "Hello, Father. Just holding things together as best I could; Barsymes told me you were busy with that madman of a priest."

"So I was. I thank you for the help. Do we have the upper hand?"

"We seem to," Katakolon said, more caution in his voice than Krispos was used to hearing there.

"Good enough," Krispos said. "Now let's see if we can keep it."

Toward midmorning, riot flared again in the quarter south of Middle Street. The soldiers Krispos had sent in the night before stayed loyal, much to his relief. Better still, the wind stayed calm, which gave Thokyodes' crew a fighting chance against the blazes set by the heretics and rioters—not identical groups; some of the brawlers arrested were out for what they reckoned piety, others just for loot.

When messengers reported that spasm spent, Krispos raised cups of wine with both Katakolon and Evripos, convinced the worst was past. Then another messenger arrived, this one a gaoler from under the government office building. "What now?" Krispos asked.

"It concerns the matter of the prisoner Digenis the priest," the fellow answered.

"Well, what about him?" Krispos said, wishing the gaoler wouldn't talk like what he was now that he'd come away from the cells and into the sun.

"Your Majesty, he has refused alimentation," the man declared. Krispos'
upraised eyebrow warned him he'd better talk straighter than that. He did
try: "Your Majesty, he won't eat his victuals. He declares his intention to
starve himself to death."

FOR THE FIRST TIME SINCE HE GREW OLD ENOUGH TO JUMP OVER
a bonfire instead of falling into one, Phostis did no leaping on Midwinter's
Day. Whatever ill-luck he'd accumulated over the past year remained unburned. He wasn't mewed up in his monklike cell in the keep of Etchmiadzin; he'd been allowed out and about for some weeks. But no fires blazed
on street corners anywhere in the town.

Dark streets on Midwinter's Day struck him as unnatural, even while
he accompanied Olyvria and—inevitably—Syagrios to one of Etchmiadzin's temples. The service was timed for sunset, which came early not
only became this was the shortest day of the year but also because the sun,
instead of descending to a smooth horizon, disappeared behind the
mountains to the west.

Night came down like an avalanche. Inside the temple, whose strong,
blocky architecture spoke of Vaspurakaner builders, darkness seemed absolute; the Thanasio: unlike the orthodox, did not celebrate the light on
Midwinter's Day but rather confronted their fear of the dark. Not a torch,
not a candle burned inside the temple.

Standing there in the midst of blackness, Phostis peered about, trying
to see something, anything. For all the good his eyes did, he might as well
have been blindfolded again. His shiver had nothing to do with the cold
that filled the temple along with night. Never had the menace of Skotos
seemed so real, so close.

Seeking assurance where sight gave none, he reached out and clasped
Olyvria's hand in his own. She squeezed back hard; he wondered if this
eerie, silent ritual was as hard on her, on all the Thanasioi, as it was on
him.

"Someone will start screaming soon," he whispered, not least to keep
himself from becoming that someone. His breathless voice seemed to echo
through the temple, though he knew even Olyvria could hardly hear him.

"Yes," she whispered back. "It happens sometimes. I remember when—"

He didn't find out what she remembered. Her words were lost in a great
exhalation of relief from the whole congregation. A priest carrying a single
candle strode up the aisle toward the altar. Every eye swung toward that
glowing point as if drawn by a lodestone.

"We bless thee, Phos, lord with the great and good mind," the priest intoned, and everyone in the temple joined in the creed with greater fervor than Phostis had ever known, "by thy grace our protector, watchful beforehand that the great test of life may be decided in our favor."

The congregation's amens came echoing back from the conical dome that surmounted the altar. Often, to Phostis, Phos' creed had become mere words to be quickly gabbled through without thinking on what they meant. Not now. In the cold and frightening dark, they, like the tiny flame from the candle the priest held on high, took on new meaning, new importance. If they were not, if light was not—what then? Only black, only ice. Phostis shivered again.

The priest moved the candle to and fro and said, "Here is the soul, adrift in a creation not its own, the sole light floating on an ocean of darkness. It moves here, it moves there, always surrounded by—things." Coming out of the gloom that prevailed even at the altar, the word had a frightening power.

"But the soul is not a—thing," the priest went on. "The soul is a spark from the infinite torch of Phos, trapped in a world made by the foe of sparks and the greater foe of greater sparks. The things that surround us distract us from the pursuit of goodness, holiness, and piety, which are all that truly matter.

"For our souls endure forever, and will be judged forever. Shall we then turn toward that which does not endure? Food turns to dung, fire to ash, fine raiment to rags, our bodies to stench and bones and then to dust. What boots it, then, whether we gorge on sweetmeats, toast our homes till we sweat in the midst of winter, drape ourselves with silks and furs, or twitch to the brief deluded passions—miscalled pleasures—that spring from the organs we better use to void ourselves of dross?"

Contemplating infinite judgment, contemplating infinite punishment for the sins he, like any mortal, had surely committed, made Phostis want to tear his grip free from Olyvria's. Anything involving base matter in any way was surely evil, surely sufficient to cast him down to the ice forevermore.

But Olyvria clung to him harder than she had before. Maybe, he told himself, she needed comfort and reassurance. Granting her that spiritual boon might outweigh his guilt for noticing how warm and smooth her skin was. He did not let go of her hand.

The priest said, "Each year, the lord with the great and good mind warns us we cannot presume his mercy will endure forever. Each year, all through fall, Phos' sun sinks lower in the sky. Each year, our prayers call it back to rise higher once more, to grant warmth and light even to the wicked figments of reality that spring from the dark heart of Skotos.

"But beware! No mercy, not even the good god's, endures forever. Phos may yet sicken on our great glut of sins. One year—maybe one year not far from now, given the wretched state of mankind; maybe even next year, maybe even *this* year—one year, I say, the sun may not turn back toward the north the day after Midwinter's Day, but rather go on sinking ever southward, sinking until only a little crimson twilight remains on the horizon, and then—nothing. No light. No hope. No blessings. Forever."

"No!" someone wailed. In an instant, the whole congregation took up the cry. Among the rest was Olyvria, her voice clear and strong. Among them, after a moment, was Phostis himself: the priest had a gift for instilling fright. Among them even was Syagrios. Phostis hadn't thought the ruffian respected Phos or feared Skotos.

Through all the outcry, Olyvria's fingers remained laced with his. He didn't really think about that; he just accepted it gratefully. Instead of feeling alone in the cold blackness that could have come straight from Skotos, he was reminded others fought the dark with him. He needed that reminder. Never in all his years of worshiping at the High Temple had he known such fear of the dark god.

The priest said, "With fasting and lamentation we may yet show Phos that, despite our failings, despite the corruption that springs from the bodies in which we dwell, we remain worthy of the sign of his light for yet another year, that we may advance farther down the gleaming path praised by the holy Thanasios. Pray now, and let the lord with the great and good mind know what is in your hearts!"

If before the temple had echoed to the shouts of the congregation, now, even louder, it was filled with the worshipers' prayers. Phostis' went up with the rest. In the riches and light of the High Temple it was easy to believe, along with the ecumenical patriarch and his plump, contented votaries, that Phos would surely vanquish Skotos at the end of days. Such sublime confidence was harder to maintain in the dark of a chilly temple with a priest preaching of light draining out of the world like water from a tub.

At first, all Phostis heard was the din of people at noisy prayer. Then, little by little, he noticed individual voices in the din. Some repeated Phos' creed over and over: Videssos' universal prayer prevailed among Thanasioi and their foes alike. Others sent up simple requests: "Give us light." "Bless my wife with a son this year, O Phos." "Make me more pious and less lustful!" "Heal my mother's sores, which no salve has aided!"

Prayers like those would not have seemed out of place back in the High

Temple. Others, though, had a different ring to them. "Destroy everything that stands in our way!" "To the ice with those who will not walk the gleaming path!" "O Phos, grant me the courage to cast aside the body that befouls my soul!" "Wreck them all, wreck them all, wreck them all!"

He did not care for those; they might have come from the throats of baying wolves rather than men. But before he could do more than notice them, the priest at the altar raised a hand. Any motion within his candle's tiny circle of light was astoundingly noticeable. The congregation fell silent at once, and with it Phostis' concerns.

The priest said, "Prayer alone does not suffice. We do not walk the gleaming path with our tongues; the road that leads beyond the sun is paved with deeds, not words. Go forth now and live as Thanasios would have had you live. Seek Phos' blessings in hunger and want, not the luxuries of this world that are but a single beat of a gnat's wings against the judgment yet to come. Go forth! This liturgy is ended."

No sooner had he spoken than acolytes bearing torches came into the worship area from the narthex to light the congregants' way out. Phostis blinked; his eyes filled with tears at what seemed the savage glare, though a moment later he realized it was not so bright after all.

He'd dropped Olyvria's hand the instant the acolytes entered—or perhaps she'd dropped his. In more light than a single candle flame, he dared not risk angering Syagrios . . . and, even more to the point, angering Livanios.

Then palace calculation surged forward unbidden in his mind. Would Livanios throw his daughter at the heir apparent to the throne? Did he seek influence through the marriage bed? Phostis filed that away for future consideration. But no matter what Livanios intended, the feel of Olyvria's hand in his had been the only warmth he'd known, physical or spiritual. through the Thanasiot service.

He'd thought the temple's interior cold, and so it had been. But there, at least, some hundreds of people crowded together had given a measure, albeit a small one, of animal warmth. Out on the night-black streets of Etchmiadzin, with the wind whipping knifelike down from the hills, Phostis rediscovered what true cold meant.

The heavy wool cloak he wore might have been made of lace, for all the good it did to keep off the wind. Even Syagrios hissed as the blast struck him. "By the good god," he muttered, "I'd not mind jumping over a bonfire tonight, or even into one, just so as I could get warm."

"You're right." The words were out of Phostis' mouth before he remembered to be surprised at agreeing with Syagrios about anything.

"Fires and displays are not the way of the gleaming path," Olyvria said. "I remember them, too, from the days before my father accepted Thanasios' way. He says it's better to make your soul safe than to worry about what happens to your body."

The priest in the temple had said the same. From him, it sank deep into Phostis' heart. From Livanios, even through Olyvria as intermediary, the words did not mean as much. The heresiarch mouthed Thanasiot slogans, but did he live by them? As far as Phostis could see, he remained sleek, well fed, and worldly.

Hypocrite. The word tolled like a warning bell on a rocky coast. Hypocrisy was the crime of which Phostis had in his mind convicted his father, most of the capital's nobles, the ecumenical patriarch, and most of the clergy, as well. The quest for unvarnished truth was what had drawn him to the Thanasioi in the first place. Finding Livanios anything but unvarnished made him doubt the perfection of the gleaming path.

He said, "I wouldn't mind seeing the time of the sun-turning as one of rejoicing as well as sorrow. After all, it does ensure life for another year."

"But life in the world means life in things which are Skotos," Olyvria said. "Where's to rejoice over that?"

"If it weren't for material things, life would come to an end, and so would mankind," Phostis countered. "Is that what you want: to fade away and vanish?"

"Not for myself." Olyvria's shiver, like Phostis' back in the temple, had little to do with the weather. "But there are those who do want exactly that. You'll see some of them soon, I think."

"They're daft, if you ask me," Syagrios said, though his voice lacked its usual biting edge. "We live in this world along with the next one."

Olyvria argued that. If there was one thing Videssians would do at any excuse or none, it was argue theology. Phostis kept out of the argument, not least because he inclined to Syagrios' side of it and did not want to offend Olyvria by saying so out loud.

The memory of her hand remained printed in his mind. It called up that other memory he had of her, the one from the chamber off the passageway under Digenis' temple back in the city. That latter memory was suited for Midwinter's Day, at least as he'd known it before. It was a time of festival, even of license. As the proverb put it, "Anything can happen on Midwinter's Day."

Had this been a holiday of the sort with which he was familiar, he might—somewhere down deep in him, in a place below words, he knew he would—have tried to get her off by herself. And he suspected, she would have gone with him, even if only for the one night.

But here in Etchmiadzin, seeking sensual pleasure on Midwinter's Day did not bear thinking about. Rejection was the mildest return he could expect. More likely was some sort of mortification of his flesh. Though he had increasing respect for the asceticism of the gleaming path, his flesh had lately suffered enough mortification to suit him.

Besides, Syagrios would make a eunuch of him—and enjoy doing it— if he got himself into trouble of that sort.

The ruffian broke off his disputation with Olyvria, saying, "However you care to have it, my lady. You know more about this business than me, that's for sure. All I know now is that this here poor old smashed nose of mine is going to freeze off if I don't get to somewheres with a fire."

"There I cannot disagree with you," Olyvria said.

"Let's us head back to the keep, then," Syagrios suggested. "It'll be warm—well, warmer—in there. 'Sides, I can dump his Majestyhood here back in his room and get me a chance to relax a bit."

To the ice with you, Syagrios. The thought stood pure and crystalline in the center of Phostis' mind. He wanted to scream it. Only a healthy regard for his own continued survival kept him from screaming it. He was, then, at most an imperfect Thanasiot. Like Olyvria, he remained enamored of the fleshly envelope his soul wore, no matter what the source of that flesh.

The narrow, muddy lanes of Etchmiadzin were almost preternaturally dark. Night travel in Videssos the city was undertaken with torchbearers and guards, if for any legitimate purpose. Only footpads there cherished the black of night. But no one in Etchmiadzin tonight carried a light or seemed concerned over becoming a robber's victim. Cries rose into the dark sky, but they were only the lamentations the priest had commanded of his congregants.

The bulk of the fortress and the stars it obscured helped mark the path back from the temple. Even the torches above the gates were out. Livanios went that far in adhering to the tenets of the Thanasioi.

Syagrios grumbled under his breath. "Don't like that," he said. "Just anybody could come wandering in, and who'd be the wiser till too late?"

"Who's in the town save our own folk and a few Vaspurakaners?" Olyvria said. "They have their own rites and leave ours alone."

"They'd better," Syagrios replied. "More of us than there is of them."

Only inside the keep did light return. Livanios' caftan-wearing advisor sat at a table gnawing the leg of a roasted fowl and whistling a cheery tune Phostis did not know. If he'd heard the order for fasting and lamentation, he was doing a good job of ignoring it.

Syagrios lit a candle from a torch set in a soot-blackened sconce. With it in one hand and his knife in the other, he urged Phostis up the spiral stairway. "Back to your room now," he said. Phostis barely had time to nod to Olyvria before the twist of the stairs made her disappear.

The corridor that led to his little chamber was midnight black. He turned to Syagrios, pointing at the candle. "May I light a lamp in my room from that?"

"Not tonight," Syagrios said. "I got to watch you instead of roisterin', so you get no more enjoyment than me."

Once inside, Phostis drew off his cloak and put it over the blanket on his pallet. He did not take off his tunic as he got under them both and huddled up in a ball to try to warm himself as fast as he could. He looked back toward the door, beyond which Syagrios surely lurked. "Roistering, is it?" he whispered. He might be a poor Thanasiot himself, but he knew a worse one.

Chapter VII

T HE MAN'S EYES TWITCHED BACK AND FORTH IN THEIR SOCK-
ets. It was like no motion Phostis had ever seen before; watching made him queasy. Voice calm but weak, the man said, "I can't see you, not really, but that's all right. It goes away in a few days, I'm told by those who have come this way before me."

"That's g-good." Phostis knew he sounded shaky. It shamed him, but he couldn't help it.

"Fear not," the man said. He'd been introduced to Phostis as Strabon. He smiled radiantly. "Soon, I know, I shall join the lord with the great and good mind and cast aside this flesh that has too long weighed me down."

Strabon had, Phostis thought, already cast aside almost all of his flesh. His face was a skull covered with skin; his neck seemed hardly thicker than a torch. Withered branches might have done for his arms, and claws for his hands. Not only had he no fat left on his bones, he had no muscle, either. He was bone and tendon and skin, nothing more. No, one more thing: the joy that lit his blind eyes.

"Soon," he repeated. "It's been six weeks, a few days over, since last I polluted my soul with aliment. Only a man who was fat to begin with will last much above eight, and never was I in the habit of glutting myself. Soon I shall fare beyond the sun and look on Phos face-to-face. Soon."

"Does—does it hurt?" Phostis asked. Beside him, Olyvria sat calmly. She'd seen these human skeletons before, often enough so now she was easy with the husk of Strabon. Syagrios had not come into the hut; Phostis heard him pacing around outside the door.

Strabon said, "No, boy, no; as I told you, fear not. Oh, my belly panged in the early days, I'll not deny, as Skotos' part of me realized I had determined to cut my essential self free of it. But no, I feel no pain, only longing to be free." He smiled again. Save for the faintest tinge of pink, his lips were invisible.

"But to linger so—" Phostis shook his head, though he knew Strabon could not see that. Then he blurted, "Could you not also have refused water, and so made a quicker end of it?"

The corners of Strabon's gash of a mouth turned down. "Some of those who are most holy do as you say. Sinner that I am, I had not the fortitude for it."

Phostis stared at him. Never in his comfortable life back at the palaces had he dreamed he'd be talking with a man in the last stages of deliberately starving himself to death. Even if he had dreamed that, could he have imagined the man would reproach himself for lack of fortitude? No; impossible.

The lids fell over Strabon's twitching eyes; he seemed to doze. "Is he not a miracle of piety?" Olyvria whispered.

"Well, yes, that he is." Phostis scratched his head. Back in Videssos the city, he'd despised the temple hierarchy for wearing bejeweled vestments and venerating Phos in temples built by riches taken—stolen—from the peasantry. Better, he'd thought, a simple but strong worship, one that sprang from within and demanded nothing of anyone save the single pious individual.

Now before him he saw personified, and indeed taken to an extreme he'd never imagined, an example of such worship. He had to respect the religious impulse that had led Strabon to make himself into a collection of twigs and branches, but he was less sure he considered it an ideal.

Yet such self-destruction was implicit in Thanasiot doctrine, for those who had the courage to follow where logic led. If the world of the senses was but a creation of Skotos', what course more logical than to remove one's precious and eternal soul from that swamp of evil and corruption?

Rather hesitantly, he turned toward Olyvria. "However holy he may be, I'd not care to imitate him. Granted, the world is not all it might be, but leaving it this way strikes me as—oh, I don't know—as running away from the fight against wickedness rather than joining it."

"Ah, but the body itself is evil, boy," Strabon said. He hadn't been asleep after all. "Because of that, any fight is foredoomed to failure." His eyes closed again.

Olyvria spoke in a low voice. "For the many, there may be much truth in what you say, Phostis. As I told you back on Midwinter's Day, I'd not have the bravery to do as Strabon does. But I thought you ought to see him, to celebrate and admire what the soul can do if it so wills."

"I see it," Phostis said. "It is indeed a marvel. But something to celebrate? Of that I'm less certain."

Olyvria looked at him severely. Had she been standing, her hands would have gone onto her hips. As it was, she breathed out in exasperation. "Even the dogma you grew up with has room for asceticism and mortifying the flesh."

"That's true," he said. "Too much care for this world and you have fat, contented priests who might as well not be priests at all. But now, seeing Strabon here, I think there may be too little care for the world, as well." His voice fell to a whisper, so he would not disturb the fitfully sleeping relic of a man. This time, Strabon did not respond.

Phostis listened to himself with some surprise. *I sound like my father,* he thought. How many times, back at the palaces, had he watched and listened to Krispos steering a middle course between schemes that might have proved spectacular successes or even more spectacular disasters? How many times had he sneered at his father for that moderation?

"What he does affects no one but himself," Olyvria said, "and will surely earn him eternity in communion with Phos."

"That's true," Phostis repeated. "What he does by himself affects him alone. But if one man and one woman in four, say, decided to walk the gleaming path in his exact footprints, that would affect those who declined to do so very much indeed. And Strabon's way, if I rightly understand it, is the one Thanasiot doctrine favors."

"For those whose spirits let them take it, yes," Olyvria said. Phostis looked from Strabon to her, then back again. He tried to envision her features ravaged by starvation, her bright eyes writhing blindly in their sockets. He'd never been the most imaginative of young men. More often than not, he felt that to be a lack. It seemed a blessing now.

Strabon coughed himself awake. He tried to say something, but the coughs went on and on, deep wet ones that wracked the sack of bones he had become. "Chest fever," Phostis whispered to Olyvria. She shrugged. If it was, he thought, the Thanasiot zealot might be dead by evening, for how could he have any strength in his body to fight off illness?

Olyvria stood to go. Phostis was far from sorry to get up with her. When he no longer saw the wasted figure lying on the bed, he felt more alive himself. Maybe that was illusion sprung from the animal part of him and from Skotos; he could not say. But he knew he would have trouble overcoming that animal part. Was his soul a prisoner of his body, as the Thanasioi proclaimed, or a partner with it? He would have to think long and hard on that.

Outside Strabon's hut, Syagrios paced up and down the muddy street, whistling a tune and spitting through his uneven teeth. Phostis watched him grin and swagger. When he tried to visualize the ruffian starving himself, his thoughts ran headlong into a blank wall. He simply could not see it happening. Syagrios was an ugly specimen, but a vivid one for all that.

"So what did you think of the boneyard?" he asked Phostis, spitting again.

Olyvria rounded on him, tight black curls flying in fury. "Show proper respect for the pious and holy Strabon!" she blazed.

"Why? Soon enough he'll be dead, and then it'll be up to Phos, not to the likes of me, to figure out what he deserves."

Olyvria opened her mouth, then closed it again. Phostis made a mental note that Syagrios, while indubitably uncouth, was far from stupid. *Too bad*, he thought. Aloud, he said, "If a few people choose to make their end that way, I don't see that it much matters to the world around them—and, as Olyvria says, they are pious and holy. But if many decide to end their lives, the Empire will shake."

"And why shouldn't the Empire shake, pray?" Olyvria asked.

Now Phostis had to pause and consider. An unshaken Empire of Videssos was almost as much of an article of faith for him as Phos' creed. And why not? For seven centuries and more, Videssos had given folk in a great swathe of the world reasonable peace and reasonable security. True, there had been disasters, as when steppe nomads took advantage of Videssian civil war to invade the north and east and form their own khaganates in the ruins of imperial provinces. True, every generation or two fought another in the long string of debilitating wars with Makuran. But, on the whole, he remained convinced life within the Empire was likelier to be happy than anywhere outside it.

But when he said as much, Olyvria answered, "So what? If life in this world is but part of Skotos' trap, what matter if you're happy as the jaws close? Better then that we should be unhappy, that we should recognize everything material as part of the lure that draws us down to the ice."

"But—" Phostis felt himself floundering. "Suppose—hmm—suppose everyone in the westlands, or most people, starved themselves to death like Strabon. What would happen after that? The Makuraners would march in unopposed and rule the land forever."

"Well, what if they did?" Olyvria said. "The pious men and women who'd abandoned the world would be safe in Phos' heaven, and the invaders would surely go to the ice when their days were done."

"Yes, and the worship of Phos would go out of the world, for the Makuraners reverence their Four Prophets, not the good god," Phostis said. "No one who worshiped Phos would be left, and Skotos would have the victory in this world. The realm beyond the sun would gain no new recruits, but the dark god would have to carve new caverns into the ice." He spat in ritual rejection of Skotos.

Olyvria frowned. The very tip of her tongue poked out of her mouth for a moment. Her voice was troubled as she said, "This argument has more weight than I would have looked for."

"No it don't," Syagrios said with a raucous laugh. "The two of you's quarreling over whether you'd like your cow's eggs better poached or fried. Truth is, a cow ain't about to lay no eggs—and whole flocks of people ain't about to starve themselves to death, neither. Come to that, is either one o' *you* ready to stop eatin' yet?"

"No," Olyvria said quietly. Phostis shook his head.

"Well, then," Syagrios said, and laughed even louder.

"But if you're not ready to leave the world behind, how can you be a proper Thanasiot?" Phostis asked with the relentless logic of the young.

"That's a bloody good question." Syagrios whacked Phostis on the back, almost hard enough to knock him sprawling into the muck that passed for a street. "You ain't as dumb as you look, kid." The day was gloomy, the sky an inverted bowl full of thick gray clouds. The gold ring in Syagrios' ear glinted nonetheless. In Etchmiadzin he did not wear it to deceive those not of his faith, for the Thanasioi ruled the town. But he did not take it out, either.

"Syagrios, to say one can be a good Thanasiot only through starvation contradicts the faith as the holy Thanasios set it forth, which you know perfectly well." Olyvria sounded as if she were holding on to patience with both hands.

Syagrios caught the warning in her voice. Suddenly he reverted to being a guardsman rather than an equal. "As you say, my lady," he answered. Had Phostis told him the same thing, the ruffian would have torn into him in argument and likely with fists and booted feet, as well.

But Phostis, though prisoner in Etchmiadzin, was not Olyvria's servitor. Moreover, he actively enjoyed theological disputation. Turning to Olyvria, he said, "But if you choose to live in Skotos' world, surely you compromise with evil, and compromise with evil takes you to the ice, not so?"

"But not everyone is or can be suited to leaving the world of his own will," Olyvria said. "The holy Thanasios teaches that those who feel they must remain in Skotos' realm may yet gain merit along two byroads of the gleaming path. In one, they may lessen the temptations of the material for themselves and for those around them."

"Those who follow that byroad would be the men your father leads," Phostis said.

Olyvria nodded. "Them among others. But it is also virtuous to content yourself with simple things: black bread instead of white, coarse cloth rather than fine. The more you do without, the less you subject yourself to Skotos."

"Yes, I see the point," Phostis said slowly. *The more you burn and destroy, also,* he thought, but kept that to himself. Instead of mentioning it, he asked, "What is the second byroad you spoke of?"

"Why, ministering to those who have chosen the path of greater abnegation," Olyvria answered. "By helping them as they advance along the gleaming path, those who stay behind bask in their reflected piety, so to speak."

"Hmm," Phostis said. At first hearing, that sounded good. But after a moment, he said, "How does that make their dealings with those of greater holiness different from any peasant's dealings with a noble?"

Olyvria gave him an exasperated glare. "It's different because the usual run of noble wallows in corruption, thinking mostly of his purse and his, ah, member, and so a peasant who serves such a man is but drawn deeper into the sensual mire. But our pious heroes reject all the lures of the world and inspire others to do likewise to the degree that is in their power."

"Hmm," Phostis said again. "Something to that, I suppose." He wondered how much. A good noble of the non-Thanasiot sort helped the peasants on his land get through hard times, defended them against raiders if he lived near a frontier, and didn't go around seducing their women. Phostis knew a good many nobles, and knew of a good many more. He wondered how maintaining one's dependents rated against the individual pursuit of piety. The good god knew for certain, but Phostis doubted whether anyone merely human did.

Before he could say as much, a familiar figure from Livanios' miniature court at the keep came stamping up the street: the fellow who seemed to be the heresiarch's chief wizard. Despite all his time in Etchmiadzin, Phostis still had not learned the man's name. Now he wore a thick wool caftan with bright vertical stripes, and on his head a fur cap with earflaps that might have come straight off the plains of Pardraya.

He touched his forehead, lips, and chest in greeting to Olyvria, gave Phostis a measuring stare, and ignored Syagrios. "He's going into Strabon's house," Phostis said. "What does he want with someone who likely won't be here two weeks from now and may not be here tomorrow?"

"He visits everyone he can who chooses to leave the world of evil things," Olyvria answered. "I don't know why; if he's as curious as most mages, perhaps he seeks to learn as much as he can about the world to come while still remaining in this one."

"Maybe." Phostis supposed one did not cease to be a mage, or a tanner, or a tailor, on becoming a Thanasiot. "What *is* he called, anyhow?"

Olyvria paused visibly before she answered. Syagrios stepped into the breach: "He doesn't like people knowin' his name, for fear they'll work magic with it."

"That's silly. He must not be much of a wizard, then," Phostis said. "My father's chief mage is named Zaidas, and he doesn't care who knows it. He says if you can't protect yourself from name magic, you have no business taking up sorcery in the first place."

"Not all wizards have the same ways," Olyvria said. Since that was too obviously true to require comment, Phostis let it go.

The fellow in the caftan came out of Strabon's house a couple of minutes later. He did not look happy, and was muttering under his breath. Not all the muttering sounded like Videssian; Phostis wondered if he was from nearby Vaspurakan. Of what was in the imperial language, Phostis caught only one phrase: "Old bastard's not ripe yet." The wizard stalked away.

"Not ripe yet?" Phostis said after he'd rounded a corner. "Not ripe for what?"

"I don't know," Syagrios said. "Me, I don't mess with mages or their business and I don't want them messin' with me."

That was a sensible attitude for anyone, and especially, Phostis thought, for somebody like Syagrios, who was likely to be "messed with" by mages when said mages were on the track of objects mysteriously vanished. Phostis smiled at his automatic contempt for the bruiser who'd become his keeper. Syagrios saw the smile and gave him a hard, suspicious stare. He did his best to look innocent, which was rendered more difficult because he was guilty.

Syagrios changed the subject. "How's about we go find some food? Standin' on my pins all mornin', me, I could hack steaks off a donkey and eat 'em raw."

"Get out of here, you beast! Out of my sight!" Olyvria snarled, her voice breaking with fury. "Out! Away! How dare you—how could you be so dense, so blockheaded—as to talk about food after we've just seen the pious Strabon dedicating himself to escaping the world and advancing along the gleaming path? Get out!"

"No," Syagrios said. "Your father told me to keep an eye on this one"— he pointed at Phostis—"and that there's just what I aim to do."

Up till then, that stolid remark had been proof against anything Olyvria would throw at it. Indeed, Olyvria had not tried to contest it. Now, though, she said, "Where will he go? Do you think he'll kidnap *me*?"

"I don't know and I don't care," Syagrios answered. "I just know what I got told to do."

"Well, I tell you to go away. I can't abide the sight or sound of you after what you just said," Olyvria said. When he shook his head, she added, "If you don't, I'll tell my father what you said just now. Do you want to undergo the penance you'd receive for mocking the holy faith?"

"I don't," Syagrios said, but he seemed suddenly doubtful. Whether he had or he hadn't, Livanios was apt to believe Olyvria rather than him. It was most unfair. All at once, Phostis understood why he himself had not had many friends as a boy. If he ran to tell his father about a quarrel, *his* father was the Avtokrator. If the Avtokrator—or Livanios now—ruled against you, to whom could you appeal?

Bitterness gusted through Phostis. The Avtokrator, in those lost boyhood days, was only too likely to rule against him, not for. His father had never truly warmed to him; from time to time he wondered what he'd done wrong, to make Krispos find fault with everything about him. He doubted he'd ever find out.

Olyvria said to Syagrios, "Go on, I tell you. I'll be responsible for seeing Phostis doesn't run out of Etchmiadzin. And I tell you this, too: if you say me nay once more, you'll be sorry for it."

"All right, then, my lady." The ruffian turned what should have been a title of respect into one of reproach. "On you the blame, and almost I hope you end up wearing it." Syagrios strode off with the straight, proud back of a man who's had the last word.

Watching him go, Phostis felt a burden lift from his spirit, as if the sun had come out to brighten a gloomy day. He also had to stifle a burst of laughter. In spite of having just come out of starving Strabon's house, he was hungry.

Since unlike Strabon he was not about to waste away and die of hunger, he kept that to himself. He didn't want Olyvria rounding on him as she had on Syagrios. If anything was more likely to bring back the watchdog, he couldn't imagine what it might be.

Olyvria was looking at him with a quizzical expression. He realized she was left as much at a loss by Syagrios' departure as was he. "What shall we do now?" she asked, perhaps hoping he could think of something.

Unfortunately, he couldn't. "I don't know," he answered. "I really haven't seen enough of Etchmiadzin to know what you *can* do around here." *Not much before the Thanasioi took over the town, and less now,* he guessed.

"Let's just amble about, then, and see where our feet take us," she said.

"That's all right with me." Short of a trip to the torturer, anything Olyvria suggested would have been all right with Phostis. He looked for grass to sprout in the streets, flowers to burst into bloom, and birds to start singing in winter, all because she'd managed to outbluff Syagrios.

Their feet led them to a street of dyers. That the men there followed the gleaming path didn't keep their shops from smelling of stale piss, just like the establishments of perfectly orthodox dyers back in Videssos the city. In the same way, Thanasiot carpenters had hands crisscrossed with scars and Thanasiot bakers faces permanently reddened from peering into hot ovens.

"It all seems so—ordinary," Phostis said after a while. *Dull* was the other word that came to mind, but he suppressed it. "For most folk, it's as if being a Thanasiot doesn't change much in their lives."

That bothered him. To his way of thinking, heresy and orthodoxy—whichever was which in this dispute—should have been easy to tell apart at a glance. But, on further reflection, he wondered why. Unless they chose Strabon's path out of the world, the Thanasioi had to make their way in it, and only so many ways of doing that were possible. The dyeshops probably stank of urine in Mashiz, too; carpenters would sometimes gouge themselves with chisels; and bakers would need to make sure their loaves didn't burn.

Olyvria said, "The difference is the gleaming path, it's standing aside from the world as well as one can, not thinking riches the only end in life, seeking to satisfy the spirit rather than the baser impulses of the body."

"I suppose so," Phostis said. They walked a little farther while he ruminated on that. Then he said, "May I ask you something? For all the ribbons on my cage, I know I'm pretty much a prisoner here, so I don't mean to make you angry, but there is something I'd like to learn, if giving the answer doesn't offend you."

Olyvria turned toward him. Her eyes were wide with curiosity, her mouth slightly open. She looked very young, and very lovely. "Ask," she said at once. "You're here to learn about the gleaming path, after all. How will you learn if you don't ask?"

"All right, I will." Phostis thought for a little while; the question he had in mind needed to be framed carefully. At last he said, "In the room in the tunnel under Digenis' temple, what you said there—"

"Aha!" Olyvria stuck out her tongue at him. "I thought it would be something about that, just from the way you went all around it like a man feeling for a goldpiece in the middle of a nettle patch."

Phostis felt his face heat. By the way Olyvria giggled, his embarrassment was also plain to the eye. Even so, he stubbornly plowed ahead; in some ways—though he would have hotly denied it—he was very much like Krispos. "What you said under there, when you tried to lure me to you, about the pleasure of love being sweet, and no sin?"

"What about it?" Olyvria lost some—though not all—of her mischievous air as she saw how serious he was.

What he really wanted to ask was how she knew—or, even more to the point, what she would have done had he lain down on the bed beside her and taken her in his arms. But he did not think he was in a position where he could safely put either of those questions. So instead he said, "If you hold to Thanasios' gleaming path as strongly as you say, how could you make such a claim? Doesn't it go straight against everything you profess to believe?"

"I could answer that any number of ways," Olyvria said. "I could tell you, for instance, that it was none of your business."

"So you could, and I would beg your pardon," he said. "I said from the start that I didn't want to offend you."

Olyvria went on as if he had not spoken: "Or I could say I was doing as Digenis and my father bade me do, and trusted them to judge the rights and wrongs of it." Her eyes twinkled again. He knew she was toying with him, but what could he do about it?

"Or," she went on, maddeningly disingenuous, "I could say Thanasios countenanced dissimulation when it serves spreading the truth, and that you have no idea what my true feelings on the subject are."

"I know I don't. That's what I was trying to find out, your true feelings on the subject." Phostis felt like an old, spavined plowhorse trying to trap a dragonfly without benefit of net. He tramped on, straight ahead, while Olyvria flitted, evaded, and occasionally flew so close to the end of his nose that his eyes crossed when he tried to see her clearly.

"Those are just some examples of what I might say," she noted, ticking them off on her fingertips. "If you'd like others, I might also say—"

As if the old plowhorse suddenly snorted and startled the beautiful, glittering insect, he broke in, "What *would* you say that's so, by the good god?"

"I'd say—" But then Olyvria shook her head and looked away from him. "No, I wouldn't say anything at all, Phostis. Better if I don't."

He wanted to shake truth from her, but she was not a saltcellar. "Why?" he howled, months of frustration boiled into a single despairing word.

"Just—better if I don't." Olyvria still held her head averted. In a small voice, she added, "I think we ought to go back to the fortress now."

Phostis didn't think that, nor anything like it, but walked with her all the same. In the inner ward stood Syagrios, talking with someone almost as disreputable-looking as he was. The ruffian left his—partner in crime?—ambled over, and attached himself to Phostis like a shadow returning from a brief holiday. In an unsettling sort of way, Phostis was almost glad to have him back. He'd certainly made a hash of his first little while in Etchmiadzin on his own.

Digenis' ROBE HAD FALLEN OPEN, DISPLAYING RIBS LIKE LADder rungs. His thighs were thinner than his knees. Even his ears seemed to be wasting away. But his eyes still blazed defiance. "To the ice with you, your false Majesty," he growled when Krispos came into his cell. "Your way would have sent me beyond the sun quicker, but I gain, I gain."

To Krispos, the firebrand priest looked more as if he lost. Lean to begin with, now he looked like a peasant in a village after three years of blighted crops. But for those eerily compelling eyes, he might have been a skeleton that refused to turn back into a man.

"By the good god," Krispos muttered when that thought struck him, "now I understand the mime troupe."

"Which one, Your Majesty?" asked Zaidas, who still labored fruitlessly to extract truth from the dwindling Digenis.

"The one with the fellow in the suit of bones," Krispos answered. "He was supposed to be a Thanasiot starving himself to death, that's what he was. Now, were the mimes heretics, too, or just mocking their beliefs?" Something else occurred to him. "And isn't it a fine note when mimes know more about what's going on with the faith than my own ecumenical patriarch?"

Digenis' mocking laugh flayed his ears. "Of Oxeites' ignorance no possible doubt can exist."

"Oh, shut up," Krispos said, though down deep he knew tractability was one of the qualities that had gained Oxeites the blue boots. *If only he'd been more tractable about letting me do what I wanted with this wretch here,* the Avtokrator thought. But Oxeites, like any good bureaucrat, protected his own.

Krispos sat down on a three-legged stool to see if Zaidas would have any better luck today. His chief wizard swore his presence inhibited nothing. Zaidas at least had courage, to be willing to labor on in the presence of his Avtokrator. What he did not have, unfortunately, was success.

He was trying something new today, Krispos saw, or maybe something so old he hoped its time had come round again. At any rate, the implements he took from his carpetbag were unfamiliar. But before the Emperor saw them in action, a panting messenger from the palaces poked his head into Digenis' cell.

"What's happened?" Krispos asked suspiciously; his orders were that he be left undisturbed in his visits here save for only the most important news . . . and the most important news was all too often bad.

"May it please Your Majesty," the messenger began, and then paused to pant some more. While he caught his breath, Krispos worried. That opening, lately, had given him good cause to worry. But the fellow surprised him, saying, "May it please Your Majesty, the eminent Iakovitzes has returned to Videssos the city from his embassy to Makuran and awaits your pleasure at the imperial residence."

"Well, by the good god, there's word that truly does please me," Krispos exclaimed. He turned to Zaidas. "Carry on here without me, and may Phos grant you good fortune. If you glean anything from this bag of bones, report it to me at once."

"Certainly, Your Majesty," Zaidas said.

Digenis laughed again. "The catamite goes off to pleasure his defiler."

"That is a lie, one of so many you spew," Krispos said coldly. The Halogai fell in around him. As he went up the stairs that led to the doorway of the government office building, he found himself laughing. He'd have to tell that one to Iakovitzes. His longtime associate would laugh, too, not least because he'd wish the lie were true. Iakovitzes never made any secret of his fondness for stalwart youths, and had tried again and again to seduce Krispos when Krispos, newly arrived in Videssos the city, was in his service.

Barsymes greeted him when he returned to the imperial residence.

"Good day, Your Majesty. I've taken the liberty of installing the eminent Iakovitzes in the small dining chamber in the south hallway. He requested hot mulled wine, which was fetched to him."

"I'll have the same," Krispos said. "I can't think of a better way to fight the winter chill."

Iakovitzes rose from his chair as Krispos came into the room where he sat. He started to prostrate himself; Krispos waved for him not to bother. With a smug nod, Iakovitzes returned to his seat. He was a well-preserved seventy, plump, his hair and beard dyed dark to make him seem younger, with a complexion on the florid side and eyes that warned—truly—he had a temper.

"Good to see you, by Phos," Krispos exclaimed. "I've wished you were here a great many times the past few months."

On the table in front of Iakovitzes lay a scribe's three-paneled writing tablet. He opened it, used a stylus to scribble rapid words on the wax, then passed Krispos the tablet. "I've wished I were back a great many times myself. I'm bloody sick of mutton."

"Sup with me this evening, then," Krispos said. "What do they say? 'When in Videssos the city, eat fish.' I'll feast you till you grow fins."

Iakovitzes made a strange gobbling noise that served him for laughter. "Make it tentacles, if you'd be so kind," he wrote. "Squid, octopus . . . lobster, come to think of it, has no tentacles, but then lobster is lobster, in itself a sufficient justification. By the good god, it makes me wish I could lick my lips."

"I wish you could, too, old friend, and taste in fullness as well," Krispos said. Iakovitzes had only the stump of his tongue; twenty years before, Harvas Black-Robe had torn it from his mouth when he was on an embassy to the evil sorcerer.

The wound—and the spell placed on it to defeat healing—had almost been the death of him. But he'd rallied, even thrived. Krispos knew a great part of his own persona would have been lost had he suffered Iakovitzes' mutilation. He wrote well enough, but never had been fluent with a pen in his hand. Iakovitzes, though, wielded pen or stylus with such vim that, reading his words, Krispos still sometimes heard the living voice that had been two decades silent.

Iakovitzes took back the tablet, wrote, and returned it to Krispos. "It's not so bad, Your Majesty: not nearly so bad as sitting down to table with a bad cold in your head, for instance. Half your taste, or maybe more, I've found, is in your nose, not in your mouth. Besides, staying in Mashiz turned into a bore. The only folk who read Videssian seemed as old and wrinkled as I am. You have no notion how hard it is to seduce a pretty boy when he can't understand you."

"Gold speaks a lot of languages," Krispos observed.

"Sometimes you're too pragmatic for your own good," Iakovitzes wrote, rolling his eyes at his sovereign's obtuseness. "There's no challenge to merely buying it; the pursuit is part of the game. Why do you think I chased you so long and hard when I knew your appetite ran only to women?"

"So that's it, eh?" Krispos said. "At the time, I thought you were just being beastly."

Iakovitzes clapped a hand over his heart and pantomimed a death scene well enough to earn him a place on a professional mime troupe. Then, miraculously recovered, he bent over his tablet and wrote rapidly: "I think I shall make my way back to Mashiz after all. There, being a representative of the enemy, I am treated with the respect I deserve. My alleged friends prefer slander." He rolled his eyes.

Krispos laughed out loud. Iakovitzes' peculiar combination of touchiness and viperish wit never failed to amuse—except when it infuriated. Sometimes it managed both at once. The Avtokrator quickly sobered. He asked, "On your way back from Makuran, did you have any trouble with the Thanasioi?"

Iakovitzes shook his head, then amplified on the tablet. "I returned by the southern route, and saw no trace. They seem to be a perversion centered in the northwest, though I gather you've had your bouts with them here in the city, too."

"Bouts indeed," Krispos said heavily. "A good windstorm and they might have burned down half this place. Not only that, interrogation by sorcery doesn't have any luck with them, and they're so drunk in their beliefs that many take torture more as an honor than a torment."

"And they have your son," Iakovitzes wrote. He spread his hands to show sympathy for Krispos.

"They have him, aye," Krispos said, "certainly in body and perhaps in spirit as well." Iakovitzes raised a questioning eyebrow; his gestures, though wordless, had grown so expressive in the years since he'd lost his tongue as to have almost the quality of speech. Krispos explained, "He was talking with a priest who turned out to be a Thanasiot. For all I know, he's taken the wretch's doctrines as his own."

"Not good," Iakovitzes wrote.

"No. And now this Digenis—the priest—is starving himself in my jail. He thinks he'll end up with Phos when he quits the world. My guess is that Skotos will punish him forevermore." The Emperor spat between his feet in despisal of the dark god.

Iakovitzes wrote, "If you ask me, asceticism is its own punishment, but I'd not heard of its being a capital offense till now." That observation made Krispos nod. It also filled all three leaves of the tablet. Iakovitzes reversed his stylus, smoothed out the wax with the blunt end, wrote again. "These days I can tell very easily when I'm talking too much—as soon as I have to start erasing, I know I've been running on. Would that those who still flap their gums enjoyed such a visible sign of prolixity."

"Ah, but if they did, they'd spend their increased silent time thinking up new ways to commit mischief," Krispos said.

"You're likely right," Iakovitzes answered. He studied Krispos for a few seconds, then reclaimed the tablet. "You're more cynical than you used to be. Is that all good? I do admit it's natural enough, for from the throne you've likely heard more drivel these last twenty years than any other man alive, but is it good?"

Krispos thought about that for some little while before he answered. In different forms, the question had arisen several times lately, as when he gave that first Thanasiot prisoner over to torture after Zaidas' magic failed to extract answers from him. He'd not have done that so readily when he was younger. Was he just another Emperor now, holding to power by whatever means came to hand?

"We're none of us what we were awhile ago," he said, but that was not an answer, and he knew it. By the way Iakovitzes raised an eyebrow, cocked his head, and waited for Krispos to go on, he knew it was no answer, too. Floundering, Krispos tried to give one: "The temples will never venerate me as holy, I daresay, but I hope the chroniclers will be able to report I governed Videssos well. I work hard at it, at any rate. If I'm harsh when I have to be, I also think I'm mild when I can be. My sons are turning into men, and not, I can say, the worst of men. Is it enough?" He heard pleading in his voice, a note he'd not found there in some years: the Avtokrator heard pleas; he did not make them.

Iakovitzes bent over the writing tablet. When the stylus was done racing back and forth, he passed the tablet to Krispos, who received it with some anxiety. He knew Iakovitzes well enough to be sure his old companion would be blunt with him. He had no trouble reading it, at any rate; constant poring over documents had kept his sight from lengthening with age as much as most men's.

"That you can ask the question after so long on the throne speaks well for you," Iakovitzes wrote. "Too many Avtokrators forget it exists within days of their anointing. As for the reply you gave, well, Videssos has had the occasional holy man on the throne, and most turned out bad, for the world is not a holy place. So long as you remember now and again what an innocent—and attractive—boy you once were, you'll not turn out too badly."

Krispos nodded slowly. "I'll take that."

"You'd better," Iakovitzes replied after more scribbling. "I flatter only when I hope to entice someone under the sheets with me, and after all our years of acquaintance I'm at last beginning to doubt I'll ever have much luck with you."

"You're incorrigible," Krispos said.

"Now that you mention it, yes," Iakovitzes wrote. He beamed, taking it for a compliment. Then he covered his mouth with a hand while he yawned; the empty cavern within was an unpleasant sight, and he made a point of not displaying it. He wrote some more. "By your leave, Your Majesty, I'll take my own leave now, to rest at home after my travels. Do you still take supper just past sunset?"

"I have enough years on me now to have become a creature of habit," Krispos answered, nodding. "And with which of your handsome grooms do you intend to rest until suppertime?"

Iakovitzes assumed a comically innocent look, then bowed his way out of the little dining chamber. Krispos guessed his barb had struck home— or at least given Iakovitzes an idea. Krispos finished his mulled wine, then set the silver goblet down beside Iakovitzes'. The wine hadn't stayed warm, but the ginger and cinnamon stirred into it nipped his tongue pleasantly.

Barsymes came in with a tray on which to carry away the goblets. Krispos said, "Iakovitzes will join me for supper this evening. Please let the cooks know he'll like seafood in as many courses as possible—he says he's tired of Makuraner mutton."

"I shall convey the eminent sir's request," Barsymes agreed gravely. "His presence will allow the kitchen staff to display their full range of talents."

"Hrmp," Krispos said in mock indignation. "I can't help being raised on a poor farm." While he enjoyed fancy dishes well enough, he more often preferred the simple fare he'd grown up with. More than one cook had complained of having his wings clipped.

Dusk was settling over the city when Iakovitzes returned, resplendent and glittering in a robe shot through with silver thread. Barsymes escorted him and Krispos to the small dining room where they'd taken wine earlier in the day. A fresh jar awaited them, cooling in a silver bucket of snow. The vestiarios poured a cup for each man. Iakovitzes wrote, "Ah, it's pale. Perhaps someone listened to me."

"Perhaps someone did, eminent sir," Barsymes said. "And now, if you will excuse me—" He glided away, to return with a bowl. "A salad of lettuce and endives, dressed with vinegar flavored by rue, dates, pepper, honey, and crushed cumin—a garnish said to promote good health—and topped with anchovies and rings of squid."

Iakovitzes rose from his chair and gave Barsymes a formal military salute, then kissed him on each beardless cheek. The vestiarios retreated in order less good than was his wont. Krispos hid a smile and attacked the salad, which proved tasty. Iakovitzes cut his portion into very small bits. He had to wash each one down with wine and put his head back to swallow.

His smile was blissful. He wrote, "Ah, squid! Were you to offer one of these tentacled lovelies to Rubyab King of Kings, Your Majesty, without doubt he would flee faster than from an invading Videssian army. The Makuraners, when it comes to food, live most insular—or perhaps I should say inlandsular—lives."

"The more fools they." Krispos ate slowly, so as not to get ahead of Iakovitzes. Barsymes cleared away the plates. Krispos said, "Tell me, eminent sir, did you ever find out what was making Rubyab's mustaches quiver with secret glee?"

"Do you know, I didn't, not to be sure of it," Iakovitzes answered. He looked thoughtful. "Terrible, isn't it, when a Makuraner outdoes me in deceit? I must be getting old. But I tell you this, Your Majesty: one way or another, it concerns us."

"I was sure it would," Krispos said. "Nothing would make Rubyab happier than buggering Videssos." He caught Iakovitzes' eye. "In the metaphorical sense, of course."

Iakovitzes gobbled laughter. "Oh, of course, Your Majesty," he wrote.

Barsymes returned with a fresh course. "Here we have leeks boiled in water and olive oil," he declared, "and then stewed in more oil and mullet broth. To accompany them, oysters in a sauce of oil, honey, wine, egg yolks, pepper, and lovage."

Iakovitzes tasted the oysters, then wrote in big letters, "I want to marry the cook."

"He is a man, eminent sir," Barsymes said.

"All the better," Iakovitzes wrote, which sent the vestiarios into rapid retreat. He presently returned with another new platter along with a fresh jar of wine. This dish held peppered mullet liver paste baked in a fish-shaped mold and then sprinkled with virgin olive oil, as well as squashes baked with mint, coriander, and cumin, and stuffed with pine nuts ground with honey and wine.

"I shan't eat for a week," Krispos declared happily.

"But Your Majesty, the main courses approach," Barsymes said in anxious tones.

Krispos corrected himself: "Two weeks. Bring 'em on." The tip of his nose was getting numb. How much wine had he drunk, anyhow? The rich flavor of the fish livers nicely complemented the squashes' sweet stuffing.

Barsymes bore away the empty mold from which the liver paste had come and the bowl that had held the squashes. Under the table, Krispos felt something on his leg, just above the knee. It turned out to be Iakovitzes' hand. "By the good god," the Avtokrator exclaimed, "you never give up, do you?"

"I'm still breathing," Iakovitzes wrote. "If I haven't stopped the one, why should I stop the other?"

"Something to that," Krispos admitted. He hadn't had much luck with the other lately, and he'd surely be too gorged after this banquet was done to try to improve that tonight. Just then Barsymes came back again, this time with a tureen and two bowls. Thinking about what the tureen might hold took Krispos' mind off other matters, a sure sign of advancing years.

The vestiarios announced, "Here we have mullets stewed in wine, with leeks, broth, and vinegar, seasoned with oregano, coriander, and crushed pepper. For your added pleasure, the stew also includes scallops and baby prawns."

After the first taste, Iakovitzes wrote, "The only thing that could further add to my pleasure would be an infinitely distensible stomach, and you may tell the cooks as much."

"I shall, eminent sir," Barsymes promised. "They will take pleasure in knowing they have pleased you."

The next course was lobster meat and spawn chopped fine, mixed with eggs, pepper, and mullet broth, wrapped in grape leaves, and then fried. After that came cuttlefish boiled in wine, honey, celery, and caraway seeds, and stuffed with boiled calves' brains and crumbled hard-cooked eggs. Only the expectant look on Barsymes' face kept Krispos from falling asleep then and there. "One entree yet to come," the vestiarios said. "I assure you, it shall be worth the wait."

"My weight's already gone up considerably," Krispos said, patting his midsection. He could have used an infinitely distensible stomach himself about then.

But Barsymes, as usual, proved right. When he set down the last tray and its serving bowl, he said, "I am bidden by the cooks to describe this dish in detail. Any lapses in the description spring from my lapses of memory, not theirs of talent. I begin: to soaked pine nuts and sea urchins, they added in a casserole layers of mallows, beets, leeks, celery, cabbage, and other vegetables I now forget. Also included are stewed chickens, pigs' brains, blood sausage, chicken gizzards, fried tunny in bits, sea nettles, stewed oysters in pieces, and fresh cheeses. It is spiced with celery seed, lovage, pepper, and asafetida. Over the top was poured milk with beaten egg. It was then stiffened in a hot-water bath, garnished with fresh mussels, and peppered once more. I am only too certain I've left out something or another; I beg you not to report my failing to the cooks."

"Phos have mercy," Krispos exclaimed, eyeing the big casserole dish with something far beyond mere respect. "Should we eat of it or worship it?" After Barsymes served Iakovitzes and him, he had his answer. "Both!" he said with his mouth full.

The feast had stretched far into the night; every so often, Barsymes fed charcoal to a brazier that kept the dining chamber tolerably warm. Iakovitzes held up his tablet. "I hope you have a wheelbarrow in which to roll me home, for I'm certain I can't walk."

"Something shall be arranged, I am certain," the vestiarios said. "Dessert will be coming shortly. I trust you will do it justice?"

Iakovitzes and Krispos both groaned. The Avtokrator said, "We'll deal with it or burst trying. I'd say it's about even money which." He'd taken an army into battle many times with better odds than those.

But the sweet scent of the steam gently rising from the pan Barsymes brought in revived his interest. "Here we have grated apricots cooked in milk until tender, then covered in honey and lightly dusted with ground cinnamon." The vestiarios bowed to Iakovitzes. "Eminent sir, the cooks apologize for their failure to include seafood in this one dish."

"Tell them I forgive their lapse," Iakovitzes wrote. "I've not yet decided whether to sprout fins or tentacles from tonight's fête."

The apricots tasted as good as they smelled. Krispos nonetheless ate them very slowly, being full far past repletion. He was only halfway through his portion when Barsymes hurried into the dining chamber. The Emperor raised an eyebrow; such a lapse was unlike the eunuch.

Barsymes said, "Forgive me, Your Majesty, but the mage Zaidas would have speech with you. It is, I gather, a matter of some urgency."

"Maybe he's here to tell me Digenis dropped dead at last," Krispos said hopefully. "Fetch him in, esteemed sir. If he'd come sooner, he could have helped the two of us commit gluttony here, not that we haven't managed well enough on our own."

When Zaidas came to the doorway, he started to prostrate himself.

Krispos waved for him not to bother. Nodding his thanks, the wizard greeted Iakovitzes, whom he knew well. "Good to have you back with us, eminent sir. You've been away too long."

"It certainly *seemed* too bloody long," Iakovitzes wrote.

Barsymes carried in a chair for the mage. "Help yourself to apricots," Krispos said. "But first tell me what brings you here so late. It must be getting close to the sixth hour of the night. Has Digenis finally gone to the ice?"

To his surprise, Zaidas answered, "No, Your Majesty, or not that I know of. It has rather to do with your son Phostis."

"You found a way to make Digenis talk?" Krispos demanded eagerly.

"Not that either, Your Majesty," the mage said. "As you know, till now I've had no success even learning the possible source of the magic that conceals the young Majesty from my search. This has not been from want of effort or diligence, I assure you. Till now, I would have described the trouble as want of skill."

"Till now?" Krispos prompted.

"As you know, Your Majesty, my wife Aulissa is a very determined lady." Zaidas gave a small, self-deprecating chuckle. "She has, in fact, determination to spare for herself and me both."

Iakovitzes reached for the stylus, but forbore. Krispos admired Aulissa's beauty and her strength of purpose while remaining content she was his mage's wife, not his own. The two of them had been happy together for many years, though. Now Krispos just said, "Go on, pray."

"Yes, Your Majesty. In any case, Aulissa, seeing my discontent at failing to penetrate the shield the Thanasiot sorcerers have thrown up to disguise Phostis' whereabouts, suggested I test that screen at odd times and in odd ways, in the hope of ascertaining its nature while it might be weakest. Having no more likely profitable notions of my own, I fell in with her plan, and this evening I saw it crowned with success."

"There's good news indeed," Krispos said. "I'm in your debt, and in Aulissa's. Tell her when you go home that I'll show I'm grateful with more than words. But for now, by the good god, tell me what you know before I get up and tear it from you."

Iakovitzes let out his gobbling laugh. "It's an idle threat, sorcerous sir," he wrote. "Neither Krispos nor I could rise for anything right now, in any sense of the word."

Zaidas' smile was nervous. "You must understand, Your Majesty, I've not broken the screen, merely peeked behind one lifted corner of it, if I may use ordinary words to describe sorcerous operations. But this I can tell you with some confidence: the magic behind the screen is of the school inspired by the Prophets Four."

"*Is* it?" Krispos said. Iakovitzes' eyebrows were eloquent of surprise. The Avtokrator added, "So the wind blows from that quarter, does it? It's not what I expected, I'll say that. Knowing how the screen was made, can you now pierce it?"

"That remains to be seen," Zaidas said, "but I can essay such piercing with more hope than previously was mine."

"Good for you!" Krispos lifted the latest wine jar from its bed of snow. It was distressingly light. "Barsymes!" he called. "I'd intended to make an end of things here, but I find we need more wine after all. Fetch us another, and a cup for Zaidas and one for yourself. Tonight the news is good."

"I shall attend to it directly, Your Majesty," Barsymes said, and he did.

OCCASIONAL SLEET RODE THE WIND OUTSIDE THE LITTLE STONE house with the thatched roof. Inside, a small fire burned on the hearth, but the chill remained. Phostis chafed his hands one against the other to keep feeling in them.

The priest who had presided over the Midwinter's Day liturgy at the main temple in Etchmiadzin bowed to the middle-aged couple who sat side by side at the table where they'd no doubt eaten together for many years. On the table rested a small loaf of black bread and two cups of wine.

"We are met here today with Laonikos and Siderina to celebrate their last meal, their last partaking of the gross substance of the world and their commencement of a new journey on Phos' gleaming path," the priest proclaimed.

Along with Phostis, Olyvria, and Syagrios, the little house was crowded with friends and relatives; the couple's son and daughter and two of Laonikos' brothers were easy to pick out by looks. Everyone, including Laonikos and Siderina, seemed happy and proud of what was about to happen. Phostis looked happy himself, but he'd learned in the palaces how to assume an expression at will. In fact, he didn't know what to think. The man and woman at that table were obviously of sound mind and as obviously eager to begin with what they thought of as the last step of their earthly existence and their first steps toward heaven. *How should I feel about that,* Phostis wondered, *when it's not a choice I'd ever make for myself?*

"Let us pray," the priest said. Phostis bent his head, sketched the sun-circle over his heart. Everyone recited Phos' creed. As he had at Etchmiadzin's temple, Phostis found the creed more moving, more sincere, here than he ever had in the High Temple. These people *meant* their prayers.

They put fervor into a round of Thanasiot hymns, too. Phostis did not know those as well as the rest of the folk gathered here; he kept stumbling over the words and then coming in again a line and a half later. The hymns had different tunes—some borrowed from the orthodox liturgy—but the same message: that loving the good god was all-important, that the next world meant more than this one, and that every earthly pleasure was from Skotos and to be shunned.

The priest turned to Laonikos and Siderina and asked, "Are you now prepared to abandon the wickedness in this world, the dark god's vessel, and to seek the light in the realm beyond the sun?"

They looked at each other, then touched hands. It was a loving gesture, but in no way a sensual one; with it they affirmed that what they did, they did together. Without hesitation, they said, "We are." Phostis could not have told which of them spoke first.

"It's so beautiful," Olyvria whispered, and Phostis had to nod. Dropping her voice still further, so only he heard, she added, "And so frightening." He nodded again.

"Take up the knife," the priest said. "Divide the bread and eat it. Take the wine and drink. Never again shall the stuff of Skotos pass your lips. Soon the bodies that are themselves sinful shall be no more and pass away; soon your souls shall know the true joy of union with the lord with the great and good mind."

Laonikos was a sturdy man with a proud hooked nose and distinctive eyebrows, tufted and bushy. Siderina might have been pretty as a girl; her face was still sweet and strong. *Soon,* Phostis thought, *they'll both look like Strabon.* The idea horrified him. It didn't seem to bother Laonikos and Siderina at all.

Laonikos cut the little loaf in half and gave one piece to his wife. The other he kept himself. He ate it in three or four bites, then tilted back the wine cup until the last drop was gone. His smile lit up the house. "It's done," he said proudly. "Phos be praised."

"Phos be praised," everyone echoed. "May the gleaming path lead you to him!"

Siderina finished her final meal a few seconds after Laonikos. She dabbed at her lips with a linen napkin. Her eyes sparkled. "Now I shan't have to fret about what to cook for supper anymore," she said. Her voice was gay and eager; she looked forward to the world to come. Her family laughed with her. Even Phostis found himself smiling, for her manifest happiness communicated itself to him no matter how much trouble he had sharing it.

The couple's son took the plate, knife, and wine cups. "The good god willing, these will inspire us to join you soon," he said.

"I hope they do," Laonikos said. He got up from the table and hugged the young man. In a moment, the whole family was embracing.

"We bless thee, Phos, lord with the great and good mind—" the priest began. Everyone joined him in prayer once more.

Phostis thought the blue-robe had intruded himself on the family's celebration. He thought his own presence an intrusion, too. Turning to Olyvria, he whispered, "We really ought to go."

"Yes, I suppose you're right," she murmured back.

"Phos bless you, friends, and may we see you along his gleaming path," Laonikos called to them as they made their way out the door. Phostis put up his hood and pulled his cloak tight around him to shield against the storm.

"Well," Olyvria said when they'd gone a few yards down the street, "what did you think of that?"

"Very much what you did," Phostis answered. "Terrifying and beautiful at the same time."

"Huh!" Syagrios said. "Where's the beauty in turning into a bag of bones?" It was the same thought Phostis had worried at before, if more pungently put.

Olyvria let out an indignant sniff. Before she could speak, Phostis said, "Seeing faith so fully realized is beautiful, even for someone like me. My own faith, I fear, is not so deep. I cling to life on earth, which is why seeing someone choose to leave it frightens me."

"We'll all leave it sooner or later, so why choose to hurry?" Syagrios said.

"For a proper Thanasiot," Olyvria said, emphasizing *proper,* "the world is corrupt from its creation, and to be shunned and abandoned as soon as possible."

Syagrios remained unmoved. "Somebody has to take care of all the bloody sods leavin' the world, or else they'll leave it faster'n they have in mind, thanks to his old man's soldiers." He jerked a thumb at Phostis. "So I'm not a sheep. I'm a sheepdog. You don't have sheepdogs, my lady, wolves get fat."

The argument was ugly but potent. Olyvria bit her lip and looked to Phostis. He felt he was called to save her from some dreadful fate, even though she and Syagrios were in truth on the same side. He flung the best rhetorical brickbat he could find: "Saving others from sin doesn't excuse sins of your own."

"Boy, you can talk about sin when you find out what it is," Syagrios said scornfully. "You're as milk-fed now as when you came out from between your mother's legs. And how do you think you got in there to come out, eh, if there'd been no heavy breathing awhile before?"

Phostis *had* thought about that, as uneasily as most people when making similar contemplations. He started to shoot back that his parents had been honestly married when he was conceived, but he wasn't even sure of that. And rumor in the palace quarter said—whispered, when he was suspected of being in earshot—Krispos and Dara had been lovers while the previous Avtokrator—and Dara's previous husband—Anthimos still held the throne. Glaring at Syagrios wasn't the response Phostis would have liked to make, but seemed the best one available.

As wet will not stick to a duck's oiled feather, so glares slid off Syagrios. He threw back his head and laughed raucously at Phostis' discomfiture. Then he spun on his heel and swaggered away through the slush, as if to say Phostis wouldn't know what to do with a chance to sin if one fell into his lap.

"Cursed ruffian," Phostis growled—but softly, so Syagrios would not hear. "By the good god, he knows enough of sin to spend eternity in the ice; the gleaming path should be ashamed to call him its own."

"He's not a Thanasiot, not really, though he'll quarrel over the workings of the faith like any Videssian." Olyvria's voice was troubled, as if she did not care for the admission she was about to make. "He's much more a creature of my father's."

"Why does that not surprise me?" Phostis freighted the words with as much irony as they would bear. Only after they had passed his lips did he wish he'd held them in. Railing at Livanios would not help him with Olyvria.

She sounded defensive as she answered, "Surely Krispos also has men to do his bidding, no matter what it may be."

"Oh, he does," Phostis said. "But he doesn't wrap himself in piety while he's about it." In some surprise, he listened to himself defending his father. This wasn't the first time he'd had good things to say about Krispos since he'd ended up in Etchmiadzin. He hadn't had many when he was back in the imperial capital under Krispos' eye—and his thumb.

Olyvria said, "My father seeks to liberate Videssos so the gleaming path may become a reality for everyone. Do you deny it's a worthy goal?"

He seeks power, like any other ambitious man, Phostis thought. Before he could say it aloud, he started to laugh. Olyvria's eyes raked him. "I wasn't laughing at you," he assured her quickly. "It's just that we sound like a couple of little squabbling children: 'My father can do this.' 'Well, *my* father can do that.' "

"Oh." She smiled back, her good humor restored. "So we do. What would you rather talk about than what our fathers can do?"

The challenging way she threw the question at him reminded him of the first time he'd seen her, in the tunnel under Videssos the city. If he was to become a proper Thanasiot, as Olyvria had put it in her argument with Syagrios, he ought to have forgotten that, or at most remembered it as a test he'd passed. But he'd discovered before he ever heard of Thanasios that he did not have a temper approaching the monastic. He did not remember just the test; he remembered *her*.

And so he did not answer in words. Instead, he reached out and slipped an arm around her waist. If she'd pulled back, he was ready to apologize profusely. He was even ready to produce a convincing stammer. But she didn't pull back. Instead, she let him draw her to him.

In Videssos the city, they would have been nothing out of the ordinary: a young man and a young woman happy with each other and not paying much attention to anything else. Even in Etchmiadzin, a few people on the street smiled as they walked by. Others, though, glowered in pious indignation at such a public display of affection. *Crabs,* he thought.

After a few steps, though, Olyvria pulled away. He thought she'd seen the disapproving faces, too. But she said, "Strolling with you like this is very pleasant, but I can't feel happy about pleasure, if you know what I mean, just after we've come away from the celebration of the Last Meal."

"Oh. That." As it has a way of doing, the wider world intruded itself on Phostis' thoughts. He remembered the joy Laonikos and Siderina had shown when they swallowed the last wine and bread they would taste on earth. "It's still hard to imagine that impinging on me. Like Syagrios, if in lesser measure, I fear I'm a creature of this world."

"In lesser measure," Olyvria agreed. "Well, so am I, if the truth be told. Maybe when I'm older the world will repel me enough to make me want to leave it, but for now, even if everything Thanasios says about it is true, I can't force my flesh to turn altogether away from it."

"Nor I," Phostis said. The fleshly world intruded again, in a different way this time: He stepped up to Olyvria and kissed her. Her lips were for a moment still and startled under his; he was a little startled himself, because he hadn't planned to do it But then her arms enfolded him as his did her. Her tongue touched his, just for a couple of heartbeats.

At that, they broke apart from each other, so fast Phostis couldn't tell which of them drew back first. "Why did you do that?" Olyvria asked in a voice that was all breath.

"Why? Because—" Phostis stopped. He didn't know why, not in the way he knew how mulberries tasted or where in Videssos the city the High Temple stood. He tried again: "Because—" Another stumble. Once more: "Because of all the folk in Etchmiadzin, you're the only one who's shown me any true kindness." That was indeed part of the truth. The rest Phostis did not care to examine quite so closely; it was as filled with carnality as the upper part of his mind was with the notion that carnality and sinfulness were one and the same.

Olyvria considered what he'd said. Slowly she nodded. "Kindness is a virtue that moves you forward on the gleaming path, a reaching out from one soul to another," she said. But her eyes slipped away from his as she spoke. He watched her lips. They seemed slightly softer, slightly fuller than they had before his touched them. He wondered if she, too, was having trouble reconciling what she believed with what she felt.

They walked on aimlessly for a while, not touching, both of them thoughtful. Then, over a low rooftop, Phostis saw the bulk of the fortress. "We'd better get back," he said. Olyvria nodded, as if relieved to have a definite goal for her feet.

As if he were a conjured demon, Syagrios popped out of a wineshop not far outside the fortress' walls. He might have started shirking his watchdog duties, but he didn't want Livanios finding out about that. The ruffian glanced mockingly at the two of them. "Well, have you settled all the doings of the lord with the great and good mind?"

"That's for Phos to do with us, not we with him," Phostis said.

Syagrios liked that; his laugh blew grapey fumes into Phostis' face. He pointed toward the gates. "Back to your cage now, and you can see how Phos settles you there."

Phostis kept walking toward the fortress. He'd learned that giving any sign Syagrios' jabs hurt guaranteed he'd keep getting them. As he went through the gates, he also noticed how much like home the fortress was becoming in his mind. *Just because it's familiar doesn't mean they can make you belong here,* he told himself.

But were they making him? He still hadn't settled that question in his own mind. If he followed Thanasios' gleaming path, oughtn't he be here of his own free will?

In the inner yard, Livanios was watching some of his recruits throw javelins. The light spears thumped into bales of hay propped against the far wall. Some missed and bounced back.

Ever alert, Livanios turned his head to see who the newcomers were. "Ah, the young Majesty," he said. Phostis didn't care for the way he used the title; it was devoid even of scornful courtesy. The heresiarch sounded as if he wondered whether Phostis, instead of proving useful, might be turning into a liability. That made Phostis nervous. If he wasn't useful to Livanios, how long would he last?

"Take him up to his chamber, Syagrios," Livanios said; he might have been speaking of a dog, or of a sack of flour.

As the door to his little cell closed behind him, Phostis realized that, if he didn't care to abandon his fleshly form as the Thanasioi advocated for their most pious folk, he might have to take some most un-Thanasiot actions. As soon as that thought crossed his mind, he remembered Olyvria's lips sweet against his. The Thanasioi would not have approved of that, not even a little.

He also remembered whose daughter Olyvria was. If he tried to escape, would she betray him? Or might she help? He stamped on the cold floor. He just did not know.

Chapter VIII

KRISPOS WAS WADING THROUGH CHANGES IN A LAW THAT dealt with tariffs on tallow imported from the northeastern land of Thatagush when Barsymes tapped at the open door of his study with one knuckle. He looked up. The vestiarios said, "May it please Your Majesty, a messenger from the mage Zaidas at the government office building."

"Maybe it *will* please me, by the good god," Krispos said. "Send him in."

The messenger quickly prostrated himself, then said, "Your Majesty, Zaidas bids me tell you that he has at last succeeded in commencing a sorcerous interrogation of the rebel priest Digenis."

"Has he? Well, to the ice with tallow."

"Your Majesty?"

"Never mind." The less the messenger knew about the dickering with Thatagush, the happier he'd be. Krispos got up and accompanied him out of the study and out of the imperial residence. Haloga guards fell in with him as he went down the broad steps outside. He felt a childish delight in having caught his parasol-bearers napping, as if he'd put one over on Barsymes.

He hadn't gone to listen to Digenis since the day of Iakovitzes' return. He'd seen no point to it: he'd already heard all the Thanasiot platitudes he could stomach, and Digenis refused to yield the truths he wanted to learn.

He was shocked at how the priest had wasted away. In his peasant days, he'd seen men and women lean with hunger after a bad harvest, but Digenis was long past leanness: everything between his skeleton and his skin seemed to have disappeared. His eyes shifted when Krispos came into his cell, but did not catch fire as they had before.

"He is very weak, Your Majesty; his will at last begins to fail," Zaidas said quietly. "Otherwise I doubt even now I could have found a way to coax answers from him."

"What have you done?" Krispos asked. "I see no apparatus for the two-mirror test."

"No." By his expression, Zaidas would have been glad never to try the two-mirror test again. "This is half magic, half healing art. I laced the water he drinks with a decoction of henbane, having first used sorcery to remove the taste so he would notice nothing out of the ordinary."

"Well done." After a moment, Krispos added, "I do hope the technique for that is not so simple as to be available to any poisoner who happens to take a dislike to his neighbor—or to me."

"No, Your Majesty," Zaidas said, smiling. "In any case, the spell, because it goes against nature, is easy to detect by sorcery. Digenis, of course, was not in a position to do so."

"And a good thing, too," Krispos said. "All right, let's see if he'll give forth the truth now. What questions have you put to him thus far?"

"None of major import. As soon as I saw he was at last receptive, I sent for you at once. I suggest you keep your questions as simple as you can. The henbane frees his mind, but also clouds it—both far more strongly than wine."

"As you say, sorcerous sir." Krispos raised his voice. "Digenis! Do you hear me, Digenis?"

"Aye, I hear you." Digenis' voice was not only weak from weeks of self-imposed starvation but also dreamy and faraway.

"Where's Phostis—my son? The son of the Avtokrator Krispos," Krispos added, in case the priest did not realize who was talking to him.

Digenis answered, "He walks the golden path to true piety, striding ever farther from the perverse materialistic heresy that afflicts too many soulblind folk throughout the Empire." The priest held his convictions all the way down to his heart, not merely on the surface of his mind. Krispos had already been sure of that.

He tried again: "Where is Phostis physically?"

"The physical is unimportant," Digenis declared. Krispos glanced over at Zaidas, who bared his teeth in an agony of frustration. But Digenis went on, "If all went as was planned, Phostis is now with Livanios."

Krispos had thought as much, but hearing the plan had been kidnap rather than murder lifted fear from his heart. Phostis could easily have been dumped in some rocky ravine with his throat cut; only the wolves and ravens would have been likely to discover him. The Avtokrator said, "What does Livanios hope to do with him? Use him as a weapon against me?"

"Phostis has a hope of assuming true piety," Digenis said. Krispos wondered if he'd confused him by asking two questions at once. After a few heartbeats, the priest resumed, "For a youth, Phostis resists carnality well. To my surprise, he declined the body of Livanios' daughter, which she offered to see if he could be tempted from the gleaming path. He could not. He may yet prove suitable for an imminent union with the good god rather than revolting and corruptible flesh."

"An imminent union?" All faiths used words in special ways. Krispos wanted to be sure he understood what Digenis was talking about. "What's an imminent union?"

"That which I am approaching now," Digenis answered. "The voluntary abandonment of the flesh to free the spirit to fly to Phos."

"You mean starving yourself to death," Krispos said. Somehow Digenis used his emaciated neck for a nod. Slow horror trickled through Krispos as he imagined Phostis wasting away like the Thanasiot priest. No matter that he and the young man quarreled, no matter even that Phostis might not be his by blood: he would not have wished such a fate on him.

Digenis began to whisper a Thanasiot hymn. Seeking to rock him out of the holy smugness he maintained even in the face of approaching death, Krispos said, "Did you know Livanios uses magic of the school of the Prophets Four to hide Phostis' whereabouts?"

"He is cursed with ambition," Digenis answered. "I knew the spoor; I recognized the stench. He prates of the golden path, but Skotos has filled his heart with greed for power."

"You worked with him, knowing he was evil by your reckoning?" That surprised Krispos; he'd expected the renegade priest to have sterner standards for himself. "And you still claim you walk Thanasios' gleaming path? Are you not a hypocrite?"

"No, for Livanios' ambition furthers the advance of the holy Thanasios' doctrines, whereas yours leads only to the further aggrandizement of Skotos," Digenis declared. "Thus evil is transmuted into good and the dark god confounded."

"Thus sincerity turns to expedience," Krispos said. He'd already gained the impression that Livanios cared more for Livanios than for the gleaming path. In a way, that made the heresiarch more dangerous, for he was liable to be more flexible than an out-and-out fanatic. But in another way, it weakened Livanios: fanatics, by the strength of their beliefs, could sometimes make their followers transcend difficulties from which an ordinary thoughtful man would flinch.

Krispos thought for a while, but could not come up with any more questions about Phostis or the rebels in the field. Turning to Zaidas, he said, "Squeeze all you can from him about the riots and the city and those involved. And then—" He paused.

"Yes, what then, Your Majesty?" the mage asked. "Shall we let him continue his decline until he stops breathing one day before long?"

"I'd sooner strike off his head and put it up on the Milestone," Krispos said grimly. "But if I did that now, with him looking as he does, all the Thanasioi in the city would have themselves a new martyr. I'd just as soon do without that, if I could. Better to let him die in quiet and disappear: the good god willing, folk will just forget about him."

"You are wise and cruel," Digenis said. "Skotos speaks through your lips."

"If I thought that were so, I'd step down from the throne and cast off my crown this instant," Krispos said. "My task is to rule the Empire as well as I can devise, and pass it on to my heir so he may do likewise. Having Videssos torn apart in religious strife doesn't seem to me to be part of that bargain."

"Yield to the truth and there will be no strife." Digenis began whispering hymns again in his dusty voice.

"This talk has no point," Krispos said. "I'd sooner build than destroy, and you Thanasioi feel the opposite. I don't want the land burned over, nor do I want it vacant of Videssians who slew themselves for piety's sake. Other folk would simply steal what we've spent centuries building. I will not have that, not while I live."

Digenis said, "The lord with the great and good mind willing, Phostis will prove a man of better sense and truer piety."

Krispos thought about that. Suppose he got his son back, but as a full-fledged fanatical Thanasiot? What then? *If that's so,* he told himself, *it's as well I had three boys, not one.* If Phostis came back a Thanasiot, he'd live out his days in a monastery, whether he went there of his own free will or not. Krispos promised himself that: he wouldn't turn the Empire over to someone more interesting in wrecking than maintaining it.

Time enough to worry about that if he ever saw Phostis again, though. He turned to Zaidas. "You've done well, sorcerous sir. Knowing what you've learned now, you should have a better chance of pinpointing Phostis' whereabouts."

"I'll bend every effort toward that end," the mage promised.

Nodding, Krispos stepped out of Digenis' cell. The head gaoler came up to him and said, "A question, Your Majesty?" Krispos raised an eyebrow and waited. The gaoler said, "That priest in there, he's getting on toward the end. What happens if he decides he doesn't care to starve himself to death and wants to start eating again?"

"I don't think that's likely to happen." If nothing else, Krispos respected Digenis' sense of purpose. "If it does, though, by all means let him eat; this refusal to take food is his affair, not mine. But notify me immediately."

"You'll want to ask him more questions, Your Majesty?" the gaoler said.

"No, no; you misunderstand. That priest is a condemned traitor. If he wants to carry out the sentence of death on himself in his own way, I am willing to permit it. But if his will falters, he'll meet the headsman on a full stomach."

"Ah," the gaoler said. "The wind sits so, eh? Very well, Your Majesty, it shall be as you say."

In his younger days, Krispos would have come back with something harsh, like *It had better be.* More secure in his power now, he headed upstairs without a backward glance. As long as the gaoler felt no other result than the one he desired was possible, that result was what Krispos would get.

The Halogai who had waited outside the government office building took their places around Krispos and those who had gone down with him into the gaol. "Is the word good, Majesty?" one of the northerners asked.

"Good enough, anyhow," the Avtokrator answered. "I know now Phostis was snatched, not killed, and I have a good notion of where he's been taken. As for getting him back—time will tell about that." *And about what sort of person he'll be when I do get him back,* he added to himself.

The guardsmen cheered, their deep-voiced shouts making passersby's heads turn to find out what news was so gladsome. Some people exclaimed to see Krispos out and about without his retinue of parasolbearers. Others exclaimed at the Halogai. The men from the north—tall, fair, gloomy, and slow-spoken—never failed to fascinate the Videssians, whose opposites they were in almost every way.

Struck by sudden curiosity, Krispos turned to one of the northerners and said, "Tell me, Trygve, what do you make of the folk of Videssos the city?"

Trygve pursed his lips and gave the matter some serious thought. At last, in his deliberate Videssian, he answered, "Majesty, the wine here is very fine, the women looser than they are in Halogaland. But everyone, I t'ink, here talks too much." Several other guardsmen nodded in solemn agreement. Since Krispos had the same opinion of the city folk, he nodded, too.

Back at the imperial residence, he gave the news from Digenis to Barsymes. The vestiarios' smile, unusually broad, filled his face full of fine wrinkles. He said, "Phos be praised that the young Majesty is thought to be alive. The other palace chamberlains, I know, will be as delighted as I am."

Down a side corridor, Krispos came upon Evripos and Katakolon arguing about something or other. He didn't ask what; when the mood struck them, they could argue over the way a lamp flame flickered. He'd had no brothers himself, only two sisters younger than he, both many years dead now. He supposed he should have been glad his sons kept their fights to words and occasional fists rather than hiring knifemen or poisoners or wizards.

Both youths glanced warily in his direction as he approached. Neither one looked conspicuously guilty, so each of them felt the righteousness of his own cause—though Evripos, these days, was developing the beginning of a pretty good stone face.

Krispos said, "Digenis has cracked at last, thank the good god. By what he said, Phostis is held in some Thanasiot stronghold, but is alive and likely to stay that way."

Now he studied Evripos and Katakolon rather than the other way round. Katakolon said, "That's good news. By the time we're done smashing the Thanasioi next summer, we should have him back again." His expression was open and happy; Krispos didn't think he was acting. He was sure he couldn't have done so well at Katakolon's age . . . but then, he hadn't been raised at court, either.

Evripos' features revealed nothing whatever. His eyes were watchful and hooded. Krispos prodded to see what lay behind the mask. "Aren't you glad to be sure your elder brother lives?"

"For blood's sake, aye, but should I rejoice to see my ambition thwarted?" Evripos said. "Would you, in my boots?"

The question cut to the root. Ambition for a better life had driven

Krispos from his farm to Videssos; while he was one of Iakovitzes' grooms, ambition had led him to wrestle a Kubrati champion and gained him the notice of the then-Emperor Anthimos' uncle Petronas, who administered Videssos in his nephew's name; ambition led him to let Petronas use him to supplant Anthimos' previous vestiarios; and then, as vestiarios himself, to take ever more power into his own hands, supplanting first Petronas and then Anthimos.

He said, "Son, I know you want the red boots. Well, so does Phostis, and I have but the one set to give. What would you have me do?"

"Give them to me, by Phos," Evripos answered. "I'd wear them better than he would."

"I have no way to be sure of that—nor do you," Krispos said. "For that matter, a day may come when Katakolon here begins to think past the end of his prick. He might prove a better ruler than either of you two. Who can say?"

"Him?" Evripos shook his head. "No, Father, forgive me, but I don't see it."

"Me?" Katakolon seemed as bemused as his brother. "I've never thought much of wearing the crown. I always figured the only way it would come to me was if Phostis and Evripos were dead. I don't want it badly enough to wish for that. And since I'm not likely to be Avtokrator, why shouldn't I enjoy myself?"

As Avtokrator and voluptuary both, Anthimos had been anything but good for the Empire. But as Emperor's brother, Katakolon would be relatively harmless if he devoted himself to pleasure. If he did lack ambition, he might even be safer as a voluptuary. The chronicles had shown Krispos that rulers had a way of turning suspicious of their closest kin: who else was likelier both to accumulate power and to use it against them?

"Maybe it's because I grew up on a farm," Krispos began, and both Evripos and Katakolon rolled their eyes. Nonetheless, the Avtokrator persisted: "Maybe that's why I think waste is a sin Phos won't forgive. We never had much; if we'd wasted anything, we would have starved. The lord with the great and good mind knows I'm glad it isn't so with you boys: being hungry is no fun. But even though you have so much, you should still work to make the most you can of your lives. Pleasure is all very well in its place, but you can do other things when you're not in bed."

Katakolon grinned. "Aye, belike: you can get drunk."

"Another sermon wasted, Father," Evripos said acidly. "How does that fit into your scheme of worths?"

Without answering, Krispos pushed past his two younger sons and down the corridor. Phostis was unenthusiastic about ruling, Evripos embittered, and Katakolon had other things on his mind. What would Videssos come to when the common fate of mankind took his own hand from the steering oar?

Men had been asking that question, on one scale or another, for as long as there were men. If the head of a family died and his relatives were less able then he, the family might fall on hard times, but the rest of the world went on. When an able Emperor passed from the scene, families past counting might suffer because of it.

"What am I supposed to do?" Krispos asked the statues and paintings and relics that lined that hallway. No answer came back to him. All he could think of was to go on himself, as well as he could for as long as he could.

And after that? After that it would be in his sons' hands, and in the good god's. He remained confident Phos would continue to watch over Videssos. Of his sons he was less certain.

R AIN POURED DOWN IN SHEETS, RAN IN WIDE, WATERY FISH-tails off the edges of roofs, and turned the inner ward of the fortress of Etchmiadzin into a thin soup of mud. Phostis closed the wooden shutter to the little slit window in his cell; with it open, things were about as wet inside as they were out in the storm.

But with it closed, the bare square room was dark as night; fitfully flickering lamps did little to cut the gloom. Phostis slept as much as he could. Inside the cell in near darkness, he had little else to do.

After a few days of the steady rain, he felt as full of sleep as a new wineskin is of wine. He went into the corridor in search of something other than food.

Syagrios was dozing on a chair down the hall. Perhaps he'd had himself magically attuned to Phostis' door, for he came alert as soon as it opened, though Phostis had been quiet with it. The ruffian yawned, stretched, and said, "I was beginning to think you'd died in there, boy. In a little while, I was going to check for a stink."

You might have found one, Phostis thought. Because the Thanasioi reckoned the body Skotos' creation, they neither lavished baths on it nor disguised its odors with sweet scents. Sometimes Phostis didn't notice the resulting stench, as he was part of it. Sometimes it oppressed him dreadfully.

He said, "I'm going downstairs. I've grown too bored even to nap anymore."

"You won't stay bored forever," Syagrios answered. "After the rain comes the clear, and when the clear comes, we go out to fight." He closed a fist and slammed it down on his leg. Syagrios was bored, too, Phostis realized: he hadn't had the chance to go out and hurt anything lately.

A couple of torches had gone out along the corridor, leaving it hardly brighter than Phostis' cell. He lit a taper from the burning torch nearest the stairway and headed down the steep stone spiral. Syagrios followed him. As always, he was sweating by the time he reached the bottom; a misstep on the stairs and he would have got there much faster than he wanted to.

Livanios' soldiers crowded the ground floor of the citadel. Some of them slept rolled in blankets, their worldly goods either under their heads in leather sacks that served for pillows or somewhere else close by. However much the Thanasioi professed to despise the things of the world, their fighters could still be tempted to take hold of things of the world that were not things of theirs.

Some of the men who were awake threw dice; there coins and other things of the world changed hands in more generally accepted fashion. Phostis had been bemused the first time he saw Thanasiot soldiers gambling. He'd watched the dice many times since and concluded the men were soldiers first and followers of the gleaming path afterward.

Off in a corner, a small knot of men gathered around a game board whereon two of their fellows dueled. Phostis made his way over to them. "If nobody's up for the next game, I challenge the winner," he said.

The players looked up from their pieces. "Hullo, friend," one of them said, a Thanasiot greeting Phostis was still getting used to. "Aye, I'll take you on after I take care of Grypas here."

"Ha!" Grypas returned to the board the prelate he'd captured from his opponent. "Guard your emperor, Astragalos; Phostis here will play *me* next."

Grypas proved right; after some further skirmishing, Astragalos' emperor, beset on all sides, found no square where he could move without threat of capture. Muttering into his beard, the soldier gave up.

Phostis sat in his place. He and Grypas returned the pieces to their proper squares on the first three rows on each man's side of the nine-by-nine board. Grypas glanced over at Phostis. "I've played you before, friend. I'm going to take winner's privilege and keep first move."

"However you like," Phostis answered. Grypas advanced the foot soldier diagonally ahead of his prelate, freeing up the wide-ranging piece for action. Phostis pushed one of his own foot soldiers forward in reply.

Grypas played like the soldier he was. He hurled men into the fight without much worry about where they would be three moves later. Phostis had learned in a subtler school. He lost a little time fortifying his emperor behind an array of goldpieces and silvers, but then started taking advantage of that safety.

Before long, Grypas was gnawing his mustache in consternation. He tried to fight back by returning to the fray pieces he'd taken from Phostis, but Phostis had not left himself as vulnerable as Astragalos had before. He beat the soldier without much trouble.

As the dejected man got up from the board, Syagrios sat down across it from Phostis. He leered at the junior Avtokrator. "All right, youngster, let's see how tough you are."

"I'll keep first move against you, by the good god," Phostis said. Around them, bets crackled back and forth. Over the long winter, they'd shown they were the two best players in the fortress. Which of them was better than the other swung from day to day.

Phostis stared over the grid at his unkempt opponent. Who would have guessed that a man with the looks of a bandit and habits to match made such a cool, precise player? But the pieces on the board cared nothing for how a man looked or even how he acted when he wasn't at the game. And Syagrios had already showed he had more wit behind that battered face than anyone who judged by it alone would guess.

The ruffian had a special knack for returning captured pieces to the board with telling effect. If he set down a horseman, you could be sure it threatened two pieces at once, both of them worth more than it. If a siege engine went into action, your emperor would be in trouble soon.

His manner at the game betrayed his origins. Whenever Phostis made a move he didn't like, he'd growl, "Oh, you son of a whore!" It had been unnerving at first; by now, Phostis took no more notice of it than of the twitches and tics of some of his opponents back in Videssos the city.

He took far fewer chances against Syagrios than he had against Grypas. In fact, he took no chances at all that he could see: give Syagrios an opening and he'd charge right through. Syagrios treated him with similar caution. The game, as a result, was slow and positional.

Finally, with returned foot soldiers paving the way, Syagrios broke up Phostis' fortress and sent his emperor scurrying for safety. When he was trapped in a corner with no hope of escape, Phostis took him off the board and said, "I surrender."

"You made me sweat there, by the good god." Syagrios thumped his chest with a big fist, then boomed out, "Who else wants a go at me?"

Astragalos said, "Let Phostis take you on again. That'll make a more even match than the rest of us are apt to give you."

Phostis had stood up. He looked around to see if anybody else wanted to play Syagrios. When no one made a move, he sat back down again. Sya-grios leered at him. "I ain't gonna give you first move, either, boy."

"I didn't expect you would," Phostis answered, altogether without ironic intent: any man who didn't look out for himself wasn't likely to find anyone to do it for him.

After a game as hard-fought as the first one, he got his revenge. Syagrios leaned over the board and punched him on the meaty part of his arm. "You're a sneaky little bastard, you know that? To the ice with whose son you are. That ain't horse manure between your ears, you know?"

"Whatever you say." Compliments from Syagrios made Phostis even more nervous than the abuse that usually filled the ruffian's mouth. Phostis stood up again and said, "You can take on the next challenger."

"Why's that?" Syagrios demanded. Quitting while you were winning was bad form.

"If I don't leave about now, you'll have to wipe up the floor under me," Phostis answered, which made Syagrios and several of the other men around the game board laugh. With the fortress of Etchmiadzin packed full of fighters, the humor there was decidedly coarse.

In better weather, Phostis would have wandered out into the inner ward to make water against the wall. There was, however, an oversuffi-ciency of water in the inner ward already. He headed off to the garderobe instead. The chamber, connected as it was to a cesspit under the keep, was so noisome that he avoided it when he could. At the moment, however, he had little choice.

Wooden stalls separated one hole in the long stone bench from another, an unusual concession to delicacy but one Phostis appreciated. Three of the four were occupied when he went in; he stepped into the fourth, which was farthest from the doorway.

As he was easing himself, he heard a couple of people come in behind him. One of them let out an unhappy grunt. "All full," he said. By the slight accent he gave his words, Phostis recognized him as Livanios' pet wizard.

The other was Livanios. "Don't worry, Artapan," he said easily. "You won't burst in the next couple of minutes, and neither shall I."

"Don't use my name," the wizard grumbled.

Livanios laughed at him. "By the good god, if we have spies in the la-trine, we're doomed before we start. Here, this fellow's coming out. You go ahead; I'll wait."

Phostis had already set his clothes to rights, but he waited, too, waited until he heard Livanios go into a stall and shut the door. Then he all but jumped out of the one he'd been in and hurried away from the garderobe. He didn't want either Livanios or Artapan to know he'd heard.

Now that he knew the wizard's name, he also recognized the accent that had tantalized him for so long. Artapan was from Makuran. Phostis wondered what a mage from Videssos' perennial enemy was doing in Livanios' camp. Why couldn't Livanios find a proper Thanasiot mage?

After a few seconds, he stopped wondering. To one raised in the palaces, to one who had, however unwillingly, soaked up a good deal of history, the answer fairly shouted at him: Artapan was there serving the interests of Rubyab King of Kings. And how could Rubyab's interest be better served than by keeping Videssos at war with itself?

Two other questions immediately sprang from that one. The first was whether Livanios knew he was being used. Maybe he didn't, maybe he was Makuran's willing cat's-paw, or maybe he was out to exploit Rubyab's help at the same time Rubyab used him. Phostis had a tough time seeing Livanios as a witless dupe. Choosing between the other two alternatives was harder.

Phostis set them aside. To him, the second question carried greater weight: if the Thanasioi were flourishing thanks to aid from Makuran, what did that say about the truth of their teachings? That one was hard enough to break teeth when you bit into it. Would Thanasios' interpretation of the faith have grown and spread without the foreign—no, no mincing words—without the enemy—help? Was it at bottom a religious movement at all, or rather a political one? If it was just political, why did it have such a strong appeal to so many Videssians?

Without even bothering to get a taper, Phostis went upstairs and into his room. All at once, he didn't care how gloomy it was in there. In fact, he hardly noticed. He sat down on the battered old stool. He had a lot to think about.

SOMEWHERE AMONG THE GEARS AND LEVERS BEHIND THE WALL of the Grand Courtroom, a servitor stood in frustrated uselessness. Much to the fellow's dismay, Krispos had ordered him not to raise the throne on high when the ambassador from Khatrish prostrated himself. "But it's the custom!" the man had wailed.

"But the reason behind the custom is to overawe foreign envoys," Krispos had answered. "It doesn't overawe Tribo—it just makes him laugh."

"But it's the custom," the servitor had repeated. To him, reasons were irrelevant. Raising the throne was what he'd always done, so raising the throne was what he had to do forever.

Even now, as Tribo approached the throne and cast himself down on his belly, Krispos wondered if the throne would rise beneath him in spite of orders. Custom died hard in the Empire, when it died at all.

To his relief, he remained at his usual elevation. As the ambassador from Khatrish got to his feet, he asked, "Mechanism in the throne break down?"

I can't win, Krispos thought. Khatrishers seemed to specialize in complicating the lives of their Videssian neighbors. Krispos did not reply: he stood—or rather sat—on the imperial dignity, though he had the feeling that would do him about as much good as the climbing throne had before.

Sure enough, Tribo let out a knowing sniff when he saw he wouldn't get an answer. He said, "May it please Your Majesty, the Thanasioi are still troubling us."

"They're still troubling us, too, in case you hadn't noticed," Krispos said dryly.

"Well, yes, but it's different for you Videssians, you see, Your Majesty. You grew the murrain your very own selves, so of course it's still spreading through your flocks. We don't take kindly to having our cows infected, too, though, if you take my meaning."

A Videssian would have used a comparison from agriculture rather than herding, but Krispos had no trouble following Tribo. "What would you have me do?" he asked. "Shut the border between our states and ban shipping, too?"

The Khatrisher envoy flinched, as Krispos had known he would: Khatrish needed trade with Videssos much more than Videssos with Khatrish. "Let's not be hasty, Your Majesty. All I want is to hear you say again that you and your ministers don't have anything to do with spreading the cursed heresy, so I can take the word to my khagan."

Barsymes and Iakovitzes stood in front of the imperial throne. Krispos could see only their backs and the sides of their faces. He often made a game of trying to figure out from that limited view what they were thinking. He guessed Iakovitzes was amused—he admired effrontery—and Barsymes outraged—the normally self-controlled eunuch was fairly quivering in his place. Krispos needed a moment to realize why: Barsymes reckoned it an insult for him to have to deny anything more than once.

His own notion of what was insulting was more flexible, even after twenty years and more on the throne. If the envoy wanted another guarantee, he could have it. Krispos said, "You can tell Nobad son of Gumush that we aren't exporting this heresy to Khatrish on purpose. We wish it would go away here, and we're trying to get rid of it. But we aren't in the habit of stirring up sectarian strife, even if it might profit us."

"I shall send exactly that word to the puissant khagan, Your Majesty, and I thank you for the reassurance," Tribo said. He glanced toward the throne. Under his shaggy beard, a frown twisted his mouth. "Your Majesty? Did you hear me, Your Majesty?"

Krispos still didn't answer. He was listening to what he'd just said, not to the ambassador from Khatrish. Videssos might fight shy of turning its neighbors topsy-turvy with religious war, but would Makuran? Didn't the Thanasiot mage who hid Phostis use spells that smelled of Mashiz? No wonder Rubyab's mustaches had twitched!

Iakovitzes spun where he stood so he faced Krispos. The assembled courtiers murmured at the breach of etiquette. Iakovitzes had a fine nose for intrigue. His upraised hand and urgent expression said he'd just smelled some. Krispos would have bet a counterfeit copper against a year's tax receipts it was the same odor that had just filled his own nostrils.

He realized he had to say something to Tribo. After a few more seconds, he managed, "Yes, I'm glad you'll reassure your sovereign we are doing everything we can to fight the Thanasiot doctrine, not to spread it. This audience now is ended."

"But, Your Majesty—" Tribo began indignantly. Then, with a glare, he bowed to inflexible Videssian custom. When the Avtokrator spoke those words, an envoy had no choice but to prostrate himself once more, back away from the throne until he had gone far enough that he could turn around, and then depart the Grand Courtroom. He left in a manifest snit; evidently he'd had a good deal more on his mind than he got the chance to say.

I'll have to make it up to him, Krispos thought; keeping Khatrish friendly was going to be all the more important in the months ahead. But for now even the urgency of that paled. As soon as Tribo left the Grand Courtroom, Krispos also made his way out, at a pace that set the tongues of the assembled nobles and prelates and ministers wagging.

Politics was a religion of its own in Videssos; before long, many of those officials would figure out what was going on. Something obviously was, or the Avtokrator would not have left so unceremoniously. For the moment, though, they were at a loss as to what.

Iakovitzes half trotted along in Krispos' wake. He knew what was going through the Emperor's mind. Barsymes plainly didn't, but he would sooner have gone before the torturers in their red leather than question

Krispos where anyone else could hear him. What he'd have to say in private about cutting short the Khatrisher's audience was liable to be pointed.

Krispos swept across the rain-slicked flags of the path that led through the cherry orchard and to the imperial residence. The cherry trees were still bare-branched, but before too long they'd grow leaves and then the pink and white blossoms that would make the orchard fragrant and lovely for a few brief weeks in spring.

As soon as he was inside, Krispos burst out, "That bastard! That sneaky, underhanded son of a snake, may he shiver in the ice for all eternity to come."

"Surely Tribo did not so offend you with his remark concerning the throne?" Barsymes asked. No, he didn't know why Krispos had left on the run.

"I'm not talking about Tribo, I'm talking about Rubyab the fornicating King of Kings," Krispos said. "Unless I've lost all of my mind, he's using the Thanasioi for his stalking horse. How can Videssos hope to deal with Makuran if we tie ourselves up in knots?"

Barsymes had been in the palaces longer than Krispos; he was anything but a stranger to devious machinations. As soon as this one was pointed out to him, he nodded emphatically. "I have no doubt but that you're right, Your Majesty. Who would have looked for such elaborate deceit from Makuran?"

Iakovitzes held up a hand to gain a pause while he wrote something in his tablet. He passed it to Krispos. "We Videssians pride ourselves as the sneakiest folk on earth, but down deep somewhere we ought to remember the Makuraners can match us. They're not barbarians we can outmaneuver in our sleep. They've proved it, to our sorrow, too many times in the past."

"That's true," Krispos said as he handed the tablet to Barsymes. The vestiarios quickly read it, then nodded his agreement. Krispos thought back over the histories and chronicles he'd read. He said, "This seems to me to be something new. Aye, the King of Kings and his folk have fooled us many times, but mainly that's meant fooling us about what Makuran intends to do. Here, though, Rubyab's seen deep into our soul, seen how to make ourselves our own worst foes. That's more dangerous than any threat Makuran has posed in a long time."

Iakovitzes wrote, "There was a time, oh, about a hundred fifty years ago, when the men from Mashiz came closer to sacking Videssos the city than any Videssian likes to think about. Of course, we'd been meddling in their affairs before then, so I suppose they were out for revenge."

"Yes, I've seen those tales, too," Krispos said, nodding. "The question, though, is what we do about it now." He eyed Iakovitzes. "Suppose I send you back to Mashiz with a formal note of protest to Rubyab King of Kings?"

"Suppose you don't, Your Majesty," Iakovitzes wrote, and underlined the words.

"One thing we ought to do is get this tale told as widely as possible," Barsymes said. "If every official and every priest in every town lets the people know Makuran is behind the Thanasioi, they'll be less inclined to go over to the heretics."

"Some of them will, anyhow," Krispos said. "Others will have heard too many pronouncements from the pulpit and from the city square to take special notice of one more. No, don't look downhearted, esteemed sir. It's a good plan, and we'll use it. I just don't want anyone here expecting miracles."

"No matter what the priests and the officials say, what we must have is victory," Iakovitzes wrote. "If we can make the Thanasioi stop hurting us, people will see us as the stronger side and pretend they never had a heretical notion in all their born days. But if we lose, the rebels' power will grow regardless of who's behind them."

"Not so long till spring, either," Krispos said. "May the good god grant us the victory you rightly say we need." He turned to Barsymes. "Summon the most holy patriarch Oxeites to the palaces, if you please. What words can do, they shall do."

"As you say, Your Majesty." The vestiarios turned to go.

"Wait." Krispos stopped him in midstride. "Before you draft the note, why don't you fetch all three of us a jar of something sweet and strong? Today, by the good god, we've earned a taste of celebration."

"So we have, Your Majesty," Barsymes said with the hint of a smile that was as much as he allowed himself. "I'll attend to that directly."

The jar of wine became two and then three. Krispos knew he would pay for it in the morning. He'd been a young man when he discovered he couldn't come close to roistering with Anthimos. Older now, he had less capacity than in those days, and less practice at carousing, too. But every so often, once or twice a year, he still enjoyed letting himself go.

Barsymes, abstemious in pleasure as in most things, bowed his way out halfway down the second jar, presumably to write the letter ordering Oxeites to appear at the palace. Iakovitzes stayed and drank: he was always game for a debauch, and held his wine better than Krispos. The only sign he gave of its effects was that the words he wrote grew large and sprawling. Syntax and venom remained unchanged.

"Why don't you write like you're drunk?" Krispos asked some time after dinner; by then he'd forgotten what he'd eaten.

Iakovitzes replied, "You drink with your mouth and then try to talk through it; no wonder you've started mumbling. My hand hasn't touched a drop."

As the night hours advanced, one of the chamberlains sent to Iakovitzes' house. A couple of his muscular grooms came to the imperial residence to escort their master home. He patted them both and went off humming a dirty song.

The hallway swayed around Krispos as he walked back from his farewells to Iakovitzes at the entrance: he felt like a beamy ship trying to cope with quickly shifting winds. In such a storm, the imperial bedchamber seemed a safe harbor.

After he closed the door behind him, he needed a few seconds to notice Drina smiling at him from the bed. The night was chilly; she had the covers drawn up to her neck. "Barsymes is up to his old tricks again," Krispos said slowly, "and he thinks I'm up to mine."

"Why not, Your Majesty?" the serving maid said. "You never know till you try." She threw off the bedclothes. The smile was all she was wearing.

Even through the haze of wine, memory stabbed at Krispos: Dara had always been in the habit of sleeping without clothes. Drina was larger, softer, simpler—his wife the Empress had always been prickly as a hedgehog. As he seldom did these days, he let himself remember how much he missed her.

Watching Drina flip away the covers like that took him back almost a quarter of a century to the night he and Dara had joined on this very bed. Even after so long, a remembered thrill of fear ran through him—had Anthimos caught them, he would not be here now, or certain vital parts of him would not. And with the fear came the memory of how excited he'd been.

The memory of past excitement—and Drina there waiting for him— were enough to summon up at least the beginning of excitement now. He pulled off his robe and tugged at the red boots. "We'll see what happens," he said. "I make no promises: I've drunk a lot of wine."

"Whatever happens is all right, Your Majesty," Drina said, laughing. "Haven't I told you before that you men worry too much about these things?"

"Women have probably been saying that since the start of time," he said as he lay down beside her. "My guess is that the next man who believes it will be the first."

But oddly, knowing she had no great expectations helped him perform better than he'd expected himself. He didn't think she was pretending when she gasped and quivered under him; he could feel her secret place clench around him, again and again. Spurred by that, he, too, gasped and quivered a few seconds later.

"There—you see, Your Majesty?" Drina said triumphantly.

"I see," Krispos said. "This was already a good day; you've made it better still."

"I'm glad." Drina let out a squeak. "I'd better get up, or else I'll leave stains on the sheet for the washerwomen to giggle at."

"Do they do that?" Krispos asked. He fell asleep in the middle of her answer.

By THE TIME SPRING DREW NEAR IN ETCHMIADZIN, PHOSTIS knew every little winding street in town. He knew where the stonecutters had their shops, and the harnessmakers, and the bakers. He knew the street on which Laonikos and Siderina were busy dying—knew it and kept away from it.

He got more and more chances to wander where he would without Syagrios. Etchmiadzin's wall was too high to jump from without breaking his neck, its single gate too well guarded for him to think of bolting through it and away. And as the weather got better, Syagrios was more and more closeted with Livanios, planning the upcoming summer's campaign.

Phostis did his best to stay out of Livanios' way. The less he reminded the heresiarch of his presence, the less likely Livanios was to think of him, think of the danger he might represent, and put him out of the way.

Just wandering, however, was beginning to pall. When he'd had Syagrios at his elbow every hour of the day and night, he was sure just getting away from the ruffian for a little while would bring peace to his soul. And so it had . . . for a little while. But the taste of freedom, however small, served only to whet his appetite for more. He was no longer a glad explorer of Etchmiadzin's back alleys. He paced them more like a wildcat searching for an opening in its cage.

He hadn't found one yet. *Maybe around the next corner,* he told himself for the hundredth time. He went round the next corner—and almost walked into Olyvria, who was coming around it the other way.

They both sidestepped in the same direction, which meant they almost bumped into each other again. Olyvria started to laugh. "Get out of my way, you," she said, miming a push at his chest.

He made as if to stumble backward from it, then bowed extravagantly. "I humbly crave your pardon, my lady; I had no intention of disturbing your glorious progress," he cried. "I pray that you find it in your heart to forgive me!"

"We'll see about that," she said darkly.

By then they were both laughing. Phostis came back up to her and slipped an arm around her waist. She snuggled against him; her chin fit nicely on the top of his shoulder. He wanted to kiss her, but held back— she was still nervous about it. From her perspective, he supposed she had reason to be.

"What are you doing here?" they both asked in the same breath. That made them laugh again.

"Nothing much," Phostis answered. "Keeping away from mischief as best I can. What about you?"

Olyvria was carrying a canvas bag. She pulled a shoe out of it and held it up so close to Phostis' face that his eyes crossed. "I broke off the heel, see?" she said. "There's a little old Vaspurakaner cobbler down this street who does wonderful work. Why not? He's been doing it longer than both of us put together have been alive. Anyway, I was taking it to him."

"May I accompany you on your journey?" he asked grandly.

"I hoped you would," she answered, and dropped the wounded shoe back into the bag. Arm in arm, they walked down the little lane.

"Oh, this place," Phostis said when they reached the cobbler's shop. "Yes, I went by here." Over the door hung a boot carved from wood. To one side of it the wall bore the word SHOON in Videssian, to the other what was presumably the same message in the square, blocky characters the "princes" of Vaspurakan used to write their language.

Phostis peered through one of the narrow windows set into the front wall, Olyvria into the other. "I don't see anyone in there," she said, frowning.

"Let's find out." Phostis reached for the latch and pulled the door open. A bell rang. The rich smell of leather filled his nose. He motioned for Olyvria to precede him into the cobbler's shop. The door swung shut behind them.

"He's *not* here," Olyvria said disappointedly. All the candles and lamps were out; even with them burning, Phostis would have found the shop too dim. Awls and punches, little hammers and trimming knives hung in neat rows on pegs behind the cobbler's bench. No one came out from the back room to answer the bell.

"Maybe he was taken ill," Phostis said. Something else ran through his mind: *Or maybe he'd rather starve himself to death than work anymore.* But no, probably not. She'd said he was a Vaspurakaner, not a Thanasiot.

"Here's a scrap of parchment." Olyvria pounced on it. "See if you can find pen and ink. I'll leave him the shoe and a note." She clicked her tongue between her teeth. "I hope he reads Videssian. I'm not sure. Someone could easily have painted that word on the wall for him."

"Here." Phostis discovered a little clay jar of ink and a reed pen below the tools. "He reads something, anyhow, or I don't think he'd have these."

"That's true. Thanks." Olyvria scribbled a couple of lines, put her broken shoe on the bench, and secured the parchment to it with a long rawhide lace. "There. That should be all right. If he can't read Videssian, he ought to know someone who can. I hope he's well."

A donkey went by outside. Its hooves made little wet sucking noises as it lifted them from the mud one after another. It let out a braying squeal of discontent at being ridden in such dreadful conditions. "Ahh, quit your bellyaching," growled the man on its back, who was plainly used to its complaints. The donkey brayed again as it squelched past the cobbler's shop.

But for the donkey, everything was still save far off in the distance, where a dog barked. Olyvria took a small step toward the door. "I suppose I should get back," she said.

"Wait," Phostis said.

She raised a questioning eyebrow. He put his arms around her and bent his face down to hers. Before their lips touched, she pulled back a little and whispered, "Are you sure?" In the murky light, the pupils of her eyes were enormous.

He wondered how she meant that, but it could have only one answer. "Yes, I'm sure."

"Well, then." Now she moved forward to kiss him.

She hesitated once more, just for a heartbeat, when his hand closed on the firm softness of her breast. But then she molded herself against him. They sank down to the rammed-earth floor of the cobbler's shop together, fumbling at each other's garments.

It was the usual clumsy first time, made more frantic than usual by fear that someone—most likely the cobbler—would walk through the door at the most inopportune moment possible. "Hurry!" Olyvria gasped.

Phostis did his best to oblige. Afterward, because he'd rushed so, he wasn't sure he'd fully satisfied her. At the time, he didn't worry about it. His mouth slid from hers to her breasts and down the rounded slope of her belly. Her hand was urgent on him. She lay on her rumpled dress. A fold of it got distractingly between them when he scrambled above her. He leaned on one elbow to yank it out of the way. He kissed her again as he slid inside.

When he was through, he sat back on his haunches, enormously pleased with the entire world. Olyvria hissed, "Get dressed, you lackwit," which brought him back to himself in a hurry. They both dressed quickly, then spent another minute or so dusting off each other's clothes. Olyvria stirred the dirt of the floor around with her foot to cover up the marks they'd left. She looked Phostis over. 'Your elbow's dirty." She licked a fingertip with a catlike dab of her tongue and rubbed it clean.

He held the door for her. They both almost bounded out of the cobbler's shop. Once out on the street again, Phostis said, "Now what?"

"I just don't know," Olyvria answered after a small pause. "I have to think." Her voice was quiet, almost toneless, as if she'd left behind all her exuberance, all her mischief, with the broken shoe. "I didn't—quite—expect to do that."

Phostis hadn't seen her at a loss before; he didn't know what to make of it. "I didn't expect to, either." He knew his grin was foolish, but he couldn't help it. "I'm glad we did, though."

She glared at him. "Of course you are. Men always are." Then she softened, a little, and let her hand rest on his arm for a moment. "I'm not angry, not really. We have to see what happens later, that's all."

Phostis knew what he would like to have happen later, but also had a good notion that mentioning it straight out would make it less likely. Instead, he spoke obliquely. "The flesh is hard to ignore."

"Isn't it?" Olyvria glanced back at the cobbler's shop. "If we . . . well, if we do that again, we'll have to find a better place for it. My heart was in my mouth every second."

"Yes, I know. Mine, too." But they'd joined anyhow. Like Olyvria, Phostis saw he was going to have to do some hard thinking about that. By every Thanasiot standard, they'd just committed a good-sized sin. He didn't feel sinful, though. He felt relaxed and happy and ready to tackle anything the world threw at him.

Olyvria might have plucked that thought right out of his brain. She said, "You don't have to worry if you're with child till the moon spins through its phases."

That sobered him. He didn't have to worry about conceiving, not directly, but if Olyvria's belly started to swell, what would Livanios do? He might force a marriage on them, if that fit into his own schemes. But if it didn't . . . He might act like any outraged father, and beat Phostis within an inch of his life or even kill him. Or he might give him over to the clergy. The priests of the Thanasioi took a very dim view of carnal pleasures. Their punishments might make him wish Livanios had personally attended to the matter—and, to add humiliation to anguish, would have the vociferous approval of most of the townsfolk.

"Whatever happens, I'll take care of you," he said at last.

"How do you propose to manage that?" she asked with a woman's bitter practicality. "You can't even take care of yourself."

Phostis flinched. He knew she spoke the truth, but having his nose rubbed in it stung. As the Avtokrator's son, he'd never really had to worry about taking care of himself. He was taken care of, simply by virtue—or fault—of his birth. Here in Etchmiadzin, he was also taken care of: as a prisoner. The amount of freedom he'd lost was smaller than it seemed at first glance.

At Krispos' insistence, he'd studied logic. He saw only one possible conclusion. "I'll have to get out. If you like, I'll take you with me."

As soon as the words left his mouth, he knew he should have kept them in there. Having her laugh at him would be bad enough. Having her tell her father would be a thousand times worse.

She didn't laugh. She said, "Don't try to run. You'd just be caught, and then you'd never get another chance."

"But how can I stay here?" he demanded. "Even under the best of circumstances, I'm"—he hesitated, but finished the thought as he'd intended—"I'm not a Thanasiot, nor likely to become one. I know that now."

"I know what you mean," Olyvria answered unhappily. Phostis noted she had not said she agreed with him. She shook her head. "I'd better go." She hurried away.

He started to call after her, but in the end did not. He kicked at the gluey ground underfoot. In the romances, all your problems were supposed to be over when you made love to the beautiful girl. Olyvria was pretty enough, no doubt about that. But as far as Phostis could see, making love to her had only complicated his life further.

He wondered why the romances were so popular if they were also so far removed from actuality. That notion disturbed him; he thought the popular should match the real. Then he realized that simple paintings in bright colors might be easier to appreciate than more highly detailed ones—and honey was sweeter than the usual mix of flavors life presented.

None of which helped him in his present complexities. Here at last he'd found a woman who, he believed, wanted him only for himself, not because of the rank he held or the advantage she might gain from sleeping with him—and who was she? Not just the woman who had kidnapped him and who was the daughter of the rebel who held him prisoner. That would have been muddle enough by itself. But there was more. For all her fencing with him about it, he knew she took Thanasiot principles seriously—a lot more seriously than Livanios, if Phostis was any judge. And Thanasios, to put it mildly, had not thought well of the flesh.

Phostis still distrusted his own flesh, too. But he was coming to the sometimes reluctant conclusion that it was part of what made him himself, not just an unfortunate adjunct to his spirit that ought to be discarded as quickly as possible.

Almost as vividly as if he were in her arms again, he remembered the feel of Olyvria's warm, sweet body pressed against him. Sometimes he was not so reluctant about that conclusion, too. He knew he wanted her again, when and as he got the chance.

Digenis would not have approved. He knew that, too. Now, though, he hadn't talked with the fiery priest, or come under the spell of his words, for several months. And he'd seen far more of the way the Thanasioi ran their lives than he had when he'd listened to Digenis back in Videssos the city. Much of it he still found admirable—much of it, but a long way from all. Reality had a way of intruding on Digenis' bright word-pictures, no less than on those of the romancers.

If Olyvria was heading back toward the fortress of Etchmiadzin, Phostis decided he ought to stay away awhile longer, so as not to make anyone there draw a connection between them. It was a nice calculation. If he just followed her back, he might arouse suspicion. If he stayed away too long, Syagrios would track him like hound after hare. He didn't want Syagrios to have to do that; it would anger the ruffian, and Phostis cherished the limited freedom he'd so slowly regained.

He had a few coins in his belt pouch, winnings at the battle game. He spent a silver piece on a leg of roasted fowl and a hard roll, then carefully put the coppers from his change back into the pouch. He'd learned about haggling: it was what you did when you were short of money. He'd got good at it. Despite Krispos' firm hand, he'd never been short of money before he ended up in Etchmiadzin.

He was chewing on the roll when Artapan strode by. The wizard, full of his own affairs, didn't notice him. Phostis decided to try to find out where he was going in such a hurry. Ever since he'd realized Artapan was from Makuran, he'd wondered just how the mage fit into Livanios' plans . . . or perhaps how Livanios fit into Artapan's plans. Maybe now he could learn.

He'd followed the wizard for half a furlong before he realized he was liable to get in trouble if Artapan did discover him dogging his tracks. He tried to be sneakier, keeping people and, once, a donkey cart between the mage and him, dodging from doorway to doorway.

After another couple of minutes, he concluded he could do just about anything short of walking up, tapping Artapan on the shoulder, and asking him for the time of day. Artapan plainly had something on his mind. He looked neither to the left nor to the right, and marched down the muddy streets of Etchmiadzin as if they were cobblestoned boulevards.

The wizard rapped on the door of a house separated from its neighbors by dank, narrow alleys. After a moment, he went inside. Phostis ducked into one of the alleys. He promptly regretted it: someone was in the habit of dumping slops there. The stink almost made him cough. He jammed a sleeve into his mouth and breathed hard through his nose till the spasm passed.

But he did not leave. A little slit window let him hear what was going on inside. He wouldn't have put a window there, but maybe it had been made before anyone started emptying chamber pots in the alley.

Artapan was saying, "How fare you today, supremely holy Tzepeas?"

The answer came in a dragging whisper: "Soon I shall be free. Skotos and his entrapping world cling hard to me; already most who abandon what is falsely called nourishment for as long as I have are on the journey behind the sun. But still I remain wrapped in the flesh that disfigures the soul."

What do you want with one who has starved himself to the point of death? Phostis almost shouted it at the Makuraner wizard. *If he's chosen to do it, let him alone with his choice.*

"You want, then, to leave this world?" Artapan's accented voice held wonder. Phostis wondered about that: the Four Prophets had their holy ascetics, too. "What will you find, do you think?"

"Light!" Just for a word, Tzepeas' voice came strong and clear, as if he were a well-fed man rather than a shivering bag of bones. As he continued, it faded again. "I shall be part of Phos' eternal light. Too long have I lingered in this sin-filled place."

"Would you seek help in leaving it?" Artapan had moved while Tzepeas was talking. Now he sounded as if he was right beside the starving Thanasiot. "I don't know," Tzepeas said. "Is it permitted?"

"Of course," the wizard answered smoothly. "But a moment and you shall meet your good god face-to-face."

"*My* good god?" Tzepeas said indignantly. "He is *the* good god, the lord with the great and good mind. He—" The zealot's voice, which had risen again, suddenly broke off. Phostis heard a couple of very faint thumps, as if a man with no muscles left was trying to struggle against someone far stronger than he.

The thumps soon ceased. Artapan began a soft chant, partly in the Makuraner tongue—which Phostis did not understand—and partly in Videssian. Phostis knew he was missing some of what the mage said, but what he heard was quite enough: unless he'd gone completely mad, he could only conclude Artapan was using Tzepeas' death energy to further his own sorceries.

Phostis' stomach lurched harder than it ever had while sailing on the Videssian Sea. He sickly wondered how many starving Thanasioi hadn't finished the course they set out to travel, but were instead shoved from it by the Makuraner wizard for his own purposes. The one was bad enough: the other struck Phostis as altogether abominable. And who would ever know?

Artapan came out of the house. Phostis flattened himself against the wall. The wizard walked on by. He wasn't quite rubbing his hands with glee, but he gave that impression. Again, he had no time to look around for details as small as Phostis.

Phostis waited until he was sure Artapan was gone, then cautiously emerged from the alley. "What do I do now?" he said out loud. His first thought was to run to Livanios with the story as fast as his legs would carry him. A version of the tale he'd tell formed in his mind: *After I'd had your daughter, I found out your pet wizard was going around killing devout Thanasioi before they could die on their own.* He shook his head. Like a lot of first thoughts, that one needed some work.

All right, suppose he managed not to mention Olyvria and also managed to convince Livanios he was telling the truth about Artapan. What then? How much good would that do him? If Livanios didn't know what the mage was up to, maybe quite a lot. But what if he did?

In that case, the only thing Phostis saw in his own future was a lot more trouble—something he'd not imagined possible when he woke up after Olyvria drugged him. And he could not tell whether Livanios knew or not.

It came down to the question he'd been asking himself ever since he learned Artapan's name: was Livanios the wizard's puppet, or the other way round? He didn't know the answer to that, either, or how to find out.

From Olyvria, he thought. But even she might well not know for certain. She'd know what her father thought, but that might not be what was so. Videssian history was littered with men who'd thought themselves in charge—until the worlds they'd made crashed down around them. Anthimos had been sure he held a firm grip on the Empire—until Krispos took it away from him.

And so, when Phostis got back to the fortress, he did not go looking for Livanios. Instead, he headed over to the corner where, as usual, several men gathered around a couple of players hunched over the game board.

The soldiers moved away from him, wrinkling their noses. One of them said, "You may have been born a toff, friend, but you smell like you've been wading in shit."

Phostis remembered the stinking alleyway where he'd stood. He should have done a better job of cleaning his shoes after he came out. Then he thought of what Artapan had done in the house by the alleyway. How was he supposed to clean that from his memory?

He looked at the soldier. "Maybe I have," he said.

Chapter IX

WALL, ROOFS, STREETS, NEW LEAVES—ALL GLISTENED WITH rain under the bright sun. It made them seem to Krispos brighter and more vivid than they really were, as if the shower—or perhaps the season—had washed the whole world clean.

The clouds that had dropped the rain on Videssos the city were now just small, gray, fluffy lumps diminishing toward the east. The rest of the sky was the glorious blue the enamelmakers kept trying—and failing—to match with glass paste.

With the wary eye of one who has had to watch the weather for the sake of his crops, Krispos looked not east at the receding rain clouds but west, whence new weather would come. He tasted the breeze between his tongue and the roof of his mouth. That it came straight off the sea gave it a salt tang he'd not had to worry about in his peasant days, but he'd learned to allow for that. He sucked in another breath, tasting that one, too.

When at last he spat it out, he'd made up his mind. "Spring is really here," he declared.

"Your Majesty has in the past been remarkably accurate with such predictions," Barsymes said, as close as he ever came to alluding to Krispos' decidedly unimperial birth.

"It matters more this year than most," Krispos said, "for as soon as I can be sure—or at least can expect—the roads will stay dry, I have to move against the Thanasioi. The less chance they have of getting loose and raiding, the better off the westlands and the whole Empire will be."

"The city has stayed quiet since Midwinter's Day, for which Phos be praised."

"Aye." Whenever Krispos prayed, he made a point of reminding the good god how grateful he was for that. He still did not completely trust the calm that had prevailed through winter and now up to the borderland of spring: he kept wondering whether he was walking on a thin crust of ice over freezing water—the images from Skotos' hell seemed particularly fitting. If the crust ever broke, he might be dragged down to doom. But so far it had held.

"I believe Your Majesty handled the matter of the priest Digenis with as much discretion as was practicable," the vestiarios said.

"Just letting him go out like a guttering taper, you mean? All he wanted to do was raise a ruction. Smothering his end in silence is the best revenge on him; if Phos is kind, the chroniclers will forget his name as the people have—so far—forgotten to rally to the cause he preached."

Barsymes looked at him out of the corners of his eyes that had seen so much. "And when you fare forth on campaign, Your Majesty, will you then leave Videssos the city ungarrisoned?"

"Oh, of course," Krispos answered, and laughed to make sure his vestiarios knew he was not in earnest. "Wouldn't that be lovely, beating the Thanasioi in the field and coming back to find my capital closed against me? It won't happen, not if I can find any way around it."

"Whom shall you name to command the city garrison?" Barsymes asked.

"Do you know, esteemed sir, I was thinking of giving the job to Evripos." Krispos spoke in a deliberately neutral tone. If Barsymes had anything to say against the appointment of his middle son, he didn't want to intimidate the eunuch into keeping his mouth shut.

Barsymes tasted the appointment with the same sort of thoughtful attention Krispos had given to the weather. After a similar pause for that consideration, the vestiarios answered, "That may serve very nicely, Your Majesty. By all accounts, the young Majesty acquitted himself well in the westlands."

"He did," Krispos agreed. "Not only that, soldiers followed where he led, which is a magic that can't be taught. I'll also leave behind some steady officer who can try to keep him from doing anything too rash if the need arises."

"That's sensible," Barsymes replied, saying by not saying that he would have reckoned Krispos daft for doing anything else. "It will be valuable experience for the young Majesty, especially if—if other matters do not eventuate as we would desire."

"Phostis still lives," Krispos said suddenly. "Zaidas' sorcery continues to confirm that, and he's fairly sure Phostis is in Etchmiadzin, where the rebels seem to have their headquarters. He's made real headway in penetrating the masking sorcery since we realized it springs from Makuran." His briefly kindled enthusiasm faded fast. "Of course, he has no way of telling what Phostis believes these days."

There lay the nut of it, as was Krispos' way, in one sentence. The Avtokrator shook his head. Phostis was so young; who could say what latest enthusiasm he'd seized on? At that same age, Krispos knew he'd had a good core of solid sense. But at just past twenty, he'd been a peasant still, and he could imagine no stronger dose of reality than that. Phostis had grown up in the palaces, where flights of fancy were far more easily sustained. And Phostis had always taken pleasure in going dead against whatever Krispos had in mind.

"What of Katakolon?" Barsymes asked.

"I'll take him with me—I'll need one spatharios, at any rate," Krispos said. "He did tolerably well in the westlands himself, and rather better than that during the Midwinter's Day riots. One thing these past few months have taught me: all my sons need such training in command as I can give them. Counting on Phos' mercy instead of providing for the times to come is foolish and wasteful."

"Few have accused Your Majesty of harboring those traits—none truthfully."

"For which, believe me, you have my thanks," Krispos said. "Find Evripos for me, would you? I've not yet told him what I have in mind."

"Of course, Your Majesty." Barsymes went back inside the imperial residence. Krispos stood and enjoyed the sunshine. The cherry trees around the residence were putting on leaves; soon, for a few glorious weeks, they'd be a riot of sweet pink and white blossoms. Krispos' thoughts drifted away from them and back toward raising troops, moving troops, supplying troops . . .

He sighed. Being Avtokrator meant having to worry about things you'd rather ignore. He wondered if the rebels he'd put down ever realized how much work the job of ruling the Empire really was. He certainly hadn't, back when he took it away from Anthimos.

If I thought Livanios wouldn't botch things, I ought to give him the crown and let him see how he likes it, he thought angrily. But he knew that would never happen: the only way Livanios would take the crown from him was by prying it out of his dead fingers.

"What is it, Father?" Evripos asked, coming up in Barsymes' wake. The wariness in his voice was different from what Krispos was used to hearing from Phostis. Phostis and he simply disagreed every chance they got. Evripos resented being born second; it made his opinions not worth serious disagreement.

Or it had made them so. Now Krispos explained what he had in mind for his son. "This is serious business," he emphasized. "If real trouble does come, I won't want you throwing out orders at random. That's why I'll leave a steady captain with you. I expect you to heed his advice on matters military."

Evripos had puffed out his chest with pride at the trust Krispos placed in him. Now he said, "But what if I think he's wrong, Father?"

Obey him anyhow, Krispos started to say. But the words did not pass his lips. He remembered when Petronas had maneuvered him into the position of vestiarios for Anthimos. The then-Avtokrator's uncle had made it very clear that he expected nothing but obedience to him from Krispos. He remembered asking Petronas a question very similar to the one he'd just heard from Evripos.

"You have command," he said slowly. "If you think your advisor is wrong, you'd better do what you reckon right. But you have to remember, son, that with command comes responsibility. If you choose to go against the officer I give you and your course goes wrong, you will answer to me. Do you understand?"

"Aye, Father, I do. You're telling me I'd better be sure—and even if I am sure, I'd better be right. Is that the meat of it?"

"That's it exactly," Krispos agreed. "I'm not putting you in this place as part of a game, Evripos. The post is not only real but also important. A mistake would be important, too, in how much damage it could do. So if you go off on your own, against the advice of a man older and wiser than you are, what you do had better not turn out badly, for your sake and the Empire's both."

With the prickliness of youth, Evripos bristled like a hedgehog. "How do you know this officer you'll appoint for me will be smarter than I am?"

"I didn't say that. You're as smart as you'll ever be, son, and I have no reason to doubt that's very smart indeed. But you're not as wise as you're going to be, say, twenty years from now. Wisdom comes from using the wits you have to think on what's happened to you during your life, and you haven't lived long enough yet to have stored up much of it."

Evripos looked eloquently unconvinced. Krispos didn't blame him; at Evripos' age, he hadn't believed experience mattered, either. Now that he had a good deal of it, he was sure he'd been wrong before—but the only way for Evripos to come to the same conclusion was with the slow passage of the years. He couldn't afford to wait for that.

His middle son said, "Suppose this officer you name suggests a course I think is wrong, but I go along with it for fear of what you've just said. And suppose it does turn out to be the wrong course. What then, Father?"

"Maybe you should be pleading your case in the courts, not commanding men in the field," Krispos said. But the question was too much to the point to be answered with a sour joke. Slowly, the Avtokrator went on, "If I put you in the post, you will be the commander. When the time comes, making the judgment will be up to you. That's the hardest burden anyone can lay on a man. If you don't care to bear it, speak up now."

"Oh, I'll bear it, Father. I just wanted to be sure I understood what you were asking of me," Evripos said.

"Good," Krispos said. "I'll give you one piece of advice and one only— I know how you won't much care to listen. It's just this: if you have to decide, do it firmly. No matter how much doubt, no matter how much fear and trembling you feel, don't let it show. Half the business of leading people is just keeping up a solid front."

"That may be worth remembering," Evripos said, as big a concession as Krispos knew he was likely to get. His son asked, "What will Katakolon be doing while I'm here in the city?"

"He'll go the westlands as my spatharios. Another campaign will do him good, I think."

"Ah." If Evripos wanted to take issue with that, he didn't find any way to manage it. After a pause a tiny bit longer than a more experienced man would have given, he nodded brusquely and changed the subject. "I hope I'll serve as you'd have me do, Father."

"I hope you will, too. I don't see any reason why you shouldn't. If the lord with the great and good mind hears my prayers, you'll have a quiet time of it. I don't really *want* you to see action here; you'd better understand that. The less fighting there is, the happier I'll be."

"Then why take the army out?" Evripos asked.

Krispos sighed. "Because sometimes it's needful, as you know very well.

If I don't go to the fighting this summer, it will come to me. Given that choice, I'd sooner do it on my own terms, or as nearly as I can."

"Aye, that makes sense," Evripos said after a moment's thought. "Sometimes the world won't let you have things all as you'd like them."

He was probably speaking from bitterness at not being first in line for the throne. Nonetheless, Krispos was moved to reach out and set a hand on his shoulder. "That's an important truth, son. You'd do well to remember it." It was, he thought, a truth Phostis hadn't fully grasped—but then Phostis, as firstborn, hadn't had the need. Each son was so different from the other two . . . "Where's Katakolon? Do you know?"

Evripos pointed. "One of the rooms down that hallway: second or third on the left, I think."

"Thanks." Later, Krispos realized he hadn't asked what his youngest son was doing. If Evripos knew, he kept his mouth shut, a useful ploy he might well have picked up from his father. Krispos walked down the hallway. The second chamber on the left, a sewing room for the serving women, was empty.

The door to the third room on the left was closed. Krispos worked the latch. He saw a tangle of bare arms and legs, heard a couple of horrified squawks, and shut the door again in a hurry. He stood chuckling in the hall until Katakolon, his robe rumpled and his face red, came out a couple of minutes later.

He let Katakolon steer him down the corridor, and was anything but surprised to hear the door open and close behind him. He didn't look back, but started to laugh. Katakolon gave him a dirty look. "What's so funny?"

"You are," Krispos answered. "I do apologize for interrupting."

Katakolon's glare got blacker, but he seemed confused as well as annoyed. "Is that all you're going to say?"

"Yes, I think so. After all, it's nothing I haven't seen before. Remember, I was Anthimos' vestiarios." He decided not to go into detail about Anthimos' orgies. Katakolon was too likely to try imitating them.

Looking at his youngest son's face, Krispos had all he could do to keep from laughing again. Katakolon was obviously having heavy going imagining his rather paunchy, gray-bearded father reveling with an Avtokrator who, even after a generation, remained a byword for debauchery of all sorts.

Krispos patted his son on the back. "You have to bear in mind, lad, that once upon a time I wasn't a creaking elder. I had the same yen for good wine and bad women as any other young man."

"Yes, Father," Katakolon said, but not as if he believed it.

Sighing, Krispos said, "If you have too much trouble picturing me with a zest for life, try to imagine Iakovitzes, say, as a young man. The exercise will do your wits good."

He gave Katakolon credit: the youth visibly did try. After a few seconds, he whistled. "He'd have been something, wouldn't he?"

"Oh, he was," Krispos said. "He's still something, come to that"

All at once, he wondered if Iakovitzes had ever tried his blandishments on Katakolon. He didn't think the old lecher would have got anywhere; like his other two sons, his youngest seemed interested only in women. If Iakovitzes had ever tried to seduce Katakolon or one of the other boys, they'd never brought Krispos the tale.

"Now let me tell you why I interrupted you at a tender moment—" Krispos explained what he had in mind for the most junior Avtokrator.

"Of course, Father. I'll come with you, and help as I can," Katakolon said when he was done; of the three boys, he was the most tractable. Even the stubborn streak he shared with his brothers and Krispos was in him good-natured. "I don't expect I'll be busy every moment, and some of the provincial lasses last summer were tastier than I'd have expected away from the capital. When do we start out?"

"As soon as the roads are dry." Dry himself, Krispos added, "You won't be devastating the local girls by leaving quite yet."

"All right," Katakolon said. "In that case, if you'll excuse me—" He started down the hall, more purpose in his stride than on any mission for his father. Krispos wondered if he'd burned that hot at seventeen. He probably had, but he had almost as much trouble believing it as Katakolon did in placing him at one of Anthimos' revels.

LIVANIOS ADDRESSED HIS ASSEMBLED FIGHTERS: "SOON WE FARE forth, both to fight and to advance along the gleaming path. We shall not go alone. By the lord with the great and good mind, I swear our trouble will not be raising men but rather making sure we are not overwhelmed by those who would join us. We shall spread across the countryside like a fire through grassland; no one and nothing can hold us back."

The men cheered. By their look, a good many of them were herders from the westlands' central plateau: lean, weather-beaten, sunbaked men intimately acquainted with grass fires. Now they carried javelins in their hands, not staves. They were not the best-disciplined troops in the world, but fanaticism went a long way toward making up for sloppy formations.

Phostis cheered when everyone else did. Standing there silent and glum would have got him noticed, and not in a way he wanted. He was trying to cultivate invisibility, the way a farmer cultivated radishes. He wished Livanios would forget he existed.

The heresiarch was in full spate: "The leeches who live in Videssos the city think they can suck our life's blood forever. We'll show them they're wrong, by the good god, and if the gleaming path leads through the smoking ruins of the palaces built from poor men's blood, why then, it does."

More cheers. Phostis didn't feel quite such a hypocrite in joining these: the ostentatious wealth the capital held was what had made him flirt with the doctrines of the Thanasioi in the first place. But Livanios' speech was a harangue and nothing more. If any Avtokrator of recent generations was sensitive to the peasant's plight, it was Krispos. Phostis was sick of hearing how his father had been taxed off his land, but he knew the experience made Krispos want not to visit it on anyone else.

"We'll hang up the fat ecclesiastics by their thumbs, too," Livanios shouted. "Whatever gold the Emperors don't get, the clerics do. Has Phos the need for fancy houses?"

"No!" the men roared back, and Phostis with them. In spite of everything, he still had some sympathy for what Thanasios had preached. He wondered if Livanios could truly say the same. And he wondered still more just how much hold Artapan had on the rebel leader. He was no closer to knowing that for certain than he had been on the day when he and Olyvria first became lovers.

Whenever she crossed his mind, his blood ran hotter. Digenis would have scolded him, or more likely given up on him as an incorrigible sinner and sensualist. He didn't care. He wanted her more with every passing day—and he knew she also wanted him.

They'd managed to join twice more since that first time: once late at night up in his little cell while the guard snored down the hall and once in a quiet corridor carved into the stone beneath the keep. Both couplings were almost as hurried and frantic as the first had been; neither was what Phostis had in mind when he thought of making love. But they inflamed him and Olyvria for more.

Was what he felt the love of which the romancers sang? He knew little firsthand of love; around the palaces, seduction and hedonism were more often on display. His own father and mother seemed to have got on well, but he'd still been a boy when Dara died. Zaidas and Aulissa were called a love match, but the wizard—aside from being Krispos' crony, which of itself made him suspect—had to be close to forty: could an old man really be in love?

Phostis couldn't tell if he was in love himself. All he knew was that he missed Olyvria desperately, that when they were apart every moment dragged as if it were an hour, that every stolen hour together somehow flashed by like a moment.

Lost in his own thoughts, he missed Livanios' last few sentences. They brought loud cheers from the assembled soldiers. Phostis cheered, too, as he had all through the heresiarch's speech.

Then one of the fighters who knew who he was turned round and slapped him on the back. "So you're going to fight with us for the gleaming path, are you, friend?" the fellow boomed. His grin had almost as many gaps as Syagrios'.

"I'm going to what?" Phostis said foolishly. It wasn't that he didn't believe his ears: more that he didn't want to.

"Sure—like Livanios said just now." The soldier wrinkled his brow, trying to recall his chief's exact words. "Take up the blade against maternalism—something like that, anyways."

"Materialism," Phostis corrected before he wondered why he bothered.

"Yeah, that's it," the soldier said happily. "Thank you, friend. By the good god, I'm right glad the Emperor's son's taken up with righteousness."

Moving as if in a daze, Phostis made his way toward the citadel. Fighters who recognized him kept coming up and congratulating him on taking up arms for the Thanasiot cause. By the time he got inside, he was sore and bruised, while his wits had taken a worse pummeling than his back.

Livanios was using his name to raise the spirits of the Thanasiot warriors: so much was clear. But life in the palace, while it left Phostis ignorant of love, made him look beneath the surface of machinations with as little effort as he used to breathe.

Not only would his name spur on the followers of the gleaming path, it would also dismay those who clove to his father. And if he fought alongside the Thanasioi, he might never be reconciled with Krispos.

Further, Livanios might arrange a hero's death for him. That would embarrass the Avtokrator as much as having him alive and fighting, and would hurt Krispos a good deal more. And it would serve Livanios' ends very well indeed.

Syagrios found Phostis. Phostis might have guessed the ruffian would come looking for him. From the nasty grin on Syagrios' face, he'd known about Livanios' scheme before the heresiarch announced it to his men. In fact, Phostis thought with the taut nerves of a man who genuinely has been persecuted, Syagrios might well have come up with it himself.

"So you're going to be a man before your mother, are you, stripling?" he said, making cut-and-thrust motions right in front of Phostis' face. "Go out there and make the gleaming path proud of you, boy."

"I'll do what I can." Phostis was aware of the ambiguity, but let it lay. He did not want to hear Syagrios speak of his mother. He wanted to smash the ruffian for presuming to speak of her. Only a well-founded apprehension that Syagrios would smash him instead kept him from trying it.

That was yet another thing the romances didn't talk about. Their heroes always beat the villains just because they were heroes. No writer of romances, Phostis was certain, had ever met Syagrios. For that matter, both sides here thought they were heroes and their foes villains. *I swear by the good god I'll never read another romance again as long as I live,* Phostis thought.

Syagrios said, "I don't know what you know about weapons, but whatever it is, you better practice it. Whoever you fight ain't gonna care that you're the Avtokrator's brat."

"I suppose not," Phostis said in a hollow voice that set Syagrios laughing anew. He'd actually had some training; his father had thought he'd find it useful. He didn't mention it. The more hopeless a dub everyone took him for, the less attention people would pay him.

He went up the black spiral stairway to his little chamber. When he opened the door, his mouth fell open in astonishment: Olyvria waited inside. He was not too surprised, however, to shut the door behind him as fast as he could. "What are you doing here?" he demanded. "Do you want to get us both caught?"

She grinned at him. "What could be safer?" she whispered back. "Everyone in the keep was down in the courtyard listening to my father."

Phostis wanted to rush to her and take her in his arms, but that brought him up short. "Yes, and do you know what your father said?" he whispered, and went on to explain exactly what Livanios had announced.

"Oh, no," Olyvria said, still in a tiny voice. "He wants you dead, then. I prayed he wouldn't."

"That's what I think, too," Phostis agreed bitterly. "But what can I do about it?"

"I don't know." Olyvria reached out to him. He hurried over to her. Her touch made him, if not forget everything else, then at least reckon it unimportant for as long as he held her. But he remembered how careful they had to be even while her thighs clasped his flanks; what should have been sighs of delight came from both of them as tiny hisses.

As they'd grown used to doing, they set their clothes to rights as fast as they could when they were through. Not for them the pleasure of lying lazily by each other afterward. "How will we get you out of here?" Phostis whispered. Before Olyvria could say anything, he found the answer for himself: "I'll go downstairs. Whoever's out there—probably Syagrios—will follow me. Once we're gone, you can come down, too."

Olyvria nodded. "Yes, that's very good. It should work; few of the rooms in this hallway have people in them, so I'm not likely to be seen till I'm safely down." She looked at him with some of her old calculation. He liked the soft looks he usually got from her these days better. But she said, "You wouldn't have found a plan so fast when we first brought you here."

"Maybe not," he admitted. "I've had to take care of a good many things I wasn't in the habit of doing for myself." He touched the very tip of her breast through her tunic, just for a moment. "Some of them I like better than others."

"You don't mean I'm your first?" That thought almost startled her into raising her voice; he made an alarmed gesture. But she was already shaking her head. "No, I couldn't have been."

"No, of course not," he said. "You're the first who matters, though."

She leaned forward and brushed her lips against his. "That's a sweet thing to say. It must not have been easy for you, growing up as you did."

He shrugged. He supposed the problem was that he just thought too much. Evripos and especially Katakolon seemed to have had no trouble enjoying themselves immensely. But all that was by the way. He got to his feet. "I'll leave you now. Listen to make sure everything's quiet before you come out." He took a step toward the door, stopped, then turned back to Olyvria. "I love you."

Her arched eyebrows lifted. "You hadn't said that before. I love you—but then you know I must, or I wouldn't be here in spite of my father."

"Yes." Phostis thought he knew that, but he'd been raised to see plots, so sometimes he found them even when they weren't there. Here, though, he had to—and wanted to—take the chance.

He stepped into the hallway. Sure enough, there sat Syagrios. The ruffian leered at him. "So you found out you can't hide in there, did you? Now what are you going to do, head down and celebrate that you got turned into a soldier?"

"As a matter of fact, yes," Phostis answered. He had the somber satisfaction of seeing Syagrios' jaw sag. After lighting a taper to keep from killing

himself on the dark stairway, he headed down toward the ground floor of
the keep. Syagrios muttered under his breath but followed. Phostis had all
he could do to keep from whistling on the stairs: letting Syagrios know
he'd put one over on him wouldn't do.

OUTSIDE THE SOUTHERN END OF THE GREAT DOUBLE WALL
that warded the landward side of Videssos the city lay a broad stretch of
meadow on which the Empire's cavalry practiced their maneuvers. Fresh
new grass poked through the mud and the dead grayish remains of last
year's growth as Krispos came out to watch his soldiers exercise.

"Don't be too hard on them too soon, Your Majesty," Sarkis urged.
"They're still ragged from being cooped up through the winter."

"I know that—we have done this business a few times before," Krispos
answered, amiably enough. "But we'll go on campaign as soon as weather
and supplies allow, and if they're still ragged then, it will cost lives and
maybe battles."

"They won't be." Sarkis put grim promise into his voice. Krispos
smiled; he'd hoped to hear that note.

A company rode hard toward upright bales of hay that simulated an
enemy. They drew up eighty or ninety yards away, plied the targets with
arrows as rapidly as they could draw bow, and then, at an officer's command, yanked out their swords and charged the imaginary foe with fierce
and sanguinary roars.

The iron blades glittering in the bright sun made a fine martial spectacle. Nonetheless, Krispos turned to Sarkis and remarked, "This whole
business of war would be a lot easier if the Thanasioi didn't fight back any
harder than those bales."

Sarkis' doughy face twitched in a grin. "Isn't it the truth, Your Majesty?
Every general wants every campaign to be a walkover, but you can make
yourself a reputation that will live forever if you get one of those in a lifetime. The trouble is, you see, the chap on the other side wants his
walkover, too, and doesn't much care to cooperate in yours. Rude and in-
considerate of him, if you ask me."

"At the very least," Krispos agreed. After the company of archers re-
assembled well beyond the hay bales, another unit approached and pelted
the targets with javelins. Farther away, a regiment split in two to get in
some more realistic mounted swordwork. They tried not to hurt one another in practices like that, but Krispos knew the healers would have some
extra work tonight.

"Their spirits seem as high as you could hope for," Sarkis said judiciously. "No hesitation about going out for another crack at the heretics, anyhow." He used the word with no irony whatever, though his own beliefs were anything but orthodox.

Krispos didn't twit him about it, not today. After some thought, he'd figured out the difference between the Vaspurakaners' heterodoxy and that of the Thanasioi. The "princes" might not want any part of that version of the faith that emanated from Videssos the city, but they also weren't interested in imposing their version on Videssos the city. Krispos could live with that.

He said, "Where do you suppose the Thanasioi will pop up this season?"

"Wherever they can make the worst nuisances of themselves," Sarkis answered at once. "Livanios proved how dangerous he is last year. He won't hurt us in a small way if he has the chance to hurt us in a big one."

Since that accorded all too well with Krispos' view of the situation, he only grunted by way of reply. Not far away, a youngster in gilded chain mail rode up to the hay-bale targets and flung light spears at them. Katakolon's aim wasn't bad, but could have been better.

Krispos cupped his hands to his mouth and yelled, "Everybody knows you can use your lance, son, but you've got to get the javelin down, too!"

Katakolon's head whipped around. He spotted his father and stuck out his tongue at him. Ribald howls rose from the horsemen who heard. Sarkis' chuckle held dry amusement. "You'll give him a reputation that way. I suppose it's what you have in mind."

"As a matter of fact, yes. If you're a lecher at my age, you're a laughingstock, but young men pride themselves on how hard they can go—so to speak."

"So to speak, indeed." Sarkis chuckled again, even more dryly than before. Then he sighed. "We ought to get some practice in ourselves. Battles take funny turns sometimes."

"So we should." Krispos sighed, too. "The good god knows I'll be sore for a long time after I start working, though. I begin to see I won't be able to go out on a campaign forever."

"You?" Sarkis ran a hand along his own corpulent frame. "Your Majesty, you're still svelte. I've put almost another me inside my mail here."

Krispos made an imperial decision. "I'll start exercising—tomorrow." The trouble with being Avtokrator was that none of the demands of the job went away when you concentrated on any one thing. You had to plug leaks everywhere at once, or some of them would get beyond the plugging stage while you weren't watching.

He went back to the palaces to make sure he didn't fall too far behind on matters of trade and commerce. He was examining customs reports from Prista, the imperial outpost on the northern shore of the Videssian Sea, when someone tapped on the door to the study. He glanced up, expecting to see Barsymes or another of the chamberlains. But it was none of them—it was Drina.

His frown was almost a scowl. She should have known better than to bother him while he was working. "Yes?" he said curtly.

Drina looked more than nervous—she looked frightened. She dropped to her knees and then to her belly in a full proskynesis. Krispos took a couple of seconds to wonder about the propriety of having the woman who warmed his bed prostrate herself before him. But by the time he decided she needn't bother, she was already rising. But she kept her eyes to the floor, her voice was small and her stammer large as she began, "May it p-please Your Majesty—"

With that start, it probably wouldn't. Krispos almost said as much. The only thing that held him back was a strong suspicion she'd flee if he pressed her too hard. Since she'd braved bearding him at his work, whatever she had on her mind was important to her. Trying at least to sound neutral, he asked, "What's troubling you, Drina?"

"Your Majesty, I'm pregnant," she blurted.

He opened his mouth to answer her, but no words came out. After a little while, he realized she didn't need to keep looking at the back of his throat. He needed two tries to close his mouth, but managed in the end. "You're telling me it's mine?" he got out at last.

Drina nodded. "Your Majesty, I didn't—I mean, I haven't—so it must—" She spread her hands, as if that would help her explain better than her tongue, which seemed as fumbling as Krispos'.

"Well, well," he said, and then again, because it let him make noise without making sense, "Well, well." Another pause and he produced a coherent sentence, then a second one: "I didn't expect that to happen. If it was the night I think it was, I didn't expect anything to happen."

"People never do, Your Majesty." Drina tried a wary smile, but still looked ready to run away. "But it does happen, or there wouldn't be any more people after a while."

The Thanasioi would like that, he thought. He shook his head. Drina was too much a creature of her body and her urges ever to make a Thanasiot, just as he was himself. "An imperial bastard," he said, more to himself than to her.

"Is it your first, Your Majesty?" she asked. Now fear and a peculiar sort of pride warred in her voice. She held her chin a little higher.

"The first time I've fathered a child since Dara died, you mean? No," Krispos said. "It happened twice before, as a matter of fact, but once the mother miscarried and the other time the babe lived but a couple of days. Phos' choice, not mine, if that's what you're wondering. Both were years ago; I thought my seed had gone cold. I hope your luck will be better."

Hearing that, she let her face open up like a flower suddenly touched by the sun. "Oh, thank you, Your Majesty!" she breathed.

"Neither you nor the child will ever want," Krispos promised. "If you don't know I care for my own, you don't know me." For the past twenty years, the whole Empire had been his own. Maybe that was why he worried so much about every detail of its life.

"Everyone knows Your Majesty is kind and generous." Drina's smile got wider still.

"Everyone doesn't know any such thing," he answered sharply. "So you don't misunderstand, here are two things I won't do: number one, I won't marry you. I won't let this babe disturb the succession if it turns out to be a boy. Trying to get me to break my word about that will be the fastest way you can think of to make me angry. Do you have that?"

"Yes," she whispered. The smile flickered.

"I'm sorry to speak so plain to you, but I want to leave you in no doubt about these matters," Krispos said. "Here is the second thing: if you have a swarm of relatives who descend on me looking for jobs with no work for high pay, they'll go home to wherever they came from with stripes on their backs. I already told you I won't stint on what I give you, and of course you may share that with whomever you like. But the fisc is not a toy and it does have a bottom. All right?"

"Your Majesty, how can the likes of me argue with whatever you choose to do?" Drina sounded frightened again.

The plain answer was that she couldn't. Krispos didn't say that; it would just have alarmed her further. What he did say was: "Go and tell Barsymes what you've just told me. Tell him I said you're to be treated with every consideration, too."

"I will, Your Majesty. Thank you. Uh, Your Majesty—"

"What now?" Krispos asked when she showed no sign of saying anything more than *uh.*

"Will you still want me?" she said, and then stood there as if she wished the mosaic floor would open and swallow her up. Like most Videssians, she was olive-skinned; Krispos thought he saw her blush anyhow.

He got up, came around the desk, and put an arm around her. "I expect so, now and again," he said. "But if you have some young man waiting under the Amphitheater for the next race, so to speak, don't be shy about saying so. I wouldn't have you do anything you don't care to." He'd watched Anthimos take advantage of so many women that moderation came easy to him: anything Anthimos did was a good bet to have been wrong.

"It's not that," Drina said quickly. "I just—worry that you'll forget about me."

"I already said I wouldn't. I do keep my word." Thinking she needed more reassurance than words, he patted her on the backside. She sighed and snuggled against him. He let her stay for a bit, then said, "Go on, go see Barsymes. He'll take care of you."

Snuffling a little, Drina went. Krispos stood in the study, listening to her footsteps fade as she walked down the hall. When he couldn't hear them anymore, he returned to his seat and to the customs reports he'd been reviewing. But he soon found he had to shove aside the parchments: he couldn't concentrate on what was in them.

"An imperial bastard," he said quietly. "*My* bastard. Well, well, what am I going to do about that?"

He was a man who believed in making plans as implicitly as he believed in Phos. Fathering a child at his age wasn't in any of those he'd made so far. *No help for it,* he told himself. *I'll have to come up with some new ones.*

He knew he might not need them; so many children never lived to grow up. As in so many things, though, better to have and not need than to need and not have. Besides, you always hoped your children lived unless you were a fanatical Thanasiot who thought all life ought to vanish from the earth and be quick about it, too.

If he had a daughter, things would stay simple. When she grew up, he'd do his best to make sure she married someone well disposed to him. That was what marriages were for, after all: joining together families that could be useful to each other.

If he had a son, now . . . He clicked his tongue between his teeth. That would complicate matters. Some Avtokrators had their bastards made into eunuchs; some had risen to high rank in the temples or at the palace. It was certainly one way of guaranteeing the boy would never challenge his legitimate sons for the throne: being physically imperfect, eunuchs could not claim imperial rank in Videssos or Makuran or any other country he knew of.

Krispos made that clicking noise again. He wasn't sure he had the stomach for that, no matter how expedient it might be. He stared down at the delicately veined marble desktop, wondering what to do. He was so lost in his thoughts, the tap on the door frame made him jump. He looked up. This time it was Barsymes.

"I am given to understand congratulations are in order, Your Majesty?" the vestiarios said carefully.

"Thank you, esteemed sir. I'm given to understand the same thing myself." Krispos managed a rueful laugh. "Life has a way of going off on its own path, not the one you'd choose for it."

"Very true. As you have requested, every care will be given to the mother-to-be. As part of that care, I gather you will want to ensure, so far as is feasible, that she does not acquire an exaggerated notion either of her own station or that of her offspring."

"You've hit in the center of the target, Barsymes. Can you imagine me, say, disinheriting the sons I have for the sake of a by-blow? Not a cook could find a better recipe for civil war after I'm gone."

"What you say is true, Your Majesty. And yet—" Barsymes stepped out into the hallway, looked right and left. Even after he was sure no one save Krispos could hear him, he lowered his voice. "And yet, Your Majesty, one of your sons may be lost to you, and you've not expressed entire satisfaction with any of them."

"But why should I expect the next one to be any better?" Krispos said. "Besides, I'd have to wait twenty years to have any idea what sort of man he is, and who says I have twenty years left? I might, aye, but the odds aren't the best. So I'd sooner discommode the one young bastard than the three older legitimate boys."

"I would not think of faulting the logic; I merely wondered if Your Majesty had fully considered the situation. I see you have: well and good." The vestiarios ran pale tongue across paler lips. "I also wondered if you were, ah, besotted with the mother of the child-to-be."

"So I'd do stupid things to keep her happy, you mean?" Krispos said. Barsymes nodded. Krispos started to laugh, but restrained himself—that would have been cruel. "No, esteemed sir. Drina's very pleasant, but I've not lost my head."

"Ah," Barsymes said again. He seldom showed much emotion, and this moment was no exception to the rule; nonetheless, Krispos thought he heard relief in that single syllable.

I've not lost my head. That might have been the watchword for his reign, and for his life. If it had left him on the cold-blooded side, it had also given the Empire of Videssos more than two decades of steady, sensible rule. There were worse exchanges.

He remembered the thought he'd had before. "Esteemed sir, may I ask a question that might perturb you? Please understand my aim is not to cause you pain, but to learn."

"Ask, Your Majesty," Barsymes replied at once. "You are the Avtokrator; you have the right."

"Very well, then. To make sure dynastic problems don't come up, Avtokrators have been known to make eunuchs of their bastard offspring. You know your life as only one who lives it can. What have you to say of it?"

The vestiarios gave the question his usual grave consideration. "The pain of the gelding does not last forever, of course. I have never known desire, so I do not particularly pine for it, though that is not true of all my kind. But being set aside forever from the general run of mankind—there is the true curse of the eunuch, Your Majesty. So far as any of us knows, it has no balm."

"Thank you, esteemed sir." Krispos put the thought in the place where bad ideas belong. He felt an urgent need to change the subject. "By the good god!" he exclaimed, as heartily as he could. Barsymes raised an interrogative eyebrow. He explained: "No matter how smoothly things go, I'll never hear the end of teasing about this from my sons. I've given them a hard time about their affairs, but now I'm the one who's gone and put a loaf in a serving maid's oven."

"I pray Your Majesty to forgive me, but you've forgotten something," Barsymes said. Now it was Krispos' turn to look puzzled. The vestiarios went on, "Think what the eminent Iakovitzes will say."

Krispos thought. After a moment, he pushed back his seat and hid under the desk. He'd seldom made Barsymes laugh, but he added one to the short list. He laughed, too, as he reemerged, but he still dreaded what would happen the next time he saw his special envoy.

PHOSTIS MADE SURE THE SWORD FIT LOOSE IN ITS SHEATH. IT was not a fancy weapon with a gold-chased hilt like the one he'd carried before he was kidnapped: just a curved blade, a leather-wrapped grip, and an iron hand guard. It would slice flesh as well as any other sword, though.

The horse they gave him wasn't fit to haul oats to the imperial stables. It was a scrawny, swaybacked gelding with scars on its knees and an evil glint in its eye. By the monster of a bit that went with the rest of its tack, it must have had a mouth made of wrought iron and a temper worthy of Skotos. But it was a horse, and the Thanasioi let him ride it. That marked a change for the better.

It would have been better still had Syagrios not joined the band to which Phostis had been attached. "What, you thought you'd be rid of me?" he boomed when Phostis could not quite hide his lack of enthusiasm. "Not so easy as that, boy."

Phostis shrugged, in control of himself again. "If nothing else, we can spar at the board game," he said.

Syagrios laughed in his face. "I never bother with that dung when I'm out fighting. It's for slack times, when there's no real blood to be spilled." His narrow eyes lit up with anticipation.

The raiders rode out of Etchmiadzin that afternoon, a party of about twenty-five heading south and east toward territory the men of the gleaming path did not control. Excitement ran high; everyone was eager to bring Thanasios' doctrines a step closer to reality by destroying the material goods of those who did not follow them.

The band's leader, a tough-looking fellow named Themistios, seemed almost as unsavory as Syagrios. He put the theology in terms no one could fail to follow: "Burn the farms, burn the monasteries, kill the animals, kill the people. They go straight to the ice. Any of us who fall, we walk the gleaming path beyond the sun and stay with Phos forever."

"The gleaming path!" the raiders bawled. "Phos bless the gleaming path!"

Phostis wondered how many such bands were sallying forth from Etchmiadzin and other Thanasiot strongholds, how many men stormed into the Empire with murder and martyrdom warring for the uppermost place in their minds. He also wondered where the main body of Livanios' men would fare. Syagrios knew. But Syagrios, however much he liked to brag and jeer, knew how to keep his mouth shut about things that mattered.

Soon Phostis' concerns became more immediate. Not least among them was seeing if he couldn't inconspicuously vanish from the raiding band. He couldn't. The horsemen kept him in their midst; Syagrios clung to him like a leech. *Maybe when the fighting starts,* he thought.

For the first day and a half of riding, they remained in territory under Thanasiot rule. Peasants waved from the fields and shouted slogans at the horsemen as they trotted past. The riders shouted back less often as time went by: muscles unused since fall were claiming their price. Phostis hadn't been so saddle sore in years.

Another day on horseback brought the raiders into country where, instead of cheering, the peasants fled at first sight of them. That occasioned argument among Phostis' companions: some wanted to scatter and destroy the peasants and their huts, while others preferred to press ahead without delay.

In the end, Themistios came down in favor of the second group. "There's a monastery outside Aptos I want to hit," he declared, "and I'm not going to waste my time with this riffraff till it's smashed. We can nail peasants on the way home." With a large, juicy target thus set before them, the raiders stopped arguing. It would have taken a very bold man to quarrel with Themistios, anyhow.

They came to the monastery a little before sunset. Some of the monks were still in the fields. Howling like demons, the Thanasioi rode them down. Swords rose, fell, and rose again smeared with scarlet. Instead of prayers to Phos, screams rose into the reddening sky.

"We'll burn the building!" Themistios shouted. "Even monks have too fornicating much." He spurred his horse straight toward the monastery gate and got inside before the startled monks could slam it shut against him. His sword forced back the first blue-robe who came running up, and a moment later more of his wolves were in there with him.

Several of the raiders carried smoldering sticks of punk. Oil-soaked torches caught quickly. Syagrios pressed one into Phostis' hand. "Here," he growled. "Do some good with this." *Or else,* his voice warned. So did the way he cocked his sword.

Phostis threw the torch at a wall. He'd hoped it would fall short, and it did, but it rolled up against the wood. Flames crackled, caught, and began to spread. Syagrios pounded him on the back, as if he'd just been initiated into the brotherhood of wreckers. Shuddering, he realized he had.

A monk waving a cudgel rushed at him, shouting something incoherent. He wanted to tell the shaven-headed holy man it was all a dreadful mistake, that he didn't want to be here and hadn't truly intended to harm the monastery. But the monk didn't care about any of that. All he wanted to do was smash the closest invader—who happened to be Phostis.

He parried the blue-robe's first wild swipe, and his second. "By the good god, cut him!" Syagrios shouted in disgust. "What do you think— he's going to get tired and go away?"

Phostis didn't quite parry the third blow. It glanced off his shin, hard enough to make him bite his lip against the pain. He realized with growing dismay that he couldn't just try to hold off the monk, not when the fellow wanted nothing more than to kill him.

The monk drew back his club for yet another swing. Phostis slashed at him, feeling the blade bite. Behind him, Syagrios roared with glee. Phostis would cheerfully have killed the ruffian for forcing him into a position where he either had to hurt the monk or get himself maimed or killed.

None of the other raiders had any such compunctions. Several had dismounted, the better to torture the monks they overcame. Screams echoed down the halls that had resounded with hymns of praise to Phos. Watching the Thanasioi at their work—or was it better called sport?—Phostis felt his stomach lurch like a horse stepping into a snow-covered hole.

"Away! Away!" Themistios shouted. "It'll burn now, and we have more to do before we head home."

What does he have in mind? Phostis thought. About the only thing that fit in with what the raiders had done at the monastery was torching a home for penniless widows and orphans. Videssos the city had several such; he wondered if Aptos was a big enough town to boast any.

He never got the chance to find out, for as he and the Thanasioi rode away from the monastery, a troop of imperial soldiers came storming after them from out of Aptos. Faint in the distance but growing louder fast, Phostis heard a wary cry he'd never imagined could sound so welcome: "Krispos! The Avtokrator Krispos! Krispos!"

A good many of the Thanasioi had bows as well as sabers. They started shooting at the imperials. The garrison troops, like most imperial cavalry, were archers, too. They shot back. The advantage lay on their side, because they wore mail shirts and helmets while almost all the Thanasioi were unarmored.

Phostis yanked his horse's head around and booted the animal toward the imperials. All he thought about was giving himself up and doing whatever penance the patriarch or some other ecclesiastic set him for his sins in the monastery. Among the things he forgot was the saber he clutched in his right fist.

To the onrushing cavalrymen, he must have looked like a fanatical Thanasiot challenging them single-handed so he could go straight from death to the gleaming path beyond the sun. An arrow whistled past his ear. Another one buried itself in the ground by the horse's forefoot. Another one hit him in the shoulder.

At first he felt only the impact, and thought a kicked-up stone had grazed him. Then he looked down and saw the pale ash shaft sticking out of him. His eyes focused on the gray goose feathers of the fletching. *How stupid,* he thought. *I've been shot by my own father's men.*

All at once, the pain struck, and with it weakness. His own blood ran hot down his chest and began to stain his tunic. He swayed in the saddle. More arrows hissed past.

Syagrios came up beside him at a gallop. "Have you gone out of your head?" he yelled. "You can't fight them all by yourself." His eyes went wide when he saw Phostis was wounded. "See what I'm telling you? We got to get out of here."

Neither Phostis' wits nor his body was working very well. Syagrios saw that, too. He grabbed the reins away from the younger man and led Phostis' horse alongside his own. The horse was nasty, and tried to balk. Syagrios was nastier, and wouldn't let it. A couple of other Thanasioi came back to cover their retreat.

The weight of armor on the imperial cavalrymen slowed them in a long chase. The raiders managed to stay in front until darkness let them give the imperials the slip. Several were hurt by then, and a couple of others lost when their horses went down.

Phostis' world focused on the burning in his shoulder. Everything else seemed far away, unimportant. He scarcely noticed when the Thanasioi halted beside a little stream, though not having to fight to stay in the saddle was a relief.

Syagrios advanced on him with a knife. "We'll have to tend to that," he said. "Here, lie flat."

No one dared light a fire. Syagrios held his head close to Phostis to see what he was doing as he cut the tunic away from the arrow. He examined the wound, made an abstracted clucking noise, and pulled something out of the pouch he wore on his belt.

"What's that?" Phostis asked.

"Arrow-drawing spoon," Syagrios answered. "Can't just pull the fornicating thing out; the point'll have barbs. Hold still and shut up. Digging in there will hurt, but you won't be as torn up inside this way. Now—"

In spite of Syagrios' injunction, Phostis groaned. Nor were his the only cries that rose to the uncaring sky as the raiders did what they could for their wounded comrades. Now darkness didn't much matter; Syagrios was working more by feel than by sight as he forced the narrow, cupped end of the spoon down along the arrow's shaft toward the head.

Phostis felt the spoon grate on something. Syagrios grunted in satisfaction. "Here we go. Now we can get it out. Wasn't too deep—you're lucky."

The taste of blood filled Phostis' mouth: he'd bitten his lip while the ruffian guddled for the arrow. He could smell his own blood, too. He choked out, "If I were lucky, it would have missed me."

"Ha," Syagrios said. "Can't say you're wrong there. Hold on, now. Here it comes, here it comes—yes!" He got the spoon out of the wound, and the arrow with it. He grunted again. "No blood spurting—just a dribble. I'd say you'll make it."

In place of a canteen, the ruffian carried a wineskin on his belt. He poured a stream of wine onto Phostis' wound. After the probing with the spoon and the drawing of the arrow, the abused flesh felt as if it were being bathed with fire. Phostis thrashed and swore and clumsily tried to hit Syagrios left-handed.

"Easy there, curse you," Syagrios said. "Just hold still. You wash out a wound with wine, it's less likely to rot. You *want* pus and fever? You may get 'em anyways, mind, but wouldn't you rather bump up your odds?"

He wadded up a rag, pressed it to Phostis' shoulder to soak up the blood that still oozed from the wound, and tied it in place with another strip of cloth. "Thank you," Phostis got out, a little slower than he should have: he still struggled with the irony of being treated by a man he despised.

"Anytime." Syagrios set a hand on his good shoulder. "I never would've thought it, but you really do want to walk the gleaming path, don't you? You laid out that monk fine as you please, and then you were ready to take on all the imperials at the same time. More brave than smart, maybe, but to the ice with smart, sometimes. You done better'n I would've dreamed."

"To the ice with smart, sometimes," Phostis repeated wearily. At last he'd found what it took to satisfy Syagrios: be too cowardly to refuse what he was ordered and then botch what he'd intended as a desertion. The moral there was too elusive for him. He let out a long, worn sigh.

"Yeah, sleep while you can," Syagrios said. "We'll have some fancy riding to do tomorrow before we're sure we've broken loose from the stinking imperials. But I've got to get you back to Etchmiadzin. Now that I know for sure you're with us, we'll have all kinds of things we can use you for."

Sleep? Phostis wouldn't have imagined it possible. Even though the worst of the agony had left his shoulder now that the arrow was out, it still ached like a rotting tooth and throbbed in time to his pulse. But as the wild excitement of the ride and the fight faded, exhaustion rolled over him like a great black tide. Rough ground, aching shoulder—no matter. He slept hard.

He woke from a dream where a wolf was alternately biting and kicking him to find Syagrios shaking him back to consciousness. The shoulder still hurt fiercely, but he managed a nod when the ruffian asked if he could ride.

He did his best to forget as much as he could of the journey back to

Etchmiadzin. However much he tried, he couldn't forget the torment of
more wine poured into his wound at every halt. The shoulder got hot, but
only right around the hole in it, so he supposed the treatment, no matter
how agonizing, did some good.

He wished a healer-priest would look at the wound, but had not seen
any such among the Thanasioi. That made theological sense: if the body,
like all things of this world, sprang from Skotos, what point to making
any special effort to preserve it? Such an attitude was easy enough to maintain as an abstract principle. When it came down to Phostis' personal
body and its pain, abstract principles got trivial fast.

The rising foothills ahead seemed welcome, not because Etchmiadzin
was the home the Thanasioi had hoped it would become for him, but because they meant the imperial soldiers would not catch him on the road
and finish the job of killing him. And, he reminded himself, Olyvria
would be back at the fortress. The aching wound kept him from being as
delighted about that as he would have been otherwise.

When the raiders drew near the valley that cupped Etchmiadzin,
Themistios rode up to Syagrios and said, "My men and I will follow the
gleaming path against the materialists now. Go as Phos wills you; we cannot follow any farther."

"I can take him in from here easy enough," Syagrios answered, nodding. "Do what you need to do, Themistios, and may the good god keep
his eyes on you and your lads."

Singing a hymn with Thanasiot lyrics, the zealots wheeled their horses
and rode back out of the holy work of slaughter and destruction. Syagrios
and Phostis kept on toward the stronghold of Etchmiadzin.

"We'll get you patched up proper, make sure that arm's all right before
we send you out again," Syagrios said as the gray stone mass of the fortress
came in view. "Might be just as well I'm here, too, in case we need to settle anything while Livanios is in the field."

"Whatever you say." All Phostis wanted was a chance to get down from
his horse and not have to mount again for, say, the next ten years.

Etchmiadzin seemed strangely spacious as he and Syagrios rode
through the muddy streets toward the fortress. Wits dulled by pain and fatigue, Phostis needed longer than he should have to figure out why. At last
he realized that most of the soldiers who had swelled the town through the
winter were off glorifying the lord with the great and good mind by laying
waste to what they reckoned the creations of his evil foe.

Only a couple of sentries stood guard at the fortress gate. The inner
ward felt empty without warriors at weapons practice or listening to one

of Livanios' orations. Most of the heresiarch's chief aides seemed to have gone with him; at least no one came out of the keep to take a report from Syagrios.

As Phostis soon discovered, that was because the keep was almost empty, too. His footsteps and Syagrios' echoed down the halls that had been crammed with soldiers. At least life did exist inside. A trooper came out of the chamber where Livanios had been wont to hold audiences as if he were Avtokrator. Seeing Phostis leaning on Syagrios, he asked the ruffian, "What happened to him?"

"What does it look like?" Syagrios growled. "He just found out he's been chosen patriarch and he can't even walk for the joy of it." The Thanasiot gaped; Phostis fought not to giggle as he watched the fellow realize Syagrios was being sarcastic. Syagrios pointed to the stained bandage on his shoulder. "He got shot in a scrape with the imperials—he did good."

"All right, but why bring him back here?" the soldier said. "He don't look like he's hurt too bad."

"You likely can't tell under all the dirt and stuff, but this is the Emperor's brat," Syagrios answered. "We need to take a little more care with him than with your regular fighter."

"Why?" Like any Videssian, the Thanasiot was ready to argue about his faith on any excuse or none. "We're all alike on the gleaming path."

"Yeah, but Phostis here has special worth," Syagrios returned. "If we use him right, he can help us put lots of new people on the gleaming path."

The soldier chewed on that: literally, for he gnawed at his lower lip while he thought. At last, grudgingly, he nodded. "The doctrine may be sound."

Syagrios turned his head to mutter into Phostis' ear, "The clincher is, I'd have chopped him into raven's meat if he said me nay." He gave his attention back to the trooper. "Is anybody left alive in the kitchens? We're starved, and not on purpose."

"Should be someone there," the fellow answered, though he frowned at Syagrios' levity.

Phostis had not had much appetite since he was wounded. Now his belly rumbled hungrily at the thought of food. Maybe that meant he was getting better.

The smell of bean porridge and onions and bread in the kitchens made his insides growl all over again. Bowls were piled in great stacks there, against a need that had for the moment gone. Only a handful of people sat at the long tables. Phostis' heart gave a lurch—one of them was Olyvria.

She looked around to see who the newcomers were. Phostis must have been as grimy as Syagrios had said, for she recognized the ruffian first. Then her eyes traveled from Phostis' face to the stained bandage on his shoulder and back again. He saw them widen. "What happened?" she exclaimed as she hurried over to the two men.

"I got shot," Phostis answered. Keeping his tone as light as he could, he went on, "I'll probably live." He couldn't say anything more, but did his silent best to urge her not to give anything away. Having Syagrios find out—or even suspect—they were lovers would be more likely fatal than the shaft the cavalryman had put into him.

They were lucky. Syagrios evidently didn't suspect, and so wasn't alert for any small clues they might have given him. He boomed, "Aye, he fought well—better'n I had any reason to think he would, my lady. He was riding toward the imperials when one of 'em got him. I drew the arrow myself and cleaned the wound. It seems to be healing well enough."

Now Olyvria looked at Phostis as if she didn't know what to make of him. She probably didn't: he hadn't gone out intending to fight, let alone well enough to draw praise from Syagrios. But self-preservation had made him swing his sword against the monk with the club, and the ruffian thought he'd been attacking the imperials, not trying to give himself up to them. The world got very strange sometimes.

"Could I please have some food before I fall over?" he asked plaintively.

Between them, Syagrios and Olyvria all but dragged him to a table, sat him down, and brought back bread, hard crumbly cheese, and wine he reckoned fit only for washing out wounded shoulders. He knocked back a hefty mug of it anyhow, and felt it mount quickly to his head. In between bites of bread and cheese, he gave Olyvria a carefully edited version of how he'd ended up on the pointed end of an arrow.

"I see," she said when he was through. He wasn't sure she did, but then he wasn't exactly sure himself of the wherefores of everything that had happened. She turned to Syagrios. Speaking carefully herself, and as if Phostis were not sitting across from her, she said, "When he was ordered to go out raiding, I thought the plan might be to expend him to bring woe to his father."

"That was in *your* father's mind, my lady," Syagrios agreed, also ignoring him, "but he doubted the lad's faith in the gleaming path. Since it's real, he becomes worth more to us alive than dead. That's what I figured, anyways."

"Let's hope you're right," Olyvria said with what Phostis hoped was a good imitation of dispassion.

He kept munching on the loaf of bread. The falser he was to what Syagrios thought him to be, the better off he did. What was the lesson there? That Syagrios was so wicked being false to him turned good? Then how to explain the way the ruffian had cared for him, brought him back to Etchmiadzin, and now poured more of that vile but potent wine into his mug?

He raised it left-handed. "Here's to—using my other arm soon."

Everyone drank.

Chapter X

SCRIBBLING ON A MAP RUINED IT FOR FUTURE USE. SO DID poking pins into it. Krispos had prevailed upon Zaidas to magic some red-painted pebbles so they behaved like lodestones and clung to their appointed places on the parchment even when it was rolled up. Now he wished he'd chosen some other color: when the map was unrolled, it looked too much as if it were suffering from smallpox.

And every time he unrolled it, he had to add more stones to show fresh outbreaks of Thanasiot violence. Messengers brought in a constant stream of such reports. Most, as had been true the summer before, were in the northwest quadrant of the westlands, but far from all. He glanced at dispatches and put down two stones in the hill country in the southeastern part of the gnarled peninsula that held the Empire's heartland.

That the map lay on a folding table in the imperial pavilion rather than his study back at the palaces consoled him little. The mere fact of being on campaign would have sufficed for some Emperors, giving them the impression—justified or not—they were doing something about the religious zealots.

But Krispos saw in his mind's eye fires rising up from the map where every red pebble was placed, heard screams of triumph and of despair. Even one of those stones should have been too many, yet several dozen measled the map.

At his side, Katakolon also stared glumly at the scarlet stones. "They're everywhere," he said, shaking his head in dismay.

"They do seem that way, don't they?" Krispos said. He liked the picture no better than his son did.

"Aye, they do." Katakolon still eyed the stippled parchment. "Which of these shows where Livanios and his main band of fighters are lurking?"

"It's a good question," the Avtokrator admitted. "The Empire would be better off for a good answer. I wish I could give you one. Trouble is, the heresiarch is using all the little raids as cover to conceal that main band. They could be almost anywhere."

Put that way, the thought was especially disquieting. His own army was only a few days out of Videssos the city. If Livanios' fanatics fell on it before it was ready to fight—Krispos shook his head. It wasn't as if he didn't have sentries posted. Anyone who tried surprising him would be roughly handled. If he started jumping at shadows, Livanios was ahead of the game.

Katakolon looked from the map to him. "So you're going to have yourself another brat, are you, Father? At your age?"

"I've already had three brats. One more won't wreck Videssos, I expect, not if the lot of you haven't managed it. And yes, at my age, as I told you back in the city. The parts do still work, you see."

"Well, yes, I suppose so, but really . . . " Katakolon seemed to think that was a complete sentence. It probably meant something like *just because they work doesn't mean you have any business going around using them.*

Krispos parried, "Maybe you'll learn something watching how I handle things. The way you go on, boy, you're going to sire enough bastards to make up your own cavalry company. Katakolon's Whoresons they could call themselves, and be ferocious-sounding and truthful at the same time."

He'd hoped to abash his youngest son—he'd long since given up trying to shame him over venery—but the idea delighted Katakolon. He clapped his hands and exclaimed, "And if I sire a company, Father, the lads can father themselves a couple of regiments, and my great-grandsons will end up being the whole Videssian army."

Every so often with Iakovitzes, Krispos had to throw his hands in the air and own himself beaten. Now he found himself doing the same with Katakolon. "You're incorrigible. Go tell Sarkis I want to see him, and try not to seduce anyone between this tent and that one."

"Haloga guards are not to my taste," Katakolon replied with dignity bordering on hauteur. "Now, if their daughters and sisters took service with Videssos—" Krispos made as if to throw a folding chair at him. Laughing, the youth ducked out of the tent. Krispos remembered the exotically blond and pink Haloga doxy at a revel of Anthimos, a generation before. Katakolon surely would have liked her very well.

Krispos forced his wits away from lickerish memories and back toward the map. As best he could tell, the Thanasioi were popping up everywhere at once. That made it hard for him to figure out how to fight them.

One of the guards stuck his head into the tent. Krispos straightened, expecting him to announce Sarkis. But instead he said, "Your Majesty, the mage Zaidas would have speech wit' you."

"Would he? Yes, of course I'll listen to what he has to say."

As usual, Zaidas started to prostrate himself; as usual, Krispos waved for him not to bother. Both men smiled at the little ritual. But the wizard's lips quickly fell from their happy curve. He said, "May it please Your Majesty, these past few days my magic has enabled me to track the whereabouts of the young Majesty Phostis."

"He's not stayed in the same place all the while?" Krispos asked. "I thought he was still at Etchmiadzin." Because Zaidas hadn't detected any motion from Phostis since he'd managed to pierce the screen of Makuraner magic, Krispos had dared hope his heir was prisoner rather than convert to the gleaming path.

"No, Your Majesty, I'm afraid not. Here, let me show you." Zaidas drew from his belt pouch a square of leather. "This is from the tanned hide of a deer, the animal having been chosen because the melting tenderness of its gaze symbolically represents the affection you feel for your kidnapped son. See these marks—here, here, here?"

Krispos saw the marks: they looked as if the deerskin had been burned here and there with the end of a hot awl. "I see them, magical sir, but I must say I don't grasp what they mean."

"As you know, I've at last been able to locate Phostis through the law of contagion. Were he remaining in Etchmiadzin, the scorch marks you see would be virtually one on top of the other. As it was, their dispersal indicates he moved some considerable distance, most probably to the south and east, and then returned to the place whence he had departed."

"I see." Krispos scowled down at the piece of deerskin. "And why do you think he's been making these—movements?"

"Your Majesty, I am sufficiently pleased to be able to infer that he *has* moved, or rather moved and returned. Why he has done so is beyond the scope of my art." Zaidas spoke with quiet determination, as if to say he did not want to know why Phostis had gone out from the Thanasiot stronghold and then back to it.

The mage was both courtier and friend; no wonder he found discretion the easier path to take. Krispos said harshly, "Magical sir, isn't the likeliest explanation that he went out on a raid with the fanatics and then rode—rode home again?"

"That is certainly a possibility which must be considered," Zaidas admitted. "And yet, many other explanations are possible."

"Possible, yes, but likely? What I said fits the facts better than anything else I can think of." Half a lifetime of judging cases had convinced Krispos that the simplest explanation was most often the right one. What could be simpler than Phostis' joining the rebels and going out to fight for them? Krispos crumbled the deerskin in his fist and threw it to the ground. "I wish that cursed Digenis were still alive so I could have the pleasure of executing him now."

"I sympathize, Your Majesty, and believe me, I fully appreciate the gravity of the problem this presents."

"Problem, yes." That was a nice, bloodless way to put it. What were you supposed to do when your son and heir turned against you? However fond he was of making plans, Krispos hadn't made one for that set of circumstances. Now, of necessity, he began to. How would Evripos shape as heir? He'd be delighted, certainly. But would he make a good Avtokrator? Krispos didn't know.

Zaidas must have been thinking along with him. The wizard said, "No need to deal with this on the instant, Your Majesty. Perhaps the campaign will reveal the full circumstances of what's gone on."

"It probably will," Krispos said gloomily. "The trouble is, the full circumstances may be ones I'd sooner not have learned."

Before Zaidas could answer that, Katakolon led Sarkis into the imperial pavilion. The youth nodded easily to the mage; Zaidas, having been around the palaces since before Katakolon was born, was familiar to him as the furniture. Sarkis sketched a salute, which Zaidas returned. They'd both prospered handsomely under Krispos; if either was jealous of the other, he hid it well.

"What's toward, Your Majesty?" Sarkis said, and then, "Anything to eat in here? I'm peckish."

Krispos pointed to a bowl of salted olives. The cavalry general picked up a handful of them and popped them into his mouth one after another, spitting the seeds on the ground. As soon as he finished his first helping, he took another.

"Here." Krispos pointed to the map. "Some things occurred to me—late, perhaps, but better late than not at all. The trouble with this campaign is that the Thanasioi know just where we are. If they don't want to meet us in the field, they don't have to. They can just divide themselves up and raid endlessly: even if we smash some of their bands, we haven't done anything to break the back of the movement."

"Truth," Sarkis mumbled around an olive. "It's the curse of fighting folk who are only one step up from hill bandits. We move slow, with horns playing and banners waving, while they bounce over the landscape like fleas on a hot griddle. Belike they have spies in camp, too, to let them know right where we are at any hour of the day or night."

"I'm sure they do," Krispos said. "Here's what I have in mind, then: suppose we detach, say, fifteen hundred men from this force, take 'em back to the coast, and put 'em on board ship. Don't tell them where to land in advance; let the drungarios in charge of the fleet pick a coastal town—Tavas, Nakoleia, or Pityos—after they've set out. The detachment would be big enough to do us some good when it landed, maybe big enough to force Livanios to concentrate quickly against it . . . at which point, the good god willing, we'd be close enough to hit him with the rest of the army. Well?" He knew he was an amateur strategist, and wasn't in the habit of giving orders for major moves till he'd talked them over with professionals.

Sarkis absently popped another olive into his mouth. "It would keep the spies from knowing what was going on, which I like. But you ought to pick out the target town in advance and give it to the drungarios as a sealed order—"

"Sealed magically, too," Zaidas put in, "to prevent scrying as well as spying."

"Aye, sealed magically, by all means," Sarkis said. "No one would see the order save you and, say, one spatharios"—he glanced over at Katakolon—"until the drungarios opened it. That way you could make sure the main army was at the right place at the right time."

"Thank you, eminent sir; you've closed a loophole. We'll do it as you suggest. What I mostly want is to make the Thanasioi react to us for once instead of the other way round. Let them counter our mischief for a change."

Krispos looked from Sarkis to Zaidas to Katakolon. They all nodded. His son asked, "Which town will you choose for the landing?"

Sarkis turned away from Katakolon so the youth would not see him smile. Krispos saw, though. Gently he answered, "I'm not going to tell you, because this tent just has cloth walls and I don't know who's walking by with his ear bent. The less we blab, the less there is for unfriendly people to learn from us."

"Oh." Katakolon still had trouble realizing this wasn't a large, elaborate game. Then he said, "Couldn't you have Zaidas create a zone of silence around the pavilion?"

"I could," Krispos said. "But I won't, because it's far more trouble than it's worth. Besides, another mage would be apt to notice the zone of silence and wonder what we were brewing up behind it. This way, everything stays nice and ordinary and no one suspects we have anything sneaky in mind—which is the best way to pull off something sneaky, assuming you want to."

"Oh," Katakolon said again.

Without warning, Syagrios came through the door into Phostis' little cubicle in the keep at Etchmiadzin. "Get your imperial backside out of bed," he growled. "You've got work to do."

Phostis' first muzzy thought on waking was relief that Olyvria wasn't lying on the pallet beside him. His next, as his head cleared a little, was curiosity. "Work?" he said. "What kind of work?" He crawled out from under the blanket, stretched, and tried to pull wrinkles out of his tunic. He'd slept on his beard wrong; parts of it were sticking out from his face like spikes.

"Come down and get some wine and porridge in you and we'll talk," Syagrios said. "No point to telling you anything now—you don't have any brains before breakfast."

Since that was more or less true, Phostis answered it with as dignified a silence as he could muster. The dignity would have been easier to maintain had he not made a hash of buckling one sandal. Syagrios laughed raucously.

On the way downstairs, the ruffian asked, "How's the arm?"

Phostis raised it and bent it at odd angles till he caught his breath at a sharp stab of pain. "It's still not perfect, not by a long shot," he answered, "but I'm getting to where I can use it well enough."

"Good," Syagrios said, and then nothing more until he and Phostis were down in the kitchens. If he'd hoped to pique Phostis' interest, he succeeded. The younger man would have gone through his morning porridge twice as fast had he not kept pestering Syagrios with questions. The ruffian, who drank more breakfast than he ate, was gleefully noncommunicative until Olyvria came in and joined the two of them at table. Seeing her made Phostis stop asking so many questions, but didn't make him eat any faster.

"Have you told him?" Olyvria asked Syagrios.

"No, he hasn't told me," Phostis said indignantly; were curiosity an itch, he would have been scratching with both hands.

Syagrios gave him an evil leer before he answered Olyvria. "Not a word. I figured I'd let him stew in his own juice a while longer."

"I think I'm done to a turn now," Phostis said. "What in the name of the lord with the great and good mind is going on? What *are* you supposed to tell me, Syagrios?" He knew he was being too eager, but couldn't help himself.

"All right, boy, you want to know that bad, you oughta know," Syagrios said. But instead of telling Phostis whatever it was he wasn't saying, he got up and, with slow deliberation, poured himself another mug of wine. Phostis looked a mute appeal to Olyvria, but she didn't say anything, either. Syagrios came swaggering back, sat down again, and noisily swigged from the mug. Only when he was through did he come to the point. "Your father, lad, is getting cute."

Phostis had heard his father described in many ways. Till that moment, *cute* had never been one of them. Cautiously, he asked, "What's he done?"

"That's just it—we don't quite know." By Syagrios' scowl, he thought he had every right to know everything Krispos did. He went on, "He's sent a force out of the Videssian Sea, same as he did last fall when we snagged you. This time, though, we don't know ahead of time which town he's gonna land at."

"Ah." Phostis hoped he sounded wise. But he wasn't all that wise, for he had to ask another question. "What has that to do with me?"

"Suppose you're an imperial soldier," Syagrios said. "That makes you pretty fornicating dumb to start with, right? All right, now suppose you land in a town and you're getting ready to do whatever they tell you to do and here comes the Avtokrator's son, saying to the ice with your officers and come on and join the gleaming path. What you gonna do then?"

"I . . . see," Phostis said slowly. And he did, too; had he been as enamored of the gleaming path as Syagrios thought he was, he could have done his father a lot of harm. But he also saw a problem. "You said you didn't know where these troops are going to land?"

"Naah, we don't." No doubt about it: Syagrios was indignant about that. He continued, "But we think—and it's only a think, worse luck— like I say, we think he's gonna try and send 'em in at Pityos. It's what Livanios would do if he wore the red boots. He likes to strike for the heart, Livanios does."

Phostis nodded; the ruffian's reasoning made sense to him, too. He said, "So you'll send me to Pityos, then? Will I go alone?"

Syagrios and Olyvria both laughed at that. She said, "No, Phostis. While we're sure enough you follow the gleaming path to send you out, we're not sure enough to send you alone. We have to be sure you will say what you're supposed to. So I shall accompany you to Pityos . . . and so will Syagrios."

"All right," he answered mildly. He had no idea how things would go once he got to Pityos; he wasn't even sure whether Olyvria was on his side or her father's. He'd find out in due course, he supposed. Either way, he intended to try to escape. Etchmiadzin was in the heart of Thanasiot country—even if he got out of town, he'd be hunted down before he could go far.

But Pityos, now, Pityos lay by the sea. He was no great sailor, but he could manage a small boat. The good god willing, he wouldn't have to. If imperial soldiers were heading into the port, all he'd have to do was go over to them rather than persuade them to come over to the gleaming path. It seemed too easy to be true.

"When will we leave?" he asked, careful now to sound casual. "I'll need a little while to think about what I'm going to say. I don't suppose I'll be talking much to the officers?"

"Not bloody likely," Syagrios agreed, rumbling laughter. "You're after the odds and sods, the poor buggers who make a living—and a bad one—from soldiering. With any luck, they'll rise up and slaughter the proud bastards who give 'em orders. Most of those midwife's mistakes have it coming, anyways." While he might not have been a proper Thanasiot as far as theology went, Syagrios had unbounded contempt for anyone in authority.

Olyvria actually answered Phostis' question: "We want to leave tomorrow. It's several days' ride down to the coast; you can work on what you'll say as we go."

"However you like." Phostis laughed. "The lord with the great and good mind knows I haven't much to pack."

"Nor should you, if you follow the gleaming path," Olyvria said.

Phostis had to work hard not to stare at her. Now she sounded the way she had when she'd first fetched him to Etchmiadzin. What had become of the passion she'd shown? Was she dissembling now because Syagrios sat next to her? Or had she seduced Phostis to win him to the gleaming path when more honest methods failed?

He simply could not tell. In a certain sense, it didn't matter. When he got to Pityos, he was going to try to escape, no matter what. If she stood in his way then, he'd do it alone. But he knew some trust would go out of him forever if the girl he loved turned out only to have been using him for her own purposes.

He hoped she'd sneak up to his cubicle that night, both because he wanted her and so he could ask her the questions he couldn't speak with Syagrios listening. But she kept to herself. When morning came, Phostis packed a spare tunic he'd come by, belted on the sword he'd left in the little room ever since he came back from the raid on Aptos, and went downstairs.

Syagrios was already down in the kitchens eating. He flipped Phostis a wide-brimmed hat of woven straw like the one that sat at a jaunty angle on his own head. When Olyvria came down, she was wearing one like it, too, and mannish tunic and trousers suitable for riding.

"Good," Syagrios said, nodding approval when he saw her. "We'll take enough food here to keep us going till we get to Pityos, then stuff it into our saddlebags and be on our way. The bread'll go stale, but who cares?"

Phostis took several loaves, some cheese, some onions, and a length of hard, dry pork sausage flavored with fennel. He paused before some round pastries dusted with powdered sugar. "What's in these?" he asked.

"Take a few; they're good," Olyvria said. "They're made from chopped dates and nuts and honey. We must have a new cook out of Vaspurakan, because that's where they come from."

"True enough," Syagrios agreed. "You ever hear a Videssian who wants them, he'll call 'em 'princes' balls.' " He guffawed. Phostis smiled. Olyvria did her best to pretend she hadn't heard.

Phostis fed his foul-tempered horse one of the pastries in the hope of sweetening its disposition. The beast tried to bite his hand. He jerked it back just in time. Syagrios laughed again. Had Phostis been in any other company, he would have named his horse for the ruffian.

The ride into Pityos was a pleasant five days. The upland plateaus still wore their bright green coat of spring grass and shrubs; another month or two would go by before the vicious summer sun began baking everything brown. Fritillaries and hairstreaks flitted from one clump of red or yellow restharrow to another, and then on to white-flowered fenugreek. Swallows and skylarks swooped after the insects.

About halfway through the first day's ride, Syagrios dismounted to go off behind a bush some little distance from the road. Without turning her head toward Phostis, Olyvria said quietly, "It will be all right."

"Will it?" he answered. He wanted to believe her, but he'd grown chary of trusting anyone. If she meant what she'd said, she'd have the chance to prove it.

Before she could reply, back came Syagrios, buttoning the top button of his fly, rebuckling his belt, and whistling a marching song with more foul verses than clean ones. He grunted as he swung himself up into the saddle. "Off we go again," he declared.

The last day and a half of the journey were through the coastal lowlands. Peasants labored in the fields, plowing, planting, and pruning grape vines. Summer felt near in the lowlands, for the weather there was already hot and sticky. Phostis' shoulder twinged more than it had in the drier climate of the plateau.

As soon as Pityos came into view, the travelers all squinted and shaded their eyes to peer ahead. Phostis wondered how he'd feel to see a forest of masts in the harbor. But unless his eyes were tricking him, though the town seemed to boast fishing boats aplenty, none of them were the big imperial merchantmen that hauled troops and horses.

Syagrios grunted suspiciously. "Your old man is up to something sneaky," he told Phostis, as if it were the latter's fault. "Maybe the ships are lying out to sea so they can come in at nightfall and take folk by surprise, or maybe he's decided to have them make land at Tavas or Nakoleia after all."

"Livanios' Makuraner mage should have been able to divine where they'd put in," Phostis said.

"Naah." Syagrios made a slashing gesture of contempt with his hand. "Livanios took him on because his sorcery fuddles Videssian wizards, but it works the other way round, too, worse luck—some days he's lucky to find his way out of bed, that one is." He paused to give Phostis a meditative stare. "How did you know he's from Makuran?"

"By his accent," Phostis answered, as innocently as he could. "And when I recognized that, I remembered I'd seen Makuraner envoys at court who wore caftans like his."

"Oh. All right." Syagrios relaxed. Phostis breathed easier, too; if he'd let Artapan's name fall from his lips, he'd have thrown himself straight into the soup pot.

The sentries lounging in front of the gates of Pityos were Thanasioi, longer on ferocity than discipline. When Syagrios greeted them in the name of the gleaming path, grins creased their grim faces in unexpected directions. They waved him and his companions into the city.

Pityos was smaller than Nakoleia; as Phostis had thought Nakoleia little better than a village, he'd expected to feel cramped in Pityos as well. But after some months in Etchmiadzin, much of that time mewed up inside the fortress, he found Pityos spacious enough to suit him.

Syagrios rented an upstairs room in a tavern near the harbor so he could keep lookout and spy imperial ships before they started spewing out their men. Olyvria stayed quiet all through the spirited haggle that got the room; Phostis couldn't tell whether the taverner thought her a beardless youth or knew she was a woman but didn't care.

The chamber got crowded when a potboy fetched in a third straw pallet, but remained roomier than Phostis' cubicle had been with him there by himself. He unslung his bedroll and, with a sigh of relief, let it fall to the mattress he'd chosen.

Syagrios leaned out the window to examine the harbor at close range. He shook his head. "Bugger me with a pinecone if I know where they are. They ought to be here, unless I miss my guess altogether." By a slight swagger, he managed to indicate how unlikely that was.

Olyvria picked up the chamber pot, which had been shoved into a corner when the new set of bedding arrived. She looked down into it, made a face, then walked over to the window as if to throw its contents out onto the street—and any unwary passersby below. Instead, when she came up behind Syagrios, she raised the chamber pot high and smashed it over his head.

The pot was of heavy earthenware; no doubt she'd hoped he would sag silently and easily into unconsciousness. But Syagrios was made of stern stuff. He staggered and groaned out, blood running down his face, turned shakily on Olyvria.

Phostis felt his heart beat—once, twice—while he gaped dumbfounded on what she'd done. Then he unfroze. He grabbed Syagrios by the shoulder and hit the ruffian in the face as hard as he could with his left fist. Syagrios lurched backward. He tried to bring up his hands to protect himself or even to grapple with Phostis, but he moved as if in the slowness of a dream. Phostis hit him again, and again. His eyes rolled up in his head; he collapsed to the floor.

Olyvria seized the knife on his belt and held it above his neck. Phostis grabbed her wrist. "Have you gone mad?" she cried.

"No. We'll take his weapons and we'll tie him up," he answered. "But I owe him enough for this"—he touched his healing shoulder—"that I don't care to slit his throat."

She made a face but didn't argue, instead turning the dagger on the linen mattress covers to cut strips of cloth for bonds. Syagrios grunted and stirred when Phostis rolled him over to tie his hands behind his back. Phostis hit him again, and also tied cloth strips over his mouth for a gag. Then he tied the ruffian's ankles together as tightly as he could.

"Give me the dagger," he said suddenly.

Olyvria pressed it into his hand. "Change your mind?"

"No." Phostis slit the money pouch Syagrios wore on his belt. Half a dozen goldpieces and a handful of silver spilled out. He scooped up the coins and stuffed them into his own belt pouch. "Now let's get out of here."

"All right," Olyvria said. "Whatever you intend to do, you'd best be quick about it. The good god only knows how long he'll lie quiet there, and he won't be pleased with us for what we've done."

That, Phostis was sure, was an understatement. "Come on," he said. They hurried out of the chamber. When they came down into the all-but-deserted taproom, the taverner raised an eyebrow but didn't say anything. Phostis walked over to him, took out a goldpiece, and set it on the bar. "You didn't see us come out. You were in the back room. You've never seen us."

The taverner's hand covered the coin. "Did somebody say something?" he asked, looking past Phostis. "This place is so empty, I'm starting to hear phantoms."

"I hope it's enough," Phostis said as he and Olyvria walked rapidly down to the harbor.

"So do I," Olyvria said. "Best if we don't have to find out. I hope you have something along those lines in mind."

"I do." Phostis took deep, happy gulps of seaside air. The salt tang and the aroma of stale fish reminded him at a level almost below consciousness of the way things smelled around the palaces. For the first time in months, he felt at home.

A fisherman leapt from the little boat he'd just tied to a pier. His catch was similarly minimal, a couple of buckets of mackerel and other, less interesting, fare. "Good day," Phostis called to him.

The fisherman was closer to sixty than fifty, and looked deathly tired. "Maybe you think so," he said. "It is a day. It is done. It is enough."

Phostis said, "I will give you two goldpieces for that boat, and another to forget you ever sold it to me." The boat could not have been worth more than a goldpiece and a half. Phostis didn't care. He had the money and he needed to be out of Pityos as fast as he could. He pressed ahead: "Does that make it a better day, if not a good one?"

He pulled out the three bright gold coins from his pouch and held them in the palm of his hand so they sparkled into the fisherman's face. The fellow stared as if he could not believe his eyes. He set down one of his buckets of fish. "Young man," he said slowly, "if you mock me, I shall thrash you, grizzled though I am. By the lord with the great and good mind I swear it."

"I don't mock," Phostis answered. "Have you hammocks aboard there, and your lines and nets?"

"Only one hammock—I fish alone," the fisherman answered, "but there are blankets so the other of you can bed down on deck. And aye, the rest of the tackle is there. See for yourself before you buy—I would not have you say I cheated you, though you must know you are cheating yourself. There's fresh water from yesterday in the tuns, too. You can sail a good ways without coming in to land, if that's what you aim to do."

"Never mind what I aim to do." The less Phostis told the fisherman, the better. He walked along the dock and peered into the boat. The nets lay neatly coiled at the bow; lines with hooks on them were wrapped between pegs on one side of the tiny cabin behind the mast. A pair of long sweeps lay on the deck. He nodded to himself and gave the fisherman the gold-pieces. "You keep it shipshape."

"And if I don't, who'll do it for me?" the man answered.

Phostis handed Olyvria down into the boat, then got in himself and put the sweeps in the oarlocks. "Would you cast off the line?" he called to the fisherman.

The fellow was still staring at the gold coins. He started slightly before he obeyed. Grunting with effort, Phostis worked the sweeps. The fishing boat slowly backed away from the pier. Its former owned seemed glad to have seen the last of it. He picked up his buckets and walked into town without a backward glance.

When Phostis had put enough distance between himself and the dock, he let down the sail from its yard. It was, like most Videssian sails, a simple square rig, not much good for sailing against the wind but fine with it. The wind blew out of the west. Phostis wanted to sail east. As long as the wind held, he'd have no problems.

He turned to Olyvria. "Do you know anything about fishing?"

"No, not much, not boats, either," she answered. "Do you?"

"Enough," he said. "I can manage the boat as long as the weather doesn't get too rough. And I can fish, too, even if the gear here isn't exactly what I'm used to. I learned from my father." It was, he thought, the first time he'd ever simply acknowledged that Krispos had taught him something worth knowing.

"Good for him and good for you." Olyvria watched the harbor of Pityos recede off to the starboard side of the stern. That means we won't starve right away?"

"I hope so," Phostis said, "though you never can tell with fish. If we have to put in to shore to feed ourselves, I still have some of Syagrios' money left." He slapped the pouch that hung from his belt.

Olyvria nodded. "That sounds fine to me. What do you plan to do? Sail along the coast until you find where the imperial fleet really is?"

"As a matter of fact, I'd intended to sail straight to Videssos the city. I can find out more about what's going on there than anywhere else, and then head straight out to the main body of the army. My father will be there, and I ought to join him. If I hadn't intended to do that, what point to leaving the Thanasioi?"

"None, I suppose." Olyvria looked back at Pityos again. Already it seemed a toy town, the buildings shrunk to the size of those a woodcarver might shape for his children to play with. Quietly, without looking back to him, she asked, "And what do you intend to do about me?"

"Why—" Phostis shut his mouth with a snap. The question was too pointed to answer before he considered it. After a moment, he went on, "I hadn't thought so far ahead yet. The most that had occurred to me was that for the next few days we'd finally be able to make love without worry about someone catching us while we were at it."

She smiled, but her eyes were still on Pityos. "Yes, we'll be able to do that, if it's what you want. But what about afterward? What happens when you go to the palaces in Videssos the city? What then, young Majesty?"

At Etchmiadzin, no one had called him that except in mockery or the false courtesy that was worse. Now Olyvria reminded him of everything to which he'd be returning: the eunuchs, the ceremonial, the rank. He also remembered, as he had not lately, that she'd kidnapped and humiliated him. She, plainly, had never forgotten. The question she'd asked him was pointed indeed.

Where she looked back across the water toward everything she was leaving, he looked out past the fishing boat's bow at what lay ahead. Slowly he said, "You stole me out of the camp, true. But if it hadn't been for you just now, I wouldn't have got free of Pityos, either. As far as I can reckon us, that puts us at quits there—but still leaves everything else between us."

"Which means?" Olyvria still sounded—*apprehensive* was the word, Phostis decided after a little thought. And no wonder. Until the fishing boat headed out onto the Videssian Sea, she'd been the dominant one, and set the terms of their dealings with each other. She'd kidnapped him, at Etchmiadzin she'd had the power of her father and the Thanasioi behind her . . . but now she'd committed herself to sailing into what literally was, or would be, his dominion. If he wanted vengeance, it was his for the taking.

"If you like," he said, "I'll put in to shore at any deserted beach you like and let you off there. I swear by the lord with the great and good mind I'll do everything in my power to keep my father from ever coming after you. Or—"

"Or what?" She fairly snapped at him. Yes, she was nervous about how things had changed.

He took a deep breath. "Or you can stay with me till we get to Videssos the city, and for as long as you care to after that. For the rest of our lives, I hope."

She studied him, wondering, no doubt, if this was but one more trap to make eventual revenge sweeter. "You mean it," she said at last, and then, "Of course I will," and then, "But what will your father say?"

"He'll probably have kittens," Phostis said cheerfully. "So what? I'm of a man's years, so he can't *make* me put you aside. And besides, people don't always remember these days—it's been a long time, after all—but my mother was Anthimos' Empress before she was my father's. Since I was born less than a year after my father took the throne, you can see his ways there weren't perfectly regular, either."

Phostis listened to that sentence again in his mind. As a matter of fact, he'd been born quite a bit less than a year after Krispos became Avtokrator. He hadn't really thought about how much less till just now. He wondered if Krispos had sired him . . . or Anthimos. By his birthdate, either was possible.

Maybe he frowned, for Olyvria said, "What's wrong?"

"Nothing," he said, and then again, more firmly, "Nothing." Anthimos wasn't around anymore to claim him and, even if Krispos never had quite warmed to him—all at once, he wondered if he saw a new reason for that—he'd named him junior Avtokrator before he was out of swaddling clothes. Krispos wouldn't dispossess him of the succession now, especially when he'd escaped from danger by his own efforts—and those of Olyvria.

She was looking off to starboard again. Land now was just a strip of green and occasional brown on the horizon there; they were too far out to sea to make out any detail. Smiling, she turned to Phostis. "If nothing's wrong, you can prove it."

He started to say, "How am I supposed to do that?" Before he got out more than a couple of words, she took off her hat, shook down her hair, and then pulled her tunic up over her head. Sure enough, he found a way to show her everything was all right.

"YOUR MAJESTY!" THAT WAS ZAIDAS, CALLING FROM OUTSIDE the imperial pavilion before the army got moving on a day full of muggy heat. "I've news, Your Majesty!"

Inside the pavilion, Krispos was wearing a decidedly unimperial pair of linen drawers and nothing more. *To the ice with ceremony,* he thought, and called, "Well, come in and tell it, then." He smiled at Zaidas' pop-eyed expression. "Never mind the proskynesis, sorcerous sir. Just brush aside the mosquito netting and let me know what you've learned."

Zaidas inhaled portentously. "May it please Your Majesty, my sorcery shows your son Phostis has traveled from Etchmiadzin down to Pityos on the coast."

"Has he?" Krispos growled. As usual with news prefaced by that formula, it pleased him not at all. "Bloody good thing I ordered the fleet to Tavas, then. The only reason I can find for him to go down to the port is to try and forestall us. But Livanios sent him to the wrong place, by Phos." He smacked one fist into the other palm. "The Thanasioi have spies among us, sure enough, but they didn't learn enough, not this time."

"No, Your Majesty," Zaidas agreed. He hesitated, then went on, "Your Majesty, I might add that Phostis' sorcerous trace, if you will forgive an inexact expression, has itself become inexact."

"More interference from that accursed Makuraner." Krispos made it statement, not question.

But Zaidas shook his head. "I think not, Your Majesty. It's almost as if the trace is attenuated by—water, perhaps. I'm puzzled to come up with any other explanation, yet the heretics would scarcely send Phostis out by sea, would they?"

"Not a chance," Krispos said, his voice flat. "Livanios isn't such a fool; I wish to Phos he were. Keep searching. The lord with the great and good mind willing, you'll come up with something that makes better sense. Believe me, sorcerous sir, I still have full confidence in you."

"More than I have in myself sometimes." Zaidas shook his head. "I'll do my best for you."

Krispos started sweating hard as soon as he put on his gilded mail shirt. He sighed; summer felt as if it were here already. He went out to stand in line with the soldiers for his morning bowl of porridge. The cooks never knew which line he'd pick. The food in all of them was better for it. This morning, for instance, the barley porridge was thick with onions and cloves of garlic, and almost every spoonful had a bit of chopped ham with an intensely smoky flavor.

He emptied the bowl. "If I'd eaten this well on my farm, I'd never have wanted to come to Videssos the city," he remarked.

Several of the soldiers nodded. Life on a farm, as Krispos knew, was seldom easy. That was one of the big reasons men left the country: if nothing else, soldiers ate regularly. But while farm work was harder day in and day out, soldiers sometimes earned their keep harder than any man who lived off the land.

The army's discipline, not bad when the men set out from the capital, had improved steadily since. Everyone knew his place, and went to it with a minimum of fuss. The cooks' kettles went back onto the supply wagons, the troopers mounted their horses, and the army pushed on through the lowlands toward Tavas.

Krispos rode at the head of the main body, a few hundred yards behind the vanguard. Peasants looked up from the fields in wonder as he went by, as if he were some kind of being altogether different from themselves. Had Anthimos' father Rhaptes ever happened to parade past the village where Krispos had grown to manhood, he was sure he would have gaped the same way.

A little before noon, a messenger on a lathered, blowing horse caught up with the army from behind. The animal gulped in great drafts of air as the fellow brought it down to a slow trot beside the Avtokrator's horse. He pulled out a sealed tube of oiled leather and handed it to Krispos. "From the city, Your Majesty."

The seal was a sunburst stamped into the sky-blue wax that was an imperial prerogative, which meant the dispatch came from Evripos. Krispos could think of only one reason why his son would send out an urgent message. Filled with foreboding, he broke the seal.

His son's script still retained some of the copybook clarity that years of quickly scribbling will erode. The words were as legible as they were unwelcome: "Evripos to his father. Greetings. Riots flared here night before last, and have grown worse rather than better since. Forces under my command are doing all they can to restore order. I shall send more news as it becomes available. Phos guard you and this city both. Farewell."

"Do you know anything of this?" Krispos asked the messenger, waving the parchment in his direction.

"No, Your Majesty, I'm sorry but I don't," the man answered. "I'm but the latest of a string of relay riders. I hear tell from the fellow who gave me the tube that there's some sort of trouble back at the city. Is that so?"

"Aye, that's so," Krispos answered grimly. He'd known the Thanasioi might try that ploy to distract him and, prepared for it as well as he could. Whether *well as he could* was *well enough* would come clear before long.

Then he thought of something else, something that chilled him: was Phostis on the sea to go to the capital and lead the rioters against loyal troops? If he was, he might throw the city into worse turmoil than even Krispos had expected. *Have to warn Evripos about that,* the Avtokrator thought.

"Is there a reply, Your Majesty?" the messenger asked.

"Yes, by the good god, there is," Krispos said. But before he could give it, another dispatch rider rode up on an abused horse and waved a message tube in his face. He didn't like the fearful look in the newcomer's eyes. "Rest easy there, you. I've never been in the habit of blaming the messenger for the word he brings."

"Aye, Your Majesty," the second rider said, but he didn't sound convinced. He thrust out the message tube as if it held poison.

Krispos took it, then asked, "You know what's in it?" The messenger nodded. Krispos said, "Speak it to me plain, then. By the lord with the great and good mind, I swear no harm nor blame shall fall on you because of it."

He'd never seen a man who so obviously wanted to be somewhere, anywhere, else. The dispatch rider licked his lips, looked this way and that, but found no escape. He sucked in a deep breath, then let it all out in five blurted words: "Your Majesty, Garsavra is fallen."

"What?" Krispos gaped at him, more in disbelief than horror. So did everyone close enough to hear. Lying where the Eriza and Arandos rivers came together, Garsavra was one of the two or three greatest towns in the westlands. The army was already west of it; they'd forded the northern reaches of the Eriza day before yesterday.

Krispos opened the message tube. It confirmed what the dispatch rider had said, and added details. Outriding news of their coming, the Thanasioi had swept down on the town at sunrise. They'd burned and killed and maimed; they'd thrown the local prelate headfirst off the roof of the temple by the central square, then set fire to the building. Few survivors would have their souls burdened by a surplus of material goods for years to come.

Krispos stared at the parchment in his left hand. He wanted to tear it into a thousand pieces. With a deliberate effort of will, he checked himself: some of the information it held might be valuable. As steadily as he could, he told the messenger, "You have my thanks for your courage in bringing this to me. What is your rank?"

"I'm on the books as a file closer, Your Majesty," the man answered.

"You're a file leader now," Krispos told him.

One of the scouts from the vanguard came riding back to the main body. He waited to catch Krispos' eye, then said, "May it please Your Majesty, we've rounded up a Thanasiot riding at us under shield of truce. He says he bears a message for you from Livanios."

Too much was falling on Krispos too fast. He had the feeling of a tavern juggler who has reached out for one plate he's tossed away, only to have all the others that were up in the air smash down on his head before he can snatch back his hand. "Bring me this Thanasiot," he said heavily. "Tell him I'll honor his truce sign, which is likely more courtesy than he'd give to one of ours. Tell him just that way."

The scout saluted and rode ahead. He came back a few minutes later with one of Livanios' irregulars. The Thanasiot carried a white-painted round target on his left arm. He smiled at Krispos' somber face and said, "I'd wager you have the news already. Am I right, friend?"

"I'm no friend of yours," Krispos said. "Give me your master's message."

The Thanasiot handed him a tube no different from those he'd had from his own couriers save in the seal: the image of a leaping flame stamped into scarlet wax. Krispos broke it and angrily threw the little pieces of wax down onto the ground. The parchment inside was sealed with the identical mark. Krispos cracked it, unrolled the parchment, and scanned the message it contained:

Livanios who treads the gleaming path to the false Avtokrator and servant of Skotos Krispos: Greetings. Know that I write this from the ruins of Garsavra, which city has been purified and cleansed of its sinful materialism by warriors true to the lord with the great and good mind. Know further that all cities of the westlands are liable to the same penalty, which Phos' soldiers may deliver at any time which suits them.

And know further, miscalled ruler destined for the ice, your corrupt and gold-bloated regime is henceforward and ever after banished from these westlands. If you would preserve even a fragment of your illicit and tyrannical rule, withdraw at once over the Cattle-Crossing, yielding this land to those who shall hold it in triumph, peace, and piety. Repent of your wealth and other sins before Phos' final judgment descends upon you. Cast aside your greed and surrender yourself to the gleaming path. I am yours in Phos. Farewell.

Krispos slowly and deliberately crumpled the parchment, then turned to the Thanasiot messenger and said, "My reply is one word: no. Take it and be thankful your life goes with it."

"I don't fear death—death liberates me from Skotos," the messenger retorted. "You call down doom on your own head." He twitched the reins, dug his heels into his horse's sides, and rode away singing a hymn.

"What did the whoreson want of you?" Sarkis asked. When Krispos told him, his fleshy face darkened with anger. "By the good god, a bragging fool ought to know better than to taunt a force that's bigger than his, especially when we stand closer to Etchmiadzin than he does."

"Maybe we stand closer to it," Krispos said bleakly. "You've said all along Livanios is no fool. Surely he'll have withdrawn after the rape of Garsavra. I don't want to chase him back to his stronghold; I want to force him to battle outside of it."

"How do you propose to do that?" Sarkis said. "The cursed Thanasioi move faster than we; they aren't even burdened by loot, because they burn it instead of carrying it along with them."

"I know." Krispos' scowl was black as winter midnight. "I suppose you were right before, though: We have to try. Livanios can't be smart all the time—I hope. If we march smartly, we may come to grips with him up on the plateau. Worth a try, anyhow."

"Aye." Sarkis nodded vigorously. "Our cavalry at Tavas can hold its own against anything the Thanasioi have around there—and now we know where their main force has been lurking."

"So we do," Krispos said. "It's a bloody big cloud for such a thin silver lining." He leaned over, spat down onto the ground as if in ritual rejection of Skotos, then began issuing the orders that would shift the army's line of march from the coast and up into the central highlands. Changing the troops' destination was the easy part. Making sure they would have food and their animals fodder along the new track was much more involved.

What with everything that came after, he forgot to send Evripos a reply.

P HOSTIS GUIDED THE FISHING BOAT UP TO THE LITTLE QUAY from which his father would row out to see what he could catch. He threw out a line, scrambled up onto the dock, and made the boat fast.

He was just helping Olyvria up onto the planks when an indignant palace servitor opened the seawall gate and exclaimed, "Here, who do you think you are? This dock's not for just anyone. It's reserved for the Avtokrator, Phos bless him, so you can kindly take your smelly little boat somewhere else."

"It's all right, Soranos," Phostis answered. "I don't think Father will mind."

He wasn't in the least put out that Soranos hadn't recognized him. He was grimy, shaggy, wearing a cheap, ragged long tunic, and sunburned. In fact, he was sunburned in some tender spots under the tunic, too, thanks to frolicking with Olyvria in broad, hot daylight. She was also sunburned; they'd shared misery and fish on the way back to the city.

The servitor put hands on hips. "Oh, your father won't mind, eh? And who, pray, is your father? Do you know yourself?"

Phostis had been wondering the same thing, but didn't let on. He said, "My father is Krispos son of Phostis, Avtokrator of the Videssians. I have, you will notice if you look closely, escaped from the Thanasioi."

Soranos started to give back another sharp answer, but paused and took a long look at Phostis. He was too swarthy to turn pale, but his jaw fell, his eyes widened, and his right hand, seemingly of its own accord, shaped the sun-circle above his heart. He prostrated himself, gabbling, "Young Majesty, it is yourself—I mean, you are yourself! A thousand pardons, I pray, I beg! Phos be praised that he has granted you safe voyage home and blessed you with liberty once again."

Beside Phostis, Olyvria snickered. He shook his head reproachfully, then told the servitor, "Get up, get up. I forgive you. Now tell me at once what's going on, why I saw so much smoke in the sky as I was sailing down the Cattle-Crossing."

"The heretics have rioted again, young Majesty; they're trying to burn the city down around our heads," Soranos answered as he rose.

"I feared that's what it was. Take me to my father at once, then."

Soranos' face assumed the exaggerated mask of regret any sensible servant donned when saying no to a member of the imperial family. "Young Majesty, I cannot. He has left the city to campaign against the Thanasioi."

"Yes, of course he has," Phostis said, annoyed at himself. Had the imperial army not been on the move, he wouldn't have been sent to Pityos— or escaped. "Who is in command here in the city, then?"

"The young Majesty Evripos, your brother."

"Oh." Phostis bit down on that like a man finding a pebble in his lentil stew. From Krispos' point of view, the appointment made sense, especially with Phostis himself absent. But he could not imagine anyone who would be less delighted than Evripos at his sudden arrival. No help for it, though. "You'd best take me to him."

"Certainly, young Majesty. But would you and your, ah, companion—" Olyvria had her hair up under her hat and was in her baggy, mannish outfit, so Soranos could not be sure if she was woman or youth. "—not care first to refresh yourselves and change into, ah, more suitable garments?"

"No." Phostis made the single word as imperious—and imperial—as he could; not till it had passed his lips did he realize he'd taken his tone from Krispos.

Whatever its source, it worked wonders. Soranos said, "Of course, young Majesty. Follow me, if you would be so kind."

Phostis followed. No one came close to him, Olyvria, and Soranos as they walked through the palace compound. People who saw them at a distance no doubt thought Soranos was escorting a couple of day laborers to some job or other.

To Phostis, the palace compound was simply home. He took no special notice of the lawns and gardens and buildings among which he strode. To Olyvria, though, they all seemed new and marvelous. Watching her try to look every which way at once, seeing her awe at the Grand Courtroom, the cherry orchard that screened the imperial residence, and the Hall of the Nineteen Couches made him view them with fresh eyes, too.

Evripos was not conducting his fight against the rioters from the palaces. He'd set up a headquarters in the plaza of Palamas. People—some soldiers, some not—hurried in and out with news, orders, what-have-you. A big Haloga gave Phostis a first-rate dubious stare. "What you want here?" he asked in accented Videssian.

"I'd like to see my brother, Herwig," Phostis answered.

Herwig glowered at him, wondering who his brother might be—and who he was himself, to presume to address an imperial guardsman by name. Then the glower faded to wonderment. "Young Majesty!" the Haloga boomed, loud enough to cause heads to turn in the makeshift pavilion.

Among those heads was Evripos'. "Well, well," he said when he saw it truly was Phostis. "Look what the dog dragged to the doorstep."

"Hello, brother," Phostis said, more cautiously than he'd expected. In the bit more than half a year since he'd set eyes on his younger brother, Evripos had gone from youth to man. His features were sharper than they had been, his beard thicker and not so soft. He wore a man's expression, too, under a coat of smoke and dirt: tired, harassed, but determined to do what he'd set out to do.

Now he gave Phostis a hostile stare. It wasn't the stare Phostis was used to, the one that came because he was older. It was because he might be an enemy. Evripos barked, "Did the cursed Thanasioi send you here to stir up more trouble?"

"If they had, would I have tied up the fishing boat I sailed here over at Father's quay?" Phostis said. "Would I have come looking for you instead of Digenis?"

"Digenis is dead, and we don't miss him a bit," Evripos said, voice still harsh. "And who knows what you'd do? One of the things I know about the bloody heretics is that they're bloody sneaky. For all I know, you could have that doxy there by you just to fool me into thinking you're not off the pleasures of the flesh."

Unlike Soranos, Evripos knew a girl when he saw one, no matter what she wore. Phostis said, "Brother, I present to you Olyvria the daughter of Livanios, who helped me escape from the Thanasioi and rejects them as much as I do, which is to say altogether."

That succeeded in startling Evripos. Then Olyvria startled Phostis: She prostrated herself before his brother, murmuring, "Your Majesty." She probably should have said *young Majesty,* but Evripos had been left in command of the city, so she wasn't really wrong—and she was dead right to err on the side of flattery.

Evripos grunted. Before he could say more than "Get up," a messenger bleeding from a cut over one eye came up and gasped something Phostis didn't follow. Evripos said, "It's not hard unless you make it so. Push one troop down from Middle Street east of where those maniacs are holed up and another west of 'em. Then crush 'em between our men."

The messenger dashed away. Off to one side in the pavilion, Phostis saw Noetos bent over a map. But Noetos was not running the show. Evripos was. Phostis had watched Krispos exercise command too often to mistake it.

He said, "What can I do to help?"

"To take things away from me, you mean?" Evripos asked suspiciously.

"No. Father gave it to you, and you seem to be doing well by it. I just got here, remember? I haven't the faintest idea what's going on. But if I can be of use, tell me how."

Evripos looked as if such cooperation were the last thing he wanted. Olyvria said, "If you like, we could speak to the mob and tell them why we care for the gleaming path no more."

"Not the least reason being that Makuran is behind the Thanasioi and supports them with a wizard and the good god only knows what all else," Phostis added.

"So you know about that, do you? We wondered, Father and I. We were afraid you knew and didn't care, afraid you'd thrown your lot in with the heretics. You hadn't seemed exactly eager when we went on campaign against them last year." Evripos' sarcasm stung like a whiplash.

"I wasn't eager then," Phostis admitted: No point denying it, for Evripos knew better. "It's different now. Fetch a mage for the two-mirror test if you don't believe me."

Evripos glowered at him. "The Thanasioi have tricks to beat the two-mirror test, as you'll recall from the delightful time Zaidas had trying to use it last year. And if Zaidas couldn't make it work, I doubt another mage would be able to, either. And so, brother of mine, I'll keep you and the heresiarch's daughter off the platform. I can't trust you, you see."

"Can't trust us how?" Phostis demanded.

"How d'you think? Suppose I let you go talk to the mob and instead of saying, 'The golden path is a midden full of dung,' you say, 'Hurrah for Thanasios! Now go out and burn the High Temple!'? That would spill the chamber pot into the stew, now wouldn't it?"

Noetos looked up from the map table and said, "Surely the young Majesty would commit no such outrage. He—"

Evripos cut him off with a sharp wave of the hand. "No." He sounded as imperial—and as much like his father—as Phostis had with the same word. "I will not take the chance. Have we not seen enough chaos in the city these past few days to fight shy of provoking more? I say again, no." He shifted his feet into a fighter's stance, as if defying Noetos to make him change his mind.

The general tamely yielded. "It shall be as you say, of course, young Majesty," he murmured, and went back to his map.

Phostis found himself furious enough to want to hit his brother over the head with the nearest hard object he could find. "You're a fool," he growled.

"And you're a blockhead," Evripos retorted. "I'm not the one who let Digenis seduce him."

"How's this, then?" Phostis said. "Suppose you summon Oxeites the patriarch here to the plaza of Palamas or anyplace else you think would be a good idea, and he can marry me to Olyvria as publicly as possible. That ought to convince people I'm not a Thanasiot—they'd sooner starve than wive . . . Curse you, Evripos, I mean it. What's so bloody funny?"

"I'm sorry," Evripos said, the first concession Phostis had got from him. "I was just thinking it's too bad Father's gone on campaign. The two of you might don the crowns of marriage side by side. Do you remember the serving maid named Drina?"

"Of course. She's a pretty little thing, but—" Phostis gaped at his grinning brother. "Father's gone all soft in the head over her?"

"I doubt that," Evripos said judiciously. "When has Father ever gone soft in the head over anyone, us included? But she is pregnant by him. We'll have ourselves a little half brother or half sister before Midwinter's Day. Relax, Phostis—you don't need to go so white. Father truly doesn't plan on marrying her. Believe me, I'm as happy at that as you are."

"Yes. A new half brother or half sister, eh? Well, well." Phostis wondered if he was only half brother to Evripos and Katakolon as it was. He'd never know, not for certain. He said, "If you're done gossiping, I'm dead serious about what I said. If you think it will help end the riots, I'll wed in as open a ceremony as the chamberlains can dream up."

Beside him, Olyvria nodded vigorously. "That might be the best way to discredit the gleaming path: let those who think of following it see that their onetime leaders are abandoning it."

"The plan is sensible, young Majesty," Noetos said.

"Mmm—maybe it is." Evripos frowned in intense concentration. A messenger interrupted with a note. Evripos read it, snapped orders, and returned to study. At last he said, "No, I will not order it. One of the drawbacks of our rank, brother, is that we aren't always free to make the matches we would. I see nothing wrong with this one, but I'm slowly finding out—" His grin was rueful and disarming at the same time. "—I don't know everything there is to know. Too much rides here for me to say aye or nay."

"What then?" Phostis demanded.

"I'll send you along the courier route to Father. Tell him your tale. If he believes you, what can I possibly say? And if he thinks this marriage of yours a good idea, then married you shall be—and at a quickstep, if I know Father. Bargain?"

"Bargain," Phostis replied at once. A couple of orders from Evripos and he and Olyvria might have disappeared for good. If Krispos ever found out, Evripos could claim they were fanatical Thanasioi. Who would contradict him, especially after he became the primary heir? "It's . . . decent of you."

"Meaning you expect me to throw you into some dungeon or other and then forget which one it was?" Evripos asked.

"Well—yes." Phostis felt his face heat at being so obvious; had he made that kind of mistake at Etchmiadzin, he never would have got out of the fortress.

"If you think the notion didn't cross my mind, you're daft." Phostis needed a moment to realize the strangled noise Evripos made was intended as laughter. His younger brother went on, "Father always taught us to fear the ice, and I guess I listened to him. If you'd gone over to the gleaming path, nothing would have made me happier than hunting you down and taking your place. Always believe that, Phostis. But stealing it after you've got loose of the Thanasioi?" He made a wry face. "It's tempting, but I can resist it."

Phostis thought of the chamber under Digenis' tunnel, and of the naked and lovely temptation Olyvria had represented. He'd passed her by—then. Now he lay in her arms whenever he could. Had he yielded to temptation? Would Evripos, with some future chance to seize the throne, spring after it rather than turning his back?

As for the first question, Phostis told himself, the situation had changed by the time he and Olyvria became lovers. She wasn't just so much flesh set out for him to enjoy; she'd become his closest friend—almost his only friend—in Etchmiadzin. Were circumstances different, he'd gladly have paid her formal court.

As for the second question . . . the future would have to answer it. Phostis knew he'd be a fool to ignore the possibility of Evripos' trying to usurp him. In the future, though, he'd have the power, not his brother—as Evripos did today. And maybe today showed they had hope, at least, of working together.

Evripos said, "Come the day, brother, we may not make such a bad team. Even if you end up with the red boots on your feet, give me something to do with soldiers and I'll do well for Videssos with them."

Not *in your service,* Phostis noted. He didn't quibble. Among the other things Krispos had taught was that the Empire came first, that anyone who didn't put it ahead of everything else didn't deserve to have his fundament warm the throne in the Grand Courtroom. The lesson made more sense to Phostis than it ever had before.

"You know what?" he said. Evripos raised a questioning eyebrow. Phostis continued, "It'll be good to see Father. It's been too long." Phostis paused again. "I don't suppose I could bring Olyvria along?"

"No," Evripos said at once, but then added, "Wait. Maybe you should. She'll know a lot about the Thanasioi—"

"She does," Phostis said, at the same time as Olyvria was saying, "I do."

"Well then," Evripos said, as if that settled things, "if you don't bring her, Father will come down on me for making you leave her behind so he can't wring her dry with questions. Take her by all means."

"I shall obey your commands, young Majesty," Phostis said with a salute.

Evripos saluted in return. "I've obeyed yours a time or two, young Majesty," he answered.

"Brothers," Olyvria said; she might have been referring to some lower form of life. Phostis and Evripos looked at each other. Grinning, they both nodded.

Chapter XI

KRISPOS SLAMMED HIS FOREHEAD WITH THE HEEL OF HIS hand, hard enough to hurt. "By the good god, I'm an idiot," he exclaimed.

"No doubt, Your Majesty," Sarkis agreed cheerfully; along with Iakovitzes, Zaidas, and Barsymes, he could say something like that without going up on charges of lèse majesté. "In which particular matter are you being an idiot today?"

"With all the hoorah over Garsavra, I clean forgot to write to Evripos and warn him to be alert for Phostis," Krispos answered. He thumped himself again, in disgust. Characteristically, he wasted no more time on reproaches. Instead, he pulled a scrap of parchment and pen and ink from pouches on his belt, scrawled a few nearly illegible lines—the motion of the horse didn't help—and then called, "Katakolon!" After a moment, he called again, louder.

"Aye, Father? How can I help you?" His youngest son brought his own horse trotting up alongside Krispos' mount.

Krispos handed him the note. "Seal this, stick it in a message tube, and get it off to Videssos the city as fast as you can."

"Just as you say." The piece of parchment was too small to roll or fold conveniently. Katakolon read it before he took it to do as Krispos had commanded. His eyes were troubled when he raised them to look at his father again. "Surely it can't be as bad as—this?"

"I don't know whether it is or not," Krispos said. "But as to whether it can be—by Phos, boy, it could be ten times worse. He might be landing in the city with a shipload of fanatics all hot to die for the gleaming path."

"Phostis?" Katakolon's voice rose. He shook his head. "I can't believe it."

"I can, which is what matters," Krispos answered. "Now get moving. I didn't give you that note to argue over it, just to have it start on its way to the city."

"Aye, Father," Katakolon said dolefully.

"You don't suppose he'll 'accidentally' lose that, do you?" Sarkis said.

"He'd better not," Krispos answered; the same thought had crossed his mind. He remembered his talk with Evripos back in the city. If his sons thought strongly enough that they were right, they would follow their own wills, not his. They were turning into men—at the most inconvenient time possible.

Had Phostis done that? When he chose to walk the gleaming path, was he making his own judgments as best he knew how, no matter how wrongheaded they seemed to Krispos? Or had he merely found someone whose lead he preferred to his father's? Krispos shook his head. He wondered if Phostis knew.

As he had so often over the years, he forced personal worries—and worries about which he could do nothing—to the back of his mind. Enough other business remained to occupy him. The army was up on the plateau now, with everyone a bit on the hungry side because supply arrangements hadn't kept up with the changed route.

Of Livanios' force there was no sign. That worried Krispos. If the Thanasioi scattered before he could smite them, what point to the campaign? How was he supposed to beat them if they turned back into harmless-looking herders and farmers and tanners and candlemakers and what-have-you? If he went back to Videssos the city, they'd be raiders again the moment his dust vanished over the horizon. He was bitterly certain of that.

The army camped for the night by a stream that wouldn't have water in it too much longer. Now, though, it would serve. The men saw to their horses before they cared for themselves. Krispos strolled through the encampment, checking to make sure his orders on that score were obeyed.

He'd served as groom first for Iakovitzes and then for Petronas after he came to the imperial city; he knew what went into tending horses.

He was sound asleep on his folding cot in the imperial tent when a Haloga called "Your Majesty" over and over until it woke him. He groaned as he made himself sit; his eyes felt as if someone had poured sand into their sockets. The guardsman said, "Your pardon, Majesty, but out here waits a courier who must see you."

"Aye, send him in," Krispos said in a voice that sounded nothing like his own.

He waved for the courier not to bother prostrating himself; the sooner the fellow was gone, he thought, the sooner he could get back to sleep. "May it please Your Majesty," the courier said, and Krispos braced himself for bad news. The man delivered it: "I have to report that the Thanasioi have fallen on and taken the city of Kyzikos."

"Kyzikos?" Still foggy, Krispos needed a moment to place the town on the map. It lay down in the coastal plain, east of Garsavra. "What's Livanios doing there?" As soon as he raised the question, the answer became obvious: "The imperial mint!"

"Aye, Your Majesty, it's taken and burned," the courier said. "The temple is burned, as well, and so is much of the central part of the city—like many towns in the western lowlands, Kyzikos has, or rather had, no wall to hold invaders at bay. And the farmland round the city is ravaged as if locusts had been at it."

"Aye," Krispos said. "A heavy blow." If Livanios' warriors could ravage Kyzikos, no place in the westlands was safe from them. And if Livanios had the gold from the mint in Kyzikos, he could work untold mischief with it, too. Gold and the Thanasioi did not normally mix, but Krispos did not think Livanios was a typical Thanasiot. If he read the heresiarch aright, Livanios cared more about Livanios than about the gleaming path.

But no matter how much damage they had done—Krispos' wits began working a little faster—they'd also made what might prove a bad mistake: they'd given the imperial army the chance to interpose itself between them and their stronghold near the border with Vaspurakan.

"If you stick your neck out too far, it gets chopped," Krispos said.

"Your Majesty?" the courier asked.

"Never mind." Clad only in his linen drawers, the Avtokrator strode out into the night. Ignoring the grunts of surprise that rose from the Haloga guards, he started bawling for his generals. If he couldn't sleep, he wouldn't let them sleep, either, not with work to be done.

Two days later, Sarkis said, for about the dozenth time, "The trick, Your Majesty, will be to make sure they don't get by us."

"Yes," Krispos said, also for the dozenth time. The westlands' central plateau was not flat like the lowlands; it was rough, broken country, gullies running into ravines running into valleys. If the imperial army didn't position itself correctly, slipping between the Thanasioi and Etchmiadzin wouldn't matter because the raiders would get past without being noticed till too late. That was probably the gamble Livanios had made when he decided to strike Kyzikos.

Sarkis found a new question to ask: "How will you choose the right spot?"

"The best way I can figure is this," Krispos said: "I'll station us near one of the central valleys and fan scouts out widely ahead of us and to either side. It's no guarantee of anything, of course, but it's what we'll do unless you have a better idea. I hope you will."

"I was thinking something along the same lines," Sarkis said. "The trouble is, it's what Livanios will think is in our minds, too."

"That's so," Krispos admitted. "But if we play the game of if-he-then-we and if-we-then-he, we're liable to get lost in the maze. I'll cut through it and just do what I think best under the circumstances."

"Against any other foe I would say you were wise, Your Majesty, but Livanios . . . Livanios never seems to do what you'd expect." Sarkis turned his head at the sound of galloping hoofbeats. So did Krispos. Sarkis said, "Looks like another courier coming up—no, two of 'em together."

"Oh, Phos, what now?" It was more a groan than a prayer. Every courier who'd ridden up to Krispos lately had brought bad news with him. How much longer could that go on?

Sure enough, the riders made straight for the imperial standard that marked Krispos' place in the line of march. *They're sending out babies,* he thought. One of the couriers had no beard. The other didn't seem much older.

Krispos braced for the call of "May it please Your Majesty" and the displeasing message that would follow it. The bearded rider spotted him under the sunburst standard, then raised a hand to his mouth to make a shout carry farther. But he didn't yell "May it please Your Majesty." Instead, he called, "Father!"

Krispos' first thought was that Katakolon was playing some kind of trick on him, and not a funny one. Then he recognized the voice. He hadn't been sure he'd ever hear that voice again, or want to. "Phostis," he whispered.

His son approached, and the other rider with him. Several Halogai quickly moved to put themselves between Phostis and Krispos—they knew where Phostis had been, and did not know what he'd become. Krispos wanted to thank them and punch them at the same time.

"It's all right, Father—I've escaped the gleaming path," Phostis said.

Before Krispos answered, one of the Halogai said, "What proof of this have you, young Majesty?" The big fair men from the north did not stand aside.

What proof could Phostis possibly have? Krispos wondered. But he produced some: "Allow me to present Olyvria, the daughter of Livanios."

By then, Krispos had figured out that Phostis' companion was a woman. To remove any doubt, she doffed her traveler's hat with a flourish and let her piled-up hair tumble out in a curly black waterfall. "Your Majesty," she said, bowing in the saddle to Krispos.

She's not just accompanying Phostis, Krispos realized. *She's* with *him.* Phostis' eyes did not want to leave her, even to look at his father. Katakolon got that mooncalf gaze, but never over the same girl for more than a couple of months. Krispos hadn't seen it on Phostis before. Olyvria looked at Phostis the same way.

Acting? Krispos didn't think so. He asked Olyvria, "Are you here of your own will, girl, or did he kidnap you?"

"As a matter of fact, Your Majesty, I kidnapped him," Olyvria answered boldly. Krispos stared; that was not the reply he'd expected. Olyvria added, "We've made other arrangements since."

"So I gather." Krispos glanced over to Phostis, who was still grinning like a besotted schoolboy. The Avtokrator made his decision. He told the Haloga guards, "Stand aside." After a moment's hesitation, they obeyed. He urged his horse up alongside Phostis', held out his arms. The two men, one young, the other vividly remembering when he had been, embraced.

Phostis pulled away. "Sorry, Father, but hugging chain mail hurts. I have so much to tell you—did you know, for instance, that Makuran is aiding the Thanasioi?"

"As things turn out, I did," Krispos said. "I'm glad to hear you tell me as much all the same—it lets me know you are to be trusted indeed."

He wondered if he should have been so frank. He watched Phostis' face freeze into the mask he'd seen so often before, the one that concealed whatever went on behind it. Minutes into their reunion, would the two of them go back to misunderstanding each other?

But Olyvria said, "I don't blame you for being wary of us, Your Majesty. Truly, though, the gleaming path lures us no more."

To Krispos' relief, Phostis' face cleared. "That's so," he said. "I've seen more along those lines than I can stomach. And Father!—is Zaidas with you?"

"Aye, he is," Krispos answered. "Why?"

"I have much to tell him—and little of it good—of Artapan, the Makuraner mage who aids Livanios' schemes."

"All that can wait till tonight when we camp," Krispos said. "For now, it's enough to see you again." *And to see you here as something besides a Thanasiot fanatic,* he thought. He kept that to himself, though Phostis would have to be a fool if he couldn't figure it out. Let the lad have his time in Phos' sun now, though. "How did you escape the zealots' clutches, then?"

Phostis and Olyvria took turns telling the tale, which, as it unfolded, seemed only fair to Krispos. Phostis didn't try to minimize what he'd done as an unwilling Thanasiot raider; if anything, he dwelt on it with pained guilt. "How are your arm and shoulder now?" Krispos asked.

"They still pain me now and again," Phostis said, working the arm. "I can use them, though. Anyhow, Father, getting wounded helped convince Syagrios I could be trusted, and prompted him to let me go to Pityos—"

Olyvria took over then with the story of how she'd smashed the chamber pot on Syagrios' head. "Fitting enough," Krispos agreed. Then Phostis told of buying the fishing boat and sailing to Videssos the city. That made Krispos laugh out loud. "There—you see? All that time you passed on the water with me wasn't wasted after all."

"I suppose not," Phostis said; he was, if nothing else, more patient around Krispos than he had been before he was kidnapped. Krispos watched his mirth fade as he continued, "I found riots in the city when I got there."

"Yes, I knew of them," Krispos said, nodding. "I knew you were on the way to the city, too; Zaidas' magic told me as much. I feared you were traveling as provocateur, not escapee. I meant to write Evripos and tell him as much, but it slipped my mind until yesterday in the midst of everything else that's been going on."

"It didn't matter," Phostis answered. "He thought of it for himself."

"Good," Krispos said, to see how Phostis would react. Phostis didn't react much at all, certainly not with the anger he would have shown a few months before. He just nodded and went on with his story. When he was finished, Krispos said, "So our troops have the upper hand?"

"They did when Olyvria and I left to join you," Phostis said. "Uh, Father . . ."

"Yes?"

"What *do* you think of the suggestion I made to Evripos, that Olyvria and I should marry at once to show the Thanasioi we've renounced their sect?"

"Imperial marriages have a way of being made for reasons of state, but till now I'd never heard of one made for reasons of doctrine," Krispos answered. "Were the emergency worse, I might send the two of you back there to be wedded forthwith. As it is, I think you can wait till the campaign is over before you marry—assuming you still want to by then."

Their expressions said they could imagine no other possibility. Krispos had a deeper imagination. If they still wanted to go through with it come fall, he didn't think he'd object—or that Phostis would listen if he tried. The lad had needed to take care of himself lately, and had discovered he could do it. Few discoveries were more important.

Krispos said, "If you two like, you can spend the night in my pavilion." Then he saw their faces and laughed at himself. "No, you'll want a tent for yourselves, won't you? I would have, at your age."

"Well, yes," Phostis said. "Thank you, Father."

"It's all right," Krispos answered. At that moment, having Phostis back not only in one piece but opposed to the gleaming path, he could have refused him very little. He did add, "Before you repair to that tent, I trust you'll do me the honor of dining on army food and bad wine in the pavilion. I'll have Zaidas there, too; you said you wanted to talk with him, didn't you, Phostis? I'll see you around sunset."

E VEN WITH OLYVRIA'S HAND WARM IN HIS, PHOSTIS APPROACHED Krispos' tent with considerable trepidation. When he set sail for Videssos the city, she'd feared he would remember he was junior Avtokrator and forget he was her lover. Now, as the bright silks of the imperial pavilion drew near, he was afraid his father would turn him into a boy again, simply by refusing to imagine he could be anything else.

The Halogai outside the entrance to the tent saluted him in imperial style, clenched right fists over their hearts. He watched them discreetly look Olyvria up and down, as men of any nation will when they see a pretty girl. One of them said something in his own language. Phostis understood it was about Olyvria but not what it meant; he had only a smattering of the Haloga tongue. He almost asked the guardsmen what it meant, but at the last minute decided not to make an issue of it—Haloga candor could be brutal.

Inside the tent waited Krispos, Katakolon, Zaidas, Sarkis, and half a dozen helpings of bread and onions and sausage and salted olives. Olyvria's smile puzzled Phostis till he remembered she was an officer's daughter. No doubt the fare looked familiar.

As they ate, Phostis and Olyvria retold their story for Zaidas; Sarkis and Katakolon had heard most of it in the afternoon. The mage, as usual, made a good audience. He clapped his hands when Olyvria again recounted knocking Syagrios out with the chamber pot, and when Phostis told how they'd decamped immediately thereafter.

"That's the way to do it," he said approvingly. "When you need to get out in a hurry, spend what you have to and leave. What's the point to saving your gold but failing of your purpose? Which reminds me . . . " He abruptly went serious and intent. "His Majesty the Avtokrator—"

"Oh, just say, 'your father' and have done," Krispos broke in. "Otherwise you'll waste half the night in useless blathering."

"As Your Majesty the Avtokrator commands," Zaidas said. Krispos made as if to throw a crust of bread at him. Grinning, Zaidas turned back to Phostis. "Your father, I should say, tells me you learned something of importance about the techniques of Livanios' Makuraner wizard."

"That's true, sorcerous sir." Phostis had to work to stay formal; he'd almost called the mage Uncle Zaidas. "One day—this was after I learned Artapan was from Makuran—I followed him and—" He described how he'd learned Artapan fortified his power with the death energies of Thanasioi who starved themselves to complete their renunciation of the world. "And if they weren't quite dead when he needed them so, he wasn't averse to holding a pillow over their heads, either."

"That's disgusting," Katakolon said, sick horror in his voice.

Zaidas, by contrast, sounded eager, like a hunting dog just catching a scent. "Tell me more," he urged.

Olyvria gave Phostis a curious look. "You never spoke to me of this before," she said.

"I know I didn't. I didn't even like to think about it. And besides, I didn't think saying anything would be safe in Etchmiadzin. Too many ears around." And even after they became lovers, he hadn't trusted her, not completely, not until she set upon Syagrios. That, though, he kept to himself.

"Go on," Zaidas said. "All the ears here are friendly."

In as much detail as he could, prompted by sharp questions from the mage, Phostis recounted following Artapan down the street, standing in the stinking alley listening to him talk with Tzepeas, and the Thanasiot's premature and assisted death. "That isn't the only time I saw him hovering over people who were on the point of starving, either," he said. "Remember, Olyvria? He kept hanging around Strabon's house while he was dying."

"He did," she said, nodding. "With Strabon and others. I never thought much about it—wizards have their ways, that's all."

Zaidas stirred in his seat, but didn't say anything. For a man of his age he was, Phostis thought, reasonably normal save for his sorcerous talent. But then, he was the only wizard Phostis knew well. Who could say what others were like?

"Did he pray as he—ended—this heretic's life?" Zaidas asked. "Either to Phos or to the Four Prophets, I mean?"

"He spoke some in Makuraner, but since I don't understand it, I don't know what he said. I'm sorry," Phostis answered.

"Can't be helped," the mage said. "It probably doesn't matter in any case. As you've noted for yourself, the transition from life to death is a powerful source of magical energy. We who follow Phos are forbidden to exploit it, lest we grow to esteem the power so much that we fall into injustice, slaying for the sake of magic alone. I was given to understand that prohibition also applied to followers of the Prophets Four, but I may be wrong. On the other hand, Artapan—that was the name, not so?—may be as much a heretic by Mashiz's standards as the Thanasioi are by ours."

Krispos said, "This would all be very interesting if we were hashing it out as an exercise at the Sorcerers' Collegium, sorcerous sir, but how does it affect us here in the wider world? Suppose Artapan is using magic fueled by death? Does that make him more dangerous? How do we counteract his magic if it does?"

Behind her hand, Olyvria whispered, "Your father drives straight for the heart of a question."

"That he does." Phostis scratched at the side of his jaw. "He gets frustrated when others don't follow as quickly, as they often don't." He wondered if that accounted for some of his father's impatience with him. But how could someone just coming into manhood be expected to stay with the schemes of a grown man with the full power of experience who was also one of the master schemers that Videssos, a nation of schemers, had ever known?

Zaidas missed the byplay and spoke straight to Krispos: "Your Majesty, a mage who uses death energy in his thaumaturgy gains strength, aye, but he also becomes more vulnerable to others' magic. That sort of compensation is nothing surprising. Wizardry, no matter what the ignorant may think, offers no free miracles. What you gain in one area, you lose in an-other."

"That's not just wizardry—that's life," Krispos said. "If you've chosen to take on a big flock of sheep, you won't be able to plant as much barley."

Sarkis chuckled. "How many years on the throne, Your Majesty, to have you still talking like a peasant? A proper Emperor now, one from the ro-mances, would say you can't war in east and west at the same time, or some such."

"To the ice with the romances," Phostis broke in. "The next one that tells a copper's worth of truth will be the first."

He caught Krispos watching him with eyebrow upraised in speculation. Unabashed, the Avtokrator gave him a sober nod. "You're learning, lad."

"I will speak for the romances," Olyvria said. "Where but in them does the prisoner escape with the heresiarch's daughter who's fallen in love with him?"

Now Sarkis laughed out loud. "By the good god, she's caught father and son in the same net." He swigged wine, refilled his mug, and swigged again.

When Krispos turned his gaze on Olyvria, amusement sparked in his eyes. He dipped his head, as if she'd made a clever move at the board game. "There is something to what you say, lady."

"No, there's not," Phostis insisted. "In what romance isn't the woman a quivering wreck who requires some bold hero to rescue her? And in which of them does *she* rescue the hero by clouting the villain with a thunder-mug?"

"It seemed the handiest thing in the room," Olyvria said amid general laughter. "Besides, you can't expect a romance to have *all* the details straight."

"You have to watch this one, brother," Katakolon said. "She's quick."

The only things Katakolon looked for in his companions were looks and willingness. No wonder he went through them like a drunkard through a wine cellar, Phostis thought. But he didn't feel like quarreling with Katakolon, not tonight. "I'll take my chances," he said, and let it go at that.

Sarkis looked at the jar of wine in front of him, yawned, and shook his head. He climbed to his feet. "I'm for bed, Your Majesty," he announced. He turned to Phostis. "Good to have you back, and your *quick* lady." He walked out into the night.

Zaidas also rose. "I'm for bed, too. Would I had the power to store up sleep as a dormouse stores fat for its winter rest. Spurred not least by what you've said tonight, young Majesty, I think I shall be engaged in serious sorcery soon, at which time I will call on all my bodily reserves. The good god grant that they suffice."

"How cozy—it's a family gathering now," Krispos said when the mage left. He was not being sardonic; he beamed from Katakolon to Phostis and on to Olyvria. That took a weight of worry from Phostis; a young man will seldom turn aside from his beloved at his father's urging, but that is not an urging he ever cares to hear.

Then Katakolon also stood up. He clapped Phostis on the back, careful to stay away from the wounded shoulder. "Wonderful you're here and mostly intact," he said. He nodded to Olyvria and Krispos, then followed Sarkis and Zaidas out of the pavilion.

"He didn't say anything about bed," Krispos said, half laughing, half sighing. "He's probably out prowling for a friendly wench among the camp followers. He'll probably find one, too."

"Now I know you believe our tale, Your Majesty," Olyvria said.

"How's that?" Krispos asked. Phostis recognized his tone; it was the one he always used when he was finding out what his sons had learned of their lessons.

"If you didn't, you'd not be sitting here with the two of us closer to you than your guards are," she answered. "We're desperate characters, after all, and if we can turn a chamber pot into a weapon, who knows what we might do with a spoon or an inkwell?"

"Who indeed?" Krispos said with a small chuckle. He turned to Phostis. "She is quick—you'd better take good care of her." He was quick himself; he didn't miss the yawn Olyvria tried to hide. "Now you'd better take her back to your tent. Riding the courier circuit is wearing—I remember."

"I'll do that, Father," Phostis said. "But may I come back here for a few minutes afterward?" Both Olyvria and Krispos looked at him in surprise. "Something I want to ask you," he said, knowing it was not an explanation.

Krispos had to know that, too, but he nodded. "Whatever you like, of course."

Olyvria asked questions all the way to the tent that had been set up for them. Phostis didn't answer any of them. He knew how much that irked her, but held his course regardless. The most he would say was, "It's nothing to do with you."

He walked back to the imperial pavilion almost as warily as he'd entered the tunnel that ran under Videssos the city. What he found here might be as dangerous as anything that had lurked there.

Salutes from the Halogai didn't make him any less nervous as he ducked his way into the pavilion. Krispos waited at the map table, a wine cup in his hand and curiosity on his face. Despite that curiosity, he waited quietly until Phostis had also filled a cup and taken a long draft. Then wine ran sweet down his throat, but gave him no extra courage. *Too bad,* he thought.

"Well," Krispos said when Phostis lowered the wine cup from his lips, "what's such a deep, dark secret that you can't speak of it in front of your lady love?"

Had Krispos sounded sarcastic, Phostis would have turned on his heel and strode out of the pavilion without answering. But he just seemed inquisitive—and friendly, too, which Phostis wasn't used to. He'd tried a dozen different ways of framing his question. When it escaped his lips, though, it did so without any fancy frame whatever: "Are you my father?"

He watched Krispos suddenly seem to freeze in place, all except his eyes, which grew very wide. Then, as if to give himself time to think, the Avtokrator lifted his cup and drained it dry. "I'd wondered what you wanted," he said at last. "I didn't expect you to ask me that."

"Are you?" Phostis pressed.

As young men will of their fathers—or those they believe their fathers—he'd always thought of Krispos as old, but old in the sense of conservative and powerful rather than actually elderly. Now, as the lines on Krispos' face deepened harshly, Phostis saw with eerie certainty what he would look like as an old man.

"*Are* you?" Phostis said again.

Krispos sighed. His shoulders sagged. He laughed for a moment, quietly and to himself. Phostis almost hit him then. Krispos walked over to the wine jar, poured himself another cup from it, then peered into the dark ruby depths. When he looked up toward Phostis, he spoke in what was almost a whisper: "Not a week's gone by, I think, since I took the crown that I haven't asked myself the same question . . . and I just don't know."

Phostis had expected a *yes* or *no,* something he could get his teeth into either way. Being left with more uncertainty was—maddening. "How can you *not* know?" he cried.

"If you thought to ask the question, son, the answer should be plain enough," Krispos said. He drank some of the wine—maybe he was looking for courage there, too. "Your mother was Anthimos' Empress; if it hadn't been for her, Anthimos would have slain me by magic the night I took the throne. She'd been his Empress for some years before she was mine, and never conceived. None of the other women he had—and believe me, he had a great flock of them—ever quickened, either. But what does that prove? Nothing for certain. I think you're likely to be mine, but that's the most I can say with any hope for truth."

Phostis did some more quiet calculating. If Krispos had sired him, he'd likely done it before he took the throne from Anthimos . . . and before he'd married Dara. He'd done it adulterously, in other words—and so had Phostis' mother.

He shied away from that thought; it was too uncomfortable to examine straight on. Instead, he said, "You always say I look like Mother."

"Oh, you do, lad—the eyes especially. That tiny fold of skin on the inner corner comes straight from her. So does the shape of your face, and so does your nose. She's the reason you don't have a great beak like mine." Krispos put thumb and forefinger on the tip of his nose.

"Unless you had nothing to do with the way my nose looks at all," Phostis said.

"There is that chance," Krispos agreed. "But if you don't take after me, you don't look like Anthimos, either. You might be handsomer if you did; nothing wrong with the way he looked. You favor Dara, though. You always have, ever since you were a baby."

In his mind's eye, Phostis had a sudden, vivid picture of Krispos studying the infant he'd been, trying to trace resemblances. "No wonder you sometimes treated me as if I were the cuckoo's egg," he said.

"Did I?" Krispos peered down into his wine cup again. He sighed deeply. "I'm sorry, son; I truly am. I've always tried to be just with you, to put aside whatever doubts I had."

"Just? I'd say you were that," Phostis answered. "But you didn't often—" He broke off. How was he supposed to explain to Krispos that justice sufficed in the courts, but families needed more? The closest he could come was to say, "You always did seem easier with Evripos and Katakolon."

"Maybe I was . . . maybe I am. Not your fault, though—the trouble's been mine." If without great warmth, Krispos had the strength to meet troubles head on. "Where do we go from here?" he asked. "What would you have of me?"

"Can you take me for what I am instead of for whose son I might be?" Phostis said. "In every way that matters, I'm yours." He told Krispos how he'd found himself imitating him while a prisoner, and how so much of what Krispos said made more sense afterward.

"I know why that is," Krispos said. Phostis made a questioning noise. Krispos went on, "It's because the only experience anyone can really learn from is his own. I was probably just wasting breath beforehand when I preached at you: you couldn't have had any idea what I was talking about. And when my words did prove of some use to you—nothing could make me prouder."

He folded Phostis into a bear hug. For a moment, resentment flared in the younger man: where had embraces like this been when he was a boy and needed them most? But he'd already worked out the answer to that for himself. He wasn't pleased with Krispos for acting as he had over the years, but now that, too, made more sense.

Phostis said, "Can we go on as we did before? Even with doubts, I can't think of anyone I'd rather have for my father than you—and that includes Anthimos."

"That cuts both ways—son," Krispos said. "With me or in spite of me, you've made yourself a man. Let's hope it's not as it was. Let's hope it's better. So it may prove, for much of the poison between us is out in the open now."

"Phos grant that it be so—Father," Phostis said. They embraced again. When they separated, Phostis found himself yawning. He said, "Now I'm going back to my tent for the night."

Krispos gave him a sly look. "Will you tell your lady what passed here?"

"One of these days, maybe," Phostis said after a little thought. "Not just yet."

"That's what I'd say in your sandals," Krispos agreed. "You think like one of mine, all right. Good night, son."

"Good night," Phostis said. He yawned again, then headed back to the tent where Olyvria was waiting. When he walked in, he found that, almost certainly against her best intentions, she'd fallen asleep. He was careful not to wake her when he lay down himself.

"ALL RIGHT, SORCEROUS SIR," KRISPOS SAID TO ZAIDAS, "HAV-ing learned what you did from my son, how do you propose to exploit it to our best advantage?"

He felt a stab when he spoke thus of Phostis, but it was not the usual stab of suspicious fear, merely one of curiosity. He was beginning to see he had a man there to reckon with, and if perchance Phostis was not his by blood, he certainly was by turn of mind. What more could any ruler—any father—want?

Zaidas said, "I will show you what I can do, Your Majesty. Not least by using the power he has gained from the transition of fanatical Thanasioi out of life and into death, this Makuraner wizard, this Artapan, has built his magic to a point where it is difficult to assail. This much, to my discomfiture, you have seen."

"Yes," Krispos said. Many times he'd resolved to treat Phostis as if he were certain of his parentage; as many times, till now, he'd failed. This time, he thought he might succeed.

"An arch has a keystone," Zaidas went on. "Take it out and the whole thing crashes to the ground. So with Artapan's magic. Take away this power he has wrongfully arrogated to himself and he will be weaker than if he never meddled where he should not have. This is what I aim to do."

Krispos recognized the didactic tone in the sorcerer's voice. It suited him: though he had no sorcerous talent himself, he was always interested in hearing how wizards did what they did. Today, moreover, it would influence how he conducted his campaign. And so he asked, "How will you manage it, sorcerous sir?"

"By opposing the power of death with the power of life," Zaidas answered. "The sorcery is prepared, Your Majesty. I shall essay it tomorrow at dawn, when the rising of Phos' sun, most powerful symbol of light and life and rebirth, shall add its influence to that of my magic. And your son, too, shall play a role, as shall Livanios' daughter Olyvria."

"Shall they?" Krispos said. "Will it endanger them? I'd not care to have Phostis restored to me only to lose him two days later in a war of sorcerers."

"No, no." Zaidas shook his head. "The good god willing—and so I believe the case to be—the procedure I have in mind will take Artapan altogether by surprise. And even if he knows Phostis has escaped and joined you here, your son gives the strong impression the Makuraner does not know his technique has been discovered."

"Until the dawn, then," Krispos said. He wanted immediate action, but Zaidas' reason for delay struck him as good. It also let the imperial army advance farther onto the westlands' central plateau—with luck, positioning the force to exploit whatever success against Artapan that Zaidas achieved.

Krispos wondered how much faith to place in his chief mage. Zaidas hadn't had much luck against the Thanasioi. Before, though, he hadn't known what he was opposing. Now he did. If he couldn't do something useful with that advantage . . . "Then he won't be any help at all," Krispos said aloud. He breathed a silent prayer for Zaidas up to the watching sky.

Red as blood, the sun crawled up over the eastern horizon. Zaidas greeted it by raising his hands to the heavens and intoning Phos' creed: "We bless thee, Phos, lord with the great and good mind, by thy grace our protector, watchful beforehand that the great test of life may be decided in our favor."

Phostis imitated the gesture and echoed the creed. He fought to stifle a yawn; yawning during the creed struck him as faintly blasphemous. But getting up well before sunrise as spring grew toward summer was anything but easy.

Beside him, Olyvria shifted from foot to foot. She looked awake enough, but nervous nonetheless. She kept stealing glances at Krispos. Being around the Avtokrator had to add to her unease. To Phostis, his father—for so he still supposed Krispos to be—was family first and ruler second; familiarity overcame awe. It was just the other way round for Olyvria.

"Get on with it," Krispos said harshly.

Used to any other man, it would have been a heads-will-roll tone. Zaidas merely nodded and said, "All in good time, Your Majesty . . . Ah, now we see the entire disk of the sun. We may proceed."

A few hundred yards away, sunrise made the imperial army begin to stir in camp. Almost all the Haloga bodyguards stood between the camp and this little hillock, to make sure no one blundered up while Zaidas was at his magic. The rest were between the sorcerer and Krispos. Phostis didn't know what their axes could do against magic gone wrong. He didn't think they knew, either, but they were ready to try.

Zaidas lighted a sliver of wood from one of the torches that had illuminated the hillock before the day began. He used the flame to light a stout candle of sky-blue wax, one fat and tall enough to have provided imperial sealing wax for the next fifty years. As the flame slid down the wick and caught in the wax, he spoke the creed again, this time softly to himself.

Candles in daylight were normally overwhelmed by the sun. Somehow this one was not. Though when seen directly its flame was no brighter than that of an ordinary candle, yet its glow caught and held on Zaidas' face, and Krispos', and Olyvria's. Though he could not see himself, Phostis supposed the light lingered on him, as well.

Zaidas said, "This light symbolizes the long and great life of the Empire of Videssos, and of the faith that it has sustained and that has sustained it across the centuries. Long may Empire and faith flourish."

From under a silk cloth he took out another candle, this one hardly better than a tiny taper, a thin layer of bright red wax around a wick.

"That's the same color as the sealing wax on that vaunting letter Livanios sent me," Krispos said.

Zaidas smiled. "Your Majesty lacks only the gift to be a first-rate wizard. Your instincts are perfectly sound." He raised his voice to the half-chanting tone he used when incanting. "This small, brief candle stands for the Thanasioi, whose foolish heresy will soon fail and be forgotten."

Almost as soon as he spoke the last words, the little red candle guttered out. A thin spiral of smoke rose from it. When the breeze blew that away, nothing showed that the candle representing the Thanasioi had ever existed. The larger light, the one symbolizing Videssos as a whole, burned on.

"Now what?" Krispos demanded. "This should be the time to settle accounts with that Makuraner mage."

"Yes, Your Majesty." Zaidas was a patient man. Sometimes even the most patient of men finds it necessary to let his patience show. He said, "I could proceed even more expeditiously if I did not have to pause and respond to inquiries and comments. Now—"

Krispos chuckled, quite unabashed. This time Zaidas ignored him. He took a large silk cloth, big enough for a wall hanging, and draped it over both Phostis and Olyvria. The cloth was of the same sky blue as the candle that stood for the Empire and the orthodox faith. The silk's fine weave let Phostis see through it mistily, as if through fog.

He watched Zaidas take up yet another cloth, this one striped in bright colors. It reminded him of the caftans Artapan had worn. No sooner had the thought crossed his mind than Zaidas declared, "Now we shall sorcerously show the wicked wizard of Makuran that he shall profit nothing from his courtship of death!" He dropped out of that impressive tone and into ordinary speech for a moment: "Now, young Majesty, comes your time to contribute to this magic. Take your intended in your arms, kiss her, and think on all you might be doing were the rest of us not standing around here making nuisances of ourselves."

Phostis stared at him through the thin silk cloth. "Are you sure that's what you want of us, Uncle Z—uh, sorcerous sir?"

"Do that alone and do it properly, young Majesty, and no one could do more this day. Think of it, if you must, as duty rather than pleasure."

Kissing Olyvria was not a duty, and Phostis refused to consider it one. Her sweet lips and tongue, the soft firmness of her body pressed against his, argued that she, too, enjoyed the task Zaidas had set them. So tightly did Phostis hold her against him that she could not have doubted what he wanted to do with her. He heard her laugh softly, back in her throat.

After a while, he opened his eyes. He'd kissed Olyvria a lot lately, and while he thoroughly enjoyed it, he'd never been part of a major conjuration before. He wanted to see what Zaidas was up to. The first thing he saw was that Olyvria's eyes were already open. That made him laugh.

Zaidas was holding the piece of striped fabric above the flame of the blue candle. He intoned, "As they celebrate life under their cloth, so may that overturn the Makuraner mage who would strengthen himself through death. Let his sorcery be consumed as Videssos' light consumes the cloth of his country." He thrust the fabric into the fire.

Phostis always regretted the silk cloth that hazed his vision; it made him doubt his own eyes. The striped square of fabric flared up brightly the moment the candle flame touched it. For that instant, it burned as if it had been soaked in oil; Phostis wondered if Zaidas could drop it fast enough to save his fingers.

But then the burning cloth flickered and almost went out. Not only that, the part that had been consumed seemed restored, so that the cloth looked bigger than it had when it burned brightest. Zaidas stumbled and almost took it out of the candle flame.

He stood steady, though, and repeated the incantation he'd used when he first put the cloth in the flame. To it he added other muttered charms that Phostis heard only indistinctly. The striped cloth began to burn again, hesitantly at first but then with greater vigor. "You have it, sorcerous sir!" Krispos breathed.

Though he spoke softly, he must have distracted Zaidas, for the flame on the cloth shrank and the cloth itself seemed to expand once more. But Zaidas rallied again. More and more of the cloth burned away. Finally, with a puff of smoke like the one from the expiring Thanasiot candle, it was gone. Zaidas stuck the thumb and forefinger of his right hand into his mouth. They shouldn't have been scorched, though—they should have been burned to the bone.

When he took the fingers out, the wizard said in a worn voice, "What magic can do, magic has done. The good god willing, I have struck Artapan a heavy blow this day."

"How shall you know whether the good god was willing?" Krispos asked.

Instead of answering directly, Zaidas swept the filmy silk cloth away from Phostis and Olyvria and said, "You two can detach yourselves from each other now."

They shook their heads at the same time and both started to laugh. That was what made them break apart. Phostis said, "We liked what we were doing."

"I noticed that, yes," Zaidas said, so dryly it might have been Krispos talking.

Krispos repeated, "How will you know whether you smote Artapan?"

"Your Majesty, I am about to find that out, for which purpose I require your eldest son once more."

"Me?" Phostis said. "What do I need to do now?"

"What I tell you." Before explaining what that was, the mage turned to Olyvria and bowed. "My lady, I am grateful for your services against the Makuraner. Your presence is not required for this next conjuration." He made it sound as if her presence was not desired. Though that miffed Phostis, Olyvria nodded and swept down the little hillock. A couple of Halogai trailed after her; the northerners seemed to have accepted her as part of the imperial family.

"Why don't you want her to watch what we're doing?" Phostis asked Zaidas.

"Because I am going to use you to help locate her father Livanios," Zaidas answered. "You were in contact with him; by the law of contagion, you remain in contact. So, for that matter, does she, but no matter how she loves you, I would not use her as the instrument of her father's betrayal."

"A nicety of sentiment the Thanasioi wouldn't give back to us," Krispos said. "But you're right to use it. Carry on, sorcerous sir."

"I shall, never fear," Zaidas answered. "I was just about to explain that Artapan's magic has up to this point shielded the Thanasioi from such direct sorcerous scrutiny. If, however, we have weakened him with the conjuration just completed, this next spell should also succeed."

"Very neat," Krispos said approvingly. "You use the same magic to learn whether the previous one worked and where the heresiarch's main force is. That's economical enough to have sprung from the brain of a treasury logothete."

"I shall construe that as a compliment, and hope it was meant so," Zaidas said, which squeezed a chuckle out of Krispos.

The conjuration the sorcerer had in mind seemed simple in the extreme. He took some loose, crumbly dirt from the top of the hillock and put it in a large, low bowl. Then he called Phostis over and had him press his hand down onto the dirt. As soon as Phostis drew back a pace, Zaidas began to chant. His left hand moved in quick passes over the bowl.

A few seconds later, hair prickled up on the back of Phostis' neck. The dirt was stirring, shifting, humping itself up into a ridge—no, not a ridge, an arrow, for one end showed an unmistakable point.

"East and a little south," Zaidas said.

"Very, very good," Krispos breathed; as usual, he was quietest when he felt most triumphant. "The mask is down, then—we can see the moves Livanios makes. Have you any idea how far away his force lies?"

"Not precisely, no," the mage answered. "By the speed with which the arrow formed, I should say he is not close. It gives but a rough measure, though."

"A rough measure is all we need for now. You and Phostis will work this magic every morning from now on, to give us the foe's bearing and your rough measure of how far away he is. Will Artapan know his magic has failed him?"

"I'm afraid so, Your Majesty," Zaidas said. "Did you see how the cloth representing Makuran tried a couple of times to reconstitute itself? That was my opponent, attempting to resist and undo my spell. But he failed as I thought he would, for the power of life is stronger than that of death."

Krispos walked over to Phostis and clapped him on the back hard enough to stagger him. "And all of it thanks to you, son. I owe you a great deal; you've done me as much good by returning and aiding me as I feared you'd do me harm had you stayed with the Thanasioi. And besides that, I'm glad you're back."

"I'm glad I'm back, too, Father," Phostis said. If Krispos claimed the relationship despite his doubts, Phostis would not quarrel with it. He went on, "And what's this I hear about your missing me so much that you decided to sire a bastard"—He carefully did not say *another bastard*—"to take my place?" The year before, he couldn't have bantered so with Krispos.

The Avtokrator looked startled, then laughed. "Which of your brothers told you that?"

"Evripos, back at Videssos the city."

"Aye, it's true. I hope he also said I didn't intend to let it compromise the rights you three enjoy, even if it is a son."

"He did," Phostis said, nodding. "But really, Father, at your age—"

"That's all of you who've said that now," Krispos broke in. "To the ice with your teasing. As you'll find out, gray in your beard doesn't stop you from being a man. It may slow you down, but it doesn't stop you." He looked defiant, as if waiting for Phostis to find that funny.

But Phostis didn't feel like provoking him any further. Having just found his way onto good terms with Krispos, he wouldn't risk throwing that away for the sake of a few minutes' amusement. He probably wouldn't have made such a calculation the year before; two or three years earlier, he was sure he wouldn't have.

What does that signify? he wondered. *Is it what they mean by growing up?* But he already was grown up. He had been for years—hadn't he? Scratching his head, he walked back to the tent he shared with Olyvria.

"DUE EAST NOW, YOUR MAJESTY," ZAIDAS REPORTED. "THEY'RE getting close, too; the arrow formed almost as soon as Phostis took his hand from the ensorceled soil."

"All right, sorcerous sir, and thank you," Krispos answered. For the last week he'd been maneuvering to place the imperial army square in the path of the withdrawing Thanasioi. "If the lord with the great and good mind is kind to us, we'll swoop down on them before they even know we're in the neighborhood."

"May it be so," Zaidas said.

"Due east, you say?" Krispos went on musingly. "They'd be somewhere not far from, hmm, Aptos, I'd say. Is that about right?"

"Given where we are now—" The mage frowned in concentration, then nodded. "Somewhere not far from there, yes."

"Uh, Father . . . ?" Phostis began in a tentative voice.

He hadn't sounded tentative since he'd escaped from the Thanasioi. Krispos gave him a curious look, wondering why he did now. "What's wrong?" he asked.

"Uh," Phostis said again. By the hangdog look on his face, he regretted having spoke up. He needed a very visible rally before he continued. "When I had to go out on that Thanasiot raiding party, Father— remember? I told you of that."

"I remember," Krispos said. He also remembered what a turn news of Phostis' movement had given him, and how much he'd feared the youth really had decided to follow the gleaming path.

"When I was on that raid," Phostis resumed, "to my shame, I had to join in attacking a monastery. I know I wounded one of the holy monks; if I hadn't, he'd have broken my bones with his cudgel. And my torch was one that helped fire the place."

"Why are you telling me this?" Krispos asked. "Oxeites the patriarch is a better one to hear it if you're after the forgiveness of your sin."

"I wasn't thinking of that so much—more of making amends," Phostis said. "By your leave, I'd like to set aside a third of my allowance for the next couple of years and devote it to the monastery."

"You don't need my leave; the gold I give you each month is yours to do with as you will," Krispos said. "But this I will say to you: I'm proud of you for having the idea." He thought for a moment. "So you'd give them eighty goldpieces a year, would you? How would it be if I matched that?"

He watched Phostis' face catch fire. "Thank you, Father! That would be wonderful."

"I'll leave my name off the money," Krispos said. "Let them think it all comes from you."

"Uh," Phostis said for a third time. "I hadn't planned on putting my name on, either."

"Really?" Krispos said. "The most holy Oxeites would tell you an anonymous gift finds twice as much favor with Phos as the other kind, for it must be given for its own sake rather than to gain acclaim. I don't know about that, but I admit it sounds reasonable. I know I'm all the prouder of you, though."

"You know, you tell me that now twice in the space of a couple of minutes, but I'm not sure you ever said it to me before," Phostis said.

Had he spoken with intent to wound, he would have infuriated Krispos. But he had the air of a man just stating a fact. And it *was* a fact; Krispos' memory confirmed that too well. He hung his head. "You shame me."

"I didn't mean to."

"I know," Krispos said. "That makes it worse."

Sarkis rode up then, rather to Krispos' relief. After saluting, the cavalry general asked, "Now that the heretics are drawing near, shall we send out scouts to learn exactly where they are?"

Instead of answering at once, Krispos turned to Phostis. "Your store of wisdom seems bigger than usual this morning. What would *you* do?"

"Urk," Phostis said.

Krispos shook a finger at him. "You have to answer without the foolish noises. When the red boots are on your feet, these are the questions you must deal with. You can't waste time, either." He studied the youth, wondering how he'd do.

As if to redeem that startled squawk, Phostis made his voice as deep and serious as he could: "Were the command mine, I'd say no. We're tracking the Thanasioi well by magic, so why let them blunder against our men before the last possible moment? If Zaidas' magic has worked as well as he hopes, Artapan should be nearly blind to us. The more surprise we have, the better."

Sarkis glanced toward Krispos. The Avtokrator spoke six words: "As he said, for his reasons." Phostis looked even more pleased at that indirect praise than he had when Krispos said he was proud of him.

"Aye, it does make sense." Sarkis chuckled. "Your Majesty, you were a pretty fair strategist yourself before you really knew what you were doing. It must run in the blood."

"Well, maybe." Krispos and Phostis said it in the same breath and in the same tone. They looked at each other. The Avtokrator started to laugh. A moment later, so did Phostis. Neither one seemed able to stop.

Now Sarkis studied them as if wondering whether they'd lost their wits. "I didn't think it was that funny," he said plaintively.

"Maybe it's not," Krispos said.

"On the other hand, maybe it is," Phostis said. Thinking back to the grueling and in the end uncertain talk they'd had a few nights before, the Avtokrator found himself nodding. If they could laugh about it, that probably boded well for the future.

"I still say you've gone mad in the morning," Sarkis rumbled. "I'll try one of you or the other this afternoon and see if you make any sense then." He rode off, beak of a nose in the air.

THE TENT WAS SMALL AND CLOSE. THE WARM NIGHT MADE IT seem even closer. So did the stink of hot tallow from the candle stuck in the ground where its flame couldn't reach anything burnable. As she had for the past several nights, Olyvria asked, "What *did* you go back to talk about with your father?"

"I don't want to tell you," Phostis said. He'd been saying that ever since he'd come back from Krispos' pavilion. It was not an answer calculated to stifle curiosity, but he knew no better to give.

"Why don't you?" Olyvria demanded. "If it had to do with me, I have a right to know."

"It had nothing to do with you." Phostis had repeated that a good many times, too. It was even true. The only trouble was, Olyvria didn't believe him.

Tonight she seemed to have decided to argue like a canon lawyer. "Well, if it has nothing to do with me, then what possible harm could there be to my knowing it?" She grinned smugly, pleased with herself; she'd put him in a logician's classic double bind.

But he refused to be bound. "If it were your business, I wouldn't have wanted the talk to be private."

"That's not right." She glared, angry now.

"I think it is." Phostis didn't want anyone wondering who his father was. He wished he didn't have to wonder himself. One person could keep a secret—Krispos had, after all. Two people might keep a secret. More than two people . . . he supposed it was possible, but it didn't seem likely.

"*Why* won't you tell me?" Olyvria tried a new tack. "You've given me no reason."

"If I tell you why I won't tell you, that would be about the same as telling you." Phostis had to listen to that sentence again in his head before he was sure it had come out the way he wanted it. He went on, "It has nothing to do with you and me."

"What you talked about may not have, but that you won't tell me certainly does." Olyvria needed a moment's hesitation, too. "What could you possibly want to keep to yourself that way?"

"It's none of your concern." Phostis ground out the words one at a time. Olyvria glowered at him. He glowered back; these arguments got him angry, too. His hissed exhale was almost a snarl. He said, "All right, by the good god, I'll tell you what: suppose you go over to the Avtokrator's pavilion and ask him. If he doesn't mind telling you what we talked about, I suppose it's all right with me."

She had spirit. He'd known that from the day he first encountered her, naked and lovely and tempting, under Videssos the city. For a moment he thought she'd do as he'd dared and storm out of the tent. He wondered what Krispos would make of that, how he'd handle it.

But even Olyvria's nerve could fray. She said, "It's not just that he's your father—he's the Avtokrator, too."

"I know," Phostis said dryly. "I've had to deal with that my whole life. You'd best get used to it, too. Phos is the only true judge, of course, but my guess is that he'll be Avtokrator a good many years yet."

Videssian history knew instances of imperial heirs who grew impatient waiting for their fathers to die and helped the process along. It also knew rather more instances of impatient imperial heirs who tried to help the process along, failed, and never, ever got a second chance. Phostis had no interest in raising a sedition against Krispos for, among others, the most practical of good reasons: he was convinced the Avtokrator would smell out the plot and use him for it as a failed rebel deserved. He counted himself lucky that Krispos had forgiven him after his involuntary sojourn among the Thanasioi.

Probing still, Olyvria said, "Is it something that discredits you or your father? Is that why you don't want to talk about it?"

"I won't answer questions like that, either," Phostis said. Not answering was another trick he'd learned from Krispos. If you started responding the questions around the edge of the one you didn't want to discuss, before long the exact shape and size of the answer to that one came clear.

"I think you're being hateful," Olyvria said.

Phostis stared down his nose at her. It wasn't quite as long and impressive as Krispos', but it served well enough. "I'm doing what I think I need to do. You're Livanios' daughter, but no one has tried to tear out of you any of his secrets that you didn't care to give. Seems to me I ought to be allowed a secret or two of my own."

"It just strikes me as foolish, that's all," Olyvria said. "How could telling whatever it is possibly hurt you?"

"Maybe it couldn't," Phostis said, though he wondered how much hay Evripos might make out of knowing how uncertain his paternity was. Then he started to laugh.

"What's funny?" Olyvria's voice turned dangerous. "You're not laughing at me, are you?"

Phostis drew the sun-circle over his heart. "By the good god, I swear I'm not." His obvious sincerity mollified Olyvria. Better still, he'd not taken a false oath. When he thought of Evripos making hay, whose perspective was he borrowing but that of Krispos the ex-peasant? Even if Krispos hadn't sired him, he'd certainly shaped the way he thought, at levels so deep Phostis rarely noticed them.

Olyvria remained mulish. "How can I trust you if you keep secrets from me?"

"If you don't think you can trust me, you should have let me put you ashore at some deserted beach." Now Phostis grew angry. "And if you still don't trust me, I daresay my father will give you a safe conduct to leave camp and go back to Etchmiadzin or wherever else you'd like."

"No, I don't want that." Olyvria studied him curiously. "You're not the same as you were last summer under the temple or even last fall after you—came to Etchmiadzin. Then you weren't sure of what you wanted or how to go about getting it. You're harder now—and don't make lewd jokes. You trust your own judgment more than you did before."

"Do I?" Phostis thought about it. "Perhaps I do. I'd better, don't you think? In the end, it's all I have."

"I hadn't thought you could be so stubborn," Olyvria said. "Now that I know, I'll have to deal with you a little differently." She laughed in small embarrassment. "Maybe I shouldn't have said that. It sounds as if I'm giving away some special womanly secret."

"No, I don't think so," Phostis said; he was happy to steer the conversation away from what he and Krispos had talked about. "Men also have to change the way they treat women as they come to know them better—or so I'm finding out, anyway."

"You don't mean *men,* you mean *you,*" Olyvria said with a catlike pounce. Phostis spread his hands, conceding the point. He didn't mind yielding on small things if that let him keep hold of the big ones. He slowly nodded—Krispos would have handled this the same way.

Someone rode up to the nearby imperial pavilion in a tearing hurry. A moment later, Krispos started yelling for Sarkis. Not long after that, the Avtokrator and his general both yelled for messengers. And not long after *that,* the whole camp started stirring, though it had to be well into the third hour of the night.

"What do you suppose that's all about?" Olyvria asked.

Phostis had an idea of what it might be about, but before he could answer, someone called from outside the tent, "Are you two decent in there?"

Olyvria looked offended. Phostis didn't—he recognized the voice. "Aye, decent enough," he called back. "Come on in, Katakolon."

His younger brother pushed aside the entry flap. "If you are decent, you've probably been listening to all the fuss outside." Katakolon's eyes gleamed with excitement.

"So we have," Phostis said. "What is it? Have scouts brought back word that they've run into the Thanasioi?"

"Oh, to the ice with you," Katakolon said indignantly. "I was hoping to bring a surprise, and here you've gone and figured it out."

"Never mind that," Phostis said. "The fuss means we fight tomorrow?"

"Aye," Katakolon answered. "We fight tomorrow."

Chapter XII

KATAKOLON POINTED TO THE RISING CLOUD OF DUST AHEAD.
"Soon now, Father," he said.

"Aye, very soon," Krispos agreed. Through the dust, the early morning sun sparkled off the iron heads of arrows and javelins, off chain mail shirts, off the polished edges of sword blades. The Thanasioi were hurrying through the pass, heading back toward Etchmiadzin after a raid that had spanned most of the length of the westlands.

Sarkis said, "Now, Your Majesty?"

Krispos tasted the moment. "Aye, now." he said.

Sarkis waved. Quietly, without the trumpet calls that usually would have ordered them into action, two regiments of cavalry rode up the pass from the imperial lines. Sarkis' grin filled his fat face. "That should give them something new to think about. If Zaidas spoke truly, they don't know we're anywhere nearby, let alone in front of them."

"I hope he spoke truly," Krispos said. "I think he did. By all the signs his magic could give, their Makuraner mage is altogether stifled."

"The good god grant it be so," Sarkis said. "I have no love for Makuraners; every so often they take it into their heads that the princes of

Vaspurakan should be forced to reverence their Prophets Four rather than Phos."

"One day, maybe, Videssos can do something about that," Krispos said. The Empire, he thought, ought to protect all those who followed the lord with the great and good mind. But Vaspurakan had lain under the rule of the King of Kings of Makuran for a couple of hundred years.

"Begging your pardon, Your Majesty, but I'd sooner we were free altogether," Sarkis said. "Likely your hierarchs would make spiritual masters no more pleasant than the men from Mashiz. Your folk would be as harsh on us as heretics as the Makuraners are on us as infidels."

"Seems to me you're both quarreling over the taste of a loaf you don't have," Katakolon said.

Krispos laughed. "You're probably right, son—no, you *are* right." Then in the distance, shouts said that the Thanasioi and the regiments Krispos had sent out to delay them were knocking heads.

This time, Krispos waved. Now trumpets and drums and pipes rang loud. The imperial force that had been aligned parallel to the direction of the pass swung in a great left wheel to block its mouth and keep the heretics from breaking through.

As the imperials raised their own dust and then as they came into view, the shouts from the Thanasioi got louder. Their red banners waved furiously. They might have been taken by surprise, but there was no quit in them. On they came, driving the lead regiments back on the main body of Krispos' force.

The Avtokrator, who now stood at his army's extreme right rather than to the fore, admired the bravery of the Thanasioi. He would have admired it even more had it been aimed at the Empire's foreign enemies rather than against him.

Phostis tapped him on the shoulder, pointing to the center of the heretics' line. "That's Livanios, Father: the fellow in the gilded shirt between those two flags there."

Krispos' eye followed Phostis' finger. "I see the man you mean. His helm is gilded, too, isn't it? For someone who leads a heresy where all men are condemned to the least they can stand, he likes imperial trappings well, doesn't he?"

"He does," Phostis agreed. "That's one of the reasons I decided I couldn't stomach the Thanasioi: too much hypocrisy there for me to stand."

"I see," Krispos said slowly. Had Livanios been a sincere fanatic rather than an opportunist, then, he might have used Phostis' self-righteousness

to draw him deep into the Thanasiot movement. But a sincerely destruc-
tive fanatic would not have gone after the imperial mint at Kyzikos. Had
Krispos needed any further explication of Livanios' character, that raid
would have given it to him.

Which was not to say he lacked courage. He threw himself into the
thick of the fighting, flinging javelins and slashing with his saber when the
battle came to close quarters.

It was, to all appearances, a fight devoid of tactical subtlety. The Thanasioi wanted to break through the imperial line; Krispos' soldiers aimed to
keep them bottled up inside the pass. They plied the heretics with arrows
from a line several men deep. Even when the first ranks had to struggle
hand to hand, those behind them kept shooting at the Thanasioi who
piled up ever tighter against the barrier the imperials had formed.

Fewer Thanasioi were archers. In any case, archery by itself would not
sweep aside Krispos' men. In spite of the galling wounds they received, the
heretics charged again and again, seeking to hew a path through their foes.
"The path!" they cried. "The gleaming path!"

Along with trying to break through in the center, the Thanasioi also
sent wave after wave of fighters against Krispos and his retinue. With their
shields, mail shirts, and heavy axes, the Halogai stood like a dam between
the Avtokrator and the fighters who sought to lay him low. But the northerners could not hold all arrows away from him. He had a shield of his
own, and needed it to protect his face.

His horse let out a frightened squeal and tried to rear. Krispos fought
the animal back under control. An arrow protruded from its rump. *Poor
beast,* he thought—it knew nothing of the differences in worship because
of which it had been wounded.

The Thanasioi charged again. This time some of them broke through
his screen of bodyguards. Phostis traded saber strokes with one, Katakolon
with another. That left Krispos facing two at once. He slashed at the one
on his right side, used his shield to hold off the blows of the one to his left,
and hoped someone would come to his aid soon.

Suddenly the horse of the Thanasiot to his right screamed, far louder
and more terribly than his own mount had a few minutes before. A
Haloga axe had bitten into its spine, just behind its rider. The horse
foundered. The Haloga raised his axe again and slew the Thanasiot.

That let Krispos turn against his other foe. He still remembered how
to use a sword himself, and slashed the fellow on the forearm. Another
Haloga guard, his axe dripping gore, bore down on the heretic. The
Thanasiot ignored him, bending every effort toward slaying the Avtokra-

tor. He paid the price for his fanaticism: the guardsman hacked him out of the saddle.

"Thanks." Krispos panted. Sweat ran down his forehead and stung his eyes. "I'm getting old for this business, much as I hate to admit it."

"No man is young enough to be happy fighting two," the Haloga said, which made him feel a little better.

Among them, his sons and the northerners had put an end to the other Thanasioi who'd broken through. Katakolon had a cut that stretched halfway across one cheek, but managed a blood-spattered smile for Krispos. "Iakovitzes won't like me so well anymore," he shouted.

"Ah, but all the girls will sigh over how brave you are," Krispos answered, which made his youngest son's smile wider.

Another Thanasiot surge. The Halogai on foot and Videssians on horseback contained it. Krispos gauged the fighting. He had not asked a great deal of his men, only that they hold their place against the onslaught of the Thanasioi. So much had they done. The heretics were bunched against them, still trying to force their way out of the valley.

"Send for Zaidas," Krispos commanded. A messenger rode off.

He soon returned with the wizard, who had not been far away. "Now, Your Majesty?" Zaidas asked.

"The time will never be better," Krispos said.

Zaidas set to work. Most of his preparations for this magic had been made ahead of time. It was not, properly speaking, battle magic, nor directed against the Thanasioi. Battle magic had a way of failing; the stress of fighting raised emotions to such a pitch that a spell which might otherwise have been fatal failed to bite at all.

"Let it come forth!" Zaidas cried, and stabbed a finger up toward the sky. From his fingertip sprang a glowing green fireball that rose high above the heaving battle line, growing and getting brighter as it climbed. A few soldiers from both sides paused for an instant to call Phos' name or sketch the sun-sign above their hearts. Most, however, were too busy fighting for their lives to exclaim over the fireball or to notice it at all.

Zaidas turned to Krispos. "What magic may do, magic has done," he said. His voice was ragged and worn; sorcery cost those who worked it dear.

Little by little, the green fireball faded. Before too long, it was gone. Watching the indecisive fight to which he had committed his army, Krispos wondered if it had been sent skyward in vain. Men should have been watching for its flare . . . but one of the lessons he'd learned after close to half a lifetime on the throne was the chasm that sometimes yawned between *should have been* and *were*.

His head went rapidly back and forth from one side of the valley to the other. "Where are they?" he demanded, not of anyone in particular but of the world at large.

As if that had been a cue, martial music rang out in the distance. Soldiers in the imperial army cheered like men possessed; the Thanasioi stared about in sudden confusion and alarm. Down into the valley from left and right rode fresh regiments of horsemen in line. "Krispos!" they cried as they bent their bows.

"Taken in both flanks, by the good god!" Sarkis exclaimed. "Your Majesty, my hat's off to you." He doffed the iron pot he wore on his head to show he meant his words literally.

"You helped come up with the plan," Krispos said. "Besides, we both ought to thank Zaidas for giving a signal the watchers from both concealed flanking parties could see and use. Better by far than trying to gauge when to come in by the sandglass or any other way I could think of."

"Very well." Sarkis took off his helmet for Zaidas, too.

The wizard's grin took years off his age and reminded Krispos of the eager, almost painfully bright youngster he'd been when he began his sorcerous service. That had been in the last campaign against Harvas, till now the hardest one Krispos had known. But civil war—and religious civil war at that—was worse than any attack from a foreign foe.

Where the Avtokrator and the general had praised his sorcery, Zaidas thought about the fighting that remained ahead. "We still have to win the battle," he said. "Fail in that and the best plan in the world counts for nothing."

Krispos studied the field. Had the Thanasioi been professional soldiers, they might have salvaged something by retreating as soon as they discovered themselves so disastrously outflanked. But all they understood of the military art was going forward no matter what. That only got them more thoroughly trapped.

For the first time since fighting began, Krispos turned loose a smile. "This is a battle we are going to win," he said.

PHOSTIS WAS ONLY A FEW FEET FROM HIS FATHER WHEN KRISPOS claimed victory. He was no practiced strategist himself, but he could see that a foe attacked on three sides at once was on the way to destruction. He was glad Olyvria had stayed back at the camp. Though she'd given herself to him without reservation, seeing all her father's hopes go down in ruin could only bring her pain.

Phostis knew pain, too, but of a purely physical sort. His shoulder ached with the effort it took to hold up a shield against arrows and saber slashes. In another couple of weeks it could have borne the burden without complaint, but not yet.

Screeching "The gleaming path!" for all they were worth, the Thanasioi mounted yet another charge. And from the midst of the fanatics' ranks, Phostis heard another cry, one not fanatical at all: "If we slay the Avtokrator, lads, it's all up for grabs!"

Fueled by desperation, fervor, and that coldly rational cry, the heretics surged against the right wing of the imperial line. As they had once before, they shot and hacked their way through the Halogai and Videssians protecting Krispos. All at once, being of high rank stopped mattering.

Off to one side of Phostis, Sarkis laid about him with a vigor that denied his bulk. To the other, Krispos and Katakolon were both engaged. Before Phostis could spur his horse to their aid, someone landed what felt like a hammer blow to his shield.

He twisted in the saddle. His foe was yelling at the top of his lungs; his was the voice that had urged the Thanasioi against Krispos. "Syagrios!" Phostis yelled.

The ruffian's face screwed into a gap-toothed grimace of hate. "You, eh?" he said. "I'd rather carve you than your old man—I owe you plenty, by the good god." He sent a vicious cut at Phostis' head.

Just staying alive through the next minute or so was as hard as anything Phostis had ever done. He didn't so much as think of attack; defense was enough and more. Intellectually, he knew that was a mistake—if all he did was try to block Syagrios' blows, sooner or later one would get through. But they came in such unrelenting torrents that he could do nothing else. Syagrios was twice his age and more, but fought with the vigor of a tireless youth.

As he slashed, he taunted Phostis: "After I'm done with you, I'll settle accounts with that little whore who crowned me. Pity you won't be around to watch, on account of it'd be worth seeing. First I'll cut her a few times, just so she hurts while I'm—" He went into deliberately obscene detail.

Fury all but blinded Phostis. The only thing that kept him from attacking wildly, foolishly, was the calculating look in Syagrios' eyes as he went through his speech. He was working to enrage, to provoke. Refusing to give him what he wanted was the best thing Phostis saw to do.

A Haloga came up on Syagrios' left side. The ruffian had no shield, but managed to turn aside the guardsman's axe with the flat of his blade. That wouldn't work every time, and he knew it. He spurred his horse away from the northerner—and from Phostis.

As he drew back, Phostis cut at him. The stroke missed. Phostis laughed. In the romances, the hero always slashed the villain into steaks. In real life, you were lucky if you didn't get hacked to bits yourself.

Since he was for the moment not beset, Phostis looked around to see how his comrades were faring. He found Krispos in the midst of a sea of shouting Thanasioi. The Avtokrator, badly beset, slashed frantically this way and that.

Phostis spurred toward him. To the Thanasioi, he was nothing—just another soldier, a nuisance, not a vital target like Krispos. He wounded three heretics from behind in quick succession. That sort of thing wasn't in the romances, either; they went on and on about glory and duels and fair fights. Real war, Phostis was discovering in a hurry, didn't concern itself with such niceties. If you stayed alive and the other fellow didn't, that was a triumph of strategy.

The Halogai also fought their way in Krispos' direction. So did all the reserves who saw he was in danger. Quite suddenly, no living Thanasioi were near the Avtokrator. Krispos' helmet had been battered so that it sat at a crazy angle on his head. He had a cut on his cheek—almost a match for Katakolon's—and another on his sword arm. His gilded mail shirt and shield were splashed with sticky red.

"Hello, everyone," he said. "Rather to my surprise, I find myself still in one piece."

Several variations of *Glad you are* rose into the air, Phostis' among them. He looked round for Syagrios, but did not see him. Real battle lacked the romances' neat resolutions, too.

Krispos went in the blink of an eye from a horseman fighting wildly for his life to the commander of a great host. "Drive them hard!" he shouted, pointing toward the center of the line. "See them waver? One good push and they'll break."

Had Zaidas not said Krispos lacked all talent for magic, Phostis might have believed him a wizard then. No sooner had he called attention to the sagging Thanasiot line than crimson banners began falling or being wrested from the hands of the heretics who bore them. The roar that went up from the imperials at that rang through the valley like a great horn call.

"How could you tell?" Phostis demanded.

"What? That?" Krispos thought for a moment, then looked sheepish. "Part of it comes from seeing a lot of fights. My eye knows the signs even if my mouth doesn't. And part of it—sometimes, don't ask me how, you can make your will reach over a whole battlefield."

"Maybe it *is* magic."

Phostis didn't realize he'd spoken out loud until Krispos nodded soberly. "Aye, it is, but not of the sort Zaidas practices. Evripos has a touch of it; I've seen that. You haven't yet had the chance to find out. You can rule without it, no doubt of that, but it makes life easier if it's there."

One more thing to worry about, Phostis thought. Then he shook his head. He needed to worry about two things, not one: whether he had the magic of leadership, and how vulnerable he would be if Evripos had it and he didn't.

At any other time, he might have occupied himself for hours, maybe days, with worries over those two. Now, with the battle swinging the imperials' way at last—could it be past noon already?—he had no leisure for fretting.

"Forward!" came the cry all along the line. Phostis was glad to press the fighting. It relieved him of having to think. As he'd found in Olyvria's arms, that could be a blessing of sorts. The only trouble was, worries didn't go away. When the fighting or the loving was done, they reared their heads again.

But not now. Shouting "Forward!" with the rest, he rode against the crumbling resistance of the Thanasioi.

KRISPOS LOOKED OUT AT VICTORY AND FOUND IT AS APPALLING as it usually is. Pierced and mangled men and horses were the building blocks of what the chroniclers would one day call a splendid triumph of arms. At the moment, it reminded Krispos of nothing so much as an open-air slaughterhouse, down to the stink of entrails and the buzz of hungry flies.

Healer-priests wandered through the carnage, now and then stooping to aid some desperately wounded man. Their calling did not let them discriminate between Krispos' followers and the Thanasioi. Once, though, Krispos saw a blue-robe stand up and walk away from someone, shaking his shaven head in bewilderment. He wondered if a dying Thanasiot had possessed the courage to tell the healer he would sooner walk the gleaming path.

Most of the heretics, though, were glad enough to get any help the imperials gave them. They held out gashed arms and legs for bandages and obeyed their captors' commands with the alacrity of men who knew they might suffer for any transgression. In short, they behaved like other prisoners of war Krispos had seen over the years.

Katakolon rode up to the Avtokrator. "Father, they've run down the heretics' baggage train. In it they found some of the gold, ah, abstracted from the mint at Kyzikos."

"Did they? That's good news," Krispos said. "How much of the gold was recovered?"

"Something less than half the amount reported taken," Katakolon answered.

"More than I expected," Krispos said. Nevertheless, he suspected the troopers who'd captured the baggage train were richer now than when they'd started their pursuit. That was part of the price the Empire paid for civil war. If he tried to squeeze the gold out of them, he'd get a name for niggardliness that might lead to another revolt a year or three down the line.

"Your Majesty!" Another messenger waved frantically. "Your Majesty, we think we have Livanios!"

The gilded mail shirt that weighed on Krispos' shoulders all at once seemed lighter. "Fetch him here," the Avtokrator ordered. Then he raised his voice. "Phostis!"

"Aye, Father?" His eldest looked worn, but so did everyone else in the army.

"Did you hear that? They think they've caught Livanios. Will you identify him for me? You've see him often enough."

Phostis thought for a moment, then shook his head. "No," he said firmly.

"What?" Krispos glared at him. "Why not?"

"He's Olyvria's father," Phostis said. "How am I to live with her if I point the finger at him for the headsman?"

"Your mother's father plotted against me when you were a baby, do you know that?" Krispos said. "I exiled him to a monastery at Prista." The outpost on the northern shore of the Videssian Sea was as grim a place of exile as the Empire had.

"But did Mother tell you of his plot?" Phostis demanded. "And would you have taken his head if he'd not been her father?"

The questions, Krispos admitted to himself, were to the point. "No and yes, in that order," he said. Even after exiling Rhisoulphos, he'd been nervous about sleeping in the same bed with Dara for a while.

"There, you see?" Phostis said. "Livanios was an officer of ours. You'll have others here who can name him for you."

Krispos thought about ordering Phostis to do as he'd said, but not for long. He had learned better than to give orders that had no hope of being obeyed—and in any case, Phostis was right. "Let it be as you say, son," the Avtokrator said.

He watched in some amusement as Phostis, obviously ready to argue more, deflated. "Thank you," the younger man said, his voice full of relief.

Krispos nodded, then called, "Who among my soldiers knows the traitor and rebel Livanios by sight?"

The question ran rapidly through the army. Before long, several men sat their horses close by Krispos. Among them was Gainas, the officer who'd sent back to Videssos the city the dispatch warning of Livanios' defection to the gleaming path.

The prisoner himself took a while to arrive. When he did, Krispos saw why: he was afoot, one of several captives with hands tied behind their backs so they could not even walk quickly. Phostis said, "The one on the left there, Father, is the mage Artapan."

"Very good," Krispos said quietly. If Artapan was in this group, then Livanios probably was, too. Phostis had, in fact, all but said he was. Here, though, the *all but* was important. Krispos turned to the men he'd assembled. "Which of them is Livanios?"

Without hesitation, they all pointed to the fellow two men away from Artapan. The captive straightened and glared at Krispos. He was doing his best to keep up a brave front. "I am Livanios. Do as you please with my body. My soul will walk the gleaming path beyond the sun and dwell with Phos forever."

"If you were so set on walking the gleaming path, why did you rob the mint at Kyzikos and not just burn it?" Phostis asked. "You didn't despise material things enough to keep from dirtying your hands with them."

"I do not claim to be the purest among the followers of the holy Thanasios," Livanios said. "Nevertheless, I follow the truth he preached."

"The only place you'll follow him, I think, is to the ice," Krispos said. "And since I've beaten you and taken you in arms against me, I don't need to argue with you." He turned to one of the Halogai. "Trygve, you're still carrying your axe. Strike off his head and have done."

"Aye, Majesty." The big blond northerner strode over to Livanios and pushed him so he went to his knees. Trygve spoke with neither cruelty nor any great compassion, merely a sense of what needed doing: "Bend your neck, you. It will be over soonest then."

Livanios started to obey, but then his eyes found Phostis. With a quick glance toward Krispos, he asked, "May I put a last question?"

Krispos thought he knew what that question would be. "Be quick about it."

"Yes, Your Majesty." Livanios did not sound sarcastic—but then, Krispos did not have to give him an easy end, and he knew it. He turned to Phostis. "D'you have my daughter? Syagrios said he thought you did, but—"

"Yes, I have her," Phostis said.

Livanios bowed his head. "I die content. My blood goes on."

Krispos did not want him having the last word. "My father-in-law died in exile up in Prista, a traitor," he said. "My son's father-in-law will die before he even properly gains that title, also a traitor. Temptation, it seems, rides Emperors' fathers-in-law hard—too hard." He gestured to Trygve.

The axe came down. It wasn't a broad-bladed, long-handled headsman's weapon, but the big man who wielded it was strong enough that that didn't matter. Krispos turned his head away from the convulsions of Livanios' corpse. Phostis, who had watched, looked green. Executions were harder to stomach than deaths in combat.

Unfortunately, they were also sometimes necessary. Krispos turned to Artapan. "If your hands were free, sirrah, I daresay you'd be making magic from his death agony there."

"I would try." Artapan's mouth twisted. "You have a strong mage at your side, Videssian Emperor. With him opposing, perhaps I'd not succeed."

"Did Rubyab King of Kings know you were a death-drinker when he sent you forth to help our heretics?" Krispos asked.

"Oh, indeed." The Makuraner magician's mouth twisted again, this time in a different way—wry amusement. "I was under sentence of death from the *Mobedham-mobedh*—the high patriarch, you would say—when the King of Kings plucked me from my cell and told me what he required. I had nothing to lose by the arrangement. Nor did he."

"True enough," Krispos said. If Artapan had failed in the mission Rubyab set him, he would die—but he was condemned to die anyhow. And if he succeeded, he would do more good for Makuran than for himself. Rubyab had never been anything but a wily foe to Videssos, but this piece of double-dealing was as devious as any Krispos had ever imagined.

He nodded again to Trygve. Artapan jerked free of his captors and tried to run. With his hands bound behind him, with so many men chasing him, he didn't get more than a couple of paces. The meaty sound of the axe striking cut off his last scream.

"Foolishness," Trygve said from where he cleaned the blade on the wizard's caftan. "Better to die well, since die he would. Livanios did it properly."

Katakolon pointed to the other two captive Thanasioi, who stood in glum and shaky silence. "Will you take their heads, too, Father?"

Krispos started to ask if they would abandon their heresy, then remembered the answer meant little: the Thanasioi felt no shame at lying to save their skins, and might keep their beliefs in secret. Instead, the Avtokrator turned to Phostis and asked, "How big are these fish we've caught?"

"Medium size," Phostis answered. "They're officers, but they weren't part of Livanios' inner circle."

"Take them away and put them with the rest of the prisoners, then," Krispos said to the guards who stood behind the captives. "I'll figure out what to do with them later."

"I've never seen—I've never imagined—so many captives." Katakolon pointed toward long rows of Thanasiot prisoners, each bound to the man in front of him by a line that wrapped round his wrists and then his neck: any effort to flee would only choke those near him. Katakolon went on, "What will you do with them all?"

"I'll figure that out later, too," Krispos said. His memory went back across two decades, to the fearsome massacres Harvas Black-Robe had worked among the captives he'd taken. Seeing those pathetic corpses, even so long ago, had burned away forever any inclination toward slaughter Krispos might have had. He could imagine no surer road to the eternal ice.

"You can't just send them back to their villages," Phostis said. "I did come to know them while I was in their hands. They'll promise anything, and then a year from now, or two, or three, they'll find themselves a new leader and start raiding again."

"I know that," Krispos said. "I'm glad to see you do, too."

Sarkis rode up. In spite of bloody bandages, the cavalry general seemed in high spirits. "We shattered 'em and scattered 'em, Your Majesty," he boomed.

"Aye, so we did." Krispos sounded less gleeful. He'd learned to think in bigger terms than battles, or even campaigns. He wanted more from this victory than the two years' respite Phostis had suggested. He scratched his nose, which wasn't as impressive as Sarkis' but did exceed the Videssian norm. "By the good god," he said softly.

"What is it?" Katakolon asked.

"My father—after whom you're named, Phostis—always said we had Vaspurakaner blood in us, even though we lived far from here, up by— and sometimes over—what used to be the border with Kubrat. My guess is that our ancestors had been resettled there on account of some crime or other."

"Very likely," Sarkis said, as if that were a matter for pride.

"We could do the same with the Thanasioi," Krispos said. "If we uproot the villages where the heresy flourishes most and transplant those people over near Opsikion in the far east, say, and up near the Istros—what used to be Kubrat still needs more folk to work the land—those Thanasioi would be likely to lose their beliefs in a generation or two among so many orthodox folk, just as a pinch of salt loses itself in a big jug of water."

"It might work," Sarkis said. "Videssos has done such things before—else, as you say, Your Majesty, your own forebears would not have ended up where they did."

"So I've read," Krispos said. "We can even run the transfer both ways, sending in orthodox villagers to loosen the hold the Thanasioi have on the region round Etchmiadzin. It will mean a great lot of work, but if the good god is willing it will put an end to the Thanasiot problem once and for all."

"Moving whole villages—thousands, tens of thousands of people—from one end of the Empire to the other? Moving more thousands back the other way?" Phostis said. "Not the work alone—think of the hardships you'll be making."

Krispos exhaled in exasperation. "Remember, these men we just beat down have sacked and ravaged Kyzikos and Garsavra just lately, Pityos last year, and the lord with the great and good mind only knows how many smaller places. How much hardship did they make? How much more would they have made if we hadn't beaten them? Put that in the balance against moving villagers around and tell me which side of the scale goes down."

"They believe in the Balance in Khatrish and Thatagush," Phostis said. "Have you beaten one heresy, Father, only to join another?"

"I wasn't talking about Phos' Balance, only the one any man with a dram of sense can form in his own mind," Krispos said irritably. Then he saw Phostis was laughing at him. "You scamp! I didn't think you'd stoop to baiting me."

As was his way, Phostis quickly turned serious again. "I'm sorry. I'll build that balance and tell you what I think."

"That's fair," Krispos said. "Meanwhile, no need to apologize. I can stand being twitted. If I couldn't, Sarkis here would have spent these last many years in a cell under the government office buildings—assuming he'd fit into one."

The cavalry commander assumed an injured expression. "If you'd gaoled me many years ago, Your Majesty, I shouldn't have attained to my present size. Not on what you feed your miscreants, I shouldn't."

"Hrmph." Krispos turned back to Phostis. "What did your balance tell you?"

"If it must be done, then it must." Phostis neither looked nor sounded happy. Krispos didn't mind that. He wasn't happy himself. He and his village had been resettled twice when he was a boy, once forcibly by Kubrati raiders, and then again after the Empire ransomed them from the nomads. He knew the hardship relocating entailed. Phostis went on, "I wish it didn't have to be done."

"So do I," Krispos said. Phostis blinked, which made Krispos snort. "Son, if you think I enjoy doing this, you're daft. But I see that it has to be done, and I don't shrink from it. Liking all of what you do when you wear the red boots is altogether different from doing what needs doing whether you like it or not."

Phostis thought about that. It was a very visible process. Krispos gave him credit for it; before he'd been snatched, he would have been more likely to dismiss out of hand anything Krispos said. At last, biting his lip, Phostis nodded. Krispos nodded back, well pleased. He'd actually managed to get a lesson home to his hardheaded son.

"COME ON, MOVE!" A SOLDIER SHOUTED, WITH THE AIR OF A man who's already shouted the same thing twenty times and expects to shout it another twenty before the day is through.

The woman in faded gray wool, her head covered by a white scarf, sent the horseman a look of hatred. Back bent under the bundle she bore, she trudged away from the thatch-roofed hut that had housed her since she wed, away from the village that had housed her family for untold generations. Tears carved tracks through the dust on her cheeks. "The good god curse you to the ice forever," she snarled.

The imperial trooper said, "If I had a goldpiece for every time I've been cursed these past weeks, I'd be rich enough to buy this whole province."

"And heartless enough to rule it," the peasant woman retorted.

To her obvious dismay, the trooper thought that was funny. Having no choice—the soldier and his comrades confronted the villagers with sabers and drawn bows and implacable purpose—she kept walking, three children trailing behind her, and then her husband, who carried an even bigger pack on his back and held lead ropes for a couple of scrawny goats.

Phostis watched the family join the stream of unwilling peasants shambling east. Soon they were gone from sight, as one drop of water loses itself in a river. For a little while longer, he could hear the goats bleating.

Then their voices, too, were lost amid murmurs and complaints and low-ing cattle and creaking axles from richer farmers' carts and the endless shuffle of feet.

This had to be the dozenth village he'd watched empty. He wondered why he kept making himself witness the process over and over again. The best answer he came up with was that he was partly responsible for what was happening to these people, and so he had the obligation to under-stand it to the fullest, no matter how pained and uncomfortable it made him.

That afternoon, as the sun sank toward the not so distant mountains of Vaspurakan, he rode with another company that descended on another village. As the peasants were forcibly assembled in the marketplace, a woman screamed, "You have no right to treat us so. We're orthodox, by the good god. This for the gleaming path!" She spat in the dust.

"Is that so?" Phostis worriedly asked the officer in charge of the com-pany.

"Young Majesty, you just wait till they're all gathered here and then you'll see for yourself," the captain answered.

The people kept coming until at last the village marketplace was full. Phostis frowned. He told the officer, "I don't see anything that makes them look either orthodox or Thanasiot."

"You don't know what to look for, then," the man replied. He waved at the glum crowd. "Do you see more men or women, young Majesty?"

Phostis hadn't noticed one way or the other. Now he examined villagers with a new eye. "More women, I'd say."

"I'd say so, too, young Majesty," the captain said, nodding. "And note the men, how many of them are either graybeards or else striplings with the down just sprouting on their cheeks and chins. Not a lot of fellows in their prime, are there? Why do you suppose that is?"

Phostis studied the shouting, sweating crowd once more. "I see what you're saying. Why, though?"

The officer glanced upward for a moment, perhaps in lieu of calling the heir to the imperial throne dense. "Young Majesty, it's on account of most of the men in their prime were in Livanios' army, and we either killed 'em or caught 'em. So you can believe that skirt is orthodox if you choose, but me, I have to doubt it."

Orthodox or heretic—and Phostis found the company commander's logic compelling—the villagers, carrying and leading what they could, shuffled away on the first stage of their journey to new homes at the far end of the Empire. Some of the company quartered themselves in aban-doned houses. Phostis went back with the rest to the main imperial camp.

The place was becoming more like a semipermanent town than the encampment of an army on the march. Krispos' men fanned out from it every day to resettle villagers who followed—or might follow—the gleaming path. Supply wagons rumbled in every day—with occasional lapses as unsubdued Thanasioi raided them—to keep the army fed. Tents were not pitched at random, but in clumps with ways—almost streets—through them. Phostis had no trouble finding his way to the tent he shared with Olyvria.

When he ducked through the flap, she was lying on her bedroll. Her eyes were closed, but came open as soon as he walked in, so he did not think she'd been asleep. "How are you?" she asked listlessly.

"Worn," he answered. "Saying you're going to resettle some peasants is one thing; it sounds simple and practical enough. But seeing what it entails—" He shook his head. "Ruling is a hard, cruel business."

"I suppose so." Olyvria sounded indifferent.

Phostis asked, "How are *you*?" She'd wept through the night when she learned her father's fate. In the days since then, she'd been like this—very quiet, more than a little withdrawn from what happened around her. He hadn't touched her, except accidentally, since he'd held her while she cried herself out that night.

Now she answered, "All right," as she had whenever he'd asked her since then. The response was as flat and unemphatic as everything else she'd said lately.

He wanted to shake her, to force some life into her. He did not think that was a good idea. Instead, he unrolled his own blanket. Under a surcoat, his mail shirt jingled as he sat down beside her. He said, "How are you really?"

"All right," she repeated, as indifferently as before. But now a small spark came into her eyes. "I'll truly be all right in time; I'm sure I will. It's just that . . . my life has turned upside down these past weeks. No, even that's not right. First it turned upside down—I turned it upside down— and then it flipped again, when, when—"

She didn't go on, not with words, but she started to cry again, as she had not done since Krispos, sparing Phostis that duty, brought her word of what he'd ordered done to Livanios. Phostis thought there might be healing in these tears. He held his arms open, hoping she would come to him. After a few seconds, she did.

When she was through, she dried her eyes on the fabric of his surcoat. "Better?" he asked, patting her back as if she were a child.

"Who can say?" she answered. "I made the choice; I have to live with it. I love you. Phostis, I do, but I hadn't thought through everything that

might happen after I got onto that fishing boat with you. My father—"
She started to cry again.

"That would have happened anyhow, I think," he said. "You didn't
have anything to do with it. Even when we were on the worst of terms—
which seemed like much of the time—I knew my father did what he did
well. I doubt the Thanasioi would have won the civil war even with us,
and if they lost it . . . . Early in his reign, my father paid a price for showing his enemies more mercy than they deserved. One of the things that set
him apart from most people is that he learns from his mistakes. He gives
rebels no second chance these days."

"But my father wasn't just a rebel," she said. "He was my father."

To that, Phostis had no good answer. Luckily for him, he didn't have to
grope for a poor one. From outside the tent, a Haloga guard called,
"Young Majesty, here's a man would have speech with you."

"I'm coming," Phostis answered. To Olyvria, he added in a low voice,
"Probably a messenger from my father. Who else would disturb me?"

He climbed to his feet. Tired as he was, the iron he wore felt doubly
heavy. He blinked against the bright afternoon sunshine as he stepped
outside, then stopped in surprise and horror. "You!" he gasped.

"You!" Syagrios roared. The ruffian wore a long-sleeved tunic to cover
the knife he'd strapped to his forearm. He flipped it into his hand now,
and stabbed Phostis in the belly with it before the Haloga guard could
spring between them.

As Phostis remembered, Syagrios was strong as a bear. He cried out
when the tip of the knife bit him and grabbed Syagrios' right arm with
both hands.

"I'll get you," Syagrios panted. "I'll get you and then I'll get that little
whore you're swiving. I'll—"

Phostis never did find out what Syagrios would do next. The guardsman's frozen surprise did not last longer than a heartbeat. Syagrios
screamed hoarsely as the Haloga's axe went into his back. He broke free of
Phostis and whirled, trying to come to grips with the northerner. The
Haloga struck him again, this time full in the face. Blood sprayed over
Phostis. Syagrios crumpled. The guardsman methodically smote him
again and again until he stopped twitching.

Olyvria burst out of the tent, a knife in her hand, her eyes wild. The
guardsman, however, needed no help. Olyvria gulped at Syagrios' dreadful
wounds. Though an officer's daughter, she wasn't altogether accustomed
to fighting's grim aftermath.

Then the Haloga turned to Phostis. "Are you yet hale, young Majesty?"

"I don't know." Phostis yanked up his mail shirt and surcoat together. He had a bleeding scratch a couple of inches above his navel, but nothing worse. He let the mail shirt fall back down with a clink of iron rings.

"Aye, here we are. Look, young Majesty." The northerner poked the mail shirt with a forefinger. "You had luck with you. The knife went into a ring—see the bright cuts here and here? It went in, but could go no farther. Had it slid between two rings, more of your gore would have spilled."

"Yes." Phostis started to shake. So much luck in life—a fingernail's breadth to either side and he'd be lying on the ground beside dead Syagrios, trying to hold his guts in. Maybe a healer-priest would have been able to save him, but he was ever so glad he didn't have to make the test. He told the guard, "My thanks for slaying him, Viggo."

The Haloga guardsman looked disgusted with himself. "I should never have let him draw near enough to stab you. I thank the gods you were not worse hurt." He lifted Syagrios' corpse by the heels and dragged it away. The ruffian's blood soaked blackly into the thirsty soil.

By then, curious and concerned faces pressed close; the fight and the outcries had raised a crowd as if by magic. Phostis waved to show he was all right. "No harm done," he called, "and the madman got what he deserved." He pointed to the trail Syagrios left behind, as if he were a snail filled with blood rather than slime. The soldiers cheered.

Phostis waved again, then ducked back into the tent. Olyvria followed. Phostis looked again at the little cut he'd taken. He didn't require much imagination to make it bigger in his mind's eye. If the knife had slipped between rings, or if he'd taken off the mail shirt, the better to comfort Olyvria . . . He shuddered. He didn't even want to think about that.

"I fought with him during the battle," he said. "I guessed he'd flee, but he must have been wild for revenge."

"You never wanted to cross Syagrios," Olyvria agreed soberly. "And—" She hesitated, then went on, "And I'd known he wanted me for a long time."

"Oh." Phostis made a sour face at that. But it made sense—how doubly mortifying and infuriating to be struck down by someone you lusted after. "No wonder he didn't run, then." His laugh was shaky. "I wish he would have—he came too close to getting his vengeance and letting the air out of me in the process."

Katakolon stuck his head into the tent. "Ah, good, you still have your clothes on," he said. "Father's right behind me, and I don't suppose you'd care to be caught as I was."

Before Phostis could do more than gape at that or ask any of the myriad questions that suggested themselves. Krispos came in. "I'm glad you're all right," he said, folding Phostis into a bear hug. When he let Phostis go, he stood back and eyed him quizzically. "Someone didn't care for you there, son."

"No, he didn't," Phostis agreed. "He helped kidnap me"—he watched Krispos, but the Avtokrator's eyes never moved toward Olyvria: discipline and style—"and he was my, I guess you'd say keeper, in Etchmiadzin. He couldn't have been very happy when I escaped."

"Your keeper, eh? So that was Syagrios?" Krispos asked.

Phostis nodded, impressed at his memory for detail. He said, "He was a bad man, but not of the worst. He played the board game well, and he drew the arrow from my shoulder when I got shot while I was along with the Thanasiot raiding party."

"A slim enough eulogy, but the best he'll get, and likely better than he deserves, too," Krispos said. "If you think I'll say I'm sorry he's gone, you can think again: good riddance, say I. I just praise the good god that you weren't hurt." He embraced Phostis again.

"I'm glad you're not ventilated, too," Katakolon said. "It's good having you back, especially in one piece." He ducked to get out of the tent. Krispos followed a moment later.

"What was that your brother said about getting caught with his clothes off?" Olyvria kept her voice low so no one but Phostis would hear, but she couldn't stop the giggle that welled up from deep inside.

"I don't know," Phostis said. "As a matter of fact, I don't think I want to know. Knowing Katakolon, it was probably something spectacular. Sometimes I think he takes after Anthimos, even if—" He'd been about to say something like *even if I'm the one Anthimos might have fathered.* That was just what he didn't want to say to Olyvria.

"Even if what?" she asked.

"Even if Anthimos was four years dead before Katakolon was born," Phostis finished, more smoothly than he would have thought possible.

"Oh." Olyvria sounded disappointed, which meant his answer had convinced her. He nodded to himself. Krispos would have approved. And he'd lived through a completely unexpected attack. He approved of that himself.

KRISPOS STUDIED THE GLOOMY STONE PILE OF ETCHMIADZIN. It had been built to hold off men at arms, but the ones its designers had in mind came from Makuran. The stone, however, knew nothing of that. It would—and did—defy Videssians as readily as any others.

The fanatics on those grim stone walls still screamed defiance at the imperial army below. Most of the territory the Thanasioi had once held was back in Krispos' hands again. Dozens of villages were empty; he'd given the orders to send streams of orthodox peasants on the way to replace those uprooted from the area. Pityos and its hinterland had fallen to Noetos' cavalry, advancing west along the coast from Nakoleia.

But if Etchmiadzin held until the advancing season made Krispos withdraw, much of what he'd accomplished was likely to unravel. The Thanasioi would still have a base from which to grow once more. He'd already seen the consequences of their growth. He didn't care for them.

Storming the fortress, though, was easier to talk about than to do. Videssian engineers had labored mightily to make it as near impregnable as they could. So far as Krispos knew, it had never fallen to the Makuraners, despite several sieges. It didn't look likely to fall to his army, either.

"If they won't fall, maybe I can trip them," Krispos muttered.

"How's that, Your Majesty?"

Krispos jumped. There beside him stood Sarkis. "I'm sorry—I didn't notice you'd come up. I was trying to work out some way to inveigle the cursed Thanasioi into coming out of Etchmiadzin without storming the place."

"Good luck to you," Sarkis said skeptically. "Hard enough to trick a foe in the confusion of the battlefield. Why should the heretics come out from their citadel for anything you do short of leaving? Even if they stand and fight and die, they think they go up their gleaming path to heaven. Next to that, any promise you can make is a small loaf."

"Aye, they're solidly against me, stiff-necked as they are." Krispos' voice was gloomy—but only for a moment. He turned to Sarkis. "They're solidly against me—for now. But tell me, eminent sir, what do you have if you put three Videssians together and tell them to talk about their faith for a day?"

"Six heresies," Sarkis answered at once. "Each one's view of his two comrades. Also a big brawl, probably a knifing or two, a couple of slit purses. Begging your pardon, Majesty, but that's how it looks to a poor stolid prince from Vaspurakan, anyhow."

"That's how it looks to me, too," Krispos said, smiling, "even if I have only a touch of princes' blood in me. I think like a Videssian, no matter whose blood I have, and I know full well that if you give Videssians a chance to argue about religion, they're sure to take it."

"I don't hold your breeding against you, Your Majesty," Sarkis said generously, "but how do you propose to get the Thanasioi squabbling among themselves when to them you're the impious heretic they've all joined together to fight?"

"It's not even my idea," Krispos said. "Phostis thought of it and gave it to Evripos."

"To Evripos?" Sarkis scratched his head. "But he's back in Videssos the city. How could anything there have to do with the Thanasioi here? Did Evripos write you a letter and—" The cavalry commander stopped. His black, black eyes sparkled. Just for a moment, through the sheath of heavy flesh, Krispos saw the eager young scout with whom he'd ridden like a madman back to the imperial capital in the days when his reign was new. He said, "Wait a minute. You're not going to—"

"Oh, yes, I am," Krispos said. "Right out there where they can all watch from the walls. If it wouldn't brew more scandal than it was worth, I'd have them consummate it out there, too, not that it hasn't been consummated already."

"You're a demon, you are—but then, you used to revel with Anthimos, now that I think of it." Sarkis let out a theatrical sigh. "Too bad you couldn't get by with that. She's a fine-looking young woman. I wouldn't mind watching that marriage consummated, not one bit I wouldn't."

"Shameless old stallion." Krispos lowered his voice. "I wouldn't, either." They both laughed.

For a day, the imperial army besieging Etchmiadzin had sent no darts, no arrows, no stones against those frowning gray walls. Instead, heralds bearing white-painted shields of truce had approached the walls, bidding the Thanasioi also desist from battle "so that you may join us in observing a celebration at noon."

The choice of words must have intrigued the heretics; they had gone along with the heralds' suggestion, at least thus far. Phostis wondered how long they would remain calm when they observed what was about to happen. *Not long,* he thought.

He'd suggested to Evripos that he marry Olyvria to help calm the rampaging Thanasioi of the city. Trust Krispos to take his suggestion and turn it into a weapon of war against the belligerent heretics here at Etchmiadzin.

"Noon" was an approximation; the only sundial in the imperial army was a little brass one that belonged to Zaidas. But men accustomed to gauging the apex of the sun's path when they were working in the fields had no trouble doing the same while on campaign. Imperial soldiers gathered to protect the wooden platform that had been built safely out of bowshot of Etchmiadzin's walls. On those walls, the Thanasioi also gathered.

A herald with a shield of truce strode from the imperial lines toward the rebel-held fortress. In a huge bass voice, he called to the Thanasioi: "His imperial Majesty the Avtokrator Krispos bids you welcome to the marriage of his son Phostis to the lady Olyvria, daughter of the late Livanios."

Phostis wished the herald had omitted *the late;* the words would hurt Olyvria. But at the same time, he understood why Krispos had told the man to include them: they would remind Etchmiadzin's defenders of the defeats their cause had already suffered.

The Thanasioi rained curses on the herald's head. A couple of them shot at him, too. He lifted the shield of truce to protect his face; he wore a helmet and a mail shirt that covered him down to the knee.

When the arrows stopped coming, the man lowered the white-faced shield and resumed: "The Avtokrator bids you ponder the import of this wedding: not only what it says about your fortune in battle, but how it reminds you of the joy that life holds and the way it continues—and should continue—from one generation to the next."

More curses—and more arrows—flew at him. Having delivered his message, he needed to stand up under them no more, but hastily drew back out of range.

The wedding party ascended to the makeshift stage. It was not a large group, certainly not the horde that would have been involved had the marriage taken place at the High Temple in Videssos the city. Ahead of Phostis and Olyvria came a healer-priest named Glavas, who would perform the ceremony. Behind them walked Krispos, Katakolon, and Zaidas. That was all.

Even Zaidas' presence was not directly required by the ceremony, though Phostis was glad to have him close by. But the wizard was there mainly because he owned a small magic that would let the voices of the people on the platform carry farther than they would have without it: Krispos wanted the Thanasioi to listen to all that passed here.

The priest said, "Let us praise the lord with the great and good mind." He recited Phos' creed. So did Phostis and Olyvria; so as well did Krispos, Katakolon, and Zaidas. Phostis also heard the watching soldiers echo the prayer they made several times every day of their lives.

"We are come together in this unusual place to celebrate an unusual union," Glavas said. "After the boon of many healthful years, the greatest gift the good god can grant his worshipers is continuance of their line. A marriage is a time of rejoicing not least because it marks hope and expectation for that continuance.

"When the marriage comes from the imperial family, more hopes ride

on it than those of the family alone. Continuance of the dynasty, generation upon generation, is our best guarantee against the disaster of civil
war."

Phostis noticed he did not mention that Krispos was the first member
of his family to hold the imperial throne, or indeed anything more than a
peasant plot. The priest went on, "And with this marriage, we also have
the chance to heal a rift that has opened among the faithful of Videssos,
to symbolize the return to their familiar faith by those who for a time
thought differently in the union of the young Majesty Phostis to Olyvria
the daughter of Livanios."

That, Phostis thought, was as conciliatory toward the Thanasioi as
Krispos could be without following the gleaming path himself. He hadn't
even had Glavas call them heretics. He wanted to make them forget their
beliefs, not stubbornly cling to them.

The priest went on for some time about the qualities bride and groom
should bring to a marriage to ensure its success. Phostis' mind wandered.
He was taken unawares when Glavas asked, "Are the two of you prepared
to cleave to these virtues, and to each other, so long as you both may live?"

From behind, Krispos nudged Phostis. He realized he had to speak first.
"Yes," he said, and was glad Zaidas' magic made his voice larger than it
was.

"Yes, for all my life—*this* is the path I will walk," Olyvria responded
firmly.

Krispos and Katakolon set on her head and Phostis' garlands of sweet-
smelling herbs—the crown of marriage that completed the ceremony. The
priest stepped down from the platform. As quickly as that, it was over.
"I'm married," Phostis said. Even to himself, he sounded surprised.

The Thanasioi on the wall screamed insults and catcalls for all they
were worth. Ignoring them, Krispos slapped Phostis on the back and said,
"So you are, son—and to a wise woman, too." He turned to Olyvria and
added, "That last touch was perfect. Phos willing, they'll do a lot of stewing over it."

Katakolon poked Phostis in the ribs. "Now you're supposed to grab her
and carry her off to your—well, to your tent it would be here."

Phostis had a well-founded suspicion that Olyvria would not permit
any such thing. He glanced over to her. Sure enough, a steely glint in her
eye warned him he'd better not try it.

"I've heard ideas that sounded more practical," Krispos said; the amusement in his voice said he'd seen that glint, too. "But do go on back to your
tent. You would anyhow—that's what the day is for—but you should do
it now, while you're still decked in the crowns of marriage."

That tickled Phostis' curiosity. He extended his arm to Olyvria. She took it. As they headed away from the hastily built platform, some of the soldiers cheered and others called lewd advice. Phostis smiled foolishly at Olyvria. She smiled back. Lewd advice from the bystanders came with every wedding celebration.

A grinning Haloga held the tent flap wide, then let it fall behind the newlyweds. "We'll not see you for a while, I think," he said.

"Will you look at that?" Olyvria exclaimed.

Phostis looked. At the top corners of their unfolded blankets, someone—maybe Krispos himself, maybe a man acting at his orders—had driven stout sticks into the ground to stimulate bedposts. "It's good luck to hang the crowns on them," Phostis said. He doffed his and carefully set it on top of one post.

Olyvria did the same on the other side. "It starts to feel real," she said.

"It is real." Phostis lowered his voice so the guardsmen outside would not hear—not that they wouldn't know perfectly well what was going on in there, but the forms had to be observed. "As long as it's real, and as long as we're here by ourselves and no battle's going on right this moment—"

"Yes? What then?" Olyvria played the game with him. She spoke quietly, too; her hands worked at the catch of the white linen dress Krispos had given her for the wedding. It came open. "What then?" she repeated softly.

Between the two of them, they figured out what then. Because Phostis was still quite a young man, they got to try again soon, and again after that. Phostis had lost track of the hour by then, though the sun still lit one side of the tent. He yawned, wiped his sweaty forehead with a sweaty forearm, and dozed off. Beside him, Olyvria had already fallen asleep.

It was dark when a horrible racket woke him. He sat up and looked around, blinking. Olyvria lay beside him, still sleeping—snoring just a little—a small smile on her face. Carefully, so as not to disturb her, he put on a robe and walked outside. A new shift of Halogai ringed his tent. "What's toward?" he asked one of them.

The northerner pointed toward Etchmiadzin. The ruddy light of campfires and torches gave him the look of a man made of bronze. "Fighting in there," he said.

"By Phos," Phostis murmured, smacking a fist into the other palm. He looked over toward the imperial pavilion not far away. Krispos was outside, too, watching. Phostis felt a surge of relief that he'd not thrown in his lot with the Thanasioi. One way or another, he was more sure now than ever, Krispos would have found a way to beat them no matter what they did.

Inside Etchmiadzin, they sounded as if they were going at each other with everything they had. *They probably were,* Phostis thought. The men and women who followed the gleaming path were fanatics—whatever views they held, they held with all their hearts and all their souls. If Krispos had managed to drive a wedge between two groups of them over the propriety of Olyvria's marriage, they'd fight each other as savagely as—maybe more savagely than—they'd opposed the imperial army.

The Haloga pointed again. "Ha! Look, young Majesty—smoke. With blazing brand they burn their burg."

Sure enough, a thick column of smoke rose from inside the walls, orange-tinted gray against the black of the night sky. Phostis tried to figure out where in the town the fire had flared. His best guess was that it wasn't far from the Vaspurakaner cobbler's shop where he and Olyvria had first made love.

Another plume of smoke sprang up, and a few minutes later yet another. A tongue of yellow fire, perhaps from a burning roof, leapt into sight above the walls like a live thing, then sullenly fell back.

Before long, more and more flames sprang into view, and not all of them died down again. Fire was a terror in any city; it could so easily race ahead of anything men were able to do to hold it back. Fire in a city at war with itself was a horror to rank with the ice in Skotos' hell: how could you hope to fight it when your hand was turned against your neighbor, your friend—and his against you?

The answer was, you couldn't. The fires in Etchmiadzin burned on and on. The air of the imperial camp grew thick with the stink of smoke and, now and again, of burned flesh. Screams rent the air, some of terror, some of agony, but most of hate. In the burning streets, the battle among the Thanasioi went on.

After a while, Olyvria came out of the tent to stand beside Phostis. She slipped her hand into his without saying anything. Silently, they watched Etchmiadzin burn. Olyvria wiped at her eyes. The smoke made Phostis' sting, too. For the sake of his own peace of mind, he assumed that smoke was why she dabbed at hers.

He yawned and said, "I'm going back inside the tent. Maybe the air will be fresher in there."

Olyvria followed him in, still without speaking. Only when they were away from the guards did she say in a low voice, "There is the dowry I bring to you and your father—Etchmiadzin."

"You knew that," he answered. "You must have known it, or you'd not have answered the priest as you did."

"I suppose I did know, in a way. But knowing in advance what a thing is and seeing what it looks like when it comes to pass are not the same. Tonight I'm finding out how different they can be." She shook her head.

Had Krispos been in the tent, Phostis suspected he would have said that was one of the lessons of growing up. Phostis couldn't put a middle-aged rasp in his voice to make that sound convincing. He asked, "If you'd known, would you have done differently?"

Olyvria stayed quiet so long, he wondered if she'd heard. At last she said, "No, I suppose I would have left things as they were, but I'd have thought about them more beforehand."

"That's fair," Phostis agreed. He yawned again. "Shall we try to get some more sleep? I don't think they're going to sally against us; they're too busy warring with each other."

"I suppose so." Olyvria lay down and closed her eyes. Phostis lay down beside her. To his surprise, he dropped off almost at once.

Olyvria must have fallen asleep, too, for she jerked up at the same time as he when a great cheer roared through the encampment. He needed a moment to realize what time it was—sunshine against the east side of the tent meant dawn had broken.

As he had the night before, he poked out his head and asked a Haloga what was going on. The northerner answered, "Those in there, they have yielded themselves. The gates are thrown wide."

"Then the war is over," Phostis blurted. When he realized what he'd said, he repeated it: "The war is over." He wanted to say it again and again; he couldn't imagine four more wonderful words.

Chapter XIII

A LINE OF MEN AND WOMEN AND CHILDREN TRUDGING WEARILY down a dirt track, carrying such belongings as they could, the cows and goats and donkeys with them as thin and worn as they were. The only difference Krispos could see between them and the uprooted Thanasioi was the direction of their journey: they were moving west, not east.

No, there was another: they'd not rebelled to give him a reason to remove them from their old homes. But the land from which war and policy had removed the Thanasioi could not stay empty. That was asking for trouble. And so peasants who lived in a relatively crowded—and safely loyal—stretch of territory between Develtos and Opsikion east of Videssos the city were taking the place of the Thanasioi whether they liked the idea or not.

Phostis rode up alongside Krispos and pointed to the villagers on the way to resettlement. "Is that justice?" he asked.

"I just put the same question to myself," Krispos answered. "I don't think the answer is clear or easy. If you asked any one of them now, no doubt they'd curse me to the skies. But after two years, who can say? I've granted them tax exemptions for that long, and put them on half rates for three years more. I'm not moving them just to fill space—I want them to thrive."

"It may work out well enough for them," Phostis persisted, "but is it justice?"

"Probably not," Krispos answered, sighing. He fought back a smile; he'd managed to surprise Phostis. "Probably not," he repeated, "but is it justice to empty a land so no crops to speak of are raised on it, so it becomes a haven for brigands and outlaws, so it tempts the Makuraners to try to gobble it up? Makuran hasn't much troubled us lately, but that's because Rubyab King of Kings sees me as strong. It hasn't always been so."

"How do you aim to pay Rubyab back for sponsoring the Thanasioi?" Phostis asked.

Krispos took the change of subject to mean that Phostis thought he had a point. He answered, "I don't know right now. A big war, like the one we fought with Makuran a century and a half ago, could leave both lands prostrate for years. I don't want that. But believe me, that's not a debt to forget. Maybe it'll be one I leave to you to repay."

Phostis responded to that with a calculating look Krispos had seldom seen on him before he was kidnapped. "Fomenting the Vaspurakaners against Mashiz is likely to be worth trying."

"Aye, maybe, if the Makuraners commit some outrage in the princes' lands, or they're troubled with foes farther west," Krispos said. "But that's not as sure a bet as it looks, because the Makuraners are always on the watch for it. The beauty of Rubyab's ploy was that it used our own people against us: Videssos has known so much religious strife over the years that for a long time I didn't see the Makuraner hand in the Thanasiot glove."

"The beauty of it?" Phostis shook his head. "I don't see how you can use that word for something that caused so much trouble and death."

"It's like an unexpected clever move at the board game," Krispos said. "The board here, though, stretches all the way across the world, and you can change the rules you play by."

"And the pieces you take off the board are real people," Phostis said, "and you can't bring them back again and play them somewhere else."

"Can't I?" Krispos said. "What do you think this resettlement is, if not capturing a piece and playing it on a better square?"

He watched Phostis chew on that. The young man said, "I suppose I should have learned to stop arguing with you. No matter how well I start out, most of the time you end up turning things your way. Experience." By the way that sounded in his mouth, it might as well have been a filthy word. It was something he lacked, at any rate, which of itself made its possession suspect.

Krispos pulled a silk handkerchief from a pocket of his surcoat and dabbed at his dripping forehead. He'd left some of the imperial army back in and around Etchmiadzin, both to watch the border with Makuraner-held Vaspurakan and to help uprooted arrivals settle in. More troops were strung out along the line of travel between west and east. With what remained, he was drawing near Videssos the city.

That meant, of course, that he and his men were passing through the coastal lowlands. In late summer, there were other places he'd sooner have been; at the moment, he would have welcomed some of Skotos' ice, so long as he did not have to meet its master. It was so hot and sticky that sweat wouldn't dry; it just clung to you and rolled greasily along your skin.

"By the good god, I wish I didn't have to wear the imperial regalia," he said. "In this country, I'd sooner be dressed like them." He pointed to the peasants working in the fields to either side of the road. Some of them were in thin linen tunics that came down about half the distance from buttocks to knee. Others didn't even bother with that, but were content to wrap a loincloth around their middles.

Phostis shook his head. "If I dressed like that, it would mean I lived here all year around. I don't think I could stand that."

"You'd best be glad someone can," Krispos said. "The soil here is wonderful, and they get plenty of rain. The crops they bring in are bigger than anywhere else in the Empire. If it weren't for the lowlands, Videssos the city wouldn't have enough to eat."

"The peasants aren't fleeing from us the way they did when we set out," Katakolon said, stopping his horse by his father and brother.

"A good thing, too," Krispos answered. "One reason we have an army is to protect them. If they think soldiers are something they need to be protected from, we aren't doing the job as we should." He knew as well as anyone else that soldiers plundered peasants when they got the chance. The trick was not giving them the chance and making the peasants know they wouldn't get it. He wouldn't have to worry about that much longer on this campaign—almost home now. He said that aloud.

Katakolon leered at him. "You needn't be in such a swivet to get back to Drina, Father. Remember, she'll be out to here by now." He held a hand a couple of feet in front of his belly.

"She's not giving birth to a foal, by the good god," Krispos said. "If she were out to *there,* I might think you meant an elephant." He glared at his youngest, but couldn't help snorting as he went on, "And I'll thank you not to twit me any more about her having my by-blow. Only fool luck I'm not paying for six or seven of yours; Phos knows it's not your lack of effort."

"He's just giving you twit for twat, Father," Phostis said helpfully.

Beset from both sides, Krispos threw his hands in the air. "The two of you will be the death of me. If Evripos were here, I'd be altogether surrounded. I expect I shall be when we get back to the palaces. That's the first decent argument I've heard for making this march take longer."

"I thought it was an indecent argument," Katakolon said, not willing to be outdone by Phostis.

"Enough, enough!" Krispos groaned. "Have mercy on your poor decrepit father. I've got softening of the brain from too many years of staring at tax receipts and edicts; you can't expect me to throw puns about the way you do."

Just then, the scouts up ahead started raising a racket. One of them rode back to the van of the main body. Saluting Krispos, he said, "Your Majesty, the sharp-eyed among us have spied the sun glinting off the temple domes of Videssos the city."

Krispos peered ahead. He wasn't particularly sharp-sighted any longer; things in the distance got blurry for him. But whether he could see them or not, knowing the temples and their domes were so close made him feel the journey was coming to its end.

"Almost home," he said again. He looked from Phostis to Katakolon, daring them to make more wisecracks. They both kept quiet. He nodded, pleased with himself: the young bulls still respected the old bull's horns.

T HE FOLK OF VIDESSOS THE CITY PACKED THE COLONNADED sidewalks of Middle Street, cheering as the triumphal procession made its way toward the plaza of Palamas. Phostis rode near the head of the procession, Olyvria at his side. He wore a gilded mail shirt and helmet to let the people know who he was—and to make sure no die-hard Thanasiot assassinated him for the greater glory of the gleaming path.

As he rode, he waved, which brought fresh applause from the crowd. He turned to Olyvria and said quietly, "I wonder how many of these same people were screaming for Thanasios and trying to burn down the city not long ago."

"A fair number, I'd say," she answered.

He nodded. "I think you're right." Rooting Thanasioi out from Videssos the city wasn't nearly so straightforward as uprooting and transplanting villages. Unless you caught someone setting fires or wrecking, how could you know what was in his heart? You couldn't; that was the long and short of it. Thanasios' followers surely lingered here. If they stayed quiet, they might go unnoticed for generations—those who cared to raise new generations, at any rate.

Middle Street showed few scars from the rioting. Countless fires burned in the city every day, for cooking and heating and at smithies and other workplaces. Whitewashed buildings were usually gray with soot in a few months' time. The soot that came from the rioters' blazes looked no different from any other after the fact.

The procession passed through the Forum of the Ox, about a third of the way from the Silver Gate in the great land wall to the plaza of Palamas. The stalls in the Forum of the Ox sold cheap goods to people who could afford no better. Most of the folk who packed the square wore either ragged tunics or gaudy finery whose "gold" threads were apt to turn green in a matter of days. Phostis would have bet that plenty of them had bawled for the gleaming path.

Now, though, they cried out Krispos' name as loudly as anyone else— and that despite some former market stalls that were now only charred ruins. "Maybe they'll come back to orthodoxy now that they've really seen what their heresy leads to," Phostis said. He spoke more softly still: "That's more or less what I did, after all."

"Maybe," Olyvria said, her voice so neutral he couldn't tell whether she agreed with him or not.

We'll know twenty years from now, he thought. Looking about as far ahead as he'd already lived felt strange, almost unnatural, to him, but he was beginning to do it. He didn't know whether that was because he'd started taking seriously the idea of ruling or simply because he was getting older.

Off to the north of Middle Street, between the Forum of the Ox and the plaza of Palamas, stood the huge mass of the High Temple. It was undamaged, not from any lack of malevolence on the part of the Thanasioi but because soldiers and ecclesiastics armed with stout staves had ringed it day and night until rioting subsided.

Phostis still felt uncomfortable as he rode past the High Temple: He looked on it as an enormous sponge that had soaked up endless gold that might have been better spent elsewhere. But he had returned to the faith that found deepest expression beneath that marvelous dome. He shook his head. Not all puzzles had neat solutions. This one, too, would have to wait for more years to do their work in defining his views.

The red granite facing of the government office building caught his eye and told him the plaza of Palamas was drawing near. Somewhere under there, in the gaol levels below ground, Digenis the priest had starved himself to death.

"Digenis might have been right to be angry about how the rich have too much, but I don't think making everyone poor is the right answer," Phostis said to Olyvria. "Still, I can't hate him, not when I met you through him."

She smiled at that, but answered, "Aren't you putting your own affairs above those of the Empire there?"

He needed a moment to realize she was teasing. "As a matter of fact, yes," he said. "Or at least one affair. Katakolon's the fellow who keeps four of them in the air at the same time." She made a face at him, which let him think he'd come out best in that little skirmish.

Up ahead, a great roar announced that Krispos had entered the packed plaza of Palamas. With the Avtokrator marched servitors armed not with weapons but with sacks of gold and silver. Many an Emperor had kept the city mob happy with largess, and Krispos had shown over and over that he was able to profit from others' examples. Letting people squabble over money flung among them might keep them from more serious uprisings like the one Videssos the city had just seen.

Sky-blue ribbons—and Haloga guardsmen—kept the crowds from swamping the route the procession took to the western edge of the plaza. Krispos had ascended to a wooden platform whose pieces were stored in a palace outbuilding against time of need. Phostis wondered how many times Krispos had mounted that platform to speak to the people of the city. *Quite a few,* he thought.

He dismounted, then reached out to help Olyvria do the same. Grooms took their horses. Hand in hand, the two of them went up onto the platform themselves.

"It's a sea of people out there," Phostis exclaimed, looking out at the restless mass. Their noise rose and fell in almost regular waves, like the surf.

For the first time, Phostis had a chance to see that part of the procession which had been behind him. A parade was not a parade without soldiers. A company of Halogai marched around Krispos, Phostis, and Olyvria, for protection and show both. Behind them came several regiments of Videssians, some mounted, others afoot. They tramped along looking neither right nor left, as if the people of the city were not worth their notice. Not only were they part of the spectacle, they also served as a reminder that Krispos had powerful forces ready at hand should rioting break out again.

The Halogai formed up in front of the platform. The rest of the troops headed past the plaza of Palamas and into the palace quarter. Some had barracks there; others would be dismissed back to the countryside after the celebration was over.

Between one regiment and the next walked dejected Thanasiot prisoners. Some of them still showed the marks of wounds; none wore anything more than ragged drawers; all had their hands tied behind their backs. The crowd jeered them and pelted them with eggs and rotten fruit and the occasional stone.

Olyvria said, "A lot of Avtokrators would have capped this parade with a massacre."

"I know," Phostis said. "But Father has seen real massacres—ask him about Harvas Black-Robe sometime. Having seen the beast, he doesn't want to give birth to it."

The prisoners took the same route out of the plaza as had the soldiers. Their fate would not be much different: they'd be sent off to live on the land with the rest of the uprooted Thanasioi, with luck in peace. Unlike the soldiers, though, they would get no choice about where they went.

Another contingent of Halogai entered the plaza of Palamas. The noise from the crowd grew quieter and took on a rougher edge. Behind the front of axe-bearing northerners rode Evripos. By the reaction, not everyone in Videssos the city was happy with the way he had put down the riots.

He rode as if blithely unaware of that, waving to the people as Krispos and Phostis had before him. The guardsmen who had surrounded him took their places with their countrymen while he climbed up to stand by Phostis and Olyvria.

Without turning his head toward Phostis, he said, "They're not pleased that I didn't give them all a kiss and send them to bed with a mug of milk and a spiced bun. Well, I wasn't any too pleased that they did their best to bring the city down around my ears."

"I can understand that," Phostis answered, also looking straight ahead.

Evripos' lip curled. "And you, brother, you come through this everyone's hero. You've married the beautiful girl, like someone out of a romance. Hardly seems fair, somehow." He did not try to hide his bitterness.

"To the ice with the romances," Phostis said, but that wasn't what was bothering Evripos, and he knew it.

The low-voiced argument stopped then, because someone else ascended to the platform: Iakovitzes, gorgeous in robes just short in imperial splendor. He would not make a speech, of course, not without a tongue, but he had served in so many different roles during Krispos' reign that excluding him would have seemed unnatural.

He smiled at Olyvria, politely enough but without real interest. As he walked past Phostis and Evripos toward Krispos, he managed to pat each of them on the behind. Olyvria's eyes went wide. The two brothers looked at Iakovitzes, looked at each other, and started to laugh. "He's been doing that for as long as we've been alive," Phostis said.

"For a lot longer than that," Evripos said. "Father always tells of how Iakovitzes tried to seduce him when he was a boy, and then later when he was a groom in Iakovitzes' service, and even after he donned the red boots."

"He knows we care nothing for men," Phostis said. "If we ever made as if we wanted to go along, the shock might kill him. He's anything but young, even if he dyes his hairs and powders over his wrinkles to try to hide his years."

"I don't think you're right, Phostis," Evripos said. "If he thought we wanted to go along, he'd have our robes up and our drawers down before we could say 'I was only joking.' "

Phostis considered. "You may have something there." On a matter like that, he was willing to concede a point to his brother.

Olyvria stared at both of them, then at Iakovitzes. "That's—terrible," she exclaimed. "Why does your father keep him around?"

She made the mistake of speaking as if Iakovitzes couldn't hear her. He strolled back toward her, smiling now in a way that said he meant mischief. Alarmed, Phostis tried to head him off. Iakovitzes opened the tablet he always carried, wrote rapidly on the wax, and showed it to Phostis. "Does she read?"

"Yes, of course she does," Phostis said, whereupon Iakovitzes pushed past him toward Olyvria, scribbling as he walked.

He handed her the tablet. She took it with some apprehension, read aloud: "His Majesty keeps me around, as you say, for two reasons: first, because I am slyer than any three men you can name, including your father before and after he lost his head; and second, because he knows I would never try to seduce any wives of the imperial family."

Iakovitzes' smile got wider, and therefore more unnerving. He took back the tablet and started away. "Wait," Olyvria said sharply. Iakovitzes turned back, stylus poised like a sting. Phostis started to step between them again. But Olyvria said, "I wanted to apologize. I was cruel without thinking."

Iakovitzes chewed on that. He scribbled again, then proffered the tablet to her with a bow. Phostis looked over her shoulder. Iakovitzes had written, "So was I, to speak of your father so. In my book, the honors—or rather, dishonors—are even."

To Phostis' relief, Olyvria said, "Let it be so." Generations of sharp wits had picked quarrels with Iakovitzes, generally to end up in disarray. Phostis was glad Olyvria did not propose to make the attempt.

Iakovitzes nodded and walked back to Krispos' side. The Avtokrator held up a hand, waited for quiet. It came slowly, but did at length arrive. Into it Krispos said, "Let us have peace: peace in Videssos the city, peace in the Empire of Videssos. Civil war is nothing the Empire needs. The lord with the great and good mind knows I undertook it unwillingly. Only when those who followed what they called the gleaming path rose in rebellion, first in the westlands and then here in Videssos the city, did I take up arms against them."

"Does that mean your father would have let the Thanasioi alone if they'd been quiet, peaceful heretics?" Olyvria asked.

"I don't know. Maybe," Phostis said. "He's never persecuted the Vaspurakaners, that's certain." Phostis puzzled over that: Krispos always said religious unity was vital to holding the Empire together, but he didn't necessarily practice what he preached. Was that hypocrisy, or just pragmatism? Phostis couldn't answer, not without more thought.

He'd missed a few sentences. Krispos was saying "—shall rebuild the city so that no one may know it has come to harm. We shall rebuild the fabric of our lives in the same fashion. It will not be quick, not all of it, but Videssos is no child, to need everything on the instant. What we do, we do for generations."

Phostis still had trouble thinking in those terms. Next year felt a long way away to him; worrying about what would happen when his grandchildren were old felt as strange as worrying about what was on the other side of the moon.

He'd fallen behind again. "—but so long as you live at peace with one another, you need not fear spies will seek you out to do you harm," Krispos declared.

"What about tax collectors?" a safely anonymous wit roared from the crowd.

Krispos took no notice of him. "People of the city," he said earnestly, "if you so choose, you can be at one another's throats for longer than you care to imagine. If you start feuds now, they may last for generations after you are gone. I pray to Phos this does not happen." He let iron show in his voice: "I do not intend to let it happen. If you try to fight among your-selves, first you must overcome the soldiers of the Empire. I say this as warning, not as threat. My view is that we have had enough of strife. May we be free of it for years to come."

He did not say "forever," Phostis noted, and wondered why. He de-cided Krispos didn't believe such things endured forever. By everything the Avtokrator had shown, he worked to build a framework for what would come after him, but did not necessarily expect that framework to become a solid wall: he knew too well that history gave no assurance of success.

"We shall rebuild, as I said, and we shall go on," Krispos said. "To-gether, we shall do as well as we can for as long as we can. The good god knows we can do no more." He stepped back on the platform, his speech done.

Applause filled the plaza of Palamas, more than polite, less than ecsta-tic. Along with Olyvria and Evripos, Phostis joined it. *As well as we can for as long as we can,* he thought. If Krispos had picked a phrase to summarize himself, he couldn't have found a better one.

T HOUGH KRISPOS WAVED FOR HIM NOT TO BOTHER, BARSYMES performed a full proskynesis. "I welcome you back to the imperial resi-dence, Your Majesty," he said from the pavement. Then, still spry, he rose as gracefully as he had prostrated himself and added, "The truth is, life is on the boring side here when you take the field."

Krispos snorted. "I'm glad to be back, then, if only to give you some-thing interesting to do."

"The cooks are also glad you've returned," the vestiarios said.

"They're looking for a chance to spread themselves, you mean," Krispos said. "Too bad. They can wait until the next time I dine with Iakovitzes; he'll appreciate it properly. As for me, I've got used to eating like a soldier. A bowl of stew, a heel of bread, and a mug of wine will suit me nicely."

Barsymes' shoulders moved slightly in what would have been a sigh in someone less exquisitely polite than the eunuch. "I shall inform the kitchens of your desires," he said. "The cooks will be disappointed, but perhaps not surprised. You have a habit of acting thus whenever you re-turn from campaign."

"Do I?" Krispos said, irked at being so predictable. He was tempted to demand a fancy feast just to keep people guessing about him. The only trouble was, he really did want stew.

Barsymes said, "Perhaps Your Majesty will not take it too much amiss if the stew be of lobster and mullet, though I know that diverges from what the army cooks ladled into your bowl."

"Perhaps I won't," Krispos admitted. "I did miss seafood." Barsymes nodded in satisfaction; Krispos might rule the Empire, but the vestiarios held sway here. Unlike some vestiarioi, he had the sense not to flaunt his power or push it beyond its limits—or perhaps he had simply decided Krispos would not let him get away with the liberties some vestiarioi had taken.

"The hour remains young," Barsymes said after a glance at the shadows. "Would Your Majesty care for an early supper?"

"Thank you, no," Krispos said. "I could plunge into the pile of parchments that no doubt reaches tall as the apex of the High Temple's dome. I will do that . . . tomorrow, or perhaps the day after. The pile won't be much taller by then. For now, though, I am going to march to the imperial bedchamber and do the one thing I couldn't in the field: relax." He paused. "No. I'm not."

"Your Majesty?" Barsymes said. "What, then?"

"I am going to the bedchamber," Krispos said. "I may even rest . . . presently. But first, please tell Drina I want to see her."

"Ah," Barsymes said; Krispos read approval in the nondescript noise. The vestiarios added, "It shall be just as you say, of course."

In the privacy of the bedchamber, Krispos took off his own boots. When his feet were free, he happily wiggled his toes. In the palaces, his doing something for himself rather than summoning a servant was as much an act of rebellion as a Thanasiot's taking a torch to a rich man's house. Barsymes had needed quite a while before he accepted that the Avtokrator was sometimes stubborn enough to insist on having his own way in such matters.

A tapping at the door sounded so tentative that Krispos wondered if he'd really heard it. He walked over and opened the door anyhow. Drina stood in the hall, looking nervous. "I'm not going to bite you," Krispos said. "It would spoil my appetite for the supper the esteemed Barsymes wants to stuff down me." She didn't laugh; he concluded she didn't get the joke. Swallowing a sigh, he waved her into the bedchamber.

She walked slowly. She was still a couple of months from giving birth, but her belly bulged quite noticeably even though she wore a loose-fitting linen smock. Krispos leaned forward over that belly to give her a light kiss, hoping to put her more at ease.

He succeeded, if not quite the way he thought he would. She smiled and said, "You didn't bump into my middle there. You know how to kiss a woman who's big with child."

"I should," Krispos said. "I've had practice, even if it was years ago. Sit if you care to; I know your feet won't be happy now. How are you feeling?"

"Well enough, thank you, Your Majesty," Drina answered, sinking with a grateful sigh into a chair. "I only lost my breakfast once or twice, and but for needing the chamber pot all the time, I'm pretty well."

Krispos paced back and forth, wondering what to say next. He hadn't been in this situation for a long time, and had never expected to find himself in it again. It wasn't as if he loved Drina, or even as if he knew her well. He wished it were that way, but it wasn't. He'd just found her convenient for relieving the lust he still sometimes felt. Now he was discovering that convenience for the moment could turn into something else over the long haul. He used that principle every day in the way he ruled; he realized he should have applied it to his own life, too.

Well, he hadn't. Now he had to make the best of it. After a couple of more back and forths, he settled on, "Is everyone treating you well?"

"Oh, yes, Your Majesty." Drina nodded eagerly. "Better than I've ever been treated before. Plenty of nice food—not that I haven't always eaten well, but more and better—and I haven't had to work too hard, especially since I started getting big." Her hands cupped her belly. She gave Krispos a very serious look. "And you warned me about putting on airs, so I haven't. I've been careful about that."

"Good. I wish everyone paid as much attention to what I say," Krispos said. Drina nodded, serious still. Even with that intent expression, even pregnant as she was, she looked very young. Suddenly he asked, "How many years do you have, Drina?"

She counted on her fingers before she answered: "Twenty-two, I think, Your Majesty, but I may be out one or two either way."

Krispos started pacing again. It wasn't that she didn't know her exact age; he wasn't precisely sure of his own. Peasants such as he and his family had been didn't worry over such things: you were as old as the work you could do. But twenty-two, more or less? She'd been born right around the time he took the throne.

"What am I to do with you?" he asked, aiming the question as much at himself, or possibly at Phos, as at her.

"Your Majesty?" Her eyes got large and frightened. "You said I'd not lack for anything . . . " Her voice trailed away, as if reminding him of his own promise took all the courage she had, and as if she'd not be surprised if he broke it.

"You won't—by the good god I swear it. " He sketched the sun-circle over his heart to reinforce his words. "But that's not what I meant."

"What then?" Drina's horizons, like his when he'd been a peasant, reached no farther than plenty of food and not too much work. "All I want to do is take care of the baby."

"You'll do that, and with as much help as you need," he said. He scratched his head. "Do you read?"

"No, Your Majesty."

"Do you want to learn how?"

"Not especially, Your Majesty," Drina said. "Can't see that I'd ever have much call to use it."

Krispos clucked disapprovingly. A veteran resettled to his village had taught him his letters before his beard sprouted, and his world was never the same again. Written words bound time and space together in a way mere talk could never match. But if Drina did not care to acquire the skill, forcing it on her would not bring her pleasure. He scratched his head again.

"Your Majesty?" she asked. He raised an eyebrow and waited for her to go on. She did, nervously: "Your Majesty, after the baby's born, will you—will you want me again?"

It was a good question, Krispos admitted to himself. From Drina's point of view, it probably looked like the most important question in the world. She wanted to know whether she'd stay close to the source of power and influence in the Empire. The trouble was, Krispos had no idea what reply to give her. He couldn't pretend, to himself or to her, that he'd fallen wildly in love, not when he was more than old enough to be her father. And even if he had fallen wildly in love with her, the result would only have been grotesque. Older men who fell in love with girls got laughed at behind their backs.

She waited for his answer. "We'll have to see," he said at last. He wished he could do better than that, but he didn't want to lie to her, either.

"Yes, Your Majesty," she said. The pained resignation in her voice cut like a knife. He wished he hadn't bedded her at all. But he hadn't the nature or temperament to make a monk. What was he supposed to do?

I should have remarried after Dara died, he thought. But he hadn't wanted to do that then, and a second wife might have created more problems—dynastic ones—than she solved. So he'd taken serving maids to bed every now and then . . . and so he had his present problem.

"I told you before that I'd settle a fine dowry on you when you find yourself someone who can give you all the love and caring you deserve," he said. "I don't think you'll find an Emperor's bastard any obstacle to that."

"No, I don't think so, either," she agreed; she was ignorant, but not stupid. "The trouble is, I don't have anyone like that in mind right now."

Not right now. She was twenty-two; *not right now* didn't look that different from *forever* to her. Nor, in fairness, could she look past her confinement. Her whole world would turn upside down once she held her baby in her arms. She'd need time to see how things had changed.

"We'll see," Krispos said again.

"All right." She accepted that; she had no choice.

Krispos knew it wasn't fair for her. Most Avtokrators would not have given that a first thought, let alone a second, but he knew about unfairness from having been on the receiving end. If he hadn't been unjustly taxed off his farm, he never would have come to Videssos the city and started on the road that led to a crown.

But what was he to do? Say he loved her when he didn't? That wouldn't be right—or fair—either. He was uneasily aware that providing for Drina and her child wasn't enough, but he didn't see what else he could do.

She wasn't a helpless maiden, not by a long shot. Her eyes twinkled as she asked, "What do the young Majesties think of all this? Evripos has known for a long time, of course; he just laughs whenever he sees me."

"Does he?" Krispos didn't know whether to be miffed or to laugh himself. "If you must know, Phostis and Katakolon seem to be of a mind that I'm a disgusting old lecher who should keep his drawers on when he goes to bed."

Drina dismissed that with one word: "Pooh."

Krispos couldn't even glow with pride, as another man might have. He'd spent too many years on the throne weighing everything he heard for flattery, doing his best not to believe all the praise that poured over him like honey, thick and sweet. He thought some of the man he had been still remained behind the imperial façade he'd built up—but how could you be sure?

He started pacing again. *Sometimes you think too much,* he told himself. He knew it was true, but it was so ingrained in him that he couldn't change. At last, too late, he told Drina, "Thank you."

"I should thank you, Your Majesty, for not ignoring me or casting me out of the palaces or putting me in a sack and throwing me into the Cattle-Crossing because my belly made me a nuisance to you," Drina said.

"You shame me," Krispos said. He saw she didn't understand, and felt bound to explain: "When I'm thanked for not being a monster, it tells me I've not been all the man I might be."

"Who is?" she said. "And you're the Avtokrator. All the things you keep in your head, Your Majesty—I'd go mad if I tried it for a day. I was just glad you saw fit to remember me at all, and do what you can for me."

Krispos pondered that. An Avtokrator could do what he chose—he needed to look no further than Anthimos' antics to be reminded of that. The power made responsibility hard to remember. Seen from that viewpoint, maybe he wasn't doing so badly after all.

"Thank you," he said to Drina again, this time with no hesitation at all.

A BOYS' CHOIR SANG HYMNS OF THANKSGIVING. THE SWEET, almost unearthly notes came echoing back from the dome of the High Temple, filling the worship area below with joyous sound.

Phostis, however, listened without joy. He knew he was no Thanasiot. All the same, the countless wealth lavished on the High Temple still struck him as excessive. And when Oxeites lifted up his hands to beseech Phos' favor, all Phostis could think of was the ecumenical patriarch's cloth-of-gold sleeves and the pearls and precious gems mounted on them.

Only because of the peace he'd made with Krispos had he come here. He recognized that celebrating his safe return to Videssos the city at the most holy shrine of the Empire's faith was politically and theologically valuable, so he endured it. That did not mean he liked it.

Beside him, though, awe turned Olyvria's face almost into that of a stranger. Her eyes flew like butterflies, landing now here, now there, marveling at the patriarch's regalia, at the moss-agate and marble columns, at the altar, at the rich woods of the pews, and most of all, inevitably, at the mosaic image of Phos, stern in judgment, that looked down on his worshipers from the dome.

"It's so marvelous," she whispered to Phostis for the third time since the service began. "Every city in the provinces says its main temple is modeled after this one. What none of them says is that all their models are toys."

Phostis grunted softly, back in his throat. What she found wondrous was cloying to him. Then, of themselves, his eyes too went up to the dome. No man could be easy meeting the gaze of that Phos: the image seemed to see inside his head, to know and note every stain on his soul. Even Thanasios would have quailed under that inspection. For the sake of the image in the dome, Phostis forgave the rest of the temple.

The choirmaster brought down his hands. The boys fell silent. Their blue silk robes shimmered in the lamplight as the echoes of their music slowly faded. Oxeites recited Phos' creed. The notables who filled the temple joined him at prayer. Those echoes also reverberated from the dome.

The patriarch said, "Not only do we seek thy blessing, Phos, we also humbly send up to thee our thanks for returning to us Phostis son of Krispos, heir to the throne of Videssos, and granting him thine aid through all the troubles he has so bravely endured."

"He's never been humble in his life, surely not since he donned the blue boots," Phostis murmured to Olyvria.

"Hush," she murmured back; the Temple had her in its spell.

Oxeites went on, "Surely, lord with the great and good mind, thou also viewest with favor the ending of the Empire's trial of heresy, and the way in which its passing was symbolized by the recent union of the young Majesty and his lovely bride."

A spattering of applause rose from the assembled worshipers, vigorously led by Krispos. Phostis was convinced Oxeites would not know a symbol if it reached up and yanked him by the beard; he suspected the Avtokrator of putting words in his patriarch's mouth.

"We thank thee, Phos, for thy blessings of peace and prosperity, and once more for the restoration of the young Majesty to the bosom of his family and to Videssos the city," Oxeites said in ringing tones.

The choir burst into song again. When the hymn was finished, the patriarch dismissed the congregation: the thanksgiving service was not a full and formal liturgy. Phostis blinked against the late summer sun as he walked down the broad, wide stairs outside the High Temple. Katakolon poked him in the ribs and said, "The only bosom you care about in your family is Olyvria's."

"By the good god, you're shameless," Phostis said. He couldn't help laughing, even so. Because Katakolon had no malice in him, he could get away with outrages that would have landed either of his brothers in trouble.

In the courtyard outside the High Temple, people of rank insufficient to get them into the thanksgiving service cheered as Phostis came down from the steps and walked over to his horse. He waved to them, all the while wondering how many had shouted for the gleaming path not long before.

The Haloga guard who held the horse's head said, "You talk to your god only a little while today." He sounded approving, or at least relieved.

Phostis handed Olyvria up onto her mount, then swung into the saddle himself. The Halogai formed up around the imperial party for the return to the palaces. Olyvria rode at Phostis' left. To his right was Evripos. His older younger brother curled his lip and said, "You're back. Hurrah." Then he looked straight ahead and seemed to concentrate solely on his horsemanship.

"Wait a minute," Phostis said harshly. "I'm sick of cracks like that from you. If you wanted me to be gone and stay gone, you had your chance to do something about it."

"I told you then, I don't have that kind of butchery in me," Evripos answered.

"Well then, quit talking to me as if you wish you did."

That made Evripos look his way again, though still without anything that could be called friendliness. "Brother of mine, just because I won't shed blood of my blood, that doesn't mean I want to clasp you to my bosom, if I can steal the patriarch's phrase."

"That's not enough," Phostis said.

"It's all I care to make it," Evripos answered.

"It's not enough, I tell you," Phostis said, which succeeded in gaining Evripos' undivided attention. Phostis went on, "One of these days, if I live, I'm going to wear the red boots. Unless Olyvria and I have a son of our own, you'll be next in line for them. Even if we do, he'd be small for a long time. The day may come when you decide blood doesn't matter, or maybe you'll think you can just shave my head and pack me off to a monastery: you'd get the throne and salve your tender conscience at the same time."

Evripos scowled. "I wouldn't do that. As you said, I had my chance."

"You wouldn't do it *now,*" Phostis returned. "What about ten years from now, or twenty, when you feel you can't stand being second in line for another heartbeat? Or what happens if I decide I can't trust you to stay in your proper place? I might strike first, little brother. Did you ever think of that?"

Evripos was good at using his face to mask his thoughts. But Phostis had watched him all his life, and saw he'd succeeded in surprising him. The surprise faded quickly. Evripos studied Phostis as closely as he was studied in turn. Slowly, he said, "You've changed." It sounded like an accusation.

"Have I, now?" Phostis tried to keep anything but the words themselves from his voice.

"Aye, you have." It *was* accusation. "Before you got kidnapped, you didn't have the slightest notion what you were for, what you wanted. You knew what you were against—"

"Anything that had to do with Father," Phostis interrupted.

"Just so," Evripos agreed with a thin smile. "But being against is easy. Finding, knowing, what you truly do want is harder."

"You know what you want," Olyvria put in.

"Of course I do," Evripos said. *The red boots* hung unspoken in the air. "But it looks like I can't have that. And now that Phostis knows what he wants, too, and what it means to him, it makes him ever so much more dangerous to me than he was before."

"So it does," Phostis said. "You can do one of two things about it, as far as I can see: you can try to take me out, which you say you don't want to do, or you can work with me. We spoke of that before I got kidnapped; maybe you remember. You scoffed at me then. Do you sing a different tune now? The second man in all the Empire can find or make a great part for himself."

"But it's not the first part," Evripos said.

"I know that's what you want," Phostis answered, saying it for his brother. "If you look one way, you see one person ahead of you. But if you look in the other direction, you see everyone else behind. Isn't that enough?"

Enough to make Evripos thoughtful, at any rate. When he answered, "It's not what I want," the words lacked the hostility with which he'd spoken before.

Krispos rode ahead of the younger members of the imperial family. As he clattered down the cobblestones in front of the government office building where Digenis had been confined, a man strolling along the sidewalk sang out, "Phos bless you, Your Majesty!" Krispos sent him a wave and kept on riding.

"*That's* what I want." Now Evripos' voice ached with envy. "Who's going to cheer a general or a minister? It's the Avtokrator who gets the glory, by the good god."

"He gets the blame, too," Phostis pointed out. "If I could, I'd give you all the glory, Evripos; for all I care, it can go straight to the ice. But there's more to running the Empire than having people cheer you in the streets. I didn't take it seriously before I got snatched, but my eyes have been opened since then."

He wondered if that would mean anything to his brother. It seemed to, for Evripos said, "So have mine. Don't forget, I was running Videssos the city while Father went on campaign. Even without the riots, I'll not deny that was a great bloody lot of work. All jots and tittles and parchments that didn't mean anything till you'd read them five times, and sometimes not then."

Phostis nodded. He often wondered if he wanted to walk in Krispos' footsteps and pore over documents into the middle of the night. That, surely, was why the Empire of Videssos had developed so large and thorough a bureaucracy over the centuries: to keep the Avtokrator from having to shoulder such burdens.

As if Krispos had spoken aloud, Phostis heard his opinion of that: *Aye, and if you let the pen-pushers and seal-stampers run affairs without checking up on them, how do you know when they're bungling things or cheating you? The good god knows we need them, and he also knows they need someone looking over them. Anthimos almost brought the Empire to ruin because he wouldn't attend to his ruling.*

"I wouldn't be Anthimos," Phostis protested, just as if Krispos *had* spoken out loud. Olyvria, Evripos, and Katakolon all gave him curious looks. He felt his cheeks heat.

Evripos said, "Well, I wouldn't, either. If I tried to live that life after Father died, I expect he'd climb out of the tomb and wring my neck with bony fingers." He dropped his voice and sent a nervous glance up ahead toward Krispos; Phostis guessed he was only half joking.

"Me, I'm just as glad I'm not likely to wear the red boots," Katakolon said. "I like a good carouse now and then; it keeps you from going stale."

"A good carouse now and then is one thing," Phostis said. "From all the tales, though, Anthimos never stopped, or even slowed down."

"A short life but a merry one," Katakolon said, grinning.

"You let Father hear that from you and your life may be short, but it won't be merry," Phostis answered. "He's not what you'd call fond of Anthimos' memory."

Katakolon looked forward again; he did not want to rouse Krispos' wrath. Phostis suddenly grasped another reason why Krispos so despised the predecessor whose throne and wife he'd taken: no doubt he'd wondered all the years since Anthimos had left behind a cuckoo's egg for him to raise as his own.

And yet, of the three young men, Phostis was probably most like Krispos in character, if perhaps more inclined to reflection and less to action. Evripos was devious in a different way, and his resentment that he hadn't been born first left him sour. And Katakolon—Katakolon had a blithe disregard for consequences that set him apart from both his brothers.

Without warning, Evripos said, "You'll give me room to make something for myself, make something of myself, when the red boots go on your feet?"

"I've said so all along," Phostis answered. "Would an oath make you happier?"

"Nothing along those lines would truly make me happy," Evripos said. "But one of the things I've seen is that sometimes there's nothing to be done about the way things are . . . or nothing that isn't worse, anyhow. Let it be as you say, brother of mine; I'll serve you, and do my best to recall that everyone else serves me as well as you."

The two of them solemnly clasped hands. Olyvria exclaimed in delight; even Katakolon looked unwontedly sober. Evripos' palm was warm in Phostis'. By her expression, Olyvria thought all the troubles between them were over. Phostis wished he thought the same. As far as he could see, he and Evripos would be watching each other for the rest of their lives, no matter what promises they made each other. That, too, came with being part of the imperial family.

Had Evripos said something like *Good to have that settled once and for all,* Phostis would have suspected him more, not less. As it was, his younger brother just flicked him a glance to see how seriously he took the gesture of reconciliation. For a moment, their eyes met. They both smiled, again for a moment only. They might not trust each other, but they understood each other.

Along with the rest of the imperial party, they rode through the plaza of Palamas and into the palace quarter. After the raucous bustle of the rest of the city, quiet enfolded them there like a cloak. Phostis felt he was coming home. That had special meaning to him after what he'd gone through the past few months.

He'd always used his bedchamber in the imperial residence as a refuge from Krispos. Now that Olyvria shared it with him, he sometimes thought he never wanted to come out again. It wasn't that they spent all their time making love, delightful though that was. But he'd also found in her somebody he liked talking with more than anyone else he'd ever known.

He let himself tip over backward onto the bed like a falling tree. The thick goose down of the mattress absorbed his weight; it was like falling into a warm, dry snowbank. With him sprawled across the middle of the bed, Olyvria sat at its foot. She said, "All of this—" She waved to show she meant not just the room, not just the palace, but also the service and the procession through the streets of the city. "—still feels unreal to me."

"You'll have the rest of your days to get used to it," Phostis answered. "A lot of it is foolish and boring to go through; even Father thinks so. But ceremony is the glue that holds Videssos together, so he does go through with it, and then grumbles when no one outside the palaces can hear him."

"That's hypocrisy." Olyvria frowned; like Phostis, she still had some Thanasiot righteousness clinging to her.

"I've told him as much," Phostis said. "He just shrugs and says things would go worse if he didn't give the people what they expected of him." Before he'd been kidnapped, he would have rolled his eyes at that. Now, after a small pause for thought, he admitted, "There may be something to it."

"I don't know." Olyvria's frown deepened. "How can you live with yourself after doing things you don't believe in year after year after year?"

"I didn't say Father doesn't believe in them. He does, for the sake of the Empire. I said he doesn't like them. It's not quite the same thing."

"Close enough, for anyone who's not a theologian and used to splitting hairs." But Olyvria changed the subject, which might have meant she yielded the point. "I'm glad you made peace with your brother—or he with you, however you want to look at it."

"So am I," Phostis said. Not wanting to deceive Olyvria about his judgment of that peace, he added, "Now we'll see how long it lasts."

She took his meaning at once. "Oh," she said in a crestfallen voice. "I'd thought you put more faith in it than that."

"Hope, yes. Faith?" He shrugged, then repeated, "We'll see how long it lasts. The good god willing, it'll hold forever. If it doesn't—"

"If it doesn't, you'll do what you have to do," Olyvria said.

"Aye, what I have to do," Phostis echoed. He'd come safe out of Etchmiadzin by that rule, but if you cared to, you could use it to justify anything. He sighed, then said, "You know what the real trouble with Thanasiot doctrine is?"

"What?" Olyvria asked. "The ecumenical patriarch could come up with a hundred without thinking."

"Oxeites does quite a lot without thinking," Phostis said. "He's not good at it."

Olyvria giggled, deliciously scandalized. "But what's yours?" she asked.

"The real trouble with Thanasiot doctrine," Phostis declared, as if pontificating before a synod, "is that it makes the world and life out to be simpler than they are. Burn and wreck and starve and you've somehow made the world a better place? But what about the people who don't want to be burned out and who like to eat till they're fat? What about the Makuraners, who would pick up the pieces if Videssos fell apart—and who tried to make it fall apart? The gleaming path takes none of them into account. It just goes on along the track it thinks right, regardless of any complications."

"That's all true enough," Olyvria said.

"In fact," Phostis went on, "following the gleaming path is almost like getting caught up in a new love affair, where you just notice everything that's good and kind about the person you love, but none of the flaws."

Olyvria gave him an unfathomable look. His analogy pleased him so much that he wondered what was troubling her until she asked, in rather a small voice, "And what does that say about us?"

"It says—uh—" Feeling his mouth hanging foolishly open, Phostis shut it. He kept it shut while he did some hard thinking. At last, much less sure of himself than he had been a moment before, he answered, "I think it says that we can't afford to take us for granted, or to think that, because we're happy now, we're always going to be happy unless we work to make that happen. The romances talk a lot about living happily ever after, but they don't say how it's done. We have to find that out for ourselves."

"I wish you'd stop poking fun at the romances, seeing as we're living one," Olyvria said, but she smiled to take any sting from her words. "Other than that, though, you make good sense. You seem to have a way of doing that."

"Thank you," he said seriously. Then he reached out and poked her in the ribs. She squawked and whipped her head around, curls flying. He drew her to him and drowned the squawk in a kiss. When at last he had to breathe, he asked her softly, "How are we doing now?"

"Now, well." This time, she kissed him. "As for the rest, ask me in twenty years."

He glanced up, just for a moment, to make sure the door was barred. "I will."

I MPERIAL CROWN HEAVY ON HIS HEAD, KRISPOS SAT ON THE throne in the Grand Courtroom, awaiting the approach of the ambassador for Khatrish. In front of the throne stood Barsymes, Iakovitzes, and Zaidas. Krispos hoped the three of them would be enough to protect him from Tribo's pungent sarcasm.

The fuzzy-bearded envoy advanced down the long central aisle of the courtroom between ranks of courtiers who scorned him as both barbarian and heretic. He managed to give the impression that their scorn amused him, which only irked them the more.

He prostrated himself at the proper place before Krispos' throne. Krispos had debated whether to have the throne rise while Tribo's head rested on the gleaming marble floor. In the end, he'd decided against it.

As before, when Tribo rose, he asked, "Has the gearing broken down, Your Majesty, or are you just not bothering?"

"I'm not bothering." Krispos swallowed a sigh. So much for the fond hope Avtokrators nursed of overawing envoys from less sophisticated lands. He inclined his head to Tribo. "I've waited in eager curiosity for your words since you requested this audience, honored ambassador."

"You're wondering how I'll get on your nerves now, you mean." Mutters rose at Tribo's undiplomatic language. By his foxy grin, he reveled in them. But when he resumed, he spoke more formally: "I am bidden by the puissant khagan Nobad son of Gumush to extend Khatrish's congratulations to Your Majesty for your victory over the Thanasiot heretics."

"The puissant khagan is gracious," Krispos said.

"The puissant khagan, for all his congratulations, is unhappy with Your Majesty," Tribo said. "You've put out the fire in your own house, but sparks caught in the thatch of ours, and they're liable to burn down the roof. We still have plenty of trouble from the Thanasioi in Khatrish."

"I'm sorry to hear that." Krispos reflected that he wasn't even lying. Just as Videssian Thanasioi had spread the heresy to Khatrish, so foreign followers of the gleaming path might one day bring it back to the Empire. Krispos resumed, "I don't know what the khagan would have me do now, though, beyond what I've already done here in my own realm."

"He thinks it hardly just for you to export your problems and then forget about them when they trouble you no more," Tribo said.

"What would he have me do?" Krispos repeated. "Shall I ship imperial troops to your ports to help your soldiers root out the heretics? Shall I send in priests I reckon orthodox to uphold the pure and true doctrines?"

Tribo made a sour face. "Shall Videssos swallow up Khatrish, you mean. Thank you, Your Majesty, but no. If I said aye to that, my khagan would likely tie me between horses and whip them to a gallop, one going one way and one the other . . . unless he paused to think up a truly interesting and creative end for me. Khatrish has been free of the imperial yoke for more than three hundred years. For reasons you may not understand, we'd sooner keep it that way."

"As you will," Krispos said. "Your land and mine are at peace, and I'm happy with that. But if you don't want our warriors and you don't want our priests, honored ambassador, what do you expect us to do about the Thanasioi in Khatrish?"

"You ought to pay us an indemnity for inflicting the heresy on us," Tribo said. "The gold would help us take care of the problem for ourselves."

Krispos shook his head. "If we'd deliberately set the Thanasioi on you, that would be a just claim. But Videssos just fought a war to put them down here: we didn't want them around, either. I'm sorry they spread to Khatrish, but it was no fault of ours. Shall I bill the puissant khagan every time the Balancer heresy you love so well shows its head here in the Empire?"

"Your Majesty, I know you imperials have a saying, 'When in Videssos the city, eat fish.' But till now I hadn't known you hid a shark's dorsal fin under those fancy robes."

"From you, honored ambassador, that's high praise indeed," Krispos said, which only made Tribo look unhappier still. The Avtokrator went on, "Does your puissant khagan have any other business for you to set before me?"

"No, Your Majesty," Tribo answered. "I shall convey to him your stubborn refusal to act as justice would dictate, and warn you that I cannot answer for the consequences."

From the Makuraner ambassador, that would have meant war. But Videssos badly outweighed Khatrish, and the two nations, despite bickering, had not fought for generations. So Krispos said, "Do tell his puissant self that I admire his gall, and that if I could afford to subsidize it, I would. As is, he'll just have to smuggle more and hope he makes it up that way."

"I shall convey your insulting and degrading remarks along with your refusal." Tribo paused. "He may take you up on that smuggling scheme."

"I know. I'll stop him if I can." Krispos mentally began framing orders for more customs inspectors and tighter vigilance along the Khatrisher border. All the same, he knew the easterners would get some untaxed amber through.

Tribo prostrated himself again, then rose and walked away from the throne backward until he'd withdrawn far enough to turn around without offending court etiquette. He was too accomplished a diplomat to do anything so rude as sticking his nose in the air as he marched off, but so accomplished a mime that he managed to create that impression without the reality.

The courtiers began streaming out after the ambassador left the Grand Courtroom. Their robes and capes of bright, glistening silk made them seem a moving field of springtime flowers.

Zaidas turned to Krispos and made small, silent clapping motions. "Well done, Your Majesty," he said. "It's not every day that the envoy from Khatrish, whoever he may be, leaves an audience in such dismay."

"Khatrishers are insolent louts with no respect for their betters," Barsymes said. "They disrupt ceremonial merely for the sake of disruption." By his tone, the offense ranked somewhere between heresy and infanticide on his scale of enormities.

"I don't mind them that much," Krispos said. "They just have a hard time taking anything seriously." He'd lost his own war against ceremonial years before; if he needed a reminder, the weight of the crown on his head gave him one. Seeing other folk strike blows against the foe—the only foe, in the Empire or out of it that had overcome him—let him dream about renewing the struggle himself one day. He was, sadly, realist enough to know he did but dream.

Iakovitzes opened his table, plucked out a stylus, and wrote busily: "I don't like Khatrishers because they're too apt to cheat when they dicker with us. Of course, they say the same of Videssos."

"And they're probably as right as we are," Zaidas murmured.

Krispos suspected Iakovitzes didn't like Khatrishers because they took the same glee he did in flouting staid Videssian custom—and sometimes upstaged him while they were at it. That was something he wouldn't say out loud, for fear of finding out he was right and wounding Iakovitzes in the process.

The Grand Courtroom continued to empty. A couple of men came forward instead of leaving; they carried rolled and sealed parchments in their outstretched right hands. Haloga guardsmen kept them from getting too close. One of the northerners glanced back at Krispos. He nodded. The Haloga took the petitions and carried them over to him. They'd go into one of the piles on his desk. He wondered when he'd have the chance to read them. *They'll reach the top one of these days,* he thought.

The petitioners walked down the long aisle toward the doorway. Krispos rose, stretched, and descended the stairs from the throne. Iakovitzes wrote another note: "You know, it might not be so bad if the Thanasioi give the Khatrishers all the trouble they can handle and a bit more besides. Let Tribo say what he will; the day may come when the khagan really has to choose between going under and calling on Videssos for aid."

"That would be excellent," Barsymes said. "Krispos brought Kubrat back under Videssian rule; why not Khatrish, as well?"

Why not? Krispos thought. Videssos had never abandoned her claim to Kubrat or Khatrish or Thatagush, all lands overwhelmed by Khamorth nomads off the plains of Pardraya three hundred years before. To restore two of them to the Empire . . . he might go down in the chronicles as Krispos the Conqueror.

That, however, assumed the Khatrishers were ripe to be conquered. "I don't see it," Krispos said, not altogether regretfully. "Khatrish somehow has a way of fumbling through troubles and coming out on the other side stronger than it has any business being. They're more easygoing about their religion than we are, too, so heresy has a harder time inciting them."

"They certainly didn't—don't—care for the Thanasioi," Zaidas said. Krispos guessed the idea of conquest appealed to him, too.

"We'll see what happens, that's all," the Avtokrator said. "If it turns to chaos, we may try going in. We'd have to be careful even so, though, to make sure the Khatrishers don't unite again—against us. Nothing like a foreign foe to make the problems you have with your neighbors look small."

"Remember also, Your Majesty, the Thanasioi dissemble," Barsymes said. "Even if the Khatrishers seem to put down the heresy of the gleaming path for the time being, it may yet spring to life a generation from now."

"A generation from now?" Krispos snorted. "Odds are that'll be Phostis' worry, not mine." A year before, the idea of passing the Empire on to his eldest—if Phostis was *his* eldest—had filled him with dread. Now . . . "I expect he'll take care of it," he said.

HARRY TURTLEDOVE is an award-winning author of science fiction and fantasy. His alternate-history works have included several short stories and novels, such as *The Guns of the South; How Few Remain* (winner of the Sidewise Award for Best Novel); the Great War epics: *American Front, Walk in Hell,* and *Breakthroughs;* the Worldwar saga: *In the Balance, Tilting the Balance, Upsetting the Balance,* and *Striking the Balance;* the Colonization books: *Second Contact, Down to Earth,* and *Aftershocks;* the American Empire novels: *Blood & Iron, The Center Cannot Hold,* and *Victorious Opposition; Settling Accounts: Return Engagement; Settling Accounts: Drive to the East;* and others. He is married to fellow novelist Laura Frankos. They have three daughters: Alison, Rachel, and Rebecca.